W. SOMERSET MAUGHAM

W. SOMERSET MAUGHAM

◆

SIXTY-FIVE SHORT STORIES

Heinemann/Octopus

This edition first published in Great Britain
by arrangement with Doubleday & Company, Inc
in 1982 jointly by

William Heinemann Inc
450 Park Avenue, New York, NY 10022

and

Octopus Books Inc
747 Third Avenue
New York, NY 10017

ISBN 0 905712 69 2

Printed in the United States of America
by R. R. Donnelley and Sons Company.

CONTENTS

INTRODUCTION

William Somerset Maugham was born in 1874 and educated at the King's School, Canterbury and Heidelberg University. He spent some time at St Thomas's Hospital as a medical student but was attracted from medicine to letters by the success of his first novel, *Liza of Lambeth* (1897), in which he drew on what he had seen in the district served by his hospital. He also drew on his medical experience in his first masterpiece, *Of Human Bondage* (1915). Upon the appearance of *The Moon and Sixpence* (1919) his reputation as a novelist was established. He was at the same time a successful playwright, his last play, *Sheppey*, appearing in 1933. Apart from short stories, his work included essays, criticism, autobiography and travel books.

A widely travelled man, he spent much of the 1914–18 war abroad in the intelligence service–the time in which he laid the basis of the 'Ashenden' stories. In the 'twenties he took up residence in the south of France and, but for the last war, lived there until his death in December 1965.

The stories published here were largely written in the three decades following the First World War. Although Maugham had written short stories early in his career, preoccupation with his other writing led to a long interval before he next took up the form, on a voyage in the South Seas in 1919, originally as a relief from other work. It is consequently an irony which he would have appreciated that many consider him to be at his best in his short stories. When he stopped writing them he made a collection of those that he wished to preserve and arranged them in the order felt to be most agreeable to the reader. This edition as far as possible preserves that arrangement.

A good part of the success of his stories derives from the technique that Maugham used. He discussed this in the preface to the first American edition of his collected short stories and compared it with the contrasting techniques of Chekhov and de Maupassant. Chekhov had markedly superior character-isation, he said, but de Maupassant did give his short stories a beginning, a middle and an end–which Maugham approved, and which is the key to his style: 'My prepossessions in the arts are on the side of law and order. I like a story that fits.' Such was his answer to critics who had applied the word 'competent' to his stories, disparagingly as they thought–and, judging by the stories' vast and continuing popularity, unwisely.

Following this principle, Maugham developed a style which was as ordered as his general plan. His sentences are short. They balance one another and are balanced in themselves. They are a highly appropriate form for his narratives, stamped as they are by their fluency and discursiveness. Moreover, it is a style equally suited to Maugham's view of his characters: a view that is largely detached, cool, at times slightly cynical but tempered constantly by a wry sense of humour–as illustrated by 'Jane'. Maugham is, however, at ease equally in pure comedy ('The Facts of Life') and in high tragedy ('The Unconquered'). His stories are with the same felicity as varied in mood as they are in setting.

Each of these stories can stand on its own. Maugham himself wrote that such a compactness of technique, character and incident may seem disconcerting in a world where at least one loose end is normally left behind; but the compactness is part of the method used by such short story writers as Maugham. As he put it in his own distinctive way, such a writer 'seeks to prove nothing. He paints a picture and sets it before you. You can take it or leave it.' Most take it.

Rain

◆

It was nearly bed-time and when they awoke next morning land would be in sight. Dr Macphail lit his pipe and, leaning over the rail, searched the heavens for the Southern Cross. After two years at the front and a wound that had taken longer to heal than it should, he was glad to settle down quietly at Apia for twelve months at least, and he felt already better for the journey. Since some of the passengers were leaving the ship next day at Pago-Pago they had had a little dance that evening and in his ears hammered still the harsh notes of the mechanical piano. But the deck was quiet at last. A little way off he saw his wife in a long chair talking with the Davidsons, and he strolled over to her. When he sat down under the light and took off his hat you saw that he had very red hair, with a bald patch on the crown, and the red, freckled skin which accompanies red hair; he was a man of forty, thin, with a pinched face, precise and rather pedantic; and he spoke with a Scots accent in a very low, quiet voice.

Between the Macphails and the Davidsons, who were missionaries, there had arisen the intimacy of shipboard, which is due to propinquity rather than to any community of taste. Their chief tie was the disapproval they shared of the men who spent their days and nights in the smoking-room playing poker or bridge and drinking. Mrs Macphail was not a little flattered to think that she and her husband were the only people on board with whom the Davidsons were willing to associate, and even the doctor, shy but no fool, half unconsciously acknowledged the compliment. It was only because he was of an argumentative mind that in their cabin at night he permitted himself to carp.

'Mrs Davidson was saying she didn't know how they'd have got through the journey if it hadn't been for us,' said Mrs Macphail, as she neatly brushed out her transformation. 'She said we were really the only people on the ship they cared to know.'

'I shouldn't have thought a missionary was such a big bug that he could afford to put on frills.'

'It's not frills. I quite understand what she means. It wouldn't have been very nice for the Davidsons to have to mix with all that rough lot in the smoking-room.'

'The founder of their religion wasn't so exclusive,' said Dr Macphail with a chuckle.

'I've asked you over and over again not to joke about religion,' answered his wife. 'I shouldn't like to have a nature like yours, Alec. You never look for the best in people.'

He gave her a sidelong glance with his pale, blue eyes, but did not reply. After many years of married life he had learned that it was more conducive to peace to leave his wife with the last word. He was undressed before she was, and climbing into the upper bunk he settled down to read himself to sleep.

When he came on deck next morning they were close to land. He looked at it with greedy eyes. There was a thin strip of silver beach rising quickly to hills covered to the top with luxuriant vegetation. The coconut trees, thick and green, came nearly to the water's edge, and among them you saw the grass houses of the Samoans; and here and there, gleaming white, a little church. Mrs Davidson came and stood beside him. She was dressed in black and wore round her neck a gold chain, from which dangled a small cross. She was a little woman, with brown, dull hair very elaborately arranged, and she had prominent blue eyes behind invisible pince-nez. Her face was long, like a sheep's, but she gave no impression of foolishness, rather of extreme alertness; she had the quick movements of a bird. The most remarkable thing about her was her voice, high, metallic, and without inflexion; it fell on the ear with a hard monotony, irritating to the nerves like the pitiless clamour of the pneumatic drill.

'This must seem like home to you,' said Dr Macphail, with his thin, difficult smile.

'Ours are low islands, you know, not like these. Coral. These are volcanic. We've got another ten days' journey to reach them.'

'In these parts that's almost like being in the next street at home,' said Dr Macphail facetiously.

'Well, that's rather an exaggerated way of putting it, but one does look at distances differently in the South Seas. So far you're right.'

Dr Macphail sighed faintly.

'I'm glad we're not stationed here,' she went on. 'They say this is a terribly difficult place to work in. The steamers' touching makes the people unsettled; and then there's the naval station; that's bad for the natives. In our district we don't have difficulties like that to contend with. There are one or two traders, of course, but we take care to make them behave, and if they don't we make the place so hot for them they're glad to go.'

Fixing the glasses on her nose she looked at the green island with a ruthless stare.

'It's almost a hopeless task for the missionaries here. I can never be sufficiently thankful to God that we are at least spared that.'

Davidson's district consisted of a group of islands to the North of Samoa; they were widely separated and he had frequently to go long distances by canoe. At these times his wife remained at their headquarters and managed the mission. Dr Macphail felt his heart sink when he considered the efficiency with which she certainly managed it. She spoke of the depravity of the natives in a voice which nothing could hush, but with a vehemently unctuous horror. Her sense of delicacy was singular. Early in their acquaintance she had said to him:

'You know, their marriage customs when we first settled in the islands were so shocking that I couldn't possibly describe them to you. But I'll tell Mrs Macphail and she'll tell you.'

Then he had seen his wife and Mrs Davidson, their deck-chairs close together, in earnest conversation for about two hours. As he walked past them backwards and forwards for the sake of exercise, he had heard Mrs Davidson's agitated whisper, like the distant flow of a mountain torrent, and he saw by his wife's open mouth and pale face that she was enjoying an alarming experience. At night in their cabin she repeated to him with bated breath all she had heard.

'Well, what did I say to you?' cried Mrs Davidson, exultant next morning. 'Did you ever hear anything more dreadful? You don't wonder that I couldn't tell you myself, do you? Even though you are a doctor.'

Mrs Davidson scanned his face. She had a dramatic eagerness to see that she had achieved the desired effect.

'Can you wonder that when we first went there our hearts sank? You'll hardly believe me when I tell you it was impossible to find a single good girl in any of the villages.'

She used the word *good* in a severely technical manner.

'Mr Davidson and I talked it over, and we made up our minds the first thing to do was to put down the dancing. The natives were crazy about dancing.'

'I was not averse to it myself when I was a young man,' said Dr Macphail.

'I guessed as much when I heard you ask Mrs Macphail to have a turn with you last night. I don't think there's any real harm if a man dances with his wife, but I was relieved that she wouldn't. Under the circumstances I thought it better that we should keep ourselves to ourselves.'

'Under what circumstances?'

Mrs Davidson gave him a quick look through her pince-nez, but did not answer his question.

'But among white people it's not quite the same,' she went on, 'though I must say I agree with Mr Davidson, who says he can't understand how a husband can stand by and see his wife in another man's arms, and as far as I'm concerned I've never danced a step since I married. But the native dancing is quite another matter. It's not only immoral in itself, but it distinctly leads to immorality. However, I'm thankful to God that we stamped it out, and I don't think I'm wrong in saying that no one has danced in our district for eight years.'

But now they came to the mouth of the harbour and Mrs Macphail joined them. The ship turned sharply and steamed slowly in. It was a great land-locked harbour big enough to hold a fleet of battleships; and all around it rose, high and steep, the green hills. Near the entrance, getting such breeze as blew from the sea, stood the governor's house in a garden. The Stars and Stripes dangled languidly from a flagstaff. They passed two or three trim bungalows, and a tennis court, and then they came to the quay with its warehouses. Mrs Davidson pointed out the schooner, moored two or three hundred yards from the side, which was to take them to Apia. There was a crowd of eager, noisy, and good-humoured natives come from all parts of the island, some from curiosity, others to barter with the travellers on their way to Sydney; and they brought pineapples and huge bunches of bananas, tapa cloths, necklaces of shells or sharks' teeth, *kava*-bowls, and models of war canoes. American sailors, neat and trim, clean-shaven and frank of face, sauntered among them, and there was a little group of officials. While their luggage was being landed the Macphails and Mrs Davidson watched the crowd. Dr Macphail looked at the yaws from which most of the children and the young boys seemed to suffer, disfiguring sores like torpid ulcers, and his professional eyes glistened when he saw for the first time in his experience cases of elephantiasis, men going about with a huge, heavy arm or dragging along a grossly disfigured leg. Men and women wore the lava-lava.

'It's a very indecent costume,' said Mrs Davidson. 'Mr Davidson thinks it should be prohibited by law. How can you expect people to be moral when they wear nothing but a strip of red cotton round their loins?'

'It's suitable enough to the climate,' said the doctor, wiping the sweat off his head.

Now that they were on land the heat, though it was so early in the morning, was already oppressive. Closed in by its hills, not a breath of air came in to Pago-Pago.

'In our islands,' Mrs Davidson went on in her high-pitched tones, 'we've practically eradicated the lava-lava. A few old men still continue to wear it, but that's all. The women have all taken to the Mother Hubbard, and the men wear trousers and singlets. At the beginning of our stay Mr Davidson said in one of his reports: the inhabitants of these islands will never be thoroughly Christianized till every boy of more than ten years is made to wear a pair of trousers.'

But Mrs Davidson had given two or three of her birdlike glances at heavy grey clouds that came floating over the mouth of the harbour. A few drops began to fall.

'We'd better take shelter,' she said.

They made their way with all the crowd to a great shed of corrugated iron, and the rain began to fall in torrents. They stood there for some time and then were joined by Mr Davidson. He had been polite enough to the Macphails during the journey, but he had not his wife's sociability, and had spent much of his time reading. He was a silent, rather sullen man, and you felt that his affability was a duty that he imposed upon himself Christianly; he was by nature reserved and even morose. His appearance was singular. He was very tall and thin, with long limbs loosely jointed; hollow cheeks, and curiously high cheek-bones; he had so cadaverous an air that it surprised you to notice how full and sensual were his lips. He wore his hair very long. His dark eyes, set deep in their sockets, were large and tragic; and his hands with their big, long fingers, were finely shaped; they gave him a look of great strength. But the most striking thing about him was the feeling he gave you of suppressed fire. It was impressive and vaguely troubling. He was not a man with whom any intimacy was possible.

He brought now unwelcome news. There was an epidemic of measles, a serious and often fatal disease among the Kanakas, on the island, and a case had developed among the crew of the schooner which was to take them on their journey. The sick man had been brought ashore and put in hospital on the quarantine station, but telegraphic instructions had been sent from Apia to say that the schooner would not be allowed to enter the harbour till it was certain no other member of the crew was affected.

'It means we shall have to stay here for ten days at least.'

'But I'm urgently needed at Apia,' said Dr Macphail.

'That can't be helped. If no more cases develop on board, the schooner will be allowed to sail with white passengers, but all native traffic is prohibited for three months.'

'Is there a hotel here?' asked Mrs Macphail.

Davidson gave a low chuckle.

'There's not.'

'What shall we do then?'

'I've been talking to the governor. There's a trader along the front who has rooms that he rents, and my proposition is that as soon as the rain lets up we should go along there and see what we can do. Don't expect comfort. You've just got to be thankful if we get a bed to sleep on and a roof over our heads.'

But the rain showed no signs of stopping, and at length with umbrellas and waterproofs they set out. There was no town, but merely a group of official buildings, a store or two, and at the back, among the coconut trees and plantains, a few native dwellings. The house they sought was about five minutes' walk from the wharf. It was a frame house of two storeys, with broad verandas on both floors and a roof of corrugated iron. The owner was a half-caste named Horn, with a native wife surrounded by little brown children, and on the ground-floor he had a store where he sold canned goods and cottons. The rooms he showed them were almost bare of furniture. In the Macphails' there was nothing but a poor, worn bed with a ragged mosquito net, a rickety chair, and a washstand. They looked round with dismay. The rain poured down without ceasing.

'I'm not going to unpack more than we actually need,' said Mrs Macphail.

Mrs Davidson came into the room as she was unlocking a portmanteau. She was very brisk and alert. The cheerless surroundings had no effect on her.

'If you'll take my advice you'll get a needle and cotton and start right in to mend the mosquito net,' she said, 'or you'll not be able to get a wink of sleep tonight.'

'Will they be very bad?' asked Dr Macphail.

'This is the season for them. When you're asked to a party at Government House at Apia you'll notice that all the ladies are given a pillowslip to put their–their lower extremities in.'

'I wish the rain would stop for a moment,' said Mrs Macphail. 'I could try to make the place comfortable with more heart if the sun were shining.'

'Oh, if you wait for that, you'll wait a long time. Pago-Pago is about the rainiest place in the Pacific. You see, the hills, and that bay, they attract the water, and one expects rain at this time of year anyway.'

She looked from Macphail to his wife, standing helplessly in different parts of the room, like lost souls, and she pursed her lips. She saw that she must take them in hand. Feckless people like that made her impatient, but her hands itched to put everything in the order which came so naturally to her.

'Here, you give me a needle and cotton and I'll mend that net of yours, while you go on with your unpacking. Dinner's at one. Dr Macphail, you'd better go down to the wharf and see that your heavy luggage has been put in a dry place. You know what these natives are, they're quite capable of storing it where the rain will beat in on it all the time.'

The doctor put on his waterproof again and went downstairs. At the door Mr Horn was standing in conversation with the quartermaster of the ship they had just arrived in and a second-class passenger whom Dr Macphail had seen several times on board. The quartermaster, a little, shrivelled man, extremely dirty, nodded to him as he passed.

'This is a bad job about the measles, doc,' he said. 'I see you've fixed yourself up already.'

Dr Macphail thought he was rather familiar, but he was a timid man and he did not take offence easily.

'Yes, we've got a room upstairs.'

'Miss Thompson was sailing with you to Apia, so I've brought her along here.'

The quartermaster pointed with his thumb to the woman standing by his side. She was twenty-seven perhaps, plump, and in a coarse fashion pretty. She wore a white dress and a large white hat. Her fat calves in white cotton stockings bulged over the tops of long white boots in glacé kid. She gave Macphail an ingratiating smile.

'The feller's tryin' to soak me a dollar and a half a day for the meanest-sized room,' she said in a hoarse voice.

'I tell you she's a friend of mine, Jo,' said the quartermaster. 'She can't pay more than a dollar, and you've sure got to take her for that.'

The trader was fat and smooth and quietly smiling.

'Well, if you put it like that, Mr Swan, I'll see what I can do about it. I'll talk to Mrs Horn and if we think we can make a reduction we will.'

'Don't try to pull that stuff with me,' said Miss Thompson. 'We'll settle this right now. You get a dollar a day for the room and not one bean more.'

Dr Macphail smiled. He admired the effrontery with which she bargained. He was the sort of man who always paid what he was asked. He preferred to be over-charged than to haggle. The trader sighed.

'Well, to oblige Mr Swan I'll take it.'

'That's the goods,' said Miss Thompson. 'Come right in and have a shot of hooch. I've got some real good rye in that grip if you'll bring it along, Mr Swan. You come along too, doctor.'

'Oh, I don't think I will, thank you,' he answered. 'I'm just going down to see that our luggage is all right.'

He stepped out into the rain. It swept in from the opening of the harbour in sheets and the opposite shore was all blurred. He passed two or three natives clad in nothing but the lava-lava, with huge umbrellas over them. They walked finely, with leisurely movements, very upright; and they smiled and greeted him in a strange tongue as they went by.

It was nearly dinner-time when he got back, and their meal was laid in the trader's parlour. It was a room designed not to live in but for purposes of prestige, and it had a musty, melancholy air. A suite of stamped plush was arranged neatly round the walls, and from the middle of the ceiling, protected from the flies by yellow tissue-paper, hung a gilt chandelier. Davidson did not come.

'I know he went to call on the governor,' said Mrs Davidson, 'and I guess he's kept him to dinner.'

A little native girl brought them a dish of Hamburger steak, and after a while the trader came up to see that they had everything they wanted.

'I see we have a fellow lodger, Mr Horn,' said Dr Macphail.

'She's taken a room, that's all,' answered the trader. 'She's getting her own board.'

He looked at the two ladies with an obsequious air.

'I put her downstairs so she shouldn't be in the way. She won't be any trouble to you.'

'Is it someone who was on the boat?' asked Mrs Macphail.

'Yes, ma'am, she was in the second cabin. She was going to Apia. She has a position as cashier waiting for her.'

'Oh!'

When the trader was gone Macphail said:

'I shouldn't think she'd find it exactly cheerful having her meals in her room.'

'If she was in the second cabin I guess she'd rather,' answered Mrs Davidson. 'I don't exactly know who it can be.'

'I happened to be there when the quartermaster brought her along. Her name's Thompson.'

'It's not the woman who was dancing with the quartermaster last night?' asked Mrs Davidson.

'That's who it must be,' said Mrs Macphail. 'I wondered at the time what she was. She looked rather fast to me.'

'Not good style at all,' said Mrs Davidson.

They began to talk of other things, and after dinner, tired with their early rise, they separated and slept. When they awoke, though the sky was still grey and the clouds hung low, it was not raining and they went for a walk on the high road which the Americans had built along the bay.

On their return they found that Davidson had just come in.

'We may be here for a fortnight,' he said irritably. 'I've argued it out with the governor, but he says there is nothing to be done.'

'Mr Davidson's just longing to get back to his work,' said his wife, with an anxious glance at him.

'We've been away for a year,' he said, walking up and down the veranda. 'The mission has been in charge of native missionaries and I'm terribly nervous that they've let things slide. They're good men, I'm not saying a word against them, God-fearing, devout, and truly Christian men – their Christianity would put many so-called Christians at home to the blush – but they're pitifully lacking in energy. They can make a stand once, they can make a stand twice, but they can't make a stand all the time. If you leave a mission in charge of a native missionary, no matter how trustworthy he seems, in course of time you'll find he's let abuses creep in.'

Mr Davidson stood still. With his tall, spare form, and his great eyes flashing out of his pale face, he was an impressive figure. His sincerity was obvious in the fire of his gestures and in his deep, ringing voice.

'I expect to have my work cut out for me. I shall act and I shall act promptly. If the tree is rotten it shall be cut down and cast into the flames.'

And in the evening after the high tea which was their last meal, while they sat in the stiff parlour, the ladies working and Dr Macphail smoking his pipe, the missionary told them of his work in the islands.

'When we went there they had no sense of sin at all,' he said. 'They broke the commandments one after the other and never knew they were doing wrong. And I think that was the most difficult part of my work, to instil into the natives the sense of sin.'

The Macphails knew already that Davidson had worked in the Solomons for five years before he met his wife. She had been a missionary in China, and they had become acquainted in Boston, where they were both spending part of their leave to attend a missionary congress. On their marriage they had been appointed to the islands in which they had laboured ever since.

In the course of all the conversations they had had with Mr Davidson one thing had shone out clearly and that was the man's unflinching courage. He was a medical missionary, and he was liable to be called at any time to one or other of the islands in the group. Even the whaleboat is not so very safe a conveyance in the stormy Pacific of the wet season, but often he would be sent for in a canoe, and then the danger was great. In cases of illness or accident he never hesitated. A dozen times he had spent the whole night baling for his life, and more than once Mrs Davidson had given him up for lost.

'I'd beg him not to go sometimes,' she said, 'or at least to wait till the weather was more settled, but he'd never listen. He's obstinate, and when he's once made up his mind, nothing can move him.'

'How can I ask the natives to put their trust in the Lord if I am afraid to do so myself?' cried Davidson. 'And I'm not, I'm not. They know that if they send for me in their trouble I'll come if it's humanly possible. And do you think the Lord is going to abandon me when I am on his business? The wind blows at his bidding and the waves toss and rage at his word.'

Dr Macphail was a timid man. He had never been able to get used to the hurtling of the shells over the trenches, and when he was operating in an advanced dressing-station the sweat poured from his brow and dimmed his spectacles in the effort he made to control his unsteady hand. He shuddered a little as he looked at the missionary.

'I wish I could say that I've never been afraid,' he said.

'I wish you could say that you believed in God,' retorted the other.

But for some reason, that evening the missionary's thoughts travelled back to the early days he and his wife had spent on the islands.

'Sometimes Mrs Davidson and I would look at one another and the tears would stream down our cheeks. We worked without ceasing, day and night, and we seemed to make no progress. I don't know what I should have done without her then. When I felt my heart sink, when I was very near despair, she gave me courage and hope.'

Mrs Davidson looked down at her work, and a slight colour rose to her thin cheeks. Her hands trembled a little. She did not trust herself to speak.

'We had no one to help us. We were alone, thousands of miles from any of our own people, surrounded by darkness. When I was broken and weary she would put her work aside and take the Bible and read to me till peace came and settled upon me like sleep upon the eyelids of a child, and when at last she closed the book she'd say: "We'll save them in spite of themselves." And I felt strong again in the Lord, and I answered: "Yes, with God's help I'll save them. I must save them."'

He came over to the table and stood in front of it as though it were a lectern.

'You see, they were so naturally depraved that they couldn't be brought to see their wickedness. We had to make sins out of what they thought were natural actions. We had to make it a sin, not only to commit adultery and to lie and thieve, but to expose their bodies, and to dance and not to come to church. I made it a sin for a girl to show her bosom and a sin for a man not to wear trousers.'

'How?' asked Dr Macphail, not without surprise.

'I instituted fines. Obviously the only way to make people realize that an action is sinful is to punish them if they commit it. I fined them if they didn't come to church, and I fined them if they danced. I fined them if they were improperly dressed. I had a tariff, and every sin had to be paid for either in money or work. And at last I made them understand.'

'But did they never refuse to pay?'

'How could they?' asked the missionary.

'It would be a brave man who tried to stand up against Mr Davidson,' said his wife, tightening her lips.

Dr Macphail looked at Davidson with troubled eyes. What he heard shocked him, but he hesitated to express his disapproval.

'You must remember that in the last resort I could expel them from their church membership.'

'Did they mind that?'

Davidson smiled a little and gently rubbed his hands.

'They couldn't sell their copra. When the men fished they got no share of the catch. It meant something very like starvation. Yes, they minded quite a lot.'

'Tell him about Fred Ohlson,' said Mrs Davidson.

The missionary fixed his fiery eyes on Dr Macphail.

'Fred Ohlson was a Danish trader who had been in the islands a good many years. He was a pretty rich man as traders go and he wasn't very pleased when we came. You see, he'd had things very much his own way. He paid the natives what he liked for their copra, and he paid in goods and whisky. He had a native wife, but he was flagrantly unfaithful to her. He was a drunkard. I gave him a chance to mend his ways, but he wouldn't take it. He laughed at me.'

Davidson's voice fell to a deep bass as he said the last words, and he was silent for a minute or two. The silence was heavy with menace.

'In two years he was a ruined man. He'd lost everything he'd saved in a quarter of a century. I broke him, and at last he was forced to come to me like a beggar and beseech me to give him a passage back to Sydney.'

'I wish you could have seen him when he came to see Mr Davidson,' said the missionary's wife. 'He had been a fine, powerful man, with a lot of fat on him, and he had a great big voice, but now he was half the size, and he was shaking all over. He'd suddenly become an old man.'

With abstracted gaze Davidson looked out into the night. The rain was falling again.

Suddenly from below came a sound, and Davidson turned and looked questioningly at his wife. It was the sound of a gramophone, harsh and loud, wheezing out a syncopated tune.

'What's that?' he asked.

Mrs Davidson fixed her pince-nez more firmly on her nose.

'One of the second-class passengers has a room in the house. I guess it comes from there.'

They listened in silence, and presently they heard the sound of dancing. Then the music stopped, and they heard the popping of corks and voices raised in animated conversation.

'I daresay she's giving a farewell party to her friends on board,' said Dr Macphail. 'The ship sails at twelve, doesn't it?'

Davidson made no remark, but he looked at his watch.

'Are you ready?' he asked his wife.

She got up and folded her work.

'Yes, I guess I am,' she answered.

'It's early to go to bed yet, isn't it?' said the doctor.

'We have a good deal of reading to do,' explained Mrs Davidson. 'Wherever we are, we read a chapter of the Bible before retiring for the night and we study it with the commentaries, you know, and discuss it thoroughly. It's a wonderful training for the mind.'

The two couples bade one another good night. Dr and Mrs Macphail were left alone. For two or three minutes they did not speak.

'I think I'll go and fetch the cards,' the doctor said at last.

Mrs Macphail looked at him doubtfully. Her conversation with the Davidsons had left her a little uneasy, but she did not like to say that she thought they had better not play cards when the Davidsons might come in at any moment. Dr Macphail brought them and she watched him, though with a vague sense of guilt, while he laid out his patience. Below the sound of revelry continued.

It was fine enough next day, and the Macphails, condemned to spend a fortnight of idleness at Pago-Pago, set about making the best of things. They went down to the quay and got out of their boxes a number of books. The doctor called on the chief surgeon of the naval hospital and went round the beds with him. They left cards on the governor. They passed Miss Thompson on the road. The doctor took off his hat, and she gave him a 'Good morning doc,' in a loud, cheerful voice. She was dressed as on the day before, in a white frock, and her shiny white boots with their high heels, her fat legs bulging over the tops of them, were strange things on that exotic scene.

'I don't think she's very suitably dressed, I must say,' said Mrs Macphail. 'She looks extremely common to me.'

When they got back to their house, she was on the veranda playing with one of the trader's dark children.

'Say a word to her,' Dr Macphail whispered to his wife. 'She's all alone here, and it seems rather unkind to ignore her.'

Mrs Macphail was shy, but she was in the habit of doing what her husband bade her.

'I think we're fellow lodgers here,' she said, rather foolishly.

'Terrible, ain't it, bein' cooped up in a one-horse burg like this?' answered Miss Thompson. 'And they tell me I'm lucky to have gotten a room. I don't see myself livin' in a native house, and that's what some have to do. I don't know why they don't have a hotel.'

They exchanged a few more words. Miss Thompson, loud-voiced and garrulous, was evidently quite willing to gossip, but Mrs Macphail had a poor stock of small talk and presently she said:

'Well, I think we must go upstairs.'

In the evening when they sat down to their high tea, Davidson on coming in said:

'I see that woman downstairs has a couple of sailors sitting there. I wonder how she's gotten acquainted with them.'

'She can't be very particular,' said Mrs Davidson.

They were all rather tired after the idle, aimless day.

'If there's going to be a fortnight of this I don't know what we shall feel like at the end of it,' said Dr Macphail.

'The only thing to do is to portion out the day to different activities,' answered the missionary. 'I shall set aside a certain number of hours to study and a certain number to exercise, rain or fine – in the wet season you can't afford to pay any attention to the rain – and a certain number to recreation.'

Dr Macphail looked at his companion with misgiving. Davidson's programme oppressed him. They were eating Hamburger steak again. It seemed the only dish the cook knew how to make. Then below the gramophone began. Davidson started nervously when he heard it, but said nothing. Men's voices floated up. Miss Thompson's guests were joining in a well-known song and presently they heard her voice too, hoarse and loud. There was a good deal of shouting and laughing. The four people upstairs, trying to make conversation, listened despite themselves to the clink of glasses and the scrape of chairs. More people had evidently come. Miss Thompson was giving a party.

'I wonder how she gets them all in,' said Mrs Macphail suddenly breaking into a medical conversation between the missionary and her husband.

It showed whither her thoughts were wandering. The twitch of Davidson's face proved that, though he spoke of scientific things, his mind was busy in the same direction. Suddenly, while the doctor was giving some experience of practice on the Flanders front, rather prosily, he sprang to his feet with a cry.

'What's the matter, Alfred?' asked Mrs Davidson.

'Of course! It never occurred to me. She's out of Iwelei.'

'She can't be.'

'She came on board at Honolulu. It's obvious. And she's carrying on her trade here. Here.'

He uttered the last word with a passion of indignation.

'What's Iwelei?' asked Mrs Macphail.

He turned his gloomy eyes on her and his voice trembled with horror.

'The plague spot of Honolulu. The Red Light district. It was a blot on our civilization.'

Iwelei was on the edge of the city. You went down side streets by the harbour, in the darkness, across a rickety bridge, till you came to a deserted road, all ruts and holes, and then suddenly you came out into the light. There was parking room for motors on each side of the road, and there were saloons, tawdry and bright, each one noisy with its mechanical piano, and there were barbers' shops and tobacconists. There was a stir in the air and a sense of expectant gaiety. You turned down a narrow alley, either to the right or to the left, for the road divided Iwelei into two parts, and you found yourself in the district. There were rows of little bungalows, trim and neatly painted in green, and the pathway between them was broad and straight. It was laid out like a garden-city. In its respectable regularity, its order and spruceness, it gave an impression of sardonic horror; for never can the search for love have been so systematized and ordered. The pathways were lit by a rare lamp, but they would have been dark except for the lights that came from the open windows of the bungalows. Men wandered about, looking at the women who sat at their windows, reading or sewing, for the most part taking no notice of the passers-by; and like the women they were of all nationalities. There were Americans, sailors from the ships in port, enlisted men off the gunboats, sombrely drunk, and soldiers from the regiments, white and black, quartered on the island; there were Japanese, walking in twos and threes; Hawaiians, Chinese in long robes, and Filipinos in preposterous hats. They were silent and as it were oppressed. Desire is sad.

'It was the most crying scandal of the Pacific,' exclaimed Davidson vehemently. 'The missionaries had been agitating against it for years, and at last the local press took it up. The police refused to stir. You know their argument. They say that vice is inevitable and consequently the best thing is to localize and control it. The truth is, they were paid. Paid. They were paid by the saloon-keepers, paid by the bullies, paid by the women themselves. At last they were forced to move.'

'I read about it in the papers that came on board in Honolulu,' said Dr Macphail.

'Iwelei, with its sin and shame, ceased to exist on the very day we arrived. The whole population was brought before the justices. I don't know why I didn't understand at once what that woman was.'

'Now you come to speak of it,' said Mrs Macphail, 'I remember seeing her come on board only a few minutes before the boat sailed. I remember thinking at the time she was cutting it rather fine.'

'How dare she come here!' cried Davidson indignantly. 'I'm not going to allow it.'

He strode towards the door.

'What are you going to do?' asked Macphail.

'What do you expect me to? I'm going to stop it. I'm not going to have this house turned into–into . . .'

He sought for a word that should not offend the ladies' ears. His eyes were flashing and his pale face was paler still in his emotion.

'It sounds as though there were three or four men down there,' said the doctor. 'Don't you think it's rather rash to go in just now?'

The missionary gave him a contemptuous look and without a word flung out of the room.

'You know Mr Davidson very little if you think the fear of personal danger can stop him in the performance of his duty,' said his wife.

She sat with her hands nervously clasped, a spot of colour on her high cheek-bones, listening to what was about to happen below. They all listened. They heard him clatter down the wooden stairs and throw open the door. The singing stopped suddenly, but the gramophone continued to bray out its vulgar tune. They heard Davidson's voice and then the noise of something heavy falling. The music stopped. He had hurled the gramophone on the floor. Then again they heard Davidson's voice, they could not make out the words, then Miss Thompson's, loud and shrill, then a confused clamour as though several people were shouting together at the top of their lungs. Mrs Davidson gave a little gasp, and she clenched her hands more tightly. Dr Macphail looked uncertainly from her to his wife. He did not want to go down, but he wondered if they expected him to. Then there was something that sounded like a scuffle. The noise now was more distinct. It might be that Davidson was being thrown out of the room. The door was slammed. There was a moment's silence and they heard Davidson come up the stairs again. He went to his room.

'I think I'll go to him,' said Mrs Davidson.

She got up and went out.

'If you want me, just call,' said Mrs Macphail, and then when the other was gone: 'I hope he isn't hurt.'

'Why couldn't he mind his own business?' said Dr Macphail.

They sat in silence for a minute or two and then they both started, for the gramophone began to play once more, defiantly, and mocking voices shouted hoarsely the words of an obscene song.

Next day Mrs Davidson was pale and tired. She complained of headache, and she looked old and wizened. She told Mrs Macphail that the missionary had not slept at all; he had passed the night in a state of frightful agitation and at five had got up and gone out. A glass of beer had been thrown over him and his clothes were stained and stinking. But a sombre fire glowed in Mrs Davidson's eyes when she spoke of Miss Thompson.

'She'll bitterly rue the day when she flouted Mr Davidson,' she said. 'Mr Davidson has a wonderful heart and no one who is in trouble has ever gone to him without being comforted, but he has no mercy for sin, and when his righteous wrath is excited he's terrible.'

'Why, what will he do?' asked Mrs Macphail.

'I don't know, but I wouldn't stand in that creature's shoes for anything in the world.'

Mrs Macphail shuddered. There was something positively alarming in the triumphant assurance of the little woman's manner. They were going out together that morning, and they went down the stairs side by side. Miss Thompson's door was open, and they saw her in a bedraggled dressing-gown, cooking something in a chafing-dish.

'Good morning,' she called. 'Is Mr Davidson better this morning?'

They passed her in silence, with their noses in the air, as if she did not exist. They flushed, however, when she burst into a shout of derisive laughter. Mrs Davidson turned on her suddenly.

'Don't you dare to speak to me,' she screamed. 'If you insult me I shall have you turned out of here.'

'Say, did I ask Mr Davidson to visit with me?'

'Don't answer her,' whispered Mrs Macphail hurriedly.

They walked on till they were out of earshot.

'She's brazen, brazen,' burst from Mrs Davidson.

Her anger almost suffocated her.

And on their way home they met her strolling towards the quay. She had all her finery on. Her great white hat with its vulgar, showy flowers was an affront. She called out cheerily to them as she went by, and a couple of American sailors who were standing there grinned as the ladies set their faces to an icy stare. They got in just before the rain began to fall again.

'I guess she'll get her fine clothes spoilt,' said Mrs Davidson with a bitter sneer.

Davidson did not come in till they were half-way through dinner. He was wet through, but he would not change. He sat, morose and silent, refusing to eat more than a mouthful, and he stared at the slanting rain. When Mrs Davidson told him of their two encounters with Miss Thompson he did not answer. His deepening frown alone showed that he had heard.

'Don't you think we ought to make Mr Horn turn her out of here?' asked Mrs Davidson. 'We can't allow her to insult us.'

'There doesn't seem to be any other place for her to go,' said Macphail.

'She can live with one of the natives.'

'In weather like this a native hut must be a rather uncomfortable place to live in.'

'I lived in one for years,' said the missionary.

When the little native girl brought in the fried bananas which formed the sweet they had every day, Davidson turned to her.

'Ask Miss Thompson when it would be convenient for me to see her,' he said.

The girl nodded shyly and went out.

'What do you want to see her for, Alfred?' asked his wife.

'It's my duty to see her. I won't act till I've given her every chance.'

'You don't know what she is. She'll insult you.'

'Let her insult me. Let her spit on me. She has an immortal soul, and I must do all that is in my power to save it.'

Mrs Davidson's ears rang still with the harlot's mocking laughter.

'She's gone too far.'

'Too far for the mercy of God?' His eyes lit up suddenly and his voice grew mellow and soft. 'Never. The sinner may be deeper in sin than the depth of hell itself, but the love of the Lord Jesus can reach him still.'

The girl came back with the message.

'Miss Thompson's compliments and as long as Rev Davidson don't come in business hours she'll be glad to see him any time.'

The party received it in stony silence, and Dr Macphail quickly effaced from his lips the smile which had come upon them. He knew his wife would be vexed with him if he found Miss Thompson's effrontery amusing.

They finished the meal in silence. When it was over the two ladies got up and took their work. Mrs Macphail was making another of the innumerable comforters which she had turned out since the beginning of the war, and the doctor lit his pipe. But Davidson remained in his chair and with abstracted eyes stared at the table. At last he got up and without a word went out of the room. They heard him go down and they heard Miss Thompson's defiant 'Come in' when he knocked at the door. He remained with her for an hour. And Dr Macphail watched the rain. It was beginning to get on his nerves. It was not like soft English rain that drops gently on the earth; it was unmerciful and somehow terrible; you felt in it the malignancy of the primitive powers of nature. It did not pour, it flowed. It was like a deluge from heaven, and it rattled on the roof of corrugated iron with a steady persistence that was maddening. It seemed to have a fury of its own. And sometimes you felt that you must scream if it did not stop, and then suddenly you felt powerless, as though your bones had suddenly become soft; and you were miserable and hopeless.

Macphail turned his head when the missionary came back. The two women looked up.

'I've given her every chance. I have exhorted her to repent. She is an evil woman.'

He paused, and Dr Macphail saw his eyes darken and his pale face grow hard and stern.

'Now I shall take the whips with which the Lord Jesus drove the usurers and the money changers out of the Temple of the Most High.'

He walked up and down the room. His mouth was close set, and his black brows were frowning.

'If she fled to the uttermost parts of the earth I should pursue her.'

With a sudden movement he turned round and strode out of the room. They heard him go downstairs again.

'What is he going to do?' asked Mrs Macphail.

'I don't know.' Mrs Davidson took off her pince-nez and wiped them. 'When he is on the Lord's work I never ask him questions.'

She sighed a little.

'What is the matter?'

'He'll wear himself out. He doesn't know what it is to spare himself.'

Dr Macphail learnt the first results of the missionary's activity from the half-caste trader in whose house they lodged. He stopped the doctor when he passed the store and came out to speak to him on the stoop. His fat face was worried. 'The Rev Davidson has been at me for letting Miss Thompson have a room here,' he said, 'but I didn't know what she was when I rented it to her. When people come and ask if I can rent them a room all I want to know is if they've the money to pay for it. And she paid me for hers a week in advance.'

Dr Macphail did not want to commit himself.

'When all's said and done it's your house. We're very much obliged to you for taking us in at all.'

Horn looked at him doubtfully. He was not certain yet how definitely Macphail stood on the missionary's side.

'The missionaries are in with one another,' he said, hesitatingly. 'If they get it in for a trader he may just as well shut up his store and quit.'

'Did he want you to turn her out?'

'No, he said so long as she behaved herself he couldn't ask me to do that. He said he wanted to be just to me. I promised she shouldn't have no more visitors. I've just been and told her.'

'How did she take it?'

'She gave me Hell.'

The trader squirmed in his old ducks. He had found Miss Thompson a rough customer.

'Oh, well, I daresay she'll get out. I don't suppose she wants to stay here if she can't have anyone in.'

'There's nowhere she can go, only a native house, and no native'll take her now, not now that the missionaries have got their knife in her.'

Dr Macphail looked at the falling rain.

'Well, I don't suppose it's any good waiting for it to clear up.'

In the evening when they sat in the parlour Davidson talked to them of his early days at college. He had had no means and had worked his way through by doing odd jobs during the vacations. There was silence downstairs. Miss Thompson was sitting in her little room alone. But suddenly the gramophone began to play. She had set it on in defiance, to cheat her loneliness, but there was no one to sing, and it had a melancholy note. It was like a cry for help. Davidson took no notice. He was in the middle of a long anecdote and without change of expression went on. The gramophone continued. Miss Thompson put on one reel after another. It looked as though the silence of the night were getting on her nerves. It was breathless and sultry. When the Macphails went to bed they could not sleep. They lay side by side with their eyes wide open, listening to the cruel singing of the mosquitoes outside their curtain.

'What's that?' whispered Mrs Macphail at last.

They heard a voice, Davidson's voice, through the wooden partition. It went on with a monotonous, earnest insistence. He was praying aloud. He was praying for the soul of Miss Thompson.

Two or three days went by. Now when they passed Miss Thompson on the road she did not greet them with ironic cordiality or smile; she passed with her nose in the air, a sulky look on her painted face, frowning, as though she did not see them. The trader told Macphail that she had tried to get lodging elsewhere, but had failed. In the evening she played through the various reels of her gramophone, but the pretence of mirth was obvious now. The ragtime had a cracked, heart-broken rhythm as though it were a one-step of despair. When she began to play on Sunday Davidson sent Horn to beg her to stop at once since it was the Lord's day. The reel was taken off and the house was silent except for the steady pattering of the rain on the iron roof.

'I think she's getting a bit worked up,' said the trader next day to Macphail. 'She don't know what Mr Davidson's up to and it makes her scared.'

Macphail had caught a glimpse of her that morning and it struck him that her arrogant expression had changed. There was in her face a hunted look. The half-caste gave him a sidelong glance.

'I suppose you don't know what Mr Davidson is doing about it?' he hazarded.

'No, I don't.'

It was singular that Horn should ask him that question, for he also had the idea that the missionary was mysteriously at work.

He had an impression that he was weaving a net around the woman, carefully, systematically, and suddenly, when everything was ready, would pull the strings tight.

'He told me to tell her,' said the trader, 'that if at any time she wanted him she only had to send and he'd come.'

'What did she say when you told her that?'

'She didn't say nothing. I didn't stop. I just said what he said I was to and then I beat it. I thought she might be going to start weepin'.'

'I have no doubt the loneliness is getting on her nerves,' said the doctor. 'And the rain–that's enough to make anyone jumpy,' he continued irritably. 'Doesn't it ever stop in this confounded place?'

'It goes on pretty steady in the rainy season. We have three hundred inches in the year. You see, it's the shape of the bay. It seems to attract the rain from all over the Pacific.'

'Damn the shape of the bay,' said the doctor.

He scratched his mosquito bites. He felt very short-tempered. When the rain stopped and the sun shone, it was like a hot-house, seething, humid, sultry, breathless, and you had a strange feeling that everything was growing with a savage violence. The natives, blithe and childlike by reputation, seemed then, with their tattooing and their dyed hair, to have something sinister in their appearance; and when they pattered along at your heels with their naked feet you looked back instinctively. You felt they might at any moment come behind you swiftly and thrust a long knife between your shoulder-blades. You could not tell what dark thought lurked behind their wide-set eyes. They had a little the look of ancient Egyptians painted on a temple wall, and there was about them the terror of what is immeasurably old.

The missionary came and went. He was busy, but the Macphails did not know what he was doing. Horn told the doctor that he saw the governor every day, and once Davidson mentioned him.

'He looks as if he had plenty of determination,' he said, 'but when you come down to brass tacks he has no backbone.'

'I suppose that means he won't do exactly what you want,' suggested the doctor facetiously.

The missionary did not smile.

'I want him to do what's right. It shouldn't be necessary to persuade a man to do that.'

'But there may be differences of opinion about what is right.'

'If a man had a gangrenous foot would you have patience with anyone who hesitated to amputate it?'

'Gangrene is a matter of fact.'

'And Evil?'

What Davidson had done soon appeared. The four of them had just finished their midday meal, and they had not yet separated for the siesta which the heat imposed on the ladies and on the doctor. Davidson had little patience with the slothful habit. The door was suddenly flung open and Miss Thompson came in. She looked round the room and then went up to Davidson.

'You low-down skunk, what have you been saying about me to the governor?'

She was spluttering with rage. There was a moment's pause. Then the missionary drew forward a chair.

'Won't you be seated, Miss Thompson? I've been hoping to have another talk with you.'

'You poor low-life bastard.'

She burst into a torrent of insult, foul and insolent. Davidson kept his grave eyes on her.

'I'm indifferent to the abuse you think fit to heap on me, Miss Thompson,' he said, 'but I must beg you to remember that ladies are present.'

Tears by now were struggling with her anger. Her face was red and swollen as though she were choking.

'What has happened?' asked Dr Macphail.

'A feller's just been in here and he says I gotter beat it on the next boat.'

Was there a gleam in the missionary's eyes? His face remained impassive.

'You could hardly expect the governor to let you stay here under the circumstances.'

'You done it,' she shrieked. 'You can't kid me. You done it.'

'I don't want to deceive you. I urged the governor to take the only possible step consistent with his obligations.'

'Why couldn't you leave me be? I wasn't doin' you no harm.'

'You may be sure that if you had I should be the last man to resent it.'

'Do you think I want to stay on in this poor imitation of a burg? I don't look no busher, do I?'

'In that case I don't see what cause of complaint you have,' he answered.

She gave an inarticulate cry of rage and flung out of the room. There was a short silence.

'It's a relief to know that the governor has acted at last,' said Davidson finally. 'He's a weak man and he shilly-shallied. He said she was only here for a fortnight anyway, and if she went on to Apia, that was under British jurisdiction and had nothing to do with him.'

The missionary sprang to his feet and strode across the room.

'It's terrible the way the men who are in authority seek to evade their responsibility. They speak as though evil that was out of sight ceased to be evil. The very existence of that woman is a scandal and it does not help matters to shift it to another of the islands. In the end I had to speak straight from the shoulder.'

Davidson's brow lowered, and he protruded his firm chin. He looked fierce and determined.

'What do you mean by that?'

'Our mission is not entirely without influence at Washington. I pointed out to the governor that it wouldn't do him any good if there was a complaint about the way he managed things here.'

'When has she got to go?' asked the doctor, after a pause.

'The San Francisco boat is due here from Sydney next Tuesday. She's to sail on that.'

That was in five days' time. It was next day, when he was coming back from the hospital where for want of something better to do Macphail spent most of his mornings, that the half-caste stopped him as he was going upstairs.

'Excuse me, Dr Macphail, Miss Thompson's sick. Will you have a look at her?'

'Certainly.'

Horn led him to her room. She was sitting in a chair idly, neither reading nor sewing, staring in front of her. She wore her white dress and the large hat with the flowers on it. Macphail noticed that her skin was yellow and muddy under her powder, and her eyes were heavy.

'I'm sorry to hear you're not well,' he said.

'Oh, I ain't sick really. I just said that, because I just had to see you. I've got to clear on a boat that's going to 'Frisco.'

She looked at him and he saw that her eyes were suddenly startled. She opened and clenched her hands spasmodically. The trader stood at the door, listening.

'So I understand,' said the doctor.

She gave a little gulp.

'I guess it ain't very convenient for me to go to 'Frisco just now. I went to see the governor yesterday afternoon, but I couldn't get to him. I saw the secretary, and he told me I'd got to take that boat and that was all there was to it. I just had to see the governor, so I waited outside his house this morning, and when he came out I spoke to him. He didn't want to speak to me, I'll say, but I wouldn't let him shake me off, and at last he said he hadn't no objection to my staying here till the next boat to Sydney if the Rev Davidson will stand for it.'

She stopped and looked at Dr Macphail anxiously.

'I don't know exactly what I can do,' he said.

'Well, I thought maybe you wouldn't mind asking him. I swear to God I won't start anything here if he'll just only let me stay. I won't go out of the house if that'll suit him. It's no more'n a fortnight.'

'I'll ask him.'

'He won't stand for it,' said Horn. 'He'll have you out on Tuesday, so you may as well make up your mind to it.'

'Tell him I can get work in Sydney, straight stuff, I mean. 'Tain't asking very much.'

'I'll do what I can.'

'And come and tell me right away, will you? I can't set down to a thing till I get the dope one way or the other.'

It was not an errand that much pleased the doctor, and, characteristically perhaps, he went about it indirectly. He told his wife what Miss Thompson had said to him and asked her to speak to Mrs Davidson. The missionary's attitude seemed rather arbitrary and it could do no harm if the girl were allowed to stay in Pago-Pago another fortnight. But he was not prepared for the result of his diplomacy. The missionary came to him straightway.

'Mrs Davidson tells me that Thompson has been speaking to you.'

Dr Macphail, thus directly tackled, had the shy man's resentment at being forced out into the open. He felt his temper rising, and he flushed.

'I don't see that it can make any difference if she goes to Sydney rather than to San Francisco, and so long as she promises to behave while she's here it's dashed hard to persecute her.'

The missionary fixed him with his stern eyes.

'Why is she unwilling to go back to San Francisco?'

'I didn't inquire,' answered the doctor with some asperity. 'And I think one does better to mind one's own business.'

Perhaps it was not a very tactful answer.

'The governor has ordered her to be deported by the first boat that leaves the island. He's only done his duty and I will not interfere. Her presence is a peril here.'

'I think you're very harsh and tyrannical.'

The two ladies looked up at the doctor with some alarm, but they need not have feared a quarrel, for the missionary smiled gently.

'I'm terribly sorry you should think that of me, Dr Macphail. Believe me, my heart bleeds for that unfortunate woman, but I'm only trying to do my duty.'

The doctor made no answer. He looked out of the window sullenly. For once it was not raining and across the bay you saw nestling among the trees the huts of a native village.

'I think I'll take advantage of the rain stopping to go out,' he said.

'Please don't bear me malice because I can't accede to your wish,' said Davidson, with a melancholy smile. 'I respect you very much, doctor, and I should be sorry if you thought ill of me.'

'I have no doubt you have a sufficiently good opinion of yourself to bear mine with equanimity,' he retorted.

'That's one on me,' chuckled Davidson.

When Dr Macphail, vexed with himself because he had been uncivil to no purpose, went downstairs, Miss Thompson was waiting for him with her door ajar.

'Well,' she said, 'have you spoken to him?'

'Yes, I'm sorry, he won't do anything,' he answered, not looking at her in his embarrassment.

But then he gave her a quick glance, for a sob broke from her. He saw that her face was white with fear. It gave him a shock of dismay. And suddenly he had an idea.

'But don't give up hope yet. I think it's a shame the way they're treating you and I'm going to see the governor myself.'

'Now?'

He nodded. Her face brightened.

'Say, that's real good of you. I'm sure he'll let me stay if you speak for me. I just won't do a thing I didn't ought all the time I'm here.'

Dr Macphail hardly knew why he had made up his mind to appeal to the governor. He was perfectly indifferent to Miss Thompson's affairs, but the missionary had irritated him, and with him temper was a smouldering thing. He found the governor at home. He was a large, handsome man, a sailor, with a grey toothbrush moustache; and he wore a spotless uniform of white drill.

'I've come to see you about a woman who's lodging in the same house as we are,' he said. 'Her name's Thompson.'

'I guess I've heard nearly enough about her, Dr Macphail,' said the governor, smiling. 'I've given her the order to get out next Tuesday and that's all I can do.'

'I wanted to ask you if you couldn't stretch a point and let her stay here till the boat comes in from San Francisco so that she can go to Sydney. I will guarantee her good behaviour.'

The governor continued to smile, but his eyes grew small and serious.

'I'd be very glad to oblige you, Dr Macphail, but I've given the order and it must stand.'

The doctor put the case as reasonably as he could, but now the governor ceased to smile at all. He listened sullenly, with averted gaze. Macphail saw that he was making no impression.

'I'm sorry to cause any lady inconvenience, but she'll have to sail on Tuesday and that's all there is to it.'

'But what difference can it make?'

'Pardon me, doctor, but I don't feel called upon to explain my official actions except to the proper authorities.'

Macphail looked at him shrewdly. He remembered Davidson's hint that he had used threats, and in the governor's attitude he read a singular embarrassment.

'Davidson's a damned busybody,' he said hotly.

'Between ourselves, Dr Macphail, I don't say that I have formed a very favourable opinion of Mr Davidson, but I am bound to confess that he was within his rights in pointing out to me the danger that the presence of a woman of Miss Thompson's character was to a place like this where a number of enlisted men are stationed among a native population.'

He got up and Dr Macphail was obliged to do so too.

'I must ask you to excuse me. I have an engagement. Please give my respects to Mrs Macphail.'

The doctor left him crestfallen. He knew that Miss Thompson would be waiting for him, and unwilling to tell her himself that he had failed, he went into the house by the back door and sneaked up the stairs as though he had something to hide.

At supper he was silent and ill-at-ease, but the missionary was jovial and animated. Dr Macphail thought his eyes rested on him now and then with triumphant good-humour. It struck him suddenly that Davidson knew of his visit to the governor and of its ill success. But how on earth could he have heard of it? There was something sinister about the power of that man. After supper he saw Horn on the veranda and, as though to have a casual word with him, went out.

'She wants to know if you've seen the governor,' the trader whispered.

'Yes. He wouldn't do anything. I'm awfully sorry, I can't do anything more.'

'I knew he wouldn't. They daren't go against the missionaries.'

'What are you talking about?' said Davidson affably, coming out to join them.

'I was just saying there was no chance of your getting over to Apia for at least another week,' said the trader glibly.

He left them, and the two men returned into the parlour. Mr Davidson devoted one hour after each meal to recreation. Presently a timid knock was heard at the door.

'Come in,' said Mrs Davidson, in her sharp voice.

The door was not opened. She got up and opened it. They saw Miss Thompson standing at the threshold. But the change in her appearance was extraordinary. This was no longer the flaunting hussy who had jeered at them in the road, but a broken, frightened woman. Her hair, as a rule so elaborately arranged, was tumbling untidily over her neck. She wore bedroom slippers and a skirt and blouse. They were unfresh and bedraggled. She stood at the door with the tears streaming down her face and did not dare to enter.

'What do you want?' said Mrs Davidson harshly.

'May I speak to Mr Davidson?' she said in a choking voice.

The missionary rose and went towards her.

'Come right in, Miss Thompson,' he said in cordial tones. 'What can I do for you?'

She entered the room.

'Say, I'm sorry for what I said to you the other day an' for–for everythin' else. I guess I was a bit lit up. I beg pardon.'

'Oh, it was nothing. I guess my back's broad enough to bear a few hard words.'

She stepped towards him with a movement that was horribly cringing.

'You've got me beat. I'm all in. You won't make me go back to 'Frisco?'

His genial manner vanished and his voice grew on a sudden hard and stern.

'Why don't you want to go back there?'

She cowered before him.

'I guess my people live there. I don't want them to see me like this. I'll go anywhere else you say.'

'Why don't you want to go back to San Francisco?'

'I've told you.'

He leaned forward, staring at her, and his great, shining eyes seemed to try to bore into her soul. He gave a sudden gasp.

'The penitentiary.'

She screamed, and then she fell at his feet, clasping his legs.

'Don't send me back there. I swear to you before God I'll be a good woman. I'll give all this up.'

She burst into a torrent of confused supplication and the tears coursed down her painted cheeks. He leaned over her and, lifting her face, forced her to look at him.

'Is that it, the penitentiary?'

'I beat it before they could get me,' she gasped. 'If the bulls grab me it's three years for me.'

He let go his hold of her and she fell in a heap on the floor, sobbing bitterly. Dr Macphail stood up.

'This alters the whole thing,' he said. 'You can't make her go back when you know this. Give her another chance. She wants to turn over a new leaf.'

'I'm going to give her the finest chance she's ever had. If she repents let her accept her punishment.'

She misunderstood the words and looked up. There was a gleam of hope in her heavy eyes.

'You'll let me go?'

'No. You shall sail for San Francisco on Tuesday.'

She gave a groan of horror and then burst into low, hoarse shrieks which sounded hardly human, and she beat her head passionately on the ground. Dr Macphail sprang to her and lifted her up.

'Come on, you mustn't do that. You'd better go to your room and lie down. I'll get you something.'

He raised her to her feet and partly dragging her, partly carrying her, got her downstairs. He was furious with Mrs Davidson and with his wife because they made no effort to help. The half-caste was standing on the landing and with his assistance he managed to get her on the bed. She was moaning and crying. She was almost insensible. He gave her a hypodermic injection. He was hot and exhausted when he went upstairs again.

'I've got her to lie down.'

The two women and Davidson were in the same positions as when he had left them. They could not have moved or spoken since he went.

'I was waiting for you,' said Davidson, in a strange, distant voice. 'I want you all to pray with me for the soul of our erring sister.'

He took the Bible off a shelf, and sat down at the table at which they had supped. It had not been cleared, and he pushed the tea-pot out of the way. In a powerful voice, resonant and deep, he read to them the chapter in which is narrated the meeting of Jesus Christ with the woman taken in adultery.

'Now kneel with me and let us pray for the soul of our dear sister, Sadie Thompson.'

He burst into a long, passionate prayer in which he implored God to have mercy on the sinful woman. Mrs Macphail and Mrs Davidson knelt with covered eyes. The doctor, taken by surprise, awkward and sheepish, knelt too. The missionary's prayer had a savage eloquence. He was extraordinarily moved, and as he spoke the tears ran down his cheeks. Outside, the pitiless rain fell, fell steadily, with a fierce malignity that was all too human.

At last he stopped. He paused for a moment and said:

'We will now repeat the Lord's prayer.'

They said it and then, following him, they rose from their knees. Mrs Davidson's face was pale and restful. She was comforted and at peace, but the Macphails felt suddenly bashful. They did not know which way to look.

'I'll just go down and see how she is now,' said Dr Macphail.

When he knocked at her door it was opened for him by Horn. Miss Thompson was in a rocking-chair, sobbing quietly.

'What are you doing there?' exclaimed Macphail. 'I told you to lie down.'

'I can't lie down. I want to see Mr Davidson.'

'My poor child, what do you think is the good of it? You'll never move him.'

'He said he'd come if I sent for him.'

Macphail motioned to the trader.

'Go and fetch him.'

He waited with her in silence while the trader went upstairs. Davidson came in.

'Excuse me for asking you to come here,' she said, looking at him sombrely.

'I was expecting you to send for me. I knew the Lord would answer my prayer.'

They stared at one another for a moment and then she looked away. She kept her eyes averted when she spoke.

'I've been a bad woman. I want to repent.'

'Thank God! Thank God! He has heard our prayers.'

He turned to the two men.

'Leave me alone with her. Tell Mrs Davidson that our prayers have been answered.'

They went out and closed the door behind them.

'Gee whizz,' said the trader.

That night Dr Macphail could not get to sleep till late, and when he heard the missionary come upstairs he looked at his watch. It was two o'clock. But even then he did not go to bed at once, for through the wooden partition that separated their rooms he heard him praying aloud, till he himself, exhausted, fell asleep.

When he saw him next morning he was surprised at his appearance. He was paler than ever, tired, but his eyes shone with inhuman fire. It looked as though he were filled with an overwhelming joy.

'I want you to go down presently and see Sadie,' he said. 'I can't hope that her body is better, but her soul—her soul is transformed.'

The doctor was feeling wan and nervous.

'You were with her very late last night,' he said.

'Yes, she couldn't bear to have me leave her.'

'You look as pleased as Punch,' the doctor said irritably.

Davidson's eyes shone with ecstasy.

'A great mercy has been vouchsafed me. Last night I was privileged to bring a lost soul to the loving arms of Jesus.'

Miss Thompson was again in the rocking-chair. The bed had not been made. The room was in disorder. She had not troubled to dress herself, but wore a dirty dressing-gown, and her hair was tied in a sluttish knot. She had given her face a dab with a wet towel, but it was all swollen and creased with crying. She looked a drab.

She raised her eyes dully when the doctor came in. She was cowed and broken.

'Where's Mr Davidson?' she asked.

'He'll come presently if you want him,' answered Macphail acidly. 'I came here to see how you were.'

'Oh, I guess I'm O.K. You needn't worry about that.'

'Have you had anything to eat?'

'Horn brought me some coffee.'

She looked anxiously at the door.

'D'you think he'll come down soon? I feel as if it wasn't so terrible when he's with me.'

'Are you still going on Tuesday?'

'Yes, he says I've got to go. Please tell him to come right along. You can't do me any good. He's the only one as can help me now.'

'Very well,' said Dr Macphail.

During the next three days the missionary spent almost all his time with Sadie Thompson. He joined the others only to have his meals. Dr Macphail noticed that he hardly ate.

'He's wearing himself out,' said Mrs Davidson pitifully. 'He'll have a breakdown if he doesn't take care, but he won't spare himself.'

She herself was white and pale. She told Mrs Macphail that she had no sleep. When the missionary came upstairs from Miss Thompson he prayed till he was exhausted, but even then he did not sleep for long. After an hour or two he got up and dressed himself, and went for a tramp along the bay. He had strange dreams.

'This morning he told me that he'd been dreaming about the mountains of Nebraska,' said Mrs Davidson.

'That's curious,' said Dr Macphail.

He remembered seeing them from the windows of the train when he crossed America. They were like huge mole-hills, rounded and smooth, and they rose from the plain abruptly. Dr Macphail remembered how it struck him that they were like a woman's breasts.

Davidson's restlessness was intolerable even to himself. But he was buoyed up by a wonderful exhilaration. He was tearing out by the roots the last vestiges of sin that lurked in the hidden corners of that poor woman's heart. He read with her and prayed with her.

'It's wonderful,' he said to them one day at supper. 'It's a true rebirth. Her soul, which was black as night, is now pure and white like the new-fallen snow. I am humble and afraid. Her remorse for all her sins is beautiful. I am not worthy to touch the hem of her garment.'

'Have you the heart to send her back to San Francisco?' said the doctor. 'Three years in an American prison. I should have thought you might have saved her from that.'

'Ah, but don't you see? It's necessary. Do you think my heart doesn't bleed for her? I love her as I love my wife and my sister. All the time that she is in prison I shall suffer all the pain that she suffers.'

'Bunkum,' cried the doctor impatiently.

'You don't understand because you're blind. She's sinned, and she must suffer. I know what she'll endure. She'll be starved and tortured and humiliated. I want her to accept the punishment of man as a sacrifice to God. I want her to accept it joyfully. She has an opportunity which is offered to very few of us. God is very good and very merciful.'

Davidson's voice trembled with excitement. He could hardly articulate the words that tumbled passionately from his lips.

'All day I pray with her and when I leave her I pray again, I pray with all my might and main, so that Jesus may grant her this great mercy. I want to put in her heart the passionate desire to be punished so that at the end, even if I offered to let her go, she would refuse. I want her to feel that the bitter punishment of prison is the thank-offering that she places at the feet of our Blessed Lord, who gave his life for her.'

The days passed slowly. The whole household, intent on the wretched, tortured woman downstairs, lived in a state of unnatural excitement. She was like a victim that was being prepared for the savage rites of a bloody idolatry. Her terror numbed her. She could not bear to let Davidson out of her sight; it was only when he was with her that she had courage, and she hung upon him with a slavish dependence. She cried a great deal, and she read the Bible, and prayed. Sometimes she was exhausted and apathetic. Then she did indeed look forward to her ordeal, for it seemed to offer an escape, direct and concrete, from the anguish she was enduring. She could not bear much longer the vague terrors which now assailed her. With her sins she had put aside all personal vanity, and she slopped about her room, unkempt and dishevelled, in her tawdry dressing-gown. She had not taken off her night-dress for four days, nor put on stockings. Her room was littered and untidy. Meanwhile the rain fell with a cruel persistence. You felt that the heavens must at last be empty of water, but still it poured down, straight and heavy, with a maddening iteration, on the iron roof. Everything was damp and clammy. There was mildew on the walls and on the boots that stood on the floor. Through the sleepless nights the mosquitoes droned their angry chant.

'If it would only stop raining for a single day it wouldn't be so bad,' said Dr Macphail.

They all looked forward to the Tuesday when the boat for San Francisco was to arrive from Sydney. The strain was intolerable. So far as Dr Macphail was concerned, his pity and his resentment were alike extinguished by his desire to be rid of the unfortunate woman. The inevitable must be accepted. He felt he would breathe more freely when the ship had sailed. Sadie Thompson was to be escorted on board by a clerk in the governor's office. This person called on the Monday evening and told Miss Thompson to be prepared at eleven in the morning. Davidson was with her.

'I'll see that everything is ready. I mean to come on board with her myself.'

Miss Thompson did not speak.

When Dr Macphail blew out his candle and crawled cautiously under his mosquito curtains, he gave a sigh of relief.

'Well, thank God that's over. By this time tomorrow she'll be gone.'

'Mrs Davidson will be glad too. She says he's wearing himself to a shadow,' said Mrs Macphail. 'She's a different woman.'

'Who?'

'Sadie. I should never have thought it possible. It makes one humble.'

Dr Macphail did not answer, and presently he fell asleep. He was tired out, and he slept more soundly than usual.

He was awakened in the morning by a hand placed on his arm, and, starting up, saw Horn by the side of his bed. The trader put his finger on his mouth to prevent any exclamation from Dr Macphail and beckoned to him to come. As a rule he wore shabby ducks, but now he was barefoot and wore only the lava-lava of the natives. He looked suddenly savage, and Dr Macphail, getting out of bed, saw that he was heavily tattooed. Horn made him a sign to come on to the veranda. Dr Macphail got out of bed and followed the trader out.

'Don't make a noise,' he whispered. 'You're wanted. Put on a coat and some shoes. Quick.'

Dr Macphail's first thought was that something had happened to Miss Thompson.

'What is it? Shall I bring my instruments?'

'Hurry, please, hurry.'

Dr Macphail crept back into the bedroom, put on a waterproof over his pyjamas, and a pair of rubber-soled shoes. He rejoined the trader, and together they tiptoed down the stairs. The door leading out to the road was open and at it were standing half a dozen natives.

'What is it?' repeated the doctor.

'Come along with me,' said Horn.

He walked out and the doctor followed him. The natives came after them in a little bunch. They crossed the road and came on to the beach. The doctor saw a group of natives standing round some object at the water's edge. They hurried along, a couple of dozen yards perhaps, and the natives opened out as the doctor came up. The trader pushed him forwards. Then he saw, lying half in the water and half out, a dreadful object, the body of Davidson. Dr Macphail bent down – he was not a man to lose his head in an emergency – and turned the body over. The throat was cut from ear to ear, and in the right hand was still the razor with which the deed was done.

'He's quite cold,' said the doctor. 'He must have been dead some time.'

'One of the boys saw him lying there on his way to work just now and came and told me. Do you think he did it himself?'

'Yes. Someone ought to go for the police.'

Horn said something in the native tongue, and two youths started off.

'We must leave him here till they come,' said the doctor.

'They mustn't take him into my house. I won't have him in my house.'

'You'll do what the authorities say,' replied the doctor sharply. 'In point of fact I expect they'll take him to the mortuary.'

They stood waiting where they were. The trader took a cigarette from a fold in his lava-lava and gave one to Dr Macphail. They smoked while they stared at the corpse. Dr Macphail could not understand.

'Why do you think he did it?' asked Horn.

The doctor shrugged his shoulders. In a little while native police came along, under the charge of a marine, with a stretcher, and immediately afterwards a couple of naval officers and a naval doctor. They managed everything in a businesslike manner.

'What about the wife?' said one of the officers.

'Now that you've come I'll go back to the house and get some things on. I'll see that it's broken to her. She'd better not see him till he's been fixed up a little.'

'I guess that's right,' said the naval doctor.

When Dr Macphail went back he found his wife nearly dressed.

'Mrs Davidson's in a dreadful state about her husband,' she said to him as soon as he appeared. 'He hasn't been to bed all night. She heard him leave Miss Thompson's room at two, but he went out. If he's been walking about since then he'll be absolutely dead.'

Dr Macphail told her what had happened and asked her to break the news to Mrs Davidson.

'But why did he do it?' she asked, horror-stricken.

'I don't know.'

'But I can't. I can't.'

'You must.'

She gave him a frightened look and went out. He heard her go into Mrs Davidson's room. He waited a minute to gather himself together and then began to shave and wash. When he was dressed he sat down on the bed and waited for his wife. At last she came.

'She wants to see him,' she said.

'They've taken him to the mortuary. We'd better go down with her. How did she take it?'

'I think she's stunned. She didn't cry. But she's trembling like a leaf.'

'We'd better go at once.'

When they knocked at her door Mrs Davidson came out. She was very pale, but dry-eyed. To the doctor she seemed unnaturally composed. No word was exchanged, and they set out in silence down the road. When they arrived at the mortuary Mrs Davidson spoke.

'Let me go in and see him alone.'

They stood aside. A native opened a door for her and closed it behind her. They sat down and waited. One or two white men came and talked to them in undertones. Dr Macphail told them again what he knew of the tragedy. At last the door was quietly opened and Mrs Davidson came out. Silence fell upon them.

'I'm ready to go back now,' she said.

Her voice was hard and steady. Dr Macphail could not understand the look in her eyes. Her pale face was very stern. They walked back slowly, never saying a word, and at last they came round the bend on the other side of which stood their house. Mrs Davidson gave a gasp, and for a moment they stopped still. An incredible sound assaulted their ears. The gramophone which had been silent for so long was playing, playing ragtime loud and harsh.

'What's that?' cried Mrs Macphail with horror.

'Let's go on,' said Mrs Davidson.

They walked up the steps and entered the hall. Miss Thompson was standing at her door, chatting with a sailor. A sudden change had taken place in her. She was no longer the cowed drudge of the last days. She was dressed in all her finery, in her white dress, with the high shiny boots over which her fat legs bulged in their cotton stockings; her hair was elaborately arranged; and she wore that enormous hat covered with gaudy flowers. Her face was painted, her eyebrows were boldly black, and her lips were scarlet. She held herself erect. She was the flaunting queen that they had known at first. As they came in she broke into a loud, jeering laugh; and then, when Mrs Davidson involuntarily stopped, she collected the spittle in her mouth and spat. Mrs Davidson cowered back, and two red spots rose suddenly to her cheeks. Then, covering her face with her hands, she broke away and ran quickly up the stairs. Dr Macphail was outraged. He pushed past the woman into her room.

'What the devil are you doing?' he cried. 'Stop that damned machine.'

He went up to it and tore the record off. She turned on him.

'Say, doc, you can that stuff with me. What the hell are you doin' in my room?'

'What do you mean?' he cried. 'What d'you mean?'

She gathered herself together. No one could describe the scorn of her expression or the contemptuous hatred she put into her answer.

'You men! You filthy, dirty pigs! You're all the same, all of you. Pigs! Pigs!'

Dr Macphail gasped. He understood.

The Fall of
Edward Barnard

◆

Bateman Hunter slept badly. For a fortnight on the boat that brought him from
Tahiti to San Francisco he had been thinking of the story he had to tell, and for
three days on the train he had repeated to himself the words in which he meant
to tell it. But in a few hours now he would be in Chicago, and doubts assailed
him. His conscience, always very sensitive, was not at ease. He was uncertain
that he had done all that was possible, it was on his honour to do much more
than the possible, and the thought was disturbing that, in a matter which so
nearly touched his own interest, he had allowed his interest to prevail over his
quixotry. Self-sacrifice appealed so keenly to his imagination that the inability
to exercise it gave him a sense of disillusion. He was like the philanthropist who
with altruistic motives builds model dwellings for the poor and finds that he has
made a lucrative investment. He cannot prevent the satisfaction he feels in the
ten per cent which rewards the bread he had cast upon the waters, but he has an
awkward feeling that it detracts somewhat from the savour of his virtue.
Bateman Hunter knew that his heart was pure, but he was not quite sure how
steadfastly, when he told her his story, he would endure the scrutiny of Isabel
Longstaffe's cool grey eyes. They were far-seeing and wise. She measured the
standards of others by her own meticulous uprightness and there could be no
greater censure than the cold silence with which she expressed her disapproval
of a conduct that did not satisfy her exacting code. There was no appeal from
her judgement, for, having made up her mind, she never changed it. But
Bateman would not have had her different. He loved not only the beauty of her
person, slim and straight, with the proud carriage of her head, but still more the
beauty of her soul. With her truthfulness, her rigid sense of honour, her fearless
outlook, she seemed to him to collect in herself all that was most admirable in
his country-women. But he saw in her something more than the perfect type of

the American girl, he felt that her exquisiteness was peculiar in a way to her environment, and he was assured that no city in the world could have produced her but Chicago. A pang seized him when he remembered that he must deal so bitter a blow to her pride, and anger flamed up in his heart when he thought of Edward Barnard.

But at last the train steamed in to Chicago and he exulted when he saw the long streets of grey houses. He could hardly bear his impatience at the thought of State and Wabash with their crowded pavements, their hustling traffic, and their noise. He was at home. And he was glad that he had been born in the most important city in the United States. San Francisco was provincial, New York was effete; the future of America lay in the development of its economic possibilities, and Chicago, by its position and by the energy of its citizens, was destined to become the real capital of the country.

'I guess I shall live long enough to see it the biggest city in the world,' Bateman said to himself as he stepped down to the platform.

His father had come to meet him, and after a hearty handshake, the pair of them, tall, slender, and well-made, with the same fine, ascetic features and thin lips, walked out of the station. Mr Hunter's automobile was waiting for them and they got in. Mr Hunter caught his son's proud and happy glance as he looked at the street.

'Glad to be back, son?' he asked.

'I should just think I was,' said Bateman.

His eyes devoured the restless scene.

'I guess there's a bit more traffic here than in your South Sea island,' laughed Mr Hunter. 'Did you like it there?'

'Give me Chicago, dad,' answered Bateman.

'You haven't brought Edward Barnard back with you.'

'No.'

'How was he?'

Bateman was silent for a moment, and his handsome, sensitive face darkened.

'I'd sooner not speak about him, dad,' he said at last.

'That's all right, my son. I guess your mother will be a happy woman today.'

They passed out of the crowded streets in the Loop and drove along the lake till they came to the imposing house, an exact copy of a château on the Loire, which Mr Hunter had built himself some years before. As soon as Bateman was alone in his room he asked for a number on the telephone. His heart leaped when he heard the voice that answered him.

'Good morning, Isabel,' he said gaily.

'Good morning, Bateman.'

'How did you recognize my voice?'

'It is not so long since I heard it last. Besides, I was expecting you.'

'When may I see you?'

'Unless you have anything better to do perhaps you'll dine with us tonight.'

'You know very well that I couldn't possibly have anything better to do.'

'I suppose that you're full of news?'

He thought he detected in her voice a note of apprehension.

'Yes,' he answered.

'Well, you must tell me tonight. Good-bye.'

She rang off. It was characteristic of her that she should be able to wait so many unnecessary hours to know what so immensely concerned her. To Bateman there was an admirable fortitude in her restraint.

At dinner, at which beside himself and Isabel no one was present but her father and mother, he watched her guide the conversation into the channels of an urbane small-talk, and it occurred to him that in just such a manner would a marquise under the shadow of the guillotine toy with the affairs of a day that would know no morrow. Her delicate features, the aristocratic shortness of her upper lip, and her wealth of fair hair suggested the marquise again, and it must have been obvious, even if it were not notorious, that in her veins flowed the best blood in Chicago. The dining-room was a fitting frame to her fragile beauty, for Isabel had caused the house, a replica of a palace on the Grand Canal at Venice, to be furnished by an English expert in the style of Louis XV; and the graceful decoration linked with the name of that amorous monarch enhanced her loveliness and at the same time acquired from it a more profound significance. For Isabel's mind was richly stored, and her conversation, however light, was never flippant. She spoke now of the Musicale to which she and her mother had been in the afternoon, of the lectures which an English poet was giving at the Auditorium, of the political situation, and of the Old Master which her father had recently bought for fifty thousand dollars in New York. It comforted Bateman to hear her. He felt that he was once more in the civilized world, at the centre of culture and distinction; and certain voices, troubling and yet against his will refusing to still their clamour, were at last silent in his heart.

'Gee, but it's good to be back in Chicago,' he said.

At last dinner was over, and when they went out of the dining-room Isabel said to her mother:

'I'm going to take Bateman along to my den. We have various things to talk about.'

'Very well, my dear,' said Mrs Longstaffe. 'You'll find your father and me in the Madame du Barry room when you're through.'

Isabel led the young man upstairs and showed him into the room of which he had so many charming memories. Though he knew it so well he could not repress the exclamation of delight which it always wrung from him. She looked round with a smile.

'I think it's a success,' she said. 'The main thing is that it's right. There's not even an ash-tray that isn't of the period.'

'I suppose that's what makes it so wonderful. Like all you do it's so superlatively right.'

They sat down in front of a log fire and Isabel looked at him with calm grave eyes.

'Now what have you to say to me?' she asked.

'I hardly know how to begin.'

'Is Edward Barnard coming back?'

'No.'

There was a long silence before Bateman spoke again, and with each of them it was filled with many thoughts. It was a difficult story he had to tell, for there were things in it which were so offensive to her sensitive ears that he could not bear to tell them, and yet in justice to her, no less than in justice to himself, he must tell her the whole truth.

It had all begun long ago when he and Edward Barnard, still at college, had met Isabel Longstaffe at the tea-party given to introduce her to society. They had both known her when she was a child and they long-legged boys, but for two years she had been in Europe to finish her education and it was with a surprised delight that they renewed acquaintance with the lovely girl who returned. Both of them fell desperately in love with her, but Bateman saw quickly that she had eyes only for Edward, and, devoted to his friend, he resigned himself to the role of confidant. He passed bitter moments, but he could not deny that Edward was worthy of his good fortune, and, anxious that nothing should impair the friendship he so greatly valued, he took care never by a hint to disclose his own feelings. In six months the young couple were engaged. But they were very young and Isabel's father decided that they should not marry at least till Edward graduated. They had to wait a year. Bateman remembered the winter at the end of which Isabel and Edward were to be married, a winter of dances and theatre-parties and of informal gaieties at which he, the constant third, was always present. He loved her no less because she would shortly be his friend's wife; her smile, a gay word she flung him, the confidence of her affection, never ceased to delight him; and he congratulated himself, somewhat complacently, because he did not envy them their happiness. Then an accident happened. A great bank failed, there was a panic on the exchange, and Edward Barnard's father found himself a ruined man. He came home one night, told his wife he was penniless, and after dinner, going into his study, shot himself.

A week later, Edward Barnard, with a tired, white face, went to Isabel and asked her to release him. Her only answer was to throw her arms round his neck and burst into tears.

'Don't make it harder for me, sweet,' he said.

'Do you think I can let you go now? I love you.'

'How can I ask you to marry me? The whole thing's hopeless. Your father would never let you. I haven't a cent.'

'What do I care? I love you.'

He told her his plans. He had to earn money at once, and George Braunschmidt, an old friend of his family, had offered to take him into his own business. He was a South Sea merchant, and he had agencies in many of the islands of the Pacific. He had suggested that Edward should go to Tahiti for a year or two, where under the best of his managers he could learn the details of that varied trade, and at the end of that time he promised the young man a position in Chicago. It was a wonderful opportunity, and when he had finished his explanations Isabel was once more all smiles.

'You foolish boy, why have you been trying to make me miserable?'

His face lit up at her words and his eyes flashed.

'Isabel, you don't mean to say you'll wait for me?'

'Don't you think you're worth it?' she smiled.

'Ah, don't laugh at me now. I beseech you to be serious. It may be for two years.'

'Have no fear. I love you, Edward. When you come back I will marry you.'

Edward's employer was a man who did not like delay and he had told him that if he took the post he offered he must sail that day week from San Francisco. Edward spent his last evening with Isabel. It was after dinner that Mr Longstaffe, saying he wanted a word with Edward, took him into the smoking-room. Mr Longstaffe had accepted good-naturedly the arrangement which his daughter had told him of and Edward could not imagine what mysterious communication he had now to make. He was not a little perplexed to see that his host was embarrassed. He faltered. He talked of trivial things. At last he blurted it out.

'I guess you've heard of Arnold Jackson,' he said, looking at Edward with a frown.

Edward hesitated. His natural truthfulness obliged him to admit a knowledge he would gladly have been able to deny.

'Yes, I have. But it's a long time ago. I guess I didn't pay very much attention.'

'There are not many people in Chicago who haven't heard of Arnold Jackson,' said Mr Longstaffe bitterly, 'and if there are they'll have no difficulty in finding someone who'll be glad to tell them. Did you know he was Mrs Longstaffe's brother?'

'Yes, I knew that.'

'Of course we've had no communication with him for many years. He left the country as soon as he was able to, and I guess the country wasn't sorry to see the last of him. We understand he lives in Tahiti. My advice to you is to give him a wide berth, but if you do hear anything about him Mrs Longstaffe and I would be very glad if you'd let us know.'

'Sure.'

'That was all I wanted to say to you. Now I daresay you'd like to join the ladies.'

There are few families that have not among their members one whom, if their neighbours permitted, they would willingly forget, and they are fortunate when the lapse of a generation or two has invested his vagaries with a romantic glamour. But when he is actually alive, if his peculiarities are not of the kind that can be condoned by the phrase, 'he is nobody's enemy but his own', a safe one when the culprit has no worse to answer for than alcoholism or wandering affections, the only possible course is silence. And it was this which the Longstaffes had adopted towards Arnold Jackson. They never talked of him. They would not even pass through the street in which he had lived. Too kind to make his wife and children suffer for his misdeeds, they had supported them for years, but on the understanding that they should live in Europe. They did everything they could to blot out all recollection of Arnold Jackson and yet were conscious that the story was as fresh in the public mind as when first the scandal burst upon a gaping world. Arnold Jackson was as black a sheep as any family could suffer from. A wealthy banker, prominent in his church, a philanthropist, a man respected by all, not only for his connexions (in his veins ran the blue blood of Chicago), but also for his upright character, he was arrested one day on a charge of fraud; and the dishonesty which the trial brought to light was not the sort which could be explained by a sudden temptation; it was deliberate and systematic. Arnold Jackson was a rogue. When he was sent to the penitentiary for seven years there were few who did not think he had escaped lightly.

When at the end of this last evening the lovers separated it was with many protestations of devotion. Isabel, all tears, was consoled a little by her certainty of Edward's passionate love. It was a strange feeling that she had. It made her wretched to part from him and yet she was happy because he adored her.

This was more than two years ago.

He had written to her by every mail since then, twenty-four letters in all, for the mail went but once a month, and his letters had been all that a lover's letters should be. They were intimate and charming, humorous sometimes, especially of late, and tender. At first they suggested that he was homesick, they were full of his desire to get back to Chicago and Isabel; and, a little anxiously, she wrote begging him to persevere. She was afraid that he might throw up his opportunity and come racing back. She did not want her lover to lack endurance and she quoted to him the lines:

> I could not love thee, dear, so much,
> Loved I not honour more.

But presently he seemed to settle down and it made Isabel very happy to observe his growing enthusiasm to introduce American methods into that forgotten corner of the world. But she knew him, and at the end of the year, which was the shortest time he could possibly stay in Tahiti, she expected to have to use all her influence to dissuade him from coming home. It was much better that he should learn the business thoroughly, and if they had been able to wait a year there seemed no reason why they should not wait another. She talked it over with Bateman Hunter, always the most generous of friends (during those first few days after Edward went she did not know what she would have done without him), and they decided that Edward's future must stand before everything. It was with relief that she found as the time passed that he made no suggestion of returning.

'He's splendid, isn't he?' she exclaimed to Bateman.

'He's white, through and through.'

'Reading between the lines of his letter I know he hates it over there, but he's sticking it out because . . .'

She blushed a little and Bateman, with the grave smile which was so attractive in him, finished the sentence for her.

'Because he loves you.'

'It makes me feel so humble,' she said.

'You're wonderful, Isabel, you're perfectly wonderful.'

But the second year passed and every month Isabel continued to receive a letter from Edward, and presently it began to seem a little strange that he did not speak of coming back. He wrote as though he were settled definitely in Tahiti, and what was more, comfortably settled. She was surprised. Then she read his letters again, all of them, several times; and now, reading between the lines indeed, she was puzzled to notice a change which had escaped her. The later letters were as tender and as delightful as the first, but the tone was different. She was vaguely suspicious of their humour, she had the instinctive mistrust of her sex for that unaccountable quality, and she discerned in them now a flippancy which perplexed her. She was not quite certain that the Edward who wrote to her now was the same Edward that she had known. One afternoon, the day after a mail had arrived from Tahiti, when she was driving with Bateman he said to her:

'Did Edward tell you when he was sailing?'

'No, he didn't mention it. I thought he might have said something to you about it.'

'Not a word.'

'You know what Edward is,' she laughed in reply, 'he has no sense of time. If it occurs to you next time you write you might ask him when he's thinking of coming.'

Her manner was so unconcerned that only Bateman's acute sensitiveness could have discerned in her request a very urgent desire. He laughed lightly.

'Yes. I'll ask him. I can't imagine what he's thinking about.'

A few days later, meeting him again, she noticed that something troubled him. They had been much together since Edward left Chicago; they were both devoted to him and each in his desire to talk of the absent one found a willing listener; the consequence was that Isabel knew every expression of Bateman's face, and his denials now were useless against her keen instinct. Something told her that his harassed look had to do with Edward and she did not rest till she had made him confess.

'The fact is,' he said at last, 'I heard in a roundabout way that Edward was no longer working for Braunschmidt and Co., and yesterday I took the opportunity to ask Mr Braunschmidt himself.'

'Well?'

'Edward left his employment with them nearly a year ago.'

'How strange he should have said nothing about it!'

Bateman hesitated, but he had gone so far now that he was obliged to tell the rest. It made him feel dreadfully embarrassed.

'He was fired.'

'In heaven's name what for?'

'It appears they warned him once or twice, and at last they told him to get out. They say he was lazy and incompetent.'

'Edward?'

They were silent for a while, and then he saw that Isabel was crying. Instinctively he seized her hand.

'Oh, my dear, don't, don't,' he said. 'I can't bear to see it.'

She was so unstrung that she let her hand rest in his. He tried to console her.

'It's incomprehensible, isn't it? It's so unlike Edward. I can't help feeling there must be some mistake.'

She did not say anything for a while, and when she spoke it was hesitatingly.

'Has it struck you that there was anything queer in his letters lately?' she asked, looking away, her eyes all bright with tears.

He did not quite know how to answer.

'I have noticed a change in them,' he admitted. 'He seems to have lost that high seriousness which I admired so much in him. One would almost think that the things that matter – well, don't matter.'

Isabel did not reply. She was vaguely uneasy.

'Perhaps in his answer to your letter he'll say when he's coming home. All we can do is to wait for that.'

Another letter came from Edward for each of them, and still he made no mention of his return; but when he wrote he could not have received Bateman's inquiry. The next mail would bring them an answer to that. The next mail came, and Bateman brought Isabel the letter he had just received; but the first glance of his face was enough to tell her that he was disconcerted. She read it through carefully and then, with slightly tightened lips, read it again.

'It's a very strange letter,' she said. 'I don't quite understand it.'

'One might almost think that he was joshing me,' said Bateman, flushing.

'It reads like that, but it must be unintentional. That's so unlike Edward.'

'He says nothing about coming back.'

'If I weren't so confident of his love I should think . . . I hardly know what I should think.'

It was then that Bateman had broached the scheme which during the afternoon had formed itself in his brain. The firm, founded by his father, in which he was now a partner, a firm which manufactured all manner of motor vehicles, was about to establish agencies in Honolulu, Sydney, and Wellington; and Bateman proposed that himself should go instead of the manager, who had been suggested. He could return by Tahiti; in fact, travelling from Wellington, it was inevitable to do so; and he could see Edward.

'There's some mystery and I'm going to clear it up. That's the only way to do it.'

'Oh, Bateman, how can you be so good and kind?' she exclaimed.

'You know there's nothing in the world I want more than your happiness, Isabel.'

She looked at him and she gave him her hands.

'You're wonderful, Bateman. I didn't know there was anyone in the world like you. How can I ever thank you?'

'I don't want your thanks. I only want to be allowed to help you.'

She dropped her eyes and flushed a little. She was so used to him that she had forgotten how handsome he was. He was as tall as Edward and as well made, but he was dark and pale of face, while Edward was ruddy. Of course she knew he loved her. It touched her. She felt very tenderly towards him.

It was from this journey that Bateman Hunter was now returned.

The business part of it took him somewhat longer than he expected and he had much time to think of his two friends. He had come to the conclusion that it could be nothing serious that prevented Edward from coming home, a pride, perhaps, which made him determined to make good before he claimed the bride he adored; but it was a pride that must be reasoned with. Isabel was unhappy. Edward must come back to Chicago with him and marry her at once. A position could be found for him in the works of the Hunter Motor Traction and Automobile Company. Bateman, with a bleeding heart, exulted at the prospect of giving happiness to the two persons he loved best in the world at the cost of his own. He would never marry. He would be godfather to the children of Edward and Isabel, and many years later when they were both dead he would tell Isabel's daughter how long, long ago he had loved her mother. Bateman's eyes were veiled with tears when he pictured this scene to himself.

Meaning to take Edward by surprise he had not cabled to announce his arrival, and when at last he landed at Tahiti he allowed a youth, who said he was the son of the house, to lead him to the Hôtel de la Fleur. He chuckled when he thought of his friend's amazement on seeing him, the most unexpected of visitors, walk into his office.

'By the way,' he asked, as they went along, 'can you tell me where I shall find Mr Edward Barnard?'

'Barnard?' said the youth. 'I seem to know the name.'

'He's an American. A tall fellow with light brown hair and blue eyes. He's been here over two years.'

'Of course. Now I know who you mean. You mean Mr Jackson's nephew.'

'Whose nephew?'

'Mr Arnold Jackson.'

'I don't think we're speaking of the same person,' answered Bateman, frigidly.

He was startled. It was queer that Arnold Jackson, known apparently to all and sundry, should live here under the disgraceful name in which he had been convicted. But Bateman could not imagine whom it was that he passed off as his nephew. Mrs Longstaffe was his only sister and he had never had a brother. The young man by his side talked volubly in an English that had something in it of the intonation of a foreign tongue, and Bateman, with a sidelong glance, saw, what he had not noticed before, that there was in him a good deal of native blood. A touch of hauteur involuntarily entered into his manner. They reached the hotel. When he had arranged about his room Bateman asked to be directed to the premises of Braunschmidt and Co. They were on the front, facing the lagoon, and, glad to feel the solid earth under his feet after eight days at sea, he sauntered down the sunny road to the water's edge. Having found the place he sought, Bateman sent in his card to the manager and was led through a lofty barn-like room, half store and half warehouse, to an office in which sat a stout, spectacled, bald-headed man.

'Can you tell me where I shall find Mr Edward Barnard? I understand he was in this office for some time.'

'That is so. I don't know just where he is.'

'But I thought he came here with a particular recommendation from Mr Braunschmidt. I know Mr Braunschmidt very well.'

The fat man looked at Bateman with shrewd, suspicious eyes. He called to one of the boys in the warehouse.

'Say, Henry, where's Barnard now, d'you know?'

'He's working at Cameron's, I think,' came the answer from someone who did not trouble to move.

The fat man nodded.

'If you turn to your left when you get out of here you'll come to Cameron's in about three minutes.'

Bateman hesitated.

'I think I should tell you that Edward Barnard is my greatest friend. I was very much surprised when I heard he'd left Braunschmidt and Co.'

The fat man's eyes contracted till they seemed like pin-points, and their scrutiny made Bateman so uncomfortable that he felt himself blushing.

'I guess Braunschmidt and Co. and Edward Barnard didn't see eye to eye on certain matters,' he replied.

Bateman did not quite like the fellow's manner, so he got up, not without dignity, and with an apology for troubling him bade him good day. He left the place with a singular feeling that the man he had just interviewed had much to tell him, but no intention of telling it. He walked in the direction indicated and soon found himself at Cameron's. It was a trader's store, such as he had passed half a dozen of on his way, and when he entered the first person he saw, in his shirt-sleeves, measuring out a length of trade cotton, was Edward. It gave him a start to see him engaged in so humble an occupation. But he had scarcely appeared when Edward, looking up, caught sight of him, and gave a joyful cry of surprise.

'Bateman! Who ever thought of seeing you here?'

He stretched his arm across the counter and wrung Bateman's hand. There was no self-consciousness in his manner and the embarrassment was all on Bateman's side.

'Just wait till I've wrapped this package.'

With perfect assurance he ran his scissors across the stuff, folded it, made it into a parcel, and handed it to the dark-skinned customer.

'Pay at the desk, please.'

Then, smiling, with bright eyes, he turned to Bateman.

'How did you show up here? Gee, I am delighted to see you. Sit down, old man. Make yourself at home.'

'We can't talk here. Come along to my hotel. I suppose you can get away?' This he added with some apprehension.

'Of course I can get away. We're not so business-like as all that in Tahiti.' He called out to a Chinese who was standing behind the opposite counter. 'Ah-Ling, when the boss comes tell him a friend of mine's just arrived from America and I've gone out to have a dram with him.'

'All-light,' said the Chinese, with a grin.

Edward slipped on a coat and, putting on his hat, accompanied Bateman out of the store. Bateman attempted to put the matter facetiously.

'I didn't expect to find you selling three and a half yards of rotten cotton to a greasy nigger,' he laughed.

'Braunschmidt fired me, you know, and I thought that would do as well as anything else.'

Edward's candour seemed to Bateman very surprising, but he thought it indiscreet to pursue the subject.

'I guess you won't make a fortune where you are,' he answered, somewhat dryly.

'I guess not. But I earn enough to keep body and soul together, and I'm quite satisfied with that.'

'You wouldn't have been two years ago.'

'We grow wiser as we grow older,' retorted Edward, gaily.

Bateman took a glance at him. Edward was dressed in a suit of shabby white ducks, none too clean, and a large straw hat of native make. He was thinner than he had been, deeply burned by the sun, and he was certainly better-looking than ever. But there was something in his appearance that disconcerted Bateman. He walked with a new jauntiness; there was a carelessness in his demeanour, a gaiety about nothing in particular, which Bateman could not precisely blame, but which exceedingly puzzled him.

'I'm blest if I can see what he's got to be so darned cheerful about,' he said to himself.

They arrived at the hotel and sat on the terrace. A Chinese boy brought them cocktails. Edward was most anxious to hear all the news of Chicago and bombarded his friend with eager questions. His interest was natural and sincere. But the odd thing was that it seemed equally divided among a multitude of subjects. He was as eager to know how Bateman's father was as what Isabel was doing. He talked of her without a shade of embarrassment, but she might just as well have been his sister as his promised wife; and before Bateman had done analysing the exact meaning of Edward's remarks he found that the conversation had drifted to his own work and the buildings his father had lately erected. He was determined to bring the conversation back to Isabel and was looking for the occasion when he saw Edward wave his hand cordially. A man was advancing towards them on the terrace, but Bateman's back was turned to him and he could not see him.

'Come and sit down,' said Edward gaily.

The new-comer approached. He was a very tall, thin man, in white ducks, with a fine head of curly white hair. His face was thin too, long, with a large, hooked nose and a beautiful, expressive mouth.

'This is my old friend Bateman Hunter. I've told you about him,' said Edward, his constant smile breaking on his lips.

'I'm pleased to meet you, Mr Hunter. I used to know your father.'

The stranger held out his hand and took the young man's in a strong, friendly grasp. It was not till then that Edward mentioned the other's name.

'Mr Arnold Jackson.'

Bateman turned white and he felt his hands grow cold. This was the forger, the convict, this was Isabel's uncle. He did not know what to say. He tried to conceal his confusion. Arnold Jackson looked at him with twinkling eyes.

'I daresay my name is familiar to you.'

Bateman did not know whether to say yes or no, and what made it more awkward was that both Jackson and Edward seemed to be amused. It was bad enough to have forced on him the acquaintance of the one man on the island he would rather have avoided, but worse to discern that he was being made a fool of. Perhaps, however, he had reached this conclusion too quickly, for Jackson, without a pause, added:

'I understand you're very friendly with the Longstaffes. Mary Longstaffe is my sister.'

Now Bateman asked himself if Arnold Jackson could think him ignorant of the most terrible scandal that Chicago had ever known. But Jackson put his hand on Edward's shoulder.

'I can't sit down, Teddie,' he said. 'I'm busy. But you two boys had better come up and dine tonight.'

'That'll be fine,' said Edward.

'It's very kind of you, Mr Jackson,' said Bateman, frigidly, 'but I'm here for so short a time; my boat sails tomorrow, you know; I think if you'll forgive me, I won't come.'

'Oh, nonsense. I'll give you a native dinner. My wife's a wonderful cook. Teddie will show you the way. Come early so as to see the sunset. I can give you both a shake-down if you like.'

'Of course we'll come,' said Edward. 'There's always the devil of a row in the hotel on the night a boat arrives and we can have a good yarn up at the bungalow.'

'I can't let you off, Mr Hunter,' Jackson continued with the utmost cordiality. 'I want to hear all about Chicago and Mary.'

He nodded and walked away before Bateman could say another word.

'We don't take refusals in Tahiti,' laughed Edward. 'Besides, you'll get the best dinner on the island.'

'What did he mean by saying his wife was a good cook? I happen to know his wife's in Geneva.'

'That's a long way off for a wife, isn't it?' said Edward. 'And it's a long time since he saw her. I guess it's another wife he's talking about.'

For some time Bateman was silent. His face was set in grave lines. But looking up he caught the amused look in Edward's eyes, and he flushed darkly.

'Arnold Jackson is a despicable rogue,' he said.

'I greatly fear he is,' answered Edward, smiling.

'I don't see how any decent man can have anything to do with him.'

'Perhaps I'm not a decent man.'

'Do you see much of him, Edward?'

'Yes, quite a lot. He's adopted me as his nephew.'

Bateman leaned forward and fixed Edward with his searching eyes.

'Do you like him?'

'Very much.'

'But don't you know, doesn't everyone here know, that he's a forger and that he's been a convict? He ought to be hounded out of civilized society.'

Edward watched a ring of smoke that floated from his cigar into the still, scented air.

'I suppose he is a pretty unmitigated rascal,' he said at last. 'And I can't flatter myself that any repentance for his misdeeds offers one an excuse for condoning them. He was a swindler and a hypocrite. You can't get away from it. I never met a more agreeable companion. He's taught me everything I know.'

'What has he taught you?' cried Bateman in amazement.

'How to live.'

Bateman broke into ironical laughter.

'A fine master. Is it owing to his lessons that you lost the chance of making a fortune and earn your living now by serving behind a counter in a ten-cent store?'

'He has a wonderful personality,' said Edward, smiling good-naturedly. 'Perhaps you'll see what I mean tonight.'

'I'm not going to dine with him if that's what you mean. Nothing would induce me to set foot within that man's house.'

'Come to oblige me, Bateman. We've been friends for so many years, you won't refuse me a favour when I ask it.'

Edward's tone had in it a quality new to Bateman. Its gentleness was singularly persuasive.

'If you put it like that, Edward, I'm bound to come,' he smiled.

Bateman reflected, moreover, that it would be as well to learn what he could about Arnold Jackson. It was plain that he had a great ascendancy over Edward, and if it was to be combated it was necessary to discover in what exactly it consisted. The more he talked with Edward the more conscious he became that a change had taken place in him. He had an instinct that it behoved him to walk warily, and he made up his mind not to broach the real purport of his visit till he saw his way more clearly. He began to talk of one thing and another, of his journey and what he had achieved by it, of politics in Chicago, of this common friend and that, of their days together at college.

At last Edward said he must get back to his work and proposed that he should fetch Bateman at five so that they could drive out together to Arnold Jackson's house.

'By the way, I rather thought you'd be living at this hotel,' said Bateman, as he strolled out of the garden with Edward. 'I understand it's the only decent one here.'

'Not I,' laughed Edward. 'It's a deal too grand for me. I rent a room just outside the town. It's cheap and clean.'

'If I remember right those weren't the points that seemed most important to you when you lived in Chicago.'

'Chicago!'

'I don't know what you mean by that, Edward. It's the greatest city in the world.'

'I know,' said Edward.

Bateman glanced at him quickly, but his face was inscrutable.

'When are you coming back to it?'

'I often wonder,' smiled Edward.

This answer, and the manner of it, staggered Bateman, but before he could ask for an explanation Edward waved to a half-caste who was driving a passing motor.

'Give us a ride down, Charlie,' he said.

He nodded to Bateman, and ran after the machine that had pulled up a few yards in front. Bateman was left to piece together a mass of perplexing impressions.

Edward called for him in a rickety trap drawn by an old mare, and they drove along a road that ran by the sea. On each side of it were plantations, coconut and vanilla; and now and then they saw a great mango, its fruit yellow and red and purple among the massy green of the leaves, now and then they had a glimpse of the lagoon, smooth and blue, with here and there a tiny islet graceful with tall palms. Arnold Jackson's house stood on a little hill and only a path led to it, so they unharnessed the mare and tied her to a tree, leaving the trap by the side of the road. To Bateman it seemed a happy-go-lucky way of doing things. But when they went up to the house they were met by a tall, handsome native woman, no longer young, with whom Edward cordially shook hands. He introduced Bateman to her.

'This is my friend Mr Hunter. We're going to dine with you, Lavina.'

'All right,' she said, with a quick smile. 'Arnold ain't back yet.'

'We'll go down and bathe. Let us have a couple of pareos.'

The woman nodded and went into the house.

'Who is that?' asked Bateman.

'Oh, that's Lavina. She's Arnold's wife.'

Bateman tightened his lips, but said nothing. In a moment the woman returned with a bundle, which she gave to Edward; and the two men, scrambling down a steep path, made their way to a grove of coconut trees on the beach. They undressed and Edward showed his friend how to make the strip of red trade cotton which is called a pareo into a very neat pair of bathing-drawers. Soon they were splashing in the warm, shallow water. Edward was in great spirits. He laughed and shouted and sang. He might have been fifteen. Bateman had never seen him so gay, and afterwards when they lay on the beach, smoking cigarettes, in the limpid air, there was such an irresistible light-heartedness in him that Bateman was taken aback.

'You seem to find life mighty pleasant,' said he.

'I do.'

They heard a soft movement and looking round saw that Arnold Jackson was coming towards them.

'I thought I'd come down and fetch you two boys back,' he said. 'Did you enjoy your bathe, Mr Hunter?'

'Very much,' said Bateman.

Arnold Jackson, no longer in spruce ducks, wore nothing but a pareo round his loins and walked barefoot. His body was deeply browned by the sun. With his long, curling white hair and his ascetic face he made a fantastic figure in the native dress, but he bore himself without a trace of self-consciousness.

'If you're ready we'll go right up,' said Jackson.

'I'll just put on my clothes,' said Bateman.

'Why, Teddie, didn't you bring a pareo for your friend?'

'I guess he'd rather wear clothes,' smiled Edward.

'I certainly would,' answered Bateman, grimly, as he saw Edward gird himself in the loincloth and stand ready to start before he himself had got his shirt on.

'Won't you find it rough walking without your shoes?' he asked Edward. 'It struck me the path was a trifle rocky.'

'Oh, I'm used to it.'

'It's a comfort to get into a pareo when one gets back from town,' said Jackson. 'If you were going to stay here I should strongly recommend you to adopt it. It's one of the most sensible costumes I have ever come across. It's cool, convenient, and inexpensive.'

They walked up to the house, and Jackson took them into a large room with white-washed walls and an open ceiling in which a table was laid for dinner. Bateman noticed that it was set for five.

'Eva, come and show yourself to Teddie's friend, and then shake us a cocktail,' called Jackson.

Then he led Bateman to a long low window.

'Look at that,' he said, with a dramatic gesture. 'Look well.'

Below them coconut trees tumbled down steeply to the lagoon, and the lagoon in the evening light had the colour, tender and varied, of a dove's breast. On a creek, at a little distance, were the clustered huts of a native village, and towards the reef was a canoe, sharply silhouetted, in which were a couple of natives fishing. Then, beyond, you saw the vast calmness of the Pacific and twenty miles away, airy and unsubstantial like the fabric of a poet's fancy, the unimaginable beauty of the island which is called Murea. It was all so lovely that Bateman stood abashed.

'I've never seen anything like it,' he said at last.

Arnold Jackson stood staring in front of him, and in his eyes was a dreamy softness. His thin, thoughtful face was very grave. Bateman, glancing at it, was once more conscious of its intense spirituality.

'Beauty,' murmured Arnold Jackson. 'You seldom see beauty face to face. Look at it well, Mr Hunter, for what you see now you will never see again, since the moment is transitory, but it will be an imperishable memory in your heart. You touch eternity.'

His voice was deep and resonant. He seemed to breathe forth the purest idealism, and Bateman had to urge himself to remember that the man who spoke was a criminal and a cruel cheat. But Edward, as though he heard a sound, turned round quickly.

'Here is my daughter, Mr Hunter.'

Bateman shook hands with her. She had dark, splendid eyes and a red mouth tremulous with laughter; but her skin was brown, and her curling hair, rippling down her shoulders, was coal-black. She wore but one garment, a Mother Hubbard of pink cotton, her feet were bare, and she was crowned with a wreath of white scented flowers. She was a lovely creature. She was like a goddess of the Polynesian spring.

She was a little shy, but not more shy than Bateman, to whom the whole situation was highly embarrassing, and it did not put him at ease to see this sylph-like thing take a shaker and with a practised hand mix three cocktails.

'Let us have a kick in them, child,' said Jackson.

She poured them out and smiling delightfully handed one to each of the men. Bateman flattered himself on his skill in the subtle art of shaking cocktails and he was not a little astonished, on tasting this one, to find that it was excellent. Jackson laughed proudly when he saw his guest's involuntary look of appreciation.

'Not bad, is it? I taught the child myself, and in the old days in Chicago I considered that there wasn't a bar-tender in the city that could hold a candle to me. When I had nothing better to do in the penitentiary I used to amuse myself by thinking out new cocktails, but when you come down to brass tacks there's nothing to beat a dry Martini.'

Bateman felt as though someone had given him a violent blow on the funny-bone and he was conscious that he turned red and then white. But before he could think of anything to say a native boy brought in a great bowl of soup and the whole party sat down to dinner. Arnold Jackson's remark seemed to have aroused in him a train of recollections, for he began to talk of his prison days. He talked quite naturally, without malice, as though he were relating his experiences at a foreign university. He addressed himself to Bateman and Bateman was confused and then confounded. He saw Edward's eyes fixed on him and there was in them a flicker of amusement. He blushed scarlet, for it struck him that Jackson was making a fool of him, and then because he felt absurd—and knew there was no reason why he should—he grew angry. Arnold Jackson was impudent—there was no other word for it—and his callousness, whether assumed or not, was outrageous. The dinner proceeded. Bateman was asked to eat sundry messes, raw fish and he knew not what, which only his civility induced him to swallow, but which he was amazed to find very good eating. Then an incident happened which to Bateman was the most mortifying experience of the evening. There was a little circlet of flowers in front of him, and for the sake of conversation he hazarded a remark about it.

'It's a wreath that Eva made for you,' said Jackson, 'but I guess she was too shy to give it to you.'

Bateman took it up in his hand and made a polite little speech of thanks to the girl.

'You must put it on,' she said, with a smile and a blush.

'I? I don't think I'll do that.'

'It's the charming custom of the country,' said Arnold Jackson.

There was one in front of him and he placed it on his hair. Edward did the same.

'I guess I'm not dressed for the part,' said Bateman, uneasily.

'Would you like a pareo?' said Eva quickly. 'I'll get you one in a minute.'

'No, thank you. I'm quite comfortable as I am.'

'Show him how to put it on, Eva,' said Edward.

At that moment Bateman hated his greatest friend. Eva got up from the table and with much laughter placed the wreath on his black hair.

'It suits you very well,' said Mrs Jackson. 'Don't it suit him, Arnold?'

'Of course it does.'

Bateman sweated at every pore.

'Isn't it a pity it's dark?' said Eva. 'We could photograph you all three together.'

Bateman thanked his stars it was. He felt that he must look prodigiously foolish in his blue serge suit and high collar—very neat and gentlemanly—with that ridiculous wreath of flowers on his head. He was seething with indignation, and he had never in his life exercised more self-control than now when he presented an affable exterior. He was furious with that old man, sitting at the head of the table, half-naked, with his saintly face and the flowers on his handsome white locks. The whole position was monstrous.

Then dinner came to an end, and Eva and her mother remained to clear away while the three men sat on the veranda. It was very warm and the air was scented with the white flowers of the night. The full moon, sailing across an unclouded sky, made a pathway on the broad sea that led to the boundless realms of Forever. Arnold Jackson began to talk. His voice was rich and musical. He talked now of the natives and of the old legends of the country. He told strange stories of the past, stories of hazardous expeditions into the unknown, of love and death, of hatred and revenge. He told of the adventurers who had discovered those distant islands, of the sailors who, settling in them, had married the daughters of great chieftains, and of the beach-combers who had led their varied lives on those silvery shores. Bateman, mortified and exasperated, at first listened sullenly, but presently some magic in the words possessed him and he sat entranced. The mirage of romance obscured the light of common day. Had he forgotten that Arnold Jackson had a tongue of silver, a tongue by which he had charmed vast sums out of the credulous public, a tongue which very nearly enabled him to escape the penalty of his crimes? No one had a sweeter eloquence, and no one had a more acute sense of climax. Suddenly he rose.

'Well, you two boys haven't seen one another for a long time. I shall leave you to have a yarn. Teddie will show you your quarters when you want to go to bed.'

'Oh, but I wasn't thinking of spending the night, Mr Jackson,' said Bateman.

'You'll find it more comfortable. We'll see that you're called in good time.'

Then with a courteous shake of the hand, stately as though he were a bishop in canonicals, Arnold Jackson took leave of his guest.

'Of course I'll drive you back to Papeete if you like,' said Edward, 'but I advise you to stay. It's bully driving in the early morning.'

For a few minutes neither of them spoke. Bateman wondered how he should begin on the conversation which all the events of the day made him think more urgent.

'When are you coming back to Chicago?' he asked, suddenly.

For a moment Edward did not answer. Then he turned rather lazily to look at his friend and smiled.

'I don't know. Perhaps never.'

'What in heaven's name do you mean?' cried Bateman.

'I'm very happy here. Wouldn't it be folly to make a change?'

'Man alive, you can't live here all your life. This is no life for a man. It's a living death. Oh, Edward, come away at once, before it's too late. I've felt that something was wrong. You're infatuated with the place, you've succumbed to evil influences, but it only requires a wrench, and when you're free from these surroundings you'll thank all the gods there be. You'll be like a dope-fiend when he's broken from his drug. You'll see then that for two years you've been breathing poisoned air. You can't imagine what a relief it will be when you fill your lungs once more with the fresh pure air of your native country.'

He spoke quickly, the words tumbling over one another in his excitement, and there was in his voice sincere and affectionate emotion. Edward was touched.

'It is good of you to care so much, old friend.'

'Come with me tomorrow, Edward. It was a mistake that you ever came to this place. This is no life for you.'

'You talk of this sort of life and that. How do you think a man gets the best out of life?'

'Why, I should have thought there could be no two answers to that. By doing his duty, by hard work, by meeting all the obligations of his state and station.'

'And what is his reward?'

'His reward is the consciousness of having achieved what he set out to do.'

'It all sounds a little portentous to me,' said Edward, and in the lightness of the night Bateman could see that he was smiling. 'I'm afraid you'll think I've degenerated sadly. There are several things I think now which I daresay would have seemed outrageous to me three years ago.'

'Have you learnt them from Arnold Jackson?' asked Bateman, scornfully.

'You don't like him? Perhaps you couldn't be expected to. I didn't when I first came. I had just the same prejudice as you. He's a very extraordinary man. You saw for yourself that he makes no secret of the fact that he was in a penitentiary. I do not know that he regrets it or the crimes that led him there. The only complaint he ever made in my hearing was that when he came out his health was impaired. I think he does not know what remorse is. He is completely unmoral. He accepts everything and he accepts himself as well. He's generous and kind.'

'He always was,' interrupted Bateman, 'on other people's money.'

'I've found him a very good friend. Is it unnatural that I should take a man as I find him?'

'The result is that you lose the distinction between right and wrong.'

'No, they remain just as clearly divided in my mind as before, but what has become a little confused in me is the distinction between the bad man and the good one. Is Arnold Jackson a bad man who does good things or a good man who does bad things? It's a difficult question to answer. Perhaps we make too much of the difference between one man and another. Perhaps even the best of us are sinners and the worst of us are saints. Who knows?'

'You will never persuade me that white is black and that black is white,' said Bateman.

'I'm sure I shan't, Bateman.'

Bateman could not understand why the flicker of a smile crossed Edward's lips when he thus agreed with him. Edward was silent for a minute.

'When I saw you this morning, Bateman,' he said then, 'I seemed to see myself as I was two years ago. The same collar, and the same shoes, the same blue suit, the same energy. The same determination. By God, I was energetic. The sleepy methods of this place made my blood tingle. I went about and everywhere I saw possibilities for development and enterprise. There were fortunes to be made here. It seemed to me absurd that the copra should be taken away from here in sacks and the oil extracted in America. It would be far more economical to do all that on the spot, with cheap labour, and save freight, and I saw already the vast factories springing up on the island. Then the way they extracted it from the coconut seemed to me hopelessly inadequate and I invented a machine which divided the nut and scooped out the meat at the rate of two hundred and forty an hour. The harbour was not large enough. I made plans to enlarge it, then to form a syndicate to buy land, put up two or three large hotels, and bungalows for occasional residents; I had a scheme for improving the steamer service in order to attract visitors from California. In twenty years, instead of this half-French, lazy little town of Papeete I saw a great American city with ten-storey buildings and street-cars, a theatre and an opera house, a stock exchange and a mayor.'

'But go ahead, Edward,' cried Bateman, springing up from the chair in excitement. 'You've got the ideas and the capacity. Why, you'll become the richest man between Australia and the States.'

Edward chuckled softly.

'But I don't want to,' he said.

'Do you mean to say you don't want money, big money, money running into millions? Do you know what you can do with it? Do you know the power it brings? And if you don't care about it for yourself think what you can do, opening new channels for human enterprise, giving occupation to thousands. My brain reels at the visions your words have conjured up.'

'Sit down, then, my dear Bateman,' laughed Edward. 'My machine for cutting the coconuts will always remain unused, and so far as I'm concerned street-cars shall never run in the idle streets of Papeete.'

Bateman sank heavily into his chair.

'I don't understand you,' he said.

'It came upon me little by little. I came to like the life here, with its ease and its leisure, and the people, with their good nature and their happy smiling faces. I began to think. I'd never had time to do that before. I began to read.'

'You always read.'

'I read for examinations. I read in order to be able to hold my own in conversation. I read for instruction. Here I learned to read for pleasure. I learned to talk. Do you know that conversation is one of the greatest pleasures in life? But it wants leisure. I'd always been too busy before. And gradually all the life that had seemed so important to me began to seem rather trivial and vulgar. What is the use of all this hustle and this constant striving? I think of Chicago now and I see a dark, grey city, all stone—it is like a prison—and a ceaseless turmoil. And what does all that activity amount to? Does one get there the best out of life? Is that what we come into the world for, to hurry to an office, and work hour after hour till night, then hurry home and dine and go to a theatre? Is that how I must spend my youth? Youth lasts so short a time, Bateman. And when I am old, what have I to look forward to? To hurry from my home in the morning to my office and work hour after hour till night, and then hurry home again, and dine and go to a theatre? That may be worth while if you make a fortune; I don't know, it depends on your nature; but if you don't, is it worth while then? I want to make more out of my life than that, Bateman.'

'What do you value in life then?'

'I'm afraid you'll laugh at me. Beauty, truth, and goodness.'

'Don't you think you can have those in Chicago?'

'Some men can, perhaps, but not I.' Edward sprang up now. 'I tell you when I think of the life I led in the old days I am filled with horror,' he cried violently. 'I tremble with fear when I think of the danger I have escaped. I never knew I had a soul till I found it here. If I had remained a rich man I might have lost it for good and all.'

'I don't know how you can say that,' cried Bateman indignantly. 'We often used to have discussions about it.'

'Yes, I know. They were about as effectual as the discussions of deaf mutes about harmony. I shall never come back to Chicago, Bateman.'

'And what about Isabel?'

Edward walked to the edge of the veranda and leaning over looked intently at the blue magic of the night. There was a slight smile on his face when he turned back to Bateman.

'Isabel is infinitely too good for me. I admire her more than any woman I have ever known. She has a wonderful brain and she's as good as she's beautiful. I respect her energy and her ambition. She was born to make a success of life. I am entirely unworthy of her.'

'She doesn't think so.'

'But you must tell her so, Bateman.'

'I?' cried Bateman. 'I'm the last person who could ever do that.'

Edward had his back to the vivid light of the moon and his face could not be seen. Is it possible that he smiled again?

'It's no good your trying to conceal anything from her, Bateman. With her quick intelligence she'll turn you inside out in five minutes. You'd better make a clean breast of it right away.'

'I don't know what you mean. Of course I shall tell her I've seen you.' Bateman spoke in some agitation. 'Honestly I don't know what to say to her.'

'Tell her that I haven't made good. Tell her that I'm not only poor, but that I'm content to be poor. Tell her I was fired from my job because I was idle and inattentive. Tell her all you've seen tonight and all I've told you.'

The idea which on a sudden flashed through Bateman's brain brought him to his feet and in uncontrollable perturbation he faced Edward.

'Man alive, don't you want to marry her?'

Edward looked at him gravely.

'I can never ask her to release me. If she wishes to hold me to my word I will do my best to make her a good and loving husband.'

'Do you wish me to give her that message, Edward? Oh, I can't. It's terrible. It's never dawned on her for a moment that you don't want to marry her. She loves you. How can I inflict such a mortification on her?'

Edward smiled again.

'Why don't you marry her yourself, Bateman? You've been in love with her for ages. You're perfectly suited to one another. You'll make her very happy.'

'Don't talk to me like that. I can't bear it.'

'I resign in your favour, Bateman. You are the better man.'

There was something in Edward's tone that made Bateman look up quickly, but Edward's eyes were grave and unsmiling. Bateman did not know what to say. He was disconcerted. He wondered whether Edward could possibly suspect that he had come to Tahiti on a special errand. And though he knew it was horrible he could not prevent the exultation in his heart.

'What will you do if Isabel writes and puts an end to her engagement with you?' he said, slowly.

'Survive,' said Edward.

Bateman was so agitated that he did not hear the answer.

'I wish you had ordinary clothes on,' he said, somewhat irritably. 'It's such a tremendously serious decision you're taking. That fantastic costume of yours makes it seem terribly casual.'

'I assure you, I can be just as solemn in a pareo and a wreath of roses, as in a high hat and a cut-away coat.'

Then another thought struck Bateman.

'Edward, it's not for my sake you're doing this? I don't know, but perhaps this is going to make a tremendous difference to my future. You're not sacrificing yourself for me? I couldn't stand for that, you know.'

'No, Bateman, I have learnt not to be silly and sentimental here. I should like you and Isabel to be happy, but I have not the least wish to be unhappy myself.'

The answer somewhat chilled Bateman. It seemed to him a little cynical. He would not have been sorry to act a noble part.

'Do you mean to say you're content to waste your life here? It's nothing less than suicide. When I think of the great hopes you had when we left college it seems terrible that you should be content to be no more than a salesman in a cheap-John store.'

'Oh, I'm only doing that for the present, and I'm gaining a great deal of valuable experience. I have another plan in my head. Arnold Jackson has a small island in the Paumotas, about a thousand miles from here, a ring of land round a lagoon. He's planted coconut there. He's offered to give it me.'

'Why should he do that?' asked Bateman.

'Because if Isabel releases me I shall marry his daughter.'

'You?' Bateman was thunderstruck. 'You can't marry a half-caste. You wouldn't be so crazy as that.'

'She's a good girl, and she has a sweet and gentle nature. I think she would make me very happy.'

'Are you in love with her?'

'I don't know,' answered Edward reflectively. 'I'm not in love with her as I was in love with Isabel. I worshipped Isabel. I thought she was the most wonderful creature I had ever seen. I was not half good enough for her. I don't feel like that with Eva. She's like a beautiful exotic flower that must be sheltered from bitter winds. I want to protect her. No one ever thought of protecting Isabel. I think she loves me for myself and not for what I may become. Whatever happens to me I shall never disappoint her. She suits me.'

Bateman was silent.

'We must turn out early in the morning,' said Edward at last. 'It's really about time we went to bed.'

Then Bateman spoke and his voice had in it a genuine distress.

'I'm so bewildered, I don't know what to say. I came here because I thought something was wrong. I thought you hadn't succeeded in what you set out to do and were ashamed to come back when you'd failed. I never guessed I should be faced with this. I'm so desperately sorry, Edward. I'm so disappointed. I hoped you would do great things. It's almost more than I can bear to think of you wasting your talents and your youth and your chance in this lamentable way.'

'Don't be grieved, old friend,' said Edward. 'I haven't failed. I've succeeded. You can't think with what zest I look forward to life, how full it seems to me and how significant. Sometimes, when you are married to Isabel, you will think of me. I shall build myself a house on my coral island and I shall live there, looking after my trees—getting the fruit out of the nuts in the same old way that they have done for unnumbered years—I shall grow all sorts of things in my garden, and I shall fish. There will be enough work to keep me busy and not enough to make me dull. I shall have my books and Eva, children, I hope, and above all, the infinite variety of the sea and the sky, the freshness of the dawn and the beauty of the sunset, and the rich magnificence of the night. I shall make a garden out of what so short a while ago was a wilderness. I shall have created something. The years will pass insensibly, and when I am an old man I hope I shall be able to look back on a happy, simple, peaceful life. In my small way I too shall have lived in beauty. Do you think it is so little to have enjoyed contentment? We know that it will profit a man little if he gain the whole world and lose his soul. I think I have won mine.'

Edward led him to a room in which there were two beds and he threw himself on one of them. In ten minutes Bateman knew by his regular breathing, peaceful as a child's, that Edward was asleep. But for his part he had no rest, he was disturbed in mind, and it was not till the dawn crept into the room, ghostlike and silent, that he fell asleep.

Bateman finished telling Isabel his long story. He had hidden nothing from her except what he thought would wound her or what made himself ridiculous. He did not tell her that he had been forced to sit at dinner with a wreath of flowers round his head and he did not tell her that Edward was prepared to marry her uncle's half-caste daughter the moment she set him free. But perhaps Isabel had keener intuitions than he knew, for as he went on with his tale her eyes grew colder and her lips closed upon one another more tightly. Now and then she looked at him closely, and if he had been less intent on his narrative he might have wondered at her expression.

'What was this girl like?' she asked when he finished. 'Uncle Arnold's daughter. Would you say there was any resemblance between her and me?'

Bateman was surprised at the question.

'It never struck me. You know I've never had eyes for anyone but you and I could never think that anyone was like you. Who could resemble you?'

'Was she pretty?' said Isabel, smiling slightly at his words.

'I suppose so. I daresay some men would say she was very beautiful.'

'Well, it's of no consequence. I don't think we need give her any more of our attention.'

'What are you going to do, Isabel?' he asked then.

Isabel looked down at the hand which still bore the ring Edward had given her on their betrothal.

'I wouldn't let Edward break our engagement because I thought it would be an incentive to him. I wanted to be an inspiration to him. I thought if anything could enable him to achieve success it was the thought that I loved him. I have done all I could. It's hopeless. It would only be weakness on my part not to recognize the facts. Poor Edward, he's nobody's enemy but his own. He was a dear, nice fellow, but there was something lacking in him, I suppose it was backbone. I hope he'll be happy.'

She slipped the ring off her finger and placed it on the table. Bateman watched her with a heart beating so rapidly that he could hardly breathe.

'You're wonderful, Isabel, you're simply wonderful.'

She smiled, and, standing up, held out her hand to him.

'How can I ever thank you for what you've done for me?' she said. 'You have done me a great service. I knew I could trust you.'

He took her hand and held it. She had never looked more beautiful.

'Oh, Isabel, I would do so much more for you than that. You know that I only ask to be allowed to love and serve you.'

'You're so strong, Bateman,' she sighed. 'It gives me such a delicious feeling of confidence.'

'Isabel, I adore you.'

He hardly knew how the inspiration had come to him, but suddenly he clasped her in his arms; she, all unresisting, smiled into his eyes.

'Isabel, you know I wanted to marry you the very first day I saw you,' he cried passionately.

'Then why on earth didn't you ask me?' she replied.

She loved him. He could hardly believe it was true. She gave him her lovely lips to kiss. And as he held her in his arms he had a vision of the works of the Hunter Motor Traction and Automobile Company growing in size and importance till they covered a hundred acres, and of the millions of motors they would turn out, and of the great collection of pictures he would form which should beat anything they had in New York. He would wear horn spectacles.

And she, with the delicious pressure of his arms about her, sighed with happiness, for she thought of the exquisite house she would have, full of antique furniture, and of the concerts she would give, and of the *thés dansants*, and the dinners to which only the most cultured people would come.

'Poor Edward,' she sighed.

Honolulu

◆

The wise traveller travels only in imagination. An old Frenchman (he was really a Savoyard) once wrote a book called *Voyage autour de ma Chambre*. I have not read it and do not even know what it is about, but the title stimulates my fancy. In such a journey I could circumnavigate the globe. An eikon by the chimneypiece can take me to Russia with its great forests of birch and its white, domed churches. The Volga is wide, and at the end of a straggling village, in the wine-shop, bearded men in rough sheepskin coats sit drinking. I stand on the little hill from which Napoleon first saw Moscow and I look upon the vastness of the city. I will go down and see the people whom I know more intimately than so many of my friends, Alyosha, and Vronsky, and a dozen more. But my eyes fall on a piece of porcelain and I smell the acrid odours of China. I am borne in a chair along a narrow causeway between the padi fields, or else I skirt a tree-clad mountain. My bearers chat gaily as they trudge along in the bright morning and every now and then, distant and mysterious, I hear the deep sound of a monastery bell. In the streets of Peking there is a motley crowd and it scatters to allow passage to a string of camels, stepping delicately, that bring skins and strange drugs from the stony deserts of Mongolia. In England, in London, there are certain afternoons in winter when the clouds hang heavy and low and the light is so bleak that your heart sinks, but then you can look out of your window, and you see the coconut trees crowded upon the beach of a coral island. The strand is silvery and when you walk along in the sunshine it is so dazzling that you can hardly bear to look at it. Overhead the mynah birds are making a great to-do, and the surf beats ceaselessly against the reef. Those are the best journeys, the journeys that you take at your own fireside, for then you lose none of your illusions.

But there are people who take salt in their coffee. They say it gives it a tang, a savour, which is peculiar and fascinating. In the same way there are certain places, surrounded by a halo of romance, to which the inevitable disillusionment which you must experience on seeing them gives a singular spice. You had expected something wholly beautiful and you get an impression which is infintely more complicated than any that beauty can give you. It is like the weakness in the character of a great man which may make him less admirable but certainly makes him more interesting.

Nothing had prepared me for Honolulu. It is so far away from Europe, it is reached after so long a journey from San Francisco, so strange and so charming associations are attached to the name, that at first I could hardly believe my eyes. I do not know that I had formed in my mind any very exact picture of what I expected, but what I found caused me a great surprise. It is a typical western city. Shacks are cheek by jowl with stone mansions: dilapidated frame houses stand next door to smart stores with plate-glass windows; electric cars rumble noisily along the streets; and motors, Fords, Buicks, Packards, line the pavement. The shops are filled with all the necessities of American civilization. Every third house is a bank and every fifth the agency of a steamship company.

Along the streets crowd an unimaginable assortment of people. The Americans, ignoring the climate, wear black coats and high, starched collars, straw hats, soft hats, and bowlers. The Kanakas, pale brown, with crisp hair, have nothing on but a shirt and a pair of trousers; but the half-breeds are very smart with flaring ties and patent-leather boots. The Japanese, with their obsequious smile, are neat and trim in white duck, while their women walk a step or two behind them, in native dress, with a baby on their backs. The Japanese children, in bright coloured frocks, their little heads shaven, look like quaint dolls. Then there are the Chinese. The men, fat and prosperous, wear their American clothes oddly, but the women are enchanting with their tightly-dressed black hair, so neat that you feel it can never be disarranged, and they are very clean in their tunics and trousers, white, or powder-blue, or black. Lastly there are the Filipinos, the men in huge straw hats, the women in bright yellow muslin with great puffed sleeves.

It is the meeting-place of East and West. The very new rubs shoulders with the immeasurably old. And if you have not found the romance you expected you have come upon something singularly intriguing. All these strange people live close to each other, with different languages and different thoughts; they believe in different gods and they have different values; two passions alone they share, love and hunger. And somehow as you watch them you have an impression of extraordinary vitality. Though the air is so soft and the sky so blue, you have, I know not why, a feeling of something hotly passionate that beats like a throbbing pulse through the crowd. Though the native policeman at the corner, standing on a platform, with a white club to direct the traffic, gives the scene an air of respectability, you cannot but feel that it is a respectability only of the surface; a little below there is darkness and mystery. It gives you just that thrill, with a little catch at the heart, that you have when at night in the forest the silence trembles on a sudden with the low, insistent beating of a drum. You are all expectant of I know not what.

If I have dwelt on the incongruity of Honolulu, it is because just this, to my mind, gives its point to the story I want to tell. It is a story of primitive superstition, and it startles me that anything of the sort should survive in a civilization which, if not very distinguished, is certainly very elaborate. I cannot get over the fact that such incredible things should happen, or at least be thought to happen, right in the middle, so to speak, of telephones, tramcars, and daily papers. And the friend who showed me Honolulu had the same incongruity which I felt from the beginning was its most striking characteristic.

He was an American named Winter and I had brought a letter of introduction to him from an acquaintance in New York. He was a man between forty and fifty, with scanty black hair, grey at the temples, and a sharp-featured, thin face. His eyes had a twinkle in them and his large horn spectacles gave him a demureness which was not a little diverting. He was tall rather than otherwise and very spare. He was born in Honolulu and his father had a large store which sold hosiery and all such goods, from tennis racquets to tarpaulins, as a man of fashion could require. It was a prosperous business and I could well understand the indignation of Winter *père* when his son, refusing to go into it, had announced his determination to be an actor. My friend spent twenty years on the stage, sometimes in New York, but more often on the road, for his gifts were small; but at last, being no fool, he came to the conclusion that it was better to sell sock-suspenders in Honolulu than to play small parts in Cleveland, Ohio. He left the stage and went into the business. I think after the hazardous existence he had lived so long, he thoroughly enjoyed the luxury of driving a large car and living in a beautiful house near the golf-course, and I am quite sure, since he was a man of parts. he managed the business competently. But he could not bring himself entirely to break his connexion with the arts and since he might no longer act he began to paint. He took me to his studio and showed me his work. It was not at all bad, but not what I should have expected from him. He painted nothing but still life, very small pictures, perhaps eight by ten; and he painted very delicately, with the utmost finish. He had evidently a passion for detail. His fruit pieces reminded you of the fruit in a picture by Ghirlandajo. While you marvelled a little at his patience, you could not help being impressed by his dexterity. I imagine that he failed as an actor because his effects, carefully studied, were neither bold nor broad enough to get across the footlights.

I was entertained by the proprietary, yet ironical air with which he showed me the city. He thought in his heart that there was none in the United States to equal it, but he saw quite clearly that his attitude was comic. He drove me round to the various buildings and swelled with satisfaction when I expressed a proper admiration for their architecture. He showed me the houses of rich men. 'That's the Stubbses' house,' he said. 'It cost a hundred thousand dollars to build. The Stubbses are one of our best families. Old man Stubbs came here as a missionary more than seventy years ago.'

He hesitated a little and looked at me with twinkling eyes through his big round spectacles.

'All our best families are missionary families,' he said. 'You're not very much in Honolulu unless your father or your grandfather converted the heathen.'

'Is that so?'

'Do you know your Bible?'

'Fairly,' I answered.

'There is a text which says: The fathers have eaten sour grapes and the children's teeth are set on edge. I guess it runs differently in Honolulu. The fathers brought Christianity to the Kanaka and the children jumped his land.'

'Heaven helps those who help themselves,' I murmured.

'It surely does. By the time the natives of this island had embraced Christianity they had nothing else they could afford to embrace. The kings gave the missionaries land as a mark of esteem, and the missionaries bought land by way of laying up treasure in heaven. It surely was a good investment. One missionary left the business – I think one may call it a business without offence – and became a land agent, but that is an exception. Mostly it was their sons who looked after the commercial side of the concern. Oh, it's a fine thing to have a father who came here fifty years ago to spread the faith.'

But he looked at his watch.

'Gee, it's stopped. That means it's time to have a cocktail.'

We sped along an excellent road, bordered with red hibiscus, and came back into the town.

'Have you been to the Union Saloon?'

'Not yet.'

'We'll go there.'

I knew it was the most famous spot in Honolulu and I entered it with a lively curiosity. You get to it by a narrow passage from King Street, and in the passage are offices, so that thirsty souls may be supposed bound for one of these just as well as for the saloon. It is a large square room, with three entrances, and opposite the bar, which runs the length of it, two corners have been partitioned off into little cubicles. Legend states that they were built so that King Kalakaua might drink there without being seen by his subjects, and it is pleasant to think that in one or other of these he may have sat over his bottle, a coal-black potentate, with Robert Louis Stevenson. There is a portrait of him, in oils, in a rich gold frame; but there are also two prints of Queen Victoria. On the walls, besides, are old line engravings of the eighteenth century, one of which, and heaven knows how it got there, is after a theatrical picture by De Wilde; and there are oleographs from the Christmas supplements of the *Graphic* and the *Illustrated London News* of twenty years ago. Then there are advertisements of whisky, gin, champagne, and beer; and photographs of baseball teams and of native orchestras.

The place seemed to belong not to the modern, hustling world that I had left in the bright street outside, but to one that was dying. It had the savour of the day before yesterday. Dingy and dimly lit, it had a vaguely mysterious air and you could imagine that it would be a fit scene for shady transactions. It suggested a more lurid time, when ruthless men carried their lives in their hands, and violent deeds diapered the monotony of life.

When I went in, the saloon was fairly full. A group of business men stood together at the bar, discussing affairs, and in a corner two Kanakas were drinking. Two or three men who might have been store-keepers were shaking dice. The rest of the company plainly followed the sea; they were captains of tramps, first mates, and engineers. Behind the bar, busily making the Honolulu cocktail for which the place was famous, served two large half-castes, in white, fat, clean-shaven and dark-skinned, with thick, curly hair and large bright eyes.

Winter seemed to know more than half the company, and when we made our way to the bar a little fat man in spectacles, who was standing by himself, offered him a drink.

'No, you have one with me, Captain,' said Winter.

He turned to me.

'I want you to know Captain Butler.'

The little man shook hands with me. We began to talk, but, my attention distracted by my surroundings, took small notice of him, and after we had each ordered a cocktail we separated. When we had got into the motor again and were driving away, Winter said to me:

'I'm glad we ran up against Butler. I wanted you to meet him. What did you think of him?'

'I don't know that I thought very much of him at all,' I answered.

'Do you believe in the supernatural?'

'I don't exactly know that I do,' I smiled.

'A very queer thing happened to him a year or two ago. You ought to have him tell you about it.'

'What sort of thing?'

Winter did not answer my question.

'I have no explanation of it myself,' he said. 'But there's no doubt about the facts. Are you interested in things like that?'

'Things like what?'

'Spells and magic and all that.'

'I've never met anyone who wasn't.'

Winter paused for a moment.

'I guess I won't tell you myself. You ought to hear it from his own lips so that you can judge. How are you fixed up for tonight?'

'I've got nothing on at all.'

'Well, I'll get hold of him between now and then and see if we can't go down to his ship.'

Winter told me something about him. Captain Butler had spent all his life on the Pacific. He had been in much better circumstances than he was now, for he had been first officer and then captain of a passenger-boat plying along the coast of California, but he had lost his ship and a number of passengers had been drowned.

'Drink, I guess,' said Winter.

Of course there had been an inquiry, which had cost him his certificate, and then he drifted further afield. For some years he had knocked about the South Seas, but he was now in command of a small schooner which sailed between Honolulu and the various islands of the group. It belonged to a Chinese to whom the fact that his skipper had no certificate meant only that he could be had for lower wages, and to have a white man in charge was always an advantage.

And now that I had heard this about him I took the trouble to remember more exactly what he was like. I recalled his round spectacles and the round blue eyes behind them, and so gradually reconstructed him before my mind. He was a little man, without angles, plump, with a round face like the full moon and a little fat round nose. He had fair short hair, and he was red-faced and clean-shaven. He had plump hands, dimpled on the knuckles, and short fat legs. He was a jolly soul, and the tragic experience he had gone through seemed to have left him unscarred. Though he must have been thirty-four or thirty-five he looked much younger. But after all I had given him but a superficial attention, and now that I knew of this catastrophe, which had obviously ruined his life, I promised myself that when I saw him again I would take more careful note of him. It is very curious to observe the differences of emotional response that you find in different people. Some can go through terrible battles, the fear of imminent death and unimaginable horrors, and preserve their soul unscathed, while with others the trembling of the moon on a solitary sea or the song of a bird in a thicket will cause a convulsion great enough to transform their entire being. Is it due to strength or weakness, want of imagination or instability of character? I do not know. When I called up in my fancy that scene of shipwreck, with the shrieks of the drowning and the terror, and then later, the ordeal of the inquiry, the bitter grief of those who sorrowed for the lost, and the harsh things he must have read of himself in the papers, the shame and the disgrace, it came to me with a shock to remember that Captain Butler had talked with the frank obscenity of a schoolboy of the Hawaiian girls and of Iwelei, the Red Light district, and of his successful adventures. He laughed readily, and one would have thought he could never laugh again. I remembered his shining, white teeth; they were his best feature. He began to interest me, and thinking of him and of his gay insouciance I forgot the particular story, to hear which I was to see him again. I wanted to see him rather to find out if I could a little more what sort of man he was.

Winter made the necessary arrangements and after dinner we went down to the water front. The ship's boat was waiting for us and we rowed out. The schooner was anchored some way across the harbour, not far from the breakwater. We came alongside, and I heard the sound of a ukulele. We clambered up the ladder.

'I guess he's in the cabin,' said Winter, leading the way.

It was a small cabin, bedraggled and dirty, with a table against one side and a broad bench all round upon which slept, I supposed, such passengers as were ill-advised enough to travel in such a ship. A petroleum lamp gave a dim light. The ukulele was being played by a native girl and Butler was lolling on the seat, half lying, with his head on her shoulder and an arm round her waist.

'Don't let us disturb you, Captain,' said Winter, facetiously.

'Come right in,' said Butler, getting up and shaking hands with us. 'What'll you have?'

It was a warm night, and through the open door you saw countless stars in a heaven that was still almost blue. Captain Butler wore a sleeveless undershirt, showing his fat white arms, and a pair of incredibly dirty trousers. His feet were bare, but on his curly head he wore a very old, a very shapeless felt hat.

'Let me introduce you to my girl. Ain't she a peach?'

We shook hands with a very pretty person. She was a good deal taller than the captain, and even the Mother Hubbard, which the missionaries of a past generation had, in the interests of decency, forced on the unwilling natives, could not conceal the beauty of her form. One could not but suspect that age would burden her with a certain corpulence, but now she was graceful and alert. Her brown skin had an exquisite translucency and her eyes were magnificent. Her black hair, very thick and rich, was coiled round her head in a massive plait. When she smiled in a greeting that was charmingly natural, she showed teeth that were small, even, and white. She was certainly a most attractive creature. It was easy to see that the captain was madly in love with her. He could not take his eyes off her; he wanted to touch her all the time. That was very easy to understand; but what seemed to me stranger was that the girl was apparently in love with him. There was a light in her eyes that was unmistakable, and her lips were slightly parted as though in a sigh of desire. It was thrilling. It was even a little moving, and I could not help feeling somewhat in the way. What had a stranger to do with this lovesick pair? I wished that Winter had not brought me. And it seemed to me that the dingy cabin was transfigured and now it seemed a fit and proper scene for such an extremity of passion. I thought I should never forget that schooner in the harbour of Honolulu, crowded with shipping, and yet, under the immensity of the starry sky, remote from all the world. I liked to think of those lovers sailing off together in the night over the empty spaces of the Pacific from one green, hilly island to another. A faint breeze of romance softly fanned my cheek.

And yet Butler was the last man in the world with whom you would have associated romance, and it was hard to see what there was in him to arouse love. In the clothes he wore now he looked podgier than ever, and his round spectacles gave his round face the look of a prim cherub. He suggested rather a curate who had gone to the dogs. His conversation was peppered with the quaintest Americanisms, and it is because I despair of reproducing these that, at whatever loss of vividness, I mean to narrate the story he told me a little later in my own words. Moreover he was unable to frame a sentence without an oath, though a good-natured one, and his speech, albeit offensive only to prudish ears, in print would seem coarse. He was a mirth-loving man, and perhaps that accounted not a little for his successful amours; since women, for the most part frivolous creatures, are excessively bored by the seriousness with which men treat them, and they can seldom resist the buffoon who makes them laugh. Their sense of humour is crude, Diana of Ephesus is always prepared to fling prudence to the winds for the red-nosed comedian who sits on his hat. I realized that Captain Butler had charm. If I had not known the tragic story of the shipwreck I should have thought he had never had a care in his life.

Our host had rung the bell on our entrance and now a Chinese cook came in with more glasses and several bottles of soda. The whisky and the captain's empty glass stood already on the table. But when I saw the Chinese I positively started, for he was certainly the ugliest man I had ever seen. He was very short, but thick-set, and he had a bad limp. He wore a singlet and a pair of trousers that had been white, but were now filthy, and, perched on a shock of bristly, grey hair, an old tweed deer-stalker. It would have been grotesque on any Chinese, but on him it was outrageous. His broad, square face was very flat as though it had been bashed in by a mighty fist, and it was deeply pitted with smallpox; but the most revolting thing in him was a very pronounced harelip which had never been operated on, so that his upper lip, cleft, went up in an angle to his nose, and in the opening was a huge yellow fang. It was horrible. He came in with the end of a cigarette at the corner of his mouth and this, I do not know why, gave him a devilish expression.

He poured out the whisky and opened a bottle of soda.

'Don't drown it, John,' said the captain.

He said nothing, but handed a glass to each of us. Then he went out.

'I saw you lookin' at my Chink,' said Butler, with a grin on his fat, shining face.

'I should hate to meet him on a dark night,' I said.

'He sure is homely,' said the captain, and for some reason he seemed to say it with a peculiar satisfaction. 'But he's fine for one thing, I'll tell the world; you just have to have a drink every time you look at him.'

But my eyes fell on a calabash that hung against the wall over the table, and I got up to look at it. I had been hunting for an old one and this was better than any I had seen outside the museum.

'It was given me by a chief over on one of the islands,' said the captain, watching me. 'I done him a good turn and he wanted to give me something good.'

'He certainly did,' I answered.

I was wondering whether I could discreetly make Captain Butler an offer for it, I could not imagine that he set any store on such an article, when, as though he read my thoughts, he said:

'I wouldn't sell that for ten thousand dollars.'

'I guess not,' said Winter. 'It would be a crime to sell it.'

'Why?' I asked.

'That comes into the story,' returned Winter. 'Doesn't it, Captain?'

'It surely does.'

'Let's hear it then.'

'The night's young yet,' he answered.

The night distinctly lost its youth before he satisfied my curiosity, and meanwhile we drank a great deal too much whisky while Captain Butler narrated his experiences of San Francisco in the old days and of the South Seas. At last the girl fell asleep. She lay curled up on the seat, with her face on her brown arm, and her bosom rose and fell gently with her breathing. In sleep she looked sullen, but darkly beautiful.

He had found her on one of the islands in the group among which, whenever there was cargo to be got, he wandered with his crazy old schooner. The Kanakas have little love for work, and the laborious Chinese, the cunning Japs, have taken the trade out of their hands. Her father had a strip of land on which he grew taro and bananas and he had a boat in which he went fishing. He was vaguely related to the mate of the schooner, and it was he who took Captain Butler up to the shabby little frame house to spend an idle evening. They took a bottle of whisky with them and the ukulele. The captain was not a shy man and when he saw a pretty girl he made love to her. He could speak the native language fluently and it was not long before he had overcome the girl's timidity. They spent the evening singing and dancing, and by the end of it she was sitting by his side and he had his arm round her waist. It happened that they were delayed on the island for several days and the captain, at no time a man to hurry, made no effort to shorten his stay. He was very comfortable in the snug little harbour and life was long. He had a swim round his ship in the morning and another in the evening. There was a chandler's shop on the water front where sailormen could get a drink of whisky, and he spent the best part of the day there, playing cribbage with the half-caste who owned it. At night the mate and he went up to the house where the pretty girl lived and they sang a song or two and told stories. It was the girl's father who suggested that he should take her away with him. They discussed the matter in a friendly fashion, while the girl, nestling against the captain, urged him by the pressure of her hands and her soft smiling glances. He had taken a fancy to her and he was a domestic man. He was a little dull sometimes at sea and it would be very pleasant to have a pretty little creature like that about the old ship. He was of a practical turn too, and he recognized that it would be useful to have someone around to darn his socks and look after his linen. He was tired of having his things washed by a Chink who tore everything to pieces; the natives washed much better, and now and then when the captain went ashore at Honolulu he liked to cut a dash in a smart duck suit. It was only a matter of arranging a price. The father wanted two hundred and fifty dollars, and the captain, never a thrifty man, could not put his hand on such a sum. But he was a generous one, and with the girl's soft face against his, he was not inclined to haggle. He offered to give a hundred and fifty dollars there and then and another hundred in three months. There was a good deal of argument and the parties could not come to any agreement that night, but the idea had fired the captain, and he could not sleep as well as usual. He kept dreaming of the lovely girl and each time he awoke it was with the pressure of her soft, sensual lips on his. He cursed himself in the morning, because a bad night at poker the last time he was at Honolulu had left him so short of ready money. And if the night before he had been in love with the girl, this morning he was crazy about her.

'See here, Bananas,' he said to the mate, 'I've got to have that girl. You go and tell the old man I'll bring the dough up tonight and she can get fixed up. I figure we'll be ready to sail at dawn.'

I have no idea why the mate was known by that eccentric name. He was called Wheeler, but though he had that English surname there was not a drop of white blood in him. He was a tall man, and well-made though inclined to stoutness, but much darker than is usual in Hawaii. He was no longer young, and his crisply curling, thick hair was grey. His upper front teeth were cased in gold. He was very proud of them. He had a marked squint and this gave him a saturnine expression. The captain, who was fond of a joke, found in it a constant source of humour and hesitated the less to rally him on the defect because he realized that the mate was sensitive about it. Bananas, unlike most of the natives, was a taciturn fellow and Captain Butler would have disliked him if it had been possible for a man of his good nature to dislike anyone. He liked to be at sea with someone he could talk to, he was a chatty, sociable creature, and it was enough to drive a missionary to drink to live there day after day with a chap who never opened his mouth. He did his best to wake the mate up, that is to say, he chaffed him without mercy, but it was poor fun to laugh by oneself, and he came to the conclusion that, drunk or sober, Bananas was no fit companion for a white man. But he was a good seaman and the captain was shrewd enough to know the value of a mate he could trust. It was not rare for him to come aboard, when they were sailing, fit for nothing but to fall into his bunk, and it was worth something to know that he could stay there till he had slept his liquor off, since Bananas could be relied on. But he was an unsociable devil, and it would be a treat to have someone he could talk to. That girl would be fine. Besides, he wouldn't be so likely to get drunk when he went ashore if he knew there was a little girl waiting for him when he came on board again.

He went to his friend the chandler and over a peg of gin asked him for a loan. There were one or two useful things a ship's captain could do for a ship's chandler, and after a quarter of an hour's conversation in low tones (there is no object in letting all and sundry know your business), the captain crammed a wad of notes in his hip-pocket, and that night, when he went back to his ship the girl went with him.

What Captain Butler, seeking for reasons to do what he had already made up his mind to, had anticipated, actually came to pass. He did not give up drinking, but he ceased to drink to excess. An evening with the boys, when he had been away from town two or three weeks, was pleasant enough, but it was pleasant too to get back to his little girl; he thought of her, sleeping so softly, and how, when he got into his cabin and leaned over her, she would open her eyes lazily and stretch out her arms for him: it was as good as a full hand. He found he was saving money, and since he was a generous man he did the right thing by the little girl: he gave her some silver-backed brushes for her long hair, and a gold chain, and a reconstructed ruby for her finger. Gee, but it was good to be alive.

A year went by, a whole year, and he was not tired of her yet. He was not a man who analysed his feelings, but this was so surprising that it forced itself upon his attention. There must be something very wonderful about that girl.

He couldn't help seeing that he was more wrapped up in her than ever, and sometimes the thought entered his mind that it might not be a bad thing if he married her.

Then, one day the mate did not come in to dinner or to tea. Butler did not bother himself about his absence at the first meal, but at the second he asked the Chinese cook:

'Where's the mate? He no come tea?'

'No wantchee,' said the Chink.

'He ain't sick?'

'No savvy.'

Next day Bananas turned up again, but he was more sullen than ever, and after dinner the captain asked the girl what was the matter with him. She smiled and shrugged her pretty shoulders. She told the captain that Bananas had taken a fancy to her and he was sore because she had told him off. The captain was a good-humoured man and he was not of a jealous nature; it struck him as exceeding funny that Bananas should be in love. A man who had a squint like that had a precious poor chance. When tea came round he chaffed him gaily. He pretended to speak in the air, so that the mate should not be certain that he knew anything, but he dealt him some pretty shrewd blows. The girl did not think him as funny as he thought himself, and afterwards she begged him to say nothing more. He was surprised at her seriousness. She told him he did not know her people. When their passion was aroused they were capable of anything. She was a little frightened. This was so absurd to him that he laughed heartily.

'If he comes bothering round you, you just threaten to tell me. That'll fix him.'

'Better fire him, I think.'

'Not on your sweet life. I know a good sailor when I see one. But if he don't leave you alone I'll give him the worst licking he's ever had.'

Perhaps the girl had a wisdom unusual in her sex. She knew that it was useless to argue with a man when his mind was made up, for it only increased his stubbornness, and she held her peace. And now on the shabby schooner, threading her way across the silent sea, among those lovely islands, was enacted a dark, tense drama of which the fat little captain remained entirely ignorant. The girl's resistance fired Bananas so that he ceased to be a man, but was simply blind desire. He did not make love to her gently or gaily, but with a black and savage ferocity. Her contempt now was changed to hatred and when he besought her she answered him with bitter, angry taunts. But the struggle went on silently, and when the captain asked her after a little while whether Bananas was bothering her, she lied.

But one night, when they were in Honolulu, he came on board only just in time. They were sailing at dawn. Bananas had been ashore, drinking some native spirit, and he was drunk. The captain, rowing up, heard sounds that surprised him. He scrambled up the ladder. He saw Bananas, beside himself, trying to wrench open the cabin door. He was shouting at the girl. He swore he would kill her if she did not let him in.

'What in hell are you up to?' cried Butler.

The mate let go the handle, gave the captain a look of savage hate, and without a word turned away.

'Stop here. What are you doing with that door?'

The mate still did not answer. He looked at him with sullen, bootless rage.

'I'll teach you not to pull any of your queer stuff with me, you dirty, cross-eyed nigger,' said the captain.

He was a good foot shorter than the mate and no match for him, but he was used to dealing with native crews, and he had his knuckle-duster handy. Perhaps it was not an instrument that a gentleman would use, but then Captain Butler was not a gentleman. Nor was he in the habit of dealing with gentlemen. Before Bananas knew what the captain was at, his right arm had shot out and his fist, with its ring of steel, caught him fair and square on the jaw. He fell like a bull under the pole-axe.

'That'll learn him,' said the captain.

Bananas did not stir. The girl unlocked the cabin door and came out.

'Is he dead?'

'He ain't.'

He called a couple of men and told them to carry the mate to his bunk. He rubbed his hands with satisfaction and his round blue eyes gleamed behind his spectacles. But the girl was strangely silent. She put her arms round him as though to protect him from invisible harm.

It was two or three days before Bananas was on his feet again, and when he came out of his cabin his face was torn and swollen. Through the darkness of his skin you saw the livid bruise. Butler saw him slinking along the deck and called him. The mate went to him without a word.

'See here, Bananas,' he said to him, fixing his spectacles on his slippery nose, for it was very hot. 'I ain't going to fire you for this, but you know now that when I hit, I hit hard. Don't forget it and don't let me have any more funny business.'

Then he held out his hand and gave the mate that good-humoured, flashing smile of his which was his greatest charm. The mate took the outstretched hand and twitched his swollen lips into a devilish grin. The incident in the captain's mind was so completely finished that when the three of them sat at dinner he chaffed Bananas on his appearance. He was eating with difficulty and, his swollen face still more distorted by pain, he looked truly a repulsive object.

That evening, when he was sitting on the upper deck, smoking his pipe, a shiver passed through the captain.

'I don't know what I should be shiverin' for on a night like this,' he grumbled. 'Maybe I've gotten a dose of fever. I've been feelin' a bit queer all day.'

When he went to bed he took some quinine, and next morning he felt better, but a little washed out, as though he were recovering from a debauch.

'I guess my liver's out of order,' he said, and he took a pill.

He had not much appetite that day and towards evening he began to feel very unwell. He tried the next remedy he knew, which was to drink two or three hot whiskies, but that did not seem to help him much, and when in the morning he surveyed himself in the glass he thought he was not looking quite the thing.

'If I ain't right by the time we get back to Honolulu I'll just give Dr Denby a call. He'll sure fix me up.'

He could not eat. He felt a great lassitude in all his limbs. He slept soundly enough, but he awoke with no sense of refreshment; on the contrary he felt a peculiar exhaustion. And the energetic little man, who could not bear the thought of lying in bed, had to make an effort to force himself out of his bunk. After a few days he found it impossible to resist the languor that oppressed him, and he made up his mind not to get up.

'Bananas can look after the ship,' he said. 'He has before now.'

He laughed a little to himself as he thought how often he had lain speechless in his bunk after a night with the boys. That was before he had his girl. He smiled at her and pressed her hand. She was puzzled and anxious. He saw that she was concerned about him and tried to reassure her. He had never had a day's illness in his life and in a week at the outside he would be as right as rain.

'I wish you'd fired Bananas,' she said. 'I've got a feeling that he's at the bottom of this.'

'Damned good thing I didn't, or there'd be no one to sail the ship. I know a good sailor when I see one.' His blue eyes, rather pale now, with the whites all yellow, twinkled. 'You don't think he's trying to poison me, little girl?'

She did not answer, but she had one or two talks with the Chinese cook, and she took great care with the captain's food. But he ate little enough now, and it was only with the greatest difficulty that she persuaded him to drink a cup of soup two or three times a day. It was clear that he was very ill, he was losing weight quickly, and his chubby face was pale and drawn. He suffered no pain, but merely grew every day weaker and more languid. He was wasting away. The round trip on this occasion lasted about four weeks and by the time they came to Honolulu the captain was a little anxious about himself. He had not been out of his bed for more than a fortnight and really he felt too weak to get up and go to the doctor. He sent a message asking him to come on board. The doctor examined him, but could find nothing to account for his condition. His temperature was normal.

'See here, Captain,' he said, 'I'll be perfectly frank with you. I don't know what's the matter with you, and just seeing you like this don't give me a chance. You come into the hospital so that we can keep you under observation. There's nothing organically wrong with you, I know that, and my impression is that a few weeks in hospital ought to put you to rights.'

'I ain't going to leave my ship.'

Chinese owners were queer customers, he said; if he left his ship because he was sick, his owner might fire him, and he couldn't afford to lose his job. So long as he stayed where he was his contract safeguarded him, and he had a first-rate mate. Besides, he couldn't leave his girl. No man could want a better nurse; if anyone could pull him through she would. Every man had to die once and he only wished to be left in peace. He would not listen to the doctor's expostulations, and finally the doctor gave in.

'I'll write you a prescription,' he said doubtfully, 'and see if it does you any good. You'd better stay in bed for a while.'

'There ain't much fear of my getting up, doc,' answered the captain. 'I feel as weak as a cat.'

But he believed in the doctor's prescription as little as did the doctor himself, and when he was alone amused himself by lighting his cigar with it. He had to get amusement out of something, for his cigar tasted like nothing on earth, and he smoked only to persuade himself that he was not too ill to. That evening a couple of friends of his, masters of tramp steamers, hearing he was sick came to see him. They discussed his case over a bottle of whisky and a box of Philippine cigars. One of them remembered how a mate of his had been taken queer just like that and not a doctor in the United States had been able to cure him. He had seen in the paper an advertisement of a patent medicine, and thought there'd be no harm in trying it. That man was as strong as ever he'd been in his life after two bottles. But his illness had given Captain Butler a lucidity which was new and strange, and while they talked he seemed to read their minds. They thought he was dying. And when they left him he was afraid.

The girl saw his weakness. This was her opportunity. She had been urging him to let a native doctor see him, and he had stoutly refused; but now she entreated him. He listened with harassed eyes. He wavered. It was very funny that the American doctor could not tell what was the matter with him. But he did not want her to think that he was scared. If he let a damned nigger come along and look at him, it was to comfort *her*. He told her to do what she liked.

The native doctor came the next night. The captain was lying alone, half awake, and the cabin was dimly lit by an oil lamp. The door was softly opened and the girl came in on tip-toe. She held the door open and someone slipped in silently behind her. The captain smiled at this mystery, but he was so weak now, the smile was no more than a glimmer in his eyes. The doctor was a little, old man, very thin and very wrinkled, with a completely bald head, and the face of a monkey. He was bowed and gnarled like an old tree. He looked hardly human, but his eyes were very bright, and in the half darkness they seemed to glow with a reddish light. He was dressed filthily in a pair of ragged dungarees, and the upper part of his body was naked. He sat down on his haunches and for ten minutes looked at the captain. Then he felt the palms of his hands and the soles of his feet. The girl watched him with frightened eyes. No word was spoken. Then he asked for something that the captain had worn. The girl gave him the old felt hat which the captain used constantly and taking it he sat down again on the floor, clasping it firmly with both hands; and rocking backwards and forwards slowly he muttered some gibberish in a very low tone.

At last he gave a little sigh and dropped the hat. He took an old pipe out of his trouser pocket and lit it. The girl went over to him and sat by his side. He whispered something to her, and she started violently. For a few minutes they talked in hurried undertones, and then they stood up. She gave him money and opened the door for him. He slid out as silently as he had come in. Then went over to the captain and leaned over him so that she could speak into his ear.

'It's an enemy praying you to death.'

'Don't talk fool stuff, girlie,' he said impatiently.

'It's truth. It's God's truth. That's why the American doctor couldn't do anything. Our people can do that. I've seen it done. I thought you were safe because you were a white man.'

'I haven't an enemy.'

'Bananas.'

'What's he want to pray me to death for?'

'You ought to have fired him before he had a chance.'

'I guess if I ain't got nothing more the matter with me than Bananas' hoodoo I shall be sitting up and taking nourishment in a very few days.'

She was silent for a while and she looked at him intently.

'Don't you know you're dying?' she said to him at last.

That was what the two skippers had thought, but they hadn't said it. A shiver passed across the captain's wan face.

'The doctor says there ain't nothing really the matter with me. I've only to lie quiet for a bit and I shall be all right.'

She put her lips to his ear as if she were afraid that the air itself might hear.

'You're dying, dying, dying. You'll pass out with the old moon.'

'That's something to know.'

'You'll pass out with the old moon unless Bananas dies before.'

He was not a timid man and he had recovered already from the shock her words, and still more her vehement, silent manner, had given him. Once more a smile flickered in his eyes.

'I guess I'll take my chance, girlie.'

'There's twelve days before the new moon.'

There was something in her tone that gave him an idea.

'See here, my girl, this is all bunk. I don't believe a word of it. But I don't want you to try any of your monkey tricks with Bananas. He ain't a beauty, but he's a first-rate mate.'

He would have said a good deal more, but he was tired out. He suddenly felt very weak and faint. It was always at that hour that he felt worse. He closed his eyes. The girl watched him for a minute and then slipped out of the cabin. The moon, nearly full, made a silver pathway over the dark sea. It shone from an unclouded sky. She looked at it with terror, for she knew that with its death the man she loved would die. His life was in her hands. She could save him, she alone could save him, but the enemy was cunning, and she must be cunning too. She felt that someone was looking at her, and without turning, by the sudden fear that seized her, knew that from the shadow the burning eyes of the mate were fixed upon her. She did not know what he could do; if he could read her thoughts she was defeated already, and with a desperate effort she emptied her mind of all content. His death alone could save her lover, and she could bring his death about. She knew that if he could be brought to look into a calabash in which was water so that a reflection of him was made, and the reflection were broken by hurtling the water, he would die as though he had been struck by lightning; for the reflection was his soul. But none knew better than he the danger, and he could be made to look only by a guile which had lulled his least suspicion. He must never think that he had an enemy who was on the watch to cause his destruction. She knew what she had to do. But the time was short, the time was terribly short. Presently she realized that the mate had gone. She breathed more freely.

Two days later they sailed, and there were ten now before the new moon. Captain Butler was terrible to see. He was nothing but skin and bone, and he could not move without help. He could hardly speak. But she dared do nothing yet. She knew that she must be patient. The mate was cunning, cunning. They went to one of the smaller islands of the group and discharged cargo, and now there were only seven days more. The moment had come to start. She brought some things out of the cabin she shared with the captain and made them into a bundle. She put the bundle in the deck cabin where she and Bananas ate their meals, and at dinner time, when she went in, he turned quickly and she saw that he had been looking at it. Neither of them spoke, but she knew what he suspected. She was making her preparations to leave the ship. He looked at her mockingly. Gradually, as though to prevent the captain from knowing what she was about, she brought everything she owned into the cabin, and some of the captain's clothes, and made them all into bundles. At last Bananas could keep silence no longer. He pointed to a suit of ducks.

'What are you going to do with that?' he asked.

She shrugged her shoulders.

'I'm going back to my island.'

He gave a laugh that distorted his grim face. The captain was dying and she meant to get away with all she could lay hands on.

'What'll you do if I say you can't take those things? They're the captain's.'
'They're no use to you,' she said.

There was a calabash hanging on the wall. It was the very calabash I had seen when I came into the cabin and which we had talked about. She took it down. It was all dusty, so she poured water into it from the water-bottle, and rinsed it with her fingers.

'What are you doing with that?'
'I can sell it for fifty dollars,' she said.
'If you want to take it you'll have to pay me.'
'What d'you want?'
'You know what I want.'

She allowed a fleeting smile to play on her lips. She flashed a quick look at him and quickly turned away. He gave a gasp of desire. She raised her shoulders in a little shrug. With a savage bound he sprang upon her and seized her in his arms. Then she laughed. She put her arms, her soft, round arms, about his neck, and surrendered herself to him voluptuously.

When the morning came she roused him out of a deep sleep. The early rays of the sun slanted into the cabin. He pressed her to his heart. Then he told her that the captain could not last more than a day or two, and the owner wouldn't so easily find another white man to command the ship. If Bananas offered to take less money he would get the job and the girl could stay with him. He looked at her with love-sick eyes. She nestled up against him. She kissed his lips, in the foreign way, in the way the captain had taught her to kiss. And she promised to stay. Bananas was drunk with happiness.

It was now or never.

She got up and went to the table to arrange her hair. There was no mirror and she looked into the calabash, seeking for her reflection. She tidied her beautiful hair. Then she beckoned to Bananas to come to her. She pointed to the calabash.

'There's something in the bottom of it,' she said.

Instinctively, without suspecting anything, Bananas looked full into the water. His face was reflected in it. In a flash she beat upon it violently, with both her hands, so that they pounded on the bottom and the water splashed up. The reflection was broken in pieces. Bananas started back with a sudden hoarse cry and he looked at the girl. She was standing there with a look of triumphant hatred on her face. A horror came into his eyes. His heavy features were twisted in agony, and with a thud, as though he had taken a violent poison, he crumpled up on the ground. A great shudder passed through his body and he was still. She leaned over him callously. She put her hand on his heart and then she pulled down his lower eye-lid. He was quite dead.

She went into the cabin in which lay Captain Butler. There was a faint colour in his cheeks and he looked at her in a startled way.

'What's happened?' he whispered.

They were the first words he had spoken for forty-eight hours.

'Nothing's happened,' she said.

'I feel all funny.'

Then his eyes closed and he fell asleep. He slept for a day and a night, and when he awoke he asked for food. In a fortnight he was well.

It was past midnight when Winter and I rowed back to shore and we had drunk innumerable whiskies and sodas.

'What do you think of it all?' asked Winter.

'What a question! If you mean, have I any explanation to suggest, I haven't.'

'The captain believes every word of it.'

'That's obvious; but, you know, that's not the part that interests me most: whether it's true or not, and what it all means; the part that interests me is that such things should happen to such people. I wonder what there is in that common-place little man to arouse such a passion in that lovely creature. As I watched her, asleep there, while he was telling the story I had some fantastic idea about the power of love being able to work miracles.'

'But that's not the girl,' said Winter.

'What on earth do you mean?'

'Didn't you notice the cook?'

'Of course I did. He's the ugliest man I ever saw.'

'That's why Butler took him. The girl ran away with the Chinese cook last year. This is a new one. He's only had her there about two months.'

'Well, I'm hanged.'

'He thinks this cook is safe. But I wouldn't be too sure in his place. There's something about a Chink, when he lays himself out to please a woman she can't resist him.'

The Ant and the Grasshopper

◆

When I was a very small boy I was made to learn by heart certain of the fables of La Fontaine, and the moral of each was carefully explained to me. Among those I learnt was *The Ant and The Grasshopper*, which is devised to bring home to the young the useful lesson that in an imperfect world industry is rewarded and giddiness punished. In this admirable fable (I apologize for telling something which everyone is politely, but inexactly, supposed to know) the ant spends a laborious summer gathering its winter store, while the grasshopper sits on a blade of grass singing to the sun. Winter comes and the ant is comfortably provided for, but the grasshopper has an empty larder: he goes to the ant and begs for a little food. Then the ant gives him her classic answer:

'What were you doing in the summer time?'

'Saving your presence, I sang, I sang all day, all night.'

'You sang. Why, then go and dance.'

I do not ascribe it to perversity on my part, but rather to the inconsequence of childhood, which is deficient in moral sense, that I could never quite reconcile myself to the lesson. My sympathies were with the grasshopper and for some time I never saw an ant without putting my foot on it. In this summary (and as I have discovered since, entirely human) fashion I sought to express my disapproval of prudence and common sense.

I could not help thinking of this fable when the other day I saw George Ramsay lunching by himself in a restaurant. I never saw anyone wear an expression of such deep gloom. He was staring into space. He looked as though the burden of the whole world sat on his shoulders. I was sorry for him: I suspected at once that his unfortunate brother had been causing trouble again. I went up to him and held out my hand.

'How are you?' I asked.

'I'm not in hilarious spirits,' he answered.

'Is it Tom again?'

He sighed.

'Yes, it's Tom again.'

'Why don't you chuck him? You've done everything in the world for him. You must know by now that he's quite hopeless.'

I suppose every family has a black sheep. Tom had been a sore trial to his for twenty years. He had begun life decently enough: he went into business, married, and had two children. The Ramsays were perfectly respectable people and there was every reason to suppose that Tom Ramsay would have a useful and honourable career. But one day, without warning, he announced that he didn't like work and that he wasn't suited for marriage. He wanted to enjoy himself. He would listen to no expostulations. He left his wife and his office. He had a little money and he spent two happy years in the various capitals of Europe. Rumours of his doings reached his relations from time to time and they were profoundly shocked. He certainly had a very good time. They shook their heads and asked what would happen when his money was spent. They soon found out: he borrowed. He was charming and unscrupulous. I have never met anyone to whom it was more difficult to refuse a loan. He made a steady income from his friends and he made friends easily. But he always said that the money you spent on necessities was boring; the money that was amusing to spend was the money you spent on luxuries. For this he depended on his brother George. He did not waste his charm on him. George was a serious man and insensible to such enticements. George was respectable. Once or twice he fell to Tom's promises of amendment and gave him considerable sums in order that he might make a fresh start. On these Tom bought a motor-car and some very nice jewellery. But when circumstances forced George to realize that his brother would never settle down and he washed his hands of him, Tom, without a qualm, began to blackmail him. It was not very nice for a respectable lawyer to find his brother shaking cocktails behind the bar of his favourite restaurant or to see him waiting on the box-seat of a taxi outside his club. Tom said that to serve in a bar or to drive a taxi was a perfectly decent occupation, but if George could oblige him with a couple of hundred pounds he didn't mind for the honour of the family giving it up. George paid.

Once Tom nearly went to prison. George was terribly upset. He went into the whole discreditable affair. Really Tom had gone too far. He had been wild, thoughtless, and selfish, but he had never before done anything dishonest, by which George meant illegal; and if he were prosecuted he would assuredly be convicted. But you cannot allow your only brother to go to gaol. The man Tom had cheated, a man called Cronshaw, was vindictive. He was determined to take the matter into court; he said Tom was a scoundrel and should be punished. It cost George an infinite deal of trouble and five hundred pounds to settle the affair. I have never seen him in such a rage as when he heard that Tom and Cronshaw had gone off together to Monte Carlo the moment they cashed the cheque. They spent a happy month there.

For twenty years Tom raced and gambled, philandered with the prettiest girls, danced, ate in the most expensive restaurants, and dressed beautifully. He always looked as if he had just stepped out of a bandbox. Though he was forty-six you would never have taken him for more than thirty-five. He was a most amusing companion and though you knew he was perfectly worthless you could not but enjoy his society. He had high spirits, an unfailing gaiety, and incredible charm. I never grudged the contributions he regularly levied on me for the necessities of his existence. I never lent him fifty pounds without feeling that I was in his debt. Tom Ramsay knew everyone and everyone knew Tom Ramsay. You could not approve of him, but you could not help liking him.

Poor George, only a year older than his scapegrace brother, looked sixty. He had never taken more than a fortnight's holiday in the year for a quarter of a century. He was in his office every morning at nine-thirty and never left it till six. He was honest, industrious, and worthy. He had a good wife, to whom he had never been unfaithful even in thought, and four daughters to whom he was the best of fathers. He made a point of saving a third of his income and his plan was to retire at fifty-five to a little house in the country where he proposed to cultivate his garden and play golf. His life was blameless. He was glad that he was growing old because Tom was growing old too. He rubbed his hands and said:

'It was all very well when Tom was young and good-looking, but he's only a year younger than I am. In four years he'll be fifty. He won't find life so easy then. I shall have thirty thousand pounds by the time I'm fifty. For twenty-five years I've said that Tom would end in the gutter. And we shall see how he likes that. We shall see if it really pays best to work or be idle.'

Poor George! I sympathized with him. I wondered now as I sat down beside him what infamous thing Tom had done. George was evidently very much upset.

'Do you know what's happened now?' he asked me.

I was prepared for the worst. I wondered if Tom had got into the hands of the police at last. George could hardly bring himself to speak.

'You're not going to deny that all my life I've been hardworking, decent, respectable, and straightforward. After a life of industry and thrift I can look forward to retiring on a small income in gilt-edged securities. I've always done my duty in that state of life in which it has pleased Providence to place me.'

'True.'

'And you can't deny that Tom has been an idle, worthless, dissolute, and dishonourable rogue. If there were any justice he'd be in the workhouse.'

'True.'

George grew red in the face.

'A few weeks ago he became engaged to a woman old enough to be his mother. And now she's died and left him everything she had. Half a million pounds, a yacht, a house in London, and a house in the country.'

George Ramsay beat his clenched fist on the table.

'It's not fair, I tell you, it's not fair. Damn it, it's not fair.'

I could not help it. I burst into a shout of laughter as I looked at George's wrathful face, I rolled in my chair, I very nearly fell on the floor. George never forgave me. But Tom often asks me to excellent dinners in his charming house in Mayfair, and if he occasionally borrows a trifle from me, that is merely from force of habit. It is never more than a sovereign.

The Pool

♦

When I was introduced to Lawson by Chaplin, the owner of the Hotel Metropole at Apia, I paid no particular attention to him. We were sitting in the lounge over an early cocktail and I was listening with amusement to the gossip of the island.

Chaplin entertained me. He was by profession a mining engineer and perhaps it was characteristic of him that he had settled in a place where his professional attainments were of no possible value. It was, however, generally reported that he was an extremely clever mining engineer. He was a small man, neither fat nor thin, with black hair, scanty on the crown, turning grey, and a small, untidy moustache; his face, partly from the sun and partly from liquor, was very red. He was but a figurehead, for the hotel, though so grandly named but a frame building of two storeys, was managed by his wife, a tall, gaunt Australian of five-and-forty, with an imposing presence and a determined air. The little man, excitable and often tipsy, was terrified of her, and the stranger soon heard of domestic quarrels in which she used her fist and her foot in order to keep him in subjection. She had been known after a night of drunkenness to confine him for twenty-four hours to his own room, and then he could be seen, afraid to leave his prison, talking somewhat pathetically from his veranda to people in the street below.

He was a character, and his reminiscences of a varied life, whether true or not, made him worth listening to, so that when Lawson strolled in I was inclined to resent the interruption. Although not midday, it was clear that he had had enough to drink, and it was without enthusiasm that I yielded to his persistence and accepted his offer of another cocktail. I knew already that Chaplin's head was weak. The next round which in common politeness I should be forced to order would be enough to make him lively, and then Mrs

Chaplin would give me black looks.

Nor was there anything attractive in Lawson's appearance. He was a little thin man, with a long, sallow face and a narrow, weak chin, a prominent nose, large and bony, and great shaggy black eyebrows. They gave him a peculiar look. His eyes, very large and very dark, were magnificent. He was jolly, but his jollity did not seem to me sincere; it was on the surface, a mask which he wore to deceive the world, and I suspected that it concealed a mean nature. He was plainly anxious to be thought a 'good sport' and he was hail-fellow-well-met; but, I do not know why, I felt that he was cunning and shifty. He talked a great deal in a raucous voice, and he and Chaplin capped one another's stories of beanos which had become legendary, stories of 'wet' nights at the English Club, of shooting expeditions where an incredible amount of whisky had been consumed, and of jaunts to Sydney of which their pride was that they could remember nothing from the time they landed till the time they sailed. A pair of drunken swine. But even in their intoxication, for by now, after four cocktails each, neither was sober, there was a great difference between Chaplin, rough and vulgar, and Lawson: Lawson might be drunk, but he was certainly a gentleman.

At last he got out of his chair, a little unsteadily.

'Well, I'll be getting along home,' he said. 'See you before dinner.'

'Missus all right?' said Chaplin.

'Yes.'

He went out. There was a peculiar note in the monosyllable of his answer which made me look up.

'Good chap,' said Chaplin flatly, as Lawson went out of the door into the sunshine. 'One of the best. Pity he drinks.'

This from Chaplin was an observation not without humour.

'And when he's drunk he wants to fight people.'

'Is he often drunk?'

'Dead drunk, three or four days a week. It's the island done it, and Ethel.'

'Who's Ethel?'

'Ethel's his wife. Married a half-caste. Old Brevald's daughter. Took her away from here. Only thing to do. But she couldn't stand it, and now they're back again. He'll hang himself one of these days, if he don't drink himself to death. Good chap. Nasty when he's drunk.'

Chaplin belched loudly.

'I'll go and put my head under the shower. I oughtn't to have had that last cocktail. It's always the last one that does you in.'

He looked uncertainly at the staircase as he made up his mind to go to the cubby hole in which was the shower, and then with unnatural seriousness got up.

'Pay you to cultivate Lawson,' he said. 'A well-read chap. You'd be surprised when he's sober. Clever too. Worth talking to.'

Chaplin had told me the whole story in these few speeches.

When I came in towards evening from a ride along the seashore Lawson was again in the hotel. He was heavily sunk in one of the cane chairs in the lounge and he looked at me with glassy eyes. It was plain that he had been drinking all the afternoon. He was torpid, and the look on his face was sullen and vindictive. His glance rested on me for a moment, but I could see that he did not recognize me. Two or three other men were sitting there, shaking dice, and they took no notice of him. His condition was evidently too usual to attract attention. I sat down and began to play.

'You're a damned sociable lot,' said Lawson suddenly.

He got out of his chair and waddled with bent knees towards the door. I do not know whether the spectacle was more ridiculous than revolting. When he had gone one of the men sniggered.

'Lawson's fairly soused today,' he said.

'If I couldn't carry my liquor better than that,' said another, 'I'd climb on the waggon and stay there.'

Who would have thought that this wretched object was in his way a romantic figure or that his life had in it those elements of pity and terror which the theorist tells us are necessary to achieve the effect of tragedy?

I did not see him again for two or three days.

I was sitting one evening on the first floor of the hotel on a veranda that overlooked the street when Lawson came up and sank into a chair beside me. He was quite sober. He made a casual remark and then, when I had replied somewhat indifferently, added with a laugh which had in it an apologetic tone:

'I was devilish soused the other day.'

I did not answer. There was really nothing to say. I pulled away at my pipe in the vain hope of keeping the mosquitoes away, and looked at the natives going home from their work. They walked with long steps, slowly, with care and dignity, and the soft patter of their naked feet was strange to hear. Their dark hair, curling or straight, was often white with lime, and then they had a look of extraordinary distinction. They were tall and finely built. Then a gang of Solomon Islanders, indentured labourers, passed by, singing; they were shorter and slighter than the Samoans, coal-black, with great heads of fuzzy hair dyed red. Now and then a white man drove past in his buggy or rode into the hotel yard. In the lagoon two or three schooners reflected their grace in the tranquil water.

'I don't know what there is to do in a place like this except to get soused,' said Lawson at last.

'Don't you like Samoa?' I asked casually, for something to say.

'It's pretty, isn't it?'

The word he chose seemed so inadequate to describe the unimaginable beauty of the island that I smiled, and smiling I turned to look at him. I was startled by the expression in those fine sombre eyes of his, an expression of intolerable anguish; they betrayed a tragic depth of emotion of which I should never have thought him capable. But the expression passed away and he smiled. His smile was simple and a little naïve. It changed his face so that I wavered in my first feeling of aversion from him.

'I was all over the place when I first came out,' he said.

He was silent for a moment.

'I went away for good about three years ago, but I came back.' He hesitated. 'My wife wanted to come back. She was born here, you know.'

'Oh yes.'

He was silent again, and then hazarded a remark about Robert Louis Stevenson. He asked me if I had been up to Vailima. For some reason he was making an effort to be agreeable to me. He began to talk of Stevenson's books, and presently the conversation drifted to London.

'I suppose Covent Garden's still going strong,' he said. 'I think I miss the opera as much as anything here. Have you seen *Tristan and Isolde*?'

He asked me the question as though the answer was really important to him, and when I said, a little casually I daresay, that I had, he seemed pleased. He began to speak of Wagner, not as a musician, but as the plain man who received from him an emotional satisfaction that he could not analyse.

'I suppose Bayreuth was the place to go really,' he said. 'I never had the money, worse luck. But of course one might do worse than Covent Garden, all the lights and the women dressed up to the nines, and the music. The first act of the *Walküre*'s all right, isn't it? And the end of *Tristan.* Golly!'

His eyes were flashing now and his face was lit up so that he hardly seemed the same man. There was a flush on his sallow, thin cheeks, and I forgot that his voice was harsh and unpleasant. There was even a certain charm about him.

'By George, I'd like to be in London tonight. Do you know the Pall Mall restaurant? I used to go there a lot. Piccadilly Circus with the shops all lit up, and the crowd. I think it's stunning to stand there and watch the buses and taxis streaming along as though they'd never stop. And I like the Strand too. What are those lines about God and Charing Cross?'

I was taken aback.

'Thompson's, d'you mean?' I asked.

I quoted them:

> 'But when so sad, thou canst not sadder,
> Cry, and upon thy so sore loss
> Shall shine the traffic of Jacob's ladder
> Pitched between Heaven and Charing Cross.'

He gave a faint sigh.

'I've read *The Hound of Heaven*. It's a bit of all right.'

'It's generally thought so,' I murmured.

'You don't meet anybody here who's read anything. They think it's swank.'

There was a wistful look on his face, and I thought I divined the feeling that made him come to me. I was a link with the world he regretted and a life that he would know no more. Because not so very long before I had been in the London which he loved, he looked upon me with awe and envy. He had not spoken for five minutes perhaps when he broke out with words that startled me by their intensity.

'I'm fed up,' he said. 'I'm fed up.'

'Then why don't you clear out?' I asked.

His face grew sullen.

'My lungs are a bit dicky. I couldn't stand an English winter now.'

At that moment another man joined us on the veranda and Lawson sank into a moody silence.

'It's about time for a dram,' said the newcomer. 'Who'll have a drop of Scotch with me? Lawson?'

Lawson seemed to arise from a distant world. He got up.

'Let's go down to the bar,' he said.

When he left me I remained with a more kindly feeling towards him than I should have expected. He puzzled and interested me. And a few days later I met his wife. I knew they had been married for five or six years, and I was surprised to see that she was still extremely young. When he married her she could not have been more than sixteen. She was adorably pretty. She was no darker than a Spaniard, small and very beautifully made, with tiny hands and feet, and a slight, lithe figure. Her features were lovely; but I think what struck me most was the delicacy of her appearance; the half-castes as a rule have a certain coarseness, they seem a little roughly formed, but she had an exquisite daintiness which took your breath away. There was something extremely civilized about her, so that it surprised you to see her in those surroundings, and you thought of those famous beauties who had set all the world talking at the Court of the Emperor Napoleon III. Though she wore but a muslin frock and a straw hat she wore them with an elegance that suggested the woman of fashion. She must have been ravishing when Lawson first saw her.

He had but lately come out from England to manage the local branch of an English bank, and, reaching Samoa at the beginning of the dry season, he had taken a room at the hotel. He quickly made the acquaintance of all and sundry. The life of the island is pleasant and easy. He enjoyed the long idle talks in the lounge of the hotel and the gay evenings at the English Club when a group of fellows would play pool. He liked Apia straggling along the edge of the lagoon, with its stores and bungalows, and its native village. Then there were week-ends when he would ride over to the house of one planter or another and spend a couple of nights on the hills. He had never before known freedom or leisure. And he was intoxicated by the sunshine. When he rode through the bush his head reeled a little at the beauty that surrounded him. The country was indescribably fertile. In parts the forest was still virgin, a tangle of strange trees, luxuriant undergrowth, and vine; it gave an impression that was mysterious and troubling.

But the spot that entranced him was a pool a mile or two away from Apia to which in the evenings he often went to bathe. There was a little river that bubbled over the rocks in a swift stream, and then, after forming the deep pool, ran on, shallow and crystalline, past a ford made by great stones where the natives came sometimes to bathe or to wash their clothes. The coconut trees, with their frivolous elegance, grew thickly on the banks, all clad with trailing plants, and they were reflected in the green water. It was just such a scene as you might see in Devonshire among the hills and yet with a difference, for it had a tropical richness, a passion, a scented languor which seemed to melt the heart. The water was fresh, but not cold; and it was delicious after the heat of the day. To bathe there refreshed not only the body but the soul.

At the hour when Lawson went, there was not a soul and he lingered for a long time, now floating idly in the water, now drying himself in the evening sun, enjoying the solitude and the friendly silence. He did not regret London then, nor the life that he had abandoned, for life as it was seemed complete and exquisite.

It was here that he first saw Ethel.

Occupied till late by letters which had to be finished for the monthly sailing of the boat next day, he rode down one evening to the pool when the light was almost failing. He tied up his horse and sauntered to the bank. A girl was sitting there. She glanced round as he came and noiselessly slid into the water. She vanished like a naiad startled by the approach of a mortal. He was surprised and amused. He wondered where she had hidden herself. He swam downstream and presently saw her sitting on a rock. She looked at him with uncurious eyes. He called out a greeting in Samoan.

'*Talofa.*'

She answered him, suddenly smiling, and then let herself into the water again. She swam easily and her hair spread out behind her. He watched her cross the pool and climb out on the bank. Like all the natives she bathed in a

Mother Hubbard, and the water had made it cling to her slight body. She wrung out her hair, and as she stood there, unconcerned, she looked more than ever like a wild creature of the water or the woods. He saw now that she was half-caste. He swam towards her and, getting out, addressed her in English.

'You're having a late swim.'

She shook back her hair and then let it spread over her shoulders in luxuriant curls.

'I like it when I'm alone,' she said.

'So do I.'

She laughed with the childlike frankness of the native. She slipped a dry Mother Hubbard over her head and, letting down the wet one, stepped out of it. She wrung it out and was ready to go. She paused a moment irresolutely and then sauntered off. The night fell suddenly.

Lawson went back to the hotel and, describing her to the men who were in the lounge shaking dice for drinks, soon discovered who she was. Her father was a Norwegian called Brevald who was often to be seen in the bar of the Hotel Metropole drinking rum and water. He was a little old man, knotted and gnarled like an ancient tree, who had come out to the islands forty years before as mate of a sailing vessel. He had been a blacksmith, a trader, a planter, and at one time fairly well-to-do; but, ruined by the great hurricane of the nineties, he had now nothing to live on but a small plantation of coconut trees. He had had four native wives and, as he told you with a cracked chuckle, more children than he could count. But some had died and some had gone out into the world, so that now the only one left at home was Ethel.

'She's a peach,' said Nelson, the super-cargo of the *Moana*. 'I've given her the glad eye once or twice, but I guess there's nothing doing.'

'Old Brevald's not that sort of a fool, sonny,' put in another, a man called Miller. 'He wants a son-in-law who's prepared to keep him in comfort for the rest of his life.'

It was distasteful to Lawson that they should speak of the girl in that fashion. He made a remark about the departing mail and so distracted their attention. But next evening he went again to the pool. Ethel was there; and the mystery of the sunset, the deep silence of the water, the lithe grace of the coconut trees, added to her beauty, giving it a profoundity, a magic, which stirred the heart to unknown emotions. For some reason that time he had the whim not to speak to her. She took no notice of him. She did not even glance in his direction. She swam about the green pool. She dived, she rested on the bank, as though she were quite alone: he had a queer feeling that he was invisible. Scraps of poetry, half forgotten, floated across his memory, and vague recollections of the Greece he had negligently studied in his school days. When she had changed her wet clothes for dry ones and sauntered away he found a scarlet hibiscus where she had been. It was a flower that she had worn in her hair when she came to bathe and, having taken it out on getting into the water, had forgotten or not cared to put in again. He took it in his hands and looked at it with a singular emotion. He had an instinct to keep it, but his sentimentality irritated him, and he flung it away. It gave him quite a little pang to see it float down the stream.

He wondered what strangeness it was in her nature that urged her to go down to this hidden pool when there was no likelihood that anyone should be there. The natives of the islands are devoted to the water. They bathe, somewhere or other, every day, once always, and often twice; but they bathe in bands, laughing and joyous, a whole family together; and you often saw a group of girls, dappled by the sun shining through the trees, with the half-castes among them, splashing about the shallows of the stream. It looked as though there were in this pool some secret which attracted Ethel against her will.

Now the night had fallen, mysterious and silent, and he let himself down in the water softly, in order to make no sound, and swam lazily in the warm darkness. The water seemed fragrant still from her slender body. He rode back to the town under the starry sky. He felt at peace with the world.

Now he went every evening to the pool and every evening he saw Ethel. Presently he overcame her timidity. She became playful and friendly. They sat together on the rocks above the pool, where the water ran fast, and they lay side by side on the ledge that overlooked it, watching the gathering dusk envelop it with mystery. It was inevitable that their meetings should become known—in the South Seas everyone seems to know everyone's business—and he was subjected to much rude chaff by the men at the hotel. He smiled and let them talk. It was not even worth while to deny their coarse suggestions. His feelings were absolutely pure. He loved Ethel as a poet might love the moon. He thought of her not as a woman but as something not of this earth. She was the spirit of the pool.

One day at the hotel, passing through the bar, he saw that old Brevald, as ever in his shabby blue overalls, was standing there. Because he was Ethel's father he had a desire to speak to him, so he went in, nodded and, ordering his own drink, casually turned and invited the old man to have one with him. They chatted for a few minutes of local affairs, and Lawson was uneasily conscious that the Norwegian was scrutinizing him with sly blue eyes. His manner was not agreeable. It was sycophantic, and yet behind the cringing air of an old man who had been worsted in his struggle with fate was a shadow of old truculence. Lawson remembered that he had once been captain of a schooner engaged in the slave trade, a blackbirder they call it in the Pacific, and he had a large hernia in the chest which was the result of a wound received in a scrap with Solomon Islanders. The bell rang for luncheon.

'Well, I must be off,' said Lawson.

'Why don't you come along to my place one time?' said Brevald, in his wheezy voice. 'It's not very grand, but you'll be welcome. You know Ethel.'

'I'll come with pleasure.'

'Sunday afternoon's the best time.'

Brevald's bungalow, shabby and bedraggled, stood among the coconut trees of the plantation, a little away from the main road that ran up to Vailima. Immediately around it grew huge plantains. With their tattered leaves they had the tragic beauty of a lovely woman in rags. Everything was slovenly and neglected. Little black pigs, thin and high-backed, rooted about, and chickens clucked noisily as they picked at the refuse scattered here and there. Three or four natives were lounging about the veranda. When Lawson asked for Brevald the old man's cracked voice called out to him, and he found him in the sitting-room smoking an old briar pipe.

'Sit down and make yerself at home,' he said. 'Ethel's just titivating.'

She came in. She wore a blouse and skirt and her hair was done in the European fashion. Although she had not the wild, timid grace of the girl who came down every evening to the pool, she seemed now more usual and consequently more approachable. She shook hands with Lawson. It was the first time he had touched her hand.

'I hope you'll have a cup of tea with us,' she said.

He knew she had been at a mission school, and he was amused, and at the same time touched, by the company manners she was putting on for his benefit. Tea was already set out on the table and in a minute old Brevald's fourth wife brought in the tea-pot. She was a handsome native, no longer very young, and she spoke but a few words of English. She smiled and smiled. Tea was rather a solemn meal, with a great deal of bread and butter and a variety of very sweet cakes, and the conversation was formal. Then a wrinkled old woman came in softly.

'That's Ethel's granny,' said old Brevald, noisily spitting on the floor.

She sat on the edge of a chair, uncomfortably, so that you saw it was unusual for her and she would have been more at ease on the ground, and remained silently staring at Lawson with fixed, shining eyes. In the kitchen behind the bungalow someone began to play the concertina and two or three voices were raised in a hymn. But they sang for the pleasure of the sounds rather than from piety.

When Lawson walked back to the hotel he was strangely happy. He was touched by the higgledy-piggledy way in which those people lived; and in the smiling good-nature of Mrs Brevald, in the little Norwegian's fantastic career, and in the shining mysterious eyes of the old grandmother he found something unusual and fascinating. It was a more natural life than any he had known, it was nearer to the friendly, fertile earth; civilization repelled him at that moment, and by mere contact with these creatures of a more primitive nature he felt a greater freedom.

He saw himself rid of the hotel which already was beginning to irk him, settled in a little bungalow of his own, trim and white, in front of the sea so that he had before his eyes always the multi-coloured variety of the lagoon. He loved the beautiful island. London and England meant nothing to him any more, he was content to spend the rest of his days in that forgotten spot, rich in the best of the world's goods, love and happiness. He made up his mind that whatever the obstacles nothing should prevent him from marrying Ethel.

But there were no obstacles. He was always welcome at the Brevalds' house. The old man was ingratiating and Mrs Brevald smiled without ceasing. He had brief glimpses of natives who seemed somehow to belong to the establishment, and once he found a tall youth in a lava-lava, his body tattooed, his hair white with lime, sitting with Brevald, and was told he was Mrs Brevald's brother's son; but for the most part they kept out of his way. Ethel was delightful with him. The light in her eyes when she saw him filled him with ecstasy. She was charming and naïve. He listened enraptured when she told him of the mission school at which she was educated, and of the sisters. He went with her to the cinema which was given once a fortnight and danced with her at the dance which followed it. They came from all parts of the island for this, since gaieties are few in Upolu; and you saw there all the society of the place, the white ladies keeping a good deal to themselves, the half-castes very elegant in American clothes, the natives, strings of dark girls in white Mother Hubbards and young men in unaccustomed ducks and white shoes. It was all very smart and gay. Ethel was pleased to show her friends the white admirer who did not leave her side. The rumour was soon spread that he meant to marry her and her friends looked at her with envy. It was a great thing for a half-caste to get a white man to marry her, even the less regular relation was better than nothing, but one could never tell what it would lead to; and Lawson's position as manager of the bank made him one of the catches of the island. If he had not been so absorbed in

Ethel he would have noticed that many eyes were fixed on him curiously, and he would have seen the glances of the white ladies and noticed how they put their heads together and gossiped.

Afterwards, when the men who lived at the hotel were having a whisky before turning in, Nelson burst out with:

'Say, they say Lawson's going to marry that girl.'

'He's a damned fool then,' said Miller.

Miller was a German-American who had changed his name from Müller, a big man, fat and bald-headed, with a round, clean-shaven face. He wore large gold-rimmed spectacles, which gave him a benign look, and his ducks were always clean and white. He was a heavy drinker, invariably ready to stay up all night with the 'boys', but he never got drunk; he was jolly and affable, but very shrewd. Nothing interfered with his business; he represented a firm in San Francisco, jobbers of the goods sold in the islands, calico, machinery and what not; and his good-fellowship was part of his stock-in-trade.

'He don't know what he's up against,' said Nelson. 'Someone ought to put him wise.'

'If you'll take my advice you won't interfere in what don't concern you,' said Miller. 'When a man's made up his mind to make a fool of himself, there's nothing like letting him.'

'I'm all for having a good time with the girls out here, but when it comes to marrying them—this child ain't taking any, I'll tell the world.'

Chaplin was there, and now he had his say.

'I've seen a lot of fellows do it, and it's no good.'

'You ought to have a talk with him, Chaplin,' said Nelson. 'You know him better than anyone else does.'

'My advice to Chaplin is to leave it alone,' said Miller.

Even in those days Lawson was not popular and really no one took enough interest in him to bother. Mrs Chaplin talked it over with two or three of the white ladies, but they contented themselves with saying that it was a pity; and when he told her definitely that he was going to be married it seemed too late to do anything.

For a year Lawson was happy. He took a bungalow at the point of the bay round which Apia is built, on the borders of a native village. It nestled charmingly among the coconut trees and faced the passionate blue of the Pacific. Ethel was lovely as she went about the little house, lithe and graceful like some young animal of the woods, and she was gay. They laughed a great deal. They talked nonsense. Sometimes one or two of the men at the hotel would come over and spend the evening, and often on a Sunday they would go for a day to some planter who had married a native; now and then one or other of the half-caste traders who had a store in Apia would give a party and they went to it. The half-castes treated Lawson quite differently now. His marriage had made him one of themselves and they called him Bertie. They put their arms through his and smacked him on the back. He liked to see Ethel at these gatherings. Her eyes shone and she laughed. It did him good to see her radiant happiness. Sometimes Ethel's relations would come to the bungalow, Old Brevald of course, and her mother, but cousins too, vague native women in Mother Hubbards and men and boys in lava-lavas, with their hair dyed red and their bodies elaborately tattooed. He would find them sitting there when he got back from the bank. He laughed indulgently.

'Don't let them eat us out of hearth and home,' he said.

'They're my own family. I can't help doing something for them when they ask me.'

He knew that when a white man marries a native or a half-caste he must expect her relations to look upon him as a gold mine. He took Ethel's face in his hands and kissed her red lips. Perhaps he could not expect her to understand that the salary which had amply sufficed for a bachelor must be managed with some care when it had to support a wife and a house. Then Ethel was delivered of a son.

It was when Lawson first held the child in his arms that a sudden pang shot through his heart. He had not expected it to be so dark. After all it had but a fourth part of native blood, and there was no reason really why it should not look just like an English baby; but, huddled together in his arms, sallow, its head covered already with black hair, with huge black eyes, it might have been a native child. Since his marriage he had been ignored by the white ladies of the colony. When he came across men in whose houses he had been accustomed to dine as a bachelor, they were a little self-conscious with him; and they sought to cover their embarrassment by an exaggerated cordiality.

'Mrs Lawson well?' they would say. 'You're a lucky fellow. Damned pretty girl.'

But if they were with their wives and met him and Ethel they would feel it awkward when their wives gave Ethel a patronizing nod. Lawson had laughed.

'They're as dull as ditchwater, the whole gang of them,' he said. 'It's not going to disturb my night's rest if they don't ask me to their dirty parties.'

But now it irked him a little.

The little dark baby screwed up its face. That was his son. He thought of the half-caste children in Apia. They had an unhealthy look, sallow and pale, and they were odiously precocious. He had seen them on the boat going to school in New Zealand, and a school had to be chosen which took children with native blood in them; they were huddled together, brazen and yet timid, with traits which set them apart strangely from white people. They spoke the native language among themselves. And when they grew up the men accepted smaller salaries because of their native blood; girls might marry a white man, but boys had no chance; they must marry a half-caste like themselves, or a native. Lawson made up his mind passionately that he would take his son away from the humiliation of such a life. At whatever cost he must get back to Europe. And when he went in to see Ethel, frail and lovely in her bed, surrounded by native women, his determination was strengthened. If he took her away among his own people she would belong more completely to him. He loved her so passionately he wanted her to be one soul and one body with him; and he was conscious that here, with those deep roots attaching her to the native life, she would always keep something from him.

He went to work quietly, urged by an obscure instinct of secrecy, and wrote to a cousin who was a partner in a shipping firm in Aberdeen, saying that his health (on account of which like so many more he had come out to the islands) was so much better, there seemed no reason why he should not return to Europe. He asked him to use what influence he could to get him a job, no matter how poorly paid, on Deeside, where the climate was particularly suitable to such as suffered from diseases of the lungs. It takes five or six weeks for letters to get from Aberdeen to Samoa, and several had to be exchanged. He had plenty of time to prepare Ethel. She was as delighted as a child. He was amused to see how she boasted to her friends that she was going to England; it was a step up for her; she would be quite English there; and she was excited at the interest the approaching departure gave her. When at length a cable came offering him a post in a bank in Kincardineshire she was beside herself with joy.

When, their long journey over, they were settled in the little Scots town with its granite houses Lawson realized how much it meant to him to live once more among his own people. He looked back on the three years he had spent in Apia as exile, and returned to the life that seemed the only normal one with a sigh of relief. It was good to play golf once more, and to fish–to fish properly, that was poor fun in the Pacific when you just threw in your line and pulled out one big sluggish fish after another from the crowded sea–and it was good to see a paper every day with that day's news, and to meet men and women of your own sort, people you could talk to; and it was good to eat meat that was not frozen and to drink milk that was not canned. They were thrown upon their own resources much more than in the Pacific, and he was glad to have Ethel exclusively to himself. After two years of marriage he loved her more devotedly than ever, he could hardly bear her out of his sight, and the need in him grew urgent for a more intimate communion between them. But it was strange that after the first excitement of arrival she seemed to take less interest in the new life than he had expected. She did not accustom herself to her surroundings. She was a little lethargic. As the fine autumn darkened into winter she complained of the cold. She lay half the morning in bed and the rest of the day on a sofa, reading novels sometimes, but more often doing nothing. She looked pinched.

'Never mind, darling,' he said. 'You'll get used to it very soon. And wait till the summer comes. It can be almost as hot as in Apia.'

He felt better and stronger than he had done for years.

The carelessness with which she managed her house had not mattered in Samoa, but here it was out of place. When anyone came he did not want the place to look untidy; and, laughing, chaffing Ethel a little, he set about putting things in order. Ethel watched him indolently. She spent long hours playing with her son. She talked to him in the baby language of her own country. To distract her, Lawson bestirred himself to make friends among the neighbours, and now and then they went to little parties where the ladies sang drawing-room ballads and the men beamed in silent good nature. Ethel was shy. She seemed to sit apart. Sometimes Lawson, seized with a sudden anxiety, would ask her if she was happy.

'Yes, I'm quite happy,' she answered.

But her eyes were veiled by some thought he could not guess. She seemed to withdraw into herself so that he was conscious that he knew no more of her than when he had first seen her bathing in the pool. He had an uneasy feeling that she was concealing something from him, and because he adored her it tortured him.

'You don't regret Apia, do you?' he asked her once.

'Oh, no–I think it's very nice here.'

An obscure misgiving drove him to make disparaging remarks about the island and the people there. She smiled and did not answer. Very rarely she received a bundle of letters from Samoa and then she went about for a day or two with a set, pale face.

'Nothing would induce me ever to go back there,' he said once. 'It's no place for a white man.'

But he grew conscious that sometimes, when he was away, Ethel cried. In Apia she had been talkative, chatting volubly about all the little details of their common life, the gossip of the place; but now she gradually became silent, and, though he increased his efforts to amuse her, she remained listless. It seemed to him that her recollections of the old life were drawing her away from him, and he was madly jealous of the island and of the sea, of Brevald, and all the dark-skinned people whom he remembered now with horror. When she spoke of Samoa he was bitter and satirical. One evening late in the spring when the birch trees were bursting into leaf, coming home from a round of golf, he found her not as usual lying on the sofa, but at the window, standing. She had evidently been waiting for his return. She addressed him the moment he came into the room. To his amazement she spoke in Samoan.

'I can't stand it. I can't live here any more. I hate it. I hate it.'

'For God's sake speak in a civilized language,' he said irritably.

She went up to him and clasped her arms around his body awkwardly, with a gesture that had in it something barbaric.

'Let's go away from here. Let's go back to Samoa. If you make me stay here I shall die. I want to go home.'

Her passion broke suddenly and she burst into tears. His anger vanished and he drew her down on his knees. He explained to her that it was impossible for him to throw up his job, which after all meant his bread and butter. His place in Apia was long since filled. He had nothing to go back to there. He tried to put it to her reasonably, the inconveniences of life there, the humiliation to which they must be exposed, and the bitterness it must cause their son.

'Scotland's wonderful for education and that sort of thing. Schools are good and cheap, and he can go to the University at Aberdeen. I'll make a real Scot of him.'

They had called him Andrew. Lawson wanted him to become a doctor. He would marry a white woman.

'I'm not ashamed of being half native,' Ethel said sullenly.

'Of course not, darling. There's nothing to be ashamed of.'

With her soft cheek against his he felt incredibly weak.

'You don't know how much I love you,' he said. 'I'd give anything in the world to be able to tell you what I've got in my heart.'

He sought her lips.

The summer came. The highland valley was green and fragrant and the hills were gay with the heather. One sunny day followed another in that sheltered spot, and the shade of the birch trees was grateful after the glare of the high road. Ethel spoke no more of Samoa and Lawson grew less nervous. He thought that she was resigned to her surroundings, and he felt that his love for her was so passionate that it could leave no room in her heart for any longing. One day the local doctor stopped him in the street.

'I say, Lawson, your missus ought to be careful how she bathes in our highland streams. It's not like the Pacific, you know.'

Lawson was surprised, and had not the presence of mind to conceal the fact.

'I didn't know she was bathing.'

The doctor laughed.

'A good many people have seen her. It makes them talk a bit, you know, because it seems a rum place to choose, the pool up above the bridge, and bathing isn't allowed there, but there's no harm in that. I don't know how she can stand the water.'

Lawson knew the pool the doctor spoke of, and suddenly it occurred to him that in a way it was just like that pool at Upolu where Ethel had been in the habit of bathing every evening. A clear highland stream ran down a sinuous course, rocky, splashing gaily, and then formed a deep, smooth pool, with a little sandy beach. Trees overshadowed it thickly, not coconut trees, but beeches, and the sun played fitfully through the leaves on the sparkling water. It gave him a shock. With his imagination he saw Ethel go there every day and undress on the bank and slip into the water, cold, colder than that of the pool she loved at home, and for a moment regain the feeling of the past. He saw her once more as the strange, wild spirit of the stream, and it seemed to him fantastically that the running water called her. That afternoon he went along to the river. He made his way cautiously among the trees and the grassy path deadened the sound of his steps. Presently he came to a spot from which he could see the pool. Ethel was sitting on the bank, looking down at the water. She sat quite still. It seemed as though the water drew her irresistibly. He wondered what strange thoughts wandered through her head. At last she got up, and for a minute or two she was hidden from his gaze; then he saw her again, wearing a Mother Hubbard, and with her little bare feet she stepped delicately over the mossy bank. She came to the water's edge, and softly, without a splash, let herself down. She swam about quietly, and there was something not quite of a human being in the way she swam. He did not know why it affected him so queerly. He waited till she clambered out. She stood for a moment with the wet folds of her dress clinging to her body, so that its shape was outlined, and then, passing her hands slowly over her breasts, gave a little sigh of delight. Then she disappeared. Lawson turned away and walked back to the village. He had a bitter pain in his heart, for he knew that she was still a stranger to him and his hungry love was destined ever to remain unsatisfied.

He did not make any mention of what he had seen. He ignored the incident completely, but he looked at her curiously, trying to divine what was in her mind. He redoubled the tenderness with which he used her. He sought to make her forget the deep longing of her soul by the passion of his love.

Then one day, when he came home, he was astonished to find her not in the house.

'Where's Mrs Lawson?' he asked the maid.

'She went into Aberdeen, Sir, with the baby,' the maid answered, a little surprised at the question. 'She said she would not be back till the last train.'

'Oh, all right.'

He was vexed that Ethel had said nothing to him about the excursion, but he was not disturbed, since of late she had been in now and again to Aberdeen, and he was glad that she should look at the shops and perhaps visit a cinema. He went to meet the last train, but when she did not come he grew suddenly frightened. He went up to the bedroom and saw at once that her toilet things were no longer in their place. He opened the wardrobe and the drawers. They were half empty. She had bolted.

He was seized with a passion of anger. It was too late that night to telephone to Aberdeen and make inquiries, but he knew already all that his inquiries might have taught him. With fiendish cunning she had chosen a time when they were making up their periodical accounts at the bank and there was no chance that he could follow her. He was imprisoned by his work. He took up a paper and saw that there was a boat sailing for Australia next morning. She must be now well on the way to London. He could not prevent the sobs that were wrung painfully from him.

'I've done everything in the world for her,' he cried, 'and she had the heart to treat me like this. How cruel, how monstrously cruel!'

After two days of misery he received a letter from her. It was written in her school-girl hand. She had always written with difficulty:

Dear Bertie
  I couldn't stand it any more. I'm going home. Good-bye.

                                                                    Ethel

She did not say a single word of regret. She did not even ask him to come too. Lawson was prostrated. He found out where the ship made its first stop, and, though he knew very well she would not come, sent a cable beseeching her to return. He waited with pitiful anxiety. He wanted her to send him just one word of love; she did not even answer. He passed through one violent phase after another. At one moment he told himself that he was well rid of her, and at the next that he would force her to return by withholding money. He was lonely and wretched. He wanted his boy and he wanted her. He knew that, whatever he pretended to himself, there was only one thing to do and that was to follow her. He could never live without her now. All his plans for the future were like a house of cards and he scattered them with angry impatience. He did not care whether he threw away his chances for the future, for nothing in the world mattered but that he should get Ethel back again. As soon as he could he went into Aberdeen and told the manager of his bank that he meant to leave at once. The manager remonstrated. The short notice was inconvenient. Lawson would not listen to reason. He was determined to be free before the next boat sailed; and it was not until he was on board of her, having sold everything he possessed, that in some measure he regained his calm. Till then to those who had come in contact with him he seemed hardly sane. His last action in England was to cable to Ethel at Apia that he was joining her.

He sent another cable from Sydney, and when at last with the dawn his boat crossed the bar at Apia and he saw once more the white houses straggling along the bay he felt an immense relief. The doctor came on board, and the agent. They were both old acquaintances and he felt kindly towards their familiar faces. He had a drink or two with them for old times' sake, and also because he was desperately nervous. He was not sure if Ethel would be glad to see him. When he got into the launch and approached the wharf he scanned anxiously the little crowd that waited. She was not there and his heart sank, but then he saw Brevald, in his old blue clothes, and his heart warmed towards him.

'Where's Ethel?' he said, as he jumped on shore.

'She's down at the bungalow. She's living with us.'

Lawson was dismayed, but he put on a jovial air.

'Well, have you got room for me? I daresay it'll take a week or two to fix ourselves up.'

'Oh, yes, I guess we can make room for you.'

After passing through the custom-house they went to the hotel and there Lawson was greeted by several of his old friends. There were a good many rounds of drinks before it seemed possible to get away and when they did go at last to Brevald's house they were both rather gay. He clasped Ethel in his arms. He had forgotten all his bitter thoughts in the joy of beholding her once more. His mother-in-law was pleased to see him, and so was the old, wrinkled beldame, her mother; natives and half-castes came in, and they all sat round, beaming on him. Brevald had a bottle of whisky and everyone who came was given a nip. Lawson sat with his little dark-skinned boy on his knees, they had taken his English clothes off him and he was stark, with Ethel by his side in a Mother Hubbard. He felt like a returning prodigal. In the afternoon he went down to the hotel again and when he got back he was more than gay, he was drunk. Ethel and her mother knew that white men got drunk now and then, it was what you expected of them, and they laughed good-naturedly as they helped him to bed.

But in a day or two he set about looking for a job. He knew that he could not hope for such a position as that which he had thrown away to go to England; but with his training he could not fail to be useful to one of the trading firms, and perhaps in the end he would not lose by the change.

'After all, you can't make money in a bank,' he said. 'Trade's the thing.'

He had hopes that he would soon make himself so indispensable that he would get someone to take him into partnership, and there was no reason why in a few years he should not be a rich man.

'As soon as I'm fixed up we'll find ourselves a shack,' he told Ethel. 'We can't go on living here.'

Brevald's bungalow was so small that they were all piled on one another, and there was no chance of ever being alone. There was neither peace nor privacy.

'Well, there's no hurry. We shall be all right here till we find just what we want.'

It took him a week to get settled and then he entered the firm of a man called Bain. But when he talked to Ethel about moving she said she wanted to stay where she was till her baby was born, for she was expecting another child. Lawson tried to argue with her.

'If you don't like it,' she said, 'go and live at the hotel.'

He grew suddenly pale.

'Ethel, how can you suggest that!'

She shrugged her shoulders.

'What's the good of having a house of our own when we can live here.'

He yielded.

When Lawson, after his work, went back to the bungalow he found it crowded with natives. They lay about smoking, sleeping, drinking *kava*; and they talked incessantly. The place was grubby and untidy. His child crawled about, playing with native children, and it heard nothing spoken but Samoan. He fell into the habit of dropping into the hotel on his way home to have a few cocktails, for he could only face the evening and the crowd of friendly natives when he was fortified with liquor. And all the time, though he loved her more passionately than ever, he felt that Ethel was slipping away from him. When the baby was born he suggested that they should get into a house of their own, but Ethel refused. Her stay in Scotland seemed to have thrown her back on her own people, now that she was once more among them, with a passionate zest, and she turned to her native ways with abandon. Lawson began to drink more. Every Saturday night he went to the English Club and got blind drunk.

He had the peculiarity that as he grew drunk he grew quarrelsome and once he had a violent dispute with Bain, his employer. Bain dismissed him, and he had to look out for another job. He was idle for two or three weeks and during these, sooner than sit in the bungalow, he lounged about in the hotel or at the English Club, and drank. It was more out of pity than anything else that Miller, the German–American, took him into his office; but he was a businessman, and though Lawson's financial skill made him valuable, the circumstances were such that he could hardly refuse a smaller salary than he had had before, and Miller did not hesitate to offer it to him. Ethel and Brevald blamed him for taking it, since Pedersen, the half-caste, offered him more. But he resented bitterly the thought of being under the orders of a half-caste. When Ethel nagged him he burst out furiously:

'I'll see myself dead before I work for a nigger.'

'You may have to,' she said.

And in six months he found himself forced to this final humiliation. The passion for liquor had been gaining on him, he was often heavy with drink, and he did his work badly. Miller warned him once or twice and Lawson was not the man to accept remonstrance easily. One day in the midst of an altercation he put on his hat and walked out. But by now his reputation was well known and he could find no one to engage him. For a while he idled, and then he had an attack of delirium tremens. When he recovered, shameful and weak, he could no longer resist the constant pressure and he went to Pedersen and asked him for a job. Pedersen was glad to have a white man in his store and Lawson's skill at figures made him useful.

From that time his degeneration was rapid. The white people gave him the cold shoulder. They were only prevented from cutting him completely by disdainful pity and by a certain dread of his angry violence when he was drunk. He became extremely susceptible and was always on the lookout for affront.

He lived entirely among the natives and half-castes, but he had no longer the prestige of the white man. They felt his loathing for them and they resented his attitude of superiority. He was one of themselves now and they did not see why he should put on airs. Brevald, who had been ingratiating and obsequious, now treated him with contempt. Ethel had made a bad bargain. There were disgraceful scenes and once or twice the two men came to blows. When there was a quarrel Ethel took the part of her family. They found he was better drunk than sober, for when he was drunk he would lie on the bed or on the floor, sleeping heavily.

Then he became aware that something was being hidden from him.

When he got back to the bungalow for the wretched, half-native supper which was his evening meal, often Ethel was not in. If he asked where she was Brevald told him she had gone to spend the evening with one or other of her friends. Once he followed her to the house Brevald had mentioned and found she was not there. On her return he asked her where she had been and she told him her father had make a mistake; she had been to so-and-so's. But he knew that she was lying. She was in her best clothes; her eyes were shining, and she looked lovely.

'Don't try any monkey tricks on me, my girl,' he said, 'or I'll break every bone in your body.'

'You drunken beast,' she said, scornfully.

He fancied that Mrs Brevald and the old grandmother looked at him maliciously and he ascribed Brevald's good humour with him, so unusual those days, to his satisfaction at having something up his sleeve against his son-in-law. And then, his suspicions aroused, he imagined that the white men gave him curious glances. When he came into the lounge of the hotel the sudden silence which fell upon the company convinced him that he had been the subject of the conversation. Something was going on and everyone knew it but himself. He was seized with furious jealousy. He believed that Ethel was carrying on with one of the white men, and he looked at one after the other with scrutinizing eyes; but there was nothing to give him even a hint. He was helpless. Because he could find no one on whom definitely to fix his suspicions, he went about like a raving maniac, looking for someone on whom to vent his wrath. Chance caused him in the end to hit upon the man who of all others least deserved to suffer from his violence. One afternoon, when he was sitting in the hotel by himself, moodily, Chaplin came in and sat down beside him. Perhaps Chaplin was the only man on the island who had any sympathy for him. They ordered drinks and chatted a few minutes about the races that were shortly to be run. Then Chaplin said:

'I guess we shall all have to fork out money for new dresses.'

Lawson sniggered. Since Mrs Chaplin held the purse-strings, if she wanted a new frock for the occasion she would certainly not ask her husband for the money.

'How is your missus?' asked Chaplin, desiring to be friendly.

'What the hell's that got to do with you?' said Lawson, knitting his dark brows.

'I was only asking a civil question.'

'Well, keep your civil questions to yourself.'

Chaplin was not a patient man; his long residence in the tropics, the whisky bottle, and his domestic affairs had given him a temper hardly more under control than Lawson's.

'Look here, my boy, when you're in my hotel you behave like a gentleman or you'll find yourself in the street before you can say knife.'

Lawson's lowering face grew dark and red.

'Let me just tell you once for all and you can pass it on to the others,' he said, panting with rage. 'If any of you fellows come messing round with my wife he'd better look out.'

'Who do you think wants to mess around with your wife?'

'I'm not such a fool as you think. I can see a stone wall in front of me as well as most men, and I warn you straight, that's all. I'm not going to put up with any hanky-panky, not on your life.'

'Look here, you'd better clear out of here, and come back when you're sober.'

'I shall clear out when I choose and not a minute before,' said Lawson.

It was an unfortunate boast, for Chaplin in the course of his experience as a hotel-keeper had acquired a peculiar skill in dealing with gentlemen whose room he preferred to their company, and the words were hardly out of Lawson's mouth before he found himself caught by the collar and arm and hustled not without force into the street. He stumbled down the steps into the blinding glare of the sun.

It was in consequence of this that he had his first violent scene with Ethel. Smarting with humiliation and unwilling to go back to the hotel, he went home that afternoon earlier than usual. He found Ethel dressing to go out. As a rule she lay about in a Mother Hubbard, barefoot, with a flower in her dark hair; but now, in white silk stockings and high-heeled shoes, she was doing up a pink muslin dress which was the newest she had.

'You're making yourself very smart,' he said. 'Where are you going?'

'I'm going to the Crossleys.'

'I'll come with you.'

'Why?' she asked coolly.

'I don't want you to gad about by yourself all the time.'

'You're not asked.'

'I don't care a damn about that. You're not going without me.'

'You'd better lie down till I'm ready.'

She thought he was drunk and if he once settled himself on the bed would quickly drop off to sleep. He sat down on a chair and began to smoke a cigarette. She watched him with increasing irritation. When she was ready he got up. It happened by an unusual chance that there was no one in the bungalow. Brevald was working on the plantation and his wife had gone into Apia. Ethel faced him.

'I'm not going with you. You're drunk.'

'That's a lie. You're not going without me.'

She shrugged her shoulders and tried to pass him, but he caught her by the arm and held her.

'Let me go, you devil,' she said, breaking into Samoan.

'Why do you want to go without me? Haven't I told you I'm not going to put up with any monkey tricks?'

She clenched her fist and hit him in the face. He lost all control of himself. All his love, all his hatred, welled up in him and he was beside himself.

'I'll teach you,' he shouted. 'I'll teach you.'

He seized a riding-whip which happened to be under his hand, and struck her with it. She screamed, and the scream maddened him so that he went on striking her, again and again. Her shrieks rang through the bungalow and he cursed her as he hit. Then he flung her on the bed. She lay there sobbing with pain and terror. He threw the whip away from him and rushed out of the room. Ethel heard him go and she stopped crying. She looked round cautiously, then she raised herself. She was sore, but she had not been badly hurt, and she looked at her dress to see if it was damaged. The native women are not unused to blows. What he had done did not outrage her. When she looked at herself in the glass and arranged her hair, her eyes were shining. There was a strange look in them. Perhaps then she was nearer loving him than she had ever been before.

But Lawson, driven forth blindly, stumbled through the plantation and suddenly exhausted, weak as a child, flung himself on the ground at the foot of a tree. He was miserable and ashamed. He thought of Ethel, and in the yielding tenderness of his love all his bones seemed to grow soft within him. He thought of the past, and of his hopes, and he was aghast at what he had done. He wanted her more than ever. He wanted to take her in his arms. He must go to her at once. He got up. He was so weak that he staggered as he walked. He went into the house and she was sitting in their cramped bedroom in front of her looking-glass.

'Oh, Ethel, forgive me. I'm so awfully ashamed of myself. I didn't know what I was doing.'

He fell on his knees before her and timidly stroked the skirt of her dress.

'I can't bear to think of what I did. It's awful. I think I was mad. There's no one in the world I love as I love you. I'd do anything to save you from pain and I've hurt you. I can never forgive myself, but for God's sake say you forgive me.'

He heard her shrieks still. It was unendurable. She looked at him silently. He tried to take her hands and the tears streamed from his eyes. In his humiliation he hid his face in her lap and his frail body shook with sobs. An expression of utter contempt came over her face. She had the native woman's disdain of a man who abased himself before a woman. A weak creature! And for a moment she had been on the point of thinking there was something in him. He grovelled at her feet like a cur. She gave him a little scornful kick.

'Get out,' she said. 'I hate you.'

He tried to hold her, but she pushed him aside. She stood up. She began to take off her dress. She kicked off her shoes and slid the stockings off her feet, then she slipped on her old Mother Hubbard.

'Where are you going?'

'What's that got to do with you? I'm going down to the pool.'

'Let me come too,' he said.

He asked as though he were a child.

'Can't you even leave me that?'

He hid his face in his hands, crying miserably, while she, her eyes hard and cold, stepped past him and went out.

From that time she entirely despised him; and though, herded together in the small bungalow, Lawson and Ethel with her two children, Brevald, his wife and her mother, and the vague relations and hangers-on who were always in and about, they had to live cheek by jowl, Lawson, ceasing to be of any account, was hardly noticed. He left in the morning after breakfast, and came back only to have supper. He gave up the struggle, and when for want of money he could not go to the English Club he spent the evening playing hearts with old Brevald and the natives. Except when he was drunk he was cowed and listless. Ethel treated him like a dog. She submitted at times to his fits of wild passion, and she was frightened by the gusts of hatred with which they were followed; but when, afterwards, he was cringing and lachrymose she had such a contempt for him that she could have spat in his face. Sometimes he was violent, but now she was prepared for him, and when he hit her she kicked and scratched and bit. They had horrible battles in which he had not always the best of it. Very soon it was known all over Apia that they got on badly. There was little sympathy for Lawson, and at the hotel the general surprise was that old Brevald did not kick him out of the place.

'Brevald's a pretty ugly customer,' said one of the men. 'I shouldn't be surprised if he put a bullet into Lawson's carcass one of these days.'

Ethel still went in the evenings to bathe in the silent pool. It seemed to have an attraction for her that was not quite human, just that attraction you might imagine that a mermaid who had won a soul would have for the cool salt waves of the sea; and sometimes Lawson went also. I do not know what urged him to go, for Ethel was obviously irritated by his presence; perhaps it was because in that spot he hoped to regain the clean rapture which had filled his heart when first he saw her; perhaps only, with the madness of those who love them that love them not, from the feeling that his obstinacy could force love. One day he strolled down there with a feeling that was rare with him now. He felt suddenly at peace with the world. The evening was drawing in and the dusk seemed to cling to the leaves of the coconut trees like a little thin cloud. A faint breeze stirred them noiselessly. A crescent moon hung just over their tops. He made his way to the bank. He saw Ethel in the water floating on her back. Her hair streamed out all round her, and she was holding in her hand a large hibiscus. He stopped a moment to admire her; she was like Ophelia.

'Hullo, Ethel,' he cried joyfully.

She made a sudden movement and dropped the red flower. It floated idly away. She swam a stroke or two till she knew there was ground within her depth and then stood up.

'Go away,' she said. 'Go away.'

He laughed.

'Don't be selfish. There's plenty of room for both of us.'

'Why can't you leave me alone? I want to be by myself.'

'Hang it all, I want to bathe,' he answered, good-humouredly.

'Go down to the bridge. I don't want you here.'

'I'm sorry for that,' he said, smiling still.

He was not in the least angry, and he hardly noticed that she was in a passion. He began to take off his coat.

'Go away,' she shrieked. 'I won't have you here. Can't you even leave me this? Go away.'

'Don't be silly, darling.'

She bent down and picked up a sharp stone and flung it quickly at him. He had no time to duck. It hit him on the temple. With a cry he put his hand to his head and when he took it away it was wet with blood. Ethel stood still, panting with rage. He turned very pale, and without a word, taking up his coat, went away. Ethel let herself fall back into the water and the stream carried her slowly down to the ford.

The stone had made a jagged wound and for some days Lawson went about with a bandaged head. He had invented a likely story to account for the accident when the fellows at the club asked him about it, but he had no occasion to use it. No one referred to the matter. He saw them cast surreptitious glances at his head, but not a word was said. The silence could only mean that they knew how he came by his wound. He was certain now that Ethel had a lover, and they all knew who it was. But there was not the smallest indication to guide him. He never saw Ethel with anyone; no one showed a wish to be with her, or treated him in a manner that seemed strange. Wild rage seized him, and having no one to vent it on he drank more and more heavily. A little while before I came to the island he had had another attack of delirium tremens.

I met Ethel at the house of a man called Caster, who lived two or three miles from Apia with a native wife. I had been playing tennis with him and when we were tired he suggested a cup of tea. We went into the house and in the untidy living-room found Ethel chatting with Mrs Caster.

'Hullo, Ethel,' he said, 'I didn't know you were here.'

I could not help looking at her with curiosity. I tried to see what there was in her to have excited in Lawson such a devastating passion. But who can explain these things? It was true that she was lovely; she reminded one of the red hibiscus, the common flower of the hedgerow in Samoa, with its grace and its languor and its passion; but what surprised me most, taking into consideration the story I knew even then a good deal of, was her freshness and simplicity. She was quiet and a little shy. There was nothing coarse or loud about her; she had not the exuberance common to the half-caste; and it was almost impossible to believe that she could be the virago that the horrible scenes between husband and wife, which were now common knowledge, indicated. In her pretty pink frock and high-heeled shoes she looked quite European. You could hardly have guessed at that dark background of native life in which she felt herself so much more at home. I did not imagine that she was at all intelligent, and I should not have been surprised if a man, after living with her for some time, had found the passion which had drawn him to her sink into boredom. It suggested itself to me that in her elusiveness, like a thought that presents itself to consciousness and vanishes before it can be captured by words, lay her peculiar charm; but perhaps that was merely fancy, and if I had known nothing about her I should have seen in her only a pretty little half-caste like another.

She talked to me of the various things which they talk of to the stranger in

Samoa, of the journey, and whether I had slid down the water rock at Papaseea, and if I meant to stay in a native village. She talked to me of Scotland, and perhaps I noticed in her a tendency to enlarge on the sumptuousness of her establishment there. She asked me naïvely if I knew Mrs This and Mrs That, with whom she had been acquainted when she lived in the north.

Then Miller, the fat German–American, came in. He shook hands all round very cordially and sat down, asking in his loud, cheerful voice for a whisky and soda. He was very fat and he sweated profusely. He took off his gold-rimmed spectacles and wiped them; you saw then that his little eyes, benevolent behind the large round glasses, were shrewd and cunning; the party had been somewhat dull till he came, but he was a good story-teller and a jovial fellow. Soon he had the two women, Ethel and my friend's wife, laughing delightedly at his sallies. He had a reputation on the island of a lady's man, and you could see how this fat, gross fellow, old and ugly, had yet the possibility of fascination. His humour was on a level with the understanding of his company, an affair of vitality and assurance, and his Western accent gave a peculiar point to what he said. At last he turned to me:

'Well, if we want to get back for dinner we'd better be getting. I'll take you along in my machine if you like.'

I thanked him and got up. He shook hands with the others, went out of the room, massive and strong in his walk, and climbed into his car.

'Pretty little thing, Lawson's wife,' I said, as we drove along.

'Too bad the way he treats her. Knocks her about. Gets my dander up when I hear of a man hitting a woman.'

We went on a little. Then he said:

'He was a darned fool to marry her. I said so at the time. If he hadn't, he'd have had the whip hand over her. He's yaller, that's what he is, yaller.'

The year was drawing to its end and the time approached when I was to leave Samoa. My boat was scheduled to sail for Sydney on the fourth of January. Christmas Day had been celebrated at the hotel with suitable ceremonies, but it was looked upon as no more than a rehearsal for New Year, and the men who were accustomed to foregather in the lounge determined on New Year's Eve to make a night of it. There was an uproarious dinner, after which the party sauntered down to the English Club, a simple little frame house, to play pool. There was a great deal of talking, laughing, and betting, but some very poor play, except on the part of Miller, who had drunk as much as any of them, all far younger than he, but had kept unimpaired the keenness of his eye and the sureness of his hand. He pocketed the young men's money with humour and urbanity. After an hour of this I grew tired and went out. I crossed the road and came to the beach. Three coconut trees grew there, like three moon maidens waiting for their lovers to ride out of the sea, and I sat at the foot of one of them, watching the lagoon and the nightly assemblage of the stars.

I do not know where Lawson had been during the evening, but between ten and eleven he came along to the club. He shambled down the dusty, empty road, feeling dull and bored, and when he reached the club, before going into the billiard-room, went into the bar to have a drink by himself. He had a shyness now about joining the company of white men when there were a lot of them together and needed a stiff dose of whisky to give him confidence. He was standing with the glass in his hand when Miller came in to him. He was in his shirt-sleeves and still held his cue. He gave the bar-tender a glance.

'Get out, Jack,' he said.

The bar-tender, a native in a white jacket and a red lava-lava, without a word slid out of the small room.

'Look here, I've been wanting to have a few words with you, Lawson,' said the big American.

'Well, that's one of the few things you can have free, gratis, and for nothing on this damned island.'

Miller fixed his gold spectacles more firmly on his nose and held Lawson with his cold determined eyes.

'See here, young fellow, I understand you've been knocking Mrs Lawson about again. I'm not going to stand for that. If you don't stop it right now I'll break every bone of your dirty little body.'

Then Lawson knew what he had been trying to find out so long. It was Miller. The appearance of the man, fat, bald-headed, with his round bare face and double chin and the gold spectacles, his age, his benign, shrewd look, like that of a renegade priest, and the thought of Ethel, so slim and virginal, filled him with a sudden horror. Whatever his faults Lawson was no coward, and without a word he hit out violently at Miller. Miller quickly warded the blow with the hand that held the cue, and then with a great swing of his right arm brought his fist down on Lawson's ear. Lawson was four inches shorter than the American and he was slightly built, frail and weakened not only by illness and the enervating tropics, but by drink. He fell like a log and lay half dazed at the foot of the bar. Miller took off his spectacles and wiped them with his handkerchief.

'I guess you know what to expect now. You've had your warning and you'd better take it.'

He took up his cue and went back into the billiard-room. There was so much noise there that no one knew what had happened. Lawson picked himself up. He put his hand to his ear, which was singing still. Then he slunk out of the club.

I saw a man cross the road, a patch of white against the darkness of the night, but did not know who it was. He came down to the beach, passed me sitting at the foot of the tree, and looked down. I saw then that it was Lawson, but since he was doubtless drunk, did not speak. He went on, walked irresolutely two or three steps, and turned back. He came up to me and bending down stared in my face.

'I thought it was you,' he said.

He sat down and took out his pipe.

'It was hot and noisy in the club,' I volunteered.

'Why are you sitting here?'

'I was waiting about for the midnight mass at the Cathedral.'

'If you like I'll come with you.'

Lawson was quite sober. We sat for a while smoking in silence. Now and then in the lagoon was the splash of some big fish, and a little way out towards the opening in the reef was the light of a schooner.

'You're sailing next week, aren't you?' he said.

'Yes.'

'It would be jolly to go home once more. But I could never stand it now. The cold, you know.'

'It's odd to think that in England now they're shivering round the fire,' I said.

There was not even a breath of wind. The balminess of the night was like a spell. I wore nothing but a thin shirt and a suit of ducks. I enjoyed the exquisite languor of the night, and stretched my limbs voluptuously.

'This isn't the sort of New Year's Eve that persuades one to make good resolutions for the future,' I smiled.

He made no answer, but I do not know what train of thought my casual remark had suggested in him, for presently he began to speak. He spoke in a low voice, without any expression, but his accents were educated, and it was a relief to hear him after the twang and the vulgar intonations which for some time had wounded my ears.

'I've made an awful hash of things. That's obvious, isn't it? I'm right down at the bottom of the pit and there's no getting out for me. "*Black as the pit from pole to pole.*"' I felt him smile as he made the quotation. 'And the strange thing is that I don't see how I went wrong.'

I held my breath, for to me there is nothing more awe-inspiring than when a man discovers to you the nakedness of his soul. Then you see that no one is so trivial or debased but that in him is a spark of something to excite compassion.

'It wouldn't be so rotten if I could see that it was all my own fault. It's true I drink, but I shouldn't have taken to that if things had gone differently. I wasn't really fond of liquor. I suppose I ought not to have married Ethel. If I'd kept her it would be all right. But I did love her so.'

His voice faltered.

'She's not a bad lot, you know, not really. It's just rotten luck. We might have been as happy as lords. When she bolted I suppose I ought to have let her go, but I couldn't do that – I was dead stuck on her then; and there was the kid.'

'Are you fond of the kid?' I asked.

'I was. There are two, you know. But they don't mean so much to me now. You'd take them for natives anywhere. I have to talk to them in Samoan.'

'Is it too late for you to start fresh? Couldn't you make a dash for it and leave the place?'

'I haven't the strength. I'm done for.'

'Are you still in love with your wife?'

'Not now. Not now.' He repeated the two words with a kind of horror in his voice. 'I haven't even got that now. I'm down and out.'

The bells of the Cathedral were ringing.

'If you really want to come to the midnight mass we'd better go along,' I said. 'Come on.'

We got up and walked along the road. The Cathedral, all white, stood facing the sea not without impressiveness, and beside it the Protestant chapels had the look of meeting-houses. In the road were two or three cars, and a great number of traps, and traps were put up against the walls at the side. People had come from all parts of the island for the service, and through the great open doors we saw that the place was crowded. The high altar was all ablaze with light. There were a few whites and a good many half-castes, but the great majority were natives. All the men wore trousers, for the Church had decided that the lava-lava is indecent. We found chairs at the back, near the open door, and sat down. Presently, following Lawson's eyes, I saw Ethel come in with a party of half-castes. They were all very much dressed up, the men in high, stiff collars and shiny boots, the women in large, gay hats. Ethel nodded and smiled to her friends as she passed up the aisle. The service began.

When it was over Lawson and I stood on one side for a while to watch the crowd stream out, then he held out his hand.

'Good night,' he said. 'I hope you'll have a pleasant journey home.'

'Oh, but I shall see you before I go.'

He sniggered.

'The question is if you'll see me drunk or sober.'

He turned and left me. I had a recollection of those very large black eyes, shining wildly under the shaggy brows. I paused irresolutely. I did not feel sleepy and I thought I would at all events go along to the club for an hour before turning in. When I got there I found the billiard-room empty, but half-a-dozen men were sitting round a table in the lounge, playing poker. Miller looked up as I came in.

'Sit down and take a hand,' he said.

'All right.'

I bought some chips and began to play. Of course it is the most fascinating game in the world and my hour lengthened out to two, and then to three. The native bar-tender, cheery and wide-awake notwithstanding the time, was at our elbow to supply us with drinks and from somewhere or other he produced a ham and a loaf of bread. We played on. Most of the party had drunk more than was good for them and the play was high and reckless. I played modestly, neither wishing to win nor anxious to lose, but I watched Miller with a fascinated interest. He drank glass for glass with the rest of the company, but remained cool and level-headed. His pile of chips increased in size and he had a neat little paper in front of him on which he had marked various sums lent to players in distress. He beamed amiably at the young men whose money he was taking. He kept up interminably his stream of jest and anecdotes, but he never missed a draw, he never let an expression of the face pass him. At last the dawn crept into the windows, gently, with a sort of deprecating shyness, as though it had no business there, and then it was day.

'Well,' said Miller. 'I reckon we've seen the old year out in style. Now let's have a round of jackpots and me for my mosquito net. I'm fifty, remember, I can't keep these late hours.'

The morning was beautiful and fresh when we stood on the veranda, and the lagoon was like a sheet of multicoloured glass. Someone suggested a dip before going to bed, but none cared to bathe in the lagoon, sticky and treacherous to the feet. Miller had his car at the door and he offered to take us down to the pool. We jumped in and drove along the deserted road. When we reached the pool it seemed as though the day had hardly risen there yet. Under the trees the water was all in shadow and the night had the effect of lurking still. We were in great spirits. We had no towels or any costume and in my prudence I wondered how we were going to dry ourselves. None of us had much on and it did not take us long to snatch off our clothes. Nelson, the little super-cargo, was stripped first.

'I'm going down to the bottom,' he said.

He dived and in a moment another man dived too, but shallow, and was out of the water before him. Then Nelson came up and scrambled to the side.

'I say, get me out,' he said.

'What's up?'

Something was evidently the matter. His face was terrified. Two fellows gave him their hands and he slithered up.

'I say, there's a man down there.'

'Don't be a fool. You're drunk.'

'Well, if there isn't I'm in for D.T.s. But I tell you there's a man down there. It just scared me out of my wits.'

Miller looked at him for a moment. The little man was all white. He was actually trembling.

'Come on, Caster,' said Miller to the big Australian, 'we'd better go down and see.'

'He was standing up,' said Nelson, 'all dressed. I saw him. He tried to catch hold of me.'

'Hold your row,' said Miller. 'Are you ready?'

They dived in. We waited on the bank, silent. It really seemed as though they were underwater longer than any men could breathe. Then Caster came up, and immediately after him, red in the face as though he were going to have a fit, Miller. They were pulling something behind them. Another man jumped in to help them, and the three together dragged their burden to the side. They shoved it up. Then we saw that it was Lawson, with a great stone tied up in his coat and bound to his feet.

'He was set on making a good job of it,' said Miller, as he wiped the water from his short-sighted eyes.

Mackintosh

◆

He splashed about for a few minutes in the sea; it was too shallow to swim in and for fear of sharks he could not go out of his depth; then he got out and went into the bath-house for a shower. The coldness of the fresh water was grateful after the heavy stickiness of the salt Pacific, so warm, though it was only just after seven, that to bathe in it did not brace you but rather increased your languor; and when he had dried himself, slipping into a bath-gown, he called out to the Chinese cook that he would be ready for breakfast in five minutes. He walked barefoot across the patch of coarse grass which Walker, the administrator, proudly thought was a lawn, to his own quarters and dressed. This did not take long, for he put on nothing but a shirt and a pair of duck trousers and then went over to his chief's house on the other side of the compound. The two men had their meals together, but the Chinese cook told him that Walker had set out on horseback at five and would not be back for another hour.

Mackintosh had slept badly and he looked with distaste at the paw-paw and the eggs and bacon which were set before him. The mosquitoes had been maddening that night; they flew about the net under which he slept in such numbers that their humming, pitiless and menacing, had the effect of a note, infinitely drawn out, played on a distant organ, and whenever he dozed off he awoke with a start in the belief that one had found its way inside his curtains. It was so hot that he lay naked. He turned from side to side. And gradually the dull roar of the breakers on the reef, so unceasing and so regular that generally you did not hear it, grew distinct on his consciousness, its rhythm hammered on his tired nerves and he held himself with clenched hands in the effort to bear it. The thought that nothing could stop that sound, for it would continue to all eternity, was almost impossible to bear, and, as though his strength were a match for the ruthless forces of nature, he had an insane impulse to do some violent thing. He felt he must cling to his self-control or he would go mad. And now, looking out of the window at the lagoon and the strip of foam which marked the reef, he shuddered with hatred of the brilliant scene. The cloudless sky was like an inverted bowl that hemmed it in. He lit his pipe and turned over the pile of Auckland papers that had come over from Apia a few days before. The newest of them was three weeks old. They gave an impression of incredible dullness.

Then he went into the office. It was a large, bare room with two desks in it and a bench along one side. A number of natives were seated on this, and a couple of women. They gossiped while they waited for the administrator, and when Mackintosh came in they greeted him.

'*Talofa-li.*'

He returned their greeting and sat down at his desk. He began to write, working on a report which the governor of Samoa had been clamouring for and which Walker, with his usual dilatoriness, had neglected to prepare. Mackintosh as he made his notes reflected vindictively that Walker was late with his report because he was so illiterate that he had an invincible distaste for anything to do with pens and paper; and now when it was at last ready, concise and neatly official, he would accept his subordinate's work without a word of appreciation, with a sneer rather or a gibe, and send it on to his own superior as though it were his own composition. He could not have written a word of it. Mackintosh thought with rage that if his chief pencilled in some insertion it would be childish in expression and faulty in language. If he remonstrated or sought to put his meaning into an intelligible phrase, Walker would fly into a passion and cry:

'What the hell do I care about grammar? That's what I want to say and that's how I want to say it.'

At last Walker came in. The natives surrounded him as he entered, trying to get his immediate attention, but he turned on them roughly and told them to sit down and hold their tongues. He threatened that if they were not quiet he would have them all turned out and see none of them that day. He nodded to Mackintosh.

'Hullo, Mac; up at last? I don't know how you can waste the best part of the day in bed. You ought to have been up before dawn like me. Lazy beggar.'

He threw himself heavily into his chair and wiped his face with a large bandana.

'By heaven, I've got a thirst.'

He turned to the policeman who stood at the door, a picturesque figure in his white jacket and lava-lava, the loincloth of the Samoan, and told him to bring *kava*. The *kava* bowl stood on the floor in the corner of the room, and the policeman filled a half coconut shell and brought it to Walker. He poured a few drops on the ground, murmured the customary words to the company, and drank with relish. Then he told the policeman to serve the waiting natives, and the shell was handed to each one in order of birth or importance and emptied with the same ceremonies.

Then he set about the day's work. He was a little man, considerably less than of middle height, and enormously stout; he had a large, fleshy face, clean-shaven, with the cheeks hanging on each side in great dew-laps, and three vast chins; his small features were all dissolved in fat; and, but for a crescent of white hair at the back of his head, he was completely bald. He reminded you of Mr Pickwick. He was grotesque, a figure of fun, and yet, strangely enough, not without dignity. His blue eyes, behind large gold-rimmed spectacles, were shrewd and vivacious, and there was a great deal of determination in his face. He was sixty, but his native vitality triumphed over advancing years. Notwithstanding his corpulence his movements were quick, and he walked with a heavy, resolute tread as though he sought to impress his weight upon the earth. He spoke in a loud, gruff voice.

It was two years now since Mackintosh had been appointed Walker's assistant. Walker, who had been for a quarter of a century administrator of Talua, one of the larger islands in the Samoan group, was a man known in person or by report through the length and breadth of the South Seas; and it was with lively curiosity that Mackintosh looked forward to his first meeting with him. For one reason or another he stayed a couple of weeks at Apia before he took up his post and both at Chaplin's hotel and at the English Club he heard innumerable stories about the administrator. He thought now with irony of his interest in them. Since then he had heard them a hundred times from Walker himself. Walker knew that he was a character and, proud of his reputation, deliberately acted up to it. He was jealous of his 'legend' and anxious that you should know the exact details of any of the celebrated stories that were told of him. He was ludicrously angry with anyone who had told them to the stranger incorrectly.

There was a rough cordiality about Walker which Mackintosh at first found not unattractive, and Walker, glad to have a listener to whom all he said was fresh, gave of his best. He was good-humoured, hearty, and considerate. To Mackintosh, who had lived the sheltered life of a government official in London till at the age of thirty-four an attack of pneumonia, leaving him with the threat of tuberculosis, had forced him to seek a post in the Pacific, Walker's existence seemed extraordinarily romantic. The adventure with which he started on his conquest of circumstance was typical of the man. He ran away to sea when he was fifteen and for over a year was employed in shovelling coal on a collier. He was an undersized boy and both men and mates were kind to him, but the captain for some reason conceived a savage dislike of him. He used the lad cruelly so that, beaten and kicked, he often could not sleep for the pain that racked his limbs. He loathed the captain with all his soul. Then he was given a tip for some race and managed to borrow twenty-five pounds from a friend he had picked up in Belfast. He put it on the horse, an outsider, at long odds. He had no means of repaying the money if he lost, but it never occurred to him that he could lose. He felt himself in luck. The horse won and he found himself with something over a thousand pounds in hard cash. Now his chance had come. He found out who was the best solicitor in the town—the collier lay then somewhere on the Irish coast—went to him, and, telling him that he heard the ship was for sale, asked him to arrange the purchase for him. The solicitor was amused at his small client, he was only sixteen and did not look so old, and, moved perhaps by sympathy, promised not only to arrange the matter for him but to see that he made a good bargain. After a little while Walker found himself the owner of the ship. He went back to her and had what he described as the most glorious moment of his life when he gave the skipper notice and told him that he must get off *his* ship in half an hour. He made the mate captain and sailed on the collier for another nine months, at the end of which he sold her at a profit.

He came out to the islands at the age of twenty-six as a planter. He was one of the few white men settled in Talua at the time of the German occupation and had then already some influence with the natives. The Germans made him administrator, a position which he occupied for twenty years, and when the island was seized by the British he was confirmed in his post. He ruled the island despotically, but with complete success. The prestige of this success was another reason for the interest that Mackintosh took in him.

But the two men were not made to get on. Mackintosh was an ugly man, with ungainly gestures, a tall thin fellow, with a narrow chest and bowed shoulders. He had sallow, sunken cheeks, and his eyes were large and sombre. He was a great reader, and when his books arrived and were unpacked Walker came over to his quarters and looked at them. Then he turned to Mackintosh with a coarse laugh.

'What in Hell have you brought all this muck for?' he asked.

Mackintosh flushed darkly.

'I'm sorry you think it muck. I brought my books because I want to read them.'

'When you said you'd got a lot of books coming I thought there'd be something for me to read. Haven't you got any detective stories?'

'Detective stories don't interest me.'

'You're a damned fool then.'

'I'm content that you should think so.'

Every mail brought Walker a mass of periodical literature, papers from New Zealand and magazines from America, and it exasperated him that Mackintosh showed his contempt for these ephemeral publications. He had no patience with the books that absorbed Mackintosh's leisure and thought it only a pose that he read Gibbon's *Decline and Fall* or Burton's *Anatomy of Melancholy*. And since he had never learned to put any restraint on his tongue, he expressed his opinion of his assistant freely. Mackintosh began to see the real man, and under the boisterous good-humour he discerned a vulgar cunning which was hateful; he was vain and domineering, and it was strange that he had notwithstanding a shyness which made him dislike people who were not quite of his kidney. He judged others, naïvely, by their language, and if it was free from the oaths and the obscenity which made up the greater part of his own conversation, he looked upon them with suspicion. In the evening the two men played piquet. He played badly but vaingloriously, crowing over his opponent when he won and losing his temper when he lost. On rare occasions a couple of planters or traders would drive over to play bridge, and then Walker showed himself in what Mackintosh considered a characteristic light. He played regardless of his partner, calling up in his desire to play the hand, and argued interminably, beating down opposition by the loudness of his voice. He constantly revoked, and when he did so said with an ingratiating whine: 'Oh, you wouldn't count it against an old man who can hardly see.' Did he know that his opponents thought it as well to keep on the right side of him and hesitated to insist on the rigour of the game? Mackintosh watched him with an icy contempt. When the game was over, while they smoked their pipes and drank whisky, they would begin telling stories. Walker told with gusto the story of his marriage. He had got so drunk at the wedding feast that the bride had fled and he had never seen her since. He had had numberless adventures, commonplace and sordid, with the women of the island and he described them with a pride in his own prowess which was an offence to Mackintosh's fastidious ears. He was a gross, sensual old man. He thought Mackintosh a poor fellow because he would not share his promiscuous amours and remained sober when the company was drunk.

He despised him also for the orderliness with which he did his official work. Mackintosh liked to do everything just so. His desk was always tidy, his papers were always neatly docketed, he could put his hand on any document that was needed, and he had at his fingers' ends all the regulations that were required for the business of their administration.

'Fudge, fudge,' said Walker. 'I've run this island for twenty years without red tape, and I don't want it now.'

'Does it make it any easier for you that when you want a letter you have to hunt half an hour for it?' answered Mackintosh.

'You're nothing but a damned official. But you're not a bad fellow; when you've been out here a year or two you'll be all right. What's wrong about you is that you won't drink. You wouldn't be a bad sort if you got soused once a week.'

The curious thing was that Walker remained perfectly unconscious of the dislike for him which every month increased in the breast of his subordinate. Although he laughed at him, as he grew accustomed to him, he began almost to like him. He had a certain tolerance for the peculiarities of others, and he accepted Mackintosh as a queer fish. Perhaps he liked him, unconsciously, because he could chaff him. His humour consisted of coarse banter and he wanted a butt. Mackintosh's exactness, his morality, his sobriety, were all fruitful subjects; his Scots name gave an opportunity for the usual jokes about Scotland; he enjoyed himself thoroughly when two or three men were there and he could make them all laugh at the expense of Mackintosh. He would say ridiculous things about him to the natives, and Mackintosh, his knowledge of Samoan still imperfect, would see their unrestrained mirth when Walker had made an obscene reference to him. He smiled good-humouredly.

'I'll say this for you, Mac,' Walker would say in his gruff loud voice, 'you can take a joke.'

'Was it a joke?' smiled Mackintosh. 'I didn't know.'

'Scots wha hae!' shouted Walker, with a bellow of laughter. 'There's only one way to make a Scotchman see a joke and that's by a surgical operation.'

Walker little knew that there was nothing Mackintosh could stand less than chaff. He would wake in the night, the breathless night of the rainy season, and brood sullenly over the gibe that Walker had uttered carelessly days before. It rankled. His heart swelled with rage, and he pictured to himself ways in which he might get even with the bully. He had tried answering him, but Walker had a gift of repartee, coarse and obvious, which gave him an advantage. The dullness of his intellect made him impervious to a delicate shaft. His self-satisfaction made it impossible to wound him. His loud voice, his bellow of laughter, were weapons against which Mackintosh had nothing to counter, and he learned that the wisest thing was never to betray his irritation. He learned to control himself. But his hatred grew till it was a monomania. He watched Walker with an insane vigilance. He fed his own self-esteem by every instance of meanness on Walker's part, by every exhibition of childish vanity, of cunning, and of vulgarity. Walker ate greedily, noisily, filthily, and Mackintosh watched him with satisfaction. He took note of the foolish things he said and of his mistakes in grammar. He knew that Walker held him in small esteem, and he found a bitter satisfaction in his chief's opinion of him; it increased his own contempt for the narrow, complacent old man. And it gave him a singular pleasure to know that Walker was entirely unconscious of the hatred he felt for him. He was a fool who liked popularity, and he blandly fancied that everyone admired him. Once Mackintosh had overheard Walker speaking of him.

'He'll be all right when I've licked him into shape,' he said. 'He's a good dog and he loves his master.'

Mackintosh silently, without a movement of his long, sallow face, laughed long and heartily.

But his hatred was not blind; on the contrary, it was peculiarly clear-sighted, and he judged Walker's capabilities with precision. He ruled his small kingdom with efficiency. He was just and honest. With opportunities to make money he was a poorer man than when he was first appointed to his post, and his only support for his old age was the pension which he expected when at last he retired from official life. His pride was that with an assistant and a half-caste clerk he was able to administer the island more competently than Upolu, the island of which Apia is the chief town, was administered with its army of functionaries. He had a few native policemen to sustain his authority, but he made no use of them. He governed by bluff and his Irish humour.

'They insisted on building a jail for me,' he said. 'What the devil do I want a jail for? I'm not going to put the natives in prison. If they do wrong I know how to deal with them.'

One of his quarrels with the higher authorities at Apia was that he claimed entire jurisdiction over the natives of his island. Whatever their crimes he would not give them up to courts competent to deal with them, and several times an angry correspondence had passed between him and the governor at Upolu. For he looked upon the natives as his children. And that was the amazing thing about this coarse, vulgar, selfish man; he loved the island on which he had lived so long with passion, and he had for the natives a strange rough tenderness which was quite wonderful.

He loved to ride about the island on his old grey mare and he was never tired of its beauty. Sauntering along the grassy roads among the coconut trees he would stop every now and then to admire the loveliness of the scene. Now and then he would come upon a native village and stop while the headman brought him a bowl of *kava*. He would look at the little group of bell-shape huts with their high thatched roofs, like beehives, and a smile would spread over his fat face. His eyes rested happily on the spreading green of the bread-fruit trees.

'By George, it's like the garden of Eden.'

Sometimes his rides took him along the coast and through the trees he had a glimpse of the wide sea, empty, with never a sail to disturb the loneliness; sometimes he climbed a hill so that a great stretch of country, with little villages nestling among the tall trees was spread out before him like the kingdom of the world, and he would sit there for an hour in an ecstasy of delight. But he had no words to express his feelings and to relieve them would utter an obscene jest; it was as though his emotion was so violent that he needed vulgarity to break the tension.

Mackintosh observed this sentiment with an icy disdain. Walker had always been a heavy drinker, he was proud of his capacity to see men half his age under the table when he spent a night in Apia, and he had the sentimentality of the toper. He could cry over the stories he read in his magazines and yet would refuse a loan to some trader in difficulties whom he had known for twenty years. He was close with his money. Once Mackintosh said to him:

'No one could accuse you of giving money away.'

He took it as a compliment. His enthusiasm for nature was but the drivelling sensibility of the drunkard. Nor had Mackintosh any sympathy for his chief's feelings towards the natives. He loved them because they were in his power, as a selfish man loves his dog, and his mentality was on a level with theirs. Their humour was obscene and he was never at a loss for the lewd remark. He understood them and they understood him. He was proud of his influence over them. He looked upon them as his children and he mixed himself in all their affairs. But he was very jealous of his authority; if he ruled them with a rod of iron, brooking no contradiction, he would not suffer any of the white men on the island to take advantage of them. He watched the missionaries suspiciously and, if they did anything of which he disapproved, was able to make life so unendurable to them that if he could not get them removed they were glad to go of their own accord. His power over the natives was so great that on his word they would refuse labour and food to their pastor. On the other hand he showed the traders no favour. He took care that they should not cheat the natives; he saw that they got a fair reward for their work and their copra and that the traders made no extravagant profit on the wares they sold them. He was merciless to a bargain that he thought unfair. Sometimes the traders would complain at Apia that they did not get fair opportunities. They suffered for it. Walker then hesitated at no calumny, at no outrageous lie, to get even with them, and they found that if they wanted not only to live at peace, but to exist at all, they had to accept the situation on his own terms. More than once the store of a trader obnoxious to him had been burned down, and there was only the appositeness of the event to show that the administrator had instigated it. Once a Swedish half-caste, ruined by the burning, had gone to him and roundly accused him of arson. Walker laughed in his face.

'You dirty dog. Your mother was a native and you try to cheat the natives. If your rotten old store is burned down it's a judgement of Providence; that's what it is, a judgement of Providence. Get out.'

And as the man was hustled out by two native policemen the administrator laughed fatly.

'A judgement of Providence.'

And now Mackintosh watched him enter upon the day's work. He began with the sick, for Walker added doctoring to his other activities, and he had a small room behind the office full of drugs. An elderly man came forward, a man with a crop of curly grey hair, in a blue lava-lava, elaborately tattooed, with the skin of his body wrinkled like a wine-skin.

'What have you come for?' Walker asked him abruptly.

In a whining voice the man said that he could not eat without vomiting and that he had pains here and pains there.

'Go to the missionaries,' said Walker. 'You know that I only cure children.'

'I have been to the missionaries and they do me no good.'

'Then go home and prepare yourself to die. Have you lived so long and still want to go on living? You're a fool.'

The man broke into querulous expostulation, but Walker, pointing to a woman with a sick child in her arms, told her to bring it to his desk. He asked her questions and looked at the child.

'I will give you medicine,' he said. He turned to the half-caste clerk. 'Go into the dispensary and bring me some calomel pills.'

He made the child swallow one there and then and gave another to the mother.

'Take the child away and keep it warm. Tomorrow it will be dead or better.'

He leaned back in his chair and lit his pipe.

'Wonderful stuff, calomel. I've saved more lives with it than all the hospital doctors at Apia put together.'

Walker was very proud of his skill, and with the dogmatism of ignorance had no patience with the members of the medical profession.

'The sort of case I like,' he said, 'is the one that all the doctors have given up as hopeless. When the doctors have said they can't cure you, I say to them, "come to me". Did I ever tell you about the fellow who had a cancer?'

'Frequently,' said Mackintosh.

'I got him right in three months.'

'You've never told me about the people you haven't cured.'

He finished this part of the work and went on to the rest. It was a queer medley. There was a woman who could not get on with her husband and a man who complained that his wife had run away from him.

'Lucky dog,' said Walker. 'Most men wish their wives would too.'

There was a long complicated quarrel about the ownership of a few yards of land. There was a dispute about the sharing out of a catch of fish. There was a complaint against a white trader because he had given short measure. Walker listened attentively to every case, made up his mind quickly, and gave his decision. Then he would listen to nothing more; if the complainant went on he was hustled out of the office by a policeman. Mackintosh listened to it all with sullen irritation. On the whole, perhaps, it might be admitted that rough justice was done, but it exasperated the assistant that his chief trusted his instinct rather than the evidence. He would not listen to reason. He browbeat the witnesses and when they did not see what he wished them to called them thieves and liars.

He left to the last a group of men who were sitting in the corner of the room. He had deliberately ignored them. The party consisted of an old chief, a tall, dignified man with short, white hair, in a new lava-lava, bearing a huge fly wisp as a badge of office, his son, and half a dozen of the important men of the village. Walker had had a feud with them and had beaten them. As was characteristic of him he meant now to rub in his victory, and because he had them down to profit by their helplessness. The facts were peculiar. Walker had a passion for building roads. When he had come to Talua there were but a few tracks here and there, but in course of time he had cut roads through the country, joining the villages together, and it was to this that a great part of the island's prosperity was due. Whereas in the old days it had been impossible to get the produce of the land, copra chiefly, down to the coast where it could be put on schooners or motor launches and so taken to Apia, now transport was easy and simple. His ambition was to make a road right round the island and a great part of it was already built.

'In two years I shall have done it, and then I can die or they can fire me, I don't care.'

His roads were the joy of his heart and he made excursions constantly to see that they were kept in order. They were simple enough, wide tracks, grass-covered, cut through the scrub or through the plantations; but trees had to be rooted out, rocks dug up or blasted, and here and there levelling had been necessary. He was proud that he had surmounted by his own skill such difficulties as they presented. He rejoiced in his disposition of them so that they were not only convenient, but showed off the beauties of the island which his soul loved. When he spoke of his roads he was almost a poet. They meandered through those lovely scenes, and Walker had taken care that here and there they should run in a straight line, giving you a green vista through the tall trees, and here and there should turn and curve so that the heart was rested by the diversity. It was amazing that this coarse and sensual man should exercise so subtle an ingenuity to get the effects which his fancy suggested to him. He had used in making his roads all the fantastic skill of a Japanese gardener. He received a grant from headquarters for the work but took a curious pride in using but a small part of it, and the year before had spent only a hundred pounds of the thousand assigned to him.

'What do they want money for?' he boomed. 'They'll only spend it on all kinds of muck they don't want; what the missionaries leave them, that is to say.'

For no particular reason, except perhaps pride in the economy of his administration and the desire to contrast his efficiency with the wasteful methods of the authorities at Apia, he got the natives to do the work he wanted for wages that were almost nominal. It was owing to this that he had lately had difficulty with the village whose chief men now were come to see him. The chief's son had been in Upolu for a year and on coming back had told his people of the large sums that were paid at Apia for the public works. In long, idle talks he had inflamed their hearts with the desire for gain. He held out to them visions of vast wealth and they thought of the whisky they could buy–it was dear, since there was a law that it must not be sold to natives, and so it cost them double what the white man had to pay for it–they thought of the great sandalwood boxes in which they kept their treasures, and the scented soap and potted salmon, the luxuries for which the Kanaka will sell his soul; so that when the administrator sent for them and told them he wanted a road made from their village to a certain point along the coast and offered them twenty pounds, they asked him a hundred. The chief's son was called Manuma. He was a tall, handsome fellow, copper-coloured, with his fuzzy hair dyed red with lime, a wreath of red berries round his neck, and behind his ear a flower like a scarlet flame against his brown face. The upper part of his body was naked, but to show that he was no longer a savage, since he had lived in Apia, he wore a pair of dungarees instead of a lava-lava. He told them that if they held together the administrator would be obliged to accept their terms. His heart was set on building the road and when he found they would not work for less he would give them what they asked. But they must not move; whatever he said they must not abate their claim; they had asked a hundred and that they must keep to. When they mentioned the figure, Walker burst into a shout of his long, deep-voiced laughter. He told them not to make fools of themselves, but to set about the work at once. Because he was in a good humour that day he promised to give them a feast when the road was finished. But when he found that no attempt was made to start work, he went to the village and asked the men what silly game they were playing. Manuma had coached them well. They were quite calm, they did not attempt to argue–and argument is a passion with the Kanaka–they merely shrugged their shoulders: they would do it for a hundred pounds, and if he would not give them that they would do no work. He could please himself. They did not care. Then Walker flew into a passion. He was ugly then. His short fat neck swelled ominously, his red face grew purple, he foamed at the mouth. He set upon the natives with invective. He knew well how to wound and how to humiliate. He was terrifying. The older men grew pale and uneasy. They hesitated. If it had not been for Manuma, with his knowledge of the great world, and their dread of his ridicule, they would have yielded. It was Manuma who answered Walker.

'Pay us a hundred pounds and we will work.'

Walker, shaking his fist at him, called him every name he could think of. He riddled him with scorn. Manuma sat still and smiled. There may have been more bravado than confidence in his smile, but he had to make a good show before the others. He repeated his words.

'Pay us a hundred pounds and we will work.'

They thought that Walker would spring on him. It would not have been the first time that he had thrashed a native with his own hands; they knew his strength, and though Walker was three times the age of the young man and six inches shorter they did not doubt that he was more than a match for Manuma. No one had ever thought of resisting the savage onslaught of the administrator. But Walker said nothing. He chuckled.

'I am not going to waste my time with a pack of fools,' he said. 'Talk it over again. You know what I have offered. If you do not start in a week, take care.'

He turned round and walked out of the chief's hut. He untied his old mare and it was typical of the relations between him and the natives that one of the elder men hung on to the off stirrup while Walker from a convenient boulder hoisted himself heavily into the saddle.

That same night when Walker according to his habit was strolling along the road that ran past his house, he heard something whizz past him and with a thud strike a tree. Something had been thrown at him. He ducked instinctively. With a shout, 'Who's that?' he ran towards the place from which the missile had come and he heard the sound of a man escaping through the bush. He knew it was hopeless to pursue in the darkness, and besides he was soon out of breath, so he stopped and made his way back to the road. He looked about for what had been thrown, but could find nothing. It was quite dark. He went quickly back to the house and called Mackintosh and the Chinese boy.

'One of those devils has thrown something at me. Come along and let's find out what it was.'

He told the boy to bring a lantern and the three of them made their way back to the place. They hunted about the ground, but could not find what they sought. Suddenly the boy gave a guttural cry. They turned to look. He held up the lantern, and there, sinister in the light that cut the surrounding darkness, was a long knife sticking into the trunk of a coconut tree. It had been thrown with such force that it required quite an effort to pull it out.

'By George, if he hadn't missed me I'd have been in a nice state.'

Walker handled the knife. It was one of those knives, made in imitation of the sailor knives brought to the islands a hundred years before by the first white men, used to divide the coconuts in two so that the copra might be dried. It was a murderous weapon, and the blade, twelve inches long, was very sharp. Walker chuckled softly.

'The devil, the impudent devil.'

He had no doubt it was Manuma who had flung the knife. He had escaped death by three inches. He was not angry. On the contrary, he was in high spirits; the adventure exhilarated him, and when they got back to the house, calling for drinks, he rubbed his hands gleefully.

'I'll make them pay for this!'

His little eyes twinkled. He blew himself out like a turkey-cock, and for the second time within half an hour insisted on telling Mackintosh every detail of the affair. Then he asked him to play piquet, and while they played he boasted of his intentions. Mackintosh listened with tightened lips.

'But why should you grind them down like this?' he asked. 'Twenty pounds is precious little for the work you want them to do.'

'They ought to be precious thankful I give them anything.'

'Hang it all, it's not your own money. The government allots you a reasonable sum. They won't complain if you spend it.'

'They're a bunch of fools at Apia.'

Mackintosh saw that Walker's motive was merely vanity. He shrugged his shoulders.

'It won't do you much good to score off the fellows at Apia at the cost of your life.'

'Bless you, they wouldn't hurt me, these people. They couldn't do without me. They worship me. Manuma is a fool. He only threw that knife to frighten me.'

The next day Walker rode over again to the village. It was called Matautu. He did not get off his horse. When he reached the chief's house he saw that the men were sitting round the floor in a circle, talking, and he guessed they were discussing again the question of the road. The Samoan huts are formed in this way: trunks of slender trees are placed in a circle at intervals of perhaps five or six feet; a tall tree is set in the middle and from this downwards slopes the thatched roof. Venetian blinds of coconut leaves can be pulled down at night or when it is raining. Ordinarily the hut is open all round so that the breeze can blow through freely. Walker rode to the edge of the hut and called out to the chief.

'Oh, there, Tangatu, your son left his knife in a tree last night. I have brought it back to you.'

He flung it down on the ground in the midst of the circle, and with a low burst of laughter ambled off.

On Monday he went out to see if they had started work. There was no sign of it. He rode through the village. The inhabitants were about their ordinary avocations. Some were weaving mats of the pandanus leaf, one old man was busy with a *kava* bowl, the children were playing, the women went about their household chores. Walker, a smile on his lips, came to the chief's house.

'*Talofa-li*,' said the chief.

'*Talofa*,' answered Walker.

Manuma was making a net. He sat with a cigarette between his lips and looked up at Walker with a smile of triumph.

'You have decided that you will not make the road?'

The chief answered.

'Not unless you pay us one hundred pounds.'

'You will regret it.' He turned to Manuma. 'And you, my lad, I shouldn't wonder if your back was very sore before you're much older.'

He rode away chuckling. He left the natives vaguely uneasy. They feared the fat sinful old man, and neither the missionaries' abuse of him nor the scorn which Manuma had learnt in Apia made them forget that he had a devilish cunning and that no man had ever braved him without in the long run suffering for it. They found out within twenty-four hours what scheme he had devised. It was characteristic. For next morning a great band of men, women, and children came into the village and the chief men said that they had made a bargain with Walker to build the road. He had offered them twenty pounds and they had accepted. Now, the cunning lay in this, that the Polynesians have rules of hospitality which have all the force of laws; an etiquette of absolute rigidity made it necessary for the people of the village not only to give lodging to the strangers, but to provide them with food and drink as long as they wished to stay. The inhabitants of Matautu were outwitted. Every morning the workers went out in a joyous band, cut down trees, blasted rocks, levelled here and there and then in the evening tramped back again, and ate and drank, ate heartily, danced, sang hymns, and enjoyed life. For them it was a picnic. But soon their hosts began to wear long faces; the strangers had enormous appetites, and the plantains and the bread-fruit vanished before their rapacity; the alligator-pear trees, whose fruit sent to Apia might sell for good money, were stripped bare. Ruin stared them in the face. And then they found that the strangers were working very slowly. Had they received a hint from Walker that they might take their time? At this rate by the time the road was finished there would not be a scrap of food in the village. And worse than this, they were a laughing-stock; when one or other of them went to some distant hamlet on an errand he found that the story had got there before him, and he was met with derisive laughter. There is nothing the Kanaka can endure less than ridicule. It was not long before much angry talk passed among the sufferers. Manuma was no longer a hero; he had to put up with a good deal of plain speaking, and one day what Walker had suggested came to pass: a heated argument turned into a quarrel and half a dozen of the young men set upon the chief's son and gave him such a beating that for a week he lay bruised and sore on the pandanus mats. He turned from side to side and could find no ease. Every day or two the administrator rode over on his old mare and watched the progress of the road. He was not a man to resist the temptation of taunting the fallen foe, and he missed no opportunity to rub into the shamed inhabitants of Matautu the bitterness of their humiliation. He broke their spirit. And one morning, putting their pride in their pockets—a figure of speech, since pockets they had not—they all set out with the strangers and started working on the road. It was urgent to get it done quickly if they wanted to save any food at all, and the whole village joined in. But they worked silently, with rage and mortification in their hearts, and even the children toiled in silence. The women wept as they carried away bundles of brushwood. When Walker saw them he laughed so much that he almost rolled out of his saddle. The news spread quickly and tickled the people of the island to death. This was the greatest joke of all, the crowning triumph of that cunning old white man whom no Kanaka had ever been able to circumvent; and they came from distant villages, with their wives and children, to look at the foolish folk who had refused twenty pounds to make the road and now were forced to work for nothing. But the harder they worked the more easily went the guests. Why should they hurry, when they were getting good food for nothing and the longer they took about the job the better the joke became? At last the wretched villagers could stand it no longer, and they were come this morning to beg the administrator to send the strangers back to their own homes. If he would do this they promised to finish the road themselves for nothing. For him it was a victory complete and unqualified. They were humbled. A look of arrogant complacence spread over his large, naked face, and he seemed to swell in his chair like a great bullfrog. There was something sinister in his appearance, so that Mackintosh shivered with disgust. Then in his booming tones he began to speak.

'Is it for my good that I make the road? What benefit do you think I get out of it? It is for you, so that you can walk in comfort and carry your copra in comfort. I offered to pay you for your work, though it was for your own sake the work was done. I offered to pay you generously. Now *you* must pay. I will send the people of Manua back to their homes if you will finish the road and pay the twenty pounds that I have to pay them.'

There was an outcry. They sought to reason with him. They told him they had not the money. But to everything they said he replied with brutal gibes. Then the clock struck.

'Dinner time,' he said. 'Turn them all out.'

He raised himself heavily from his chair and walked out of the room. When Mackintosh followed him, he found him already seated at table, a napkin tied round his neck, holding his knife and fork in readiness for the meal the Chinese cook was about to bring. He was in high spirits.

'I did 'em down fine,' he said, as Mackintosh sat down. 'I shan't have much trouble with the roads after this.'

'I suppose you were joking,' said Mackintosh icily.

'What do you mean by that?'

'You're not really going to make them pay twenty pounds?'

'You bet your life I am.'

'I'm not sure you've got any right to.'

'Ain't you? I guess I've got the right to do any damned thing I like on this island.'

'I think you've bullied them quite enough.'

Walker laughed fatly. He did not care what Mackintosh thought.

'When I want your opinion I'll ask for it.'

Mackintosh grew very white. He knew by bitter experience that he could do nothing but keep silence, and the violent effort at self-control made him sick and faint. He could not eat the food that was before him and with disgust he watched Walker shovel meat into his vast mouth. He was a dirty feeder, and to sit at table with him needed a strong stomach. Mackintosh shuddered. A tremendous desire seized him to humiliate that gross and cruel man; he would give anything in the world to see him in the dust, suffering as much as he had made others suffer. He had never loathed the bully with such loathing as now.

The day wore on. Mackintosh tried to sleep after dinner, but the passion in his heart prevented him; he tried to read, but the letters swam before his eyes. The sun beat down pitilessly, and he longed for rain; but he knew that rain would bring no coolness; it would only make it hotter and more steamy. He was a native of Aberdeen and his heart yearned suddenly for the icy winds that whistled through the granite streets of that city. Here he was a prisoner, imprisoned not only by that placid sea, but by his hatred for that horrible old man. He pressed his hands to his aching head. He would like to kill him. But he pulled himself together. He must do something to distract his mind, and since he could not read he thought he would set his private papers in order. It was a job which he had long meant to do and which he had constantly put off. He unlocked the drawer of his desk and took out a handful of letters. He caught sight of his revolver. An impulse, no sooner realized than set aside, to put a bullet through his head and so escape from the intolerable bondage of life flashed through his mind. He noticed that in the damp air the revolver was slightly rusted, and he got an oil-rag and began to clean it. It was while he was thus occupied that he grew aware of someone slinking round the door. He looked up and called:

'Who is there?'

There was a moment's pause, then Manuma showed himself.

'What do you want?'

The chief's son stood for a moment, sullen and silent, and when he spoke it was with a strangled voice.

'We can't pay twenty pounds. We haven't the money.'

'What am I to do?' said Mackintosh. 'You heard what Mr Walker said.'

Manuma began to plead, half in Samoan and half in English. It was a sing-song whine, with the quavering intonations of a beggar, and it filled Mackintosh with disgust. It outraged him that the man should let himself be so crushed. He was a pitiful object.

'I can do nothing,' said Mackintosh irritably. 'You know that Mr Walker is master here.'

Manuma was silent again. He still stood in the doorway.

'I am sick,' he said at last. 'Give me some medicine.'

'What is the matter with you?'

'I do not know. I am sick. I have pains in my body.'

'Don't stand there,' said Mackintosh sharply. 'Come in and let me look at you.'

Manuma entered the little room and stood before the desk.

'I have pains here and here.'

He put his hands to his loins and his face assumed an expression of pain. Suddenly Mackintosh grew conscious that the boy's eyes were resting on the revolver which he had laid on the desk when Manuma appeared in the doorway. There was a silence between the two which to Mackintosh was endless. He seemed to read the thoughts which were in the Kanaka's mind. His heart beat violently. And then he felt as though something possessed him so that he acted under the compulsion of a foreign will. Himself did not make the movements of his body, but a power that was strange to him. His throat was suddenly dry, and he put his hand to it mechanically in order to help his speech. He was impelled to avoid Manuma's eyes.

'Just wait here,' he said, his voice sounded as though someone had seized him by the windpipe, 'and I'll fetch you something from the dispensary.'

He got up. Was it his fancy that he staggered a little? Manuma stood silently, and though he kept his eyes averted, Mackintosh knew that he was looking dully out of the door. It was this other person that possessed him that drove him out of the room, but it was himself that took a handful of muddled papers and threw them on the revolver in order to hide it from view. He went to the dispensary. He got a pill and poured out some blue draught into a small bottle, and then came out into the compound. He did not want to go back into his own bungalow, so he called to Manuma.

'Come here.'

He gave him the drugs and instructions how to take them. He did not know what it was that made it impossible for him to look at the Kanaka. While he was speaking to him he kept his eyes on his shoulder. Manuma took the medicine and slunk out of the gate.

Mackintosh went into the dining-room and turned over once more the old newspapers. But he could not read them. The house was very still. Walker was upstairs in his room asleep, the Chinese cook was busy in the kitchen, the two policemen were out fishing. The silence that seemed to brood over the house was unearthly, and there hammered in Mackintosh's head the question whether the revolver still lay where he had placed it. He could not bring himself to look. The uncertainty was horrible, but the certainty would be more horrible still. He sweated. At last he could stand the silence no longer, and he made up his mind to go down the road to the trader's, a man named Jervis, who had a store about a mile away. He was a half-caste, but even that amount of white blood made him possible to talk to. He wanted to get away from his bungalow, with the desk littered with untidy papers, and underneath them something, or nothing. He walked along the road. As he passed the fine hut of a chief a greeting was called out to him. Then he came to the store. Behind the counter sat the trader's daughter, a swarthy broad-featured girl in a pink blouse and a white drill skirt. Jervis hoped he would marry her. He had money, and he had told Mackintosh that his daughter's husband would be well-to-do. She flushed a little when she saw Mackintosh.

'Father's just unpacking some cases that have come in this morning. I'll tell him you're here.'

He sat down and the girl went out behind the shop. In a moment her mother waddled in, a huge old woman, a chiefess, who owned much land in her own right; and gave him her hand. Her monstrous obesity was an offence, but she managed to convey an impression of dignity. She was cordial without obsequiousness; affable, but conscious of her station.

'You're quite a stranger, Mr Mackintosh. Teresa was saying only this morning: "Why, we never see Mr Mackintosh now."'

He shuddered a little as he thought of himself as that old native's son-in-law. It was notorious that she ruled her husband, notwithstanding his white blood, with a firm hand. Hers was the authority and hers the business head. She might be no more than Mrs Jervis to the white people, but her father had been a chief of the blood royal, and his father and his father's father had ruled as kings. The trader came in, small beside his imposing wife, a dark man with a black beard going grey, in ducks, with handsome eyes and flashing teeth. He was very British, and his conversation was slangy, but you felt he spoke English as a foreign tongue; with his family he used the language of his native mother. He was a servile man, cringing and obsequious.

'Ah, Mr Mackintosh, this is a joyful surprise. Get the whisky, Teresa; Mr Mackintosh will have a gargle with us.'

He gave all the latest news of Apia, watching his guest's eyes the while, so that he might know the welcome thing to say.

'And how is Walker? We've not seen him just lately. Mrs Jervis is going to send him a sucking-pig one day this week.'

'I saw him riding home this morning,' said Teresa.

'Here's how,' said Jervis, holding up his whisky.

Mackintosh drank. The two women sat and looked at him, Mrs Jervis in her black Mother Hubbard, placid and haughty, and Teresa anxious to smile whenever she caught his eye, while the trader gossiped insufferably.

'They were saying in Apia it was about time Walker retired. He ain't so young as he was. Things have changed since he first come to the islands and he ain't changed with them.'

'He'll go too far,' said the old chiefess. 'The natives aren't satisfied.'

'That was a good joke about the road,' laughed the trader. 'When I told them about it in Apia they fair split their sides with laughing. Good old Walker.'

Mackintosh looked at him savagely. What did he mean by talking of him in that fashion? To a half-caste trader he was Mr Walker. It was on his tongue to utter a harsh rebuke for the impertinence. He did not know what held him back.

'When he goes I hope you'll take his place, Mr Mackintosh,' said Jervis. 'We all like you on the island. You understand the natives. They're educated now, they must be treated differently to the old days. It wants an educated man to be administrator now. Walker was only a trader same as I am.'

Teresa's eyes glistened.

'When the time comes if there's anything anyone can do here, you bet your bottom dollar we'll do it. I'd get all the chiefs to go over to Apia and make a petition.'

Mackintosh felt horribly sick. It had not struck him that if anything happened to Walker it might be he who would succeed him. It was true that no one in his official position knew the island so well. He got up suddenly and scarcely taking his leave walked back to the compound. And now he went straight to his room. He took a quick look at his desk. He rummaged among the papers.

The revolver was not there.

His heart thumped violently against his ribs. He looked for the revolver everywhere. He hunted in the chairs and in the drawers. He looked desperately, and all the time he knew he would not find it. Suddenly he heard Walker's gruff, hearty voice.

'What the devil are you up to, Mac?'

He started. Walker was standing in the doorway and instinctively he turned round to hide what lay upon his desk.

'Tidying up?' quizzed Walker. 'I've told 'em to put the grey in the trap. I'm going down to Tafoni to bathe. You'd better come along.'

'All right,' said Mackintosh.

So long as he was with Walker nothing could happen. The place they were bound for was about three miles away, and there was a fresh-water pool, separated by a thin barrier of rock from the sea, which the administrator had blasted out for the natives to bathe in. He had done this at spots round the island, wherever there was a spring; and the fresh water, compared with the sticky warmth of the sea, was cool and invigorating. They drove along the silent grassy road, splashing now and then through fords, where the sea had forced its way in, past a couple of native villages, the bell-shaped huts spaced out roomily and the white chapel in the middle, and at the third village they got out of the trap, tied up the horse, and walked down to the pool. They were accompanied by four or five girls and a dozen children. Soon they were all splashing about, shouting and laughing, while Walker, in a lava-lava, swam to and fro like an unwieldy porpoise. He made lewd jokes with the girls, and they amused themselves by diving under him and wriggling away when he tried to catch them. When he was tired he lay down on a rock, while the girls and the children surrounded him; it was a happy family; and the old man, huge, with his crescent of white hair and his shining bald crown, looked like some old sea god. Once Mackintosh caught a queer soft look in his eyes.

'They're dear children,' he said. 'They look upon me as their father.'

And then without a pause he turned to one of the girls and made an obscene remark which sent them all into fits of laughter. Mackintosh started to dress. With his thin legs and thin arms he made a grotesque figure, a sinister Don Quixote, and Walker began to make coarse jokes about him. They were acknowledged with little smothered laughs. Mackintosh struggled with his shirt. He knew he looked absurd, but he hated being laughed at. He stood silent and glowering.

'If you want to get back in time for dinner you ought to come soon.'

'You're not a bad fellow, Mac. Only you're a fool. When you're doing one thing you always want to do another. That's not the way we live.'

But all the same he raised himself slowly to his feet and began to put on his clothes. They sauntered back to the village, drank a bowl of *kava* with the chief, and then, after a joyful farewell from all the lazy villagers, drove home.

After dinner, according to his habit, Walker, lighting his cigar, prepared to go for a stroll. Mackintosh was suddenly seized with fear.

'Don't you think it's rather unwise to go out at night by yourself just now?'

Walker stared at him with his round blue eyes.

'What the devil do you mean?'

'Remember the knife the other night. You've got those fellows' backs up.'

'Pooh! They wouldn't dare.'

'Someone dared before.'

'That was only a bluff. They wouldn't hurt me. They look upon me as a father. They know that whatever I do is for their own good.'

Mackintosh watched him with contempt in his heart. The man's self-complacency outraged him, and yet something, he knew not what, made him insist.

'Remember what happened this morning. It wouldn't hurt you to stay at home just tonight. I'll play piquet with you.'

'I'll play piquet with you when I come back. The Kanaka isn't born yet who can make me alter my plans.'

'You'd better let me come with you.'

'You stay where you are.'

Mackintosh shrugged his shoulders. He had given the man full warning. If he did not heed it that was his own lookout. Walker put on his hat and went out. Mackintosh began to read; but then he thought of something; perhaps it would be as well to have his own whereabouts quite clear. He crossed over to the kitchen and, inventing some pretext, talked for a few minutes with the cook. Then he got out the gramophone and put a record on it, but while it ground out its melancholy tune, some comic song of a London music-hall, his ear was strained for a sound away there in the night. At his elbow the record reeled out its loudness, the words were raucous, but notwithstanding he seemed to be surrounded by an unearthly silence. He heard the dull roar of the breakers against the reef. He heard the breeze sigh, far up, in the leaves of the coconut trees. How long would it be? It was awful.

He heard a hoarse laugh.

'Wonders will never cease. It's not often you play yourself a tune, Mac.'

Walker stood at the window, red-faced, bluff and jovial.

'Well, you see I'm alive and kicking. What were you playing for?'

Walker came in.

'Nerves a bit dicky, eh? Playing a tune to keep your pecker up?'

'I was playing your requiem.'

'What the devil's that?'

''Alf o' bitter an' a pint of stout.'

'A rattling good song too. I don't mind how often I hear it. Now I'm ready to take your money off you at piquet.'

They played and Walker bullied his way to victory, bluffing his opponent, chaffing him, jeering at his mistakes, up to every dodge, browbeating him, exulting. Presently Mackintosh recovered his coolness, and standing outside himself, as it were, he was able to take a detached pleasure in watching the overbearing old man and in his own cold reserve. Somewhere Manuma sat quietly and awaited his opportunity.

Walker won game after game and pocketed his winnings at the end of the evening in high good-humour.

'You'll have to grow a little bit older before you stand much chance against me, Mac. The fact is I have a natural gift for cards.'

'I don't know that there's much gift about it when I happen to deal you fourteen aces.'

'Good cards come to good players,' retorted Walker. 'I'd have won if I'd had your hands.'

He went on to tell long stories of the various occasions on which he had played cards with notorious sharpers and to their consternation had taken all their money from them. He boasted. He praised himself. And Mackintosh listened with absorption. He wanted now to feed his hatred; and everything Walker said, every gesture, made him more detestable. At last Walker got up.

'Well, I'm going to turn in,' he said with a loud yawn. 'I've got a long day tomorrow.'

'What are you going to do?'

'I'm driving over to the other side of the island. I'll start at five, but I don't expect I shall get back to dinner till late.'

They generally dined at seven.

'We'd better make it half past seven then.'

'I guess it would be as well.'

Mackintosh watched him knock the ashes out of his pipe. His vitality was rude and exuberant. It was strange to think that death hung over him. A faint smile flickered in Mackintosh's cold, gloomy eyes.

'Would you like me to come with you?'

'What in God's name should I want that for? I'm using the mare and she'll have enough to do to carry me; she don't want to drag you over thirty miles of road.'

'Perhaps you don't quite realize what the feeling is at Matautu. I think it would be safer if I came with you.'

Walker burst out into contemptuous laughter.

'You'd be a fine lot of use in a scrap. I'm not a great hand at getting the wind up.'

Now the smile passed from Mackintosh's eyes to his lips. It distorted them painfully.

'*Quem deus vult perdere prius dementat.*'

'What the hell is that?' said Walker.

'Latin,' answered Mackintosh as he went out.

And now he chuckled. His mood had changed. He had done all he could and the matter was in the hands of fate. He slept more soundly than he had done for weeks. When he awoke next morning he went out. After a good night he found a pleasant exhilaration in the freshness of the early air. The sea was a more vivid blue, the sky more brilliant, than on most days, the trade wind was fresh, and there was a ripple on the lagoon as the breeze brushed over it like velvet brushed the wrong way. He felt himself stronger and younger. He entered upon the day's work with zest. After luncheon he slept again, and as evening drew on he had the bay saddled and sauntered through the bush. He seemed to see it all with new eyes. He felt more normal. The extraordinary thing was that he was able to put Walker out of his mind altogether. So far as he was concerned he might never have existed.

He returned late, hot after his ride, and bathed again. Then he sat on the veranda, smoking his pipe, and looked at the day declining over the lagoon. In the sunset the lagoon, rosy and purple and green, was very beautiful. He felt at peace with the world and with himself. When the cook came out to say that dinner was ready and to ask whether he should wait, Mackintosh smiled at him with friendly eyes. He looked at his watch.

'It's half past seven. Better not wait. One can't tell when the boss'll be back.'

The boy nodded, and in a moment Mackintosh saw him carry across the yard a bowl of steaming soup. He got up lazily, went into the dining-room, and ate his dinner. Had it happened? The uncertainty was amusing and Mackintosh chuckled in the silence. The food did not seem so monotonous as usual, and even though there was Hamburger steak, the cook's invariable dish when his poor invention failed him, it tasted by some miracle succulent and spiced. After dinner he strolled over lazily to his bungalow to get a book. He liked the intense stillness, and now that the night had fallen the stars were blazing in the sky. He shouted for a lamp and in a moment the Chink pattered over on his bare feet, piercing the darkness with a ray of light. He put the lamp on the desk and noiselessly slipped out of the room. Mackintosh stood rooted to the floor, for there, half hidden by untidy papers, was his revolver. His heart throbbed painfully, and he broke into a sweat. It was done then.

He took up the revolver with a shaking hand. Four of the chambers were empty. He paused a moment and looked suspiciously out into the night, but there was no one there. He quickly slipped four cartridges into the empty chambers and locked the revolver in his drawer.

He sat down to wait.

An hour passed, a second hour passed. There was nothing. He sat at his desk as though he were writing, but he neither wrote nor read. He merely listened. He strained his ears for a sound travelling from a far distance. At last he heard hesitating footsteps and knew it was the Chinese cook.

'Ah-Sung,' he called.

The boy came to the door.

'Boss velly late,' he said. 'Dinner no good.'

Mackintosh stared at him, wondering whether he knew what had happened, and whether, when he knew, he would realize on what terms he and Walker had been. He went about his work, sleek, silent, and smiling, and who could tell his thoughts?

'I expect he's had dinner on the way, but you must keep the soup hot at all events.'

The words were hardly out of his mouth when the silence was suddenly broken into by a confusion, cries, and a rapid patter of naked feet. A number of natives ran into the compound, men and women and children; they crowded round Mackintosh and they all talked at once. They were unintelligible. They were excited and frightened and some of them were crying. Mackintosh pushed his way through them and went to the gateway. Though he had scarcely understood what they said he knew quite well what had happened. And as he reached the gate the dog-cart arrived. The old mare was being led by a tall Kanaka, and in the dog-cart crouched two men, trying to hold Walker up. A little crowd of natives surrounded it.

The mare was led into the yard and the natives surged in after it. Mackintosh shouted to them to stand back and the two policemen, appearing suddenly from God knows where, pushed them violently aside. By now he had managed to understand that some lads, who had been fishing, on their way back to their village had come across the cart on the home side of the ford. The mare was nuzzling about the herbage and in the darkness they could just see the great white bulk of the old man sunk between the seat and the dashboard. At first they thought he was drunk and they peered in, grinning, but then they heard him groan, and guessed that something was amiss. They ran to the village and called for help. It was when they returned, accompanied by half a hundred people, that they discovered Walker had been shot.

With a sudden thrill of horror Mackintosh asked himself whether he was already dead. The first thing at all events was to get him out of the cart, and that, owing to Walker's corpulence, was a difficult job. It took four strong men to lift him. They jolted him and he uttered a dull groan. He was still alive. At last they carried him into the house, up the stairs, and placed him on his bed. Then Mackintosh was able to see him, for in the yard, lit only by half a dozen hurricane lamps, everything had been obscured. Walker's white ducks were stained with blood, and the men who had carried him wiped their hands, red and sticky, on their lava-lavas. Mackintosh held up the lamp. He had not expected the old man to be so pale. His eyes were closed. He was breathing still, his pulse could be just felt but it was obvious that he was dying. Mackintosh had not bargained for the shock of horror that convulsed him. He saw that the native clerk was there, and in a voice hoarse with fear told him to go into the dispensary and get what was necessary for a hypodermic injection. One of the policemen had brought up the whisky, and Mackintosh forced a little into the old man's mouth. The room was crowded with natives. They sat about the floor, speechless now and terrified, and every now and then one wailed aloud. It was very hot, but Mackintosh felt cold, his hands and his feet were like ice, and he had to make a violent effort not to tremble in all his limbs. He did not know what to do. He did not know if Walker was bleeding still, and if he was, how he could stop the bleeding.

The clerk brought the hypodermic needle.

'You give it to him,' said Mackintosh. 'You're more used to that sort of thing than I am.'

His head ached horribly. It felt as though all sorts of little savage things were beating inside it, trying to get out. They watched for the effect of the injection. Presently Walker opened his eyes slowly. He did not seem to know where he was.

'Keep quiet,' said Mackintosh. 'You're at home. You're quite safe.'

Walker's lips outlined a shadowy smile.

'They've got me,' he whispered.

'I'll get Jervis to send his motor-boat to Apia at once. We'll get a doctor out by tomorrow afternoon.'

There was a long pause before the old man answered.

'I shall be dead by then.'

A ghastly expression passed over Mackintosh's pale face. He forced himself to laugh.

'What rot! You keep quiet and you'll be as right as rain.'

'Give me a drink,' said Walker. 'A stiff one.'

With shaking hand Mackintosh poured out whisky and water, half and half, and held the glass while Walker drank greedily. It seemed to restore him. He gave a long sigh and a little colour came into his great fleshy face. Mackintosh felt extraordinarily helpless. He stood and stared at the old man.

'If you'll tell me what to do I'll do it,' he said.

'There's nothing to do. Just leave me alone. I'm done for.'

He looked dreadfully pitiful as he lay on the great bed, a huge, bloated, old man; but so wan, so weak, it was heart-rending. As he rested, his mind seemed to grow clearer.

'You were right, Mac,' he said presently. 'You warned me.'

'I wish to God I'd come with you.'

'You're a good chap, Mac, only you don't drink.'

There was another long silence, and it was clear that Walker was sinking. There was an internal haemorrhage and even Mackintosh in his ignorance could not fail to see that his chief had but an hour or two to live. He stood by the side of the bed stock-still. For half an hour perhaps Walker lay with his eyes closed, then he opened them.

'They'll give you my job,' he said, slowly. 'Last time I was in Apia I told them you were all right. Finish my road. I want to think that'll be done. All round the island.'

'I don't want your job. You'll get all right.'

Walker shook his head wearily.

'I've had my day. Treat them fairly, that's the great thing. They're children. You must always remember that. You must be firm with them, but you must be kind. And you must be just. I've never made a bob out of them. I haven't saved a hundred pounds in twenty years. The road's the great thing. Get the road finished.'

Something very like a sob was wrung from Mackintosh.

'You're a good fellow, Mac. I always liked you.'

He closed his eyes, and Mackintosh thought that he would never open them again. His mouth was so dry that he had to get himself something to drink. The Chinese cook silently put a chair for him. He sat down by the side of the bed and waited. He did not know how long a time passed. The night was endless. Suddenly one of the men sitting there broke into uncontrollable sobbing, loudly, like a child, and Mackintosh grew aware that the room was crowded by this time with natives. They sat all over the floor on their haunches, men and women, staring at the bed.

'What are all these people doing here?' said Mackintosh. 'They've got no right. Turn them out, turn them out, all of them.'

His words seemed to rouse Walker, for he opened his eyes once more, and now they were all misty. He wanted to speak, but he was so weak that Mackintosh had to strain his ears to catch what he said.

'Let them stay. They're my children. They ought to be here.'

Mackintosh turned to the natives.

'Stay where you are. He wants you. But be silent.'

A faint smile came over the old man's white face.

'Come nearer,' he said.

Mackintosh bent over him. His eyes were closed and the words he said were like a wind sighing through the fronds of the coconut trees.

'Give me another drink. I've got something to say.'

This time Mackintosh gave him his whisky neat. Walker collected his strength in a final effort of will.

'Don't make a fuss about this. In ninety-five when there were troubles white men were killed, and the fleet came and shelled the villages. A lot of people were killed who'd had nothing to do with it. They're damned fools at Apia. If they make a fuss they'll only punish the wrong people. I don't want anyone punished.'

He paused for a while to rest.

'You must say it was an accident. No one's to blame. Promise me that.'

'I'll do anything you like,' whispered Mackintosh.

'Good chap. One of the best. They're children. I'm their father. A father don't let his children get into trouble if he can help it.'

A ghost of a chuckle came out of his throat. It was astonishingly weird and ghastly.

'You're a religious chap, Mac. What's that about forgiving them? You know.'

For a while Mackintosh did not answer. His lips trembled.

'Forgive them, for they know not what they do?'

'That's right. Forgive them. I've loved them, you know, always loved them.'

He sighed. His lips faintly moved, and now Mackintosh had to put his ears quite close to them in order to hear.

'Hold my hand,' he said.

Mackintosh gave a gasp. His heart seemed wrenched. He took the old man's hand, so cold and weak, a coarse, rough hand, and held it in his own. And thus he sat until he nearly started out of his seat, for the silence was suddenly broken by a long rattle. It was terrible and unearthly. Walker was dead. Then the natives broke out with loud cries. The tears ran down their faces, and they beat their breasts.

Mackintosh disengaged his hand from the dead man's and staggering like one drunk with sleep he went out of the room. He went to the locked drawer in his writing-desk and took out the revolver. He walked down to the sea and walked into the lagoon; he waded out cautiously, so that he should not trip against a coral rock, till the water came to his arm-pits. Then he put a bullet through his head.

An hour later half a dozen slim brown sharks were splashing and struggling at the spot where he fell.

The
Three Fat Women
of Antibes

♦

One was called Mrs Richman and she was a widow. The second was called Mrs
Sutcliffe; she was American and she had divorced two husbands. The third was
called Miss Hickson and she was a spinster. They were all in the comfortable
forties and they were all well off. Mrs Sutcliffe had the odd first name of Arrow.
When she was young and slender she had liked it well enough. It suited her and
the jests it occasioned though too often repeated were very flattering; she was
not disinclined to believe that it suited her character too: it suggested
directness, speed, and purpose. She liked it less now that her delicate features
had grown muzzy with fat, that her arms and shoulders were so substantial and
her hips so massive. It was increasingly difficult to find dresses to make her look
as she liked to look. The jests her name gave rise to now were made behind her
back and she very well knew that they were far from obliging. But she was by no
means resigned to middle age. She still wore blue to bring out the colour of
her eyes and, with the help of art, her fair hair had kept its lustre. What she
liked about Beatrice Richman and Frances Hickson was that they were both
so much fatter than she, it made her look quite slim; they were both of them
older and much inclined to treat her as a little young thing. It was not
disagreeable. They were good-natured women and they chaffed her pleasantly
about her beaux; they had both given up the thought of that kind of nonsense,
indeed Miss Hickson had never given it a moment's consideration, but they
were sympathetic to her flirtations. It was understood that one of these days
Arrow would make a third man happy.

'Only you mustn't get any heavier, darling,' said Mrs Richman.

'And for goodness' sake make certain of his bridge,' said Miss Hickson.

They saw for her a man of about fifty, but well-preserved and of
distinguished carriage, an admiral on the retired list and a good golfer, or a

widower without encumbrances, but in any case with a substantial income. Arrow listened to them amiably, and kept to herself the fact that this was not at all her idea. It was true that she would have liked to marry again, but her fancy turned to a dark slim Italian with flashing eyes and a sonorous title or to a Spanish don of noble lineage; and not a day more than thirty. There were times when, looking at herself in her mirror, she was certain she did not look any more than that herself.

They were great friends, Miss Hickson, Mrs Richman, and Arrow Sutcliffe. It was their fat that had brought them together and bridge that had cemented their alliance. They had met first at Carlsbad, where they were staying at the same hotel and were treated by the same doctor who used them with the same ruthlessness. Beatrice Richman was enormous. She was a handsome woman, with fine eyes, rouged cheeks, and painted lips. She was very well content to be a widow with a handsome fortune. She adored her food. She liked bread and butter, cream, potatoes, and suet puddings, and for eleven months of the year ate pretty well everything she had a mind to, and for one month went to Carlsbad to reduce. But every year she grew fatter. She upbraided the doctor, but got no sympathy from him. He pointed out to her various plain and simple facts.

'But if I'm never to eat a thing I like, life isn't worth living,' she expostulated.

He shrugged his disapproving shoulders. Afterwards she told Miss Hickson that she was beginning to suspect he wasn't so clever as she had thought. Miss Hickson gave a great guffaw. She was that sort of woman. She had a deep bass voice, a large flat sallow face from which twinkled little bright eyes; she walked with a slouch, her hands in her pockets, and when she could do so without exciting attention smoked a long cigar. She dressed as like a man as she could.

'What the deuce should I look like in frills and furbelows?' she said. 'When you're as fat as I am you may just as well be comfortable.'

She wore tweeds and heavy boots and whenever she could went about bareheaded. But she was as strong as an ox and boasted that few men could drive a longer ball than she. She was plain of speech, and she could swear more variously than a stevedore. Though her name was Frances she preferred to be called Frank. Masterful, but with tact, it was her jovial strength of character that held the three together. They drank their waters together, had their baths at the same hour, they took their strenuous walks together, pounded about the tennis court with a professional to make them run, and ate at the same table their sparse and regulated meals. Nothing impaired their good humour but the scales, and when one or other of them weighed as much on one day as she had the day before neither Frank's coarse jokes, the *bonhomie* of Beatrice, nor Arrow's pretty kittenish ways sufficed to dispel the gloom. Then drastic measures were resorted to, the culprit went to bed for twenty-four hours and nothing passed her lips but the doctor's famous vegetable soup which tasted like hot water in which a cabbage had been well rinsed.

Never were three women greater friends. They would have been independent of anyone else if they had not needed a fourth at bridge. They were fierce, enthusiastic players and the moment the day's cure was over, they sat down at the bridge table. Arrow, feminine as she was, played the best game of the three, a hard, brilliant game, in which she showed no mercy and never conceded a point or failed to take advantage of a mistake. Beatrice was solid and reliable. Frank was dashing; she was a great theorist, and had all the authorities at the tip of her tongue. They had long arguments over the rival systems. They bombarded one another with Culbertson and Sims. It was obvious that not one of them ever played a card without fifteen good reasons, but it was also obvious from the subsequent conversation that there were fifteen equally good reasons why she should not have played it. Life would have been perfect, even with the prospect of twenty-four hours of that filthy soup when the doctor's rotten (Beatrice) bloody (Frank) lousy (Arrow) scales pretended one hadn't lost an ounce in two days, if only there had not been this constant difficulty of finding someone to play with them who was in their class.

It was for this reason that on the occasion with which this narrative deals Frank invited Lena Finch to come and stay with them at Antibes. They were spending some weeks there on Frank's suggestion. It seemed absurd to her, with her common sense, that immediately the cure was over Beatrice who always lost twenty pounds should be giving way to her ungovernable appetite put it all on again. Beatrice was weak. She needed a person of strong will to watch her diet. She proposed then that on leaving Carlsbad they should take a house at Antibes, where they could get plenty of exercise–everyone knew that nothing slimmed you like swimming–and as far as possible could go on with the cure. With a cook of their own they could at least avoid things that were obviously fattening. There was no reason why they should not all lose several pounds more. It seemed a very good idea. Beatrice knew what was good for her, and she could resist temptation well enough if temptation was not put right under her nose. Besides, she liked gambling, and a flutter at the Casino two or three times a week would pass the time very pleasantly. Arrow adored Antibes, and she would be looking her best after a month at Carlsbad. She could just pick and choose among the young Italians, the passionate Spaniards, the gallant Frenchmen, and the long-limbed English who sauntered about all day in bathing trunks and gay-coloured dressing-gowns. The plan worked very well. They had a grand time. Two days a week they ate nothing but hard-boiled eggs and raw tomatoes and they mounted the scales every morning with light hearts. Arrow got down to eleven stone and felt just like a girl; Beatrice and Frank by standing in a certain way just avoided the thirteen. The machine they had bought registered kilogrammes, and they got extraordinarily clever at translating them in the twinkling of an eye to pounds and ounces.

But the fourth at bridge continued to be the difficulty. This person played like a fool, the other was so slow that it drove you frantic, one was quarrelsome, another was a bad loser, a third was next door to a crook. It was strange how hard it was to find exactly the player you wanted.

One morning when they were sitting in pyjamas on the terrace overlooking the sea, drinking their tea (without milk or sugar) and eating a rusk prepared by Dr Hudebert and guaranteed not to be fattening, Frank looked up from her letters.

'Lena Finch is coming down to the Riviera,' she said.

'Who's she?' asked Arrow.

'She married a cousin of mine. He died a couple of months ago and she's just recovering from a nervous breakdown. What about asking her to come here for a fortnight?'

'Does she play bridge?' asked Beatrice.

'You bet your life she does,' boomed Frank in her deep voice. 'And a damned good game too. We should be absolutely independent of outsiders.'

'How old is she?' asked Arrow.

'Same age as I am.'

'That sounds all right.'

It was settled. Frank, with her usual decisiveness, stalked out as soon as she had finished her breakfast to send a wire, and three days later Lena Finch arrived. Frank met her at the station. She was in deep but not obtrusive mourning for the recent death of her husband. Frank had not seen her for two years. She kissed her warmly and took a good look at her.

'You're very thin, darling,' she said.

Lena smiled bravely.

'I've been through a good deal lately. I've lost a lot of weight.'

Frank sighed, but whether from sympathy with her cousin's sad loss, or from envy, was not obvious.

Lena was not, however, depressed, and after a quick bath was quite ready to accompany Frank to Eden Roc. Frank introduced the stranger to her two friends and they sat down in what was known as the Monkey House. It was an enclosure covered with glass overlooking the sea, with a bar at the back, and it was crowded with chattering people in bathing costumes, pyjamas, or dressing-gowns, who were seated at the tables having drinks. Beatrice's soft heart went out to the lorn window, and Arrow, seeing that she was pale, quite ordinary to look at, and probably forty-eight, was prepared to like her very much. A waiter approached them.

'What will you have, Lena dear?' Frank asked.

'Oh, I don't know, what you all have, a dry Martini or a White Lady.'

Arrow and Beatrice gave her a quick look. Everyone knows how fattening cocktails are.

'I daresay you're tired after your journey,' said Frank kindly.

She ordered a dry Martini for Lena and a mixed lemon and orange juice for herself and her two friends.

'We find alcohol isn't very good in all this heat,' she explained.

'Oh, it never affects me at all,' Lena answered airily. 'I like cocktails.'

Arrow went very slightly pale under her rouge (neither she nor Beatrice ever wet their faces when they bathed and they thought it absurd of Frank, a woman of her size, to pretend she liked diving) but she said nothing. The conversation was gay and easy, they all said the obvious things with gusto, and presently they strolled back to the villa for luncheon.

In each napkin were two little antifat rusks. Lena gave a bright smile as she put them by the side of her plate.

'May I have some bread?' she asked.

The grossest indecency would not have fallen on the ears of those three women with such a shock. Not one of them had eaten bread for ten years. Even Beatrice, greedy as she was, drew the line there. Frank, the good hostess, recovered herself first.

'Of course, darling,' she said and turning to the butler asked him to bring some.

'And some butter,' said Lena in that pleasant easy way of hers.

There was a moment's embarrassed silence.

'I don't know if there's any in the house,' said Frank, 'but I'll inquire. There may be some in the kitchen.'

'I adore bread and butter, don't you?' said Lena, turning to Beatrice.

Beatrice gave a sickly smile and an evasive reply. The butler brought a long crisp roll of French bread. Lena slit it in two and plastered it with the butter which was miraculously produced. A grilled sole was served.

'We eat very simply here,' said Frank. 'I hope you won't mind.'

'Oh, no, I like my food very plain,' said Lena as she took some butter and spread it over her fish. 'As long as I can have bread and butter and potatoes and cream I'm quite happy.'

The three friends exchanged a glance. Frank's great sallow face sagged a little and she looked with distaste at the dry, insipid sole on her plate. Beatrice came to the rescue.

'It's such a bore, we can't get cream here,' she said. 'It's one of the things one has to do without on the Riviera.'

'What a pity,' said Lena.

The rest of the luncheon consisted of lamb cutlets, with the fat carefully removed so that Beatrice should not be led astray, and spinach boiled in water, with stewed pears to end up with. Lena tasted her pears and gave the butler a look of inquiry. That resourceful man understood her at once and though powdered sugar had never been served at that table before handed her without a moment's hesitation a bowl of it. She helped herself liberally. The other three pretended not to notice. Coffee was served and Lena took three lumps of sugar in hers.

'You have a very sweet tooth,' said Arrow in a tone which she struggled to keep friendly.

'We think saccharine so much more sweetening,' said Frank, as she put a tiny tablet of it into her coffee.

'Disgusting stuff,' said Lena.

Beatrice's mouth drooped at the corners, and she gave the lump sugar a yearning look.

'Beatrice,' boomed Frank sternly.

Beatrice stifled a sigh, and reached for the saccharine.

Frank was relieved when they could sit down to the bridge table. It was plain to her that Arrow and Beatrice were upset. She wanted them to like Lena and she was anxious that Lena should enjoy her fortnight with them. For the first rubber Arrow cut with the newcomer.

'Do you play Vanderbilt or Culbertson?' she asked her.

'I have no conventions,' Lena answered in a happy-go-lucky way, 'I play by the light of nature.'

'I play strict Culbertson,' said Arrow acidly.

The three fat women braced themselves to the fray. No conventions indeed! They'd learn her. When it came to bridge even Frank's family feeling was forgotten and she settled down with the same determination as the others to trim the stranger in their midst. But the light of nature served Lena very well. She had a natural gift for the game and great experience. She played with imagination, quickly, boldly, and with assurance. The other players were in too high a class not to realize very soon that Lena knew what she was about, and since they were all thoroughly good-natured, generous women, they were gradually mollified. This was real bridge. They all enjoyed themselves. Arrow and Beatrice began to feel more kindly towards Lena, and Frank, noticing this, heaved a fat sigh of relief. It was going to be a success.

After a couple of hours they parted, Frank and Beatrice to have a round of golf, and Arrow to take a brisk walk with a young Prince Roccamare whose acquaintance she had lately made. He was very sweet and young and good-looking. Lena said she would rest.

They met again just before dinner.

'I hope you've been all right, Lena dear,' said Frank. 'I was rather conscience-stricken at leaving you with nothing to do all this time.'

'Oh, don't apologize. I had a lovely sleep and then I went down to Juan and had a cocktail. And d'you know what I discovered? You'll be so pleased. I found a dear little tea-shop where they've got the most beautiful thick fresh cream. I've ordered half a pint to be sent every day. I thought it would be my little contribution to the household.'

Her eyes were shining. She was evidently expecting them to be delighted.

'How very kind of you,' said Frank, with a look that sought to quell the indignation that she saw on the faces of her two friends. 'But we never eat cream. In this climate it makes one so bilious.'

'I shall have to eat it all myself then,' said Lena cheerfully.

'Don't you ever think of your figure?' Arrow asked with icy deliberation.

'The doctor said I must eat.'

'Did he say you must eat bread and butter and potatoes and cream?'

'Yes. That's what I thought you meant when you said you had simple food.'

'You'll get simply enormous,' said Beatrice.

Lena laughed gaily.

'No, I shan't. You see, nothing ever makes me fat. I've always eaten everything I wanted to and it's never had the slightest effect on me.'

The stony silence that followed this speech was only broken by the entrance of the butler.

'*Mademoiselle est servie*,' he announced.

They talked the matter over late that night, after Lena had gone to bed, in Frank's room. During the evening they had been furiously cheerful, and they had chaffed one another with a friendliness that would have taken in the keenest observer. But now they dropped the mask. Beatrice was sullen, Arrow was spiteful and Frank was unmanned.

'It's not very nice for me to sit there and see her eat all the things I particularly like,' said Beatrice plaintively.

'It's not very nice for any of us,' Frank snapped back.

'You should never have asked her here,' said Arrow.

'How was I to know?' cried Frank.

'I can't help thinking that if she really cared for her husband she would hardly eat so much,' said Beatrice. 'He's only been buried two months. I mean, I think you ought to show some resect for the dead.'

'Why can't she eat the same as we do?' asked Arrow viciously. 'She's a guest.'

'Well, you heard what she said. The doctor told her she must eat.'

'Then she ought to go to a sanatorium.'

'It's more than flesh and blood can stand, Frank,' moaned Beatrice.

'If I can stand it you can stand it.'

'She's your cousin, she's not our cousin,' said Arrow. 'I'm not going to sit there for fourteen days and watch that woman make a hog of herself.'

'It's so vulgar to attach all this importance to food,' Frank boomed, and her voice was deeper than ever. 'After all the only thing that counts really is spirit.'

'Are you calling *me* vulgar, Frank?' asked Arrow with flashing eyes.

'No, of course she isn't,' interrupted Beatrice.

'I wouldn't put it past you to go down in the kitchen when we're all in bed and have a good square meal on the sly.'

Frank sprang to her feet.

'How dare you say that, Arrow! I'd never ask anybody to do what I'm not prepared to do myself. Have you known me all these years and do you think me capable of such a mean thing?'

'How is it you never take off any weight then?'

Frank gave a gasp and burst into a flood of tears.

'What a cruel thing to say! I've lost pounds and pounds.'

She wept like a child. Her vast body shook and great tears splashed on her mountainous bosom.

'Darling, I didn't mean it,' cried Arrow.

She threw herself on her knees and enveloped what she could of Frank in her own plump arms. She wept and the mascara ran down her cheeks.

'D'you mean to say I don't look thinner?' Frank sobbed. 'After all I've gone through.'

'Yes, dear, of course you do,' cried Arrow through her tears. 'Everybody's noticed it.'

Beatrice, though naturally of a placid disposition, began to cry gently. It was very pathetic. Indeed, it would have been a hard heart that failed to be moved by the sight of Frank, that lion-hearted woman, crying her eyes out. Presently, however, they dried their tears and had a little brandy and water, which every doctor had told them was the least fattening thing they could drink, and then they felt much better. They decided that Lena should have the nourishing food that had been ordered her and they made a solemn resolution not to let it disturb their equanimity. She was certainly a first-rate bridge player and after all it was only for a fortnight. They would do whatever they could to make her stay enjoyable. They kissed one another warmly and separated for the night feeling strangely uplifted. Nothing should interfere with the wonderful friendship that had brought so much happiness into their three lives.

But human nature is weak. You must not ask too much of it. They ate grilled fish while Lena ate macaroni sizzling with cheese and butter; they ate grilled cutlets and boiled spinach while Lena ate *pâté de foie gras*; twice a week they ate hard-boiled eggs and raw tomatoes, while Lena ate peas swimming in cream and potatoes cooked in all sorts of delicious ways. The chef was a good chef and he leapt at the opportunity afforded him to send up one dish more rich, tasty and succulent than the other.

'Poor Jim,' sighed Lena, thinking of her husband, 'he loved French cooking.'

The butler disclosed the fact that he could make half a dozen kinds of cocktail and Lena informed them that the doctor had recommended her to drink burgundy at luncheon and champagne at dinner. The three fat women persevered. They were gay, chatty and even hilarious (such is the natural gift that women have for deception) but Beatrice grew limp and forlorn, and Arrow's tender blue eyes acquired a steely glint. Frank's deep voice grew more raucous. It was when they played bridge that the strain showed itself. They had always been fond of talking over their hands, but their discussion had been friendly. Now a distinct bitterness crept in and sometimes one pointed out a mistake to another with quite unnecessary frankness. Discussion turned to argument and argument to altercation. Sometimes the session ended in angry silence. Once Frank accused Arrow of deliberately letting her down. Two or three times Beatrice, the softest of the three, was reduced to tears. On another occasion Arrow flung down her cards and swept out of the room in a pet. Their tempers were getting frayed. Lena was the peacemaker.

'I think it's such a pity to quarrel over bridge,' she said. 'After all, it's only a game.'

It was all very well for her. She had had a square meal and half a bottle of champagne. Besides, she had phenomenal luck. She was winning all their money. The score was put down in a book after each session, and hers mounted up day after day with unfailing regularity. Was there no justice in the world? They began to hate one another. And though they hated her too they could not resist confiding in her. Each of them went to her separately and told her how detestable the others were. Arrow said she was sure it was bad for her to see so much of women so much older than herself. She had a good mind to sacrifice her share of the lease and go to Venice for the rest of the summer. Frank told Lena that with her masculine mind it was too much to expect that she could be satisfied with anyone so frivolous as Arrow and so frankly stupid as Beatrice.

'I must have intellectual conversation,' she boomed. 'When you have a brain like mine you've got to consort with your intellectual equals.'

Beatrice only wanted peace and quiet.

'Really I hate women,' she said. 'They're so unreliable; they're so malicious.'

By the time Lena's fortnight drew to its close the three fat women were barely on speaking terms. They kept up appearances before Lena, but when she was not there made no pretences. They had got past quarrelling. They ignored one another, and when this was not possible treated each other with icy politeness.

Lena was going to stay with friends on the Italian Riviera and Frank saw her off by the same train as that by which she had arrived. She was taking away with her a lot of their money.

'I don't know how to thank you,' she said, as she got into the carriage. 'I've had a wonderful visit.'

If there was one thing that Frank Hickson prided herself on more than on being a match for any man it was that she was a gentlewoman, and her reply was perfect in its combination of majesty and graciousness.

'We've all enjoyed having you here, Lena,' she said. 'It's been a real treat.'

But when she turned away from the departing train she heaved such a vast sigh of relief that the platform shook beneath her. She flung back her massive shoulders and strode home to the villa.

'Ouf!' she roared at intervals. 'Ouf!'

She changed into her one-piece bathing-suit, put on her espadrilles and a man's dressing-gown (no nonsense about it), and went to Eden Roc. There was still time for a bathe before luncheon. She passed through the Monkey House, looking about her to say good morning to anyone she knew, for she felt on a sudden at peace with mankind, and then stopped dead still. She could not believe her eyes. Beatrice was sitting at one of the tables, by herself; she wore the pyjamas she had bought at Molyneux's a day or two before, she had a string of pearls round her neck, and Frank's quick eyes saw that she had just had her hair waved; her cheeks, her eyes, her lips were made up. Fat, nay vast, as she was, none could deny that she was an extremely handsome woman. But what was she doing? With the slouching gait of the Neanderthal man which was Frank's characteristic walk she went up to Beatrice. In her black bathing-dress Frank looked like the huge cetacean which the Japanese catch in the Torres Straits and which the vulgar call a sea-cow.

'Beatrice, what are you doing?' she cried in her deep voice.

It was like the roll of thunder in the distant mountains. Beatrice looked at her coolly.

'Eating,' she answered.

'Damn it, I can see you're eating.'

In front of Beatrice was a plate of *croissants* and a plate of butter, a pot of strawberry jam, coffee, and a jug of cream. Beatrice was spreading butter thick on the delicious hot bread, covering this with jam, and then pouring the thick cream over all.

'You'll kill yourself,' said Frank.

'I don't care,' mumbled Beatrice with her mouth full.

'You'll put on pounds and pounds.'

'Go to hell!'

She actually laughed in Frank's face. My God, how good those *croissants* smelt!

'I'm disappointed in you, Beatrice. I thought you had more character.'

'It's your fault. That blasted woman. You would have her down. For a fortnight I've watched her gorge like a hog. It's more than flesh and blood can stand. I'm going to have one square meal if I bust.'

The tears welled up to Frank's eyes. Suddenly she felt very weak and womanly. She would have liked a strong man to take her on his knee and pet her and cuddle her and call her little baby names. Speechless she sank down on a chair by Beatrice's side. A waiter came up. With a pathetic gesture she waved towards the coffee and *croissants.*

'I'll have the same,' she sighed.

She listlessly reached out her hand to take a roll, but Beatrice snatched away the plate.

'No, you don't,' she said. 'You wait till you get your own.'

Frank called her a name which ladies seldom apply to one another in affection. In a moment the waiter brought her *croissants*, butter, jam, and coffee.

'Where's the cream, you fool?' she roared like a lioness at bay.

She began to eat. She ate gluttonously. The place was beginning to fill up with bathers coming to enjoy a cocktail or two after having done their duty by the sun and the sea. Presently Arrow strolled along with Prince Roccamare. She had on a beautiful silk wrap which she held tightly round her with one hand in order to look as slim as possible and she bore her head high so that he should not see her double chin. She was laughing gaily. She felt like a girl. He had just told her (in Italian) that her eyes made the blue of the Mediterranean look like pea-soup. He left her to go into the men's room to brush his sleek black hair and they arranged to meet in five minutes for a drink. Arrow walked on to the women's room to put a little more rouge on her cheeks and a little more red on her lips. On her way she caught sight of Frank and Beatrice. She stopped. She could hardly believe her eyes.

'My God!' she cried. 'You beasts. You hogs.' She seized a chair. 'Waiter.'

Her appointment went clean out of her head. In the twinkling of an eye the waiter was at her side.

'Bring me what these ladies are having,' she ordered.

Frank lifted her great heavy head from her plate.

'Bring me some *pâté de foie gras,*' she boomed.

'Frank!' cried Beatrice.

'Shut up.'

'All right. I'll have some too.'

The coffee was brought and the hot rolls and cream and the *pâté de foie gras* and they set to. They spread the cream on the *pâté* and they ate it. They devoured great spoonfuls of jam. They crunched the delicious crisp bread voluptuously. What was love to Arrow then? Let the Prince keep his palace in Rome and his castle in the Apennines. They did not speak. What they were about was much too serious. They ate with solemn, ecstatic fervour.

'I haven't eaten potatoes for twenty-five years,' said Frank in a far-off brooding tone.

'Waiter,' cried Beatrice, 'bring fried potatoes for three.'

'*Très bien, Madame.*'

The potatoes were brought. Not all the perfumes of Arabia smelt so sweet. They ate them with their fingers.

'Bring me a dry Martini,' said Arrow.

'You can't have a dry Martini in the middle of a meal, Arrow,' said Frank.

'Can't I? You wait and see.'

'All right then. Bring me a double dry Martini,' said Frank.

'Bring three double dry Martinis,' said Beatrice.

They were brought and drunk at a gulp. The women looked at one another and sighed. The misunderstandings of the last fortnight dissolved and the sincere affection each had for the others welled up again in their hearts. They could hardly believe that they had ever contemplated the possibility of severing a friendship that had brought them so much solid satisfaction. They finished the potatoes.

'I wonder if they've got any chocolate éclairs,' said Beatrice.

'Of course they have.'

And of course they had. Frank thrust one whole into her huge mouth, swallowed it and seized another, but before she ate it she looked at the other two and plunged a vindictive dagger into the heart of the monstrous Lena.

'You can say what you like, but the truth is she played a damned rotten game of bridge, really.'

'Lousy,' agreed Arrow.

But Beatrice suddenly thought she would like a meringue.

The
Facts of Life

◆

It was Henry Garnet's habit on leaving the city of an afternoon to drop in at his club and play bridge before going home to dinner. He was a pleasant man to play with. He knew the game well and you could be sure that he would make the best of his cards. He was a good loser; and when he won was more inclined to ascribe his success to his luck than to his skill. He was indulgent, and if his partner made a mistake could be trusted to find an excuse for him. It was surprising then on this occasion to hear him telling his partner with unnecessary sharpness that he had never seen a hand worse played; and it was more surprising still to see him not only make a grave error himself, an error of which you would never have thought him capable, but when his partner, not unwilling to get a little of his own back, pointed it out, insist against all reason and with considerable heat that he was perfectly right. But they were all old friends, the men he was playing with, and none of them took his ill-humour very seriously. Henry Garnet was a broker, a partner in a firm of repute, and it occurred to one of them that something had gone wrong with some stock he was interested in.

'How's the market today?' he asked.

'Booming. Even the suckers are making money.'

It was evident that stocks and shares had nothing to do with Henry Garnet's vexation; but something was the matter; that was evident too. He was a hearty fellow, who enjoyed excellent health; he had plenty of money; he was fond of his wife, and devoted to his children. As a rule he had high spirits, and he laughed easily at the nonsense they were apt to talk while they played; but today he sat glum and silent. His brows were crossly puckered and there was a sulky look about his mouth. Presently, to ease the tension, one of the others mentioned a subject upon which they all knew Henry Garnet was glad to speak.

'How's your boy, Henry? I see he's done pretty well in the tournament.'

Henry Garnet's frown grew darker.

'He's done no better than I expected him to.'

'When does he come back from Monte?'

'He got back last night.'

'Did he enjoy himself?'

'I suppose so; all I know is that he made a damned fool of himself.'

'Oh. How?'

'I'd rather not talk about it if you don't mind.'

The three men looked at him with curiosity. Henry Garnet scowled at the green baize.

'Sorry, old boy. You call.'

The game proceeded in a strained silence. Garnet got his bid, and when he played his cards so badly that he went three down not a word was said. Another rubber was begun and in the second game Garnet denied a suit.

'Having none?' his partner asked him.

Garnet's irritability was such that he did not even reply, and when at the end of the hand it appeared that he had revoked, and that his revoke cost the rubber, it was not to be expected that his partner should let his carelessness go without remark.

'What's the devil's the matter with you, Henry?' he said. 'You're playing like a fool.'

Garnet was disconcerted. He did not so much mind losing a big rubber himself, but he was sore that his inattention should have made his partner lose too. He pulled himself together.

'I'd better not play any more. I thought a few rubbers would calm me, but the fact is I can't give my mind to the game. To tell you the truth I'm in a hell of a temper.'

They all burst out laughing.

'You don't have to tell us that, old boy. It's obvious.'

Garnet gave them a rueful smile.

'Well, I bet you'd be in a temper if what's happened to me had happened to you. As a matter of fact I'm in a damned awkward situation, and if any of you fellows can give me any advice how to deal with it I'd be grateful.'

'Let's have a drink and you tell us all about it. With a K.C., a Home Office official and an eminent surgeon—if we can't tell you how to deal with a situation, nobody can.'

The K.C. got up and rang the bell for a waiter.

'It's about that damned boy of mine,' said Henry Garnet.

Drinks were ordered and brought. And this is the story that Henry Garnet told them.

The boy of whom he spoke was his only son. His name was Nicholas and of course he was called Nicky. He was eighteen. The Garnets had two daughters besides, one of sixteen and the other of twelve, but however unreasonable it seemed, for a father is generally supposed to like his daughters best, and though he did all he could not to show his preference, there was no doubt that the greater share of Henry Garnet's affection was given to his son. He was kind, in a chaffing, casual way, to his daughters, and gave them handsome presents on their birthdays and at Christmas; but he doted on Nicky. Nothing was too good for him. He thought the world of him. He could hardly take his eyes off him. You could not blame him, for Nicky was a son that any parent might have been proud of. He was six foot two, lithe but muscular, with broad shoulders and a slim waist, and he held himself gallantly erect; he had a charming head, well placed on the shoulders, with pale brown hair that waved slightly, blue eyes with long dark lashes under well-marked eyebrows, a full red mouth, and a tanned, clean skin. When he smiled he showed very regular and very white teeth. He was not shy, but there was a modesty in his demeanour that was attractive. In social intercourse he was easy, polite, and quietly gay. He was the offspring of nice, healthy, decent parents, he had been well brought up in a good home, he had been sent to a good school, and the general result was as engaging a specimen of young manhood as you were likely to find in a long time. You felt that he was as honest, open, and virtuous as he looked. He had never given his parents a moment's uneasiness. As a child he was seldom ill and never naughty. As a boy he did everything that was expected of him. His school reports were excellent. He was wonderfully popular, and he ended his career, with a creditable number of prizes, as head of the school and captain of the football team. But this was not all. At the age of fourteen Nicky had developed an unexpected gift for lawn tennis. This was a game that his father not only was fond of, but played very well, and when he discerned in the boy the promise of a tennis-player he fostered it. During the holidays he had him taught by the best professionals and by the time he was sixteen he had won a number of tournaments for boys of his age. He could beat his father so badly that only parental affection reconciled the older player to the poor show he put up. At eighteen Nicky went to Cambridge and Henry Garnet conceived the ambition that before he was through with the university he should play for it. Nicky had all the qualifications for becoming a great tennis-player. He was tall, he had a long reach, he was quick on his feet, and his timing was perfect. He realized instinctively where the ball was coming and, seemingly without hurry, was there to take it. He had a powerful serve, with a nasty break that made it difficult to return, and his forehand drive, low, long, and accurate, was deadly. He was not so good on the backhand and his volleying was wild, but all through the summer before he went to Cambridge Henry Garnet made him work on these points under the best teacher in England. At the back of his mind, though he did not even mention it to Nicky, he cherished a further ambition, to see his son play at Wimbledon, and who could tell, perhaps be chosen to represent his country in the Davis Cup. A great lump came into Henry Garnet's throat as he saw in fancy his son leap over the net to shake hands with the American champion whom he had just defeated, and walk off the court to the deafening plaudits of the multitude.

As an assiduous frequenter of Wimbledon Henry Garnet had a good many friends in the tennis world, and one evening he found himself at a City dinner sitting next to one of them, a Colonel Brabazon, and in due course began talking to him of Nicky and what chance there might be of his being chosen to play for his university during the following season.

'Why don't you let him go down to Monte Carlo and play in the spring tournament there?' said the Colonel suddenly.

'Oh, I don't think he's good enough for that. He's not nineteen yet, he only went up to Cambridge last October; he wouldn't stand a chance against all those cracks.'

'Of course, Austin and von Cramm and so on would knock spots off him, but he might snatch a game or two; and if he got up against some of the smaller fry there's no reason why he shouldn't win two or three matches. He's never been up against any of the first-rate players and it would be wonderful practice for him. He'd learn a lot more than he'll ever learn in the seaside tournaments you enter him for.'

'I wouldn't dream of it. I'm not going to let him leave Cambridge in the middle of a term. I've always impressed upon him that tennis is only a game and it mustn't interfere with work.'

Colonel Brabazon asked Garnet when the term ended.

'That's all right. He'd only have to cut about three days. Surely that could be arranged. You see, two of the men we were depending on have let us down, and we're in a hole. We want to send as good a team as we can. The Germans are sending their best players and so are the Americans.'

'Nothing doing, old boy. In the first place Nicky's not good enough, and secondly, I don't fancy the idea of sending a kid like that to Monte Carlo without anyone to look after him. If I could get away myself I might think of it, but that's out of the question.'

'I shall be there. I'm going as the non-playing captain of the English team. I'll keep an eye on him.'

'You'll be busy, and besides, it's not a responsibility I'd like to ask you to take. He's never been abroad in his life, and to tell you the truth, I shouldn't have a moment's peace all the time he was there.'

They left it at that and presently Henry Garnet went home. He was so flattered by Colonel Brabazon's suggestion that he could not help telling his wife.

'Fancy his thinking Nicky's as good as that. He told me he'd seen him play and his style was fine. He only wants more practice to get into the first flight. We shall see the kid playing in the semi-finals at Wimbledon yet, old girl.'

To his surprise Mrs Garnet was not so much opposed to the notion as he would have expected.

'After all the boy's eighteen. Nicky's never got into mischief yet and there's no reason to suppose he will now.'

'There's his work to be considered; don't forget that. I think it would be a very bad precedent to let him cut the end of term.'

'But what can three days matter? It seems a shame to rob him of a chance like that. I'm sure he'd jump at it if you asked him.'

'Well, I'm not going to. I haven't sent him to Cambridge just to play tennis. I know he's steady, but it's silly to put temptation in his way. He's much too young to go to Monte Carlo by himself.'

'You say he won't have a chance against these crack players, but you can't tell.'

Henry Garnet sighed a little. On the way home in the car it had struck him that Austin's health was uncertain and that von Cramm had his off-days. Supposing, just for the sake of argument, that Nicky had a bit of luck like that—then there would be no doubt that he would be chosen to play for Cambridge. But of course that was all nonsense.

'Nothing doing, my dear. I've made up my mind and I'm not going to change it.'

Mrs Garnet held her peace. But next day she wrote to Nicky, telling him what had happened, and suggested to him what she would do in his place if, wanting to go, he wished to get his father's consent. A day or two later Henry Garnet received a letter from his son. He was bubbling over with excitement. He had seen his tutor, who was a tennis-player himself, and the Provost of his college, who happened to know Colonel Brabazon, and no objection would be made to his leaving before the end of term; they both thought it an opportunity that shouldn't be missed. He didn't see what harm he could come to, and if only, just this once, his father would stretch a point, well, next term, he promised faithfully, he'd work like blazes. It was a very pretty letter. Mrs Garnet watched her husband read it at the breakfast table; she was undisturbed by the frown on his face. He threw it over to her.

'I don't know why you thought it necessary to tell Nicky something I told you in confidence. It's too bad of you. Now you've thoroughly unsettled him.'

'I'm sorry. I thought it would please him to know that Colonel Brabazon had such a high opinion of him. I don't see why one should only tell people the disagreeable things that are said about them. Of course I made it quite clear that there could be no question of his going.'

'You've put me in an odious position. If there's anything I hate it's for the boy to look upon me as a spoil-sport and a tyrant.'

'Oh, he'll never do that. He may think you rather silly and unreasonable, but I'm sure he'll understand that it's only for his own good that you're being so unkind.'

'Christ,' said Henry Garnet.

His wife had a great inclination to laugh. She knew the battle was won. Dear, oh dear, how easy it was to get men to do what you wanted. For appearance sake Henry Garnet held out for forty-eight hours, but then he yielded, and a fortnight later Nicky came to London. He was to start for Monte Carlo next morning, and after dinner, when Mrs Garnet and her elder daughter had left them, Henry took the opportunity to give his son some good advice.

'I don't feel quite comfortable about letting you go off to a place like Monte Carlo at your age practically by yourself,' he finished, 'but there it is and I can only hope you'll be sensible. I don't want to play the heavy father, but there are three things especially that I want to warn you against: one is gambling, don't gamble; the second is money, don't lend anyone money; and the third is women, don't have anything to do with women. If you don't do any of those three things you can't come to much harm, so remember them well.'

'All right, father,' Nicky smiled.

'That's my last word to you. I know the world pretty well and believe me, my advice is sound.'

'I won't forget it. I promise you.'

'That's a good chap. Now let's go up and join the ladies.'

Nicky beat neither Austin nor von Cramm in the Monte Carlo tournament, but he did not disgrace himself. He snatched an unexpected victory over a Spanish player and gave one of the Austrians a closer match than anyone had thought possible. In the mixed doubles he got into the semi-finals. His charm conquered everyone and he vastly enjoyed himself. It was generally allowed that he showed promise, and Colonel Brabazon told him that when he was a little older and had had more practice with first-class players he would be a credit to his father. The tournament came to an end and the day following he was to fly back to London. Anxious to play his best he had lived very carefully, smoking little and drinking nothing, and going to bed early; but on his last evening he thought he would like to see something of the life in Monte Carlo of which he had heard so much. An official dinner was given to the tennis-players and after dinner with the rest of them he went into the Sporting Club. It was the first time he had been there. Monte Carlo was very full and the rooms were crowded. Nicky had never before seen roulette played except in the pictures; in a maze he stopped at the first table he came to; chips of different sizes were scattered over the green cloth in what looked like a hopeless muddle; the croupier gave the wheel a sharp turn and with a flick threw in the little white ball. After what seemed an endless time the ball stopped and another croupier with a broad, indifferent gesture raked in the chips of those who had lost.

Presently Nicky wandered over to where they were playing *trente et quarante*, but he couldn't understand what it was all about and he thought it dull. He saw a crowd in another room and sauntered in. A big game of baccarat was in progress and he was immediately conscious of the tension. The players were protected from the thronging bystanders by a brass rail; they sat round the table, nine on each side, with the dealer in the middle and the croupier facing him. Big money was changing hands. The dealer was a member of the Greek Syndicate. Nicky looked at his impassive face. His eyes were watchful, but his expression never changed whether he won or lost. It was a terrifying, strangely impressive sight. It gave Nicky, who had been thriftily brought up, a peculiar thrill to see someone risk a thousand pounds on the turn of a card and when he lost make a little joke and laugh. It was all terribly exciting. An acquaintance came up to him.

'Been doing any good?' he asked.

'I haven't been playing.'

'Wise of you. Rotten game. Come and have a drink.'

'All right.'

While they were having it Nicky told his friends that this was the first time he had ever been in the rooms.

'Oh, but you must have one little flutter before you go. It's idiotic to leave Monte without having tried your luck. After all it won't hurt you to lose a hundred francs or so.'

'I don't suppose it will, but my father wasn't any too keen on my coming at all and one of the three things he particularly advised me not to do was to gamble.'

But when Nicky left his companion he strolled back to one of the tables where they were playing roulette. He stood for a while looking at the losers' money being raked-in by the croupier and the money that was won paid out to the winners. It was impossible to deny that it was thrilling. His friend was right, it did seem silly to leave Monte without putting something on the table just once. It would be an experience, and at his age you had to have all the experience you could get. He reflected that he hadn't promised his father not to gamble, he'd promised him not to forget his advice. It wasn't quite the same, was it? He took a hundred-franc note out of his pocket and rather shyly put it on number eighteen. He chose it because that was his age. With a wildly beating heart he watched the wheel turn; the little white ball whizzed about like a small demon of mischief; the wheel went round more slowly, the little white ball hesitated, it seemed about to stop, it went on again; Nicky could hardly believe his eyes when it fell into number eighteen. A lot of chips were passed over to him and his hands trembled as he took them. It seemed to amount to a lot of money. He was so confused that he never thought of putting anything on the following round; in fact he had no intention of playing any more, once was enough; and he was surprised when eighteen again came up. There was only one chip on it.

'By George, you've won again,' said a man who was standing near to him.

'Me? I hadn't got anything on.'

'Yes, you had. Your original stake. They always leave it on unless you ask for it back. Didn't you know?'

Another packet of chips was handed over to him. Nicky's head reeled. He counted his gains: seven thousand francs. A queer sense of power seized him; he felt wonderfully clever. This was the easiest way of making money that he had ever heard of. His frank, charming face was wreathed in smiles. His bright eyes met those of a woman standing by his side. She smiled.

'You're in luck,' she said.

She spoke English, but with a foreign accent.

'I can hardly believe it. It's the first time I've ever played.'

'That explains it. Lend me a thousand francs, will you? I've lost everything I've got. I'll give it you back in half an hour.'

'All right.'

She took a large red chip from his pile and with a word of thanks disappeared. The man who had spoken to him before grunted.

'You'll never see that again.'

Nicky was dashed. His father had particularly advised him not to lend anyone money. What a silly thing to do! And to somebody he'd never seen in his life. But the fact was, he felt at that moment such a love for the human race that it had never occurred to him to refuse. And that big red chip, it was almost impossible to realize that it had any value. Oh well, it didn't matter, he still had six thousand francs, he'd just try his luck once or twice more and if he didn't win he'd go home. He put a chip on sixteen, which was his elder sister's age, but it didn't come up; then on twelve, which was his younger sister's, and that didn't come up either; he tried various numbers at random, but without success. It was funny, he seemed to have lost his knack. He thought he would try just once more and then stop; he won. He had made up all his losses and had something over. At the end of an hour, after various ups and downs, having experienced such thrills as he had never known in his life, he found himself with so many chips that they would hardly go in his pockets. He decided to go. He went to the changers' office and he gasped when twenty thousand-franc notes were spread out before him. He had never had so much money in his life. He put it in his pocket and was turning away when the woman to whom he had lent the thousand francs came up to him.

'I've been looking for you everywhere,' she said. 'I was afraid you'd gone. I was in a fever, I didn't know what you'd think of me. Here's your thousand francs and thank you so much for the loan.'

Nicky, blushing scarlet, stared at her with amazement. How he had misjudged her! His father had said, don't gamble; well, he had, and he'd made twenty thousand francs; and his father had said, don't lend anyone money; well, he had, he'd lent quite a lot to a total stranger, and she'd returned it. The fact was that he wasn't nearly such a fool as his father thought: he'd had an instinct that he could lend her money with safety, and you see, his instinct was right. But he was so obviously taken aback that the little lady was forced to laugh.

'What is the matter with you?' she asked.

'To tell you the truth I never expected to see the money back.'

'What did you take me for? Did you think I was a—cocotte?'

Nicky reddened to the roots of his wavy hair.

'No, of course not.'

'Do I look like one?'

'Not a bit.'

She was dressed very quietly, in black, with a string of gold beads round her neck; her simple frock showed off a neat, slight figure; she had a pretty little face and a trim head. She was made up, but not excessively, and Nicky supposed that she was not more than three or four years older than himself. She gave him a friendly smile.

'My husband is in the administration in Morocco, and I've come to Monte Carlo for a few weeks because he thought I wanted a change.'

'I was just going,' said Nicky because he couldn't think of anything else to say.

'Already!'

'Well, I've got to get up early tomorrow. I'm going back to London by air.'

'Of course. The tournament ended today, didn't it? I saw you play, you know, two or three times.'

'Did you? I don't know why you should have noticed me.'

'You've got a beautiful style. And you looked very sweet in your shorts.'

Nicky was not an immodest youth, but it did cross his mind that perhaps she had borrowed that thousand francs in order to scrape acquaintance with him.

'Do you ever go to the Knickerbocker?' she asked.

'No. I never have.'

'Oh, but you mustn't leave Monte Carlo without having been there. Why don't you come and dance a little? To tell you the truth, I'm starving with hunger and I should adore some bacon and eggs.'

Nicky remembered his father's advice not to have anything to do with women, but this was different; you had only to look at the pretty little thing to know at once that she was perfectly respectable. Her husband was in what corresponded, he supposed, to the Civil Service. His father and mother had friends who were Civil Servants and they and their wives sometimes came to dinner. It was true that the wives were neither so young nor so pretty as this one, but she was just as ladylike as they were. And after winning twenty thousand francs he thought it wouldn't be a bad idea to have a little fun.

'I'd love to go with you,' he said. 'But you won't mind if I don't stay very long. I've left instructions at my hotel that I'm to be called at seven.'

'We'll leave as soon as ever you like.'

Nicky found it very pleasant at the Knickerbocker. He ate his bacon and eggs with appetite. They shared a bottle of champagne. They danced, and the little lady told him he danced beautifully. He knew he danced pretty well, and of course she was easy to dance with. As light as a feather. She laid her cheek against his and when their eyes met there was in hers a smile that made his heart go pit-a-pat. A coloured woman sang in a throaty, sensual voice. The floor was crowded.

'Have you ever been told that you're very good-looking?' she asked.

'I don't think so,' he laughed. 'Gosh,' he thought, 'I believe she's fallen for me.'

Nicky was not such a fool as to be unaware that women often liked him, and when she made that remark he pressed her to him a little more closely. She closed her eyes and a faint sigh escaped her lips.

'I suppose it wouldn't be quite nice if I kissed you before all these people,' he said.

'What do you think they would take me for?'

It began to grow late and Nicky said that really he thought he ought to be going.

'I shall go too,' she said. 'Will you drop me at my hotel on your way?'

Nicky paid the bill. He was rather surprised at its amount, but with all that money he had in his pocket he could afford not to care, and they got into a taxi. She snuggled up to him and he kissed her. She seemed to like it.

'By Jove,' he thought, 'I wonder if there's anything doing.'

It was true that she was a married woman, but her husband was in Morocco, and it certainly did look as if she'd fallen for him. Good and proper. It was true also that his father had warned him to have nothing to do with women, but, he reflected again, he hadn't actually promised he wouldn't, he'd only promised not to forget his advice. Well, he hadn't; he was bearing it in mind that very minute. But circumstances alter cases. She was a sweet little thing; it seemed silly to miss the chance of an adventure when it was handed to you like that on a tray. When they reached the hotel he paid off the taxi.

'I'll walk home,' he said. 'The air will do me good after the stuffy atmosphere of that place.'

'Come up a moment,' she said. 'I'd like to show you the photo of my little boy.'

'Oh, have you got a little boy?' he exclaimed, a trifle dashed.

'Yes, a sweet little boy.'

He walked upstairs after her. He didn't in the least want to see the photograph of her little boy, but he thought it only civil to pretend he did. He was afraid he'd made a fool of himself; it occurred to him that she was taking him up to look at the photograph in order to show him in a nice way that he'd made a mistake. He'd told her he was eighteen.

'I suppose she thinks I'm just a kid.'

He began to wish he hadn't spent all that money on champagne at the night-club.

But she didn't show him the photograph of her little boy after all. They had no sooner got into her room than she turned to him, flung her arms round his neck, and kissed him full on the lips. He had never in all his life been kissed so passionately.

'Darling,' she said.

For a brief moment his father's advice once more crossed Nicky's mind and then he forgot it.

Nicky was a light sleeper and the least sound was apt to wake him. Two or three hours later he awoke and for a moment could not imagine where he was. The room was not quite dark, for the door of the bathroom was ajar, and the light in it had been left on. Suddenly he was conscious that someone was moving about the room. Then he remembered. He saw that it was his little friend, and he was on the point of speaking when something in the way she was behaving stopped him. She was walking very cautiously, as though she were afraid of waking him; she stopped once or twice and looked over at the bed. He wondered what she was after. He soon saw. She went over to the chair on which he had placed his clothes and once more looked in his direction. She waited for what seemed to him an interminable time. The silence was so intense that Nicky thought he could hear his own heart beating. Then, very slowly, very quietly, she took up his coat, slipped her hand into the inside pocket and drew out all those beautiful thousand-franc notes that Nicky had been so proud to win. She put the coat back and placed some other clothes on it so that it should look as though it had not been disturbed, then, with the bundle of notes in her hand, for an appreciable time stood once more stock-still. Nicky had repressed an instinctive impulse to jump up and grab her, it was partly surprise that had kept him quiet, partly the notion that he was in a strange hotel, in a foreign country, and if he made a row he didn't know what might happen. She looked at him. His eyes were partly closed and he was sure that she thought he was asleep. In the silence she could hardly fail to hear his regular breathing. When she had reassured herself that her movements had not disturbed him she stepped, with infinite caution, across the room. On a small table in the window a cineraria was growing in a pot. Nicky watched her now with his eyes wide open. The plant was evidently placed quite loosely in the pot, for taking it by the stalks she lifted it out; she put the banknotes in the bottom of the pot and replaced the plant. It was an excellent hiding-place. No one could have guessed that anything was concealed under that richly-flowering plant. She pressed the earth down with her fingers and then, very slowly, taking care not to make the smallest noise, crept across the room and slipped back into bed.

'*Chèri,*' she said, in a caressing voice.

Nicky breathed steadily, like a man immersed in deep sleep. The little lady turned over on her side and disposed herself to slumber. But though Nicky lay so still his thoughts worked busily. He was extremely indignant at the scene he had just witnessed, and to himself he spoke his thoughts with vigour.

'She's nothing but a damned tart. She and her dear little boy and her husband in Morocco. My eye! She's a rotten thief, that's what she is. Took me for a mug. If she thinks she's going to get away with anything like that, she's mistaken.'

He had already made up his mind what he was going to do with the money he had so cleverly won. He had long wanted a car of his own, and had thought it rather mean of his father not to have given him one. After all, a feller doesn't always want to drive about in the family bus. Well, he'd just teach the old man a lesson and buy one himself. For twenty thousand francs, two hundred pounds roughly, he could get a very decent second-hand car. He meant to get the money back, but just then he didn't quite know how. He didn't like the idea of kicking up a row, he was a stranger, in a hotel he knew nothing of; it might very well be that the beastly woman had friends there, he didn't mind facing anyone in a fair fight, but he'd look pretty foolish if someone pulled a gun on him. He reflected besides, very sensibly, that he had no proof the money was his. If it came to a showdown and she swore it was hers, he might very easily find himself hauled off to a police-station. He really didn't know what to do. Presently by her regular breathing he knew that the little lady was asleep. She must have fallen asleep with an easy mind, for she had done her job without a hitch. It infuriated Nicky that she should rest so peacefully while he lay awake worried to death. Suddenly an idea occurred to him. It was such a good one that it was only by the exercise of all his self-control that he prevented himself from jumping out of bed and carrying it out at once. Two could play at her game. She'd stolen his money; well, he'd steal it back again, and they'd be all square. He made up his mind to wait quite quietly until he was sure that deceitful woman was sound asleep. He waited for what seemed to him a very long time. She did not stir. Her breathing was as regular as a child's.

'Darling,' he said at last.

No answer. No movement. She was dead to the world. Very slowly, pausing after every movement, very silently, he slipped out of bed. He stood still for a while, looking at her to see whether he had disturbed her. Her breathing was as regular as before. During the time he was waiting he had taken note carefully of the furniture in the room so that in crossing it he should not knock against a chair or a table and make a noise. He took a couple of steps and waited, he took a couple of steps more; he was very light on his feet and made no sound as he walked; he took fully five minutes to get to the window, and here he waited again. He started, for the bed slightly creaked, but it was only because the sleeper turned in her sleep. He forced himself to wait till he had counted one hundred. She was sleeping like a log. With infinite care he seized the cineraria by the stalks and gently pulled it out of the pot; he put his other hand in, his heart beat nineteen to the dozen as his fingers touched the notes, his hand closed on them and he slowly drew them out. He replaced the plant and in turn carefully pressed down the earth. While he was doing all this he had kept one eye on the form lying in the bed. It remained still. After another pause he crept softly to the chair on which his clothes were lying. He first put the bundle of notes in his coat pocket and then proceeded to dress. It took him a good quarter of an hour, because he could afford to make no sound. He had been wearing a soft shirt with his dinner jacket, and he congratulated himself on this, because it was easier to put on silently than a stiff one. He had some difficulty in tying his tie without a looking-glass, but he very wisely reflected that it didn't really matter if it wasn't tied very well. His spirits were rising. The whole thing now began to seem rather a lark. At length he was completely dressed except for his shoes, which he took in his hand; he thought he would put them on when he got into the passage. Now he had to cross the room to get to the door. He reached it so quietly that he could not have disturbed the lightest sleeper. But the door had to be unlocked. He turned the key very slowly; it creaked.

'Who's that?'

The little woman suddenly sat up in bed. Nicky's heart jumped to his mouth. He made a great effort to keep his head.

'It's only me. It's six o'clock and I've got to go. I was trying not to wake you.'

'Oh, I forgot.'

She sank back on to the pillow.

'Now that you're awake I'll put on my shoes.'

He sat down on the edge of the bed and did this.

'Don't make a noise when you go out. The hotel people don't like it. Oh, I'm so sleepy.'

'You go right off to sleep again.'

'Kiss me before you go.' He bent down and kissed her. 'You're a sweet boy and a wonderful lover. *Bon voyage.*'

Nicky did not feel quite safe till he got out of the hotel. The dawn had broken. The sky was unclouded, and in the harbour the yachts and the fishing-boats lay motionless on the still water. On the quay fishermen were getting ready to start on their day's work. The streets were deserted. Nicky took a long breath of the sweet morning air. He felt alert and well. He also felt as pleased as Punch. With a swinging stride, his shoulders well thrown back, he walked up the hill and along the gardens in front of the Casino—the flowers in that clear light had a dewy brilliance that was delicious—till he came to his hotel. Here the day had already begun. In the hall porters with mufflers round their necks and berets on their heads were busy sweeping. Nicky went up to his room and had a hot bath. He lay in it and thought with satisfaction that he was not such a mug as some people might think. After his bath he did his exercises, dressed, packed, and went down to breakfast. He had a grand appetite. No continental breakfast for him! He had grapefruit, porridge, bacon and eggs, rolls fresh from the oven, so crisp and delicious they melted in your mouth, marmalade, and three cups of coffee. Though feeling perfectly well before, he felt better after that. He lit the pipe he had recently learnt to smoke, paid his bill and stepped into the car that was waiting to take him to the aerodrome on the other side of Cannes. The road as far as Nice ran over the hills and below him was the blue sea and the coast-line. He couldn't help thinking it damned pretty. They passed through Nice, so gay and friendly in the early morning, and presently they came to a long stretch of straight road that ran by the sea. Nicky had paid his bill, not with the money he had won the night before, but with the money his father had given him; he had changed a thousand francs to pay for supper at the Knickerbocker, but that deceitful little woman had returned him the thousand francs he had lent her, so that he still had twenty thousand-franc notes in his pocket. He thought he would like to have a look at them. He had so nearly lost them that they had a double value for him. He took them out of his hip-pocket into which for safety's sake he had stuffed them when he put on the suit he was travelling in, and counted them one by one. Something very strange had happened to them. Instead of there being twenty notes as there should have been there were twenty-six. He couldn't understand it at all. He counted them twice more. There was no doubt about it; somehow or other he had twenty-six thousand francs instead of the twenty he should have had. He couldn't make it out. He asked himself if it was possible that he had won more at the Sporting Club than he had realized. But no, that was out of the question; he distinctly remembered the man at the desk laying the notes out in four rows of five, and he had counted them himself. Suddenly the explanation occurred to him; when he had put his hand into the flower-pot, after taking out the cineraria, he had grabbed everything he felt there. The flower-pot was the little hussy's money-box and he had taken out not only his own money, but her savings as well. Nicky leant back in the car and burst into a roar of laughter. It was the funniest thing he had ever heard in his life. And when he thought of her going to the flower-pot some time later in the morning when she awoke, expecting to find the money she had so cleverly got away with, and finding, not only that it wasn't there, but that her own had gone too, he laughed more than ever. And so far as he was concerned there was nothing to do about it; he neither knew her name, nor the name of the hotel to which she had taken him. He couldn't return her money even if he wanted to.

'It serves her damned well right,' he said.

This then was the story that Henry Garnet told his friends over the bridge-table, for the night before, after dinner when his wife and daughter had left them to their port, Nicky had narrated it in full.

'And you know what infuriated me is that he's so damned pleased with himself. Talk of a cat swallowing a canary. And d'you know what he said to me when he'd finished? He looked at me with those innocent eyes of his and said: "You know, father, I can't help thinking there was something wrong about the advice you gave me. You said, don't gamble; well, I did, and I made a packet; you said, don't lend money; well, I did, and I got it back; and you said, don't have anything to do with women; well, I did, and made six thousand francs on the deal."'

It didn't make it any better for Henry Garnet that his three companions burst out laughing.

'It's all very well for you fellows to laugh, but you know, I'm in a damned awkward position. The boy looked up to me, he respected me, he took whatever I said as gospel truth, and now, I saw it in his eyes, he just looks upon me as a drivelling old fool. It's no good my saying one swallow doesn't make a summer; he doesn't see that it was just a fluke, he thinks the whole thing was due to his own cleverness. It may ruin him.'

'You do look a bit of a damned fool, old man,' said one of the others. 'There's no denying that, is there?'

'I know I do, and I don't like it. It's so dashed unfair. Fate has no right to play one tricks like that. After all, you must admit that my advice was good.'

'Very good.'

'And the wretched boy ought to have burnt his fingers. Well, he hasn't. You're all men of the world, you tell me how I'm to deal with the situation now.'

But they none of them could.

'Well, Henry, if I were you I wouldn't worry,' said the lawyer. 'My belief is that your boy's born lucky, and in the long run that's better than to be born clever or rich.'

Gigolo and Gigolette

◆

The bar was crowded. Sandy Westcott had had a couple of cocktails and he was beginning to feel hungry. He looked at his watch. He had been asked to dinner at half past nine and it was nearly ten. Eva Barrett was always late and he would be lucky if he got anything to eat by ten-thirty. He turned to the barman to order another cocktail and caught sight of a man who at that moment came up to the bar.

'Hullo, Cotman,' he said. 'Have a drink?'

'I don't mind if I do, sir.'

Cotman was a nice-looking fellow, of thirty perhaps, short, but with so good a figure that he did not look it, very smartly dressed in a double-breasted dinner jacket, a little too much waisted, and a butterfly tie a good deal too large. He had a thick mat of black, wavy hair, very sleek and shiny, brushed straight back from his forehead, and large flashing eyes. He spoke with great refinement, but with a Cockney accent.

'How's Stella?' asked Sandy.

'Oh, she's all right. Likes to have a lay-down before the show, you know. Steadies the old nerves, she says.'

'I wouldn't do that stunt of hers for a thousand pounds.'

'I don't suppose you would. No one can do it but her, not from that height, I mean, and only five foot of water.'

'It's the most sick-making thing I've ever seen.'

Cotman gave a little laugh. He took this as a compliment. Stella was his wife. Of course she did the trick and took the risk, but it was he who had thought of the flames, and it was the flames that had taken the public fancy and made the turn the huge success it was. Stella dived into a tank from the top of a ladder sixty feet high, and as he said, there were only five feet of water in the tank. Just before she dived they poured enough petrol on to cover the surface and he set it alight; the flames soared up and she dived straight into them.

'Paco Espinel tells me it's the biggest draw the Casino has ever had,' said Sandy.

'I know. He told me they'd served as many dinners in July as they generally do in August. And that's you, he says to me.'

'Well, I hope you're making a packet.'

'Well, I can't exactly say that. You see, we've got our contract and naturally we didn't know it was going to be a riot, but Mr Espinel's talking of booking us for next month, and I don't mind telling you he's not going to get us on the same terms or anything like it. Why, had a letter from an agent only this morning saying they wanted us to go to Deauville.'

'Here are my people,' said Sandy.

He nodded to Cotman and left him. Eva Barrett sailed in with the rest of her guests. She had gathered them together downstairs. It was a party of eight.

'I knew we should find you here, Sandy,' she said. 'I'm not late, am I?'

'Only half an hour.'

'Ask them what cocktails they want and then we'll dine.'

While they were standing at the bar, emptying now, for nearly everyone had gone down to the terrace for dinner, Paco Espinel passed through and stopped to shake hands with Eva Barrett. Paco Espinel was a young man who had run through his money and now made his living by arranging the turns with which the Casino sought to attract visitors. It was his duty to be civil to the rich and great. Mrs Chaloner Barrett was an American widow of vast wealth; she not only entertained expensively, but also gambled. And after all, the dinners and suppers and the two cabaret shows that accompanied them were only provided to induce people to lose their money at the tables.

'Got a good table for me, Paco?' said Eva Barrett.

'The best.' His eyes, fine, dark Argentine eyes, expressed his admiration of Mrs Barrett's opulent, ageing charms. This also was business. 'You've seen Stella?'

'Of course. Three times. It's the most terrifying thing I've ever seen.'

'Sandy comes every night.'

'I want to be in at the death. She's bound to kill herself one of these nights and I don't want to miss that if I can help it.'

Paco laughed.

'She's been such a success, we're going to keep her on another month. All I ask is that she shouldn't kill herself till the end of August. After that she can do as she likes.'

'Oh, God, have I got to go on eating trout and roast chicken every night till the end of August?' cried Sandy.

'You brute, Sandy,' said Eva Barrett. 'Come on, let's go in to dinner. I'm starving.'

Paco Espinel asked the barman if he'd seen Cotman. The barman said he'd had a drink with Mr Westcott.

'Oh, well, if he comes in here again, tell him I want a word with him.'

Mrs Barrett paused at the top of the steps that led down to the terrace long enough for the press representative, a little haggard woman with an untidy head, to come up with her note-book. Sandy whispered the names of the guests. It was a representative Riviera party. There was an English Lord and his Lady, long and lean both of them, who were prepared to dine with anyone who would give them a free meal. They were certain to be as tight as drums before midnight. There was a gaunt Scotch woman, with a face like a Peruvian mask that has been battered by the storms of ten centuries, and her English husband. Though a broker by profession, he was bluff, military, and hearty. He gave you an impression of such integrity that you were almost more sorry for him than for yourself when the good thing he had put you on to as a special favour turned out to be a dud. There was an Italian countess who was neither Italian nor a countess, but played a beautiful game of bridge, and there was a Russian prince who was ready to make Mrs Barrett a princess and in the meantime sold champagne, motor-cars, and Old Masters on commission. A dance was in progress, and Mrs Barrett, waiting for it to end, surveyed with a look which her short upper lip made scornful the serried throng on the dance floor. It was a gala night and the dining tables were crowded together. Beyond the terrace the sea was calm and silent. The music stopped and the head waiter, affably smiling, came up to guide her to her table. She swept down the steps with majestic gait.

'We shall have quite a good view of the dive,' she said as she sat down.

'I like to be next door to the tank,' said Sandy, 'so that I can see her face.'

'Is she pretty?' asked the Countess.

'It's not that. It's the expression of her eyes. She's scared to death every time she does it.'

'Oh, I don't believe that,' said the City gentleman, Colonel Goodhart by name, though no one had ever discovered how he came by the title. 'I mean, the whole bally stunt's only a trick. There's no danger really, I mean.'

'You don't know what you're talking about. Diving from that height in as little water as that, she's got to turn like a flash the moment she touches the water. And if she doesn't do it right she's bound to bash her head against the bottom and break her back.'

'That's just what I'm telling you, old boy,' said the Colonel, 'it's a trick. I mean, there's no argument.'

'If there's no danger there's nothing to it, anyway,' said Eva Barrett. 'It's over in a minute. Unless she's risking her life it's the biggest fraud of modern times. Don't say we've come to see this over and over again and it's only a fake.'

'Pretty well everything is. You can take my word for that.'

'Well, you ought to know,' said Sandy.

If it occurred to the Colonel that this might be a nasty dig he admirably concealed it. He laughed.

'I don't mind saying I know a thing or two,' he admitted. 'I mean, I've got my eyes peeled all right. You can't put much over on me.'

The tank was on the far left of the terrace, and behind it, supported by stays, was an immensely tall ladder at the top of which was a tiny platform. After two or three dances more, when Eva Barrett's party were eating asparagus, the music stopped and the lights were lowered. A spot was turned on the tank. Cotman was visible in the brilliance. He ascended half a dozen steps so that he was on a level with the top of the tank.

'Ladies and gentlemen,' he cried out, in a loud clear voice, 'you are now going to see the most marvellous feat of the century. Madam Stella, the greatest diver in the world, is about to dive from a height of sixty feet into a lake of flames five foot deep. This is a feat that has never been performed before, and Madam Stella is prepared to give one hundred pounds to anyone who will attempt it. Ladies and gentlemen, I have the honour to present Madam Stella.'

A little figure appeared at the top of the steps that led on to the terrace, ran quickly up to the tank, and bowed to the applauding audience. She wore a man's silk dressing-gown and on her head a bathing-cap. Her thin face was made up as if for the stage. The Italian countess looked at her through her *face-à-main.*

'Not pretty,' she said.

'Good figure,' said Eva Barrett. 'You'll see.'

Stella slipped out of her dressing-gown and gave it to Cotman. He went down the steps. She stood for a moment and looked at the crowd. They were in darkness and she could only see vague white faces and white shirt-fronts. She was small, beautifully made, with legs long for her body and slim hips. Her bathing costume was very scanty.

'You're quite right about the figure, Eva,' said the Colonel. 'Bit undeveloped, of course, but I know you girls think that's quite the thing.'

Stella began to climb the ladder and the spot-light followed her. It seemed an incredible height. An attendant poured petrol on the surface of the water. Cotman was handed a flaming torch. He watched Stella reach the top of the ladder and settle herself on the platform.

'Ready?' he cried.

'Yes.'

'Go,' he shouted.

And as he shouted he seemed to plunge the burning torch into the water. The flames sprang up, leaping high, and really terrifying to look at. At the same moment Stella dived. She came down like a streak of lightning and plunged through the flames, which subsided a moment after she had reached the water. A second later she was at the surface and jumped out to a roar, a storm of applause. Cotman wrapped the dressing-gown round her. She bowed and bowed. The applause went on. Music struck up. With a final wave of the hand she ran down the steps and between the tables to the door. The lights went up and the waiters hurried along with their neglected service.

Sandy Westcott gave a sigh. He did not know whether he was disappointed or relieved.

'Top hole,' said the English peer.

'It's a bally fake,' said the Colonel, with his British pertinacity. 'I bet you anything you like.'

'It's over so quickly,' said her English ladyship. 'I mean, you don't get your money's worth really.'

Anyhow it wasn't her money. That it never was. The Italian countess leaned forward. She spoke fluent English, but with a strong accent.

'Eva, my darling, who are those extraordinary people at the table near the door under the balcony?'

'Packet of fun, aren't they?' said Sandy. 'I simply haven't been able to take my eyes off them.'

Eva Barrett glanced at the table the Countess indicated, and the Prince, who sat with his back to it, turned round to look.

'They can't be true,' cried Eva. 'I must ask Angelo who they are.'

Mrs Barrett was the sort of woman who knew the head waiters of all the principal restaurants in Europe by their first names. She told the waiter who was at that moment filling her glass to send Angelo to her.

It was certainly an odd pair. They were sitting by themselves at a small table. They were very old. The man was big and stout, with a mass of white hair, great bushy white eyebrows, and an enormous white moustache. He looked like the late King Humbert of Italy, but much more like a king. He sat bolt upright. He wore full evening dress, with a white tie and a collar that has been out of fashion for hard on thirty years. His companion was a little old lady in a black satin ball dress, cut very low, and tight at the waist. Round her neck were several chains of coloured beads. She wore what was obviously a wig, and a very ill-fitting one at that; it was very elaborate, all curls and sausages, and raven black. She was outrageously made-up, bright blue under the eyes and on the eyelids, the eyebrows heavily black, a great patch of very pink rouge on each cheek, and the lips a livid scarlet. The skin hung loosely on her face in deep wrinkles. She had large bold eyes and they darted eagerly from table to table. She was taking everything in, and every other minute called the old man's attention to someone or other. The appearance of the couple was so fantastic in that fashionable crowd, the men in dinner jackets, the women in thin, pale-coloured frocks, that many eyes were turned on them. The staring did not seem to incommode the old lady. When she felt certain persons were looking at her she raised her eyebrows archly, smiled and rolled her eyes. She seemed on the point of acknowledging applause.

Angelo hurried up to the good customer that Eva Barrett was.

'You wished to see me, my lady?'

'Oh, Angelo, we're simply dying to know who those absolutely marvellous people are at the next table to the door.'

Angelo gave a look and then assumed a deprecating air. The expression of his face, the movement of his shoulders, the turn of his spine, the gesture of his hands, probably even the twiddle of his toes, all indicated a half-humorous apology.

'You must overlook them, my lady.' He knew of course that Mrs Barrett had no right to be thus addressed, just as he knew that the Italian countess was neither Italian nor a countess and that the English lord never paid for a drink if anyone else would pay for it, but he also knew that to be thus addressed did not displease her. 'They begged me to give them a table because they wanted to see Madam Stella do her dive. They were in the profession themselves once. I know they're not the sort of people one expects to see dining here, but they made such a point of it I simply hadn't the heart to refuse.'

'But I think they're a perfect scream. I adore them.'

'I've known them for many years. The man indeed is a compatriot of mine.' The head waiter gave a condescending little laugh. 'I told them I'd give them a table on the condition that they didn't dance. I wasn't taking any risks, my lady.'

'Oh, but I should have loved to see them dance.'

'One has to draw the line somewhere, my lady,' said Angelo gravely.

He smiled, bowed again and withdrew.

'Look,' cried Sandy, 'they're going.'

The funny old couple were paying their bill. The old man got up and put round his wife's neck a large white, but not too clean, feather boa. She rose. He gave her his arm, holding himself very erect, and she, small in comparison, tripped out beside him. Her black satin dress had a long train, and Eva Barrett (who was well over fifty) screamed with joy.

'Look, I remember my mother wearing a dress like that when I was in the schoolroom.'

The comic pair walked, still arm in arm, through the spacious rooms of the

Casino till they came to the door. The old man addressed a commissionaire.
'Be so good as to direct me to the artistes' dressing-rooms. We wish to pay
our respects to Madam Stella.'
The commissionaire gave them a look and summed them up. They were not
people with whom it was necessary to be very polite.
'You won't find her there.'
'She has not gone? I thought she gave a second performance at two?'
'That's true. They might be in the bar.'
'It won't 'urt us just to go an' 'ave a look, Carlo,' said the old lady.
'Right-o, my love,' he answered with a great roll of the R.
They walked slowly up the great stairs and entered the bar. It was empty but
for the deputy-barman and a couple sitting in two arm-chairs in the corner.
The old lady released her husband's arm and tripped up with outstretched
hands.
''Ow are you, dear? I felt I just 'ad to come and congratulate you, bein'
English same as you are. And in the profession meself. It's a grand turn, my
dear, it deserves to be a success.' She turned to Cotman. 'And this is your
'usband?'
Stella got out of her arm-chair and a shy smile broke on her lips as she
listened with some confusion to the voluble old lady.
'Yes, that's Syd.'
'Pleased to meet you,' he said.
'And this is mine,' said the old lady, with a little dig of the elbow in the
direction of the tall white-haired man. 'Mr Penezzi. 'E's a count really, and I'm
the Countess Penezzi by rights, but when we retired from the profession we
dropped the title.'
'Will you have a drink?' said Cotman.
'No, you 'ave one with us,' said Mrs Penezzi, sinking into an arm-chair.
'Carlo, you order.'
The barman came, and after some discussion three bottles of beer were
ordered. Stella would not have anything.
'She never has anything till after the second show,' explained Cotman.
Stella was slight and small, about twenty-six, with light brown hair, cut short
and waved, and grey eyes. She had reddened her lips, but wore little rouge on
her face. Her skin was pale. She was not very pretty, but she had a neat little
face. She wore a very simple evening frock of white silk. The beer was brought
and Mr Penezzi, evidently not very talkative, took a long swig.
'What was your line?' asked Syd Cotman, politely.
Mrs Penezzi gave him a rolling glance of her flashing, made-up eyes and
turned to her husband.
'Tell 'em who I am, Carlo,' she said.
'The 'uman cannon-ball,' he announced.
Mrs Penezzi smiled brightly and with a quick, birdlike glance looked from
one to the other. They stared at her in dismay.
'Flora,' she said. 'The 'uman cannon-ball.'
She so obviously expected them to be impressed that they did not quite know
what to do. Stella gave her Syd a puzzled look. He came to the rescue.
'It must have been before our time.'
'Naturally it was before your time. Why, we retired from the profession
definitely the year poor Queen Victoria died. It made quite a sensation when we
did too. But you've 'eard of me, of course.' She saw the blank look on their

faces; her tone changed a little. 'But I was the biggest draw in London. At the Old Aquarium, that was. All the swells came to see me. The Prince of Wales and I don't know who all. I was the talk of the town. Isn't that true, Carlo?' 'She crowded the Aquarium for a year.' 'It was the most spectacular turn they'd ever 'ad there. Why, only a few years ago I went up and introduced meself to Lady de Bathe. Lily Langtry, you know. She used to live down 'ere. She remembered me perfectly. She told me she'd seen me ten times.'

'What did you do?' asked Stella.

'I was fired out of a cannon. Believe me, it was a sensation. And after London I went all over the world with it. Yes, my dear, I'm an old woman now and I won't deny it. Seventy-eight Mr Penezzi is and I shall never see seventy again, but I've 'ad me portrait on every 'oardin' in London. Lady de Bathe said to me: My dear, you was as celebrated as I was. But you know what the public is, give 'em a good thing and they go mad over it, only they want change; 'owever good it is, they get sick of it and then they won't go and see it any more. It'll 'appen to you, my dear, same as it 'appened to me. It comes to all of us. But Mr Penezzi always 'ad 'is 'ead screwed on 'is shoulders the right way. Been in the business since 'e was so 'igh. Circus, you know. Ringmaster. That's 'ow I first knew 'im. I was in a troupe of acrobacks. Trapeze act, you know. 'E's a fine-lookin' man now, but you should 'ave seen 'im then, in 'is Russian boots, and ridin' breeches, and a tight-fittin' coat with frogs all down the front of it, crackin' 'is long whip as 'is 'orses galloped round the ring, the 'andsomest man I ever see in my life.'

Mr Penezzi did not make any remark, but thoughtfully twisted his immense white moustache.

'Well, as I was tellin' you, 'e was never one to throw money about and when the agents couldn't get us bookin's any more 'e said, let's retire. An 'e was quite right, after 'avin' been the biggest star in London, we couldn't go back to circus work any more, I mean, Mr Penezzi bein' a count really, 'e 'ad 'is dignity to think of, so we come down 'ere and we bought a 'ouse and started a pension. It always 'ad been Mr Penezzi's ambition to do something like that. Thirty-five years we been 'ere now. We 'aven't done so badly not until the last two or three years, and the slump came, though visitors are very different from what they was when we first started, the things they want, electric-light and runnin' water in their bedrooms and I don't know what all. Give them a card, Carlo. Mr Penezzi does the cookin' 'imself, and if ever you want a real 'ome from 'ome, you'll know where to find it. I like professional people and we'd 'ave a rare lot to talk about, you and me, dearie. Once a professional always a professional, I say.'

At that moment the head barman came back from his supper. He caught sight of Syd.

'Oh, Mr Cotman, Mr Espinel was looking for you, wants to see you particularly.'

'Oh, where is he?'

'You'll find him around somewhere.'

'We'll be going,' said Mrs Penezzi, getting up. 'Come and 'ave lunch with us one day, will you? I'd like to show you my old photographs and me press cuttin's. Fancy you not 'avin' 'eard of the 'uman cannon-ball. Why, I was as well known as the Tower of London.'

Mrs Penezzi was not vexed at finding that these young people had never even heard of her. She was simply amused.

They bade one another good-bye, and Stella sank back again into her chair.

'I'll just finish my beer,' said Syd, 'and then I'll go and see what Paco wants. Will you stay here, ducky, or would you like to go to your dressing-room?'

Stella's hands were tightly clenched. She did not answer. Syd gave her a look and then quickly glanced away.

'Perfect riot, that old girl,' he went on, in his hearty way. 'Real figure of fun. I suppose it's true what she said. It's difficult to believe, I must say. Fancy 'er drawing all London, what, forty years ago? And the funny thing is, her thinking anybody remembered. Seemed as though she simply couldn't understand us not having heard of her even.'

He gave Stella another glance, from the corner of his eye so that she should not see he was looking at her, and he saw she was crying. He faltered. The tears were rolling down her pale face. She made no sound.

'What's the matter, darling?'

'Syd, I can't do it again tonight,' she sobbed.

'Why on earth not?'

'I'm afraid.'

He took her hand.

'I know you better than that,' he said. 'You're the bravest little woman in the world. Have a brandy, that'll pull you together.'

'No, that'd only make it worse.'

'You can't disappoint your public like that.'

'That filthy public. Swine who eat too much and drink too much. A pack of chattering fools with more money than they know what to do with. I can't stick them. What do they care if I risk my life?'

'Of course, it's the thrill they come for, there's no denying that,' he replied uneasily. 'But you know and I know, there's no risk, not if you keep your nerve.'

'But I've lost my nerve, Syd. I shall kill myself.'

She had raised her voice a little, and he looked round quickly at the barman. But the barman was reading the *Éclaireur de Nice* and paying no attention.

'You don't know what it looks like from up there, the top of the ladder, when I look down at the tank. I give you my word, tonight I thought I was going to faint. I tell you I can't do it again tonight, you've got to get me out of it, Syd.'

'If you funk it tonight it'll be worse tomorrow.'

'No, it won't. It's having to do it twice kills me. The long wait and all that. You go and see Mr Espinel and tell him I can't give two shows a night. It's more than my nerves'll stand.'

'He'll never stand for that. The whole supper trade depends on you. It's only to see you they come in then at all.'

'I can't help it, I tell you I can't go on.'

He was silent for a moment. The tears still streamed down her pale little face and he saw that she was quickly losing control of herself. He had felt for some days that something was up and he had been anxious. He had tried not to give her an opportunity to talk. He knew obscurely that it was better for her not to put into words what she felt. But he had been worried. For he loved her.

'Anyhow Espinel wants to see me,' he said.

'What about?'

'I don't know. I'll tell him you can't give the show more than once a night and see what he says. Will you wait here?'

'No, I'll go along to the dressing-room.'

Ten minutes later he found her there. He was in great spirits and his step was jaunty. He burst open the door.

'I've got grand news for you, honey. They're keeping us on next month at twice the money.'

He sprang forward to take her in his arms and kiss her, but she pushed him away.

'Have I got to go on again tonight?'

'I'm afraid you must. I tried to make it only one show a night, but he wouldn't hear of it. He says it's quite essential you should do the supper turn. And after all, for double the money, it's worth it.'

She flung herself down on the floor and this time burst into a storm of tears.

'I can't, Syd, I can't. I shall kill myself.'

He sat down on the floor and raised her head and took her in his arms and petted her.

'Buck up, darling. You can't refuse a sum like that. Why, it'll keep us all the winter and we shan't have to do a thing. After all there are only four more days to the end of July and then it's only August.'

'No, no, no. I'm frightened. I don't want to die, Syd. I love you.'

'I know you do, darling, and I love you. Why, since we married I've never looked at another woman. We've never had money like this before and we shall never get it again. You know what these things are, we're a riot now, but we can't expect it to go on for ever. We've got to strike while the iron's hot.'

'D'you want me to die, Syd?'

'Don't talk so silly. Why, where should I be without you? You mustn't give way like this. You've got your self-respect to think of. You're famous all over the world.'

'Like the human cannon-ball was,' she cried with a laugh of fury.

'That damned old woman,' he thought.

He knew that was the last straw. Bad luck, Stella taking it like that.

'That was an eye-opener to me,' she went on. 'What do they come and see me over and over again for? On the chance they'll see me kill myself. And a week after I'm dead they'll have forgotten even my name. That's what the public is. When I looked at that painted old hag I saw it all. Oh, Syd, I'm so miserable.' She threw her arms round his neck and pressed her face to his. 'Syd, it's no good, I can't do it again.'

'Tonight, d'you mean? If you really feel like that about it, I'll tell Espinel you've had a fainting fit. I daresay it'll be all right just for once.'

'I don't mean tonight, I mean never.'

She felt him stiffen a little.

'Syd dear, don't think I'm being silly. It's not just today, it's been growing on me. I can't sleep at night thinking of it, and when I do drop off I see myself standing at the top of the ladder and looking down. Tonight I could hardly get up it, I was trembling so, and when you lit the flames and said go, something seemed to be holding me back. I didn't even know I'd jumped. My mind was a blank till I found myself on the platform and heard them clapping. Syd, if you loved me you wouldn't want me to go through such torture.'

He sighed. His own eyes were wet with tears. For he loved her devotedly.

'You know what it means,' he said. 'The old life. Marathons and all.'

'Anything's better than this.'

The old life. They both remembered it. Syd had been a dancing gigolo since he was eighteen, he was very good-looking in his dark Spanish way and full of life, old women and middle-aged women were glad to pay to dance with him, and he was never out of work. He had drifted from England to the Continent and there he had stayed, going from hotel to hotel, to the Riviera in the winter, to watering-places in France in the summer. It wasn't a bad life they led, there were generally two or three of them together, the men, and they shared a room in cheap lodgings. They didn't have to get up till late and they only dressed in time to go to the hotel at twelve to dance with stout women who wanted to get their weight down. Then they were free till five, when they went to the hotel again and sat at a table, the three of them together, keeping a sharp eye open for anyone who looked a likely client. They had their regular customers. At night they went to the restaurant and the house provided them with quite a decent meal. Between the courses they danced. It was good money. They generally got fifty or a hundred francs from anyone they danced with. Sometimes a rich woman, after dancing a good deal with one of them for two or three nights, would give him as much as a thousand francs. Sometimes a middle-aged woman would ask one to spend a night with her, and he would get two hundred and fifty francs for that. There was always the chance of a silly old fool losing her head, and then there were platinum and sapphire rings, cigarette-cases, clothes, and a wristwatch to be got. One of Syd's friends had married one of them, who was old enough to be his mother, but she gave him a car and money to gamble with, and they lived in a beautiful villa at Biarritz. Those were the good days when everybody had money to burn. The slump came and hit the gigolos hard. The hotels were empty, and the clients didn't seem to want to pay for the pleasure of dancing with a nice-looking young fellow. Often and often Syd passed a whole day without earning the price of a drink, and more than once a fat old girl who weighed a ton had had the nerve to give him ten francs. His expenses didn't go down, for he had to be smartly dressed or the manager of the hotel made remarks, washing cost a packet, and you'd be surprised the amount of linen he needed; then shoes, those floors were terribly hard on shoes, and they had to look new. He had his room to pay for and his lunch.

It was then he met Stella. It was at Évian, and the season was disastrous. She was a swimming instructress. She was Australian, and a beautiful diver. She gave exhibitions every morning and afternoon. At night she was engaged to dance at the hotel. They dined together at a little table in the restaurant apart from the guests, and when the band began to play they danced together to induce the customers to come on to the floor. But often no one followed them and they danced by themselves. Neither of them got anything much in the way of paying partners. They fell in love with one another, and at the end of the season got married.

They had never regretted it. They had gone through hard times. Even though for business reasons (elderly ladies didn't so much like the idea of dancing with a married man when his wife was there) they concealed their marriage, it was not so easy to get a hotel job for the pair of them, and Syd was far from being able to earn enough to keep Stella, even in the most modest pension, without working. The gigolo business had gone to pot. They went to Paris and learnt a dancing act, but the competition was fearful and cabaret engagements were very hard to get. Stella was a good ballroom dancer, but the rage was for acrobatics, and however much they practised she never managed to do anything startling. The public was sick of the apache turn. They were out of a job for weeks at a time. Syd's wrist-watch, his gold cigarette-case, his platinum ring, all went up the spout. At last they found themselves in Nice reduced to such straits that Syd had to pawn his evening clothes. It was a catastrophe. They were forced to enter for the Marathon that an enterprising manager was starting. Twenty-four hours a day they danced, resting every hour for fifteen minutes. It was frightful. Their legs ached, their feet were numb. For long periods they were unconscious of what they were doing. They just kept time to the music, exerting themselves as little as possible. They made a little money, people gave them sums of a hundred francs, or two hundred, to encourage them, and sometimes to attract attention they roused themselves to give an exhibition dance. If the public was in a good humour this might bring in a decent sum. They grew terribly tired. On the eleventh day Stella fainted and had to give up. Syd went on by himself, moving, moving without pause, grotesquely, without a partner. That was the worst time they had ever had. It was the final degradation. It had left with them a recollection of horror and misery.

But it was then that Syd had his inspiration. It had come to him while he was slowly going round the hall by himself. Stella always said she could dive in a saucer. It was just a trick.

'Funny how ideas come,' he said afterwards. 'Like a flash of lightning.'

He suddenly remembered having seen a boy set fire to some petrol that had been spilt on the pavement, and the sudden blaze-up. For of course it was the flames on the water and the spectacular dive into them that had caught the public fancy. He stopped dancing there and then; he was too excited to go on. He talked it over with Stella, and she was enthusiastic. He wrote to an agent who was a friend of his; everyone liked Syd, he was a nice little man, and the agent put up the money for the apparatus. He got them an engagement at a circus in Paris, and the turn was a success. They were made. Engagements followed here and there, Syd bought himself an entire outfit of new clothes, and the climax came when they got a booking for the summer casino on the coast. It was no exaggeration of Syd's when he said that Stella was a riot.

'All our troubles are over, old girl,' he said fondly. 'We can put a bit by now for a rainy day, and when the public's sick of this I'll just think of something else.'

And now, without warning, at the top of their boom, Stella wanted to chuck it. He didn't know what to say to her. It broke his heart to see her so unhappy. He loved her more now even than when he had married her. He loved her because of all they'd gone through together; after all, for five days once they'd had nothing to eat but a hunk of bread each and a glass of milk, and he loved her because she'd taken him out of all that; he had good clothes to wear again and his three meals a day. He couldn't look at her; the anguish in her dear grey eyes was more than he could bear. Timidly she stretched out her hand and touched his. He gave a deep sigh.

'You know what it means, honey. Our connexion in the hotels has gone west, and the business is finished, anyway. What there is'll go to people younger than us. You know what these old women are as well as I do; it's a boy they want, and besides, I'm not tall enough really. It didn't matter so much when I was a kid. It's no good saying I don't look my age because I do.'

'Perhaps we can get into pictures.'

He shrugged his shoulders. They'd tried that before when they were down and out.

'I wouldn't mind what I did. I'd serve in a shop.'

'D'you think jobs can be had for the asking?'

She began to cry again.

'Don't, honey. It breaks my heart.'

'We've got a bit put by.'

'I know we have. Enough to last us six months. And then it'll mean starvation. First popping the bits and pieces, and then the clothes'll have to go, same as they did before. And then dancing in lowdown joints for our supper and fifty francs a night. Out of a job for weeks together. And Marathons whenever we hear of one. And how long will the public stand for them?'

'I know you think I'm unreasonable, Syd.'

He turned and looked at her now. There were tears in her eyes. He smiled, and the smile he gave her was charming and tender.

'No, I don't, ducky. I want to make you happy. After all, you're all I've got. I love you.'

He took her in his arms and held her. He could feel the beating of her heart. If Stella felt like that about it, well, he must just make the best of it. After all, supposing she were killed? No, no, let her chuck it and be damned to the money. She made a little movement.

'What is it, honey?'

She released herself and stood up. She went over to the dressing-table.

'I expect it's about time for me to be getting ready,' she said.

He started to his feet.

'You're not going to do a show tonight?'

'Tonight, and every night till I kill myself. What else is there? I know you're right, Syd. I can't go back to all that other, stinking rooms in fifth-rate hotels and not enough to eat. Oh, that Marathon. Why did you bring that up? Being tired and dirty for days at a time and then having to give up because flesh and blood just couldn't stand it. Perhaps I can go on another month and then there'll be enough to give you a chance of looking round.'

'No, darling. I can't stand for that. Chuck it. We'll manage somehow. We starved before; we can starve again.'

She slipped out of her clothes, and for a moment stood naked but for her stockings, looking at herself in the glass. She gave her reflection a hard smile.

'I mustn't disappoint my public,' she sniggered.

The
Voice of the Turtle

◆

For some time I could not make up my mind if I liked Peter Melrose or not. He
had had a novel published that had caused some stir among the rather dreary
but worthy people who are always on the lookout for new talent. Elderly
gentlemen with nothing much to do but go to luncheon parties praised it with
girlish enthusiasm, and wiry little women who didn't get on with their
husbands thought it showed promise. I read a few reviews. They contradicted
one another freely. Some of the critics claimed that with this first novel the
author had sprung into the front rank of English novelists: others reviled it. I
did not read it. I have learnt by experience that when a book makes a sensation
it is just as well to wait a year before you read it. It is astonishing how many
books then you need not read at all. But it chanced that one day I met Peter
Melrose. With some misgiving I had accepted an invitation to a sherry party. It
was in the top flat of a converted house in Bloomsbury, and I was a trifle out of
breath when I had climbed four flights of stairs. My hostesses were two women,
much over life-size, in early middle life, the sort of women who know all about
the insides of motor-cars and like a good tramp in the rain, but very feminine
for all that, fond of eating out of paper bags. The drawing-room, which they
called 'our workshop', though being of independent means neither had ever
done a stroke of work in her life, was large and bare, furnished with rustless-
steel chairs, which looked as though they could with difficulty support the very
substantial weight of their owners, glass-topped tables, and a vast divan
covered with zebra-skin. On the walls were book-shelves, and pictures by the
better-known English imitators of Cézanne, Braque, and Picasso. In the
shelves, besides a number of 'curious' books of the eighteenth century (for
pornography is ageless) there were only the works of living authors, mostly first

editions, and it was indeed to sign some of my own that I had been asked to the party.

It was quite small. There was but one other woman, who might have been a younger sister of my hostesses, for, though stout, she was not quite so stout, though tall, not quite so tall, and though hearty, not quite so hearty. I did not catch her name, but she answered to that of Boofuls. The only man besides myself was Peter Melrose. He was quite young, twenty-two or twenty-three, of the middle height, but with an ungainly figure that made him look squat. He had a reddish skin that seemed to fit over the bones of his face too tightly, a rather large semitic nose, though he was not a Jew, and alert green eyes under bushy eyebrows. His brown hair, cut very short, was scurfy. He was dressed in the brown Norfolk jacket and grey flannel trousers that are worn by the art students who wander hatless along King's Road, Chelsea. An uncouth young man. Nor was there much to attract in his manner. He was self-assertive, disputatious and intolerant. He had a hearty contempt for his fellow-writers which he expressed with zest. The satisfaction he gave me by his breezy attacks on reputations which for my part I considered exaggerated, but prudently held my tongue about, was only lessened by the conviction that no sooner was my back turned than he would tear my own to shreds. He talked well. He was amusing and sometimes witty. I should have laughed at his sallies more easily if those three ladies had not been so unreasonably convulsed by them. They roared with laughter at what he said, whether it was funny or whether it was inept. He said many silly things, for he talked without stopping, but he also said some very clever ones. He had a point of view, crude and not so original as he thought, but sincere. But the most striking thing about him was his eager, impetuous vitality; it was like a hot flame that burnt him with an unendurable fury. It even shed a glow on those about him. He had something, if only that, and when I left it was with a slight sense of curiosity at what would come of him. I did not know if he had talent; so many young things can write a clever novel—that means nothing; but it seemed to me that as a man he was not quite like everybody else. He was the sort of person who at thirty, when time had softened his asperity and experience had taught him that he was not quite so intelligent as he thought, would turn into an interesting and agreeable fellow. But I never expected to see him again.

It was with surprise that I received two or three days later a copy of his novel with a very flattering dedication. I read it. It was obviously autobiographical. The scene was a small town in Sussex, and the characters of the upper middle class that strives to keep up appearances on an inadequate income. The humour was rather brutal and rather vulgar. It grated on me, for it consisted chiefly of mockery at people because they were old and poor. Peter Melrose did not know how hard those misfortunes are to bear, and that the efforts made to cope with them are more deserving of sympathy than of derision. But there were descriptions of places, little pictures of a room or impressions of the countryside, which were excellently done. They showed tenderness and a sense of the spiritual beauty of material things. The book was written easily, without affectation, and with a pleasant feeling for the sound of words. But what made it indeed somewhat remarkable, so that I understood why it had attracted attention, was the passion that quivered in the love story of which the plot, such as it was, consisted. It was, as is the modern fashion, more than a trifle coarse and, again in the modern fashion, it tailed off vaguely, without any particular result, so that everything was left in the end pretty much as it had been in the beginning; but you did get the impression of young love, idealistic and yet vehemently sexual; it was so vivid and so deeply felt that it took your breath away. It seemed to throb on the printed page like the pulse of life. It had no reticence. It was absurd, scandalous, and beautiful. It was like a force of nature. That was passion all right. There is nothing, anywhere, so moving and so awe-inspiring.

I wrote to Peter Melrose and told him what I thought of his book, then suggested that we might lunch together. He rang me up next day and we made a date.

I found him unaccountably shy when we sat down opposite one another at a table in a restaurant. I gave him a cocktail. He talked glibly enough, but I could not help seeing that he was ill at ease. I gained the impression that his self-assurance was a pose assumed to conceal, from himself, maybe, a diffidence that tortured him. His manners were brusque and awkward. He would say a rude thing and then laugh nervously to cover his own embarrassment. Though he pretended to be so sure of himself he wanted all the time to be reassured by you. By irritating you, by saying the things he thought would annoy, he tried to force from you some admission, tacit it might be, that he was as wonderful as he longed to think himself. He wanted to despise the opinion of his fellows, and nothing was more important to him. I thought him rather an odious young man, but I did not mind that. It is very natural that clever young men should be rather odious. They are conscious of gifts that they do not know how to use. They are exasperated with the world that will not recognize their merit. They have something to give, and no hand is stretched out to receive it. They are impatient for the fame they regard as their due. No, I do not mind odious young men; it is when they are charming that I button up the pockets of my sympathy.

Peter Melrose was extremely modest about his book. He blushed through his reddish skin when I praised what I liked in it, and accepted my strictures with a humility that was almost embarrassing. He had made very little money out of it, and his publishers were giving him a small monthly allowance in advance of royalties on the next one. This he had just started, but he wanted to get away to write it in peace, and knowing I lived on the Riviera he asked me if I could tell him of a quiet place where he could bathe and live cheaply. I suggested that he should come and spend a few days with me so that he could look about till he found something to suit him. His green eyes sparkled when I proposed this and he flushed.

'Shouldn't I be an awful nuisance?'

'No. I shall be working. All I can offer you is three meals a day and a room to sleep in. It'll be very dull, but you can do exactly what you like.'

'It sounds grand. May I let you know if I decide to come?'

'Of course.'

We separated, and a week or two later I went home. This was in May. Early in June I received a letter from Peter Melrose asking, if I had really meant what I said when I invited him to spend a few days with me, whether he might arrive on such and such a date. Well, at the time I had meant it, but now, a month later, I remembered that he was an arrogant and ill-bred youth, whom I had seen but twice and wasn't in the least interested in, and I didn't mean it any longer. It seemed to me very likely that he would be bored stiff. I lived a very quiet life and saw few people. And I thought it would be a great strain on my nerves if he were as rude as I knew he could be, and I as his host felt it behoved me to keep my temper. I saw myself driven beyond endurance, and ringing the bell to have his clothes packed and the car brought round to take him away within half an hour. But there was nothing to do about it. It would save him the cost of board and lodging to spend a short period with me, and if he was tired and unhappy as he said in his letter it might be that it would do him good. I sent him a wire and shortly afterwards he arrived.

He looked very hot and grubby in his grey flannel trousers and brown tweed coat when I met him at the station, but after a swim in the pool he changed into white shorts and a Cochet shirt. He looked then quite absurdly young. He had never been out of England before. He was excited. It was touching to see his delight. He seemed, amid those unaccustomed surroundings, to lose his sense of himself, and he was simple, boyish and modest. I was agreeably surprised. In the evening, after dinner, sitting in the garden, with only the croaking of the little green frogs to break the silence, he began talking to me of his novel. It was a romantic story about a young writer and a celebrated *prima donna*. The theme was reminiscent of Ouida, the last thing I should have expected this hard-boiled youth to write, and I was tickled; it was odd how the fashion completed the circle and returned generation after generation to the same themes. I had no doubt that Peter Melrose would treat it in a very modern way, but there it was, the same old story as had entranced sentimental readers in the three-volume novels of the eighties. He proposed to set it in the beginning of the Edwardian era, which to the young has already acquired the fantastic, far-away feeling of a past age. He talked and talked. He was not unpleasant to listen to. He had no notion that he was putting into fiction his own day-dreams, the comic and touching day-dreams of a rather unattractive, obscure young man who sees himself beloved, to the admiration of the whole world, by an incredibly beautiful, celebrated, and magnificent woman. I always enjoyed the novels of Ouida, and Peter's idea did not at all displease me. With his charming gift of description, his vivid, ingenuous way of looking at material things, fabrics, pieces of furniture, walls, trees, flowers, and his power of representing the passion of life, the passion of love, that thrilled every fibre of his own uncouth body, I had a notion that he might well produce something exuberant, absurd, and poetical. But I asked him a question.

'Have you ever known a *prima donna*?'

'No, but I've read all the autobiographies and memoirs that I could find. I've gone into it pretty thoroughly. Not only the obvious things, you know, but I've hunted around in all sorts of byways to get the revealing touch or the suggestive anecdote.'

'And have you got what you wanted?'

'I think so.'

He began to describe his heroine to me. She was young and beautiful, wilful it is true and with a quick temper, but magnanimous. A woman on the grand scale. Music was her passion; there was music not only in her voice, but in her gestures and in her inmost thoughts. She was devoid of envy, and her appreciation of art was such that when another singer had done her an injury she forgave her when she heard her sing a role beautifully. She was of a wonderful generosity, and would give away everything she possessed when a story of misfortune touched her soft heart. She was a great lover, prepared to sacrifice the world for the man she loved. She was intelligent and well-read. She was tender, unselfish, and disinterested. In fact she was much too good to be true.

'I think you'd better meet a *prima donna*,' I said at last.

'How can I?'

'Have you ever heard of La Falterona?'

'Of course I have. I've read her memoirs.'

'She lives just along the coast. I'll ring her up and ask her to dinner.'

'Will you really? It would be wonderful.'

'Don't blame me if you don't find her quite what you expect.'

'It's the truth I want.'

Everyone has heard of La Falterona. Not even Melba had a greater reputation. She had ceased now to sing in opera, but her voice was still lovely, and she could fill a concert hall in any part of the world. She went for long tours every winter, and in summer rested in a villa by the sea. On the Riviera people are neighbours if they live thirty miles from one another, and for some years I had seen a good deal of La Falterona. She was a woman of ardent temperament, and she was celebrated not only for her singing, but for her love affairs: she never minded talking about them, and I had often sat entranced for hours while with the humour which to me was her most astonishing characteristic she regaled me with lurid tales of royal or very opulent adorers. I was satisfied that there was at least a measure of truth in them. She had been married, for short periods, three or four times, and in one of these unions had annexed a Neapolitan prince. Thinking that to be known as La Falterona was grander than any title, she did not use his name (to which indeed she had no right, since after divorcing him she had married somebody else) but her silver, her cutlery, and her dinner-service were heavily decorated with a coat of arms and a crown, and her servants invariably addressed her as *madame la princesse*. She claimed to be a Hungarian, but her English was perfect; she spoke it with a slight accent (when she remembered), but with an intonation suggestive, I had been told, of Kansas City. This she explained by saying that her father was a political exile who had fled to America when she was no more than a child; but she did not seem quite sure whether he was a distinguished scientist who had got into trouble for his liberal views, or a Magyar of high rank who had brought down on his head the imperial wrath because he had had a love affair with an Archduchess. It depended on whether she was just an artist among artists, or a great lady among persons of noble birth.

With me she was not natural, for that she could never have been if she had tried, but franker than with anyone else. She had a natural and healthy contempt for the arts. She genuinely looked upon the whole thing as a gigantic bluff, and deep down in her heart was an amused sympathy for all the people who were able to put it over on the public. I will admit that I looked forward to the encounter between Peter Melrose and La Falterona with a good deal of sardonic amusement.

She liked coming to dine with me because she knew the food was good. It was the only meal she ate in the day, for she took great care of her figure, but she liked that one to be succulent and ample. I asked her to come at nine, knowing that was the earliest hour she dreamt of eating, and ordered dinner for half past. She turned up at a quarter to ten. She was dressed in apple-green satin, cut very low in front, with no back at all, and she wore a string of huge pearls, a number of expensive-looking rings, and on her left arm diamond and emerald bracelets from the wrist to the elbow. Two or three of them were certainly real. On her raven-black hair was a thin circlet of diamonds. She could not have looked more splendid if she had been going to a ball at Stafford House in the old days. We were in white ducks.

'How grand you are,' I said. 'I told you it wasn't a party.'

She flashed a look of her magnificent black eyes at Peter.

'Of course it's a party. You told me your friend was a writer of talent. I am only an interpreter.' She ran one finger down her flashing bracelets. 'This is the homage I pay to the creative artist.'

I did not utter the vulgar monosyllable that rose to my lips, but offered her what I knew was her favourite cocktail. I was privileged to call her Maria, and she always called me Master. This she did, first because she knew it made me feel a perfect fool, and secondly because, though she was in point of fact not more than two or three years younger than I, it made it quite clear that we belonged to different generations. Sometimes, however, she also called me you dirty swine. This evening she certainly might very well have passed for thirty-five. She had those rather large features which somehow do not seem to betray age. On the stage she was a beautiful woman, and even in private life, notwithstanding her big nose, large mouth, and fleshy face, a good-looking one. She wore a brown make-up, with dark rouge, and her lips were vividly scarlet. She looked very Spanish and, I suspected, felt it, for her accent at the beginning of dinner was quite Sevillian. I wanted her to talk so that Peter should get his money's worth, and I knew there was but one subject in the world that she could talk about. She was in point of fact a stupid woman who had acquired a line of glib chatter which made people on first meeting her think she was as brilliant as she looked; but it was merely a performance she gave, and you soon discovered that she not only did not know what she was talking about, but was not in the least interested in it. I do not think she had ever read a book in her life. Her knowledge of what was going on in the world was confined to what she was able to gather by looking at the pictures in the illustrated press. Her passion for music was complete bunkum. Once at a concert to which I went with her she slept all through the Fifth Symphony, and I was charmed to hear her during the interval telling people that Beethoven stirred her so much that she hesitated to come and hear him, for with those glorious themes singing through her head, it meant that she wouldn't sleep a wink all night. I could well believe she would lie awake, for she had had so sound a nap during the Symphony that it could not but interfere with her night's rest.

But there was one subject in which her interest never failed. She pursued it with indefatigable energy. No obstacle prevented her from returning to it; no chance word was so remote that she could not use it as a stepping-stone to come back to it, and in effecting this she displayed a cleverness of which one would never have thought her capable. On this subject she could be witty, vivacious, philosophic, tragic and inventive. It enabled her to exhibit all the resources of her ingenuity. There was no end to its ramifications, and no limit to its variety. This subject was herself. I gave her an opening at once and then all I had to do was to make suitable interjections. She was in great form. We were dining on the terrace and a full moon was obligingly shining on the sea in front of us. Nature, as though she knew what was proper to the occasion, had set just the right scene. The view was framed by two tall black cypresses, and all round us on the terrace the orange trees in full flower exhaled their heady perfume. There was no wind, and the candles on the table flamed with a steady softness. It was a light that exactly suited La Falterona. She sat between us, eating heartily and thoroughly appreciating the champagne, and she was enjoying herself. She gave the moon a glance. On the sea was a broad pathway of silver.

'How beautiful nature is,' she said. 'My God, the scenery one has to play in.

How can they expect one to sing? You know, really, the sets at Covent Garden are a disgrace. The last time I sang Juliet I just told them I wouldn't go on unless they did something about the moon.'

Peter listened to her in silence. He ate her words. She was better value than I had dared to hope. She got a little tight not only on the champagne but on her own loquaciousness. To listen to her you would have thought she was a meek and docile creature against whom the whole world was in conspiracy. Her life had been one long bitter struggle against desperate odds. Managers treated her vilely, impresarios played foul tricks on her, singers combined to ruin her, critics bought by the money of her enemies wrote scandalous things about her, lovers for whom she had sacrificed everything used her with base ingratitude; and yet, by the miracle of her genius and her quick wits, she had discomfited them all. With joyous glee, her eyes flashing, she told us how she had defeated their machinations and what disaster had befallen the wretches who stood in her way. I wondered how she had the nerve to tell the disgraceful stories she told. Without the smallest consciousness of what she was doing she showed herself vindictive and envious, hard as nails, incredibly vain, cruel, selfish, scheming, and mercenary. I stole a glance now and then at Peter. I was tickled at the confusion he must be experiencing when he compared his ideal picture of the *prima donna* with the ruthless reality. She was a woman without heart. When at last she left us I turned to Peter with a smile.

'Well,' I said, 'at all events you've got some good material.'

'I know, and it all fits in so beautifully,' he said with enthusiasm.

'Does it?' I exclaimed, taken aback.

'She's exactly like my woman. She'll never believe that I'd sketched out the main lines of the character before I'd ever seen her.'

I stared at him in amazement.

'The passion for art. The disinterestedness. She had that same nobility of soul that I saw in my mind's eye. The small-minded, the curious, the vulgar put every obstacle in her way and she sweeps them all aside by the greatness of her purpose and the purity of her ends.' He gave a little happy laugh. 'Isn't it wonderful how nature copies art? I swear to you, I've got her to the life.'

I was about to speak; I held my tongue; though I shrugged a spiritual shoulder I was touched. Peter had seen in her what he was determined to see. There was something very like beauty in his illusion. In his own way he was a poet. We went to bed, and two or three days later, having found a pension to his liking, he left me.

In course of time his book appeared, and like most second novels by young people it had but a very moderate success. The critics had overpraised his first effort and now were unduly censorious. It is of course a very different thing to write a novel about yourself and the people you have known from childhood and to write one about persons of your own invention. Peter's was too long. He had allowed his gift for word-painting to run away with him, the humour was still rather vulgar; but he had reconstructed the period with skill, and the romantic story had that same thrill of real passion which in his first book had so much impressed me.

After the dinner at my house I did not see La Falterona for more than a year. She went for a long tour in South America and did not come down to the Riviera till late in the summer. One night she asked me to dine with her. We were alone but for her companion-secretary, an Englishwoman, Miss Glaser by name, whom La Falterona bullied and ill-treated, hit and swore at, but whom she could not do without. Miss Glaser was a haggard person of fifty, with grey hair and a sallow, wrinkled face. She was a queer creature. She knew everything there was to be known about La Falterona. She both adored and hated her. Behind her back she could be extremely funny at her expense, and the imitation she gave in secret of the great singer with her admirers was the most richly comic thing I have ever heard. But she watched over her like a mother. It was she who, sometimes by wheedling, sometimes by sheer plainness of speech, caused La Falterona to behave herself something like a human being. It was she who had written the singer's exceedingly inaccurate memoirs.

La Falterona wore pale-blue satin pyjamas (she liked satin) and, presumably to rest her hair, a green silk wig; except for a few rings, a pearl necklace, a couple of bracelets, and a diamond brooch at her waist, she wore no jewellery. She had much to tell me of her triumphs in South America. She talked on and on. She had never been in more superb voice and the ovations she had received were unparalleled. The concert halls were sold out for every performance, and she had made a packet.

'Is it true or is it not true, Glaser?' cried Maria with a strong South American accent.

'Most of it,' said Miss Glaser.

La Falterona had the objectionable habit of addressing her companion by her surname. But it must long since have ceased to annoy the poor woman, so there was not much point in it.

'Who was that man we met in Buenos Aires?'

'Which man?'

'You fool, Glaser. You remember perfectly. The man I was married to once.'

'Pepe Zapata,' Miss Glaser replied without a smile.

'He was broke. He had the impudence to ask me to give him back a diamond necklace he'd given me. He said it had belonged to his mother.'

'It wouldn't have hurt you to give it him,' said Miss Glaser. 'You never wear it.'

'Give it him back?' cried La Falterona, and her astonishment was such that she spoke the purest English. 'Give it him back? You're crazy.'

She looked at Miss Glaser as though she expected her there and then to have an attack of acute mania. She got up from the table, for we had finished our dinner.

'Let us go outside,' she said. 'If I hadn't the patience of an angel I'd have sacked that woman long ago.'

La Falterona and I went out, but Miss Glaser did not come with us. We sat on the veranda. There was a magnificent cedar in the garden, and its dark branches were silhouetted against the starry sky. The sea, almost at our feet, was marvellously still. Suddenly La Falterona gave a start.

'I almost forgot. Glaser, you fool,' she shouted, 'why didn't you remind me?' And then again to me: 'I'm furious with you.'

'I'm glad you didn't remember till after dinner,' I answered.

'That friend of yours and his book.'

I didn't immediately grasp what she was talking about.

'What friend and what book?'

'Don't be so stupid. An ugly little man with a shiny face and a bad figure. He wrote a book about me.'

'Oh! Peter Melrose. But it's not about you.'

'Of course it is. Do you take me for a fool? He had the impudence to send it me.'

'I hope you had the decency to acknowledge it.'

'Do you think I have the time to acknowledge all the books twopenny-halfpenny authors send me? I expect Glaser wrote to him. You had no right to ask me to dinner to meet him. I came to oblige you, because I thought you liked me for myself, I didn't know I was just being made use of. It's awful that one can't trust one's oldest friends to behave like gentlemen. I'll never dine with you again so long as I live. Never, never, never.'

She was working herself into one of her tantrums, so I interrupted her before it was too late.

'Come off it, my dear,' I said. 'In the first place the character of the singer in that book, which I suppose is the one you're referring to . . .'

'You don't suppose I'm referring to the charwoman, do you?'

'Well, the character of the singer was roughed out before he'd even seen you, and besides, it isn't in the least like you.'

'How d'you mean, it's not like me? All my friends have recognized me. I mean, it's the most obvious portrait.'

'Mary,' I expostulated.

'My name is Maria and no one knows it better than you, and if you can't call me Maria you can call me Madame Falterona or Princess.'

I paid no attention to this.

'Did you read the book?'

'Of course I read it. When everyone told me it was about me.'

'But the boy's heroine, the *prima donna*, is twenty-five.'

'A woman like me is ageless.'

'She's musical to her finger-tips, gentle as a dove, and a miracle of unselfishness; she's frank, loyal, and disinterested. Is that the opinion you have of yourself?'

'And what is *your* opinion of me?'

'Hard as nails, absolutely ruthless, a born intriguer, and as self-centred as they make 'em.'

She then called me a name which a lady does not habitually apply to a gentleman who, whatever his faults, has never had his legitimacy called in question. But though her eyes flashed I could see that she was not in the least angry. She accepted my description of her as complimentary.

'And what about the emerald ring? Are you going to deny that I told him that?'

The story of the emerald ring was this: La Falterona was having a passionate love-affair with the Crown Prince of a powerful state and he had made her a present of an emerald of immense value. One night they had a quarrel, high words passed, and some reference being made to the ring she tore it off her finger and flung it in the fire. The Crown Prince, being a man of thrifty habit, with a cry of consternation, threw himself on his knees and began raking out the coals till he recovered the ring. La Falterona watched him scornfully as he grovelled on the floor. She didn't give much away herself, but she could not bear economy in others. She finished the story with these splendid words:

'After that I *couldn't* love him.'

The incident was picturesque and had taken Peter's fancy. He had used it very neatly.

'I told you both about that in the greatest confidence and I've never told it to a soul before. It's a scandalous breach of confidence to have to put it into a book. There are no excuses either for him or for you.'

'But I've heard you tell the story dozens of times. And it was told me by Florence Montgomerie about herself and the Crown Prince Rudolf. It was one of her favourite stories too. Lola Montez used to tell it about herself and the King of Bavaria. I have little doubt that Nell Gwyn told it about herself and Charles II. It's one of the oldest stories in the world.'

She was taken aback, but only for an instant.

'I don't see anything strange in its having happened more than once. Everyone knows that women are passionate and that men are as mean as cat's-meat. I could show you the emerald if you liked. I had to have it reset, of course.'

'With Lola Montez it was pearls,' I said ironically. 'I believe they were considerably damaged.'

'Pearls?' She gave that brilliant smile of hers. 'Have I ever told you about Benjy Riesenbaum and the pearls? You might make a story out of it.'

Benjy Riesenbaum was a person of great wealth, but it was common knowledge that for a long time he had been the Falterona's lover. In fact it was he who had bought her the luxurious little villa in which we were now sitting.

'He'd given me a very handsome string in New York. I was singing at the Metropolitan, and at the end of the season we travelled back to Europe together. You never knew him, did you?'

'No.'

'Well, he wasn't bad in some ways, but he was insanely jealous. We had a row on the boat because a young Italian officer was paying me a good deal of attention. Heaven knows, I'm the easiest woman in the world to get on with, but I will not be bullied by any man. After all, I have my self-respect to think of. I told him where he got off, if you understand what I mean, and he slapped my face. On deck if you please. I don't mind telling you I was mad. I tore the string of pearls off my neck and flung it in the sea. "They cost fifty thousand dollars," he gasped. He went white. I drew myself up to my full height. "I only valued them because I loved you," I said. And I turned on my heel.'

'You were a fool,' I said.

'I wouldn't speak to him for twenty-four hours. At the end of that time I had him eating out of my hand. When we got to Paris the first thing he did was to go to Cartier's and buy me another just as good.'

She began to giggle.

'Did you say I was a fool? I'd left the real string in the bank in New York, because I knew I was going back next season. It was an imitation one that I threw in the sea.'

She started to laugh, and her laugh was rich and joyous and like a child's. That was the sort of trick that thoroughly appealed to her. She chortled with glee.

'What fools men are,' she gasped. 'And you, you thought I'd throw a real string into the sea.'

She laughed and laughed. At last she stopped. She was excited.

'I want to sing. Glaser, play an accompaniment.'

A voice came from the drawing-room.

'You can't sing after all that food you walloped down.'

'Shut up, you old cow. Play something, I tell you.'

There was no reply, but in a moment Miss Glaser began to play the opening bars of one of Schumann's songs. It was no strain on the voice, and I guessed that Miss Glaser knew what she was doing when she chose it. La Falterona began to sing, in an undertone, but as she heard the sounds come from her lips and found that they were clear and pure she let herself go. The song finished. There was silence. Miss Glaser had heard that La Falterona was in magnificent voice, and she sensed that she wished to sing again. The *prima donna* was standing in the window, with her back to the lighted room, and she looked out at the darkly shining sea. The cedar made a lovely pattern against the sky. The night was soft and balmy. Miss Glaser played a couple of bars. A cold shiver ran down my spine. La Falterona gave a little start as she recognized the music, and I felt her gather herself together:

> *Mild und leise wie er lächelt*
> *Wie das Auge er öffnet.*

It was Isolde's death song. She had never sung in Wagner, fearing the strain on her voice, but this, I suppose, she had often sung in concerts. It did not matter now that instead of an orchestral accompaniment she had only the thin tinkle of a piano. The notes of the heavenly melody fell upon the still air and travelled over the water. In that too romantic scene, in that starry night, the effect was shattering. La Falterona's voice, even now, was exquisite in its quality, mellow and crystalline; and she sang with wonderful emotion, so tenderly, with such tragic, beautiful anguish that my heart melted within me. I had a most awkward lump in my throat when she finished, and looking at her I saw that tears were streaming down her face. I did not want to speak. She stood quite still looking out at that ageless sea.

What a strange woman! I thought then that I would sooner have her as she was, with her monstrous faults, than as Peter Melrose saw her, a pattern of all the virtues. But then people blame me because I rather like people who are a little worse than is reasonable. She was hateful, of course, but she was irresistible.

The
Unconquered

◆

He came back into the kitchen. The man was still on the floor, lying where he had hit him, and his face was bloody. He was moaning. The woman had backed against the wall and was staring with terrified eyes at Willi, his friend, and when he came in she gave a gasp and broke into loud sobbing. Willi was sitting at the table, his revolver in his hand, with a half empty glass of wine beside him. Hans went up to the table, filled his glass and emptied it at a gulp.

'You look as though you'd had trouble, young fellow,' said Willi with a grin.

Hans's face was blood-stained and you could see the gashes of five sharp finger-nails. He put his hand gingerly to his cheek.

'She'd have scratched my eyes out if she could, the bitch. I shall have to put some iodine on. But she's all right now. You go along.'

'I don't know. Shall I? It's getting late.'

'Don't be a fool. You're a man, aren't you? What if it is getting late? We lost our way.'

It was still light and the westering sun streamed into the kitchen windows of the farm-house. Willi hesitated a moment. He was a little fellow, dark and thin-faced, a dress designer in civil life, and he didn't want Hans to think him a cissy. He got up and went towards the door through which Hans had come. When the woman saw what he was going to do she gave a shriek and sprang forwards.

'*Non, non,*' she cried.

With one step Hans was in front of her. He seized her by the shoulders and flung her violently back. She tottered and fell. He took Willi's revolver.

'Stop still, both of you,' he rasped in French, but with his guttural German accent. He nodded his head towards the door. 'Go on. I'll look after them.'

Willi went out, but in a moment was back again.

'She's unconscious.'

'Well, what of it?'

'I can't. It's no good.'

'Stupid, that's what you are. *Ein Weibchen.* A woman.'

Willi flushed.

'We'd better be getting on our way.'

Hans shrugged a scornful shoulder.

'I'll just finish the bottle of wine and then we'll go.'

He was feeling at ease and it would have been pleasant to linger. He had been on the job since morning and after so many hours on his motor-cycle his limbs ached. Luckily they hadn't far to go, only to Soissons–ten or fifteen kilometres. He wondered if he'd have the luck to get a bed to sleep in. Of course all this wouldn't have happened if the girl hadn't been a fool. They had lost their way, he and Willi, they had stopped a peasant working in a field and he had deliberately misled them, and they found themselves on a side road. When they came to the farm they stopped to ask for a direction. They'd asked very politely, for orders were to treat the French population well as long as they behaved themselves. The door was opened for them by the girl and she said she didn't know the way to Soissons, so they pushed in; then the woman, her mother, Hans guessed, told them. The three of them, the farmer, his wife and daughter, had just finished supper and there was a bottle of wine on the table. It reminded Hans that he was as thirsty as the devil. The day had been sweltering and he hadn't had a drink since noon. He asked them for a bottle of wine and Willi had added that they would pay them well for it. Willi was a good little chap, but soft. After all, they were the victors. Where was the French army? In headlong flight. And the English, leaving everything behind, had scuttled like rabbits back to their island. The conquerors took what they wanted, didn't they? But Willi had worked at a Paris dressmaker's for two years. It's true he spoke French well, that's why he had his present job, but it had done something to him. A decadent people. It did a German no good to live among them.

The farmer's wife put a couple of bottles of wine on the table and Willi took twenty francs out of his pocket and gave it to her. She didn't even say thank you. Hans's French wasn't as good as Willi's, but he could make himself understood, and he and Willi spoke it together all the time. Willi corrected his mistakes. It was because Willi was so useful to him in this way that he had made him his friend, and he knew that Willi admired him. He admired him because he was so tall, slim, and broad-shouldered, because his curly hair was so fair and his eyes so blue. He never lost an opportunity to practise his French, and he tried to talk now, but those three French people wouldn't meet him half-way. He told them that he was a farmer's son himself and when the war was over was going back to the farm. He had been sent to school in Munich because his mother wanted him to go into business, but his heart wasn't in it, and so after matriculating he had gone to an agricultural college.

'You came here to ask your way and now you know it,' said the girl. 'Drink up your wine and go.'

He had hardly looked at her before. She wasn't pretty, but she had fine dark eyes and a straight nose. Her face was very pale. She was plainly dressed, but somehow she didn't look quite like what she evidently was. There was a sort of distinction about her. Ever since the war started he'd heard fellows talk about the French girls. They had something the German girls hadn't. Chic, Willi said it was, but when he asked him just what he meant by that Willi could only say that you had to see it to understand. Of course he'd heard others say that they were mercenary and hard as nails. Well, they'd be in Paris in a week and he'd find out for himself. They said the High Command had already arranged for houses for the men to go to.

'Finish your wine and let's go,' said Willi.

But Hans was feeling comfortable and didn't want to be hurried.

'You don't look like a farmer's daughter,' he said to the girl.

'And so what?' she answered.

'She's a teacher,' said her mother.

'Then you've had a good education.' She shrugged her shoulders, but he went on good-humouredly in his bad French. 'You ought to understand that this is the best thing that has ever happened to the French people. We didn't declare war. You declared war. And now we're going to make France a decent country. We're going to put order into it. We're going to teach you to work. You'll learn obedience and discipline.'

She clenched her fists and looked at him, her eyes black with hatred. But she did not speak.

'You're drunk, Hans,' said Willi.

'I'm as sober as a judge. I'm only telling them the truth and they may just as well know it at once.'

'He's right,' she cried out, unable any longer to contain herself. 'You're drunk. Now go. Go.'

'Oh, you understand German, do you? All right, I'll go. But you must give me a kiss first.'

She took a step back to avoid him, but he seized her wrist.

'Father,' she cried. 'Father.'

The farmer flung himself on the German. Hans let go of her and with all his might hit him in the face. He crumpled up on the floor. Then, before she could escape him, he caught the girl in his arms. She gave him a swinging blow on the cheek. . . . He chuckled grimly.

'Is that how you take it when a German soldier wants to kiss you? You'll pay for this.'

With his great strength he pinioned her arms and was dragging her out of the door, but her mother rushed at him and catching him by the clothes tried to pull him away. With one arm holding the girl close to him, with the flat of his other hand he gave the woman a great push and she staggered back to the wall.

'Hans, Hans,' cried Willi.

'Shut up, damn you.'

He put his hands over the girl's mouth to stop her shrieking and carried her out of the room. That was how it had happened and you had to admit that she'd brought it on herself. She shouldn't have slapped him. If she'd given him the kiss he'd asked for he'd have gone away. He gave a glance at the farmer still lying where he had fallen and he could hardly help laughing at his funny face. There was a smile in his eyes when he looked at the woman cowering against the wall. Was she afraid it was her turn next? Not likely. He remembered a French proverb.

'*C'est le premier pas qui coûte.* There's nothing to cry about, old woman. It had to come sooner or later.' He put his hand to his hip pocket and pulled out a wallet. 'Look, here's a hundred francs so that mademoiselle can buy herself a new dress. There's not much left of that one.' He placed the note on the table and put his helmet back on his head. 'Let's go.'

They slammed the door behind them and got on their motor-cycles. The woman went into the parlour. Her daughter was lying on the divan. She was lying as he had left her and she was weeping bitterly.

Three months later Hans found himself in Soissons again. He had been in Paris with the conquering army and had ridden through the Arc de Triomphe on his motor-cycle. He had advanced with the army first to Tours and then to Bordeaux. He'd seen very little fighting. The only French soldiers he'd seen were prisoners. The campaign had been the greatest spree he could ever have imagined. After the armistice he had spent a month in Paris. He'd sent picture postcards to his family in Bavaria and bought them all presents. Willi, because he knew the city like the palm of his hand, had stayed on, but he and the rest of his unit were sent to Soissons to join the force that was holding it. It was a nice little town and he was comfortably billeted. Plenty to eat and champagne for less than a mark a bottle in German money. When he was ordered to proceed there it had occurred to him that it would be fun to go and have a look at the girl he'd had. He'd take her a pair of silk stockings to show there was no ill-feeling. He had a good bump of locality and he thought he would be able to find the farm without difficulty. So one afternoon, when he had nothing to do, he put the silk stockings in his pocket and got on his machine. It was a lovely autumn day, with hardly a cloud in the sky, and it was pretty, undulating country that he rode through. It had been fine and dry for so long that, though it was September, not even the restless poplars gave sign that the summer was drawing to an end. He took one wrong turning, which delayed him, but for all that he got to the place he sought in less than half an hour. A mongrel dog barked at him as he walked up to the door. He did not knock, but turned the handle and stepped in. The girl was sitting at the table peeling potatoes. She sprang to her feet when she saw the uniformed man.

'What d'you want?' Then she recognized him. She backed to the wall, clutching the knife in her hands. 'It's you. *Cochon.*'

'Don't get excited. I'm not going to hurt you. Look. I've brought you some silk stockings.'

'Take them away and take yourself off with them.'

'Don't be silly. Drop that knife. You'll only get hurt if you try to be nasty. You needn't be afraid of me.'

'I'm not afraid of you,' she said.

She let the knife fall to the floor. He took off his helmet and sat down. He reached out with his foot and drew the knife towards him.

'Shall I peel some of your potatoes for you?' She did not answer. He bent down for the knife and then took a potato out of the bowl and went to work on it. Her face hard, her eyes hostile, she stood against the wall and watched him. He smiled at her disarmingly. 'Why do you look so cross? I didn't do you much harm, you know. I was excited, we all were, they'd talked of the invincible French army and the Maginot line . . .' he finished the sentence with a chuckle. 'And the wine went to my head. You might have fared worse. Women have told me that I'm not a bad-looking fellow.'

She looked him up and down scornfully.

'Get out of here.'

'Not until I choose.'

'If you don't go my father will go to Soissons and complain to the general.'

'Much he'll care. Our orders are to make friends with the population. What's your name?'

'That's not your business.'

There was a flush in her cheeks now and her angry eyes were blazing. She was prettier than he remembered her. He hadn't done so badly. She had a refinement that suggested the city-dweller rather than the peasant. He remembered her mother saying she was a teacher. Because she was almost a lady it amused him to torment her. He felt strong and healthy. He passed his hand through his curly blond hair, and giggled when he thought that many girls would have jumped at the chance she had had. His face was so deeply tanned by the summer that his eyes were startlingly blue.

'Where are your father and mother?'

'Working in the fields.'

'I'm hungry. Give me a bit of bread and cheese and a glass of wine. I'll pay.'

She gave a harsh laugh.

'We haven't seen cheese for three months. We haven't enough bread to stay our hunger. The French took our horses a year ago and now the Boches have taken our cows, our pigs, our chickens, everything.'

'Well, they paid you for them.'

'Can we eat the worthless paper they gave us?'

She began to cry.

'Are you hungry?'

'Oh, no,' she answered bitterly, 'we can eat like kings on potatoes and bread and turnips and lettuce. Tomorrow my father's going to Soissons to see if he can buy some horse meat.'

'Listen, Miss. I'm not a bad fellow. I'll bring you a cheese, and I think I can get hold of a bit of ham.'

'I don't want your presents. I'll starve before I touch the food you swine have stolen from us.'

'We'll see,' he said good-humouredly.

He put on his hat, got up, and with an *Au revoir, mademoiselle*, walked out.

He wasn't supposed to go joy-riding round the country and he had to wait to be sent on an errand before he was able to get to the farm again. It was ten days later. He walked in as unceremoniously as before and this time he found the farmer and his wife in the kitchen. It was round about noon and the woman was stirring a pot on the stove. The man was seated at table. They gave him a glance when he came in, but there was no surprise in it. Their daughter had evidently told them of his visit. They did not speak. The woman went on with her cooking, and the man, a surly look on his face, stared at the oil-cloth on the table. But it required more than this to disconcert the good-humoured Hans.

'*Bonjour, la compagnie*,' he said cheerfully. 'I've brought you a present.'

He undid the package he had with him and set out a sizeable piece of Gruyère cheese, a piece of pork, and a couple of tins of sardines. The woman turned round and he smiled when he saw the light of greed in her eyes. The man looked at the foodstuff sullenly. Hans gave him his sunny grin.

'I'm sorry we had a misunderstanding the first time I came here. But you shouldn't have interfered.'

At that moment the girl came in.

'What are you doing here?' she cried harshly. Then her eyes fell on the things he had brought. She swept them together and flung them at him. 'Take them away. Take them.'

But her mother sprang forward.

'Annette, you're crazy.'

'I won't take his presents.'

'It's our own food that they've stolen from us. Look at the sardines. They're Bordeaux sardines.'

She picked the things up. Hans looked at the girl with a mocking smile in his light blue eyes.

'Annette's your name, is it? A pretty name. Do you grudge your parents a little food? You said you hadn't had cheese for three months. I couldn't get any ham; I did the best I could.'

The farmer's wife took the lump of meat in her hands and pressed it to her bosom. You felt that she could have kissed it. Tears ran down Annette's cheeks.

'The shame of it,' she groaned.

'Oh, come now, there's no shame in a bit of Gruyère and a piece of pork.'

Hans sat down and lit a cigarette. Then he passed the packet over to the old man. The farmer hesitated for a moment, but the temptation was too strong for him; he took one and handed back the packet.

'Keep it,' said Hans. 'I can get plenty more.' He inhaled the smoke and blew a cloud of it from his nostrils. 'Why can't we be friends? What's done can't be undone. War is war, and, well, you know what I mean. I know Annette's an educated girl and I want her to think well of me. I expect we shall be in Soissons for quite a while and I can bring you something now and then to help out. You know, we do all we can to make friends with the townspeople, but they won't let us. They won't even look at us when we pass them in the street. After all, it was an accident, what happened that time I came here with Willi. You needn't be afraid of me. I'll respect Annette as if she was my own sister.'

'Why do you want to come here? Why can't you leave us alone?' asked Annette.

He really didn't know. He didn't like to say that he wanted a little human friendship. The silent hostility that surrounded them all at Soissons got on his nerves so that sometimes he wanted to go up to a Frenchman who looked at him as if he wasn't there and knock him down, and sometimes it affected him so that he was almost inclined to cry. It would be nice if he had some place to go where he was welcome. He spoke the truth when he said he had no desire for Annette. She wasn't the sort of woman he fancied. He liked women to be tall and full-breasted, blue-eyed, and fair-haired like himself; he liked them to be strong and hefty and well-covered. That refinement which he couldn't account for, that thin fine nose and those dark eyes, the long pale face—there was something intimidating about the girl, so that if he hadn't been excited by the great victories of the German armies, if he hadn't been so tired and yet so elated, if he hadn't drunk all that wine on an empty stomach, it would never have crossed his mind that he could have anything to do with her.

For a fortnight after that Hans couldn't get away. He'd left the food at the farm and he had no doubt that the old people had wolfed it. He wondered if Annette had eaten it too; he wouldn't have been surprised to discover that the moment his back was turned she had set to with the others. These French people, they couldn't resist getting something for nothing. They were weak and decadent. She hated him, yes, God, how she hated him, but pork was pork, and cheese was cheese. He thought of her quite a lot. It tantalized him that she should have such a loathing for him. He was used to being liked by women. It would be funny if one of these days she fell in love with him. He'd been her first lover and he'd heard the students at Munich over their beer saying that it was her first lover a woman loved, after that it was love. When he'd set his mind on

getting a girl he'd never failed yet. Hans laughed to himself and a sly look came
into his eyes.

At last he got his chance to go to the farm. He got hold of cheese and butter,
sugar, a tin of sausages, and some coffee, and set off on his motor-cycle. But
that time he didn't see Annette. She and her father were at work in the fields.
The old woman was in the yard and her face lit up when she saw the parcel he
was bringing. She led him into the kitchen. Her hands trembled a little as she
untied the string and when she saw what he had brought her eyes filled with
tears.

'You're very good,' she said.

'May I sit down?' he asked politely.

'Of course.' She looked out of the window and Hans guessed that she wanted
to make sure that Annette was not coming. 'Can I offer you a glass of wine.'

'I'd be glad of it.'

He was sharp enough to see that her greed for food had made her, if not
friendly to him, at least willing to come to terms with him. That look out of the
window made them almost fellow conspirators.

'Did you like the pork?' he asked.

'It was a treat.'

'I'll try to bring you some more next time I come. Did Annette like it?'

'She wouldn't touch a thing you'd left. She said she'd rather starve.'

'Silly.'

'That's what I said to her. As long as the food is there, I said, there's nothing
to be gained by not eating it.'

They chatted quite amicably while Hans sipped his wine. He discovered that
she was called Madame Périer. He asked her whether there were any other
members of the family. She sighed. No, they'd had a son, but he'd been
mobilized at the beginning of the war and he'd died. He hadn't been killed, he'd
got pneumonia and died in the hospital at Nancy.

'I'm sorry,' said Hans.

'Perhaps he's better off than if he'd lived. He was like Annette in many ways.
He could never have borne the shame of defeat.' She sighed again. 'Oh, my
poor friend, we've been betrayed.'

'Why did you want to fight for the Poles? What were they to you?'

'You're right. If we had let your Hitler take Poland he would have left us
alone.'

When Hans got up to go he said he would come again soon.

'I shan't forget the pork.'

Then Hans had a lucky break; he was given a job that took him twice a week
to a town in the vicinity so that he was able to get to the farm much oftener. He
took care never to come without bringing something. But he made no headway
with Annette. Seeking to ingratiate himself with her, he used the simple wiles
that he had discovered went down with women; but they only excited her
derision. Thin-lipped and hard, she looked at him as though he were dirt. On
more than one occasion she made him so angry that he would have liked to take
her by the shoulders and shake the life out of her. Once he found her alone, and
when she got up to go he barred her passage.

'Stop where you are. I want to talk to you.'

'Talk. I am a woman and defenceless.'

'What I want to say is this: for all I know I may be here for a long time.
Things aren't going to get easier for you French, they're going to get harder. I

can be useful to you. Why don't you be reasonable like your father and mother?'
It was true that old Périer had come round. You couldn't say that he was
cordial, he was indeed cold and gruff, but he was civil. He had even asked Hans
to bring him some tobacco, and when he wouldn't accept payment for it had
thanked him. He was pleased to hear the news of Soissons and grabbed the
paper that Hans brought him. Hans, a farmer's son, could talk about the farm as
one who knew. It was a good farm, not too big and not too small, well watered,
for a sizeable brook ran through it, and well wooded, with arable land and
pasture. Hans listened with understanding sympathy when the old man
bewailed himself because without labour, without fertilizers, his stock taken
from him, it was all going to rack and ruin.
'You ask me why I can't be reasonable like my father and mother,' said
Annette.
She pulled her dress tight and showed herself to him. He couldn't believe his
eyes. What he saw caused such a convulsion in his soul as he had never known.
The blood rushed to his cheeks.
'You're pregnant.'
She sank back on her chair and leaning her head on her hands began to weep
as though her heart would break.
'The shame of it. The shame.'
He sprang towards her to take her in his arms.
'My sweet,' he cried.
But she sprang to her feet and pushed him away.
'Don't touch me. Go away. Go away. Haven't you done me enough harm
already?'
She flung out of the room. He waited by himself for a few minutes. He was
bewildered. His thoughts in a whirl, he rode slowly back to Soissons, and when
he went to bed he couldn't get to sleep for hours. He could think of nothing but
Annette and her swollen body. She had been unbearably pathetic as she sat
there at the table crying her eyes out. It was his child she bore in her womb. He
began to feel drowsy, and then with a start he was once more wide awake, for
suddenly it came to him, it came to him with the shattering suddenness of gun-
fire: he was in love with her. It was such a surprise, such a shock that he couldn't
cope with it. Of course he'd thought of her a lot, but never in that way, he'd
thought it would be a great joke if he made her fall in love with him, it would be
a triumph if the time came when she offered what he had taken by force; but not
for a moment had it occurred to him that she was anything to him but a woman
like another. She wasn't his type. She wasn't very pretty. There was nothing to
her. Why should he have all of a sudden this funny feeling for her? It wasn't a
pleasant feeling either, it was a pain. But he knew what it was all right; it was
love, and it made him feel happier than he had ever felt in his life. He wanted to
take her in his arms, he wanted to pet her, he wanted to kiss those tear-stained
eyes of hers. He didn't desire her, he thought, as a man desires a woman, he
wanted to comfort her, wanted her to smile at him – strange, he had never seen
her smile, he wanted to see her eyes – fine eyes they were, beautiful eyes – soft
with tenderness.
For three days he could not leave Soissons and for three days, three days and
three nights, he thought of Annette and the child she would bear. Then he was
able to go to the farm. He wanted to see Madame Périer by herself, and luck was
with him, for he met her on the road some way from the house. She had been
gathering sticks in the wood and was going home with a great bundle on her

back. He stopped his motor-cycle. He knew that the friendliness she showed him was due only to the provisions he brought with him, but he didn't care; it was enough that she was mannerly, and that she was prepared to be so as long as she could get something out of him. He told her he wanted to talk to her and asked her to put her bundle down. She did as he bade. It was a grey, cloudy day, but not cold.

'I know about Annette,' he said.

She started.

'How did you find out? She was set on your not knowing.'

'She told me.'

'That was a pretty job of work you did that evening.'

'I didn't know. Why didn't you tell me sooner?'

She began to talk, not bitterly, not blaming him even, but as though it were a misfortune of nature, like a cow dying in giving birth to a calf or a sharp spring frost nipping the fruit trees and ruining the crop, a misfortune that human kind must accept with resignation and humility. After that dreadful night Annette had been in bed for days with a high fever. They thought she was going out of her mind. She would scream for hours on end. There were no doctors to be got. The village doctor had been called to the colours. Even in Soissons there were only two doctors left, old men both of them, and how could they get to the farm even if it had been possible to send for them? They weren't allowed to leave the town. Even when the fever went down Annette was too ill to leave her bed, and when she got up she was so weak, so pale, it was pitiful. The shock had been terrible, and when a month went by, and another month, without her being unwell she paid no attention. She had always been irregular. It was Madame Périer who first suspected that something was wrong. She questioned Annette. They were terrified, both of them, but they weren't certain and they said nothing to Périer. When the third month came it was impossible to doubt any longer. Annette was pregnant.

They had an old Citroën in which before the war Madame Périer had taken the farm produce into the market at Soissons two mornings a week, but since the German occupation they had had nothing to sell that made the journey worth while. Petrol was almost unobtainable. But now they got it out and drove into town. The only cars to be seen were the military cars of the Germans. German soldiers lounged about. There were German signs in the streets, and on public buildings proclamations in French signed by the Officer Commanding. Many shops were closed. They went to the old doctor they knew, and he confirmed their suspicions. But he was a devout Catholic and would not help them. When they wept he shrugged his shoulders.

'You're not the only one,' he said. '*Il faut souffrir.*'

They knew about the other doctor too and went to see him. They rang the bell and for a long time no one answered. At last the door was opened by a sad-faced woman in black, but when they asked to see the doctor she began to cry. He had been arrested by the Germans because he was a freemason, and was held as a hostage. A bomb had exploded in a café frequented by German officers and two had been killed and several wounded. If the guilty were not handed over before a certain date he was to be shot. The woman seemed kindly and Madame Périer told her of their trouble.

'The brutes,' she said. She looked at Annette with compassion 'My poor child.'

She gave them the address of a midwife in the town and told them to say that they had come from her. The midwife gave them some medicine. It made Annette so ill that she thought she was going to die, but it had no further effect. Annette was still pregnant.

That was the story that Madame Périer told Hans. For a while he was silent. 'It's Sunday tomorrow,' he said then. 'I shall have nothing to do. I'll come and we'll talk. I'll bring something nice.'

'We have no needles. Can you bring some?'

'I'll try.'

She hoisted the bundle of sticks on her back and trudged down the road. Hans went back to Soissons. He dared not use his motor-cycle, so next day he hired a push-bike. He tied his parcel of food on the carrier. It was a larger parcel than usual because he had put a bottle of champagne into it. He got to the farm when the gathering darkness made it certain that they would all be home from work. It was warm and cosy in the kitchen when he walked in. Madame Périer was cooking and her husband was reading a *Paris-Soir*. Annette was darning stockings.

'Look, I've brought you some needles,' he said, as he undid his parcel. 'And here's some material for you, Annette.'

'I don't want it.'

'Don't you?' he grinned. 'You'll have to begin making things for the baby.'

'That's true, Annette,' said her mother, 'and we have nothing.' Annette did not look up from her sewing. Madame Périer's greedy eyes ran over the contents of the parcel. 'A bottle of champagne.'

Hans chuckled.

'I'll tell you what that's for presently. I've had an idea.' He hesitated for a moment, then drew up a chair and sat down facing Annette. 'I don't know quite how to begin. I'm sorry for what I did that night, Annette. It wasn't my fault, it was the circumstances. Can't you forgive me?'

She threw him a look of hatred.

'Never. Why don't you leave me alone? Isn't it enough that you've ruined my life?'

'Well, that's just it. Perhaps I haven't. When I knew you were going to have a baby it had a funny effect on me. It's all different now. It's made me so proud.'

'Proud?' she flung at him viciously.

'I want you to have the baby, Annette. I'm glad you couldn't get rid of it.'

'How dare you say that?'

'But listen to me. I've been thinking of nothing else since I knew. The war will be over in six months. We shall bring the English to their knees in the spring. They haven't got a chance. And then I shall be demobilized and I'll marry you.'

'You? Why?'

He blushed under his tan. He could not bring himself to say it in French, so he said it in German. He knew she understood it.

'*Ich liebe dich.*'

'What does he say?' asked Madame Périer.

'He says he loves me.'

Annette threw back her head and broke into a peal of harsh laughter. She laughed louder and louder and she couldn't stop and tears streamed from her eyes. Madame Périer slapped her sharply on both cheeks.

'Don't pay any attention,' she said to Hans. 'It's hysteria. Her condition, you know.'

Annette gasped. She gained control over herself.

'I brought the bottle of champagne to celebrate our engagement,' said Hans.

'That's the bitterest thing of all,' said Annette, 'that we were beaten by fools, by such fools.'

Hans went on speaking in German.

'I didn't know I loved you till that day when I found out that you were going to have a baby. It came like a clap of thunder, but I think I've loved you all the time.'

'What does he say?' asked Madame Périer.

'Nothing of importance.'

He fell back into French. He wanted Annette's parents to hear what he had to say.

'I'd marry you now, only they wouldn't let me. And don't think I'm nothing at all. My father's well-to-do and we're well thought of in our commune. I'm the eldest son and you'd want for nothing.'

'Are you a Catholic?' asked Madame Périer.

'Yes, I'm a Catholic.'

'That's something.'

'It's pretty, the country where we live and the soil's good. There's not better farming land between Munich and Innsbruck, and it's our own. My grandfather bought it after the war of '70. And we've got a car and a radio, and we're on the telephone.'

Annette turned to her father.

'He has all the tact in the world, this gentleman,' she cried ironically. She eyed Hans. 'It would be a nice position for me, the foreigner from the conquered country with a child born out of wedlock. It offers me a chance of happiness, doesn't it? A fine chance.'

Périer, a man of few words, spoke for the first time.

'No. I don't deny that it's a fine gesture you're making. I went through the last war and we all did things we wouldn't have done in peace time. Human nature is human nature. But now that our son is dead, Annette is all we have. We can't let her go.'

'I thought you might feel that way,' said Hans, 'and I've got my answer to that. I'll stay here.'

Annette gave him a quick look.

'What do you mean?' asked Madame Périer.

'I've got another brother. He can stay and help my father. I like this country. With energy and initiative a man could make a good thing of your farm. When the war's over a lot of Germans will be settling here. It's well known that you haven't got enough men in France to work the land you've got. A fellow gave us a lecture the other day at Soissons. He said that a third of the farms were left uncultivated because there aren't the men to work them.'

Périer and his wife exchanged glances and Annette saw that they were wavering. That was what they'd wanted since their son had died, a son-in-law who was strong and hefty and could take over when they grew too old to do more than potter about.

'That changes the case,' said Madame Périer. 'It's a proposition to consider.'

'Hold your tongue,' cried Annette roughly. She leant forward and fixed her burning eyes on the German. 'I'm engaged to a teacher who worked in the boys' school in the town where I taught, we were to be married after the war. He's not strong and big like you, or handsome; he's small and frail. His only beauty is the intelligence that shines in his face, his only strength is the greatness of his soul. He's not a barbarian, he's civilized; he has a thousand years of civilization behind him. I love him. I love him with all my heart and soul.'

Hans's face grew sullen. It had never occurred to him that Annette might care for anyone else.

'Where is he now?'

'Where do you suppose he is? In Germany. A prisoner and starving. While you eat the fat of our land. How many times have I got to tell you that I hate you? You ask me to forgive you. Never. You want to make reparation. You fool.' She threw her head back and there was a look of intolerable anguish on her face. 'Ruined. Oh, he'll forgive me. He's tender. But I'm tortured by the thought that one day the suspicion may come to him that perhaps I hadn't been forced–that perhaps I'd given myself to you for butter and cheese and silk stockings. I shouldn't be the only one. And what would our life be with that child between us, your child, a German child? Big like you, and blond like you, and blue-eyed like you. Oh, my God, why do I have to suffer this?'

She got up and went swiftly out of the kitchen. For a minute the three were left in silence. Hans looked ruefully at his bottle of champagne. He sighed and rose to his feet. When he went out Madame Périer accompanied him.

'Did you mean it when you said you would marry her?' she asked him, speaking in a low voice.

'Yes. Every word. I love her.'

'And you wouldn't take her away? You'd stay here and work on the farm?'

'I promise you.'

'Evidently my old man can't last for ever. At home you'd have to share with your brother. Here you'd share with nobody.'

'There's that too.'

'We never were in favour of Annette marrying that teacher, but our son was alive then and he said, if she wants to marry him, why shouldn't she? Annette was crazy about him. But now that our son's dead, poor boy, it's different. Even if she wanted to, how could she work the farm alone?'

'It would be a shame if it was sold. I know how one feels about one's own land.'

They had reached the road. She took his hand and gave it a little squeeze.

'Come again soon.'

Hans knew that she was on his side. It was a comfort to him to think that as he rode back to Soissons. It was a bother that Annette was in love with somebody else. Fortunately he was a prisoner; long before he was likely to be released the baby would be born. That might change her: you could never tell with a woman. Why, in his village there'd been a woman who was so much in love with her husband that it had been a joke, and then she had a baby and after that she couldn't bear the sight of him. Well, why shouldn't the contrary happen too? And now that he'd offered to marry her she must see that he was a decent sort of fellow. God, how pathetic she'd looked with her head flung back, and how well she'd spoken! What language! An actress on the stage couldn't have expressed herself better, and yet it had all sounded so natural. You had to admit that, these French people knew how to talk. Oh, she was clever. Even when she lashed him with that bitter tongue it was a joy to listen to her. He hadn't had a bad education himself, but he couldn't hold a candle to her. Culture, that's what she had.

'I'm a donkey,' he said out loud as he rode along. She'd said he was big and strong and handsome. Would she have said that if it hadn't meant something to her? And she'd talked of the baby having fair hair and blue eyes like his own. If that didn't mean that his colouring had made an impression on her he was a Dutchman. He chuckled. 'Give me time. Patience, and let nature go to work.'

The weeks went by. The C.O. at Soissons was an elderly, easy-going fellow and in view of what the spring had in store for them he was content not to drive his men too hard. The German papers told them that England was being wrecked by the Luftwaffe and the people were in a panic. Submarines were sinking British ships by the score and the country was starving. Revolution was imminent. Before summer it would be all over and the Germans would be masters of the world. Hans wrote home and told his parents that he was going to marry a French girl and with her a fine farm. He proposed that his brother should borrow money to buy him out of his share of the family property so that he could increase the size of his own holding while land, owing to the war and the exchange, could still be bought for a song. He went over the farm with Périer. The old man listened quietly when Hans told him his ideas: the farm would have to be restocked and as a German he would have a pull; the motor tractor was old, he would get a fine new one from Germany, and a motor plough. To make a farm pay you had to take advantage of modern inventions. Madame Périer told him afterwards that her husband had said he wasn't a bad lad and seemed to know a lot. She was very friendly with him now and insisted that he should share their midday meal with them on Sundays. She translated his name into French and called him Jean. He was always ready to give a hand, and as time went on and Annette could do less and less it was useful to have a man about who didn't mind doing a job of work.

Annette remained fiercely hostile. She never spoke to him except to answer his direct questions and as soon as it was possible went to her own room. When it was so cold that she couldn't stay there she sat by the side of the kitchen stove, sewing or reading, and took no more notice of him than if he hadn't been there. She was in radiant health. There was colour in her cheeks and in Hans's eyes she was beautiful. Her approaching maternity had given her a strange dignity and he was filled with exultation when he gazed upon her. Then one day when he was on his way to the farm he saw Madame Périer in the road waving to him to stop. He put his brakes on hard.

'I've been waiting for an hour. I thought you'd never come. You must go back. Pierre is dead.'

'Who's Pierre?'

'Pierre Gavin. The teacher Annette was going to marry.'

Hans's heart leapt. What luck! Now he'd have his chance.

'Is she upset?'

'She's not crying. When I tried to say something she bit my head off. If she saw you today she's capable of sticking a knife into you.'

'It's not my fault if he died. How did you hear?'

'A prisoner, a friend of his, escaped through Switzerland and he wrote to Annette. We got the letter this morning. There was a mutiny in the camp because they weren't given enough to eat, and the ringleaders were shot. Pierre was one of them.'

Hans was silent. He could only think it served the man right. What did they think that a prison camp was—the Ritz?

'Give her time to get over the shock,' said Madame Périer. 'When she's calmer I'll talk to her. I'll write you a letter when you can come again.'

'All right. You will help me, won't you?'

'You can be sure of that. My husband and I, we're agreed. We talked it over and we came to the conclusion that the only thing to do was to accept the situation. He's no fool, my husband, and he says the best chance for France now is to collaborate. And take it all in all I don't dislike you. I shouldn't wonder if you didn't make Annette a better husband than that teacher. And with the baby coming and all.'

'I want it to be a boy,' said Hans.

'It's going to be a boy. I know for certain. I've seen it in the coffee grounds and I've put out the cards. The answer is a boy every time.'

'I almost forgot, here are some papers for you,' said Hans, as he turned his cycle and prepared to mount.

He handed her three numbers of *Paris-Soir*. Old Périer read every evening. He read that the French must be realistic and accept the new order that Hitler was going to create in Europe. He read that the German submarines were sweeping the sea. He read that the General Staff had organized to the last detail the campaign that would bring England to her knees and that the Americans were too unprepared, too soft and too divided to come to her help. He read that France must take the heaven-sent opportunity and by loyal collaboration with the Reich regain her honoured position in the new Europe. And it wasn't Germans who wrote it all; it was Frenchmen. He nodded his head with approval when he read that the plutocrats and the Jews would be destroyed and the poor man in France would at last come into his own. They were quite right, the clever fellows who said that France was essentially an agricultural country and its backbone was its industrious farmers. Good sense, that was.

One evening, when they were finishing their supper, ten days after the news had come of Pierre Gavin's death, Madame Périer, by arrangement with her husband, said to Annette:

'I wrote a letter to Hans a few days ago telling him to come here tomorrow.'

'Thank you for the warning. I shall stay in my room.'

'Oh, come, daughter, the time has passed for foolishness. You must be realistic. Pierre is dead. Hans loves you and wants to marry you. He's a fine-looking fellow. Any girl would be proud of him as a husband. How can we restock the farm without his help? He's going to buy a tractor and a plough with his own money. You must let bygones be bygones.'

'You're wasting your breath, Mother. I earned my living before, I can earn my living again. I hate him. I hate his vanity and his arrogance. I could kill him: his death wouldn't satisfy me. I should like to torture him as he's tortured me. I think I should die happy if I could find a way to wound him as he's wounded me.'

'You're being very silly, my poor child.'

'Your mother's right, my girl,' said Périer. 'We've been defeated and we must accept the consequences. We're got to make the best arrangement we can with the conquerors. We're cleverer than they are and if we play our cards well we shall come out on top. France was rotten. It's the Jews and the plutocrats who ruined the country. Read the papers and you'll see for yourself!'

'Do you think I believe a word in that paper? Why do you think he brings it to you except that it's sold to the Germans? The men who write in it–traitors, traitors. Oh God, may I live to see them torn to pieces by the mob. Bought, bought every one of them–bought with German money. The swine.'

Madame Périer was getting exasperated.

'What have you got against the boy? He took you by force–yes, he was drunk at the time. It's not the first time that's happened to a woman and it won't be the last time. He hit your father and he bled like a pig, but does your father bear him malice?'

'It was an unpleasant incident, but I've forgotten it,' said Périer.

Annette burst into harsh laughter.

'You should have been a priest. You forgive injuries with a spirit truly Christian.'

'And what is there wrong about that?' asked Madame Périer angrily. 'Hasn't he done everything he could to make amends? Where would your father have got his tobacco all these months if it hadn't been for him? If we haven't gone hungry it's owing to him.'

'If you'd had any pride, if you'd had any sense of decency, you'd have thrown his presents in his face.'

'You've profited by them, haven't you?'

'Never. Never.'

'It's a lie and you know it. You've refused to eat the cheese he brought and the butter and the sardines. But the soup you've eaten, you know I put the meat in it that he brought; and the salad you ate tonight, if you didn't have to eat it dry, it's because he brought me oil.'

Annette sighed deeply. She passed her hand over her eyes.

'I know. I tried not to, I couldn't help myself, I was so hungry. Yes, I knew his meat went into the soup and I ate it. I knew the salad was made with his oil. I wanted to refuse it; I had such a longing for it, it wasn't I that ate it, it was a ravenous beast within me.'

'That's neither here nor there. You ate it.'

'With shame. With despair. They broke our strength first with their tanks and their planes, and now when we're defenceless they're breaking our spirit by starving us.'

'You get nowhere by being theatrical, my girl. For an educated woman you have really no sense. Forget the past and give a father to your child, to say nothing of a good workman for the farm who'll be worth two hired men. That is sense.'

Annette shrugged her shoulders wearily and they lapsed into silence. Next day Hans came. Annette gave him a sullen look, but neither spoke nor moved. Hans smiled.

'Thank you for not running away,' he said.

'My parents asked you to come and they've gone down to the village. It suits me because I want to have a definite talk with you. Sit down.'

He took off his coat and his helmet and drew a chair to the table.

'My parents want me to marry you. You've been clever; with your presents, with your promises, you've got round them. They believe all they read in the papers you bring them. I want to tell you that I will never marry you. I wouldn't have thought it possible that I could hate a human being as I hate you.'

'Let me speak in German. You understand enough to know what I'm saying.'

'I ought to. I taught it. For two years I was governess to two little girls in Stuttgart.'

He broke into German, but she went on speaking French.

'It's not only that I love you, I admire you. I admire your distinction and your grace. There's something about you I don't understand. I respect you. Oh, I can see that you don't want to marry me now even if it were possible. But Pierre is dead.'

'Don't speak of him,' she cried violently. 'That would be the last straw.'

'I only want to tell you that for your sake I'm sorry he died.'

'Shot in cold blood by his German jailers.'

'Perhaps in time you'll grieve for him less. You know, when someone you love dies, you think you'll never get over it, but you do. Won't it be better then to have a father for your child?'

'Even if there were nothing else do you think I could ever forget that you are a German and I'm a Frenchwoman? If you weren't as stupid as only a German can be you'd see that that child must be a reproach to me as long as I live. Do you think I have no friends? How could I ever look them in the face with the child I had with a German soldier? There's only one thing I ask you; leave me alone with my disgrace. Go, go–for God's sake go and never come again.'

'But he's my child too. I want him.'

'You?' she cried in astonishment. 'What can a by-blow that you got in a moment of savage drunkenness mean to you?'

'You don't understand. I'm so proud and so happy. It was when I knew you were going to have a baby that I knew I loved you. At first I couldn't believe it; it was such a surprise to me. Don't you see what I mean? That child that's going to be born means everything in the world to me. Oh, I don't know how to put it; it's put feelings in my heart that I don't understand myself.'

She looked at him intently and there was a strange gleam in her eyes. You would have said it was a look of triumph. She gave a short laugh.

'I don't know whether I more loathe the brutality of you Germans or despise your sentimentality.'

He seemed not to have heard what she said.

'I think of him all the time.'

'You've made up your mind it'll be a boy?'

'I know it'll be a boy. I want to hold him in my arms and I want to teach him to walk. And then when he grows older I'll teach him all I know. I'll teach him to ride and I'll teach him to shoot. Are there fish in your brook? I'll teach him to fish. I'm going to be the proudest father in the world.'

She stared at him with hard, hard eyes. Her face was set and stern. An idea, a terrible idea was forming itself in her mind. He gave her a disarming smile.

'Perhaps when you see how much I love our boy, you'll come to love me too. I'll make you a good husband, my pretty.'

She said nothing. She merely kept on gazing at him sullenly.

'Haven't you one kind word for me?' he said.

She flushed. She clasped her hands tightly together.

'Others may despise me. I will never do anything that can make me despise myself. You are my enemy and you will always be my enemy. I only live to see the deliverance of France. It'll come, perhaps not next year or the year after, perhaps not for thirty years, but it'll come. The rest of them can do what they like, I will never come to terms with the invaders of my country. I hate you and I hate this child that you've given me. Yes, we've been defeated. Before the end comes you'll see that we haven't been conquered. Now go. My mind's made up and nothing on God's earth can change it.'

He was silent for a minute or two.

'Have you made arrangements for a doctor? I'll pay all the expenses.'

'Do you suppose we want to spread our shame through the whole countryside? My mother will do all that's necessary.'

'But supposing there's an accident?'

'And supposing you mind your own business!'

He sighed and rose to his feet. When he closed the door behind him she watched him walk down the pathway that led to the road. She realized with rage that some of the things he said had aroused in her heart a feeling that she had never felt for him before.

'O God, give me strength,' she cried.

Then, as he walked along, the dog, an old dog they'd had for years, ran up to him barking angrily. He had tried for months to make friends with the dog, but it had never responded to his advances; when he tried to pat it, it backed away growling and showing its teeth. And now as the dog ran towards him, irritably giving way to his feeling of frustration, Hans gave it a savage brutal kick and the dog was flung into the bushes and limped yelping away.

'The beast,' she cried. 'Lies, lies, lies. And I was weak enough to be almost sorry for him.'

There was a looking-glass hanging by the side of the door and she looked at herself in it. She drew herself up and smiled at her reflection. But rather than a smile it was a fiendish grimace.

It was now March. There was a bustle of activity in the garrison at Soissons. There were inspections and there was intensive training. Rumour was rife. There was no doubt they were going somewhere, but the rank and file could only guess where. Some thought they were being got ready at last for the invasion of England, others were of opinion that they would be sent to the Balkans, and others again talked of the Ukraine. Hans was kept busy. It was not till the second Sunday afternoon that he was able to get out to the farm. It was a cold grey day, with sleet that looked as though it might turn to snow falling in sudden windy flurries. The country was grim and cheerless.

'You!' cried Madame Périer when he went in. 'We thought you were dead.'

'I couldn't come before. We're off any day now. We don't know when.'

'The baby was born this morning. It's a boy.'

Hans's heart gave a great leap in his breast. He hung his arms round the old woman and kissed her on both cheeks.

'A Sunday child, he ought to be lucky. Let's open the bottle of champagne. How's Annette?'

'She's as well as can be expected. She had a very easy time. She began to have pains last night and by five o'clock this morning it was all over.'

Old Périer was smoking his pipe sitting as near the stove as he could get. He smiled quietly at the boy's enthusiasm.

'One's first child, it has an effect on one,' he said.

'He has quite a lot of hair and it's as fair as yours; and blue eyes just like you said he'd have,' said Madame Périer. 'I've never seen a lovelier baby. He'll be just like his papa.'

'Oh, my God, I'm so happy,' cried Hans. 'How beautiful the world is! I want to see Annette.'

'I don't know if she'll see you. I don't want to upset her on account of the milk.'

'No, no, don't upset her on my account. If she doesn't want to see me it doesn't matter. But let me see the baby just for a minute.'

'I'll see what I can do. I'll try to bring it down.'

Madame Périer went out and they heard her heavy tread clumping up the stairs. But in a moment they heard her clattering down again. She burst into the kitchen.

'They're not there. She isn't in her room. The baby's gone.'

Périer and Hans cried out and without thinking what they were doing all three of them scampered upstairs. The harsh light of the winter afternoon cast over the shabby furniture, the iron bed, the cheap wardrobe, the chest of drawers, a dismal squalor. There was no one in the room.

'Where is she?' screamed Madame Périer. She ran into the narrow passage, opening doors, and called the girl's name. 'Annette, Annette. Oh, what madness!'

'Perhaps in the sitting-room.'

They ran downstairs to the unused parlour. An icy air met them as they opened the door. They opened the door of a storeroom.

'She's gone out. Something awful has happened.'

'How could she have got out?' asked Hans sick with anxiety.

'Through the front door, you fool.'

Périer went up to it and looked.

'That's right. The bolt's drawn back.'

'Oh, my God, my God, what madness,' cried Madame Périer. 'It'll kill her.'

'We must look for her,' said Hans. Instinctively, because that was the way he always went in and out, he ran back into the kitchen and the others followed him. 'Which way?'

'The brook,' the old woman gasped.

He stopped as though turned to stone with horror. He stared at the old woman aghast.

'I'm frightened,' she cried. 'I'm frightened.'

Hans flung open the door, and as he did so Annette walked in. She had nothing on but her nightdress and a flimsy rayon dressing-gown. It was pink, with pale blue flowers. She was soaked, and her hair, dishevelled, clung damply to her head and hung down her shoulders in bedraggled wisps. She was deathly white. Madame Périer sprang towards her and took her in her arms.

'Where have you been? Oh, my poor child, you're wet through. What madness!'

But Annette pushed her away. She looked at Hans.

'You've come at the right moment, you.'

'Where's the baby?' cried Madame Périer.

'I had to do it at once. I was afraid if I waited I shouldn't have the courage.'

'Annette, what have you done?'

'I've done what I had to do. I took it down to the brook and held it under water till it was dead.' .

Hans gave a great cry, the cry of an animal wounded to death; he covered his face with his hands, and staggering like a drunken man flung out of the door. Annette sank into a chair, and leaning her forehead on her two fists burst into passionate weeping.

The Escape

♦

I have always been convinced that if a woman once made up her mind to marry a man nothing but instant flight could save him. Not always that; for once a friend of mine, seeing the inevitable loom menacingly before him, took ship from a certain port (with a tooth-brush for all his luggage, so conscious was he of his danger and the necessity for immediate action) and spent a year travelling round the world; but when, thinking himself safe (women are fickle, he said, and in twelve months she will have forgotten all about me), he landed at the selfsame port the first person he saw gaily waving to him from the quay was the little lady from whom he had fled. I have only once known a man who in such circumstances managed to extricate himself. His name was Roger Charing. He was no longer young when he fell in love with Ruth Barlow and he had had sufficient experience to make him careful; but Ruth Barlow had a gift (or should I call it a quality?) that renders most men defenceless, and it was this that dispossessed Roger of his commonsense, his prudence, and his worldly wisdom. He went down like a row of ninepins. This was the gift of pathos. Mrs Barlow, for she was twice a widow, had splendid dark eyes and they were the most moving I ever saw; they seemed to be ever on the point of filling with tears; they suggested that the world was too much for her, and you felt that, poor dear, her sufferings had been more than anyone should be asked to bear. If, like Roger Charing, you were a strong, hefty fellow with plenty of money, it was almost inevitable that you should say to yourself: I must stand between the hazards of life and this helpless little thing, oh, how wonderful it would be to take the sadness out of those big and lovely eyes! I gathered from Roger that everyone had treated Mrs Barlow very badly. She was apparently one of those unfortunate persons with whom nothing by any chance goes right. If she married a husband he beat her; if she employed a broker he cheated her; if she engaged a cook she drank. She never had a little lamb but it was sure to die.

When Roger told me that he had at last persuaded her to marry him, I wished him joy.

'I hope you'll be good friends,' he said. 'She's a little afraid of you, you know; she thinks you're callous.'

'Upon my word I don't know why she should think that.'

'You do like her, don't you?'

'Very much.'

'She's had a rotten time, poor dear. I feel so dreadfully sorry for her.'

'Yes,' I said.

I couldn't say less. I knew she was stupid and I thought she was scheming. My own belief was that she was as hard as nails.

The first time I met her we had played bridge together and when she was my partner she twice trumped my best card. I behaved like an angel, but I confess that I thought if the tears were going to well up into anybody's eyes they should have been mine rather than hers. And when, having by the end of the evening lost a good deal of money to me, she said she would send me a cheque and never did, I could not but think that I and not she should have worn a pathetic expression when next we met.

Roger introduced her to his friends. He gave her lovely jewels. He took her here, there, and everywhere. Their marriage was announced for the immediate future. Roger was very happy. He was committing a good action and at the same time doing something he had very much a mind to. It is an uncommon situation and it is not surprising if he was a trifle more pleased with himself than was altogether becoming.

Then, on a sudden, he fell out of love. I do not know why. It could hardly have been that he grew tired of her conversation, for she had never had any conversation. Perhaps it was merely that this pathetic look of hers ceased to wring his heart-strings. His eyes were opened and he was once more the shrewd man of the world he had been. He became acutely conscious that Ruth Barlow had made up her mind to marry him and he swore a solemn oath that nothing would induce him to marry Ruth Barlow. But he was in a quandary. Now that he was in possession of his senses he saw with clearness the sort of woman he had to deal with and he was aware that, if he asked her to release him, she would (in her appealing way) assess her wounded feelings at an immoderately high figure. Besides, it is always awkward for a man to jilt a woman. People are apt to think he has behaved badly.

Roger kept his own counsel. He gave neither by word nor gesture an indication that his feelings towards Ruth Barlow had changed. He remained attentive to all her wishes; he took her to dine at restaurants, they went to the play together, he sent her flowers; he was sympathetic and charming. They had made up their minds that they would be married as soon as they found a house that suited them, for he lived in chambers and she in furnished rooms; and they set about looking at desirable residences. The agents sent Roger orders to view and he took Ruth to see a number of houses. It was very hard to find anything that was quite satisfactory. Roger applied to more agents. They visited house after house. They went over them thoroughly, examining them from the cellars in the basement to the attics under the roof. Sometimes they were too large and sometimes they were too small; sometimes they were too far from the centre of things and sometimes they were too close; sometimes they were too expensive and sometimes they wanted too many repairs; sometimes they were too stuffy and sometimes they were too airy; sometimes they were too dark and sometimes they were too bleak. Roger always found a fault that made the house unsuitable. Of course he was hard to please; he could not bear to ask his dear Ruth to live in any but the perfect house, and the perfect house wanted finding. House-hunting is a tiring and a tiresome business and presently Ruth began to grow peevish. Roger begged her to have patience; somewhere, surely, existed the very house they were looking for, and it only needed a little perseverance and they would find it. They looked at hundreds of houses; they climbed thousands of stairs; they inspected innumerable kitchens. Ruth was exhausted and more than once lost her temper.

'If you don't find a house soon,' she said, 'I shall have to reconsider my position. Why, if you go on like this we shan't be married for years.'

'Don't say that,' he answered, 'I beseech you to have patience. I've just received some entirely new lists from agents I've only just heard of. There must be at least sixty houses on them.'

They set out on the chase again. They looked at more houses and more houses. For two years they looked at houses. Ruth grew silent and scornful: her pathetic, beautiful eyes acquired an expression that was almost sullen. There are limits to human endurance. Mrs Barlow had the patience of an angel, but at last she revolted.

'Do you want to marry me or do you not?' she asked him.

There was an unaccustomed hardness in her voice, but it did not affect the gentleness of his reply.

'Of course I do. We'll be married the very moment we find a house. By the way, I've just heard of something that might suit us.'

'I don't feel well enough to look at any more houses just yet.'

'Poor dear, I was afraid you were looking rather tired.'

Ruth Barlow took to her bed. She would not see Roger and he had to content himself with calling at her lodgings to inquire and sending her flowers. He was as ever assiduous and gallant. Every day he wrote and told her that he had heard of another house for them to look at. A week passed and then he received the following letter:

Roger

    I do not think you really love me. I have found someone who is anxious to take care of me and I am going to be married to him today.

                                                                                    Ruth

He sent back his reply by special messenger:

Ruth

    Your news shatters me. I shall never get over the blow, but of course your happiness must be my first consideration. I send you herewith seven orders to view; they arrived by this morning's post and I am quite sure you will find among them a house that will exactly suit you.

                                                                                    Roger

Mr Know-All

◆

I was prepared to dislike Max Kelada even before I knew him. The war had just finished and the passenger traffic in the ocean-going liners was heavy. Accommodation was very hard to get and you had to put up with whatever the agents chose to offer you. You could not hope for a cabin to yourself and I was thankful to be given one in which there were only two berths. But when I was told the name of my companion my heart sank. It suggested closed port-holes and the night air rigidly excluded. It was bad enough to share a cabin for fourteen days with anyone (I was going from San Francisco to Yokohama), but I should have looked upon it with less dismay if my fellow-passenger's name had been Smith or Brown.

When I went on board I found Mr Kelada's luggage already below. I did not like the look of it; there were too many labels on the suitcases, and the wardrobe trunk was too big. He had unpacked his toilet things, and I observed that he was a patron of the excellent Monsieur Coty; for I saw on the washing-stand his scent, his hair-wash, and his brilliantine. Mr Kelada's brushes, ebony with his monogram in gold, would have been all the better for a scrub. I did not at all like Mr Kelada. I made my way into the smoking-room. I called for a pack of cards and began to play patience. I had scarcely started before a man came up to me and asked me if he was right in thinking my name was so-and-so.

'I am Mr Kelada,' he added, with a smile that showed a row of flashing teeth, and sat down.

'Oh, yes, we're sharing a cabin, I think.'

'Bit of luck, I call it. You never know who you're going to be put in with. I was jolly glad when I heard you were English. I'm all for us English sticking together when we're abroad, if you understand what I mean.'

I blinked.

'Are you English?' I asked, perhaps tactlessly.

'Rather. You don't think I look an American, do you? British to the backbone, that's what I am.'

To prove it, Mr Kelada took out of his pocket a passport and airily waved it under my nose.

King George has many strange subjects. Mr Kelada was short and of a sturdy build, clean-shaven and dark-skinned, with a fleshy, hooked nose and very large, lustrous and liquid eyes. His long black hair was sleek and curly. He spoke with a fluency in which there was nothing English and his gestures were exuberant. I felt pretty sure that a closer inspection of that British passport would have betrayed the fact that Mr Kelada was born under a bluer sky than is generally seen in England.

'What will you have?' he asked me.

I looked at him doubtfully. Prohibition was in force and to all appearances the ship was bone-dry. When I am not thirsty I do not know which I dislike more, ginger-ale or lemon-squash. But Mr Kelada flashed an oriental smile at me.

'Whisky and soda or a dry Martini, you have only to say the word.'

From each of his hip-pockets he fished a flask and laid them on the table before me. I chose the Martini, and calling the steward he ordered a tumbler of ice and a couple of glasses.

'A very good cocktail,' I said.

'Well, there are plenty more where that came from, and if you've got any friends on board, you tell them you've got a pal who's got all the liquor in the world.'

Mr Kelada was chatty. He talked of New York and of San Francisco. He discussed plays, pictures, and politics. He was patriotic. The Union Jack is an impressive piece of drapery, but when it is flourished by a gentleman from Alexandria or Beirut, I cannot but feel that it loses somewhat in dignity. Mr Kelada was familiar. I do not wish to put on airs, but I cannot help feeling that it is seemly in a total stranger to put mister before my name when he addresses me. Mr Kelada, doubtless to set me at my ease, used no such formality. I did not like Mr Kelada. I had put aside the cards when he sat down, but now, thinking that for this first occasion our conversation had lasted long enough, I went on with my game.

'The three on the four,' said Mr Kelada.

There is nothing more exasperating when you are playing patience than to be told where to put the card you have turned up before you have had a chance to look for yourself.

'It's coming out, it's coming out,' he cried. 'The ten on the knave.'

With rage and hatred in my heart I finished. Then he seized the pack.

'Do you like card tricks?'

'No, I hate card tricks,' I answered.

'Well, I'll just show you this one.'

He showed me three. Then I said I would go down to the dining-room and get my seat at table.

'Oh, that's all right,' he said. 'I've already taken a seat for you. I thought that as we were in the same state-room we might just as well sit at the same table.'

I did not like Mr Kelada.

I not only shared a cabin with him and ate three meals a day at the same table, but I could not walk round the deck without his joining me. It was impossible to snub him. It never occurred to him that he was not wanted. He was certain that you were as glad to see him as he was to see you. In your own house you might have kicked him downstairs and slammed the door in his face without the suspicion dawning on him that he was not a welcome visitor. He was a good mixer, and in three days knew everyone on board. He ran everything. He managed the sweeps, conducted the auctions, collected money for prizes at the sports, got up quoit and golf matches, organized the concert, and arranged the fancy-dress ball. He was everywhere and always. He was certainly the best-hated man in the ship. We called him Mr Know-All, even to his face. He took it as a compliment. But it was at meal times that he was most intolerable. For the better part of an hour then he had us at his mercy. He was hearty, jovial, loquacious and argumentative. He knew everything better than anybody else, and it was an affront to his overweening vanity that you should disagree with him. He would not drop a subject, however unimportant, till he had brought you round to his way of thinking. The possibility that he could be mistaken never occurred to him. He was the chap who knew. We sat at the doctor's table. Mr Kelada would certainly have had it all his own way, for the doctor was lazy and I was frigidly indifferent, except for a man called Ramsay who sat there also. He was as dogmatic as Mr Kelada and resented bitterly the Levantine's cocksureness. The discussions they had were acrimonious and interminable.

Ramsay was in the American Consular Service, and was stationed at Kobe. He was a great heavy fellow from the Middle West, with loose fat under a tight skin, and he bulged out of his ready-made clothes. He was on his way back to resume his post, having been on a flying visit to New York to fetch his wife, who had been spending a year at home. Mrs Ramsay was a very pretty little thing, with pleasant manners and a sense of humour. The Consular Service is ill paid, and she was dressed always very simply; but she knew how to wear her clothes. She achieved an effect of quiet distinction. I should not have paid any particular attention to her but that she possessed a quality that may be common enough in women, but nowadays is not obvious in their demeanour. You could not look at her without being struck by her modesty. It shone in her like a flower on a coat.

One evening at dinner the conversation by chance drifted to the subject of pearls. There had been in the papers a good deal of talk about the culture pearls which the cunning Japanese were making, and the doctor remarked that they must inevitably diminish the value of real ones. They were very good already; they would soon be perfect. Mr Kelada, as was his habit, rushed the new topic. He told us all that was to be known about pearls. I do not believe Ramsay knew anything about them at all, but he could not resist the opportunity to have a fling at the Levantine, and in five minutes we were in the middle of a heated argument. I had seen Mr Kelada vehement and voluble before, but never so voluble and vehement as now. At last something that Ramsay said stung him, for he thumped the table and shouted:

'Well, I ought to know what I am talking about. I'm going to Japan just to look into this Japanese pearl business. I'm in the trade and there's not a man in it who won't tell you that what I say about pearls goes. I know all the best pearls in the world, and what I don't know about pearls isn't worth knowing.'

Here was news for us, for Mr Kelada, with all his loquacity, had never told anyone what his business was. We only knew vaguely that he was going to Japan on some commercial errand. He looked round the table triumphantly.

'They'll never be able to get a culture pearl that an expert like me can't tell with half an eye.' He pointed to a chain that Mrs Ramsay wore. 'You take my word for it, Mrs Ramsay, that chain you're wearing will never be worth a cent less than it is now.'

Mrs Ramsay in her modest way flushed a little and slipped the chain inside her dress. Ramsay leaned forward. He gave us all a look and a smile flickered in his eyes.

'That's a pretty chain of Mrs Ramsay's, isn't it?'

'I noticed it at once,' answered Mr Kelada. 'Gee, I said to myself, those are pearls all right.'

'I didn't buy it myself, of course. I'd be interested to know how much you think it cost.'

'Oh, in the trade somewhere round fifteen thousand dollars. But if it was bought on Fifth Avenue I shouldn't be surprised to hear that anything up to thirty thousand was paid for it.'

Ramsay smiled grimly.

'You'll be surprised to hear that Mrs Ramsay bought that string at a department store the day before we left New York, for eighteen dollars.'

Mr Kelada flushed.

'Rot. It's not only real, but it's as fine a string for its size as I've ever seen.'

'Will you bet on it? I'll bet you a hundred dollars it's imitation.'

'Done.'

'Oh, Elmer, you can't bet on a certainty,' said Mrs Ramsay.

She had a little smile on her lips and her tone was gently deprecating.

'Can't I? If I get a chance of easy money like that I should be all sorts of a fool not to take it.'

'But how can it be proved?' she continued. 'It's only my word against Mr Kelada's.'

'Let me look at the chain, and if it's imitation I'll tell you quickly enough. I can afford to lose a hundred dollars,' said Mr Kelada.

'Take it off, dear. Let the gentleman look at it as much as he wants.'

Mrs Ramsay hesitated a moment. She put her hands to the clasp.

'I can't undo it,' she said. 'Mr Kelada will just have to take my word for it.'

I had a sudden suspicion that something unfortunate was about to occur, but I could think of nothing to say.

Ramsay jumped up.

'I'll undo it.'

He handed the chain to Mr Kelada. The Levantine took a magnifying glass from his pocket and closely examined it. A smile of triumph spread over his smooth and swarthy face. He handed back the chain. He was about to speak. Suddenly he caught sight of Mrs Ramsay's face. It was so white that she looked as though she were about to faint. She was staring at him with wide and terrified eyes. They held a desperate appeal; it was so clear that I wondered why her husband did not see it.

Mr Kelada stopped with his mouth open. He flushed deeply. You could almost *see* the effort he was making over himself.

'I was mistaken,' he said. 'It's a very good imitation, but of course as soon as I looked through my glass I saw that it wasn't real. I think eighteen dollars is just about as much as the damned thing's worth.'

He took out his pocket-book and from it a hundred-dollar note. He handed it to Ramsay without a word.

'Perhaps that'll teach you not to be so cocksure another time, my young friend,' said Ramsay as he took the note.

I noticed that Mr Kelada's hands were trembling.

The story spread over the ship as stories do, and he had to put up with a good deal of chaff that evening. It was a fine joke that Mr Know-All had been caught out. But Mrs Ramsay retired to her state-room with a headache.

Next morning I got up and began to shave. Mr Kelada lay on his bed smoking a cigarette. Suddenly there was a small scraping sound and I saw a letter pushed under the door. I opened the door and looked out. There was nobody there. I picked up the letter and saw that it was addressed to Max Kelada. The name was written in block letters. I handed it to him.

'Who's this from?' He opened it. 'Oh!'

He took out of the envelope, not a letter, but a hundred-dollar note. He looked at me and again he reddened. He tore the envelope into little bits and gave them to me.

'Do you mind just throwing them out of the port-hole?'

I did as he asked, and then I looked at him with a smile.

'No one likes being made to look a perfect damned fool,' he said.

'Were the pearls real?'

'If I had a pretty little wife I shouldn't let her spend a year in New York while I stayed at Kobe,' said he.

At that moment I did not entirely dislike Mr Kelada. He reached out for his pocket-book and carefully put in it the hundred-dollar note.

The Romantic Young Lady

One of the many inconveniences of real life is that it seldom gives you a complete story. Some incident has excited your interest, the people who are concerned in it are in the devil's own muddle, and you wonder what on earth will happen next. Well, generally nothing happens. The inevitable catastrophe you foresaw wasn't inevitable after all, and high tragedy, without any regard to artistic decency, dwindles into drawing-room comedy. Now, growing old has many disadvantages, but it has this compensation (among, let us admit, not a few others), that sometimes it gives you the opportunity of seeing what was the outcome of certain events you had witnessed long ago. You had given up the hope of ever knowing what was the end of the story, and then, when you least expected it, it is handed to you on a platter.

These reflections occurred to me when, having escorted the Marquesa de San Esteban to her car, I went back into the hotel and sat down again in the lounge. I ordered a cocktail, lit a cigarette, and composed myself to order my recollections. The hotel was new and splendid, it was like every other first-class hotel in Europe, and I had been regretting that for the sake of its modern plumbing I had deserted the old-fashioned, picturesque Hotel de Madrid to which I generally went when I stayed in Seville. It was true that from my hotel I had a view of the noble river, the Guadalquivir, but that did not make up for the *thés dansants* that filled the bar-lounge two or three days a week with a fashionable crowd whose exuberant conversation almost drowned the strident din of a jazz orchestra.

I had been out all the afternoon, and coming in found myself in the midst of a seething mob. I went to the desk and asked for my key so that I might go straight up to my room. But the porter, handing it to me, said that a lady had been asking for me.

'For me?'

'She wants to see you very much. It's the Marquesa de San Esteban.'

I knew no one of that name.

'It must be some mistake.'

As I said the words, looking rather vaguely around, a lady came up to me with outstretched hands and a bright smile on her lips. To the best of my knowledge I had never seen her before in my life. She seized my hands, both of them, and shook them warmly. She spoke in fluent French.

'How very nice to see you again after all these years. I saw by the paper that you were staying here and I said to myself: I must look him up. How many years is it since we danced together? I daren't think. Do you still dance? I do. And I'm a grandmother. I'm fat of course, I don't care, and it keeps me from getting fatter.'

She talked with such a rush that it took my breath away to listen to her. She was a stout, more than middle-aged woman, very much made up, with dark red hair, obviously dyed, cut short; and she was dressed in the height of Parisian fashion, which never suits Spanish women very well. But she had a gay, fruity laugh that made you feel you wanted to laugh too. It was quite obvious that she thoroughly enjoyed life. She was a fine figure of a woman and I could well believe that in youth she had been beautiful. But I could not place her.

'Come and drink a glass of champagne with me and we will talk of old times. Or will you have a cocktail? Our dear old Seville had changed, you see. *Thés dansants* and cocktails. It's just like Paris and London now. We've caught up. We're a civilized people.'

She led me to a table near the space where they were dancing and we sat down. I could not go on pretending I was at ease; I thought I should only get into a fearful mess.

'It's terribly stupid of me, I'm afraid,' I said, 'but I don't seem able to remember ever having known anyone of your name in the old days in Seville.'

'San Esteban?' she interrupted before I could go on. 'Naturally. My husband came from Salamanca. He was in the diplomatic service. I'm a widow. You knew me as Pilar Carreon. Of course having my hair red changes me a little, but otherwise I don't think I've altered much.'

'Not at all,' I said quickly. 'It was only the name that bothered me.'

Of course now I remembered her, but I was concerned at the moment only with the effort to conceal from her the mingled consternation and amusement that filled me as I realized that the Pilar Carreon I had danced with at the Countess de Marbella's parties and at the Fair had turned into this stout, flaunting dowager. I could not get over it. But I had to watch my step. I wondered if she knew how well I recollected the story that had shaken Seville to its foundations, and I was glad when after she had finally bidden me an effusive farewell I was able to recall it at ease.

In those days, forty years ago, Seville had not become a prosperous commercial city. It had quiet, white streets, paved with cobbles, with a multitude of churches on the belfries of which storks built their nests. Bull-fighters, students, and loungers sauntered in the Sierpes all day long. Life was easy. This of course, was before the time of motor-cars, and the Sevillan would live in penury, practising every possible economy, in order to have a carriage. For this luxury he was willing to sacrifice the necessities of life. Everyone who had any claim to gentility drove up and down the Delicias, the park-like gardens by the Guadalquivir, every blessed afternoon from five till seven. You saw carriages of all sorts, from fashionable London victorias to old broken-down shays that seemed as though they would fall to pieces, magnificent horses and wretched hacks whose tragic end in the bull-ring was near at hand. But there was one equipage that could not fail to attract the stranger's attention. It was a victoria, very smart and new, drawn by two beautiful mules; and the coachman and the footman wore the national costume of Andalusia in pale grey. It was the most splendid turn-out Seville had ever known, and it belonged to the Countess de Marbella. She was a Frenchwoman married to a Spaniard, who had enthusiastically adopted the manners and customs of her husband's country, but with a Parisian elegance that gave them a peculiar distinction. The rest of the carriages went at a snail's pace so that their occupants could see and be seen, but the countess, behind her mules, dashed up between the two crawling lines at a fast trot, went to the end of the Delicias and back twice and then drove away. The proceeding savoured somewhat of royalty. When you looked at her gracefully seated in that swift victoria, her head handsomely poised, her hair of too brilliant a gold to be natural, you did not wonder that her French vivacity and determination had given her the position she held. She made the fashion. Her decrees were law. But the countess had too many adorers not to have as many enemies, and the most determined of these was the widowed Duchess de Dos Palos, whose birth and social consequence made her claim as a right the first place in Society which the Frenchwoman had won by grace, wit and character.

Now the duchess had an only daughter. This was Doña Pilar. She was twenty when I first knew her and she was very beautiful. She had magnificent eyes and a skin that, however hard you tried to find a less hackneyed way to describe it, you could only call peach-like. She was very slim, rather tall for a Spanish girl, with a red mouth and dazzlingly white teeth. She wore her abundant, shining black hair dressed very elaborately in the Spanish style of the period. She was infinitely alluring. The fire in her black eyes, the warmth of her smile, the seductiveness of her movements suggested so much passion that it really wasn't quite fair. She belonged to the generation which was straining to break the old conventions that had kept the Spanish girl of good family hidden away till it was time for her to be married. I often played tennis with her and I used to dance with her at the Countess de Marbella's parties. The duchess considered the Frenchwoman's parties, with champagne and a sit-down supper, ostentatious, and when she opened her own great house to Society, which was only twice a year, it was to give them lemonade and biscuits. But she bred fighting-bulls, as her husband had done, and on the occasions when the young bulls were tried out, she gave picnic luncheons to which her friends were asked, very gay and informal, but with a sort of feudal state which fascinated my romantic imagination. Once, when the duchess's bulls were to fight at a *corrida* in Seville, I rode in with them at night as one of the men escorting Doña Pilar dressed in a costume that reminded one of a picture by Goya, who headed the cavalcade. It was a charming experience to ride through the night, on those prancing Andalusian horses, with the six bulls, surrounded by oxen thundering along behind.

A good many men, rich or noble and sometimes both, had asked Doña Pilar's hand in marriage, but, notwithstanding her mother's remonstrances, she had refused them. The duchess had been married at fifteen and it seemed to her really indecent that her daughter at twenty should be still single. The duchess asked her what she was waiting for; it was absurd to be too difficult. It was her duty to marry. But Pilar was stubborn. She found reasons to reject every one of her suitors.

Then the truth came out.

During the daily drives in the Delicias which the duchess, accompanied by her daughter, took in a great old-fashioned landau, they passed the countess as she was twice swiftly driven up and down the promenade. The ladies were on such bad terms that they pretended not to see one another, but Pilar could not keep her eyes off that smart carriage and the two beautiful grey mules and, not wishing to catch the countess's somewhat ironic glance, her own fell on the coachman who drove her. He was the handsomest man in Seville and in his beautiful uniform he was a sight to see. Of course no one knew exactly what happened, but apparently the more Pilar looked at the coachman the more she liked the look of him, and somehow or other, for all this part of the story remained a mystery, the pair met. In Spain the classes are strangely mingled and the butler may have in his veins much nobler blood than the master. Pilar learnt, not I think without satisfaction, that the coachman belonged to the ancient family of León, than which there is none in Andalusia more distinguished; and really so far as birth went there was little to choose between them. Only her life had been passed in a ducal mansion, while fate had forced him to earn his living on the box of a victoria. Neither could regret this, since only in that exalted place could he have attracted the attention of the most difficult young woman in Seville. They fell madly in love with one another. It so happened that just then a young man called the Marqués de San Esteban, whom they had met at San Sebastian the summer before, wrote to the duchess and asked for Pilar's hand in marriage. He was extremely eligible and the two families had formed alliances from time to time ever since the reign of Philip II. The duchess was determined not to stand any more nonsense, and when she told Pilar of the proposal added that she had shilly-shallied long enough. She must either marry him or she should go into a convent.

'I'm not going to do either the one or the other,' said Pilar.

'What are you going to do then? I have given you a home long enough.'

'I'm going to marry José León.'

'Who is he?'

Pilar hesitated for a moment and it may be, it is indeed to be hoped, that she blushed a little.

'He's the countess's coachman.'

'What countess?'

'The Countess de Marbella.'

I remembered the duchess well and I am sure that when roused she stuck at little. She raged, she implored, she cried, she argued. There was a terrific scene. People said that she slapped her daughter and pulled her hair, but I have an impression that Pilar in such a pass was capable of hitting back. She repeated that she loved José León and he loved her. She was determined to marry him. The duchess called a family council. The matter was put before them and it was decided that to save them all from disgrace Pilar should be taken away to the country and kept there till she had recovered from her infatuation. Pilar got wind of the scheme and put a stop to it by slipping out of the window of her room one night when everyone was asleep and going to live with her lover's parents. They were respectable persons who inhabited a small apartment on the unfashionable side of the Guadalquivir, in the quarter called Triana.

After that no concealment was possible. The fat was in the fire and the clubs along the Sierpes buzzed with the scandal. Waiters were kept busy bringing trays of little glasses of Manzanilla to the members from the neighbouring wine-shops. They gossiped and laughed over the scandal, and Pilar's rejected suitors were the recipients of many congratulations. What an escape! The duchess was in despair. She could think of nothing better to do than go to the Archbishop, her trusted friend and former confessor, and beg him himself to reason with the infatuated girl. Pilar was summoned to the episcopal palace, and the good old man, used to intervening in family quarrels, did his utmost to show her the folly of her course. But she would not be persuaded. Nothing that anyone could say would induce her to forsake the man she loved. The duchess, waiting in an adjoining room, was sent for and made a final appeal to her daughter. In vain. Pilar returned to her humble lodging and the duchess in tears was left alone with the Archbishop. The Archbishop was no less astute than he was pious, and when he saw that the distracted woman was in a fit state to listen to him, advised her as a last resource to go to the Countess de Marbella. She was the cleverest woman in Seville and it might be that she could do something.

At first the duchess indignantly refused. She would never suffer the humiliation of appealing to her greatest enemy. Sooner might the ancient house of Dos Palos fall in ruin. The Archbishop was accustomed to dealing with tiresome women. He set himself with gentle cunning to induce her to change her mind and presently she consented to throw herself on the Frenchwoman's mercy. With rage in her heart she sent a message asking if she might see her, and that afternoon was ushered into her drawing-room. The countess of course had been one of the first to hear the story, but she listened to the unhappy mother as though she had not known a thing about it. She relished the situation enormously. It was the crowning triumph to have the vindictive duchess on her knees before her. But she was at heart a good-natured woman and she had a sense of humour.

'It's a most unfortunate situation,' she said. 'And I'm sorry that one of my servants should be the occasion of it. But I don't exactly see what I can do.'

The duchess would have liked to slap her painted face and her voice trembled a little with the effort she made to control her anger.

'It is not for my own sake I'm asking you to help. It's for Pilar's. I know, we all know, that you are the cleverest woman in the city. It seemed to me, it seemed to the Archbishop, that if there was a way out, your quick wit would find it.'

The countess knew she was being grossly flattered. She did not mind. She liked it.

'You must let me think.'

'Of course, if he'd been a gentleman I could have sent for my son and he would have killed him, but the Duke of Dos Palos cannot fight a duel with the Countess de Marbella's coachman.'

'Perhaps not.'

'In the old days it would have been so simple. I should merely have hired a couple of ruffians and had the brute's throat cut one night in the street. But with all these laws they have nowadays decent people have no way of protecting themselves from insult.'

'I should deplore any method of settling the difficulty that deprived me of the services of an excellent coachman,' murmured the countess.

'But if he married my daughter he cannot continue to be your coachman,' cried the duchess indignantly.

'Are you going to give Pilar an income for them to live on?'

'Me? Not a peseta. I told Pilar at once that she should get nothing from me. They can starve for all I care.'

'Well, I should think rather than do that he will prefer to stay on as my coachman. There are very nice rooms over my stables.'

The duchess went pale. The duchess went red.

'Forget all that has passed between us. Let us be friends. You can't expose me to such a humiliation. If I've ever done things to affront you I ask you on my knees to forgive me.'

The duchess cried.

'Dry your eyes, Duchess,' the Frenchwoman said at last. 'I will do what I can.'

'Is there anything you can do?'

'Perhaps. Is it true that Pilar has and will have no money of her own?'

'Not a penny if she marries without my consent.'

The countess gave her one of her brightest smiles.

'There is a common impression that southern people are romantic and northern people matter-of-fact. The reverse is true. It is the northerners who are incurably romantic. I have lived long enough among you Spaniards to know that you are nothing if not practical.'

The duchess was too broken to resent openly these unpleasant remarks, but, oh, how she hated the woman! The Countess de Marbella rose to her feet.

'You shall hear from me in the course of the day.'

She firmly dismissed her visitor.

The carriage was ordered for five o'clock and at ten minutes to, the countess, dressed for her drive, sent for José. When he came into the drawing-room, wearing his pale grey livery with such an air, she could not deny that he was very good to look upon. If he had not been her own coachman–well, it was not the moment for ideas of that sort. He stood before her, holding himself easily, but with a gallant swagger. There was nothing servile in his bearing.

'A Greek god,' the countess murmured to herself. 'It is only Andalusia that can produce such types.' And then aloud: 'I hear that you are going to marry the daughter of the Duchess of Dos Palos.'

'If the countess does not object.'

She shrugged her shoulders.

'Whoever you marry is a matter of complete indifference to me. You know of course that Doña Pilar will have no fortune.'

'Yes, madam. I have a good place and I can keep my wife. I love her.'

'I can't blame you for that. She is a beautiful girl. But I think it only right to tell you that I have a rooted objection to married coachmen. On your wedding-day you leave my service. That is all I had to say to you. You can go.'

She began to look at the daily paper that had just arrived from Paris, but José, as she expected, did not stir. He stared down at the floor. Presently the countess looked up.

'What are you waiting for?'

'I never knew madam would send me away,' he answered in a troubled tone.

'I have no doubt you'll find another place.'

'Yes, but . . .'

'Well, what is it?' she asked sharply.

He sighed miserably.

'There's not a pair of mules in the whole of Spain to come up to ours. They're almost human beings. They understand every word I say to them.'

The countess gave him a smile that would have turned the head of anyone who was not madly in love already.

'I'm afraid you must choose between me and your betrothed.'

He shifted from one foot to the other. He put his hand to his pocket to get himself a cigarette, but then, remembering where he was, restrained the gesture. He glanced at the countess and that peculiar shrewd smile came over his face which those who have lived in Andalusia know so well.

'In that case, I can't hesitate. Pilar must see that this alters my position entirely. One can get a wife any day of the week, but a place like this is found only once in a lifetime. I should be a fool to throw it up for a woman.'

That was the end of the adventure. José León continued to drive the Countess de Marbella, but she noticed when they sped up and down the Delicias that henceforward as many eyes were turned on her handsome coachman as on her latest hat: and a year later Pilar married the Marqués de San Esteban.

A
Man
From Glasgow

◆

It is not often that anyone entering a great city for the first time has the luck to witness such an incident as engaged Shelley's attention when he drove into Naples. A youth ran out of a shop pursued by a man armed with a knife. The man overtook him and with one blow in the neck laid him dead on the road. Shelley had a tender heart. He didn't look upon it as a bit of local colour; he was seized with horror and indignation. But when he expressed his emotions to a Calabrian priest who was travelling with him, a fellow of gigantic strength and stature, the priest laughed heartily and attempted to quiz him. Shelley says he never felt such an inclination to beat anyone.

I have never seen anything so exciting as that, but the first time I went to Algeciras I had an experience that seemed to me far from ordinary. Algeciras was then an untidy, neglected town. I arrived somewhat late at night and went to an inn on the quay. It was rather shabby, but it had a fine view of Gibraltar, solid and matter-of-fact, across the bay. The moon was full. The office was on the first floor, and a slatternly maid, when I asked for a room, took me upstairs. The landlord was playing cards. He seemed little pleased to see me. He looked me up and down, curtly gave me a number, and then, taking no further notice of me, went on with his game.

When the maid had shown me to my room I asked her what I could have to eat.

'What you like,' she answered.

I knew well enough the unreality of the seeming profusion.

'What have you got in the house?'

'You can have eggs and ham.'

The look of the hotel had led me to guess that I should get little else. The maid led me to a narrow room with white-washed walls and a low ceiling in which was a long table laid already for the next day's luncheon. With his back to the door sat a tall man, huddled over a *brasero*, the round brass dish of hot ashes which is erroneously supposed to give sufficient warmth for the temperate winter of Andalusia. I sat down at table and waited for my scanty meal. I gave the stranger an idle glance. He was looking at me, but meeting my eyes he quickly turned away. I waited for my eggs. When at last the maid brought them he looked up again.

'I want you to wake me in time for the first boat,' he said.

'*Si, señor.*'

His accent told me that English was his native tongue, and the breadth of his build, his strongly marked features, led me to suppose him a northerner. The hardy Scot is far more often found in Spain than the Englishman. Whether you go to the rich mines of Rio Tinto, or to the *bodegas* of Jerez, to Seville or to Cadiz, it is the leisurely speech of beyond the Tweed that you hear. You will meet Scotsmen in the olive groves of Carmona, on the railway between Algeciras and Bobadilla, and even in the remote cork woods of Merida.

I finished eating and went over to the dish of burning ashes. It was midwinter and the windy passage across the bay had chilled my blood. The man pushed his chair away as I drew mine forwards.

'Don't move,' I said. 'There's heaps of room for two.'

I lit a cigar and offered one to him. In Spain the Havana from Gib is never unwelcome.

'I don't mind if I do,' he said, stretching out his hand.

I recognized the singing speech of Glasgow. But the stranger was not talkative, and my efforts at conversation broke down before his monosyllables. We smoked in silence. He was even bigger than I had thought, with great broad shoulders and ungainly limbs; his face was sunburned, his hair short and grizzled. His features were hard; mouth, ears and nose were large and heavy and his skin much wrinkled. His blue eyes were pale. He was constantly pulling his ragged, grey moustache. It was a nervous gesture that I found faintly irritating. Presently I felt that he was looking at me, and the intensity of his stare grew so irksome that I glanced up expecting him, as before, to drop his eyes. He did, indeed, for a moment, but then raised them again. He inspected me from under his long, bushy eyebrows.

'Just come from Gib?' he asked suddenly.

'Yes.'

'I'm going tomorrow–on my way home. Thank God.'

He said the last two words so fiercely that I smiled.

'Don't you like Spain?'

'Oh, Spain's all right.'

'Have you been here long?'

'Too long. Too long.'

He spoke with a kind of gasp. I was surprised at the emotion my casual inquiry seemed to excite in him. He sprang to his feet and walked backwards and forwards. He stamped to and fro like a caged beast pushing aside a chair that stood in his way, and now and again repeated the words in a groan. 'Too long. Too long.' I sat still. I was embarrassed. To give myself countenance I stirred the *brasero* to bring the hotter ashes to the top, and he stood suddenly still, towering over me, as though my movement had brought back my existence to his notice. Then he sat down heavily in his chair.

'D'you think I'm queer?' he asked.

'Not more than most people,' I smiled.

'You don't see anything strange in me?'

He leant forward as he spoke so that I might see him well.

'No.'

'You'd say so if you did, wouldn't you?'

'I would.'

I couldn't quite understand what all this meant. I wondered if he was drunk. For two or three minutes he didn't say anything and I had no wish to interrupt the silence.

'What's your name?' he asked suddenly. I told him.

'Mine's Robert Morrison.'

'Scotch?'

'Glasgow. I've been in this blasted country for years. Got any baccy?'

I gave him my pouch and he filled his pipe. He lit it from a piece of burning charcoal.

'I can't stay any longer. I've stayed too long. Too long.'

He had an impulse to jump up again and walk up and down, but he resisted it, clinging to his chair. I saw on his face the effort he was making. I judged that his restlessness was due to chronic alcoholism. I find drunks very boring, and I made up my mind to take an early opportunity of slipping off to bed.

'I've been managing some olive groves,' he went on. 'I'm here working for the Glasgow and South of Spain Olive Oil Company Limited.'

'Oh, yes.'

'We've got a new process for refining oil, you know. Properly treated, Spanish oil is every bit as good as Lucca. And we can sell it cheaper.'

He spoke in a dry, matter-of-fact, business-like way. He chose his words with Scotch precision. He seemed perfectly sober.

'You know, Ecija is more or less the centre of the olive trade, and we had a Spaniard there to look after the business. But I found he was robbing us right and left, so I had to turn him out. I used to live in Seville; it was more convenient for shipping the oil. However, I found I couldn't get a trustworthy man to be at Ecija, so last year I went there myself. D'you know it?'

'No.'

'The firm has got a big estate two miles from the town, just outside the village of San Lorenzo, and it's got a fine house on it. It's on the crest of a hill, rather pretty to look at, all white, you know, and straggling, with a couple of storks perched on the roof. No one lived there, and I thought it would save the rent of a place in town if I did.'

'It must have been a bit lonely,' I remarked.

'It was.'

Robert Morrison smoked on for a minute or two in silence. I wondered whether there was any point in what he was telling me.

I looked at my watch.

'In a hurry?' he asked sharply.

'Not particularly. It's getting late.'

'Well, what of it?'

'I suppose you didn't see many people?' I said, going back.

'Not many. I lived there with an old man and his wife who looked after me, and sometimes I used to go down to the village and play *tresillo* with Fernández, the chemist, and one or two men who met at his shop. I used to shoot a bit and ride.'

'It doesn't sound such a bad life to me.'

'I'd been there two years last spring. By God, I've never known such heat as we had in May. No one could do a thing. The labourers just lay about in the shade and slept. Sheep died and some of the animals went mad. Even the oxen couldn't work. They stood around with their backs all humped up and gasped for breath. That blasted sun beat down and the glare was so awful, you felt your eyes would shoot out of your head. The earth cracked and crumbled, and the crops frizzled. The olives went to rack and ruin. It was simply hell. One couldn't get a wink of sleep. I went from room to room, trying to get a breath of air. Of course I kept the windows shut and had the floors watered, but that didn't do any good. The nights were just as hot as the days. It was like living in an oven.

'At last I thought I'd have a bed made up for me downstairs on the north side of the house in a room that was never used because in ordinary weather it was damp. I had an idea that I might get a few hours' sleep there at all events. Anyhow it was worth trying. But it was no damned good; it was a washout. I turned and tossed and my bed was so hot that I couldn't stand it. I got up and opened the doors that led to the veranda and walked out. It was a glorious night. The moon was so bright that I swear you could read a book by it. Did I tell you the house was on the crest of a hill? I leant against the parapet and looked at the olive-trees. It was like the sea. I suppose that's what made me think of home. I thought of the cool breeze in the fir-trees and the racket of the streets in Glasgow. Believe it or not, I could smell them, and I could smell the sea. By God, I'd have given every bob I had in the world for an hour of that air. They say it's a foul climate in Glasgow. Don't you believe it. I like the rain and the grey sky and that yellow sea and the waves. I forgot that I was in Spain, in the middle of the olive country, and I opened my mouth and took a long breath as though I were breathing in the sea-fog.

'And then all of a sudden I heard a sound. It was a man's voice. Not loud, you know, low. It seemed to creep through the silence like – well, I don't know what it was like. It surprised me. I couldn't think who could be down there in the olives at that hour. It was past midnight. It was a chap laughing. A funny sort of laugh. I suppose you'd call it a chuckle. It seemed to crawl up the hill–disjointedly.'

Morrison looked at me to see how I took the odd word he used to express a sensation that he didn't know how to describe.

'I mean, it seemed to shoot up in little jerks, something like shooting stones out of a pail. I leant forward and stared. With the full moon it was almost as light as day, but I'm dashed if I could see a thing. The sound stopped, but I kept on looking at where it had come from in case somebody moved. And in a minute it started off again, but louder. You couldn't have called it a chuckle any more, it was a real belly laugh. It just rang through the night. I wondered it didn't wake my servants. It sounded like someone who was roaring drunk.

'"Who's there?" I shouted.

'The only answer I got was a roar of laughter. I don't mind telling you I was getting a bit annoyed. I had half a mind to go down and see what it was all about. I wasn't going to let some drunken swine kick up a row like that on my place in the middle of the night. And then suddenly there was a yell. By God, I was startled. Then cries. The man had laughed with a deep bass voice, but his cries were–shrill, like a pig having his throat cut.

'"My God," I cried.

'I jumped over the parapet and ran down towards the sound. I thought somebody was being killed. There was silence and then one piercing shriek. After that sobbing and moaning. I'll tell you what it sounded like, it sounded like someone at the point of death. There was a long groan and then nothing. Silence. I ran from place to place. I couldn't find anyone. At last I climbed the hill again and went back to my room.

'You can imagine how much sleep I got that night. As soon as it was light, I looked out of the window in the direction from which the row had come and I was surprised to see a little white house in a sort of dale among the olives. The ground on that side didn't belong to us and I'd never been through it. I hardly ever went to that part of the house and so I'd never seen the house before. I asked José who lived there. He told me that a madman had inhabited it, with his brother and a servant.'

'Oh, was that the explanation?' I said. 'Not a very nice neighbour.'

The Scot bent over quickly and seized my wrist. He thrust his face into mine and his eyes were starting out of his head with terror.

'The madman had been dead for twenty years,' he whispered.

He let go my wrist and leant back in his chair panting.

'I went down to the house and walked all round it. The windows were barred and shuttered and the door was locked. I knocked. I shook the handle and rang the bell. I heard it tinkle, but no one came. It was a two-storey house and I looked up. The shutters were tight closed, and there wasn't a sign of life anywhere.'

'Well, what sort of condition was the house in?' I asked.

'Oh, rotten. The whitewash had worn off the walls and there was practically no paint left on the door or the shutters. Some of the tiles off the roof were lying on the ground. They looked as though they'd been blown away in a gale.'

'Queer,' I said.

'I went to my friend Fernández, the chemist, and he told me the same story as José. I asked about the madman and Fernández said that no one ever saw him. He was more or less comatose ordinarily, but now and then he had an attack of acute mania and then he could be heard from ever so far laughing his head off and then crying. It used to scare people. He died in one of his attacks and his keepers cleared out at once. No one had ever dared to live in the house since.

'I didn't tell Fernández what I'd heard. I thought he'd only laugh at me. I stayed up that night and kept watch. But nothing happened. There wasn't a sound. I waited about till dawn and then I went to bed.'

'And you never heard anything more?'

'Not for a month. The drought continued and I went on sleeping in the lumber-room at the back. One night I was fast asleep, when something seemed to happen to me; I don't exactly know how to describe it, it was a funny feeling as though someone had given me a little nudge, to warn me, and suddenly I was wide awake. I lay there in my bed and then in the same way as before I heard a long, low gurgle, like a man enjoying an old joke. It came from away down in the valley and it got louder. It was a great bellow of laughter. I jumped out of bed and went to the window. My legs began to tremble. It was horrible to stand there and listen to the shouts of laughter that rang through the night. Then there was the pause, and after that a shriek of pain and that ghastly sobbing. It didn't sound human. I mean, you might have thought it was an animal being tortured. I don't mind telling you I was scared stiff. I couldn't have moved if I'd wanted to. After a time the sounds stopped, not suddenly, but dying away little by little. I strained my ears, but I couldn't hear a thing. I crept back to bed and hid my face.

'I remembered then that Fernández had told me that the madman's attacks only came at intervals. The rest of the time he was quite quiet. Apathetic, Fernández said. I wondered if the fits of mania came regularly. I reckoned out how long it had been between the two attacks I'd heard. Twenty-eight days. It didn't take me long to put two and two together; it was quite obvious that it was the full moon that set him off. I'm not a nervous man really and I made up my mind to get to the bottom of it, so I looked out in the calendar which day the moon would be full next and that night I didn't go to bed. I cleaned my revolver and loaded it. I prepared a lantern and sat down on the parapet of my house to wait. I felt perfectly cool. To tell you the truth, I was rather pleased with myself because I didn't feel scared. There was a bit of a wind, and it whistled about the roof. It rustled over the leaves of the olive trees like waves swishing on the pebbles of the beach. The moon shone on the white walls of the house in the hollow. I felt particularly cheery.

'At last I heard a little sound, the sound I knew, and I almost laughed. I was right; it was the full moon and the attacks came as regular as clockwork. That was all to the good. I threw myself over the wall into the olive grove and ran straight to the house. The chuckling grew louder as I came near. I got to the house and looked up. There was no light anywhere. I put my ears to the door and listened. I heard the madman simply laughing his bloody head off. I beat on the door with my fist and I pulled the bell. The sound of it seemed to amuse him. He roared with laughter. I knocked again, louder and louder, and the more I knocked the more he laughed. Then I shouted at the top of my voice.

'"Open the blasted door, or I'll break it down."

'I stepped back and kicked the latch with all my might. I flung myself at the door with the whole weight of my body. It cracked. Then I put all my strength into it and the damned thing smashed open.

'I took the revolver out of my pocket and held my lantern in the other hand. The laughter sounded louder now that the door was opened. I stepped in. The stink nearly knocked me down. I mean, just think, the windows hadn't been opened for twenty years. The row was enough to raise the dead, but for a moment I didn't know where it was coming from. The walls seemed to throw the sound backwards and forwards. I pushed open a door by my side and went into a room. It was bare and white and there wasn't a stick of furniture in it. The sound was louder and I followed it. I went into another room, but there was nothing there. I opened a door and found myself at the foot of a staircase. The madman was laughing just over my head. I walked up, cautiously, you know, I wasn't taking any risks, and at the top of the stairs there was a passage. I walked along it, throwing my light ahead of me, and I came to a room at the end. I stopped. He was in there. I was only separated from the sound by a thin door.

'It was awful to hear it. A shiver passed through me and I cursed myself because I began to tremble. It wasn't like a human being at all. By Jove, I very nearly took to my heels and ran. I had to clench my teeth to force myself to stay. But I simply couldn't bring myself to turn the handle. And then the laughter was cut, cut with a knife you'd have said, and I heard a hiss of pain. I hadn't heard that before, it was too low to carry to my place, and then a gasp.

'"Ay!" I heard the man speak in Spanish. "You're killing me. Take it away. O God, help me!"

'He screamed. The brutes were torturing him. I flung open the door and burst in. The draught blew a shutter back and the moon streamed in so bright that it dimmed my lantern. In my ears, as clearly as I hear you speak and as close, I heard the wretched chap's groans. It was awful, moaning and sobbing, and frightful gasps. No one could survive that. He was at the point of death. I tell you I heard his broken, choking cries right in my ears. And the room was empty.'

Robert Morrison sank back in his chair. That huge solid man had strangely the look of a lay figure in a studio. You felt that if you pushed him he would fall over in a heap on to the floor.

'And then?' I asked.

He took a rather dirty handkerchief out of his pocket and wiped his forehead.

'I felt I didn't much want to sleep in that room on the north side, so, heat or no heat, I moved back to my own quarters. Well, exactly four weeks later, about two in the morning, I was waked up by the madman's chuckle. It was almost at my elbow. I don't mind telling you that my nerve was a bit shaken by then, so next time the blighter was due to have an attack, next time the moon was full, I mean, I got Fernández to come and spend the night with me. I didn't tell him anything. I kept him up playing cards till two in the morning, and then I heard it again. I asked him if he heard anything. "Nothing," he said. "There's somebody laughing," I said. "You're drunk, man," he said, and he began laughing too. That was too much. "Shut up, you fool," I said. The laughter grew louder and louder. I cried out. I tried to shut it out by putting my hands to my ears, but it wasn't a damned bit of good. I heard it and I heard the scream of pain. Fernández thought I was mad. He didn't dare say so, because he knew I'd have killed him. He said he'd go to bed, and in the morning I found he'd slunk away. His bed hadn't been slept in. He'd taken himself off when he left me.

'After that I couldn't stop in Ecija. I put a factor there and went back to Seville. I felt myself pretty safe there, but as the time came near I began to get scared. Of course I told myself not to be a damned fool, but, you know, I damned well couldn't help myself. The fact is, I was afraid the sounds had followed me, and I knew if I heard them in Seville I'd go on hearing them all my life. I've got as much courage as any man, but damn it all, there are limits to everything. Flesh and blood couldn't stand it. I knew I'd go stark staring mad. I got in such a state that I began drinking, the suspense was so awful, and I used to lie awake counting the days. And at last I knew it'd come. And it came. I heard those sounds in Seville–sixty miles away from Ecija.'

I didn't know what to say. I was silent for a while.

'When did you hear the sounds last?' I asked.

'Four weeks ago.'

I looked up quickly. I was startled.

'What d'you mean by that? It's not full moon tonight?'

He gave me a dark, angry look. He opened his mouth to speak and then stopped as though he couldn't. You would have said his vocal cords were paralysed, and it was with a strange croak that at last he answered.

'Yes, it is.'

He stared at me and his pale blue eyes seemed to shine red. I have never seen in a man's face a look of such terror. He got up quickly and stalked out of the room, slamming the door behind him.

I must admit that I didn't sleep any too well that night myself.

Before the Party

◆

Mrs Skinner liked to be in good time. She was already dressed, in black silk as befitted her age and the mourning she wore for her son-in-law, and now she put on her toque. She was a little uncertain about it, since the egrets' feathers which adorned it might very well arouse in some of the friends she would certainly meet at the party acid expostulations; and of course it was shocking to kill those beautiful white birds, in the mating season too, for the sake of their feathers; but there they were, so pretty and stylish, and it would have been silly to refuse them, and it would have hurt her son-in-law's feelings. He had brought them all the way from Borneo and he expected her to be so pleased with them. Kathleen had made herself rather unpleasant about them, she must wish she hadn't now, after what had happened, but Kathleen had never really liked Harold. Mrs Skinner, standing at her dressing-table, placed the toque on her head, it was after all the only nice hat she had, and put in a pin with a large jet knob. If anybody spoke to her about the ospreys she had her answer.

'I know it's dreadful,' she would say, 'and I wouldn't dream of buying them, but my poor son-in-law brought them back the last time he was home on leave.'

That would explain her possession of them and excuse their use. Everyone had been very kind. Mrs Skinner took a clean handkerchief from a drawer and sprinkled a little eau de Cologne on it. She never used scent, and she had always thought it rather fast, but eau de Cologne was so refreshing. She was very nearly ready now, and her eyes wandered out of the window behind her looking-glass. Canon Heywood had a beautiful day for his garden-party. It was warm and the sky was blue; the trees had not yet lost the fresh green of the spring. She smiled as she saw her little granddaughter in the strip of garden behind the house busily raking her very own flower-bed. Mrs Skinner wished Joan were not quite so pale, it was a mistake to have kept her so long in the tropics; and she was so grave for her age, you never saw her run about; she played quiet games of her own invention and watered her garden. Mrs Skinner gave the front of her dress a little pat, took up her gloves, and went downstairs.

Kathleen was at the writing-table in the window busy with lists she was making, for she was honorary secretary of the Ladies' Golf Club, and when there were competitions had a good deal to do. But she too was ready for the party.

'I see you've put on your jumper after all,' said Mrs Skinner.

They had discussed at luncheon whether Kathleen should wear her jumper or her black chiffon. The jumper was black and white, and Kathleen thought it rather smart, but it was hardly mourning. Millicent, however, was in favour of it.

'There's no reason why we should all look as if we'd just come from a funeral,' she said. 'Harold's been dead eight months.'

To Mrs Skinner it seemed rather unfeeling to talk like that. Millicent was strange since her return from Borneo.

'You're not going to leave off your weeds yet, darling?' she asked.

Millicent did not give a direct answer.

'People don't wear mourning in the way they used,' she said. She paused a little and when she went on there was a tone in her voice which Mrs Skinner thought quite peculiar. It was plain that Kathleen noticed it too, for she gave her sister a curious look. 'I'm sure Harold wouldn't wish me to wear mourning for him indefinitely.'

'I dressed early because I wanted to say something to Millicent,' said Kathleen in reply to her mother's observation.

'Oh?'

Kathleen did not explain. But she put her lists aside and with knitted brows read for the second time a letter from a lady who complained that the committee had most unfairly marked down her handicap from twenty-four to eighteen. It requires a good deal of tact to be honorary secretary to a ladies' golf club. Mrs Skinner began to put on her new gloves. The sun-blinds kept the room cool and dark. She looked at the great wooden hornbill, gaily painted, which Harold had left in her safekeeping; and it seemed a little odd and barbaric to her, but he had set much store on it. It had some religious significance and Canon Heywood had been greatly struck by it. On the wall, over the sofa, were Malay weapons, she forgot what they were called, and here and there on occasional tables pieces of silver and brass which Harold at various times had sent to them. She had liked Harold and involuntarily her eyes sought his photograph which stood on the piano with photographs of her two daughters, her grandchild, her sister, and her sister's son.

'Why, Kathleen, where's Harold's photograph?' she asked.

Kathleen looked round. It no longer stood in its place.

'Someone's taken it away,' said Kathleen.

Surprised and puzzled, she got up and went over to the piano. The photographs had been rearranged so that no gap should show.

'Perhaps Millicent wanted to have it in her bedroom,' said Mrs Skinner.

'I should have noticed it. Besides, Millicent has several photographs of Harold. She keeps them locked up.'

Mrs Skinner had thought it very peculiar that her daughter should have no photographs of Harold in her room. Indeed she had spoken of it once, but Millicent had made no reply. Millicent had been strangely silent since she came back from Borneo, and had not encouraged the sympathy Mrs Skinner would have been so willing to show her. She seemed unwilling to speak of her great loss. Sorrow took people in different ways. Her husband had said the best thing was to leave her alone. The thought of him turned her ideas to the party they were going to.

'Father asked if I thought he ought to wear a top-hat,' she said. 'I said I thought it was just as well to be on the safe side.'

It was going to be quite a grand affair. They were having ices, strawberry and vanilla, from Boddy, the confectioner, but the Heywoods were making the iced coffee at home. Everyone would be there. They had been asked to meet the Bishop of Hong Kong, who was staying with the Canon, an old college friend of his, and he was going to speak on the Chinese missions. Mrs Skinner, whose daughter had lived in the East for eight years and whose son-in-law had been Resident of a district in Borneo, was in a flutter of interest. Naturally it meant more to her than to people who had never had anything to do with the Colonies and that sort of thing.

'What can they know of England who only England know?' as Mr Skinner said.

He came into the room at that moment. He was a lawyer, as his father had been before him, and he had offices in Lincoln's Inn Fields. He went up to London every morning and came down every evening. He was only able to accompany his wife and daughters to the Canon's garden-party because the Canon had very wisely chosen a Saturday to have it on. Mr Skinner looked very well in his tail-coat and pepper-and-salt trousers. He was not exactly dressy, but he was neat. He looked like a respectable family solicitor, which indeed he was; his firm never touched work that was not perfectly above board, and if a client went to him with some trouble that was not quite nice, Mr Skinner would look grave.

'I don't think this is the sort of case that we very much care to undertake,' he said. 'I think you'd do better to go elsewhere.'

He drew towards him his writing-block and scribbled a name and address on it. He tore off a sheet of paper and handed it to his client.

'If I were you I think I would go and see these people. If you mention my name I believe they'll do anything they can for you.'

Mr Skinner was clean-shaven and very bald. His pale lips were tight and thin, but his blue eyes were shy. He had no colour in his cheeks and his face was much lined.

'I see you've put on your new trousers,' said Mrs Skinner.

'I thought it would be a good opportunity,' he answered. 'I was wondering if I should wear a buttonhole.'

'I wouldn't, father,' said Kathleen. 'I don't think it's awfully good form.'

'A lot of people will be wearing them,' said Mrs Skinner.

'Only clerks and people like that,' said Kathleen. 'The Heywoods have had to ask everybody, you know. And besides, we are in mourning.'

'I wonder if there'll be a collection after the Bishop's address,' said Mr Skinner.

'I should hardly think so,' said Mrs Skinner.

'I think it would be rather bad form,' agreed Kathleen.

'It's as well to be on the safe side,' said Mr Skinner. 'I'll give for all of us. I was wondering if ten shillings would be enough or if I must give a pound.'

'If you give anything I think you ought to give a pound, father,' said Kathleen.

'I'll see when the time comes. I don't want to give less than anyone else, but on the other hand I see no reason to give more than I need.'

Kathleen put away her papers in the drawer of the writing-table and stood up. She looked at her wrist-watch.

'Is Millicent ready?' asked Mrs Skinner.

'There's plenty of time. We're only asked at four, and I don't think we ought to arrive much before half past. I told Davis to bring the car round at four-fifteen.'

Generally Kathleen drove the car, but on grand occasions like this Davis, who was the gardener, put on his uniform and acted as chauffeur. It looked better when you drove up, and naturally Kathleen didn't much want to drive herself when she was wearing her new jumper. The sight of her mother forcing her fingers one by one into her new gloves reminded her that she must put on her own. She smelt them to see if any odour of the cleaning still clung to them. It was very slight. She didn't believe anyone would notice. She didn't believe anyone would notice.

At last the door opened and Millicent came in. She wore her widow's weeds. Mrs Skinner never could get used to them, but of course she knew that Millicent must wear them for a year. It was a pity they didn't suit her; they suited some people. She had tried on Millicent's bonnet once, with its white band and long veil, and thought she looked very well in it. Of course she hoped dear Alfred would survive her, but if he didn't she would never go out of weeds. Queen Victoria never had. It was different for Millicent; Millicent was a much younger woman; she was only thirty-six: it was very sad to be a widow at thirty-six. And there wasn't much chance of her marrying again. Kathleen wasn't very likely to marry now, she was thirty-five; last time Millicent and Harold had come home she had suggested that they should have Kathleen to stay with them; Harold had seemed willing enough, but Millicent said it wouldn't do. Mrs Skinner didn't know why not. It would give her a chance. Of course they didn't want to get rid of her, but a girl ought to marry, and somehow all the men they knew at home were married already. Millicent said the climate was trying. It was true she was a bad colour. No one would think now that Millicent had been the prettier of the two. Kathleen had fined down as she grew older, of course some people said she was too thin, but now that she had cut her hair, with her cheeks red from playing golf in all weathers, Mrs Skinner thought her quite pretty. No one could say that of poor Millicent; she had lost her figure completely; she had never been tall, and now that she had filled out she looked stocky. She was a good deal too fat; Mrs Skinner supposed it was due to the tropical heat that prevented her from taking exercise. Her skin was sallow and muddy; and her blue eyes, which had been her best feature, had gone quite pale.

'She ought to do something about her neck,' Mrs Skinner reflected. 'She's becoming dreadfully jowly.'

She had spoken of it once or twice to her husband. He remarked that Millicent wasn't as young as she was; that might be, but she needn't let herself go altogether. Mrs Skinner made up her mind to talk to her daughter seriously, but of course she must respect her grief, and she would wait till the year was up. She was just as glad to have this reason to put off a conversation the thought of which made her slightly nervous. For Millicent was certainly changed. There was something sullen in her face which made her mother not quite at home with her. Mrs Skinner liked to say aloud all the thoughts that passed through her head, but Millicent when you made a remark (just to say something, you know) had an awkward habit of not answering, so that you wondered whether she had heard. Sometimes Mrs Skinner found it so irritating, that not to be quite sharp with Millicent she had to remind herself that poor Harold had only been dead eight months.

The light from the window fell on the widow's heavy face as she advanced silently, but Kathleen stood with her back to it. She watched her sister for a moment.

'Millicent, there's something I want to say to you,' she said. 'I was playing golf with Gladys Heywood this morning.'

'Did you beat her?' asked Millicent.

Gladys Heywood was the Canon's only unmarried daughter.

'She told me something about you which I think you ought to know.'

Millicent's eyes passed beyond her sister to the little girl watering flowers in the garden.

'Have you told Annie to give Joan her tea in the kitchen, mother?' she said.

'Yes, she'll have it when the servants have theirs.'

Kathleen looked at her sister coolly.

'The Bishop spent two or three days at Singapore on his way home,' she went on. 'He's very fond of travelling. He's been to Borneo, and he knows a good many of the people that you know.'

'He'll be interested to see you, dear,' said Mrs Skinner. 'Did he know poor Harold?'

'Yes, he met him at Kuala Solor. He remembers him very well. He says he was shocked to hear of his death.'

Millicent sat down and began to put on her black gloves. It seemed strange to Mrs Skinner that she received these remarks with complete silence.

'Oh, Millicent,' she said, 'Harold's photo has disappeared. Have you taken it?'

'Yes, I put it away.'

'I should have thought you'd like to have it out.'

Once more Millicent said nothing. It really was an exasperating habit.

Kathleen turned slightly in order to face her sister.

'Millicent, why did you tell us that Harold died of fever?'

The widow made no gesture, she looked at Kathleen with steady eyes, but her sallow skin darkened with a flush. She did not reply.

'What *do* you mean, Kathleen?' asked Mr Skinner, with surprise.

'The Bishop says that Harold committed suicide.'

Mrs Skinner gave a startled cry, but her husband put out a deprecating hand.

'Is it true, Millicent?'

'It is.'

'But why didn't you tell us?'

Millicent paused for an instant. She fingered idly a piece of Brunei brass which stood on the table by her side. That too had been a present from Harold.

'I thought it better for Joan that her father should be thought to have died of fever. I didn't want her to know anything about it.'

'You've put us in an awfully awkward position,' said Kathleen, frowning a little. 'Gladys Heywood said she thought it rather nasty of me not to have told her the truth. I had the greatest difficulty in getting her to believe that I knew absolutely nothing about it. She said her father was rather put out. He says, after all the years we've known one another, and considering that he married you, and the terms we've been on, and all that, he does think we might have had confidence in him. And at all events, if we didn't want to tell him the truth we needn't have told him a lie.'

'I must say I sympathize with him there,' said Mr Skinner, acidly.

'Of course I told Gladys that we weren't to blame. We only told them what you told us.'

'I hope it didn't put you off your game,' said Millicent.

'Really, my dear, I think that is a most improper observation,' exclaimed her father.

He rose from his chair, walked over to the empty fireplace, and from force of habit stood in front of it with parted coat-tails.

'It was my business,' said Millicent, 'and if I chose to keep it to myself I didn't see why I shouldn't.'

'It doesn't look as if you had any affection for your mother if you didn't even tell her,' said Mrs Skinner.

Millicent shrugged her shoulders.

'You might have known it was bound to come out,' said Kathleen.

'Why? I didn't expect that two gossiping old parsons would have nothing else to talk about than me.'

'When the Bishop said he'd been to Borneo it's only natural that the Heywoods should ask him if he knew you and Harold.'

'All that's neither here nor there,' said Mr Skinner. 'I think you should certainly have told us the truth, and we could have decided what was the best thing to do. As a solicitor I can tell you that in the long run it only makes things worse if you attempt to hide them.'

'Poor Harold,' said Mrs Skinner, and the tears began to trickle down her raddled cheeks. 'It seems dreadful. He was always a good son-in-law to me. Whatever induced him to do such a dreadful thing?'

'The climate.'

'I think you'd better give us all the facts, Millicent,' said her father.

'Kathleen will tell you.'

Kathleen hesitated. What she had to say really was rather dreadful. It seemed terrible that such things should happen to a family like theirs.

'The Bishop says he cut his throat.'

Mrs Skinner gasped and she went impulsively up to her bereaved daughter. She wanted to fold her in her arms.

'My poor child,' she sobbed.

But Millicent withdrew herself.

'Please don't fuss me, mother. I really can't stand being mauled about.'

'Really, Millicent,' said Mr Skinner, with a frown.

He did not think she was behaving very nicely.

Mrs Skinner dabbed her eyes carefully with her handkerchief and with a sigh and a little shake of the head returned to her chair. Kathleen fidgeted with the long chain she wore round her neck.

'It does seem rather absurd that I should have to be told the details of my brother-in-law's death by a friend. It makes us all look such fools. The Bishop wants very much to see you, Millicent; he wants to tell you how much he feels for you.' She paused, but Millicent did not speak. 'He says that Millicent had been away with Joan and when she came back she found poor Harold lying dead on his bed.'

'It must have been a great shock,' said Mr Skinner.

Mrs Skinner began to cry again, but Kathleen put her hand gently on her shoulder.

'Don't cry, mother,' she said. 'It'll make your eyes red and people will think it so funny.'

They were all silent while Mrs Skinner, drying her eyes, made a successful effort to control herself. It seemed very strange to her that this very moment she should be wearing in her toque the ospreys that poor Harold had given her.

'There's something else I ought to tell you,' said Kathleen.

Millicent looked at her sister again, without haste, and her eyes were steady, but watchful. She had the look of a person who is waiting for a sound which he is afraid of missing.

'I don't want to say anything to wound you, dear,' Kathleen went on, 'but there's something else and I think you ought to know it. The Bishop says that Harold drank.'

'Oh, my dear, how dreadful!' cried Mrs Skinner. 'What a shocking thing to say. Did Gladys Heywood tell you? What did you say?'

'I said it was entirely untrue.'

'This is what comes of making secrets of things,' said Mr Skinner, irritably. 'It's always the same. If you try and hush a thing up all sorts of rumours get about which are ten times worse than the truth.'

'They told the Bishop in Singapore that Harold had killed himself while he was suffering from delirium tremens. I think for all our sakes you ought to deny that, Millicent.'

'It's such a dreadful thing to have said about anyone who's dead,' said Mrs Skinner. 'And it'll be so bad for Joan when she grows up.'

'But what is the foundation of this story, Millicent?' asked her father. 'Harold was always very abstemious.'

'Here,' said the widow.

'Did he drink?'

'Like a fish.'

The answer was so unexpected, and the tone so sardonic, that all three of them were startled.

'Millicent, how can you talk like that of your husband when he's dead?' cried her mother, clasping her neatly gloved hands. 'I can't understand you. You've been so strange since you came back. I could never have believed that a girl of mine could take her husband's death like that.'

'Never mind about that, mother,' said Mr Skinner. 'We can go into all that later.'

He walked to the window and looked out at the sunny little garden, and then walked back into the room. He took his pince-nez out of his pocket, and though he had no intention of putting them on, wiped them with his handkerchief. Millicent looked at him and in her eyes, unmistakably, was a look of irony which was quite cynical. Mr Skinner was vexed. He had finished his week's work and he was a free man till Monday morning. Though he had told his wife that this garden-party was a great nuisance and he would much sooner have tea quietly in his own garden, he had been looking forward to it. He did not care very much about Chinese missions, but it would be interesting to meet the Bishop. And now this! It was not the kind of thing he cared to be mixed up in; it was most unpleasant to be told on a sudden that his son-in-law was a drunkard and a suicide. Millicent was thoughtfully smoothing her white cuffs. Her coolness irritated him; but instead of addressing her he spoke to his younger daughter.

'Why don't you sit down, Kathleen? Surely there are plenty of chairs in the room.'

Kathleen drew forward a chair and without a word seated herself. Mr Skinner stopped in front of Millicent and faced her.

'Of course I see why you told us Harold had died of fever. I think it was a mistake, because that sort of thing is bound to come out sooner or later. I don't know how far what the Bishop has told the Heywoods coincides with the facts, but if you will take my advice you will tell us everything as circumstantially as you can, then we can see. We can't hope that it will go no further now that Canon Heywood and Gladys know. In a place like this people are bound to talk. It will make it easier for all of us if we at all events know the exact truth.'

Mrs Skinner and Kathleen thought he put the matter very well. They waited for Millicent's reply. She had listened with an impassive face; that sudden flush had disappeared and it was once more, as usual, pasty and sallow.

'I don't think you'll much like the truth if I tell it you,' she said.

'You must know that you can count on our sympathy and understanding,' said Kathleen gravely.

Millicent gave her a glance and the shadow of a smile flickered across her set mouth. She looked slowly at the three of them. Mrs Skinner had an uneasy impression that she looked at them as though they were mannequins at a dressmaker's. She seemed to live in a different world from theirs and to have no connexion with them.

'You know, I wasn't in love with Harold when I married him,' she said reflectively.

Mrs Skinner was on the point of making an exclamation when a rapid gesture of her husband, barely indicated, but after so many years of married life perfectly significant, stopped her. Millicent went on. She spoke with a level voice, slowly, and there was little change of expression in her tone.

'I was twenty-seven, and no one else seemed to want to marry me. It's true he was forty-four, and it seemed rather old, but he had a very good position, hadn't he? I wasn't likely to get a better chance.'

Mrs Skinner felt inclined to cry again, but she remembered the party.

'Of course I see now why you took his photograph away,' she said dolefully.

'Don't, mother,' exclaimed Kathleen.

It had been taken when he was engaged to Millicent and was a very good photograph of Harold. Mrs Skinner had always thought him quite a fine man. He was heavily built, tall and perhaps a little too fat, but he held himself well, and his presence was imposing. He was inclined to be bald, even then, but men did go bald very early nowadays, and he said that topees, sun-helmets, you know, were very bad for the hair. He had a small dark moustache, and his face was deeply burned by the sun. Of course his best feature was his eyes; they were brown and large, like Joan's. His conversation was interesting. Kathleen said he was pompous, but Mrs Skinner didn't think him so, she didn't mind it if a man laid down the law; and when she saw, as she very soon did, that he was attracted by Millicent she began to like him very much. He was always very attentive to Mrs Skinner, and she listened as though she were really interested when he spoke of his district, and told her of the big game he had killed. Kathleen said he had a pretty good opinion of himself, but Mrs Skinner came of a generation which accepted without question the good opinion that men had of themselves. Millicent saw very soon which way the wind blew, and though she said nothing to her mother, her mother knew that if Harold asked her she was going to accept him.

Harold was staying with some people who had been thirty years in Borneo and they spoke well of the country. There was no reason why a woman shouldn't live there comfortably; of course the children had to come home when they were seven; but Mrs Skinner thought it unnecessary to trouble about that yet. She asked Harold to dine, and she told him they were always in to tea. He seemed to be at a loose end, and when his visit to his old friends was drawing to a close, she told him they would be very much pleased if he would come and spend a fortnight with them. It was towards the end of this that Harold and Millicent became engaged. They had a very pretty wedding, they went to Venice for their honeymoon, and then they started for the East. Millicent wrote from various ports at which the ship touched. She seemed happy.

'People were very nice to me at Kuala Solor,' she said. Kuala Solor was the chief town of the state of Sembulu. 'We stayed with the Resident and everyone asked us to dinner. Once or twice I heard men ask Harold to have a drink, but he refused; he said he had turned over a new leaf now he was a married man. I didn't know why they laughed. Mrs Gray, the Resident's wife, told me they were all so glad Harold was married. She said it was dreadfully lonely for a bachelor on one of the outstations. When we left Kuala Solor Mrs Gray said good-bye to me so funnily that I was quite surprised. It was as if she was solemnly putting Harold in my charge.'

They listened to her in silence. Kathleen never took her eyes off her sister's impassive face; but Mr Skinner stared straight in front of him at the Malay arms, krises and parangs, which hung on the wall above the sofa on which his wife sat.

'It wasn't till I went back to Kuala Solor a year and a half later, that I found out why their manner had seemed so odd.' Millicent gave a queer little sound like the echo of a scornful laugh. 'I knew then a good deal that I hadn't known before. Harold came to England that time in order to marry. He didn't much mind who it was. Do you remember how we spread ourselves out to catch him, mother? We needn't have taken so much trouble.'

'I don't know what you mean, Millicent,' said Mrs Skinner, not without acerbity, for the insinuation of scheming did not please her. 'I saw he was attracted by you.'

Millicent shrugged her heavy shoulders.

'He was a confirmed drunkard. He used to go to bed every night with a bottle of whisky and empty it before morning. The Chief Secretary told him he'd have to resign unless he stopped drinking. He said he'd give him one more chance. He could take his leave then and go to England. He advised him to marry so that when he got back he'd have someone to look after him. Harold married me because he wanted a keeper. They took bets in Kuala Solor on how long I'd make him stay sober.'

'But he was in love with you,' Mrs Skinner interrupted. 'You don't know how he used to speak to me about you, and at that time you're speaking of, when you went to Kuala Solor to have Joan, he wrote me such a charming letter about you.'

Millicent looked at her mother again and a deep colour dyed her sallow skin. Her hands, lying on her lap, began to tremble a little. She thought of those firs months of her married life. The government launch took them to the mouth of the river, and they spent the night at the bungalow which Harold said jokingly was their seaside residence. Next day they went up-stream in a prahu. From the novels she had read she expected the rivers of Borneo to be dark and strangely sinister, but the sky was blue, dappled with little white clouds, and the green of the mangroves and the nipahs, washed by the flowing water, glistened in the sun. On each side stretched the pathless jungle, and in the distance, silhouetted against the sky, was the rugged outline of a mountain. The air in the early morning was fresh and buoyant. She seemed to enter upon a friendly, fertile land, and she had a sense of spacious freedom. They watched the banks for monkeys sitting on the branches of the tangled trees, and once Harold pointed out something that looked like a log and said it was a crocodile. The Assistant Resident, in ducks and a topee, was at the landing-stage to meet them, and a dozen trim little soldiers were lined up to do them honour. The Assistant Resident was introduced to her. His name was Simpson.

'By Jove, sir,' he said to Harold. 'I'm glad to see you back. It's been deuced lonely without you.'

The Resident's bungalow, surrounded by a garden in which grew wildly all manner of gay flowers, stood on the top of a low hill. It was a trifle shabby and the furniture was sparse, but the rooms were cool and of generous size.

'The kampong is down there,' said Harold, pointing.

Her eyes followed his gesture, and from among the coconut trees rose the beating of a gong. It gave her a queer little sensation in the heart.

Though she had nothing much to do the days passed easily enough. At dawn a boy brought them their tea and they lounged about the veranda, enjoying the fragrance of the morning (Harold in a singlet and a sarong, she in a dressing-gown) till it was time to dress for breakfast. Then Harold went to his office and she spent an hour or two learning Malay. After tiffin he went back to his office while she slept. A cup of tea revived them both, and they went for a walk or played golf on the nine-hole links which Harold had made on a level piece of cleared jungle below the bungalow. Night fell at six and Mr Simpson came along to have a drink. They chatted till their late dinner hour, and sometimes Harold and Mr Simpson played chess. The balmy evenings were enchanting. The fireflies turned the bushes just below the veranda into coldly-sparkling, tremulous beacons, and flowering trees scented the air with sweet odours. After dinner they read the papers which had left London six weeks before and presently went to bed. Millicent enjoyed being a married woman, with a house of her own, and she was pleased with the native servants, in their gay sarongs, who went about the bungalow, with bare feet, silent but friendly. It gave her a pleasant sense of importance to be the wife of the Resident. Harold impressed her by the fluency with which he spoke the language, by his air of command, and by his dignity. She went into the court-house now and then to hear him try cases. The multifariousness of his duties and the competent way in which he performed them aroused her respect. Mr Simpson told her that Harold understood the natives as well as any man in the country. He had the combination of firmness, tact, and good-humour which was essential in dealing with that timid, revengeful, and suspicious race. Millicent began to feel a certain admiration for her husband.

They had been married nearly a year when two English naturalists came to stay with them for a few days on their way to the interior. They brought a pressing recommendation from the governor, and Harold said he wanted to do them proud. Their arrival was an agreeable change. Millicent asked Mr Simpson to dinner (he lived at the Fort and only dined with them on Sunday nights) and after dinner the men sat down to play bridge. Millicent left them presently and went to bed, but they were so noisy that for some time she could not get to sleep. She did not know at what hour she was awakened by Harold staggering into the room. She kept silent. He made up his mind to have a bath before getting into bed; the bath-house was just below their room, and he went down the steps that led to it. Apparently he slipped, for there was a great clatter, and he began to swear. Then he was violently sick. She heard him sluice the buckets of water over himself and in a little while, walking very cautiously this time, he crawled up the stairs and slipped into bed. Millicent pretended to be asleep. She was disgusted. Harold was drunk. She made up her mind to speak about it in the morning. What would the naturalists think of him? But in the morning Harold was so dignified that she hadn't quite the determination to refer to the matter. At eight Harold and she, with their two guests, sat down to breakfast. Harold looked round the table.

'Porridge,' he said. 'Millicent, your guests might manage a little Worcester sauce for breakfast, but I don't think they'll much fancy anything else. Personally I shall content myself with a whisky and soda.'

The naturalists laughed, but shamefacedly.

'Your husband's a terror,' said one of them.

'I should not think I had properly performed the duties of hospitality if I sent you sober to bed on the first night of your visit,' said Harold, with his round, stately way of putting things.

Millicent, smiling acidly, was relieved to think that her guests had been as drunk as her husband. The next evening she sat up with them and the party broke up at a reasonable hour. But she was glad when the strangers went on with their journey. Their life resumed its placid course. Some months later Harold went on a tour of inspection of his district and came back with a bad attack of malaria. This was the first time she had seen the disease of which she had heard so much, and when he recovered it did not seem strange to her that Harold was very shaky. She found his manner peculiar. He would come back from the office and stare at her with glazed eyes; he would stand on the veranda, swaying slightly, but still dignified, and make long harangues about the political situation in England; losing the thread of his discourse, he would look at her with an archness which his natural stateliness made somewhat disconcerting and say:

'Pulls you down dreadfully, this confounded malaria. Ah, little woman, you little know the strain it puts upon a man to be an empire builder.'

She thought that Mr Simpson began to look worried, and once or twice, when they were alone, he seemed on the point of saying something to her which his shyness at the last moment prevented. The feeling grew so strong that it made her nervous, and one evening when Harold, she knew not why, had remained later than usual at the office she tackled him.

'What have you got to say to me, Mr Simpson?' she broke out suddenly.

He blushed and hesitated.

'Nothing. What makes you think I have anything in particular to say to you?'

Mr Simpson was a thin, weedy youth of four and twenty, with a fine head of waving hair which he took great pains to plaster down very flat. His wrists were swollen and scarred with mosquito bites. Millicent looked at him steadily.

'If it's something to do with Harold don't you think it would be kinder to tell me frankly?'

He grew scarlet now. He shuffled uneasily on his rattan chair. She insisted. 'I'm afraid you'll think it awful cheek,' he said at last. 'It's rotten of me to say anything about my chief behind his back. Malaria's a rotten thing, and after one's had a bout of it one feels awfully down and out.'

He hesitated again. The corners of his mouth sagged as if he were going to cry. To Millicent he seemed like a little boy.

'I'll be as silent as the grave,' she said with a smile, trying to conceal her apprehension. 'Do tell me.'

'I think it's a pity your husband keeps a bottle of whisky at the office. He's apt to take a nip more often than he otherwise would.'

Mr Simpson's voice was hoarse with agitation. Millicent felt a sudden coldness shiver through her. She controlled herself, for she knew that she must not frighten the boy if she were to get out of him all there was to tell. He was unwilling to speak. She pressed him, wheedling, appealing to his sense of duty, and at last she began to cry. Then he told her that Harold had been drunk more or less for the last fortnight, the natives were talking about it, and they said that soon he would be as bad as he had been before his marriage. He had been in the habit of drinking a good deal too much then, but details of that time, notwithstanding all her attempts, Mr Simpson resolutely declined to give her.

'Do you think he's drinking now?' she asked.

'I don't know.'

Millicent felt herself on a sudden hot with shame and anger. The Fort, as it was called because the rifles and the ammunition were kept there, was also the court-house. It stood opposite the Resident's bungalow in a garden of its own. The sun was just about to set and she did not need a hat. She got up and walked across. She found Harold sitting in the office behind the large hall in which he administered justice. There was a bottle of whisky in front of him. He was smoking cigarettes and talking to three or four Malays who stood in front of him listening with obsequious and at the same time scornful smiles. His face was red.

The natives vanished.

'I came to see what you were doing,' she said.

He rose, for he always treated her with elaborate politeness, and lurched. Feeling himself unsteady he assumed an elaborate stateliness of demeanour.

'Take a seat, my dear, take a seat. I was detained by press of work.'

She looked at him with angry eyes.

'You're drunk,' she said.

He stared at her, his eyes bulging a little, and a haughty look gradually traversed his large and fleshy face.

'I haven't the remotest idea what you mean,' he said.

She had been ready with a flow of wrathful expostulation, but suddenly she burst into tears. She sank into a chair and hid her face. Harold looked at her for an instant, then the tears began to trickle down his own cheeks; he came towards her with outstretched arms and fell heavily on his knees. Sobbing, he clasped her to him.

'Forgive me, forgive me,' he said. 'I promise you it shall not happen again. It was that damned malaria.'

'It's so humiliating,' she moaned.

He wept like a child. There was something very touching in the self-abasement of that big dignified man. Presently Millicent looked up. His eyes, appealing and contrite, sought hers.

'Will you give me your word of honour that you'll never touch liquor again?'

'Yes, yes. I hate it.'

It was then she told him that she was with child. He was overjoyed.

'That is the one thing I wanted. That'll keep me straight.'

They went back to the bungalow. Harold bathed himself and had a nap. After dinner they talked long and quietly. He admitted that before he married her he had occasionally drunk more than was good for him; in outstations it was easy to fall into bad habits. He agreed to everything that Millicent asked. And during the months before it was necessary for her to go to Kuala Solor for her confinement, Harold was an excellent husband, tender, thoughtful, proud, and affectionate; he was irreproachable. A launch came to fetch her, she was to leave him for six weeks, and he promised faithfully to drink nothing during her absence. He put his hands on her shoulders.

'I never break a promise,' he said in his dignified way. 'But even without it, can you imagine that while you are going through so much, I should do anything to increase your troubles?'

Joan was born. Millicent stayed at the Resident's, and Mrs Gray, his wife, a kindly creature of middle age, was very good to her. The two women had little to do during the long hours they were alone but to talk, and in course of time Millicent learnt everything there was to know of her husband's alcoholic past. The fact which she found most difficult to reconcile herself to was that Harold had been told that the only condition upon which he would be allowed to keep his post was that he should bring back a wife. It caused in her a dull feeling of resentment. And when she discovered what a persistent drunkard he had been, she felt vaguely uneasy. She had a horrid fear that during her absence he would not have been able to resist the craving. She went home with her baby and a nurse. She spent a night at the mouth of the river and sent a messenger in a canoe to announce her arrival. She scanned the landing-stage anxiously as the launch approached it. Harold and Mr Simpson were standing there. The trim little soldiers were lined up. Her heart sank, for Harold was swaying slightly, like a man who seeks to keep his balance on a rolling ship, and she knew he was drunk.

It wasn't a very pleasant home-coming. She had almost forgotten her mother and father and her sister who sat there silently listening to her. Now she roused herself and became once more aware of their presence. All that she spoke of seemed very far away.

'I knew that I hated him then,' she said. 'I could have killed him.'

'Oh, Millicent, don't say that,' cried her mother. 'Don't forget that he's dead, poor man.'

Millicent looked at her mother, and for a moment a scowl darkened her impassive face. Mr Skinner moved uneasily.

'Go on,' said Kathleen.

'When he found out that I knew all about him he didn't bother very much more. In three months he had another attack of D.T.s.'

'Why didn't you leave him?' said Kathleen.

'What would have been the good of that? He would have been dismissed from the service in a fortnight. Who was to keep me and Joan? I had to stay. And when he was sober I had nothing to complain of. He wasn't in the least in love with me, but he was fond of me; I hadn't married him because I was in love with him, but because I wanted to be married. I did everything I could to keep liquor from him; I managed to get Mr Gray to prevent whisky being sent from Kuala Solor, but he got it from the Chinese. I watched him as a cat watches a mouse. He was too cunning for me. In a little while he had another outbreak. He neglected his duties. I was afraid complaints would be made. We were two days from Kuala Solor and that was our safeguard, but I suppose something was said, for Mr Gray wrote a private letter of warning to me. I showed it to Harold. He stormed and blustered, but I saw he was frightened, and for two or three months he was quite sober. Then he began again. And so it went on till our leave became due.

'Before we came to stay here I begged and prayed him to be careful. I didn't want any of you to know what sort of a man I had married. All the time he was in England he was all right and before we sailed I warned him. He'd grown to be very fond of Joan, and very proud of her, and she was devoted to him. She always liked him better than she liked me. I asked him if he wanted to have his child grow up, knowing that he was a drunkard, and I found out that at last I'd got a hold on him. The thought terrified him. I told him that *I* wouldn't allow it, and if he ever let Joan see him drunk I'd take her away from him at once. Do you know, he grew quite pale when I said it. I fell on my knees that night and thanked God, because I'd found a way of saving my husband.

'He told me that if I would stand by him he would have another try. We made up our minds to fight the thing together. And he tried so hard. When he felt as though he *must* drink he came to me. You know he was inclined to be rather pompous; with me he was so humble, he was like a child; he depended on me. Perhaps he didn't love me when he married me, but he loved me then, me and Joan. I'd hated him, because of the humiliation, because when he was drunk and tried to be dignified and impressive he was loathsome; but now I got a strange feeling in my heart. It wasn't love, but it was a queer, shy tenderness. He was something more than my husband, he was like a child that I'd carried under my heart for long and weary months. He was so proud of me and, you know, I was proud too. His long speeches didn't irritate me any more, and I only thought his stately ways rather funny and charming. At last we won. For two years he never touched a drop. He lost his craving entirely. He was even able to joke about it.

'Mr Simpson had left us then and we had another young man called Francis.

'"I'm a reformed drunkard, you know, Francis," Harold said to him once. "If it hadn't been for my wife I'd have been sacked long ago. I've got the best wife in the world, Francis."

'You don't know what it meant to me to hear him say that. I felt that all I'd gone through was worth while. I was so happy.'

She was silent. She thought of the broad, yellow and turbid river on whose banks she had lived so long. The egrets, white and gleaming in the tremulous sunset, flew down the stream in a flock, flew low and swift, and scattered. They were like a ripple of snowy notes, sweet and pure and spring-like, which an unseen hand drew forth, a divine arpeggio, from an unseen harp. They fluttered along between the green banks, wrapped in the shadows of evening, like the happy thoughts of a contented mind.

'Then Joan fell ill. For three weeks we were very anxious. There was no doctor nearer than Kuala Solor and we had to put up with the treatment of a native dispenser. When she grew well again I took her down to the mouth of the river in order to give her a breath of sea air. We stayed there a week. It was the first time I had been separated from Harold since I went away to have Joan. There was a fishing village, on piles, not far from us, but really we were quite alone. I thought a great deal about Harold, so tenderly, and all at once I knew that I loved him. I was so glad when the prahu came to fetch us back, because I wanted to tell him. I thought it would mean a good deal to him. I can't tell you how happy I was. As we rowed up-stream the headman told me that Mr Francis had had to go up-country to arrest a woman who had murdered her husband. He had been gone a couple of days.

'I was surprised that Harold was not on the landing-stage to meet me; he was always very punctilious about that sort of thing; he used to say that husband and wife should treat one another as politely as they treated acquaintances; and I could not imagine what business had prevented him. I walked up the little hill on which the bungalow stood. The ayah brought Joan behind me. The bungalow was strangely silent. There seemed to be no servants about, and I could not make it out; I wondered if Harold hadn't expected me so soon and was out. I went up the steps. Joan was thirsty and the ayah took her to the servants' quarters to give her something to drink. Harold was not in the sitting-room. I called him, but there was no answer. I was disappointed because I should have liked him to be there. I went into our bedroom. Harold wasn't out after all; he was lying on the bed asleep. I was really very much amused, because he always pretended he never slept in the afternoon. He said it was an unnecessary habit that we white people got into. I went up to the bed softly. I thought I would have a joke with him. I opened the mosquito curtains. He was lying on his back, with nothing on but a sarong, and there was an empty whisky bottle by his side. He was drunk.

'It had begun again. All my struggles for so many years were wasted. My dream was shattered. It was all hopeless. I was seized with rage.'

Millicent's face grew once again darkly red and she clenched the arms of the chair she sat in.

'I took him by the shoulders and shook him with all my might. "You beast," I cried, "you beast." I was so angry I don't know what I did, I don't know what I said. I kept on shaking him. You don't know how loathsome he looked, that large fat man, half naked; he hadn't shaved for days, and his face was bloated and purple. He was breathing heavily. I shouted at him, but he took no notice. I tried to drag him out of bed, but he was too heavy. He lay there like a log. "Open your eyes," I screamed. I shook him again. I hated him. I hated him all the more because for a week I'd loved him with all my heart. He'd let me down. He'd let me down. I wanted to tell him what a filthy beast he was. I could make no impression on him. "You shall open your eyes,' I cried. I was determined to make him look at me.'

The widow licked her dry lips. Her breath seemed hurried. She was silent.

'If he was in that state I should have thought it best to have let him go on sleeping,' said Kathleen.

'There was a parang on the wall by the side of the bed. You know how fond Harold was of curios.'

'What's a parang?' said Mrs Skinner.

'Don't be silly, mother,' her husband replied irritably. 'There's one on the wall immediately behind you.'

He pointed to the Malay sword on which for some reason his eyes had been unconsciously resting. Mrs Skinner drew quickly into the corner of the sofa, with a little frightened gesture, as though she had been told that a snake lay curled up beside her.

'Suddenly the blood spurted out from Harold's throat. There was a great red gash right across it.'

'Millicent,' cried Kathleen, springing up and almost leaping towards her, 'what in God's name do you mean?'

Mrs Skinner stood staring at her with wide startled eyes, her mouth open.

'The parang wasn't on the wall any more. It was on the bed. Then Harold opened his eyes. They were just like Joan's.'

'I don't understand,' said Mr Skinner. 'How could he have committed suicide if he was in the state you describe?'

Kathleen took her sister's arm and shook her angrily.

'Millicent, for God's sake explain.'

Millicent released herself.

'The parang was on the wall, I told you. I don't know what happened. There was all the blood, and Harold opened his eyes. He died almost at once. He never spoke, but he gave a sort of gasp.'

At last Mr Skinner found his voice.

'But, you wretched woman, it was murder.'

Millicent, her face mottled with red, gave him such a look of scornful hatred that he shrank back. Mrs Skinner cried out.

'Millicent, you didn't do it, did you?'

Then Millicent did something that made them all feel as though their blood were turned to ice in their veins. She chuckled.

'I don't know who else did,' she said.

'My God,' muttered Mr Skinner.

Kathleen had been standing bolt upright with her hands to her heart, as though its beating were intolerable.

'And what happened then?' she said.

'I screamed. I went to the window and flung it open. I called for the ayah. She came across the compound with Joan. "Not Joan," I cried. "Don't let her come." She called the cook and told him to take the child. I cried to her to hurry. And when she came I showed her Harold. "The Tuan's killed himself!" I cried. She gave a scream and ran out of the house.

'No one would come near. They were all frightened out of their wits. I wrote a letter to Mr Francis, telling him what had happened and asking him to come at once.'

'How do you mean you told him what had happened?'

'I said, on my return from the mouth of the river, I'd found Harold with his throat cut. You know, in the tropics you have to bury people quickly. I got a Chinese coffin, and the soldiers dug a grave behind the Fort. When Mr Francis came, Harold had been buried for nearly two days. He was only a boy. I could do anything I wanted with him. I told him I'd found the parang in Harold's hand and there was no doubt he'd killed himself in an attack of delirium tremens. I showed him the empty bottle. The servants said he'd been drinking hard ever since I left to go to the sea. I told the same story at Kuala Solor. Everyone was very kind to me, and the government granted me a pension.'

For a little while nobody spoke. At last Mr Skinner gathered himself together.

'I am a member of the legal profession. I'm a solicitor. I have certain duties.

We've always had a most respectable practice. You've put me in a monstrous position.'

He fumbled, searching for the phrases that played at hide and seek in his scattered wits. Millicent looked at him with scorn.

'What are you going to do about it?'

'It was murder, that's what it was; do you think I can possibly connive at it?'

'Don't talk nonsense, father,' said Kathleen sharply. 'You can't give up your own daughter.'

'You've put me in a monstrous position,' he repeated.

Millicent shrugged her shoulders again.

'You made me tell you. And I've borne it long enough by myself. It was time that all of you bore it too.'

At that moment the door was opened by the maid.

'Davis has brought the car round, sir,' she said.

Kathleen had the presence of mind to say something, and the maid withdrew.

'We'd better be starting,' said Millicent.

'I can't go to the party now,' cried Mrs Skinner, with horror. 'I'm far too upset. How can we face the Heywoods? And the Bishop will want to be introduced to you.'

Millicent made a gesture of indifference. Her eyes held their ironical expression.

'We must go, mother,' said Kathleen. 'It would look so funny if we stayed away.' She turned on Millicent furiously. 'Oh, I think the whole thing is such frightfully bad form.'

Mrs Skinner looked helplessly at her husband. He went to her and gave her his hand to help her up from the sofa.

'I'm afraid we must go, mother,' he said.

'And me with the ospreys in my toque that Harold gave me with his own hands,' she moaned.

He led her out of the room, Kathleen followed close on their heels, and a step or two behind came Millicent.

'You'll get used to it, you know,' she said quietly. 'At first I thought of it all the time, but now I forget it for two or three days together. It's not as if there was any danger.'

They did not answer. They walked through the hall and out of the front door. The three ladies got into the back of the car and Mr Skinner seated himself beside the driver. They had no self-starter; it was an old car, and Davis went to the bonnet to crank it up. Mr Skinner turned round and looked petulantly at Millicent.

'I ought never to have been told,' he said. 'I think it was most selfish of you.'

Davis took his seat and they drove off to the Canon's garden-party.

The
Vessel
of Wrath

♦

There are few books in the world that contain more meat than the *Sailing Directions* published by the Hydrographic Department by order of the Lords Commissioners of the Admiralty. They are handsome volumes, bound (very flimsily) in cloth of different colours, and the most expensive of them is cheap. For four shillings you can buy the *Yangtse Kiang Pilot*, 'containing a description of, and sailing directions for, the Yangtse Kiang from the Wusung river to the highest navigable point, including the Han Kiang, the Kialing Kiang, and the Min Kiang'; and for three shillings you can get Part III of the *Eastern Archipelago Pilot*, 'comprising the N.E. end of Celebes, Molucca and Gilolo passages, Banda and Arafura Seas, and North, West, and South-West coasts of New Guinea'. But it is not very safe to do so if you are a creature of settled habits that you have no wish to disturb or if you have an occupation that holds you fast to one place. These business-like books take you upon enchanted journeys of the spirit; and their matter-of-fact style, the admirable order, the concision with which the material is set before you, the stern sense or the practical that informs every line, cannot dim the poetry that, like the spice-laden breeze that assails your senses with a more than material languor when you approach some of those magic islands of the Eastern seas, blows with so sweet a fragrance through the printed pages. They tell you the anchorages and the landing places, what supplies you can get at each spot, and where you can get water; they tell you the lights and buoys, tides, winds, and weather that you will find there. They give you brief information about the population and the trade. And it is strange when you think how sedately it is all set down, with no words wasted, that so much else is given you besides. What? Well, mystery and beauty, romance and the glamour of the unknown. It is no common book that offers you casually turning its pages such a paragraph as this: 'Supplies. A few jungle fowl are preserved, the island is also the resort of vast numbers of sea birds. Turtle are found in the lagoon, as well as quantities of various fish, including grey mullet, shark, and dog-fish; the seine cannot be used with any effect; but there is a fish which may be taken on a rod. A small store of tinned provisions and spirits is kept in a hut for the relief of shipwrecked persons. Good water may be obtained from a well near the landing-place.' Can the imagination want more material than this to go on a journey through time and space?

In the volume from which I have copied this passage, the compilers with the same restraint have described the Alas Islands. They are composed of a group or chain of islands, 'for the most part low and wooded, extending about 75 miles east and west, and 40 miles north and south'. The information about them, you are told, is very slight; there are channels between the different groups, and several vessels have passed through them, but the passages have not been thoroughly explored, and the positions of many of the dangers not yet determined; it is therefore advisable to avoid them. The population of the group is estimated at about 8,000, of whom 200 are Chinese and 400 Mohammedans. The rest are heathen. The principal island is called Baru, it is surrounded by a reef, and here lives a Dutch Contrôleur. His white house with its red roof on the top of a little hill is the most prominent object that the vessels of the Royal Netherlands Steam Packet Company see when every other month on their way up to Macassar and every four weeks on their way down to Merauke in Dutch New Guinea they touch at the island.

At a certain moment of the world's history the Contrôleur was Mynheer Evert Gruyter and he ruled the people who inhabited the Alas Islands with firmness tempered by a keen sense of the ridiculous. He had thought it a very good joke to be placed at the age of twenty-seven in a position of such consequence, and at thirty he was still amused by it. There was no cable communication between his islands and Batavia, and the mail arrived after so long a delay that even if he asked advice, by the time he received it, it was useless, and so he equably did what he thought best and trusted to his good fortune to keep out of trouble with the authorities. He was very short, not more than five feet four in height, and extremely fat; he was of a florid complexion. For coolness' sake he kept his head shaved and his face was hairless. It was round and red. His eyebrows were so fair that you hardly saw them; and he had little twinkling blue eyes. He knew that he had no dignity, but for the sake of his position made up for it by dressing very dapperly. He never went to his office, nor sat in court, nor walked abroad but in spotless white. His stengahshifter, with its bright brass buttons, fitted him very tightly and displayed the shocking fact that, young though he was, he had a round and protruding belly. His good-humoured face shone with sweat and he constantly fanned himself with a palm-leaf fan.

But in his house Mr Gruyter preferred to wear nothing but a sarong and then with his white podgy little body he looked like a fat funny boy of sixteen. He was an early riser and his breakfast was always ready for him at six. It never varied. It consisted of a slice of papaia, three cold fried eggs, Edam cheese, sliced thin, and a cup of black coffee. When he had eaten it, he smoked a large Dutch cigar, read the papers if he had not read them through and through already, and then dressed to go down to his office.

One morning while he was thus occupied his head boy came into his bedroom and told him that Tuan Jones wanted to know if he could see him. Mr

Gruyter was standing in front of a looking-glass. He had his trousers on and was admiring his smooth chest. He arched his back in order to throw it out and throw in his belly and with a good deal of satisfaction gave his breast three or four resounding slaps. It was a manly chest. When the boy brought the message he looked at his own eyes in the mirror and exchanged a slightly ironic smile with them. He asked himself what the devil his visitor could want. Evert Gruyter spoke English, Dutch, and Malay with equal facility, but he thought in Dutch. He liked to do this. It seemed to him a pleasantly ribald language.

'Ask the tuan to wait and say I shall come directly.' He put on his tunic, over his naked body, buttoned it up, and strutted into the sitting-room. The Rev. Owen Jones got up.

'Good morning, Mr Jones,' said the Contrôleur. 'Have you come in to have a peg with me before I start my day's work?'

Mr Jones did not smile.

'I've come to see you upon a very distressing matter, Mr Gruyter,' he answered.

The Contrôleur was not disconcerted by his visitor's gravity nor depressed by his words. His little blue eyes beamed amiably.

'Sit down, my dear fellow, and have a cigar.'

Mr Gruyter knew quite well that the Rev. Owen Jones neither drank nor smoked, but it tickled something prankish in his nature to offer him a drink and a smoke whenever they met. Mr Jones shook his head.

Mr Jones was in charge of the Baptist Mission on the Alas Islands. His headquarters were at Baru, the largest of them, with the greatest population, but he had meeting-houses under the care of native helpers in several other islands of the group. He was a tall, thin, melancholy man, with a long face, sallow and drawn, of about forty. His brown hair was already white on the temples and it receded from the forehead. This gave him a look of somewhat vacuous intellectuality. Mr Gruyter both disliked and respected him. He disliked him because he was narrow-minded and dogmatic. Himself a cheerful pagan who liked the good things of the flesh and was determined to get as many of them as his circumstances permitted, he had no patience with a man who disapproved of them all. He thought the customs of the country suited its inhabitants and had no patience with the missionary's energetic efforts to destroy a way of life that for centuries had worked very well. He respected him because he was honest, zealous, and good. Mr Jones, an Australian of Welsh descent, was the only qualified doctor in the group and it was a comfort to know that if you fell ill you need not rely only on a Chinese practitioner, and none knew better than the Contrôleur how useful to all Mr Jones's skill had been and with what charity he had given it. On the occasion of an epidemic of influenza the missionary had done the work of ten men and no storm short of a typhoon could prevent him from crossing to one island or another if his help was needed.

He lived with his sister in a little white house about half a mile from the village, and when the Contrôleur had arrived came on board to meet him and begged him to stay till he could get his own house in order. The Contrôleur had accepted and soon saw for himself with what simplicity the couple lived. It was more than he could stand. Tea at three sparse meals a day, and when he lit his cigar Mr Jones politely but firmly asked him to be good enough not to smoke, since both his sister and he strongly disapproved of it. In twenty-four hours Mr Gruyter moved into his own house. He fled, with panic in his heart, as though from a plague-stricken city. The Contrôleur was fond of a joke and he liked to laugh; to be with a man who took your nonsense in deadly earnest and never even smiled at your best story was more than flesh and blood could stand. The Rev. Owen Jones was a worthy man, but as a companion he was impossible. His sister was worse. Neither had a sense of humour, but whereas the missionary was of a melancholy turn, doing his duty so conscientiously, with the obvious conviction that everything in the world was hopeless, Miss Jones was resolutely cheerful. She grimly looked on the bright side of things. With the ferocity of an avenging angel she sought out the good in her fellow-men. Miss Jones taught in the mission school and helped her brother in his medical work. When he did operations she gave the anaesthetic and was matron, dresser, and nurse of the tiny hospital which on his own initiative Mr Jones had added to the mission. But the Contrôleur was an obstinate little fellow and he never lost his capacity of extracting amusement from the Rev. Owen's dour struggle with the infirmities of human nature, and Miss Jones's ruthless optimism. He had to get his fun where he could. The Dutch boats came in three times in two months for a few hours and then he could have a good old crack with the captain and chief engineer, and once in a blue moon a pearling lugger came in from Thursday Island or Port Darwin and for two or three days he had a grand time. They were rough fellows, the pearlers, for the most part, but they were full of guts, and they had plenty of liquor on board, and good stories to tell, and the Contrôleur had them up to his house and gave them a fine dinner, and the party was only counted a success if they were all too drunk to get back on the lugger again that night. But beside the missionary the only white man who lived on Baru was Ginger Ted, and he, of course, was a disgrace to civilization. There was not a single thing to be said in his favour. He cast discredit on the white race. All the same, but for Ginger Ted the Contrôleur sometimes thought he would find life on the island of Baru almost more than he could bear.

Oddly enough it was on account of this scamp that Mr Jones, when he should have been instructing the pagan young in the mysteries of the Baptist faith, was paying Mr Gruyter this early visit.

'Sit down, Mr Jones,' said the Contrôleur. 'What can I do for you?'

'Well, I've come to see you about the man they call Ginger Ted. What are you going to do now?'

'Why, what's happened?'

'Haven't you heard? I thought the sergeant would have told you.'

'I don't encourage the members of my staff to come to my private house unless the matter is urgent,' said the Contrôleur rather grandly. 'I am unlike you, Mr Jones, I only work in order to have leisure, and I like to enjoy my leisure without disturbance.'

But Mr Jones did not care much for small talk and he was not interested in general reflections.

'There was a disgraceful row in one of the Chinese shops last night. Ginger Ted wrecked the place and half killed a Chinaman.'

'Drunk again, I suppose,' said the Contrôleur placidly.

'Naturally. When is he anything else? They sent for the police and he assaulted the sergeant. They had to have six men to get him to the jail.'

'He's a hefty fellow,' said the Contrôleur.

'I suppose you'll send him to Macassar.'

Evert Gruyter returned the missionary's outraged look with a merry twinkle. He was no fool and he knew already what Mr Jones was up to. It gave him considerable amusement to tease him a little.

'Fortunately my powers are wide enough to enable me to deal with the situation myself,' he answered.

'You have power to deport anyone you like, Mr Gruyter, and I'm sure it would save a lot of trouble if you got rid of the man altogether.'

'I have the power of course, but I am sure you would be the last person to wish me to use it arbitrarily.'

'Mr Gruyter, the man's presence here is a public scandal. He's never sober from morning till night; it's notorious that he has relations with one native woman after another.'

'That is an interesting point, Mr Jones. I had always heard that alcoholic excess, though it stimulated sexual desire, prevented its gratification. What you tell me about Ginger Ted does not seem to bear out this theory.'

The missionary flushed a dull red.

'These are physiological matters which at the moment I have no wish to go into,' he said, frigidly. 'The behaviour of this man does incalculable damage to the prestige of the white race, and his example seriously hampers the efforts that are made in other quarters to induce the people of these islands to lead a less vicious life. He's an out-and-out bad lot.'

'Pardon my asking, but have you made any attempts to reform him?'

'When he first drifted here I did my best to get in touch with him. He repelled all my advances. When there was that first trouble I went to him and talked to him straight from the shoulder. He swore at me.'

'No one has a greater appreciation than I of the excellent work that you and other missionaries do on these islands, but are you sure that you always exercise your calling with all the tact possible?'

The Contrôleur was rather pleased with this phrase. It was extremely courteous and yet contained a reproof that he thought worth administering. The missionary looked at him gravely. His sad brown eyes were full of sincerity.

'Did Jesus exercise tact when he took a whip and drove the money-changers from the Temple? No, Mr Gruyter. Tact is the subterfuge the lax avail themselves of to avoid doing their duty.'

Mr Jones's remark made the Contrôleur feel suddenly that he wanted a bottle of beer. The missionary leaned forward earnestly.

'Mr Gruyter, you know this man's transgressions just as well as I do. It's unnecessary for me to remind you of them. There are no excuses for him. Now he really has overstepped the limit. You'll never have a better chance than this. I beg you to use the power you have and turn him out once for all.'

The Contrôleur's eyes twinkled more brightly than ever. He was having a lot of fun. He reflected that human beings were much more amusing when you did not feel called upon in dealing with them to allot praise or blame.

'But, Mr Jones, do I understand you right? Are you asking me to give you an assurance to deport this man before I've heard the evidence against him and listened to his defence?'

'I don't know what his defence can be.'

The Contrôleur rose from his chair and really he managed to get quite a little dignity into his five feet four inches.

'I am here to administer justice according to the laws of the Dutch Government. Permit me to tell you that I am exceedingly surprised that you should attempt to influence me in my judicial functions.'

The missionary was a trifle flustered. It had never occurred to him that this little whipper-snapper of a boy, ten years younger than himself, would dream of adopting such an attitude. He opened his mouth to explain and apologize, but the Contrôleur raised a podgy little hand.

'It is time for me to go to my office, Mr Jones. I wish you good morning.'

The missionary, taken aback, bowed and without another word walked out of the room. He would have been surprised to see what the Contrôleur did when his back was turned. A broad grin broke on his lips and he put his thumb to his nose and cocked a snook at the Rev. Owen Jones.

A few minutes later he went down to his office. His head clerk, who was a Dutch half-caste, gave him his version of the previous night's row. It agreed pretty well with Mr Jones's. The court was sitting that day.

'Will you take Ginger Ted first, sir?' asked the clerk.

'I see no reason to do that. There are two or three cases held over from the last sitting. I will take him in his proper order.'

'I thought perhaps as he was a white man you would like to see him privately, sir.'

'The majesty of the law knows no difference between white and coloured, my friend,' said Mr Gruyter, somewhat pompously.

The court was a big square room with wooden benches on which, crowded together, sat natives of all kinds, Polynesians, Bugis, Chinese, Malays, and they all rose when a door was opened and a sergeant announced the arrival of the Contrôleur. He entered with his clerk and took his place on a little dais at a table of varnished pitch pine. Behind him was a large engraving of Queen Wilhelmina. He dispatched half a dozen cases and then Ginger Ted was brought in. He stood in the dock, handcuffed, with a warder on either side of him. The Contrôleur looked at him with a grave face, but he could not keep the amusement out of his eyes.

Ginger Ted was suffering from a hang-over. He swayed a little as he stood and his eyes were vacant. He was a man still young, thirty perhaps, of somewhat over the middle height, rather fat, with a bloated red face and a shock of curly red hair. He had not come out of the tussle unscathed. He had a black eye and his mouth was cut and swollen. He wore khaki shorts, very dirty and ragged, and his singlet had been almost torn off his back. A great rent showed the thick mat of red hair with which his chest was covered, but showed also the astonishing whiteness of his skin. The Contrôleur looked at the charge sheet. He called the evidence. When he had heard it, when he had seen the Chinaman whose head Ginger Ted had broken with a bottle, when he had heard the agitated story of the sergeant who had been knocked flat when he tried to arrest him, when he had listened to the tale of the havoc wrought by Ginger Ted who in his drunken fury had smashed everything he could lay hands on, he turned and addressed the accused in English.

'Well, Ginger, what have you got to say for yourself?'

'I was blind. I don't remember a thing about it. If they say I half killed 'im I suppose I did. I'll pay the damage if they'll give me time.'

'You will, Ginger,' said the Contrôleur, 'but it's me who'll give you time.'

He looked at Ginger Ted for a minute in silence. He was an unappetizing object. A man who had gone completely to pieces. He was horrible. It made you shudder to look at him and if Mr Jones had not been so officious, at that moment the Contrôleur would certainly have ordered him to be deported.

'You've been a trouble ever since you came to the islands, Ginger. You're a disgrace. You're incorrigibly idle. You've been picked up in the street dead drunk time and time again. You've kicked up row after row. You're hopeless. I told you the last time you were brought here that if you were arrested again I should deal with you severely. You've gone the limit this time and you're for it. I sentence you to six months' hard labour.'

'Me?'

'You.'

'By God, I'll kill you when I come out.'

He burst into a string of oaths both filthy and blasphemous. Mr Gruyter listened scornfully. You can swear much better in Dutch than in English and there was nothing that Ginger Ted said that he could not have effectively capped.

'Be quiet,' he ordered. 'You make me tired.'

The Contrôleur repeated his sentence in Malay and the prisoner was led struggling away.

Mr Gruyter sat down to tiffin in high good-humour. It was astonishing how amusing life could be if you exercised a little ingenuity. There were people in Amsterdam and even in Batavia and Surabaya, who looked upon his island home as a place of exile. They little knew how agreeable it was and what fun he could extract from unpromising material. They asked him whether he did not miss the club and the races and the cinema, the dances that were held once a week at the Casino and the society of Dutch ladies. Not at all. He liked comfort. The substantial furniture of the room in which he sat had a satisfying solidity. He liked reading French novels of a frivolous nature and he appreciated the sensation of reading one after the other without the uneasiness occasioned by the thought that he was wasting his time. It seemed to him a great luxury to waste time. When his young man's fancy turned to thoughts of love his head boy brought to the house a little dark-skinned bright-eyed creature in a sarong. He took care to form no connexion of a permanent nature. He thought that change kept the heart young. He enjoyed freedom and was not weighed down by a sense of responsibility. He did not mind the heat. It made a sluice over with cold water half a dozen times a day a pleasure that had almost an aesthetic quality. He played the piano. He wrote letters to his friends in Holland. He felt no need for the conversation of intellectual persons. He liked a good laugh, but he could get that out of a fool just as well as out of a professor of philosophy. He had a notion that he was a very wise little man.

Like all good Dutchmen in the Far East he began his lunch with a small glass of Hollands gin. It has a musty acrid flavour, and the taste for it must be acquired, but Mr Gruyter preferred it to any cocktail. When he drank it he felt besides that he was upholding the traditions of his race. Then he had *rijsttafel*. He had it every day. He heaped a soup-plate high with rice, and then, his three boys waiting on him, helped himself to the curry that one handed him, to the fried egg that another brought, and to the condiment presented by the third. Then each one brought another dish, of bacon, or bananas, or pickled fish, and presently his plate was piled high in a huge pyramid. He stirred it all together and began to eat. He ate slowly and with relish. He drank a bottle of beer.

He did not think while he was eating. His attention was applied to the mass in front of him and he consumed it with a happy concentration. It never palled on him. And when he had emptied the great plate it was a compensation to think that next day he would have *rijsttafel* again. He grew tired of it as little as the rest of us grow tired of bread. He finished his beer and lit his cigar. The boy brought him a cup of coffee. He leaned back in his chair then and allowed himself the luxury of reflection.

It tickled him to have sentenced Ginger Ted to the richly deserved punishment of six months' hard labour, and he smiled when he thought of him working on the roads with the other prisoners. It would have been silly to deport from the island the one man with whom he could occasionally have a heart-to-heart talk, and besides, the satisfaction it would have given the missionary would have been bad for that gentleman's character. Ginger Ted was a scamp and a scallywag, but the Contrôleur had a kindly feeling for him. They had drunk many a bottle of beer in one another's company, and when the pearl fishers from Port Darwin came in and they all made a night of it, they had got gloriously tight together. The Contrôleur liked the reckless way in which Ginger Ted squandered the priceless treasure of life.

Ginger Ted had wandered in one day on the ship that was going up from Merauke to Macassar. The captain did not know how he had found his way there, but he had travelled steerage with the natives, and he stopped off at the Alas Islands because he liked the look of them. Mr Gruyter had a suspicion that their attraction consisted perhaps in their being under the Dutch flag and so out of British jurisdiction. But his papers were in order, so there was no reason why he should not stay. He said that he was buying pearl-shell for an Australian firm, but it soon appeared that his commercial undertakings were not serious. Drink, indeed, took up so much of his time that he had little left over for other pursuits. He was in receipt of two pounds a week, paid monthly, which came regularly to him from England. The Contrôleur guessed that this sum was paid only so long as he kept well away from the persons who sent it. It was anyway too small to permit him any liberty of movement. Ginger Ted was reticent. The Contrôleur discovered that he was an Englishman, this he learnt from his passport, which described him as Edward Wilson, and that he had been in Australia. But why he had left England and what he had done in Australia he had no notion. Nor could he ever quite tell to what class Ginger Ted belonged. When you saw him in a filthy singlet and a pair of ragged trousers, a battered topee on his head, with the pearl fishers and heard his conversation, coarse, obscene, and illiterate, you thought he must be a sailor before the mast who had deserted his ship, or a labourer, but when you saw his handwriting you were surprised to find that it was that of a man not without at least some education, and on occasion when you got him alone, if he had had a few drinks but was not yet drunk, he would talk of matters that neither a sailor nor a labourer would have been likely to know anything about. The Contrôleur had a certain sensitiveness and he realized that Ginger Ted did not speak to him as an inferior to a superior but as an equal. Most of his remittance was mortgaged before he received it, and the Chinamen to whom he owed money were standing at his elbow when the monthly letter was delivered to him, but with what was left he proceeded to get drunk. It was then that he made trouble, for when drunk he grew violent and was then likely to commit acts that brought him into the hands of the police. Hitherto Mr Gruyter had contented himself with keeping him in jail till he was sober and giving him a talking to. When he was out of money he cadged what drink he could from anyone who would give it him. Rum, brandy, arak, it was all the same to him. Two or three times Mr Gruyter had got him work on plantations run by Chinese in one or other of the islands, but he could not stick to it, and in a few weeks was back again at Baru on the beach. It was a miracle how he kept body and soul together. He had, of course, a way with him. He picked up the various dialects spoken on the islands, and knew how to make the natives laugh. They despised him, but they respected his physical strength, and they liked his company. He was as a result never at a loss for a meal or a mat to sleep on. The strange thing was, and it was this that chiefly outraged the Rev. Owen Jones, that he could do anything he liked with a woman. The Contrôleur could not imagine what it was they saw in him. He was casual with them and rather brutal. He took what they gave him, but seemed incapable of gratitude. He used them for his pleasure and then flung them indifferently away. Once or twice this had got him into trouble, and Mr Gruyter had had to sentence an angry father for sticking a knife in Ginger Ted's back one night, and a Chinese woman had sought to poison herself by swallowing opium because he had deserted her. Once Mr Jones came to the Contrôleur in a great state because the beachcomber had seduced one of his converts. The Contrôleur agreed that it was very deplorable, but could only advise Mr Jones to keep a sharp eye on these young persons. The Contrôleur liked it less when he discovered that a girl whom he fancied a good deal himself and had been seeing for several weeks had all the time been according her favours also to Ginger Ted. When he thought of this particular incident he smiled again at the thought of Ginger Ted doing six months' hard labour. It is seldom in this life that in the process of doing your bounden duty you can get back on a fellow who has played you a dirty trick.

A few days later Mr Gruyter was taking a walk, partly for exercise and partly to see that some job he wanted done was being duly proceeded with, when he passed a gang of prisoners working under the charge of a warder. Among them he saw Ginger Ted. He wore the prison sarong, a dingy tunic called in Malay a *baju*, and his own battered topee. They were repairing the road, and Ginger Ted was wielding a heavy pick. The way was narrow and the Contrôleur saw that he must pass within a foot of him. He remembered his threats. He knew that Ginger Ted was a man of violent passion, and the language he had used in the dock made it plain that he had not seen what a good joke it was of the Contrôleur's to sentence him to six months' hard labour. If Ginger Ted suddenly attacked him with the pick, nothing on God's earth could save him. It was true that the warder would immediately shoot him down, but meanwhile the Contrôleur's head would be bashed in. It was with a funny little feeling in the pit of his stomach that Mr Gruyter walked through the gang of prisoners. They were working in pairs a few feet from one another. He set his mind on neither hastening his pace nor slackening it. As he passed Ginger Ted, the man swung his pick into the ground and looked up at the Contrôleur and as he caught his eye winked. The Contrôleur checked the smile that rose to his lips and with official dignity strode on. But that wink, so lusciously full of sardonic humour, filled him with satisfaction. If he had been the Caliph of Bagdad instead of a junior official in the Dutch Civil Service, he could forthwith have released Ginger Ted, sent slaves to bath and perfume him, and having clothed him in a golden robe entertained him to a sumptuous repast.

Ginger Ted was an exemplary prisoner and in a month or two the Contrôleur, having occasion to send a gang to do some work on one of the outlying islands, included him in it. There was no jail there, so the ten fellows he sent, under the charge of a warder, were billeted on the natives and after their day's work lived like free men. The job was sufficient to take up the rest of Ginger Ted's sentence. The Contrôleur saw him before he left.

'Look here, Ginger,' he said to him, 'here's ten guilder for you so that you can buy yourself tobacco when you're gone.'

'Couldn't you make it a bit more? There's eight pounds a month coming in regularly.'

'I think that's enough. I'll keep the letters that come for you, and when you get back you'll have a tidy sum. You'll have enough to take you anywhere you want to go.'

'I'm very comfortable here,' said Ginger Ted.

'Well, the day you come back, clean yourself up and come over to my house. We'll have a bottle of beer together.'

'That'll be fine. I guess I'll be ready for a good crack then.'

Now chance steps in. The island to which Ginger Ted had been sent was called Maputiti, and like all the rest of them it was rocky, heavily wooded, and surrounded by a reef. There was a village among coconuts on the sea-shore opposite the opening of the reef and another village on a brackish lake in the middle of the island. Of this some of the inhabitants had been converted to Christianity. Communication with Baru was effected by a launch that touched at the various islands at irregular intervals. It carried passengers and produce. But the villagers were seafaring folk, and if they had to communicate urgently with Baru, manned a prahu and sailed the fifty miles or so that separated them from it. It happened that when Ginger Ted's sentence had but another fortnight to run the Christian headman of the village on the lake was taken suddenly ill. The native remedies availed him nothing and he writhed in agony. Messengers were sent to Baru imploring the missionary's help; but as ill luck would have it Mr Jones was suffering at the moment from an attack of malaria. He was in bed and unable to move. He talked the matter over with his sister.

'It sounds like acute appendicitis,' he told her.

'You can't go, Owen,' she said.

'I can't let the man die.'

Mr Jones had a temperature of a hundred and four. His head was aching like mad. He had been delirious all night. His eyes were shining strangely and his sister felt that he was holding on to his wits by a sheer effort of will.

'You couldn't operate in the state you're in.'

'No, I couldn't. Then Hassan must go.'

Hassan was the dispenser.

'You couldn't trust Hassan. He'd never dare to do an operation on his own responsibility. And they'd never let him. I'll go. Hassan can stay here and look after you.'

'You can't remove an appendix.'

'Why not? I've seen you do it. I've done lots of minor operations.'

Mr Jones felt he didn't quite understand what she was saying.

'Is the launch in?'

'No, it's gone to one of the islands. But I can go in the prahu the men came in.'

'You? I wasn't thinking of you. You can't go.'

'I'm going, Owen.'

'Going where?' he said.

She saw that his mind was wandering already. She put her hand soothingly on his dry forehead. She gave him a dose of medicine. He muttered something and she realized that he did not know where he was. Of course she was anxious about him, but she knew that his illness was not dangerous, and she could leave him safely to the mission boy who was helping her nurse him and to the native dispenser. She slipped out of the room. She put her toilet things, a night-dress, and a change of clothes into a bag. A little chest with surgical instruments, bandages, and antiseptic dressings was kept always ready. She gave them to the two natives who had come over from Maputiti, and telling the dispenser what she was going to do gave him instructions to inform her brother when he was able to listen. Above all he was not to be anxious about her. She put on her topee and sallied forth. The mission was about half a mile from the village. She walked quickly. At the end of the jetty the prahu was waiting. Six men manned it. She took her place in the stern and they set off with a rapid stroke. Within the reef the sea was calm, but when they crossed the bar they came upon a long swell. But this was not the first journey of the sort Miss Jones had taken and she was confident of the seaworthiness of the boat she was in. It was noon and the sun beat down from a sultry sky. The only thing that harassed her was that they could not arrive before dark, and if she found it necessary to operate at once she could count only on the light of hurricane lamps.

Miss Jones was a woman of hard on forty. Nothing in her appearance would have prepared you for such determination as she had just shown. She had an odd drooping gracefulness, which suggested that she might be swayed by every breeze; it was almost an affectation; and it made the strength of character which you soon discovered in her seem positively monstrous. She was flat-chested, tall, and extremely thin. She had a long sallow face and she was much afflicted with prickly heat. Her lank brown hair was drawn back straight from her forehead. She had rather small eyes, grey in colour, and because they were somewhat too close they gave her face a shrewish look. Her nose was long and thin and a trifle red. She suffered a good deal from indigestion. But this infirmity availed nothing against her ruthless determination to look upon the bright side of things. Firmly persuaded that the world was evil and men unspeakably vicious, she extracted any little piece of decency she could find in them with the modest pride with which a conjurer extracts a rabbit from a hat. She was quick, resourceful, and competent. When she arrived on the island she saw that there was not a moment to lose if she was to save the headman's life. Under the greatest difficulties, showing a native how to give the anaesthetic, she operated, and for the next three days nursed the patient with anxious assiduity. Everything went very well and she realized that her brother could not have made a better job of it. She waited long enough to take out the stitches and then prepared to go home. She could flatter herself that she had not wasted her time. She had given medical attention to such as needed it, she had strengthened the small Christian community in its faith, admonished such as were lax, and cast the good seed in places where it might be hoped under divine providence to take root.

The launch, coming from one of the other islands, put in somewhat late in the afternoon, but it was full moon and they expected to reach Baru before midnight. They brought her things down to the wharf and the people who were seeing her off stood about repeating their thanks. Quite a little crowd collected. The launch was loaded with sacks of copra, but Miss Jones was used to its strong smell and it did not incommode her. She made herself as comfortable a place to sit in as she could, and waiting for the launch to start, chatted with her grateful flock. She was the only passenger. Suddenly a group of natives emerged from the trees that embowered the little village on the lagoon and she saw that among them was a white man. He wore a prison sarong and a baju. He had long red hair. She at once recognized Ginger Ted. A policeman was with him. They shook hands and Ginger Ted shook hands with the villagers who accompanied him. They bore bundles of fruit and a jar which Miss Jones guessed contained native spirit, and these they put in the launch. She discovered to her surprise that Ginger Ted was coming with her. His term was up and instructions had arrived that he was to be returned to Baru in the launch. He gave her a glance, but did not nod –indeed Miss Jones turned away her head–and stepped in. The mechanic started his engine and in a moment they were jug-jugging through the channel in the lagoon. Ginger Ted clambered on to a pile of sacks and lit a cigarette.

Miss Jones ignored him. Of course she knew him very well. Her heart sank when she thought that he was going to be once more in Baru, creating a scandal and drinking, a peril to the women and a thorn in the flesh of all decent people. She knew the steps her brother had taken to have him deported and she had no patience with the Contrôleur, who would not see a duty that stared him so plainly in the face. When they had crossed the bar and were in the open sea Ginger Ted took the stopper out of the jar of arak and putting his mouth to it took a long pull. Then he handed the jar to the two mechanics who formed the crew. One was a middle-aged man and the other a youth.

'I do not wish you to drink anything while we are on the journey,' said Miss Jones sternly to the elder one.

He smiled at her and drank.

'A little arak can do no one any harm,' he answered. He passed the jar to his companion, who drank also.

'If you drink again I shall complain to the Contrôleur,' said Miss Jones.

The elder man said something she could not understand, but which she suspected was very rude, and passed the jar back to Ginger Ted. They went along for an hour or more. The sea was like glass and the sun set radiantly. It set behind one of the islands and for a few minutes changed it into a mystic city of the skies. Miss Jones turned round to watch it and her heart was filled with gratitude for the beauty of the world.

'And only man is vile,' she quoted to herself.

They went due east. In the distance was a little island which she knew they passed close by. It was uninhabited. A rocky islet thickly grown with virgin forest. The boatman lit his lamps. The night fell and immediately the sky was thick with stars. The moon had not yet risen. Suddenly there was a slight jar and the launch began to vibrate strangely. The engine rattled. The head mechanic calling to his mate to take the helm, crept under the housing. They seemed to be going more slowly. The engine stopped. She asked the youth what was the matter, but he did not know. Ginger Ted got down from the top of the copra sacks and slipped under the housing. When he reappeared she would have liked to ask him what had happened, but her dignity prevented her. She sat still and occupied herself with her thoughts. There was a long swell and the launch rolled slightly. The mechanic emerged once more into view and started the engine. Though it rattled like mad they began to move. The launch vibrated from stem to stern. They went very slowly. Evidently something was amiss, but Miss Jones was exasperated rather than alarmed. The launch was supposed to do six knots, but now it was just crawling along; at that rate they would not get into Baru till long, long after midnight. The mechanic, still busy under the housing, shouted out something to the man at the helm. They spoke in Bugi, of which Miss Jones knew very little. But after a while she noticed that they had changed their course and seemed to be heading for the little uninhabited island a good deal to the lee of which they should have passed.

'Where are we going?' she asked the helmsman with sudden misgiving.

He pointed to the islet. She got up and went to the housing and called to the man to come out.

'You're not going there? Why? What's the matter?'

'I can't get to Baru,' he said.

'But you must. I insist. I order you to go to Baru.'

The man shrugged his shoulders. He turned his back on her and slipped once more under the housing. Then Ginger Ted addressed her.

'One of the blades of the propeller has broken off. He thinks he can get as far as that island. We shall have to stay the night there and he'll put on a new propeller in the morning when the tide's out.'

'I can't spend the night on an uninhabited island with three men,' she cried.

'A lot of women would jump at it.'

'I insist on going to Baru. Whatever happens we must get there tonight.'

'Don't get excited, old girl. We've got to beach the boat to put a new propeller on, and we shall be all right on the island.'

'How dare you speak to me like that! I think you're very insolent.'

'You'll be O.K. We've got plenty of grub and we'll have a snack when we land. You have a drop of arak and you'll feel like a house on fire.'

'You're an impertinent man. If you don't go to Baru I'll have you all put in prison.'

'We're not going to Baru. We can't. We're going to that island and if you don't like it you can get out and swim.'

'Oh, you'll pay for this.'

'Shut up, you old cow,' said Ginger Ted.

Miss Jones gave a gasp of anger. But she controlled herself. Even out there, in the middle of the ocean, she had too much dignity to bandy words with that vile wretch. The launch, the engine rattling horribly, crawled on. It was pitch dark now, and she could no longer see the island they were making for. Miss Jones, deeply incensed, sat with lips tight shut and a frown on her brow; she was not used to being crossed. Then the moon rose and she could see the bulk of Ginger Ted sprawling on the top of the piled sacks of copra. The glimmer of his cigarette was strangely sinister. Now the island was vaguely outlined against the sky. They reached it and the boatman ran the launch on to the beach. Suddenly Miss Jones gave a gasp. The truth had dawned on her and her anger changed to fear. Her heart beat violently. She shook in every limb. She felt dreadfully faint. She saw it all. Was the broken propeller a put-up job or was it an accident? She could not be certain; anyhow, she knew that Ginger Ted would seize the opportunity. Ginger Ted would rape her. She knew his character. He was mad about women. That was what he had done, practically, to the girl at the mission, such a good little thing she was and an excellent sempstress; they would have prosecuted him for that and he would have been sentenced to years of imprisonment only very unfortunately the innocent child had gone back to him several times and indeed had only complained of his ill usage when he left her for somebody else. They had gone to the Contrôleur about it, but he had refused to take any steps, saying in that coarse way of his that even if what the girl said was true, it didn't look very much as though it had been an altogether unpleasant experience. Ginger Ted was a scoundrel. And she was a white woman. What chance was there that he would spare her? None. She knew men. But she must pull herself together. She must keep her wits about her. She must have courage. She was determined to sell her virtue dearly, and if he killed her – well, she would rather die than yield. And if she died she would rest in the arms of Jesus. For a moment a great light blinded her eyes and she saw the mansions of her Heavenly Father. They were a grand and sumptuous mixture of a picture palace and a railway station. The mechanics and Ginger Ted jumped out of the launch and, waist-deep in water, gathered round the broken propeller. She took advantage of their preoccupation to get her case of surgical instruments out of the box. She took out the four scalpels it contained and secreted them in her clothing. If Ginger Ted touched her she would not hesitate to plunge a scalpel in his heart.

'Now then, miss, you'd better get out,' said Ginger Ted. 'You'll be better off on the beach than in the boat.'

She thought so too. At least here she would have freedom of action. Without a word she clambered over the copra sacks. He offered her his hand.

'I don't want your help,' she said coldly.

'You can go to hell,' he answered.

It was a little difficult to get out of the boat without showing her legs, but by the exercise of considerable ingenuity she managed it.

'Damned lucky we've got something to eat. We'll make a fire and then you'd better have a snack and a nip of arak.'

'I want nothing. I only want to be left alone.'

'It won't hurt me if you go hungry.'

She did not answer. She walked, with head erect, along the beach. She held the largest scalpel in her closed fist. The moon allowed her to see where she was going. She looked for a place to hide. The thick forest came down to the very edge of the beach; but, afraid of its darkness (after all, she was but a woman), she dared not plunge into its depth. She did not know what animals lurked there or what dangerous snakes. Besides, her instinct told her that it was better to keep those three bad men in sight; then if they came towards her she would be prepared. Presently she found a little hollow. She looked round. They seemed to be occupied with their own efforts and they could not see her. She slipped in. There was a rock between them and her so that she was hidden from them and yet could watch them. She saw them go to and from the boat carrying things. She saw them build a fire. It lit them luridly and she saw them sit around it and eat, and she saw the jar of arak passed from one to the other. They were all going to get drunk. What would happen to her then? It might be that she could cope with Ginger Ted, though his strength terrified her, but against three she would be powerless. A mad idea came to her to go to Ginger Ted and fall on her knees before him and beg him to spare her. He must have some spark of decent feeling in him and she had always been so convinced that there was good even in the worst of men. He must have had a mother. Perhaps he had a sister. Ah, but how could you appeal to a man blinded with lust and drunk with arak? She began to feel terribly weak. She was afraid she was going to cry. That would never do. She needed all her self-control. She bit her lip. She watched them, like a tiger watching his prey; no, not like that, like a lamb watching three hungry wolves. She saw them put more wood on the fire, and Ginger Ted, in his sarong, silhouetted by the flames. Perhaps after he had had his will of her he would pass her on to the others. How could she go back to her brother when such a thing had happened to her? Of course he would be sympathetic, but would he ever feel quite the same to her again? It would break his heart. And perhaps he would think that she ought to have resisted more. For his sake perhaps it would be better if she said nothing about it. Naturally the men would say nothing. It would mean twenty years in prison for them. But then supposing she had a baby. Miss Jones instinctively clenched her hands with horror and nearly cut herself with the scalpel. Of course it would only infuriate them if she resisted.

'What shall I do?' she cried. 'What have I done to deserve this?'

She flung herself down on her knees and prayed to God to save her. She prayed long and earnestly. She reminded God that she was a virgin and just mentioned, in case it had slipped the divine memory, how much St Paul had valued that excellent state. And then she peeped round the rock again. The three men appeared to be smoking and the fire was dying down. Now was the time that Ginger Ted's lewd thoughts might be expected to turn to the woman who was at his mercy. She smothered a cry, for suddenly he got up and walked in her direction. She felt all her muscles grow taut, and though her heart was beating furiously she clenched the scalpel firmly in her hand. But it was for another purpose that Ginger Ted had got up. Miss Jones blushed and looked away. He strolled slowly back to the others and sitting down again raised the jar of arak to his lips. Miss Jones, crouching behind the rock, watched with straining eyes. The conversation round the fire grew less and presently she divined, rather than saw, that the two natives wrapped themselves in blankets and composed themselves to slumber. She understood. This was the moment Ginger Ted had been waiting for. When they were fast asleep he would get up cautiously and without a sound, in order not to wake the others, creep stealthily towards her. Was it that he was unwilling to share her with them or did he know that his deed was so dastardly that he did not wish them to know of it? After all, he was a white man and she was a white woman. He could not have sunk so low as to allow her to suffer the violence of natives. But his plan, which was so obvious to her, had given her an idea; when she saw him coming she would scream, she would scream so loudly that it would wake the two mechanics. She remembered now that the elder, though he had only one eye, had a kind face. But Ginger Ted did not move. She was feeling terribly tired. She began to fear that she would not have the strength now to resist him. She had gone through too much. She closed her eyes for a minute.

When she opened them it was broad daylight. She must have fallen asleep and, so shattered was she by emotion, have slept till long after dawn. It gave her quite a turn. She sought to rise, but something caught in her legs. She looked and found that she was covered with two empty copra sacks. Someone had come in the night and put them over her. Ginger Ted! She gave a little scream. The horrible thought flashed through her mind that he had outraged her in her sleep. No. It was impossible. And yet he had had her at his mercy. Defenceless. And he had spared her. She blushed furiously. She raised herself to her feet, feeling a little stiff, and arranged her disordered dress. The scalpel had fallen from her hand and she picked it up. She took the two copra sacks and emerged from her hiding-place. She walked towards the boat. It was floating in the shallow water of the lagoon.

'Come on, Miss Jones,' said Ginger Ted. 'We've finished. I was just going to wake you up.'

She could not look at him, but she felt herself as red as a turkey cock.

'Have a banana?' he said.

Without a word she took it. She was very hungry, and ate it with relish.

'Step on this rock and you'll be able to get in without wetting your feet.'

Miss Jones felt as though she could sink into the ground with shame, but she did as he told her. He took hold of her arm–good heavens his hand was like an iron vice, never, never could she have struggled with him–and helped her into the launch. The mechanic started the engine and they slid out of the lagoon. In three hours they were at Baru.

That evening, having been officially released, Ginger Ted went to the Contrôleur's house. He wore no longer the prison uniform but the ragged singlet and the khaki shorts in which he had been arrested. He had had his hair cut and it fitted his head now like a little curly red cap. He was thinner. He had lost his bloated flabbiness and looked younger and better. Mr Gruyter, a friendly grin on his round face, shook hands with him and asked him to sit down. The boy brought two bottles of beer.

'I'm glad to see you hadn't forgotten my invitation, Ginger,' said the Contrôleur.

'Not likely. I've been looking forward to this for six months.'

'Here's luck, Ginger Ted.'

'Same to you, Contrôleur.'

They emptied their glasses and the Contrôleur clapped his hands. The boy brought two more bottles.

'Well, you don't bear me any malice for the sentence I gave you, I hope.'

'No bloody fear. I was mad for a minute, but I got over it. I didn't have half a bad time, you know. Nice lot of girls on that island, Contrôleur. You ought to give 'em a look over one of these days.'

'You're a bad lot, Ginger.'

'Terrible.'

'Good beer, isn't it?'

'Fine.'

'Let's have some more.'

Ginger Ted's remittance had been arriving every month and the Contrôleur now had fifty pounds for him. When the damage he had done to the Chinaman's shop was paid for there would still be over thirty.

'That's quite a lot of money, Ginger. You ought to do something useful with it.'

'I mean to,' answered Ginger. 'Spend it.'

The Contrôleur sighed.

'Well, that's what money's for, I guess.'

The Contrôleur gave his guest the news. Not much had happened during the last six months. Time on the Alas Islands did not matter very much and the rest of the world did not matter at all.

'Any wars anywhere?' asked Ginger Ted.

'No. Not that I've noticed. Harry Jervis found a pretty big pearl. He says he's going to ask a thousand quid for it.'

'I hope he gets it.'

'And Charlie McCormack's married.'

'He always was a bit soft.'

Suddenly the boy appeared and said Mr Jones wished to know if he might come in. Before the Contrôleur could give an answer Mr Jones walked in.

'I won't detain you long,' he said. 'I've been trying to get hold of this good man all day and when I heard he was here I thought you wouldn't mind my coming.'

'How is Miss Jones?' asked the Contrôleur politely. 'None the worse for her night in the open, I trust.'

'She's naturally a bit shaken. She had a temperature and I've insisted on her going to bed, but I don't think it's serious.'

The two men had got up on the missionary's entrance, and now the missionary went up to Ginger Ted and held out his hand.

'I want to thank you. You did a great and noble thing. My sister is right, one should always look for the good in their fellow-men; I am afraid I misjudged you in the past; I beg your pardon.'

He spoke very solemnly. Ginger Ted looked at him with amazement. He had not been able to prevent the missionary taking his hand. He still held it.

'What the hell are you talking about?'

'You had my sister at your mercy and you spared her. I thought you were all evil and I am ashamed. She was defenceless. She was in your power. You had pity on her. I thank you from the bottom of my heart. Neither my sister nor I will ever forget. God bless and guard you always.'

Mr Jones's voice shook a little and he turned his head away. He released Ginger Ted's hand and strode quickly to the door. Ginger Ted watched him with a blank face.

'What the blazes does he mean?' he asked.

The Contrôleur laughed. He tried to control himself, but the more he did the more he laughed. He shook and you saw the folds of his fat belly ripple under the sarong. He leaned back in his long chair and rolled from side to side. He did not laugh only with his face, he laughed with his whole body, and even the muscles of his podgy legs shook with mirth. He held his aching ribs. Ginger Ted looked at him frowning, and because he did not understand what the joke was he grew angry. He seized one of the empty beer bottles by the neck.

'If you don't stop laughing, I'll break your bloody head open,' he said.

The Contrôleur mopped his face. He swallowed a mouthful of beer. He sighed and groaned because his sides were hurting him.

'He's thanking you for having respected the virtue of Miss Jones,' he spluttered at last.

'Me?' cried Ginger Ted.

The thought took quite a long time to travel through his head, but when at last he got it he flew into a violent rage. There flowed from his mouth such a stream of blasphemous obscenities as would have startled a marine.

'That old cow,' he finished. 'What does he take me for?'

'You have the reputation of being rather hot stuff with the girls, Ginger,' giggled the little Contrôleur.

'I wouldn't touch her with the fag-end of a barge-pole. It never entered my head. The nerve. I'll wring his blasted neck. Look here, give me my money, I'm going to get drunk.'

'I don't blame you,' said the Contrôleur.

'That old cow,' repeated Ginger Ted. 'That old cow.'

He was shocked and outraged. The suggestion really shattered his sense of decency.

The Contrôleur had the money at hand and having got Ginger Ted to sign the necessary papers gave it to him.

'Go and get drunk, Ginger Ted,' he said, 'but I warn you, if you get into mischief it'll be twelve months next time.'

'I shan't get into mischief,' said Ginger Ted sombrely. He was suffering from a sense of injury. 'It's an insult,' he shouted at the Contrôleur. 'That's what it is, it's a bloody insult.'

He lurched out of the house, and as he went he muttered to himself: 'Dirty swine, dirty swine.' Ginger Ted remained drunk for a week. Mr Jones went to see the Contrôleur again.

'I'm very sorry to hear that poor fellow has taken up his evil course again,' he said. 'My sister and I are dreadfully disappointed. I'm afraid it wasn't very wise to give him so much money at once.'

'It was his own money. I had no right to keep it back.'

'Not a legal right, perhaps, but surely a moral right.'

He told the Contrôleur the story of that fearful night on the island. With her feminine instinct, Miss Jones had realized that the man, inflamed with lust, was determined to take advantage of her, and, resolved to defend herself to the last, had armed herself with a scalpel. He told the Contrôleur how she had prayed and wept and how she had hidden herself. Her agony was indescribable, and she knew that she could never have survived the shame. She rocked to and fro and every moment she thought he was coming. And there was no help anywhere and at last she had fallen asleep; she was tired out, poor thing, she had undergone more than any human being could stand, and then when she awoke she found that he had covered her with copra sacks. He had found her asleep, and surely it was her innocence, her very helplessness that had moved him, he hadn't the heart to touch her; he covered her gently with two copra sacks and crept silently away.

'It shows you that deep down in him there is something sterling. My sister feels it's our duty to save him. We must do something for him.'

'Well, in your place I wouldn't try till he's got through all his money,' said the Contrôleur, 'and then if he's not in jail you can do what you like.'

But Ginger Ted didn't want to be saved. About a fortnight after his release from prison he was sitting on a stool outside a Chinaman's shop looking vacantly down the street when he saw Miss Jones coming along. He stared at her for a minute and once more amazement seized him. He muttered to himself and there can be little doubt that his mutterings were disrespectful. But then he noticed that Miss Jones had seen him and he quickly turned his head away; he was conscious, notwithstanding, that she was looking at him. She was walking briskly, but she sensibly diminished her pace as she approached him. He thought she was going to stop and speak to him. He got up quickly and went into the shop. He did not venture to come out for at least five minutes. Half an hour later Mr Jones himself came along and he went straight up to Ginger Ted with outstretched hand.

'How do you do, Mr Edward? My sister told me I should find you here.'

Ginger Ted gave him a surly look and did not take the proffered hand. He made no answer.

'We'd be so very glad if you'd come to dinner with us next Sunday. My sister's a capital cook and she'll make you a real Australian dinner.'

'Go to hell,' said Ginger Ted.

'That's not very gracious,' said the missionary, but with a little laugh to show that he was not affronted. 'You go and see the Contrôleur from time to time, why shouldn't you come and see us? It's pleasant to talk to white people now and then. Won't you let bygones be bygones? I can assure you of a very cordial welcome.'

'I haven't got clothes fit to go out in,' said Ginger Ted sulkily.

'Oh, never mind about that. Come as you are.'

'I won't.'

'Why not? You must have a reason.'

Ginger Ted was a blunt man. He had no hesitation in saying what we should all like to when we receive unwelcome invitations.

'I don't want to.'

'I'm sorry. My sister will be very disappointed.'

Mr Jones, determined to show that he was not in the least offended, gave him a breezy nod and walked on. Forty-eight hours later there mysteriously arrived at the house in which Ginger Ted lodged a parcel containing a suit of ducks, a tennis shirt, a pair of socks, and some shoes. He was unaccustomed to receiving presents and next time he saw the Contrôleur asked him if it was he who had sent the things.

'Not on your life,' replied the Contrôleur. 'I'm perfectly indifferent to the state of your wardrobe.'

'Well, then, who the hell can have?'

'Search me.'

It was necessary from time to time for Miss Jones to see Mr Gruyter on business and shortly after this she came to see him one morning in his office. She was a capable woman and though she generally wanted him to do something he had no mind to, she did not waste his time. He was a little surprised then to discover that she had come on a very trivial errand. When he told her that he could not take cognizance of the matter in question, she did not as was her habit try to convince him, but accepted his refusal as definite. She got up to go and then as though it were an afterthought said:

'Oh, Mr Gruyter, my brother is very anxious that we should have the man they call Ginger Ted to supper with us and I've written him a little note inviting him for the day after tomorrow. I think he's rather shy, and I wonder if you'd come with him.'

'That's very kind of you.'

'My brother feels that we ought to do something for the poor fellow.'

'A woman's influence and all that sort of thing,' said the Contrôleur demurely.

'Will you persuade him to come? I'm sure he will if you make a point of it, and when he knows the way he'll come again. It seems such a pity to let a young man like that go to pieces altogether.'

The Contrôleur looked up at her. She was several inches taller than he. He thought her very unattractive. She reminded him strangely of wet linen hung on a clothes-line to dry. His eyes twinkled, but he kept a straight face.

'I'll do my best,' he said.

'How old is he?' she asked.

'According to his passport he's thirty-one.'

'And what is his real name?'

'Wilson.'

'Edward Wilson,' she said softly.

'It's astonishing that after the life he's led he should be so strong,' murmured the Contrôleur. 'He has the strength of an ox.'

'Those red-headed men sometimes are very powerful,' said Miss Jones, but spoke as though she were choking.

'Quite so,' said the Contrôleur.

Then for no obvious reason Miss Jones blushed. She hurriedly said goodbye to the Contrôleur and left his office.

'*Godverdomme!*' said the Contrôleur.

He knew now who had sent Ginger Ted the new clothes.

He met him during the course of the day and asked him whether he had heard from Miss Jones. Ginger Ted took a crumpled ball of paper out of his pocket and gave it to him. It was the invitation. It ran as follows:

Dear Mr Wilson

My brother and I would be so very glad if you would come and have supper with us next Thursday at 7.30. The Contrôleur has kindly promised to come. We have some new records from Australia which I am sure you will like. I am afraid I was not very nice to you last time we met, but I did not know you so well then, and I am big enough to admit it when I have committed an error. I hope you will forgive me and let me be your friend,

Yours sincerely,
Martha Jones

The Contrôleur noticed that she addressed him as Mr Wilson and referred to his own promise to go, so that when she told him she had already invited Ginger Ted she had a little anticipated the truth.

'What are you going to do?'

'I'm not going, if that's what you mean. Damned nerve.'

'You must answer the letter.'

'Well, I won't.'

'Now look here, Ginger, you put on those new clothes and you come as a favour to me. I've got to go and, damn it all, you can't leave me in the lurch. It won't hurt you just once.'

Ginger Ted looked at the Contrôleur suspiciously, but his face was serious and his manner sincere: he could not guess that within him the Dutchman bubbled with laughter.

'What the devil do they want me for?'

'I don't know. The pleasure of your society, I suppose.'

'Will there be any booze?'

'No, but come up to my house at seven, and we'll have a tiddly before we go.'

'Oh, all right,' said Ginger Ted sulkily.

The Contrôleur rubbed his little fat hands with joy. He was expecting a great deal of amusement from the party. But when Thursday came and seven o'clock, Ginger Ted was dead drunk and Mr Gruyter had to go alone. He told the missionary and his sister the plain truth. Mr Jones shook his head.

'I'm afraid it's no good, Martha, the man's hopeless.'

For a moment Miss Jones was silent and the Contrôleur saw two tears trickle down her long thin nose. She bit her lip.

'No one is hopeless. Everyone has some good in him. I shall pray for him every night. It would be wicked to doubt the power of God.'

Perhaps Miss Jones was right in this, but the divine providence took a very funny way of effecting its ends. Ginger Ted began to drink more heavily than ever. He was so troublesome that even Mr Gruyter lost patience with him. He made up his mind that he could not have the fellow on the island any more and resolved to deport him on the next boat that touched at Baru. Then a man died under mysterious circumstances after having been for a trip to one of the islands and the Contrôleur learnt that there had been several deaths on the same island. He sent the Chinese who was the official doctor of the group to look into the matter, and very soon received intelligence that the deaths were due to cholera. Two more took place at Baru and the certainty was forced upon him that there was an epidemic.

The Contrôleur cursed freely. He cursed in Dutch, he cursed in English, and he cursed in Malay. Then he drank a bottle of beer and smoked a cigar. After that he took thought. He knew the Chinese doctor would be useless. He was a nervous little man from Java and the natives would refuse to obey his orders. The Contrôleur was efficient and knew pretty well what must be done, but he could not do everything single-handed. He did not like Mr Jones, but just then he was thankful that he was at hand, and he sent for him at once. He was accompanied by his sister.

'You know what I want to see you about, Mr Jones,' he said abruptly.

'Yes. I've been expecting a message from you. That is why my sister has come with me. We are ready to put all our resources at your disposal. I need not tell you that my sister is as competent as a man.'

'I know. I shall be very glad of her assistance.'

They set to without further delay to discuss the steps that must be taken. Hospital huts would have to be erected and quarantine stations. The inhabitants of the various villages on the islands must be forced to take proper precautions. In a good many cases the infected villages drew their water from the same well as the uninfected, and in each case this difficulty would have to be dealt with according to circumstances. It was necessary to send round people to give orders and make sure that they were carried out. Negligence must be ruthlessly punished. The worst of it was that the natives would not obey other natives, and orders given by native policemen, themselves unconvinced of their efficacy, would certainly be disregarded. It was advisable for Mr Jones to stay at Baru, where the population was largest and his medical attention most wanted; and what with the official duties that forced him to keep in touch with headquarters, it was impossible for Mr Gruyter to visit all the other islands himself. Miss Jones must go; but the natives of some of the outlying islands were wild and treacherous; the Contrôleur had had a good deal of trouble with them. He did not like the idea of exposing her to danger.

'I'm not afraid,' she said.

'I daresay. But if you have your throat cut I shall get into trouble, and besides, we're so short-handed I don't want to risk losing your help.'

'Then let Mr Wilson come with me. He knows the natives better than anyone and can speak all their dialects.'

'Ginger Ted?' The Contrôleur stared at her. 'He's just getting over an attack of D.T.s.'

'I know,' she answered.

'You know a great deal, Miss Jones.'

Even though the moment was so serious Mr Gruyter could not but smile. He gave her a sharp look, but she met it coolly.

'There's nothing like responsibility for bringing out what there is in a man, and I think something like this may be the making of him.'

'Do you think it would be wise to trust yourself for days at a time to a man of such infamous character?' said the missionary.

'I put my trust in God,' she answered gravely.

'Do you think he'd be any use?' asked the Contrôleur. 'You know what he is.'

'I'm convinced of it.' Then she blushed. 'After all, no one knows better than I that he's capable of self-control.'

The Contrôleur bit his lip.

'Let's send for him.'

He gave a message to the sergeant and in a few minutes Ginger Ted stood before them. He looked ill. He had evidently been much shaken by his recent attack and his nerves were all to pieces. He was in rags and he had not shaved for a week. No one could have looked more disreputable.

'Look here, Ginger,' said the Contrôleur, 'it's about this cholera business. We've got to force the natives to take precautions and we want you to help us.'

'Why the hell should I?'

'No reason at all. Except philanthropy.'

'Nothing doing, Contrôleur. I'm not a philanthropist.'

'That settles that. That was all. You can go.'

But as Ginger Ted turned to the door Miss Jones stopped him.

'It was my suggestion, Mr Wilson. You see, they want me to go to Labobo and Sakunchi, and the natives there are so funny I was afraid to go alone. I thought if you came I should be safer.'

He gave her a look of extreme distaste.

'What do you suppose I care if they cut your throat?'

Miss Jones looked at him and her eyes filled with tears. She began to cry. He stood and watched her stupidly.

'There's no reason why you should.' She pulled herself together and dried her eyes. 'I'm being silly. I shall be all right. I'll go alone.'

'It's damned foolishness for a woman to go to Labobo.'

She gave him a little smile.

'I daresay it is, but you see, it's my job and I can't help myself. I'm sorry if I offended you by asking you. You must forget about it. I daresay it wasn't quite fair to ask you to take such a risk.'

For quite a minute Ginger Ted stood and looked at her. He shifted from one foot to the other. His surly face seemed to grow black.

'Oh, hell, have it your own way,' he said at last. 'I'll come with you. When d'you want to start?'

They set out next day, with drugs and disinfectants, in the Government launch. Mr Gruyter as soon as he had put the necessary work in order was to start off in a prahu in the other direction. For four months the epidemic raged. Though everything possible was done to localize it, one island after another was attacked. The Contrôleur was busy from morning to night. He had no sooner got back to Baru from one or other of the islands to do what was necessary there than he had to set off again. He distributed food and medicine. He cheered the terrified people. He supervised everything. He worked like a dog. He saw nothing of Ginger Ted, but he heard from Mr Jones that the experiment was working out beyond all hopes. The scamp was behaving himself. He had a way with the natives; and by cajolery, firmness, and on occasion the use of his fist, managed to make them take the steps necessary for their own safety. Miss Jones could congratulate herself on the success of the scheme. But the Contrôleur was too tired to be amused. When the epidemic had run its course he rejoiced because out of a population of eight thousand only six hundred had died.

Finally he was able to give the district a clean bill of health.

One evening he was sitting in his sarong on the veranda of his house and he read a French novel with the happy consciousness that once more he could take things easy. His head boy came in and told him that Ginger Ted wished to see him. He got up from his chair and shouted to him to come in. Company was just what he wanted. It had crossed the Contrôleur's mind that it would be pleasant to get drunk that night, but it is dull to get drunk alone, and he had regretfully put the thought aside. And heaven had sent Ginger Ted in the nick of time. By

God, they would make a night of it. After four months they deserved a bit of fun. Ginger Ted entered. He was wearing a clean suit of white ducks. He was shaved. He looked another man.

'Why, Ginger, you look as if you'd been spending a month at a health resort instead of nursing a pack of natives dying of cholera. And look at your clothes. Have you just stepped out of a band-box?'

Ginger Ted smiled rather sheepishly. The head boy brought two bottles of beer and poured them out.

'Help yourself, Ginger,' said the Contrôleur as he took his glass.

'I don't think I'll have any, thank you.'

The Contrôleur put down his glass and looked at Ginger Ted with amazement.

'Why, what's the matter? Aren't you thirsty?'

'I don't mind having a cup of tea.'

'A cup of what?'

'I'm on the wagon. Martha and I are going to be married.'

'Ginger!'

The Contrôleur's eyes popped out of his head. He scratched his shaven pate. 'You can't marry Miss Jones,' he said. 'No one could marry Miss Jones.'

'Well, I'm going to. That's what I've come to see you about. Owen's going to marry us in chapel, but we want to be married by Dutch law as well.'

'A joke's a joke, Ginger. What's the idea?'

'She wanted it. She fell for me that night we spent on the island when the propeller broke. She's not a bad old girl when you get to know her. It's her last chance, if you understand what I mean, and I'd like to do something to oblige her. And she wants someone to take care of her, there's no doubt about that.'

'Ginger, Ginger, before you can say knife she'll make you into a damned missionary.'

'I don't know that I'd mind that so much if we had a little mission of our own. She says I'm a bloody marvel with the natives. She says I can do more with a native in five minutes than Owen can do in a year. She says she's never known anyone with the magnetism I have. It seems a pity to waste a gift like that.'

The Contrôleur looked at him without speaking and slowly nodded his head three or four times. She'd nobbled him all right.

'I've converted seventeen already,' said Ginger Ted.

'You? I didn't know you believed in Christianity.'

'Well, I don't know that I did exactly, but when I talked to 'em and they just came into the fold like a lot of blasted sheep, well, it gave me quite a turn. Blimey, I said, I daresay there's something in it after all.'

'You should have raped her, Ginger. I wouldn't have been hard on you. I wouldn't have given you more than three years and three years is soon over.'

'Look here, Contrôleur, don't you ever let on that the thought never entered my head. Women are touchy, you know, and she'd be as sore as hell if she knew that.'

'I guessed she'd got her eye on you, but I never thought it would come to this.' The Contrôleur in an agitated manner walked up and down the veranda. 'Listen to me, old boy,' he said after an interval of reflection, 'we've had some grand times together and a friend's a friend. I'll tell you what I'll do, I'll lend you the launch and you can go and hide on one of the islands till the next ship comes along and then I'll get 'em to slow down and take you on board. You've only got one chance now and that's to cut and run.'

Ginger Ted shook his head.

'It's no good, Contrôleur, I know you mean well, but I'm going to marry the blasted woman, and that's that. You don't know the joy of bringing all them bleeding sinners to repentance, and Christ! that girl can make a treacle pudding. I haven't eaten a better one since I was a kid.'

The Contrôleur was very much disturbed. The drunken scamp was his only companion on the islands and he did not want to lose him. He discovered that he had even a certain affection for him. Next day he went to see the missionary.

'What's this I hear about your sister marrying Ginger Ted?' he asked him. 'It's the most extraordinary thing I've ever heard in my life.'

'It's true nevertheless.'

'You must do something about it. It's madness.'

'My sister is of full age and entitled to do as she pleases.'

'But you don't mean to tell me you approve of it. You know Ginger Ted. He's a bum and there are no two ways about it. Have you told her the risk she's running? I mean, bringing sinners to repentance and all that sort of thing's all right, but there are limits. And does the leopard ever change his spots?'

Then for the first time in his life the Contrôleur saw a twinkle in the missionary's eye.

'My sister is a very determined woman, Mr Gruyter,' he replied. 'From that night they spent on the island he never had a chance.'

The Contrôleur gasped. He was as surprised as the prophet when the Lord opened the mouth of the ass, and she said unto Balaam, What have I done unto thee, that thou hast smitten me these three times? Perhaps Mr Jones was human after all.

'*Allejezus!*' muttered the Contrôleur.

Before anything more could be said Miss Jones swept into the room. She was radiant. She looked ten years younger. Her cheeks were flushed and her nose was hardly red at all.

'Have you come to congratulate me, Mr Gruyter?' she cried, and her manner was sprightly and girlish. 'You see, I was right after all. Everyone has some good in them. You don't know how splendid Edward has been all through this terrible time. He's a hero. He's a saint. Even I was surprised.'

'I hope you'll be very happy, Miss Jones.'

'I know I shall. Oh, it would be wicked of me to doubt it. For it is the Lord who has brought us together.'

'Do you think so?'

'I know it. Don't you see? Except for the cholera Edward would never have found himself. Except for the cholera we should never have learnt to know one another. I have never seen the hand of God more plainly manifest.'

The Contrôleur could not but think that it was rather a clumsy device to bring those two together that necessitated the death of six hundred innocent persons, but not being well versed in the ways of omnipotence he made no remark.

'You'll never guess where we're going for our honeymoon,' said Miss Jones, perhaps a trifle archly.

'Java.'

'No, if you'll lend us the launch, we're going to that island where we were marooned. It has very tender recollections for both of us. It was there that I first guessed how fine and good Edward was. It's there I want him to have his reward.'

The Contrôleur caught his breath. He left quickly, for he thought that unless he had a bottle of beer at once he would have a fit. He was never so shocked in his life.

Louise

◆

I could never understand why Louise bothered with me. She disliked me and I knew that behind my back, in that gentle way of hers, she seldom lost the opportunity of saying a disagreeable thing about me. She had too much delicacy ever to make a direct statement, but with a hint and a sigh and a little flutter of her beautiful hands she was able to make her meaning plain. She was a mistress of cold praise. It was true that we had known one another almost intimately, for five-and-twenty years, but it was impossible for me to believe that she could be affected by the claims of old association. She thought me a coarse, brutal, cynical, and vulgar fellow. I was puzzled at her not taking the obvious course and dropping me. She did nothing of the kind; indeed, she would not leave me alone; she was constantly asking me to lunch and dine with her and once or twice a year invited me to spend a week-end at her house in the country. At last I thought that I had discovered her motive. She had an uneasy suspicion that I did not believe in her; and if that was why she did not like me, it was also why she sought my acquaintance: it galled her that I alone should look upon her as a comic figure and she could not rest till I acknowledged myself mistaken and defeated. Perhaps she had an inkling that I saw the face behind the mask and because I alone held out was determined that sooner or later I too should take the mask for the face. I was never quite certain that she was a complete humbug. I wondered whether she fooled herself as thoroughly as she fooled the world or whether there was some spark of humour at the bottom of her heart. If there was it might be that she was attracted to me, as a pair of crooks might be attracted to one another, by the knowledge that we shared a secret that was hidden from everybody else.

I knew Louise before she married. She was then a frail, delicate girl with large and melancholy eyes. Her father and mother worshipped her with an anxious adoration, for some illness, scarlet fever I think, had left her with a weak heart and she had to take the greatest care of herself. When Tom Maitland proposed to her they were dismayed, for they were convinced that she was much too delicate for the strenuous state of marriage. But they were not too well off and Tom Maitland was rich. He promised to do everything in the world for Louise and finally they entrusted her to him as a sacred charge. Tom Maitland was a big, husky fellow, very good-looking and a fine athlete. He doted on Louise. With her weak heart he could not hope to keep her with him long and he made up his mind to do everything he could to make her few years on earth happy. He gave up the games he excelled in, not because she wished him to, she was glad that he should play golf and hunt, but because by a coincidence she had a heart attack whenever he proposed to leave her for a day. If they had a difference of opinion she gave in to him at once, for she was the most submissive wife a man could have, but her heart failed her and she would be laid up, sweet and uncomplaining, for a week. He would not be such a brute as to cross her. Then they would have quite a little tussle about which should yield and it was only with difficulty that at last he persuaded her to have her own way. On one occasion seeing her walk eight miles on an expedition that she particularly wanted to make, I suggested to Tom Maitland that she was stronger than one would have thought. He shook his head and sighed.

'No, no, she's dreadfully delicate. She's been to all the best heart specialists in the world and they all say that her life hangs on a thread. But she has an unconquerable spirit.'

He told her that I had remarked on her endurance.

'I shall pay for it tomorrow,' she said to me in her plaintive way. 'I shall be at death's door.'

'I sometimes think that you're quite strong enough to do the things you want to,' I murmured.

I had noticed that if a party was amusing she could dance till five in the morning, but if it was dull she felt very poorly and Tom had to take her home early. I am afraid she did not like my reply, for though she gave me a pathetic little smile I saw no amusement in her large blue eyes.

'You can't very well expect me to fall down dead just to please you,' she answered.

Louise outlived her husband. He caught his death of cold one day when they were sailing and Louise needed all the rugs there were to keep her warm. He left her a comfortable fortune and a daughter. Louise was inconsolable. It was wonderful that she managed to survive the shock. Her friends expected her speedily to follow poor Tom Maitland to the grave. Indeed they already felt dreadfully sorry for Iris, her daughter, who would be left an orphan. They redoubled their attentions towards Louise. They would not let her stir a finger; they insisted on doing everything in the world to save her trouble. They had to, because if she was called upon to do anything tiresome or inconvenient her heart went back on her and there she was at death's door. She was entirely lost without a man to take care of her, she said, and she did not know how, with her delicate health, she was going to bring up her dear Iris. Her friends asked why she did not marry again. Oh, with her heart it was out of the question, though of course she knew that dear Tom would have wished her to, and perhaps it would be the best thing for Iris if she did; but who would want to be bothered with a wretched invalid like herself? Oddly enough more than one young man showed himself quite ready to undertake the charge and a year after Tom's death she allowed George Hobhouse to lead her to the altar. He was a fine, upstanding fellow and he was not at all badly off. I never saw anyone so grateful as he for the privilege of being allowed to take care of this frail little thing.

'I shan't live to trouble you long,' she said.

He was a soldier and an ambitious one, but he resigned his commission. Louise's health forced her to spend the winter at Monte Carlo and the summer at Deauville. He hesitated a little at throwing up his career, and Louise at first would not hear of it; but at last she yielded as she always yielded, and he prepared to make his wife's last few years as happy as might be.

'It can't be very long now,' she said. 'I'll try not to be troublesome.'

For the next two or three years Louise managed, notwithstanding her weak heart, to go beautifully dressed to all the most lively parties, to gamble very heavily, to dance and even to flirt with tall slim young men. But George Hobhouse had not the stamina of Louise's first husband and he had to brace himself now and then with a stiff drink for his day's work as Louise's second husband. It is possible that the habit would have grown on him, which Louise would not have liked at all, but very fortunately (for her) the war broke out. He rejoined his regiment and three months later was killed. It was a great shock to Louise. She felt, however, that in such a crisis she must not give way to a private grief; and if she had a heart attack nobody heard of it. In order to distract her mind she turned her villa at Monte Carlo into a hospital for convalescent officers. Her friends told her that she would never survive the strain.

'Of course it will kill me,' she said, 'I know that. But what does it matter? I must do my bit.'

It didn't kill her. She had the time of her life. There was no convalescent home in France that was more popular. I met her by chance in Paris. She was lunching at the Ritz with a tall and very handsome young Frenchman. She explained that she was there on business connected with the hospital. She told me that the officers were too charming to her. They knew how delicate she was and they wouldn't let her do a single thing. They took care of her, well–as though they were all her husbands. She sighed.

'Poor George, who would ever have thought that I with my heart should survive him?'

'And poor Tom!' I said.

I don't know why she didn't like my saying that. She gave me her plaintive smile and her beautiful eyes filled with tears.

'You always speak as though you grudged me the few years that I can expect to live.'

'By the way, your heart's much better, isn't it?'

'It'll never be better. I saw a specialist this morning and he said I must be prepared for the worst.'

'Oh, well, you've been prepared for that for nearly twenty years now, haven't you?'

When the war came to an end Louise settled in London. She was now a woman of over forty, thin and frail still, with large eyes and pale cheeks, but she did not look a day more than twenty-five. Iris, who had been at school and was now grown up, came to live with her.

'She'll take care of me,' said Louise. 'Of course, it'll be hard on her to live with such a great invalid as I am, but it can only be for such a little while, I'm sure she won't mind.'

Iris was a nice girl. She had been brought up with the knowledge that her mother's health was precarious. As a child she had never been allowed to make a noise. She had always realized that her mother must on no account be upset. And though Louise told her now that she would not hear of her sacrificing herself for a tiresome old woman the girl simply would not listen. It wasn't a question of sacrificing herself, it was a happiness to do what she could for her poor dear mother. With a sigh her mother let her do a great deal.

'It pleases the child to think she's making herself useful,' she said.

'Don't you think she ought to go out and about more?' I asked.

'That's what I'm always telling her. I can't get her to enjoy herself. Heaven knows, I never want anyone to put themselves out on my account.'

And Iris, when I remonstrated with her, said: 'Poor dear mother, she wants me to go and stay with friends and go to parties, but the moment I start off anywhere she has one of her heart attacks, so I much prefer to stay at home.'

But presently she fell in love. A young friend of mine, a very good lad, asked her to marry him and she consented. I liked the child and was glad that she was to be given at last the chance to lead a life of her own. She had never seemed to suspect that such a thing was possible. But one day the young man came to me in great distress and told me that his marriage was indefinitely postponed. Iris felt that she could not desert her mother. Of course it was really no business of mine, but I made the opportunity to go and see Louise. She was always glad to receive her friends at tea-time and now that she was older she cultivated the society of painters and writers.

'Well, I hear that Iris isn't going to be married,' I said after a little.

'I don't know about that. She's not going to be married quite as soon as I could have wished. I've begged her on my bended knees not to consider me, but she absolutely refuses to leave me.'

'Don't you think it's rather hard on her?'

'Dreadfully. Of course it can only be for a few months, but I hate the thought of anyone sacrificing themselves for me.'

'My dear Louise, you've buried two husbands, I can't see the least reason why you shouldn't bury at least two more.'

'Do you think that's funny?' she asked me in a tone that she made as offensive as she could.

'I suppose it's never struck you as strange that you're always strong enough to do anything you want to and that your weak heart only prevents you from doing things that bore you?'

'Oh, I know, I know what you've always thought of me. You've never believed that I had anything the matter with me, have you?'

I looked at her full and square.

'Never. I think you've carried out for twenty-five years a stupendous bluff. I think you're the most selfish and monstrous woman I have ever known. You ruined the lives of those two wretched men you married and now you're going to ruin the life of your daughter.'

I should not have been surprised if Louise had had a heart attack then. I fully expected her to fly into a passion. She merely gave me a gentle smile.

'My poor friend, one of these days you'll be so dreadfully sorry you said this to me.'

'Have you quite determined that Iris shall not marry this boy?'

'I've begged her to marry him. I know it'll kill me, but I don't mind. Nobody cares for me. I'm just a burden to everybody.'

'Did you tell her it would kill you?'

'She made me.'

'As if anyone ever made you do anything that you were not yourself quite determined to do.'

'She can marry her young man tomorrow if she likes. If it kills me, it kills me.'

'Well, let's risk it, shall we?'

'Haven't you got any compassion for me?'

'One can't pity anyone who amuses one as much as you amuse me,' I answered.

A faint spot of colour appeared on Louise's pale cheeks and though she smiled still her eyes were hard and angry.

'Iris shall marry in a month's time,' she said, 'and if anything happens to me I hope you and she will be able to forgive yourselves.'

Louise was as good as her word. A date was fixed, a trousseau of great magnificence was ordered, and invitations were issued. Iris and the very good lad were radiant. On the wedding-day, at ten o'clock in the morning, Louise, that devilish woman, had one of her heart attacks—and died. She died gently forgiving Iris for having killed her.

The
Promise

◆

My wife is a very unpunctual woman, so when, having arranged to lunch with her at Claridge's, I arrived there ten minutes late and did not find her I was not surprised. I ordered a cocktail. It was the height of the season and there were but two or three vacant tables in the lounge. Some of the people after an early meal were drinking their coffee, others like myself were toying with a dry Martini; the women in their summer frocks looked gay and charming and the men debonair; but I could see no one whose appearance sufficiently interested me to occupy the quarter of an hour I was expecting to wait. They were slim and pleasant to look upon, well dressed and carelessly at ease, but they were for the most part of a pattern and I observed them with tolerance rather than with curiosity. But it was two o'clock and I felt hungry. My wife tells me that she can wear neither a turquoise nor a watch, for the turquoise turns green and the watch stops; and this she attributes to the malignity of fate. I have nothing to say about the turquoise, but I sometimes think the watch might go if she wound it. I was engaged with these reflections when an attendant came up and with that hushed significance that hotel attendants affect (as though their message held a more sinister meaning than their words suggested) told me that a lady had just telephoned to say that she had been detained and could not lunch with me.

I hesitated. It is not very amusing to eat in a crowded restaurant by oneself, but it was late to go to a club and I decided that I had better stay where I was. I strolled into the dining-room. It has never given me any particular satisfaction (as it appears to do to so many elegant persons) to be known by name to the head waiters of fashionable restaurants, but on this occasion I should certainly have been glad to be greeted by less stony an eye. The *maître d'hôtel* with a set and hostile face told me that every table was occupied. I looked helplessly round the

large and stately room and on a sudden to my pleasure caught sight of someone
I knew. Lady Elizabeth Vermont was an old friend. She smiled and noticing
that she was alone I went up to her.

'Will you take pity on a hungry man and let me sit with you?' I asked.

'Oh, do. But I've nearly finished.'

She was at a little table by the side of a massive column and when I took my
place I found that notwithstanding the crowd we sat almost in privacy.

'This is a bit of luck for me,' I said. 'I was on the point of fainting from
hunger.'

She had a very agreeable smile; it did not light up her face suddenly, but
seemed rather to suffuse it by degrees with charm. It hesitated for a moment
about her lips and then slowly travelled to those great shining eyes of hers and
there softly lingered. No one surely could say that Elizabeth Vermont was cast
in the common mould. I never knew her when she was a girl, but many have
told me that then she was so lovely, it brought the tears to one's eyes, and I
could well believe it; for now, though fifty, she was still incomparable. Her
ravaged beauty made the fresh and blooming comeliness of youth a trifle
insipid. I do not like these painted faces that look all alike; and I think women
are foolish to dull their expression and obscure their personality with powder,
rouge, and lipstick. But Elizabeth Vermont painted not to imitate nature, but to
improve it; you did not question the means but applauded the result. The
flaunting boldness with which she used cosmetics increased rather than
diminished the character of that perfect face. I suppose her hair was dyed; it
was black and sleek and shining. She held herself upright as though she had
never learned to loll and she was very slim. She wore a dress of black satin, the
lines and simplicity of which were admirable, and about her neck was a long
rope of pearls. Her only other jewel was an enormous emerald which guarded
her wedding-ring, and its sombre fire emphasized the whiteness of her hand.
But it was in her hands with their reddened nails that she most clearly betrayed
her age; they had none of a girl's soft and dimpled roundness; and you could not
but look at them with a certain dismay. Before very long they would look like
the talons of a bird of prey.

Elizabeth Vermont was a remarkable woman. Of great birth, for she was the
daughter of the seventh Duke of St Erth, she married at the age of eighteen a
very rich man and started at once upon a career of astounding extravagance,
lewdness, and dissipation. She was too proud to be cautious, too reckless to
think of consequences, and within two years her husband in circumstances of
appalling scandal divorced her. She married then one of the three co-
respondents named in the case and eighteen months later ran away from him.
Then followed a succession of lovers. She became notorious for her profligacy.
Her startling beauty and her scandalous conduct held her in the public eye and
it was never very long but that she gave the gossips something to talk about. Her
name stank in the nostrils of decent people. She was a gambler, a spendthrift,
and a wanton. But though unfaithful to her lovers she was constant to her
friends and there always remained a few who would never allow, whatever she
did, that she was anything but a very nice woman. She had candour, high
spirits, and courage. She was never a hypocrite. She was generous and sincere.
It was at this period of her life that I came to know her; for great ladies, now that
religion is out of fashion, when they are very much blown upon take a flattering
interest in the arts. When they receive the cold shoulder from members of their
own class they condescend sometimes to the society of writers, painters, and

musicians. I found her an agreeable companion. She was one of those blessed persons who say quite fearlessly what they think (thus saving much useful time), and she had a ready wit. She was always willing to talk (with a diverting humour) of her lurid past. Her conversation, though uninstructed, was good, because, notwithstanding everything, she was an honest woman.

Then she did a very surprising thing. At the age of forty, she married a boy of twenty-one. Her friends said it was the maddest act of all her life, and some who had stuck to her through thick and thin, now for the boy's sake, because he was nice and it seemed shameful thus to take advantage of his inexperience, refused to have anything more to do with her. It really was the limit. They prophesied disaster, for Elizabeth Vermont was incapable of sticking to any man for more than six months, nay, they hoped for it, since it seemed the only chance for the wretched youth that his wife should behave so scandalously that he must leave her. They were all wrong. I do not know whether time was responsible for a change of heart in her, or whether Peter Vermont's innocence and simple love touched her, but the fact remains that she made him an admirable wife. They were poor, and she was extravagant, but she became a thrifty housewife; she grew on a sudden so careful of her reputation that the tongue of scandal was silenced. His happiness seemed her only concern. No one could doubt that she loved him devotedly. After being the subject of so much conversation for so long Elizabeth Vermont ceased to be talked about. It looked as though her story were told. She was a changed woman, and I amused myself with the notion that when she was a very old lady, with many years of perfect respectability behind her, the past, the lurid past, would seem to belong not to her but to someone long since dead whom once she had vaguely known. For women have an enviable faculty of forgetting.

But who can tell what the fates have in store? In the twinkling of an eye all was changed. Peter Vermont, after ten years of an ideal marriage, fell madly in love with a girl called Barbara Canton. She was a nice girl, the youngest daughter of Lord Robert Canton who was at one time Under-Secretary for Foreign Affairs, and she was pretty in a fair and fluffy way. Of course she was not for a moment to be compared with Lady Elizabeth. Many people knew what had happened, but no one could tell whether Elizabeth Vermont had any inkling of it, and they wondered how she would meet a situation that was so foreign to her experience. It was always she who had discarded her lovers; none had deserted her. For my part I thought she would make short work of little Miss Canton; I knew her courage and her adroitness. All this was in my mind now while we chatted over our luncheon. There was nothing in her demeanour, as gay, charming, and frank as usual, to suggest that anything troubled her. She talked as she always talked, lightly but with good sense and a lively perception of the ridiculous, of the various topics which the course of conversation brought forward. I enjoyed myself. I came to the conclusion that by some miracle she had no notion of Peter's changed feelings, and I explained this to myself by the supposition that her love for him was so great, she could not conceive that his for her might be less.

We drank our coffee and smoked a couple of cigarettes, and she asked me the time.

'A quarter to three.'

'I must ask for my bill.'

'Won't you let me stand you lunch?'

'Of course,' she smiled.

'Are you in a hurry?'

'I'm meeting Peter at three.'

'Oh, how is he?'

'He's very well.'

She gave a little smile, that tardy and delightful smile of hers, but I seemed to discern in it a certain mockery. For an instant she hesitated and she looked at me with deliberation.

'You like curious situations, don't you?' she said. 'You'd never guess the errand I'm bound on. I rang up Peter this morning and asked him to meet me at three. I'm going to ask him to divorce me.'

'You're not,' I cried. I felt myself flush and did not know what to say. 'I thought you got on so well together.'

'Do you think it's likely that I shouldn't know what all the world knows? I'm really not such a fool as all that.'

She was not a woman to whom it was possible to say what one did not believe and I could not pretend that I did not know what she meant. I remained silent for a second or two.

'Why should you allow yourself to be divorced?'

'Robert Canton is a stuffy old thing. I very much doubt if he'd let Barbara marry Peter if I divorced him. And for me, you know, it isn't of the smallest consequence: one divorce more or less . . .'

She shrugged her pretty shoulders.

'How do you know he wants to marry her?'

'He's head over ears in love with her.'

'Has he told you so?'

'No. He doesn't even know that I know. He's been so wretched, poor darling. He's been trying so hard not to hurt my feelings.'

'Perhaps it's only a momentary infatuation,' I hazarded. 'It may pass.'

'Why should it? Barbara's young and pretty. She's quite nice. They're very well suited to one another. And besides, what good would it do if it did pass? They love each other now and the present in love is all that matters. I'm nineteen years older than Peter. If a man stops loving a woman old enough to be his mother do you think he'll ever come to love her again? You're a novelist, you must know more about human nature than that.'

'Why should you make this sacrifice?'

'When he asked me to marry him ten years ago I promised him that when he wanted his release he should have it. You see there was so great a disproportion between our ages I thought that was only fair.'

'And are you going to keep a promise that he hasn't asked you to keep?'

She gave a little flutter of those long thin hands of hers and now I felt that there was something ominous in the dark glitter of that emerald.

'Oh, I must, you know. One must behave like a gentleman. To tell you the truth, that's why I'm lunching here today. It was at this table that he proposed to me; we were dining together, you know, and I was sitting just where I am now. The nuisance is that I'm just as much in love with him now as I was then.' She paused for a minute and I could see that she clenched her teeth. 'Well, I suppose I ought to go. Peter hates one to keep him waiting.'

She gave me a sort of little helpless look and it struck me that she simply could not bring herself to rise from her chair. But she smiled and with an abrupt gesture sprang to her feet.

'Would you like me to come with you?'

'As far as the hotel door,' she smiled.

We walked through the restaurant and the lounge and when we came to the entrance a porter swung round the revolving doors. I asked if she would like a taxi.

'No, I'd sooner walk, it's such a lovely day.' She gave me her hand. 'It's been so nice to see you. I shall go abroad tomorrow, but I expect to be in London all the autumn. Do ring me up.'

She smiled and nodded and turned away. I watched her walk up Davies Street. The air was still bland and springlike, and above the roofs little white clouds were sailing leisurely in a blue sky. She held herself very erect and the poise of her head was gallant. She was a slim and lovely figure so that people looked at her as they passed. I saw her bow graciously to some acquaintance who raised his hat, and I thought that never in a thousand years would it occur to him that she had a breaking heart. I repeat, she was a very honest woman.

The Yellow Streak

◆

The two prahus were dropping easily down-stream, one a few yards ahead of the other, and in the first sat the two white men. After seven weeks on the rivers they were glad to know that they would lodge that night in a civilized house. To Izzart, who had been in Borneo since the war, the Dyak houses and their feasts were of course an old story; but Campion, though new to the country and at first amused by the strangeness, hankered too now for chairs to sit on and a bed to sleep in. The Dyaks were hospitable, but no one could say that there was much comfort to be found in their houses, and there was a monotony in the entertainment they offered a guest which presently grew somewhat wearisome. Every evening, as the travellers reached the landing-place, the headman, bearing a flag, and the more important members of the household came down to the river to fetch them. They were led up to the long-house–a village really under one roof, built on piles, to which access was obtained by climbing up the trunk of a tree rudely notched into steps–and to the beating of drums and gongs walked up and down the whole length of it in long procession. On both sides serried throngs of brown people sat on their haunches and stared silently as the white men passed. Clean mats were unrolled and the guests seated themselves. The headman brought a live chicken and, holding it by the legs, waved it three times over their heads, called the spirits loudly to witness and uttered an invocation. Then various persons brought eggs. Arak was drunk. A girl, a very small shy thing with the grace of a flower but with something hieratic in her immobile face, held a cup to the white man's lips till it was empty and then a great shout arose. The men began to dance, one after the other, each treading his little measure, with his shield and his parang, to the accompaniment of drum and gong. After this had gone on for some time the visitors were taken into one of the rooms that led off the long platform on which was led the common life of the household and found their supper prepared for them. The girls fed them with Chinese spoons. Then everyone grew a little drunk and they all talked till the early hours of the morning.

But now their journey was done and they were on their way to the coast. They had started at dawn. The river then was very shallow and ran clear and bright over a shingly bottom; the trees leaned over it so that above there was only a strip of blue sky; but now it had broadened out, and the men were poling no longer but paddling. The trees, bamboos, wild sago like huge bunches of ostrich feathers, trees with enormous leaves and trees with feathery foliage like the acacia, coconut trees and areca palms, with their long straight white stems, the trees on the banks were immensely and violently luxuriant. Here and there, gaunt and naked, was the bare skeleton of a tree struck by lightning or dead of old age, and its whiteness against all that green was vivid. Here and there, rival kings of the forest, tall trees soared above the common level of the jungle. Then there were the parasites; in the fork of two branches great tufts of lush green leaves, or flowering creepers that covered the spreading foliage like a bride's veil; sometimes they wound round a tall trunk, a sheath of splendour, and threw long flowering arms from branch to branch. There was something thrilling in the passionate wildness of that eager growth; it had the daring abandon of the maenad rioting in the train of the god.

The day wore on, and now the heat was no longer so oppressive. Campion looked at the shabby silver watch on his wrist. It could not be long now before they reached their destination.

'What sort of a chap is Hutchinson?' he asked.

'I don't know him. I believe he's a very good sort.'

Hutchinson was the Resident in whose house they were to spend the night, and they had sent on a Dyak in a canoe to announce their arrival.

'Well, I hope he's got some whisky. I've drunk enough arak to last me a lifetime.'

Campion was a mining engineer whom the Sultan on his way to England had met at Singapore, and finding him at a loose end had commissioned to go to Sembulu and see whether he could discover any mineral which might be profitably worked. He sent Willis, the Resident at Kuala Solor, instructions to afford him every facility, and Willis had put him in the care of Izzart because Izzart spoke both Malay and Dyak like a native. This was the third trip they had made into the interior, and now Campion was to go home with his reports. They were to catch the *Sultan Ahmed*, which was due to pass the mouth of the river at dawn on the next day but one, and with any luck they should reach Kuala Solor on the same afternoon. They were both glad to get back to it. There was tennis and golf there, and the club with its billiard tables, food which was relatively good, and the comforts of civilization. Izzart was glad, too, that he would have other society than Campion's. He gave him a sidelong glance. He was a little man with a big, bald head, and though certainly fifty, strong and wiry; he had quick, shining blue eyes and a stubbly, grey moustache. He was seldom without an old briar pipe between his broken and discoloured teeth. He was neither clean nor neat, his khaki shorts were ragged and his singlet torn; he was wearing now a battered topee. He had knocked about the world since he was eighteen and had been in South Africa, in China and in Mexico. He was good company; he could tell a story well, and he was prepared to drink and drink again with anyone he met. They had got on very well together, but Izzart had never felt quite at home with him. Though they joked and laughed together, got drunk together, Izzart felt that there was no intimacy between them; for all the cordiality of their relations they remained nothing but acquaintances. He was very sensitive to the impression he made on others, and behind Campion's joviality he had felt a certain coolness; those shining blue eyes had summed him up; and it vaguely irritated Izzart that Campion had formed an opinion of him, and he did not quite know what it was. He was exasperated by the possibility that this common little man did not think entirely well of him. He desired to be liked and admired. He wanted to be popular. He wished the people he met to take an inordinate fancy to him, so that he could either reject them or a trifle condescendingly bestow his friendship on them. His inclination was to be familiar with all and sundry, but he was held back by the fear of a rebuff; sometimes he had been uneasily conscious that his effusiveness surprised the persons he lavished it on.

By some chance he had never met Hutchinson, though of course he knew all about him just as Hutchinson knew all about *him*, and they would have many common friends to talk of. Hutchinson had been at Winchester, and Izzart was glad that he could tell him that he had been at Harrow. . . .

The prahu rounded a bend in the river and suddenly, standing on a slight eminence, they saw the bungalow. In a few minutes they caught sight of the landing-stage and on it, among a little group of natives, a figure in white waving to them.

Hutchinson was a tall, stout man with a red face. His appearance led you to expect that he was breezy and self-confident, so that it was not a little surprising to discover quickly that he was diffident and even a trifle shy. When he shook hands with his guests – Izzart introduced himself and then Campion – and led them up the pathway to the bungalow, though he was plainly anxious to be civil it was not hard to see that he found it difficult to make conversation. He took them out on to the veranda and here they found on the table glasses and whisky and soda. They made themselves comfortable on long chairs. Izzart, conscious of Hutchinson's slight embarrassment with strangers, expanded; he was very hearty and voluble. He began to speak of their common acquaintances at Kuala Solor, and he managed very soon to slip in casually the information that he had been at Harrow.

'You were at Winchester, weren't you?' he asked.

'Yes.'

'I wonder if you knew George Parker. He was in my regiment. He was at Winchester. I daresay he was younger than you.'

Izzart felt that it was a bond between them that they had been at these particular schools, and it excluded Campion, who obviously had enjoyed no such advantage. They drank two or three whiskies. Izzart in half an hour began to call his host Hutchie. He talked a good deal about 'my regiment' in which he had got his company during the war, and what good fellows his brother officers were. He mentioned two or three names which could hardly be unknown to Hutchinson. They were not the sort of people that Campion was likely to have come across, and he was not sorry to administer to him a neat snub when he claimed acquaintance with someone he spoke of.

'Billie Meadows? I knew a fellow called Billie Meadows in Sinaloa many years ago,' said Campion.

'Oh, I shouldn't think it could be the same,' said Izzart, with a smile. 'Billie's by way of being a peer of the realm. He's the Lord Meadows who races. Don't you remember, he owned Spring Carrots?'

Dinner time was approaching, and after a wash and brush-up they drank a couple of gin pahits. They sat down. Hutchinson had not been to Kuala Solor for the best part of a year, and had not seen another white man for three months. He was anxious to make the most of his visitors. He could give them no wine, but there was plenty of whisky and after dinner he brought out a precious bottle of Benedictine. They were very gay. They laughed and talked a great deal. Izzart was getting on famously. He thought he had never liked a fellow more than Hutchinson, and he pressed him to come down to Kuala Solor as soon as he could. They would have a wonderful beano. Campion was left out of the conversation by Izzart with the faintly malicious intention of putting him in his place, and by Hutchinson through shyness; and presently, after yawning a good deal, he said he would go to bed. Hutchinson showed him to his room, and when he returned Izzart said to him:

'You don't want to turn in yet, do you?'

'Not on your life. Let's have another drink.'

They sat and talked. They both grew a little drunk. Presently Hutchinson told Izzart that he lived with a Malay girl, and had a couple of children by her. He had told them to keep out of sight while Campion was there.

'I expect she's asleep now,' said Hutchinson, with a glance at the door which Izzart knew led into his room, 'but I'd like you to see the kiddies in the morning.'

Just then a faint wail was heard and Hutchinson with a 'Hullo, the little devil's awake', went to the door and opened it. In a moment or two he came out of the room with a child in his arms. A woman followed him.

'He's cutting his teeth,' said Hutchinson. 'It makes him restless.'

The woman wore a sarong and a thin white jacket and she was barefoot. She was young, with fine dark eyes, and she gave Izzart when he spoke to her a bright and pleasant smile. She sat down and lit a cigarette. She answered the civil questions Izzart put to her without embarrassment, but also without effusion. Hutchinson asked her if she would have a whisky and soda, but she refused. When the two men began to talk again in English she sat on quite quietly, faintly rocking herself in her chair, and occupied with none could tell what calm thoughts.

'She's a very good girl,' said Hutchinson. 'She looks after the house and she's no trouble. Of course it's the only thing to do in a place like this.'

'I shall never do it myself,' said Izzart. 'After all, one may want to get married and then it means all sorts of botherations.'

'But who wants to get married? What a life for a white woman. I wouldn't ask a white woman to live here for anything in the world.'

'Of course it's a matter of taste. If I have any kiddies I'm going to see that they have a white mother.'

Hutchinson looked down at the little dark-skinned child he held in his arms. He gave a faint smile.

'It's funny how you get to like them,' he said. 'When they're your own it doesn't seem to matter that they've got a touch of the tar-brush.'

The woman gave the child a look, and getting up said she would take it back to bed.

'I should think we'd better all turn in,' said Hutchinson. 'God knows what the time is.'

Izzart went to his room and threw open the shutters which his boy Hassan, whom he was travelling with, had closed. Blowing out the candle so that it should not attract the mosquitoes, he sat down at the window and looked at the soft night. The whisky he had drunk made him feel very wide awake, and he was not inclined to go to bed. He took off his ducks, put on a sarong and lit a cheroot. His good-humour was gone. It was the sight of Hutchinson looking fondly at the half-caste child which had upset him.

'They've got no right to have them,' he said to himself. 'They've got no chance in the world. Ever.'

He passed his hands reflectively along his bare and hairy legs. He shuddered a little. Though he had done everything he could to develop the calves, his legs were like broomsticks. He hated them. He was uneasily conscious of them all the time. They were like a native's. Of course they were the very legs for a top-boot. In his uniform he had looked very well. He was a tall, powerful man, over six feet high, and he had a neat black moustache and neat black hair. His dark eyes were fine and mobile. He was a good-looking fellow and he knew it, and he dressed well, shabbily when shabbiness was good form, and smartly when the occasion demanded. He had loved the army, and it was a bitter blow to him when, at the end of the war, he could not remain in it. His ambitions were simple. He wanted to have two thousand a year, give smart little dinners, go to parties, and wear a uniform. He hankered after London.

Of course his mother lived there, and his mother cramped his style. He wondered how on earth he could produce her if ever he got engaged to the girl of good family (with a little money) whom he was looking for to make his wife. Because his father had been dead so long and during the later part of his career was stationed in the most remote of the Malay States, Izzart felt fairly sure that no one in Sembulu knew anything about her, but he lived in terror lest someone, running across her in London, should write over to tell people that she was a half-caste. She had been a beautiful creature when Izzart's father, an engineer in the government service, had married her; but now she was a fat old woman with grey hair who sat about all day smoking cigarettes. Izzart was twelve years old when his father died and then he could speak Malay much more fluently than English. An aunt offered to pay for his education and Mrs Izzart accompanied her son to England. She lived habitually in furnished apartments, and her rooms with their Oriental draperies and Malay silver were overheated and stuffy. She was for ever in trouble with her landladies because she would leave cigarette-ends about. Izzart hated the way she made friends with them: she would be shockingly familiar with them for a time, then there would be a falling-out, and after a violent scene she would flounce out of the house. Her only amusement was the pictures, and to these she went every day in the week. At home she wore an old and tawdry dressing-gown, but when she went out she dressed herself—but, oh, how untidily—in extravagant colours, so that it was a mortification to her dapper son. He quarrelled with her frequently, she made him impatient and he was ashamed of her; and yet he felt for her a deep tenderness; it was almost a physical bond between them, something stronger than the ordinary feeling of mother and son, so that notwithstanding the failings that exasperated him she was the only person in the world with whom he felt entirely at home.

It was owing to his father's position and his own knowledge of Malay, for his mother always spoke it to him, that after the war, finding himself with nothing to do, he had managed to enter the service of the Sultan of Sembulu. He had been a success. He played games well, he was strong and a good athlete; in the rest-house at Kuala Solor were the cups which he had won at Harrow for running and jumping, and to these he had added since others for golf and tennis. With his abundant fund of small-talk he was an asset at parties and his cheeriness made things go. He ought to have been happy and he was wretched. He wanted so much to be popular, and he had an impression, stronger than ever at this moment, that popularity escaped him. He wondered whether by any chance the men at Kuala Solor with whom he was so hail-fellow-well-met suspected that he had native blood in him. He knew very well what to expect if they ever found out. They wouldn't say he was gay and friendly then, they would say he was damned familiar; and they would say he was inefficient and careless, as the half-castes were, and when he talked of marrying a white woman they would snigger. Oh, it was so unfair! What difference could it make, that drop of native blood in his veins, and yet because of it they would always be on the watch for the expected failure at the critical moment. Everyone knew that you couldn't rely on Eurasians, sooner or later they would let you down; he knew it too, but now he asked himself whether they didn't fail because failure was expected of them. They were never given a chance, poor devils.

But a cock crew loudly. It must be very late and he was beginning to feel chilly. He got into bed. When Hassan brought him his tea next morning he had a racking headache, and when he went into breakfast he could not look at the porridge and the bacon and eggs which were set before him. Hutchinson too was feeling none too well.

'I fancy we made rather a night of it,' said his host, with a smile to conceal his faint embarrassment.

'I feel like hell,' said Izzart.

'I'm going to breakfast off a whisky and soda myself,' added Hutchinson.

Izzart asked for nothing better, and it was with distaste that they watched Campion eat with healthy appetite a substantial meal. Campion chaffed them.

'By God, Izzart, you're looking green about the gills,' he said. 'I never saw such a filthy colour.'

Izzart flushed. His swarthiness was always a sensitive point with him. But he forced himself to give a cheery laugh.

'You see, I had a Spanish grandmother,' he answered, 'and when I'm under the weather it always comes out. I remember at Harrow I fought a boy and licked him, because he called me a damned half-caste.'

'You are dark,' said Hutchinson. 'Do Malays ever ask you if you have any native blood in you?'

'Yes, damn their impudence.'

A boat with their kit had started early in the morning in order to get to the mouth of the river before them, and tell the skipper of the *Sultan Ahmed*, if by chance he arrived before he was due, that they were on their way. Campion and Izzart were to set out immediately after tiffin in order to arrive at the place where they were to spend the night before the Bore passed. A Bore is a tidal wave that, by reason of a peculiarity in the lie of the land, surges up certain rivers, and there happened to be one on the river on which they were travelling. Hutchinson had talked to them of it the night before and Campion, who had never seen such a thing, was much interested.

'This is one of the best in Borneo. It's worth looking at,' said Hutchinson.

He told them how the natives, waiting the moment, rode it and were borne up the river on its crest at a breathless and terrifying speed. He had done it once himself.

'Never no more for me,' he said. 'I was scared out of my wits.'

'I should like to try it once,' said Izzart.

'It's exciting enough, but my word, when you're in a flimsy dug-out and you know that if the native doesn't get the right moment you'll be flung in that seething torrent and you won't have a chance in a million . . . no, it's not my idea of sport.'

'I've shot a good many rapids in my day,' said Campion.

'Rapids be damned. You wait till you see the Bore. It's one of the most terrifying things I know. D'you know that at least a dozen natives are drowned in it in this river alone every year?'

They lounged about on the veranda most of the morning and Hutchinson showed them the court-house. Then gin pahits were served. They drank two or three. Izzart began to feel himself, and when at length tiffin was ready he found that he had an excellent appetite. Hutchinson had boasted of his Malay curry and when the steaming, succulent dishes were placed before them they all set to ravenously. Hutchinson pressed them to drink.

'You've got nothing to do but sleep. Why shouldn't you get drunk?'

He could not bear to let them go so soon, it was good after so long to have white men to talk to, and he lingered over the meal. He urged them to eat. They would have a filthy meal that night at the long-house and nothing to drink but arak. They had better make hay while the sun shone. Campion suggested once or twice that they should start, but Hutchinson, and Izzart too, for now he was feeling very happy and comfortable, assured him there was plenty of time. Hutchinson sent for his precious bottle of Benedictine. They had made a hole in it last night; they might as well finish it before they went.

When at last he walked down with them to the river they were all very merry and none of them was quite steady on his legs. Over the middle of the boat was an attap awning, and under this Hutchinson had had a mattress laid. The crew were prisoners who had been marched down from the jail to row the white men, and they wore dingy sarongs with the prison mark. They waited at their oars. Izzart and Campion shook hands with Hutchinson and threw themselves down on the mattress. The boat pushed off. The turbid river, wide and placid, glistened in the heat of that brilliant afternoon like polished brass. In the distance ahead of them they could see the bank with its tangle of green trees. They felt drowsy, but Izzart at least found a curious enjoyment in resisting for a little while the heaviness that was creeping over him, and he made up his mind that he would not let himself fall asleep till he had finished his cheroot. At last the stub began to burn his fingers and he flung it into the river.

'I'm going to have a wonderful snooze,' he said.

'What about the Bore?' asked Campion.

'Oh, that's all right. We needn't worry about that.'

He gave a long and noisy yawn. His limbs felt like lead. He had one moment in which he was conscious of his delicious drowsiness and then he knew nothing more. Suddenly he was awakened by Campion shaking him.

'I say, what's that?'

'What's what?'

He spoke irritably, for sleep was still heavy upon him, but with his eyes he followed Campion's gesture. He could hear nothing, but a good way off he saw two or three white-crested waves following one another. They did not look very alarming.

'Oh, I suppose that's the Bore.'

'What are we going to do about it?' cried Campion.

Izzart was scarcely yet quite awake. He smiled at the concern in Campion's voice.

'Don't worry. These fellows know all about it. They know exactly what to do. We may get a bit splashed.'

But while they were saying these few words the Bore came nearer, very quickly, with a roar like the roar of an angry sea, and Izzart saw that the waves were much higher than he had thought. He did not like the look of them and he tightened his belt so that his shorts should not slip down if the boat were upset. In a moment the waves were upon them. It was a great wall of water that seemed to tower over them, and it might have been ten or twelve feet high, but you could measure it only with your horror. It was quite plain that no boat could weather it. The first wave dashed over them, drenching them all, half filling the boat with water, and then immediately another wave struck them. The boatman began to shout. They pulled madly at their oars and the steersman yelled an order. But in that surging torrent they were helpless, and it was frightening to see how soon they lost all control of the boat. The force of the water turned it broadside on and it was carried along, helter skelter, upon the crest of the Bore. Another great wave dashed over them and the boat began to sink. Izzart and Campion scrambled out of the covered place in which they had been lying and suddenly the boat gave way under their feet and they found themselves struggling in the water. It surged and stormed around them. Izzart's first impulse was to swim for the shore, but his boy, Hassan, shouted to him to cling to the boat. For a minute or two they all did this.

'Are you all right?' Campion shouted to him.

'Yes, enjoying the bath,' said Izzart.

He imagined that the waves would pass by as the Bore ascended the river, and in a few minutes at the outside they would find themselves in calm water once more. He forgot that they were being carried along on its crest. The waves dashed over them. They clung to the gunwale and the base of the structure which supported the attap awning. Then a larger wave caught the boat as it turned over, falling upon them so that they lost their hold; there seemed nothing but a slippery bottom to cling to and Izzart's hands slithered helplessly on the greasy surface. But the boat continued to turn and he made a desperate grab at the gunwale, only to feel it slip out of his hands as the turn went on, then he caught the framework of the awning, and still it turned, turned slowly right round and once more he sought for a hand-hold on the bottom. The boat went round and round with a horrible regularity. He thought this must be because everyone was clinging to one side of it, and he tried to make the crew go round to the other. He could not make them understand. Everyone was shouting and the waves beat against them with a dull and angry roar. Each time the boat rolled over on them Izzart was pushed under water, only to come up again as the gunwale and the framework of the awning gave him something to cling to. The struggle was awful. Presently he began to get terribly out of breath, and he felt his strength leaving him. He knew that he could not hold on much longer, but he did not feel frightened, for his fatigue by now was so great that he did not very much care what happened. Hassan was by his side and he told him he was growing very tired. He thought the best thing was to make a dash for the shore, it did not look more than sixty yards away, but Hassan begged him not to. Still they were being carried along amid those seething, pounding waves. The boat went round and round and they scrambled over it like squirrels in a cage. Izzart swallowed a lot of water. He felt he was very nearly done. Hassan could not help him, but it was a comfort that he was there, for Izzart knew that his boy, used to the water all his life, was a powerful swimmer. Then, Izzart did not know why, for a minute or two the boat held bottom downwards, so that he was able to hold on to the gunwale. It was a precious thing to be able to get his breath. At that moment two dug-outs, with Malays in them riding the Bore, passed swiftly by them. They shouted for help, but the Malays averted their faces and went on. They saw the white men, and did not want to be concerned in any trouble that might befall them. It was agonizing to see them go past, callous and indifferent in their safety. But on a sudden the boat rolled round again, round and round slowly, and the miserable, exhausting scramble repeated itself. It took the heart out of you. But the short respite had helped Izzart, and he was able to struggle a little longer. Then once more he found himself so terribly out of breath that he thought his chest would burst. His strength was all gone, and he did not know now whether he had enough to try to swim for the shore. Suddenly he heard a cry.

'Izzart, Izzart. Help. Help.'

It was Campion's voice. It was a scream of agony. It sent a shock all through Izzart's nerves. Campion, Campion, what did he care for Campion? Fear seized him, a blind animal fear, and it gave him a new strength. He did not answer.

'Help me, quick, quick,' he said to Hassan.

Hassan understood him at once. By a miracle one of the oars was floating quite close to them and he pushed it into Izzart's reach. He placed a hand under Izzart's arm and they struck away from the boat. Izzart's heart was pounding and his breath came with difficulty. He felt horribly weak. The waves beat in his face. The bank looked dreadfully far away. He did not think he could ever reach it. Suddenly the boy cried that he could touch bottom and Izzart put down his legs; but he could feel nothing; he swam a few more exhausted strokes, his eyes fixed on the bank, and then, trying again, felt his feet sink into thick mud. He was thankful. He floundered on and there was the bank within reach of his hands, black mud in which he sank to his knees; he scrambled up, desperate to get out of the cruel water, and when he came to the top he found a little flat with tall rank grass all about it. He and Hassan sank down on it and lay for a while stretched out like dead men. They were so tired that they could not move. They were covered with black mud from head to foot.

But presently Izzart's mind began to work, and a pang of anguish on a sudden shook him. Campion was drowned. It was awful. He did not know how he was going to explain the disaster when he got back to Kuala Solor. They would blame him for it; he ought to have remembered the Bore and told the steersman to make for the bank and tie up the boat when he saw it coming. It wasn't his fault, it was the steersman's, he knew the river; why in God's name hadn't he had the sense to get into safety? How could he have expected that it was possible to ride that horrible torrent? Izzart's limbs shook as he remembered the wall of seething water that rushed down upon them. He must get the body and take it back to Kuala Solor. He wondered whether any of the crew were drowned too. He felt too weak to move, but Hassan now rose and wrung the water out of his sarong; he looked over the river and quickly turned to Izzart.

'Tuan, a boat is coming.'

The lalang grass prevented Izzart from seeing anything.

'Shout to them,' he said.

Hassan slipped out of view and made his way along the branch of a tree that overhung the water; he cried out and waved. Presently Izzart heard voices. There was a rapid conversation between the boy and the occupants of the boat, and then the boy came back.

'They saw us capsize, Tuan,' he said, 'and they came as soon as the Bore passed. There's a long-house on the other side. If you will cross the river they will give us sarongs and food and we can sleep there.'

Izzart for a moment felt that he could not again trust himself on the face of the treacherous water.

'What about the other tuan?' he asked.

'They do not know.'

'If he's drowned they must find the body.'

'Another boat has gone up-stream.'

Izzart did not know what to do. He was numb. Hassan put his arm round his shoulder and raised him to his feet. He made his way through the thick grass to the edge of the water, and there he saw a dug-out with two Dyaks in it. The river now once more was calm and sluggish; the great wave had passed on and no one would have dreamed that so short a while before the placid surface was like a stormy sea. The Dyaks repeated to him what they had already told the boy. Izzart could not bring himself to speak. He felt that if he said a word he would burst out crying. Hassan helped him to get in, and the Dyaks began to pull across. He fearfully wanted something to smoke, but his cigarettes and his matches, both in a hip-pocket, were soaking. The passage of the river seemed endless. The night fell and when they reached the bank the first stars were shining. He stepped ashore and one of the Dyaks took him up to the long-house. But Hassan seized the paddle he had dropped and with the other pushed out into the stream. Two or three men and some children came down to meet Izzart and he climbed to the house amid a babel of conversation. He went up the ladder and was led with greetings and excited comment to the space where the young men slept. Rattan mats were hurriedly laid to make him a couch and he sank down on them. Someone brought him a jar of arak and he took a long drink; it was rough and fiery, burning his throat, but it warmed his heart. He slipped off his shirt and trousers and put on a dry sarong which someone lent him. By chance he caught sight of the yellow new moon lying on her back, and it gave him a keen, almost a sensual, pleasure. He could not help thinking that he might at that moment be a corpse floating up the river with the tide. The moon had never looked to him more lovely. He began to feel hungry and he asked for rice. One of the women went into a room to prepare it. He was more himself now, and he began to think again of the explanations he would make at Kuala Solor. No one could really blame him because he had gone to sleep; he certainly wasn't drunk, Hutchinson would bear him out there, and how was he to suspect that the steersman would be such a damned fool? It was just rotten luck. But he couldn't think of Campion without a shudder. At last a platter of rice was brought him, and he was just about to start eating when a man ran hurriedly along and came up to him.

'The tuan's come,' he cried.

'What tuan?'

He jumped up. There was a commotion about the doorway and he stepped forward. Hassan was coming quickly towards him out of the darkness, and then he heard a voice.

'Izzart. Are you there?'

Campion advanced towards him.

'Well, here we are again. By God, that was a pretty near thing, wasn't it? You seem to have made yourself nice and comfortable. My heavens, I could do with a drink.'

His dank clothes clung round him, and he was muddy and dishevelled. But he was in excellent spirits.

'I didn't know where the hell they were bringing me. I'd made up my mind that I should have to spend the night on the bank. I thought you were drowned.'

'Here's some arak,' said Izzart.

Campion put his mouth to the jar and drank and spluttered and drank again. 'Muck, but by God it's strong.' He looked at Izzart with a grin of his broken and discoloured teeth. 'I say, old man, you look as though you'd be all the better for a wash.'

'I'll wash later.'

'All right, so will I. Tell them to get me a sarong. How did you get out?' He did not wait for an answer. 'I thought I was done for. I owe my life to these two sportsmen here.' He indicated with a cheery nod two of the Dyak prisoners whom Izzart vaguely recognized as having been part of their crew. 'They were hanging on to that blasted boat on each side of me and somehow they cottoned on to it that I was down and out. I couldn't have lasted another minute. They made signs to me that we could risk having a shot at getting to the bank, but I didn't think I had the strength. By George, I've never been so blown in all my life. I don't know how they managed it, but somehow they got hold of the mattress we'd been lying on, and they made it into a roll. They're sportsmen they are. I don't know why they didn't just save themselves without bothering about me. They gave it me. I thought it a damned poor lifebelt, but I saw the force of the proverb about a drowning man clutching at a straw. I caught hold of the damned thing and between them somehow or other they dragged me ashore.'

The danger from which he had escaped made Campion excited and voluble; but Izzart hardly listened to what he said. He heard once more, as distinctly as though the words rang now through the air, Campion's agonized cry for help, and he felt sick with terror. The blind panic raced down his nerves. Campion was talking still, but was he talking to conceal his thoughts? Izzart looked into those bright blue eyes and sought to read the sense behind the flow of words. Was there a hard glint in them or something of cynical mockery? Did he know that Izzart, leaving him to his fate, had cut and run? He flushed deeply. After all, what was there that he could have done? At such a moment it was each for himself and the devil take the hindmost. But what would they say in Kuala Solor if Campion told them that Izzart had deserted him? He ought to have stayed, he wished now with all his heart that he had, but then, then it was stronger than himself, he couldn't. Could anyone blame him? No one who had seen that fierce and seething torrent. Oh, the water and the exhaustion, so that he could have cried!

'If you're as hungry as I am you'd better have a tuck in at this rice,' he said.

Campion ate voraciously, but when Izzart had taken a mouthful or two he found that he had no appetite. Campion talked and talked. Izzart listened suspiciously. He felt that he must be alert and he drank more arak. He began to feel a little drunk.

'I shall get into the devil of a row at K. S.' he said tentatively.

'I don't know why.'

'I was told off to look after you. They won't think it was very clever of me to let you get nearly drowned.'

'It wasn't your fault. It was the fault of the damned fool of a steersman. After all, the important thing is that we're saved. By George, I thought I was finished once. I shouted out to you. I don't know if you heard me.'

'No, I didn't hear anything. There was such a devil of a row, wasn't there?'

'Perhaps you'd got away before. I don't know exactly when you did get away.'

Izzart looked at him sharply. Was it his fancy that there was an odd look in Campion's eyes?

'There was such an awful confusion,' he said. 'I was just about down and out. My boy threw me over an oar. He gave me to understand you were all right. He told me you'd got ashore.'

The oar! He ought to have given Campion the oar and told Hassan, the strong swimmer, to give *him* his help. Was it his fancy again that Campion gave him a quick and searching glance?

'I wish I could have been of more use to you,' said Izzart.

'Oh, I'm sure you had enough to do to look after yourself,' answered Campion.

The headman brought them cups of arak, and they both drank a great deal. Izzart's head began to spin and he suggested that they should turn in. Beds had been prepared for them and mosquito nets fixed. They were to set out at dawn on the rest of their journey down the river. Campion's bed was next to his, and in a few minutes he heard him snoring. He had fallen asleep the moment he lay down. The young men of the long-house and the prisoners of the boat's crew went on talking late into the night. Izzart's head now was aching horribly and he could not think. When Hassan roused him as day broke it seemed to him that he had not slept at all. Their clothes had been washed and dried, but they were bedraggled objects as they walked along the narrow pathway to the river where the prahu was waiting for them. They rowed leisurely. The morning was lovely and the great stretch of placid water gleamed in the early light.

'By George, it's fine to be alive,' said Campion.

He was grubby and unshaved. He took long breaths, and his twisted mouth was half open with a grin. You could tell that he found the air singularly good to breathe. He was delighted with the blue sky and the sunshine and the greenness of the trees. Izzart hated him. He was sure that this morning there was a difference in his manner. He did not know what to do. He had a mind to throw himself on his mercy. He had behaved like a cad, but he was sorry, he would give anything to have the chance again, but anyone might have done what he did, and if Campion gave him away he was ruined. He could never stay in Sembulu; his name would be mud in Borneo and the Straits Settlements. If he made his confession to Campion he could surely get Campion to promise to hold his tongue. But would he keep his promise? He looked at him, a shifty little man: how could he be relied on? Izzart thought of what he had said the night before. It wasn't the truth, of course, but who could know that? At all events who could prove that he hadn't honestly thought that Campion was safe? Whatever Campion said, it was only his word against Izzart's; he could laugh and shrug his shoulders and say that Campion had lost his head and didn't know what he was talking about. Besides, it wasn't certain that Campion hadn't accepted his story; in that frightful struggle for life he could be very sure of nothing. He had a temptation to go back to the subject, but he was afraid if he did that he would excite suspicion in Campion's mind. He *must* hold his tongue. That was his only chance of safety. And when they got to K.S. he would get in his story first.

'I should be completely happy now,' said Campion, 'if I only had something to smoke.'

'We shall be able to get some stinkers on board.'

Campion gave a little laugh.

'Human beings are very unreasonable,' he said. 'At the first moment I was so glad to be alive that I thought of nothing else, but now I'm beginning to regret the loss of my notes and my photographs and my shaving tackle.'

Izzart formulated the thought which had lurked at the back of his mind, but which all through the night he had refused to admit into his consciousness.

'I wish to God he'd been drowned. Then I'd have been safe.'

'There she is,' cried Campion suddenly.

Izzart looked round. They were at the mouth of the river and there was the *Sultan Ahmed* waiting for them. Izzart's heart sank: he had forgotten that she had an English skipper and that he would have to be told the story of their adventure. What would Campion say? The skipper was called Bredon, and Izzart had met him often at Kuala Solor. He was a little bluff man, with a black moustache, and a breezy manner.

'Hurry up,' he called out to them, as they rowed up, 'I've been waiting for you since dawn.' But when they climbed on board his face fell. 'Hullo, what's the matter with you?'

'Give us a drink and you shall hear all about it,' said Campion, with his crooked grin.

'Come along.'

They sat down under the awning. On a table were glasses, a bottle of whisky and soda-water. The skipper gave an order and in a few minutes they were noisily under way.

'We were caught in the Bore,' said Izzart.

He felt he must say something. His mouth was horribly dry notwithstanding the drink.

'Were you, by Jove? You're lucky not to have been drowned. What happened?'

He addressed himself to Izzart because he knew him, but it was Campion who answered. He related the whole incident, accurately, and Izzart listened with strained attention. Campion spoke in the plural when he told the early part of the story, and then, as he came to the moment when they were thrown into the water, changed to the singular. At first it was what *they* had done and now it was what happened to *him*. He left Izzart out of it. Izzart did not know whether to be relieved or alarmed. Why did he not mention him? Was it because in that mortal struggle for life he had thought of nothing but himself or—did he *know*?

'And what happened to you?' said Captain Bredon, turning to Izzart.

Izzart was about to answer when Campion spoke.

'Until I got over to the other side of the river I thought he was drowned. I don't know how he got out. I expect he hardly knows himself.'

'It was touch and go,' said Izzart with a laugh.

Why had Campion said that? He caught his eye. He was sure now that there was a gleam of amusement in it. It was awful not to be certain. He was frightened. He was ashamed. He wondered if he could not so guide the conversation, either now or later, as to ask Campion whether that was the story he was going to tell in Kuala Solor. There was nothing in it to excite anyone's suspicions. But if nobody else knew, Campion knew. He could have killed him.

'Well, I think you're both of you damned lucky to be alive,' said the skipper.

It was but a short run to Kuala Solor, and as they steamed up the Sembulu river Izzart moodily watched the banks. On each side were the mangroves and the nipahs washed by the water, and behind, the dense green of the jungle; here and there, among fruit trees, were Malay houses on piles. Night fell as they docked. Goring, of the police, came on board and shook hands with them. He was living at the rest-house just then, and as he set about his work of seeing the native passengers he told them they would find another man, Porter by name, staying there too. They would all meet at dinner. The boys took charge of their kit, and Campion and Izzart strolled along. They bathed and changed, and at half past eight the four of them assembled in the common-room for gin pahits.

'I say, what's this Bredon tells me about your being nearly drowned?' said Goring as he came in.

Izzart felt himself flush, but before he could answer Campion broke in, and it seemed certain to Izzart that he spoke in order to give the story as he chose. He felt hot with shame. Not a word was spoken in disparagement of him, not a word was said of him at all; he wondered if those two men who listened, Goring and Porter, thought it strange that he should be left out. He looked at Campion intently as he proceeded with his narration; he told it rather humorously; he did not disguise the danger in which they had been, but he made a joke of it, so that the two listeners laughed at the quandary in which they found themselves.

'A thing that's tickled me since,' said Campion, 'is that when I got over to the other bank I was black with mud from head to foot. I felt I really ought to jump in the river and have a wash, but you know I felt I'd been in that damned river as much as ever I wanted, and I said to myself; No, by George, I'll go dirty. And when I got into the long-house and saw Izzart as black as I was, I knew he'd felt just like I did.'

They laughed and Izzart forced himself to laugh too. He noticed that Campion had told the story in precisely the same words as he had used when he told it to the skipper of the *Sultan Ahmed*. There could be only one explanation of that; he knew, he knew everything, and had made up his mind exactly what story to tell. The ingenuity with which Campion gave the facts and yet left out what must be to Izzart's discredit was devilish. But why was he holding his hand? It wasn't in him not to feel contempt and resentment for the man who had callously deserted him in that moment of dreadful peril. Suddenly, in a flash of inspiration Izzart understood: he was keeping the truth to tell to Willis, the Resident. Izzart had gooseflesh as he thought of confronting Willis. He could deny, but would his denials serve him? Willis was no fool, and he would get at Hassan; Hassan could not be trusted to be silent; Hassan would give him away. Then he would be done for. Willis would suggest that he had better go home.

He had a racking headache, and after dinner he went to his room, for he wanted to be alone so that he could devise a plan of action. And then a thought came to him which made him go hot and cold: he knew that the secret which he had guarded so long was a secret to nobody. He was on a sudden certain of it. Why should he have those bright eyes and that swarthy skin? Why should he speak Malay with such ease and have learned Dyak so quickly? Of course they knew. What a fool he was ever to think that they believed that story of his, about the Spanish grandmother! They must have laughed up their sleeves when he told it, and behind his back they had called him a damned nigger. And now another thought came to him, torturing, and he asked himself whether it was on account of that wretched drop of native blood in him that when he heard Campion cry out his nerve failed him. After all, anyone might at that moment have been seized with panic; and why in God's name should he sacrifice his life to save a man's whom he cared nothing for? It was insane. But of course in K. S. they would say it was only what they expected; they would make no allowances.

At last he went to bed, but when, after tossing about recklessly for God knows how long, he fell asleep, he was awakened by a fearful dream; he seemed to be once more in that raging torrent, with the boat turning, turning; and then there was the desperate clutching at the gunwale, and the agony as it slipped out of his hands, and the water that roared over him. He was wide awake before dawn. His only chance was to see Willis and get his story in first; and he thought over carefully what he was going to say, and chose the very words he meant to use.

He got up early, and in order not to see Campion went out without breakfast. He walked along the high road till such time as he knew the Resident would be in his office, and then walked back again. He sent in his name and was ushered into Willis's room. He was a little elderly man with thin grey hair and a long yellow face.

'I'm glad to see you back safe and sound,' he said shaking hands with Izzart. 'What's this I hear about your being nearly drowned?'

Izzart, in clean ducks, his topee spotless, was a fine figure of a man. His black hair was neatly brushed, and his moustache was trimmed. He had an upright and soldierly bearing.

'I thought I'd better come and tell you at once, sir, as you told me to look after Campion.'

'Fire away.'

Izzart told his story. He made light of the danger. He gave Willis to understand that it had not been very great. They would never have been upset if they had not started so late.

'I tried to get Campion away earlier, but he'd had two or three drinks and the fact is, he didn't want to move.'

'Was he tight?'

'I don't know about that,' smiled Izzart good-humouredly. 'I shouldn't say he was cold sober.'

He went on with his story. He managed to insinuate that Campion had lost his head a little. Of course it was a very frightening business to a man who wasn't a decent swimmer: he, Izzart, had been more concerned for Campion than for himself; he knew the only chance was to keep cool, and the moment they were upset he saw that Campion had got the wind up.

'You can't blame him for that,' said the Resident.

'Of course I did everything I possibly could for him, sir, but the fact is, there wasn't anything much I could do.'

'Well, the great thing is that you both escaped. It would have been very awkward for all of us if he'd been drowned.'

'I thought I'd better come and tell you the facts before you saw Campion, sir. I fancy he's inclined to talk rather wildly about it. There's no use exaggerating.'

'On the whole your stories agree pretty well,' said Willis, with a little smile.

Izzart looked at him blankly.

'Haven't you seen Campion this morning? I heard from Goring that there'd been some trouble, and I looked in last night on my way home from the Fort after dinner. You'd already gone to bed.'

Izzart felt himself trembling, and he made a great effort to preserve his composure.

'By the way, you got away first, didn't you?'

'I don't really know, sir. You see, there was a lot of confusion.'

'You must have if you got over to the other side before he did.'

'I suppose I did then.'

'Well, thanks for coming to tell me,' said Willis, rising from his chair.

As he did so he knocked some books on the floor. They fell with a sudden thud. The unexpected sound made Izzart start violently, and he gave a gasp. The Resident looked at him quickly.

'I say, your nerves are in a pretty state.'

Izzart could not control his trembling.

'I'm very sorry, sir,' he murmured.

'I expect it's been a shock. You'd better take it easy for a few days. Why don't you get the doctor to give you something?'

'I didn't sleep very well last night.'

The Resident nodded as though he understood. Izzart left the room, and as he passed out some man he knew stopped and congratulated him on his escape. They all knew of it. He walked back to the rest-house. And as he walked, he repeated to himself the story he had told the Resident. Was it really the same story that Campion had told? He had never suspected that the Resident had already heard it from Campion. What a fool he had been to go to bed! He should never have let Campion out of his sight. Why had the Resident listened without telling him that he already knew? Now Izzart cursed himself for having suggested that Campion was drunk and had lost his head. He had said this in order to discredit him, but he knew now that it was a stupid thing to do. And why had Willis said that about his having got away first? Perhaps he was holding his hand too; perhaps he was going to make inquiries; Willis was very shrewd. But what exactly had Campion said? He must know that; at whatever cost he must know. Izzart's mind was seething, so that he felt he could hardly keep a hold on his thoughts, but he must keep calm. He felt like a hunted animal. He did not believe that Willis liked him; once or twice in the office he had blamed him because he was careless; perhaps he was just waiting till he got all the facts. Izzart was almost hysterical.

He entered the rest-house and there, sitting on a long chair, with his legs stretched out, was Campion. He was reading the papers which had arrived during their absence in the jungle. Izzart felt a blind rush of hatred well up in him as he looked at the little, shabby man who held him in the hollow of his hand.

'Hullo,' said Campion, looking up. 'Where have you been?'

To Izzart it seemed that there was in his eyes a mocking irony. He clenched his hands, and his breath came fast.

'What have you been saying to Willis about me?' he asked abruptly.

The tone in which he put the unexpected question was so harsh that Campion gave him a glance of faint surprise.

'I don't think I've been saying anything very much about you. Why?'

'He came here last night.'

Izzart looked at him intently. His brows were drawn together in an angry frown as he tried to read Campion's thoughts.

'I told him you'd gone to bed with a headache. He wanted to know about our mishap.'

'I've just seen him.'

Izzart walked up and down the large and shaded room; now, though it was still early, the sun was hot and dazzling. He felt himself in a net. He was blind with rage; he could have seized Campion by the throat and strangled him, and yet, because he did not know what he had to fight against, he felt himself powerless. He was tired and ill, and his nerves were shaken. On a sudden the anger which had given him a sort of strength left him, and he was filled with despondency. It was as though water and not blood ran through his veins; his heart sank and his knees seemed to give way. He felt that if he did not take care, he would begin to cry. He was dreadfully sorry for himself.

'Damn you, I wish to God I'd never set eyes on you,' he cried pitifully.

'What on earth's the matter?' asked Campion, with astonishment.

'Oh, don't pretend. We've been pretending for two days, and I'm fed up with it.' His voice rose shrilly, it sounded odd in that robust and powerful man. 'I'm fed up with it. I cut and run. I left you to drown. I know I behaved like a skunk. I couldn't help it.'

Campion rose slowly from his chair.

'What *are* you talking about?'

His tone was so genuinely surprised that it gave Izzart a start. A cold shiver ran down his spine.

'When you called for help I was panic-stricken. I just caught hold of an oar and got Hassan to help me get away.'

'That was the most sensible thing you could do.'

'I couldn't help you. There wasn't a thing I could do.'

'Of course not. It was damned silly of me to shout. It was waste of breath, and breath was the very thing I wanted.'

'Do you mean to say you didn't know?'

'When those fellows got me the mattress, I thought you were still clinging to the boat. I had an idea that I got away before you did.'

Izzart put both his hands to his head, and gave a hoarse cry of despair.

'My God, what a fool I've been.'

The two men stood for a while staring at one another. The silence seemed endless.

'What are you going to do now?' asked Izzart at last.

'Oh, my dear fellow, don't worry. I've been frightened too often myself to blame anyone who shows the white feather. I'm not going to tell a soul.'

'Yes, but you *know*.'

'I promise you, you can trust me. Besides, my job's done here and I'm going home. I want to catch the next boat to Singapore.' There was a pause, and Campion looked for a while reflectively at Izzart. 'There's only one thing I'd like to ask you: I've made a good many friends here, and there are one or two things I'm a little sensitive about; when you tell the story of our upset, I should be grateful if you wouldn't make out that I had behaved badly. I wouldn't like the fellows here to think that I'd lost my nerve.'

Izzart flushed darkly. He remembered what he had said to the Resident. It almost looked as though Campion had been listening over his shoulder. He cleared his throat.

'I don't know why you think I should do that.'

Campion chuckled good-naturedly, and his blue eyes were gay with amusement.

'The yellow streak,' he replied, and then, with a grin that showed his broken and discoloured teeth: 'Have a cheroot, dear boy.'

The
Force
of Circumstance

◆

She was sitting on the veranda waiting for her husband to come in for luncheon. The Malay boy had drawn the blinds when the morning lost its freshness, but she had partly raised one of them so that she could look at the river. Under the breathless sun of midday it had the white pallor of death. A native was paddling along in a dug-out so small that it hardly showed above the surface of the water. The colours of the day were ashy and wan. They were but the various tones of the heat. (It was like an Eastern melody, in the minor key, which exacerbates the nerves by its ambiguous monotony; and the ear awaits impatiently a resolution, but waits in vain.) The cicadas sang their grating song with a frenzied energy; it was as continual and monotonous as the rustling of a brook over the stones; but on a sudden it was drowned by the loud singing of a bird, mellifluous and rich; and for an instant, with a catch at her heart, she thought of the English blackbird.

Then she heard her husband's step on the gravel path behind the bungalow, the path that led to the court-house in which he had been working, and she rose from her chair to greet him. He ran up the short flight of steps, for the bungalow was built on piles, and at the door the boy was waiting to take his topee. He came into the room which served them as a dining-room and parlour, and his eyes lit up with pleasure as he saw her.

'Hulloa, Doris. Hungry?'

'Ravenous.'

'It'll only take me a minute to have a bath and then I'm ready.'

'Be quick,' she smiled.

He disappeared into his dressing-room and she heard him whistling cheerily while, with the carelessness with which she was always remonstrating, he tore off his clothes and flung them on the floor. He was twenty-nine, but he was still a school-boy; he would never grow up. That was why she had fallen in love with him, perhaps, for no amount of affection could persuade her that he was good-looking. He was a little round man, with a red face like the full moon, and blue eyes. He was rather pimply. She had examined him carefully and had been forced to confess to him that he had not a single feature which she could praise. She had told him often that he wasn't her type at all.

'I never said I was a beauty,' he laughed.

'I can't think what it is I see in you.'

But of course she knew perfectly well. He was a gay, jolly little man, who took nothing very solemnly, and he was constantly laughing. He made her laugh too. He found life an amusing rather than a serious business, and he had a charming smile. When she was with him she felt happy and good-tempered. And the deep affection which she saw in those merry blue eyes of his touched her. It was very satisfactory to be loved like that. Once, sitting on his knees, during their honeymoon she had taken his face in her hands and said to him:

'You're an ugly, little fat man, Guy, but you've got charm. I can't help loving you.'

A wave of emotion swept over her and her eyes filled with tears. She saw his face contorted for a moment with the extremity of his feeling and his voice was a little shaky when he answered.

'It's a terrible thing for me to have married a woman who's mentally deficient,' he said.

She chuckled. It was the characteristic answer which she would have liked him to make.

It was hard to realize that nine months ago she had never even heard of him. She had met him at a small place by the seaside where she was spending a month's holiday with her mother. Doris was a secretary to a Member of Parliament. Guy was home on leave. They were staying at the same hotel, and he quickly told her all about himself. He was born in Sembulu, where his father had served for thirty years under the second Sultan, and on leaving school he had entered the same service. He was devoted to the country.

'After all, England's a foreign land to me,' he told her. 'My home's Sembulu.'

And now it was her home too. He asked her to marry him at the end of the month's holiday. She had known he was going to, and had decided to refuse him. She was her widowed mother's only child and she could not go so far away from her, but when the moment came she did not quite know what happened to her, she was carried off her feet by an unexpected emotion, and she accepted him. They had been settled now for four months in the little outstation of which he was in charge. She was very happy.

She told him once that she had quite made up her mind to refuse him.

'Are you sorry you didn't?' he asked, with a merry smile in his twinkling blue eyes.

'I should have been a perfect fool if I had. What a bit of luck that fate or chance or whatever it was stepped in and took the matter entirely out of my hands!'

Now she heard Guy clatter down the steps to the bath-house. He was a noisy fellow and even with bare feet he could not be quiet. But he uttered an exclamation. He said two or three words in the local dialect and she could not understand. Then she heard someone speaking to him, not aloud, but in a sibilant whisper. Really it was too bad of people to waylay him when he was going to have his bath. He spoke again and though his voice was low she could hear that he was vexed. The other voice was raised now; it was a woman's. Doris supposed it was someone who had a complaint to make. It was like a Malay woman to come in that surreptitious way. But she was evidently getting very little from Guy, for she heard him say: Get out. That at all events she understood, and then she heard him bolt the door. There was a sound of the water he was throwing over himself (the bathing arrangements still amused her, the bath-houses were under the bedrooms, on the ground; you had a large tub of water and you sluiced yourself with a little tin pail) and in a couple of minutes he was back again in the dining-room. His hair was still wet. They sat down to luncheon.

'It's lucky I'm not a suspicious or a jealous person,' she laughed. 'I don't know that I should altogether approve of your having animated conversations with ladies while you're having your bath.'

His face, usually so cheerful, had borne a sullen look when he came in, but now it brightened.

'I wasn't exactly pleased to see her.'

'So I judged by the tone of your voice. In fact, I thought you were rather short with the young person.'

'Damned cheek, waylaying me like that!'

'What did she want?'

'Oh, I don't know. It's a woman from the kampong. She's had a row with her husband or something.'

'I wonder if it's the same one who was hanging about this morning.'

He frowned a little.

'Was there someone hanging about?'

'Yes, I went into your dressing-room to see that everything was nice and tidy, and then I went down to the bath-house. I saw someone slink out of the door as I went down the steps and when I looked out I saw a woman standing there.'

'Did you speak to her?'

'I asked her what she wanted and she said something, but I couldn't understand.'

'I'm not going to have all sorts of stray people prowling about here,' he said. 'They've got no right to come.'

He smiled, but Doris, with the quick perception of a woman in love, noticed that he smiled only with his lips, not as usual with his eyes also, and wondered what it was that troubled him.

'What have you been doing this morning?' he asked.

'Oh, nothing much. I went for a little walk.'

'Through the kampong?'

'Yes. I saw a man send a chained monkey up a tree to pick coconuts, which rather thrilled me.'

'It's rather a lark, isn't it?'

'Oh, Guy, there were two little boys watching him who were much whiter than the others. I wondered if they were half-castes. I spoke to them, but they didn't know a word of English.'

'There are two or three half-caste children in the kampong,' he answered.

'Who do they belong to?'

'Their mother is one of the village girls.'

'Who is their father?'

'Oh, my dear, that's the sort of question we think it a little dangerous to ask out here.' He paused. 'A lot of fellows have native wives, and then when they go home or marry they pension them off and send them back to their village.'

Doris was silent. The indifference with which he spoke seemed a little callous to her. There was almost a frown on her frank, open, pretty English face when she replied.

'But what about the children?'

'I have no doubt they're properly provided for. Within his means, a man generally sees that there's enough money to have them decently educated. They get jobs as clerks in a government office, you know; they're all right.'

She gave him a slightly rueful smile.

'You can't expect me to think it's a very good system.'

'You mustn't be too hard,' he smiled back.

'I'm not hard. But I'm thankful you never had a Malay wife. I should have hated it. Just think if those two little brats were yours.'

The boy changed their plates. There was never much variety in their menu. They started luncheon with river fish, dull and insipid, so that a good deal of tomato ketchup was needed to make it palatable, and then went on to some kind of stew. Guy poured Worcester Sauce over it.

'The old Sultan didn't think it was a white woman's country,' he said presently. 'He rather encouraged people to–keep house with native girls. Of course things have changed now. The country's perfectly quiet and I suppose we know better how to cope with the climate.'

'But, Guy, the eldest of those boys wasn't more than seven or eight and the other was about five.'

'It's awfully lonely on an outstation. Why, often one doesn't see another white man for six months on end. A fellow comes out here when he's only a boy.' He gave her that charming smile of his which transfigured his round, plain face. 'There are excuses, you know.'

She always found that smile irresistible. It was his best argument. Her eyes grew once more soft and tender.

'I'm sure there are.' She stretched her hand across the little table and put it on his. 'I'm very lucky to have caught you so young. Honestly, it would upset me dreadfully if I were told that you had lived like that.'

He took her hand and pressed it.

'Are you happy here, darling?'

'Desperately.'

She looked very cool and fresh in her linen frock. The heat did not distress her. She had no more than the prettiness of youth, though her brown eyes were fine; but she had a pleasing frankness of expression, and her dark, short hair was neat and glossy. She gave you the impression of a girl of spirit and you felt sure that the Member of Parliament for whom she worked had in her a very competent secretary.

'I loved the country at once,' she said. 'Although I'm alone so much I don't think I've ever once felt lonely.'

Of course she had read novels about the Malay Archipelago and she had formed an impression of a sombre land with great ominous rivers and a silent, impenetrable jungle. When a little coasting steamer set them down at the mouth of the river, where a large boat, manned by a dozen Dyaks, was waiting to take them to the station, her breath was taken away by the beauty, friendly rather than awe-inspiring, of the scene. It had a gaiety, like the joyful singing of birds in the trees, which she had never expected. On each bank of the river were mangroves and nipah palms, and behind them the dense green of the forest. In the distance stretched blue mountains, range upon range, as far as the eye could see. She had no sense of confinement nor of gloom, but rather of openness and wide spaces where the exultant fancy could wander with delight. The green glittered in the sunshine and the sky was blithe and cheerful. The gracious land seemed to offer her a smiling welcome.

They rowed on, hugging a bank, and high overhead flew a pair of doves. A flash of colour, like a living jewel, dashed across their path. It was a kingfisher. Two monkeys, with their dangling tails, sat side by side on a branch. On the horizon, over there on the other side of the broad and turbid river, beyond the jungle, was a row of little white clouds, the only clouds in the sky, and they looked like a row of ballet-girls, dressed in white, waiting at the back of the stage, alert and merry, for the curtain to go up. Her heart was filled with joy; and now, remembering it all, her eyes rested on her husband with a grateful, assured affection.

And what fun it had been to arrange their living-room! It was very big. On the floor, when she arrived, was torn and dirty matting; on the walls of unpainted wood hung (much too high up) photogravures of Academy pictures, Dyak shields, and parangs. The tables were covered with Dyak cloth in sombre colours, and on them stood pieces of Brunei brass-ware, much in need of cleaning, empty cigarette tins, and bits of Malay silver. There was a rough wooden shelf with cheap editions of novels and a number of old travel books in battered leather; and another shelf was crowded with empty bottles. It was a bachelor's room, untidy but stiff; and though it amused her she found it intolerably pathetic. It was a dreary, comfortless life that Guy had led there, and she threw her arms round his neck and kissed him.

'You poor darling,' she laughed.

She had deft hands and she soon made the room habitable. She arranged this and that, and what she could not do with she turned out. Her wedding-presents helped. Now the room was friendly and comfortable. In glass vases were lovely orchids and in great bowls huge masses of flowering shrubs. She felt an inordinate pride because it was her house (she had never in her life lived in anything but a poky flat) and she had made it charming for him.

'Are you pleased with me?' she asked when she had finished.

'Quite,' he smiled.

The deliberate understatement was much to her mind. How jolly it was that they should understand each other so well! They were both of them shy of displaying emotion, and it was only at rare moments that they used with one another anything but ironic banter.

They finished luncheon and he threw himself into a long chair to have a sleep. She went towards her room. She was a little surprised that he drew her to him as she passed and, making her bend down, kissed her lips. They were not in the habit of exchanging embraces at odd hours of the day.

'A full tummy is making you sentimental, my poor lamb,' she chaffed him.

'Get out and don't let me see you again for at least two hours.'

'Don't snore.'

She left him. They had risen at dawn and in five minutes were fast asleep.

Doris was awakened by the sound of her husband's splashing in the bath-house. The walls of the bungalow were like a sounding board and not a thing that one of them did escaped the other. She felt too lazy to move, but she heard the boy bring the tea things in, so she jumped up and ran down into her own bath-house. The water, not cold but cool, was deliciously refreshing. When she came into the sitting-room Guy was taking the rackets out of the press, for they played tennis in the short cool of the evening. The night fell at six.

The tennis-court was two or three hundred yards from the bungalow and after tea, anxious not to lose time, they strolled down to it.

'Oh, look' said Doris, 'there's that girl that I saw this morning.'

Guy turned quickly. His eyes rested for a moment on a native woman, but he did not speak.

'What a pretty sarong she's got,' said Doris. 'I wonder where it comes fom.'

They passed her. She was slight and small, with the large, dark, starry eyes of her race and a mass of raven hair. She did not stir as they went by, but stared at them strangely. Doris saw then that she was not quite so young as she had at first thought. Her features were a trifle heavy and her skin was dark, but she was very pretty. She held a small child in her arms. Doris smiled a little as she saw it, but no answering smile moved the woman's lips. Her face remained impassive. She did not look at Guy, she looked only at Doris, and he walked on as though he did not see her. Doris turned to him.

'Isn't that baby a duck?'

'I didn't notice.'

She was puzzled by the look of his face. It was deathly white, and the pimples which not a little distressed her were more than commonly red.

'Did you notice her hands and feet? She might be a duchess.'

'All natives have good hands and feet,' he answered, but not jovially as was his wont; it was as though he forced himself to speak.

But Doris was intrigued.

'Who is she, d'you know?'

'She's one of the girls in the kampong.'

They had reached the court now. When Guy went up to the net to see that it was taut he looked back. The girl was still standing where they had passed her. Their eyes met.

'Shall I serve?' said Doris.

'Yes, you've got the balls on your side.'

He played very badly. Generally he gave her fifteen and beat her, but today she won easily. And he played silently. Generally he was a noisy player, shouting all the time, cursing his foolishness when he missed a ball and chaffing her when he placed one out of her reach.

'You're off your game, young man,' she cried.

'Not a bit,' he said.

He began to slam the balls, trying to beat her, and sent one after the other into the net. She had never seen him with that set face. Was it possible that he was a little out of temper because he was not playing well? The light fell, and they ceased to play. The woman whom they had passed stood in exactly the same position as when they came and once more, with expressionless face, she watched them go.

The blinds on the veranda were raised now, and on the table between their two long chairs were bottles and soda-water. This was the hour at which they had the first drink of the day and Guy mixed a couple of gin slings. The river stretched widely before them, and on the further bank the jungle was wrapped in the mystery of the approaching night. A native was silently rowing up-stream, standing at the bow of the boat, with two oars.

'I played like a fool,' said Guy, breaking a silence. 'I'm feeling a bit under the weather.'

'I'm sorry. You're not going to have fever, are you?'

'Oh, no. I shall be all right tomorrow.'

Darkness closed in upon them. The frogs croaked loudly and, now and then they heard a few short notes from some singing bird of the night. Fireflies flitted across the veranda and they made the trees that surrounded it look like Christmas trees lit with tiny candles. They sparkled softly. Doris thought she heard a little sigh. It vaguely disturbed her. Guy was always so full of gaiety.

'What is it, old man?' she said gently. 'Tell mother.'

'Nothing. Time for another drink,' he answered breezily.

Next day he was as cheerful as ever and the mail came. The coasting steamer passed the mouth of the river twice a month, once on its way to the coalfields and once on its way back. On the outward journey it brought mail, which Guy sent a boat down to fetch. Its arrival was the excitement of their uneventful lives. For the first day or two they skimmed rapidly all that had come, letters, English papers and papers from Singapore, magazines and books, leaving for the ensuing weeks a more exact perusal. They snatched the illustrated papers from one another. If Doris had not been so absorbed she might have noticed that there was a change in Guy. She would have found it hard to describe and harder still to explain. There was in his eyes a sort of watchfulness and in his mouth a slight droop of anxiety.

Then, perhaps a week later, one morning when she was sitting in the shaded room studying a Malay grammar (for she was industriously learning the language) she heard a commotion in the compound. She heard the house boy's voice, he was speaking angrily, the voice of another man, perhaps it was the water-carrier's, and then a woman's, shrill and vituperative. There was a scuffle. She went to the window and opened the shutters. The water-carrier had hold of a woman's arm and was dragging her along, while the house boy was pushing her from behind with both hands. Doris recognized her at once as the woman she had seen one morning loitering in the compound and later in the day outside the tennis-court. She was holding a baby against her breast. All three were shouting angrily.

'Stop,' cried Doris. 'What are you doing?'

At the sound of her voice the water-carrier let go suddenly and the woman, still pushed from behind, fell to the ground. There was a sudden silence and the house boy looked sullenly into space. The water-carrier hesitated a moment and then slunk away. The woman raised herself slowly to her feet, arranged the baby on her arm, and stood impassive, staring at Doris. The boy said something to her which Doris could not have heard even if she had understood: the woman by no change of face showed that his words meant anything to her; but she slowly strolled away. The boy followed her to the gate of the compound. Doris called to him as he walked back, but he pretended not to hear. She was growing angry now and she called more sharply.

'Come here at once,' she cried.

Suddenly, avoiding her wrathful glance, he came towards the bungalow. He came in and stood at the door. He looked at her sulkily.

'What were you doing with that woman?' she asked abruptly.

'Tuan say she no come here.'

'You mustn't treat a woman like that. I won't have it. I shall tell the tuan exactly what I saw.'

The boy did not answer. He looked away, but she felt that he was watching her through his long eyelashes. She dismissed him.

'That'll do.'

Without a word he turned and went back to the servants' quarters. She was exasperated and she found it impossible to give her attention once more to the Malay exercises. In a little while the boy came in to lay the cloth for luncheon. On a sudden he went to the door.

'What is it?' she asked.

'Tuan just coming.'

He went out to take Guy's hat from him. His quick ears had caught the footsteps before they were audible to her. Guy did not as usual come up the steps immediately; he paused, and Doris at once surmised that the boy had gone down to meet him in order to tell him of the morning's incident. She shrugged her shoulders. The boy evidently wanted to get his story in first. But she was astonished when Guy came in. His face was ashy.

'Guy, what on earth's the matter?'

He flushed a sudden hot red.

'Nothing. Why?'

She was so taken aback that she let him pass into his room without a word of what she had meant to speak of at once. It took him longer than usual to have his bath and change his clothes and luncheon was served when he came in.

'Guy,' she said, as they sat down, 'that woman we saw the other day was here again this morning.'

'So I've heard,' he answered.

'The boys were treating her brutally. I had to stop them. You must really speak to them about it.'

Though the Malay understood every word she said, he made no sign that he heard. He handed her the toast.

'She's been told not to come here. I gave instructions that if she showed herself again she was to be turned out.'

'Were they obliged to be so rough?'

'She refused to go. I don't think they were any rougher than they could help.'

'It was horrible to see a woman treated like that. She had a baby in her arms.'

'Hardly a baby. It's three years old.'

'How d'you know?'

'I know all about her. She hasn't the least right to come here pestering everybody.'

'What does she want?'

'She wants to do exactly what she did. She wants to make a disturbance.'

For a little while Doris did not speak. She was surprised at her husband's tone. He spoke tersely. He spoke as though all this were no concern of hers. She thought him a little unkind. He was nervous and irritable.

'I doubt if we shall be able to play tennis this afternoon,' he said. 'It looks to me as though we were going to have a storm.'

The rain was falling when she awoke and it was impossible to go out. During tea Guy was silent and abstracted. She got her sewing and began to work. Guy sat down to read such of the English papers as he had not yet gone through from cover to cover; but he was restless; he walked up and down the large room and then went out on the veranda. He looked at the steady rain. What was he thinking of? Doris was vaguely uneasy.

It was not till after dinner that he spoke. During the simple meal he had exerted himself to be his usual gay self, but the exertion was apparent. The rain had ceased and the night was starry. They sat on the veranda. In order not to attract insects they had put out the lamp in the sitting-room. At their feet, with a mighty, formidable sluggishness, silent, mysterious, and fatal, flowed the river. It had the terrible deliberation and the relentlessness of destiny.

'Doris, I've got something to say to you,' he said suddenly.

His voice was very strange. Was it her fancy that he had difficulty in keeping it quite steady? She felt a little pang in her heart because he was in distress, and she put her hand gently into his. He drew it away.

'It's rather a long story. I'm afraid it's not a very nice one and I find it rather difficult to tell. I'm going to ask you not to interrupt me, or to say anything, till I've finished.'

In the darkness she could not see his face, but she felt that it was haggard. She did not answer. He spoke in a voice so low that it hardly broke the silence of the night.

'I was only eighteen when I came out here. I came straight from school. I spent three months in Kuala Solor, and then I was sent to a station up the Sembulu river. Of course there was a Resident there and his wife. I lived in the court-house, but I used to have my meals with them and spend the evening with them. I had an awfully good time. Then the fellow who was here fell ill and had to go home. We were short of men on account of the war and I was put in charge of this place. Of course I was very young, but I spoke the language like a native, and they remembered my father. I was as pleased as punch to be on my own.'

He was silent while he knocked the ashes out of his pipe and refilled it. When he lit a match Doris, without looking at him, noticed that his hand was unsteady.

'I'd never been alone before. Of course at home there'd been father and mother and generally an assistant. And then at school naturally there were always fellows about. On the way out on the boat, there were people all the time, and at K.S., and the same at my first post. The people there were almost like my own people. I seemed always to live in a crowd. I like people. I'm a noisy blighter. I like to have a good time. All sorts of things make me laugh and you must have somebody to laugh with. But it was different here. Of course it was all right in the day time; I had my work and I could talk to the Dyaks. Although they were head-hunters in those days and now and then I had a bit of trouble with them, they were an awfully decent lot of fellows. I got on very well with them. Of course I should have liked a white man to gas to, but they were better than nothing, and it was easier for me because they didn't look upon me quite as a stranger. I liked the work too. It was rather lonely in the evening to sit on the veranda and drink a gin and bitters by myself, but I could read. And the boys were about. My own boy was called Abdul. He'd known my father. When I got tired of reading I could give him a shout and have a bit of a jaw with him.

'It was the nights that did for me. After dinner the boys shut up and went away to sleep in the kampong. I was all alone. There wasn't a sound in the bungalow except now and then the croak of the chik-chak. It used to come out of the silence, suddenly, so that it made me jump. Over in the kampong I heard the sound of a gong or fire-crackers. They were having a good time, they weren't so far away, but I had to stay where I was. I was tired of reading. I couldn't have been more of a prisoner if I'd been in jail. Night after night it was the same. I tried drinking three or four whiskies, but it's poor fun drinking alone, and it didn't cheer me up; it only made me feel rather rotten next day. I tried going to bed immediately after dinner, but I couldn't sleep. I used to lie in bed, getting hotter and hotter, and more wide awake, till I didn't know what to do with myself. By George, those nights were long. D'you know, I got so low, I was so sorry for myself that sometimes–it makes me laugh now when I think of it, but I was only nineteen and a half–sometimes I used to cry.

'Then, one evening, after dinner, Abdul had cleared away and was just going off, when he gave a little cough. He said, wasn't I lonely in the house all night by myself? "Oh, no, that's all right," I said. I didn't want him to know what a damned fool I was, but I expect he knew all right. He stood there without speaking, and I knew he wanted to say something to me. "What is it?" I said. "Spit it out." Then he said that if I'd like to have a girl to come and live with me he knew one who was willing. She was a very good girl and he could recommend her. She'd be no trouble and it would be someone to have about the bungalow. She'd mend my things for me. . . . I felt awfully low. It had been raining all day and I hadn't been able to get any exercise. I knew I shouldn't sleep for hours. It wouldn't cost me very much money, he said, her people were poor and they'd be quite satisfied with a small present. Two hundred Straits dollars. "You look," he said. "If you don't like her you send her away." I asked him where she was. "She's here," he said. "I call her." He went to the door. She'd been waiting on the steps with her mother. They came in and sat down on the floor. I gave them some sweets. She was shy, of course, but cool enough, and when I said something to her she gave me a smile. She was very young, hardly more than a child, they said she was fifteen. She was awfully pretty, and she had her best clothes on. We began to talk. She didn't say much, but she laughed a lot when I chaffed her. Abdul said I'd find she had plenty to say for herself when she got to know me. He told her to come and sit by me. She giggled and refused, but her mother told her to come, and I made room for her on the chair. She blushed and laughed, but she came, and then she snuggled up to me. The boy laughed too. "You see, she's taken to you already," he said. "Do you want her to stay?" he asked. "Do you want to?" I said to her. She hid her face, laughing, on my shoulder. She was very soft and small. "Very well," I said, "let her stay."'

Guy leaned forward and helped himself to a whisky and soda.

'May I speak now?' asked Doris.

'Wait a minute, I haven't finished yet. I wasn't in love with her, not even at the beginning. I only took her so as to have somebody about the bungalow. I think I should have gone mad if I hadn't, or else taken to drink. I was at the end of my tether. I was too young to be quite alone. I was never in love with anyone but you.' He hesitated a moment. 'She lived here till I went home last year on leave. It's the woman you've seen hanging about.'

'Yes, I guessed that. She had a baby in her arms. Is that your child?'

'Yes. It's a little girl.'

'Is it the only one?'

'You saw the two small boys the other day in the kampong. You mentioned them.'

'She has three children then?'

'Yes.'

'It's quite a family you've got.'

She felt the sudden gesture which her remark forced from him, but she did not speak.

'Didn't she know that you were married till you suddenly turned up here
with a wife?' asked Doris.

'She knew I was going to be married.'

'When?'

'I sent her back to the village before I left here. I told her it was all over. I gave
her what I'd promised. She always knew it was only a temporary arrangement.
I was fed up with it. I told her I was going to marry a white woman.'

'But you hadn't even seen me then.'

'No, I know. But I'd made up my mind to marry when I was home.' He
chuckled in his old manner. 'I don't mind telling you that I was getting rather
despondent about it when I met you. I fell in love with you at first sight and
then I knew it was either you or nobody.'

'Why didn't you tell me? Don't you think it would have been only fair to give
me a chance of judging for myself? It might have occurred to you that it would
be rather a shock to a girl to find out that her husband had lived for ten years
with another girl and had three children.'

'I couldn't expect you to understand. The circumstances out here are
peculiar. It's the regular thing. Five men out of six do it. I thought perhaps it
would shock you and I didn't want to lose you. You see, I was most awfully in
love with you. I am now, darling. There was no reason that you should ever
know. I didn't expect to come back here. One seldom goes back to the same
station after home leave. When we came here I offered her money if she'd go to
some other village. First she said she would and then she changed her mind.'

'Why have you told me now?'

'She's been making the most awful scenes. I don't know how she found out
that you knew nothing about it. As soon as she did she began to blackmail me.
I've had to give her an awful lot of money. I gave orders that she wasn't to be
allowed in the compound. This morning she made that scene just to attract
your attention. She wanted to frighten me. It couldn't go on like that. I thought
the only thing was to make a clean breast of it.'

There was a long silence as he finished. At last he put his hand on hers.

'You do understand, Doris, don't you? I know I've been to blame.'

She did not move her hand. He felt it cold beneath his.

'Is she jealous?'

'I daresay there were all sorts of perks when she was living here, and I don't
suppose she much likes not getting them any longer. But she was never in love
with me any more than I was in love with her. Native women never do really
care for white men, you know.'

'And the children?'

'Oh, the children are all right. I've provided for them. As soon as the boys are
old enough I shall send them to school at Singapore.'

'Do they mean nothing to you at all?'

He hesitated.

'I want to be quite frank with you. I should be sorry if anything happened to
them. When the first one was expected I thought I'd be much fonder of it than I
ever had been of its mother. I suppose I should have been if it had been white.
Of course, when it was a baby it was rather funny and touching, but I had no
particular feeling that it was mine. I think that's what it is; you see, I have no
sense of their belonging to me. I've reproached myself sometimes, because it
seemed rather unnatural, but the honest truth is that they're no more to me
than if they were somebody else's children. Of course a lot of slush is talked

about children by people who haven't got any.'

Now she had heard everything. He waited for her to speak, but she said nothing. She sat motionless.

'Is there anything more you want to ask me, Doris?' he said at last.

'No I've got rather a headache. I think I shall go to bed.' Her voice was as steady as ever. 'I don't quite know what to say. Of course it's been all very unexpected. You must give me a little time to think.'

'Are you very angry with me?'

'No. Not at all. Only–only I must be left to myself for a while. Don't move. I'm going to bed.'

She rose from her long chair and put her hand on his shoulder.

'It's so very hot tonight. I wish you'd sleep in your dressing-room. Good night.'

She was gone. He heard her lock the door of her bedroom.

She was pale next day and he could see that she had not slept. There was no bitterness in her manner, she talked as usual, but without ease; she spoke of this and that as though she were making conversation with a stranger. They had never had a quarrel, but it seemed to Guy that so would she talk if they had had a disagreement and the subsequent reconciliation had left her still wounded. The look in her eyes puzzled him; he seemed to read in them a strange fear. Immediately after dinner she said:

'I'm not feeling very well tonight. I think I shall go straight to bed.'

'Oh, my poor darling, I'm so sorry,' he cried.

'It's nothing. I shall be all right in a day or two.'

'I shall come in and say good night to you later.'

'No, don't do that. I shall try and get straight off to sleep.'

'Well, then, kiss me before you go.'

He saw that she flushed. For an instant she seemed to hesitate; then, with averted eyes, she leaned towards him. He took her in his arms and sought her lips, but she turned her face away and he kissed her cheek. She left him quickly and again he heard the key turn softly in the lock of her door. He flung himself heavily on the chair. He tried to read, but his ear was attentive to the smallest sound in his wife's room. She had said she was going to bed, but he did not hear her move. The silence in there made him unaccountably nervous. Shading the lamp with his hand he saw that there was a glimmer under her door; she had not put out her light. What on earth was she doing? He put down his book. It would not have surprised him if she had been angry and had made a scene, or if she had cried; he could have coped with that; but her calmness frightened him. And then what was that fear which he had seen so plainly in her eyes? He thought once more over all he had said to her on the previous night. He didn't know how else he could have put it. After all, the chief point was that he'd done the same as everybody else, and it was all over long before he met her. Of course as things turned out he had been a fool, but anyone could be wise after the event. He put his hand to his heart. Funny how it hurt him there.

'I suppose that's the sort of thing people mean when they say they're heartbroken,' he said to himself. 'I wonder how long it's going on like this?'

Should he knock at the door and tell her he must speak to her? It was better to have it out. He *must* make her understand. But the silence scared him. Not a sound! Perhaps it was better to leave her alone. Of course it had been a shock. He must give her as long as she wanted. After all, she knew how devotedly he loved her. Patience, that was the only thing; perhaps she was fighting it out with herself; he must give her time; he must have patience. Next morning he asked her if she had slept better.

'Yes, much,' she said.

'Are you very angry with me?' he asked piteously.

She looked at him with candid, open eyes.

'Not a bit.'

'Oh my dear, I'm so glad. I've been a brute and a beast. I know it's been hateful for you. But do forgive me. I've been so miserable.'

'I do forgive you. I don't even blame you.'

He gave her a little rueful smile, and there was in his eyes the look of a whipped dog.

'I haven't much liked sleeping by myself the last two nights.'

She glanced away. Her face grew a trifle paler.

'I've had the bed in my room taken away. It took up so much space. I've had a little camp bed put there instead.'

'My dear, what are you talking about?'

Now she looked at him steadily.

'I'm not going to live with you as your wife again.'

'Never?'

She shook her head. He looked at her in a puzzled way. He could hardly believe he had heard aright and his heart began to beat painfully.

'But that's awfully unfair to me, Doris.'

'Don't you think it was a little unfair to me to bring me out here in the circumstances?'

'But you just said you didn't blame me.'

'That's quite true. But the other's different. I can't do it.'

'But how are we going to live together like that?'

She stared at the floor. She seemed to ponder deeply.

'When you wanted to kiss me on the lips last night I—it almost made me sick.'

'Doris.'

She looked at him suddenly and her eyes were cold and hostile.

'That bed I slept on, is that the bed in which she had her children?' She saw him flush deeply. 'Oh, it's horrible. How could you?' She wrung her hands, and her twisting, tortured fingers looked like little writhing snakes. But she made a great effort and controlled herself. 'My mind is quite made up. I don't want to be unkind to you, but there are some things that you can't ask me to do. I've thought it all over. I've been thinking of nothing else since you told me, night and day, till I'm exhausted. My first instinct was to get up and go. At once. The steamer will be here in two or three days.'

'Doesn't it mean anything to you that I love you?'

'Oh, I know you love me. I'm not going to do that. I want to give us both a chance. I have loved you so, Guy.' Her voice broke, but she did not cry. 'I don't want to be unreasonable. Heaven knows, I don't want to be unkind. Guy, will you give me time?'

'I don't know quite what you mean.'

'I just want you to leave me alone. I'm frightened by the feelings that I have.'

He had been right then; she was afraid.

'What feelings?'

'Please don't ask me. I don't want to say anything to wound you. Perhaps I shall get over them. Heaven knows, I want to. I'll try, I promise you. I'll try. Give me six months. I'll do everything in the world for you, but just that one thing.' She made a little gesture of appeal. 'There's no reason why we shouldn't be happy enough together. If you really love me you'll–you'll have patience.'

He sighed deeply.

'Very well,' he said. 'Naturally I don't want to force you to do anything you don't like. It shall be as you say.'

He sat heavily for a little, as though, on a sudden grown old, it was an effort to move; then he got up.

'I'll be getting along to the office.'

He took his topee and went out.

A month passed. Women conceal their feelings better than men and a stranger visiting them would never have guessed that Doris was in any way troubled. But in Guy the strain was obvious; his round, good-natured face was drawn, and in his eyes was a hungry, harassed look. He watched Doris. She was gay and she chaffed him as she had been used to do; they played tennis together; they chatted about one thing and another. But it was evident that she was merely playing a part, and at last, unable to contain himself, he tried to speak again of his connexions with the Malay woman.

'Oh, Guy, there's no object in going back on all that,' she answered breezily. 'We've said all we had to say about it and I don't blame you for anything.'

'Why do you punish me then?'

'My poor boy, I don't want to punish you. It's not my fault if . . .' she shrugged her shoulders. 'Human nature is very odd.'

'I don't understand.'

'Don't try.'

The words might have been harsh, but she softened them with a pleasant, friendly smile. Every night when she went to bed she leaned over Guy and lightly kissed his cheek. Her lips only touched it. It was as though a moth had just brushed his face in its flight.

A second month passed, then a third, and suddenly the six months which had seemed so interminable were over. Guy asked himself whether she remembered. He gave a strained attention now to everything she said, to every look on her face and to every gesture of her hands. She remained impenetrable. She had asked him to give her six months; well, he had.

The coasting steamer passed the mouth of the river, dropped their mail, and went on its way. Guy busily wrote the letters which it would pick up on the return journey. Two or three days passed by. It was a Tuesday and the prahu was to start at dawn on Thursday to await the steamer. Except at meal time when Doris exerted herself to make conversation they had not of late talked very much together; and after dinner as usual they took their books and began to read; but when the boy had finished clearing away and was gone for the night Doris put down hers.

'Guy, I have something I want to say to you,' she murmured.

His heart gave a sudden thud against his ribs and he felt himself change colour.

'Oh, my dear, don't look like that, it's not so very terrible,' she laughed.

But he thought her voice trembled a little.

'Well?'

'I want you to do something for me.'

'My darling, I'll do anything in the world for you.'

He put out his hand to take hers, but she drew it away.

'I want you to let me go home.'

'You?' he cried, aghast. 'When? Why?'

'I've borne it as long as I can. I'm at the end of my tether.'

'How long do you want to go for? For always?'

'I don't know. I think so.' She gathered determination. 'Yes, for always.'

'Oh, my God!'

His voice broke and she thought he was going to cry.

'Oh, Guy, don't blame me. It really is not my fault. I can't help myself.'

'You asked me for six months. I accepted your terms. You can't say I've made a nuisance of myself.'

'No, no.'

'I've tried not to let you see what a rotten time I was having.'

'I know. I'm very grateful to you. You've been awfully kind to me. Listen, Guy, I want to tell you again that I don't blame you for a single thing you did. After all, you were only a boy, and you did no more than the others; I know what the loneliness is here. Oh, my dear, I'm so dreadfully sorry for you. I knew all that from the beginning. That's why I asked you for six months. My common sense tells me that I'm making a mountain out of a molehill. I'm unreasonable; I'm being unfair to you. But, you see, common sense has nothing to do with it; my whole soul is in revolt. When I see the woman and her children in the village I just feel my legs shaking. Everything in this house; when I think of that bed I slept in it gives me goose-flesh. . . . You don't know what I've endured.'

'I think I've persuaded her to go away. And I've applied for a transfer.'

'That wouldn't help. She'll be there always. You belong to them, you don't belong to me. I think perhaps I could have stood it if there'd only been one child, but three; and the boys are quite big boys. For ten years you lived with her.' And now she came out with what she had been working up to. She was desperate. 'It's a physical thing, I can't help it, it's stronger than I am. I think of those thin black arms of hers round you and it fills me with a physical nausea. I think of you holding those little black babies in your arms. Oh, it's loathsome. The touch of you is odious to me. Each night, when I've kissed you, I've had to brace myself up to it. I've had to clench my hands and force myself to touch your cheek.' Now she was clasping and unclasping her fingers in a nervous agony, and her voice was out of control. 'I know it's I who am to blame now. I'm a silly, hysterical woman. I thought I'd get over it. I can't, and now I never shall. I've brought it all on myself; I'm willing to take the consequences; if you say I must stay here, I'll stay, but if I stay I shall die. I beseech you to let me go.'

And now the tears which she had restrained so long overflowed and she wept broken-heartedly. He had never seen her cry before.

'Of course I don't want to keep you here against your will,' he said hoarsely.

Exhausted, she leaned back in her chair. Her features were all twisted and awry. It was horribly painful to see the abandonment of grief on that face which was habitually so placid.

'I'm so sorry, Guy. I've broken your life, but I've broken mine too. And we might have been so happy.'

'When do you want to go? On Thursday?'

'Yes.'

She looked at him piteously. He buried his face in his hands. At last he looked up.

'I'm tired out,' he muttered.

'May I go?'

'Yes.'

For two minutes perhaps they sat there without a word. She started when the chik-chak gave its piercing, hoarse, and strangely human cry. Guy rose and went out on to the veranda. He leaned against the rail and looked at the softly flowing water. He heard Doris go into her room.

Next morning, up earlier than usual, he went to her door and knocked.

'Yes?'

'I have to go up-river today. I shan't be back till late.'

'All right.'

She understood. He had arranged to be away all day in order not to be about while she was packing. It was heartbreaking work. When she had packed her clothes she looked round the sitting-room at the things that belonged to her. It seemed dreadful to take them. She left everything but the photograph of her mother. Guy did not come in till ten o'clock at night.

'I'm sorry I couldn't get back to dinner,' he said. 'The headman at the village I had to go to had a lot of things for me to attend to.'

She saw his eyes wander about the room and notice that her mother's photograph no longer stood in its place.

'Is everything quite ready?' he asked. 'I've ordered the boatman to be at the steps at dawn.'

'I told the boy to wake me at five.'

'I'd better give you some money.' He went to his desk and wrote out a cheque. He took some notes from a drawer. 'Here's some cash to take you as far as Singapore and at Singapore you'll be able to change the cheque.'

'Thank you.'

'Would you like me to come to the mouth of the river with you?'

'Oh, I think it would be better if we said good-bye here.'

'All right. I think I shall turn in. I've had a long day and I'm dead beat.'

He did not even touch her hand. He went into his room. In a few minutes she heard him throw himself on his bed. For a little while she sat looking for the last time round that room in which she had been so happy and so miserable. She sighed deeply. She got up and went into her own room. Everything was packed except the one or two things she needed for the night.

It was dark when the boy awakened them. They dressed hurriedly and when they were ready breakfast was waiting for them. Presently they heard the boat row up to the landing-stage below the bungalow, and then the servants carried down her luggage. It was a poor pretence they made of eating. The darkness thinned away and the river was ghostly. It was not yet day, but it was no longer night. In the silence the voices of the natives at the landing-stage were very clear. Guy glanced at his wife's untouched plate.

'If you've finished we might stroll down. I think you ought to be starting.'

She did not answer. She rose from the table. She went into her room to see that nothing had been forgotten and then side by side with him walked down the steps. A little winding path led them to the river. At the landing-stage the native guards in their smart uniform were lined up and they presented arms as Guy and Doris passed. The head boatman gave her his hand as she stepped into the boat. She turned and looked at Guy. She wanted desperately to say one last word of comfort, once more to ask for his forgiveness, but she seemed to be struck dumb.

He stretched out his hand.

'Well, good-bye, I hope you'll have a jolly journey.'

They shook hands.

Guy nodded to the head boatman and the boat pushed off. The dawn now was creeping along the river mistily, but the night lurked still in the dark trees of the jungle. He stood at the landing-stage till the boat was lost in the shadows of the morning. With a sigh he turned away. He nodded absent-mindedly when the guard once more presented arms. But when he reached the bungalow he called the boy. He went round the room picking out everything that had belonged to Doris.

'Pack all these things up,' he said. 'It's no good leaving them about.'

Then he sat down on the veranda and watched the day advance gradually like a bitter, an unmerited, and an overwhelming sorrow. At last he looked at his watch. It was time for him to go to the office.

In the afternoon he could not sleep, his head ached miserably, so he took his gun and went for a tramp in the jungle. He shot nothing, but he walked in order to tire himself out. Towards sunset he came back and had two or three drinks, and then it was time to dress for dinner. There wasn't much use in dressing now; he might just as well be comfortable; he put on a loose native jacket and a sarong. That was what he had been accustomed to wear before Doris came. He was barefoot. He ate his dinner listlessly and the boy cleared away and went. He sat down to read the *Tatler*. The bungalow was very silent. He could not read and let the paper fall on his knees. He was exhausted. He could not think and his mind was strangely vacant. The chik-chak was noisy that night and its hoarse and sudden cry seemed to mock him. You could hardly believe that this reverberating sound came from so small a throat. Presently he heard a discreet cough.

'Who's there?' he cried.

There was a pause. He looked at the door. The chik-chak laughed harshly. A small boy sidled in and stood on the threshold. It was a little half-caste boy in a tattered singlet and a sarong. It was the elder of his two sons.

'What do you want?' said Guy.

The boy came forward into the room and sat down, tucking his legs away under him.

'Who told you to come here?'

'My mother sent me. She says, do you want anything?'

Guy looked at the boy intently. The boy said nothing more. He sat and waited, his eyes cast down shyly. Then Guy in deep and bitter reflection buried his face in his hands. What was the use? It was finished. Finished! He surrendered. He sat back in his chair and sighed deeply.

'Tell your mother to pack up her things and yours. She can come back.'

'When?' asked the boy, impassively.

Hot tears trickled down Guy's funny, round spotty face.

'Tonight.'

Flotsam and Jetsam

◆

Norman Grange was a rubber-planter. He was up before daybreak to take the roll-call of his labour and then walked over the estate to see that the tapping was properly done. This duty performed, he came home, bathed and changed, and now with his wife opposite him he was eating the substantial meal, half breakfast and half luncheon, which in Borneo is called brunch. He read as he ate. The dining-room was dingy. The worn electro-plate, the shabby cruet, the chipped dishes betokened poverty, but a poverty accepted with apathy. A few flowers would have brightened the table, but there was apparently no one to care how things looked. When Grange had finished he belched, filled his pipe and lit it, rose from the table and went out on to the veranda. He took no more notice of his wife than if she had not been there. He lay down in a long rattan chair and went on reading. Mrs Grange reached over for a tin of cigarettes and smoked while she sipped her tea. Suddenly she looked out, for the house boy came up the steps and accompanied by two men went up to her husband. One was a Dyak and the other Chinese. Strangers seldom came and she could not imagine what they wanted. She got up and went to the door to listen. Though she had lived in Borneo for so many years she knew no more Malay than was necessary to get along with the boys, and she only vaguely understood what was said. She gathered from her husband's tone that something had happened to annoy him. He seemed to be asking questions first of the Chink and then of the Dyak; it looked as though they were pressing him to do something he didn't want to do; at length, however, with a frown on his face he raised himself from his chair and followed by the men walked down the steps. Curious to see where he was going she slipped out on to the veranda. He had taken the path that led down to the river. She shrugged her thin shoulders and went to her room. Presently she gave a violent start, for she heard her husband call her.

'Vesta.'

She came out.

'Get a bed ready. There's a white man in a prahu at the landing-stage. He's damned ill.'

'Who is he?'

'How the hell should I know? They're just bringing him up.'

'We can't have anyone to stay here.'

'Shut up and do as I tell you.'

He left her on that and again went down to the river. Mrs Grange called the boy and told him to put sheets on the bed in the spare room. Then she stood at the top of the steps and waited. In a little while she saw her husband coming back and behind him a huddle of Dyaks carrying a man on a mattress. She stood aside to let them pass and caught a glimpse of a white face.

'What shall I do?' she asked her husband.

'Get out and keep quiet.'

'Polite, aren't you?'

The sick man was taken into the room, and in two or three minutes the Dyaks and Grange came out.

'I'm going to see about his kit. I'll have it brought up. His boy's looking after him and there's no cause for you to butt in!'

'What's the matter with him?'

'Malaria. His boatmen are afraid he's going to die and won't take him on. His name's Skelton.'

'He isn't going to die, is he?'

'If he does we'll bury him.'

But Skelton didn't die. He woke next morning to find himself in a room, in bed and under a mosquito-net. He couldn't think where he was. It was a cheap iron bed and the mattress was hard, but to lie on it was a relief after the discomfort of the prahu. He could see nothing of the room but a chest of drawers, roughly made by a native carpenter, and a wooden chair. Opposite was a doorway, with a blind down, and this he guessed led on to a veranda.

'Kong,' he called.

The blind was drawn aside and his boy came in. The Chinaman's face broke into a grin when he saw that his master was free from fever.

'You more better, Tuan. Velly glad.'

'Where the devil am I?'

Kong explained.

'Luggage all right?' asked Skelton.

'Yes, him all light.'

'What's the name of this fellow—the tuan whose house this is?'

'Mr Norman Grange.'

To confirm what he said he showed Skelton a little book in which the owner's name was written. It was Grange. Skelton noticed that the book was Bacon's *Essays*. It was curious to find it in a planter's house away up a river in Borneo.

'Tell him I'd be glad to see him.'

'Tuan out. Him come presently.'

'What about my having a wash? And by God, I want a shave.'

He tried to get out of bed, but his head swam and with a bewildered cry he sank back. But Kong shaved and washed him, and changed the shorts and singlet in which he had been lying ever since he fell ill for a sarong and a baju. After that he was glad to lie still. But presently Kong came in and said that the tuan of the house was back. There was a knock on the door and a large stoutish man stepped in.

'I hear you're better,' he said.

'Oh, much. It's terribly kind of you to have taken me in like this. It seems awful, planting myself on you.'

Grange answered a trifle harshly.

'That's all right. You were pretty bad, you know. No wonder those Dyaks wanted to get rid of you.'

'I don't want to impose myself on you longer than I need. If I could hire a launch here, or a prahu, I could get off this afternoon.'

'There's no launch to hire. You'd better stay a bit. You must be as weak as a rat.'

'I'm afraid I shall be a frightful bother.'

'I don't see why. You've got your own boy and he'll look after you.'

Grange had just come in from his round of the estate and wore dirty shorts, a khaki shirt open at the neck, and an old, battered terai hat. He looked as shabby as a beachcomber. He took off his hat to wipe his sweating brow; he had close-cropped grey hair; his face was red, a broad, fleshy face, with a large mouth under a stubble of grey moustache, a short, pugnacious nose and small, mean eyes.

'I wonder if you could let me have something to read,' said Skelton.

'What sort of thing?'

'I don't mind so long as it's lightish.'

'I'm not much of a novel reader myself, but I'll send you in two or three books. My wife can provide you with novels. They'll be trash, because that's all she reads. But it may suit you.'

With a nod he withdrew. Not a very likeable man. But he was obviously very poor, the room in which Skelton lay, something in Grange's appearance, indicated that; he was probably manager of an estate on a cut salary, and it was not unlikely that the expense of a guest and his servant was unwelcome. Living in that remote spot, and so seeing white men but seldom, it might be that he was ill at ease with strangers. Some people improve unbelievably on acquaintance. But his hard, shifty little eyes were disconcerting; they gave the lie to the red face and the massive frame which otherwise might have persuaded you that this was a jolly sort of fellow with whom you could quickly make friends.

After a while, the house boy came in with a parcel of books. There were half a dozen novels by authors he had never heard of, and a glance told him they were slop; these must be Mrs Grange's; and then there was a Boswell's *Johnson*, Borrow's *Lavengro*, and Lamb's *Essays*. It was an odd choice. They were not the books you would have expected to find in a planter's house. In most planters' houses there is not more than a shelf or two of books and for the most part they're detective stories. Skelton had a disinterested curiosity in human creatures, and he amused himself now by trying to make out from the books Norman Grange had sent, from the look of him, and from the few words they had exchanged, what sort of a man he could be. Skelton was a little surprised that his host did not come to see him again that day; it looked as though he were going to content himself with giving his uninvited guest board and lodging, but were not sufficiently interested in him to seek his company. Next morning he felt well enough to get up, and with Kong's help settled himself in a long chair on the veranda. It badly needed a coat of paint. The bungalow stood on the brow of a hill, about fifty yards from the river; and on the opposite bank, looking very small across that great stretch of water, you could see native houses on piles nestling among the greenery. Skelton had not yet the activity of mind to read steadily, and after a page or two, his thoughts wandering, he found himself content to watch idly the sluggish flow of the turbid stream. Suddenly he heard a step. He saw the little elderly woman come towards him, and knowing that this must be Mrs Grange tried to get up.

'Don't move,' she said. 'I only came to see if you had everything you wanted.'

She wore a blue cotton dress, simple enough, but more suited to a young girl than to a woman of her age; her short hair was tousled, as though on getting out of bed she had scarcely troubled to pass a comb through it, and dyed a vivid yellow, but badly, and the roots showed white. Her skin was raddled and dry, and there was a great dab of rouge on each cheek-bone, put on however so clumsily that you could not for a moment take it for a natural colour, and a smear of lipstick on her mouth. But the strangest thing about her was a tic she had that made her jerk her head as though she were beckoning you to an inner room. It seemed to come at regular intervals, perhaps three times a minute, and her left hand was in almost constant movement; it was not quite a tremble, it was a rapid twirl as though she wanted to draw your attention to something behind her back. Skelton was startled by her appearance and embarrassed by her tic.

'I hope I'm not making myself too great a nuisance,' he said. 'I think I shall be well enough to make a move tomorrow or the day after.'

'It's not often we see anybody in a place like this, you know. It's a treat to have someone to talk to.'

'Won't you sit down? I'll tell my boy to bring you a chair.'

'Norman said I was to leave you alone.'

'I haven't spoken to a white person for two years. I've been longing for a good old talk.'

Her head twitched violently, more quickly than usual, and her hand gave that queer spasmodic gesture.

'He won't be back for another hour. I'll get a chair.'

Skelton told her who he was and what he had been doing, but he discovered that she had questioned his boy and already knew all about him.

'You must be crazy to get back to England?' she asked.

'I shan't be sorry.'

Suddenly Mrs Grange seemed to be attacked by what one could only describe as a nerve storm. Her head twitched so madly, her hand shook with such fury, that it was disconcerting. You could only look away.

'I haven't been to England for sixteen years,' she said.

'You don't mean that? Why, I thought all you planters went home every five years at the longest.'

'We can't afford it; we're broke to the wide. Norman put all the money he had into this plantation, and it hasn't really paid for years. It only just brings in enough to keep us from starvation. Of course it doesn't matter to Norman. He isn't English really.'

'He looks English enough.'

'He was born in Sarawak. His father was in the government service. If he's anything he's a native of Borneo.'

Then, without warning, she began to cry. It was horribly painful to see the tears running down the raddled, painted cheeks of that woman with the constant tic. Skelton knew neither what to say nor what to do. He did what was probably the best thing, he kept silent. She dried her eyes.

'You must think me a silly old fool. I sometimes wonder that after all these years I can still cry. I suppose it's in my nature. I always could cry very easy when I was on the stage.'

'Oh, were you on the stage?'

'Yes, before I married. That's how I met Norman. We were playing in Singapore and he was there on holiday. I don't suppose I shall ever see England any more. I shall stay here till I die and every day of my life I shall look at that beastly river. I shall never get away now. Never.'

'How did you happen to find yourself in Singapore?'

'Well, it was soon after the war, I couldn't get anything to suit me in London, I'd been on the stage a good many years and I was fed up with playing small parts: the agents told me a fellow called Victor Palace was taking a company out East. His wife was playing lead, but I could play seconds. They'd got half a dozen plays, comedies, you know, and farces. The salary wasn't much, but they were going to Egypt and India, the Malay States and China and then down to Australia. It was a chance to see the world and I accepted. We didn't do badly in Cairo and I think we made money in India, but Burma wasn't much good, and Siam was worse; Penang was a disaster and so were the rest of the Malay States. Well, one day Victor called us together and said he was bust, he hadn't got the money for our fares to Hong Kong, and the tour was a wash-out and he was very sorry but we'd have to get back home as best we could. Of course we told him he couldn't do that to us. You never heard such a row. Well, the long and short of it was that he said we could have the scenery and the props if we thought they was any good to us, but as to money it was no use asking for it because he damned well hadn't got it. And next day we found out that him and his wife, without saying a word to anybody, had got on a French boat and skipped. I was in a rare state, I can tell you. I had a few pounds I'd saved out of me salary, and that was all; somebody told me if we was absolutely stranded the government would have to send us home, but only steerage, and I didn't much fancy that. We got the Press to put our plight before the public and someone came along with the proposition that we should give a benefit performance. Well, we did, but it wasn't much without Victor or his wife, and by the time we'd paid the expenses we weren't any better off than we'd been before. I was at my wits' end, I don't mind telling you. It was then that Norman proposed to me. The funny thing is that I hardly knew him. He'd taken me for a drive round the island and we'd had tea two or three times at the Europe and danced. Men don't often do things for you without wanting something in return, and I thought he expected to get a little bit of fun, but I'd had a good deal of experience and I thought he'd be clever if he got round me. But when he asked me to marry him, well, I was so surprised, I couldn't hardly believe me own ears. He said he'd got his own estate in Borneo and it only wanted a little patience and he'd make a packet. And it was on the banks of a fine river and all round was the jungle. He made it sound very romantic. I was getting on, you know, I was thirty, it wasn't going to be any easier to get work as time went on, and it was tempting to have a house of me own and all that. Never to have to hang around agents' offices no more. Never to have to lay awake no more and wonder how you was going to pay next week's rent. He wasn't a bad-looking chap in those days, brown and big and virile. No one could say I was willing to marry anybody just to . . .' Suddenly she stopped. 'There he is. Don't say you've seen me.'

She picked up the chair she had been sitting in and quickly slipped away with it into the house. Skelton was bewildered. Her grotesque appearance, the painful tears, her story told with that incessant twitching; and then her obvious fear when she heard her husband's voice in the compound, and her hurried escape; he could make nothing of it.

In a few minutes Norman Grange stumped along the veranda.

'I hear you're better,' he said.

'Much, thanks.'

'If you care to join us at brunch I'll have a place laid for you.'

'I'd like it very much.'

'All right. I'm just going to have a bath and a change.'

He walked away. Presently a boy came along and told Skelton his tuan was waiting for him. Skelton followed him into a small sitting-room, with the jalousies drawn to keep out the heat, an uncomfortable, overcrowded room with a medley of furniture, English and Chinese, and occasional tables littered with worthless junk. It was neither cosy nor cool. Grange had changed into a sarong and baju and in the native dress looked coarse but powerful. He introduced Skelton to his wife. She shook hands with him as though she had never seen him before and uttered a few polite words of greeting. The boy announced that their meal was ready and they went into the dining-room.

'I hear that you've been in this bloody country for some time,' said Grange.

'Two years. I'm an anthropologist and I wanted to study the manners and customs of tribes that haven't had any contact with civilization.'

Skelton felt that he should tell his host how it had come about that he had been forced to accept a hospitality which he could not but feel was grudgingly offered. After leaving the village that had been his headquarters he had journeyed by land for ten days till he reached the river. There he had engaged a couple of prahus, one for himself and his luggage and the other for Kong, his Chinese servant, and the camp equipment, to take him to the coast. The long trek across country had been hard going and he found it very comfortable to lie on a mattress under an awning of rattan matting and take his ease. All the time he had been away Skelton had been in perfect health, and as he travelled down the river he could not but think that he was very lucky; but even as the thought passed through his mind, it occurred to him that if he happened just then to congratulate himself on his good fortune in this respect, it was because he did not feel quite so well as usual. It was true that he had been forced to drink a great deal of arak the night before at the long-house where he had put up, but he was used to it and that hardly accounted for his headache. He had a general sense of malaise. He was wearing nothing but shorts and a singlet, and he felt chilly; it was curious because the sun was shining fiercely and when he put his hand on the gunwale of the prahu the heat was hardly bearable. If he had had a coat handy he would have put it on. He grew colder and colder and presently his teeth began to chatter; he huddled up on his mattress, shivering all over in a desperate effort to get warm. He could not fail to guess what was the matter.

'Christ,' he groaned. 'Malaria.'

He called the headman, who was steering the prahu.

'Get Kong.'

The headman shouted to the second prahu and ordered his own paddlers to stop. In a moment the two boats were side by side and Kong stepped in.

'I've got fever, Kong,' gasped Skelton. 'Get me the medicine chest and, for God's sake, blankets. I'm freezing to death.'

Kong gave his master a big dose of quinine and piled on him what coverings they had. They started off again.

Skelton was too ill to be taken ashore when they tied up for the night and so passed it in the prahu. All next day and the day after he was very ill. Sometimes one or other of the crew came and looked at him, and often the headman stayed for quite a long while staring at him thoughtfully.

'How many days to the coast?' Skelton asked the boy.

'Four, five.' He paused for a minute. 'Headman, he no go coast. He say, he wantchee go home.'

'Tell him to go to hell.'

'Headman say, you velly sick, you die. If you die and he go coast he catchee trouble.'

'I'm not thinking of dying,' said Skelton. 'I shall be all right. It's just an ordinary go of malaria.'

Kong did not answer. The silence irritated Skelton. He knew that the Chinese had something in mind that he did not like to say.

'Spit it out, you fool,' he cried.

Skelton's heart sank when Kong told him the truth. When they reached their resting-place that night the headman was going to demand his money and slip away with the two prahus before dawn. He was too frightened to carry a dying man farther. Skelton had no strength to take the determined attitude that might have availed him; he could only hope by the offer of more money to persuade the headman to carry out his agreement. The day passed in long arguments between Kong and the headman, but when they tied up for the night the headman came to Skelton and told him sulkily that he would go no farther. There was a long-house near by where he might get lodging till he grew better. He began to unload the baggage. Skelton refused to move. He got Kong to give him his revolver and swore to shoot anyone who came near him.

Kong, the crew, and the headman went up to the long-house and Skelton was left alone. Hour after hour he lay there, the fever burning his body and his mouth parched, while muddled thoughts hammered away in his brain. Then there were lights and the sound of men talking. The Chinese boy came with the headman and another man, whom Skelton had not yet seen, from the neighbouring long-house. He did his best to understand what Kong was telling him. It appeared that a few hours down-stream there lived a white man, and to his house, if that would satisfy Skelton, the headman was willing to take him.

'More better you say yes,' said Kong. 'Maybe white man has launch, then we go down to coast chop-chop.'

'Who is he?'

'Planter,' said Kong. 'This fellow say, him have rubber estate.'

Skelton was too tired to argue further. All he wanted just then was to sleep. He accepted the compromise.

'To tell you the truth,' he finished, 'I don't remember much more till I woke up yesterday morning to find myself an uninvited guest in your house.'

'I don't blame those Dyaks, you know,' said Grange. 'When I came down to the prahu and saw you, I thought you were for it.'

Mrs Grange sat silent while Skelton told his story, her head and her hand twitching regularly, as though by the action of some invisible clockwork, but when her husband addressed her, asking for the Worcester Sauce, and that was the only time he spoke to her, she was seized with such a paroxysm of involuntary movement that it was horrible to see. She passed him what he asked for without a word. Skelton got an uncomfortable impression that she was terrified of Grange. It was odd, because to all appearance he was not a bad sort. He was knowledgeable and far from stupid; and though you could not have said that his manner was cordial, it was plain that he was ready to be of what service he could.

They finished their meal and separated to rest through the heat of the day.

'See you again at six for a sun-downer,' said Grange.

When Skelton had had a good sleep, a bath, and a read, he went out on to the veranda. Mrs Grange came up to him. It looked as though she had been waiting.

'He's back from the office. Don't think it's funny if I don't speak to you. If he thought I liked having you here he'd turn you out tomorrow.'

She said these words in a whisper and slipped back into the house. Skelton was startled. It was a strange house he had come into in a strange manner. He went into the overcrowded sitting-room and there found his host. He had been worried by the evident poverty of the establishment and he felt that the Granges could ill afford even the small expense he must be putting them to. But he had already formed the impression that Grange was a quick-tempered, susceptible man and he did not know how he would take an offer to help. He made up his mind to risk it.

'Look here,' he said to him, 'it looks as though I might have to inflict myself on you for several days. I'd be so much more comfortable if you'd let me pay for my board and lodging.'

'Oh, that's all right, your lodging costs nothing, the house belongs to the mortgagees, and your board doesn't come to much.'

'Well, there are drinks anyway and I've had to come down on your stores of tobacco and cigarettes.'

'It's not more than once a year that anyone comes up here, and then it's only the D.O. or someone like that—besides, when one's as broke as I am nothing matters much.'

'Well, then, will you take my camp equipment? I shan't be wanting it any more, and if you'd like one of my guns, I'd be only too glad to leave it with you.'

Grange hesitated. There was a glimmer of cupidity in those small, cunning eyes of his.

'If you'd let me have one of your guns you'd pay for your board and lodging over and over again.'

'That's settled, then.'

They began to talk over the whisky and sparkler with which, following the Eastern habit, they celebrated the setting of the sun. Discovering that they both played chess they had a game. Mrs Grange did not join them till dinner. The meal was dull. An insipid soup, a tasteless river fish, a tough piece of steak, and a caramel pudding. Norman Grange and Skelton drank beer; Mrs Grange water. She never of her own will uttered a word. Skelton had again the uncomfortable impression that she was scared to death of her husband. Once or twice, Skelton from common politeness sought to bring her into the conversation, addressing himself to her, telling her a story or asking her a question, but it evidently distressed her so much, her head twitched so violently, her hand was agitated by gestures so spasmodic that he thought it kinder not to insist. When the meal was over she got up. 'I'll leave you gentlemen to your port,' she said.

Both the men got up as she left the room. It was rather absurd, and somehow sinister, to see this social pretence in those poverty-stricken surroundings on a Borneo river.

'I may add that there is no port. There might be a little Benedictine left.'

'Oh, don't bother.'

They talked for a while and Grange began to yawn. He got up every morning before sunrise and by nine o'clock at night could hardly keep his eyes open.

'Well, I'm going to turn in,' he said.

He nodded to Skelton and without further ceremony left him. Skelton went to bed, but he could not sleep. Though the heat was oppressive, it was not the heat that kept him awake. There was something horrible about that house and those two people who lived in it. He didn't know what it was that affected him with this peculiar uneasiness, but this he knew, that he would be heartily thankful to be out of it and away from them. Grange had talked a good deal about himself, but he knew no more of him than he had learned at the first glance. To all appearances he was just the commonplace planter who had fallen upon evil days. He had bought his land immediately after the war and had planted trees; but by the time they were bearing the slump had come and since then it had been a constant struggle to keep going. The estate and the house were heavily mortgaged, and now that rubber was once more selling profitably all he made went to the mortgagees. That was an old story in Malaya. What made Grange somewhat unusual was that he was a man without a country. Born in Borneo, he had lived there with his parents till he was old enough to go to school in England; at seventeen he had come back and had never left it since except to go to Mesopotamia during the war. England meant nothing to him. He had neither relations nor friends there. Most planters, like civil servants, have come from England, go back on leave now and then, and look forward to settling down there when they retire. But what had England to offer Norman Grange?

'I was born here,' he said, 'and I shall die here. I'm a stranger in England. I don't like their ways over there and I don't understand the things they talk about. And yet I'm a stranger here too. To the Malays and the Chinese I'm a white man, though I speak Malay as well as they do, and a white man I shall always be.' Then he said a significant thing. 'Of course if I'd had any sense I'd have married a Malay girl and had half a dozen half-caste kids. That's the only solution really for us chaps who were born and bred here.'

Grange's bitterness was greater than could be explained by his financial embarrassment. He had little good to say of any of the white men in the colony. He seemed to think that they despised him because he was native-born. He was a sour, disappointed fellow, and a conceited one. He had shown Skelton his books. There were not many of them, but they were the best on the whole that English literature can show; he had read them over and over again; but it looked as though he had learnt from them neither charity nor loving-kindness, it looked as though their beauty had left him unmoved; and to know them so well had only made him self-complacent. His exterior, which was so hearty and English, seemed to have little relation to the man within; you could not resist the suspicion that it masked a very sinister being.

Early next morning, to enjoy the cool of the day, Skelton, with his pipe and a book, was sitting on the veranda outside his room. He was still very weak, but felt much better. In a little while Mrs Grange joined him. She held in her hand a large album.

'I thought I'd like to show you some of me old photos and me notices. You mustn't think I always looked like what I do now. He's off on his round and he won't be back for two or three hours yet.'

Mrs Grange, in the same blue dress she had worn the day before, her hair as untidy, appeared strangely excited.

'It's all I have to remind me of the past. Sometimes when I can't bear life any more I look at my album.'

She sat by Skelton's side as he turned the pages. The notices were from provincial papers, and the references to Mrs Grange, whose stage name had been apparently Vesta Blaise, were carefully underlined. From the photographs, you could see that she had been pretty enough in an undistinguished way. She had acted in musical comedy and revue, in farce and comedy, and taking the photographs and the notices together it was easy to tell that here had been the common, dreary, rather vulgar career of the girl with no particular talent who has taken to the stage on the strength of a pretty face and a good figure. Her head twitching, her hand shaking, Mrs Grange looked at the photographs and read the notices with as much interest as if she had never seen them before.

'You've got to have influence on the stage, and I never had any,' she said. 'If I'd only had my chance I know I'd have made good. I had bad luck, there's no doubt about that.'

It was all sordid and somewhat pathetic.

'I daresay you're better off as you are,' said Skelton.

She snatched the book from him and shut it with a bang. She had a paroxysm so violent that it was really frightening to look at her.

'What d'you mean by that? What d'you know about the life I lead here? I'd have killed myself years ago only I know he wants me to die. That's the only way I can get back on him, by living, and I'm going to live; I'm going to live as long as he does. Oh, I hate him. I've often thought I'd poison him, but I was afraid. I didn't know how to do it really, and if he died the Chinks would foreclose and I'd be turned out. And where should I go then? I haven't a friend in the world.'

Skelton was aghast. It flashed through his mind that she was crazy. He hadn't a notion what to say. She gave him a keen look.

'I suppose it surprises you to hear me talk like that. I mean it, you know, every word of it. He'd like to kill me too, but he daren't either. And he knows how to do it all right. He knows how the Malays kill people. He was born here. There's nothing he doesn't know about the country.'

Skelton forced himself to speak.

'You know, Mrs Grange, I'm a total stranger. Don't you think it's rather unwise to tell me all sorts of things there's no need for me to know? After all, you live a very solitary life. I daresay you get on one another's nerves. Now that things are looking up perhaps you'll be able to take a trip to England.'

'I don't want to go to England. I'd be ashamed to let them see me like I am now. D'you know how old I am? Forty-six. I look sixty and I know it. That's why I showed you those photos, so as you might see I wasn't always like what I am now. Oh, my God, how I've wasted my life! They talk of the romance of the East. They can have it. I'd rather be a dresser in a provincial theatre, I'd rather be one of the sweepers that keep it clean, than what I am now. Until I came here I'd never been alone in my life, I'd always lived in a crowd; you don't know what it is to have nobody to talk to from year's end to year's end. To have to keep it all bottled up. How would you like to see no one, week in and week out, day after day for sixteen years, except the man you hate most in the world? How would you like to live for sixteen years with a man who hates you so he can't bear to look at you?'

'Oh, come, it can't be as bad as that.'

'I'm telling you the truth. Why should I tell you a lie? I shall never see you again; what do I care what you think of me? And if you tell them what I've said when you get down to the coast, what's the odds? They'll say: "God, you don't mean to say you stayed with those people? I pity you. He's an outsider and she's crazy; got a tic; they say it looks as if she was always trying to wipe the blood off her dress. They were mixed up in a damned funny business, but no one ever really knew the ins and outs of it; it all happened a long time ago and the country was pretty wild in those days." A damned funny business and no mistake. I'd tell you for two pins. That would be a bit of dirt for them at the club. You wouldn't have to pay for a drink for days. Damn them. Oh, Christ, how I hate this country. I hate that river. I hate this house. I hate that damned rubber. I loathe the filthy natives. And that's all I've got to look forward to till I die—till I die without a doctor to take care of me, without a friend to hold me hand.'

She began to cry hysterically. Mrs Grange had spoken with a dramatic intensity of which Skelton would never have thought her capable. Her coarse irony was as painful as her anguish. Skelton was young, he was not yet thirty, and he did not know how to deal with the difficult situation. But he could not keep silent.

'I'm terribly sorry, Mrs Grange. I wish I could do something to help you.'

'I'm not asking for your help. No one can help me.'

Skelton was distressed. From what she said he could not but suspect that she had been concerned in a mysterious and perhaps dreadful occurrence, and it might be that to tell him about it without fear of consequences was just the relief she needed.

'I don't want to butt into what's no business of mine, but, Mrs Grange, if you think it would ease your mind to tell me—what you were referring to just now, I mean what you said was a damned funny business, I promise you on my word of honour that I'll never repeat it to a living soul.'

She stopped crying quite suddenly and gave him a long, intent look. She hesitated. He had an impression that the desire to speak was almost irresistible. But she shook her head and sighed.

'It wouldn't do any good. Nothing can do me any good.'

She got up and abruptly left him.

The two men sat down to brunch by themselves.

'My wife asks you to excuse her,' said Grange. 'She's got one of her sick headaches and she's staying in bed today.'

'Oh, I'm sorry.'

Skelton had a notion that in the searching look that Grange gave him was mistrust and animosity. It flashed through his mind that somehow he had discovered that Mrs Grange had been talking to him and perhaps had said things that should have been left unsaid. Skelton made an effort at conversation, but his host was taciturn, and they ended the meal in a silence that was only broken by Grange when he got up.

'You seem pretty fit today and I don't suppose you want to stay in this God-forsaken place longer than you must. I've sent over the river to arrange for a couple of prahus to take you down to the coast. They'll be here at six tomorrow morning.'

Skelton felt sure then that he was right; Grange knew or guessed that his wife had spoken too freely, and he wanted to be rid as soon as possible of the dangerous visitor.

'That's terribly kind of you,' Skelton answered, smiling. 'I'm as fit as a fiddle.'

But in Grange's eyes was no answering smile. They were coldly hostile.

'We might have another game of chess later on,' said he.

'All right. When d'you get back from your office?'

'I haven't got much to do there today. I shall be about the house.'

Skelton wondered if it were only his fancy that there was something very like a threat in the tone in which Grange uttered these words. It looked as though he were going to make sure that his wife and Skelton should not again be left alone. Mrs Grange did not come to dinner. They drank their coffee and smoked their cheroots. Then Grange, pushing back his chair, said:

'You've got to make an early start tomorrow. I daresay you'd like to turn in. I shall have started out on my round by the time you go, so I'll say good-bye to you now.'

'Let me get my guns. I want you to take the one you like best.'

'I'll tell the boy to fetch them.'

The guns were brought and Grange made his choice. He gave no sign that he was pleased with the handsome gift.

'You quite understand that this gun's worth a damned sight more than what your food and drink and smoke have run me into?' he said.

'For all I know you saved my life. I don't think an old gun is an over-generous return for that.'

'Oh, well, if you like to look at it that way, I suppose it's your own business. Thank you very much all the same.'

They shook hands and parted.

Next morning, while the baggage was being stowed away in the prahus, Skelton asked the house boy whether, before starting, he could say good-bye to Mrs Grange. The house boy said he would go and see. He waited a little while. Mrs Grange came out of her room on to the veranda. She was wearing a pink dressing-gown, shabby, rumpled, and none too clean, of Japanese silk, heavily trimmed with cheap lace. The powder was thick on her face, her cheeks were rouged and her lips scarlet with lipstick. Her head seemed to twitch more violently than usual and her hand was agitated by that strange gesture. When first Skelton saw it he had thought that it suggested a wish to call attention to something behind her back, but now, after what she had told him yesterday, it did indeed look as though she was constantly trying to brush something off her dress. Blood, she had said.

'I didn't want to go without thanking you for all your kindness to me,' he said.

'Oh, that's all right.'

'Well, good-bye.'

'I'll walk down with you to the landing-stage.'

They hadn't far to go. The boatmen were still arranging the luggage. Skelton looked across the river where you could see some native houses.

'I suppose these men come from over there. It looks quite a village.'

'No, only those few houses. There used to be a rubber estate there, but the company went broke and it was abandoned.'

'D'you ever go over there?'

'Me?' cried Mrs Grange. Her voice rose shrill and her head, her hand, were on a sudden convulsed by a paroxysm of involuntary movement. 'No. Why should I?'

Skelton could not imagine why that simple question, asked merely for something to say, should so greatly upset her. But by now all was in order and he shook hands with her. He stepped into the boat and comfortably settled down. They pushed off. He waved to Mrs Grange. As the boat slid into the current she cried out with a harsh, strident scream:

'Give my regards to Leicester Square.'

Skelton heaved a great sigh of relief as with their powerful strokes the paddlers took him farther and farther away from that dreadful house and from those two unhappy and yet repellent people. He was glad now that Mrs Grange had not told him the story that was on the tip of her tongue to tell. He did not want some tragic tale of sin or folly to connect him with them in a recollection that he could not escape. He wanted to forget them as one forgets a bad dream.

But Mrs Grange watched the two prahus till a bend of the river took them out of sight. She walked slowly up to the house and went into her bedroom. The light was dim because the blinds were drawn to keep out the heat, but she sat down at her dressing-table and stared at herself in the glass. Norman had had the dressing-table made for her soon after they were married. It had been made by a native carpenter, of course, and they had had the mirror sent from Singapore, but it was made to her own design, of the exact size and shape she wanted, with plenty of room for all her toilet things and her make-up. It was the dressing-table she had hankered after for donkey's years and had never had. She remembered still how pleased she was when first she had it. She threw her arms round her husband's neck and kissed him.

'Oh, Norman, you are good to me,' she said. 'I'm a lucky little girl to have caught a chap like you, aren't I?'

But then everything delighted her. She was amused by the river life and the life of the jungle, the teeming growth of the forest, the birds with their gay plumage and the brilliant butterflies. She set about giving the house a woman's touch; she put out all her own photographs and she got vases to put flowers in; she routed around and got a lot of knick-knacks to place here and there. 'They make a room look homey,' she said. She wasn't in love with Norman, but she liked him all right; and it was lovely to be married; it was lovely to have nothing to do from morning till night, except play the gramophone, or patience, and read novels. It was lovely to think one hadn't got to bother about one's future. Of course it was a bit lonely sometimes, but Norman said she'd get used to that, and he'd promised that in a year, or two at the outside, he'd take her to England for three months. It would be a lark to show him off to her friends. She felt that what had caught him was the glamour of the stage and she'd made herself out a good deal more successful than she really had been. She wanted him to realize that she'd made a sacrifice when she'd thrown up her career to become a planter's wife. She'd claimed acquaintance with a good many stars that in point of fact she'd never even spoken to. That would need a bit of handling when they went home, but she'd manage it; after all, poor Norman knew no more about the stage than a babe unborn, if she couldn't cod a simple fellow like that, after twelve years on the stage, well, she'd wasted her time, that's all she could say. Things went all right the first year. At one moment she thought she was going to have a baby. They were both disappointed when it turned out not to be true. Then she began to grow bored. It seemed to her that she'd done the same damned thing day after day for ever and it frightened her to think that she'd have to go on doing the same damned thing day after day for ever more. Norman said he couldn't leave the plantation that year. They had a bit of a scene. It was then that he'd said something that scared her.

'I hate England,' he said. 'If I had my way I'd never set foot in the damned country again.'

Living this lonely life Mrs Grange got into the habit of talking out loud to herself. Shut up in her room she could be heard chattering away hour after hour; and now, dipping the puff in her powder and plastering her face with it, she addressed her reflection in the mirror exactly as though she were talking to another person.

'That ought to have warned me. I should have insisted on going by myself, and who knows, I might have got a job when I got to London. With all the experience I had and everything. Then I'd have written to him and said I wasn't coming back.' Her thoughts turned to Skelton. 'Pity I didn't tell him,' she continued. 'I had half a mind to. P'raps he was right, p'raps it would have eased me mind. I wonder what he'd have said.' She imitated his Oxford accent. 'I'm so terribly sorry, Mrs Grange. I wish I could help you.' She gave a chuckle which was almost a sob. 'I'd have liked to tell him about Jack. Oh, Jack.'

It was when they had been married for two years that they got a neighbour. The price of rubber at that time was so high that new estates were being put under cultivation and one of the big companies had bought a great tract of land on the opposite bank of the river. It was a rich company and everything was done on a lavish scale. The manager they had put in had a launch at his disposal so that it was no trouble for him to pop over and have a drink whenever he felt inclined. Jack Carr his name was. He was quite a different sort of chap from Norman; for one thing he was a gentleman, he'd been to a public school and a university; he was about thirty-five, tall, not beefy like Norman, but slight, he had the sort of figure that looked lovely in evening dress; and he had crisply curling hair and a laughing look in his eyes. Just her type. She took to him at once. It was a treat, having someone you could talk about London to, and the theatre. He was gay and easy. He made the sort of jokes you could understand. In a week or two she felt more at home with him than she did with her husband after two years. There had always been something about Norman that she hadn't quite been able to get to the bottom of. He was crazy about her, of course, and he'd told her a lot about himself, but she had a funny feeling that there was something he kept from her, not because he wanted to, but—well, you couldn't hardly explain it, because it was so alien, you might say, that he couldn't put it into words. Later, when she knew Jack better, she mentioned it to him, and Jack said it was because he was country-born; even though he hadn't a drop of native blood in his veins, something of the country had gone to the making of him so that he wasn't white really; he had an Eastern streak in him. However hard he tried he could never be quite English.

She chattered away aloud, in that empty house, for the two boys, the cook and the house boy, were in their own quarters, and the sound of her voice, ringing along the wooden floors, piercing the wooden walls, was like the uncanny, unhuman gibber of new wine fermenting in a vat. She spoke just as though Skelton were there, but so incoherently that if he had been, he would have had difficulty in following the story she told. It did not take her long to discover that Jack Carr wanted her. She was excited. She'd never been promiscuous, but in all those years she'd been on the stage naturally there'd been episodes. You couldn't hardly have put up with being on tour month after month if you didn't have a bit of fun sometimes. Of course now she wasn't going to give in too easily, she didn't want to make herself cheap, but what with the life she led, she'd be a fool if she missed the chance; and as far as Norman was concerned, well, what the eye didn't see the heart didn't grieve over. They understood one another all right, Jack and her; they knew it was bound to happen sooner or later, it was only a matter of waiting for the opportunity; and the opportunity came. But then something happened that they hadn't bargained for: they fell madly in love with one another. If Mrs Grange really had been telling the story to Skelton it might have seemed as unlikely to him as it did to them. They were two very ordinary people, he a jolly, good-natured, commonplace planter, and she a small-part actress far from clever, not even very young, with nothing to recommend her but a neat figure and a prettyish face. What started as a casual affair turned without warning into a devastating passion, and neither of them was of a texture to sustain its exorbitant compulsion. They longed to be with one another; they were restless and miserable apart. She'd been finding Norman a bore for some time, but she'd put up with him because he was her husband; now he irritated her to frenzy because he stood between her and Jack. There was no question of their going off together, Jack Carr had nothing but his salary, and he couldn't throw up a job he'd been only too glad to get. It was difficult for them to meet. They had to run awful risks. Perhaps the chances they had to take, the obstacles they had to surmount, were fuel to their love; a year passed and it was as overwhelming as at the beginning; it was a year of agony and bliss, of fear and thrill. Then she discovered that she was pregnant. She had no doubt that Jack Carr was the father and she was wildly happy. It was true life was difficult, so difficult sometimes that she felt she just couldn't cope with it, but there'd be a baby, his baby, and that would make everything easy. She was going to Kuching for her confinement. It happened about then that Jack Carr had to go to Singapore on business and was to be away for several weeks; but he promised to get back before she left and he said he'd send word by a native the moment he arrived. When at last the message came she felt sick with the anguish of her joy. She had never wanted him so badly.

'I hear that Jack is back,' she told her husband at dinner. 'I shall go over tomorrow morning and get the things he promised to bring me.'

'I wouldn't do that. He's pretty sure to drop in towards sundown and he'll bring them himself.'

'I can't wait. I'm crazy to have them.'

'All right. Have it your own way.'

She couldn't help talking about him. For some time now they had seemed to have little to say to one another, Norman and she, but that night, in high spirits, she chattered away as she had done during the first months of their marriage. She always rose early, at six, and next morning she went down to the river and had a bathe. There was a little dent in the bank just there, with a tiny sandy beach, and it was delicious to splash about in the cool, transparent water. A kingfisher stood on the branch of a tree overhanging the pool and its reflection was brilliantly blue in the water. Lovely. She had a cup of tea and then stepped into a dug-out. A boy paddled her across the river. It took a good half-hour. As they got near she scanned the bank; Jack knew she would come at the earliest opportunity; he must be on the lookout. Ah, there he was. The delicious pain in her heart was almost unbearable. He came down to the landing-stage and helped her to get out of the boat. They walked hand in hand up the pathway and when they were out of sight of the boy who had paddled her over and of prying eyes from the house, they stopped. He put his arms round her and she yielded with ecstasy to his embrace. She clung to him. His mouth sought hers. In that kiss was all the agony of their separation and all the bliss of their reunion. The miracle of love transfused them so that they were unconscious of time and place. They were not human any more, but two spirits united by a divine fire. No thought passed through their minds. No words issued from their lips. Suddenly there was a brutal shock, like a blow, and immediately, almost simultaneously, a deafening noise. Horrified, not understanding, she clung to Jack more tightly and his grip on her was spasmodic, so that she gasped; then she felt that he was bearing her over.

'Jack.'

She tried to hold him up. His weight was too great for her and as he fell to the ground she fell with him. Then she gave a great cry, for she felt a gush of heat, and his blood sputtered over her. She began to scream. A rough hand seized her and dragged her to her feet. It was Norman. She was distraught. She could not understand.

'Norman, what have you done?'

'I've killed him.'

She stared at him stupidly. She pushed him aside.

'Jack. Jack.'

'Shut up. I'll go and get help. It was an accident.'

He walked quickly up the pathway. She fell to her knees and took Jack's head in her arms.

'Darling,' she moaned. 'Oh, my darling.'

Norman came back with some coolies and they carried him up to the house. That night she had a miscarriage and was so ill that for days it looked as if she would die. When she recovered she had the nervous tic that she'd had ever since. She expected that Norman would send her away; but he didn't, he had to keep her to allay suspicion. There was some talk among the natives, and after a while the District Officer came up and asked a lot of questions; but the natives were frightened of Norman, and the D.O. could get nothing out of them. The Dyak boy who paddled her over had vanished. Norman said something had gone wrong with his gun and Jack was looking at it to see what was the matter and it went off. They bury people quickly in that country and by the time they might have dug him up there wouldn't have been much left to show that Norman's story wasn't true. The D.O. hadn't been satisfied.

'It all looks damned fishy to me,' he said, 'but in the absence of any evidence, I suppose I must accept your version.'

She would have given anything to get away, but with that nervous affliction she had no ghost of a chance any longer of earning a living. She had to stay–or starve; and Norman had to keep her–or hang. Nothing had happened since then and now nothing ever would happen. The endless years one after another dragged out their weary length.

Mrs Grange on a sudden stopped talking. Her sharp ears had caught the sound of a footstep on the path and she knew that Norman was back from his round. Her head twitching furiously, her hand agitated by that sinister, uncontrollable gesture, she looked in the untidy mess of her dressing-table for her precious lipstick. She smeared it on her lips, and then, she didn't know why, on a freakish impulse daubed it all over her nose till she looked like a red-nose comedian in a music-hall. She looked at herself in the glass and burst out laughing.

'To hell with life!' she shouted.

The
Alien Corn

◆

I had known the Blands a long time before I discovered that they had any
connexion with Ferdy Rabenstein. Ferdy must have been nearly fifty when I
first knew him and at the time of which I write he was well over seventy. He had
altered little. His hair, coarse but abundant and curly, was white, but he had
kept his figure and held himself as gallantly as ever. It was not hard to believe
that in youth he had been as beautiful as people said. He had still his fine
Semitic profile and the lustrous black eyes that had caused havoc in so many a
Gentile breast. He was very tall, lean, with an oval face and a clear skin. He
wore his clothes very well and in evening dress, even now, he was one of the
handsomest men I had ever seen. He wore then large black pearls in his shirt-
front and platinum and sapphire rings on his fingers. Perhaps he was rather
flashy, but you felt it was so much in character that it would have ill become him
to be anything else.

'After all, I am an Oriental,' he said. 'I can carry a certain barbaric
magnificence.'

I have often thought that Ferdy Rabenstein would make an admirable
subject for a biography. He was not a great man, but within the limits he set
himself he made of his life a work of art. It was a masterpiece in little, like a
Persian miniature, and derived its interest from its perfection. Unfortunately
the materials are scanty. They would consist of letters that may very well have
been destroyed and the recollections of people who are old now and will soon be
dead. His memory is extraordinary, but he would never write his memoirs, for
he looks upon his past as a source of purely private entertainment; and he is a
man of the most perfect discretion. Nor do I know anyone who could do justice
to the subject but Max Beerbohm. There is no one else in this hard world of
today who can look upon the trivial with such tender sympathy and wring such a

delicate pathos from futility. I wonder that Max, who must have known Ferdy much better than I, and long before, was never tempted to exercise his exquisite fancy on such a theme. He was born for Max to write about. And who should have illustrated the elegant book that I see in my mind's eye but Aubrey Beardsley? Thus would have been erected a monument of triple brass and the ephemera imprisoned to succeeding ages in the amber's translucency.

Ferdy's conquests were social and his venue was the great world. He was born in South Africa and did not come to England till he was twenty. For some time he was on the Stock Exchange, but on the death of his father he inherited a considerable fortune, and retiring from business devoted himself to the life of a man about town. At that period English society was still a closed body and it was not easy for a Jew to force its barriers, but to Ferdy they fell like the walls of Jericho. He was handsome, he was rich, he was a sportsman and he was good company. He had a house in Curzon Street, furnished with the most beautiful French furniture, and a French chef, and a brougham. It would be interesting to know the first steps in his wonderful career: they are lost in the dark abysm of time. When I first met him he had been long established as one of the smartest men in London: this was at a very grand house in Norfolk to which I had been asked as a promising young novelist by the hostess who took an interest in letters, but the company was very distinguished and I was over-awed. We were sixteen, and I felt shy and alone among these Cabinet Ministers, great ladies, and peers of the realm who talked of people and things of which I knew nothing. They were civil to me, but indifferent, and I was conscious that I was somewhat of a burden to my hostess. Ferdy saved me. He sat with me, walked with me, and talked with me. He discovered that I was a writer and we discussed the drama and the novel: he learnt that I had lived much on the Continent and he talked to me pleasantly of France, Germany, and Spain. He seemed really to seek my society. He gave me the flattering impression that he and I stood apart from the other members of the company and by our conversation upon affairs of the spirit made that of the rest of them, the political situation, the scandal of somebody's divorce, and the growing disinclination of pheasants to be killed, seem a little ridiculous. But if Ferdy had at the bottom of his heart a feeling of ever so faint a contempt for the hearty British gentry that surrounded us I am sure that it was only to me that he allowed an inkling of it to appear, and looking back I cannot but wonder whether it was not after all a suave and very delicate compliment that he paid me. I think of course that he liked to exercise his charm and I dare say the obvious pleasure his conversation gave me gratified him, but he could have had no motive for taking so much trouble over an obscure novelist other than his real interest in art and letters. I felt that he and I at bottom were equally alien in that company, I because I was a writer and he because he was a Jew, but I envied the ease with which he bore himself. He was completely at home. Everyone called him Ferdy. He seemed to be always in good spirits. He was never at a loss for a quip, a jest, or a repartee. They liked him in that house because he made them laugh, but never made them uncomfortable by talking over their heads. He brought a faint savour of Oriental romance into their lives, but so cleverly that they only felt more English. You could never be dull when he was by and with him present you were safe from the fear of the devastating silences that sometimes overwhelm a British company. A pause looked inevitable and Ferdy Rabenstein had broken into a topic that interested everyone. An invaluable asset to any party. He had an inexhaustible fund of Jewish stories. He was a very good mimic and he assumed the Yiddish accent and reproduced the Jewish gestures to perfection; his head sank into his body, his face grew cunning, his voice oily, and he was a rabbi or an old clothes merchant or a smart commercial traveller or a fat procuress in Frankfort. It was as good as a play. Because he was himself a Jew and insisted on it you laughed without reserve, but for my own part not without an under-current of discomfort. I was not quite sure of a sense of humour that made such cruel fun of his own race. I discovered afterwards that Jewish stories were his speciality and I seldom met him anywhere without hearing him tell sooner or later the last he had heard.

But the best story he told me on this occasion was not a Jewish one. It struck me so that I have never forgotten it, but for one reason or another I have never had occasion to tell it again. I give it here because it is a curious little incident concerning persons whose names at least will live in the social history of the Victorian Era and I think it would be a pity if it were lost. He told me then that once when quite a young man he was staying in the country in a house where Mrs Langtry, at that time at the height of her beauty and astounding reputation, was also a guest. It happened to be within driving distance of that in which lived the Duchess of Somerset, who had been Queen of Beauty at the Eglinton Tournament, and knowing her slightly, it occurred to him that it would be interesting to bring the two women together. He suggested it to Mrs Langtry, who was willing, and forthwith wrote to the Duchess asking if he might bring the celebrated beauty to call on her. It was fitting, he said, that the loveliest women of this generation (this was in the eighties) should pay her respects to the loveliest woman of the last. 'Bring her by all means,' answered the Duchess, 'but I warn you that it will be a shock to her.' They drove over in a carriage and pair, Mrs Langtry in a close-fitting blue bonnet with long satin strings, which showed the fine shape of her head and made her blue eyes even bluer, and were received by a little ugly old hag who looked with irony out of her beady eyes at the radiant beauty who had come to see her. They had tea, they talked, and they drove home again. Mrs Langtry was very silent and when Ferdy looked at her he saw that she was quietly weeping. When they got back to the house she went to her room and would not come down to dinner that night. For the first time she had realized that beauty dies.

Ferdy asked me for my address and a few days after I got back to London invited me to dinner. There were only six of us, an American woman married to an English peer, a Swedish painter, an actress, and a well-known critic. We ate very good food and drank excellent wine. The conversation was easy and intelligent. After dinner Ferdy was persuaded to play the piano. He only played Viennese waltzes, I discovered later that they were his speciality, and the light, tuneful, and sensual music seemed to accord well with his discreet flamboyance. He played without affectation, with a lilt, and he had a graceful touch. This was the first of a good many dinners I had with him, he would ask me two or three times a year, and as time passed I met him more and more frequently at other people's houses. I rose in the world and perhaps he came down a little. Of late years I had sometimes found him at parties where other Jews were and I fancied that I read in his shining liquid eyes, resting for a moment on these members of his race, a certain good-natured amusement at the thought of what the world was coming to. There were people who said he was a snob, but I do not think he was; it just happened that in his early days he had never met any but the great. He had a real passion for art and in his commerce with those that produced it was at his best. With them he had never that faint air of persiflage which when he was with very grand persons made you suspect that he was never quite the dupe of their grandeur. His taste was perfect and many of his friends were glad to avail themselves of his knowledge. He was one of the first to value old furniture and he rescued many a priceless piece from the attics of ancestral mansions and gave it an honourable place in the drawing-room. It amused him to saunter round the auction rooms and he was always willing to give his advice to great ladies who desired at once to acquire a beautiful thing and make a profitable investment. He was rich and good-natured. He liked to patronize the arts and would take a great deal of trouble to get commissions for some young painter whose talent he admired or an engagement to play at a rich man's house for a violinist who could in no other way get a hearing. But he never let his rich man down. His taste was too good to deceive and civil though he might be to the mediocre he would not lift a finger to help them. His own musical parties, very small and carefully chosen, were a treat.

He never married.

'I am a man of the world,' he said, 'and I flatter myself that I have no prejudices, *tous les goûts sont dans la nature*, but I do not think I could bring myself to marry a Gentile. There's no harm in going to the opera in a dinner jacket, but it just would never occur to me to do so.'

'Then why didn't you marry a Jewess?'

(I did not hear this conversation, but the lively and audacious creature who thus tackled him told me of it.)

'Oh, my dear, our women are so prolific. I could not bear the thought of peopling the world with a little Ikey and a little Jacob and a little Rebecca and a little Leah and a little Rachel.'

But he had had affairs of note and the glamour of past romance still clung to him. He was in his youth of an amorous complexion. I have met old ladies who told me that he was irresistible, and when in reminiscent mood they talked to me of this woman and that who had completely lost her head over him, I divined that, such was his beauty, they could not find it in their hearts to blame them. It was interesting to hear of great ladies that I had read of in the memoirs of the day or had met as respectable dowagers garrulous over their grandsons at Eton or making a mess of a hand at bridge and bethink myself that they had been consumed with sinful passion for the handsome Jew. Ferdy's most notorious amour was with the Duchess of Hereford, the loveliest, the most gallant and dashing of the beauties of the end of Queen Victoria's reign. It lasted for twenty years. He had doubtless flirtations meanwhile, but their relations were stable and recognized. It was proof of his marvellous tact that when at last they ended he exchanged an ageing mistress for a loyal friend. I remember meeting the pair not so very long ago at luncheon. She was an old woman, tall and of a commanding presence, but with a mask of paint on a ravaged face. We were lunching at the Carlton and Ferdy, our host, came a few minutes late. He offered us a cocktail and the Duchess told him we had already had one.

'Ah, I wondered why your eyes were so doubly bright,' he said.

The old raddled woman flushed with pleasure.

My youth passed, I grew middle-aged, I wondered how soon I must begin to describe myself as elderly; I wrote books and plays, I travelled, I underwent experiences, I fell in love and out of it; and still I kept meeting Ferdy at parties. War broke out and was waged, millions of men were killed, and the face of the world was changed. Ferdy did not like the war. He was too old to take part in it, and his German name was awkward, but he was discreet and took care not to expose himself to humiliation. His old friends were faithful to him and he lived in a dignified but not too strict seclusion. But then peace came and with courage he set himself to making the best of changed conditions. Society was mixed now, parties were rowdy, but Ferdy fitted himself to the new life. He still told his funny Jewish stories, he still played charmingly the waltzes of Strauss, he still went round auction rooms and told the new rich what they ought to buy. I went to live abroad, but whenever I was in London I saw Ferdy and now there was something a little uncanny in him. He did not give in. He had never known a day's illness. He seemed never to grow tired. He still dressed beautifully. He was interested in everybody. His mind was alert and people asked him to dinner, not for old times' sake, but because he was worth his salt. He still gave charming little concerts at his house in Curzon Street.

It was when he invited me to one of these that I made the discovery that started the recollections of him I have here set down. We were dining at a house in Hill Street, a large party, and the women having gone upstairs Ferdy and I found ourselves side by side. He told me that Lea Makart was coming to play for him on the following Friday evening and he would be glad if I would come.

'I'm awfully sorry,' I said, 'but I'm going down to the Blands.'

'What Blands?'

'They live in Sussex at a place called Tilby.'

'I didn't know you knew them.'

He looked at me rather strangely. He smiled. I didn't know what amused him.

'Oh, yes, I've known them for years. It's a very nice house to stay at.'

'Adolf is my nephew.'

'Sir Adolphus?'

'It suggests one of the bucks of the Regency, doesn't it? But I will not conceal from you that he was named Adolf.'

'Everyone I know calls him Freddy.'

'I know, and I understand that Miriam, his wife, only answers to the name of Muriel.'

'How does he happen to be your nephew?'

'Because Hannah Rabenstein, my sister, married Alfons Bleikogel, who ended life as Sir Alfred Bland, first Baronet, and Adolf, their only son, in due course became Sir Adolphus Bland, second Baronet.'

'Then Freddy Bland's mother, the Lady Bland who lives in Portland Place, is your sister?'

'Yes, my sister Hannah. She was the eldest of the family. She's eighty, but in full possession of her faculties and a remarkable woman.'

'I've never met her.'

'I think your friends the Blands would just as soon you didn't. She has never lost her German accent.'

'Do you never see them?' I asked.

'I haven't spoken to them for twenty years. I am such a Jew and they are so English.' He smiled. 'I could never remember that their names were Freddy and Muriel. I used to come out with an Adolf or a Miriam at awkward moments. And they didn't like my stories. It was better that we should not meet. When the war broke out and I would not change my name it was the last straw. It was too late, I could never have accustomed my friends to think of me as anything but Ferdy Rabenstein; I was quite content. I was not ambitious to be a Smith, a Brown or a Robinson.'

Though he spoke facetiously, there was in his tone the faintest possible derision and I felt, hardly felt even, the sensation was so shadowy, that, as it had often vaguely seemed to me before, there was in the depth of his impenetrable heart a cynical contempt for the Gentiles he had conquered.

'Then you don't know the two boys?' I said.

'No.'

'The eldest is called George, you know. I don't think he's so clever as Harry, the other one, but he's an engaging youth. I think you'd like him.'

'Where is he now?'

'Well, he's just been sent down from Oxford. I suppose he's at home. Harry's still at Eton.'

'Why don't you bring George to lunch with me?'

'I'll ask him. I should think he'd love to come.'

'It has reached my ears that he's been a little troublesome.'

'Oh, I don't know. He wouldn't go into the army, which is what they wanted. They rather fancied the Guards. And so he went to Oxford instead. He didn't work and he spent a great deal of money and he painted the town red. It was all quite normal.'

'What was he sent down for?'

'I don't know. Nothing of any consequence.'

At that moment our host rose and we went upstairs. When Ferdy bade me good night he asked me not to forget about his great-nephew.

'Ring me up,' he said. 'Wednesday would suit me. Or Friday.'

Next day I went down to Tilby. It was an Elizabethan mansion standing in a spacious park, in which roamed fallow deer, and from its windows you had wide views of rolling downs. It seemed to me that as far as the eye could reach the land belonged to the Blands. His tenants must have found Sir Adolphus a wonderful landlord, for I never saw farms kept in such order, the barns and cow-sheds were spick and span and the pigsties were a picture; the public-houses looked like Old English water-colours and the cottages he had built on the estate combined admirably picturesqueness and convenience. It must have cost him a pot of money to run the place on these lines. Fortunately he had it. The park with its grand old trees (and its nine-hole golf course) was tended like a garden, and the wide-stretching gardens were the pride of the neighbourhood. The magnificent house, with its steep roofs and mullioned windows, had been restored by the most celebrated architect in England and furnished by Lady Bland, with taste and knowledge, in a style that perfectly fitted it.

'Of course it's very simple,' she said. 'Just an English house in the country.'

The dining-room was adorned with old English sporting pictures and the Chippendale chairs were of incredible value. In the drawing-room were portraits by Reynolds and Gainsborough and landscapes by Old Crome and Richard Wilson. Even in my bedroom with its four-post bed were water-colours by Birket Foster. It was very beautiful and a treat to stay there, but though it would have distressed Muriel Bland beyond anything to know it, it entirely missed oddly enough the effect she had sought. It did not give you for a moment the impression of an English house. You had the feeling that every object had been bought with a careful eye to the general scheme. You missed the full Academy portraits that hung in the dining-room beside a Carlo Dolci that an ancestor had brought back from the Grand Tour, and the water-colours painted by a great-aunt that cluttered up the drawing-room so engagingly. There was no ugly Victorian sofa that had always been there and that it never occurred to anybody to take away and no needlework chairs that an unmarried daughter had so painstakingly worked at about the time of the Great Exhibition. There was beauty but no sentiment.

And yet how comfortable it was and how well looked after you were! And what a cordial greeting the Blands gave you! They seemed really to like people. They were generous and kindly. They were never happier than when they were entertaining the county, and though they had not owned the property for more than twenty years they had established themselves firmly in the favour of their neighbours. Except perhaps in their splendour and the competent way in which the estate was run there was nothing to suggest that they had not been settled there for centuries.

Freddy had been at Eton and Oxford. He was now in the early fifties. He was quiet in manner, courtly, very clever, I imagine, but a trifle reserved. He had great elegance, but it was not an English elegance; he had grey hair and a short pointed grey beard, fine dark eyes and an aquiline nose. He was just above middle height; I don't think you would have taken him for a Jew, but rather for a foreign diplomat of some distinction. He was a man of character, but gave you, strangely enough, notwithstanding the success he had had in life, an impression of faint melancholy. His successes had been financial and political; in the world of sport, for all his perseverance, he had never shone. For many years he had followed hounds, but he was a bad rider and I think it must have been a relief to him when he could persuade himself that middle age and pressure of business forced him to give up hunting. He had excellent shooting and gave grand parties for it, but he was a poor shot; and despite the course in his park he never succeeded in being more than an indifferent golfer. He knew only too well how much these things meant in England and his incapacity was a bitter disappointment to him. However George would make up for it.

George was scratch at golf, and though tennis was not his game he played much better than the average; the Blands had had him taught to shoot as soon as he was old enough to hold a gun and he was a fine shot; they had put him on a pony when he was two, and Freddy, watching him mount his horse, knew that out hunting when the boy came to a fence he felt exhilaration and not that sickening feeling in the pit of his stomach, which, though he had chased the fox with such grim determination, had always made the sport a torture to him. George was so tall and slim, his curly hair, of a palish brown, was so fine, his eyes were so blue, he was the perfect type of the young Englishman. He had the engaging candour of the breed. His nose was straight, though perhaps a trifle fleshy, and his lips were perhaps a little full and sensual, but he had beautiful teeth, and his smooth skin was like ivory. George was the apple of his father's eye. He did not like Harry, his second son, so well. He was rather stocky, broad-shouldered and strong for his age, but his black eyes, shining with cleverness, his coarse dark hair, and his big nose revealed his race. Freddy was severe with him, and often impatient, but with George he was all indulgence. Harry would go into the business, he had brains and push, but George was the heir. George would be an English gentleman.

George had offered to motor me down in the roadster his father had given him as a birthday present. He drove very fast and we arrived before the rest of the guests. The Blands were sitting on the lawn and tea was laid out under a magnificent cedar.

'By the way,' I said presently, 'I saw Ferdy Rabenstein the other day and he wants me to bring George to lunch with him.'

I had not mentioned the invitation to George on the way because I thought that if there had been a family coldness I had better address his parents as well.

'Who in God's name is Ferdy Rabenstein?' said George.

How brief is human glory! A generation back such a question would have seemed grotesque.

'He's by way of being your great-uncle,' I replied.

A glance had passed from father to mother when I first spoke.

'He's a horrid old man,' said Muriel.

'I don't think it's in the least necessary for George to resume relationships that were definitely severed before he was born,' said Freddy with decision.

'Anyhow I've delivered the message,' said I, feeling somewhat snubbed.

'I don't want to see the old blighter,' said George.

The conversation was broken off by the arrival of other guests and in a little while George went off to play golf with one of his Oxford friends.

It was not till next day that the matter was referred to again. I had played an unsatisfactory round with Freddy Bland in the morning and several sets of what is known as country-house tennis in the afternoon and was sitting alone with Muriel on the terrace. In England we have so much bad weather that it is only fair that a beautiful day should be more beautiful than anywhere in the world and this June evening was perfect. The blue sky was cloudless and the air was balmy; before us stretched green rolling downs, and woods, and in the distance you saw the red roofs of a little village church. It was a day when to be alive was sufficient happiness. Detached lines of poetry hovered vaguely in my memory. Muriel and I had been chatting desultorily.

'I hope you didn't think it rather horrid of us to refuse to let George lunch with Ferdy,' she said suddenly. 'He's such a fearful snob, isn't he?'

'D'you think so? He's always been very nice to me.'

'We haven't been on speaking terms for twenty years. Freddy never forgave him for his behaviour during the war. So unpatriotic, I thought, and one really must draw the line somewhere. You know, he absolutely refused to drop his horrible German name. With Freddy in Parliament and running munitions and all that sort of thing it was quite impossible. I don't know why he should want to see George. He can't mean anything to him.'

'He's an old man. George and Harry are his great-nephews. He must leave his money to someone.'

'We'd rather not have his money,' said Muriel coldly.

Of course I didn't care a row of pins whether George went to lunch with Ferdy Rabenstein, and I was quite willing to let the matter drop, but evidently the Blands had talked it over and Muriel felt that some explanation was due to me.

'Of course you know that Freddy has Jewish blood in him,' she said.

She looked at me sharply. Muriel was rather a big blonde woman and she spent a great deal of time trying to keep down the corpulence to which she was predisposed. She had been very pretty when young, and even now was a comely person; but her round blue eyes, slightly prominent, her fleshy nose, the shape of her face and the back of her neck, her exuberant manner, betrayed her race. No Englishwoman, however fair-haired, ever looked like that. And yet her observation was designed to make me take it for granted that she was a Gentile. I answered discreetly:

'So many people have nowadays.'

'I know. But there's no reason to dwell on it, is there? After all, we're absolutely English; no one could be more English than George, in appearance and manner and everything; I mean, he's such a fine sportsman and all that sort of thing, I can't see any object of his knowing Jews just because they happen to be distant connexions of his.'

'It's very difficult in England now not to know Jews, isn't it?'

'Oh, I know, in London one does meet a good many, and I think some of them are very nice. They're so artistic. I don't go so far as to say that Freddy and I deliberately avoid them, of course I wouldn't do that, but it just happens that we don't really know any of them very well. And down here, there simply aren't any to know.'

I could not but admire the convincing manner in which she spoke. It would not have surprised me to be told that she really believed every word she said.

'You say that Ferdy might leave George his money. Well, I don't believe it's so very much anyway; it was quite a comfortable fortune before the war, but that's nothing nowadays. Besides we're hoping that George will go in for politics when he's a little older, and I don't think it would do him any good in the constituency to inherit money from a Mr Rabenstein.'

'Is George interested in politics?' I asked, to change the conversation.

'Oh, I do hope so. After all, there's the family constituency waiting for him. It's a safe Conservative seat and one can't expect Freddy to go on with the grind of the House of Commons indefinitely.'

Muriel was grand. She talked already of the constituency as though twenty generations of Blands had sat for it. Her remark, however, was my first intimation that Freddy's ambition was not satisfied.

'I suppose Freddy would go to the House of Lords when George was old enough to stand.'

'We've done a good deal for the party,' said Muriel.

Muriel was a Catholic and she often told you that she had been educated in a convent–'Such sweet women, those nuns, I always said that if I had a daughter I should have sent her to a convent too'–but she liked her servants to be Church of England, and on Sunday evenings we had what was called supper because the fish was cold and there was ice-cream, so that they could go to church, and we were waited on by two footmen instead of four. It was still light when we finished and Freddy and I, smoking our cigars, walked up and down the terrace in the gloaming. I suppose Muriel had told him of her conversation with me, and it may be that his refusal to let George see his great-uncle still troubled him, but being subtler than she he attacked the question more indirectly. He told me that he had been very much worried about George. It had been a great disappointment that he had refused to go into the army.

'I should have thought he'd have loved the life,' he said.

'And he would certainly have looked marvellous in his Guards uniform.'

'He would, wouldn't he?' returned Freddy, ingenuously. 'I wonder he could resist that.'

He had been completely idle at Oxford; although his father had given him a very large allowance, he had got monstrously into debt; and now he had been sent down. But though he spoke so tartly I could see that he was not a little proud of his scapegrace son, he loved him with oh, such an unEnglish love, and in his heart it flattered him that George had cut such a dash.

'Why should you worry?' I said. 'You don't really care if George has a degree or not.'

Freddy chuckled.

'No, I don't suppose I do really. I always think the only important thing about Oxford is that people know you were there, and I dare say that George isn't any wilder than the other young men in his set. It's the future I'm thinking of. He's so damned idle. He doesn't seem to want to do anything but have a good time.'

'He's young, you know.'

'He's not interested in politics, and though he's so good at games he's not even very keen on sport. He seems to spend most of his time strumming the piano.'

'That's a harmless amusement.'

'Oh, yes, I don't mind that, but he can't go on loafing indefinitely. You see, all this will be his one day.' Freddy gave a sweeping gesture that seemed to embrace the whole county, but I knew that he did not own it all yet. 'I'm very anxious that he should be fit to assume his responsibilities. His mother is very ambitious for him, but I only want him to be an English gentleman.'

Freddy gave me a sidelong glance as though he wanted to say something but hesitated in case I thought it ridiculous; but there is one advantage in being a writer that, since people look upon you as of no account, they will often say things to you that they would not to their equals. He thought he would risk it.

'You know, I've got an idea that nowhere in the world now is the Greek ideal of life so perfectly cultivated as by the English country gentleman living on his estates. I think his life has the beauty of a work of art.'

I could not but smile when I reflected that it was impossible for the English country gentleman in these days to do anything of the sort without a packet of money safely invested in American Bonds, but I smiled with sympathy. I thought it rather touching that this Jewish financier should cherish so romantic a dream.

'I want him to be a good landlord. I want him to take his part in the affairs of the country. I want him to be a thorough sportsman.'

'Poor mutt,' I thought, but said: 'Well, what are your plans for George now?'

'I think he has a fancy for the diplomatic service. He's suggested going to Germany to learn the language.'

'A very good idea, I should have thought.'

'For some reason he's got it into his head that he wants to go to Munich.'

'A nice place.'

Next day I went back to London and shortly after my arrival rang up Ferdy.

'I'm sorry, but George isn't able to come to lunch on Wednesday.'

'What about Friday?'

'Friday's no good either.' I thought it useless to beat about the bush. 'The fact is, his people aren't keen on his lunching with you.'

There was a moment's silence. Then:

'I see. Well, will you come on Wednesday anyway?'

'Yes, I'd like to,' I answered.

So on Wednesday at half past one I strolled round to Curzon Street. Ferdy received me with the somewhat elaborate graciousness that he cultivated. He made no reference to the Blands. We sat in the drawing-room and I could not help reflecting what an eye for beautiful objects that family had. The room was more crowded than the fashion of today approves, and the gold snuff-boxes in vitrines, the French china, appealed to a taste that was not mine; but they were no doubt choice pieces; and the Louise XV suite, with its beautiful *petit point*, must have been worth an enormous lot of money. The pictures on the walls by Lancret, Pater, and Watteau did not greatly interest me, but I recognized their intrinsic excellence. It was a proper setting for this aged man of the world. It fitted his period. Suddenly the door opened and George was announced. Ferdy saw my surprise and gave me a little smile of triumph.

'I'm very glad you were able to come after all,' he said as he shook George's hand.

I saw him in a glance take in his great-nephew whom he saw today for the first time. George was very well dressed. He wore a short black coat, striped trousers, and the grey double-breasted waistcoat which at that time was the mode. You could only wear it with elegance if you were tall and thin and your belly was slightly concave. I felt sure that Ferdy knew exactly who George's tailor was and what haberdasher he went to and approved of them. George, so smart and trim, wearing his clothes so beautifully, certainly looked very handsome. We went down to luncheon. Ferdy had the social graces at his fingers' ends and he put the boy at his ease, but I saw that he was carefully appraising him; then, I do not know why, he began to tell some of his Jewish stories. He told them with gusto and with all his wonderful mimicry. I saw George flush, and though he laughed at them, I could see that it was with embarrassment. I wondered what on earth had induced Ferdy to be so tactless. But he was watching George and he told story after story. It looked as though he would never stop. I wondered if for some reason I could not grasp he was taking a malicious pleasure in the boy's obvious discomfiture. At last we went upstairs and to make things easier I asked Ferdy to play the piano. He played us three or four little waltzes. He had lost none of his exquisite lightness nor his sense of their lilting rhythm. Then he turned to George.

'Do you play?' he asked him.

'A little.'

'Won't you play something?'

'I'm afraid I only play classical music. I don't think it would interest you.'

Ferdy smiled slightly, but did not insist. I said it was time for me to go and George accompanied me.

'What a filthy old Jew,' he said as soon as we were in the street. 'I hated those stories of his.'

'They're his great stunt. He always tells them.'

'Would you if you were a Jew?'

I shrugged my shoulders.

'How is it you came to lunch after all?' I asked George.

He chuckled. He was a light-hearted creature, with a sense of humour, and he shook off the slight irritation his great-uncle had caused him.

'He went to see Granny. You don't know Granny, do you?'

'No.'

'She treats daddy like a kid in Etons. Granny said I was to go to lunch with great-uncle Ferdy and what Granny says goes.'

'I see.'

A week or to later George went to Munich to learn German. I happened then to go on a journey and it was not till the following spring that I was again in London. Soon after my arrival I found myself sitting next to Muriel Bland at dinner. I asked after George.

'He's still in Germany,' she said.

'I see in the papers that you're going to have a great beano at Tilby for his coming of age.'

'We're going to entertain the tenants and they're making George a presentation.'

She was less exuberant than usual, but I did not pay much attention to the fact. She led a strenuous life and it might be that she was tired. I knew she liked to talk of her son, so I continued.

'I suppose George has been having a grand time in Germany,' I said.

She did not answer for a moment and I gave her a glance. I was surprised to see that her eyes were filled with tears.

'I'm afraid George has gone mad,' she said.

'What *do* you mean?'

'We've been so frightfully worried. Freddy's so angry, he won't even discuss it. I don't know what we're going to do.'

Of course it immediately occurred to me that George, who, I supposed, like most young Englishmen sent to learn the language, had been put with a German family, had fallen in love with the daughter of the house and wanted to marry her. I had a pretty strong suspicion that the Blands were intent on his making a very grand marriage.

'Why, what's happened?' I asked.

'He wants to become a pianist.'

'A what?'

'A professional pianist.'

'What on earth put that idea in his head?'

'Heaven knows. We didn't know anything about it. We thought he was working for his exam. I went out to see him. I thought I'd like to know that he was getting on all right. Oh, my dear. He looks like nothing on earth. And he used to be so smart; I could have cried. He told me he wasn't going in for the exam, and had never had any intention of doing so; he'd only suggested the diplomatic service so that we'd let him go to Germany and he'd be able to study music.'

'But has he any talent?'

'Oh, that's neither here nor there. Even if he had the genius of Paderewski we couldn't have George traipsing around the country playing at concerts. No one can deny that I'm very artistic, and so is Freddy, we love music and we've always known a lot of artists, but George will have a very great position, it's out of the question. We've set our hearts on his going into Parliament. He'll be very rich one day. There's nothing he can't aspire to.'

'Did you point all that out to him?'

'Of course I did. He laughed at me. I told him he'd break his father's heart. He said his father could always fall back on Harry. Of course I'm devoted to Harry, and he's as clever as a monkey, but it was always understood that he was to go into the business; even though I am his mother I can see that he hasn't got the advantages that George has. Do you know what he said to me? He said that if his father would settle five pounds a week on him he would resign everything in Harry's favour and Harry could be his father's heir and succeed to the baronetcy and everything. It's too ridiculous. He said that if the Crown Prince of Roumania could abdicate a throne he didn't see why he couldn't abdicate a baronetcy. But you can't do that. Nothing can prevent him from being third baronet and if Freddy should be granted a peerage from succeeding to it at Freddy's death. Do you know, he even wants to drop the name of Bland and take some horrible German name.'

I could not help asking what.

'Bleikogel or something like that,' she answered.

That was a name I recognized. I remembered Ferdy telling me that Hannah Rabenstein had married Alfons Bleikogel who became eventually Sir Alfred Bland, first Baronet. It was all very strange. I wondered what had happened to the charming, so typically English boy I had seen only a few months before.

'Of course when I came home and told Freddy he was furious. I've never seen him so angry. He foamed at the mouth. He wired to George to come back immediately and George wired back to say he couldn't on account of his work.'

'Is he working?'

'From morning till night. That's the maddening part of it. He never did a stroke of work in his life. Freddy used to say he was born idle.'

'H'm.'

'Then Freddy wired to say that if he didn't come he'd stop his allowance and George wired back: "Stop it." That put the lid on. You don't know what Freddy can be when his back is up.'

I knew that Freddy had inherited a large fortune, but I knew also that he had immensely increased it, and I could well imagine that behind the courteous and amiable Squire of Tilby there was a ruthless man of affairs. He had been used to having his own way and I could believe that when crossed he would be hard and cruel.

'We'd been making George a very handsome allowance, but you know how frightfully extravagant he was. We didn't think he'd be able to hold out long and in point of fact within a month he wrote to Ferdy and asked him to lend him a hundred pounds. Ferdy went to my mother-in-law, she's his sister, you know, and asked her what it meant. Though they hadn't spoken for twenty years Freddy went to see him and begged him not to send George a penny, and he promised he wouldn't. I don't know how George has been making both ends meet. I'm sure Freddy's right, but I can't help being rather worried. If I hadn't given Freddy my word of honour that I wouldn't send him anything I think I'd have slipped a few notes in a letter in case of accident. I mean, it's awful to think that perhaps he hasn't got enough to eat.'

'It'll do him no harm to go short for a bit.'

'We were in an awful hole, you know. We'd made all sorts of preparations for his coming of age, and I'd issued hundreds of invitations. Suddenly George said he wouldn't come. I was simply frantic. I wrote and wired. I would have gone over to Germany only Freddy wouldn't let me. I practically went down on my bended knees to George. I begged him not to put us in such a humiliating position. I mean, it's the sort of thing it's so difficult to explain. Then my mother-in-law stepped in. You don't know her, do you? She's an extraordinary old woman. You'd never think she was Freddy's mother. She was German originally, but of very good family.'

'Oh?'

'To tell you the truth I'm rather frightened of her. She tackled Freddy and then she wrote to George herself. She said that if he'd come home for his twenty-first birthday she'd pay any debts he had in Munich and we'd all give a patient hearing to anything he had to say. He agreed to that and we're expecting him one day next week. But I'm not looking forward to it, I can tell you.'

She gave a deep sigh. When we were walking upstairs after dinner Freddy addressed me.

'I see Muriel has been telling you about George. The damned fool! I have no
patience with him. Fancy wanting to be a pianist. It's so ungentlemanly.'

'He's very young, you know,' I said soothingly.

'He's had things too easy for him. I've been much too indulgent. There's
never been a thing he wanted that I haven't given him. I'll learn him.'

The Blands had a discreet apprehension of the uses of advertisement and I
gathered from the papers that the celebrations at Tilby of George's twenty-first
birthday were conducted in accordance with the usage of English county
families. There was a dinner-party and a ball for the gentry and a collation and a
dance in marquees on the lawn for the tenants. Expensive bands were brought
down from London. In the illustrated papers were pictures of George
surrounded by his family being presented with a solid silver tea-set by the
tenantry. They had subscribed to have his portrait painted, but since his
absence from the country had made it impossible for him to sit, the tea-service
had been substituted. I read in the columns of the gossip writers that his father
had given him a hunter, his mother a gramophone that changed its own
records, his grandmother the dowager Lady Bland an *Encyclopaedia
Britannica*, and his great-uncle Ferdinand Rabenstein a *Virgin and Child* by
Pellegrino da Modena. I could not help observing that these gifts were bulky
and not readily convertible into cash. From Ferdy's presence at the festivities I
concluded that George's unaccountable vagary had effected a reconciliation
between uncle and nephew. I was right. Ferdy did not at all like the notion of
his great-nephew becoming a professional pianist. At the first hint of danger to
its prestige the family drew together and a united front was presented to
oppose George's designs. Since I was not there I only know from hearsay what
happened when the birthday celebrations were over. Ferdy told me something
and so did Muriel, and later George gave me his version. The Blands had very
much the impression that when George came home and found himself
occupying the centre of the stage, when, surrounded by splendour, he saw for
himself once more how much it meant to be the heir of a great estate, he would
weaken. They surrounded him with love. They flattered him. They hung on
his words. They counted on the goodness of his heart and thought that if they
were very kind to him he would not have the courage to cause them pain. They
seemed to take it for granted that he had no intention of going back to Germany
and in conversation included him in all their plans. George did not say very
much. He seemed to be enjoying himself. He did not open a piano. Things
looked as though they were going very well. Peace descended on the troubled
house. Then one day at luncheon when they were discussing a garden-party to
which they had all been asked for one day of the following week, George said
pleasantly:

'Don't count on me. I shan't be here.'

'Oh, George, why not?' asked his mother.

'I must get back to my work. I'm leaving for Munich on Monday.'

There was an awful pause. Everyone looked for something to say, but was
afraid of saying the wrong thing, and at last it seemed impossible to break it.
Luncheon was finished in silence. Then George went into the garden and the
others, old Lady Bland and Ferdy, Muriel and Sir Adolphus, into the
morning-room. There was a family council. Muriel wept. Freddy flew into a
temper. Presently from the drawing-room they heard the sound of someone
playing a nocturne of Chopin. It was George. It was as though now he had

announced his decision he had gone for comfort, rest, and strength to the instrument he loved. Freddy sprang to his feet.

'Stop that noise,' he cried. 'I won't have him play the piano in my house.'

Muriel rang for a servant and gave him a message.

'Will you tell Mr Bland that her ladyship has a bad headache and would he mind not playing the piano.'

Ferdy, the man of the world, was deputed to have a talk with George. He was authorized to make him certain promises if he would give up the idea of becoming a pianist. If he did not wish to go into the diplomatic service his father would not insist, but if he would stand for Parliament he was prepared to pay his election expenses, give him a flat in London, and make him an allowance of five thousand a year. I must say it was a handsome offer. I do not know what Ferdy said to the boy. I suppose he painted to him the life that a young man could lead in London on such an income. I am sure he made it very alluring. It availed nothing. All George asked was five pounds a week to be able to continue his studies and to be left alone. He was indifferent to the position that he might some day enjoy. He didn't want to hunt. He didn't want to shoot. He didn't want to be a Member of Parliament. He didn't want to be a millionaire. He didn't want to be a baronet. He didn't want to be a peer. Ferdy left him defeated and in a state of considerable exasperation.

After dinner that evening there was a battle royal. Freddy was a quick-tempered man, unused to opposition, and he gave George the rough side of his tongue. I gather that it was very rough indeed. The women who sought to restrain his violence were sternly silenced. Perhaps for the first time in his life Freddy would not listen to his mother. George was obstinate and sullen. He had made up his mind and if his father didn't like it he could lump it. Freddy was peremptory. He forbade George to go back to Germany. George answered that he was twenty-one and his own master. He would go where he chose. Freddy swore he would not give him a penny.

'All right, I'll earn money.'

'You! You've never done a stroke of work in your life. What do you expect to do to earn money?'

'Sell old clothes,' grinned George.

There was a gasp from all of them. Muriel was so taken aback that she said a stupid thing.

'Like a Jew?'

'Well, aren't I a Jew? And aren't you a Jewess and isn't daddy a Jew? We're all Jews, the whole gang of us, and everyone knows it and what the hell's the good of pretending we're not?'

Then a very dreadful thing happened. Freddy burst suddenly into tears. I'm afraid he didn't behave very much like Sir Adolphus Bland, Bart, M.P., and the good old English gentleman he so much wanted to be, but like an emotional Adolf Bleikogel who loved his son and wept with mortification because the great hopes he had set on him were brought to nothing and the ambition of his life was frustrated. He cried noisily with great loud sobs and pulled his beard and beat his breast and rocked to and fro. Then they all began to cry, old Lady Bland and Muriel, and Ferdy, who sniffed and blew his nose and wiped the tears streaming down his face, and even George cried. Of course it was very painful, but to our rough Anglo-Saxon temperament I am afraid it must seem also a trifle ridiculous. No one tried to console anybody else. They just sobbed and sobbed. It broke up the party.

But it had no result on the situation. George remained obdurate. His father would not speak to him. There were more scenes. Muriel sought to excite his pity; he was deaf to her piteous entreaties, he did not seem to mind if he broke her heart, he did not care two hoots if he killed his father. Ferdy appealed to him as a sportsman and a man of the world. George was flippant and indeed personally offensive. Old Lady Bland with her guttural German accent and strong common sense argued with him, but he would not listen to reason. It was she, however, who at last found a way out. She made George acknowledge that it was no use to throw away all the beautiful things the world laid at his feet unless he had talent. Of course he thought he had, but he might be mistaken. It was not worth while to be a second-rate pianist. His only excuse, his only justification, was genius. If he had genius his family had no right to stand in his way.

'You can't expect me to show genius already,' said George. 'I shall have to work for years.'

'Are you sure you are prepared for that?'

'It's my only wish in the world. I'll work like a dog. I only want to be given my chance.'

This was the proposition she made. His father was determined to give him nothing and obviously they could not let the boy starve. He had mentioned five pounds a week. Well, she was willing to give him that herself. He could go back to Germany and study for two years. At the end of that time he must come back and they would get some competent and disinterested person to hear him play and if then that person said he showed promise of becoming a first-rate pianist no further obstacles would be placed in his way. He would be given every advantage, help, and encouragement. If on the other hand that person decided that his natural gifts were not such as to ensure ultimate success he must promise faithfully to give up all thoughts of making music his profession and in every way accede to his father's wishes. George could hardly believe his ears.

'Do you mean that, Granny?'

'I do.'

'But will daddy agree?'

'I vill see dat he does,' she answered.

George seized her in his arms and impetuously kissed her on both cheeks.

'Darling,' he cried.

'Ah, but de promise?'

He gave her his solemn word of honour that he would faithfully abide by the terms of the arrangement. Two days later he went back to Germany. Though his father consented unwillingly to his going, and indeed could not help doing so, he would not be reconciled to him and when he left refused to say good-bye to him.

I imagine that in no manner could he have caused himself such pain. I permit myself a trite remark. It is strange that men, inhabitants for so short a while of an alien and inhuman world, should go out of their way to cause themselves so much unhappiness.

George had stipulated that during his two years of study his family should not visit him, so that when Muriel heard some months before he was due to come home that I was passing through Munich on my way to Vienna, whither business called me, it was not unnatural that she should ask me to look him up. She was anxious to have first-hand information about him. She gave me

George's address and I wrote ahead, telling him I was spending a day in Munich, and asked him to lunch with me. His answer awaited me at the hotel. He said he worked all day and could not spare the time to lunch with me, but if I would come to his studio about six he would like to show me that and if I had nothing better to do would love to spend the evening with me. So soon after six I went to the address he gave me. He lived on the second floor of a large block of flats and when I came to his door I heard the sound of piano-playing. It stopped when I rang and George opened the door for me. I hardly recognized him. He had grown very fat. His hair was extremely long, it curled all over his head in picturesque confusion; and he had certainly not shaved for three days. He wore a grimy pair of Oxford bags, a tennis shirt, and slippers. He was not very clean and his finger-nails were rimmed with black. It was a startling change from the spruce, slim youth so elegantly dressed in such beautiful clothes that I had last seen. I could not but think it would be a shock to Ferdy to see him now. The studio was large and bare; on the walls were three or four unframed canvases of a highly cubist nature, there were several arm-chairs much the worse for wear, and a grand piano. Books were littered about and old newspapers and art magazines. It was dirty and untidy and there was a frowzy smell of stale beer and stale smoke.

'Do you live here alone?' I asked.

'Yes, I have a woman who comes in twice a week and cleans up. But I make my own breakfast and lunch.'

'Can you cook?'

'Oh, I only have bread and cheese and a bottle of beer for lunch. I dine at a *Bierstube*.'

It was pleasant to discover that he was very glad to see me. He seemed in great spirits and extremely happy. He asked after his relations and we talked of one thing and another. He had a lesson twice a week and for the rest of the time practised. He told me that he worked ten hours a day.

'That's a change,' I said.

He laughed.

'Daddy said I was born tired. I wasn't really lazy. I didn't see the use of working at things that bored me.'

I asked him how he was getting on with the piano. He seemed to be satisfied with his progress and I begged him to play to me.

'Oh, not now, I'm all in, I've been at it all day. Let's go out and dine and come back here later and then I'll play. I generally go to the same place, there are several students I know there, and it's rather fun.'

Presently we set out. He put on socks and shoes and a very old golf coat, and we walked together through the wide quiet streets. It was a brisk cold day. His step was buoyant. He looked round him with a sigh of delight.

'I love Munich,' he said. 'It's the only city in the world where there's art in the very air you breathe. After all, art is the only thing that matters, isn't it? I loathe the idea of going home.'

'All the same I'm afraid you'll have to.'

'I know. I'll go all right, but I'm not going to think about it till the time comes.'

'When you do, you might do worse than get a haircut. If you don't mind my saying so you look almost too artistic to be convincing.'

'You English, you're such Philistines,' he said.

He took me to a rather large restaurant in a side street, crowded even at that

early hour with people dining, and furnished heavily in the German medieval
style. A table covered with a red cloth, well away from the air, was reserved for
George and his friends and when we went to it four or five youths were at it.
There was a Pole studying Oriental languages, a student of philosophy, a
painter (I suppose the author of George's cubist pictures), a Swede, and a
young man who introduced himself to me, clicking his heels, as Hans Reiting,
Dichter, namely Hans Reiting, poet. Not one of them was more than twenty-
two and I felt a trifle out of it. They all addressed George as *du* and I noticed
that his German was extremely fluent. I had not spoken it for some time and
mine was rusty, so that I could not take much part in the lively conversation.
But nevertheless I thoroughly enjoyed myself. They ate sparingly, but drank a
good deal of beer. They talked of art and women. They were very revolutionary
and though gay very much in earnest. They were contemptuous of everyone
you had ever heard of, and the only point on which they all agreed was that in
this topsy-turvy world only the vulgar could hope for success. They argued
points of technique with animation, and contradicted one another, and shouted
and were obscene. They had a grand time.

At about eleven George and I walked back to his studio. Munich is a city that
frolics demurely and except about the Marienplatz the streets were still and,
empty. When we got in he took off his coat and said:

'Now I'll play to you.'

I sat in one of the dilapidated arm-chairs and a broken spring stuck into my
behind, but I made myself as comfortable as I could. George played Chopin. I
know very little of music and that is one of the reasons for which I have found
this story difficult to write. When I go to a concert at the Queen's Hall and in
the intervals read the programme it is all Greek to me. I know nothing of
harmony and counterpoint. I shall never forget how humiliated I felt once
when, having come to Munich for a Wagner festival, I went to a wonderful
performance of *Tristan und Isolde* and never heard a note of it. The first few
bars sent me off and I began to think of what I was writing, my characters leapt
into life and I heard their long conversations, I suffered their pains and was a
party to their joy; the years swept by and all sorts of things happened to me, the
spring brought me its rapture and in the winter I was cold and hungry; and I
loved and I hated and I died. I suppose there were intervals in which I walked
round and round the garden and probably ate *Schinken-Brödchen* and drank
beer, but I have no recollection of them. The only thing I know is that when the
curtain for the last time fell I woke with a start. I had had a wonderful time, but
I could not help thinking it was very stupid of me to come such a long way and
spend so much money if I couldn't pay attention to what I heard and saw.

I knew most of the things George played. They were the familiar pieces of
concert programmes. He played with a great deal of dash. Then he played
Beethoven's *Appassionata*. I used to play it myself when I played the piano
(very badly) in my far distant youth and I still knew every note of it. Of course it
is a classic and a great work, it would be foolish to deny it, but I confess that at
this time of day it leaves me cold. It is like *Paradise Lost,* splendid, but a trifle
stolid. This too George played with vigour. He sweated profusely. At first I
could not make out what was the matter with his playing, something did not
seem to me quite right, and then it struck me that the two hands did not exactly
synchronize, so that there was ever so slight an interval between the bass and
the treble; but I repeat, I am ignorant of these things; what disconcerted me
might have been merely the effect of his having drunk a good deal of beer that

evening or indeed only my fancy. I said all I could think of to praise him.

'Of course I know I need a lot more work. I'm only a beginner, but I know I can do it. I feel it in my bones. It'll take me ten years, but then I shall be a pianist.'

He was tired and came away from the piano. It was after midnight and I suggested going, but he would not hear of it. He opened a couple of bottles of beer and lit his pipe. He wanted to talk.

'Are you happy here?' I asked him.

'Very,' he answered gravely. 'I'd like to stay for ever. I've never had such fun in my life. This evening, for instance. Wasn't it grand?'

'It was very jolly. But one can't go on leading the student's life. Your friends here will grow older and go away.'

'Others'll come. There are always students here and people like that.'

'Yes, but you'll grow older too. Is there anything more lamentable than the middle-aged man who tries to go on living the undergraduate's life? The old fellow who wants to be a boy among boys, and tries to persuade himself that they'll accept him as one of themselves—how ridiculous he is. It can't be done.'

'I feel so at home here. My poor father wants me to be an English gentleman. It gives me gooseflesh. I'm not a sportsman. I don't care a damn for hunting and shooting and playing cricket. I was only acting.'

'You gave a very natural performance.'

'It wasn't till I came here that I knew it wasn't real. I loved Eton, and Oxford was a riot, but all the same I knew I didn't belong. I played the part all right, because acting's in my blood, but there was always something in me that wasn't satisfied. The house in Grosvenor Square is a freehold and daddy paid a hundred and eighty thousand pounds for Tilby; I don't know if you understand what I mean, I felt they were just furnished houses we'd taken for the season and one of these days we'd pack up and the real owners would come back.'

I listened to him attentively, but I wondered how much he was describing what he had obscurely felt and how much he imagined now in his changed circumstances that he had felt.

'I used to hate hearing great-uncle Ferdy tell his Jewish stories. I thought it so damned mean. I understand now; it was a safety valve. My God, the strain of being a man about town. It's easier for daddy, he can play the old English squire at Tilby, but in the City he can be himself. He's all right. I've taken the make-up off and my stage clothes and at last I can be my real self too. What a relief! You know, I don't like English people. I never really know where I am with you. You're so dull and conventional. You never let yourselves go. There's no freedom in you, freedom of the soul, and you're such funks. There's nothing in the world you're so frightened of as doing the wrong thing.'

'Don't forget that you're English yourself, George,' I murmured.

He laughed.

'I? I'm not English. I haven't got a drop of English blood in me. I'm a Jew and you know it, and a German Jew into the bargain. I don't want to be English. I want to be a Jew. My friends are Jews. You don't know how much more easy I feel with them. I can be myself. We did everything we could to avoid Jews at home; Mummy, because she was blonde, thought she could get away with it and pretended she was a Gentile. What rot! D'you know, I have a lot of fun wandering about the Jewish parts of Munich and looking at the people. I went to Frankfort once, there are a lot of them there, and I walked about and looked at the frowzy old men with their hooked noses and the fat women with their false hair. I felt such a sympathy for them, I felt I belonged to them, I could have kissed them. When they looked at me I wondered if they knew that I was one of them. I wish to God I knew Yiddish. I'd like to become friends with them, and go into their houses and eat Kosher food and all that sort of thing. I wanted to go to a synagogue, but I was afraid I'd do the wrong thing and be kicked out. I like the smell of the Ghetto and the sense of life, and the mystery and the dust and the squalor and the romance. I shall never get the longing for it out of my head now. That's the real thing. All the rest is only pretence.'

'You'll break your father's heart,' I said.

'It's his or mine. Why can't he let me go? There's Harry. Harry would love to be squire of Tilby. He'd be an English gentleman all right. You know, mummy's set her heart on my marrying a Christian. Harry would love to. He'll found the good old English family all right. After all, I ask so little. I only want five pounds a week, and they can keep the title and the park and the Gainsboroughs and the whole bag of tricks.'

'Well, the fact remains that you gave your solemn word of honour to go back after two years.'

'I'll go back all right,' he said sullenly. 'Lea Makart has promised to come and hear me play.'

'What'll you do if she says you're no good?'

'Shoot myself,' he said gaily.

'What nonsense,' I answered in the same tone.

'Do *you* feel at home in England?'

'No,' I said, 'but then I don't feel at home anywhere else.'

But he was quite naturally not interested in me.

'I loathe the idea of going back. Now that I know what life has to offer I wouldn't be an English country gentleman for anything in the world. My God, the boredom of it!'

'Money's a very nice thing and I've always understood it's very pleasant to be an English peer.'

'Money means nothing to me. I want none of the things it can buy, and I don't happen to be a snob.'

It was growing very late and I had to get up early next day. It seemed unnecessary for me to pay too much attention to what George said. It was the sort of nonsense a young man might very well indulge in when thrown suddenly among painters and poets. Art is strong wine and needs a strong head to carry it. The divine fire burns most efficiently in those who temper its fury with horse sense. After all, George was not twenty-three yet. Time teaches. And when all was said and done his future was no concern of mine. I bade him good night and walked back to my hotel. The stars were shining in the indifferent sky. I left Munich in the morning.

I did not tell Muriel on my return to London what George had said to me, or what he looked like, but contented myself with assuring her that he was well and happy, working very hard, and seemed to be leading a virtuous and sober life. Six months later he came home. Muriel asked me to go down to Tilby for the week-end; Ferdy was bringing Lea Makart to hear George play and he particularly wished me to be there. I accepted. Muriel met me at the station.

'How did you find George?' I asked.

'He's very fat, but he seems in great spirits. I think he's pleased to be back again. He's been very sweet to his father.'

'I'm glad of that.'

'Oh, my dear, I do hope Lea Makart will say he's no good. It'll be such a relief to all of us.'

'I'm afraid it'll be a terrible disappointment to him.'

'Life is full of disappointments,' said Muriel crisply. 'But one learns to put up with them.'

I gave her a smile of amusement. We were sitting in a Rolls, and there was a footman as well as a chauffeur on the box. She wore a string of pearls that had probably cost forty thousand pounds. I recollected that in the birthday honours Sir Adolphus Bland had not been one of the three gentlemen on whom the King had been pleased to confer a peerage.

Lea Makart was able to make only a flying visit. She was playing that evening at Brighton and would motor over to Tilby on the Sunday morning for luncheon. She was returning to London the same day because she had a concert in Manchester on the Monday. George was to play in the course of the afternoon.

He's practising very hard,' his mother told me. 'That's why he didn't come with me to meet you.'

We turned in at the park gates and drove up the imposing avenue of elms that led to the house. I found that there was no party.

I met the dowager Lady Bland for the first time. I had always been curious to see her. I had had in my mind's eye a somewhat sensational picture of an old, old Jewish woman who lived alone in her grand house in Portland Place, and, with a finger in every pie, ruled her family with a despotic hand. She did not disappoint me. She was of commanding presence, rather tall, and stout without being corpulent. Her countenance was markedly Hebraic. She wore a rather heavy moustache and a wig of a peculiarly metallic brown. Her dress was very grand, of black brocade, and she had a row of large diamond stars on her breast and round her neck a chain of diamonds. Diamond rings gleamed on her wrinkled hands. She spoke in a rather harsh voice and with a strong German accent. When I was introduced to her she fixed me with shining eyes. She summed me up with dispatch and to my fancy at all events made no attempt to conceal from me that the judgement she formed was unfavourable.

'You have known my brother Ferdinand for many years, is it not so?' she said, rolling a guttural R. 'My brother Ferdinand has always moved in very good society. Where is Sir Adolphus, Muriel? Does he know your guest is arrived? And will you not send for George? If he does not know his pieces by now he will not know them by tomorrow.'

Muriel explained that Freddy was finishing a round of golf with his secretary and that she had had George told I was there. Lady Bland looked as though she thought Muriel's replies highly unsatisfactory and turned again to me.

'My daughter-in-law tells me you have been in Italy?'

'Yes, I've only just come back.'

'It is a beautiful country. How is the King?'

I said I did not know.

'I used to know him when he was a little boy. He was not very strong then. His mother, Queen Margherita, was a great friend of mine. They thought he would never marry. The Duchess of Aosta was very angry when he fell in love with that Princess of Montenegro.'

She seemed to belong to some long-past period of history, but she was very alert and I imagine that little escaped her beady eyes. Freddy, very spruce in plus-fours, presently came in. It was amusing and yet a little touching to see this grey-bearded man, as a rule somewhat domineering, so obviously on his best behaviour with the old lady. He called her Mamma. Then George came in. He was as fat as ever, but he had taken my advice and had his hair cut; he was losing his boyish looks, but he was a powerful and well-set-up young man. It was good to see the pleasure he took in his tea. He ate quantities of sandwiches and great hunks of cake. He had still a boy's appetite. His father watched him with a tender smile and as I looked at him I could not be surprised at the attachment which they all so obviously felt for him. He had an ingenuousness, a charm, and an enthusiasm which were certainly very pleasant. There was about him a generosity of demeanour, a frankness, and a natural cordiality which could not but make people take to him. I do not know whether it was owing to a hint from his grandmother or merely of his own good nature, but it was plain that he was going out of his way to be nice to his father; and in his father's soft eyes, in the way he hung upon the boy's words, in his pleased, proud, and happy look, you felt how bitterly the estrangement of the last two years had weighed on him. He adored George.

We played golf in the morning, a three-ball match, since Muriel, having to go to Mass, could not join us, and at one Ferdy arrived in Lea Makart's car. We sat down to luncheon. Of course Lea Makart's reputation was well known to me. She was acknowledged to be the greatest woman pianist in Europe. She was a very old friend of Ferdy's, who with his interest and patronage had greatly helped her at the beginning of her career, and it was he who had arranged for her to come and give her opinion of George's chances. At one time I went as often as I could to hear her play. She had no affectations; she played as a bird sings, without any appearance of effort, very naturally, and the silvery notes dripped from her light fingers in a curiously spontaneous manner, so that it gave you the impression that she was improvising those complicated rhythms. They used to tell me that her technique was wonderful. I could never make up my mind how much the delight her playing gave me was due to her person. In those days she was the most ethereal thing you could imagine, and it was surprising that a creature so sylphlike should be capable of so much power. She was very slight, pale, with enormous eyes and magnificent black hair, and at the piano she had a childlike wistfulness that was most appealing. She was very beautiful in a hardly human way and when she played, a little smile on her closed lips, she seemed to be remembering things she had heard in another world. Now, however, a woman in the early forties, she was sylphlike no more; she was stout and her face had broadened; she had no longer that lovely remoteness, but the authority of her long succession of triumphs. She was brisk, business-like, and somewhat overwhelming. Her vitality lit her with a natural spotlight as his sanctity surrounds the saint with a halo. She was not interested in anything very much but her own affairs, but since she had humour and knew the world she was able to invest them with gaiety. She held the conversation, but did not absorb it. George talked little. Every now and then she gave him a glance, but did not try to draw him in. I was the only Gentile at the table. All but old Lady Bland spoke perfect English, yet I could not help feeling that they did not speak like English people; I think they rounded their vowels more than we do, they certainly spoke louder, and the words seemed not to fall, but to gush from their lips. I think if I had been in another room where I could hear the tone but not the words of their speech I should have thought it was in a foreign language that they were conversing. The effect was slightly disconcerting.

Lea Makart wished to set out for London at about six, so it was arranged that George should play at four. Whatever the result of the audition, I felt that I, a stranger in the circle which her departure must render exclusively domestic, would be in the way and so, pretending an early engagement in town next morning, I asked her if she would take me with her in her car.

At a little before four we all wandered into the drawing-room. Old Lady Bland sat on a sofa with Ferdy; Freddy, Muriel, and I made ourselves comfortable in arm-chairs; and Lea Makart sat by herself. She chose instinctively a high-backed Jacobean chair that had somewhat the air of a throne, and in a yellow dress, with her olive skin, she looked very handsome. She had magnificent eyes. She was very much made up and her mouth was scarlet.

George gave no sign of nervousness. He was already seated at the piano when I went in with his father and mother, and he watched us quietly settling ourselves down. He gave me the shadow of a smile. When he saw that we were all at our ease he began to play. He played Chopin. He played two waltzes that were familiar to me, a polonaise and an *étude*. He played with a great deal of brio. I wish I knew music well enough to give an exact description of his playing. It had strength, and a youthful exuberance, but I felt that he missed what to me is the peculiar charm of Chopin, the tenderness, the nervous melancholy, the wistful gaiety and the slightly faded romance that reminds me always of an Early Victorian keepsake. And again I had the vague sensation, so slight that it almost escaped me, that the two hands did not quite synchronize. I looked at Ferdy and saw him give his sister a look of faint surprise. Muriel's eyes were fixed on the pianist, but presently she dropped them and for the rest of the time stared at the floor. His father looked at him too, and his eyes were steadfast, but unless I was much mistaken he went pale and his face betrayed something like dismay. Music was in the blood of all of them, all their lives they had heard the greatest pianists in the world, and they judged with instinctive precision. The only person whose face betrayed no emotion was Lea Makart. She listened very attentively. She was as still as an image in a niche.

At last he stopped and turning round on his seat faced her. He did not speak.

'What is it you want me to tell you?' she asked.

They looked into one another's eyes.

'I want you to tell me whether I have any chance of becoming in time a pianist in the first rank.'

'Not in a thousand years.'

For a moment there was dead silence. Freddy's head sank and he looked down at the carpet at his feet. His wife put out her hand and took his. But George continued to look steadily at Lea Makart.

'Ferdy has told me the circumstances,' she said at last. 'Don't think I'm influenced by them. Nothing of this is very important.' She made a great sweeping gesture that took in the magnificent room with the beautiful things it contained and all of us. 'If I thought you had in you the makings of an artist I shouldn't hesitate to beseech you to give up everything for art's sake. Art is the only thing that matters. In comparison with art, wealth and rank and power are not worth a straw.' She gave us a look so sincere that it was void of insolence.

'We are the only people who count. We give the world significance. You are only our raw material.'

I was not too pleased to be included with the rest under that heading, but that is neither here nor there.

'Of course I can see that you've worked very hard. Don't think it's been wasted. It will always be a pleasure to you to be able to play the piano and it will enable you to appreciate great playing as no ordinary person can hope to do. Look at your hands. They're not a pianist's hands.'

Involuntarily I glanced at George's hands. I had never noticed them before. I was astounded to see how podgy they were and how short and stumpy the fingers.

'Your ear is not quite perfect. I don't think you can ever hope to be more than a very competent amateur. In art the difference between the amateur and the professional is immeasurable.'

George did not reply. Except for his pallor no one would have known that he was listening to the blasting of all his hopes. The silence that fell was quite awful. Lea Makart's eyes suddenly filled with tears.

'But don't take my opinion alone,' she said. 'After all, I'm not infallible. Ask somebody else. You know how good and generous Paderewski is. I'll write to him about you and you can go down and play to him. I'm sure he'll hear you.'

George now gave a little smile. He had very good manners and whatever he was feeling did not want to make the situation too difficult for others.

'I don't think that's necessary, I am content to accept your verdict. To tell you the truth it's not so very different from my master's in Munich.'

He got up from the piano and lit a cigarette. It eased the strain. The others moved a little in their chairs. Lea Makart smiled at George.

'Shall I play to you?' she said.

'Yes, do.'

She got up and went to the piano. She took off the rings with which her fingers were laden. She played Bach. I do not know the names of the pieces, but I recognized the stiff ceremonial of the frenchified little German courts and the sober, thrifty comfort of the burghers, and the dancing on the village green, the green trees that looked like Christmas trees, and the sunlight on the wide German country, and a tender cosiness; and in my nostrils there was a warm scent of the soil and I was conscious of a sturdy strength that seemed to have its roots deep in mother earth, and of an elemental power that was timeless and had no home in space. She played beautifully, with a soft brilliance that made you think of the full moon shining at dusk in the summer sky. With another part of me I watched the others and I saw how intensely they were conscious of the experience. They were rapt. I wished with all my heart that I could get from music the wonderful exaltation that possessed them. She stopped, a smile hovered on her lips, and she put on her rings. George gave a little chuckle.

'That clinches it, I fancy,' he said.

The servants brought in tea and after tea Lea Makart and I bade the company farewell and got into the car. We drove up to London. She talked all the way, if not brilliantly at all events with immense gusto; she told me of her early years in Manchester and of the struggle of her beginnings. She was very interesting. She never even mentioned George; the episode was of no consequence, it was finished and she thought of it no more.

We little knew what was happening at Tilby. When we left George went out on the terrace and presently his father joined him. Freddy had won the day, but he was not happy. With his more than feminine sensitiveness he felt all that George was feeling, and George's anguish simply broke his heart. He had never loved his son more than then. When he appeared George greeted him with a little smile. Freddy's voice broke. In a sudden and overwhelming emotion he found it in him to surrender the fruits of his victory.

'Look here, old boy,' he said, 'I can't bear to think that you've had such a disappointment. Would you like to go back to Munich for another year and then see?'

George shook his head.

'No, it wouldn't be any good. I've had my chance. Let's call it a day.'

'Try not to take it too hard.'

'You see, the only thing in the world I want is to be a pianist. And there's nothing doing. It's a bit thick if you come to think of it.'

George, trying so hard to be brave, smiled wanly.

'Would you like to go round the world? You can get one of your Oxford pals to go with you and I'll pay all the expenses. You've been working very hard for a long time.'

'Thanks awfully, daddy, we'll talk about it. I'm just going for a stroll now.'

'Shall I come with you?'

'I'd rather go alone.'

Then George did a strange thing. He put his arm round his father's neck, and kissed him on the lips. He gave a funny little moved laugh and walked away. Freddy went back to the drawing-room. His mother, Ferdy, and Muriel were sitting there.

'Freddy, why don't you marry the boy?' said the old lady. 'He is twenty-three. It would take his mind off his troubles and when he is married and has a baby he will soon settle down like everybody else.'

'Whom is he to marry, mamma?' asked Sir Adolphus, smiling.

'That's not so difficult. Lady Frielinghausen came to see me the other day with her daughter Violet. She is a very nice maiden and she will have money of her own. Lady Frielinghausen gave me to understand that her Sir Jacob would come down very handsome if Violet made a good match.'

Muriel flushed.

'I hate Lady Frielinghausen. George is much too young to marry. He can afford to marry anyone he likes.'

Old Lady Bland gave her daughter a strange look.

'You are a very foolish girl, Miriam,' she said, using the name Muriel had long discarded. 'As long as I am here I shall not allow you to commit a foolishness.'

She knew as well as if Muriel had said it in so many words that she wanted George to marry a Gentile, but she knew also that so long as she was alive neither Freddy nor his wife would dare to suggest it.

But George did not go for a walk. Perhaps because the shooting season was about to open he took it into his head to go into the gun-room. He began to clean the gun that his mother had given him on his twentieth birthday. No one had used it since he went to Germany. Suddenly the servants were startled by a report. When they went into the gun-room they found George lying on the floor shot through the heart. Apparently the gun had been loaded and George while playing about with it had accidentally shot himself. One reads of such accidents in the paper often.

The
Creative Impulse

◆

I suppose that very few people know how Mrs Albert Forrester came to write
The Achilles Statue; and since it has been acclaimed as one of the great novels of
our time I cannot but think that a brief account of the circumstances that gave it
birth must be of interest to all serious students of literature; and indeed, if, as
the critics say, this is a book that will live, the following narrative, serving a
better purpose than to divert an idle hour, may be regarded by the historian of
the future as a curious footnote to the literary annals of our day.

Everyone of course remembers the success that attended the publication of
The Achilles Statue. Month after month printers were kept busy printing,
binders were kept busy binding, edition after edition; and the publishers, both
in England and America, were hard put to it to fulfil the pressing orders of the
booksellers. It was promptly translated into every European tongue and it has
been recently announced that it will soon be possible to read it in Japanese and
in Urdu. But it had previously appeared serially in magazines on both sides of
the Atlantic and from the editors of these Mrs Albert Forrester's agent had
wrung a sum that can only be described as thumping. A dramatization of the
work was made, which ran for a season in New York, and there is little doubt
that when the play is produced in London it will have an equal success. The
film rights have been sold at a great price. Though the amount that Mrs Albert
Forrester is reputed (in literary circles) to have made is probably exaggerated,
there can be no doubt that she will have earned enough money from this one
book to save her for the rest of her life from any financial anxiety.

It is not often that a book meets with equal favour from the public and the
critics, and that she, of all persons, had (if I may so put it) squared the circle
must have proved the more gratifying to Mrs Albert Forrester, since, though
she had received the commendation of the critics in no grudging terms (and

indeed had come to look upon it as her due) the public had always remained strangely insensible to her merit. Each work she published, a slender volume beautifully printed and bound in white buckram, was hailed as a masterpiece, always to the length of a column, and in the weekly reviews which you see only in the dusty library of a very long-established club even to the extent of a page; and well-read persons read and praised it. But well-read persons apparently do not buy books, and she did not sell. It was indeed a scandal that so distinguished an author, with an imagination so delicate and a style so exquisite, should remain neglected of the vulgar. In America she was almost completely unknown; and though Mr Carl van Vechten had written an article berating the public for its obtuseness, the public remained callous. Her agent, a warm admirer of her genius, had blackmailed an American publisher into taking two of her books by refusing, unless he did so, to let him have others (trashy novels doubtless) that he badly wanted, and they had been duly published. The reception they received from the press was flattering and showed that in America the best minds were sensitive to her talent; but when it came to the third book the American publisher (in the coarse way publishers have) told the agent that any money he had to spare he preferred to spend on synthetic gin.

Since *The Achilles Statue* Mrs Albert Forrester's previous books have been republished (and Mr Carl van Vechten has written another article pointing out sadly, but firmly, that he had drawn the attention of the reading world to the merits of this exceptional writer fully fifteen years ago), and they have been so widely advertised that they can scarcely have escaped the cultured reader's attention. It is unnecessary, therefore, for me to give an account of them; and it would certainly be no more than cold potatoes after those two subtle articles by Mr Carl van Vechten. Mrs Albert Forrester began to write early. Her first work (a volume of elegies) appeared when she was a maiden of eighteen; and from then on she published, every two or three years, for she had too exalted a conception of her art to hurry her production, a volume either of verse or prose. When *The Achilles Statue* was written she had reached the respectable age of fifty-seven, so that it will be readily surmised that the number of her works was considerable. She had given the world half a dozen volumes of verse, published under Latin titles, such as *Felicitas*, *Pax Maris*, and *Aes Triplex*, all of the graver kind, for her muse, disinclined to skip on a light, fantastic toe, trod a somewhat solemn measure. She remained faithful to the Elegy, and the Sonnet claimed much of her attention; but her chief distinction was to revive the Ode, a form of poetry that the poets of the present day somewhat neglect; and it may be asserted with confidence that her *Ode to President Fallières* will find a place in every anthology of English verse. It is admirable not only for the noble sonority of its rhythms, but also for its felicitous description of the pleasant land of France. Mrs Albert Forrester wrote of the valley of the Loire with its memories of du Bellay, of Chartres and the jewelled windows of its cathedral, of the sun-swept cities of Provence, with a sympathy all the more remarkable since she had never penetrated further into France than Boulogne, which she visited shortly after her marriage on an excursion steamer from Margate. But the physical mortification of being extremely seasick and the intellectual humiliation of discovering that the inhabitants of that popular seaside resort could not understand her fluent and idiomatic French made her determine not to expose herself a second time to experiences that were at once undignified and unpleasant; and she never again embarked on the treacherous element which she, however, sang (*Pax Maris*) in numbers both grave and sweet.

There are some fine passages too in the *Ode to Woodrow Wilson*, and I regret that, owing to a change in her sentiments towards that no doubt excellent man, the author decided not to reprint it. But I think it must be admitted that Mrs Albert Forrester's most distinguished work was in prose. She wrote several volumes of brief, but perfectly constructed, essays on such subjects as Autumn in Sussex, Queen Victoria, Death, Spring in Norfolk, Georgian Architecture, Monsieur de Diaghileff, and Dante; she also wrote works, both erudite and whimsical, on the Jesuit Architecture of the Seventeenth Century and on the Literary Aspect of the Hundred Years War. It was her prose that gained her that body of devoted admirers, fit though few, as with her rare gift of phrase she herself put it that proclaimed her the greatest master of the English language that this century has seen. She admitted herself that it was her style, sonorous yet racy, polished yet eloquent, that was her strong point; and it was only in her prose that she had occasion to exhibit the delicious, but restrained, humour that her readers found so irresistible. It was not a humour of ideas, nor even a humour of words; it was much more subtle than that, it was a humour of punctuation: in a flash of inspiration she had discovered the comic possibilities of the semi-colon, and of this she had made abundant and exquisite use. She was able to place it in such a way that if you were a person of culture with a keen sense of humour, you did not exactly laugh through a horse-collar, but you giggled delightedly, and the greater your culture the more delightedly you giggled. Her friends said that it made every other form of humour coarse and exaggerated. Several writers had tried to imitate her; but in vain: whatever else you might say about Mrs Albert Forrester you were bound to admit that she was able to get every ounce of humour out of the semi-colon and no one else could get within a mile of her.

Mrs Albert Forrester lived in a flat not far from the Marble Arch, which combined the advantage of a good address and a moderate rent. It had a handsome drawing-room on the street and a large bedroom for Mrs Albert Forrester, a darkish dining-room at the back, and a small poky bedroom, next door to the kitchen, for Mr Albert Forrester, who paid the rent. It was in the handsome drawing-room that Mrs Albert Forrester every Tuesday afternoon received her friends. It was a severe and chaste apartment. On the walls was a paper designed by William Morris himself, and on this, in plain black frames, mezzotints collected before mezzotints grew expensive; the furniture was of the Chippendale period, but for the roll-top desk, vaguely Louis XVI in character, at which Mrs Albert Forrester wrote her works. This was pointed out to visitors the first time they came to see her, and there were few who looked at it without emotion. The carpet was thick and the lights discreet. Mrs Albert Forrester sat in a straight-backed grandfather's chair covered with red damask. There was nothing ostentatious about it, but since it was the only comfortable chair in the room it set her apart as it were and above her guests. Tea was dispensed by a female of uncertain age, silent and colourless, who was never introduced to anyone but who was known to look upon it as a privilege to be allowed to save Mrs Albert Forrester from the irksome duty of pouring out tea. She was thus able to devote herself entirely to conversation, and it must be admitted that her conversation was excellent. It was not sprightly; and since it is difficult to indicate punctuation in speech it may have seemed to some slightly lacking in humour, but it was of wide range, solid, instructive, and interesting. Mrs Albert Forrester was well acquainted with social science, jurisprudence, and theology. She had read much and her memory was retentive. She had a pretty gift for quotation, which is a serviceable substitute for wit, and having for thirty years known more or less intimately a great many distinguished people she had a great many interesting anecdotes to tell, which she placed with tact and which she did not repeat more than was pardonable. Mrs Albert Forrester had the gift of attracting the most varied persons and you were liable at one and the same time to meet in her drawing-room an ex-Prime Minister, a newspaper proprietor, and the ambassador of a First Class Power. I always imagined that these great people came because they thought that here they rubbed shoulders with Bohemia, but with a Bohemia sufficiently neat and clean for them to be in no danger that the dirt would come off on them. Mrs Albert Forrester was deeply interested in politics and I myself heard a Cabinet Minister tell her frankly that she had a masculine intelligence. She had been opposed to Female Suffrage, but when it was at last granted to women she began to dally with the idea of going into Parliament. Her difficulty was that she did not know which party to choose.

'After all,' she said, with a playful shrug of her somewhat massive shoulders, 'I cannot form a party of one.'

Like many serious patriots, in her inability to know for certain which way the cat would jump she held her political opinions in suspense; but of late she had been definitely turning towards Labour as the best hope of the country, and if a safe seat were offered her it was felt fairly certain that she would not hesitate to come out into the open as a champion of the oppressed proletariat.

Her drawing-room was always open to foreigners, to Czecho-Slovaks, Italians, and Frenchmen, if they were distinguished, and to Americans even if they were obscure. But she was not a snob and you seldom met there a duke unless he was of a peculiarly serious turn and a peeress only if in addition to her rank she had the passport of some small social solecism such as having been divorced, written a novel, or forged a cheque, which might give her claim to Mrs Albert Forrester's catholic sympathies. She did not much care for painters, who were shy and silent; and musicians did not interest her: even if they consented to play, and if they were celebrated they were too often reluctant, their music was a hindrance to conversation: if people wanted music they could go to a concert; for her part she preferred the more subtle music of the soul. But her hospitality to writers, especially if they were promising and little known, was warm and constant. She had an eye for budding talent and there were few of the famous writers who from time to time drank a dish of tea with her whose first efforts she had not encouraged and whose early steps she had not guided. Her own position was too well assured for her to be capable of envy, and she had heard the word genius attached to her name too often to feel a trace of jealousy because the talents of others brought them a material success that was denied to her.

Mrs Albert Forrester, confident in the judgement of posterity, could afford to be disinterested. With these elements then it is no wonder that she had succeeded in creating something as near the French salon of the eighteenth century as our barbarous nation has ever reached. To be invited to 'eat a bun and drink a cup of tea on Tuesday' was a privilege that few failed to recognize; and when you sat on your Chippendale chair in the discreetly lit but austere room, you could not but feel that you were living literary history. The American Ambassador once said to Mrs Albert Forrester:

'A cup of tea with you, Mrs Forrester, is one of the richest intellectual treats which it has ever been my lot to enjoy.'

It was indeed on occasion a trifle overwhelming. Mrs Albert Forrester's taste was so perfect, she so inevitably admired the right thing and made the just observation about it, that sometimes you almost gasped for air. For my part I found it prudent to fortify myself with a cocktail or two before I exposed myself to the rarefied atmosphere of her society. Indeed, I very nearly found myself for ever excluded from it, for one afternoon, presenting myself at the door, instead of asking the maid who opened it: 'Is Mrs Forrester at home?' I asked: 'Is there Divine Service today?'

Of course it was said in pure inadvertence, but it was unfortunate that the maid sniggered, and one of Mrs Albert Forrester's most devoted admirers, Ellen Hannaway, happened to be at the moment in the hall taking off her goloshes. She told my hostess what I had said before I got into the drawing-room, and as I entered Mrs Albert Forrester fixed me with an eagle eye.

'Why did you ask if there was Divine Service today?' she inquired.

I explained that I was absent-minded, but Mrs Albert Forrester held me with a gaze that I can only describe as compelling.

'Do you mean to suggest that my parties are . . .' she searched for a word. 'Sacramental?'

I did not know what she meant, but did not like to show my ignorance before so many clever people, and I decided that the only thing was to seize my trowel and the butter.

'Your parties are like you, dear lady, perfectly beautiful and perfectly divine.'

A little tremor passed through Mrs Albert Forrester's substantial frame. She was like a man who enters suddenly a room filled with hyacinths; the perfume is so intoxicating that he almost staggers. But she relented.

'If you were trying to be facetious,' she said, 'I should prefer you to exercise your facetiousness on my guests rather than on my maids. . . . Miss Warren will give you some tea.'

Mrs Albert Forrester dismissed me with a wave of the hand, but she did not dismiss the subject, since for the next two or three years whenever she introduced me to someone she never failed to add:

'You must make the most of him, he only comes here as a penance. When he comes to the door he always asks: Is there Divine Service today? So amusing, isn't he?'

But Mrs Albert Forrester did not confine herself to weekly tea-parties: every Saturday she gave a luncheon of eight persons; this according to her opinion being the perfect number for general conversation and her dining-room conveniently holding no more. If Mrs Albert Forrester flattered herself upon anything it was not that her knowledge of English prosody was unique, but that her luncheons were celebrated. She chose her guests with care, and an invitation to one of them was more than a compliment, it was a consecration. Over the luncheon-table it was possible to keep the conversation on a higher level than in the mixed company of a tea-party and few can have left her dining-room without taking away with them an enhanced belief in Mrs Albert Forrester's ability and a brighter faith in human nature. She only asked men, since, stout enthusiast for her sex as she was and glad to see women on other occasions, she could not but realize that they were inclined at table to talk exclusively to their next-door neighbours and thus hinder the general exchange of ideas that made her own parties an entertainment not only of the body but of the soul. For it must be said that Mrs Albert Forrester gave you uncommonly good food, excellent wine, and a first-rate cigar. Now to anyone who has partaken of literary hospitality this must appear very remarkable, since literary persons for the most part think highly and live plainly; their minds are occupied with the things of the spirit and they do not notice that the roast mutton is underdone and the potatoes cold: the beer is all right, but the wine has a sobering effect, and it is unwise to touch the coffee. Mrs Albert Forrester was pleased enough to receive compliments on the fare she provided.

'If people do me the honour to break bread with me,' she said, 'it is only fair that I should give them as good food as they can get at home.'

But if the flattery was excessive she deprecated it.

'You really embarrass me when you give me a meed of praise which is not my due. You must praise Mrs Bulfinch.'

'Who is Mrs Bulfinch?'

'My cook.'

'She's a treasure then, but you're not going to ask me to believe that she's responsible for the wine.'

'Is it good? I'm terribly ignorant of such things; I put myself entirely in the hands of my wine merchant.'

But if mention was made of the cigars Mrs Albert Forrester beamed.

'Ah, for them you must compliment Albert. It is Albert who chooses the cigars and I am given to understand that no one knows more about a cigar than Albert.'

She looked at her husband, who sat at the end of the table, with the proud bright eyes of a pedigree hen (a Buff Orpington for choice) looking at her only chick. Then there was a quick flutter of conversation as the guests, anxious to be civil to their host and relieved at length to find an occasion, expressed their appreciation of his peculiar merit.

'You're very kind,' he said. 'I'm glad you like them.'

Then he would give a little discourse on cigars, explaining the excellencies he sought and regretting the deterioration in quality which had followed on the commercialization of the industry. Mrs Albert Forrester listened to him with a complacent smile, and it was plain that she enjoyed this little triumph of his. Of course you cannot go on talking of cigars indefinitely and as soon as she perceived that her guests were growing restive she broached a topic of more general, and it may be of more significant, interest. Albert subsided into silence. But he had had his moment.

It was Albert who made Mrs Forrester's luncheons to some less attractive than her tea-parties, for Albert was a bore; but though without doubt perfectly conscious of the fact, she made a point that he should come to them and in fact had fixed upon Saturdays (for the rest of the week he was busy) in order that he should be able to. Mrs Albert Forrester felt that her husband's presence on these festive occasions was an unavoidable debt that she paid to her own self-respect. She would never by a negligence admit to the world that she had married a man who was not spiritually her equal, and it may be that in the silent watches of the nights she asked herself where indeed such could have been found. Mrs Albert Forrester's friends were troubled by no such reticence and they said it was dreadful that such a woman should be burdened with such a man. They asked each other how she had ever come to marry him and (being mostly celibate) answered despairingly that no one ever knew why anybody married anybody else.

It was not that Albert was a verbose and aggressive bore; he did not button-hole you with interminable stories or pester you with pointless jokes; he did not crucify you on a platitude or hamstring you with a commonplace; he was just dull. A cipher. Clifford Boyleston, for whom the French Romantics had no secrets and who was himself a writer of merit, had said that when you looked into a room into which Albert had just gone there was nobody there. This was thought very clever by Mrs Albert Forrester's friends, and Rose Waterford, the well-known novelist and the most fearless of women, had ventured to repeat it to Mrs Albert Forrester. Though she pretended to be annoyed, she had not been able to prevent the smile that rose to her lips. Her behaviour towards Albert could not but increase the respect in which her friends held her. She insisted that whatever in their secret hearts they thought of him, they should treat him with the decorum that was due to her husband. Her own demeanour was admirable. If he chanced to make an observation she listened to him with a pleasant expression and when he fetched her a book that she wanted or gave her his pencil to make a note of an idea that had occurred to her, she always thanked him. Nor would she allow her friends pointedly to neglect him, and though, being a woman of tact, she saw that it would be asking too much of the world if she took him about with her always, and she went out much alone, yet her friends knew that she expected them to ask him to dinner at least once a year. He always accompanied her to public banquets when she was going to make a speech, and if she delivered a lecture she took care that he should have a seat on the platform.

Albert was, I believe, of average height, but perhaps because you never thought of him except in connexion with his wife (of imposing dimensions) you only thought of him as a little man. He was spare and frail and looked older than his age. This was the same as his wife's. His hair, which he kept very short, was white and meagre, and he wore a stubby white moustache; his was a face, thin and lined, without a noticeable feature; and his blue eyes, which once might have been attractive, were now pale and tired. He was always very neatly dressed in pepper-and-salt trousers, which he chose always of the same pattern, a black coat, and a grey tie with a small pearl pin in it. He was perfectly unobtrusive, and when he stood in Mrs Albert Forrester's drawing-room to receive the guests whom she had asked to luncheon you noticed him as little as you noticed the quiet and gentlemanly furniture. He was well mannered and it was with a pleasant, courteous smile that he shook hands with them.

'How do you do? I'm very glad to see you,' he said if they were friends of some standing. 'Keeping well, I hope?'

But if they were strangers of distinction coming for the first time to the house, he went to the door as they entered the drawing-room, and said:

'I am Mrs Albert Forrester's husband. I will introduce you to my wife.'

Then he led the visitor to where Mrs Albert Forrester stood with her back to the light, and she with a glad and eager gesture advanced to make the stranger welcome.

It was agreeable to see the demure pride he took in his wife's literary reputation and the self-effacement with which he furthered her interests. He was always there when he was wanted and never when he wasn't. His tact, if not deliberate, was instinctive. Mrs Albert Forrester was the first to acknowledge his merits.

'I really don't know what I should do without him,' she said. 'He's invaluable to me. I read him everything I write and his criticisms are often very useful.'

'Molière and his cook,' said Miss Waterford.

'Is that funny, dear Rose?' asked Mrs Forrester, somewhat acidly. When Mrs Albert Forrester did not approve of a remark, she had a way that put many persons to confusion of asking you whether it was a joke which she was too dense to see. But it was impossible to embarrass Miss Waterford. She was a lady who in the course of a long life had had many affairs, but only one passion, and this was for printer's ink. Mrs Albert Forrester tolerated rather than approved her.

'Come, come, my dear,' she replied, 'you know very well that he wouldn't exist without you. He wouldn't know us. It must be wonderful to him to come in contact with all the best brains and the most distinguished people of our day.'

'It may be that the bee would perish without the hive which shelters it, but the bee nevertheless has a significance of its own.'

And since Mrs Albert Forrester's friends, though they knew all about art and literature, knew little about natural history, they had no reply to this observation. She went on:

'He doesn't interfere with me. He knows subconsciously when I don't want to be disturbed and, indeed, when I am following out a train of thought I find his presence in the room a comfort rather than a hindrance to me.'

'Like a Persian cat,' said Miss Waterford.

'But like a very well-trained, well-bred, and well-mannered Persian cat,' answered Mrs Forrester severely, thus putting Miss Waterford in her place.

But Mrs Albert Forrester had not finished with her husband.

'We who belong to the intelligentsia,' she said, 'are apt to live in a world too exclusively our own. We are interested in the abstract rather than in the concrete, and sometimes I think that we survey the bustling world of human affairs in too detached a manner and from too serene a height. Do you not think that we stand in danger of becoming a little inhuman? I shall always be grateful to Albert because he keeps me in contact with the man in the street.'

It was on account of this remark, to which none of her friends could deny the rare insight and subtlety that characterized so many of her utterances, that for some time Albert was known in her immediate circle as The Man in the Street. But this was only for a while, and it was forgotten. He then became known as The Philatelist. It was Clifford Boyleston, with his wicked wit, who invented the name. One day, his poor brain exhausted by the effort to sustain a conversation with Albert, he had asked in desperation:

'Do you collect stamps?'

'No,' answered Albert mildly. 'I'm afraid I don't.'

But Clifford Boyleston had no sooner asked the question than he saw its possibilities. He had written a book on Baudelaire's aunt by marriage, which had attracted the attention of all who were interested in French literature, and was well known in his exhaustive studies of the French spirit to have absorbed a goodly share of the Gallic quickness and the Gallic brilliancy. He paid no attention to Albert's disclaimer, but at the first opportunity informed Mrs Albert Forrester's friends that he had at last discovered Albert's secret. He collected stamps. He never met him afterwards without asking him:

'Well, Mr Forrester, how is the stamp collection?' Or: 'Have you been buying any stamps since I saw you last?'

It mattered little that Albert continued to deny that he collected stamps, the invention was too apt not to be made the most of; Mrs Albert Forrester's friends insisted that he did, and they seldom spoke to him without asking him how he was getting on. Even Mrs Albert Forrester, when she was in a specially gay humour, would sometimes speak of her husband as The Philatelist. The name really did seem to fit Albert like a glove. Sometimes they spoke of him thus to his face and they could not but appreciate the good nature with which he took it; he smiled unresentfully and presently did not even protest that they were mistaken.

Of course Mrs Albert Forrester had too keen a social sense to jeopardize the success of her luncheons by allowing her more distinguished guests to sit on either side of Albert. She took care that only her older and more intimate friends should do this, and when the appointed victims came in she would say to them:

'I know you won't mind sitting by Albert, will you?'

They could only say that they would be delighted, but if their faces too plainly expressed their dismay she would pat their hands playfully and add:

'Next time you shall sit by me. Albert is so shy with strangers and you know so well how to deal with him.'

They did: they simply ignored him. So far as they were concerned the chair in which he sat might as well have been empty. There was no sign that it annoyed him to be taken no notice of by persons who after all were eating food he paid for, since the earnings of Mrs Forrester could certainly not have provided her guests with spring salmon and forced asparagus. He sat quiet and silent, and if he opened his mouth it was only to give a direction to one of the maids. If a guest were new to him he would let his eyes rest on him in a stare that would have been embarrassing if it had not been so childlike. He seemed to be asking himself what this strange creature was; but what answer his mild scrutiny gave him he never revealed. When the conversation grew animated he would look from one speaker to the other, but again you could not tell from his thin, lined face what he thought of the fantastic notions that were bandied across the table.

Clifford Boyleston said that all the wit and wisdom he heard passed over his head like water over a duck's back. He had given up trying to understand and now only made a semblance of listening. But Harry Oakland, the versatile critic, said that Albert was taking it all in; he found it all too, too marvellous, and with his poor, muddled brain he was trying desperately to make head or tail of the wonderful things he heard. Of course in the City he must boast of the distinguished persons he knew, perhaps there he was a light of learning and letters, an authority on the ideal; it would be perfectly divine to hear what he made of it all. Harry Oakland was one of Mrs Albert Forrester's staunchest admirers, and had written a brilliant and subtle essay on her style. With his refined and even beautiful features he looked like a San Sebastian who had had an accident with a hair-restorer; for he was uncommonly hirsute. He was a very young man, not thirty, but he had been in turn a dramatic critic, and a critic of fiction, a musical critic, and a critic of painting. But he was getting a little tired of art and threatened to devote his talents in future to the criticism of sport.

Albert, I should explain, was in the city and it was a misfortune that Mrs Forrester's friends thought she bore with meritorious fortitude that he was not even rich. There would have been something romantic in it if he had been a merchant prince who held the fate of nations in his hand or sent argosies, laden with rare spices, to those ports of the Levant the names of which have provided many a poet with so rich and rare a rhyme. But Albert was only a currant merchant and was supposed to make no more than just enabled Mrs Albert Forrester to conduct her life with distinction and even with liberality. Since his occupation kept him in his office till six o'clock he never managed to get to Mrs Albert Forrester's Tuesdays till the most important visitors were gone. By the time he arrived, there were seldom more than three or four of her more intimate friends in the drawing-room, discussing with freedom and humour the guests who had departed, and when they heard Albert's key in the front door they realized with one accord that it was late. In a moment he opened the door in his hesitating way and looked mildly in. Mrs Albert Forrester greeted him with a bright smile.

'Come in, Albert, come in. I think you know everybody here.'

Albert entered and shook hands with his wife's friends.

'Have you just come from the City?' she asked eagerly, though she knew there was nowhere else he could have come from. 'Would you like a cup of tea?'

'No, thank you, my dear. I had tea in my office.'

Mrs Albert Forrester smiled still more brightly and the rest of the company thought she was perfectly wonderful with him.

'Ah, but I know you like a second cup. I will pour it out for you myself.'

She went to the tea-table and, forgetting that the tea had been stewing for an hour and a half and was stone cold, poured him out a cup and added milk and sugar. Albert took it with a word of thanks, and meekly stirred it, but when Mrs Forrester resumed the conversation which his appearance had interrupted, without tasting it put it quietly down. His arrival was the signal for the party finally to break up, and one by one the remaining guests took their departure. On one occasion, however, the conversation was so absorbing and the point at issue so important that Mrs Albert Forrester would not hear of their going.

'It must be settled once for all. And after all,' she remarked in a manner that for her was almost arch, 'this is a matter on which Albert may have something to say. Let us have the benefit of his opinion.'

It was when women were beginning to cut their hair and the subject of discussion was whether Mrs Albert Forrester should or should not shingle. Mrs Albert Forrester was a woman of authoritative presence. She was large-boned and her bones were well covered; had she not been so tall and strong it might have suggested itself to you that she was corpulent. But she carried her weight gallantly. Her features were a little larger than life-size and it was this that gave her face doubtless the look of virile intellectuality that it certainly possessed. Her skin was dark and you might have thought that she had in her veins some trace of Levantine blood: she admitted that she could not but think there was in her a gypsy strain and that would account, she felt, for the wild and lawless passion that sometimes characterized her poetry. Her eyes were large and black and bright, her nose like the great Duke of Wellington's, but more fleshy, and her chin square and determined. She had a big mouth, with full red lips, which owed nothing to cosmetics, for of these Mrs Albert Forrester had never deigned to make use; and her hair, thick, solid, and grey, was piled on top of her head in such a manner as to increase her already commanding height. She was in appearance an imposing, not to say an alarming, female.

She was always very suitably dressed in rich materials of sombre hue and she looked every inch a woman of letters; but in her discreet way (being after all human and susceptible to vanity) she followed the fashions and the cut of her gowns was modish. I think for some time she had hankered to shingle her hair, but she thought it more becoming to do it at the solicitation of her friends than on her own initiative.

'Oh, you must, you must,' said Harry Oakland, in his eager, boyish way. 'You'd look too, too wonderful.'

Clifford Boyleston, who was now writing a book on Madame de Maintenon, was doubtful. He thought it a dangerous experiment.

'I think,' he said, wiping his eye-glasses with a cambric handkerchief, 'I think when one has made a type one should stick to it. What would Louis XIV have been without his wig?'

'I'm hesitating,' said Mrs Forrester. 'After all, we must move with the times. I am of my day and I do not wish to lag behind. America, as Wilhelm Meister said, is here and now.' She turned brightly to Albert. 'What does my lord and master say about it? What is your opinion, Albert? To shingle or not to shingle, that is the question.'

'I'm afraid my opinion is not of great importance, my dear,' he answered mildly.

'To me it is of the greatest importance,' answered Mrs Albert Forrester, flatteringly.

She could not but see how beautifully her friends thought she treated The Philatelist.

'I insist,' she proceeded, 'I insist. No one knows me as you do, Albert. Will it suit me?'

'It might,' he answered. 'My only fear is that with your—statuesque appearance short hair would perhaps suggest—well, shall we say, the Isle of Greece where burning Sappho loved and sung.'

There was a moment's embarrassed pause. Rose Waterford smothered a giggle, but the others preserved a stony silence. Mrs Forrester's smile froze on her lips. Albert had dropped a brick.

'I always thought Byron a very mediocre poet,' said Mrs Albert Forrester at last.

The company broke up. Mrs Albert Forrester did not shingle, nor indeed was the matter ever again referred to.

It was towards the end of another of Mrs Albert Forrester's Tuesdays that the event occurred that had so great an influence on her literary career.

It had been one of her most successful parties. The leader of the Labour Party had been there and Mrs Albert Forrester had gone as far as she could without definitely committing herself to intimate to him that she was prepared to throw in her lot with Labour. The time was ripe and if she was ever to adopt a political career she must come to a decision. A member of the French Academy had been brought by Clifford Boyleston and, though she knew he was wholly unacquainted with English, it had gratified her to receive his affable compliment on her ornate and yet pellucid style. The American Ambassador had been there and a young Russian prince whose authentic Romanoff blood alone prevented him from looking a gigolo. A duchess who had recently divorced her duke and married a jockey had been very gracious; and her strawberry leaves, albeit sere and yellow, undoubtedly added tone to the assembly. There had been quite a galaxy of literary lights. But now all, all were gone but Clifford Boyleston, Harry Oakland, Rose Waterford, Oscar Charles, and Simmons. Oscar Charles was a little, gnome-like creature, young but with the wizened face of a cunning monkey, with gold spectacles, who earned his living in a government office but spent his leisure in the pursuit of literature. He wrote little articles for the sixpenny weeklies and had a spirited contempt for the world in general. Mrs Albert Forrester liked him, thinking he had talent, but though he always expressed the keenest admiration for her style (it was indeed he who had named her the mistress of the semi-colon), his acerbity was so general that she also somewhat feared him. Simmons was her agent; a round-faced man who wore glasses so strong that his eyes behind them looked strange and misshapen. They reminded you of the eyes of some uncouth crustacean that you had seen in an aquarium. He came regularly to Mrs Albert Forrester's parties, partly because he had the greatest admiration for her genius and partly because it was convenient for him to meet prospective clients in her drawing-room.

Mrs Albert Forrester, for whom he had long laboured with but a trifling recompense, was not sorry to put him in the way of earning an honest penny, and she took care to introduce him, with warm expressions of gratitude, to anyone who might be supposed to have literary wares to sell. It was not without pride that she remembered that the notorious and vastly lucrative memoirs of Lady St Swithin had been first mooted in her drawing-room.

They sat in a circle of which Mrs Albert Forrester was the centre and discussed brightly and, it must be confessed, somewhat maliciously the various persons who had been that day present. Miss Warren, the pallid female who had stood for two hours at the tea-table, was walking silently round the room collecting cups that had been left here and there. She had some vague employment, but was always able to get off in order to pour out tea for Mrs Albert Forrester, and in the evening she typed Mrs Albert Forrester's manuscripts. Mrs Albert Forrester did not pay her for this, thinking quite rightly that as it was she did a great deal for the poor thing; but she gave her the seats for the cinema that were sent her for nothing and often presented her with articles of clothing for which she had no further use.

Mrs Albert Forrester in her rather deep, full voice was talking in a steady flow and the rest were listening to her with attention. She was in good form and the words that poured from her lips could have gone straight down on paper without alteration. Suddenly there was a noise in the passage as though something heavy had fallen and then the sound of an altercation. Mrs Albert Forrester stopped and a slight frown darkened her really noble brow.

'I should have thought they knew by now that I will not have this devastating racket in the flat. Would you mind ringing the bell, Miss Warren, and asking what is the reason of this tumult?'

Miss Warren rang the bell and in a moment the maid appeared. Miss Warren at the door, in order not to interrupt Mrs Albert Forrester, spoke to her in undertones. But Mrs Albert Forrester somewhat irritably interrupted herself.

'Well, Carter, what is it? Is the house falling down or has the Red Revolution at last broken out?'

'If you please, ma'am, it's the new cook's box,' answered the maid. 'The porter dropped it as he was bringing it in and the cook got all upset about it.'

'What do you mean by "the new cook"?'

'Mrs Bulfinch went away this afternoon, ma'am,' said the maid.

Mrs Albert Forrester stared at her.

'This is the first I've heard of it. Had Mrs Bulfinch given notice? The moment Mr Forrester comes in tell him that I wish to speak to him.'

'Very good, ma'am.'

The maid went out and Miss Warren slowly returned to the tea-table. Mechanically, though nobody wanted them, she poured out several cups of tea.

'What a catastrophe!' cried Miss Waterford.

'You must get her back,' said Clifford Boyleston. 'She's a treasure, that woman, a remarkable cook, and she gets better and better every day.'

But at that moment the maid came in again with a letter on a small plated salver and handed it to her mistress.

'What is this?' said Mrs Albert Forrester.

'Mr Forrester said I was to give you this letter when you asked for him, ma'am,' said the maid.

'Where is Mr Forrester then?'

'Mr Forrester's gone, ma'am,' answered the maid as though the question surprised her.

'Gone? That'll do. You can go.'

The maid left the room and Mrs Albert Forrester, with a look of perplexity on her large face, opened the letter. Rose Waterford has told me that her first thought was that Albert, fearful of his wife's displeasure at the departure of Mrs Bulfinch, had thrown himself in the Thames. Mrs Albert Forrester read the letter and a look of consternation crossed her face.

'Oh, monstrous,' she cried. 'Monstrous! Monstrous!'

'What is it, Mrs Forrester?'

Mrs Albert Forrester pawed the carpet with her foot like a restive, high-spirited horse pawing the ground, and crossing her arms with a gesture that is indescribable (but that you sometimes see in a fishwife who is going to make the very devil of a scene) bent her looks upon her curious and excessively startled friends.

'Albert has eloped with the cook.'

There was a gasp of dismay. Then something terrible happened. Miss Warren, who was standing behind the tea-table, suddenly choked. Miss Warren, who never opened her mouth and whom no one ever spoke to, Miss Warren, whom not one of them, though he had seen her every week for three years, would have recognized in the street, Miss Warren suddenly burst into uncontrollable laughter. With one accord, aghast, they turned and stared at her. They felt as Balaam must have felt when his ass broke into speech. She positively shrieked with laughter. There was a nameless horror about the sight, as though something had on a sudden gone wrong with a natural phenomenon, and you were just as startled as though the chairs and tables without warning began to skip about the floor in an antic dance. Miss Warren tried to contain herself, but the more she tried the more pitilessly the laughter shook her, and seizing a handkerchief she stuffed it in her mouth and hurried from the room. The door slammed behind her.

'Hysteria,' said Clifford Boyleston.

'Pure hysteria, of course,' said Harry Oakland.

But Mrs Albert Forrester said nothing.

The letter had dropped at her feet and Simmons, the agent, picked it up and handed it to her. She would not take it

'Read it,' she said. 'Read it aloud.'

Mr Simmons pushed his spectacles up on his forehead and holding the letter very close to his eyes read as follows:

My Dear—
  Mrs Bulfinch is in need of a change and has decided to leave, and as I do not feel inclined to stay on here without her I am going too. I have had all the literature I can stand and I am fed up with art. Mrs Bulfinch does not care about marriage, but if you care to divorce me she is willing to marry me. I hope you will find the new cook satisfactory. She has excellent references. It may save you trouble if I inform you that Mrs Bulfinch and I are living at 411 Kennington Road, S.E.

                                                                  Albert

No one spoke. Mr Simmons slipped his spectacles back on to the bridge of his nose. The fact was that none of them, brilliant as they were and accustomed to find topics of conversation to suit every occasion, could think of an appropriate remark. Mrs Albert Forrester was not the kind of woman to whom you could offer condolences and each was too much afraid of the other's ridicule to venture upon the obvious. At last Clifford Boyleston came bravely to the rescue.

'One doesn't know what to say,' he observed.

There was another silence and then Rose Waterford spoke.

'What does Mrs Bulfinch look like?' she asked.

'How should I know?' answered Mrs Albert Forrester, somewhat peevishly. 'I never looked at her. Albert always engaged the servants, she just came in for a moment so that I could see if her aura was satisfactory.'

'But you must have seen her every morning when you did the housekeeping.'

'Albert did the housekeeping. It was his own wish, so that I might be free to devote myself to my work. In this life one has to limit oneself.'

'Did Albert order your luncheons?' asked Clifford Boyleston.

'Naturally. It was his province.'

Clifford Boyleston slightly raised his eyebrows. What a fool he had been never to guess that it was Albert who was responsible for Mrs Forrester's beautiful food! And of course it was owing to him that the excellent Chablis was always just sufficiently chilled to run coolly over the tongue, but never so cold as to lose its bouquet and its savour.

'He certainly knew good food and good wine.'

'I always told you he had his points,' answered Mrs Albert Forrester, as though he were reproaching her. 'You all laughed at him. You would not believe me when I told you that I owed a great deal to him.'

There was no answer to this and once more silence, heavy and ominous, fell on the party. Suddenly Mr Simmons flung a bombshell.

'You must get him back.'

So great was her surprise that if Mrs Albert Forrester had not been standing against the chimney-piece she would undoubtedly have staggered two paces to the rear.

'What on earth do you mean?' she cried. 'I will never see him again as long as I live. Take him back? Never. Not even if he came and begged me on his bended knees.'

'I didn't say take him back; I said, get him back.'

But Mrs Albert Forrester paid no attention to the misplaced interruption.

'I have done everything for him. What would he be without me? I ask you. I have given him a position which never in his remotest dreams could he have aspired to.'

None could deny that there was something magnificent in the indignation of Mrs Albert Forrester, but it appeared to have little effect on Mr Simmons.

'What are you going to live on?'

Mrs Albert Forrester flung him a glance totally devoid of amiability.

'God will provide,' she answered in freezing tones.

'I think it very unlikely,' he returned.

Mrs Albert Forrester shrugged her shoulders. She wore an outraged expression. But Mr Simmons made himself as comfortable as he could on his chair and lit a cigarette.

'You know you have no warmer admirer of your art than me,' he said.

'Than I,' corrected Clifford Boyleston.

'Or than you,' went on Mr Simmonds blandly. 'We all agree that there is no one writing now whom you need fear comparison with. Both in prose and verse you are absolutely first class. And your style–well, everyone knows your style.'

'The opulence of Sir Thomas Browne with the limpidity of Cardinal Newman,' said Clifford Boyleston. 'The raciness of John Dryden with the precision of Jonathan Swift.'

The only sign that Mrs Albert Forrester heard was the smile that hesitated for a brief moment at the corners of her tragic mouth.

'And you have humour.'

'Is there anyone in the world,' cried Miss Waterford, 'who can put such a wealth of wit and satire and comic observation into a semi-colon?'

'But the fact remains that you don't sell,' pursued Mr Simmons imperturbably. 'I've handled your work for twenty years and I tell you frankly that I shouldn't have grown fat on my commission, but I've handled it because now and again I like to do what I can for good work. I've always believed in you and I've hoped that sooner or later we might get the public to swallow you. But if you think you can make your living by writing the sort of stuff you do I'm bound to tell you that you haven't a chance.'

'I have come into the world too late,' said Mrs Albert Forrester. 'I should have lived in the eighteenth century when the wealthy patron rewarded a dedication with a hundred guineas.'

'What do you suppose the currant business brings in?'

Mrs Albert Forrester gave a little sigh.

'A pittance. Albert always told me he made about twelve hundred a year.'

'He must be a very good manager. But you couldn't expect him on that income to allow you very much. Take my word for it, there's only one thing for you to do and that's to get him back.'

'I would rather live in a garret. Do you think I'm going to submit to the affront he has put upon me? Would you have me battle for his affections with my cook? Do not forget that there is one thing which is more valuable to a woman like me than her ease and that is her dignity.'

'I was just coming to that,' said Mr Simmons coldly.

He glanced at the others and those strange, lopsided eyes of his looked more than ever monstrous and fish-like.

'There is no doubt in my mind,' he went on, 'that you have a very distinguished and almost unique position in the world of letters. You stand for something quite apart. You never prostituted your genius for filthy lucre and you have held high the banner of pure art. You're thinking of going into Parliament. I don't think much of politics myself, but there's no denying that it would be a good advertisement and if you get in I daresay we could get you a lecture tour in America on the strength of it. You have ideals and this I can say, that even the people who've never read a word you've written respect you. But in your position there's one thing you can't afford to be and that's a joke.'

Mrs Albert Forrester gave a distinct start.

'What on earth do you mean by that?'

'I know nothing about Mrs Bulfinch and for all I know she's a very respectable woman, but the fact remains that a man doesn't run away with his cook without making his wife ridiculous. If it had been a dancer or a lady of title I daresay it wouldn't have done you any harm, but a cook would finish you. In a week you'd have all London laughing at you, and if there's one thing that kills an author or a politician it is ridicule. You must get your husband back and you must get him back pretty damned quick.'

A dark flush settled on Mrs Albert Forrester's face, but she did not immediately reply. In her ears there rang on a sudden the outrageous and unaccountable laughter that had sent Miss Warren flying from the room.

'We're all friends here and you can count on our discretion.'

Mrs Forrester looked at her friends and she thought that in Rose Waterford's eyes there was already a malicious gleam. On the wizened face of Oscar Charles was a whimsical look. She wished that in a moment of abandon she had not betrayed her secret. Mr Simmons, however, knew the literary world and allowed his eyes to rest on the company.

'After all you are the centre and head of their set. Your husband has not only run away from you but also from them. It's not too good for them either. The fact is that Albert Forrester has made you all look a lot of damned fools.'

'All,' said Clifford Boyleston. 'We're all in the same boat. He's quite right, Mrs Forrester. The Philatelist must come back.'

'*Et tu, Brute.*'

Mr Simmons did not understand Latin and if he had would probably not have been moved by Mrs Albert Forrester's exclamation. He cleared his throat.

'My suggestion is that Mrs Albert Forrester should go and see him tomorrow, fortunately we have his address, and beg him to reconsider his decision. I don't know what sort of things a woman says on these occasions, but Mrs Forrester has tact and imagination and she must say them. If Mr Forrester makes any conditions she must accept them. She must leave no stone unturned.'

'If you play your cards well there is no reason why you shouldn't bring him back here with you tomorrow evening,' said Rose Waterford lightly.

'Will you do it, Mrs Forrester?'

For two minutes, at least, turned away from them, she stared at the empty fireplace; then, drawing herself to her full height, she faced them.

'For my art's sake, not for mine. I will not allow the ribald laughter of the Philistine to besmirch all that I hold good and true and beautiful.'

'Capital,' said Mr Simmons, rising to his feet. 'I'll look in on my way home tomorrow and I hope to find you and Mr Forrester billing and cooing side by side like a pair of turtle-doves.'

He took his leave, and the others, anxious not to be left alone with Mrs Albert Forrester and her agitation, in a body followed his example.

It was latish in the afternoon next day when Mrs Albert Forrester, imposing in black silk and a velvet toque, set out from her flat in order to get a bus from the Marble Arch that would take her to Victoria Station. Mr Simmons had explained to her by telephone how to reach the Kennington Road with expedition and economy. She neither felt nor looked like Delilah. At Victoria she took the tram that runs down the Vauxhall Bridge Road. When she crossed the river she found herself in a part of London more noisy, sordid, and bustling than that to which she was accustomed, but she was too much occupied with her thoughts to notice the varied scene. She was relieved to find that the tram went along the Kennington Road and asked the conductor to put her down a few doors from the house she sought. When it did and rumbled on leaving her alone in the busy street, she felt strangely lost, like a traveller in an Eastern tale set down by a djinn in an unknown city. She walked slowly, looking to right and left, and notwithstanding the emotions of indignation and embarrassment that fought for the possession of her somewhat opulent bosom, she could not but reflect that here was the material for a very pretty piece of prose. The little houses held about them the feeling of a bygone age when here it was still almost country, and Mrs Albert Forrester registered in her retentive memory a note that she must look into the literary associations of the Kennington Road. Number four hundred and eleven was one of a row of shabby houses that stood some way back from the street; in front of it was a narrow strip of shabby grass, and a paved way led up to a latticed wooden porch that badly needed a coat of paint. This and the straggling, stunted creeper that grew over the front of the house gave it a falsely rural air which was strange and even sinister in that road down which thundered a tumultuous traffic. There was something equivocal about the house that suggested that here lived women to whom a life of pleasure had brought an inadequate reward.

The door was opened by a scraggy girl of fifteen with long legs and a tousled head.

'Does Mrs Bulfinch live here, do you know?'

'You've rung the wrong bell. Second floor.' The girl pointed to the stairs and at the same time screamed shrilly: 'Mrs Bulfinch, a party to see you. Mrs Bulfinch.'

Mrs Albert Forrester walked up the dingy stairs. They were covered with torn carpet. She walked slowly, for she did not wish to get out of breath. A door opened as she reached the second floor and she recognized her cook.

'Good afternoon, Bulfinch,' said Mrs Albert Forrester, with dignity. 'I wish to see your master.'

Mrs Bulfinch hesitated for the shadow of a second, then held the door wide open.

'Come in, ma'am.' She turned her head. 'Albert, here's Mrs Forrester to see you.'

Mrs Forrester stepped by quickly and there was Albert sitting by the fire in a leather-covered, but rather shabby, arm-chair, with his feet in slippers, and in shirtsleeves. He was reading the evening paper and smoking a cigar. He rose to his feet as Mrs Albert Forrester came in. Mrs Bulfinch followed her visitor into the room and closed the door.

'How are you, my dear?' said Albert cheerfully. 'Keeping well, I hope.'

'You'd better put on your coat, Albert,' said Mrs Bulfinch. 'What *will* Mrs Forrester think of you, finding you like that? I never.'

She took the coat, which was hanging on a peg, and helped him into it; and like a woman familiar with the peculiarities of masculine dress pulled down his waistcoat so that it should not ride over his collar.

'I received your letter, Albert,' said Mrs Forrester.

'I supposed you had, or you wouldn't have known my address, would you?'

'Won't you sit down, ma'am?' said Mrs Bulfinch, deftly dusting a chair, part of a suite covered in plum-covered velvet, and pushing it forwards.

Mrs Albert Forrester with a slight bow seated herself.

'I should have preferred to see you alone, Albert,' she said.

His eyes twinkled.

'Since anything you have to say concerns Mrs Bulfinch as much as it concerns me I think it much better that she should be present.'

'As you wish.'

Mrs Bulfinch drew up a chair and sat down. Mrs Albert Forrester had never seen her but with a large apron over a print dress. She was wearing now an open-work blouse of white silk, a black skirt, and high-heeled, patent-leather shoes with silver buckles. She was a woman of about five-and-forty, with reddish hair and a reddish face, not pretty, but with a good-natured look, and buxom. She reminded Mrs Albert Forrester of a serving-wench, somewhat overblown, in a jolly picture by an old Dutch master.

'Well, my dear, what have you to say to me?' asked Albert.

Mrs Albert Forrester gave him her brightest and most affable smile. Her great black eyes shone with tolerant good-humour.

'Of course you know that this is perfectly absurd, Albert. I think you must be out of your mind.'

'Do you, my dear? Fancy that.'

'I'm not angry with you, I'm only amused, but a joke's a joke and should not be carried too far. I've come to take you home.'

'Was my letter not quite clear?'

'Perfectly. I ask no questions and I will make no reproaches. We will look upon this as a momentary aberration and say no more about it.'

'Nothing will induce me ever to live with you again, my dear,' said Albert in, however, a perfectly friendly fashion.

'You're not serious?'

'Quite.'

'Do you love this woman?'

Mrs Albert Forrester still smiled with an eager and somewhat metallic brightness. She was determined to take the matter lightly. With her intimate sense of values she realized that the scene was comic. Albert looked at Mrs Bulfinch and a smile broke out on his withered face.

'We get on very well together, don't we, old girl?'

'Not so bad,' said Mrs Bulfinch.

Mrs Albert Forrester raised her eyebrows; her husband had never in all their married life called *her* 'old girl': nor indeed would she have wished it.

'If Bulfinch has any regard or respect for you she must know that the thing is impossible. After the life you've led and the society you've moved in she can hardly expect to make you permanently happy in miserable furnished lodgings.'

'They're not furnished lodgings, ma'am,' said Mrs Bulfinch. 'It's all me own furniture. You see, I'm very independent-like and I've always liked to have a home of me own. So I keep these rooms on whether I'm in a situation or whether I'm not, and so I always have some place to go back to.'

'And a very nice cosy little place it is,' said Albert.

Mrs Albert Forrester looked about her. There was a kitchen range in the fireplace on which a kettle was simmering and on the mantelshelf was a black marble clock flanked by black marble candelabra. There was a large table covered with a red cloth, a dresser, and a sewing-machine. On the walls were photographs and framed pictures from Christmas supplements. A door at the back, covered with a red plush portière, led into what, considering the size of the house, Mrs Albert Forrester (who in her leisure moments had made a somewhat extensive study of architecture) could not but conclude was the only bedroom. Mrs Bulfinch and Albert lived in a contiguity that allowed no doubt about their relations.

'Have you not been happy with me, Albert?' asked Mrs Forrester in a deeper tone.

'We've been married for thirty-five years, my dear. It's too long. It's a great deal too long. You're a good woman in your way, but you don't suit me. You're literary and I'm not. You're artistic and I'm not.'

'I've always taken care to make you share in all my interests. I've taken great pains that you shouldn't be overshadowed by my success. You can't say that I've ever left you out of things.'

'You're a wonderful writer, I don't deny it for a moment, but the truth is I don't like the books you write.'

'That, if I may be permitted to say so, merely shows that you have very bad taste. All the best critics admit their power and their charm.'

'And I don't like your friends. Let me tell you a secret, my dear. Often at your parties I've had an almost irresistible impulse to take off all my clothes just to see what would happen.'

'Nothing would have happened,' said Mrs Albert Forrester with a slight frown. 'I should merely have sent for the doctor.'

'Besides you haven't the figure for that, Albert,' said Mrs Bulfinch.

Mr Simmons had hinted to Mrs Albert Forrester that if the need arose she must not hesitate to use the allurements of her sex in order to bring back her erring husband to the conjugal roof, but she did not in the least know how to do this. It would have been easier, she could not but reflect, had she been in evening dress.

'Does the fidelity of five-and-thirty years count for nothing? I have never looked at another man, Albert. I'm used to you. I shall be lost without you.'

'I've left all my menus with the new cook, ma'am. You've only got to tell her how many to luncheon and she'll manage,' said Mrs Bulfinch. 'She's very reliable and she has as light a hand with pastry as anyone I ever knew.'

Mrs Albert Forrester began to be discouraged. Mrs Bulfinch's remark, well meant no doubt, made it difficult to bring the conversation on to the plane on which emotion could be natural.

'I'm afraid you're only wasting your time, my dear,' said Albert. 'My decision is irrevocable. I'm not very young any more and I want someone to take care of me. I shall of course make you as good an allowance as I can. Corinne wants me to retire.'

'Who is Corinne?' asked Mrs Forrester with the utmost surprise.

'It's my name,' said Mrs Bulfinch. 'My mother was half French.'

'That explains a great deal,' replied Mrs Forrester, pursing her lips, for though she admired the literature of our neighbours she knew that their morals left much to be desired.

'What I say is, Albert's worked long enough, and it's about time he started enjoying himself. I've got a little bit of property at Clacton-on-Sea. It's a very healthy neighbourhood and the air is wonderful. We could live there very comfortable. And what with the beach and the pier there's always something to do. They're a very nice lot of people down there. If you don't interfere with nobody, nobody'll interfere with you.'

'I discussed the matter with my partners today and they're willing to buy me out. It means a certain sacrifice. When everything is settled I shall have an income of nine hundred pounds a year. There are three of us, so it gives us just three hundred a year apiece.'

'How am I to live on that?' cried Mrs Albert Forrester. 'I have my position to keep up.'

'You have a fluent, a fertile, and a distinguished pen, my dear.'

Mrs Albert Forrester impatiently shrugged her shoulders.

'You know very well that my books don't bring me in anything but reputation. The publishers always say that they lose by them and in fact they only publish them because it gives them prestige.'

It was then that Mrs Bulfinch had the idea that was to have consequences of such magnitude.

'Why don't you write a good thrilling detective story?' she asked.

'Me?' exclaimed Mrs Albert Forrester, for the first time in her life regardless of grammar.

'It's not a bad idea,' said Albert. 'It's not a bad idea at all.'

'I should have the critics down on me like a thousand bricks.'

'I'm not so sure of that. Give the highbrow the chance of being lowbrow without demeaning himself and he'll be so grateful to you, he won't know what to do.'

'For this relief much thanks,' murmured Mrs Albert Forrester reflectively.

'My dear, the critics'll eat it. And written in your beautiful English they won't be afraid to call it a masterpiece.'

'The idea is preposterous. It's absolutely foreign to my genius. I could never hope to please the masses.'

'Why not? The masses want to read good stuff, but they dislike being bored. They all know your name, but they don't read you, because you bore them. The fact is, my dear, you're dull.'

'I don't know how you can say that, Albert,' replied Mrs Albert Forrester, with as little resentment as the equator might feel if someone called it chilly. 'Everyone knows and acknowledges that I have an exquisite sense of humour and there is nobody who can extract so much good wholesome fun from a semi-colon as I can.'

'If you can give the masses a good thrilling story and let them think at the same time that they are improving their minds you'll make a fortune.'

'I've never read a detective story in my life,' said Mrs Albert Forrester. 'I once heard of a Mr Barnes of New York and I was told that he had written a book called *The Mystery of a Hansom Cab*. But I never read it.'

'Of course you have to have the knack,' said Mrs Bulfinch. 'The first thing to remember is that you don't want any lovemaking, it's out of place in a detective story, what you want is murder, and sleuth-hounds, and you don't want to be able to guess who done it till the last page.'

'But you must play fair with your reader, my dear,' said Albert. 'It always annoys me when suspicion has been thrown on the secretary or the lady of the title and it turns out to be the second footman who's never done more than say, "The carriage is at the door." Puzzle your reader as much as you can, but don't make a fool of him.'

'I love a good detective story,' said Mrs Bulfinch. 'Give me a lady in evening dress, just streaming with diamonds, lying on the library floor with a dagger in her heart, and I know I'm going to have a treat.'

'There's no accounting for tastes,' said Albert. 'Personally, I prefer a respectable family solicitor, with side-whiskers, gold watch-chain, and a benign appearance, lying dead in Hyde Park.'

'With his throat cut?' asked Mrs Bulfinch eagerly.

'No, stabbed in the back. There's something peculiarly attractive to the reader in the murder of a middle-aged gentleman of spotless reputation. It is pleasant to think that the most apparently blameless of us have a mystery in our lives.'

'I see what you mean, Albert,' said Mrs Bulfinch. 'He was the repository of a fatal secret.'

'We can give you all the tips, my dear,' said Albert, smiling mildly at Mrs Albert Forrester. 'I've read hundreds of detective stories.'

'You!'

'That's what first brought Corinne and me together. I used to pass them on to her when I'd finished them.'

'Many's the time I've heard him switch off the electric light as the dawn was creeping through the window and I couldn't help smiling to myself as I said: "There, he's finished it at last, now he can have a good sleep."'

Mrs Albert Forrester rose to her feet. She drew herself up.

'Now I see what a gulf separates us,' she said, and her fine contralto shook a little. 'You have been surrounded for thirty years with all that was best in English literature and you read hundreds of detective novels.'

'Hundreds and hundreds,' interrupted Albert with a smile of satisfaction.

'I came here willing to make any reasonable concession so that you should come back to your home, but now I wish it no longer. You have shown me that we have nothing in common and never had. There is an abyss between us.'

'Very well, my dear,' said Albert gently, 'I will submit to your decision. But you think over the detective story.'

'I will arise and go now,' she murmured, 'and go to Innisfree.'

'I'll just show you downstairs,' said Mrs Bulfinch. 'One has to be careful of the carpet if one doesn't exactly know where the holes are.'

With dignity, but not without circumspection, Mrs Albert Forrester walked downstairs and when Mrs Bulfinch opened the door and asked her if she would like a taxi she shook her head.

'I shall take the tram.'

'You need not be afraid that I won't take good care of Mr Forrester, ma'am,' said Mrs Bulfinch pleasantly. 'He shall have every comfort. I nursed Mr Bulfinch for three years during his last illness and there's very little I don't know about invalids. Not that Mr Forrester isn't very strong and active for his years. And of course he'll have a hobby. I always think a man should have a hobby. He's going to collect postage-stamps.'

Mrs Albert Forrester gave a little start of surprise. But just then a tram came in sight and, as a woman (even the greatest of them) will, she hurried at the risk of her life into the middle of the road and waved frantically. It stopped and she climbed in. She did not know how she was going to face Mr Simmons. He would be waiting for her when she got home. Clifford Boyleston would prob- ably be there too. They would all be there and she would have to tell them that she had miserably failed. At that moment she had no warm feeling of friendship for her little group of devoted admirers. Wondering what the time was, she looked up at the man sitting opposite her to see whether he was the kind of person she could modestly ask, and suddenly started; for sitting there was a middle-aged gentleman of the most respectable appearance, with side-whiskers, a benign expression, and a gold watch-chain. It was the very man whom Albert had described lying dead in Hyde Park and she could not but jump to the conclusion that he was a family solicitor. The coincidence was extraordinary and really it looked as though the hand of fate were beckoning to her. He wore a silk hat, a black coat, and pepper-and-salt trousers, he was somewhat corpulent, of a powerful build, and by his side was a despatch-case. When the tram was half-way down the Vauxhall Bridge Road he asked the conductor to stop and she saw him go down a small, mean street. Why? Ah, why? When it reached Victoria, so deeply immersed in thought was she, until the conductor somewhat roughly told her where she was, she did not move. Edgar Allan Poe had written detective stories. She took a bus. She sat inside, buried in reflection, but when it arrived at Hyde Park Corner she suddenly made up her mind to get out. She couldn't sit still any longer. She felt she must walk. She entered the gates, walking slowly, and looked about her with an air that was at once intent and abstracted. Yes, there was Edgar Allan Poe; no one could deny that. After all he had invented the genre, and everyone knew how great his influence had been on the Parnassians. Or was it the Symbolists? Never mind. Baudelaire and all that. As she passed the Achilles Statue she stopped for a minute and looked at it with raised eyebrows.

At length she reached her flat and opening the door saw several hats in the hall. They were all there. She went into the drawing-room.

'Here she is at last,' cried Miss Waterford.

Mrs Albert Forrester advanced, smiling with animation, and shook the proffered hands. Mr Simmons and Clifford Boyleston were there, Harry Oakland and Oscar Charles.

'Oh, you poor things, have you had no tea?' she cried brightly. 'I haven't an idea what the time is, but I know I'm fearfully late.'

'Well?' they said. 'Well?'

'My dears, I've got something quite wonderful to tell you. I've had an inspiration. Why should the devil have all the best tunes?'

'What *do* you mean?'

She paused in order to give full effect to the surprise she was going to spring upon them. Then she flung it at them without preamble.

'I'M GOING TO WRITE A DETECTIVE STORY.'

They stared at her with open mouths. She held up her hand to prevent them from interrupting her, but indeed no one had the smallest intention of doing so.

'I am going to raise the detective story to the dignity of Art. It came to me suddenly in Hyde Park. It's a murder story and I shall give the solution on the very last page. I shall write it in an impeccable English, and since it's occurred to me lately that perhaps I've exhausted the possibilities of the semi-colon, I am going to take up the colon. No one yet has explored its potentialities. Humour and mystery are what I aim at. I shall call it *The Achilles Statue.*'

'What a title!' cried Mr Simmons, recovering himself before any of the others. 'I can sell the serial rights on the title and your name alone.'

'But what about Albert?' asked Clifford Boyleston.

'Albert?' echoed Mrs Forrester. 'Albert?'

She looked at him as though for the life of her she could not think what he was talking about. Then she gave a little cry as if she had suddenly remembered.

'Albert! I knew I'd gone out on some errand and it absolutely slipped my memory. I was walking through Hyde Park and I had this inspiration. What a fool you'll all think me!'

'Then you haven't seen Albert?'

'My dear, I forgot all about him.' She gave an amused laugh. 'Let Albert keep his cook. I can't bother about Albert now. Albert belongs to the semi-colon period. I am going to write a detective story.' ·

'My dear, you're too, too wonderful,' said Harry Oakland.

Virtue

There are few things better than a good Havana. When I was young and very poor and smoked a cigar only when somebody gave me one, I determined that if ever I had money I would smoke a cigar every day after luncheon and after dinner. This is the only resolution of my youth that I have kept. It is the only ambition I have achieved that has never been embittered by disillusion. I like a cigar that is mild, but full-flavoured, neither so small that it is finished before you have become aware of it nor so large as to be irksome, rolled so that it draws without consciousness of effort on your part, with a leaf so firm that it doesn't become messy on your lips, and in such condition that it keeps its savour to the very end. But when you have taken the last pull and put down the shapeless stump and watched the final cloud of smoke dwindle blue in the surrounding air it is impossible, if you have a sensitive nature, not to feel a certain melancholy at the thought of all the labour, the care and pains that have gone, the thought, the trouble, the complicated organization that have been required to provide you with half an hour's delight. For this men have sweltered long years under tropical suns and ships have scoured the seven seas. These reflections become more poignant still when you are eating a dozen oysters (with half a bottle of dry white wine), and they become almost unbearable when it comes to a lamb cutlet. For these are animals and there is something that inspires awe in the thought that since the surface of the earth became capable of supporting life from generation to generation for millions upon millions of years creatures have come into existence to end at last upon a plate of crushed ice or on a silver grill. It may be that a sluggish fancy cannot grasp the dreadful solemnity of eating an oyster and evolution has taught us that the bivalve has through the ages kept itself to itself in a manner that inevitably alienates sympathy. There is an aloofness in it that is offensive to the aspiring spirit of man and a self-complacency that is obnoxious to his vanity. But I do not know how anyone can look upon a lamb cutlet without thoughts too deep for tears: here man himself has taken a hand and the history of the race is bound up with the tender morsel on your plate.

And sometimes even the fate of human beings is curious to consider. It is strange to look upon this man or that, the quiet ordinary persons of every day, the bank clerk, the dustman, the middle-aged girl in the second row of the chorus, and think of the interminable history behind them and of the long, long series of hazards by which from the primeval slime the course of events has brought them at this moment to such and such a place. When such tremendous vicissitudes have been needed to get them here at all one would have thought some huge significance must be attached to them; one would have thought that what befell them must matter a little to the Life Spirit or whatever else it is that has produced them. An accident befalls them. The thread is broken. The story that began with the world is finished abruptly and it looks as though it meant nothing at all. A tale told by an idiot. And is it not odd that this event, of an importance so dramatic, may be brought about by a cause so trivial?

An incident of no moment, that might easily not have happened, has consequences that are incalculable. It looks as though blind chance ruled all things. Our smallest actions may affect profoundly the whole lives of people who have nothing to do with us. The story I have to tell would never have happened if one day I had not walked across the street. Life is really very fantastic and one has to have a peculiar sense of humour to see the fun of it.

I was strolling down Bond Street one spring morning and having nothing much to do till lunch-time thought I would look in at Sotheby's, the auction rooms, to see whether there was anything on show that interested me. There was a block in the traffic and I threaded my way through the cars. When I reached the other side I ran into a man I had known in Borneo coming out of a hatter's.

'Hullo, Morton,' I said. 'When did you come home?'

'I've been back about a week.'

He was a District Officer. The Governor had given me a letter of introduction to him and I wrote and told him I meant to spend a week at the place he lived at and should like to put up at the government rest-house. He met me on the ship when I arrived and asked me to stay with him. I demurred. I did not see how I could spend a week with a total stranger, I did not want to put him to the expense of my board, and besides I thought I should have more freedom if I were on my own. He would not listen to me.

'I've got plenty of room,' he said, 'and the rest-house is beastly. I haven't spoken to a white man for six months and I'm fed to the teeth with my own company.'

But when Morton had got me and his launch had landed us at the bungalow and he had offered me a drink he did not in the least know what to do with me. He was seized on a sudden with shyness, and his conversation, which had been fluent and ready, ran dry. I did my best to make him feel at home (it was the least I could do, considering that it was his own house) and asked him if he had any new records. He turned on the gramophone and the sound of rag-time gave him confidence.

His bungalow overlooked the river and his living-room was a large veranda. It was furnished in the impersonal fashion that characterized the dwellings of government officials who were moved here and there at little notice according to the exigencies of the service. There were native hats as ornaments on the walls and the horns of animals, blow-pipes, and spears. In the book-shelf were detective novels and old magazines. There was a cottage piano with yellow keys. It was very untidy, but not uncomfortable.

Unfortunately I cannot very well remember what he looked like. He was young, twenty-eight, I learnt later, and he had a boyish and attractive smile. I spent an agreeable week with him. We went up and down the river and we climbed a mountain. We had tiffin one day with some planters who lived twenty miles away and every evening we went to the club. The only members were the manager of a kutch factory and his assistants, but they were not on speaking terms with one another and it was only on Morton's representations that they must not let him down when he had a visitor that we could get up a rubber of bridge. The atmosphere was strained. We came back to dinner, listened to the gramophone, and went to bed. Morton had little office work and one would have thought the time hung heavy on his hands, but he had energy and high spirits; it was his first post of the sort and he was happy to be independent. His only anxiety was lest he should be transferred before he had finished a road he was building. This was the joy of his heart. It was his own idea and he had wheedled the government into giving him the money to make it; he had surveyed the country himself and traced the path. He had solved unaided the technical problems that presented themselves. Every morning, before he went to his office, he drove out in a rickety old Ford to where the coolies were working and watched the progress that had been made since the day before. He thought of nothing else. He dreamt of it at night. He reckoned that it would be finished in a year and he did not want to take his leave till then. He could not have worked with more zest if he had been a painter or a sculptor creating a work of art. I think it was this eagerness that made me take a fancy to him. I liked his zeal. I liked his ingenuousness. And I was impressed by the passion for achievement that made him indifferent to the solitariness of his life, to promotion, and even to the thought of going home. I forget how long the road was, fifteen or twenty miles, I think, and I forget what purpose it was to serve. I don't believe Morton cared very much. His passion was the artist's and his triumph was the triumph of man over nature. He learnt as he went along. He had the jungle to contend against, torrential rains that destroyed the labour of weeks, accidents of topography; he had to collect his labour and hold it together; he had inadequate funds. His imagination sustained him. His labours gained a sort of epic quality and the vicissitudes of the work were a great saga that unrolled itself with an infinity of episodes.

His only complaint was that the day was too short. He had office duties, he was judge and tax collector, father and mother (at twenty-eight) of the people in his district; he had now and then to make tours that took him away from home. Unless he was on the spot nothing was done. He would have liked to be there twenty-four hours a day driving the reluctant coolies to further effort. It so happened that shortly before I arrived an incident had occurred that filled him with jubilation. He had offered a contract to a Chinese to make a certain section of the road and the Chinese had asked more than Morton could afford to pay. Notwithstanding interminable discussions they had been unable to arrive at an agreement and Morton with rage in his heart saw his work held up. He was at his wits' end. Then going down to his office one morning, he heard that there had been a row in one of the Chinese gambling houses the night before. A coolie had been badly wounded and his assailant was under arrest. This assailant was the contractor. He was brought into court, the evidence was clear, and Morton sentenced him to eighteen months' hard labour.

'Now he'll have to build the blasted road for nothing,' said Morton, his eyes glistening when he told me the story.

We saw the fellow at work one morning, in the prison sarong, unconcerned. He was taking his misfortune in good part.

'I've told him I'll remit the rest of his sentence when the road's finished,' said Morton, 'and he's as pleased as Punch. Bit of a snip for me, eh, what?'

When I left Morton I asked him to let me know when he came to England and he promised to write to me as soon as he landed. On the spur of the moment one gives these invitations and one is perfectly sincere about them. But when one is taken at one's word a slight dismay seizes one. People are so different at home from what they are abroad. There they are easy, cordial, and natural. They have interesting things to tell you. They are immensely kind. You are anxious when your turn comes to do something in return for the hospitality you have received. But it is not easy. The persons who were so entertaining in their own surroundings are very dull in yours. They are constrained and shy. You introduce them to your friends and your friends find them a crashing bore. They do their best to be civil, but sigh with relief when the strangers go and the conversation can once more run easily in its accustomed channels. I think the residents in far places early in their careers understand the situation pretty well, as the result maybe of bitter and humiliating experiences, for I have found that they seldom take advantage of the invitation which on some outstation on the edge of the jungle has been so cordially extended to them and by them as cordially accepted. But Morton was different. He was a young man and single. It is generally the wives that are the difficulty; other women look at their drab clothes, in a glance take in their provincial air, and freeze them with their indifference. But a man can play bridge and tennis, and dance. Morton had charm. I had had no doubt that in a day or two he would find his feet.

'Why didn't you let me know you were back?' I asked him.

'I thought you wouldn't want to be bothered with me,' he smiled.

'What nonsense!'

Of course now as we stood in Bond Street on the kerb and chatted for a minute he looked strange to me. I had never seen him in anything but khaki shorts and a tennis shirt, except when we got back from the club at night and he put on a pyjama jacket and a sarong for dinner. It is as comfortable a form of evening dress as has ever been devised. He looked a bit awkward in his blue serge suit. His face against a white collar was very brown.

'How about the road?' I asked him.

'Finished. I was afraid I'd have to postpone my leave, we struck one or two snags towards the end, but I made 'em hustle and the day before I left I drove the Ford to the end and back without stopping.'

I laughed. His pleasure was charming.

'What have you been doing with yourself in London?'

'Buying clothes.'

'Been having a good time?'

'Marvellous. A bit lonely, you know, but I don't mind that. I've been to a show every night. The Palmers, you know, I think you met them in Sarawak, were going to be in town and we were going to do the play together, but they had to go to Scotland because her mother's ill.'

His words, said so breezily, cut me to the quick. His was the common experience. It was heartbreaking. For months, for long months before it was due, these people planned their leave, and when they got off the ship they were in such spirits they could hardly contain themselves. London. Shops and clubs and theatres and restaurants. London. They were going to have the time of their lives. London. It swallowed them. A strange turbulent city, not hostile but indifferent, and they were lost in it. They had no friends. They had nothing in common with the acquaintances they made. They were more lonely than in the jungle. It was a relief when at a theatre they ran across someone they had known in the East (and perhaps been bored stiff by or disliked) and they could fix up an evening together and have a good laugh and tell one another what a grand time they were having and talk of common friends and at last confide to one another a little shyly that they would not be sorry when their leave was up and they were once again in harness. They went to see their families and of course they were glad to see them, but it wasn't the same as it had been, they did feel a bit out of it, and when you came down to brass tacks the life people led in England was deadly. It was grand fun to come home, but you couldn't live there any more, and sometimes you thought of your bungalow overlooking the river and your tours of the district and what a lark it was to run over once in a blue moon to Sandakan or Kuching or Singapore.

And because I remembered what Morton had looked forward to when, the road finished and off his chest, he went on leave, I could not but feel a pang when I thought of him dining by himself in a dismal club where he knew nobody or alone in a restaurant in Soho and then going off to see a play with no one by his side with whom he could enjoy it and no one to have a drink with during the interval. And at the same time I reflected that even if I had known he was in London I could have done nothing much for him, for during the last week I had not had a moment free. That very evening I was dining with friends and going to a play, and the next day I was going abroad.

'What are you doing tonight?' I asked him.

'I'm going to the Pavilion. It's packed jammed full, but there's a fellow over the road who's wonderful and he's got me a ticket that had been returned. You can often get one seat, you know, when you can't get two.'

'Why don't you come and have supper with me? I'm taking some people to the Haymarket and we're going on to Ciro's afterwards.'

'I'd love to.'

We arranged to meet at eleven and I left him to keep an engagement.

I was afraid the friends I had asked him to meet would not amuse Morton very much, for they were distinctly middle-aged, but I could not think of anyone young that at this season of the year I should be likely to get hold of at the last moment. None of the girls I knew would thank me for asking her to supper to dance with a shy young man from Malaya. I could trust the Bishops to do their best for him, and after all it must be jollier for him to have supper in a club with a good band where he could see pretty women dancing than to go home to bed at eleven because he had nowhere else in the world to go. I had known Charlie Bishop first when I was a medical student. He was then a thin fellow with sandy hair and blunt features; he had fine eyes, dark and gleaming, but he wore spectacles. He had a round, merry, red face. He was very fond of the girls. I suppose he had a way with him, for, with no money and no looks, he managed to pick up a succession of young persons who gratified his roving desires. He was clever and bumptious, argumentative and quick-tempered. He had a caustic tongue. Looking back, I should say he was a rather disagreeable young man, but I do not think he was a bore. Now, half-way through the fifties, he was inclined to be stout and he was very bald, but his eyes behind the gold-rimmed spectacles were still bright and alert. He was dogmatic and somewhat conceited, argumentative still and caustic, but he was good-natured and amusing. After you have known a person so long his idiosyncrasies cease to trouble you. You accept them as you accept your own physical defects. He was by profession a pathologist and now and then he sent me a slim book he had just published. It was severe and extremely technical and grimly illustrated with photographs of bacteria. I did not read it. I gathered from what I sometimes heard that Charlie's views on the subjects with which he dealt were unsound. I do not believe that he was very popular with the other members of his profession, he made no secret of the fact that he looked upon them as a set of incompetent idiots; but he had his job, it brought him in six or eight hundred a year, I think, and he was completely indifferent to other people's opinion of him.

I liked Charlie Bishop because I had known him for thirty years, but I liked Margery, his wife, because she was very nice. I was extremely surprised when he told me he was going to be married. He was hard on forty at the time and so fickle in his affections that I had made up my mind he would remain single. He was very fond of women, but he was not in the least sentimental, and his aims were loose. His views on the female sex would in these idealistic days be thought crude. He knew what he wanted and he asked for it, and if he couldn't get it for love or money he shrugged his shoulders and went his way. To be brief, he did not look to women to gratify his ideal but to provide him with fornication. It was odd that though small and plain he found so many who were prepared to grant his wishes. For his spiritual needs he found satisfaction in unicellular organisms. He had always been a man who spoke to the point, and when he told me he was going to marry a young woman called Margery Hobson I did not hesitate to ask him why. He grinned.

'Three reasons. First, she won't let me go to bed with her without. Second, she makes me laugh like a hyena. And third, she's alone in the world, without a single relation, and she must have someone to take care of her.'

'The first reason is just swank and the second is eyewash. The third is the real one and it means that she's got you by the short hairs.'

His eyes gleamed softly behind his large spectacles.

'I shouldn't be surprised if you weren't dead right.'

'She's not only got you by the short hairs but you're as pleased as Punch that she has.'

'Come and lunch tomorrow and have a look at her. She's easy on the eye.'

Charlie was a member of a cock-and-hen club which at that time I used a good deal and we arranged to lunch there. I found Margery a very attractive young woman. She was then just under thirty. She was a lady. I noticed the fact with satisfaction, but with a certain astonishment, for it had not escaped my notice that Charlie was attracted as a rule by women whose breeding left something to be desired. She was not beautiful, but comely, with fine dark hair and fine eyes, a good colour and a look of health. She had a pleasant frankness and an air of candour that were very taking. She looked honest, simple, and dependable. I took an immediate liking to her. She was easy to talk to and though she did not say anything very brilliant she understood what other people were talking about; she was quick to see a joke and she was not shy. She gave you the impression of being competent and business-like. She had a happy placidity that suggested a good temper and an excellent digestion.

They seemed extremely pleased with one another. I had asked myself when I first saw her why Margery was marrying this irritable little man, baldish already and by no means young, but I discovered very soon that it was because she was in love with him. They chaffed one another a good deal and laughed a lot and every now and then their eyes met more significantly and they seemed to exchange a little private message. It was really rather touching.

A week later they were married at a registrar's office. It was a very successful marriage. Looking back now after sixteen years I could not but chuckle sympathetically at the thought of the lark they had made of their life together. I had never known a more devoted couple. They had never had very much money. They never seemed to want any. They had no ambitions. Their life was a picnic that never came to an end. They lived in the smallest flat I ever saw, in Panton Street, a small bedroom, a small sitting-room, and a bathroom that served also as a kitchen. But they had no sense of home, they ate their meals in restaurants, and only had breakfast in the flat. It was merely a place to sleep in. It was comfortable, though a third person coming in for a whisky and soda crowded it, and Margery with the help of a charwoman kept it as neat as Charlie's untidiness permitted, but there was not a single thing in it that had a personal note. They had a tiny car and whenever Charlie had a holiday they took it across the Channel and started off, with a bag each for all their luggage, to drive wherever the fancy took them. Breakdowns never disturbed them, bad weather was part of the fun, a puncture was no end of a joke, and if they lost their way and had to sleep out in the open they thought they were having the time of their lives.

Charlie continued to be irascible and contentious, but nothing he did ever disturbed Margery's lovely placidity. She could calm him with a word. She still made him laugh. She typed his monographs on obscure bacteria and corrected the proofs of his articles in the scientific magazines. Once I asked them if they ever quarrelled.

'No,' she said, 'we never seem to have anything to quarrel about. Charlie has the temper of an angel.'

'Nonsense,' I said, 'he's an overbearing, aggressive, and cantankerous fellow. He always has been.'

She looked at him and giggled and I saw that she thought I was being funny.

'Let him rave,' said Charlie. 'He's an ignorant fool and he uses words of whose meaning he hasn't the smallest idea.'

They were sweet together. They were very happy in one another's company and were never apart if they could help it. Even after the long time they had been married Charlie used to get into the car every day at luncheon-time to come west and meet Margery at a restaurant. People used to laugh at them, not unkindly, but perhaps with a little catch in the throat, because when they were asked to go and spend a week-end in the country Margery would write to the hostess and say they would like to come if they could be given a double bed. They had slept together for so many years that neither of them could sleep alone. It was often a trifle awkward. Husbands and wives as a rule not only demanded separate rooms, but were inclined to be peevish if asked to share the same bathroom. Modern houses were not arranged for domestic couples, but among their friends it became an understood thing that if you wanted the Bishops you must give them a room with a double bed. Some people of course thought it a little indecent, and it was never convenient, but they were a pleasant pair to have to stay and it was worth while to put up with their crankiness. Charlie was always full of spirits and in his caustic way extremely amusing, and Margery was peaceful and easy. They were no trouble to entertain. Nothing pleased them more than to be left to go out together for a long ramble in the country.

When a man marries, his wife sooner or later estranges him from his old friends, but Margery on the contrary increased Charlie's intimacy with them. By making him more tolerant she made him a more agreeable companion. They gave you the impression not of a married couple, but, rather amusingly, of two middle-aged bachelors living together; and when Margery, as was the rule, found herself the only woman among half a dozen men, ribald, argumentative, and gay, she was not a bar to good-fellowship but an asset. Whenever I was in England I saw them. They generally dined at the club of which I have spoken and if I happened to be alone I joined them.

When we met that evening for a snack before going to the play I told them I had asked Morton to come to supper.

'I'm afraid you'll find him rather dull,' I said. 'But he's a very decent sort of boy and he was awfully kind to me when I was in Borneo.'

'Why didn't you let me know sooner?' cried Margery. 'I'd have brought a girl along.'

'What do you want a girl for?' said Charlie. 'There'll be you.'

'I don't think it can be much fun for a young man to dance with a woman of my advanced years,' said Margery.

'Rot. What's your age got to do with it?' He turned to me. 'Have you ever danced with anyone who danced better?'

I had, but she certainly danced very well. She was light on her feet and she had a good sense of rhythm.

'Never,' I said heartily.

Morton was waiting for us when we reached Ciro's. He looked very sunburned in his evening clothes. Perhaps it was because I knew that they had been wrapped away in a tin box with mothballs for four years that I felt he did not look quite at home in them. He was certainly more at ease in khaki shorts. Charlie Bishop was a good talker and liked to hear himself speak. Morton was shy. I gave him a cocktail and ordered some champagne. I had a feeling that he would be glad to dance, but was not quite sure whether it would occur to him to ask Margery. I was acutely conscious that we all belonged to another generation.

'I think I should tell you that Mrs Bishop is a beautiful dancer,' I said.

'Is she?' He flushed a little. 'Will you dance with me?'

She got up and they took the floor. She was looking peculiarly nice that evening, not at all smart, and I do not think her plain black dress had cost more than six guineas, but she looked a lady. She had the advantage of having extremely good legs and at that time skirts were still being worn very short. I suppose she had a little make-up on, but in contrast with the other women there she looked very natural. Shingled hair suited her; it was not even touched with white and it had an attractive sheen. She was not a pretty woman, but her kindliness, her wholesome air, her good health gave you, if not the illusion that she was, at least the feeling that it didn't at all matter. When she came back to the table her eyes were bright and she had a heightened colour.

'How does he dance?' asked her husband.

'Divinely.'

'You're very easy to dance with,' said Morton.

Charlie went on with his discourse. He had a sardonic humour and he was interesting because he was himself so interested in what he said. But he spoke of things that Morton knew nothing about and though he listened with a civil show of interest I could see that he was too much excited by the gaiety of the scene, the music, and the champagne to give his attention to conversation. When the music struck up again his eyes immediately sought Margery's. Charlie caught the look and smiled.

'Dance with him, Margery. Good for my figure to see you take exercise.'

They set off again and for a moment Charlie watched her with fond eyes.

'Margery's having the time of her life. She loves dancing and it makes me puff and blow. Not a bad youth.'

My little party was quite a success and when Morton and I, having taken leave of the Bishops, walked together towards Piccadilly Circus he thanked me warmly. He had really enjoyed himself. I said good-bye to him. Next morning I went abroad.

I was sorry not to have been able to do more for Morton and I knew that when I returned he would be on his way back to Borneo. I gave him a passing thought now and then, but by the autumn when I got home he had slipped my memory. After I had been in London a week or so I happened to drop in one night at the club to which Charlie Bishop also belonged. He was sitting with three or four men I knew and I went up. I had not seen any of them since my return. One of them, a man called Bill Marsh, whose wife, Janet, was a great friend of mine, asked me to have a drink.

'Where have you sprung from?' asked Charlie. 'Haven't seen you about lately.'

I noticed at once that he was drunk. I was astonished. Charlie had always liked his liquor, but he carried it well and never exceeded. In years gone by, when we were very young, he got tight occasionally, but probably more than anything to show what a great fellow he was, and it is unfair to bring up against a man the excesses of his youth. But I remembered that Charlie had never been very nice when he was drunk: his natural aggressiveness was exaggerated then and he talked too much and too loud; he was very apt to be quarrelsome. He was very dogmatic now, laying down the law and refusing to listen to any of the objections his rash statements called forth. The others knew he was drunk and were struggling between the irritation his cantankerousness aroused in them and the good-natured tolerance which they felt his condition demanded. He was not an agreeable object. A man of that age, bald and fattish, with spectacles, is disgusting drunk. He was generally rather dapper, but he was untidy now and there was tobacco ash all over him. Charlie called the waiter and ordered another whisky. The waiter had been at the club for thirty years.

'You've got one in front of you, sir.'

'Mind your own damned business,' said Charlie Bishop. 'Bring me a double whisky right away or I'll report you to the secretary for insolence.'

'Very good, sir,' said the waiter.

Charlie emptied his glass at a gulp, but his hand was unsteady and he spilled some of the whisky over himself.

'Well, Charlie, old boy, we'd better be toddling along,' said Bill Marsh. He turned to me. 'Charlie's staying with us for a bit.'

I was more surprised still. But I felt that something was wrong and thought it safer not to say anything.

'I'm ready,' said Charlie. 'I'll just have another drink before I go. I shall have a better night if I do.'

It did not look to me as though the party would break up for some time, so I got up and announced that I meant to stroll home.

'I say,' said Bill, as I was about to go, 'you wouldn't come and dine with us tomorrow night, would you, just me and Janet and Charlie?'

'Yes, I'll come with pleasure,' I said.

It was evident that something was up.

The Marshes lived in a terrace on the East side of Regent's Park. The maid who opened the door for me asked me to go in to Mr Marsh's study. He was waiting for me there.

'I thought I'd better have a word with you before you went upstairs,' he said as he shook hands with me. 'You know Margery's left Charlie?'

'No!'

'He's taken it very hard. Janet thought it was so awful for him alone in that beastly little flat that we asked him to stay here for a bit. We've done everything we could for him. He's been drinking like a fish. He hasn't slept a wink for a fortnight.'

'But she hasn't left him for good?'

I was astounded.

'Yes. She's crazy about a fellow called Morton.'

'Morton. Who's he?'

It never struck me it was my friend from Borneo.

'Damn it all, you introduced him and a pretty piece of work you did. Let's go upstairs. I thought I'd better put you wise.'

He opened the door and we went out. I was thoroughly confused.

'But look here,' I said.

'Ask Janet. She knows the whole thing. It beats me. I've got no patience with Margery, and he must be a mess.'

He preceded me into the drawing-room. Janet Marsh rose as I entered and came forward to greet me. Charlie was sitting at the window, reading the evening paper; he put it aside as I went up to him and shook his hand. He was quite sober and he spoke in his usual rather perky manner, but I noticed that he looked very ill. We had a glass of sherry and went down to dinner. Janet was a woman of spirit. She was tall and fair and good to look at. She kept the conversation going with alertness. When she left us to drink a glass of port it was with instructions not to stay more than ten minutes. Bill, as a rule somewhat taciturn, exerted himself now to talk. I tumbled to the game. I was hampered by my ignorance of what exactly had happened, but it was plain that the Marshes wanted to prevent Charlie from brooding, and I did my best to interest him. He seemed willing to play his part, he was always fond of holding forth, and he discussed, from the pathologist's standpoint, a murder that was just then absorbing the public. But he spoke without life. He was an empty shell, and one had the feeling that though for the sake of his host he forced himself to speak, his thoughts were elsewhere. It was a relief when a knocking on the floor above indicated to us that Janet was getting impatient. This was an occasion when a woman's presence eased the situation. We went upstairs and played family bridge. When it was time for me to go Charlie said he would walk with me as far as the Marylebone Road.

'Oh, Charlie, it's so late, you'd much better go to bed,' said Janet.

'I shall sleep better if I have a stroll before turning in,' he replied.

She gave him a worried look. You cannot forbid a middle-aged professor of pathology from going for a little walk if he wants to. She glanced brightly at her husband.

'I daresay it'll do Bill no harm.'

I think the remark was tactless. Women are often a little too managing. Charlie gave her a sullen look.

'There's absolutely no need to drag Bill out,' he said with some firmness.

'I haven't the smallest intention of coming,' said Bill, smiling. 'I'm tired out and I'm going to hit the hay.'

I fancy we left Bill Marsh and his wife to a little argument.

'They've been frightfully kind to me,' said Charlie, as we walked along by the railings. 'I don't know what I should have done without them. I haven't slept for a fortnight.'

I expressed regret but did not ask the reason, and we walked for a little in silence. I presumed that he had come with me in order to talk to me of what had happened, but I felt that he must take his own time. I was anxious to show my sympathy, but afraid of saying the wrong things; I did not want to seem eager to extract confidences from him. I did not know how to give him a lead. I was sure he did not want one. He was not a man given to beating about the bush. I imagined that he was choosing his words. We reached the corner.

'You'll be able to get a taxi at the church,' he said. 'I'll walk on a bit further. Good night.'

He nodded and slouched off. I was taken aback. There was nothing for me to do but to stroll on till I found a cab. I was having my bath next morning when a telephone call dragged me out of it, and with a towel round my wet body I took up the receiver. It was Janet.

'Well, what do you think of it all?' she said. 'You seem to have kept Charlie up pretty late last night. I heard him come home at three.'

'He left me at the Marylebone Road,' I answered. 'He said nothing to me at all.'

'Didn't he?'

There was something in Janet's voice that suggested that she was prepared to have a long talk with me. I suspected she had a telephone by the side of her bed.

'Look here,' I said quickly. 'I'm having my bath.'

'Oh, have you got a telephone in your bathroom?' she answered eagerly, and I think with envy.

'No, I haven't.' I was abrupt and firm. 'And I'm dripping all over the carpet.'

'Oh!' I felt disappointment in her tone and a trace of irritation. 'Well, when can I see you? Can you come here at twelve?'

It was inconvenient, but I was not prepared to start an argument.

'Yes, good-bye.'

I rang off before she could say anything more. In heaven when the blessed use the telephone they will say what they have to say and not a word beside.

I was devoted to Janet, but I knew that there was nothing that thrilled her more than the misfortunes of her friends. She was only too anxious to help them, but she wanted to be in the thick of their difficulties. She was the friend in adversity. Other people's business was meat and drink to her. You could not enter upon a love affair without finding her somehow your confidante nor be mixed up in a divorce case without discovering that she too had a finger in the pie. Withal she was a very nice woman. I could not help then chuckling in my heart when at noon I was shown into Janet's drawing-room and observed the subdued eagerness with which she received me. She was very much upset by the catastrophe that had befallen the Bishops, but it was exciting, and she was tickled to death to have someone fresh whom she could tell all about it. Janet had just that business-like expectancy that a mother has when she is discussing with the family doctor her married daughter's first confinement. Janet was conscious that the matter was very serious, and she would not for a moment have been thought to regard it flippantly, but she was determined to get every ounce of value out of it.

'I mean, no one could have been more horrified than I was when Margery told me she'd finally made up her mind to leave Charlie,' she said, speaking with the fluency of a person who has said the same thing in the same words a dozen times at least. 'They were the most devoted couple I'd ever known. It was a perfect marriage. They got on like a house on fire. Of course Bill and I are devoted to one another, but we have awful rows now and then. I mean, I could kill him sometimes.'

'I don't care a hang about your relations with Bill,' I said. 'Tell me about the Bishops. That's what I've come here for.'

'I simply felt I must see you. After all you're the only person who can explain it.'

'Oh, God, don't go on like that. Until Bill told me last night I didn't know a thing about it.'

'That was my idea. It suddenly dawned on me that perhaps you didn't know and I thought you might put your foot in it too awfully.'

'Supposing you began at the beginning,' I said.

'Well, you're the beginning. After all you started the trouble. You introduced the young man. That's why I was so crazy to see you. You know all about him. I never saw him. All I know is what Margery has told me about him.'

'At what time are you lunching?' I asked.

'Half past one.'

'So am I. Get on with the story.'

But my remark had given Janet an idea.

'Look here, will you get out of your luncheon if I get out of mine? We could have a snack here. I'm sure there's some cold meat in the house, and then we needn't hurry. I don't have to be at the hairdresser's till three.'

'No, no, no,' I said. 'I hate the notion of that. I shall leave here at twenty minutes past one at the latest.'

'Then I shall just have to race through it. What do *you* think of Gerry?'

'Who's Gerry?'

'Gerry Morton. His name's Gerald.'

'How should I know that?'

'You stayed with him. Weren't there any letters lying about?'

'I daresay, but I didn't happen to read them,' I answered somewhat tartly.

'Oh, don't be so stupid. I meant the envelopes. What's he like?'

'All right. Rather the Kipling type, you know. Very keen on his work. Hearty. Empire-builder and all that sort of thing.'

'I don't mean that,' cried Janet, not without impatience. 'I mean, what does he look like?'

'More or less like everybody else, I think. Of course I should recognize him if I saw him again, but I can't picture him to myself very distinctly. He looks clean.'

'Oh, my God,' said Janet. 'Are you a novelist or are you not? What's the colour of his eyes?'

'I don't know.'

'You must know. You can't spend a week with anyone without knowing if their eyes are blue or brown. Is he fair or dark?'

'Neither.'

'Is he tall or short?'

'Average, I should say.'

'Are you trying to irritate me?'

'No. He's just ordinary. There's nothing in him to attract your attention. He's neither plain nor good-looking. He looks quite decent. He looks a gentleman.'

'Margery says he has a charming smile and a lovely figure.'

'I dare say.'

'He's absolutely crazy about her.'

'What makes you think that?' I asked dryly.

'I've seen his letters.'

'Do you mean to say she's shown them to you?'

'Why, of course.'

It is always difficult for a man to stomach the want of reticence that women betray in their private affairs. They have no shame. They will talk to one another without embarrassment of the most intimate matters. Modesty is a masculine virtue. But though a man may know this theoretically, each time he is confronted with women's lack of reserve he suffers a new shock. I wondered what Morton would think if he knew that not only were his letters read by Janet Marsh as well as by Margery, but that she had been kept posted from day to day with the progress of his infatuation. According to Janet he had fallen in love with Margery at first sight. The morning after they had met at my little supper party at Ciro's he had rung up and asked her to come and have tea with him at some place where they could dance. While I listened to Janet's story I was conscious of course that she was giving me Margery's view of the circumstances and I kept an open mind. I was interested to observe that Janet's sympathies were with Margery. It was true that when Margery left her husband it was her idea that Charlie should come to them for two or three weeks rather than stay on in miserable loneliness in the deserted flat and she had been extraordinarily kind to him. She lunched with him almost every day, because he had been accustomed to lunch every day with Margery; she took him for walks in Regent's Park and made Bill play golf with him on Sundays. She listened with wonderful patience to the story of his unhappiness and did what she could to console him. She was terribly sorry for him. But all the same she was definitely on Margery's side and when I expressed my disapproval of her she came down on me like a thousand of bricks. The affair thrilled her. She had been in it from the beginning when Margery, smiling, flattered, and a little doubtful, came and told her that she had a young man to the final scene when Margery, exasperated and distraught, announced that she could not stand the strain any more and had packed her things and moved out of the flat.

'Of course, at first I couldn't believe my ears,' she said. 'You know how Charlie and Margery were. They simply lived in one another's pockets. One couldn't help laughing at them, they were so devoted to one another. I never thought him a very nice little man and heaven knows he wasn't very attractive physically, but one couldn't help liking him because he was so awfully nice to

Margery. I rather envied her sometimes. They had no money and they lived in a hugger-mugger sort of way, but they were frightfully happy. Of course I never thought anything would come of it. Margery was rather amused. "Naturally I don't take it very seriously," she told me, "but it is rather fun to have a young man at my time of life. I haven't had any flowers sent me for years. I had to tell him not to send any more because Charlie would think it so silly. He doesn't know a soul in London and he loves dancing and he says I dance like a dream. It's miserable for him going to the theatre by himself all the time and we've done two or three matinées together. It's pathetic to see how grateful he is when I say I'll go out with him." "I must say," I said, "he sounds rather a lamb." "He is," she said. "I knew you'd understand. You don't blame me, do you?" "Of course not, darling," I said, "surely you know me better than that. I'd do just the same in your place."'

Margery made no secret of her outings with Morton and her husband chaffed her good-naturedly about her beau. But he thought him a very civil, pleasant-spoken young man and was glad that Margery had someone to play with while he was busy. It never occurred to him to be jealous. The three of them dined together several times and went to a show. But presently Gerry Morton begged Margery to spend an evening with him alone; she said it was impossible, but he was persuasive, he gave her no peace; and at last she went to Janet and asked her to ring up Charlie one day and ask him to come to dinner and make a fourth at bridge. Charlie would never go anywhere without his wife, but the Marshes were old friends, and Janet made a point of it. She invented some cock-and-bull story that made it seem important that he should consent. Next day Margery and she met. The evening had been wonderful. They had dined at Maidenhead and danced there and then had driven home through the summer night.

'He says he's crazy about me,' Margery told her.

'Did he kiss you?' asked Janet.

'Of course,' Margery chuckled. 'Don't be silly, Janet. He is awfully sweet and, you know, he has such a nice nature. Of course I don't believe half the things he says to me.'

'My dear, you're not going to fall in love with him.'

'I have,' said Margery.

'Darling, isn't it going to be rather awkward?'

'Oh, it won't last. After all he's going back to Borneo in the autumn.'

'Well, one can't deny that it's made you look years younger.'

'I know, and I feel years younger.'

Soon they were meeting every day. They met in the morning and walked in the Park together or went to a picture gallery. They separated for Margery to lunch with her husband and after lunch met again and motored into the country or to some place on the river. Margery did not tell her husband. She very naturally thought he would not understand.

'How was it you never met Morton?' I asked Janet.

'Oh, she didn't want me to. You see, we belong to the same generation, Margery and I. I can quite understand that.'

'I see.'

'Of course I did everything I could. When she went out with Gerry she was always supposed to be with me.'

I am a person who likes to cross a 't' and dot an 'i'.

'Were they having an affair?' I asked.

'Oh, no. Margery isn't that sort of woman at all.'

'How do you know?'

'She would have told me.'

'I suppose she would.'

'Of course I asked her. But she denied it point-blank and I'm sure she was telling me the truth. There's never been anything of that sort between them at all.'

'It seems rather odd to me.'

'Well, you see, Margery is a very good woman.'

I shrugged my shoulders.

'She was absolutely loyal to Charlie. She wouldn't have deceived him for anything in the world. She couldn't bear the thought of having any secret from him. As soon as she knew she was in love with Gerry she wanted to tell Charlie. Of course I begged her not to. I told her it wouldn't do any good and it would only make Charlie miserable. And after all, the boy was going away in a couple of months, it didn't seem much good to make a lot of fuss about a thing that couldn't possibly last.'

But Gerry's imminent departure was the cause of the crash. The Bishops had arranged to go abroad as usual and proposed to motor through Belgium, Holland, and the North of Germany. Charlie was busy with maps and guides. He collected information from friends about hotels and roads. He looked forward to his holiday with the bubbling excitement of a schoolboy. Margery listened to him discussing it with a sinking heart. They were to be away four weeks and in September Gerry was sailing. She could not bear to lose so much of the short time that remained to them and the thought of the motor tour filled her with exasperation. As the interval grew shorter and shorter she grew more and more nervous. At last she decided that there was only one thing to do.

'Charlie, I don't want to come on this trip,' she interrupted him suddenly, one day when he was talking to her of some restaurant he had just heard of. 'I wish you'd get someone else to go with you.'

He looked at her blankly. She was startled at what she had said and her lips trembled a little.

'Why, what's the matter?'

'Nothing's the matter. I don't feel like it. I want to be by myself for a bit.'

'Are you ill?'

She saw the sudden fear in his eyes. His concern drove her beyond her endurance.

'No. I've never been better in my life. I'm in love.'

'You? Whom with?'

'Gerry.'

He looked at her in amazement. He could not believe his ears. She mistook his expression.

'It's no good blaming me. I can't help it. He's going away in a few weeks. I'm not going to waste the little time he has left.'

He burst out laughing.

'Margery, how can you make such a damned fool of yourself? You're old enough to be his mother.'

She flushed.

'He's just as much in love with me as I am with him.'

'Has he told you so?'

'A thousand times.'

'He's a bloody liar, that's all.'

He chuckled. His fat stomach rippled with mirth. He thought it a huge joke. I daresay Charlie did not treat his wife in the proper way. Janet seemed to think he should have been tender and compassionate. *He should have understood.* I saw the scene that was in her mind's eye, the stiff upper lip, the silent sorrow, and the final renunciation. Women are always sensitive to the beauty of the self-sacrifice of others. Janet would have sympathized also if he had flown into a violent passion, broken one or two pieces of furniture (which he would have had to replace), or given Margery a sock in the jaw. But to laugh at her was unpardonable. I did not point out that it is very difficult for a rather stout and not very tall professor of pathology, aged fifty-five, to act all of a sudden like a cave-man. Anyhow, the excursion to Holland was given up and the Bishops stayed in London through August. They were not very happy. They lunched and dined together every day because they had been in the habit of doing so for so many years and the rest of the time Margery spent with Gerry. The hours she passed with him made up for all she had to put up with and she had to put up with a good deal. Charlie had a ribald and sarcastic humour and he made himself very funny at her expense and at Gerry's. He persisted in refusing to take the matter seriously. He was vexed with Margery for being so silly, but apparently it never occurred to him that she might have been unfaithful to him. I commented upon this to Janet.

'He never suspected it even,' she said. 'He knew Margery much too well.'

The weeks passed and at last Gerry sailed. He went from Tilbury and Margery saw him off. When she came back she cried for forty-eight hours. Charlie watched her with increasing exasperation. His nerves were much frayed.

'Look here, Margery,' he said at last, 'I've been very patient with you, but now you must pull yourself together. This is getting past a joke.'

'Why can't you leave me alone?' she cried. 'I've lost everything that made life lovely to me.'

'Don't be such a fool,' he said.

I do not know what else he said. But he was unwise enough to tell her what he thought of Gerry and I gather that the picture he drew was virulent. It started the first violent scene they had ever had. She had borne Charlie's jibes when she knew that she would see Gerry in an hour or next day, but now that she had lost him for ever she could bear them no longer. She had held herself in for weeks: now she flung her self-control to the winds. Perhaps she never knew exactly what she said to Charlie. He had always been irascible and at last he hit her. They were both frightened when he had. He seized a hat and flung out of the flat. During all that miserable time they had shared the same bed, but when he came back, in the middle of the night, he found that she had made herself up a shake-down on the sofa in the sitting-room.

'You can't sleep there,' he said. 'Don't be so silly. Come to bed.'

'No, I won't, let me alone.'

For the rest of the night they wrangled, but she had her way and now made up her bed every night on the sofa. But in that tiny flat they could not get away from one another; they could not even get out of sight or out of hearing of one another. They had lived in such intimacy for so many years that it was an instinct for them to be together. He tried to reason with her. He thought her incredibly stupid and argued with her interminably in the effort to show her how wrong-headed she was. He could not leave her alone. He would not let her sleep, and he talked half through the night till they were both exhausted. He thought he could talk her out of love. For two or three days at a time they would not speak to one another. Then one day, coming home, he found her crying bitterly; the sight of her tears distracted him; he told her how much he loved her and sought to move her by the recollection of all the happy years they had spent together. He wanted to let bygones be bygones. He promised never to refer to Gerry again. Could they not forget the nightmare they had been through? But the thought of all that a reconciliation implied revolted her. She told him she had a racking headache and asked him to give her a sleeping draught. She pretended to be still asleep when he went out next morning, but the moment he was gone she packed up her things and left. She had a few trinkets that she had inherited and by selling them she got a little money. She took a room at a cheap boarding-house and kept her address a secret from Charlie.

It was when he found she had left him that he went all to pieces. The shock of her flight broke him. He told Janet that his loneliness was intolerable. He wrote to Margery imploring her to come back, and asked Janet to intercede for him; he was willing to promise anything; he abased himself. Margery was obdurate.

'Do you think she'll ever go back?' I asked Janet.

'She says not.'

I had to leave then, for it was nearly half past one and I was bound for the other end of London.

Two or three days later I got a telephone message from Margery asking if I could see her. She suggested coming to my rooms. I asked her to tea. I tried to be nice to her; her affairs were no business of mine, but in my heart I thought her a very silly woman and I dare say my manner was cold. She had never been handsome and the passing years had changed her little. She had still those fine dark eyes and her face was astonishingly unlined. She was very simply dressed and if she wore make-up it was so cunningly put on that I did not perceive it. She had still the charm she had always had of perfect naturalness and of a kindly humour.

'I want you to do something for me if you will,' she began without beating about the bush.

'What is it?'

'Charlie is leaving the Marshes today and going back to the flat. I'm afraid his first few days there will be rather difficult; it would be awfully nice of you if you'd ask him to dinner or something.'

'I'll have a look at my book.'

'I'm told he's been drinking heavily. It's such a pity. I wish you could give him a hint.'

'I understand he's had some domestic worries of late,' I said, perhaps acidly.

Margery flushed. She gave me a pained look. She winced as though I had struck her.

'Of course you've known him ever so much longer than you've known me. It's natural that you should take his part.'

'My dear, to tell you the truth I've known him all these years chiefly on your account. I have never very much liked him, but I thought you were awfully nice.'

She smiled at me and her smile was very sweet. She knew that I meant what I said.

'Do you think I was a good wife to him?'

'Perfect.'

'He used to put people's backs up. A lot of people didn't like him, but I never found him difficult.'

'He was awfully fond of you.'

'I know. We had a wonderful time together. For sixteen years we were perfectly happy.' She paused and looked down. 'I had to leave him. It became quite impossible. That cat-and-dog life we were leading was too awful.'

'I never see why two persons should go on living together if they don't want to.'

'You see, it was awful for us. We'd always lived in such close intimacy. We could never get away from one another. At the end I hated the sight of him.'

'I don't suppose the situation was easy for either of you.'

'It wasn't my fault that I fell in love. You see, it was quite a different love from the one I'd felt for Charlie. There was always something maternal in that and protective. I was so much more reasonable than he was. He was unmanageable, but I could always manage him. Gerry was different.' Her voice grew soft and her face was transfigured with glory. 'He gave me back my youth. I was a girl to him and I could depend on his strength and be safe in his care.'

'He seemed to me a very nice lad,' I said slowly. 'I imagine he'll do well. He was very young for the job he had when I ran across him. He's only twenty-nine now, isn't he?'

She smiled softly. She knew quite well what I meant.

'I never made any secret of my age to him. He says it doesn't matter.'

I knew this was true. She was not the woman to have lied about her age. She had found a sort of fierce delight in telling him the truth about herself.

'How old are you?'

'Forty-four.'

'What are you going to do now?'

'I've written to Gerry and told him I've left Charlie. As soon as I hear from him I'm going out to join him.'

I was staggered.

'You know, it's a very primitive little colony he's living in. I'm afraid you'll find your position rather awkward.'

'He made me promise that if I found my life impossible after he left I'd go to him.'

'Are you sure you're wise to attach so much importance to the things a young man says when he's in love?'

Again that really beautiful look of exaltation came into her face.

'Yes, when the young man happens to be Gerry.'

My heart sank. I was silent for a moment. Then I told her the story of the road Gerry Morton had built. I dramatized it, and I think I made it rather effective.

'What did you tell me that for?' she asked when I finished.

'I thought it rather a good story.'

She shook her head and smiled.

'No, you wanted to show me that he was very young and enthusiastic, and so keen on his work that he hadn't much time to waste on other interests. I wouldn't interfere with his work. You don't know him as I do. He's incredibly romantic. He looks upon himself as a pioneer. I've caught from him something of his excitement at the idea of taking part in the opening up of a new country. It *is* rather splendid, isn't it? It makes life here seem very humdrum and commonplace. But of course it's very lonely there. Even the companionship of a middle-aged woman may be worth having.'

'Are you proposing to marry him?' I asked.

'I leave myself in his hands. I want to do nothing that he does not wish.'

She spoke with so much simplicity, there was something so touching in her self-surrender, that when she left me I no longer felt angry with her. Of course I thought her very foolish, but if the folly of men made one angry one would pass one's life in a state of chronic ire. I thought all would come right. She said Gerry was romantic. He was, but the romantics in this workaday world only get away with their nonsense because they have at bottom a shrewd sense of reality: the mugs are the people who take their vapourings at their face value. The English are romantic; that is why other nations think them hypocritical; they are not: they set out in all sincerity for the Kingdom of God, but the journey is arduous and they have reason to pick up any gilt-edged investment that offers itself by the way. The British soul, like Wellington's armies, marches on its belly. I supposed that Gerry would go through a bad quarter of an hour when he received Margery's letter. My sympathies were not deeply engaged in the matter and I was only curious to see how he would extricate himself from the pass he was in. I thought Margery would suffer a bitter disappointment; well, that would do her no great harm, and then she would go back to her husband and I had no doubt the pair of them, chastened, would live in peace, quiet, and happiness for the rest of their lives.

The event was different. It happened that it was quite impossible for me to make any sort of engagement with Charlie Bishop for some days, but I wrote to him and asked him to dine with me one evening in the following week. I proposed, though with misgiving, that we should go to a play; I knew he was drinking like a fish, and when tight he was noisy. I hoped he would not make a nuisance of himself in the theatre. We arranged to meet at our club and dine at seven because the piece we were going to began at a quarter past eight. I arrived. I waited. He did not come. I rang up his flat, but could get no reply, so concluded that he was on his way. I hate missing the beginning of a play and I waited impatiently in the hall so that when he came we could go straight upstairs. To save time I had ordered dinner. The clock pointed to half past seven, then a quarter to eight; I did not see why I should wait for him any longer, so walked up to the dining-room and ate my dinner alone. He did not appear. I put a call through from the dining-room to the Marshes and presently was told by a waiter that Bill Marsh was at the end of the wire.

'I say, do you know anything about Charlie Bishop?' I said. 'We were dining together and going to a play and he hasn't turned up.'

'He died this afternoon.'

'What?'

My exclamation was so startled that two or three people within earshot looked up. The dining-room was full and the waiters were hurrying to and fro. The telephone was on the cashier's desk and a wine waiter came up with a bottle of hock and two long-stemmed glasses on a tray and gave the cashier a chit. The portly steward showing two men to a table jostled me.

'Where are you speaking from?' asked Bill.

I suppose he heard the clatter that surrounded me. When I told him he asked me if I could come round as soon as I had finished my dinner. Janet wanted to speak to me.

'I'll come at once,' I said.

I found Janet and Bill sitting in the drawing-room. He was reading the paper and she was playing patience. She came forward swiftly when the maid showed me in. She walked with a sort of spring, crouching a little, on silent feet, like a panther stalking his prey. I saw at once that she was in her element. She gave me her hand and turned her face away to hide her eyes brimming with tears. Her voice was low and tragic.

'I brought Margery here and put her to bed. The doctor has given her a sedative. She's all in. Isn't it awful?' She gave a sound that was something between a gasp and a sob. 'I don't know why these things always happen to me.'

The Bishops had never kept a servant but a charwoman went in every morning, cleaned the flat, and washed up the breakfast things. She had her own key. That morning she had gone in as usual and done the sitting-room. Since his wife had left him Charlie's hours had been irregular and she was not surprised to find him asleep. But the time passed and she knew he had his work to go to. She went to the bedroom door and knocked. There was no answer. She thought she heard him groaning. She opened the door softly. He was lying in bed, on his back, and was breathing stertorously. He did not wake. She called him. Something about him frightened her. She went to the flat on the same landing. It was occupied by a journalist. He was still in bed when she rang, and opened the door to her in pyjamas.

'Beg pardon, sir,' she said, 'but would you just come and 'ave a look at my gentleman. I don't think he's well.'

The journalist walked across the landing and into Charlie's flat. There was an empty bottle of veronal by the bed.

'I think you'd better fetch a policeman,' he said.

A policeman came and rang through to the police station for an ambulance. They took Charlie to Charing Cross Hospital. He never recovered consciousness. Margery was with him at the end.

'Of course there'll have to be an inquest,' said Janet. 'But it's quite obvious what happened. He'd been sleeping awfully badly for the last three or four weeks and I suppose he'd been taking veronal. He must have taken an overdose by accident.'

'Is that what Margery thinks?' I asked.

'She's too upset to think anything, but I told her I was positive he hadn't committed suicide. I mean, he wasn't that sort of a man. Am I right, Bill?'

'Yes, dear,' he answered.

'Did he leave any letter?'

'No, nothing. Oddly enough Margery got a letter from him this morning, well, hardly a letter, just a line. "I'm so lonely without you, darling." That's all. But of course that means nothing and she's promised to say nothing about it at the inquest. I mean, what is the use of putting ideas in people's heads? Everyone knows that you never can tell with veronal, I wouldn't take it myself for anything in the world, and it was quite obviously an accident. Am I right, Bill?'

'Yes, dear,' he answered.

I saw that Janet was quite determined to believe that Charlie Bishop had not committed suicide, but how far in her heart she believed what she wanted to believe I was not sufficiently expert in female psychology to know. And of course it might be that she was right. It is unreasonable to suppose that a middle-aged scientist should kill himself because his middle-aged wife leaves him and it is extremely plausible that, exasperated by sleeplessness, and in all probability far from sober, he took a larger dose of the sleeping-draught than he realized. Anyhow that was the view the coroner took of the matter. It was indicated to him that of late Charles Bishop had given way to habits of intemperance which had caused his wife to leave him, and it was quite obvious that nothing was further from his thoughts than to put an end to himself. The coroner expressed his sympathy with the widow and commented very strongly on the dangers of sleeping-draughts.

I hate funerals, but Janet begged me to go to Charlie's. Several of his colleagues at the hospital had intimated their desire to come, but at Margery's wish they were dissuaded; and Janet and Bill, Margery and I were the only persons who attended it. We were to fetch the hearse from the mortuary and they offered to call for me on their way. I was on the look-out for the car and when I saw it drive up went downstairs, but Bill got out and met me just inside the door.

'Half a minute,' he said. 'I've got something to say to you. Janet wants you to come back afterwards and have tea. She says it's no good Margery moping and after tea we'll play a few rubbers of bridge. Can you come?'

'Like this?' I asked.

I had a tail coat on and a black tie and my evening dress trousers.

'Oh, that's all right. It'll take Margery's mind off.'

'Very well.'

But we did not play bridge after all. Janet, with her fair hair, was very smart in her deep mourning and she played the part of the sympathetic friend with amazing skill. She cried a little, wiping her eyes delicately so as not to disturb the black on her eyelashes, and when Margery sobbed broken-heartedly put her arm tenderly through hers. She was a very present help in trouble. We returned to the house. There was a telegram for Margery. She took it and went upstairs. I presumed it was a message of condolence from one of Charlie's friends who had just heard of his death. Bill went to change and Janet and I went up to the drawing-room and got the bridge table out. She took off her hat and put it on the piano.

'It's no good being hypocritical,' she said. 'Of course Margery has been frightfully upset, but she must pull herself together now. A rubber of bridge will help her to get back to her normal state. Naturally I'm dreadfully sorry about poor Charlie, but as far as he was concerned I don't believe he'd ever have got over Margery's leaving him and one can't deny that it has made things much easier for her. She wired to Gerry this morning.'

'What about?'

'To tell him about poor Charlie.'

At that moment the maid came to the room.

'Will you go up to Mrs Bishop, please, ma'am? She wants to see you.'

'Yes, of course.'

She went out of the room quickly and I was left alone. Bill joined me presently and we had a drink. At last Janet came back. She handed a telegram to me. It read as follows:

For God's sake await letter. Gerry

'What do you think it means?' she asked me.

'What it says,' I replied.

'Idiot! Of course I've told Margery that it doesn't mean anything, but she's rather worried. It must have crossed her cable telling him that Charles was dead. I don't think she feels very much like bridge after all. I mean, it would be rather bad form to play on the very day her husband has been buried.'

'Quite,' I said.

'Of course he may wire in answer to the cable. He's sure to do that, isn't he? The only thing we can do now is to sit tight and wait for his letter.'

I saw no object in continuing the conversation. I left. In a couple of days Janet rang me up to tell me that Margery had received a telegram of condolence from Morton. She repeated it to me:

Dreadfully distressed to hear sad news. Deeply sympathize with your great grief. Love. Gerry

'What do you think of it?' she asked me.

'I think it's very proper.'

'Of course he couldn't say he was as pleased as Punch, could he?'

'Not with any delicacy.'

'And he did put in *love*.'

I imagined how those women had examined the two telegrams from every point of view and scrutinized every word to press from it every possible shade of meaning. I almost heard their interminable conversations.

'I don't know what'll happen to Margery if he lets her down now,' Janet went on. 'Of course it remains to be seen if he's a gentleman.'

'Rot,' I said and rang off quickly.

In the course of the following days I dined with the Marshes a couple of times. Margery looked tired. I guessed that she awaited the letter that was on the way with sickening anxiety. Grief and fear had worn her to a shadow, she seemed very fragile now and she had acquired a spiritual look that I had never seen in her before. She was very gentle, very grateful for every kindness shown her, and in her smile, unsure and a little timid, was an infinite pathos. Her helplessness was very appealing. But Morton was several thousand miles away. Then one morning Janet rang me up.

'The letter has come. Margery says I can show it to you. Will you come round?'

Her tense voice told me everything. When I arrived Janet gave it to me. I read it. It was a very careful letter and I guessed that Morton had written it a good many times. It was very kind and he had evidently taken great pains to avoid saying anything that could possibly wound Margery; but what transpired was his terror. It was obvious that he was shaking in his shoes. He had felt apparently that the best way to cope with the situation was to be mildly facetious and he made very good fun of the white people in the colony. What would they say if Margery suddenly turned up? He would be given the order of the boot pretty damn quick. People thought the East was free and easy; it wasn't, it was more suburban than Clapham. He loved Margery far too much to bear the thoughts of those horrible women out there turning up their noses at her. And besides he had been sent to a station ten days from anywhere; she couldn't live in his bungalow exactly and of course there wasn't a hotel, and his work took him out into the jungle for days at a time. It was no place for a woman anyhow. He told her how much she meant to him, but she mustn't bother about him and he couldn't help thinking it would be better if she went back to her husband. He would never forgive himself if he thought he had come between her and Charlie. Yes, I am quite sure it had been a difficult letter to write.

'Of course he didn't know then that Charlie was dead. I've told Margery that changes everything.'

'Does she agree with you?'

'I think she's being rather unreasonable. What do you make of the letter?'

'Well, it's quite plain that he doesn't want her.'

'He wanted her badly enough two months ago.'

'It's astonishing what a change of air and a change of scene will do for you. It must seem to him already like a year since he left London. He's back among his old friends and his old interests. My dear, it's no good Margery kidding herself; the life there has taken him back and there's no place for her.'

'I've advised her to ignore the letter and go straight out to him.'

'I hope she's too sensible to expose herself to a very terrible rebuff.'

'But then what's to happen to her? Oh, it's too cruel. She's the best woman in the world. She has real goodness.'

'It's funny if you come to think of it, it's her goodness that has caused all the trouble. Why on earth didn't she have an affair with Morton? Charlie would have known nothing about it and wouldn't have been a penny the worse. She and Morton could have had a grand time and when he went away they could have parted with the consciousness that a pleasant episode had come to a graceful end. It would have been a jolly recollection, and she could have gone back to Charlie satisfied and rested and continued to make him the excellent wife she had always been.'

Janet pursed her lips. She gave me a look of disdain.

'There is such a thing as virtue, you know.'

'Virtue be damned. A virtue that only causes havoc and unhappiness is worth nothing. You can call it virtue if you like. I call it cowardice.'

'The thought of being unfaithful to Charlie while she was living with him revolted her. There are women like that, you know.'

'Good gracious, she could have remained faithful to him in spirit while she was being unfaithful to him in the flesh. That is a feat of legerdemain that women find it easy to accomplish.'

'What an odious cynic you are.'

'If it's cynical to look truth in the face and exercise common sense in the affairs of life, then certainly I'm a cynic and odious if you like. Let's face it, Margery's a middle-aged woman, Charlie was fifty-five and they'd been married for sixteen years. It was natural enough that she should lose her head over a young man who made a fuss of her. But don't call it love. It was physiology. She was a fool to take anything he said seriously. It wasn't himself speaking, it was his starved sex, he'd suffered from sexual starvation, at least as far as white women are concerned, for four years; it's monstrous that she should seek to ruin his life by holding him to the wild promises he made then. It was an accident that Margery took his fancy; he wanted her, and because he couldn't get her wanted her more. I dare say he thought it love; believe me, it was only letch. If they'd gone to bed together Charlie would be alive today. It's her damned virtue that caused the whole trouble.'

'How stupid you are. Don't you see that she couldn't help herself? She just doesn't happen to be a loose woman.'

'I prefer a loose woman to a selfish one and a wanton to a fool.'

'Oh, shut up. I didn't ask you to come here in order to make yourself absolutely beastly.'

'What did you ask me to come here for?'

'Gerry is your friend. You introduced him to Margery. If she's in the soup it's on his account. But *you* are the cause of the whole trouble. It's your duty to write to him and tell him he must do the right thing by her.'

'I'm damned if I will,' I said.

'Then you'd better go.'

I started to do so.

'Well, at all events it's a mercy that Charlie's life was insured,' said Janet.

Then I turned on her.

'And you have the nerve to call me a cynic.'

I will not repeat the opprobious word I flung at her as I slammed the door behind me. But Janet is all the same a very nice woman. I often think it would be great fun to be married to her.

The
Closed Shop

◆

Nothing would induce me to tell the name of the happy country in which the
incidents occurred that I am constrained to relate; but I see no harm in
admitting that it is a free and independent state on the continent of America.
This is vague enough in all conscience and can give rise to no diplomatic
incident. Now the president of this free and independent state had an eye to a
pretty woman and there came to his capital, a wide and sunny town with a
plaza, a cathedral that was not without dignity, and a few old Spanish houses, a
young person from Michigan of such a pleasing aspect that his heart went out to
her. He lost no time in declaring his passion and was gratified to learn that it was
returned, but he was mortified to discover that the young person regarded his
possession of a wife and her possession of a husband as a bar to their union. She
had a feminine weakness for marriage. Though it seemed unreasonable to the
president, he was not the man to refuse a pretty woman the gratification of her
whim and promised to make such arrangements as would enable him to offer
her wedlock. He called his attorneys together and put the matter before them.
He had long thought, he said, that for a progressive country their marriage laws
were remarkably out of date and he proposed therefore radically to amend
them. The attorneys retired and after a brief interval devised a divorce law that
was satisfactory to the president. But the state of which I write was always
careful to do things in a constitutional way, for it was a highly civilized,
democratic, and reputable country. A president who respects himself and his
oath of office cannot promulgate a law, even if it is to his own interest, without
adhering to certain forms, and these things take time; the president had barely
signed the decree that made the new divorce law valid when a revolution broke
out and he was very unfortunately hanged on a lamp-post in the *plaza* in front
of the cathedral that was not without dignity. The young person of pleasing

aspect left town in a hurry, but the law remained. Its terms were simple. On the payment of one hundred dollars gold and after a residence of thirty days a man could divorce his wife or a wife her husband without even apprising the other party of the intended step. Your wife might tell you that she was going to spend a month with her aged mother and one morning at breakfast when you looked through your mail you might receive a letter from her informing you that she had divorced you and was already married to another.

Now it was not long before the happy news spread here and there that at a reasonable distance from New York was a country, the capital of which had an equable climate and tolerable accommodation, where a woman could release herself, expeditiously and with economy, from the irksome bonds of matrimony. The fact that the operation could be performed without the husband's knowledge saved her from those preliminary and acrimonious discussions that are so wearing to the nerves. Every woman knows that however much a man may argue about a proposition he will generally accept a fact with resignation. Tell him you want a Rolls-Royce and he will say he can't afford it, but buy it and he will sign his cheque like a lamb. So in a very short time beautiful women in considerable numbers began to come down to the pleasant, sunny town; tired business women and women of fashion, women of pleasure and women of leisure; they came from New York, Chicago, and San Francisco, they came from Georgia and they came from Dakota, they came from all the states in the Union. The passenger accommodation on the ships of the United Fruit Line was only just adequate to the demand, and if you wanted a stateroom to yourself you had to engage it six months in advance. Prosperity descended upon the capital of this enterprising state and in a very little while there was not a lawyer in it who did not own a Ford car. Don Agosto, the proprietor of the Grand Hotel, went to the expense of building several bathrooms, but he did not grudge it; he was making a fortune, and he never passed the lamp-post on which the outgoing president had been hanged without giving it a jaunty wave of his hand.

'He was a great man,' he said. 'One day they will erect a statue to him.'

I have spoken as though it were only women who availed themselves of this convenient and reasonable law, and this might indicate that in the United States it is they rather than men who desire release from the impediment of Holy Matrimony. I have no reason to believe that this is so. Though it was women in great majority who travelled to this country to get a divorce, I ascribe this to the fact that it is always easy for them to get away for six weeks (a week there, a week back, and thirty days to establish a domicile) but it is difficult for men to leave their affairs so long. It is true that they could go there during their summer holidays, but then the heat is somewhat oppressive; and besides, there are no golf links; it is reasonable enough to suppose that many a man will hesitate to divorce his wife when he can only do it at the cost of a month's golf. There were of course two or three males spending their thirty days at the Grand Hotel, but they were generally, for a reason that is obscure, commercial travellers. I can but imagine that by the nature of their avocations they were able at one and the same time to pursue freedom and profit.

Be this as it may, the fact remains that the inmates of the Grand Hotel were for the most part women, and very gay it was in the patio at luncheon and at dinner when they sat at little square tables under the arches discussing their matrimonial troubles and drinking champagne. Don Agosto did a roaring trade with the generals and colonels (there were more generals than colonels in the army of this state), the lawyers, bankers, merchants, and the young sparks of the town who came to look at these beautiful creatures. But the perfect is seldom realized in this world. There is always something that is not quite right and women engaged in getting rid of their husbands are very properly in an agitated condition. It makes them at times hard to please. Now it must be confessed that this delightful little city, notwithstanding its manifold advantages, somewhat lacked places of amusement. There was but one cinema and this showed films that had been wandering too long from their happy home in Hollywood. In the daytime you could have consultations with your lawyer, polish your nails, and do a little shopping, but the evenings were intolerable. There were many complaints that thirty days was a long time and more than one impatient young thing asked her lawyer why they didn't put a little pep into their law and do the whole job in eight and forty hours. Don Agosto, however, was a man of resource, and presently he had an inspiration: he engaged a troupe of wandering Guatemalecans who played the marimba. There is no music in the world that sets the toes so irresistibly tingling and in a little while everyone in the patio began dancing. It is of course obvious that twenty-five beautiful women cannot dance with three commercial travellers, but there were all these generals and colonels and there were all the young sparks of the town. They danced divinely and they had great liquid black eyes. The hours flew, the days tripped one upon the heels of the other so quickly that the month passed before you realized it, and more than one of Don Agosto's guests when she bade him farewell confessed that she would willingly have stayed longer. Don Agosto was radiant. He liked to see people enjoy themselves. The marimba band was worth twice the money he paid for it, and it did his heart good to see his ladies dance with the gallant officers and the young men of the town. Since Don Agosto was thrifty he always turned off the electric light on the stairs and in the passages at ten o'clock at night and the gallant officers and the young men of the town improved their English wonderfully.

Everything went as merrily as a marriage bell, if I may use a phrase that, however hackneyed, in this connexion is irresistible, till one day Madame Coralie came to the conclusion that she had had enough of it. For one man's meat is another man's poison. She dressed herself and went to call on her friend Carmencita. After she had in a few voluble words stated the purpose of her visit, Carmencita called a maid and told her to run and fetch La Gorda. They had a matter of importance which they wished to discuss with her. La Gorda, a woman of ample proportions with a heavy moustache, soon joined them, and over a bottle of Malaga the three of them held a momentous conversation. The result of it was that they indited a letter to the president asking for an audience. The new president was a hefty young man in the early thirties who, a few years before, had been a stevedore in the employment of an American firm, and he had risen to his present exalted station by a natural eloquence and an effective use of his gun when he wanted to make a point or emphasize a statement. When one of his secretaries placed the letter before him he laughed.

'What do those three old faggots want with me?'

But he was a good-natured fellow and accessible. He did not forget that he had been elected by the people, as one of the people, to protect the people. He had also during his early youth been employed for some months by Madame Coralie to run errands. He told his secretary that he would see them at ten o'clock next morning. They went at the appointed hour to the palace and were led up a noble stairway to the audience chamber; the official who conducted them knocked softly on the door; a barred judas was opened and a suspicious eye appeared. The president had no intention of suffering the fate of his predecessor if he could help it and no matter who his visitors were did not receive them without precaution. The official gave the three ladies' names, the door was opened, but not too wide, and they slipped in. It was a handsome room and various secretaries at little tables, in their shirtsleeves and with a revolver on each hip, were busy typing. One or two other young men, heavily armed, were lying on sofas reading the papers and smoking cigarettes. The president, also in his shirtsleeves, with a revolver in his belt, was standing with his thumbs in the sleeve-holes of his waistcoat. He was tall and stout, of a handsome and even dignified presence.

'*Qué tal?*' he cried, jovially, with a flash of his white teeth. 'What brings you here, *señoras?*'

'How well you're looking, Don Manuel,' said La Gorda. 'You are a fine figure of a man.'

He shook hands with them, and his staff, ceasing their strenuous activity, leaned back and cordially waved their hands to the three ladies. They were old friends, and the greetings, if a trifle sardonic, were hearty. I must disclose the fact now (which I could without doubt do in a manner so discreet that I might be misunderstood; but if you have to say something you may just as well say it plainly as not) that these three ladies were the Madams of the three principal brothels in the capital of this free and independent state. La Gorda and Carmencita were of Spanish origin and were very decently dressed in black, with black silk shawls over their heads, but Madame Coralie was French and she wore a toque. They were all of mature age and of modest demeanour.

The president made them sit down, and offered them madeira and cigarettes, but they refused.

'No, thank you, Don Manuel,' said Madame Coralie. 'It is on business that we have come to see you.'

'Well, what can I do for you?'

La Gorda and Carmencita looked at Madame Coralie and Madame Coralie looked at La Gorda and Carmencita. They nodded and she saw that they expected her to be their spokeswoman.

'Well, Don Manuel, it is like this. We are three women who have worked hard for many years and not a breath of scandal has ever tarnished our good names. There are not in all the Americas three more distinguished houses than ours and they are a credit to this beautiful city. Why, only last year I spent five hundred dollars to supply my *sala principal* with plate-glass mirrors. We have always been respectable and we have paid our taxes with regularity. It is hard now that the fruits of our labours should be snatched away from us. I do not hesitate to say that after so many years of honest and conscientious attention to business it is unjust that we should have to submit to such treatment.'

The president was astounded.

'But, Coralie, my dear, I do not know what you mean. Has anyone dared to claim money from you that the law does not sanction or that I know nothing about?'

He gave his secretaries a suspicious glance. They tried to look innocent, but though they were, only succeeded in looking uneasy.

'It is the law we complain of. Ruin stares us in the face.'

'Ruin?'

'So long as this new divorce law is in existence we can do no business and we may just as well shut up our beautiful houses.'

Then Madame Coralie explained in a manner so frank that I prefer to paraphrase her speech that owing to this invasion of the town by beautiful ladies from a foreign land the three elegant houses on which she and her two friends paid rates and taxes were utterly deserted. The young men of fashion preferred to spend their evenings at the Grand Hotel where they received for soft words entertainment which at the regular establishments they could only have got for hard cash.

'You cannot blame them,' said the president.

'I don't,' cried Madame Coralie. 'I blame the women. They have no right to come and take the bread out of our mouths. Don Manuel, you are one of the people, you are not one of these aristocrats; what will the country say if you allow us to be driven out of business by blacklegs? I ask you is it just, is it honest?'

'But what can I do?' said the president. 'I cannot lock them up in their rooms for thirty days. How am I to blame if these foreigners have no sense of decency?'

'It's different for a poor girl,' said La Gorda. 'She has her way to make. But that these women do that sort of thing when they're not obliged to, no, that I shall never understand.'

'It is a bad and wicked law,' said Carmencita.

The president sprang to his feet and threw his arms akimbo.

'You are not going to ask me to abrogate a law that has brought peace and plenty to this country. I am of the people and I was elected by the people, and the prosperity of my fatherland is very near my heart. Divorce is our staple industry and the law shall be repealed only over my dead body.'

'Oh, *María Santísima,* that it should come to this,' said Carmencita. 'And me with two daughters in a convent in New Orleans. Ah, in this business one often has unpleasantness, but I always consoled myself by thinking that my daughters would marry well, and when the time came for me to retire they would inherit my business. Do you think I can keep them in a convent in New Orleans for nothing?'

'And who is going to keep my son at Harvard if I have to close my house, Don Manuel?' asked La Gorda.

'As for myself,' said Madame Coralie, 'I do not care. I shall return to France. My dear mother is eighty-seven years of age and she cannot live very much longer. It will be a comfort to her if I spend her last remaining years by her side. But it is the injustice of it that hurts. You have spent many happy evenings in my house, Don Manuel, and I am wounded that you should let us be treated like this. Did you not tell me yourself that it was the proudest day of your life when you entered as an honoured guest the house in which you had once been employed as errand boy?'

'I do not deny it. I stood champagne all round.' Don Manuel walked up and down the large hall, shrugging his shoulders as he went, and now and then, deep in thought, he gesticulated. 'I am of the people, elected by the people,' he cried, 'and the fact is, these women are blacklegs.' He turned to his secretaries with a dramatic gesture. 'It is a stain on my administration. It is against all my principles to allow unskilled foreign labour to take the bread out of the mouths of honest and industrious people. These ladies are quite right to come to me and appeal for my protection. I will not allow the scandal to continue.'

It was of course a pointed and effective speech, but all who heard it knew that it left things exactly where they were. Madame Coralie powdered her nose and gave it, a commanding organ, a brief look in her pocket mirror.

'Of course I know what human nature is,' she said, 'and I can well understand that time hangs heavily on the hands of these creatures.'

'We could build a golf-course,' hazarded one of the secretaries. 'It is true that this would only occupy them by day.'

'If they want men why can't they bring them with them?' said La Gorda.

'*Caramba!*' cried the president, and with that stood on a sudden quite still. 'There is the solution.'

He had not reached his exalted station without being a man of insight and resource. He beamed.

'We will amend the law. Men shall come in as before without let or hindrance, but women only accompanied by their husbands or with their written consent.' He saw the look of consternation which his secretaries gave him, and he waved his hand. 'But the immigration authorities shall receive instructions to interpret the word husband with the widest latitude.'

'*Maria Santisima!*' cried Madame Coralie. 'If they come with a friend he will take care that no one else interferes with them and our customers will return to the houses where for so long they have been so hospitably entertained. Don Manuel, you are a great man and one of these days they will erect a statue to you.'

It is often the simplest expedients that settle the most formidable difficulties. The law was briefly amended according to the terms of Don Manuel's suggestion and, whereas prosperity continued to pour its blessings on the wide and sunny capital of this free and independent state, Madame Coralie was enabled profitably to pursue her useful avocations, Carmencita's two daughters completed their expensive education in the convent at New Orleans, and La Gorda's son successfully graduated at Harvard.

The Dream

◆

It chanced that in August 1917 the work upon which I was then engaged obliged me to go from New York to Petrograd, and I was instructed for safety's sake to travel by way of Vladivostok. I landed there in the morning and passed an idle day as best I could. The trans-Siberian train was due to start, so far as I remember, at about nine in the evening. I dined at the station restaurant by myself. It was crowded and I shared a small table with a man whose appearance entertained me. He was a Russian, a tall fellow, but amazingly stout, and he had so vast a paunch that he was obliged to sit well away from the table. His hands, small for his size, were buried in rolls of fat. His hair, long, dark, and thin, was brushed carefully across his crown in order to conceal his baldness, and his huge sallow face, with its enormous double chin, clean-shaven, gave you an impression of indecent nakedness. His nose was small, a funny little button upon that mass of flesh, and his black shining eyes were small too. But he had a large, red, and sensual mouth. He was dressed neatly enough in a black suit. It was not worn but shabby; it looked as if it had been neither pressed nor brushed since he had had it.

The service was bad and it was almost impossible to attract the attention of a waiter. We soon got into conversation. The Russian spoke good and fluent English. His accent was marked but not tiresome. He asked me many questions about myself and my plans, which—my occupation at the time making caution necessary—I answered with a show of frankness but with dissimulation. I told him I was a journalist. He asked me whether I wrote fiction and when I confessed that in my leisure moments I did, he began to talk of the later Russian novelists. He spoke intelligently. It was plain that he was a man of education.

By this time we had persuaded the waiter to bring us some cabbage soup, and my acquaintance pulled a small bottle of vodka from his pocket which he invited me to share. I do not know whether it was the vodka or the natural loquaciousness of his race that made him communicative, but presently he told me, unasked, a good deal about himself. He was of noble birth, it appeared, a lawyer by profession, and a radical. Some trouble with the authorities had made it necessary for him to be much abroad, but now he was on his way home. Business had detained him at Vladivostok, but he expected to start for Moscow in a week and if I went there he would be charmed to see me.

'Are you married?' he asked me.

I did not see what business it was of his, but I told him that I was. He sighed a little.

'I am a widower,' he said. 'My wife was a Swiss, a native of Geneva. She was a very cultivated woman. She spoke English, German, and Italian perfectly. French, of course, was her native tongue. Her Russian was much above the average for a foreigner. She had scarcely the trace of an accent.'

He called a waiter who was passing with a tray full of dishes and asked him, I suppose–for then I knew hardly any Russian–how much longer we were going to wait for the next course. The waiter, with a rapid but presumably reassuring exclamation, hurried on, and my friend sighed.

'Since the revolution the waiting in restaurants has become abominable.'

He lighted his twentieth cigarette and I, looking at my watch, wondered whether I should get a square meal before it was time for me to start.

'My wife was a very remarkable woman,' he continued. 'She taught languages at one of the best schools for the daughters of noblemen in Petrograd. For a good many years we lived together on perfectly friendly terms. She was, however, of a jealous temperament and unfortunately she loved me to distraction.'

It was difficult for me to keep a straight face. He was one of the ugliest men I had ever seen. There is sometimes a certain charm in the rubicund and jovial fat man, but this saturnine obesity was repulsive.

'I do not pretend that I was faithful to her. She was not young when I married her and we had been married for ten years. She was small and thin, and she had a bad complexion. She had a bitter tongue. She was a woman who suffered from a fury of possession, and she could not bear me to be attracted to anyone but her. She was jealous not only of the women I knew, but of my friends, my cat, and my books. On one occasion in my absence she gave away a coat of mine merely because I liked none of my coats so well. But I am of an equable temperament. I will not deny that she bored me, but I accepted her acrimonious disposition as an act of God and no more thought of rebelling against it than I would against bad weather or a cold in the head. I denied her accusations as long as it was possible to deny them, and when it was impossible I shrugged my shoulders and smoked a cigarette.

'The constant scenes she made me did not very much affect me. I led my own life. Sometimes, indeed, I wondered whether it was passionate love she felt for me or passionate hate. It seemed to me that love and hate were very near allied.

'So we might have continued to the end of the chapter if one night a very curious thing had not happened. I was awakened by a piercing scream from my wife. Startled, I asked her what was the matter. She told me that she had had a fearful nightmare; she had dreamt that I was trying to kill her. We lived at the top of a large house and the well round which the stairs climbed was broad. She had dreamt that just as we had arrived at our own floor I had caught hold of her and attempted to throw her over the balusters. It was six storeys to the stone floor at the bottom and it meant certain death.

'She was much shaken. I did my best to soothe her. But next morning, and for two or three days after, she referred to the subject again and, notwithstanding my laughter, I saw that it dwelt in her mind. I could not help thinking of it either, for this dream showed me something that I had never suspected. She thought I hated her, she thought I would gladly be rid of her; she knew of course that she was insufferable, and at some time or other the idea had evidently occurred to her that I was capable of murdering her. The thoughts of men are incalculable and ideas enter our minds that we should be ashamed to confess. Sometimes I had wished that she might run away with a lover, sometimes that a painless and sudden death might give me my freedom; but never, never had the idea come to me that I might deliberately rid myself of an intolerable burden.

'The dream made an extraordinary impression upon both of us. It frightened my wife, and she became for a little less bitter and more tolerant. But when I walked up the stairs to our apartment it was impossible for me not to look over the balusters and reflect how easy it would be to do what she had dreamt. The balusters were dangerously low. A quick gesture and the thing was done. It was hard to put the thought out of my mind. Then some months later my wife awakened me one night. I was very tired and I was exasperated. She was white and trembling. She had had the dream again. She burst into tears and asked me if I hated her. I swore by all the saints of the Russian calendar that I loved her. At last she went to sleep again. It was more than I could do. I lay awake. I seemed to see her falling down the well of the stairs, and I heard her shriek and the thud as she struck the stone floor. I could not help shivering.'

The Russian stopped and beads of sweat stood on his forehead. He had told the story well and fluently so that I had listened with attention. There was still some vodka in the bottle; he poured it out and swallowed it at a gulp.

'And how did your wife eventually die?' I asked after a pause.

He took out a dirty handkerchief and wiped his forehead.

'By an extraordinary coincidence she was found late one night at the bottom of the stairs with her neck broken.'

'Who found her?'

'She was found by one of the lodgers who came in shortly after the catastrophe.'

'And where were you?'

I cannot describe the look he gave me of malicious cunning. His little black eyes sparkled.

'I was spending the evening with a friend of mine. I did not come in till an hour later.'

At that moment the waiter brought us the dish of meat that we had ordered, and the Russian fell upon it with good appetite. He shovelled the food into his mouth in enormous mouthfuls.

I was taken aback. Had he really been telling me in this hardly veiled manner that he had murdered his wife? That obese and sluggish man did not look like a murderer; I could not believe that he would have had the courage. Or was he making a sardonic joke at my expense?

In a few minutes it was time for me to go and catch my train. I left him and I have not seen him since. But I have never been able to make up my mind whether he was serious or jesting.

The Colonel's Lady

◆

All this happened two or three years before the outbreak of the war.

The Peregrines were having breakfast. Though they were alone and the table was long they sat at opposite ends of it. From the walls George Peregrine's ancestors, painted by the fashionable painters of the day, looked down upon them. The butler brought in the morning post. There were several letters for the colonel, business letters, *The Times*, and a small parcel for his wife Evie. He looked at his letters and then, opening *The Times*, began to read it. They finished breakfast and rose from the table. He noticed that his wife hadn't opened the parcel.

'What's that?' he asked.

'Only some books.'

'Shall I open it for you?'

'If you like.'

He hated to cut string and so with some difficulty untied the knots.

'But they're all the same,' he said when he had unwrapped the parcel. 'What on earth d'you want six copies of the same book for?' He opened one of them. 'Poetry.' Then he looked at the title-page. *When Pyramids Decay*, he read, by E. K. Hamilton. Eva Katherine Hamilton: that was his wife's maiden name. He looked at her with smiling surprise. 'Have you written a book, Evie? You are a slyboots.'

'I didn't think it would interest you very much. Would you like a copy?'

'Well, you know poetry isn't much in my line, but–yes, I'd like a copy; I'll read it. I'll take it along to my study. I've got a lot to do this morning.'

He gathered up *The Times*, his letters, and the book, and went out. His study was a large and comfortable room, with a big desk, leather arm-chairs, and what he called 'trophies of the chase' on the walls. On the bookshelves were works of reference, books on farming, gardening, fishing, and shooting, and books on the last war, in which he had won an M.C. and a D.S.O. For before his marriage he had been in the Welsh Guards. At the end of the war he retired and settled down to the life of a country gentleman in the spacious house, some twenty miles from Sheffield, which one of his forebears had built in the reign of George III. George Peregrine had an estate of some fifteen hundred acres which he managed with ability; he was a Justice of the Peace and performed his duties conscientiously. During the season he rode to hounds two days a week. He was a good shot, a golfer, and though now a little over fifty could still play a hard game of tennis. He could describe himself with propriety as an all-round sportsman.

He had been putting on weight lately, but was still a fine figure of a man; tall, with grey curly hair, only just beginning to grow thin on the crown, frank blue eyes, good features, and a high colour. He was a public-spirited man, chairman of any number of local organizations and, as became his class and station, a loyal member of the Conservative Party. He looked upon it as his duty to see to the welfare of the people on his estate and it was a satisfaction to him to know that Evie could be trusted to tend the sick and succour the poor. He had built a cottage hospital on the outskirts of the village and paid the wages of a nurse out of his own pocket. All he asked of the recipients of his bounty was that at elections, county or general, they should vote for his candidate. He was a friendly man, affable to his inferiors, considerate with his tenants, and popular with the neighbouring gentry. He would have been pleased and at the same time slightly embarrassed if someone had told him he was a jolly good fellow. That was what he wanted to be. He desired no higher praise.

It was hard luck that he had no children. He would have been an excellent father, kindly but strict, and would have brought up his sons as gentlemen's sons should be brought up, sent them to Eton, you know, taught them to fish, shoot, and ride. As it was, his heir was a nephew, son of his brother killed in a motor accident, not a bad boy, but not a chip off the old block, no, sir, far from it; and would you believe it, his fool of a mother was sending him to a co-educational school. Evie had been a sad disappointment to him. Of course she was a lady, and she had a bit of money of her own; she managed the house uncommonly well and she was a good hostess. The village people adored her. She had been a pretty little thing when he married her, with a creamy skin, light brown hair, and a trim figure, healthy too, and not a bad tennis player; he couldn't understand why she'd had no children; of course she was faded now, she must be getting on for five and forty; her skin was drab, her hair had lost its sheen, and she was as thin as a rail. She was always neat and suitably dressed, but she didn't seem to bother how she looked, she wore no make-up and didn't even use lipstick; sometimes at night when she dolled herself up for a party you could tell that once she'd been quite attractive, but ordinarily she was–well, the sort of woman you simply didn't notice. A nice woman, of course, a good wife, and it wasn't her fault if she was barren, but it was tough on a fellow who wanted an heir of his own loins; she hadn't any vitality, that's what was the matter with her. He supposed he'd been in love with her when he asked her to marry him, at least sufficiently in love for a man who wanted to marry and settle down, but with time he discovered that they had nothing much in common. She didn't care about hunting, and fishing bored her. Naturally they'd drifted apart. He had to do her the justice to admit that she'd never bothered him. There'd been no scenes. They had no quarrels. She seemed to take it for granted that he should go his own way. When he went up to London now and then she never wanted to come with him. He had a girl there, well, she wasn't exactly a girl, she was thirty-five if she was a day, but she was blonde and luscious and he only had to wire ahead of time and they'd dine, do a show, and spend the night together. Well, a man, a healthy normal man had to have some fun in his life. The thought crossed his mind that if Evie hadn't been such a good woman she'd have been a better wife; but it was not the sort of thought that he welcomed and he put it away from him.

George Peregrine finished his *Times* and being a considerate fellow rang the bell and told the butler to take it to Evie. Then he looked at his watch. It was half past ten and at eleven he had an appointment with one of his tenants. He had half an hour to spare.

'I'd better have a look at Evie's book,' he said to himself.

He took it up with a smile. Evie had a lot of highbrow books in her sitting-room, not the sort of books that interested him, but if they amused her he had no objection to her reading them. He noticed that the volume he now held in his hand contained no more than ninety pages. That was all to the good. He shared Edgar Allan Poe's opinion that poems should be short. But as he turned the pages he noticed that several of Evie's had long lines of irregular length and didn't rhyme. He didn't like that. At his first school, when he was a little boy, he remembered learning a poem that began: *The boy stood on the burning deck,* and later, at Eton, one that started: *Ruin seize thee, ruthless king*; and then there was *Henry V*; they'd had to take that, one half. He stared at Evie's pages with consternation.

'That's not what I call poetry,' he said.

Fortunately it wasn't all like that. Interspersed with the pieces that looked so odd, lines of three or four words and then a line of ten or fifteen, there were little poems, quite short, that rhymed, thank God, with the lines all the same length. Several of the pages were just headed with the word *Sonnet*, and out of curiosity he counted the lines; there were fourteen of them. He read them. They seemed all right, but he didn't quite know what they were all about. He repeated to himself: *Ruin seize thee, ruthless king.*

'Poor Evie,' he sighed.

At that moment the farmer he was expecting was ushered into the study, and putting the book down he made him welcome. They embarked on their business.

'I read your book, Evie,' he said as they sat down to lunch. 'Jolly good. Did it cost you a packet to have it printed?'

'No, I was lucky. I sent it to a publisher and he took it.'

'Not much money in poetry, my dear,' he said in his good-natured, hearty way.

'No, I don't suppose there is. What did Bannock want to see you about this morning?'

Bannock was the tenant who had interrupted his reading of Evie's poems.

'He's asked me to advance the money for a pedigree bull he wants to buy. He's a good man and I've half a mind to do it.'

George Peregrine saw that Evie didn't want to talk about her book and he was not sorry to change the subject. He was glad she had used her maiden name on the title-page; he didn't suppose anyone would ever hear about the book, but he was proud of his own unusual name and he wouldn't have liked it if some damned penny-a-liner had made fun of Evie's effort in one of the papers.

During the few weeks that followed he thought it tactful not to ask Evie any questions about her venture into verse, and she never referred to it. It might have been a discreditable incident that they had silently agreed not to mention. But then a strange thing happened. He had to go to London on business and he took Daphne out to dinner. That was the name of the girl with whom he was in the habit of passing a few agreeable hours whenever he went to town.

'Oh, George,' she said, 'is that your wife who's written a book they're all talking about?'

'What on earth d'you mean?'

'Well, there's a fellow I know who's a critic. He took me out to dinner the other night and he had a book with him. "Got anything for me to read?" I said. "What's that?" "Oh, I don't think that's your cup of tea," he said. "It's poetry. I've just been reviewing it." "No poetry for me," I said. "It's about the hottest stuff I ever read," he said. "Selling like hot cakes. And it's damned good."'

'Who's the book by?' asked George.

'A woman called Hamilton. My friend told me that wasn't her real name. He said her real name was Peregrine. "Funny," I said, "I know a fellow called Peregrine." "Colonel in the army," he said. "Lives near Sheffield."'

'I'd just as soon you didn't talk about me to your friends,' said George with a frown of vexation.

'Keep your shirt on, dearie. Who d'you take me for? I just said: "It's not the same one."' Daphne giggled. 'My friend said: "They say he's a regular Colonel Blimp."'

George had a keen sense of humour.

'You could tell them better than that,' he laughed. 'If my wife had written a book I'd be the first to know about it, wouldn't I?'

'I suppose you would.'

Anyhow the matter didn't interest her and when the colonel began to talk of other things she forgot about it. He put it out of his mind too. There was nothing to it, he decided, and that silly fool of a critic had just been pulling Daphne's leg. He was amused at the thought of her tackling that book because she had been told it was hot stuff and then finding it just a lot of bosh cut up into unequal lines.

He was a member of several clubs and next day he thought he'd lunch at one in St James's Street. He was catching a train back to Sheffield early in the afternoon. He was sitting in a comfortable arm-chair having a glass of sherry before going into the dining-room when an old friend came up to him.

'Well, old boy, how's life?' he said. 'How d'you like being the husband of a celebrity?'

George Peregrine looked at his friend. He thought he saw an amused twinkle in his eyes.

'I don't know what you're talking about,' he answered.

'Come off it, George. Everyone knows E. K. Hamilton is your wife. Not often a book of verse has a success like that. Look here, Henry Dashwood is lunching with me. He'd like to meet you.'

'Who the devil is Henry Dashwood and why should he want to meet me?'

'Oh, my dear fellow, what do you do with yourself all the time in the country? Henry's about the best critic we've got. He wrote a wonderful review of Evie's book. D'you mean to say she didn't show it you?'

Before George could answer his friend had called a man over. A tall, thin man, with a high forehead, a beard, a long nose, and a stoop, just the sort of man whom George was prepared to dislike at first sight. Introductions were effected. Henry Dashwood sat down.

'Is Mrs Peregrine in London by any chance? I should very much like to meet her,' he said.

'No, my wife doesn't like London. She prefers the country,' said George stiffly.

'She wrote me a very nice letter about my review. I was pleased. You know, we critics get more kicks than halfpence. I was simply bowled over by her book. It's so fresh and original, very modern without being obscure. She seems to be as much at her ease in free verse as in the classical metres.' Then because he was a critic he thought he should criticize. 'Sometimes her ear is a trifle at fault, but you can say the same of Emily Dickinson. There are several of those short lyrics of hers that might have been written by Landor.'

All this was gibberish to George Peregrine. The man was nothing but a disgusting highbrow. But the colonel had good manners and he answered with proper civility: Henry Dashwood went on as though he hadn't spoken.

'But what makes the book so outstanding is the passion that throbs in every line. So many of these young poets are so anaemic, cold, bloodless, dully intellectual, but here you have real naked, earthy passion; of course deep, sincere emotion like that is tragic—ah, my dear Colonel, how right Heine was when he said that the poet makes little songs out of his great sorrows. You know, now and then, as I read and re-read those heart-rending pages I thought of Sappho.'

This was too much for George Peregrine and he got up.

'Well, it's jolly nice of you to say such nice things about my wife's little book. I'm sure she'll be delighted. But I must bolt, I've got to catch a train and I want to get a bite of lunch.'

'Damned fool,' he said irritably to himself as he walked upstairs to the dining-room.

He got home in time for dinner and after Evie had gone to bed he went into his study and looked for her book. He thought he'd just glance through it again to see for himself what they were making such a fuss about, but he couldn't find it. Evie must have taken it away.

'Silly,' he muttered.

He'd told her he thought it jolly good. What more could a fellow be expected to say? Well, it didn't matter. He lit his pipe and read the *Field* till he felt sleepy. But a week or so later it happened that he had to go into Sheffield for the day. He lunched there at his club. He had nearly finished when the Duke of Haverel came in. This was the great local magnate and of course the colonel knew him, but only to say how d'you do to; and he was surprised when the Duke stopped at his table.

'We're so sorry your wife couldn't come to us for the week-end,' he said, with a sort of shy cordiality. 'We're expecting rather a nice lot of people.'

George was taken aback. He guessed that the Haverels had asked him and Evie over for the week-end and Evie, without saying a word to him about it, had refused. He had the presence of mind to say he was sorry too.

'Better luck next time,' said the Duke pleasantly and moved on.

Colonel Peregrine was very angry and when he got home he said to his wife:

'Look here, what's this about our being asked over to Haverel? Why on earth did you say we couldn't go? We've never been asked before and it's the best shooting in the county.'

'I didn't think of that. I thought it would only bore you.'

'Damn it all, you might at least have asked me if I wanted to go.'

'I'm sorry.'

He looked at her closely. There was something in her expression that he didn't quite understand. He frowned.

'I suppose *I* was asked?' he barked.

Evie flushed a little.

'Well, in point of fact you weren't.'

'I call it damned rude of them to ask you without asking me.'

'I suppose they thought it wasn't your sort of party. The Duchess is rather fond of writers and people like that, you know. She's having Henry Dashwood, the critic, and for some reason he wants to meet me.'

'It was damned nice of you to refuse, Evie.'

'It's the least I could do,' she smiled. She hesitated a moment. 'George, my publishers want to give a little dinner party for me one day towards the end of the month and of course they want you to come too.'

'Oh, I don't think that's quite my mark. I'll come up to London with you if you like. I'll find someone to dine with.'

Daphne.

'I expect it'll be very dull, but they're making rather a point of it. And the day after, the American publisher who's taken my book is giving a cocktail party at Claridge's. I'd like you to come to that if you wouldn't mind.'

'Sounds like a crashing bore, but if you really want me to come I'll come.'

'It would be sweet of you.'

George Peregrine was dazed by the cocktail party. There were a lot of people. Some of them didn't look so bad, a few of the women were decently turned out, but the men seemed to him pretty awful. He was introduced to everyone as Colonel Peregrine, E. K. Hamilton's husband, you know. The men didn't seem to have anything to say to him, but the women gushed.

'You *must* be proud of your wife. Isn't it *wonderful*? You know, I read it right through at a sitting, I simply couldn't put it down, and when I'd finished I started again at the beginning and read it right through a second time. I was simply *thrilled.*'

The English publisher said to him:

'We've not had a success like this with a book of verse for twenty years. I've never seen such reviews.'

The American publisher said to him:

'It's swell. It'll be a smash hit in America. You wait and see.'

The American publisher had sent Evie a great spray of orchids. Damned ridiculous, thought George. As they came in, people were taken up to Evie, and it was evident that they said flattering things to her, which she took with a pleasant smile and a word or two of thanks. She was a trifle flushed with the excitement, but seemed quite at her ease. Though he thought the whole thing a lot of stuff and nonsense George noted with approval that his wife was carrying it off in just the right way.

'Well, there's one thing,' he said to himself, 'you can see she's a lady and that's a damned sight more than you can say of anyone else here.'

He drank a good many cocktails. But there was one thing that bothered him. He had a notion that some of the people he was introduced to looked at him in rather a funny sort of way, he couldn't quite make out what it meant, and once when he strolled by two women who were sitting together on a sofa he had the impression that they were talking about him and after he passed he was almost certain they tittered. He was very glad when the party came to an end.

In the taxi on their way back to their hotel Evie said to him:

'You were wonderful, dear. You made quite a hit. The girls simply raved about you: they thought you so handsome.'

'Girls,' he said bitterly. 'Old hags.'

'Were you bored, dear?'

'Stiff.'

She pressed his hand in a gesture of sympathy.

'I hope you won't mind if we wait and go down by the afternoon train. I've got some things to do in the morning.'

'No, that's all right. Shopping?'

'I do want to buy one or two things, but I've got to go and be photographed. I hate the idea, but they think I ought to be. For America, you know.'

He said nothing. But he thought. He thought it would be a shock to the American public when they saw the portrait of the homely, desiccated little women who was his wife. He'd always been under the impression that they liked glamour in America.

He went on thinking, and next morning when Evie had gone out he went to his club and up to the library. There he looked up recent numbers of *The Times Literary Supplement*, the *New Statesman*, and the *Spectator*. Presently he found reviews of Evie's book. He didn't read them very carefully, but enough to see that they were extremely favourable. Then he went to the bookseller's in Piccadilly where he occasionally bought books. He'd made up his mind that he had to read this damned thing of Evie's properly, but he didn't want to ask her what she'd done with the copy she'd given him. He'd buy one for himself. Before going in he looked in the window and the first thing he saw was a display of *When Pyramids Decay*. Damned silly title! He went in. A young man came forward and asked if he could help him.

'No, I'm just having a look round.' It embarrassed him to ask for Evie's book and he thought he'd find it for himself and then take it to the salesman. But he couldn't see it anywhere and at last, finding the young man near him, he said in a carefully casual tone: 'By the way, have you got a book called *When Pyramids Decay*?'

'The new edition came in this morning. I'll get a copy.'

In a moment the young man returned with it. He was a short, rather stout young man, with a shock of untidy carroty hair and spectacles. George Peregrine, tall, upstanding, very military, towered over him.

'Is this a new edition then?' he asked.

'Yes, sir. The fifth. It might be a novel the way it's selling.'

George Peregrine hesitated a moment.

'Why d'you suppose it's such a success? I've always been told no one reads poetry.'

'Well, it's good, you know. I've read it meself.' The young man, though obviously cultured, had a slight Cockney accent, and George quite instinctively adopted a patronizing attitude. 'It's the story they like. Sexy, you know, but tragic.'

George frowned a little. He was coming to the conclusion that the young man was rather impertinent. No one had told him anything about there being a story in the damned book and he had not gathered that from reading the reviews. The young man went on:

'Of course it's only a flash in the pan, if you know what I mean. The way I look at it, she was sort of inspired like by a personal experience, like Housman was with *The Shropshire Lad*. She'll never write anything else.'

'How much is the book?' said George coldly to stop his chatter. 'You needn't wrap it up, I'll just slip it into my pocket.'

The November morning was raw and he was wearing a greatcoat.

At the station he bought the evening papers and magazines and he and Evie settled themselves comfortably in opposite corners of a first-class carriage and read. At five o'clock they went along to the restaurant car to have tea and chatted a little. They arrived. They drove home in the car which was waiting for them. They bathed, dressed for dinner, and after dinner Evie, saying she was tired out, went to bed. She kissed him, as was her habit, on the forehead. Then he went into the hall, took Evie's book out of his greatcoat pocket and going into the study began to read it. He didn't read verse very easily and though he read with attention, every word of it, the impression he received was far from clear. Then he began at the beginning again and read it a second time. He read with increasing malaise, but he was not a stupid man and when he had finished he had a distinct understanding of what it was all about. Part of the book was in free verse, part in conventional metres, but the story it related was coherent and plain to the meanest intelligence. It was the story of a passionate love affair between an older woman, married, and a young man. George Peregrine made out the steps of it as easily as if he had been doing a sum in simple addition.

Written in the first person, it began with the tremulous surprise of the woman, past her youth, when it dawned upon her that the young man was in love with her. She hesitated to believe it. She thought she must be deceiving herself. And she was terrified when on a sudden she discovered that she was passionately in love with him. She told herself it was absurd; with the disparity of age between them nothing but unhappiness could come to her if she yielded to her emotion. She tried to prevent him from speaking but the day came when he told her that he loved her and forced her to tell him that she loved him too. He begged her to run away with him. She couldn't leave her husband, her home; and what life could they look forward to, she an ageing woman, he so young? How could she expect his love to last? She begged him to have mercy on her. But his love was impetuous. He wanted her, he wanted her with all his heart, and at last trembling, afraid, desirous, she yielded to him. Then there was a period of ecstatic happiness. The world, the dull, humdrum world of every day, blazed with glory. Love songs flowed from her pen. The woman worshipped the young, virile body of her lover. George flushed darkly when she praised his broad chest and slim flanks, the beauty of his legs and the flatness of his belly.

Hot stuff, Daphne's friend had said. It was that all right. Disgusting.

There were sad little pieces in which she lamented the emptiness of her life when as must happen he left her, but they ended with a cry that all she had to suffer would be worth it for the bliss that for a while had been hers. She wrote of the long, tremulous nights they passed together and the languor that lulled them to sleep in one another's arms. She wrote of the rapture of brief stolen moments when, braving all danger, their passion overwhelmed them and they surrendered to its call.

She thought it would be an affair of a few weeks, but miraculously it lasted. One of the poems referred to three years having gone by without lessening the love that filled their hearts. It looked as though he continued to press her to go away with him, far away, to a hill town in Italy, a Greek island, a walled city in Tunisia, so that they could be together always, for in another of the poems she besought him to let things be as they were. Their happiness was precarious. Perhaps it was owing to the difficulties they had to encounter and the rarity of their meetings that their love had retained for so long its first enchanting ardour. Then on a sudden the young man died. How, when or where George could not discover. There followed a long, heartbroken cry of bitter grief, grief she could not indulge in, grief that had to be hidden. She had to be cheerful, give dinner-parties and go out to dinner, behave as she had always behaved, though the light had gone out of her life and she was bowed down with anguish. The last poem of all was a set of four short stanzas in which the writer, sadly resigned to her loss, thanked the dark powers that rule man's destiny that she had been privileged at least for a while to enjoy the greatest happiness that we poor human beings can ever hope to know.

It was three o'clock in the morning when George Peregrine finally put the book down. It had seemed to him that he heard Evie's voice in every line, over and over again he came upon turns of phrase he had heard her use, there were details that were as familiar to him as to her: there was no doubt about it; it was her own story she had told, and it was as plain as anything could be that she had had a lover and her lover had died. It was not anger so much that he felt, nor horror or dismay, though he was dismayed and he was horrified, but amazement. It was as inconceivable that Evie should have had a love affair, and a wildly passionate one at that, as that the trout in a glass case over the chimney-piece in his study, the finest he had ever caught, should suddenly wag its tail. He understood now the meaning of the amused look he had seen in the eyes of that man he had spoken to at the club, he understood why Daphne when she was talking about the book had seemed to be enjoying a private joke, and why those two women at the cocktail party had tittered when he strolled past them.

He broke out into a sweat. Then on a sudden he was seized with fury and he jumped up to go and awake Evie and ask her sternly for an explanation. But he stopped at the door. After all, what proof had he? A book. He remembered that he'd told Evie he thought it jolly good. True, he hadn't read it, but he'd pretended he had. He would look a perfect fool if he had to admit that.

'I must watch my step,' he muttered.

He made up his mind to wait for two or three days and think it all over. Then he'd decide what to do. He went to bed, but he couldn't sleep for a long time.

'Evie,' he kept on saying to himself. 'Evie, of all people.'

They met at breakfast next morning as usual. Evie was as she always was, quiet, demure, and self-possessed, a middle-aged woman who made no effort to look younger than she was, a woman who had nothing of what he still called It. He looked at her as he hadn't looked at her for years. She had her usual placid serenity. Her pale blue eyes were untroubled. There was no sign of guilt on her candid brow. She made the same little casual remarks she always made.

'It's nice to get back to the country again after those two hectic days in London. What are you going to do this morning?'

It was incomprehensible.

Three days later he went to see his solicitor. Henry Blane was an old friend of George's as well as his lawyer. He had a place not far from Peregrine's and for years they had shot over one another's preserves. For two days a week he was a country gentleman and for the other five a busy lawyer in Sheffield. He was a tall, robust fellow, with a boisterous manner and a jovial laugh, which suggested that he liked to be looked upon essentially as a sportsman and a good fellow and only incidentally as a lawyer. But he was shrewd and wordly-wise. 'Well, George, what's brought you here today?' he boomed as the colonel was shown into his office. 'Have a good time in London? I'm taking my missus up for a few days next week. How's Evie?'

'It's about Evie I've come to see you,' said Peregrine, giving him a suspicious look. 'Have you read her book?'

His sensitivity had been sharpened during those last days of troubled thought and he was conscious of a faint change in the lawyer's expression. It was as though he were suddenly on his guard.

'Yes, I've read it. Great success, isn't it? Fancy Evie breaking out into poetry. Wonders will never cease.'

George Peregrine was inclined to lose his temper.

'It's made me look a perfect damned fool.'

'Oh, what nonsense, George! There's no harm in Evie's writing a book. You ought to be jolly proud of her.'

'Don't talk such rot. It's her own story. You know it and everyone else knows it. I suppose I'm the only one who doesn't know who her lover was.'

'There is such a thing as imagination, old boy. There's no reason to suppose the whole thing isn't made up.'

'Look here, Henry, we've known one another all our lives. We've had all sorts of good times together. Be honest with me. Can you look me in the face and tell me you believe it's a made-up story?'

Harry Blane moved uneasily in his chair. He was disturbed by the distress in old George's voice.

'You've got no right to ask me a question like that. Ask Evie.'

'I daren't,' George answered after an anguished pause. 'I'm afraid she'd tell me the truth.'

There was an uncomfortable silence.

'Who was the chap?'

Harry Blane looked at him straight in the eye.

'I don't know, and if I did I wouldn't tell you.'

'You swine. Don't you see what a position I'm in? Do you think it's very pleasant to be made absolutely ridiculous?'

The lawyer lit a cigarette and for some moments silently puffed it.

'I don't see what I can do for you,' he said at last.

'You've got private detectives you employ, I suppose. I want you to put them on the job and let them find everything out.'

'It's not very pretty to put detectives on one's wife, old boy; and besides, taking for granted for a moment that Evie had an affair, it was a good many years ago and I don't suppose it would be possible to find out a thing. They seem to have covered their tracks pretty carefully.'

'I don't care. You put the detectives on. I want to know the truth.'

'I won't, George. If you're determined to do that you'd better consult someone else. And look here, even if you got evidence that Evie had been unfaithful to you what would you do with it? You'd look rather silly divorcing your wife because she'd committed adultery ten years ago.'

'At all events I could have it out with her.'

'You can do that now, but you know just as well as I do that if you do she'll leave you. D'you want her to do that?'

George gave him an unhappy look.

'I don't know. I always thought she'd been a damned good wife to me. She runs the house perfectly, we never have any servant trouble; she's done wonders with the garden and she's splendid with all the village people. But damn it, I have my self-respect to think of. How can I go on living with her when I know that she was grossly unfaithful to me?'

'Have you always been faithful to her?'

'More or less, you know. After all, we've been married for nearly twenty-four years and Evie was never much for bed.'

The solicitor slightly raised his eyebrows, but George was too intent on what he was saying to notice.

'I don't deny that I've had a bit of fun now and then. A man wants it. Women are different.'

'We only have men's word for that,' said Harry Blane, with a faint smile.

'Evie's absolutely the last woman I'd have suspected of kicking over the traces. I mean, she's a very fastidious, reticent woman. What on earth made her write the damned book?'

'I suppose it was a very poignant experience and perhaps it was a relief to her to get it off her chest like that.'

'Well, if she had to write it why the devil didn't she write it under an assumed name?'

'She used her maiden name. I suppose she thought that was enough, and it would have been if the book hadn't had this amazing boom.'

George Peregrine and the lawyer were sitting opposite one another with a desk between them. George, his elbow on the desk, his cheek on his hand, frowned at his thought.

'It's so rotten not to know what sort of a chap he was. One can't even tell if he was by way of being a gentleman. I mean, for all I know he may have been a farm-hand or a clerk in a lawyer's office.'

Harry Blane did not permit himself to smile and when he answered there was in his eyes a kindly, tolerant look.

'Knowing Evie so well I think the probabilities are that he was all right. Anyhow I'm sure he wasn't a clerk in my office.'

'It's been a shock to me,' the colonel sighed. 'I thought she was fond of me. She couldn't have written that book unless she hated me.'

'Oh, I don't believe that. I don't think she's capable of hatred.'

'You're not going to pretend that she loves me.'

'No.'

'Well, what does she feel for me?'

Harry Blane leaned back in his swivel chair and looked at George reflectively.

'Indifference, I should say.'

The colonel gave a little shudder and reddened.

'After all, you're not in love with her, are you?'

George Peregrine did not answer directly.

'It's been a great blow to me not to have any children, but I've never let her see that I think she's let me down. I've always been kind to her. Within reasonable limits I've tried to do my duty by her.'

The lawyer passed a large hand over his mouth to conceal the smile that trembled on his lips.

'It's been such an awful shock to me,' Peregrine went on. 'Damn it all, even ten years ago Evie was no chicken and God knows, she wasn't much to look at. It's so ugly.' He sighed deeply. 'What would *you* do in my place?'

'Nothing.'

George Peregrine drew himself bolt upright in his chair and he looked at Harry with the stern set face that he must have worn when he inspected his regiment.

'I can't overlook a thing like this. I've been made a laughing-stock. I can never hold up my head again.'

'Nonsense,' said the lawyer sharply, and then in a pleasant, kindly manner, 'Listen, old boy: the man's dead; it all happened a long while back. Forget it. Talk to people about Evie's book, rave about it, tell 'em how proud you are of her. Behave as though you had so much confidence in her, you *knew* she could never have been unfaithful to you. The world moves so quickly and people's memories are so short. They'll forget.'

'I shan't forget.'

'You're both middle-aged people. She probably does a great deal more for you than you think and you'd be awfully lonely without her. I don't think it matters if you don't forget. It'll be all to the good if you can get it into that thick head of yours that there's a lot more in Evie than you ever had the gumption to see.'

'Damn it all, you talk as if I was to blame.'

'No, I don't think you were to blame, but I'm not so sure that Evie was either. I don't suppose she wanted to fall in love with this boy. D'you remember those verses right at the end? The impression they gave me was that though she was shattered by his death, in a strange sort of way she welcomed it. All through she'd been aware of the fragility of the tie that bound them. He died in the full flush of his first love and had never known that love so seldom endures; he'd only known its bliss and beauty. In her own bitter grief she found solace in the thought that he'd been spared all sorrow.'

'All that's a bit above my head, old boy. I see more or less what you mean.'

George Peregrine stared unhappily at the inkstand on the desk. He was silent and the lawyer looked at him with curious, yet sympathetic, eyes.

'Do you realize what courage she must have had never by a sign to show how dreadfully unhappy she was?' he said gently.

Colonel Peregrine sighed.

'I'm broken, I suppose you're right; it's no good crying over spilt milk and it would only make things worse if I made a fuss.'

'Well?'

George Peregrine gave a pitiful little smile.

'I'll take your advice. I'll do nothing. Let them think me a damned fool and to hell with them. The truth is, I don't know what I'd do without Evie. But I'll tell you what, there's one thing I shall never understand till my dying day: What in the name of heaven did the fellow ever see in her?'

Miss King

◆

It was not till the beginning of September that Ashenden, a writer by profession, who had been abroad at the outbreak of the war, managed to get back to England. He chanced soon after his arrival to go to a party and was there introduced to a middle-aged colonel whose name he did not catch. He had some talk with him. As he was about to leave, this officer came up to him and asked:

'I say, I wonder if you'd mind coming to see me. I'd rather like to have a chat with you.'

'Certainly,' said Ashenden. 'Whenever you like.'

'What about tomorrow at eleven?'

'All right.'

'I'll just write down my address. Have you a card on you?'

Ashenden gave him one and on this the colonel scribbled in pencil the name of a street and the number of a house. When Ashenden walked along next morning to keep his appointment he found himself in a street of rather vulgar red-brick houses in a part of London that had once been fashionable, but was now fallen in the esteem of the house-hunter who wanted a good address. On the house at which Ashenden had been asked to call there was a board up to announce that it was for sale, the shutters were closed, and there was no sign that anyone lived in it. He rang the bell and the door was opened by a non-commissioned officer so promptly that he was startled. He was not asked his business, but led immediately into a long room at the back, once evidently a dining-room, the florid decoration of which looked oddly out of keeping with the office furniture, shabby and sparse, that was in it. It gave Ashenden the impression of a room in which the brokers had taken possession. The colonel, who was known in the Intelligence Department, as Ashenden later discovered, by the letter R. rose when he came in and shook hands with him. He was a man somewhat above the middle height, lean, with a yellow, deeply lined face, thin grey hair, and a toothbrush moustache. The thing immediately noticeable about him was the closeness with which his blue eyes were set. He only just escaped a squint. They were hard and cruel eyes, and very wary; and they gave him a cunning, shifty look. Here was a man that you could neither like nor trust at first sight. His manner was pleasant and cordial.

He asked Ashenden a good many questions and then, without further to-do, suggested that he had particular qualifications for the secret service. Ashenden was acquainted with several European languages and his profession was excellent cover; on the pretext that he was writing a book he could without attracting attention visit any neutral country. It was while they were discussing this point that R. said:

'You know, you ought to get material that would be very useful to you in your work.'

'I shouldn't mind that,' said Ashenden.

'I'll tell you an incident that occurred only the other day and I can vouch for its truth. I thought at the time it would make a damned good story. One of the French ministers went down to Nice to recover from a cold and he had some very important documents with him that he kept in a dispatch-case. They were very important indeed. Well, a day or two after he arrived he picked up a yellow-haired lady at some restaurant or other where there was dancing, and he got friendly with her. To cut a long story short, he took her back to his hotel—of course it was a very imprudent thing to do—and when he came to himself in the morning the lady and the dispatch-case had disappeared. They had one or two drinks up in his room and his theory is that when his back was turned the woman slipped a drug into his glass.'

R. finished and looked at Ashenden with a gleam in his close-set eyes.

'Dramatic, isn't it?' he asked.

'Do you mean to say that happened the other day?'

'The week before last.'

'Impossible,' cried Ashenden. 'Why, we've been putting that incident on the stage for sixty years, we've written it in a thousand novels. Do you mean to say that life has only just caught up with us?'

R. was a trifle disconcerted.

'Well, if necessary, I could give you names and dates, and believe me, the Allies have been put to no end of trouble by the loss of the documents that the dispatch-case contained.'

'Well, sir, if you can't do better than that in the secret service,' sighed Ashenden, 'I'm afraid that as a source of inspiration to the writer of fiction it's a wash-out. We really *can't* write that story much longer.'

It did not take them long to settle things and when Ashenden rose to go he had already made careful note of his instructions. He was to start for Geneva next day. The last words that R. said to him, with a casualness that made them impressive, were:

'There's just one thing I think you ought to know before you take on this job. And don't forget it. If you do well you'll get no thanks and if you get into trouble you'll get no help. Does that suit you?'

'Perfectly.'

'Then I'll wish you good afternoon.'

Ashenden was on his way back to Geneva. The night was stormy and the wind blew cold from the mountains, but the stodgy little steamer plodded sturdily through the choppy waters of the lake. A scudding rain, just turning into sleet, swept the deck in angry gusts, like a nagging woman who cannot leave a subject alone. Ashenden had been to France in order to write and dispatch a report. A day or two before, about five in the afternoon, an Indian agent of his had come to see him in his rooms; it was only by a lucky chance that he was in, for he had no appointment with him, and the agent's instructions were to come to the hotel only in a case of urgent importance. He told Ashenden that a Bengali in the German service had recently come from Berlin with a black cane trunk in which were a number of documents interesting to the British Government. At that time the Central Powers were doing their best to foment such an agitation in India as would make it necessary for Great Britain to keep her troops in the country and perhaps send others from France. It had been found possible to get the Bengali arrested in Berne on a charge that would keep him out of harm's way for a while, but the black cane trunk could not be found. Ashenden's agent was a very brave and very clever fellow and he mixed freely with such of his countrymen as were disaffected to the interests of Great Britain. He had just discovered that the Bengali before going to Berne had, for greater safety, left the trunk in the cloak-room at Zürich station, and now that he was in gaol, awaiting trial, was unable to get the *bulletin* by which it might be obtained into the hands of any of his confederates. It was a matter of great urgency for the German Intelligence Department to secure the contents of the trunk without delay, and since it was impossible for them to get hold of it by the ordinary official means, they had decided to break into the station that very night and steal it. It was a bold and ingenious scheme and Ashenden felt a pleasant exhilaration (for a great deal of his work was uncommonly dull) when he heard of it. He recognized the dashing and unscrupulous touch of the head of the German secret service at Berne. But the burglary was arranged for two o'clock on the following morning and there was not a moment to lose. He could trust neither the telegraph nor the telephone to communicate with the British officer at Berne, and since the Indian agent could not go (he was taking his life in his hands by coming to see Ashenden and if he were noticed leaving his room it might easily be that he would be found one day floating in the lake with a knife-thrust in his back), there was nothing for it but to go himself.

There was a train to Berne that he could just catch and he put on his hat and coat as he ran downstairs. He jumped into a cab. Four hours later he rang the bell of the headquarters of the Intelligence Department. His name was known there but to one person, and it was for him that Ashenden asked. A tall tired-looking man, whom he had not met before, came out and without a word led him into an office. Ashenden told him his errand. The tall man looked at his watch.

'It's too late for us to do anything ourselves. We couldn't possibly get to Zürich in time.'

He reflected.

'We'll put the Swiss authorities on the job. They can telephone, and when your friends attempt their little burglary, I have no doubt they'll find the station well guarded. Anyhow, you had better get back to Geneva.'

He shook hands with Ashenden and showed him out. Ashenden was well aware that he would never know what happened then. Being no more than a tiny rivet in a vast and complicated machine, he never had the advantage of seeing a completed action. He was concerned with the beginning or the end of it, perhaps, or with some incident in the middle, but what his own doings led to he had seldom a chance of discovering. It was as unsatisfactory as those modern novels that give you a number of unrelated episodes and expect you by piecing them together to construct in your mind a connected narrative.

Notwithstanding his fur coat and his muffler, Ashenden was chilled to the bone. It was warm in the saloon and there were good lights to read by, but he thought it better not to sit there in case some habitual traveller, recognizing him, wondered why he made these constant journeys between Geneva in Switzerland and Thonon in France; and so, making the best of what shelter could be found, he passed the tedious time in the darkness of the deck. He looked in the direction of Geneva, but could see no lights, and the sleet, turning into snow, prevented him from recognizing the landmarks. Lake Leman, on fine days so trim and pretty, artificial like a piece of water in a French garden, in this tempestuous weather was as secret and as menacing as the sea. He made up his mind that, on getting back to his hotel, he would have a fire lit in his sitting-room, a hot bath, and dinner comfortably by the fireside in pyjamas and a dressing-gown. The prospect of spending an evening by himself with his pipe and a book was so agreeable that it made the misery of that journey across the lake positively worth while. Two sailors tramped past him heavily, their heads bent down to save themselves from the sleet that blew in their faces, and one of them shouted to him: *Nous arrivons*; they went to the side and withdrew a bar to allow passage for the gangway, and looking again Ashenden through the howling darkness saw mistily the lights of the quay. A welcome sight. In two or three minutes the steamer was made fast and Ashenden, muffled to the eyes, joined himself to the little knot of passengers that waited to step ashore. Though he made the journey so often—it was his duty to cross the lake into France once a week to deliver his reports and to receive instructions—he had always a faint sense of trepidation when he stood among the crowd at the gangway and waited to land. There was nothing on his passport to show that he had been in France; the steamer went round the lake touching French soil at two places, but going from Switzerland to Switzerland, so that his journey might have been to Vevey or to Lausanne; but he could never be sure that the secret police had not taken note of him, and if he had been followed and seen to land in France, the fact that there was no stamp on his passport would be difficult to explain. Of course he had his story ready, but he well knew that it was not a very convincing one, and though it might be impossible for the Swiss authorities to prove that he was anything but a casual traveller, he might nevertheless spend two or three days in gaol, which would be uncomfortable, and then be firmly conducted to the frontier, which would be mortifying. The Swiss knew well that their country was the scene of all manner of intrigues; agents of the secret service, spies, revolutionaries, and agitators infested the hotels of the principal towns and, jealous of their neutrality, they were determined to prevent conduct that might embroil them with any of the belligerent powers.

There were as usual two police officers on the quay to watch the passengers disembark and Ashenden, walking past them with as unconcerned an air as he could assume, was relieved when he had got safely by. The darkness swallowed him up and he stepped out briskly for his hotel. The wild weather with a scornful gesture had swept all the neatness from the trim promenade. The shops were closed and Ashenden passed only an occasional pedestrian who sidled along, scrunched up, as though he fled from the blind wrath of the unknown. You had a feeling in that black and bitter night that civilization, ashamed of its artificiality, cowered before the fury of elemental things. It was hail now that blew in Ashenden's face, and the pavement was wet and slippery so that he had to walk with caution. The hotel faced the lake. When he reached it and a page-boy opened the door for him, he entered the hall with a flurry of wind that sent the papers on the porter's desk flying into the air. Ashenden was dazzled by the light. He stopped to ask the porter if there were letters for him. There was nothing, and he was about to get into the lift when the porter told him that two gentlemen were waiting in his room to see him. Ashenden had no friends in Geneva.

'Oh?' he answered, not a little surprised. 'Who are they?'

He had taken care to get on friendly terms with the porter and his tips for trifling services had been generous. The porter gave a discreet smile.

'There is no harm in telling you. I think they are members of the police.'

'What do they want?' asked Ashenden.

'They did not say. They asked me where you were, and I told them you had gone for a walk. They said they would wait till you came back.'

'How long have they been there?'

'An hour.'

Ashenden's heart sank, but he took care not to let his face betray his concern.

'I'll go up and see them,' he said. The liftman stood aside to let him step into the lift, but Ashenden shook his head. 'I'm so cold,' he said, 'I'll walk up.'

He wished to give himself a moment to think, but as he ascended the three flights slowly his feet were like lead. There could be small doubt why two police officers were so bent upon seeing him. He felt on a sudden dreadfully tired. He did not feel he could cope with a multitude of questions. And if he were arrested as a secret agent he must spend at least the night in a cell. He longed more than ever for a hot bath and a pleasant dinner by his fireside. He had half a mind to turn tail and walk out of the hotel, leaving everything behind him; he had his passport in his pocket and he knew by heart the hours at which trains started for the frontier: before the Swiss authorities had made up their minds what to do he would be in safety. But he continued to trudge upstairs. He did not like the notion of abandoning his job so easily; he had been sent to Geneva, knowing the risks, to do work of a certain kind, and it seemed to him that he had better go through with it. Of course it would not be very nice to spend two years in a Swiss prison, but the chance of this was, like assassination to kings, one of the inconveniences of his profession. He reached the landing of the third floor and walked to his room. Ashenden had in him, it seems, a strain of flippancy (on account of which, indeed, the critics had often reproached him) and as he stood for a moment outside the door his predicament appeared to him on a sudden rather droll. His spirits went up and he determined to brazen the thing out. It was with a genuine smile on his lips that he turned the handle and entering the room faced his visitors.

'Good evening, gentlemen,' said he.

The room was brightly lit, for all the lights were on, and a fire burned in the hearth. The air was grey with smoke, since the strangers, finding it long to wait for him, had been smoking strong and inexpensive cigars. They sat in their greatcoats and bowler-hats as though they had only just that moment come in; but the ashes in the little tray on the table would alone have suggested that they had been long enough there to make themselves familiar with their surroundings. They were two powerful men, with black moustaches, on the stout side, heavily built, and they reminded Ashenden of Fafner and Fasolt, the giants in *The Rhinegold;* their clumsy boots, the massive way they sat in their chairs, and the ponderous alertness of their expression made it obvious that they were members of the detective force. Ashenden gave his room an enveloping glance. He was a neat creature and saw at once that his things, though not in disorder, were not as he had left them. He guessed that an examination had been made of his effects. That did not disturb him, for he kept in his room no document that would compromise him; his code he had learned by heart and destroyed before leaving England, and such communications as reached him from Germany were handed to him by third parties and transmitted without delay to the proper places. There was nothing he need fear in a search, but the impression that it had been made confirmed his suspicion that he had been denounced to the authorities as a secret agent.

'What can I do for you, gentlemen?' he asked affably. 'It's warm in here, wouldn't you like to take off your coats—and hats?'

It faintly irritated him that they should sit there with their hats on.

'We're only staying a minute,' said one of them. 'We were passing and as the *concierge* said you would be in at once, we thought we would wait.'

He did not remove his hat. Ashenden unwrapped his scarf and disembarrassed himself of his heavy coat.

'Won't you have a cigar?' he asked, offering the box to the two detectives in turn.

'I don't mind if I do,' said the first, Fafner, taking one, upon which the second, Fasolt, helped himself without a word, even of thanks.

The name on the box appeared to have a singular effect on their manners, for both now took off their hats.

'You must have had a very disagreeable walk in this bad weather,' said Fafner, as he bit half an inch off the end of his cigar and spat it in the fire-place.

Now it was Ashenden's principle (a good one in life as well as in the Intelligence Department) always to tell as much of the truth as he conveniently could; so he answered as follows:

'What do you take me for? I wouldn't go out in such weather if I could help it. I had to go to Vevey today to see an invalid friend and I came back by boat. It was bitter on the lake.'

'We come from the police,' said Fafner casually.

Ashenden thought they must consider him a perfect idiot if they imagined he had not guessed that, but it was not a piece of information to which it was discreet to reply with a pleasantry.

'Oh, really,' he said.

'Have you your passport on you?'

'Yes. In these war-times I think a foreigner is wise always to keep his passport on him.'

'Very wise.'

Ashenden handed the man the nice new passport, which gave no information about his movements other than that he had come from London three months before and had since then crossed no frontier. The detective looked at it carefully and passed it on to his colleague.

'It appears to be all in order,' he said.

Ashenden, standing in front of the fire to warm himself, a cigarette between his lips, made no reply. He watched the detectives warily, but with an expression, he flattered himself, of amiable unconcern. Fasolt handed back the passport to Fafner, who tapped it reflectively with a thick forefinger.

'The chief of police told us to come here,' he said, and Ashenden was conscious that both of them now looked at him with attention, 'to make a few inquiries of you.'

Ashenden knew that when you have nothing apposite to say it is better to hold your tongue; and when a man has made a remark that calls to his mind for an answer, he is apt to find silence a trifle disconcerting. Ashenden waited for the detective to proceed. He was not quite sure, but it seemed to him that he hesitated.

'It appears that there have been a good many complaints lately of the noise that people make when they come out of the Casino late at night. We wish to know if you personally have been troubled by the disturbance. It is evident that as your rooms look on the lake and the revellers pass your windows, if the noise is serious, you must have heard it.'

For an instant Ashenden was dumbfounded. What balderdash was this the detective was talking to him (boom, boom, he heard the big drum as the giant lumbered on the scene), and why on earth should the chief of police send to him to find out if his beauty sleep had been disturbed by vociferous gamblers? It looked very like a trap. But nothing is so foolish as to ascribe profundity to what on the surface is merely inept; it is a pitfall into which many an ingenuous reviewer has fallen headlong. Ashenden had a confident belief in the stupidity of the human animal, which in the course of his life had stood him in good stead. It flashed across him that if the detective asked him such a question it was because he had no shadow of proof that he was engaged in any illegal practice. It was clear that he had been denounced, but no evidence had been offered, and the search of his rooms had been fruitless. But what a silly excuse was this to make for a visit and what a poverty of invention it showed! Ashenden immediately thought of three reasons the detectives might have given for seeking an interview with him and he wished that he were on terms sufficiently familiar with them to make the suggestions. This was really an insult to the intelligence. These men were even stupider than he thought; but Ashenden had always a soft corner in his heart for the stupid and now he looked upon them with a feeling of unexpected kindliness. He would have liked to pat them gently. But he answered the question with gravity.

'To tell you the truth, I am a very sound sleeper (the result doubtless of a pure heart and an easy conscience), and I have never heard a thing.'

Ashenden looked at them for the faint smile that he thought his remark deserved, but their countenances remained stolid. Ashenden, as well as an agent of the British Government, was a humorist, and he stifled the beginnings of a sigh. He assumed a slightly imposing air and adopted a more serious tone.

'But even if I had been awakened by noisy people I should not dream of complaining. At a time when there is so much trouble, misery, and unhappiness in the world, I cannot but think it very wrong to disturb the amusement of persons who are lucky enough to be able to amuse themselves.'

'*En effet*,' said the detective. 'But the fact remains that people have been disturbed and the chief of police thought the matter should be inquired into.'

His colleague, who had hitherto preserved a silence that was positively sphinx-like, now broke it.

'I noticed by your passport that you are an author, *monsieur*,' he said.

Ashenden in reaction from his previous perturbation was feeling exceedingly debonair and he answered with good-humour:

'It is true. It is a profession full of tribulation, but it has now and then its compensations.'

'*La gloire,*' said Fafner politely.

'Or shall we say notoriety?' hazarded Ashenden.

'And what are you doing in Geneva?'

The question was put so pleasantly that Ashenden felt it behoved him to be on his guard. A police officer amiable is more dangerous to the wise than a police officer aggressive.

'I am writing a play,' said Ashenden.

He waved his hand to the papers on his table. Four eyes followed his gesture. A casual glance told him that the detectives had looked and taken note of his manuscripts.

'And why should you write a play here rather than in your own country?'

Ashenden smiled upon them with even more affability than before, since this was a question for which he had long been prepared, and it was a relief to give the answer. He was curious to see how it would go down.

'*Mais, monsieur,* there is the war. My country is in turmoil, it would be impossible to sit there quietly and write a play.'

'Is it a comedy or a tragedy?'

'Oh, a comedy, and a light one at that,' replied Ashenden. 'The artist needs peace and quietness. How do you expect him to preserve that detachment of spirit that is demanded by creative work unless he can have perfect tranquillity? Switzerland has the good fortune to be neutral, and it seemed to me that in Geneva I should find the very surroundings I wanted.'

Fafner nodded slightly to Fasolt, but whether to indicate that he thought Ashenden an imbecile or whether in sympathy with his desire for a safe retreat from a turbulent world, Ashenden had no means of knowing. Anyhow the detective evidently came to the conclusion that he could learn nothing more from talking to Ashenden, for his remarks grew now desultory and in a few minutes he rose to go.

When Ashenden, having warmly shaken their hands, closed the door behind the pair he heaved a great sigh of relief. He turned on the water for his bath, as hot as he thought he could possibly bear it, and as he undressed reflected comfortably over his escape.

The day before, an incident had occurred that had left him on his guard There was in his service a Swiss, known in the Intelligence Department as Bernard, who had recently come from Germany, and Ashenden, desiring to see him, had instructed him to go to a certain café at a certain time. Since he had not seen him before, so that there might be no mistake he had informed him through an intermediary what question he himself would ask and what reply he was to give. He chose the luncheon hour for the meeting, since the café was unlikely to be crowded, and it chanced that on entering he saw but one man of about the age he knew Bernard to be. He was by himself, and going up to him Ashenden casually put to him the pre-arranged question. The pre-arranged answer was given, and sitting down beside him, Ashenden ordered himself a Dubonnet. The spy was a stocky little fellow, shabbily dressed, with a bullet-shaped head, close-cropped, fair, with shifty blue eyes and a sallow skin. He did not inspire confidence, and but that Ashenden knew by experience how hard it was to find men willing to go into Germany he would have been surprised that his predecessor had engaged him. He was a German-Swiss and spoke French with a strong accent. He immediately asked for his wages and these Ashenden passed over to him in an envelope. They were in Swiss francs. He gave a general account of his stay in Germany and answered Ashenden's careful questions. He was by calling a waiter and had found a job in a restaurant near one of the Rhine bridges, which gave him good opportunity to get information that was required of him. His reasons for coming to Switzerland for a few days were plausible and there could apparently be no difficulty in his crossing the frontier on his return. Ashenden expressed his satisfaction with his behaviour, gave him his orders and was prepared to finish the interview.

'Very good,' said Bernard. 'But before I go back to Germany I want two thousand francs.'

'Do you?'

'Yes, and I want them now, before you leave this café. It's a sum I have to pay, and I've got to have it.'

'I'm afraid I can't give it to you.'

A scowl made the man's face even more unpleasant to look at than it was before.

'You've got to.'

'What makes you think that?'

The spy leaned forward and, not raising his voice, but speaking so that only Ashenden could hear, burst out angrily:

'Do you think I'm going on risking my life for that beggarly sum you give me? Not ten days ago a man was caught at Mainz and shot. Was that one of your men?'

'We haven't got anyone at Mainz,' said Ashenden, carelessly, and for all he knew it was true. He had been puzzled not to receive his usual communications from that place and Bernard's information might afford the explanation. 'You knew exactly what you were to get when you took on the job, and if you weren't satisfied you needn't have taken it. I have no authority to give you a penny more.'

'Do you see what I've got here?' said Bernard.

He took a small revolver out of his pocket and fingered it significantly.

'What are you going to do with it? Pawn it?'

With an angry shrug of the shoulders he put it back in his pocket. Ashenden reflected that had he known anything of the technique of the theatre Bernard would have been aware that it was useless to make a gesture that had no ulterior meaning.

'You refuse to give me the money?'

'Certainly.'

The spy's manner, which at first had been obsequious, was now somewhat truculent, but he kept his head and never for a moment raised his voice. Ashenden could see that Bernard, however big a ruffian, was a reliable agent, and he made up his mind to suggest to R. that his salary should be raised. The scene diverted him. A little way off two fat citizens of Geneva, with black beards, were playing dominoes, and on the other side a young man with spectacles was with great rapidity writing sheet after sheet of an immensely long letter. A Swiss family (who knows, perhaps Robinson by name), consisting of a father and mother and four children, were sitting round a table making the best of two small cups of coffee. The *caissière* behind the counter, an imposing brunette with a large bust encased in black silk, was reading the local paper. The surroundings made the melodramatic scene in which Ashenden was engaged perfectly grotesque. His own play seemed to him much more real.

Bernard smiled. His smile was not engaging.

'Do you know that I have only to go to the police and tell them about you to have you arrested? Do you know what a Swiss prison is like?'

'No, I've often wondered lately. Do you?'

'Yes, and you wouldn't much like it.'

One of the things that had bothered Ashenden was the possibility that he would be arrested before he finished his play. He disliked the notion of leaving it half done for an indefinite period. He did not know whether he would be treated as a political prisoner or as a common criminal and he had a mind to ask Bernard whether in the latter case (the only one Bernard was likely to know anything about) he would be allowed writing materials. He was afraid Bernard would think the inquiry an attempt to laugh at him. But he was feeling comparatively at ease and was able to answer Bernard's threat without heat.

'You could of course get me sentenced to two years' imprisonment.'

'At least.'

'No, that is the maximum, I understand, and I think it is quite enough. I won't conceal from you that I should find it extremely disagreeable. But not nearly so disagreeable as you would.'

'What could you do?'

'Oh, we'd get you somehow. And after all, the war won't last for ever. You are a waiter, you want your freedom of action. I promise you that if I get into any trouble, you will never be admitted into any of the Allied countries for the rest of your life. I can't help thinking it would cramp your style.'

Bernard did not reply, but looked down sulkily at the marble-topped table. Ashenden thought this was the moment to pay for the drinks and go.

'Think it over, Bernard,' he said. 'If you want to go back to your job, you have your instructions, and your usual wages shall be paid through the usual channels.'

The spy shrugged his shoulders, and Ashenden, though not knowing in the least what was the result of their conversation, felt that it behoved him to walk out with dignity. He did so.

And now as he carefully put one foot into the bath, wondering if he could bear it, he asked himself what Bernard had in the end decided on. The water was just not scalding and he gradually let himself down into it. On the whole it seemed to him that the spy had thought it would be as well to go straight, and the source of his denunciation must be looked for elsewhere. Perhaps in the hotel itself. Ashenden lay back, and as his body grew used to the heat of the water gave a sigh of satisfaction.

'Really,' he reflected, 'there are moments in life when all this to-do that has led from the primeval slime to myself seems almost worth while.'

Ashenden could not but think he was lucky to have wriggled out of the fix he had found himself in that afternoon. Had he been arrested and in due course sentenced, R., shrugging his shoulders, would merely have called him a damned fool and set about looking for someone to take his place. Already Ashenden knew his chief well enough to be aware that when he had told him that if he got into trouble he need look for no help he meant exactly what he said.

Ashenden, lying comfortably in his bath, was glad to think that in all probability he would be able to finish his play in peace. The police had drawn a blank and though they might watch him from now on with some care, it was unlikely that they would take a further step until he had at least roughed out his third act. It behoved him to be prudent (only a fortnight ago his colleague at Lausanne had been sentenced to a term of imprisonment), but it would be foolish to be alarmed: his predecessor in Geneva, seeing himself, with an exaggerated sense of his own importance, shadowed from morning till night, had been so affected by the nervous strain that it had been found necessary to withdraw him. Twice a week Ashenden had to go to the market to receive instructions that were brought to him by an old peasant woman from French Savoy who sold butter and eggs. She came in with the other market-women and the search at the frontier was perfunctory. It was barely dawn when they crossed and the officials were only too glad to have done quickly with these chattering noisy women and get back to their warm fires and their cigars. Indeed this old lady looked so bland and innocent, with her corpulence, her fat red face, and her smiling good-natured mouth, it would have been a very astute detective who could imagine that if he took the trouble to put his hand deep down between those voluminous breasts of hers, he would find a little piece of paper that would land in the dock an honest old woman (who kept her son out of the trenches by taking this risk) and an English writer approaching middle age. Ashenden went to the market about nine when the housewives of Geneva for the most part had done their provisioning, stopped in front of the basket by the side of which, rain or wind, hot or cold, sat that indomitable creature and bought half a pound of butter. She slipped the note into his hand when he was given change for ten francs and he sauntered away. His only moment of risk was when he walked back to his hotel with the paper in his pocket, and after this scare he made up his mind to shorten as much as possible the period during which it could be found on him.

Ashenden sighed, for the water was no longer quite so hot; he could not reach the tap with his hand nor could he turn it with his toes (as every properly regulated tap should turn) and if he got up enough to add more hot water he might just as well get out altogether. On the other hand he could not pull out the plug with his foot in order to empty the bath and so force himself to get out, nor could he find himself the will-power to step out of it like a man. He had often heard people tell him that he possessed character and he reflected that people judge hastily in the affairs of life because they judge on insufficient evidence: they had never seen him in a hot, but diminishingly hot, bath. His mind, however, wandered back to his play, and telling himself jokes and repartees that he knew by bitter experience would never look so neat on paper nor sound so well on the stage as they did then, he abstracted his mind from the fact that his bath was growing almost tepid, when he heard a knock at the door. Since he did not want anyone to enter, he had the presence of mind not to say come in, but the knocking was repeated.

'Who is it?' he cried irascibly.

'A letter.'

'Come in then. Wait a minute.'

Ashenden heard his bedroom door open and getting out of the bath flung a towel round him and went in. A page-boy was waiting with a note. It needed only a verbal answer. It was from a lady staying in the hotel asking him to play bridge after dinner and was signed in the continental fashion Baronne de Higgins. Ashenden, longing for a cosy meal in his own room, in slippers and with a book leaned up against a reading-lamp, was about to refuse when it occurred to him that in the circumstances it might be discreet to show himself in the dining-room that night. It was absurd to suppose that in that hotel the news would not have spread that he had been visited by the police and it would be as well to prove to his fellow guests that he was not disconcerted. It had passed through his mind that it might be someone in the hotel who had denounced him and indeed the name of the sprightly baroness had not failed to suggest itself to him. If it was she who had given him away there would be a certain humour in playing bridge with her. He gave the boy a message that he would be pleased to come and proceeded slowly to don his evening clothes.

The Baroness von Higgins was an Austrian, who on settling in Geneva during the first winter of the war had found it convenient to make her name look as French as possible. She spoke English and French perfectly. Her surname, so far from Teutonic, she owed to her grandfather, a Yorkshire stable-boy, who had been taken over to Austria by a Prince Blankenstein early in the nineteenth century. He had had a charming and romantic career; a very good-looking man, he attracted the attention of one of the archduchesses and then made such good use of his opportunities that he ended his life as a baron and minister plenipotentiary to an Italian court. The baroness, his only descendant, after an unhappy marriage, the particulars of which she was fond of relating to her acquaintance, had resumed her maiden name. She mentioned not infrequently the fact that her grandfather had been an ambassador, but never that he had been a stable-boy and Ashenden had learned this interesting detail from Vienna; for as he grew friendly with her he had thought it necessary to get a few particulars about her past, and he knew among other things that her private income did not permit her to live on the somewhat lavish scale on which she was living in Geneva. Since she had so many advantages for espionage, it was fairly safe to suppose that an alert secret service had enlisted her services and Ashenden took it for granted that she was engaged somehow on the same kind of work as himself. It increased if anything the cordiality of his relations with her.

When he went into the dining-room it was already full. He sat down at his table and feeling jaunty after his adventure ordered himself (at the expense of the British Government) a bottle of champagne. The baroness gave him a flashing, brilliant smile. She was a woman of more than forty, but in a hard and glittering manner extremely beautiful. She was a high-coloured blonde with golden hair of a metallic lustre, lovely no doubt but not attractive, and Ashenden had from the first reflected that it was not the sort of hair you would like to find in your soup. She had fine features, blue eyes, a straight nose, and a pink and white skin, but her skin was stretched over her bones a trifle tightly; she was generously *décolletée* and her white and ample bosom had the quality of marble. There was nothing in her appearance to suggest the yielding tenderness that the susceptible find so alluring. She was magnificently gowned, but scantily bejewelled, so that Ashenden, who knew something of these matters, concluded that the superior authority had given her *carte blanche* at a dressmaker's but had not thought it prudent or necessary to provide her with rings or pearls. She was notwithstanding so showy that but for R.'s story of the minister, Ashenden would have thought the sight of her alone must have aroused in anyone on whom she desired to exercise her wiles the sense of prudence.

While he waited for his dinner to be served, Ashenden cast his eyes over the company. Most of the persons gathered were old friends by sight. At that time Geneva was a hot-bed of intrigue and its home was the hotel at which Ashenden was staying. There were Frenchmen there, Italians and Russians, Turks,

Rumanians, Greeks, and Egyptians. Some had fled their country, some doubtless represented it. There was a Bulgarian, an agent of Ashenden, whom for greater safety he had never even spoken to in Geneva; he was dining that night with two fellow countrymen and in a day or so, if he was not killed in the interval, might have a very interesting communication to make. Then there was a little German prostitute, with china-blue eyes and a doll-like face, who made frequent journeys along the lake and up to Berne, and in the exercise of her profession got little titbits of information over which doubtless they pondered with deliberation in Berlin. She was of course of a different class from the baroness and hunted much easier game. But Ashenden was surprised to catch sight of Count von Holzminden and wondered what on earth he was doing there. This was the German agent in Vevey and he came over to Geneva only on occasion. Once Ashenden had seen him in the old quarter of the city, with its silent houses and deserted streets, talking at a corner to a man whose appearance very much suggested the spy and he would have given a great deal to hear what they said to one another. It had amused him to come across the Count, for in London before the war he had known him fairly well. He was of great family and indeed related to the Hohenzollerns. He was fond of England; he danced well, rode well, and shot well; people said he was more English than the English. He was a tall, thin fellow, in well-cut clothes, with a close-cropped Prussian head, and that peculiar bend of the body—as though he were just about to bow to a royalty—that you feel, rather than see, in those who have spent their lives about a court. He had charming manners and was much interested in the Fine Arts. But now Ashenden and he pretended they had never seen one another before. Each of course knew on what work the other was engaged and Ashenden had had a mind to chaff him about it—it seemed absurd when he had dined with a man off and on for years and played cards with him, to act as though he did not know him from Adam—but refrained in case the German looked upon his behaviour as further proof of the British frivolity in face of war. Ashenden was perplexed: Holzminden had never set foot in that hotel before and it was unlikely that he had done so now without good reason.

Ashenden asked himself whether this event had anything to do with the unusual presence in the dining-room of Prince Ali. At that juncture it was imprudent to ascribe any occurrence, however accidental it looked, to the hazard of coincidence. Prince Ali was an Egyptian, a near relation of the Khedive, who had fled his country when the Khedive was deposed. He was a bitter enemy of the English and was known to be actively engaged in stirring up trouble in Egypt. The week before, the Khedive in great secrecy had passed three days at the hotel and the pair of them had held constant meetings in the prince's apartments. He was a little fat man with a heavy black moustache. He was living with his two daughters and a certain pasha, Mustapha by name, who was his secretary and managed his affairs. The four of them were now dining together; they drank a great deal of champagne, but sat in a stolid silence. The two princesses were emancipated young women who spent their nights dancing in restaurants with the bloods of Geneva. They were short and stout, with fine black eyes and heavy sallow faces; and they were dressed with a rich loudness that suggested the Fish-market at Cairo rather than the Rue de la Paix. His Highness usually ate upstairs but the princesses dined every evening in the public dining-room: they were chaperoned vaguely by a little old English-woman, a Miss King, who had been their governess; but she sat at a table by herself and they appeared to pay no attention to her. Once Ashenden, going along a corridor, had come upon the elder of the two fat princesses berating the governess in French with a violence that took his breath away. She was shouting at the top of her voice and suddenly smacked the old woman's face. When she caught sight of Ashenden she gave him a furious look and flinging into her room slammed the door. He walked on as though he had noticed nothing.

On his arrival Ashenden had tried to scrape acquaintance with Miss King, but she had received his advances not merely with frigidity but with churlishness. He had begun by taking off his hat when he met her, and she had given him a stiff bow, then he had addressed her and she had answered with such brevity that it was evident that she wished to have nothing much to do with him. But it was not his business to be discouraged, so with what assurance he could muster he took the first opportunity to enter into conversation with her. She drew herself up and said in French, but with an English accent:

'I don't wish to make acquaintance with strangers.'

She turned her back on him and, next time he saw her, cut him dead.

She was a tiny woman, just a few little bones in a bag of wrinkled skin, and her face was deeply furrowed. It was obvious that she wore a wig, it was of a mousy brown, very elaborate and not always set quite straight, and she was heavily made up, with great patches of scarlet on her withered cheeks and brilliantly red lips. She dressed fantastically in gay clothes that looked as though they had been bought higgledy-piggledy from an old-clothes shop and in the day-time she wore enormous, extravagantly girlish hats. She tripped along in very small smart shoes with very high heels. Her appearance was so grotesque that it created consternation rather than amusement. People turned in the street and stared at her with open mouths.

Ashenden was told that Miss King had not been to England since she was first engaged as governess of the prince's mother and he could not but be amazed to think of all she must have seen during those long years in the harems of Cairo. It was impossible to guess how old she was. How many of those short Eastern lives must have run their course under her eyes and what dark secrets must she have known! Ashenden wondered where she came from; an exile from her own country for so long, she must possess in it neither family nor friends: he knew that her sentiments were anti-English and if she had answered him so rudely he surmised that she had been told to be on her guard against him. She never spoke anything but French. Ashenden wondered what it was she thought of as she sat there, at luncheon and dinner by herself. He wondered if ever she read. After meals she went straight upstairs and was never seen in the public sitting-rooms. He wondered what she thought of those two emancipated princesses who wore garish frocks and danced with strange men in second-rate cafés. But when Miss King passed him on her way out of the dining-room it seemed to Ashenden that her mask of a face scowled. She appeared actively to dislike him. Her gaze met his and the pair of them looked at one another for a moment: he imagined that she tried to put into her stare an unspoken insult. It would have been pleasantly absurd in that painted, withered visage if it had not been for some reason rather oddly pathetic.

But now the Baroness de Higgins, having finished her dinner, gathered up her handkerchief and her bag, and with waiters bowing on either side sailed down the spacious room. She stopped at Ashenden's table. She looked magnificent.

'I'm so glad you can play bridge tonight,' she said in perfect English, with no more than a trace of German accent. 'Will you come to my sitting-room when you are ready and have your coffee?'

'What a lovely dress,' said Ashenden.

'It is frightful. I have nothing to wear, I don't know what I shall do now that I cannot go to Paris. Those horrible Prussians,' and her r's grew guttural as she raised her voice, 'why did they want to drag my poor country into this terrible war?'

She gave a sigh, and a flashing smile, and sailed on. Ashenden was among the last to finish and when he left the dining-room it was almost empty. As he walked past Count Holzminden, Ashenden feeling very gay hazarded the shadow of a wink. The German agent could not be quite sure of it and if he suspected it might rack his brains to discover what mystery it portended. Ashenden walked up to the second floor and knocked at the baroness's door.

'*Entrez, entrez,*' she said and flung it open.

She shook both his hands with cordiality and drew him into the room. He saw that the two persons who were to make the four had already arrived. They were Prince Ali and his secretary. Ashenden was astounded.

'Allow me to introduce Mr Ashenden to Your Highness,' said the baroness, speaking in her fluent French.

Ashenden bowed and took the proffered hand. The prince gave him a quick look, but did not speak. Madame de Higgins went on:

'I do not know if you have met the Pasha.'

'I am delighted to make your acquaintance, Mr Ashenden,' said the prince's secretary, warmly shaking his hand. 'Our beautiful baroness has talked to us of your bridge and His Highness is devoted to the game. *N'est-ce pas, Altesse?*'

'*Oui, oui,*' said the prince.

Mustapha Pasha was a huge fat fellow, of forty-five perhaps, with large mobile eyes and a big black moustache. He wore a dinner jacket with a large diamond in his shirt-front and the *tarboosh* of his country. He was exceedingly voluble, and the words tumbled out of his mouth tumultuously, like marbles out of a bag. He took pains to be extremely civil to Ashenden. The prince sat in silence, looking at Ashenden quietly from under his heavy eyelids. He seemed shy.

'I have not seen you at the club, *Monsieur,*' said the pasha. 'Do you not like baccarat?'

'I play but seldom.'

'The baroness, who has read everything, tells me that you are a remarkable writer. Unfortunately I do not read English.'

The baroness paid Ashenden some very fulsome compliments to which he listened with a proper and grateful politeness, and then, having provided her guests with coffee and liqueurs, she produced the cards. Ashenden could not but wonder why he had been asked to play. He had (he flattered himself) few illusions about himself, and so far as bridge was concerned none. He knew that he was a good player of the second class, but he had played often enough with the best players in the world to know that he was not in the same street with them. The game played now was contract, with which he was not very familiar, and the stakes were high; but the game was obviously but a pretext and Ashenden had no notion what other game was being played under the rose. It might be that knowing he was a British agent the prince and his secretary had desired to see him in order to find out what sort of person he was. Ashenden had felt for a day or two that something was in the air and this meeting confirmed his suspicions, but he had not the faintest notion of what nature this something was. His spies had told him of late nothing that signified. He was now persuaded that he owed that visit of the Swiss police to the kindly intervention of the baroness and it looked as though the bridge-party had been arranged when it was discovered that the detectives had been able to do nothing. The notion was mysterious, but diverting, and as Ashenden played one rubber after another, joining in the incessant conversation, he watched what was said by himself no less closely than what was said by the others. The war was spoken of a good deal and the baroness and the pasha expressed very anti-German sentiments. The baroness's heart was in England whence her family (the stable-boy from Yorkshire) had sprung, and the pasha looked upon Paris as his spiritual home. When the pasha talked of Montmartre and its life by night the prince was roused from his silence.

'*C'est une bien belle ville, Paris,*' he said.

'The Prince has a beautiful apartment there,' said his secretary, 'with beautiful pictures and life-sized statues.'

Ashenden explained that he had the greatest sympathy for the national aspirations of Egypt and that he looked upon Vienna as the most pleasing capital in Europe. He was as friendly to them as they were to him. But if they were under the impression that they would get any information out of him that they had not already seen in the Swiss papers he had a notion that they were mistaken. At one moment he had a suspicion that he was being sounded upon the possibility of selling himself. It was done so discreetly that he could not be quite sure, but he had a feeling that a suggestion floated in the air that a clever writer could do his country a good turn and make a vast amount of money for himself if he cared to enter into an arrangement that would bring to a troubled world the peace that every humane man must so sincerely desire. It was plain that nothing very much would be said that first evening, but Ashenden as evasively as he could, more by general amiability than by words, tried to indicate that he was willing to hear more of the subject. While he talked with the pasha and the beautiful Austrian he was conscious that the watchful eyes of Prince Ali were upon him, and had an uneasy suspicion that they read too much of his thoughts. He felt rather than knew that the prince was an able and astute man. It was possible that after he left them the prince would tell the other two that they were wasting their time and there was nothing to be done with Ashenden.

Soon after midnight, a rubber having been finished, the prince rose from the table.

'It is getting late,' he said, 'and Mr Ashenden has doubtless much to do tomorrow. We must not keep him up.'

Ashenden looked upon this as a signal to take himself off. He left the three together to discuss the situation and retired not a little mystified. He could only trust that they were no less puzzled than he. When he got to his room he suddenly realized that he was dog-tired. He could hardly keep his eyes open while he undressed, and the moment he flung himself into bed he fell asleep.

He would have sworn that he had not been asleep five minutes when he was dragged back to wakefulness by a knocking at the door. He listened for a moment.

'Who is it?'

'It's the maid. Open. I have something to say to you.'

Cursing, Ashenden turned on his light, ran a hand through his thinning and rumpled hair (for like Julius Caesar he disliked exposing an unbecoming baldness) and unlocked and opened the door. Outside it stood a tousled Swiss maid. She wore no apron and looked as though she had thrown on her clothes in a hurry.

'The old English lady, the governess of the Egyptian princesses, is dying and she wants to see you.'

'Me?' said Ashenden. 'It's impossible. I don't know her. She was all right this evening.'

He was confused and spoke his thoughts as they came to him.

'She asks for you. The doctor says, will you come. She cannot last much longer.'

'It must be a mistake. She can't want me.'

'She said your name and the number of your room. She says quick, quick.'

Ashenden shrugged his shoulders. He went back into his room to put on slippers and a dressing-gown, and as an afterthought dropped a small revolver into his pocket. Ashenden believed much more in his acuteness than in a firearm, which is apt to go off at the wrong time and make a noise, but there are moments when it gives you confidence to feel your fingers round its butt, and this sudden summons seemed to him exceedingly mysterious. It was ridiculous to suppose that those two cordial stout Egyptian gentlemen were laying some sort of trap for him, but in the work upon which Ashenden was engaged the dullness of routine was apt now and again to slip quite shamelessly into the melodrama of the sixties. Just as passion will make use brazenly of the hackneyed phrase, so will chance show itself insensitive to the triteness of the literary convention.

Miss King's room was two floors higher than Ashenden's, and as he accompanied the chamber-maid along the corridor and up the stairs he asked her what was the matter with the old governess. She was flurried and stupid.

'I think she has had a stroke. I don't know. The night-porter woke me and said Monsieur Bridet wanted me to get up at once.'

Monsieur Bridet was the assistant-manager.

'What is the time?' asked Ashenden.

'It must be three o'clock.'

They arrived at Miss King's door and the maid knocked. It was opened by Monsieur Bridet. He had evidently been roused from his sleep; he wore slippers on his bare feet, grey trousers and a frock-coat over his pyjamas. He looked absurd. His hair as a rule plastered neatly on his head stood on end. He was extremely apologetic.

'A thousand excuses for disturbing you, Monsieur Ashenden, but she kept asking for you and the doctor said you should be sent for.'

'It doesn't matter at all.'

Ashenden walked in. It was a small back room and all the lights were on. The windows were closed and the curtains drawn. It was intensely hot. The doctor, a bearded, grizzled Swiss, was standing at the bedside. Monsieur Bridet, notwithstanding his costume and his evident harassment, found in himself the presence of mind to remain the attentive manager, and with ceremony effected the proper introduction.

'This is Mr Ashenden, for whom Miss King has been asking. Dr Arbos of the Faculty of Medicine of Geneva.'

Without a word the doctor pointed to the bed. On it lay Miss King. It gave Ashenden a shock to look at her. She wore a large white cotton nightcap (on entering Ashenden had noticed the brown wig on a stand on the dressing-table) tied under the chin, and a white, voluminous nightdress that came high up in the neck. Nightcap and nightdress belonged to a past age and reminded you of Cruikshank's illustrations to the novels of Charles Dickens. Her face was greasy still with the cream she had used before going to bed to remove her make-up, but she had removed it summarily and there were streaks of black on her eyebrows and of red on her cheeks. She looked very small, lying in the bed, no larger than a child, and immensely old.

'She must be well over eighty,' thought Ashenden.

She did not look human, but like a doll, the caricature of an old, old witch that an ironic toymaker had amused himself with modelling. She lay perfectly still on her back, the tiny little body hardly marked under the flatness of the blanket, her face even smaller than usual because she had removed her teeth; and you would have thought she was dead but for the black eyes, strangely large in the shrunken mask, that stared unblinkingly. Ashenden thought their expression changed when she saw him.

'Well, Miss King, I'm sorry to see you like this,' he said with forced cheerfulness.

'She cannot speak,' said the doctor. 'She had another little stroke when the maid went to fetch you. I have just given her an injection. She may partly recover the use of her tongue in a little while. She has something to say to you.'

'I will gladly wait,' said Ashenden.

He fancied that in those dark eyes he saw a look of relief. For a moment or two the four of them stood round the bed and stared at the dying woman.

'Well, if there is nothing I can do I may just as well go back to bed,' said Monsieur Bridet then.

'*Allez, mon ami*,' said the doctor. 'You can do nothing.'

Monsieur Bridet turned to Ashenden.

'May I have a word with you?' he asked.

'Certainly.'

The doctor noticed a sudden fear in Miss King's eyes.

'Do not be alarmed,' he said kindly. 'Monsieur Ashenden is not going. He will stay as long as you wish.'

The assistant-manager took Ashenden to the door and partly closed it so that those within should not hear his undertones.

'I can count on your discretion, Monsieur Ashenden, can I not? It is a very disagreeable thing to have anyone die in a hotel. The other guests do not like it and we must do all we can to prevent their knowing. I shall have the body removed the first possible moment and I shall be extremely obliged if you will not say that there has been a death.'

'You can have every confidence in me,' said Ashenden.

'It is very unfortunate that the manager should be away for the night. I am afraid he will be exceedingly displeased. Of course if it had been possible I would have sent for an ambulance and had her taken to the hospital, but the doctor said she might die before we got her downstairs and absolutely refused to let me. It is not my fault if she dies in the hotel.'

'Death so often chooses its moments without consideration,' murmured Ashenden.

'After all she is an old woman, she should have died years ago. What did this Egyptian prince want to have a governess of that age for? He ought to have sent her back to her own country. These Orientals, they are always giving trouble.'

'Where is the prince now?' asked Ashenden. 'She has been in his service for many years. Ought you not to wake him?'

'He is not in the hotel. He went out with his secretary. He may be playing baccarat. I do not know. Anyhow I cannot send all over Geneva to find him.'

'And the princesses?'

'They have not come in. They seldom return to the hotel till dawn. They are mad about dancing. I do not know where they are; in any case they would not thank me for dragging them away from their diversions because their governess has had a stroke. I know what they are. The night-porter will tell them when they arrive and then they can please themselves. She does not want them. When the night-porter fetched me and I went into her room I asked where His Highness was and she cried with all her strength: no, no.'

'She could talk then?'

'Yes, after a fashion, but the thing that surprised me was that she spoke in English. She always insisted on talking French. You know, she hated the English.'

'What did she want with me?'

'That I cannot tell you. She said she had something that she must say to you at once. It is funny, she knew the number of your room. At first when she asked for you I would not let them send. I cannot have my clients disturbed in the middle of the night because a crazy old woman asks for them. You have the right to your sleep, I imagine. But when the doctor came he insisted. She gave us no peace and when I said she must wait till morning she cried.'

Ashenden looked at the assistant-manager. He seemed to find nothing at all touching in the scene he related.

'The doctor asked who you were and when I told him he said that perhaps she wished to see you because you were a compatriot.'

'Perhaps,' said Ashenden dryly.

'Well, I shall try to get a little sleep. I shall give the night-porter orders to wake me when everything is over. Fortunately the nights are long now and if everything goes well we may be able to get the body away before it is light.'

Ashenden went back into the room and immediately the dark eyes of the dying woman fixed upon him. He felt that it was incumbent upon him to say something, but as he spoke he reflected on the foolish way in which one speaks to the sick.

'I'm afraid you're feeling very ill, Miss King.'

It seemed to him that a flash of anger crossed her eyes and Ashenden could not but imagine that she was exasperated by his futile words.

'You do not mind waiting?' asked the doctor.

'Of course not.'

It appeared that the night-porter had been roused by the ringing of the telephone from Miss King's room, but on listening could get no one to speak. The bell continued to ring, so he went upstairs and knocked at the door. He entered with his pass-key and found Miss King lying on the floor. The telephone had fallen too. It looked as though, feeling ill, she had taken off the receiver to call for help and then collapsed. The night-porter hurried to fetch the assistant-manager and together they had lifted her back into bed. Then the maid was wakened and the doctor sent for. It gave Ashenden a queer feeling to listen to the doctor giving him these facts in Miss King's hearing. He spoke as though she could not understand his French. He spoke as though she were already dead.

Then the doctor said:

'Well, there is really nothing more that I can do. It is useless for me to stay. I can be rung up if there is any change.'

Ashenden, knowing that Miss King might remain in that condition for hours, shrugged his shoulders.

'Very well.'

The doctor patted her raddled cheek as though she were a child.

'You must try to sleep. I will come back in the morning.'

He packed up the dispatch-case in which he had his medical appliances, washed his hands, and shuffled himself into a heavy coat. Ashenden accompanied him to the door and as he shook hands the doctor gave his prognosis in a pout of his bearded mouth. Ashenden, coming back, looked at the maid. She sat on the edge of a chair, uneasily, as though in the presence of death she feared to presume. Her broad, ugly face was bloated with fatigue.

'There's no use in your staying up,' Ashenden said to her. 'Why don't you go to bed?'

'*Monsieur* wouldn't like to remain here alone. Somebody must stay with him.'

'But good heavens, why? You have your day's work to do tomorrow.'

'In any case I have to get up at five.'

'Then try to get a little sleep now. You can give me a look in when you get up. *Allez.*'

She rose heavily to her feet.

'As the gentleman wishes. But I will stay very willingly.'

Ashenden smiled and shook his head.

'*Bonsoir, ma pauvre mademoiselle,*' said the maid.

She went out and Ashenden was left alone. He sat by the bedside and again his eyes met Miss King's. It was embarrassing to encounter that unshrinking stare.

'Don't worry yourself, Miss King. You've had a slight stroke. I'm sure your speech will come back to you in a minute.'

He felt certain then that he saw in those dark eyes a desperate effort to speak. He could not be mistaken. The mind was shaken by desire, but the paralysed body was incapable of obedience. For her disappointment expressed itself quite plainly, tears came to her eyes and ran down her cheeks. Ashenden took out his handkerchief and dried them.

'Don't distress yourself, Miss King. Have a little patience and I'm sure you'll be able to say anything you want.'

He did not know if it was his fancy that he read in her eyes now the despairing thought that she had not the time to wait. Perhaps it was only that he ascribed to her the notions that came to himself. On the dressing-table were the governess's poor little toilet things, silver-backed embossed brushes and a silver mirror, in a corner stood a shabby black trunk, and on the top of the wardrobe a large hat-box in shiny leather. It all looked poor and mean in that trim hotel room, with its suite in highly varnished rosewood. The glare was intolerable.

'Wouldn't you be more comfortable if I turned out some of the lights?' asked Ashenden.

He put out all the lamps but the one by the bedside and then sat down again. He had a longing to smoke. Once more his eyes were held by those other eyes in which was all that remained alive of that old, old woman. He felt certain that she had something that she wanted urgently to say to him. But what was it? What was it? Perhaps she had asked him only because feeling death near, she had had a sudden yearning, she the exile of so many years, to die with someone of her own people, so long forgotten, by her side. That was what the doctor thought. But why should she have sent for him? There were other English people in the hotel. There was an old pair, a retired Indian Civilian and his wife, to whom it seemed more natural that she should turn. No one could be more of a stranger to her than Ashenden.

'Have you got something to say to me, Miss King?'

He tried to read an answer in her eyes. They continued to stare at him meaningly, but what the meaning was he had no notion.

'Don't be afraid I shall go. I will stay as long as you want me.'

Nothing, nothing. The black eyes, and as he looked at them they seemed to glow mysteriously as though there were fire behind them, the eyes continued to hold him with that insistent stare. Then Ashenden asked himself if she had sent for him because she knew that he was a British agent. Was it possible that at that last moment she had had some unexpected revulsion of feeling from everything that had signified to her for so many years? Perhaps at the moment of death a love for her country, a love that had been dead for half a century, awakened again in her–('I'm silly to fancy these idiotic things,' thought Ashenden, 'it's cheap and tawdry fiction')–and she had been seized with a desire to do something for what was after all her own. No one was quite himself just then and patriotism (in peace-time an attitude best left to politicians, publicists, and fools, but in the dark days of war an emotion that can wring the heart-strings), patriotism made one do odd things. It was curious that she had been unwilling to see the prince and his daughters. Did she on a sudden hate them? Did she feel herself a traitor on their account and now at the last hour wish to make amends? ('It's all very improbable, she's just a silly old maid who ought to have died years ago.') But you couldn't ignore the improbable. Ashenden, his common sense protesting, became strangely convinced that she had some secret that she wished to impart to him. She had sent for him knowing who he was because he could make use of it. She was dying and feared nothing. But was it really important? Ashenden leaned forward trying more eagerly to read what her eyes had to say. Perhaps it was only some trivial thing that was important only in her addled old brain. Ashenden was sick of the people who saw spies in every inoffensive passer-by and plots in the most innocent combination of circumstances. It was a hundred to one that if Miss King recovered her speech she would tell him something that could be of no use to anybody.

But how much must that old woman know! With her sharp eyes and sharp ears she must have had the chance to discover matters that were closely hidden from persons that seemed less insignificant. Ashenden thought again how he had the impression that something of real consequence was being prepared round about him. It was curious that Holzminden should have come to the hotel that day; and why had Prince Ali and the pasha, those wild gamblers, wasted an evening in playing contract-bridge with him? It might be that some new plan was in question, it might be that the very greatest affairs were afoot, and perhaps what the old woman had to say might make all the difference in the world. It might mean defeat or victory. It might mean anything. And there she lay powerless to speak. For a long time Ashenden stared at her in silence.

'Has it got anything to do with the war, Miss King?' he said on a sudden, loudly.

Something passed through her eyes and a tremor shot across her little old face. It was a distinct movement. Something strange and horrible was happening and Ashenden held his breath. The tiny frail body was suddenly convulsed and that old woman, as though by a final desperate effort of will, raised herself up in the bed. Ashenden sprang forward to support her.

'England,' she said, just that one word, in a harsh cracked voice, and fell back in his arms.

When he laid her down on the pillow, he saw that she was dead.

The
Hairless Mexican

◆

'Do you like macaroni?' said R.

'What do you mean by macaroni?' answered Ashenden. 'It is like asking me if I like poetry. I like Keats and Wordsworth and Verlaine and Goethe. When you say macaroni, do you mean *spaghetti, tagliatelli, vermicelli, fettuccini, tufali, farfalli,* or just macaroni?'

'Macaroni,' replied R., a man of few words.

'I like all simple things, boiled eggs, oysters and caviare, *truite au bleu,* grilled salmon, roast lamb (the saddle by preference), cold grouse, treacle tart, and rice pudding. But of all simple things the only one I can eat day in and day out, not only without disgust but with the eagerness of an appetite unimpaired by excess, is macaroni.'

'I am glad of that because I want you to go down to Italy.'

Ashenden had come from Geneva to meet R. at Lyons and having got there before him had spent the afternoon wandering about the dull, busy and prosaic streets of that thriving city. They were sitting now in a restaurant on the *place* to which Ashenden had taken R. on his arrival because it was reputed to give you the best food in that part of France. But since in so crowded a resort (for the Lyonese like a good dinner) you never knew what inquisitive ears were pricked up to catch any useful piece of information that might fall from your lips, they had contented themselves with talking of indifferent things. They had reached the end of an admirable repast.

'Have another glass of brandy?' said R.

'No, thank you,' answered Ashenden, who was of an abstemious turn.

'One should do what one can to mitigate the rigours of war,' remarked R. as he took the bottle and poured out a glass for himself and another for Ashenden.

Ashenden, thinking it would be affectation to protest, let the gesture pass, but felt bound to remonstrate with his chief on the unseemly manner in which he held the bottle.

'In my youth I was always taught that you should take a woman by the waist and a bottle by the neck,' he murmured.

'I am glad you told me. I shall continue to hold a bottle by the waist and give women a wide berth.'

Ashenden did not know what to reply to this and so remained silent. He sipped his brandy and R. called for his bill. It was true that he was an important person, with power to make or mar quite a large number of his fellows, and his opinions were listened to by those who held in their hands the fate of empires; but he could never face the business of tipping a waiter without an embarrassment that was obvious in his demeanour. He was tortured by the fear of making a fool of himself by giving too much or of exciting the waiter's icy scorn by giving too little. When the bill came he passed some hundred-franc notes over to Ashenden and said:

'Pay him, will you? I can never understand French figures.'

The groom brought them their hats and coats.

'Would you like to go back to the hotel?' asked Ashenden.

'We might as well.'

It was early in the year, but the weather had suddenly turned warm, and they walked with their coats over their arms. Ashenden knowing that R. liked a sitting-room had engaged one for him, and to this, when they reached the hotel, they went. The hotel was old-fashioned and the sitting-room was vast. It was furnished with a heavy mahogany suite upholstered in green velvet and the chairs were set primly round a large table. On the walls, covered with a dingy paper, were large steel engravings of the battles of Napoleon, and from the ceiling hung an enormous chandelier once used for gas, but now fitted with electric bulbs. It flooded the cheerless room with a cold, hard light.

'This is very nice,' said R., as they went in.

'Not exactly cosy,' suggested Ashenden.

'No, but it looks as though it were the best room in the place. It all looks very *good* to me.'

He drew one of the green velvet chairs away from the table and, sitting down, lit a cigar. He loosened his belt and unbuttoned his tunic.

'I always thought I liked a cheroot better than anything,' he said, 'but since the war I've taken quite a fancy to Havanas. Oh well, I suppose it can't last for ever.' The corners of his mouth flickered with the beginning of a smile. 'It's an ill wind that blows nobody any good.'

Ashenden took two chairs, one to sit on and one for his feet, and when R. saw him he said: 'That's not a bad idea,' and swinging another chair out from the table with a sigh of relief put his boots on it.

'What room is that next door?' he asked.

'That's your bedroom.'

'And on the other side?'

'A banqueting hall.'

R. got up and strolled slowly about the room and when he passed the windows, as though in idle curiosity, peeped through the heavy rep curtains that covered them, and then returning to his chair once more comfortably put his feet up.

'It's just as well not to take any more risk than one need,' he said.

He looked at Ashenden reflectively. There was a slight smile on his thin lips, but the pale eyes, too closely set together, remained cold and steely. R.'s stare would have been embarrassing if Ashenden had not been used to it. He knew that R. was considering how he would broach the subject that he had in mind. The silence must have lasted for two or three minutes.

'I'm expecting a fellow to come and see me tonight,' he said at last. 'His train gets in about ten.' He gave his wrist-watch a glance. 'He's known as the Hairless Mexican.'

'Why?'

'Because he's hairless and because he's a Mexican.'

'The explanation seems perfectly satisfactory,' said Ashenden.

'He'll tell you all about himself. He talks nineteen to the dozen. He was on his uppers when I came across him. It appears that he was mixed up in some revolution in Mexico and had to get out with nothing but the clothes he stood up in. They were rather the worse for wear when I found him. If you want to please him you call him General. He claims to have been a general in Huerta's army, at least I think it was Huerta; anyhow he says that if things had gone right he would be Minister of War now and no end of a big bug. I've found him very useful. Not a bad chap. The only thing I really have against him is that he will use scent.'

'And where do I come in?' asked Ashenden.

'He's going down to Italy. I've got rather a ticklish job for him to do and I want you to stand by. I'm not keen on trusting him with a lot of money. He's a gambler and he's a bit too fond of the girls. I suppose you came from Geneva on your Ashenden passport?'

'Yes.'

'I've got another for you, a diplomatic one, by the way, in the name of Somerville with visas for France and Italy. I think you and he had better travel together. He's an amusing cove when he gets going, and I think you ought to know one another.'

'What is the job?'

'I haven't yet quite made up my mind how much it's desirable for you to know about it.'

Ashenden did not reply. They eyed one another in a detached manner, as though they were strangers who sat together in a railway carriage and each wondered who and what the other was.

'In your place I'd leave the General to do most of the talking. I wouldn't tell him more about yourself than you find absolutely necessary. He won't ask you any questions, I can promise you that, I think he's by way of being a gentleman after his own fashion.'

'By the way, what is his real name?'

'I always call him Manuel. I don't know that he likes it very much, his name is Manuel Carmona.'

'I gather by what you have not said that he's an unmitigated scoundrel.'

R. smiled with his pale blue eyes.

'I don't know that I'd go quite as far as that. He hasn't had the advantages of a public-school education. His ideas of playing the game are not quite the same as yours or mine. I don't know that I'd leave a gold cigarette-case about when he was in the neighbourhood, but if he lost money to you at poker and had pinched your cigarette-case he would immediately pawn it to pay you. If he had half a chance he'd seduce your wife, but if you were up against it he'd share his last crust with you. The tears will run down his face when he hears Gounod's *Ave*

Maria on the gramophone, but if you insult his dignity he'll shoot you like a dog. It appears that in Mexico it's an insult to get between a man and his drink and he told me himself that once when a Dutchman who didn't know passed between him and the bar he whipped out his revolver and shot him dead.'

'Did nothing happen to him?'

'No, it appears that he belongs to one of the best families. The matter was hushed up and it was announced in the papers that the Dutchman had committed suicide. He did practically. I don't believe the Hairless Mexican has a great respect for human life.'

Ashenden, who had been looking intently at R., started a little and he watched more carefully than ever his chief's tired, lined, and yellow face. He knew that he did not make this remark for nothing.

'Of course a lot of nonsense is talked about the value of human life. You might just as well say that the counters you use at poker have an intrinsic value. Their value is what you like to make it; for a general giving battle, men are merely counters and he's a fool if he allows himself for sentimental reasons to look upon them as human beings.'

'But, you see, they're counters that feel and think and if they believe they're being squandered they are quite capable of refusing to be used any more.'

'Anyhow, that's neither here nor there. We've had information that a man called Constantine Andreadi is on his way from Constantinople with certain documents that we want to get hold of. He's a Greek. He's an agent of Enver Pasha and Enver has great confidence in him. He's given him verbal messages that are too secret and too important to be put on paper. He's sailing from the Piraeus, on a boat called the *Ithaca*, and will land at Brindisi on his way to Rome. He's to deliver his dispatches at the German Embassy and impart what he has to say personally to the ambassador.'

'I see.'

At this time Italy was still neutral; the Central Powers were straining every nerve to keep her so; the Allies were doing what they could to induce her to declare war on their side.

'We don't want to get into trouble with the Italian authorities, it might be fatal, but we've got to prevent Andreadi from getting to Rome.'

'At any cost?' asked Ashenden.

'Money's no object,' answered R., his lips twisting into a sardonic smile.

'What do you propose to do?'

'I don't think you need bother your head about that.'

'I have a fertile imagination,' said Ashenden.

'I want you to go down to Naples with the Hairless Mexican. He's very keen on getting back to Cuba. It appears that his friends are organizing a show and he wants to be as near at hand as possible so that he can hop over to Mexico when things are ripe. He needs cash. I've brought money down with me, in American dollars, and I shall give it to you tonight. You'd better carry it on your person.'

'Is it much?'

'It's a good deal, but I thought it would be easier for you if it wasn't bulky, so I've got it in thousand-dollar notes. You will give the Hairless Mexican the notes in return for the documents that Andreadi is bringing.'

A question sprang to Ashenden's lips, but he did not ask it. He asked another instead.

'Does this fellow understand what he has to do?'

'Perfectly.'

There was a knock at the door. It opened and the Hairless Mexican stood before them.

'I have arrived. Good evening, Colonel. I am enchanted to see you.'

R. got up.

'Had a nice journey, Manuel? This is Mr Somerville, who's going to Naples with you, General Carmona.'

'Pleased to meet you, sir.'

He shook Ashenden's hand with such force that he winced.

'Your hands are like iron, General,' he murmured.

The Mexican gave them a glance.

'I had them manicured this morning. I do not think they were very well done. I like my nails much more highly polished.'

They were cut to a point, stained bright red, and to Ashenden's mind shone like mirrors. Though it was not cold the General wore a fur coat with an astrakhan collar and with his every movement a wave of perfume was wafted to your nose.

'Take off your coat, General, and have a cigar,' said R.

The Hairless Mexican was a tall man, and though thinnish gave you the impression of being very powerful; he was smartly dressed in a blue serge suit, with a silk handkerchief neatly tucked in the breast pocket of his coat, and he wore a gold bracelet on his wrist. His features were good, but a little larger than life-size, and his eyes were brown and lustrous. He was quite hairless. His yellow skin had the smoothness of a woman's and he had no eyebrows nor eyelashes; he wore a pale brown wig, rather long, and the locks were arranged in artistic disorder. This and the unwrinkled sallow face, combined with his dandified dress, gave him an appearance that was at first glance a trifle horrifying. He was repulsive and ridiculous, but you could not take your eyes from him. There was a sinister fascination in his strangeness.

He sat down and hitched up his trousers so that they should not bag at the knee.

'Well, Manuel, have you been breaking any hearts today?' said R. with his sardonic joviality.

The General turned to Ashenden.

'Our good friend, the Colonel, envies me my successes with the fair sex. I tell him he can have just as many as I if he will only listen to me. Confidence, that is all you need. If you never fear a rebuff you will never have one.'

'Nonsense, Manuel, one has to have your way with the girls. There's something about you that they can't resist.'

The Hairless Mexican laughed with a self-satisfaction that he did not try to disguise. He spoke English very well, with a Spanish accent, but with an American intonation.

'But since you ask me, Colonel, I don't mind telling you that I got into conversation on the train with a little woman who was coming to Lyons to see her mother-in-law. She was not very young and she was thinner than I like a woman to be, but she was possible, and she helped me to pass an agreeable hour.'

'Well, let's get to business,' said R.

'I am at your service, Colonel.' He gave Ashenden a glance. 'Is Mr Somerville a military man?'

'No,' said R., 'he's an author.'

'It takes all sorts to make a world, as you say. I am happy to make your acquaintance, Mr Somerville. I can tell you many stories that will interest you; I am sure that we shall get on well together. You have a sympathetic air. I am very sensitive to that. To tell you the truth I am nothing but a bundle of nerves and if I am with a person who is antipathetic to me I go all to pieces.'

'I hope we shall have a pleasant journey,' said Ashenden.

'When does our friend arrive at Brindisi?' asked the Mexican, turning to R.

'He sails from the Piraeus in the *Ithaca* on the fourteenth. It's probably some old tub, but you'd better get down to Brindisi in good time.'

'I agree with you.'

R. got up and with his hands in his pockets sat on the edge of the table. In his rather shabby uniform, his tunic unbuttoned, he looked a slovenly creature beside the neat and well-dressed Mexican.

'Mr Somerville knows practically nothing of the errand on which you are going and I do not desire to tell him anything. I think you had much better keep your own counsel. He is instructed to give you the funds you need for your work, but your actions are your own affair. If you need his advice of course you can ask for it.'

'I seldom ask other people's advice and never take it.'

'And should you make a mess of things I trust you to keep Mr Somerville out of it. He must on no account be compromised.'

'I am a man of honour, Colonel,' answered the Hairless Mexican with dignity, 'and I would sooner let myself be cut in a thousand pieces than betray my friends.'

'That is what I have already told Mr Somerville. On the other hand, if everything pans out O.K. Mr Somerville is instructed to give you the sum we agreed on in return for the papers I spoke to you about. In what manner you get them is no business of his.'

'That goes without saying. There is only one thing I wish to make quite plain; Mr Somerville understands of course that I have not accepted the mission with which you have entrusted me on account of the money?'

'Quite,' replied R. gravely, looking him straight in the eyes.

'I am with the Allies body and soul, I cannot forgive the Germans for outraging the neutrality of Belgium, and if I accept the money that you have offered me it is because I am first and foremost a patriot. I can trust Mr Somerville implicitly, I suppose?'

R. nodded. The Mexican turned to Ashenden.

'An expedition is being arranged to free my unhappy country from the tyrants that exploit and ruin it and every penny that I receive will go on guns and cartridges. For myself I have no need of money; I am a soldier and I can live on a crust and a few olives. There are only three occupations that befit a gentleman, war, cards, and women; it costs nothing to sling a rifle over your shoulder and take to the mountains—and that is real warfare, not this manoeuvring of battalions and firing of great guns—women love me for myself, and I generally win at cards.'

Ashenden found the flamboyance of this strange creature, with his scented handkerchief and his gold bracelet, very much to his taste. This was far from being just the man in the street (whose tyranny we rail at but in the end submit to) and to the amateur of the baroque in human nature he was a rarity to be considered with delight. He was a purple patch on two legs. Notwithstanding his wig and his hairless big face, he had undoubtedly an air; he was absurd, but he did not give you the impression that he was a man to be trifled with. His self-complacency was magnificent.

'Where is your kit, Manuel?' asked R.

It was possible that a frown for an instant darkened the Mexican's brow at the abrupt question that seemed a little contemptuously to brush to one side his eloquent statement, but he gave no other sign of displeasure. Ashenden suspected that he thought the Colonel a barbarian insensitive to the finer emotions.

'I left it at the station.'

'Mr Somerville has a diplomatic passport so that he can get it through with his own things at the frontier without examination if you like.'

'I have very little, a few suits and some linen, but perhaps it would be as well if Mr Somerville would take charge of it. I bought half a dozen suits of silk pyjamas before I left Paris.'

'And what about you?' asked R., turning to Ashenden.

'I've only got one bag. It's in my room.'

'You'd better have it taken to the station while there's someone about. Your train goes at one ten.'

'Oh?'

This was the first Ashenden had heard that they were to start that night.

'I think you'd better get down to Naples as soon as possible.'

'Very well.'

R. got up.

'I'm going to bed. I don't know what you fellows want to do.'

'I shall take a walk about Lyons,' said the Hairless Mexican. 'I am interested in life. Lend me a hundred francs, Colonel, will you? I have no change on me.'

R. took out his pocket-book and gave the General the note he asked for. Then to Ashenden:

'What are you going to do? Wait here?'

'No,' said Ashenden, 'I shall go to the station and read.'

'You'd both of you better have a whisky and soda before you go, hadn't you? What about it, Manuel?'

'It is very kind of you, but I never drink anything but champagne and brandy.'

'Mixed?' asked R. dryly.

'Not necessarily,' returned the other with gravity.

R. ordered brandy and soda and when it came, whereas he and Ashenden helped themselves to both, the Hairless Mexican poured himself out three parts of a tumbler of neat brandy and swallowed it in two noisy gulps. He rose to his feet and put on his coat with the astrakhan collar, seized in one hand his bold black hat and, with the gesture of a romantic actor giving up the girl he loves to one more worthy of her, held out the other to R.

'Well, Colonel, I will bid you good night and pleasant dreams. I do not expect that we shall meet again so soon.'

'Don't make a hash of things, Manuel, and if you do, keep your mouth shut.'

'They tell me that in one of your colleges where the sons of gentlemen are trained to become naval officers it is written in letters of gold: There is no such word as impossible in the British Navy. I do not know the meaning of the word failure.'

'It has a good many synonyms,' retorted R.

'I will meet you at the station, Mr Somerville,' said the Hairless Mexican, and with a flourish left them.

R. looked at Ashenden with that little smile of his that always made his face look so dangerously shrewd.

'Well, what d'you think of him?'

'You've got me beat,' said Ashenden. 'Is he a mountebank? He seems as vain as a peacock. And with that frightful appearance can he really be the lady's man he pretends? What makes you think you can trust him?'

R. gave a low chuckle and he washed his thin, old hands with imaginary soap. 'I thought you'd like him. He's quite a character, isn't he? I think we can trust him.' R.'s eyes suddenly grew opaque. 'I don't believe it would pay him to double-cross us.' He paused for a moment. 'Anyhow we've got to risk it. I'll give you the tickets and the money and then you can take yourself off; I'm all in and I want to go to bed.'

Ten minutes later Ashenden set out for the station with his bag on a porter's shoulder.

Having nearly two hours to wait he made himself comfortable in the waiting-room. The light was good and he read a novel. When the time drew near for the arrival of the train from Paris that was to take them direct to Rome, and the Hairless Mexican did not appear, Ashenden, beginning to grow a trifle anxious, went out on the platform to look for him. Ashenden suffered from that distressing malady known as train fever: an hour before his train was due he began to have apprehensions lest he should miss it; he was impatient with the porters who would never bring his luggage down from his room in time and he could not understand why the hotel bus cut it so fine; a block in the street would drive him to frenzy and the languid movements of the station porters infuriate him. The whole world seemed in a horrid plot to delay him; people got in his way as he passed through the barriers; others, a long string of them, were at the ticket-office getting tickets for other trains than his and they counted their change with exasperating care; his luggage took an interminable time to register; and then if he was travelling with friends they would go to buy newspapers, or would take a walk along the platform, and he was certain they would be left behind, they would stop to talk to a casual stranger or suddenly be seized with a desire to telephone and disappear at a run. In fact the universe conspired to make him miss every train he wanted to take and he was not happy unless he was settled in his corner, his things on the rack above him, with a good half-hour to spare. Sometimes by arriving at the station too soon he had caught an earlier train than the one he had meant to, but that was nerve-racking and caused him all the anguish of very nearly missing it.

The Rome express was signalled and there was no sign of the Hairless Mexican; it came in and he was not to be seen. Ashenden became more and more harassed. He walked quickly up and down the platform, looked in all the waiting-rooms, went to the *consigne* where the luggage was left; he could not find him. There were no sleeping-cars, but a number of people got out and he took two seats in a first-class carriage. He stood by the door, looking up and down the platform and up at the clock; it was useless to go if his travelling companion did not turn up, and Ashenden made up his mind to take his things out of the carriage as the porter cried *en voiture*; but, by George! he would give the brute hell when he found him. There were three minutes more, then two minutes, then one; at that late hour there were few persons about and all who were travelling had taken their seats. Then he saw the Hairless Mexican,

followed by two porters with his luggage and accompanied by a man in a
bowler-hat, walk leisurely on to the platform. He caught sight of Ashenden and
waved to him.

'Ah, my dear fellow, there you are, I wondered what had become of you.'

'Good God, man, hurry up or we shall miss the train.'

'I never miss a train. Have you got good seats? The *chef de gare* has gone for
the night; this is his assistant.'

The man in the bowler-hat took it off when Ashenden nodded to him.

'But this is an ordinary carriage. I am afraid I could not travel in that.' He
turned to the stationmaster's assistant with an affable smile. 'You must do
better for me than that, *mon cher*.'

'*Certainement, mon général*, I will put you into a *salon-lit*. Of course.'

The assistant stationmaster led them along the train and opened the door of
an empty compartment where there were two beds. The Mexican eyed it with
satisfaction and watched the porters arrange the luggage.

'That will do very well. I am much obliged to you.' He held out his hand to
the man in the bowler-hat. 'I shall not forget you and next time I see the
Minister I will tell him with what civility you have treated me.'

'You are too good, General. I shall be very grateful.'

A whistle was blown and the train started.

'This is better than an ordinary first-class carriage, I think, Mr Somerville,'
said the Mexican. 'A good traveller should learn how to make the best of things.'

But Ashenden was still extremely cross.

'I don't know why the devil you wanted to cut it so fine. We should have
looked a pair of damned fools if we'd missed the train.'

'My dear fellow, there was never the smallest chance of that. When I arrived
I told the stationmaster that I was General Carmona, Commander-in-Chief of
the Mexican Army, and that I had to stop off in Lyons for a few hours to hold a
conference with the British Field-Marshal. I asked him to hold the train for me
if I was delayed and suggested that my government might see its way to
conferring an order on him. I have been to Lyons before, I like the girls here;
they have not the *chic* of the Parisians, but they have something, there is no
denying that they have something. Will you have a mouthful of brandy before
you go to sleep?'

'No, thank you,' said Ashenden morosely.

'I always drink a glass before going to bed, it settles the nerves.'

He looked in his suit-case and without difficulty found a bottle. He put it to
his lips and had a long drink, wiped his mouth with the back of his hand and lit a
cigarette. Then he took off his boots and lay down. Ashenden dimmed the
light.

'I have never yet made up my mind,' said the Hairless Mexican reflectively,
'whether it is pleasanter to go to sleep with the kisses of a beautiful woman on
your mouth or with a cigarette between your lips. Have you ever been to
Mexico? I will tell you about Mexico tomorrow. Good night.'

Soon Ashenden heard from his steady breathing that he was asleep and in a
little while himself dozed off. Presently he woke. The Mexican, deep in
slumber, lay motionless; he had taken off his fur coat and was using it as a
blanket; he still wore his wig. Suddenly there was a jolt and the train with a
noisy grinding of brakes stopped; in the twinkling of an eye, before Ashenden
could realize that anything had happened, the Mexican was on his feet with his
hand to his hip.

'What is it?' he cried.

'Nothing. Probably only a signal against us.'

The Mexican sat down heavily on his bed. Ashenden turned on the light.

'You wake quickly for such a sound sleeper,' he said.

'You have to in my profession.'

Ashenden would have liked to ask him whether this was murder, conspiracy, or commanding armies, but was not sure that it would be discreet. The General opened his bag and took out the bottle.

'Will you have a nip?' he asked. 'There is nothing like it when you wake suddenly in the night.'

When Ashenden refused he put the bottle once more to his lips and poured a considerable quantity of liquor down his throat. He sighed and lit a cigarette. Although Ashenden had seen him now drink nearly a bottle of brandy, and it was probable that he had had a good deal more when he was going about the town, he was certainly quite sober. Neither in his manner nor in his speech was there any indication that he had drunk during the evening anything but lemonade.

The train started and Ashenden again fell asleep. When he awoke it was morning and turing round lazily he saw that the Mexican was awake too. He was smoking a cigarette. The floor by his side was strewn with burnt-out butts and the air was thick and grey. He had begged Ashenden not to insist on opening a window, for he said the night air was dangerous.

'I did not get up, because I was afraid of waking you. Will you do your toilet first or shall I?'

'I'm in no hurry,' said Ashenden.

'I am an old campaigner, it will not take me long. Do you wash your teeth every day?'

'Yes,' said Ashenden.

'So do I. It is a habit I learned in New York. I always think that a fine set of teeth are an adornment to a man.'

There was a wash-basin in the compartment and the General scrubbed his teeth, with gurglings and garglings, energetically. Then he got a bottle of eau-de-Cologne from his bag, poured some of it on a towel and rubbed it over his face and hands. He took a comb and carefully arranged his wig; either it had not moved in the night or else he had set it straight before Ashenden awoke. He got another bottle out of his bag, with a spray attached to it, and squeezing a bulb covered his shirt and coat with a fine cloud of scent, did the same to his handkerchief, and then with a beaming face, like a man who has done his duty by the world and is well pleased, turned to Ashenden and said:

'Now I am ready to brave the day. I will leave my things for you, you need not be afraid of the eau-de-Cologne, it is the best you can get in Paris.'

'Thank you very much,' said Ashenden. 'All I want is soap and water.'

'Water? I never use water except when I have a bath. Nothing can be worse for the skin.'

When they approached the frontier, Ashenden, remembering the General's instinctive gesture when he was suddenly awakened in the night, said to him:

'If you've got a revolver on you I think you'd better give it to me. With my diplomatic passport they're not likely to search me, but they might take it into their heads to go through you and we don't want to have any bothers.'

'It is hardly a weapon, it is only a toy,' returned the Mexican, taking out of his hip-pocket a fully loaded revolver of formidable dimensions. 'I do not like parting with it even for an hour, it gives me the feeling that I am not fully dressed. But you are quite right, we do not want to take any risks; I will give you my knife as well. I would always rather use a knife than a revolver; I think it is a more elegant weapon.'

'I dare say it is only a matter of habit,' answered Ashenden. 'Perhaps you are more at home with a knife.'

'Anyone can pull a trigger, but it needs a man to use a knife.'

To Ashenden it looked as though it were in a single movement that he tore open his waistcoat and from his belt snatched and opened a long knife of murderous aspect. He handed it to Ashenden with a pleased smile on his large, ugly, and naked face.

'There's a pretty piece of work for you, Mr Somerville. I've never seen a better bit of steel in my life, it takes an edge like a razor and it's strong; you can cut a cigarette-paper with it and you can hew down an oak. There is nothing to get out of order and when it is closed it might be the knife a schoolboy uses to cut notches in his desk.'

He shut it with a click and Ashenden put it along with the revolver in his pocket.

'Have you anything else?'

'My hands,' replied the Mexican with arrogance, 'but those I dare say the Custom officials will not make trouble about.'

Ashenden remembered the iron grip he had given him when they shook hands and slightly shuddered. They were large and long and smooth; there was not a hair on them or on the wrists, and with the pointed, rosy, manicured nails there was really something sinister about them.

Ashenden and General Carmona went through the formalities at the frontier independently and when they returned to their carriage Ashenden handed back to his companion the revolver and the knife. He sighed.

'Now I feel more comfortable. What do you say to a game of cards?'

'I should like it,' said Ashenden.

The Hairless Mexican opened his bag again and from a corner extracted a greasy pack of French cards. He asked Ashenden whether he played *écarté* and when Ashenden told him that he did not suggested piquet. This was a game that Ashenden was not unfamiliar with, so they settled the stakes and began. Since both were in favour of quick action, they played the game of four hands, doubling the first and last. Ashenden had good enough cards, but the General seemed notwithstanding always to have better. Ashenden kept his eyes open and he was not careless of the possibility that his antagonist might correct the inequalities of chance, but he saw nothing to suggest that everything was not above board. He lost game after game. He was capoted and rubiconed. The score against him mounted up and up till he had lost something like a thousand francs, which at that time was a tidy sum. The General smoked innumerable cigarettes. He made them himself with a twist of the finger, a lick of his tongue and incredible celerity. At last he flung himself against the back of his seat.

'By the way, my friend, does the British Government pay your card losses when you are on a mission?' he asked.

'It certainly doesn't.'

'Well, I think you have lost enough. If it went down on your expense account I would have proposed playing till we reached Rome, but you are sympathetic to me. If it is your own money I do not want to win any more of it.'

He picked up the cards and put them aside. Ashenden somewhat ruefully took out a number of notes and handed them to the Mexican. He counted them and with his usual neatness put them carefully folded into his pocket-book. Then, leaning forward, he patted Ashenden almost affectionately on the knee.

'I like you, you are modest and unassuming, you have not the arrogance of your countrymen, and I am sure that you will take my advice in the spirit in which it is meant. Do not play piquet with people you don't know.'

Ashenden was somewhat mortified and perhaps his face showed it, for the Mexican seized his hand.

'My dear fellow, I have not hurt your feelings? I would not do that for the world. You do not play piquet worse than most piquet players. It is not that. If we were going to be together longer I would teach you how to win at cards. One plays cards to win money and there is no sense in losing.'

'I thought it was only in love and war that all things were fair,' said Ashenden, with a chuckle.

'Ah, I am glad to see you smile. That is the way to take a loss. I see that you have good humour and good sense. You will go far in life. When I get back to Mexico and am in possession of my estates again you must come and stay with me. I will treat you like a king. You shall ride my best horses, we will go to bullfights together, and if there are girls you fancy you have only to say the word and you shall have them.'

He began telling Ashenden of the vast territories, the *haciendas* and the mines in Mexico, of which he had been dispossessed. He told him of the feudal state in which he lived. It did not matter whether what he said was true or not, for those sonorous phrases of his were fruity with the rich-distilled perfumes of romance. He described a spacious life that seemed to belong to another age and his eloquent gestures brought before the mind's eye tawny distances and vast green plantations, great herds of cattle and in the moonlit night the song of the blind singers that melted in the air and the twanging of guitars.

'Everything I lost, everything. In Paris I was driven to earn a pittance by giving Spanish lessons or showing Americans—*Americanos del Norte*, I mean—the night life of the city. I who have flung away a thousand *duros* on a dinner have been forced to beg my bread like a blind Indian. I who have taken pleasure in clasping a diamond bracelet round the wrist of a beautiful woman have been forced to accept a suit of clothes from a hag old enough to be my mother. Patience. Man is born to trouble as the sparks fly upward, but misfortune cannot last for ever. The time is ripe and soon we shall strike our blow.'

He took up the greasy pack of cards and set them out in a number of little piles.

'Let us see what the cards say. They never lie. Ah, if I had only had greater faith in them I should have avoided the only action of my life that has weighed heavily on me. My conscience is at ease. I did what any man would do under the circumstances, but I regret that necessity forced upon me an action that I would willingly have avoided.'

He looked through the cards, set some of them on one side on a system Ashenden did not understand, shuffled the remainder and once more put them in little piles.

'The cards warned me, I will never deny that, their warning was clear and definite. Love and a dark woman, danger, betrayal and death. It was as plain as the nose on your face. Any fool would have known what it meant and I have been using the cards all my life. There is hardly an action that I make without consulting them. There are no excuses. I was besotted. Ah, you of the Northern races do not know what love means, you do not know how it can prevent you from sleeping, how it can take your appetite for food away so that you dwindle as if from a fever, you do not understand what a frenzy it is so that you are like a mad-man and you will stick at nothing to satisfy your desire. A man like me is capable of every folly and every crime when he is in love, *si*, *Señor*, and of heroism. He can scale mountains higher than Everest and swim seas broader than the Atlantic. He is god, he is devil. Women have been my ruin.'

Once more the Hairless Mexican glanced at the cards, took some out of the little piles and left others in. He shuffled them again.

'I have been loved by multitudes of women. I do not say it in vanity. I offer no explanation. It is mere matter of fact. Go to Mexico City and ask them what they know of Manuel Carmona and of his triumphs. Ask them how many women have resisted Manuel Carmona.'

Ashenden, frowning a little, watched him reflectively. He wondered whether R., that shrewd fellow who chose his instruments with such a sure instinct, had not this time made a mistake, and he was uneasy. Did the Hairless Mexican really believe that he was irresistible or was he merely a blatant liar? In the course of his manipulations he had thrown out all the cards in the pack but four, and these now lay in front of him face downwards and side by side. He touched them one by one but did not turn them up.

'There is fate,' he said, 'and no power on earth can change it. I hesitate. This is a moment that ever fills me with apprehension and I have to steel myself to turn over the cards that may tell me that disaster awaits me. I am a brave man, but sometimes I have reached this stage and not had the courage to look at the four vital cards.'

Indeed now he eyed the backs of them with an anxiety he did not try to hide.

'What was I saying to you?'

'You were telling me that women found your fascinations irresistible,' replied Ashenden dryly.

'Once all the same I found a woman who resisted me. I saw her first in a house, a *casa de mujeres* in Mexico City, she was going down the stairs as I went up; she was not very beautiful, I had had a hundred more beautiful, but she had something that took my fancy and I told the old woman who kept the house to send her to me. You will know her when you go to Mexico City; they call her La Marqueza. She said that the girl was not an inmate, but came there only from time to time and had left. I told her to have her there next evening and not to let her go till I came. But I was delayed and when I arrived La Marqueza told me that the girl had said she was not used to being kept waiting and had gone. I am a good-natured fellow and I do not mind if women are capricious and teasing, that is part of their charm, so with a laugh I sent her a note of a hundred *duros* and promised that on the following day I would be punctual. But when I went, on the minute, La Marqueza handed me back my hundred *duros* and told me the girl did not fancy me. I laughed at her impertinence. I took off the diamond ring I was wearing and told the old woman to give her that and see whether it would induce her to change her mind. In the morning La Marqueza brought me in return for my ring—a red carnation. I did not know whether to be amused or angry. I am not used to being thwarted in my passions, I never hesitate to spend money (what is it for but to squander on pretty women?), and I told La Marqueza to go to the girl and say that I would give her a thousand *duros* to dine with me that night. Presently she came back with the answer that the girl would come on the condition that I allowed her to go home immediately after dinner. I accepted with a shrug of the shoulders. I did not think she was serious. I thought that she was saying that only to make herself more desired. She came to dinner at my house. Did I say she was not beautiful? She was the most beautiful, the most exquisite creature I had ever met. I was intoxicated. She had charm and she had wit. She had all the *gracia* of the Andalusian. In one word she was adorable. I asked her why she had treated me so casually and she laughed in my face. I laid myself out to be agreeable. I exercised all my skill. I surpassed myself. But when we finished dinner she rose from her seat and bade me good night. I asked her where she was going. She said I had promised to let her go and she trusted me as a man of honour to keep my word. I expostulated, I reasoned, I raved, I stormed. She held me to my word. All I could induce her to do was to consent to dine with me the following night on the same terms.

'You will think I was a fool, I was the happiest man alive; for seven days I paid her a thousand silver *duros* to dine with me. Every evening I waited for her with my heart in my mouth, as nervous as a *novillero* at his first bull-fight, and every evening she played with me, laughed at me, coquetted with me and drove me frantic. I was madly in love with her. I have never loved anyone so much before or since. I could think of nothing else. I was distracted. I neglected everything. I am a patriot and I love my country. A small band of us had got together and made up our minds that we could no longer put up with the misrule from which we were suffering. All the lucrative posts were given to other people, we were being made to pay taxes as though we were tradesmen, and we were exposed to abominable affronts. We had money and men. Our plans were made and we were ready to strike. I had an infinity of things to do, meetings to go to, ammunition to get, orders to give, I was so besotted over this woman that I could attend to nothing.

'You would have thought that I should be angry with her for making such a fool of me, me who had never known what it was not to gratify my smallest whim; I did not believe that she refused me to inflame my desires, I believed that she told the plain truth when she said that she would not give herself to me until she loved me. She said it was for me to make her love me. I thought her an angel. I was ready to wait. My passion was so consuming that sooner or later, I felt, it must communicate itself to her; it was like a fire on the prairie that devours everything around it; and at last—at last she said she loved me. My emotion was so terrific that I thought I should fall down and die. Oh, what rapture! Oh, what madness! I would have given her everything I possessed in the world, I would have torn down the stars from heaven to deck her hair; I wanted to do something to prove to her the extravagance of my love, I wanted to do the impossible, the incredible, I wanted to give her myself, my soul, my honour, all, all I had and all I was; and that night when she lay in my arms I told her of our plot and who we were that were concerned in it. I felt her body stiffen with attention, I was conscious of a flicker of her eyelids, there was something, I hardly knew what, the hand that stroked my face was dry and cold; a sudden suspicion seized me and all at once I remembered what the cards had told me: love and a dark woman, danger, betrayal, and death. Three times they'd said it and I wouldn't heed. I made no sign that I had noticed anything. She nestled up against my heart and told me that she was frightened to hear such things and asked me if So-and-so was concerned. I answered her. I wanted to make sure. One after the other, with infinite cunning, between her kisses she cajoled me into giving every detail of the plot, and now I was certain, as certain as I am that you sit before me, that she was a spy. She was a spy of the President's and she had been set to allure me with her devilish charm and now she had wormed out of me all our secrets. The lives of all of us were in her hands and I knew that if she left that room in twenty-four hours we should be dead men. And I loved her, I loved her; oh, words cannot tell you the agony of desire that burned my heart; love like that is no pleasure; it is pain, pain, but the exquisite pain that transcends all pleasure. It is that heavenly anguish that the saints speak of when they are seized with a divine ecstasy. I knew that she must not leave the room alive and I feared that if I delayed my courage would fail me.

'"I think I shall sleep," she said.

'"Sleep, my dove," I answered.

'"*Alma de mi corazon*," she called me. "Soul of my heart." They were the last words she spoke. Those heavy lids of hers, dark like a grape and faintly humid, those heavy lids of hers closed over her eyes and in a little while I knew by the regular movement of her breast against mine that she slept. You see, I loved her, I could not bear that she should suffer; she was a spy, yes, but my heart bade me spare her the terror of knowing what must happen. It is strange, I felt no anger because she had betrayed me, I should have hated her because of her vileness; I could not, I only felt that my soul was enveloped in night. Poor thing, poor thing. I could have cried in pity for her. I drew my arm very gently from around her, my left arm that was, my right was free, and raised myself on my hand. But she was so beautiful, I turned my face away when I drew the knife with all my strength across her lovely throat. Without awaking she passed from sleep to death.'

He stopped and stared frowning at the four cards that still lay, their backs upward, waiting to be turned up.

'It was in the cards. Why did I not take their warning? I will not look at them. Damn them. Take them away.'

With a violent gesture he swept the whole pack on to the floor.

'Though I am a free-thinker I had masses said for her soul.' He leaned back and rolled himself a cigarette. He inhaled a long breathful of smoke. He shrugged his shoulders. 'The Colonel said you were a writer. What do you write?'

'Stories,' replied Ashenden.

'Detective stories?'

'No.'

'Why not? They are the only ones I read. If I were a writer I should write detective stories.'

'They are very difficult. You need an incredible amount of invention. I devised a murder story once, but the murder was so ingenious that I could never find a way of bringing it home to the murderer, and, after all, one of the conventions of the detective story is that the mystery should in the end be solved and the criminal brought to justice.'

'If your murder is as ingenious as you think the only means you have of proving the murderer's guilt is by the discovery of his motives. When once you have found a motive the chances are that you will hit upon evidence that till then had escaped you. If there is no motive the most damning evidence will be inconclusive. Imagine for instance that you went up to a man in a lonely street on a moonless night and stabbed him to the heart. Who would ever think of you? But if he was your wife's lover, or your brother, or had cheated or insulted you, then a scrap of paper, a bit of string or a chance remark would be enough to hang you. What were your movements at the time he was killed? Are there not a dozen people who saw you before and after? But if he was a total stranger you would never for a moment be suspected. It was inevitable that Jack the Ripper should escape unless he was caught in the act.'

Ashenden had more than one reason to change the conversation. They were parting at Rome and he thought it necessary to come to an understanding with his companion about their respective movements. The Mexican was going to Brindisi and Ashenden to Naples. He meant to lodge at the Hotel de Belfast, which was a large second-rate hotel near the harbour frequented by commercial travellers and the thriftier kind of tripper. It would be as well to let the General have the number of his room so that he could come up if necessary without inquiring of the porter, and at the next stopping-place Ashenden got an envelope from the station-buffet and made him address it in his own writing to himself at the post-office in Brindisi. All Ashenden had to do then was to scribble a number on a sheet of paper and post it.

The Hairless Mexican shrugged his shoulders.

'To my mind all these precautions are rather childish. There is absolutely no risk. But whatever happens you may be quite sure that I will not compromise you.'

'This is not the sort of job which I'm very familiar with,' said Ashenden. 'I'm content to follow the Colonel's instructions and know no more about it than it's essential I should.'

'Quite so. Should the exigencies of the situation force me to take a drastic step and I get into trouble I shall of course be treated as a political prisoner. Sooner or later Italy is bound to come into the war on the side of the Allies and I shall be released. I have considered everything. But I beg you very seriously to have no more anxiety about the outcome of our mission than if you were going for a picnic on the Thames.'

But when at last they separated and Ashenden found himself alone in a carriage on the way to Naples he heaved a great sigh of relief. He was glad to be rid of that chattering, hideous, and fantastic creature. He was gone to meet Constantine Andreadi at Brindisi and if half of what he had told Ashenden was true, Ashenden could not but congratulate himself that he did not stand in the Greek spy's shoes. He wondered what sort of man he was. There was a grimness in the notion of his coming across the blue Ionian, with his confidential papers and his dangerous secrets, all unconscious of the noose into which he was putting his head. Well, that was war, and only fools thought it could be waged with kid gloves on.

Ashenden arrived in Naples and, having taken a room at the hotel, wrote its number on a sheet of paper in block letters and posted it to the Hairless Mexican. He went to the British Consulate, where R. had arranged to send any instructions he might have for him, and found that they knew about him and everything was in order. Then he put aside these matters and made up his mind to amuse himself. Here in the South the spring was well advanced and in the busy streets the sun was hot. Ashenden knew Naples pretty well. The Piazza di San Ferdinando, with its bustle, the Piazza del Plebiscito, with its handsome church, stirred in his heart pleasant recollections. The Strada di Chiara was as noisy as ever. He stood at corners and looked up the narrow alleys that climbed the hill precipitously, those alleys of high houses with the washing set out to dry on lines across the streets like pennants flying to mark a feast-day: and he sauntered along the shore, looking at the burnished sea with Capri faintly outlined against the bay, till he came to Posilippo, where there was an old, rambling, and bedraggled *palazzo* in which in his youth he had spent many a romantic hour. He observed the curious little pain with which the memories of the past wrung his heart-strings. Then he took a fly drawn by a small and scraggy pony and rattled back over the stones to the Galleria, where he sat in the cool and drank an *americano* and looked at the people who loitered there, talking, for ever talking with vivacious gestures, and, exercising his fancy sought from their appearance to divine their reality.

For three days Ashenden led the idle life that fitted so well the fantastical, untidy, and genial city. He did nothing from morning till night but wander at random, looking, not with the eye of the tourist who seeks for what ought to be seen, nor with the eye of the writer who looks for his own (seeing in a sunset a melodious phrase or in a face the inkling of a character), but with that of the tramp to whom whatever happens is absolute. He went to the museum to look at the statue of Agrippina the Younger, which he had particular reasons for remembering with affection, and took the opportunity to see once more the Titian and the Brueghel in the picture gallery. But he always came back to the church of Santa Chiara. Its grace, its gaiety, the airy persiflage with which it seemed to treat religion and at the back of this its sensual emotion; its extravagance, its elegance of line; to Ashenden it seemed to express, as it were in one absurd and grandiloquent metaphor, the sunny, dusty, lovely city and its bustling inhabitants. It said that life was charming and sad; it's a pity one hadn't any money but money wasn't everything, and anyway why bother when we are here today and gone tomorrow, and it was all very exciting and amusing, and after all we must make the best of things: *facciamo una piccola combinazione.*

But on the fourth morning, when Ashenden, having just stepped out of his bath, was trying to dry himself on a towel that absorbed no moisture, his door was quickly opened and a man slipped into his room.

'What d'you want?' cried Ashenden.

'It's all right. Don't you know me?'

'Good Lord, it's the Mexican. What have you done to yourself?'

He had changed his wig and wore now a black one, close-cropped, that fitted on his head like a cap. It entirely altered the look of him and though this was still odd enough, it was quite different from that which he had borne before. He wore a shabby grey suit.

'I can only stop a minute. He's getting shaved.'

Ashenden felt his cheeks suddenly redden.

'You found him then?'

'That wasn't difficult. He was the only Greek passenger on the ship. I went on board when she got in and asked for a friend who had sailed from the Piraeus. I said I had come to meet a Mr George Diogenidis. I pretended to be much puzzled at his not coming, and I got into conversation with Andreadi. He's travelling under a false name. He calls himself Lombardos. I followed him when he landed and do you know the first thing he did? He went into a barber's and had his beard shaved. What do you think of that?'

'Nothing. Anyone might have his beard shaved.'

'That is not what I think. He wanted to change his appearance. Oh, he's cunning. I admire the Germans, they leave nothing to chance, he's got his whole story pat, but I'll tell you that in a minute.'

'By the way, you've changed your appearance too.'

'Ah, yes, this is a wig I'm wearing; it makes a difference, doesn't it?'

'I should never have known you.'

'One has to take precautions. We are bosom friends. We had to spend the day in Brindisi and he cannot speak Italian. He was glad to have me help him and we travelled up together. I have brought him to this hotel. He says he is going to Rome tomorrow, but I shall not let him out of my sight; I do not want him to give me the slip. He says that he wants to see Naples and I have offered to show him everything there is to see.'

'Why isn't he going to Rome today?'

'That is part of the story. He pretends he is a Greek business man who has made money during the war. He says he was the owner of two coasting steamers and has just sold them. Now he means to go to Paris and have his fling. He says he has wanted to go to Paris all his life and at last has the chance. He is close. I tried to get him to talk. I told him I was a Spaniard and had been to Brindisi to arrange communications with Turkey about war material. He listened to me and I saw he was interested, but he told me nothing and of course I did not think it wise to press him. He has the papers on his person.'

'How do you know?'

'He is not anxious about his grip, but he feels every now and then round his middle. They're either in a belt or in the lining of his vest.'

'Why the devil did you bring him to this hotel?'

'I thought it would be more convenient. We may want to search his luggage.'

'Are you staying here too?'

'No, I am not such a fool as that. I told him I was going to Rome by the night train and would not take a room. But I must go, I promised to meet him outside the barber's in fifteen minutes.'

'All right.'

'Where shall I find you tonight if I want you?'

Ashenden for an instant eyed the Hairless Mexican, then with a slight frown looked away.

'I shall spend the evening in my room.'

'Very well. Will you just see that there's nobody in the passage?'

Ashenden opened the door and looked out. He saw no one. The hotel in point of fact at that season was nearly empty. There were few foreigners in Naples and trade was bad.

'It's all right,' said Ashenden.

The Hairless Mexican walked boldly out. Ashenden closed the door behind him. He shaved and slowly dressed. The sun was shining as brightly as usual on the square and the people who passed, the shabby little carriages with their scrawny horses, had the same air as before, but they did not any longer fill Ashenden with gaiety. He was not comfortable. He went out and called as was his habit at the Consulate to ask if there was a telegram for him. Nothing. Then he went to Cook's and looked out the trains to Rome: there was one soon after midnight and another at five in the morning. He wished he could catch the first. He did not know what were the Mexican's plans; if he really wanted to get to Cuba he would do well to make his way to Spain, and, glancing at the notices in the office, Ashenden saw that next day there was a ship sailing from Naples to Barcelona.

Ashenden was bored with Naples. The glare in the streets tired his eyes, the dust was intolerable, the noise was deafening. He went to the Galleria and had a drink. In the afternoon he went to a cinema. Then, going back to his hotel, he told the clerk that since he was starting so early in the morning he preferred to pay his bill at once, and he took his luggage to the station, leaving in his room only a dispatch-case in which were the printed part of his code and a book or two. He dined. Then returning to the hotel he sat down to wait for the Hairless Mexican. He could not conceal from himself the fact that he was exceedingly nervous. He began to read, but the book was tiresome, and he tried another; his attention wandered and he glanced at his watch. It was desperately early; he took up his book again, making up his mind that he would not look at his watch till he had read thirty pages, but though he ran his eyes conscientiously down one page after another he could not tell more than vaguely what it was he read. He looked at the time again. Good God, it was only half past ten. He wondered where the Hairless Mexican was, and what he was doing; he was afraid he would make a mess of things. It was a horrible business. Then it struck him that he had better shut the window and draw the curtains. He smoked innumerable cigarettes. He looked at his watch and it was a quarter past eleven. A thought struck him and his heart began to beat against his chest; out of curiosity he counted his pulse and was surprised to find that it was normal. Though it was a warm night and the room was stuffy his hands and feet were icy. What a nuisance it was, he reflected irritably, to have an imagination that conjured up pictures of things that you didn't in the least want to see! From his standpoint as a writer he had often considered murder, and his mind went to that fearful description of one in *Crime and Punishment*. He did not want to think of this topic, but it forced itself upon him; his book dropped to his knees and staring at the wall in front of him (it had a brown wall-paper with a pattern of dingy roses) he asked himself how, if one had to, one would commit a murder in Naples. Of course there was the Villa, the great leafy garden facing the bay in which stood the aquarium; that was deserted at night and very dark; things happened there that did not bear the light of day and prudent persons after dusk avoided its sinister paths. Beyond Posilippo the road was very solitary and there were byways that led up the hill in which by night you would never meet a soul, but how would you induce a man who had any nerves to go there? You might suggest a row in the bay, but the boatman who hired the boat would see you; it was doubtful indeed if he would let you go on the water alone; there were disreputable hotels down by the harbour where no questions were asked of persons who arrived late at night without luggage; but here again the waiter who showed you your room had the chance of a good look at you and you had on entering to sign an elaborate questionnaire.

Ashenden looked once more at the time. He was very tired. He sat now not even trying to read, his mind a blank.

Then the door opened softly and he sprang to his feet. His flesh crept. The Hairless Mexican stood before him.

'Did I startle you?' he asked smiling. 'I thought you would prefer me not to knock.'

'Did anyone see you come in?'

'I was let in by the night-watchman; he was asleep when I rang and didn't even look at me. I'm sorry I'm so late, but I had to change.'

The Hairless Mexican wore now the clothes he had travelled down in and his fair wig. It was extraordinary how different he looked. He was bigger and more flamboyant; the very shape of his face was altered. His eyes were shining and he seemed in excellent spirits. He gave Ashenden a glance.

'How white you are, my friend! Surely you're not nervous?'

'Have you got the documents?'

'No. He hadn't got them on him. This is all he had.'

He put down on the table a bulky pocket-book and a passport.

'I don't want them,' said Ashenden quickly. 'Take them.'

With a shrug of the shoulders the Hairless Mexican put the things back in his pocket.

'What was in his belt? You said he kept feeling round his middle.'

'Only money. I've looked through the pocket-book. It contains nothing but private letters and photographs of women. He must have locked the documents in his grip before coming out with me this evening.'

'Damn,' said Ashenden.

'I've got the key of his room. We'd better go and look through his luggage.'

Ashenden felt a sensation of sickness in the pit of his stomach. He hesitated. The Mexican smiled not unkindly.

'There's no risk, *amigo*,' he said, as though he were reassuring a small boy, 'but if you don't feel happy, I'll go alone.'

'No, I'll come with you,' said Ashenden.

'There's no one awake in the hotel and Mr Andreadi won't disturb us. Take off your shoes if you like.'

Ashenden did not answer. He frowned because he noticed that his hands were slightly trembling. He unlaced his shoes and slipped them off. The Mexican did the same.

'You'd better go first,' he said. 'Turn to the left and go straight along the corridor. It's number thirty-eight.'

Ashenden opened the door and stepped out. The passage was dimly lit. It exasperated him to feel so nervous when he could not but be aware that his companion was perfectly at ease. When they reached the door the Hairless Mexican inserted the key, turned the lock, and went in. He switched on the light. Ashenden followed him and closed the door. He noticed that the shutters were shut.

'Now we're all right. We can take our time.'

He took a bunch of keys out of his pocket, tried one or two and at last hit upon the right one. The suitcase was filled with clothes.

'Cheap clothes,' said the Mexican contemptuously as he took them out. 'My own principle is that it's always cheaper in the end to buy the best. After all one is a gentleman or one isn't a gentleman.'

'Are you obliged to talk?' said Ashenden.

'A spice of danger affects people in different ways. It only excites me, but it puts you in a bad temper, *amigo*.'

'You see, I'm scared and you're not,' replied Ashenden with candour.

'It's merely a matter of nerves.'

Meanwhile he felt the clothes, rapidly but with care, as he took them out. There were no papers of any sort in the suitcase. Then he took out his knife and slit the lining. It was a cheap piece and the lining was gummed to the material of which the suitcase was made. There was no possibility of anything being concealed in it.

'They're not here. They must be hidden in the room.'

'Are you sure he didn't deposit them in some office? At one of the consulates, for example?'

'He was never out of my sight for a moment except when he was getting shaved.'

The Hairless Mexican opened the drawers and the cupboard. There was no carpet on the floor. He looked under the bed, in it, and under the mattress. His dark eyes shot up and down the room, looking for a hiding-place, and Ashenden felt that nothing escaped him.

'Perhaps he left them in charge of the clerk downstairs?'

'I should have known it. And he wouldn't dare. They're not here. I can't understand it.'

He looked about the room irresolutely. He frowned in the attempt to guess at a solution of the mystery.

'Let's get out of here,' said Ashenden.

'In a minute.'

The Mexican went down on his knees, quickly and neatly folded the clothes, and packed them up again. He locked the bag and stood up. Then, putting out the light, he slowly opened the door and looked out. He beckoned to Ashenden and slipped into the passage. When Ashenden had followed him he stopped and locked the door, put the key in his pocket, and walked with Ashenden to his room. When they were inside it and the bolt drawn Ashenden wiped his clammy hands and his forehead.

'Thank God, we're out of that!'

'There wasn't really the smallest danger. But what are we to do now? The Colonel will be angry that the papers haven't been found.'

'I'm taking the five o'clock train to Rome. I shall wire for instructions there.'

'Very well, I will come with you.'

'I should have thought it would suit you better to get out of the country more quickly. There's a boat tomorrow that goes to Barcelona. Why don't you take that and if necessary I can come to see you there?'

The Hairless Mexican gave a little smile.

'I see that you are anxious to be rid of me. Well, I won't thwart a wish that your inexperience in these matters excuses. I will go to Barcelona. I have a visa for Spain.'

Ashenden looked at his watch. It was a little after two. He had nearly three hours to wait. His companion comfortably rolled himself a cigarette.

'What do you say to a little supper?' he asked. 'I'm as hungry as a wolf.'

The thought of food sickened Ashenden, but he was terribly thirsty. He did not want to go out with the Hairless Mexican, but neither did he want to stay in that hotel by himself.

'Where could one go at this hour?'

'Come along with me. I'll find you a place.'

Ashenden put on his hat and took his dispatch-case in his hand. They went downstairs. In the hall the porter was sleeping soundly on a mattress on the floor. As they passed the desk, walking softly in order not to wake him, Ashenden noticed in the pigeon-hole belonging to his room a letter. He took it out and saw that it was addressed to him. They tiptoed out of the hotel and shut the door behind them. They then walked quickly away. Stopping after a hundred yards or so under a lamp-post Ashenden took the letter out of his pocket and read; it came from the Consulate and said: *The enclosed telegram arrived tonight and in case it is urgent I am sending it round to your hotel by messenger.* It had apparently been left some time before midnight while Ashenden was sitting in his room. He opened the telegram and saw that it was in code.

'Well, it'll have to wait,' he said, putting it back in his pocket.

The Hairless Mexican walked as though he knew his way through the deserted streets and Ashenden walked by his side. At last they came to a tavern in a blind alley, noisome and evil, and this the Mexican entered.

'It's not the Ritz,' he said, 'but at this hour of the night it's only in a place like this that we stand a chance of getting something to eat.'

Ashenden found himself in a long sordid room at one end of which a wizened young man sat at a piano; there were tables standing out from the wall on each side and against them benches. A number of persons, men and women, were sitting about. They were drinking beer and wine. The women were old, painted, and hideous; and their harsh gaiety was at once noisy and lifeless. When Ashenden and the Hairless Mexican came in they all stared and when they sat down at one of the tables Ashenden looked away in order not to meet the leering eyes, just ready to break into a smile, that sought his insinuatingly. The wizened pianist strummed a tune and several couples got up and began to dance. Since there were not enough men to go round some of the women danced together. The General ordered two plates of spaghetti and a bottle of Capri wine. When the wine was brought he drank a glassful greedily and then waiting for the *pasta* eyed the women who were sitting at the other tables.

'Do you dance?' he asked Ashenden. 'I'm going to ask one of these girls to have a turn with me.'

He got up and Ashenden watched him go up to one who had at least flashing eyes and white teeth to recommend her; she rose and he put his arm round her. He danced well. Ashenden saw him begin talking; the woman laughed and presently the look of indifference with which she had accepted his offer changed to one of interest. Soon they were chatting gaily. The dance came to an end and putting her back at her table he returned to Ashenden and drank another glass of wine.

'What do you think of my girl?' he asked. 'Not bad, is she? It does one good to dance. Why don't you ask one of them? This is a nice place, is it not? You can always trust me to find anything like this. I have an instinct.'

The pianist started again. The woman looked at the Hairless Mexican and when with his thumb he pointed to the floor she jumped up with alacrity. He buttoned up his coat, arched his back, and standing up by the side of the table waited for her to come to him. He swung her off, talking smiling, and already he was on familiar terms with everyone in the room. In fluent Italian, with his Spanish accent, he exchanged badinage with one and the other. They laughed at his sallies. Then the waiter brought two heaped platefuls of macaroni and when the Mexican saw them he stopped dancing without ceremony and, allowing his partner to get back to her table as she chose, hurried to his meal.

'I'm ravenous,' he said. 'And yet I ate a good dinner. Where did you dine? You're going to eat some macaroni, aren't you?'

'I have no appetite,' said Ashenden.

But he began to eat and to his surprise found that he was hungry. The Hairless Mexican ate with huge mouthfuls, enjoying himself vastly; his eyes shone and he was loquacious. The woman he had danced with had in that short time told him all about herself and he repeated now to Ashenden what she had said. He stuffed huge pieces of bread into his mouth. He ordered another bottle of wine.

'Wine?' he cried scornfully. 'Wine is not a drink, only champagne; it does not even quench your thirst. Well, *amigo*, are you feeling better?'

'I'm bound to say I am,' smiled Ashenden.

'Practice, that is all you want, practice.'

He stretched out his hand to pat Ashenden on the arm.

'What's that?' cried Ashenden with a start. 'What's that stain on your cuff?'
The Hairless Mexican gave his sleeve a glance.
'That? Nothing. It's only blood. I had a little accident and cut myself.'
Ashenden was silent. His eyes sought the clock that hung over the door.
'Are you anxious about your train? Let me have one more dance and then I'll
accompany you to the station.'

The Mexican got up and with his sublime self-assurance seized in his arms
the woman who sat nearest to him and danced away with her. Ashenden
watched him moodily. He was a monstrous, terrible figure, with that blond wig
and his hairless face, but he moved with a matchless grace; his feet were small
and seemed to hold the ground like the pads of a cat or a tiger; his rhythm was
wonderful and you could not but see that the bedizened creature he danced
with was intoxicated by his gestures. There was music in his toes and in the
long arms that held her so firmly, and there was music in those long legs that
seemed to move strangely from the hips. Sinister and grotesque though he was,
there was in him now a feline elegance, even something of beauty, and you felt a
secret, shameful fascination. To Ashenden he suggested one of those
sculptures of the pre-Aztec hewers of stone, in which there is barbarism and
vitality, something terrible and cruel, and yet withal a brooding and significant
loveliness. All the same he would gladly have left him to finish the night by
himself in that sordid dance-hall, but he knew that he must have a business
conversation with him. He did not look forward to it without misgiving. He had
been instructed to give Manuel Carmona certain sums in return for certain
documents. Well, the documents were not forthcoming, and as for the
rest—Ashenden knew nothing about that; it was no business of his. The
Hairless Mexican waved gaily as he passed him.
'I will come the moment the music stops. Pay the bill and then I shall be
ready.'

Ashenden wished he could have seen into his mind. He could not even make
a guess at its workings. Then the Mexican, with his scented handkerchief
wiping the sweat from his brow, came back.
'Have you had a good time, General?' Ashenden asked him.
'I always have a good time. Poor white trash, but what do I care? I like to feel
the body of a woman in my arms and see her eyes grow languid and her lips part
as her desire for me melts the marrow in her bones like butter in the sun. Poor
white trash, but women.'

They sallied forth. The Mexican proposed that they should walk and in that
quarter, at that hour, there would have been little chance of finding a cab; but the
sky was starry. It was a summer night and the air was still. The silence walked
beside them like the ghost of a dead man. When they neared the station the
houses seemed on a sudden to take on a greyer, more rigid line, and you felt that
the dawn was at hand. A little shiver trembled through the night. It was a
moment of apprehension and the soul for an instant was anxious; it was as
though, inherited down the years in their countless millions, it felt a witless fear
that perhaps another day would not break. But they entered the station and the
night once more enwrapped them. One or two porters lolled about like stagehands after the curtain has rung down and the scene is struck. Two soldiers in
dim uniforms stood motionless.

The waiting-room was empty, but Ashenden and the Hairless Mexican went
to sit in the most retired part of it.
'I still have an hour before my train goes. I'll just see what this cable's about.'

He took it out of his pocket and from the dispatch-case got his code. He was not then using a very elaborate one. It was in two parts, one contained in a slim book, and the other, given him on a sheet of paper and destroyed by him before he left allied territory, committed to memory. Ashenden put on his spectacles and set to work. The Hairless Mexican sat in a corner of the seat, rolling himself cigarettes and smoking; he sat there placidly, taking no notice of what Ashenden did, and enjoyed his well-earned repose. Ashenden deciphered the groups of numbers one by one and as he got it out jotted down each word on a piece of paper. His method was to abstract his mind from the sense till he had finished, since he had discovered that if you took notice of the words as they came along you often jumped to a conclusion and sometimes were led into error. So he translated quite mechanically, without paying attention to the words as he wrote them one after the other. When at last he had done he read the complete message. It ran as follows:

Constantine Andreadi has been detained by illness at Piraeus. He will be unable to sail. Return Geneva and await instructions.

At first Ashenden could not understand. He read it again. He shook from head to foot. Then, for once robbed of his self-possession, he blurted out, in a hoarse, agitated, and furious whisper:

'You bloody fool, you've killed the wrong man.'

The Traitor

◆

When Ashenden, given charge of a number of spies working from Switzerland, was first sent there, R., wishing him to see the sort of reports that he would be required to obtain, handed him the communications, a sheaf of typewritten documents, of a man known in the secret service as Gustav.

'He's the best fellow we've got,' said R. 'His information is always very full and circumstantial. I want you to give his reports your very best attention. Of course Gustav is a clever little chap, but there's no reason why we shouldn't get just as good reports from the other agents. It's merely a question of explaining exactly what we want.'

Gustav, who lived at Basle, represented a Swiss firm with branches at Frankfurt, Mannheim, and Cologne, and by virtue of his business was able to go in and out of Germany without risk. He travelled up and down the Rhine, and gathered material about the movement of troops, the manufacture of munitions, the state of mind of the country (a point on which R. laid stress), and other matters upon which the Allies desired information. His frequent letters to his wife hid an ingenious code and the moment she received them in Basle she sent them to Ashenden in Geneva, who extracted from them the important facts and communicated these in the proper quarter. Every two months Gustav came home and prepared one of the reports that served as models to the other spies in this particular section of the secret service.

His employers were pleased with Gustav and Gustav had reason to be pleased with his employers. His services were so useful that he was not only paid more highly than the others, but for particular scoops had received from time to time a handsome bonus.

This went on for more than a year. Then something aroused R.'s quick suspicions; he was a man of an amazing alertness, not so much of mind, as of instinct, and he had suddenly a feeling that some hanky-panky was going on. He said nothing definite to Ashenden (whatever R. surmised he was disposed to keep to himself), but told him to go to Basle, Gustav being then in Germany, and have a talk with Gustav's wife. He left it to Ashenden to decide the tenor of the conversation.

Having arrived at Basle, and leaving his bag at the station, for he did not yet know whether he would have to stay or not, he took a tram to the corner of the street in which Gustav lived and, with a quick look to see that he was not followed, walked along to the house he sought. It was a block of flats that gave you the impression of decent poverty and Ashenden conjectured that they were inhabited by clerks and small tradespeople. Just inside the door was a cobbler's shop and Ashenden stopped.

'Does Herr Grabow live here?' he asked in his none too fluent German.

'Yes, I saw him go up a few minutes ago. You'll find him in.'

Ashenden was startled, for he had but the day before received through Gustav's wife a letter addressed from Mannheim in which Gustav by means of his code gave the numbers of certain regiments that had just crossed the Rhine. Ashenden thought it unwise to ask the cobbler the question that rose to his lips, so thanked him and went up to the third floor, on which he knew already that Gustav lived. He rang the bell and heard it tinkle within. In a moment the door was opened by a dapper little man with a close shaven round head and spectacles. He wore carpet slippers.

'Herr Grabow?' asked Ashenden.

'At your service,' said Gustav.

'May I come in?'

Gustav was standing with his back to the light and Ashenden could not see the look on his face. He felt a momentary hesitation and gave the name under which he received Gustav's letters from Germany.

'Come in, come in. I am very glad to see you.'

Gustav led the way into the stuffy little room, heavy with carved oak furniture, and on the large table covered with a table-cloth of green velveteen was a typewriter. Gustav was apparently engaged in composing one of his invaluable reports. A woman was sitting at the open window darning socks, but at a word from Gustav rose, gathered up her things and left. Ashenden had disturbed a pretty picture of connubial bliss.

'Sit down, please. How very fortunate that I was in Basle! I have long wanted to make your acquaintance. I have only just this minute returned from Germany.' He pointed to the sheets of paper by the typewriter. 'I think you will be pleased with the news I bring. I have some very valuable information.' He chuckled. 'One is never sorry to earn a bonus.'

He was very cordial, but to Ashenden his cordiality rang false. Gustav kept his eyes, smiling behind the glasses, fixed watchfully on Ashenden, and it was possible that they held a trace of nervousness.

'You must have travelled quickly to get here only a few hours after your letter, sent here and then sent on by your wife, reached me in Geneva.'

'That is very probable. One of the things I had to tell you is that the Germans suspect that information is getting through by means of commercial letters and so they have decided to hold up all mail at the frontier for eight-and-forty hours.'

'I see,' said Ashenden amiably. 'And was it on that account that you took the precaution of dating your letter forty-eight hours after you sent it?'

'Did I do that? That was very stupid of me. I must have mistaken the day of the month.'

Ashenden looked at Gustav with a smile. That was very thin; Gustav, a business man, knew too well how important in his particular job was the exactness of a date. The circuitous routes by which it was necessary to get information from Germany made it difficult to transmit news quickly and it was essential to know precisely on what days certain events had taken place.

'Let me look at your passport a minute,' said Ashenden.

'What do you want with my passport?'

'I want to see when you went into Germany and when you came out.'

'But you do not imagine that my comings and goings are marked on my passport? I have methods of crossing the frontiers.'

Ashenden knew a good deal of this matter. He knew that both the Germans and the Swiss guarded the frontier with severity.

'Oh? Why should you not cross in the ordinary way? You were engaged because your connexion with a Swiss firm supplying necessary goods to Germany made it easy for you to travel backwards and forwards without suspicion. I can understand that you might get past the German sentries with the connivance of the Germans, but what about the Swiss?'

Gustav assumed a look of indignation.

'I do not understand you. Do you mean to suggest that I am in the service of the Germans? I give you my word of honour . . . I will not allow my integrity to be impugned.'

'You would not be the only one to take money from both sides and provide information of value to neither.'

'Do you pretend that my information is of no value? Why then have you given me more bonuses than any other agent has received? The Colonel has repeatedly expressed the highest satisfaction with my services.'

It was Ashenden's turn now to be cordial.

'Come, come, my dear fellow, do not try to ride the high horse. You do not wish to show me your passport and I will not insist. You are not under the impression that we leave the statements of our agents without corroboration or that we are so foolish as not to keep track of their movements? Even the best of jokes cannot bear an indefinite repetition. I am in peace-time a humorist by profession and I tell you that from bitter experience.' Now Ashenden thought the moment had arrived to attempt his bluff; he knew something of the excellent but difficult game of poker. 'We have information that you have not been to Germany now, nor since you were engaged by us, but have sat here quietly in Basle, and all your reports are merely due to your fertile imagination.'

Gustav looked at Ashenden and saw a face expressive of nothing but tolerance and good-humour. A smile slowly broke on his lips and he gave his shoulders a little shrug.

'Did you think I was such a fool as to risk my life for fifty pounds a month? I love my wife.'

Ashenden laughed outright.

'I congratulate you. It is not everyone who can flatter himself that he has made a fool of our secret service for a year.'

'I had the chance of earning money without any difficulty. My firm stopped sending me into Germany at the beginning of the war, but I learned what I could from the other travellers. I kept my ears open in restaurants and beer-cellars, and I read the German papers. I got a lot of amusement out of sending you reports and letters.'

'I don't wonder,' said Ashenden.

'What are you going to do?'

'Nothing. What can we do? You are not under the impression that we shall continue to pay you a salary?'

'No, I cannot expect that.'

'By the way, if it is not indiscreet, may I ask if you have been playing the same game with the Germans?'

'Oh, no,' Gustav cried vehemently. 'How can you think it? My sympathies are absolutely pro-Ally. My heart is entirely with you.'

'Well, why not?' asked Ashenden. 'The Germans have all the money in the world and there is no reason why you should not get some of it. We could give you information from time to time that the Germans would be prepared to pay for.'

Gustav drummed his fingers on the table. He took up a sheet of the now useless report.

'The Germans are dangerous people to meddle with.'

'You are a very intelligent man. And after all, even if your salary is stopped, you can always earn a bonus by bringing us news that can be useful to us. But it will have to be substantiated; in future we pay only by results.'

'I will think of it.'

For a moment or two Ashenden left Gustav to his reflections. He lit a cigarette and watched the smoke he had inhaled fade into the air. He thought too.

'Is there anything particular you want to know?' asked Gustav suddenly.

Ashenden smiled.

'It would be worth a couple of thousand Swiss francs to you if you could tell me what the Germans are doing with a spy of theirs in Lucerne. He is an Englishman and his name is Grantley Caypor.'

'I have heard the name,' said Gustav. He paused a moment. 'How long are you staying here?'

'As long as necessary. I will take a room at the hotel and let you know the number. If you have anything to say to me you can be sure of finding me in my room at nine every morning and at seven every night.'

'I should not risk coming to the hotel. But I can write.'

'Very well.'

Ashenden rose to go and Gustav accompanied him to the door.

'We part without ill-feeling then?' he asked.

'Of course. Your reports will remain in our archives as models of what a report should be.'

Ashenden spent two or three days visiting Basle. It did not much amuse him. He passed a good deal of time in the book-shops turning over the pages of books that would have been worth reading if life were a thousand years long. Once he saw Gustav in the street. On the fourth morning a letter was brought up with his coffee. The envelope was that of a commercial firm unknown to him and inside it was a typewritten sheet. There was no address and no signature. Ashenden wondered if Gustav was aware that a typewriter could betray its owner as certainly as a handwriting. Having twice carefully read the letter, he held the paper up to the light to see the watermark (he had no reason for doing this except that the sleuths of detective novels always did it), then struck a match and watched it burn. He scrunched up the charred fragments in his hand.

He got up, for he had taken advantage of his situation to breakfast in bed, packed his bag and took the next train to Berne. From there he was able to send a code telegram to R. His instructions were given to him verbally two days later, in the bedroom of his hotel at an hour when no one was likely to be seen walking along a corridor, and within twenty-four hours, though by a circuitous route, he arrived at Lucerne.

Having taken a room at the hotel at which he had been instructed to stay, Ashenden went out; it was a lovely day, early in August, and the sun shone in an unclouded sky. He had not been to Lucerne since he was a boy and but vaguely remembered a covered bridge, a great stone lion and a church in which he had sat, bored yet impressed, while they played an organ; and now, wandering along a shady quay (and the lake looked just as tawdry and unreal as it looked on the picture-postcards) he tried not so much to find his way about a half-forgotten scene as to re-form in his mind some recollection of the shy and eager lad, so impatient for life (which he saw not in the present of his adolescence but only in the future of his manhood) who so long ago had wandered there. But it seemed to him that the most vivid of his memories was not of himself, but of the crowd; he seemed to remember sun and heat and people; the train was crowded and so was the hotel, the lake steamers were packed and on the quays and in the streets you threaded your way among the throng of holiday-makers. They were fat and old and ugly and odd, and they stank. Now, in war-time, Lucerne was as deserted as it must have been before the world at large discovered that Switzerland was the playground of Europe. Most of the hotels were closed, the streets were empty, the rowing boats for hire rocked idly at the water's edge and there was none to take them, and in the avenues by the lake the only persons to be seen were serious Swiss taking their neutrality, like a dachshund, for a walk with them. Ashenden felt exhilarated by the solitude and, sitting down on a bench that faced the water, surrendered himself deliberately to the sensation. It was true that the lake was absurd, the water was too blue, the mountains too snowy, and its beauty, hitting you in the face, exasperated rather than thrilled; but all the same there was something pleasing in the prospect, an artless candour, like one of Mendelssohn's *Songs Without Words,* that made Ashenden smile with complacency. Lucerne reminded him of wax flowers under glass cases and cuckoo clocks and fancy-work in Berlin wool. So long at all events as the fine weather lasted he was prepared to enjoy himself. He did not see why he should not at least try to combine pleasure to himself with profit to his country. He was travelling with a brand-new passport in his pocket, under a borrowed name, and this gave him an agreeable sense of owning a new personality. He was often slightly tired of himself and it diverted him for a while to be merely a creature of R.'s facile invention. The experience he had just enjoyed appealed to his acute sense of the absurd. R., it is true, had not seen the fun of it: what humour R. possessed was of a sardonic turn and he had no facility for taking in good part a joke at his own expense. To do that you must be able to look at yourself from the outside and be at the same time spectator and actor in the pleasant comedy of life. R. was a soldier and regarded introspection as unhealthy, un-English, and unpatriotic.

Ashenden got up and strolled slowly to his hotel. It was a small German hotel, of the second class, spotlessly clean, and his bed-room had a nice view; it was furnished with brightly varnished pitch-pine, and though on a cold wet day it would have been wretched, in that warm and sunny weather it was gay and pleasing. There were tables in the hall and he sat down at one of these and ordered a bottle of beer. The landlady was curious to know why in that dead season he had come to stay and he was glad to satisfy her curiosity. He told her that he had recently recovered from an attack of typhoid and had come to Lucerne to get back his strength. He was employed in the Censorship Department and was taking the opportunity to brush up his rusty German. He asked her if she could recommend to him a German teacher. The landlady was a blonde and blowzy Swiss, good-humoured and talkative, so that Ashenden felt pretty sure that she would repeat in the proper quarter the information he gave her. It was his turn now to ask a few questions. She was voluble on the subject of the war on account of which the hotel, usually in that month so full that rooms had to be found for visitors in neighbouring houses, was nearly empty. A few people came in from outside to eat their meals *en pension* but she had only two lots of resident guests. One was an old Irish couple who lived in Vevey and passed their summers in Lucerne and the other was an Englishman and his wife. She was a German and they were obliged on that account to live in a neutral country. Ashenden took care to show little curiosity about them–he recognized in the description Grantley Caypor–but of her own accord she told him that they spent most of the day walking about the mountains. Herr Caypor was a botanist and much interested in the flora of the country. His lady was a very nice woman and she felt her position keenly. Ah, well, the war could not last for ever. The landlady bustled away and Ashenden went upstairs.

Dinner was at seven, and, wishing to be in the dining-room before anyone else so that he could take stock of his fellow-guests as they entered, he went down as soon as he heard the bell. It was a very plain, stiff, white-washed room, with chairs of the same shiny pitch-pine as in his bedroom, and on the walls were oleographs of Swiss lakes. On each little table was a bunch of flowers. It was all neat and clean and presaged a bad dinner. Ashenden would have liked to make up for it by ordering a bottle of the best Rhine wine to be found in the hotel, but did not venture to draw attention to himself by extravagance (he saw on two or three tables half-empty bottles of table hock, which made him surmise that his fellow guests drank thriftily), and so contented himself with ordering a pint of lager. Presently one or two persons came in, single men with some occupation in Lucerne and obviously Swiss, and sat down each at his own little table and untied the napkins that at the end of luncheon they had neatly tied up. They propped newspapers against their water-jugs and read while they somewhat noisily ate their soup. Then entered a very old tall bent man, with white hair and a drooping white moustache, accompanied by a little old white-haired lady in black. These were certainly the Irish colonel and his wife of whom the landlady had spoken. They took their seats and the colonel poured out a thimbleful of wine for his wife and a thimbleful for himself. They waited in silence for their dinner to be served to them by the buxom, hearty maid.

At last the persons arrived for whom Ashenden had been waiting. He was doing his best to read a German book and it was only by an exercise of self-control that he allowed himself only for one instant to raise his eyes as they came in. His glance showed him a man of about forty-five with short dark hair, somewhat grizzled, of middle height, but corpulent, with a broad red clean-shaven face. He wore a shirt open at the neck, with a wide collar, and a grey suit. He walked ahead of his wife, and of her Ashenden only caught the impression of a German woman self-effaced and dusty. Grantley Caypor sat down and began in a loud voice explaining to the waitress that they had taken an immense walk. They had been up some mountain the name of which meant nothing to Ashenden, but which excited in the maid expressions of astonishment and enthusiasm. Then Caypor, still in fluent German but with a marked English accent, said that they were so late they had not even gone up to wash, but had just rinsed their hands outside. He had a resonant voice and a jovial manner.

'Serve me quick, we're starving with hunger, and bring beer, bring three bottles. *Lieber Gott*, what a thirst I have!'

He seemed to be a man of exuberant vitality. He brought into that dull, overclean dining-room the breath of life, and everyone in it appeared on a sudden more alert. He began to talk to his wife, in English, and everything he said could be heard by all; but presently she interrupted him with a remark made in an undertone. Caypor stopped and Ashenden felt that his eyes were turned in his direction. Mrs Caypor had noticed the arrival of a stranger and had drawn her husband's attention to it. Ashenden turned the page of the book he was pretending to read, but he felt that Caypor's gaze was fixed intently upon him. When he addressed his wife again it was in so low a tone that Ashenden could not even tell what language he used, but when the maid brought them their soup Caypor, his voice still low, asked her a question. It was plain that he was inquiring who Ashenden was. Ashenden could catch of the maid's reply but the one word *länder*.

One or two people finished their dinner and went out picking their teeth. The old Irish colonel and his old wife rose from their table and he stood aside to let her pass. They had eaten their meal without exchanging a word. She walked slowly to the door; but the colonel stopped to say a word to a Swiss who might have been a local attorney, and when she reached it she stood there, bowed and with a sheep-like look, patiently waiting for her husband to come and open it for her. Ashenden realized that she had never opened a door for herself. She did not know how to. In a minute the colonel with his old, old gait came to the door and opened it; she passed out and he followed. The little incident offered a key to their whole lives, and from it Ashenden began to reconstruct their histories, circumstances, and characters; but he pulled himself up; he could not allow himself the luxury of creation. He finished his dinner.

When he went into the hall he saw tied to the leg of a table a bull-terrier and in passing mechanically put down his hand to fondle the dog's drooping, soft ears. The landlady was standing at the foot of the stairs.

'Whose is this lovely beast?' asked Ashenden.

'He belongs to Herr Caypor. Fritzi, he is called. Herr Caypor says he has a longer pedigree than the King of England.'

Fritzi rubbed himself against Ashenden's leg and with his nose sought the palm of his hand. Ashenden went upstairs to fetch his hat, and when he came down saw Caypor standing at the entrance of the hotel talking with the landlady. From the sudden silence and their constrained manner he guessed that Caypor had been making inquiries about him. When he passed between them, into the street, out of the corner of his eye he saw Caypor give a suspicious stare. That frank, jovial red face bore then a look of shifty cunning.

Ashenden strolled along till he found a tavern where he could have his coffee in the open and to compensate himself for the bottle of beer that his sense of duty had urged him to drink at dinner ordered the best brandy the house provided. He was pleased at last to have come face to face with the man of whom he had heard so much and in a day or two hoped to become acquainted with him. It is never very difficult to get to know anyone who has a dog. But he was in no hurry; he would let things take their course; with the object he had in view he could not afford to be hasty.

Ashenden reviewed the circumstances. Grantley Caypor was an Englishman, born according to his passport in Birmingham, and he was forty-two years of age. His wife, to whom he had been married for eleven years, was of German birth and parentage. That was public knowledge. Information about his antecedents was contained in a private document. He had started life, according to this, in a lawyer's office in Birmingham and then had drifted into journalism. He had been connected with an English paper in Cairo and with another in Shanghai. There he got into trouble for attempting to get money on false pretences and was sentenced to a short term of imprisonment. All trace of him was lost for two years after his release, when he reappeared in a shipping office in Marseilles. From there, still in the shipping business, he went to Hamburg, where he married, and to London. In London he set up for himself in the export business, but after some time failed and was made a bankrupt. He returned to journalism. At the outbreak of war he was once more in the shipping business, and in August 1914 was living quietly with his German wife at Southampton. In the beginning of the following year he told his employers that owing to the nationality of his wife the position was intolerable; they had no fault to find with him and, recognizing that he was in an awkward fix, granted his request that he should be transferred to Genoa. Here he remained till Italy entered the war, but then gave notice and with his papers in perfect order crossed the border and took up his residence in Switzerland.

All this indicated a man of doubtful honesty and unsettled disposition, with no background and of no financial standing; but the facts were of no importance to anyone till it was discovered that Caypor, certainly from the beginning of the war and perhaps sooner, was in the service of the German Intelligence Department. He had a salary of forty pounds a month. But though dangerous and wily no steps would have been taken to deal with him if he had contented himself with transmitting such news as he was able to get in Switzerland. He could do no great harm there and it might even be possible to make use of him to convey information that it was desirable to let the enemy have. He had no notion that anything was known of him. His letters, and he received a good many, were closely censored; there were few codes that the people who dealt with such matters could not in the end decipher and it might be that sooner or later through him it would be possible to lay hands on the organization that still flourished in England. But then he did something that drew R.'s attention to him. Had he known it none could have blamed him for shaking in his shoes: R. was not a very nice man to get on the wrong side of. Caypor scraped acquaintance in Zürich with a young Spaniard, Gomez by name, who had lately entered the British secret service, by his nationality inspired him with confidence, and managed to worm out of him the fact that he was engaged in espionage. Probably the Spaniard, with a very human desire to seem important, had done no more than talk mysteriously; but on Caypor's information he was watched when he went to Germany and one day caught just as he was posting a letter in a code that was eventually deciphered. He was tried, convicted, and shot. It was bad enough to lose a useful and disinterested agent, but it entailed besides the changing of a safe and simple code. R. was not pleased. But R. was not the man to let any desire of revenge stand in the way of his main object, and it occurred to him that if Caypor was merely betraying his country for money it might be possible to get him to take more money to betray his employers. The fact that he had succeeded in delivering into their hands an agent of the Allies must seem to them an earnest of his good faith. He might be very useful. But R. had no notion what kind of man Caypor was, he had lived his shabby, furtive life obscurely, and the only photograph that existed of him was one taken for a passport. Ashenden's instructions were to get acquainted with Caypor and see whether there was any chance that he would work honestly for the British: if he thought there was, he was entitled to sound him and if his suggestions were met with favour to make certain propositions. It was a task that needed tact and a knowledge of men. If on the other hand Ashenden came to the conclusion that Caypor could not be bought, he was to watch and report his movements. The information he had obtained from Gustav was vague, but important; there was only one point in it that was interesting, and this was that the head of the German Intelligence Department in Berne was growing restive at Caypor's lack of activity. Caypor was asking for a higher salary and Major von P. had told him that he must earn it. It might be that he was urging him to go to England. If he could be induced to cross the frontier Ashenden's work was done.

'How the devil do you expect *me* to persuade him to put his head in a noose?' asked Ashenden.

'It won't be a noose, it'll be a firing squad.' said R.

'Caypor's clever.'

'Well, be cleverer, damn your eyes.'

Ashenden made up his mind that he would take no steps to make Caypor's acquaintance, but allow the first advances to be made by him. If he was being pressed for results it must surely occur to him that it would be worth while to get into conversation with an Englishman who was employed in the Censorship Department. Ashenden was prepared with a supply of information that it could not in the least benefit the Central Powers to possess. With a false name and a false passport he had little to fear that Caypor would guess that he was a British agent.

Ashenden did not have to wait long. Next day he was sitting in the doorway of the hotel, drinking a cup of coffee and already half asleep after a substantial *Mittagessen,* when the Caypors came out of the dining-room. Mrs Caypor went upstairs and Caypor released his dog. The dog bounded along and in a friendly fashion leaped up against Ashenden.

'Come here, Fritzi,' cried Caypor, and then to Ashenden: 'I'm so sorry. But he's quite gentle.'

'Oh, that's all right. He won't hurt me.'

Caypor stopped at the doorway.

'He's a bull-terrier. You don't often see them on the Continent.' He seemed while he spoke to be taking Ashenden's measure; he called to the maid: 'A coffee please, *Fräulein.* You've just arrived, haven't you?'

'Yes, I came yesterday.'

'Really? I didn't see you in the dining-room last night. Are you making a stay?'

'I don't know. I've been ill and I've come here to recuperate.'

The maid came with the coffee and seeing Caypor talking to Ashenden put the tray on the table at which he was sitting. Caypor gave a laugh of faint embarrassment.

'I don't want to force myself upon you. I don't know why the maid put my coffee on your table.'

'Please sit down,' said Ashenden.

'It's very good of you. I've lived so long on the Continent that I'm always forgetting that my countrymen are apt to look upon it as confounded cheek if you talk to them. Are you English, by the way, or American?'

'English,' said Ashenden.

Ashenden was by nature a very shy person, and he had in vain tried to cure himself of a failing that at his age was unseemly, but on occasion he knew how to make effective use of it. He explained now in a hesitating and awkward manner the facts that he had the day before told the landlady and that he was convinced she had already passed on to Caypor.

'You couldn't have come to a better place than Lucerne. It's an oasis of peace in this war-weary world. When you're here you might almost forget that there is such a thing as a war going on. That is why I've come here. I'm a journalist by profession.'

'I couldn't help wondering if you wrote,' said Ashenden, with an eagerly timid smile.

It was clear that he had not learnt that 'oasis of peace in a war-weary world' at the shipping office.

'You see, I married a German lady,' said Caypor gravely.

'Oh, really?'

'I don't think anyone could be more patriotic than I am. I'm English through and through and I don't mind telling you that in my opinion the British Empire is the greatest instrument for good that the world has ever seen, but having a German wife I naturally see a good deal of the reverse of the medal. You don't have to tell me that the Germans have faults, but frankly I'm not prepared to admit that they're devils incarnate. At the beginning of the war my poor wife had a very rough time in England and I for one couldn't have blamed her if she'd felt rather bitter about it. Everyone thought she was a spy. It'll make you laugh when you know her. She's the typical German *Hausfrau* who cares for nothing but her house and her husband and our only child Fritzi.' Caypor fondled his dog and gave a little laugh. 'Yes, Fritzi, you are our child, aren't you? Naturally it made my position very awkward. I was connected with some very important papers, and my editors weren't quite comfortable about it. Well, to cut a long story short I thought the most dignified course was to resign and come to a neutral country till the storm blew over. My wife and I never discuss the war, though I'm bound to tell you that it's more on my account than hers, she's much more tolerant than I am and she's more willing to look upon this terrible business from my point of view than I am from hers.'

'That is strange,' said Ashenden. 'As a rule women are so much more rabid than men.'

'My wife is a very remarkable person. I should like to introduce you to her. By the way, I don't know if you know my name. Grantley Caypor.'

'My name is Somerville,' said Ashenden.

He told him then of the work he had been doing in the Censorship Department, and he fancied that into Caypor's eyes came a certain intentness. Presently he told him that he was looking for someone to give him conversation-lessons in German so that he might rub up his rusty knowledge of the language; and as he spoke a notion flashed across his mind; he gave Caypor a look and saw that same notion had come to him. It had occurred to them at the same instant that it would be a very good plan for Ashenden's teacher to be Mrs Caypor.

'I asked our landlady if she could find me someone and she said she thought she could. I must ask her again. It ought not be very hard to find a man who is prepared to come and talk German to me for an hour a day.'

'I wouldn't take anyone on the landlady's recommendation,' said Caypor. 'After all you want someone with a good North-German accent and she only talks Swiss. I'll ask my wife if she knows anyone. My wife's a very highly educated woman and you could trust her recommendation.'

'That's very kind of you.'

Ashenden observed Grantley Caypor at his ease. He noticed how the small, grey-green eyes, which last night he had not been able to see, contradicted the red good-humoured frankness of the face. They were quick and shifty, but when the mind behind them was seized by an unexpected notion they were suddenly still. It gave one a peculiar feeling of the working of the brain. They were not eyes that inspired confidence; Caypor did that with his jolly, good-natured smile, the openness of his broad, weather-beaten face, his comfortable obesity and the cheeriness of his loud deep voice. He was doing his best now to be agreeable. While Ashenden talked to him, a little shyly still but gaining confidence from that breezy, cordial manner, capable of putting anyone at his ease, it intrigued him to remember that the man was a common spy. It gave a tang to his conversation to reflect that he had been ready to sell his country for no more than forty pounds a month. Ashenden had known Gomez, the young Spaniard whom Caypor had betrayed. He was a high-spirited youth, with a love of adventure, and he had undertaken his dangerous mission not for the money he earned by it, but from a passion for romance. It amused him to outwit the clumsy German and it appealed to his sense of the absurd to play a part in a shilling shocker. It was not very nice to think of him now six feet underground in a prison yard. He was young and he had a certain grace of gesture. Ashenden wondered whether Caypor had felt a qualm when he delivered him up to destruction.

'I suppose you know a little German?' asked Caypor, interested in the stranger.

'Oh, yes, I was a student in Germany, and I used to talk it fluently, but that is long ago and I have forgotten. I can still read it very comfortably.'

'Oh, yes, I noticed you were reading a German book last night.'

Fool! It was only a little while since he had told Ashenden that he had not seen him at dinner. He wondered whether Caypor had observed the slip. How difficult it was never to make one! Ashenden must be on his guard; the thing that made him most nervous was the thought that he might not answer readily enough to his assumed name of Somerville. Of course there was always the chance that Caypor had made the slip on purpose to see by Ashenden's face whether he noticed anything. Caypor got up.

'There is my wife. We go for a walk up one of the mountains every afternoon. I can tell you some charming walks. The flowers even now are lovely.'

'I'm afraid I must wait till I'm a bit stronger,' said Ashenden, with a little sigh.

He had naturally a pale face and never looked as robust as he was. Mrs Caypor came downstairs and her husband joined her. They walked down the road, Fritzi bounding round them, and Ashenden saw that Caypor immediately began to speak with volubility. He was evidently telling his wife the results of his interview with Ashenden. Ashenden looked at the sun shining so gaily on the lake; the shadow of a breeze fluttered the green leaves of the trees; everything invited a stroll: he got up, went to his room and throwing himself on his bed had a very pleasant sleep.

He went in to dinner that evening as the Caypors were finishing, for he had wandered melancholy about Lucerne in the hope of finding a cocktail that would enable him to face the potato salad that he foresaw, and on their way out of the dining-room Caypor stopped and asked him if he would drink coffee with them. When Ashenden joined them in the hall Caypor got up and introduced him to his wife. She bowed stiffly and no answering smile came to her face to respond to Ashenden's civil greeting. It was not hard to see that her attitude was definitely hostile. It put Ashenden at his ease. She was a plainish woman, nearing forty, with a muddy skin and vague features; her drab hair was arranged in a plait round her head like that of Napoleon's Queen of Prussia; and she was squarely built, plump rather than fat, and solid. But she did not look stupid; she looked on the contrary, a woman of character, and Ashenden, who had lived enough in Germany to recognize the type, was ready to believe that though capable of doing the housework, cooking the dinner, and climbing a mountain, she might be also prodigiously well-informed. She wore a white blouse that showed a sunburned neck, a black skirt and heavy walking boots. Caypor addressing her in English told her in his jovial way, as though she did not know it already, what Ashenden had told him about himself. She listened grimly.

'I think you told me you understood German,' said Caypor, his big red face wreathed in polite smiles but his little eyes darting about restlessly.

'Yes, I was for some time a student in Heidelberg.'

'Really?' said Mrs Caypor in English, an expression of faint interest for a moment chasing away the sullenness from her face. 'I know Heidelberg very well. I was at school there for one year.'

Her English was correct, but throaty, and the mouthing emphasis she gave her words was disagreeable. Ashenden was diffuse in praise of the old university town and the beauty of the neighbourhood. She heard him, from the standpoint of her Teutonic superiority, with toleration rather than with enthusiasm.

'It is well known that the valley of the Neckar is one of the beauty places of the whole world,' she said.

'I have not told you, my dear,' said Caypor then, 'that Mr Somerville is looking for someone to give him conversation lessons while he is here. I told him that perhaps you could suggest a teacher.'

'No, I know no one whom I could conscientiously recommend,' she answered. 'The Swiss accent is hateful beyond words. It could do Mr Somerville only harm to converse with a Swiss.'

'If I were in your place, Mr Somerville, I would try and persuade my wife to give you lessons. She is, if I may say so, a very cultivated and highly educated woman.'

'*Ach*, Grantley, I have not the time. I have my own work to do.'

Ashenden saw that he was being given his opportunity. The trap was prepared and all he had to do was to fall in. He turned to Mrs Caypor with a manner that he tried to make shy, deprecating and modest.

'Of course it would be too wonderful if you would give me lessons. I should look upon it as a real privilege. Naturally I wouldn't want to interfere with your work. I am just here to get well, with nothing in the world to do, and I would suit my time entirely to your convenience.'

He felt a flash of satisfaction pass from one to the other and in Mrs Caypor's blue eyes he fancied that he saw a dark glow.

'Of course it would be a purely business arrangement,' said Caypor. 'There's no reason that my good wife shouldn't earn a litle pin-money. Would you think ten francs an hour too much?'

'No,' said Ashenden. 'I should think myself lucky to get a first-rate teacher for that.'

'What do you say, my dear? Surely you can spare an hour, and you would be doing this gentleman a kindness. He would learn that all Germans are not the devilish fiends that they think them in England.'

On Mrs Caypor's brow was an uneasy frown and Ashenden could not but think with apprehension of that hour's conversation a day that he was going to exchange with her. Heaven only knew how he would have to rack his brain for subjects of discourse with that heavy and morose woman. Now she made a visible effort.

'I shall be very pleased to give Mr Somerville conversation lessons.'

'I congratulate you, Mr Somerville,' said Caypor noisily. 'You're in for a treat. When will you start, tomorrow at eleven?'

'That would suit me very well if it suits Mrs Caypor.'

'Yes, that is as good an hour as another,' she answered.

Ashenden left them to discuss the happy outcome of their diplomacy. But when, punctually at eleven next morning, he heard a knock at his door (for it had been arranged that Mrs Caypor should give him his lesson in his room) it was not without trepidation that he opened it. It behoved him to be frank, a trifle indiscreet, but obviously wary of a German woman, sufficiently intelligent, and impulsive. Mrs Caypor's face was dark and sulky. She plainly hated having anything to do with him. But they sat down and she began, somewhat peremptorily, to ask him questions about his knowledge of German literature. She corrected his mistakes with exactness and when he put before her some difficulty in German construction explained it with clearness and precision. It was obvious that though she hated giving him a lesson she meant to give it conscientiously. She seemed to have not only an aptitude for teaching, but a love of it, and as the hour went on she began to speak with greater earnestness. It was already only by an effort that she remembered that he was a brutal Englishman. Ashenden, noticing the unconscious struggle within her, found himself not a little entertained; and it was with truth that, when later in the day Caypor asked him how the lesson had gone, he answered that it was highly satisfactory; Mrs Caypor was an excellent teacher and a most interesting person.

'I told you so. She's the most remarkable woman I know.'

And Ashenden had a feeling that when in his hearty, laughing way Caypor said this he was for the first time entirely sincere.

In a day or two Ashenden guessed that Mrs Caypor was giving him lessons only in order to enable Caypor to arrive at a closer intimacy with him, for she confined herself strictly to matters of literature, music, and painting; and when Ashenden, by way of experiment, brought the conversation round to the war, she cut him short.

'I think that is a topic that we had better avoid, Herr Somerville,' she said.

She continued to give her lessons with the greatest thoroughness, and he had his money's worth, but every day she came with the same sullen face and it was only in the interest of teaching that she lost for a moment her instinctive dislike of him. Ashenden exercised in turn, but in vain, all his wiles. He was ingratiating, ingenuous, humble, grateful, flattering, simple, and timid. She remained coldly hostile. She was a fanatic. Her patriotism was aggressive, but disinterested, and obsessed with the notion of the superiority of all things German she loathed England with a virulent hatred because in that country she saw the chief obstacle to their diffusion. Her ideal was a German world in which the rest of the nations under a hegemony greater than that of Rome should enjoy the benefits of German science and German art and German culture. There was in the conception a magnificent impudence that appealed to Ashenden's sense of humour. She was no fool. She had read much, in several languages, and she could talk of the books she had read with good sense. She had a knowledge of modern painting and modern music that not a little impressed Ashenden. It was amusing once to hear her before luncheon play one of those silvery little pieces of Debussy; she played it disdainfully because it was French and so light, but with an angry appreciation of its grace and gaiety. When Ashenden congratulated her she shrugged her shoulders.

'The decadent music of a decadent nation,' she said. Then with powerful hands she struck the first resounding chords of a sonata by Beethoven; but she stopped. 'I cannot play, I am out of practice, and you English, what do you know of music? You have not produced a composer since Purcell!'

'What do you think of that statement?' Ashenden, smiling, asked Caypor, who was standing near.

'I confess its truth. The little I know of music my wife taught me. I wish you could hear her play when she is in practice.' He put his fat hand, with its square, stumpy fingers, on her shoulder. 'She can wring your heartstrings with pure beauty.'

'*Dummer Kerl*,' she said, in a soft voice, 'Stupid fellow,' and Ashenden saw her mouth for a moment quiver, but she quickly recovered. 'You English, you cannot paint, you cannot model, you cannot write music.'

'Some of us can at times write pleasing verses,' said Ashenden, with good-humour, for it was not his business to be put out, and, he did not know why, two lines occurring to him he said them:

'Whither, O splendid ship, thy white sails crowding,
  Leaning across the bosom of the urgent West?'

'Yes,' said Mrs Caypor, with a strange gesture, 'you can write poetry. I wonder why.'

And to Ashenden's surprise she went on, in her guttural English, to recite the next two lines of the poem he had quoted.

'Come, Grantley, *Mittagessen* is ready, let us go into the dining-room.'

They left Ashenden reflective.

Ashenden admired goodness, but was not outraged by wickedness. People sometimes thought him heartless because he was more often interested in others than attached to them, and even in the few to whom he was attached his eyes saw with equal clearness the merits and the defects. When he liked people it was not because he was blind to their faults, he did not mind their faults but accepted them with a tolerant shrug of the shoulders, or because he ascribed to them excellencies that they did not possess; and since he judged his friends with candour they never disappointed him and so he seldom lost one. He asked from none more than he could give. He was able to pursue his study of the Caypors without prejudice and without passion. Mrs Caypor seemed to him more of a piece and therefore the easier of the two to understand; she obviously detested him; though it was necessary for her to be civil to him her antipathy was strong enough to wring from her now and then an expression of rudeness; and had she been safely able to do so she would have killed him without a qualm. But in the pressure of Caypor's chubby hand on his wife's shoulder and in the fugitive trembling of her lips Ashenden had divined that this unprepossessing woman and that mean fat man were joined together by a deep and sincere love. It was touching. Ashenden assembled the observations that he had been making for the past few days and little things that he had noticed but to which he had attached no significance returned to him. It seemed to him that Mrs Caypor loved her husband because she was of a stronger character than he and because she felt his dependence on her; she loved him for his admiration of her, and you might guess that till she met him this dumpy, plain woman with her dullness, good sense, and want of humour could not have much enjoyed the admiration of men; she enjoyed his heartiness and his noisy jokes, and his high spirits stirred her sluggish blood; he was a great big bouncing boy and he would never be anything else and she felt like a mother towards him; she had made him what he was, and he was her man and she was his woman, and she loved him, notwithstanding his weakness (for with her clear head she must always have been conscious of that), she loved him, *ach, was*, as Isolde loved Tristan. But then there was the espionage. Even Ashenden with all his tolerance for human frailty could not but feel that to betray your country for money is not a very pretty proceeding. Of course she knew of it, indeed it was probably through her that Caypor had first been approached; he would never have undertaken such work if she had not urged him to it. She loved him and she was an honest and an upright woman. By what devious means had she persuaded herself to force her husband to adopt so base and dishonourable a calling? Ashenden lost himself in a labyrinth of conjecture as he tried to piece together the actions of her mind.

Grantley Caypor was another story. There was little to admire in him, but at that moment Ashenden was not looking for an object of admiration; but there was much that was singular and much that was unexpected in that gross and vulgar fellow. Ashenden watched with entertainment the suave manner in which the spy tried to inveigle him in his toils. It was a couple of days after his first lesson that Caypor after dinner, his wife having gone upstairs, threw himself heavily into a chair by Ashenden's side. His faithful Fritzi came up to him and put his long muzzle with its black nose on his knee.

'He has no brain,' said Caypor, 'but a heart of gold. Look at those little pink eyes. Did you ever see anything so stupid? And what an ugly face, but what incredible charm!'

'Have you had him long?' asked Ashenden.

'I got him in 1914 just before the outbreak of war. By the way, what do you think of the news today? Of course my wife and I never discuss the war. You can't think what a relief to me it is to find a fellow-countryman to whom I can open my heart.'

He handed Ashenden a cheap Swiss cigar and Ashenden, making a rueful sacrifice to duty, accepted it.

'Of course they haven't got a chance, the Germans,' said Caypor, 'not a dog's chance. I knew they were beaten the moment we came in.'

His manner was earnest, sincere, and confidential. Ashenden made a commonplace rejoinder.

'It's the greatest grief of my life that owing to my wife's nationality I was unable to do any war work. I tried to enlist the day war broke out, but they wouldn't have me on account of my age, but I don't mind telling you, if the war goes on much longer, wife or no wife, I'm going to do something. With my knowledge of languages I ought to be of some service in the Censorship Department. That's where you were, wasn't it?'

That was the mark at which he had been aiming and in answer now to his well-directed questions Ashenden gave him the information that he had already prepared. Caypor drew his chair a little nearer and dropped his voice.

'I'm sure you wouldn't tell me anything that anyone shouldn't know, but after all these Swiss are absolutely pro-German and we don't want to give anyone the chance of overhearing.'

Then he went on another tack. He told Ashenden a number of things that were of a certain secrecy.

'I wouldn't tell this to anybody else, you know, but I have one or two friends who are in pretty influential positions, and they know they can trust me.'

Thus encouraged, Ashenden was a little more deliberately indiscreet and when they parted both had reason to be satisfied. Ashenden guessed that Caypor's typewriter would be kept busy next morning and that extremely energetic Major in Berne would shortly receive a most interesting report.

One evening, going upstairs after dinner, Ashenden passed an open bathroom. He caught sight of the Caypors.

'Come in,' cried Caypor in his cordial way. 'We're washing our Fritzi.'

The bull-terrier was constantly getting himself very dirty, and it was Caypor's pride to see him clean and white. Ashenden went in. Mrs Caypor with her sleeves turned up and a large white apron was standing at one end of the bath, while Caypor, in a pair of trousers and a singlet, his fat, freckled arms bare, was soaping the wretched hound.

'We have to do it at night,' he said, 'because the Fitzgeralds use this bath and they'd have a fit if they knew we washed the dog in it. We wait till they go to bed. Come along, Fritzi, show the gentleman how beautifully you behave when you have your face scrubbed.'

The poor brute, woebegone but faintly wagging his tail to show that however foul was this operation performed on him he bore no malice to the god who did it, was standing in the middle of the bath in six inches of water. He was soaped all over and Caypor, talking the while, shampooed him with his great fat hands.

'Oh, what a beautiful dog he's going to be when he's as white as the driven snow. His master will be as proud as Punch to walk out with him and all the little lady-dogs will say: Good gracious, who's that beautiful aristocratic-looking bull-terrier walking as though he owned the whole of Switzerland? Now stand still while you have your ears washed. You couldn't bear to go out into the street with dirty ears, could you? like a nasty little Swiss schoolboy. *Noblesse oblige.* Now the black nose. Oh, and all the soap is going into his little pink eyes and they'll smart.'

Mrs Caypor listened to this nonsense with a good-humoured sluggish smile on her broad, plain face, and presently gravely took a towel.

'Now he's going to have a ducking. Upsie-daisy.'

Caypor seized the dog by the fore-legs and ducked him once and ducked him twice. There was a struggle, a flurry and a splashing. Caypor lifted him out of the bath.

'Now go to mother and she'll dry you.'

Mrs Caypor sat down and taking the dog between her strong legs rubbed him till the sweat poured off her forehead. And Fritzi, a little shaken and breathless, but happy it was all over, stood, with his sweet stupid face, white and shining. 'Blood will tell,' cried Caypor exultantly. 'He knows the names of no less than sixty-four of his ancestors, and they were all nobly born.'

Ashenden was faintly troubled. He shivered a little as he walked upstairs.

Then, one Sunday, Caypor told him that he and his wife were going on an excursion and would eat their luncheon at some little mountain restaurant; and he suggested that Ashenden, each paying his share, should come with them. After three weeks at Lucerne Ashenden thought that his strength would permit him to venture the exertion. They started early, Mrs Caypor businesslike in her walking boots and Tyrolese hat and alpenstock, and Caypor in stockings and plus-fours looking very British. The situation amused Ashenden and he was prepared to enjoy his day; but he meant to keep his eyes open; it was not inconceivable that the Caypors had discovered what he was and it would not do to go too near a precipice; Mrs Caypor would not hesitate to give him a push and Caypor for all his jolliness was an ugly customer. But on the face of it there was nothing to mar Ashenden's pleasure in the golden morning. The air was fragrant. Caypor was full of conversation. He told funny stories. He was gay and jovial. The sweat rolled off his great red face and he laughed at himself because he was so fat. To Ashenden's astonishment he showed a peculiar knowledge of the mountain flowers. Once he went out of the way to pick one he saw a little distance from the path and brought it back to his wife. He looked at it tenderly.

'Isn't it lovely?' he cried, and his shifty grey-green eyes for a moment were as candid as a child's. 'It's like a poem by Walter Savage Landor.'

'Botany is my husband's favourite science,' said Mrs Caypor. 'I laugh at him sometimes. He is devoted to flowers. Often when we have hardly had enough money to pay the butcher he has spent everything in his pocket to bring me a bunch of roses.'

'*Qui fleurit sa maison fleurit son coeur,*' said Grantley Caypor.

Ashenden had once or twice seen Caypor, coming in from a walk, offer Mrs Fitzgerald a nosegay of mountain flowers with an elephantine courtesy that was not entirely displeasing; and what he had just learned added a certain significance to the pretty little action. His passion for flowers was genuine and when he gave them to the old Irish lady he gave her something he valued. It showed a real kindness of heart. Ashenden had always thought botany a tedious science, but Caypor, talking exuberantly as they walked along, was able to impart to it life and interest. He must have given it a good deal of study.

'I've never written a book,' he said. 'There are too many books already and any desire to write I have is satisfied by the more immediately profitable and quite ephemeral composition of an article for a daily paper. But if I stay here much longer I have half a mind to write a book about the wild flowers of Switzerland. Oh, I wish you'd been here a little earlier. They were marvellous. But one wants to be a poet for that, and I'm only a poor newspaper-man.'

It was curious to observe how he was able to combine real emotion with false fact.

When they reached the inn, with its view of the mountains and the lake, it was good to see the sensual pleasure with which he poured down his throat a bottle of ice-cold beer. You could not but feel sympathy for a man who took so much delight in simple things. They lunched deliciously off scrambled eggs and mountain trout. Even Mrs Caypor was moved to an unwonted gentleness by her surroundings; the inn was in an agreeably rural spot, it looked like a picture of a Swiss chalet in a book of early nineteenth-century travels; and she treated Ashenden with something less than her usual hostility. When they arrived she had burst into loud German exclamations on the beauty of the scene, and now, softened perhaps too by food and drink, her eyes, dwelling on the grandeur before her, filled with tears. She stretched out her hand.

'It is dreadful and I am ashamed, notwithstanding this horrible and unjust war I can feel in my heart at the moment nothing but happiness and gratitude.'

Caypor took her hand and pressed it and, an unusual thing with him, addressing her in German, called her little pet-names. It was absurd, but touching. Ashenden, leaving them to their emotions, strolled through the garden and sat down on a bench that had been prepared for the comfort of the tourist. The view was of course spectacular, but it captured you; it was like a piece of music that was obvious and meretricious, but for the moment shattered your self-control.

And as Ashenden lingered idly in that spot he pondered over the mystery of Grantley Caypor's treachery. If he liked strange people he had found in him one who was strange beyond belief. It would be foolish to deny that he had amiable traits. His joviality was not assumed, he was without pretence a hearty fellow, and he had real good nature. He was always ready to do a kindness. Ashenden had often watched him with the old Irish colonel and his wife who were the only other residents of the hotel; he would listen good-humouredly to the old man's tedious stories of the Egyptian war, and he was charming with her. Now that Ashenden had arrived at terms of some familiarity with Caypor he found that he regarded him less with repulsion than with curiosity. He did not think that he had become a spy merely for the money; he was a man of modest tastes and what he had earned in a shipping-office must have sufficed to so good a manager as Mrs Caypor; and after war was declared there was no lack of remunerative work for men over the military age. It might be that he was one of those men who prefer devious ways to straight for some intricate pleasure they get in fooling their fellows; and that he had turned spy, not from hatred of the country that had imprisoned him, not even from love of his wife, but from a desire to score off the big-wigs who never even knew of his existence. It might be that it was vanity that impelled him, a feeling that his talents had not received the recognition they merited, or just a puckish, impish desire to do mischief. He was a crook. It is true that only two cases of dishonesty had been brought home to him, but if he had been caught twice it might be surmised that he had often been dishonest without being caught. What did Mrs Caypor think of this? They were so united that she must be aware of it. Did it make her ashamed, for her own uprightness surely none could doubt, or did she accept it as an inevitable kink in the man she loved? Did she do all she could to prevent it or did she close her eyes to something she could not help?

How much easier life would be if people were all black or all white and how much simpler it would be to act in regard to them! Was Caypor a good man who loved evil or a bad man who loved good? And how could such unreconcilable elements exist side by side and in harmony within the same heart? For one thing was clear, Caypor was disturbed by no gnawing of conscience; he did his mean and despicable work with gusto. He was a traitor who enjoyed his treachery. Though Ashenden had been studying human nature more or less consciously all his life, it seemed to him that he knew as little about it now in middle age as he had done when he was a child. Of course R. would have said to him: Why the devil do you waste your time with such nonsense? The man's a dangerous spy and your business is to lay him by the heels.

That was true enough. Ashenden had decided that it would be useless to attempt to make any arrangement with Caypor. Though doubtless he would have no feeling about betraying his employers he could certainly not be trusted. His wife's influence was too strong. Besides, notwithstanding what he had from time to time told Ashenden, he was in his heart convinced that the Central Powers must win the war, and he meant to be on the winning side. Well, then Caypor must be laid by the heels, but how he was to effect that Ashenden had no notion. Suddenly he heard a voice.

'There you are. We've been wondering where you had hidden yourself.'

He looked around and saw the Caypors strolling towards him. They were walking hand in hand.

'So this is what has kept you so quiet,' said Caypor as his eyes fell on the view. 'What a spot!'

Mrs Caypor clasped her hands.

'*Ach Gott, wie schön!*' she cried. '*Wie schön.* When I look at that blue lake and those snowy mountains I feel inclined, like Goethe's Faust, to cry to the passing moment: Tarry.'

'This is better than being in England with the excursions and alarums of war, isn't it?' said Caypor.

'Much,' said Ashenden.

'By the way, did you have any difficulty in getting out?'

'No, not the smallest.'

'I'm told they make rather a nuisance of themselves at the frontier nowadays.'

'I came through without the smallest difficulty. I don't fancy they bother much about the English. I thought the examination of passports was quite perfunctory.'

A fleeting glance passed between Caypor and his wife. Ashenden wondered what it meant. It would be strange if Caypor's thoughts were occupied with the chances of a journey to England at the very moment when he was himself reflecting on its possibility. In a little while Mrs Caypor suggested that they had better be starting back and they wandered together in the shade of trees down the mountain paths.

Ashenden was watchful. He could do nothing (and his inactivity irked him) but wait with his eyes open to seize the opportunity that might present itself. A couple of days later an incident occurred that made him certain something was in the wind. In the course of his morning lesson Mrs Caypor remarked:

'My husband has gone to Geneva today. He had some business to do there.'

'Oh,' said Ashenden, 'will he be gone long?'

'No, only two days.'

It is not everyone who can tell a lie and Ashenden had the feeling, he hardly knew why, that Mrs Caypor was telling one then. Her manner perhaps was not quite as indifferent as you would have expected when she was mentioning a fact that could be of no interest to Ashenden. It flashed across his mind that Caypor had been summoned to Berne to see the redoubtable head of the German secret service. When he had the chance he said casually to the waitress:

'A little less work for you to do, *Fräulein.* I hear that Herr Caypor has gone to Berne.'

'Yes. But he'll be back tomorrow.'

That proved nothing, but it was something to go upon. Ashenden knew in Lucerne a Swiss who was willing in emergency to do odd jobs, and looking him up, asked him to take a letter to Berne. It might be possible to pick up Caypor and trace his movements. Next day Caypor appeared once more with his wife at the dinner-table, but merely nodded to Ashenden and afterwards both went straight upstairs. They looked troubled. Caypor, as a rule so animated, walked with bowed shoulders and looked neither to the right nor to the left. Next morning Ashenden received a reply to his letter: Caypor had seen Major von P. It was possible to guess what the Major had said to him. Ashenden well knew how rough he could be; he was a hard man and brutal, clever and unscrupulous, and he was not accustomed to mince his words. They were tired of paying Caypor a salary to sit still in Lucerne and do nothing; the time was come for him to go to England. Guess-work? Of course it was guess-work, but in that trade it mostly was; you had to deduce the animal from its jaw-bone. Ashenden knew from Gustav that the Germans wanted to send someone to England. He drew a long breath; if Caypor went he would have to get busy.

When Mrs Caypor came in to give him his lesson she was dull and listless. She looked tired and her mouth was set obstinately. It occurred to Ashenden that the Caypors had spent most of the night talking. He wished he knew what they had said. Did she urge him to go or did she try to dissuade him? Ashenden watched them again at luncheon. Something was the matter, for they hardly spoke to one another and as a rule they found plenty to talk about. They left the room early, but when Ashenden went out he saw Caypor sitting in the hall by himself.

'Hullo,' he cried jovially, but surely the effort was patent, 'how are you getting on? I've been to Geneva.'

'So I heard,' said Ashenden.

'Come and have your coffee with me. My poor wife's got a headache. I told her she'd better go and lie down.' In his shifty green eyes was an expression that Ashenden could not read. 'The fact is, she's rather worried, poor dear; I'm thinking of going to England.'

Ashenden's heart gave a sudden leap against his ribs, but his face remained impassive:

'Oh, are you going for long? We shall miss you.'

'To tell you the truth, I'm fed up with doing nothing. The war looks as though it were going on for years and I can't sit here indefinitely. Besides, I can't afford it, I've got to earn my living. I may have a German wife, but I am an Englishman, hang it all, and I want to do my bit. I could never face my friends again if I just stayed here in ease and comfort till the end of the war and never attempted to do a thing to help the country. My wife takes her German point of view and I don't mind telling you that she's a bit upset. You know what women are.'

Now Ashenden knew what it was that he saw in Caypor's eyes. Fear. It gave him a nasty turn. Caypor didn't want to go to England, he wanted to stay safely in Switzerland; Ashenden knew now what the major had said to him when he went to see him in Berne. He had got to go or lose his salary. What was it that his wife had said when he told her what had happened? He had wanted her to press him to stay, but, it was plain, she hadn't done that; perhaps he had not dared tell her how frightened he was; to her he had always been gay, bold, adventurous, and devil-may-care; and now, the prisoner of his own lies, he had not found it in him to confess himself the mean and sneaking coward he was.

'Are you going to take your wife with you?' asked Ashenden.

'No, she'll stay here.'

It had been arranged very neatly. Mrs Caypor would receive his letters and forward the information they contained to Berne.

'I've been out of England so long that I don't quite know how to set about getting war-work. What would you do in my place?'

'I don't know; what sort of work are you thinking of?'

'Well, you know, I imagine I could do the same thing as you did. I wonder if there's anyone in the Censorship Department that you could give me a letter of introduction to.'

It was only by a miracle that Ashenden saved himself from showing by a smothered cry or by a broken gesture how startled he was; but not by Caypor's request, but what had just dawned upon him. What an idiot he had been! He had been disturbed by the thought that he was wasting his time at Lucerne, he was doing nothing, and though in fact, as it turned out, Caypor was going to England it was due to no cleverness of his. He could take to himself no credit for the result. And now he saw that he had been put in Lucerne, told how to describe himself and given the proper information, so that what actually had occurred should occur. It would be a wonderful thing for the German secret service to get an agent into the Censorship Department; and by a happy accident there was Grantley Caypor, the very man for the job, on friendly terms with someone who had worked there. What a bit of luck! Major von P. was a man of culture and, rubbing his hands, he must surely have murmured: *stultum facit fortuna quem vult perdere.* It was a trap of that devilish R. and the grim major at Berne had fallen into it. Ashenden had done his work just by sitting still and doing nothing. He almost laughed as he thought what a fool R. had made of him.

'I was on very good terms with the chief of my department, I could give you a note to him if you liked.'

'That would be just the thing.'

'But of course I must give the facts. I must say I've met you here and only known you a fortnight.'

'Of course. But you'll say what else you can for me, won't you?'

'Oh, certainly.'

'I don't know yet if I can get a visa. I'm told they're rather fussy.'

'I don't see why. I shall be very sick if they refuse me one when I want to go back.'

'I'll go and see how my wife is getting on,' said Caypor suddenly, getting up. 'When will you let me have that letter?'

'Whenever you like. Are you going at once?'

'As soon as possible.'

Caypor left him. Ashenden waited in the hall for a quarter of an hour so that there should appear in him no sign of hurry. Then he went upstairs and prepared various communications. In one he informed R. that Caypor was going to England; in another he made arrangements through Berne that wherever Caypor applied for a visa it should be granted to him without question; and these he dispatched forthwith. When he went down to dinner he handed Caypor a cordial letter of introduction.

Next day but one Caypor left Lucerne.

Ashenden waited. He continued to have his hour's lesson with Mrs Caypor and under her conscientious tuition began now to speak German with ease.

They talked of Goethe and Winckelmann, of art and life and travel. Fritzi sat quietly by her chair.

'He misses his master,' she said, pulling his ears. 'He only really cares for him, he suffers me only as belonging to him.'

After his lesson Ashenden went every morning to Cook's to ask for his letters. It was here that all communications were addressed to him. He could not move till he received instructions, but R. could be trusted not to leave him idle long; and meanwhile there was nothing for him to do but have patience. Presently he received a letter from the consul in Geneva to say that Caypor had there applied for his visa and had set out for France. Having read this Ashenden went on for a little stroll by the lake and on his way back happened to see Mrs Caypor coming out of Cook's office. He guessed that she was having her letters addressed there too. He went up to her.

'Have you had news of Herr Caypor?' he asked her.

'No,' she said. 'I suppose I could hardly expect to yet.'

He walked along by her side. She was disappointed, but not yet anxious; she knew how irregular at that time was the post. But next day during the lesson he could not but see that she was impatient to have done with it. The post was delivered at noon and at five minutes to she looked at her watch and him. Though Ashenden knew very well that no letter would ever come for her he had not the heart to keep her on tenter-hooks.

'Don't you think that's enough for the day? I'm sure you want to go down to Cook's,' he said.

'Thank you. That is very amiable of you.'

When a little later he went there himself he found her standing in the middle of the office. Her face was distraught. She addressed him wildly.

'My husband promised to write from Paris. I am sure there is a letter for me, but these stupid people say there's nothing. They're so careless, it's a scandal.'

Ashenden did not know what to say. While the clerk was looking through the bundle to see if there was anything for him she came up to the desk again.

'When does the next post come in from France?' she asked.

'Sometimes there are letters about five.'

'I'll come then.'

She turned and walked rapidly away. Fritzi followed her with his tail between his legs. There was no doubt of it, already the fear had seized her that something was wrong. Next morning she looked dreadful; she could not have closed her eyes all night; and in the middle of the lesson she started up from her chair.

'You must excuse me, Herr Somerville. I cannot give you a lesson today. I am not feeling well.'

Before Ashenden could say anything she had flung nervously from the room, and in the evening he got a note from her to say that she regretted that she must discontinue giving him conversation lessons. She gave no reason. Then Ashenden saw no more of her; she ceased coming in to meals; except to go morning and afternoon to Cook's she spent apparently the whole day in her room. Ashenden thought of her sitting there hour after hour with that hideous fear gnawing at her heart. Who could help feeling sorry for her? The time hung heavy on his hands too. He read a good deal and wrote a little, he hired a canoe and went for long leisurely paddles on the lake; and at last one morning the clerk at Cook's handed him a letter. It was from R. It had all the appearance of a business communication, but between the lines he read a good deal.

Dear Sir, [it began] The goods, with accompanying letter, dispatched by you from Lucerne have been duly delivered. We are obliged to you for executing our instructions with such promptness.

It went on in this strain. R. was exultant. Ashenden guessed that Caypor had been arrested and by now had paid the penalty of his crime. He shuddered. He remembered a dreadful scene. Dawn. A cold grey dawn, with a drizzling rain falling. A man, blindfolded, standing against a wall, an officer very pale giving an order, a volley, and then a young soldier, one of the firing-party, turning round and holding on to his gun for support, vomiting. The officer turning paler still, and he, Ashenden, feeling dreadfully faint. How terrified Caypor must have been! It was awful when the tears ran down their faces. Ashenden shook himself. He went to the ticket-office and obedient to his orders bought himself a ticket for Geneva.

As he was waiting for his change Mrs Caypor came in. He was shocked at the sight of her. She was blowzy and dishevelled and there were heavy rings round her eyes. She was deathly pale. She staggered up to the desk and asked for a letter. The clerk shook his head.

'I'm sorry, madam, there's nothing yet.'

'But look, look. Are you sure? Please look again.'

The misery in her voice was heartrending. The clerk with a shrug of the shoulders took out the letters from a pigeon-hole and sorted them once more.

'No, there's nothing, madam.'

She gave a hoarse cry of despair and her face was distorted with anguish.

'Oh, God, oh, God,' she moaned.

She turned away, the tears streaming from her weary eyes, and for a moment she stood there like a blind man groping and not knowing which way to go. Then a fearful thing happened. Fritzi, the bull-terrier, sat down on his haunches and threw back his head and gave a long, long melancholy howl. Mrs Caypor looked at him with terror; her eyes seemed really to start from her head. The doubt, the gnawing doubt that had tortured her during those dreadful days of suspense, was a doubt to her no longer. She knew. She staggered blindly into the street.

His Excellency

♦

When Ashenden was sent to X and looked about him he could not but see that his situation was equivocal. X was the capital of an important belligerent state; but a state divided against itself; there was a large party antagonistic to the war and revolution was possible if not imminent. Ashenden was instructed to see what under the circumstances could best be done; he was to suggest a policy and, if it was approved by the exalted personages who had sent him, to carry it out. A vast amount of money was put at his disposal. The Ambassadors of Great Britain and the United States had been directed to afford him such facilities as were at their command, but Ashenden had been told privately to keep himself to himself; he was not to make difficulties for the official representatives of the two powers by divulging to them facts that might be inconvenient for them to know; and since it might be necessary for him to give support under cover to a party that was at daggers drawn with that in office and with which the relations of the United States and Great Britain were extremely cordial it was just as well that Ashenden should keep his own counsel. The exalted personages did not wish the ambassadors to suffer the affront of discovering that an obscure agent had been sent to work at cross-purposes with them. On the other hand it was thought just as well to have a representative in the opposite camp, who in the event of a sudden upheaval would be at hand with adequate funds and in the confidence of the new leaders of the country.

But ambassadors are sticklers for their dignity and they have a keen nose to scent any encroachment on their authority. When Ashenden on his arrival at X paid an official call on Sir Herbert Witherspoon, the British ambassador, he was received with a politeness to which no exception could be taken, but with a frigidity that would have sent a little shiver down the spine of a polar bear. Sir Herbert was a diplomat *de carrière* and he cultivated the manner of his profession to a degree that filled the observer with admiration. He did not ask Ashenden anything about his mission because he knew that Ashenden would reply evasively, but he allowed him to see that it was a perfectly foolish one. He talked with acidulous tolerance of the exalted personages who had sent Ashenden to X. He told Ashenden that he had instructions to meet any demands for help that he made and stated that if Ashenden at any time desired to see him he had only to say so.

'I have received the somewhat singular request to dispatch telegrams for you in a private code which I understand has been given to you and to hand over to you telegrams in code as they arrive.'

'I hope they will be few and far between, sir,' answered Ashenden. 'I know nothing so tedious as coding and decoding.'

Sir Herbert paused for an instant. Perhaps that was not quite the answer he expected. He rose.

'If you will come into the Chancellery I will introduce you to the Counsellor and to the Secretary to whom you can take your telegrams.'

Ashenden followed him out of the room, and after handing him over to the Counsellor the ambassador gave him a limp hand to shake.

'I hope I shall have the pleasure of seeing you again one of these days,' he said, and with a curt nod left him.

Ashenden bore his reception with composure. It was his business to remain in obscurity and he did not wish any official attentions to attract notice to him. But when on the afternoon of the same day he made his call at the American Embassy he discovered why Sir Herbert Witherspoon had shown him so much coldness. The American ambassador was Mr Wilbur Schäfer; he came from Kansas City and had been given his post when few suspected that a war was on the point of breaking out, as a reward for political services. He was a big stout man, no longer young, for his hair was white, but well-preserved and exceedingly robust. He had a square, red face, clean-shaven, with a little snub nose and a determined chin. His face was very mobile and he twisted it continually into odd and amusing grimaces. It looked as though it were made out of the red india-rubber from which they make hot-water bottles. He greeted Ashenden with cordiality. He was a hearty fellow.

'I suppose you've seen Sir Herbert. I reckon you've got his dander up. What do they mean in Washington and London by telling us to dispatch your code telegrams without knowing what they're all about? You know, they've got no right to do that.'

'Oh, Your Excellency, I think it was only done to save time and trouble,' said Ashenden.

'Well, what is this mission anyway?'

This of course was a question that Ashenden was not prepared to answer, but not thinking it politic to say so, he determined to give a reply from which the ambassador could learn little. He had already made up his mind from the look of him that Mr Schäfer, though doubtless possessed of the gifts that enable a man to swing a presidential election this way or that, had not, at least nakedly for all men to see, the acuteness that his position perhaps demanded. He gave you the impression of a bluff, good-humoured creature who liked good cheer. Ashenden would have been wary when playing poker with him, but where the matter in hand was concerned felt himself fairly safe. He began to talk in a loose, vague way of the world at large and before he had gone far managed to ask the ambassador his opinion of the general situation. It was as the sound of the trumpet to the war-horse: Mr Schäfer made him a speech that lasted without a break for twenty-five minutes, and when at last he stopped in exhaustion, Ashenden with warm thanks for his friendly reception was able to take his leave.

Making up his mind to give both the ambassadors a wide berth, he set about his work and presently devised a plan of campaign. But by chance he was able to do Sir Herbert Witherspoon a good turn and so was thrown again into contact with him. It has been suggested that Mr Schäfer was more of a politician than a diplomat and it was his position rather than his personality that gave weight to his opinions. He looked upon the eminence to which he had risen as an opportunity to enjoy the good things of life and his enthusiasm led him to lengths that his constitution could ill support. His ignorance of foreign affairs would in any case have made his judgement of doubtful value, but his state at meetings of the Allied ambassadors so often approached the comatose that he seemed hardly capable of forming a judgement at all. He was known to have succumbed to the fascination of a Swedish lady of undoubted beauty, but of antecedents that from the point of view of a secret service agent were suspect. Her relations with Germany were such as to make her sympathy with the Allies dubious. Mr Schäfer saw her every day and was certainly much under her influence. Now it was noticed that there was from time to time a leakage of very secret information and the question arose whether Mr Schäfer did not in these daily interviews inadvertently say things that were promptly passed on to the headquarters of the enemy. No one could have doubted Mr Schäfer's honesty and patriotism, but it was permissible to be uncertain of his discretion. It was an awkward matter to deal with, but the concern was as great in Washington as in London and Paris, and Ashenden was instructed to deal with it. He had of course not been sent to X without help to do the work he was expected to do, and among his assistants was an astute, powerful, and determined man, a Galician Pole, named Herbartus. After consultation with him it happened by one of those fortunate coincidences that occasionally come about in the secret service that a maid in the service of the Swedish lady fell ill and in her place the countess (for such she was) was very luckily able to engage an extremely respectable person from the neighbourhood of Cracow. The fact that before the war she had been secretary to an eminent scientist made her doubtless no less competent a housemaid.

The result of this was that Ashenden received every two or three days a neat report upon the goings-on at this charming lady's apartment, and though he learned nothing that could confirm the vague suspicions that had arisen he learned something else of no little importance. From conversations held at the cosy little *tête-à-tête* dinners that the countess gave the ambassador it appeared that His Excellency was harbouring a bitter grievance against his English colleague. He complained that the relations between himself and Sir Herbert were deliberately maintained on a purely official level. In his blunt way he said he was sick of the frills that damned Britisher put on. He was a he-man and a hundred-per-cent American and he had no more use for protocol and etiquette than for a snowball in hell. Why didn't they get together, like a couple of regular fellows, and have a good old crack? Blood was thicker than water, he'd say, and they'd do more towards winning the war by sitting down in their shirtsleeves and talking things out over a bottle of rye than by all their diplomacy and white spats. Now it was obviously very undesirable that there should not exist between the two ambassadors a perfect cordiality, so Ashenden thought it well to ask Sir Herbert whether he might see him.

He was ushered into Sir Herbert's library.

'Well, Mr Ashenden, what can I do for you? I hope you're quite satisfied with everything. I understand that you've been keeping the telegraph lines busy.'

Ashenden, as he sat down, gave the ambassador a glance. He was beautifully dressed in a perfectly cut tail-coat that fitted his slim figure like a glove, in his black silk tie was a handsome pearl, there was a perfect line in his grey trousers, with their quiet and distinguished stripe, and his neat, pointed shoes looked as though he had never worn them before. You could hardly imagine him sitting in his shirt-sleeves over a whisky highball. He was a tall, thin man, with exactly the figure to show off modern clothes, and he sat in his chair, rather upright, as though he were sitting for an official portrait. In his cold and uninteresting way he was really a very handsome fellow. His neat grey hair was parted on one side, his pale face was clean-shaven, he had a delicate, straight nose and grey eyes under grey eyebrows, his mouth in youth might have been sensual and well-shaped, but now it was set to an expression of sarcastic determination and the lips were pallid. It was the kind of face that suggested centuries of good breeding, but you could not believe it capable of expressing emotion. You would never expect to see it break into the hearty distortion of laughter, but at the most be for a moment frigidly kindled by an ironic smile.

Ashenden was uncommonly nervous.

'I'm afraid you'll think I'm meddling in what doesn't concern me, sir. I'm quite prepared to be told to mind my own business.'

'We'll see. Pray go on.'

Ashenden told his story and the ambassador listened attentively. He did not turn his cold, grey eyes from Ashenden's face, and Ashenden knew that his embarrassment was obvious.

'How did you find out all this?'

'I have means of getting hold of little bits of information that are sometimes useful,' said Ashenden.

'I see.'

Sir Herbert maintained his steady gaze, but Ashenden was surprised to see on a sudden in the steely eyes a little smile. The bleak, supercilious face became for an instant quite attractive.

'There is another little bit of information that perhaps you'd be good enough to give me. What does one do to be a regular fellow?'

'I am afraid one can do nothing, Your Excellency,' replied Ashenden gravely. 'I think it is a gift of God.'

The light vanished from Sir Herbert's eyes, but his manner was slightly more urbane than when Ashenden was brought into the room. He rose and held out his hand.

'You did quite right to come and tell me this, Mr Ashenden. I have been very remiss. It is inexcusable on my part to offend that inoffensive old gentleman. But I will do my best to repair my error. I will call at the American Embassy this afternoon.'

'But not in too great state, sir, if I may venture a suggestion.'

The ambassador's eyes twinkled. Ashenden began to think him almost human.

'I can do nothing but in state, Mr Ashenden. That is one of the misfortunes of my temperament.' Then as Ashenden was leaving he added: 'Oh, by the way,

I wonder if you'd care to come to dinner with me tomorrow night. Black tie. At eight-fifteen.'

He did not wait for Ashenden's assent, but took it for granted, and with a nod of dismissal sat down once more at his great writing-table.

Ashenden looked forward with misgiving to the dinner to which Sir Herbert Witherspoon had invited him. The black tie suggested a small party, perhaps only Lady Anne, the ambassador's wife, whom Ashenden did not know, or one or two young secretaries. It did not presage a hilarious evening. It was possible that they might play bridge after dinner, but Ashenden knew that professional diplomats do not play bridge with skill: it may be supposed that they find it difficult to bend their great minds to the triviality of a parlour game. On the other hand he was interested to see a little more of the ambassador in circumstances of less formality. For it was evident that Sir Herbert Witherspoon was not an ordinary person. He was in appearance and manner a perfect specimen of his class and it is always entertaining to come upon good examples of a well-known type. He was exactly what you expected an ambassador to be. If any of his characteristics had been ever so slightly exaggerated he would have been a caricature. He escaped being ridiculous only by a hair's breadth and you watched him with a kind of breathlessness as you might watch a tight-rope dancer doing perilous feats at a dizzy height. He was certainly a man of character. His rise in the diplomatic service had been rapid and though doubtless it helped him to be connected by marriage with powerful families his rise had been due chiefly to his merit. He knew how to be determined when determination was necessary and conciliatory when conciliation was opportune. His manners were perfect; he could speak half a dozen languages with ease and accuracy; he had a clear and logical brain. He was never afraid to think out his thoughts to the end, but was wise enough to suit his actions to the exigencies of the situation. He had reached his post at X at the early age of fifty-three and had borne himself in the exceedingly difficult conditions created by the war and contending parties within the state with tact, confidence, and once at least with courage. For on one occasion, a riot having arisen, a band of revolutionaries forced their way into the British Embassy and Sir Herbert from the head of his stairs had harangued them and notwithstanding revolvers flourished at him had persuaded them to go to their homes. He would end his career in Paris. That was evident. He was a man whom you could not but admire but whom it was not easy to like. He was a diplomat of the school of those Victorian ambassadors to whom could confidently be entrusted great affairs and whose self-reliance, sometimes it must be admitted tinctured with arrogance, was justified by its results.

When Ashenden drove up to the doors of the Embassy they were flung open and he was received by a stout and dignified English butler and three footmen. He was ushered up that magnificent flight of stairs on which had taken place the dramatic incident just related and shown into an immense room, dimly lit with shaded lamps, in which at the first glance he caught sight of large pieces of stately furniture and over the chimney-piece an immense portrait in coronation robes of King George IV. But there was a bright fire blazing on the hearth and from a deep sofa by the side of it his host, as his name was announced, slowly rose. Sir Herbert looked very elegant as he came towards him. He wore his dinner jacket, the most difficult costume for a man to look well in, with notable distinction.

'My wife has gone to a concert, but she'll come in later. She wants to make your acquaintance. I haven't asked anybody else. I thought I would give myself the pleasure of enjoying your company *en tête-à-tête.*'

Ashenden murmured a civil rejoinder, but his heart sank. He wondered how he was to pass at least a couple of hours alone with this man who made him he was bound to confess, feel extremely shy.

The door was opened again and the butler and a footman entered bearing very heavy silver salvers.

'I always have a glass of sherry before my dinner,' said the ambassador, 'but in case you have acquired the barbarous custom of drinking cocktails I can offer you what I believe is called a dry Martini.'

Shy though he might be, Ashenden was not going to give in to this sort of thing with complete tameness.

'I move with the times,' he replied. 'To drink a glass of sherry when you can get a dry Martini is like taking a stage-coach when you can travel by the Orient Express.'

A little desultory conversation after this fashion was interrupted by the throwing open of two great doors and the announcement that His Excellency's dinner was served. They went into the dining-room. This was a vast apartment in which sixty people might have comfortably dined, but there was now only a small round table in it so that Sir Herbert and Ashenden sat intimately. There was an immense mahogany sideboard on which were massive pieces of gold plate, and above it, facing Ashenden, was a fine picture by Canaletto. Over the chimney-piece was a threequarter-length portrait of Queen Victoria as a girl with a little gold crown on her small, prim head. Dinner was served by the corpulent butler and the three very tall English footmen. Ashenden had the impression that the ambassador enjoyed in his well-bred way the sensation of ignoring the pomp in which he lived. They might have been dining in one of the great country houses of England; it was a ceremony they performed, sumptuous without ostentation, and it was saved from a trifling absurdity only because it was in a tradition; but the experience gained for Ashenden a kind of savour from the thought that dwelt with him that on the other side of the wall was a restless, turbulent population that might at any moment break into bloody revolution, while not two hundred miles away men in the trenches were sheltering in their dug-outs from the bitter cold and the pitiless bombardment.

Ashenden need not have feared that the conversation would proceed with difficulty and the notion he had had that Sir Herbert had asked him in order to question him about his secret mission was quickly dispelled. The ambassador behaved to him as though he were a travelling Englishman who had presented a letter of introduction and to whom he desired to show civility. You would hardly have thought that a war was raging, for he made to it only such references as showed that he was not deliberately avoiding a distressing subject. He spoke of art and literature, proving himself to be a diligent reader of catholic taste, and when Ashenden talked to him, from personal acquaintance, of the writers whom Sir Herbert knew only through their works, he listened with the friendly condescension which the great ones of the earth affect towards the artist. (Sometimes, however, they paint a picture or write a book, and then the artist gets a little of his own back.) He mentioned in passing a character in one of Ashenden's novels, but did not make any other reference to the fact that his guest was a writer. Ashenden admired his urbanity. He disliked people to talk to him of his books, in which indeed, once written, he took small interest, and it made him self-conscious to be praised or blamed to his face. Sir Herbert Witherspoon flattered his self-esteem by showing that he had read him, but spared his delicacy by withholding his opinion of what he had read. He spoke too of the various countries in which during his career he had been stationed and of various persons, in London and elsewhere, that he and Ashenden knew in common. He talked well, not without a pleasant irony that might very well have passed for humour, and intelligently. Ashenden did not find his dinner dull, but neither did he find it exhilarating. He would have been more interested if the ambassador had not so invariably said the right, wise, and sensible thing upon every topic that was introduced. Ashenden was finding it something of an effort to keep up with this distinction of mind and he would have liked the conversation to get into its shirt-sleeves, so to speak, and put its feet on the table. But of this there was no chance and Ashenden once or twice caught himself wondering how soon after dinner he could decently take his leave. At eleven he had an appointment with Herbartus at the Hotel de Paris.

The dinner came to an end and coffee was brought in. Sir Herbert knew good food and good wine and Ashenden was obliged to admit that he had fared excellently. Liqueurs were served with the coffee, and Ashenden took a glass of brandy.

'I have some very old Benedictine,' said the ambassador. 'Won't you try it?'

'To tell you the honest truth I think brandy is the only liqueur worth drinking.'

'I'm not sure that I don't agree with you. But in that case I must give you something better than that.'

He gave an order to the butler, who presently brought in a cobwebbed bottle and two enormous glasses.

'I don't really want to boast,' said the ambassador as he watched the butler pour the golden liquid into Ashenden's glass, 'but I venture to think that if you like brandy you'll like this. I got it when I was counsellor for a short time in Paris.'

'I've had a good deal to do lately with one of your successors then.'

'Byring?'

'Yes.'

'What do you think of the brandy?'

'I think it's marvellous.'

'And of Byring?'

The question came so oddly on the top of the other that it sounded faintly comic.

'Oh, I think he's a damned fool.'

Sir Herbert leaned back in his chair, holding the huge glass with both hands in order to bring out the aroma, and looked slowly round the stately and spacious room. The table had been cleared of superfluous things. There was a bowl of roses between Ashenden and his host. The servants switched off the electric light as they finally left the room and it was lit now only by the candles that were on the table and by the fire. Notwithstanding its size it had an air of sober comfort. The ambassador's eyes rested on the really distinguished portrait of Queen Victoria that hung over the chimney-piece.

'I wonder,' he said at last.

'He'll have to leave the diplomatic service.'

'I'm afraid so.'

Ashenden gave him a quick glance of inquiry. He was the last man from whom he would have expected sympathy for Byring.

'Yes, in the circumstances,' he proceeded, 'I suppose it's inevitable that he should leave the service. I'm sorry. He's an able fellow and he'll be missed. I think he had a career before him.'

'Yes, that is what I've heard. I'm told that at the F.O. they thought very highly of him.'

'He has many of the gifts that are useful in this rather dreary trade,' said the ambassador, with a slight smile, in his cold and judicial manner. 'He's handsome, he's a gentleman, he has nice manners, he speaks excellent French, and he has a good head on his shoulders. He'd have done well.'

'It seems a pity that he should waste such golden opportunities.'

'I understand he's going into the wine business at the end of the war. Oddly enough he's going to represent the very firm from whom I got this brandy.'

Sir Herbert raised the glass to his nose and inhaled the fragrance. Then he looked at Ashenden. He had a way of looking at people, when he was thinking of something else perhaps, that suggested that he thought them somewhat peculiar but rather disgusting insects.

'Have you ever seen the woman?' he asked.

'I dined with her and Byring at Larue's.'

'How very interesting. What is she like?'

'Charming.'

Ashenden tried to describe her to his host, but meanwhile with another part of his mind he recollected the impression she had made on him at the restaurant when Byring had introduced him to her. He had been not a little interested to meet a woman of whom for some years he had heard so much. She called herself Rose Auburn, but what her real name was few knew. She had gone to Paris originally as one of a troupe of dancers, called the Glad Girls, who performed at the Moulin Rouge, but her astonishing beauty had soon caused her to be noticed and a wealthy French manufacturer fell in love with her. He gave her a house and loaded her with jewels, but could not long meet the demands she made upon him, and she passed in rapid succession from lover to lover. She became in a short time the best-known courtesan in France. Her expenditure was prodigal and she ruined her admirers with cynical unconcern. The richest men found themselves unable to cope with her extravagance. Ashenden, before the war, had seen her once at Monte Carlo lose a hundred and eighty thousand francs at a sitting and that then was an important sum. She sat at the big table, surrounded by curious onlookers, throwing down packets of thousand-franc notes with a self-possession that would have been admirable if it had been her own money that she was losing.

When Ashenden met her she had been leading this riotous life, dancing and gambling all night, racing most afternoons a week, for twelve or thirteen years and she was no longer very young; but there was hardly a line on that lovely brow, scarcely a crow's-foot round those liquid eyes, to betray the fact. The most astonishing thing about her was that notwithstanding this feverish and unending round of senseless debauchery she had preserved an air of virginity. Of course she cultivated the type. She had an exquisitely graceful and slender figure, and her innumerable frocks were always made with a perfect simplicity. Her brown hair was very plainly done. With her oval face, charming little nose, and large blue eyes she had all the air of one or other of Anthony Trollope's charming heroines. It was the keepsake style raised to such rareness that it made you catch your breath. She had a lovely skin, very white and red, and if she painted it was not from necessity but from wantonness. She irradiated a sort of dewy innocence that was as attractive as it was unexpected.

Ashenden had heard of course that Byring for a year or more had been her lover. Her notoriety was such that a hard light of publicity was shed on everyone with whom she had any affair, but in this instance the gossips had more to say than usual because Byring had no money to speak of and Rose Auburn had never been known to grant her favours for anything that did not in some way represent hard cash. Was it possible that she loved him? It seemed incredible and yet what other explanation was there? Byring was a young man with whom any woman might have fallen in love. He was somewhere in the thirties, very tall and good-looking with a singular charm of manner and of an appearance so debonair that people turned round in the street to look at him; but unlike most handsome men he seemed entirely unaware of the impression he created. When it became known that Byring was the *amant de cœur* (a prettier phrase than our English fancy man) of this famous harlot he became an object of admiration to many women and of envy to many men; but when a rumour spread abroad that he was going to marry her consternation seized his friends and ribald laughter everyone else. It became known that Byring's chief had asked him if it was true and he had admitted it. Pressure was put upon him to relinquish a plan that could only end in disaster. It was pointed out to him that the wife of a diplomat has social obligations that Rose Auburn could not fulfil. Byring replied that he was prepared to resign his post whenever by so doing he would not cause inconvenience. He brushed aside every expostulation and every argument; he was determined to marry.

When first Ashenden met Byring he did not very much take to him. He found him slightly aloof. But as the hazards of his work brought him from time to time into contact with him he discerned that the distant manner was due merely to shyness and as he came to know him better he was charmed by the uncommon sweetness of his disposition. Their relations, however, remained purely official so that it was a trifle unexpected when Byring one day asked him to dinner to meet Miss Auburn, and he could not but wonder whether it was because already people were beginning to turn the cold shoulder on him. When he went he discovered that the invitation was due to the lady's curiosity. But the surprise he got on learning that she had found time to read (with admiration, it appeared) two or three of his novels was not the only surprise he got that evening. Leading on the whole a quiet and studious life he had never had occasion to penetrate into the world of the higher prostitution and the great courtesans of the period were known to him only by name. It was somewhat astonishing to Ashenden to discover that Rose Auburn differed so little in air and manner from the smart women of Mayfair with whom through his books he had become more or less intimately acquainted. She was perhaps a little more anxious to please (indeed one of her agreeable traits was the interest she took in whomever she was talking to), but she was certainly no more made-up and her conversation was as intelligent. It lacked only the coarseness that society has lately affected. Perhaps she felt instinctively that those lovely lips should never disfigure themselves with foul words; perhaps only she was at heart still a trifle suburban. It was evident that she and Byring were madly in love with one another. It was really moving to see their mutual passion. When Ashenden took his leave of them, as he shook hands with her (and she held his hand a moment and with her blue, starry eyes looked into his) she said to him:

'You will come and see us when we're settled in London, won't you? You know we're going to be married.'

'I heartily congratulate you,' said Ashenden.

'And him?' she smiled, and her smile was like an angel's; it had the freshness of dawn and the tender rapture of a southern spring.

'Have you never looked at yourself in the glass?'

Sir Herbert Witherspoon watched him intently while Ashenden (he thought not without a trace of humour) was describing the dinner-party. No flicker of a smile brightened his cold eyes.

'Do you think it'll be a success?' he asked now.

'No.'

'Why not?'

The question took Ashenden aback.

'A man not only marries his wife, he marries her friends. Do you realize the sort of people Byring will have to mix with, painted women of tarnished reputation and men who've gone down in the social scale, parasites and adventurers? Of course they'll have money, her pearls must be worth a hundred thousand pounds, and they'll be able to cut a dash in the smart Bohemia of London. Do you know the gold fringe of society? When a woman of bad character marries she earns the admiration of her set, she has worked the trick, she's caught a man and become respectable, but he, the man, only earns its ridicule. Even her own friends, the old hags with their gigolos and the abject men who earn a shabby living by introducing the unwary to tradesmen on a ten per cent commission, even they despise him. He is the mug. Believe me, to conduct yourself gracefully in such a position you need either great dignity of character or an unparalleled effrontery. Besides, do you think there's a chance of its lasting? Can a woman who's led that wild career settle down to domestic life? In a little while she'll grow bored and restless. And how long does love last? Don't you think Byring's reflections will be bitter when, caring for her no longer, he compares what he is with what he might have been?'

Witherspoon helped himself to another drop of his old brandy. Then he looked up at Ashenden with a curious expression.

'I'm not sure if a man isn't wiser to do what he wants very much to do and let the consequences take care of themselves.'

'It must be very pleasant to be an ambassador,' said Ashenden.

Sir Herbert smiled thinly.

'Byring rather reminds me of a fellow I knew when I was a very junior clerk at the F.O. I won't tell you his name because he's by way of being very well-known now and highly respected. He's made a great success of his career. There is always something a little absurd in success.'

Ashenden slightly raised his eyebrows at this statement, somewhat unexpected in the mouth of Sir Herbert Witherspoon, but did not say anything.

'He was one of my fellow-clerks. He was a brilliant creature, I don't think anyone ever denied that, and everyone prophesied from the beginning that he would go far. I venture to say that he had pretty well all the qualifications necessary for a diplomatic career. He was of a family of soldiers and sailors, nothing very grand, but eminently respectable, and he knew how to behave in the great world without bumptiousness or timidity. He was well-read. He took an interest in painting. I dare say he made himself a trifle ridiculous; he wanted to be in the movement, he was very anxious to be modern, and at a time when little was known of Gauguin and Cézanne he raved over their pictures. There was perhaps a certain snobbishness in his attitude, a desire to shock and astonish the conventional, but at heart his admiration of the arts was genuine and sincere. He adored Paris and whenever he had the chance ran over and put up at a little hotel in the Latin Quarter, where he could rub shoulders with painters and writers. As is the habit with gentry of that sort they patronized him a little because he was nothing but a diplomat and laughed at him a little because he was evidently a gentleman. But they liked him because he was always ready to listen to their speeches, and when he praised their works they were even willing to admit that, although a philistine, he had a certain instinct for the Right Stuff.'

Ashenden noted the sarcasm and smiled at the fling at his own profession. He wondered what this long description was leading to. The ambassador seemed to linger over it partly because he liked it, but also because for some reason he hesitated to come to the point.

'But my friend was modest. He enjoyed himself enormously and he listened open-mouthed when these young painters and unknown scribblers tore to pieces established reputations and talked with enthusiasm of persons of whom the sober but cultured secretaries in Downing Street had never even heard. At the back of his mind he knew that they were rather a common, second-rate lot, and when he went back to his work in London it was with no regret, but with the feeling that he had been witnessing an odd and diverting play; now the curtain had fallen he was quite ready to go home. I haven't told you that he was ambitious. He knew that his friends expected him to do considerable things and he had no notion of disappointing them. He was perfectly conscious of his abilities. He meant to succeed. Unfortunately he was not rich, he had only a few hundreds a year, but his father and mother were dead and he had neither brother nor sister. He was aware that this freedom from close ties was an asset. His opportunity to make connexions that would be of use to him was unrestricted. Do you think he sounds a very disagreeable young man?'

'No,' said Ashenden in answer to the sudden question. 'Most clever young men are aware of their cleverness, and there is generally a certain cynicism in their calculations with regard to the future. Surely young men should be ambitious.'

'Well, on one of these little trips to Paris my friend became acquainted with a talented young Irish painter called O'Malley. He's an R.A. now and paints highly-paid portraits of Lord Chancellors and Cabinet Ministers. I wonder if you remember one he did of my wife, which was exhibited a couple of years ago.'

'No, I don't. But I know his name.'

'My wife was delighted with it. His art always seems to me very refined and agreeable. He's able to put on canvas the distinction of his sitters in a very remarkable way. When he paints a woman of breeding, you know that it is a woman of breeding and not a trollop.'

'It is a charming gift,' said Ashenden. 'Can he also paint a slut and make her look like one?'

'He could. Now doubtless he would scarcely wish to. He was living then in a small and dirty studio in the rue du Cherche Midi with a little Frenchwoman of the character you describe and he painted several portraits of her which were extremely like.'

It seemed to Ashenden that Sir Herbert was going into somewhat excessive detail, and he asked himself whether the friend of whom he was telling a story that till now seemed to lead no-whither was in point of fact himself. He began to give it more of his attention.

'My friend liked O'Malley. He was good company, the type of the agreeable rattle, and he had a truly Irish gift of the gab. He talked incessantly and in my friend's opinion brilliantly. He found it very amusing to go and sit in the studio while O'Malley was painting and listen to him chattering away about the technique of his art. O'Malley was always saying that he would paint a portrait of him and his vanity was tickled. O'Malley thought him far from plain and said it would do him good to exhibit the portrait of someone who at least looked like a gentleman.'

'By the way, when was all this?' asked Ashenden.

'Oh, thirty years ago. . . . They used to talk of their future and when O'Malley said the portrait he was going to paint of my friend would look very well in the National Portrait Gallery, my friend had small doubt in the back of his mind, whatever he modestly said, that it would eventually find its way there. One evening when my friend–shall we call him Brown?–was sitting in the studio and O'Malley, desperately taking advantage of the last light of day, was trying to get finished for the Salon that portrait of his mistress which is now in the Tate Gallery, O'Malley asked him if he would like to come and dine with them. He was expecting a friend of hers, she was called Yvonne by the way, and he would be glad if Brown would make a fourth. This friend of Yvonne's was an acrobat and O'Malley was anxious to get her to pose for him in the nude. Yvonne said she had a marvellous figure. She had seen O'Malley's work and was willing enough to sit and dinner was to be devoted to settling the matter. She was not performing then, but was about to open at the Gaietés Montparnasses and with her days free was not disinclined to oblige a friend and earn a little money. The notion amused Brown, who had never met an acrobat, and he accepted. Yvonne suggested that he might find her to his taste and if he did she could promise him that he would not find her very difficult to persuade. With his grand air and English clothes she would take him for a *milord anglais*. My friend laughed. He did not take the suggestion very seriously. "*On ne sait jamais,*" he said. Yvonne looked at him with mischievous eyes. He sat on. It was Easter time and cold, but the studio was comfortably warm, and though it was small and everything was higgledy-piggledy and the dust lay heavy on the rim of the window, it was most friendly and cosy. Brown had a tiny flat in Waverton Street, in London, with very good mezzotints on the walls and several pieces of early Chinese pottery here and there, and he wondered to himself why his tasteful sitting-room had none of the comforts of home nor the romance that he found in that disorderly studio.

'Presently there was a ring at the door and Yvonne ushered in her friend. Her name, it appeared, was Alix, and she shook hands with Brown, uttering a stereotyped phrase, with the mincing politeness of a fat woman in a *bureau de tabac*. She wore a long cloak in imitation mink and an enormous scarlet hat. She looked incredibly vulgar. She was not even pretty. She had a broad flat face, a wide mouth and an upturned nose. She had a great deal of hair, golden, but obviously dyed, and large china-blue eyes. She was heavily made-up.'

Ashenden began to have no doubt that Witherspoon was narrating an experience of his own, for otherwise he could never have remembered after thirty years what hat the young woman wore and what coat, and he was amused at the ambassador's simplicity in thinking that so thin a subterfuge could disguise the truth. Ashenden could not but guess how the story would end and it tickled him to think that this cold, distinguished, and exquisite person should ever have had anything like an adventure.

'She began to talk away to Yvonne, and my friend noticed that she had one feature that oddly enough he found very attractive: she had a deep and husky voice as though she were just recovering from a bad cold and, he didn't know why, it seemed to him exceedingly pleasant to listen to. He asked O'Malley if that was her natural voice and O'Malley said she had had it as long as ever he had known her. He called it a whisky voice. He told her what Brown said about it and she gave him a smile of her wide mouth and said it wasn't due to drink, it was due to standing so much on her head. That was one of the inconveniences of her profession. Then the four of them went to a beastly little restaurant off the boulevard St Michel where for two francs fifty including wine my friend ate a dinner that seemed to him more delicious than any he had ever eaten at the Savoy or Claridge's. Alix was a very chatty young person and Brown listened with amusement, with amazement even, while in her rich, throaty voice she talked of the varied incidents of the day. She had a great command of slang, and, though he could not understand half of it, he was immensely tickled with its picturesque vulgarity. It was pungent of the heated asphalt, the zinc bars of cheap taverns, and racy of the crowded squares in the poorer districts of Paris. There was an energy in those apt and vivid metaphors that went like champagne to his anaemic head. She was a guttersnipe, yes, that's what she was, but she had a vitality that warmed you like a blazing fire. He was conscious that Yvonne had told her that he was an unattached Englishman, with plenty of money; he saw the appraising glance she gave him and then, pretending that he had noticed nothing, he caught the phrase, *il n'est pas mal.* It faintly amused him: he had a notion himself that he was not so bad. There were places, indeed, where they went farther than that. She did not pay much attention to him, in point of fact they were talking of things of which he was ignorant and he could do little more than show an intelligent interest, but now and again she gave him a long look, passing her tongue quickly round her lips, that suggested to him that he only had to ask for her to give. He shrugged a mental shoulder. She looked healthy and young, she had an agreeable vivacity, but beyond her husky voice there was nothing particularly attractive in her. But the notion of having a little affair in Paris did not displease him, it was life, and the thought that she was a music-hall artiste was mildly diverting: in middle age it would doubtless amuse him to remember that he had enjoyed the favours of an acrobat. Was it la Rochefoucauld or Oscar Wilde who said that you should commit errors in youth in order to have something to regret in old age? At the end of dinner (and they sat over their coffee and brandy till late), they went out into the street and Yvonne proposed that he should take Alix home. He said he would be delighted. Alix said it was not far and they walked. She told him that she had a little apartment, of course mostly she was on tour, but she liked to have a place of her own, a woman, you know, had to be in her furniture, without that she received no consideration; and presently they reached a shabby house in a bedraggled street. She rang the bell for the *concierge* to open the door. She did not press him to enter. He did not know if she looked upon it as a matter of course. He was seized with timidity. He racked his brains, but could not think of a single thing to say. Silence fell upon them. It was absurd. With a little click the door opened; she looked at him expectantly; she was puzzled; a wave of shyness swept over him. Then she held out her hand, thanked him for bringing her to the door, and bade him good night. His heart beat nervously. If she had asked him to come in he would have gone. He wanted some sign that she would like him to. He shook her hand, said good night, raised his hat and walked away.

He felt a perfect fool. He could not sleep; he tossed from side to side of his bed, thinking what a noodle she must take him for, and he could hardly wait for the day that would permit him to take steps to efface the contemptible impression he must have made on her. His pride was lacerated. Wanting to lose no time he went round to her house at eleven to ask her to lunch with him, but she was out; he sent round some flowers and later in the day called again. She had been in, but was gone out once more. He went to see O'Malley on the chance of finding her, but she was not there, and O'Malley facetiously asked him how he had fared. To save his face he told him that he had come to the conclusion that she did not mean very much to him and so like a perfect gentleman he had left her. But he had an uneasy feeling that O'Malley saw through his story. He sent her a *pneumatique* asking her to dine with him next day. She did not answer. He could not understand it, he asked the porter of his hotel a dozen times if there was nothing for him, and at last, almost in desperation, just before dinner went to her house. The *concierge* told him she was in and he went up. He was very nervous, inclined to be angry because she had treated his invitation so cavalierly, but at the same time anxious to appear at his ease. He climbed the four flights of stairs, dark and smelly, and rang at the door to which he had been directed. There was a pause, he heard sounds within and rang again. Presently she opened. He had an absolute certitude that she did not in the least know who he was. He was taken aback, it was a blow to his vanity; but he assumed a cheerful smile.

"'I came to find out if you were going to dine with me tonight. I sent you a *pneumatique.*"

'Then she recognized him. But she stood at the door and did not ask him in.

"'Oh, no, I can't dine with you tonight. I have a terrible megrim and I am going to bed. I couldn't answer your *pneumatique,* I mislaid it, and I'd forgotten your name. Thank you for the flowers. It was nice of you to send them."

"'Then won't you come and dine with me tomorrow night?"

"'*Justement*, I have an engagement tomorrow night. I'm sorry."

'There was nothing more to say. He had not the nerve to ask her anything else and so bade her good night and went. He had the impression that she was not vexed with him, but that she had entirely forgotten him. It was humiliating. When he went back to London without having seen her again, it was with a curious sense of dissatisfaction. He was not in the least in love with her, he was annoyed with her, but he could not get her quite out of his mind. He was honest enough to realize that he was suffering from nothing more than a wounded vanity.

'During that dinner at the little restaurant off the Boul' Mich' she had mentioned that her troupe was going to London in the spring, and in one of his letters to O'Malley he slipped in casually a phrase to the effect that if his young friend Alix happened to be coming to town he (O'Malley) might let him know and he would look her up. He would like to hear from her own ingenuous lips what she thought of the nude O'Malley had painted of her. When the painter some time afterwards wrote and told him that she was appearing a week later at the Metropolitan in the Edgware Road, he felt a sudden rush of blood to his head. He went to see her play. If he had not taken the precaution to go earlier in the day and look at the programme he would have missed her, for her turn was the first on the list. There were two men, a stout one and a thin one, with large black moustaches, and Alix. They were dressed in ill-fitting pink tights with green satin trunks. The men did various exercises on twin trapezes while Alix tripped about the stage, giving them handkerchiefs to wipe their hands on, and occasionally turned a somersault. When the fat man raised the thin one on his shoulders she climbed up and stood on the shoulders of the second, kissing her hand to the audience. They did tricks with safety bicycles. There is often grace, and even beauty, in the performance of clever acrobats, but this one was so crude, so vulgar that my friend felt positively embarrassed. There is something shameful in seeing grown men publicly make fools of themselves. Poor Alix, with a fixed and artificial smile on her lips, in her pink tights and green satin trunks, was so grotesque that he wondered how he could have let himself feel a moment's annoyance because when he went to her apartment she had not recognized him. It was with a shrug of the shoulders, condescendingly, that he went round to the stage door afterwards and gave the doorkeeper a shilling to take her his card. In a few minutes she came out. She seemed delighted to see him.

'"Oh, how good it is to see the face of someone you know in this sad city," she said. "Ah, now you can give me that dinner you asked me to in Paris. I'm dying of hunger. I never eat before the show. Imagine that they should have given us such a bad place on the programme. It's an insult. But we shall see the agent tomorrow. If they think they can put upon us like that they are mistaken. *Ah, non, non et non!* And what an audience! No enthusiasm, no applause, nothing."

'My friend was staggered. Was it possible that she took her performance seriously? He almost burst out laughing. But she still spoke with that throaty voice that had such a queer effect on his nerves. She was dressed all in red and wore the same red hat in which he had first seen her. She looked so flashy that he did not fancy the notion of asking her to a place where he might be seen, and so suggested Soho. There were hansoms still in those days, and the hansom was more conducive to love-making, I imagine, than is the taxi of the present time. My friend put his arm round Alix's waist and kissed her. It left her calm, but on the other hand did not wildly excite him. While they ate a late dinner he made himself very gallant and she played up to him agreeably; but when they got up to go and he proposed that she should come round to his rooms in Waverton Street she told him that a friend had come over from Paris with her and that she had to meet him at eleven: she had only been able to dine with Brown because her companion had a business engagement. Brown was exasperated, but did not want to show it, and when, as they walked down Wardour Street (for she said she wanted to go to the Café Monico), pausing in front of a pawnbroker's to look at the jewellery in the window, she went into ecstasies over a bracelet of sapphires and diamonds that Brown thought incredibly vulgar, he asked her if she would like it.

'"But it's marked fifteen pounds," she said.

'He went in and bought it for her. She was delighted. She made him leave her just before they came to Piccadilly Circus.

'"Now listen, *mon petit*," she said, "I cannot see you in London because of my friend, he is jealous as a wolf, that is why I think it is more prudent for you to go now, but I am playing at Boulogne next week, why do you not come over? I shall be alone there. My friend has to go back to Holland, where he lives."

'"All right," said Brown, "I'll come."

'When he went to Boulogne—he had two days' leave—it was with the one idea of salving the wound to his pride. It was odd that he should care. I dare say to you it seems inexplicable. He could not bear the notion that Alix looked upon him as a fool, and he felt that when once he had removed that impression from her he would never bother about her again. He thought of O'Malley too, and of Yvonne. She must have told them, and it galled him to think that people whom in his heart he despised should laugh at him behind his back. Do you think he was very contemptible?'

'Good gracious, no,' said Ashenden. 'All sensible people know that vanity is the most devastating, the most universal, and the most ineradicable of the passions that afflict the soul of man, and it is only vanity that makes him deny its power. It is more consuming than love. With advancing years, mercifully, you can snap your fingers at the terror and the servitude of love, but age cannot free you from the thraldom of vanity. Time can assuage the pangs of love, but only death can still the anguish of wounded vanity. Love is simple and seeks no subterfuge, but vanity cozens you with a hundred disguises. It is part and parcel of every virtue: it is the mainspring of courage and the strength of ambition; it gives constancy to the lover and endurance to the stoic; it adds fuel to the fire of the artist's desire for fame and is at once the support and the compensation of the honest man's integrity; it leers even cynically in the humility of the saint. You cannot escape it, and should you take pains to guard against it, it will make use of those very pains to trip you up. You are defenceless against its onslaught because you know not on what unprotected side it will attack you. Sincerity cannot protect you from its snare nor humour from its mockery.'

Ashenden stopped, not because he had said all he had to say, but because he was out of breath. He noticed also that the ambassador, desiring to talk rather than to listen, heard him with a politeness that was strained. But he had made this speech not so much for his host's edification as for his own entertainment.

'It is vanity finally that makes man support his abominable lot.'

For a minute Sir Herbert was silent. He looked straight in front of him as though his thoughts lingered distressfully on some far horizon of memory.

'When my friend came back from Boulogne he knew that he was madly in love with Alix and he had arranged to meet her again in a fortnight's time when she would be performing at Dunkirk. He thought of nothing else in the interval, and the night before he was to start, he only had thirty-six hours this time, he could not sleep, so devouring was the passion that consumed him. Then he went over for a night to Paris to see her, and once when she was disengaged for a week he persuaded her to come to London. He knew that she did not love him. He was just a man among a hundred others and she made no secret of the fact that he was not her only lover. He suffered agonies of jealousy but knew that it would only excite her ridicule or her anger if he showed it. She had not even a fancy for him. She liked him because he was a gentleman and well dressed. She was quite willing to be his mistress so long as the claims he made on her were not irksome. But that was all. His means were not large enough to enable him to make her any serious offers, but even if they had been, liking her freedom, she would have refused.'

'But what about the Dutchman?' asked Ashenden.

'The Dutchman? He was a pure invention. She made him up on the spur of the moment because for one reason or another she did not just then want to be bothered with Brown. What should one lie more or less matter to her? Don't think he didn't struggle against his passion. He knew it was madness; he knew that a permanent connexion between them could only lead to disaster for him. He had no illusions about her; she was common, coarse, and vulgar. She could talk of none of the things that interested him, nor did she try, she took it for granted that he was concerned with her affairs and told him interminable stories of her quarrels with fellow-performers, her disputes with managers, and her wrangles with hotel-keepers. What she said bored him to death, but the sound of her throaty voice made his heart beat so that sometimes he thought he would suffocate.'

Ashenden sat uneasily in his chair. It was a Sheraton chair very good to look at, but hard and straight; and he wished that Sir Herbert had had the notion of going back to the other room where there was a comfortable sofa. It was quite plain now that the story he was telling was about himself, and Ashenden felt a certain indelicacy in the man's stripping his soul before him so nakedly. He did not desire this confidence to be forced upon him. Sir Herbert Witherspoon meant nothing to him. By the light of the shaded candles Ashenden saw that he was deathly pale and there was a wildness in his eyes that in that cold and composed man was strangely disconcerting. He poured himself out a glass of water; his throat was dry so that he could hardly speak. But he went on pitilessly.

'At last my friend managed to pull himself together. He was disgusted by the sordidness of his intrigue; there was no beauty in it, nothing but shame; and it was leading to nothing. His passion was as vulgar as the woman for whom he felt it. Now it happened that Alix was going to spend six months in the North of Africa with her troupe and for that time at least it would be impossible for him to see her. He made up his mind that he must seize the opportunity and make a definite break. He knew bitterly that it would mean nothing to her. In three weeks she would have forgotten him.

'And then there was something else. He had come to know very well some people, a man and his wife, whose social and political connexions were extremely important. They had an only daughter and, I don't know why, she fell in love with him. She was everything that Alix was not, pretty in the real English way, with blue eyes and pink and white cheeks, tall and fair; she might have stepped out of one of du Maurier's pictures in *Punch*. She was clever and well-read, and since she had lived all her life in political circles she could talk intelligently of the sort of things that interested him. He had reason to believe that if he asked her to marry him she would accept. I have told you that he was ambitious. He knew that he had great abilities and he wanted the chance to use them. She was related to some of the greatest families in England and he would have been a fool not to realize that a marriage of this kind must make his path infinitely easier. The opportunity was golden. And what a relief to think that he could put behind him definitely that ugly little episode, and what a happiness, instead of that wall of cheerful indifference and matter-of-fact good nature against which in his passion for Alix he had vainly battered his head, what a happiness to feel that to someone else he really meant something! How could he help being flattered and touched when he saw her face light up as he came into the room? He wasn't in love with her, but he thought her charming, and he wanted to forget Alix and the vulgar life into which she had led him. At last he made up his mind. He asked her to marry him and was accepted. Her family was delighted. The marriage was to take place in the autumn, since her father had to go on some political errand to South America and was taking his wife and daughter with him. They were to be gone the whole summer. My friend Brown was transferring from the F.O. to the diplomatic service and had been promised a post at Lisbon. He was to go there immediately.

'He saw his fiancée off. Then it happened that owing to some hitch the man

whom Brown was going to replace was kept at Lisbon three months longer and
so for that period my friend found himself at a loose end. And just when he was
making up his mind what to do with himself he received a letter from Alix. She
was coming back to France and had a tour booked; she gave him a long list of
the places she was going to, and in her casual, friendly way said that they would
have fun if he could manage to run over for a day or two. An insane, a criminal
notion seized him. If she had shown any eagerness for him to come he might have
resisted, it was her airy, matter-of-fact indifference that took him. On a sudden
he longed for her. He did not care if she was gross and vulgar, he had got her in
his bones, and it was his last chance. In a little while he was going to be married.
It was now or never. He went down to Marseilles and met her as she stepped off
the boat that had brought her from Tunis. His heart leaped at the pleasure she
showed on seeing him. He knew he loved her madly. He told her that he was
going to be married in three months and asked her to spend the last of his
freedom with him. She refused to abandon her tour. How could she leave her
companions in the lurch? He offered to compensate them, but she would not
hear of it; they could not find someone to take her place at a moment's notice,
nor could they afford to throw over a good engagement that might lead to
others in the future; they were honest people, and they kept their word, they
had their duty to their managers and their duty to their public. He was
exasperated; it seemed absurd that his whole happiness should be sacrificed to
that wretched tour. And at the end of the three months? What was to happen to
her then? Oh, no, he was asking something that wasn't reasonable. He told her
that he adored her. He did not know till then how insanely he loved her. Well,
then, she said, why did he not come with her and make the tour with them? She
would be glad of his company; they could have a good time together and at the
end of three months he could go and marry his heiress and neither of them
would be any the worse. For a moment he hesitated, but now that he saw her
again he could not bear the thought of being parted from her so soon. He
accepted. And then she said:

'"But listen, my little one, you mustn't be silly, you know. The managers
won't be too pleased with me if I make a lot of *chichi*, I have to think of my
future, and they won't be so anxious to have me back if I refuse to please old
customers of the house. It won't be very often, but it must be understood that
you are not to make me scenes if now and then I give myself to someone whose
fancy I take. It will mean nothing, that is business, you will be my *amant de
cœur*."

'He felt a strange, excruciating pain in his heart, and I think he went so pale
that she thought he was going to faint. She looked at him curiously.

'"Those are the terms," she said. "You can either take them or leave them."

'He accepted.'

Sir Herbert Witherspoon leaned forward in his chair and he was so white
that Ashenden thought too that he was going to faint. His skin was drawn over
his skull so that his face looked like a death's head, but the veins on his forehead
stood out like knotted cords. He had lost all reticence. And Ashenden once
more wished that he would stop, it made him shy and nervous to see the man's
naked soul: no one has the right to show himself to another in that destitute
state. He was inclined to cry:

'Stop, stop. You mustn't tell me any more. You'll be so ashamed.'

But the man had lost all shame.

'For three months they travelled together from one dull provincial town to another, sharing a filthy little bedroom in frowzy hotels; Alix would not let him take her to good hotels, she said she had not the clothes for them and she was more comfortable in the sort of hotel she was used to; she did not want her companions in the business to say that she was putting on side. He sat interminable hours in shabby cafés. He was treated as a brother by members of the troupe, they called him by his Christian name and chaffed him coarsely and slapped him on the back. He ran errands for them when they were busy with their work. He saw the good-humoured contempt in the eyes of managers and was obliged to put up with the familiarity of stagehands. They travelled third-class from place to place and he helped to carry the luggage. He with whom reading was a passion never opened a book because Alix was bored by reading and thought that anyone who did was just giving himself airs. Every night he went to the music-hall and watched her go through that grotesque and ignoble performance. He had to fall in with her pathetic fancy that it was artistic. He had to congratulate her when it had gone well and condole with her when some feat of agility had gone amiss. When she had finished he went to a café and waited for her while she changed, and sometimes she would come in rather hurriedly and say:

'"Don't wait for me tonight, *mon chou*, I'm busy."

'And then he would undergo agonies of jealousy. He would suffer as he never knew a man could suffer. She would come back to the hotel at three or four in the morning. She wondered why he was not asleep. Sleep! How could he sleep with that misery gnawing at his heart? He had promised he would not interfere with her. He did not keep his promise. He made her terrific scenes. Sometimes he beat her. Then she would lose her patience and tell him she was sick of him, she would pack her things to go, and then he would go grovelling to her, promising anything, any submission, vowing to swallow any humiliation, if she would not leave him. It was horrible and degrading. He was miserable. Miserable? No, he was happier than he'd ever been in his life. It was the gutter that he wallowed in, but he wallowed in it with delight. Oh, he was so bored with the life he'd led hitherto, and this one seemed to him amazing and romantic. This was reality. And that frowzy, ugly woman with the whisky voice, she had such a splendid vitality, such a zest for life that she seemed to raise his own to some more vivid level. It really did seem to him to burn with a pure, gem-like flame. Do people still read Pater?'

'I don't know,' said Ashenden. 'I don't.'

'There was only three months of it. Oh, how short the time seemed and how quickly the weeks sped by! Sometimes he had wild dreams of abandoning everything and throwing in his lot with the acrobats. They had come to have quite a liking for him and they said he could easily train himself to take a part in the turn. He knew they said it more in jest than in earnest, but the notion vaguely tickled him. But these were only dreams and he knew that nothing would come of them. He never really chaffered with the thought that when the three months came to an end he would not return to his own life with its obligations. With his mind, that cold, logical mind of his, he knew it would be absurd to sacrifice everything for a woman like Alix; he was ambitious, he wanted power; and besides, he could not break the heart of that poor child who loved and trusted him. She wrote to him once a week. She was longing to get back, the time seemed endless to her and he, he had a secret wish that something would happen to delay her arrival. If he could only have a little more time! Perhaps if he had six months he would have got over his infatuation.

Already sometimes he hated Alix.

'The last day came. They seemed to have little to say to one another. They were both sad; but he knew that Alix only regretted the breaking of an agreeable habit, in twenty-four hours she would be as gay and full of spirits with her stray companion as though he had never crossed her path; he could only think that next day he was going to Paris to meet his fiancée and her family. They spent their last night in one another's arms weeping. If she'd asked him then not to leave her it may be that he would have stayed; but she didn't, it never occurred to her, she accepted his going as a settled thing, and she wept not because she loved him, she wept because he was unhappy.

'In the morning she was sleeping so soundly that he had not the heart to wake her to say good-bye. He slipped out very quietly, with his bag in his hand, and took the train to Paris.'

Ashenden turned away his head, for he saw two tears form themselves in Witherspoon's eyes and roll down his cheeks. He did not even try to hide them. Ashenden lit another cigar.

'In Paris they cried out when they saw him. They said he looked like a ghost. He told them he'd been ill and hadn't said anything about it in order not to worry them. They were very kind. A month later he was married. He did very well for himself. He was given opportunities to distinguish himself and he distinguished himself. His rise was spectacular. He had the well-ordered and distinguished establishment that he had wanted. He had the power for which he had craved. He was loaded with honours. Oh, he made a success of life and there were hundreds who envied him. It was all ashes. He was bored, bored to distraction, bored by that distinguished, beautiful lady he had married, bored by the people his life forced him to live with; it was a comedy he was playing and sometimes it seemed intolerable to live for ever and ever behind a mask, sometimes he felt he couldn't bear it. But he bore it. Sometimes he longed for Alix so fiercely that he felt it would be better to shoot himself than to suffer such anguish. He never saw her again. Never. He heard from O'Malley that she had married and left her troupe. She must be a fat old woman now and it doesn't matter any more. But he had wasted his life. And he never even made that poor creature whom he married happy. How could he go on hiding from her year after year that he had nothing to give her but pity? Once in his agony he told her about Alix and she tortured him ever after with her jealousy. He knew that he should never have married her; in six months she would have got over her grief if he had told her he could not bear to, and in the end would have happily married somebody else. So far as she was concerned his sacrifice was vain. He was terribly conscious that he had only one life and it seemed so sad to think that he had wasted it. He could never surmount his immeasurable regret. He laughed when people spoke of him as a strong man: he was as weak and unstable as water. And that's why I tell you that Byring is right. Even though it only lasts five years, even though he ruins his career, even though this marriage of his ends in disaster, it will have been worth while. He will have been satisfied. He will have fulfilled himself.'

At that moment the door opened and a lady came in. The ambassador glanced at her and for an instant a look of cold hatred crossed his face, but it was only for an instant; then, rising from the table, he composed his ravaged features to an expression of courteous suavity. He gave the incomer a haggard smile.

'Here is my wife. This is Mr Ashenden.'

'I couldn't imagine where you were. Why didn't you go and sit in your study? I'm sure Mr Ashenden's been dreadfully uncomfortable.'

She was a tall, thin woman of fifty, rather drawn and faded, but she looked as though she had once been pretty. It was obvious that she was very well-bred. She vaguely reminded you of an exotic plant, reared in a hot-house, that had begun to lose its bloom. She was dressed in black.

'What was the concert like?' asked Sir Herbert.

'Oh, not bad at all. They gave a Brahms Concerto and the Fire-music from the *Walküre*, and some Hungarian dances of Dvořák. I thought them rather showy.' She turned to Ashenden. 'I hope you haven't been bored all alone with my husband. What have you been talking about? Art and Literature?'

'No, its raw material,' said Ashenden.

He took his leave.

Mr Harrington's Washing

◆

When Ashenden went on deck and saw before him a low-lying coast and a white town he felt a pleasant flutter of excitement. It was early and the sun had not long risen, but the sea was glassy and the sky was blue; it was warm already and one knew that the day would be sweltering. Vladivostok. It really gave one the sensation of being at the end of the world. It was a long journey that Ashenden had made from New York to San Francisco, across the Pacific in a Japanese boat to Yokohama, then from Tsuruki in a Russian boat, he the only Englishman on board, up the Sea of Japan. From Vladivostok he was to take the Trans-Siberian to Petrograd. It was the most important mission that he had ever had and he was pleased with the sense of responsibility that it gave him. He had no one to give him orders, unlimited funds (he carried in a belt next to his skin bills of exchange for a sum so enormous that he was staggered when he thought of them), and though he had been set to do something that was beyond human possibility he did not know this and was prepared to set about his task with confidence. He believed in his own astuteness. Though he had both esteem and admiration for the sensibility of the human race, he had little respect for their intelligence: man has always found it easier to sacrifice his life than to learn the multiplication table.

Ashenden did not much look forward to ten days on a Russian train, and in Yokohama he had heard rumours that in one or two places bridges had been blown up and the line cut. He was told that the soldiers, completely out of hand, would rob him of everything he possessed and turn him out on the steppe to shift for himself. It was a cheerful prospect. But the train was certainly starting and whatever happened later (and Ashenden had always a feeling that things never turned out as badly as you expected) he was determined to get a place on it. His intention on landing was to go at once to the British Consulate and find out what arrangements had been made for him; but as they neared the shore and he was able to discern the untidy and bedraggled town he felt not a little forlorn. He knew but a few words of Russian. The only man on the ship who spoke English was the purser and though he promised Ashenden to do anything he could to help him, Ashenden had the impression that he must not too greatly count upon him. It was a relief then, when they docked, to have a young man, small and with a mop of untidy hair, obviously a Jew, come up to him and ask if his name was Ashenden.

'Mine is Benedict. I'm the interpreter at the British Consulate. I've been told to look after you. We've got a place on the train tonight.'

Ashenden's spirits went up. They landed. The little Jew looked after his luggage and had his passport examined and then, getting into a car that waited for them, they drove off to the Consulate.

'I've had instructions to offer you every facility,' said the Consul, 'and you've only got to tell me what you want. I've fixed you up all right on the train, but God knows if you'll ever get to Petrograd. Oh, by the way, I've got a travelling companion for you. He's a man called Harrington, an American, and he's going to Petrograd for a firm in Philadelphia. He's trying to fix up some deal with the Provisional Government.'

'What's he like?' asked Ashenden.

'Oh, he's all right. I wanted him to come with the American Consul to luncheon, but they've gone for an excursion in the country. You must get to the station a couple of hours before the train starts. There's always an awful scrimmage and if you're not there in good time someone will pinch your seat.'

The train started at midnight and Ashenden dined with Benedict at the station restaurant, which was, it appeared, the only place in that slatternly town where you could get a decent meal. It was crowded. The service was intolerably slow. Then they went on to the platform, where, though they had still two hours to spare, there was already a seething mob. Whole families, sitting on piles of luggage, seemed to be camped there. People rushed to and fro, or stood in little groups violently arguing. Women screamed. Others were silently weeping. Here two men were engaged in a fierce quarrel. It was a scene of indescribable confusion. The light in the station was wan and cold and the white faces of all those people were like the white faces of the dead waiting, patient or anxious, distraught or penitent, for the judgement of the last day. The train was made up and most of the carriages were already filled to overflowing. When at last Benedict found that in which Ashenden had his place a man sprang out of it excitedly.

'Come in and sit down,' he said. 'I've had the greatest difficulty in keeping your seat. A fellow wanted to come in here with a wife and two children. My Consul has just gone off with him to see the stationmaster.'

'This is Mr Harrington,' said Benedict.

Ashenden stepped into the carriage. It had two berths in it. The porter stowed his luggage away. He shook hands with his travelling companion.

Mr John Quincy Harrington was a very thin man of somewhat less than middle height. He had a yellow, bony face, with large, pale-blue eyes, and when he took off his hat to wipe his brow wet from perturbation he had endured he showed a large, bald skull; it was very bony and the ridges and protuberances stood out disconcertingly. He wore a bowler-hat, a black coat and waistcoat, and a pair of striped trousers; a very high white collar, and a neat, unobtrusive tie. Ashenden did not know precisely how you should dress in order to take a ten days' journey across Siberia, but he could not but think that Mr Harrington's costume was eccentric. He spoke with precision in a high-pitched voice and in an accent that Ashenden recognized as that of New England.

In a minute the stationmaster came accompanied by a bearded Russian, suffering evidently from profound emotion, and followed by a lady holding two children by the hand. The Russian, tears running down his face, was talking with quivering lips to the stationmaster, and his wife between her sobs was apparently telling him the story of her life. When they arrived at the carriage the altercation became more violent and Benedict joined in with his fluent Russian. Mr Harrington did not know a word of the language, but being obviously of an excitable turn broke in and explained in voluble English that these seats had been booked by the Consuls of Great Britain and the United States respectively, and though he didn't know about the King of England, he could tell them straight and they could take it from him that the President of the United States would never permit an American citizen to be done out of a seat on the train that he had duly paid for. He would yield to force, but to nothing else, and if they touched him he would register a complaint with the Consul at once. He said all this and a great deal more to the stationmaster, who of course had no notion what he was talking about, but with much emphasis and a good deal of gesticulation made him in reply a passionate speech. This roused Mr Harrington to the utmost pitch of indignation, for shaking his fist in the stationmaster's face, his own pale with fury, he cried out:

'Tell him I don't understand a word he says and I don't want to understand. If the Russians want us to look upon them as a civilized people, why don't they talk a civilized language? Tell him that I am Mr John Quincy Harrington and I'm travelling on behalf of Messrs Crew and Adams of Philadelphia with a special letter of introduction to Mr Kerensky and if I'm not left in peaceful possession of this carriage Mr Crewe will take the matter up with the Administration in Washington.'

Mr Harrington's manner was so truculent and his gestures so menacing that the stationmaster, throwing up the sponge, turned on his heel without another word and walked moodily away. He was followed by the bearded Russian and his wife arguing heatedly with him and the two apathetic children. Mr Harrington jumped back into the carriage.

'I'm terribly sorry to have to refuse to give up my seat to a lady with two children,' he said. 'No one knows better than I the respect due to a woman and a mother, but I've got to get to Petrograd by this train if I don't want to lose a very important order and I'm not going to spend ten days in a corridor for all the mothers in Russia.'

'I don't blame you,' said Ashenden.

'I am a married man and I have two children myself. I know that travelling with your family is a difficult matter, but there's nothing that I know to prevent you from staying at home.'

When you are shut up with a man for ten days in a railway carriage you can hardly fail to learn most of what there is to know about him, and for ten days (for eleven to be exact) Ashenden spent twenty-four hours a day with Mr Harrington. It is true that they went into the dining-room three times a day for their meals, but they sat opposite to one another; it is true that the train stopped for an hour morning and afternoon so that they were able to have a tramp up and down the platform, but they walked side by side. Ashenden made acquaintance with some of his fellow-travellers and sometimes they came into the compartment to have a chat, but if they only spoke French or German Mr Harrington would watch them with acidulous disapproval and if they spoke English he would never let them get a word in. For Mr Harrington was a talker. He talked as though it were a natural function of the human being, automatically, as men breathe or digest their food; he talked not because he had something to say, but because he could not help himself, in a high-pitched, nasal voice, without inflexion, at one dead level of tone. He talked with precision, using a copious vocabulary and forming his sentences with deliberation; he never used a short word when a longer one would do; he never paused. He went on and on. It was not a torrent, for there was nothing impetuous about it, it was like a stream of lava pouring irresistibly down the side of a volcano. It flowed with a quiet and steady force that overwhelmed everything that was in its path.

Ashenden thought he had never known as much about anyone as he knew about Mr Harrington, and not only about him, with all his opinions, habits, and circumstances, but about his wife and his wife's family, his children and their schoolfellows, his employers and the alliances they had made for three or four generations with the best families in Philadelphia. His own family had come from Devonshire early in the eighteenth century and Mr Harrington had been to the village where the graves of his forebears were still to be seen in the churchyard. He was proud of his English ancestry, but proud too of his American birth, though to him America was a little strip of land along the Atlantic coast and Americans were a small number of persons of English or Dutch origin whose blood had never been sullied by foreign admixture. He looked upon the Germans, Swedes, Irish, and the inhabitants of Central and Eastern Europe who for the last hundred years have descended upon the United States, as interlopers. He turned his attention away from them as a maiden lady who lived in a secluded manor might avert her eyes from the factory chimneys that had trespassed upon her retirement.

When Ashenden mentioned a man of vast wealth who owned some of the finest pictures in America Mr Harrington said:

'I've never met him. My great-aunt Maria Penn Warmington always said his grandmother was a very good cook. My great-aunt Maria was terribly sorry when she left her to get married. She said she never knew anyone who could make an apple pancake as she could.'

Mr Harrington was devoted to his wife, and he told Ashenden at unbelievable length how cultivated and what a perfect mother she was. She had delicate health and had undergone a great number of operations all of which he described in detail. He had had two operations himself, one on his tonsils and one to remove his appendix and he took Ashenden day by day through his experiences. All his friends had had operations and his knowledge of surgery was encyclopedic. He had two sons, both at school, and he was seriously considering whether he would not be well-advised to have them operated on. It was curious that one of them should have enlarged tonsils, and he was not at all happy about the appendix of the other. They were more devoted to one another than he had ever seen two brothers be, and a very good friend of his, the brightest surgeon in Philadelphia, had offered to operate on them both together so that they should not be separated. He showed Ashenden photographs of the boys and their mother. This journey of his to Russia was the first time in their lives that he had been separated from them, and every morning he wrote a long letter to his wife telling her everything that had happened and a good deal of what he had said during the day. Ashenden watched him cover sheet after sheet of paper with his neat, legible, and precise handwriting.

Mr Harrington had read all the books on conversation and knew its technique to the last detail. He had a little book in which he noted down the stories he heard and he told Ashenden that when he was going out to dinner he always looked up half a dozen so that he should not be at a loss. They were marked with a G if they could be told in general society and with an M (for men) if they were more fit for rough masculine ears. He was a specialist in that peculiar form of anecdote that consists in narrating a long serious incident, piling detail upon detail, till a comic end is reached. He spared you nothing, and Ashenden, foreseeing the point long before it arrived, would clench his hands and knit his brows in the strenuous effort not to betray his impatience and at last force from his unwilling mouth a grim and hollow laugh. If someone came into the compartment in the middle Mr Harrington would greet him with cordiality.

'Come right in and sit down. I was just telling my friend a story. You must listen to it, it's one of the funniest things you ever heard.'

Then he would begin again from the very beginning and repeat it word for word, without altering a single apt epithet, till he reached the humorous end. Ashenden suggested once that they should see whether they could find two people on the train who played cards so that they might while away the time with a game of bridge, but Mr Harrington said he never touched cards and when Ashenden in desperation began to play patience he pulled a wry face.

'It beats me how an intelligent man can waste his time card-playing, and of all the unintellectual pursuits I have ever seen it seems to me that solitaire is the worst. It kills conversation. Man is a social animal and he exercises the highest part of his nature when he takes part in social intercourse.'

'There is a certain elegance in wasting time,' said Ashenden. 'Any fool can waste money, but when you waste time you waste what is priceless. Besides,' he added with bitterness, 'you can still talk.'

'How can I talk when your attention is taken up by whether you are going to get a black seven to put on a red eight? Conversation calls forth the highest powers of the intellect and if you have made a study of it you have the right to expect that the person you're talking to will give you the fullest attention he is capable of.'

He did not say this acrimoniously, but with the good-humoured patience of a man who has been much tried. He was just stating a plain fact and Ashenden could take it or leave it. It was the claim of the artist to have his work taken seriously.

Mr Harrington was a diligent reader. He read pencil in hand, underlining passages that attracted his attention, and on the margin making in his neat writing comments on what he read. This he was fond of discussing and when Ashenden himself was reading and felt on a sudden that Mr Harrington, book in one hand and pencil in the other, was looking at him with his large pale eyes he began to have violent palpitations of the heart. He dared not look up, he dared not even turn the page, for he knew that Mr Harrington would regard this as ample excuse to break into a discourse, but remained with his eyes fixed desperately on a single word, like a chicken with its beak to a chalk line, and only ventured to breathe when he realized that Mr Harrington, having given up the attempt, had resumed his reading. He was then engaged on a History of the American Constitution in two volumes, and for recreation was perusing a stout volume that purported to contain all the great speeches of the world. For Mr Harrington was an after-dinner speaker and had read all the best books on speaking in public. He knew exactly how to get on good terms with his audience, just where to put in the serious words that touched their hearts, how to catch their attention by a few apt stories, and finally with what degree of eloquence, suiting the occasion, to deliver his peroration.

Mr Harrington was very fond of reading aloud. Ashenden had had frequent occasion to observe the distressing propensity of Americans for this pastime. In hotel drawing-rooms at night after dinner he had often seen the father of a family seated in a retired corner and surrounded by his wife, his two sons, and his daughter, reading to them. On ships crossing the Atlantic he had sometimes watched with awe the tall, spare gentleman of commanding aspect who sat in the centre of fifteen ladies no longer in their first youth and in a resonant voice read to them the history of Art. Walking up and down the promenade deck he had passed honeymooning couples lying on deck-chairs and caught the unhurried tones of the bride as she read to her young husband the pages of a popular novel. It had always seemed to him a curious way of showing affection. He had had friends who had offered to read to him and he had known women who had said they loved being read to, but he had always politely refused the invitation and firmly ignored the hint. He liked neither reading aloud nor being read aloud to. In his heart he thought the national predilection for this form of entertainment the only flaw in the perfection of the American character. But the immortal gods love a good laugh at the expense of human beings and now delivered him, bound and helpless, to the knife of the high priest. Mr Harrington flattered himself that he was a very good reader and he explained to Ashenden the theory and practice of the art. Ashenden learned that there were two schools, the dramatic and the natural: in the first you imitated the voices of those who spoke (if you were reading a novel), and when the heroine wailed you wailed and when emotion choked her you choked too; but in the other you read as impassively as though you were reading the price-list of a mail-order house in Chicago. This was the school Mr Harrington belonged to. In the seventeen years of his married life he had read aloud to his wife, and to his sons as soon as they were old enough to appreciate them, the novels of Sir Walter Scott, Jane Austen, Dickens, the Brontë sisters, Thackeray, George Eliot, Nathaniel Hawthorne, and W.D. Howells. Ashenden came to the conclusion that it was second nature with Mr Harrington to read aloud, and to prevent him from doing so made him as uneasy as cutting off his tobacco made the confirmed smoker. He would take you unawares.

'Listen to this,' he would say, 'you must listen to this,' as though he were suddenly struck by the excellence of a maxim or the neatness of a phrase. 'Now just tell me if you don't think this is remarkably well put. It's only three lines.'

He read them and Ashenden was willing to give him a moment's attention, but having finished them, without pausing for a moment to take breath, he went on. He went right on and on. In his measured high-pitched voice, without emphasis or expression, he read page after page. Ashenden fidgeted, crossed and uncrossed his legs, lit cigarettes and smoked them, sat first in one position, then in another. Mr Harrington went on and on. The train went leisurely through the interminable steppes of Siberia. They passed villages and crossed rivers. Mr Harrington went on and on. When he finished a great speech by Edmund Burke he put down the book in triumph.

'Now that in my opinion is one of the finest orations in the English language.

It is certainly a part of our common heritage that we can look upon with genuine pride.'

'Doesn't it seem to you a little ominous that the people to whom Edmund Burke made that speech are all dead?' asked Ashenden gloomily.

Mr Harrington was about to reply that this was hardly to be wondered at since the speech was made in the eighteenth century, when it dawned upon him that Ashenden (bearing up wonderfully under affliction as any unprejudiced person could not fail to admit) was making a joke. He slapped his knee and laughed heartily.

'Gee, that's a good one,' he said. 'I'll write that down in my little book. I see exactly how I can bring it in one time when I have to speak at our luncheon club.'

Mr Harrington was a highbrow; but that appellation, invented by the vulgar as a term of abuse, he had accepted like the instrument of a saint's martyrdom, the gridiron of Saint Laurence for instance or the wheel of Saint Catherine, as an honorific title. He gloried in it.

'Emerson was a highbrow,' he said. 'Longfellow was a highbrow. Oliver Wendell Holmes was a highbrow. James Russell Lowell was a highbrow.'

Mr Harrington's study of American literature had taken him no farther down the years than the period during which those eminent, but not precisely thrilling, authors flourished.

Mr Harrington was a bore. He exasperated Ashenden, and enraged him; he got on his nerves, and drove him to frenzy. But Ashenden did not dislike him. His self-satisfaction was enormous but so ingenuous that you could not resent it; his conceit was so childlike that you could only smile at it. He was so well-meaning, so thoughtful, so deferential, so polite that though Ashenden would willingly have killed him he could not but own that in that short while he had conceived for Mr Harrington something very like affection. His manners were perfect, formal, a trifle elaborate perhaps (there is no harm in that, for good manners are the product of an artificial state of society and so can bear a touch of the powdered wig and the lace ruffle), but though natural to his good breeding they gained a pleasant significance from his good heart. He was ready to do anyone a kindness and seemed to find nothing too much trouble if he could thereby oblige his fellow-man. He was eminently *serviable*. And it may be that this is a word for which there is no exact translation because the charming quality it denotes is not very common among our practical people. When Ashenden was ill for a couple of days Mr Harrington nursed him with devotion. Ashenden was embarrassed by the care he took of him and though racked with pain could not help laughing at the fussy attention with which Mr Harrington took his temperature, from his neatly packed valise extracted a whole regiment of tabloids and firmly doctored him; and he was touched by the trouble he gave himself to get from the dining-car the things that he thought Ashenden could eat. He did everything in the world for him but stop talking.

It was only when he was dressing that Mr Harrington was silent, for then his maidenly mind was singly occupied with the problem of changing his clothes before Ashenden without indelicacy. He was extremely modest. He changed his linen every day, neatly taking it out of his suitcase and neatly putting back what was soiled; but he performed miracles of dexterity in order during the process not to show an inch of bare skin. After a day or two Ashenden gave up the struggle to keep neat and clean in that dirty train, with one lavatory for the whole carriage, and soon was as grubby as the rest of the passengers; but Mr Harrington refused to yield to the difficulties. He performed his toilet with deliberation notwithstanding the impatient persons who rattled the door-handle, and returned from the lavatory every morning washed, shining, and smelling of soap. Once dressed, in his black coat, striped trousers, and well-polished shoes, he looked as spruce as though he had just stepped out of his tidy little red-brick house in Philadelphia and was about to board the street-car that would take him downtown to his office. At one point of the journey it was announced that an attempt had been made to blow up a bridge and that there were disturbances at the next station over the river; it might be that the train would be stopped and the passengers turned adrift or taken prisoner. Ashenden, thinking he might be separated from his luggage, took the precaution to change into his thickest clothes so that if he had to pass the winter in Siberia he need suffer as little as necessary from the cold; but Mr Harrington would not listen to reason; he made no preparations for the possible experience and Ashenden had the conviction that if he spent three months in a Russian prison he would still preserve that smart and natty appearance. A troop of Cossacks boarded the train and stood on the platform of each carriage with their guns loaded, and the train rattled gingerly over the damaged bridge; then they came to the station at which they had been warned of danger, put on steam and dashed straight through it. Mr Harrington was mildly satirical when Ashenden changed back into a light summer suit.

Mr Harrington was a keen business man. It was obvious that it would need someone very astute to overreach him, and Ashenden was sure that his employers had been well-advised to send him on this errand. He would safeguard their interests with all his might and if he succeeded in driving a bargain with the Russians it would be a hard one. His loyalty to his firm demanded that. He spoke of the partners with affectionate reverence. He loved them and was proud of them; but he did not envy them because their wealth was great. He was quite content to work on a salary and thought himself adequately paid; so long as he could educate his boys and leave his widow enough to live on, what was money to him? He thought it a trifle vulgar to be rich. He looked upon culture as more important than money. He was careful of it and after every meal put down in his note-book exactly what it had cost him. His firm might be certain that he would not charge a penny more for his expenses than he had spent. But having discovered that poor people came to the station at the stopping places of the train to beg and seeing that the war had really brought them to destitution he took care before each halt to supply himself with ample small change and in a shame-faced way, mocking himself for being taken in by such impostors, distributed everything in his pocket.

'Of course I know they don't deserve it,' he said, 'and I don't do it for them. I do it entirely for my own peace of mind. I should feel so terribly badly if I thought some man really was hungry and I'd refused to give him the price of a meal.'

Mr Harrington was absurd, but lovable. It was inconceivable that anyone should be rude to him, it would have seemed as dreadful as hitting a child; and Ashenden, chafing inwardly but with a pretence of amiability, suffered meekly and with a truly Christian spirit the affliction of the gentle, ruthless creature's society. It took eleven days at that time to get from Vladivostok to Petrograd, and Ashenden felt that he could not have borne another day. If it had been twelve he would have killed Mr Harrington.

When at last (Ashenden tired and dirty, Mr Harrington neat, sprightly and sententious) they reached the outskirts of Petrograd and stood at the window looking at the crowded houses of the city, Mr Harrington turned to Ashenden and said:

'Well, I never would have thought that eleven days in the train would pass so quickly. We've had a wonderful time. I've enjoyed your company and I know you've enjoyed mine. I'm not going to pretend I don't know that I'm a pretty good conversationalist. But now we've come together like this we must take care to stay together. We must see as much of one another as we can while I'm in Petrograd.'

'I shall have a great deal to do,' said Ashenden. 'I'm afraid my time won't be altogether my own.'

'I know,' answered Mr Harrington cordially. 'I expect to be pretty busy myself, but we can have breakfast together anyway and we'll meet in the evening and compare notes. It would be too bad if we drifted apart now.'

'Too bad,' sighed Ashenden.

When Ashenden found himself alone in his bedroom for the first time, he sat down and looked about him. It had seemed an age. He had not the energy to start immediately to unpack. How many of these hotel bedrooms had he known since the beginning of the war, grand or shabby, in one place and one land after another! It seemed to him that he had been living in his luggage for as long as he could remember. He was weary. He asked himself how he was going to set about the work that he had been sent to do. He felt lost in the immensity of Russia and very solitary. He had protested when he was chosen for this mission, it looked too large an order, but his protests were ignored. He was chosen not because those in authority thought him particularly suited for the job, but because there was no one to be found who was more suited. There was a knock at the door and Ashenden, pleased to make use of the few words of the language he knew, called out in Russian. The door was opened. He sprang to his feet.

'Come in, come in,' he cried. 'I'm awfully glad to see you.'

Three men entered. He knew them by sight, since they had travelled in the same ship with him from San Francisco to Yokohama, but following their instructions no communications had passed between them and Ashenden. They were Czechs, exiled from their country for their revolutionary activity and long settled in America, who had been sent over to Russia to help Ashenden in his mission and put him in touch with Professor Z., whose authority over the Czechs in Russia was absolute. Their chief was a certain Dr Egon Orth, a tall thin man, with a little grey head; he was minister to some church in the Middle West and a doctor of divinity; but had abandoned his cure to work for the liberation of his country, and Ashenden had the impression that he was an intelligent fellow who would not put too fine a point on matters of conscience. A parson with a fixed idea has this advantage over common men, that he can persuade himself of the Almighty's approval for almost any goings-on. Dr Orth had a merry twinkle in his eye and a dry humour.

Ashenden had had two secret interviews with him in Yokohama and had learnt that Professor Z., though eager to free his country from the Austrian rule and, since he knew that this could only come about by the downfall of the Central Powers, with the Allies, body and soul, yet had scruples; he would not do things that outraged his conscience, all must be straightforward and above board, and so some things that it was necessary to do had to be done without his knowledge. His influence was so great that his wishes could not be disregarded, but on occasion it was felt better not to let him know too much of what was going on.

Dr Orth had arrived in Petrograd a week before Ashenden and now put before him what he had learned of the situation. It seemed to Ashenden that it was critical and if anything was to be done it must be done quickly. The army was dissatisfied and mutinous, the Government under the weak Kerensky was tottering and held power only because no one else had the courage to seize it, famine was staring the country in the face, and already the possibility had to be considered that the Germans would march on Petrograd. The Ambassadors of Great Britain and the United States had been apprised of Ashenden's coming, but his mission was secret even from them, and there were particular reasons why he could demand no assistance from them. He arranged with Dr Orth to make an appointment with Professor Z. so that he could learn his views and explain to him that he had the financial means to support any scheme that seemed likely to prevent the catastrophe that the Allied governments foresaw of Russia's making a separate peace. But he had to get in touch with influential persons in all classes. Mr Harrington with his business proposition and his letters to Ministers of State would be thrown in contact with members of the Government and Mr Harrington wanted an interpreter. Dr Orth spoke Russian almost as well as his own language and it struck Ashenden that he would be admirably suited to the post. He explained the circumstances to him and it was arranged that while Ashenden and Mr Harrington were at luncheon Dr Orth should come in, greeting Ashenden as though he had not seen him before, and be introduced to Mr Harrington; then Ashenden, guiding the conversation, would suggest to Mr Harrington that the heavens had sent in Dr Orth the ideal man for his purpose.

But there was another person on whom Ashenden had fixed as possibly useful to him and now he said:

'Have you ever heard of a woman called Anastasia Alexandrovna Leonidov? She's the daughter of Alexander Denisiev.'

'I know all about him of course.'

'I have reason to believe she's in Petrograd. Will you find out where she lives and what she's doing?'

'Certainly.'

Dr Orth spoke in Czech to one of the two men who accompanied him. They were sharp-looking fellows, both of them, one was tall and fair and the other was short and dark, but they were younger than Dr Orth, and Ashenden understood that they were there to do as he bade them. The man nodded, got up, shook hands with Ashenden and went out.

'You shall have all the information possible this afternoon.'

'Well, I think there's nothing more we can do for the present,' said Ashenden. 'To tell you the truth I haven't had a bath for eleven days and I badly want one.'

Ashenden had never quite made up his mind whether the pleasure of reflection was better pursued in a railway carriage or in a bath. So far as the act of invention was concerned he was inclined to prefer a train that went smoothly and not too fast, and many of his best ideas had come to him when he was thus traversing the plains of France; but for the delight of reminiscence or the entertainment of embroidery upon a theme already in his head he had no doubt that nothing could compare with a hot bath. He considered now, wallowing in soapy water like a water-buffalo in a muddy pond, the grim pleasantry of his relations with Anastasia Alexandrovna Leonidov.

In these stories no more than the barest suggestion has been made that Ashenden was capable on occasions of the passion ironically called tender. The specialists in this matter, those charming creatures who make a business of what philosophers know is but a diversion, assert that writers, painters, and musicians, all in short who are connected with the arts, in the relation of love cut no very conspicuous figure. There is much cry but little wool. They rave or sigh, make phrases and strike many a romantic attitude, but in the end, loving art or themselves (which with them is one and the same thing) better than the object of their emotion, offer a shadow when the said object, with the practical common sense of the sex, demands a substance. It may be so and this may be the reason (never before suggested) why women in their souls look upon art with such a virulent hatred. Be this as it may Ashenden in the last twenty years had felt his heart go pit-a-pat because of one charming person after another. He had had a good deal of fun and had paid for it with a great deal of misery, but even when suffering most acutely from the pangs of unrequited love he had been able to say to himself, albeit with a wry face, after all, it's grist to the mill.

Anastasia Alexandrovna Leonidov was the daughter of a revolutionary who had escaped from Siberia after being sentenced to penal servitude for life and had settled in England. He was an able man and had supported himself for thirty years by the activity of a restless pen and had even made himself a distinguished position in English letters. When Anastasia Alexandrovna reached a suitable age she married Vladimir Semenovich Leonidov, also an exile from his native country, and it was after she had been married to him for some years that Ashenden made her acquaintance. It was at the time when Europe discovered Russia. Everyone was reading the Russian novelists, the Russian dancers captivated the civilized world, and the Russian composers set shivering the sensibility of persons who were beginning to want a change from Wagner. Russian art seized upon Europe with the virulence of an epidemic of influenza. New phrases became the fashion, new colours, new emotions, and the highbrows described themselves without a moment's hesitation as members of the intelligentsia. It was a difficult word to spell but an easy one to say. Ashenden fell like the rest, changed the cushions of his sitting-room, hung an icon on the wall, read Chekhov and went to the ballet.

Anastasia Alexandrovna was by birth, circumstances, and education very much a member of the intelligentsia. She lived with her husband in a tiny house near Regent's Park and here all the literary folk in London might gaze with humble reverence at pale-faced bearded giants who leaned against the wall like caryatids taking a day off; they were revolutionaries to a man and it was a miracle that they were not in the mines of Siberia. Women of letters tremulously put their lips to a glass of vodka. If you were lucky and greatly favoured you might shake hands there with Diaghilev, and now and again, like a peach-blossom wafted by the breeze, Pavlova herself hovered in and out. At this time Ashenden's success had not been so great as to affront the highbrows, he had very distinctly been one of them in his youth, and though some already looked askance, others (optimistic creatures with a faith in human nature) still had hopes of him. Anastasia Alexandrovna told him to his face that he was a member of the intelligentsia. Ashenden was quite ready to believe it. He was in a state when he was ready to believe anything. He was thrilled and excited. It seemed to him that at last he was about to capture that illusive spirit of romance that he had so long been chasing. Anastasia Alexandrovna had fine eyes and a good, though for these days too voluptuous, figure, high cheek-bones and a snub nose (this was very Tartar), a wide mouth full of large square teeth, and a pale skin. She dressed somewhat flamboyantly. In her dark melancholy eyes Ashenden saw the boundless steppes of Russia, and the Kremlin with its pealing bells, and the solemn ceremonies of Easter at St Isaac's, and forests of silver beeches, and the Nevsky Prospekt; it was astonishing how much he saw in her eyes. They were round and shining and slightly protuberant like those of a Pekinese. They talked together of Alyosha in the *Brothers Karamazov*, of Natasha in *War and Peace*, of Anna Karenina, and of *Fathers and Sons*.

Ashenden soon discovered that her husband was quite unworthy of her and presently learned that she shared his opinion. Vladimir Semenovich was a little man with a large, long head that looked as though it had been pulled like a piece of liquorice, and he had a great shock of unruly Russian hair. He was a gentle, unobtrusive creature and it was hard to believe that the Czarist government had really feared his revolutionary activities. He taught Russian and wrote for papers in Moscow. He was amiable and obliging. He needed these qualities, for Anastasia Alexandrovna was a woman of character: when she had a toothache Vladimir Semenovich suffered the agonies of the damned, and when her heart was wrung by the suffering of her unhappy country Vladimir Semenovich might well have wished he had never been born. Ashenden could not help admitting that he was a poor thing, but he was so harmless that he conceived quite a liking for him, and when in due course he had disclosed his passion to Anastasia Alexandrovna and to his joy found it was returned he was puzzled to know what to do about Vladimir Semenovich. Neither Anastasia Alexandrovna nor he felt that they could live another minute out of one another's pockets, and Ashenden feared that, with her revolutionary views and all that, she would never consent to marry him; but somewhat to his surprise, and very much to his relief, she accepted the suggestion with alacrity.

'Would Vladimir Semenovich let himself be divorced, do you think?' he asked, as he sat on the sofa, leaning against cushions the colour of which reminded him of raw meat just gone bad, and held her hand.

'Vladimir adores me,' she answered. 'It'll break his heart.'

'He's a nice fellow, I shouldn't like him to be very unhappy. I hope he'll get over it.'

'He'll never get over it. That is the Russian spirit. I know that when I leave him he'll feel that he has lost everything that made life worth living for him. I've never known anyone so wrapped up in a woman as he is in me. But of course he wouldn't want to stand in the way of my happiness. He's far too great for that. He'll see that when it's a question of my own self-development I haven't the right to hesitate. Vladimir will give me my freedom without question.'

At that time the divorce law in England was even more complicated and absurd than it is now and in case she was not acquainted with its peculiarities Ashenden explained to Anastasia Alexandrovna the difficulties of the case. She put her hand gently on his.

'Vladimir would never expose me to the vulgar notoriety of the divorce court. When I tell him that I have decided to marry you he will commit suicide.'

'That would be terrible,' said Ashenden.

He was startled, but thrilled. It was really very much like a Russian novel and he saw the moving and terrible pages, pages and pages, in which Dostoyevsky would have described the situation. He knew the lacerations his characters would have suffered, the broken bottles of champagne, the visits to the gipsies, the vodka, the swoonings, the catalepsy, and the long, long speeches everyone would have made. It was all very dreadful and wonderful and shattering.

'It would make us horribly unhappy,' said Anastasia Alexandrovna, 'but I don't know what else he could do. I couldn't ask him to live without me. He would be like a ship without a rudder or a car without a carburettor. I know Vladimir so well. He will commit suicide.'

'How?' asked Ashenden, who had the realist's passion for the exact detail.

'He will blow his brains out.'

Ashenden remembered *Rosmersholm*. In his day he had been an ardent Ibsenite and had even flirted with the notion of learning Norwegian so that he might, by reading the master in the original, get at the secret essence of his thought. He had once seen Ibsen in the flesh drink a glass of Munich beer.

'But do you think we could ever pass another easy hour if we had the death of that man on our conscience?' he asked. 'I have a feeling that he would always be between us.'

'I know we shall suffer, we shall suffer dreadfully,' said Anastasia Alexandrovna, 'but how can we help it? Life is like that. We must think of Vladimir. There is his happiness to be considered too. He will prefer to commit suicide.'

She turned her face away and Ashenden saw that the heavy tears were coursing down her cheeks. He was much moved. For he had a soft heart and it was dreadful to think of poor Vladimir lying there with a bullet in his brain.

These Russians, what fun they have!

But when Anastasia Alexandrovna had mastered her emotion she turned to him gravely. She looked at him with her humid, round, and slightly protuberant eyes.

'We must be quite sure that we're doing the right thing,' she said. 'I should never forgive myself if I'd allowed Vladimir to commit suicide and then found I'd made a mistake. I think we ought to make sure that we really love one another.'

'But don't you know?' exclaimed Ashenden in a low, tense voice. 'I know.'

'Let's go over to Paris for a week and see how we get on. Then we shall know.'

Ashenden was a trifle conventional and the suggestion took him by surprise. But only for a moment. Anastasia was wonderful. She was very quick and she saw the hesitation that for an instant troubled him.

'Surely you have no bourgeois prejudices?' she said.

'Of course not,' he assured her hurriedly, for he would much sooner have been thought knavish than bourgeois, 'I think it's a splendid idea.'

'Why should a woman hazard her whole life on a throw? It's impossible to know what a man is really like till you've lived with him. It's only fair to give her the opportunity to change her mind before it's too late.'

'Quite so,' said Ashenden.

Anastasia Alexandrovna was not a woman to let the grass grow under her feet and so having made their arrangements forthwith on the following Saturday they started for Paris.

'I shall not tell Vladimir that I am going with you,' she said. 'It would only distress him.'

'It would be a pity to do that,' said Ashenden.

'And if at the end of the week I come to the conclusion that we've made a mistake he need never know anything about it.'

'Quite so,' said Ashenden.

They met at Victoria Station.

'What class have you got?' she asked him.

'First.'

'I'm glad of that. Father and Vladimir travel third on account of their principles, but I always feel sick on a train and I like to be able to lean my head on somebody's shoulder. It's easier in a first-class carriage.'

When the train started Anastasia Alexandrovna said she felt dizzy, so she took off her hat and leaned her head on Ashenden's shoulder. He put his arm round her waist.

'Keep quite still, won't you?' she said.

When they got on to the boat she went down to the ladies' cabin and at Calais was able to eat a very hearty meal, but when they got into the train she took off her hat again and rested her head on Ashenden's shoulder. He thought he would like to read and took up a book.

'Do you mind not reading?' she said. 'I have to be held and when you turn the pages it makes me feel all funny.'

Finally they reached Paris and went to a little hotel on the Left Bank that Anastasia Alexandrovna knew of. She said it had atmosphere. She could not bear those great big grand hotels on the other side; they were hopelessly vulgar and bourgeois.

'I'll go anywhere you like,' said Ashenden, 'as long as there's a bathroom.'

She smiled and pinched his cheek.

'How adorably English you are. Can't you do without a bathroom for a week? My dear, my dear, you have so much to learn.'

They talked far into the night about Maxim Gorki and Karl Marx, human destiny, love, and the brotherhood of man; and drank innumerable cups of Russian tea, so that in the morning Ashenden would willingly have breakfasted in bed and got up for luncheon; but Anastasia Alexandrovna was an early riser. When life was so short and there was so much to do it was a sinful thing to have breakfast a minute after half past eight. They sat down in a dingy little dining-room the windows of which showed no signs of having been opened for a month. It was full of atmosphere. Ashenden asked Anastasia Alexandrovna what she would have for breakfast.

'Scrambled eggs,' she said.

She ate heartily. Ashenden had already noticed that she had a healthy appetite. He supposed it was a Russian trait; you could not picture Anna Karenina making her midday meal off a bath-bun and a cup of coffee, could you?

After breakfast they went to the Louvre and in the afternoon they went to the Luxembourg. They dined early in order to go to the Comédie Française; then they went to a Russian cabaret where they danced. When next morning at eight-thirty they took their places in the dining-room and Ashenden asked Anastasia Alexandrovna what she fancied, her reply was:

'Scrambled eggs.'

'But we had scrambled eggs yesterday,' he expostulated.

'Let's have them again today,' she smiled.

'All right.'

They spent the day in the same manner except that they went to the Carnavalet instead of the Louvre and the Musée Guimet instead of the

Luxembourg. But when the morning after in answer to Ashenden's inquiry Anastasia Alexandrovna again asked for scrambled eggs, his heart sank.

'But we had scrambled eggs yesterday and the day before,' he said.

'Don't you think that's a very good reason to have them again today?'

'No, I don't.'

'Is it possible that your sense of humour is a little deficient this morning?' she asked. 'I eat scrambled eggs every day. It's the only way I like them.'

'Oh, very well. In that case of course we'll have scrambled eggs.'

But the following morning he could not face them.

'Will you have scrambled eggs as usual?' he asked her.

'Of course,' she smiled affectionately, showing him two rows of large square teeth.

'All right, I'll order them for you; I shall have mine fried.'

The smile vanished from her lips.

'Oh?' She paused a moment. 'Don't you think that's rather inconsiderate? Do you think it's fair to give the cook unnecessary work? You English, you're all the same, you look upon servants as machines. Does it occur to you that they have hearts like yours, the same feelings and the same emotions? How can you be surprised that the proletariat are seething with discontent when the bourgeoisie like you are so monstrously selfish?'

'Do you really think that there'll be a revolution in England if I have my eggs in Paris fried rather than scrambled?'

She tossed her pretty head in indignation.

'You don't understand. It's the principle of the thing. You think it's a jest, of course I know you're being funny, I can laugh at a joke as well as anyone, Chekhov was well-known in Russia as a humorist; but don't you see what is involved? Your whole attitude is wrong. It's a lack of feeling. You wouldn't talk like that if you had been through the events of 1905 in Petersburg. When I think of the crowds in front of the Winter Palace kneeling in the snow while the Cossacks charged them, women and children! No, no, no.'

Her eyes filled with tears and her face was all twisted with pain. She took Ashenden's hand.

'I know you have a good heart. It was just thoughtless on your part and we won't say anything more about it. You have imagination. You're very sensitive. I know. You'll have your eggs done in the same way as mine, won't you?'

'Of course,' said Ashenden.

He ate scrambled eggs for breakfast every morning after that. The waiter said: '*Monsieur aime les oeufs brouillés.*' At the end of the week they returned to London. He held Anastasia Alexandrovna in his arms, her head resting on his shoulder, from Paris to Calais and again from Dover to London. He reflected that the journey from New York to San Francisco took five days. When they arrived at Victoria and stood on the platform waiting for a cab she looked at him with her round, shining, and slightly protuberant eyes.

'We've had a wonderful time, haven't we?' she said.

'Wonderful.'

'I've quite made up my mind. The experiment has justified itself. I'm quite willing to marry you whenever you like.'

But Ashenden saw himself eating scrambled eggs every morning for the rest of his life. When he had put her in a cab, he called another for himself, went to the Cunard office, and took a berth on the first ship that was going to America.

No immigrant, eager for freedom and a new life, ever looked upon the statue of Liberty with more heartfelt thankfulness than did Ashenden, when on that bright and sunny morning his ship steamed into the harbour of New York.

Some years had passed since then and Ashenden had not seen Anastasia Alexandrovna again. He knew that on the outbreak of the revolution in March she and Vladimir Semenovich had gone to Russia. It might be that they would be able to help him, in a way Vladimir Semenovich owed him his life, and he made up his mind to write to Anastasia Alexandrovna to ask if he might come to see her.

When Ashenden went down to lunch he felt somewhat rested. Mr Harrington was waiting for him and they sat down. They ate what was put before them.

'Ask the waiter to bring us some bread,' said Mr Harrington.

'Bread?' replied Ashenden. 'There's no bread.'

'I can't eat without bread,' said Mr Harrington.

'I'm afraid you'll have to. There's no bread, no butter, no sugar, no eggs, no potatoes. There's fish and meat and green vegetables, and that's all.'

Mr Harrington's jaw dropped.

'But this is war,' he said.

'It looks very much like it.'

Mr Harrington was for a moment speechless; then he said: 'I'll tell you what I'm going to do, I'm going to get through with my business as quick as I can and then I'm going to get out of this country. I'm sure Mrs Harrington wouldn't like me to go without sugar or butter. I've got a very delicate stomach. The firm would never have sent me here if they'd thought I wasn't going to have the best of everything.'

In a little while Dr Egon Orth came in and gave Ashenden an envelope. On it was written Anastasia Alexandrovna's address. He introduced him to Mr Harrington. It was soon clear that he was pleased with Dr Egon Orth and so without further to-do he suggested that here was the perfect interpreter for him.

'He talks Russian like a Russian. But he's an American citizen so that he won't do you down. I've known him a considerable time and I can assure you that he's absolutely trustworthy.'

Mr Harrington was pleased with the notion and after luncheon Ashenden left them to settle the matter by themselves. He wrote a note to Anastasia Alexandrovna and presently received an answer to say that she was going to a meeting, but would look in at his hotel about seven. He awaited her with apprehension. Of course he knew now that he had not loved her, but Tolstoy and Dostoyevsky, Rimsky-Korsakov, Stravinsky, and Bakst; but he was not quite sure if the point had occurred to her. When between eight and half past she arrived he suggested that she should join Mr Harrington and him at dinner. The presence of a third party, he thought, would prevent any awkwardness their meeting might have; but he need not have had any anxiety, for five minutes after they had sat down to a plate of soup it was borne in upon him that the feelings of Anastasia Alexandrovna towards him were as cool as were his towards her. It gave him a momentary shock. It is very hard for a man, however modest, to grasp the possibility that a woman who has once loved him may love him no longer, and though of course he did not imagine that Anastasia Alexandrovna had languished for five years with a hopeless passion for him, he did think that by a heightening of colour, a flutter of the eyelashes, or a quiver of the lips she would betray the fact that she had still a soft place in her heart for him. Not at all. She talked to him as though he were a friend she was very glad to see again after an absence of a few days, but whose intimacy with her was purely social. He asked after Vladimir Semenovich.

'He has been a disappointment to me,' she said. 'I never thought he was a clever man, but I thought he was an honest one. He's going to have a baby.'

Mr Harrington who was about to put a piece of fish into his mouth, stopped, his fork in the air, and stared at Anastasia Alexandrovna with astonishment. In extenuation it must be explained that he had never read a Russian novel in his life. Ashenden, slightly perplexed too, gave her a questioning look.

'I'm not the mother,' she said with a laugh. 'I am not interested in that sort of thing. The mother is a friend of mine and a well-known writer on Political Economy. I do not think her views are sound, but I should be the last to deny that they deserve consideration. She has a good brain, quite a good brain.' She turned to Mr Harrington. 'Are you interested in Political Economy?'

For once in his life Mr Harrington was speechless. Anastasia Alexandrovna gave them her views on the subject and they began to speak on the situation in Russia. She seemed to be on intimate terms with the leaders of the various political parties and Ashenden made up his mind to sound her on the possibility of her working with him. His infatuation had not blinded him to the fact that she was an extremely intelligent woman. After dinner he told Mr Harrington that he wished to talk business with Anastasia Alexandrovna and took her to a retired corner of the lounge. He told her all he thought necessary and found her interested and anxious to help. She had a passion for intrigue and a desire for power. When he hinted that he had command of large sums of money she saw at once that through him she might acquire an influence in the affairs of Russia. It tickled her vanity. She was immensely patriotic, but like many patriots she had an impression that her own aggrandizement tended to the good of her country. When they parted they had come to a working agreement.

'That was a very remarkable woman,' said Mr Harrington next morning when they met at breakfast.

'Don't fall in love with her,' smiled Ashenden.

This, however, was not a matter on which Mr Harrington was prepared to jest.

'I have never looked at a woman since I married Mrs Harrington,' he said. 'That husband of hers must be a bad man.'

'I could do with a plate of scrambled eggs,' said Ashenden, irrelevantly, for their breakfast consisted of a cup of tea without milk and a little jam instead of sugar.

With Anastasia Alexandrovna to help him and Dr Orth in the background, Ashenden set to work. Things in Russia were going from bad to worse. Kerensky, the head of the Provisional Government, was devoured by vanity and dismissed any minister who gave evidence of a capacity that might endanger his own position. He made speeches. He made endless speeches. At one moment there was a possibility that the Germans would make a dash for Petrograd. Kerensky made speeches. The food shortage grew more serious, the winter was approaching and there was no fuel. Kerensky made speeches. In the background the Bolsheviks were active, Lenin was hiding in Petrograd, it was said that Kerensky knew where he was, but dared not arrest him. He made speeches.

It amused Ashenden to see the unconcern with which Mr Harrington wandered through this turmoil. History was in the making and Mr Harrington minded his own business. It was uphill work. He was made to pay bribes to secretaries and underlings under the pretence that the ear of great men would be granted to him. He was kept waiting for hours in antechambers and then sent away without ceremony. When at last he saw the great men he found they had nothing to give him but idle words. They made him promises and in a day or two he discovered that the promises meant nothing. Ashenden advised him to throw in his hand and return to America; but Mr Harrington would not hear of it; his firm had sent him to do a particular job, and by gum, he was going to do it or perish in the attempt. Then Anastasia Alexandrovna took him in hand. A singular friendship had arisen between the pair. Mr Harrington thought her a very remarkable and deeply wronged woman; he told her all about his wife and two sons, he told her all about the Constitution of the United States; she on her side told him all about Vladimir Semenovich, and she told him about Tolstoy, Turgenev, and Dostoyevsky. They had great times together. He said he couldn't manage to call her Anastasia Alexandrovna, it was too much of a mouthful; so he called her Delilah. And now she placed her inexhaustible energy at his service and they went together to the persons who might be useful to him. But things were coming to a head. Riots broke out and the streets were growing dangerous. Now and then armoured cars filled with discontented reservists careered wildly along the Nevsky Prospekt and in order to show that they were not happy took pot-shots at the passers by. On one occasion when Mr Harrington and Anastasia Alexandrovna were in a tram together shots peppered the windows and they had to lie down on the floor for safety. Mr Harrington was highly indignant.

'An old fat woman was lying right on top of me and when I wriggled to get out Delilah caught me a clip on the side of the head and said: Stop still, you fool. I don't like your Russian ways, Delilah.'

'Anyhow you stopped still,' she giggled.

'What you want in this country is a little less art and a little more civilization.'

'You are bourgeoisie, Mr Harrington, you are not a member of the intelligentsia.'

'You are the first person who's ever said that, Delilah. If I'm not a member of the intelligentsia I don't know who is,' retorted Mr Harrington with dignity.

Then one day when Ashenden was working in his room there was a knock at the door and Anastasia Alexandrovna stalked in, followed somewhat sheepishly by Mr Harrington. Ashenden saw that she was excited.

'What's the matter?' he asked.

'Unless this man goes back to America he'll get killed. You really must talk to him. If I hadn't been there something very unpleasant might have happened to him.'

'Not at all, Delilah,' said Mr Harrington, with asperity. 'I'm perfectly capable of taking care of myself and I wasn't in the smallest danger.'

'What is it all about?' asked Ashenden.

'I'd taken Mr Harrington to the Lavra of Alexander Nevsky to see Dostoyevsky's grave,' said Anastasia Alexandrovna, 'and on our way back we saw a soldier being rather rough with an old woman.'

'Rather rough!' cried Mr Harrington. 'There was an old woman walking along the pavement with a basket of provisions on her arm. Two soldiers came up behind her and one of them snatched the basket from her and walked off with it.

She burst out screaming and crying. I don't know what she was saying, but I can guess, and the other soldier took his gun and with the butt-end of it hit her over the head. Isn't that right, Delilah?'

'Yes,' she answered, unable to help smiling. 'And before I could prevent it Mr Harrington jumped out of the cab and ran up to the soldier who had the basket, wrenched it from him and began to abuse the pair of them like pickpockets. At first they were so taken aback they didn't know what to do and then they got in a rage. I ran after Mr Harrington and explained to them that he was a foreigner and drunk.'

'Drunk?' cried Mr Harrington.

'Yes, drunk. Of course a crowd collected. It looked as though it wasn't going to be very nice.'

Mr Harrington smiled with those large, pale-blue eyes of his.

'It sounded to me as though you were giving them a piece of your mind, Delilah. It was as good as a play to watch you.'

'Don't be stupid, Mr Harrington,' cried Anastasia, in a sudden fury, stamping her foot. 'Don't you know that those soldiers might very easily have killed you and me too, and not one of the bystanders would have raised a finger to help us?'

'Me? I'm an American citizen, Delilah. They wouldn't dare touch a hair of my head.'

'They'd have difficulty in finding one,' said Anastasia Alexandrovna, who when she was in a temper had no manners. 'But if you think Russian soldiers are going to hesitate to kill you because you're an American citizen you'll get a big surprise one of these days.'

'Well, what happened to the old woman?' asked Ashenden.

'The soldiers went off after a little and we went back to her.'

'Still with the basket?'

'Yes. Mr Harrington clung on to that like grim death. She was lying on the ground with the blood pouring from her head. We got her into the cab and when she could speak enough to tell us where she lived we drove her home. She was bleeding dreadfully and we had some difficulty in staunching the blood.'

Anastasia Alexandrovna gave Mr Harrington an odd look and to his surprise Ashenden saw him turn scarlet.

'What's the matter now?'

'You see, we had nothing to bind her up with. Mr Harrington's handkerchief was soaked. There was only one thing about me that I could get off quickly and so I took off my . . .'

But before she could finish Mr Harrington interrupted her.

'You need not tell Mr Ashenden what you took off. I'm a married man and I know ladies wear them, but I see no need to refer to them in general society.'

Anastasia Alexandrovna giggled.

'Then you must kiss me, Mr Harrington. If you don't I shall say.'

Mr Harrington hesitated a moment, considering evidently the pros and cons of the matter, but saw that Anastasia Alexandrovna was determined.

'Go on then, you may kiss me, Delilah, though I'm bound to say I don't see what pleasure it can be to you.'

She put her arms round his neck and kissed him on both cheeks, then without a word of warning burst into a flood of tears.

'You're a brave little man, Mr Harrington. You're absurd but magnificent,' she sobbed.

Mr Harrington was less surprised than Ashenden would have expected him to be. He looked at Anastasia with a thin, quizzical smile and gently patted her. 'Come, come, Delilah, pull yourself together. It gave you a nasty turn, didn't it? You're quite upset. I shall have terrible rheumatism in my shoulder if you go on weeping all over it.'

The scene was ridiculous and touching. Ashenden laughed, but he had the beginnings of a lump in his throat.

When Anastasia Alexandrovna had left them Mr Harrington sat in a brown study.

'They're very queer, these Russians. Do you know what Delilah did?' he said, suddenly. 'She stood up in the cab, in the middle of the street, with people passing on both sides, and took her pants off. She tore them in two and gave me one to hold while she made a bandage of the other. I was never so embarrassed in my life.'

'Tell me what gave you the idea of calling her Delilah?' smiled Ashenden.

Mr Harrington reddened a little.

'She's a very fascinating woman, Mr Ashenden. She's been deeply wronged by her husband and I naturally felt a great deal of sympathy for her. These Russians are very emotional people and I did not want her to mistake my sympathy for anything else. I told her I was very much attached to Mrs Harrington.'

'You're not under the impression that Delilah was Potiphar's wife?' asked Ashenden.

'I don't know what you mean by that, Mr Ashenden,' replied Mr Harrington. 'Mrs Harrington has always given me to understand that I'm very fascinating to women, and I thought if I called our little friend Delilah it would make my position quite clear.'

'I don't think Russia's any place for you, Mr Harrington,' said Ashenden smiling. 'If I were you I'd get out of it as quick as I could.'

'I can't go now. I've got them to agree to my terms at last and we're going to sign next week. Then I shall pack my grip and go.'

'I wonder if your signatures will be worth the paper they're written on,' said Ashenden.

He had at length devised a plan of campaign. It took him twenty-four hours' hard work to code a telegram in which he put his scheme before the persons who had sent him to Petrograd. It was accepted and he was promised all the money he needed. Ashenden knew he could do nothing unless the Provisional Government remained in power for another three months; but winter was at hand and food was getting scarcer every day. The army was mutinous. The people clamoured for peace. Every evening at the Europe Ashenden drank a cup of chocolate with Professor Z. and discussed with him how best to make use of his devoted Czechs. Anastasia Alexandrovna had a flat in a retired spot and here he had meetings with all manner of persons. Plans were drawn up. Measures were taken. Ashenden argued, persuaded, promised. He had to overcome the vacillation of one and wrestle with the fatalism of another. He had to judge who was resolute and who was self-sufficient, who was honest and who was infirm of purpose. He had to curb his impatience with the Russian verbosity; he had to be good-tempered with people who were willing to talk of everything but the matter in hand; he had to listen sympathetically to ranting and rodomontade. He had to beware of treachery. He had to humour the vanity of fools and elude the greed of the ambitious. Time was pressing. The rumours grew hot and many of the activities of the Bolsheviks. Kerensky ran hither and thither like a frightened hen.

Then the blow fell. On the night of 7 November 1917 the Bolsheviks rose. Kerensky's ministers were arrested, and the Winter Palace was sacked by the mob; the reins of power were seized by Lenin and Trotsky.

Anastasia Alexandrovna came to Ashenden's room at the hotel early in the morning. Ashenden was coding a telegram. He had been up all night, first at the Smolny, and then at the Winter Palace. He was tired out. Her face was white and her shining brown eyes were tragic.

'Have you heard?' she asked Ashenden.

He nodded.

'It's all over then. They say Kerensky has fled. They never even showed fight.' Rage seized her. 'The buffoon!' she screamed.

At that moment there was a knock at the door and Anastasia Alexandrovna looked at it with sudden apprehension.

'You know the Bolsheviks have got a list of people they've decided to execute. My name is on it, and it may be that yours is too.'

'If it's they and they want to come in they only have to turn the handle,' said Ashenden, smiling, but with ever so slightly odd a feeling at the pit of his stomach. 'Come in.'

The door was opened and Mr Harrington stepped into the room. He was as dapper as ever, in his short black coat and striped trousers, his shoes neatly polished and a derby on his bald head. He took it off when he saw Anastasia Alexandrovna.

'Oh, fancy finding you here so early. I looked in on my way out, I wanted to tell you my news. I tried to find you yesterday evening, but couldn't. You didn't come in to dinner.'

'No, I was at a meeting,' said Ashenden.

'You must both congratulate me, I got my signatures yesterday, and my business is done.'

Mr Harrington beamed on them, the picture of self-satisfaction, and he arched himself like a bantam-cock who has chased away all rivals. Anastasia Alexandrovna burst into a sudden shriek of hysterical laughter. He stared at her in perplexity.

'Why, Delilah, what is the matter?' he said.

Anastasia laughed till the tears ran from her eyes and then began to sob in earnest. Ashenden explained.

'The Bolsheviks have overthrown the Government. Kerensky's ministers are in prison. The Bolsheviks are out to kill. Delilah says her name is on the list. Your minister signed your documents yesterday because he knew it did not matter what he did then. Your contracts are worth nothing. The Bolsheviks are going to make peace with Germany as soon as they can.'

Anastasia Alexandrovna had recovered her self-control as quickly as she had lost it.

'You had better get out of Russia as soon as you can, Mr Harrington. It's no place for a foreigner now and it may be that in a few days you won't be able to.'

Mr Harrington looked from one to the other.

'O my,' he said. 'O my!' It seemed inadequate. 'Are you going to tell me that that Russian minister was just making a fool of me?'

Ashenden shrugged his shoulders.

'How can one tell what he was thinking of? He may have a keen sense of humour and perhaps he thought it funny to sign a fifty-million-dollar contract yesterday when there was every chance of his being stood against the wall and shot today. Anastasia Alexandrovna's right, Mr Harrington, you'd better take the first train that'll get you to Sweden.'

'And what about you?'

'There's nothing for me to do here any more. I'm cabling for instructions and I shall go as soon as I get leave. The Bolsheviks have got ahead of us and the people I was working with will have their work cut out to save their lives.'

'Boris Petrovich was shot this morning,' said Anastasia Alexandrovna with a frown.

They both looked at Mr Harrington and he stared at the floor. His pride in this achievement of his was shattered and he sagged like a pricked balloon. But in a minute he looked up. He gave Anastasia Alexandrovna a little smile and for the first time Ashenden noticed how attractive and kindly his smile was. There was something peculiarly disarming about it.

'If the Bolsheviks are after you, Delilah, don't you think you'd better come with me? I'll take care of you and if you like to come to America I'm sure Mrs Harrington would be glad to do anything she could for you.'

'I can see Mrs Harrington's face if you arrived in Philadelphia with a Russian refugee,' laughed Anastasia Alexandrovna. 'I'm afraid it would need more explaining than you could ever manage. No, I shall stay here.'

'But if you're in danger?'

'I'm a Russian. My place is here. I will not leave my country when most my country needs me.'

'That is bunk, Delilah,' said Mr Harrington very quietly.

Anastasia Alexandrovna had spoken with deep emotion, but now with a little start she shot a sudden quizzical look at him.

'I know it is, Samson,' she answered. 'To tell you the truth I think we're all going to have a hell of a time, God knows what's going to happen, but I want to see; I wouldn't miss a minute of it for the world.'

Mr Harrington shook his head.

'Curiosity is the bane of your sex, Delilah,' he said.

'Go along and do your packing, Mr Harrington,' said Ashenden, smiling, 'and then we'll take you to the station. The train will be besieged.'

'Very well, I'll go. And I shan't be sorry either. I haven't had a decent meal since I came here and I've done a thing I never thought I should have to do in my life, I've drunk my coffee without sugar and when I've been lucky enough to get a little piece of black bread I've had to eat it without butter. Mrs Harrington will never believe me when I tell her what I've gone through. What this country wants is organization.'

When he left them Ashenden and Anastasia Alexandrovna talked over the situation. Ashenden was depressed because all his careful schemes had come to nothing, but Anastasia Alexandrovna was excited and she hazarded every sort of guess about the outcome of this new revolution. She pretended to be very serious, but in her heart she looked upon it all very much as a thrilling play. She wanted more and more things to happen. Then there was another knock at the door and before Ashenden could answer Mr Harrington burst in.

'Really the service at this hotel is a scandal,' he cried heatedly, 'I've been ringing my bell for fifteen minutes and I can't get anyone to pay the smallest attention to me.'

'Service?' exclaimed Anastasia Alexandrovna. 'There is not a servant left in the hotel.'

'But I want my laundry. They promised to let me have it back last night.'

'I'm afraid you haven't got much chance of getting it now,' said Ashenden.

'I'm not going to leave without my laundry. Four shirts, two union suits, a pair of pyjamas, and four collars. I wash my handkerchiefs and socks in my room. I want my laundry and I'm not going to leave this hotel without it.'

'Don't be a fool,' cried Ashenden. 'What you've got to do is to get out of here while the going's good. If there are no servants to get it you'll just have to leave your washing behind you.'

'Pardon me, sir, I shall do nothing of the kind. I'll go and fetch it myself. I've suffered enough at the hands of this country and I'm not going to leave four perfectly good shirts to be worn by a lot of dirty Bolsheviks. No, sir, I do not leave Russia till I have my laundry.'

Anastasia Alexandrovna stared at the floor for a moment; then with a little smile looked up. It seemed to Ashenden that there was something in her that responded to Mr Harrington's futile obstinacy. In her Russian way she understood that Mr Harrington could not leave Petrograd without his washing. His insistence had given it the value of a symbol.

'I'll go downstairs and see if I can find anybody about who knows where the laundry is, and if I can I'll go with you and you can bring your washing away with you.'

Mr Harrington unbent. He answered with that sweet and disarming smile of his.

'That's terribly kind of you, Delilah. I don't mind if it's ready or not, I'll take it just as it is.'

Anastasia Alexandrovna left them.

'Well, what do you think of Russia and the Russians now, Mr Harrington?' asked Ashenden.

'I'm fed up with them. I'm fed up with Tolstoy, I'm fed up with Turgenev and Dostoyevsky, I'm fed up with Chekhov. I'm fed up with the Intelligentsia. I hanker after people who know their mind from one minute to another, who mean what they say an hour after they've said it, whose word you can rely on; I'm sick of fine phrases, and oratory and attitudinizing.'

Ashenden, bitten by the prevailing ill, was about to make a speech when he was interrupted by a rattle as of peas on a drum. In the city, so strangely silent, it sounded abrupt and odd.

'What's that?' asked Mr Harrington.

'Rifle-firing. On the other side of the river, I should think.'

Mr Harrington gave a funny little look. He laughed, but his face was a trifle pale; he did not like it, and Ashenden did not blame him.

'I think it's high time I got out. I shouldn't so much mind for myself, but I've got a wife and children to think of. I haven't had a letter from Mrs Harrington for so long I'm a bit worried.' He paused an instant. 'I'd like you to know Mrs Harrington, she's a very wonderful woman. She's the best wife a man ever had. Until I came here I'd not been separated from her for more than three days since we were married.'

Anastasia Alexandrovna came back and told them that she had found the address.

'It's about forty minutes' walk from here and if you'll come now I'll go with you,' she said.

'I'm ready.'

'You'd better look out,' said Ashenden. 'I don't believe the streets are very healthy today.'

Anastasia Alexandrovna looked at Mr Harrington.

'I must have my laundry, Delilah,' he said. 'I should never rest in peace if I left it behind me and Mrs Harrington would never let me hear the last of it.'

'Come on then.'

They set out and Ashenden went on with the dreary business of translating into a very complicated code the shattering news he had to give. It was a long message, and then he had to ask for instructions upon his own movements. It was a mechanical job and yet it was one in which you could not allow your attention to wander. The mistake of a single figure might make a whole sentence incomprehensible.

Suddenly his door was burst open and Anastasia Alexandrovna flung into the room. She had lost her hat and was dishevelled. She was panting. Her eyes were starting out of her head and she was obviously in a state of great excitement.

'Where's Mr Harrington?' she cried. 'Isn't he here?'

'No.'

'Is he in his bedroom?'

'I don't know. Why, what's the matter? We'll go and look if you like. Why didn't you bring him along with you?'

They walked down the passage and knocked at Mr Harrington's door; there was no answer; they tried the handle; the door was locked.

'He's not there.'

They went back to Ashenden's room. Anastasia Alexandrovna sank into a chair.

'Give me a glass of water, will you? I'm out of breath. I've been running.'

She drank the water Ashenden poured out for her. She gave a sudden sob.

'I hope he's all right. I should never forgive myself if he was hurt. I was hoping he would have got here before me. He got his washing all right. We found the place. There was only an old woman there and they didn't want to let us take it, but we insisted. Mr Harrington was furious because it hadn't been touched. It was exactly as he had sent it. They'd promised it last night and it was still in the bundle that Mr Harrington had made himself. I said that was Russia and Mr Harrington said he preferred coloured people. I'd led him by side streets because I thought it was better, and we started to come back again. We passed at the top of a street and at the bottom of it I saw a little crowd. There was a man addressing them.

'"Let's go and hear what he's saying," I said.

'I could see they were arguing. It looked exciting. I wanted to know what was happening.

'"Come along, Delilah," he said. "Let us mind our own business."

'"You go back to the hotel and do your packing. I'm going to see the fun," I said.

'I ran down the street and he followed me. There were about two or three hundred people there and a student was addressing them. There were some working-men and they were shouting at him. I love a row and I edged my way into the crowd. Suddenly we heard the sound of shots and before you could realize what was happening two armoured cars came dashing down the street. There were soldiers in them and they were firing as they went. I don't know why. For fun, I suppose, or because they were drunk. We all scattered like a lot of rabbits. We just ran for our lives. I lost Mr Harrington. I can't make out why he isn't here. Do you think something has happened to him?'

Ashenden was silent for a while.

'We'd better go out and look for him,' he said. 'I don't know why the devil he couldn't leave his washing.'

'I understand, I understand so well.'

'That's a comfort,' said Ashenden irritably. 'Let's go.'

He put on his hat and coat, and they walked downstairs. The hotel seemed strangely empty. They went out into the street. There was hardly anyone to be seen. They walked along. The trams were not running and the silence in the great city was uncanny. The shops were closed. It was quite startling when a motor-car dashed by at breakneck speed. The people they passed looked frightened and downcast. When they had to go through a main thoroughfare they hastened their steps. A lot of people were there and they stood about irresolutely as though they did not know what to do next. Reservists in their shabby grey were walking down the middle of the roadway in little bunches. They did not speak. They looked like sheep looking for their shepherd. Then they came to the street down which Anastasia Alexandrovna had run, but they entered it from the opposite end. A number of windows had been broken by the wild shooting. It was quite empty. You could see where the people had scattered, for strewn about were articles they had dropped in their haste, books, a man's hat, a lady's bag, and a basket. Anastasia Alexandrovna touched Ashenden's arm to draw his attention: sitting on the pavement, her head bent right down to her lap, was a woman and she was dead. A little way on two men had fallen together. They were dead too. The wounded, one supposed, had managed to drag themselves away or their friends had carried them. Then they found Mr Harrington. His derby had rolled in the gutter. He lay on his face, in a pool of blood, his bald head, with its prominent bones, very white; his neat black coat smeared and muddy. But his hand was clenched tight on the parcel that contained four shirts, two union suits, a pair of pyjamas, and four collars. Mr Harrington had not let his washing go.

Lord
Mountdrago

◆

Dr Audlin looked at the clock on his desk. It was twenty minutes to six. He was surprised that his patient was late, for Lord Mountdrago prided himself on his punctuality; he had a sententious way of expressing himself which gave the air of an epigram to a commonplace remark, and he was in the habit of saying that punctuality is a compliment you pay to the intelligent and a rebuke you administer to the stupid. Lord Mountdrago's appointment was for five-thirty.

There was in Dr Audlin's appearance nothing to attract attention. He was tall and spare, with narrow shoulders and something of a stoop; his hair was grey and thin; his long, sallow face deeply lined. He was not more than fifty, but he looked older. His eyes, pale-blue and rather large, were weary. When you had been with him for a while you noticed that they moved very little; they remained fixed on your face, but so empty of expression were they that it was no discomfort. They seldom lit up. They gave no clue to his thoughts nor changed with the words he spoke. If you were of an observant turn it might have struck you that he blinked much less often than most of us. His hands were on the large side, with long, tapering fingers; they were soft, but firm, cool but not clammy. You could never have said what Dr Audlin wore unless you had made a point of looking. His clothes were dark. His tie was black. His dress made his sallow lined face paler, and his pale eyes more wan. He gave you the impression of a very sick man.

Dr Audlin was a psycho-analyst. He had adopted the profession by accident and practised it with misgiving. When the war broke out he had not been long qualified and was getting experience at various hospitals; he offered his services to the authorities, and after a time was sent out to France. It was then that he discovered his singular gift. He could allay certain pains by the touch of his cool, firm hands, and by talking to them often induce sleep in men who were suffering from sleeplessness. He spoke slowly. His voice had no particular colour, and its tone did not alter with the words he uttered, but it was musical, soft, and lulling. He told the men that they must rest, that they mustn't worry, that they must sleep; and rest stole into their jaded bones, tranquillity pushed their anxieties away, like a man finding a place for himself on a crowded bench, and slumber fell on their tired eyelids like the light rain of spring upon the fresh-turned earth. Dr Audlin found that by speaking to men with that low, monotonous voice of his, by looking at them with his pale, quiet eyes, by stroking their weary foreheads with his long firm hands, he could soothe their perturbations, resolve the conflicts that distracted them, and banish the phobias that made their lives a torment. Sometimes he effected cures that seemed miraculous. He restored speech to a man who, after being buried under the earth by a bursting shell, had been struck dumb, and he gave back the use of his limbs to another who had been paralysed after a crash in a plane. He could not understand his powers; he was of a sceptical turn, and though they say that in circumstances of this kind the first thing is to believe in yourself, he never quite succeeded in doing that; and it was only the outcome of his activities, patent to the most incredulous observer, that obliged him to admit that he had some faculty, coming from he knew not where, obscure and uncertain, that enabled him to do things for which he could offer no explanation. When the war was over he went to Vienna and studied there, and afterwards to Zürich; and then settled down in London to practise the art he had so strangely acquired. He had been practising now for fifteen years, and had attained, in the speciality he followed, a distinguished reputation. People told one another of the amazing things he had done, and though his fees were high, he had as many patients as he had time to see. Dr Audlin knew that he had achieved some very extraordinary results; he had saved men from suicide, others from the lunatic asylum, he had assuaged griefs that embittered useful lives, he had turned unhappy marriages into happy ones, he had eradicated abnormal instincts and thus delivered not a few from a hateful bondage, he had given health to the sick in spirit; he had done all this, and yet at the back of his mind remained the suspicion that he was little more than a quack.

It went against his grain to exercise a power that he could not understand, and it offended his honesty to trade on the faith of the people he treated when he had no faith in himself. He was rich enough now to live without working, and the work exhausted him; a dozen times he had been on the point of giving up practice. He knew all that Freud and Jung and the rest of them had written. He was not satisfied; he had an intimate conviction that all their theory was hocus-pocus, and yet there the results were, incomprehensible, but manifest. And what had he not seen of human nature during the fifteen years that patients had been coming to his dingy back room in Wimpole Street? The revelations that had been poured into his ears, sometimes only too willingly, sometimes with shame, with reservations, with anger, had long ceased to surprise him. Nothing could shock him any longer. He knew by now that men were liars, he knew how extravagant was their vanity; he knew far worse than that about them; but he knew that it was not for him to judge or to condemn. But year by year as these terrible confidences were imparted to him his face grew a little greyer, its lines a little more marked, and his pale eyes more weary. He seldom laughed, but now and again when for relaxation he read a novel he smiled. Did their authors really think the men and women they wrote of were like that? If they only knew how much more complicated they were, how much more unexpected, what irreconcilable elements coexisted within their souls and what dark and sinister contentions afflicted them!

It was a quarter to six. Of all the strange cases he had been called upon to deal with Dr Audlin could remember none stranger than that of Lord Mountdrago. For one thing the personality of his patient made it singular. Lord Mountdrago was an able and a distinguished man. Appointed Secretary of Foreign Affairs when still under forty, now after three years in office he had seen his policy prevail. It was generally acknowledged that he was the ablest politician in the Conservative Party and only the fact that his father was a peer, on whose death he would no longer be able to sit in the House of Commons, made it impossible for him to aim at the premiership. But if in these democratic times it is out of the question for a Prime Minister of England to be in the House of Lords, there was nothing to prevent Lord Mountdrago from continuing to be Secretary for Foreign Affairs in successive Conservative administrations and so for long directing the foreign policy of his country.

Lord Mountdrago had many good qualities. He had intelligence and industry. He was widely travelled, and spoke several languages fluently. From early youth he had specialized in foreign affairs, and had conscientiously made himself acquainted with the political and economic circumstances of other countries. He had courage, insight, and determination. He was a good speaker, both on the platform and in the House, clear, precise, and often witty. He was a brilliant debater and his gift of repartee was celebrated. He had a fine presence: he was a tall, handsome man, rather bald and somewhat too stout, but this gave him solidity and an air of maturity that were of service to him. As a young man he had been something of an athlete and had rowed in the Oxford boat, and he was known to be one of the best shots in England. At twenty-four he had married a girl of eighteen whose father was a duke and her mother a great American heiress, so that she had both position and wealth, and by her he had had two sons. For several years they had lived privately apart, but in public united, so that appearances were saved, and no other attachment on either side had given the gossips occasion to whisper. Lord Mountdrago indeed was too ambitious, too hard-working, and it must be added too patriotic, to be tempted by any pleasures that might interfere with his career. He had, in short, a great deal to make him a popular and successful figure. He had unfortunately great defects.

He was a fearful snob. You would not have been surprised at this if his father had been the first holder of the title. That the son of an ennobled lawyer, a manufacturer, or a distiller should attach an inordinate importance to his rank is understandable. The earldom held by Lord Mountdrago's father was created by Charles II, and the barony held by the first Earl dated from the Wars of the Roses. For three hundred years the successive holders of the title had allied themselves with the noblest families of England. But Lord Mountdrago was as conscious of his birth as a *nouveau riche* is conscious of his money. He never missed an opportunity of impressing it upon others. He had beautiful manners when he chose to display them, but this he did only with people whom he regarded as his equals. He was coldly insolent to those whom he looked upon as his social inferiors. He was rude to his servants and insulting to his secretaries. The subordinate officials in the government offices to which he had been successively attached feared and hated him. His arrogance was horrible. He knew that he was a great deal cleverer than most of the persons he had to do with, and never hesitated to apprise them of the fact. He had no patience with the infirmities of human nature. He felt himself born to command and was irritated with people who expected him to listen to their arguments or wished to hear the reasons for his decisions. He was immeasurably selfish. He looked upon any service that was rendered him as a right due to his rank and intelligence and therefore deserving of no gratitude. It never entered his head that he was called upon to do anything for others. He had many enemies: he despised them. He knew no one who merited his assistance, his sympathy, or his compassion. He had no friends. He was distrusted by his chiefs, because they doubted his loyalty; he was unpopular with his party, because he was over-bearing and discourteous; and yet his merit was so great, his patriotism so evident, his intelligence so solid, and his management of affairs so brilliant that they had to put up with him. And what made it possible to do this was that on occasion he could be enchanting; when he was with persons whom he considered his equals, or whom he wished to captivate, in the company of foreign dignitaries or women of distinction, he could be gay, witty, and debonair; his manners then reminded you that in his veins ran the same blood as had run in the veins of Lord Chesterfield; he could tell a story with point, he could be natural, sensible, and even profound. You were surprised at the extent of his knowledge and the sensitiveness of his taste. You thought him the best company in the world; you forgot that he had insulted you the day before and was quite capable of cutting you dead the next.

Lord Mountdrago almost failed to become Dr Audlin's patient. A secretary rang up the doctor and told him that his lordship, wishing to consult him, would be glad if he would come to his house at ten o'clock on the following morning. Dr Audlin answered that he was unable to go to Lord Mountdrago's house, but would be pleased to give him an appointment at his consulting-room at five o'clock on the next day but one. The secretary took the message and presently rang back to say that Lord Mountdrago insisted on seeing Dr Audlin in his own house and the doctor could fix his own fee. Dr Audlin replied that he only saw patients in his consulting-room and expressed his regret that unless Lord Mountdrago was prepared to come to him he could not give him his attention. In a quarter of an hour a brief message was delivered to him that his lordship would come not next day but one, but next day, at five.

When Lord Mountdrago was then shown in he did not come forward, but stood at the door and insolently looked the doctor up and down. Dr Audlin perceived that he was in a rage; he gazed at him, silently, with still eyes. He saw a big heavy man, with greying hair, receding on the forehead so that it gave nobility to his brow, a puffy face with bold regular features and an expression of haughtiness. He had somewhat the look of one of the Bourbon sovereigns of the eighteenth century.

'It seems that it is as difficult to see you as a Prime Minister, Dr Audlin. I'm an extremely busy man.'

'Won't you sit down?' said the doctor.

His face showed no sign that Lord Mountdrago's speech in any way affected him. Dr Audlin sat in his chair at the desk. Lord Mountdrago still stood and his frown darkened.

'I think I should tell you that I am His Majesty's Secretary for Foreign Affairs,' he said acidly.

'Won't you sit down?' the doctor repeated.

Lord Mountdrago made a gesture, which might have suggested that he was about to turn on his heel and stalk out of the room; but if that was his intention he apparently thought better of it. He seated himself. Dr Audlin opened a large book and took up his pen. He wrote without looking at his patient.

'How old are you?'

'Forty-two.'

'Are you married?'

'Yes.'

'How long have you been married?'

'Eighteen years.'

'Have you any children?'

'I have two sons.'

Dr Audlin noted down the facts as Lord Mountdrago abruptly answered his questions. Then he leaned back in his chair and looked at him. He did not speak; he just looked, gravely, with pale eyes that did not move.

'Why have you come to see me?' he asked at length.

'I've heard about you. Lady Canute is a patient of yours, I understand. She tells me you've done her a certain amount of good.'

Dr Audlin did not reply. His eyes remained fixed on the other's face, but they were so empty of expression that you might have thought he did not even see him.

'I can't do miracles,' he said at length. Not a smile, but the shadow of a smile flickered in his eyes. 'The Royal College of Physicians would not approve of it if I did.'

Lord Mountdrago gave a brief chuckle. It seemed to lessen his hostility. He spoke more amiably.

'You have a very remarkable reputation. People seem to believe in you.'

'Why have you come to me?' repeated Dr Audlin.

Now it was Lord Mountdrago's turn to be silent. It looked as though he found it hard to answer. Dr Audlin waited. At last Lord Mountdrago seemed to make an effort. He spoke.

'I'm in perfect health. Just as a matter of routine I had myself examined by my own doctor the other day, Sir Augustus Fitzherbert, I dare say you've heard of him, and he tells me I have the physique of a man of thirty. I work hard, but I'm never tired, and I enjoy my work. I smoke very little and I'm an extremely moderate drinker. I take a sufficiency of exercise and I lead a regular life. I am a perfectly sound, normal, healthy man. I quite expect you to think it very silly and childish of me to consult you.'

Dr Audlin saw that he must help him.

'I don't know if I can do anything to help you. I'll try. You're distressed?'

Lord Mountdrago frowned.

'The work that I'm engaged in is important. The decisions I am called upon to make can easily affect the welfare of the country and even the peace of the world. It is essential that my judgement should be balanced and my brain clear. I look upon it as my duty to eliminate any cause of worry that may interfere with my usefulness.'

Dr Audlin had never taken his eyes off him. He saw a great deal. He saw behind his patient's pompous manner and arrogant pride an anxiety that he could not dispel.

'I asked you to be good enough to come here because I know by experience that it's easier for someone to speak openly in the dingy surroundings of a doctor's consulting-room than in his accustomed environment.'

'They're certainly dingy,' said Lord Mountdrago acidly. He paused. It was evident that this man who had so much self-assurance, so quick and decided a mind that he was never at a loss, at this moment was embarrassed. He smiled in order to show the doctor that he was at his ease, but his eyes betrayed his disquiet. When he spoke again it was with unnatural heartiness.

'The whole thing's so trivial that I can hardly bring myself to bother you with it. I'm afraid you'll just tell me not to be a fool and waste your valuable time.'

'Even things that seem very trivial may have their importance. They can be a symptom of a deep-seated derangement. And my time is entirely at your disposal.'

Dr Audlin's voice was low and grave. The monotone in which he spoke was strangely soothing. Lord Mountdrago at length made up his mind to be frank.

'The fact is I've been having some very tiresome dreams lately. I know it's silly to pay any attention to them, but—well, the honest truth is that I'm afraid they've got on my nerves.'

'Can you describe any of them to me?'

Lord Mountdrago smiled, but the smile that tried to be careless was only rueful.

'They're so idotic, I can hardly bring myself to narrate them.'

'Never mind.'

'Well, the first I had was about a month ago. I dreamt that I was at a party at Connemara House. It was an official party. The King and Queen were to be there and of course decorations were worn. I was wearing my ribbon and my star. I went into a sort of cloakroom they have to take off my coat. There was a little man there called Owen Griffiths, who's a Welsh Member of Paliament, and to tell you the truth, I was surprised to see him. He's very common, and I said to myself: "Really, Lydia Connemara is going too far, whom will she ask next?" I thought he looked at me rather curiously, but I didn't take any notice of him; in fact I cut the little bounder and walked upstairs. I suppose you've never been there?'

'Never.'

'No, it's not the sort of house you'd ever be likely to go to. It's a rather vulgar house, but it's got a very fine marble staircase, and the Connemaras were at the top receiving their guests. Lady Connemara gave me a look of surprise when I shook hands with her, and began to giggle; I didn't pay much attention, she's a very silly, ill-bred woman and her manners are no better than those of her ancestor whom King Charles II made a duchess. I must say the reception rooms at Connemara House are stately. I walked through, nodding to a number of people and shaking hands; then I saw the German Ambassador talking with one of the Austrian Archdukes. I particularly wanted to have a word with him, so I went up and held out my hand. The moment the Archduke saw me he burst into a roar of laughter. I was deeply affronted. I looked him up and down sternly, but he only laughed the more. I was about to speak to him rather sharply, when there was a sudden hush and I realized that the King and Queen had come. Turning my back on the Archduke, I stepped forward, and then, quite suddenly, I noticed that I hadn't got any trousers on. I was in short silk drawers, and I wore scarlet sock-suspenders. No wonder Lady Connemara had giggled; no wonder the Archduke had laughed! I can't tell you what that moment was. An agony of shame. I awoke in a cold sweat. Oh, you don't know the relief I felt to find it was only a dream.'

'It's the kind of dream that's not so very uncommon,' said Dr Audlin.

'I dare say not. But an odd thing happened next day. I was in the lobby of the House of Commons, when that fellow Griffiths walked slowly past me. He deliberately looked down at my legs and then he looked me full in the face and I was almost certain he winked. A ridiculous thought came to me. He'd been there the night before and seen me make that ghastly exhibition of myself and was enjoying the joke. But of course I knew that was impossible because it was only a dream. I gave him an icy glare and he walked on. But he was grinning his head off.'

Lord Mountdrago took his handkerchief out of his pocket and wiped the palms of his hands. He was making no attempt now to conceal his perturbation. Dr Audlin never took his eyes off him.

'Tell me another dream.'

'It was the night after, and it was even more absurd than the first one. I dreamt that I was in the House. There was a debate on foreign affairs which not only the country, but the world, had been looking forward to with the gravest concern. The government had decided on a change in their policy which vitally affected the future of the Empire. The occasion was historic. Of course the House was crowded. All the ambassadors were there. The galleries were packed. It fell to me to make the important speech of the evening. I had prepared it carefully. A man like me has enemies, there are a lot of people who resent my having achieved the position I have at an age when even the cleverest men are content with situations of relative obscurity, and I was determined that my speech should not only be worthy of the occasion, but should silence my detractors. It excited me to think that the whole world was hanging on my lips. I rose to my feet. If you've ever been in the House you'll know how members chat to one another during a debate, rustle papers and turn over reports. The silence was the silence of the grave when I began to speak. Suddenly I caught sight of that odious little bounder on one of the benches opposite, Griffiths the Welsh member; he put out his tongue at me. I don't know if you've ever heard a vulgar music-hall song called *A Bicycle Made for Two*. It was very popular a great many years ago. To show Griffiths how completely I despised him I began to sing it. I sang the first verse right through. There was a moment's surprise, and when I finished they cried "Hear, hear," on the opposite benches. I put up my hand to silence them and sang the second verse. The House listened to me in stony silence and I felt the song wasn't going down very well. I was vexed, for I have a good baritone voice, and I was determined that they should do me justice. When I started the third verse the members began to laugh; in an instant the laughter spread; the ambassadors, the strangers in the Distinguished Strangers' Gallery, the ladies in the Ladies' Gallery, the reporters, they shook, they bellowed, they held their sides, they rolled in their seats; everyone was overcome with laughter except the ministers on the Front Bench immediately behind me. In that incredible, in that unprecedented uproar, they sat petrified. I gave them a glance, and suddenly the enormity of what I had done fell upon me. I had made myself the laughing-stock of the whole world. With misery I realized that I should have to resign. I woke and knew it was only a dream.'

Lord Mountdrago's grand manner had deserted him as he narrated this, and now having finished he was pale and trembling. But with an effort he pulled himself together. He forced a laugh to his shaking lips.

'The whole thing was so fantastic that I couldn't help being amused. I didn't give it another thought, and when I went into the House on the following afternoon I was feeling in very good form. The debate was dull, but I had to be there, and I read some documents that required my attention. For some reason I chanced to look up and I saw that Griffiths was speaking. He has an unpleasant Welsh accent and an unprepossessing appearance. I couldn't imagine that he had anything to say that it was worth my while to listen to, and I was about to return to my papers when he quoted two lines from *A Bicycle Made for Two*. I couldn't help glancing at him and I saw that his eyes were fixed on me with a grin of bitter mockery. I faintly shrugged my shoulders. It was comic that a scrubby little Welsh member should look at me like that. It was an odd coincidence that he should quote two lines from that disastrous song that I'd sung all through in my dream. I began to read my papers again, but I don't mind telling you that I found it difficult to concentrate on them. I was a little puzzled. Owen Griffiths had been in my first dream, the one at Connemara House, and I'd received a very definite impression afterwards that he knew the sorry figure I'd cut. Was it a mere coincidence that he had just quoted those two lines? I asked myself if it was possible that he was dreaming the same dreams as I was. But of course the idea was preposterous and I determined not to give it a second thought.'

There was a silence. Dr Audlin looked at Lord Mountdrago and Lord Mountdrago looked at Dr Audlin.

'Other people's dreams are very boring. My wife used to dream occasionally and insist on telling me her dreams next day with circumstantial detail. I found it maddening.'

Dr Audlin faintly smiled.

'You're not boring me.'

'I'll tell you one more dream I had a few days later. I dreamt that I went into a public-house at Limehouse. I've never been to Limehouse in my life and I don't think I've ever been in a public-house since I was at Oxford, and yet I saw the street and the place I went into as exactly as if I were at home there. I went into a room, I don't know whether they call it the saloon bar or the private bar; there was a fireplace and a large leather arm-chair on one side of it, and on the other a small sofa; a bar ran the whole length of the room and over it you could see into the public bar. Near the door was a round marble-topped table and two arm-chairs beside it. It was a Saturday night and the place was packed. It was brightly lit, but the smoke was so thick that it made my eyes smart. I was dressed like a rough, with a cap on my head and a handkerchief round my neck. It seemed to me that most of the people there were drunk. I thought it rather amusing. There was a gramophone going, or the radio, I don't know which, and in front of the fireplace two women were doing a grotesque dance. There was a little crowd round them, laughing, cheering, and singing. I went up to have a look and some man said to me: "'Ave a drink, Bill?" There were glasses on the table full of a dark liquid which I understand is called brown ale. He gave me a glass and not wishing to be conspicuous I drank it. One of the women who were dancing broke away from the other and took hold of the glass. "'Ere, what's the idea?" she said. "That's my beer you're putting away." "Oh, I'm so sorry," I said, "this gentleman offered it me and I very naturally thought it was his to offer." "All right, mate," she said, "I don't mind. You come an' 'ave a dance with me." Before I could protest she'd caught hold of me and we were dancing together. And then I found myself sitting in the arm-chair with the woman on my lap and we were sharing a glass of beer. I should tell you that sex has never played any great part in my life. I married young because in my position it was desirable that I should marry, but also in order to settle once for all the question of sex. I had the two sons I had made up my mind to have, and then I put the whole matter on one side. I've always been too busy to give much thought to that kind of thing, and living so much in the public eye as I do it would have been madness to do anything that might give rise to scandal. The greatest asset a politician can have is a blameless record as far as women are concerned. I have no patience with the men who smash up their careers for women. I only despise them. The woman I had on my knees was drunk; she wasn't pretty and she wasn't young; in fact, she was just a blowsy old prostitute. She filled me with disgust, and yet when she put her mouth to mine and kissed me, though her breath stank of beer and her teeth were decayed, though I loathed myself, I wanted her – I wanted her with all my soul. Suddenly I heard a voice. "That's right, old boy, have a good time." I looked up and there was Owen Griffiths. I tried to spring out of the chair, but that horrible woman wouldn't let me. "Don't you pay no attention to 'im," she said, "'e's only one of them nosy-parkers." "You go to it," he said. "I know Moll. She'll give you your money's worth all right." You know, I wasn't so much annoyed at his seeing me in that absurd situation as angry that he should address me as "old boy". I pushed the woman aside and stood up and faced him. "I don't know you and I don't want to know you," I said. "I know you all right," he said. "And my advice to you, Molly, is, see that you get your money, he'll bilk you if he can." There was a bottle of beer on the table close by. Without a word I seized it by the neck and hit him over the head with it as hard as I could. I made such a violent gesture that it woke me up.'

'A dream of that sort is not incomprehensible,' said Dr Audlin. 'It is the revenge nature takes on persons of unimpeachable character.'

'The story's idiotic. I haven't told it you for its own sake. I've told it you for what happened next day. I wanted to look up something in a hurry and I went into the library of the House. I got the book and began reading. I hadn't noticed when I sat down that Griffiths was sitting in a chair close by me. Another of the Labour Members came in and went up to him. "Hullo, Owen," he said to him, "you're looking pretty dicky today." "I've got an awful headache," he answered. "I feel as if I'd been cracked over the head with a bottle."'

Now Lord Mountdrago's face was grey with anguish.

'I knew then that the idea I'd had and dismissed as preposterous was true. I knew that Griffiths was dreaming my dreams and that he remembered them as well as I did.'

'It may also have been a coincidence.'

'When he spoke he didn't speak to his friend, he deliberately spoke to me. He looked at me with sullen resentment.'

'Can you offer any suggestion why this same man should come into your dreams?'

'None.'

Dr Audlin's eyes had not left his patient's face and he saw that he lied. He had a pencil in his hand and he drew a straggling line or two on his blotting-paper. It often took a long time to get people to tell the truth, and yet they knew that unless they told it he could do nothing for them.

'The dream you've just described to me took place just over three weeks ago. Have you had any since?'

'Every night.'

'And does this man Griffiths come into them all?'

'Yes.'

The doctor drew more lines on his blotting-paper. He wanted the silence, the drabness, the dull light of that little room to have its effect on Lord Mountdrago's sensibility. Lord Mountdrago threw himself back in his chair and turned his head away so that he should not see the other's grave eyes.

'Dr Audlin, you must do something for me. I'm at the end of my tether. I shall go mad if this goes on. I'm afraid to go to sleep. Two or three nights I haven't. I've sat up reading and when I felt drowsy put on my coat and walked till I was exhausted. But I must have sleep. With all the work I have to do I must be at concert pitch; I must be in complete control of all my faculties. I need rest; sleep brings me none. I no sooner fall asleep than my dreams begin, and he's always there, that vulgar little cad, grinning at me, mocking me, despising me. It's a monstrous persecution. I tell you, doctor, I'm not the man of my dreams; it's not fair to judge me by them. Ask anyone you like. I'm an honest, upright, decent man. No one can say anything against my moral character either private or public. My whole ambition is to serve my country and maintain its greatness. I have money, I have rank, I'm not exposed to many of the temptations of lesser men, so that it's no credit to me to be incorruptible; but this I can claim, that no honour, no personal advantage, no thought of self would induce me to swerve by a hair's breadth from my duty. I've sacrificed everything to become the man I am. Greatness is my aim. Greatness is within my reach and I'm losing my nerve. I'm not that mean, despicable, cowardly, lewd creature that horrible little man sees. I've told you three of my dreams; they're nothing; that man has seen me do things that are so beastly, so horrible, so shameful, that even if my life depended on it I wouldn't tell them. And he remembers them. I can hardly meet the derision and disgust I see in his eyes and I even hesitate to speak because I know my words can seem to him nothing but utter humbug. He's seen me do things that no man with any self-respect would do, things for which men are driven out of the society of their fellows and sentenced to long terms of imprisonment; he's heard the foulness of my speech; he's seen me not only ridiculous, but revolting. He despises me and he no longer pretends to conceal it. I tell you that if you can't do something to help me I shall either kill myself or kill him.'

'I wouldn't kill him if I were you,' said Dr Audlin, coolly, in that soothing voice of his. 'In this country the consequences of killing a fellow-creature are awkward.'

'I shouldn't be hanged for it, if that's what you mean. Who would know that I'd killed him? That dream of mine has shown me how. I told you, the day after I'd hit him over the head with a beer-bottle he had such a headache that he couldn't see straight. He said so himself. That shows that he can feel with his waking body what happens to his body asleep. It's not with a bottle I shall hit him next time. One night, when I'm dreaming, I shall find myself with a knife in my hand or a revolver in my pocket, I must because I want to so intensely, and then I shall seize my opportunity. I'll stick him like a pig; I'll shoot him like a dog. In the heart. And then I shall be free of this fiendish persecution.'

Some people might have thought that Lord Mountdrago was mad; after all the years during which Dr Audlin had been treating the diseased souls of men he knew how thin a line divides those whom we call sane from those whom we call insane. He knew how often in men who to all appearance were healthy and normal, who were seemingly devoid of imagination, and who fulfilled the duties of common life with credit to themselves and with benefit to their fellows, when you gained their confidence, when you tore away the mask they wore to the world, you found not only hideous abnormality, but kinks so strange, mental extravagances so fantastic, that in that respect you could call them lunatic. If you put them in an asylum not all the asylums in the world would be large enough. Anyhow, a man was not certifiable because he had strange dreams and they had shattered his nerve. The case was singular, but it was only an exaggeration of others that had come under Dr Audlin's observation; he was doubtful, however, whether the methods of treatment that he had so often found efficacious would here avail.

'Have you consulted any other member of my profession?' he asked.

'Only Sir Augustus. I merely told him that I suffered from nightmares. He said I was overworked and recommended me to go for a cruise. That's absurd. I can't leave the Foreign Office just now when the international situation needs constant attention. I'm indispensable, and I know it. On my conduct at the present juncture my whole future depends. He gave me sedatives. They had no effect. He gave me tonics. They were worse than useless. He's an old fool.'

'Can you give any reason why it should be this particular man who persists in coming into your dreams?'

'You asked me that question before. I answered it.'

That was true. But Dr Audlin had not been satisfied with the answer.

'Just now you talked of persecution. Why should Owen Griffiths want to persecute you?'

'I don't know.'

Lord Mountdrago's eyes shifted a little. Dr Audlin was sure that he was not speaking the truth.

'Have you ever done him an injury?'

'Never.'

Lord Mountdrago made no movement, but Dr Audlin had a queer feeling that he shrank into his skin. He saw before him a large, proud man who gave the impression that the questions put to him were an insolence, and yet for all that, behind that façade, was something shifting and startled that made you think of a frightened animal in a trap. Dr Audlin leaned forward and by the power of his eyes forced Lord Mountdrago to meet them.

'Are you quite sure?'

'Quite sure. You don't seem to understand that our ways lead along different paths. I don't wish to harp on it, but I must remind you that I am a Minister of the Crown and Griffiths is an obscure member of the Labour Party. Naturally there's no social connection between us; he's a man of very humble origin, he's not the sort of person I should be likely to meet at any of the houses I go to; and politically our respective stations are so far separated that we could not possibly have anything in common.'

'I can do nothing for you unless you tell me the complete truth.'

Lord Mountdrago raised his eyebrows. His voice was rasping.

'I'm not accustomed to having my word doubted, Dr Audlin. If you're going to do that I think to take up any more of your time can only be a waste of mine. If you will kindly let my secretary know what your fee is he will see that a cheque is sent to you.'

For all the expression that was to be seen on Dr Audlin's face you might have thought that he simply had not heard what Lord Mountdrago said. He continued to look steadily into his eyes and his voice was grave and low.

'Have you done anything to this man that *he* might look upon as an injury?'

Lord Mountdrago hesitated. He looked away, and then, as though there were in Dr Audlin's eyes a compelling force that he could not resist, looked back. He answered sulkily:

'Only if he was a dirty, second-rate little cad.'

'But that is exactly what you've described him to be.'

Lord Mountdrago sighed. He was beaten. Dr Audlin knew that the sigh meant he was going at last to say what he had till then held back. Now he had no longer to insist. He dropped his eyes and began again drawing vague geometrical figures on his blotting-paper. The silence lasted two or three minutes.

'I'm anxious to tell you everything that can be of any use to you. If I didn't mention this before, it's only because it was so unimportant that I didn't see how it could possibly have anything to do with the case. Griffiths won a seat at the last election and he began to make a nuisance of himself almost at once. His father's a miner, and he worked in a mine himself when he was a boy; he's been a schoolmaster in the board schools and a journalist. He's that half-baked, conceited intellectual, with inadequate knowledge, ill-considered ideas, and impracticable plans, that compulsory education has brought forth from the working-classes. He's a scrawny, grey-faced man, who looks half-starved, and he's always very slovenly in appearance; heaven knows members nowadays don't bother much about their dress, but his clothes are an outrage to the dignity of the House. They're ostentatiously shabby, his collar's never clean and his tie's never tied properly; he looks as if he hadn't had a bath for a month and his hands are filthy. The Labour Party have two or three fellows on the Front Bench who've got a certain ability, but the rest of them don't amount to much. In the kingdom of the blind the one-eyed man is king: because Griffiths is glib and has a lot of superficial information on a number of subjects, the Whips on his side began to put him up to speak whenever there was a chance. It appeared that he fancied himself on foreign affairs, and he was continually asking me silly, tiresome questions. I don't mind telling you that I made a point of snubbing him as soundly as I thought he deserved. From the beginning I hated the way he talked, his whining voice and his vulgar accent; he had nervous mannerisms that intensely irritated me. He talked rather shyly, hesitatingly, as though it were torture to him to speak and yet he was forced on by some inner passion, and often he used to say some very disconcerting things. I'll admit that now and again he had a sort of tub-thumping eloquence. It had a certain influence over the ill-regulated minds of the members of his party. They were impressed by his earnestness and they weren't, as I was, nauseated by his sentimentality. A certain sentimentality is the common coin of political debate. Nations are governed by self-interest, but they prefer to believe that their aims are altruistic, and the politician is justified if with fair words and fine phrases he can persuade the electorate that the hard bargain he is driving for his country's advantage tends to the good of humanity. The mistake people like Griffiths make is to take these fair words and fine phrases at their face value. He's a crank, and a noxious crank. He calls himself an idealist. He has at his tongue's end all the tedious blather that the intelligentsia have been boring us with for years. Non-resistance. The brotherhood of man. You know the hopeless rubbish. The worst of it was that it impressed not only his own party, it even shook some of the sillier, more sloppy-minded members of ours. I heard rumours that Griffiths was likely to get office when a Labour Government came in; I even heard it suggested that he might get the Foreign Office. The notion was grotesque but not impossible. One day I had occasion to wind up a debate on foreign affairs which Griffiths had opened. He'd spoken for an hour. I thought it a very good opportunity to cook his goose, and by God, sir, I cooked it. I tore his speech to pieces. I pointed out the faultiness of his reasoning and emphasized the deficiency of his knowledge. In the House of Commons the most devastating weapon is ridicule: I mocked him; I bantered him; I was in good form that day and the House rocked with laughter. Their laughter excited me and I excelled myself. The Opposition sat glum and silent, but even some of them couldn't help laughing once or twice; it's not intolerable, you know, to see a colleague, perhaps a rival, made a fool of. And if ever a man was made a fool of I made a fool of Griffiths. He shrank down in a seat, I saw his face go white, and presently he buried it in his hands. When I sat down I'd killed him. I'd destroyed his prestige for ever; he had no more chance of getting office when a Labour Government came in than the policeman at the door. I heard afterwards that his father, the old miner, and his mother had come up from Wales, with various supporters of his in the constituency, to watch the triumph they expected him to have. They had seen only his utter humiliation. He'd won the constituency by the narrowest margin. An incident like that might very easily lose him his seat. But that was no business of mine.'

'Should I be putting it too strongly if I said you had ruined his career?' asked Dr Audlin.

'I don't suppose you would.'

'That is a very serious injury you've done him.'

'He brought it on himself.'

'Have you never felt any qualms about it?'

'I think perhaps if I'd known that his father and mother were there I might have let him down a little more gently.'

There was nothing further for Dr Audlin to say, and he set about treating his patient in such a manner as he thought might avail. He sought by suggestion to make him forget his dreams when he awoke; he sought to make him sleep so deeply that he would not dream. He found Lord Mountdrago's resistance impossible to break down. At the end of an hour he dismissed him. Since then he had seen Lord Mountdrago half a dozen times. He had done him no good. The frightful dreams continued every night to harass the unfortunate man, and it was clear that his general condition was growing rapidly worse. He was worn out. His irritability was uncontrollable. Lord Mountdrago was angry because he received no benefit from his treatment, and yet continued it, not only because it seemed his only hope, but because it was a relief to him to have someone with whom he could talk openly. Dr Audlin came to the conclusion at last that there was only one way in which Lord Mountdrago could achieve deliverance, but he knew him well enough to be assured that of his own free will he would never, never take it. If Lord Mountdrago was to be saved from the breakdown that was threatening he must be induced to take a step that must be abhorrent to his pride of birth and his self-complacency. Dr Audlin was convinced that to delay was impossible. He was treating his patient by suggestion, and after several visits found him more susceptible to it. At length he managed to get him into a condition of somnolence. With his low, soft, monotonous voice he soothed his tortured nerves. He repeated the same words over and over again. Lord Mountdrago lay quite still, his eyes closed; his breathing was regular, and his limbs were relaxed. Then Dr Audlin in the same quiet tone spoke the words he had prepared.

'You will go to Owen Griffiths and say that you are sorry that you caused him that great injury. You will say that you will do whatever lies in your power to undo the harm that you have done him.'

The words acted on Lord Mountdrago like the blow of a whip across his face. He shook himself out of his hypnotic state and sprang to his feet. His eyes blazed with passion and he poured forth upon Dr Audlin a stream of angry vituperation such as even he had never heard. He swore at him. He cursed him. He used language of such obscenity that Dr Audlin, who had heard every sort of foul word, sometimes from the lips of chaste and distinguished women, was surprised that he knew it.

'Apologize to that filthy little Welshman? I'd rather kill myself.'

'I believe it to be the only way in which you can regain your balance.'

Dr Audlin had not often seen a man presumably sane in such a condition of uncontrollable fury. He grew red in the face and his eyes bulged out of his head. He did really foam at the mouth. Dr Audlin watched him coolly, waiting for the storm to wear itself out, and presently he saw that Lord Mountdrago, weakened by the strain to which he had been subjected for so many weeks, was exhausted.

'Sit down,' he said then, sharply.

Lord Mountdrago crumpled up into a chair.

'Christ, I feel all in. I must rest a minute and then I'll go.'

For five minutes perhaps they sat in complete silence. Lord Mountdrago was a gross, blustering bully, but he was also a gentleman. When he broke the silence he had recovered his self-control.

'I'm afraid I've been very rude to you. I'm ashamed of the things I've said to you and I can only say you'd be justified if you refused to have anything more to do with me. I hope you won't do that. I feel that my visits to you do help me. I think you're my only chance.'

'You mustn't give another thought to what you said. It was of no consequence.'

'But there's one thing you mustn't ask me to do, and that is to make excuses to Griffiths.'

'I've thought a great deal about your case. I don't pretend to understand it, but I believe that your only chance of release is to do what I proposed. I have a notion that we're none of us one self, but many, and one of the selves in you has risen up against the injury you did Griffiths and has taken on the form of Griffiths in your mind and is punishing you for what you cruelly did. If I were a priest I should tell you that it is your conscience that has adopted the shape and lineaments of this man to scourge you to repentance and persuade you to reparation.'

'My conscience is clear. It's not my fault if I smashed the man's career. I crushed him like a slug in my garden. I regret nothing.'

It was on these words that Lord Mountdrago had left him. Reading through his notes, while he waited, Dr Audlin considered how best he could bring his patient to the state of mind that, now that his usual methods of treatment had failed, he thought alone could help him. He glanced at his clock. It was six. It was strange that Lord Mountdrago did not come. He knew he had intended to because a secretary had rung up that morning to say that he would be with him at the usual hour. He must have been detained by pressing work. This notion gave Dr Audlin something else to think of: Lord Mountdrago was quite unfit for work and in no condition to deal with important matters of state. Dr Audlin wondered whether it behoved him to get in touch with someone in authority, the Prime Minister or the Permanent Under-Secretary for Foreign Affairs, and impart to him his conviction that Lord Mountdrago's mind was so unbalanced that it was dangerous to leave affairs of moment in his hands. It was a ticklish thing to do. He might cause needless trouble and get roundly snubbed for his pains. He shrugged his shoulders.

'After all,' he reflected, 'the politicians have made such a mess of the world during the last five-and-twenty years, I don't suppose it makes much odds if they're mad or sane.'

He rang the bell.

'If Lord Mountdrago comes now will you tell him that I have another appointment at six-fifteen and so I'm afraid I can't see him.'

'Very good, sir.'

'Has the evening paper come yet?'

'I'll go and see.'

In a moment the servant brought it in. A huge headline ran across the front page: Tragic Death of Foreign Minister.

'My God!' cried Dr Audlin.

For once he was wrenched out of his wonted calm. He was shocked, horribly shocked, and yet he was not altogether surprised. The possibility that Lord Mountdrago might commit suicide had occurred to him several times, for that it was suicide he could not doubt. The paper said that Lord Mountdrago had been waiting in a Tube station, standing on the edge of the platform, and as the train came in was seen to fall on the rail. It was supposed that he had had a sudden attack of faintness. The paper went on to say that Lord Mountdrago had been suffering for some weeks from the effects of overwork, but had felt it impossible to absent himself while the foreign situation demanded his unremitting attention. Lord Mountdrago was another victim of the strain that modern politics placed upon those who played the more important parts in it. There was a neat little piece about the talents and industry, the patriotism and vision, of the deceased statesman, followed by various surmises upon the Prime Minister's choice of his successor. Dr Audlin read all this. He had not liked Lord Mountdrago. The chief emotion that his death caused in him was dissatisfaction with himself because he had been able to do nothing for him.

Perhaps he had done wrong in not getting into touch with Lord Mountdrago's doctor. He was discouraged, as always when failure frustrated his conscientious efforts, and repulsion seized him for the theory and practice of this empiric doctrine by which he earned his living. He was dealing with dark and mysterious forces that it was perhaps beyond the powers of the human mind to understand. He was like a man blindfold trying to feel his way to he knew not whither. Listlessly he turned the pages of the paper. Suddenly he gave a great start, and an exclamation once more was forced from his lips. His eyes had fallen on a small paragraph near the bottom of a column. Sudden Death of an M.P., he read. Mr Owen Griffiths, member for so-and-so, had been taken ill in Fleet Street that afternoon and when he was brought to Charing Cross Hospital life was found to be extinct. It was supposed that death was due to natural causes, but an inquest would be held. Dr Audlin could hardly believe his eyes. Was it possible that the night before Lord Mountdrago had at last in his dream found himself possessed of the weapon, knife or gun, that he had wanted, and had killed his tormentor, and had that ghostly murder, in the same way as the blow with the bottle had given him a racking headache on the following day, taken effect a certain number of hours later on the waking man? Or was it, more mysterious and more frightful, that when Lord Mountdrago sought relief in death, the enemy he had so cruelly wronged, unappeased, escaping from his own mortality, had pursued him to some other sphere there to torment him still? It was strange. The sensible thing was to look upon it merely as an odd coincidence. Dr Audlin rang the bell.

'Tell Mrs Milton that I'm sorry I can't see her this evening. I'm not well.'

It was true; he shivered as though of an ague. With some kind of spiritual sense he seemed to envisage a bleak, a horrible void. The dark night of the soul engulfed him, and he felt a strange, primeval terror of he knew not what.

Sanatorium

♦

For the first six weeks that Ashenden was at the sanatorium he stayed in bed. He saw nobody but the doctor who visited him morning and evening, the nurses who looked after him, and the maid who brought him his meals. He had contracted tuberculosis of the lungs, and since at the time there were reasons that made it difficult for him to go to Switzerland the specialist he saw in London had sent him up to a sanatorium in the north of Scotland. At last the day came that he had been patiently looking forward to when the doctor told him he could get up; and in the afternoon his nurse, having helped him to dress, took him down to the veranda, placed cushions behind him, wrapped him up in rugs, and left him to enjoy the sun that was streaming down from a cloudless sky. It was mid-winter. The sanatorium stood on the top of a hill and from it you had a spacious view of the snow-clad country. There were people lying all along the veranda in deck-chairs, some chatting with their neighbours and some reading. Every now and then one would have a fit of coughing and you noticed that at the end of it he looked anxiously at his handkerchief. Before the nurse left Ashenden she turned with a kind of professional briskness to the man who was lying in the next chair.

'I want to introduce Mr Ashenden to you,' she said. And then to Ashenden: 'This is Mr McLeod. He and Mr Campbell have been here longer than anyone else.'

On the other side of Ashenden was lying a pretty girl, with red hair and bright blue eyes; she had on no make-up, but her lips were very red and the colour on her cheeks was high. It emphasized the astonishing whiteness of her skin. It was lovely even when you realized that its delicate texture was due to illness. She wore a fur coat and was wrapped up in rugs, so that you could see nothing of her body, but her face was extremely thin, so thin that it made her nose, which wasn't really large, look a trifle prominent. She gave Ashenden a friendly look, but did not speak, and Ashenden, feeling rather shy among all those strange people, waited to be spoken to.

'First time they've let you get up, is it?' said McLeod.

'Yes.'

'Where's your room?'

Ashenden told him.

'Small. I know every room in the place. I've been here for seventeen years. I've got the best room here and so I damned well ought to have. Campbell's been trying to get me out of it, he wants it himself, but I'm not going to budge; I've got a right to it, I came here six months before he did.'

McLeod lying there, gave you the impression that he was immensely tall; his skin was stretched tight over his bones, his cheeks and temples hollow, so that you could see the formation of his skull under it; and in that emaciated face, with its great bony nose, the eyes were preternaturally large.

'Seventeen years is a long time,' said Ashenden, because he could think of nothing else to say.

'Time passes very quickly. I like it here. At first, after a year or two, I went away in the summer, but I don't any more. It's my home now. I've got a brother and two sisters; but they're married and now they've got families; they don't want me. When you've been here a few years and you go back to ordinary life, you feel a bit out of it, you know. Your pals have gone their own ways and you've got nothing in common with them any more. It all seems an awful rush. Much ado about nothing, that's what it is. It's noisy and stuffy. No, one's better off here. I shan't stir again till they carry me out feet first in my coffin.'

The specialist had told Ashenden that if he took care of himself for a reasonable time he would get well, and he looked at McLeod with curiosity.

'What do you do with yourself all day long?' he asked.

'Do? Having T.B. is a whole-time job, my boy. There's my temperature to take and then I weigh myself. I don't hurry over my dressing. I have breakfast, I read the papers and go for a walk. Then I have my rest. I lunch and play bridge. I have another rest and then I dine. I play a bit more bridge and I go to bed. They've got quite a decent library here, we get all the new books, but I don't really have much time for reading. I talk to people. You meet all sorts here, you know. They come and they go. Sometimes they go because they think they're cured, but a lot of them come back, and sometimes they go because they die. I've seen a lot of people out and before I go I expect to see a lot more.'

The girl sitting on Ashenden's other side suddenly spoke.

'I should tell you that few persons can get a heartier laugh out of a hearse than Mr McLeod,' she said.

McLeod chuckled.

'I don't know about that, but it wouldn't be human nature if I didn't say to myself: Well, I'm just as glad it's him and not me they're taking for a ride.'

It occurred to him that Ashenden didn't know the pretty girl, so he introduced him.

'By the way, I don't think you've met Mr Ashenden—Miss Bishop. She's English, but not a bad girl.'

'How long have *you* been here?' asked Ashenden.

'Only two years. This is my last winter. Dr Lennox says I shall be all right in a few months and there's no reason why I shouldn't go home.'

'Silly, I call it,' said McLeod. 'Stay where you're well off, that's what I say.'

At that moment a man, leaning on a stick, came walking slowly along the veranda.

'Oh, look, there's Major Templeton,' said Miss Bishop, a smile lighting up her blue eyes; and then, as he came up: 'I'm glad to see you up again.'

'Oh, it was nothing. Only a bit of a cold. I'm quite all right now.'

The words were hardly out of his mouth when he began to cough. He leaned heavily on his stick. But when the attack was over he smiled gaily.

'Can't get rid of this damned cough,' he said. 'Smoking too much. Dr Lennox says I ought to give it up, but it's no good–I can't.'

He was a tall fellow, good-looking in a slightly theatrical way, with a dusky, sallow face, fine very dark eyes, and a neat black moustache. He was wearing a fur coat with an astrakhan collar. His appearance was smart and perhaps a trifle showy. Miss Bishop made Ashenden known to him. Major Templeton said a few civil words in an easy, cordial way, and then asked the girl to go for a stroll with him; he had been ordered to walk to a certain place in the wood behind the sanatorium and back again. McLeod watched them as they sauntered off.

'I wonder if there's anything between those two,' he said. 'They do say Templeton was a devil with the girls before he got ill.'

'He doesn't look up to much in that line just now,' said Ashenden.

'You never can tell. I've seen a lot of rum things here in my day. I could tell you no end of stories if I wanted to.'

'You evidently do, so why don't you?'

McLeod grinned.

'Well, I'll tell you one. Three or four years ago there was a woman here who was pretty hot stuff. Her husband used to come and see her every other week-end, he was crazy about her, used to fly up from London; but Dr Lennox was pretty sure she was carrying on with somebody here, but he couldn't find out who. So one night when we'd all gone to bed he had a thin coat of paint put down just outside her room and next day he had everyone's slippers examined. Neat, wasn't it? The fellow whose slippers had paint on them got the push. Dr Lennox has to be particular, you know. He doesn't want the place to get a bad name.'

'How long has Templeton been here?'

'Three or four months. He's been in bed most of the time. He's for it all right. Ivy Bishop'll be a damned fool if she gets stuck on him. She's got a good chance of getting well. I've seen so many of them, you know, I can tell. When I look at a fellow I make up my mind at once whether he'll get well or whether he won't, and if he won't I can make a pretty shrewd guess how long he'll last. I'm very seldom mistaken. I give Templeton about two years myself.'

McLeod gave Ashenden a speculative look, and Ashenden, knowing what he was thinking, though he tried to be amused, could not help feeling somewhat concerned. There was a twinkle in McLeod's eyes. He plainly knew what was passing through Ashenden's mind.

'You'll get all right. I wouldn't have mentioned it if I hadn't been pretty sure of that. I don't want Dr Lennox to hoof me out for putting the fear of God into his bloody patients.'

Then Ashenden's nurse came to take him back to bed. Even though he had only sat out for an hour, he was tired, and was glad to find himself once more between the sheets. Dr Lennox came in to see him in the course of the evening. He looked at his temperature chart.

'That's not so bad,' he said.

Dr Lennox was small, brisk, and genial. He was a good enough doctor, an excellent business man, and an enthusiastic fisherman. When the fishing season began he was inclined to leave the care of his patients to his assistants; the patients grumbled a little, but were glad enough to eat the young salmon he brought back to vary their meals. He was fond of talking, and now, standing at the end of Ashenden's bed, he asked him, in his broad Scots, whether he had got into conversation with any of the patients that afternoon. Ashenden told him the nurse had introduced him to McLeod. Dr Lennox laughed.

'The oldest living inhabitant. He knows more about the sanatorium and its inmates than I do. How he gets his information I haven't an idea, but there's not a thing about the private lives of anyone under this roof that he doesn't know. There's not an old maid in the place with a keener nose for a bit of scandal. Did he tell you about Campbell?'

'He mentioned him.'

'He hates Campbell, and Campbell hates him. Funny, when you come to think of it, those two men, they've been here for seventeen years and they've got about one sound lung between them. They loathe the sight of one another. I've had to refuse to listen to the complaints about one another that they come to me with. Campbell's room is just below McLeod's and Campbell plays the fiddle. It drives McLeod wild. He says he's been listening to the same tunes for fifteen years, but Campbell says McLeod doesn't know one tune from another. McLeod wants me to stop Campbell playing, but I can't do that, he's got a perfect right to play so long as he doesn't play in the silence hours. I've offered to change McLeod's room, but he won't do that. He says Campbell only plays to drive him out of the room because it's the best in the house, and he's damned if he's going to have it. It's queer, isn't it, that two middle-aged men should think it worth while to make life hell for one another? Neither can leave the other alone. They have their meals at the same table, they play bridge together; and not a day passes without a row. Sometimes I've threatened to turn them both out if they don't behave like sensible fellows. That keeps them quiet for a bit. They don't want to go. They've been here so long, they've got no one any more who gives a damn for them, and they can't cope with the world outside. Campbell went away for a couple of months' holiday some years ago. He came back after a week; he said he couldn't stand the racket, and the sight of so many people in the streets scared him.'

It was a strange world into which Ashenden found himself thrown when, his health gradually improving, he was able to mix with his fellow patients. One morning Dr Lennox told him he could thenceforward lunch in the dining-room. This was a large, low room, with great window space; the windows were always wide open and on fine days the sun streamed in. There seemed to be a great many people and it took him some time to sort them out. They were of all kinds, young, middle-aged, and old. There were some, like McLeod and Campbell, who had been at the sanatorium for years and expected to die there. Others had only been there for a few months. There was one middle-aged spinster called Miss Atkin who had been coming every winter for a long time and in the summer went to stay with friends and relations. She had nothing much the matter with her any more, and might just as well have stayed away altogether, but she liked the life. Her long residence had given her a sort of position, she was honorary librarian and hand in glove with the matron. She was always ready to gossip with you, but you were soon warned that everything you said was passed on. It was useful to Dr Lennox to know that his patients were getting on well together and were happy, that they did nothing imprudent and followed his instructions. Little escaped Miss Atkin's sharp eyes, and from her it went to the matron and so to Dr Lennox. Because she had been coming for so many years, she sat at the same table as McLeod and Campbell, together with an old general who had been put there on account of his rank. The table was in no way different from any other, and it was not more advantageously placed, but because the oldest residents sat there it was looked upon as the most desirable place to sit, and several elderly women were bitterly resentful because Miss Atkin, who went away for four or five months every summer, should be given a place there while they who spent the whole year in the sanatorium sat at other tables. There was an old Indian Civilian who had been at the sanatorium longer than anyone but McLeod and Campbell; he was a man who in his day had ruled a province, and he was waiting irascibly for either McLeod or Campbell to die so that he might take his place at the first table. Ashenden made the acquaintance of Campbell. He was a long, big-boned fellow with a bald head, so thin that you wondered how his limbs held together; and when he sat crumpled in an arm-chair he gave you the uncanny impression of a manikin in a puppet-show. He was brusque, touchy, and bad-tempered. The first thing he asked Ashenden was:

'Are you fond of music?'

'Yes.'

'No one here cares a damn for it. I play the violin. But if you like it, come to my room one day and I'll play to you.'

'Don't you go,' said McLeod, who heard him. 'It's torture.'

'How can you be so rude?' cried Miss Atkin. 'Mr Campbell plays very nicely.'

'There's no one in this beastly place that knows one note from another,' said Campbell.

With a derisive chuckle McLeod walked off. Miss Atkin tried to smooth things down.

'You mustn't mind what McLeod said.'

'Oh, I don't. I'll get back on him all right.'

He played the same tune over and over again all that afternoon. McLeod banged on the floor, but Campbell went on. He sent a message by a maid to say that he had a headache and would Mr Campbell mind not playing; Campbell replied that he had a perfect right to play and if Mr McLeod didn't like it he could lump it. When next they met high words passed.

Ashenden was put at a table with the pretty Miss Bishop, with Templeton, and with a London man, an accountant, called Henry Chester. He was a stocky, broad-shouldered, wiry little fellow, and the last person you would ever have thought would be attacked by T.B. It had come upon him as a sudden and unexpected blow. He was a perfectly ordinary man, somewhere between thirty and forty, married, with two children. He lived in a decent suburb. He went up to the City every morning and read the morning paper; he came down from the City every evening and read the evening paper. He had no interests except his business and his family. He liked his work; he made enough money to live in comfort, he put by a reasonable sum every year, he played golf on Saturday afternoon and on Sunday, he went every August for a three weeks' holiday to the same place on the east coast; his children would grow up and marry, then he would turn his business over to his son and retire with his wife to a little house in the country where he could potter about till death claimed him at a ripe old age. He asked nothing more from life than that, and it was a life that thousands upon thousands of his fellow-men lived with satisfaction. He was the average citizen. Then this thing happened. He had caught cold playing golf, it had gone to his chest, and he had had a cough that he couldn't shake off. He had always been strong and healthy, and had no opinion of doctors; but at last at his wife's persuasion he had consented to see one. It was a shock to him, a fearful shock, to learn that there was tubercle in both his lungs and that his only chance of life was to go immediately to a sanatorium. The specialist he saw then told him that he might be able to go back to work in a couple of years, but two years had passed and Dr Lennox advised him not to think of it for at least a year more. He showed him the bacilli in his sputum, and in an X-ray photograph the actively-diseased patches in his lungs. He lost heart. It seemed to him a cruel and unjust trick that fate had played upon him. He could have understood it if he had led a wild life, if he had drunk too much, played around with women, or kept late hours. He would have deserved it then. But he had done none of these things. It was monstrously unfair. Having no resources in himself, no interest in books, he had nothing to do but think of his health. It became an obsession. He watched his symptoms anxiously. They had to deprive him of a thermometer because he took his temperature a dozen times a day. He got it into his head that the doctors were taking his case too indifferently, and in order to force their attention used every method he could devise to make the thermometer register a temperature that would alarm; and when his tricks were foiled he grew sulky and querulous. But he was by nature a jovial, friendly creature, and when he forgot himself he talked and laughed gaily; then on a sudden he remembered that he was a sick man and you would see in his eyes the fear of death.

At the end of every month his wife came up to spend a day or two in a lodging house near by. Dr Lennox did not much like the visits that relatives paid the patients, it excited and unsettled them. It was moving to see the eagerness with which Henry Chester looked forward to his wife's arrival; but it was strange to notice that once she had come he seemed less pleased than one would have expected. Mrs Chester was a pleasant, cheerful little woman, not pretty, but neat, as commonplace as her husband, and you only had to look at her to know that she was a good wife and mother, a careful housekeeper, a nice, quiet body who did her duty and interfered with nobody. She had been quite happy in the dull, domestic life they had led for so many years, her only dissipation a visit to the pictures, her great thrill the sales in the big London shops; and it had never occurred to her that it was monotonous. It completely satisfied her. Ashenden liked her. He listened with interest while she prattled about her children and her house in the suburbs, her neighbours and her trivial occupations. On one occasion he met her in the road. Chester for some reason connected with his treatment had stayed in and she was alone. Ashenden suggested that they should walk together. They talked for a little of indifferent things. Then she suddenly asked him how he thought her husband was.

'I think he seems to be getting on all right.'

'I'm so terribly worried.'

'You must remember it's a slow, long business. One has to have patience.'

They walked on a little and then he saw she was crying.

'You mustn't be unhappy about him,' said Ashenden gently.

'Oh, you don't know what I have to put up with when I come here. I know I ought not to speak about it, but I must. I can trust you, can't I?'

'Of course.'

'I love him. I'm devoted to him. I'd do anything in the world I could for him. We've never quarrelled, we've never even differed about a single thing. He's beginning to hate me and it breaks my heart.'

'Oh, I can't believe that. Why, when you're not here he talks of you all the time. He couldn't talk more nicely. He's devoted to you.'

'Yes, that's when I'm not here. It's when I'm here, when he sees me well and strong, that it comes over him. You see, he resents it so terribly that he's ill and I'm well. He's afraid he's going to die and he hates me because I'm going to live. I have to be on my guard all the time; almost everything I say, if I speak of the children, if I speak of the future, exasperates him, and he says bitter, wounding things. When I speak of something I've had to do to the house or a servant I've had to change it irritates him beyond endurance. He complains that I treat him as if he didn't count any more. We used to be so united, and now I feel there's a great wall of antagonism between us. I know I shouldn't blame him, I know it's only his illness, he's a dear good man really, and kindness itself, normally he's the easiest man in the world to get on with; and now I simply dread coming here and I go with relief. He'd be terribly sorry if I had T.B. but I know that in his heart of hearts it would be a relief. He could forgive me, he could forgive fate, if he thought I was going to die too. Sometimes he tortures me by talking about what I shall do when he's dead, and when I get hysterical and cry out to him to stop, he says I needn't grudge him a little pleasure when he'll be dead so soon and I can go on living for years and years and have a good time. Oh, it's so frightful to think that this love we've had for one another all these years should die in this sordid, miserable way.'

Mrs Chester sat down on a stone by the roadside and gave way to passionate weeping. Ashenden looked at her with pity, but could find nothing to say that might comfort her. What she had told him did not come quite as a surprise.

'Give me a cigarette,' she said at last. 'I mustn't let my eyes get all red and swollen, or Henry'll know I've been crying and he'll think I've had bad news about him. Is death so horrible? Do we all fear death like that?'

'I don't know,' said Ashenden.

'When my mother was dying she didn't seem to mind a bit. She knew it was coming and she even made little jokes about it. But she was an old woman.'

Mrs Chester pulled herself together and they set off again. They walked for a while in silence.

'You won't think any the worse of Henry for what I've told you?' she said at last.

'Of course not.'

'He's been a good husband and a good father. I've never known a better man in my life. Until this illness I don't think an unkind or ungenerous thought ever passed through his head.'

The conversation left Ashenden pensive. People often said he had a low opinion of human nature. It was because he did not always judge his fellows by the usual standards. He accepted, with a smile, a tear, or a shrug of the shoulders, much that filled others with dismay. It was true that you would never have expected that good-natured, commonplace little chap to harbour such bitter and unworthy thoughts; but who has ever been able to tell to what depths man may fall or to what heights rise? The fault lay in the poverty of his ideals. Henry Chester was born and bred to lead an average life, exposed to the normal vicissitudes of existence, and when an unforeseeable accident befell him he had no means of coping with it. He was like a brick made to take its place with a million others in a huge factory, but by chance with a flaw in it so that it is inadequate to its purpose. And the brick too, if it had a mind, might cry: What have I done that I cannot fulfil my modest end, but must be taken away from all these other bricks that support me and thrown on the dust-heap? It was no fault of Henry Chester's that he was incapable of the conceptions that might have enabled him to bear his calamity with resignation. It is not everyone who can find solace in art or thought. It is the tragedy of our day that these humble souls have lost their faith in God, in whom lay hope, and their belief in a resurrection that might bring them the happiness that has been denied them on earth; and have found nothing to put in their place.

There are people who say that suffering ennobles. It is not true. As a general rule it makes man petty, querulous, and selfish; but here in this sanatorium there was not much suffering. In certain stages of tuberculosis the slight fever that accompanies it excites rather than depresses, so that the patient feels alert and, upborne by hope, faces the future blithely; but for all that the idea of death haunts the subconscious. It is a sardonic theme song that runs through a sprightly operetta. Now and again the gay, melodious arias, the dance measures, deviate strangely into tragic strains that throb menacingly down the nerves; the petty interests of every day, the small jealousies and trivial concerns are as nothing; pity and terror make the heart on a sudden stand still and the awfulness of death broods as the silence that precedes a tropical storm broods over the tropical jungle. After Ashenden had been for some time at the sanatorium there came a boy of twenty. He was in the navy, a sub-lieutenant in a submarine, and he had what they used to call in novels galloping consumption. He was a tall, good-looking youth, with curly brown hair, blue eyes, and a very sweet smile. Ashenden saw him two or three times lying on the terrace in the sun and passed the time of day with him. He was a cheerful lad. He talked of musical shows and film stars; and he read the paper for the football results and the boxing news. Then he was put to bed and Ashenden saw him no more. His relations were sent for and in two months he was dead. He died uncomplaining. He understood what was happening to him as little as an animal. For a day or two there was the same malaise in the sanatorium as there is in a prison when a man has been hanged; and then, as though by universal consent, in obedience to an instinct of self-preservation, the boy was put out of mind: life, with its three meals a day, its golf on the miniature course, its regulated exercise, its prescribed rests, its quarrels and jealousies, its scandal-mongering and petty vexations, went on as before. Campbell, to the exasperation of McLeod, continued to play the prize-song and 'Annie Laurie' on his fiddle. McLeod continued to boast of his bridge and gossip about other people's health and morals. Miss Atkin continued to backbite. Henry Chester continued to complain that the doctors gave him insufficient attention and railed against fate because, after the model life he had led, it had played him such a dirty trick. Ashenden continued to read, and with amused tolerance to watch the vagaries of his fellow-creatures.

He became intimate with Major Templeton. Templeton was perhaps a little more than forty years of age. He had been in the Grenadier Guards, but had resigned his commission after the war. A man of ample means, he had since then devoted himself entirely to pleasure. He raced in the racing season, shot in the shooting season, and hunted in the hunting season. When this was over he went to Monte Carlo. He told Ashenden of the large sums he had made and lost at baccarat. He was very fond of women and if his stories could be believed they were very fond of him. He loved good food and good drink. He knew by their first names the head waiters of every restaurant in London where you ate well. He belonged to half a dozen clubs. He had led for years a useless, selfish, worthless life, the sort of life which maybe it will be impossible for anyone to live in the future, but he had lived it without misgiving and had enjoyed it. Ashenden asked him once what he would do if he had his time over again and he answered that he would do exactly what he had done. He was an amusing talker, gay and pleasantly ironic, and he dealt with the surface of things, which was all he knew, with a light, easy, and assured touch. He always had a pleasant word for the dowdy spinsters in the sanatorium and a joking one for the peppery old gentlemen, for he combined good manners with a natural kindliness. He knew his way about the superficial world of the people who have more money than they know what to do with as well as he knew his way about Mayfair. He was the kind of man who would always have been willing to take a bet, to help a friend, and to give a tenner to a rogue. If he had never done much good in the world he had never done much harm. He amounted to nothing. But he was a more agreeable companion than many of more sterling character and of more admirable qualities. He was very ill now. He was dying and he knew it. He took it with the same easy, laughing nonchalance as he had taken all the rest. He'd had a thundering good time, he regretted nothing, it was rotten tough luck getting T.B. but to hell with it, no one can live for ever, and when you came to think of it, he might have been killed in the war or broken his bloody neck in a point-to-point. His principle all through life had been, when you've made a bad bet, pay up and forget about it. He'd had a good run for his money and he was ready to call it a day. It had been a damned good party while it lasted, but every party's got to come to an end, and next day it doesn't matter much if you went home with the milk or if you left while the fun was in full swing.

Of all those people in the sanatorium he was probably from the moral standpoint the least worthy, but he was the only one who genuinely accepted the inevitable with unconcern. He snapped his fingers in the face of death, and you could choose whether to call his levity unbecoming or his insouciance gallant.

The last thing that ever occurred to him when he came to the sanatorium was that he might fall more deeply in love there than he had ever done before. His amours had been numerous, but they had been light; he had been content with the politely mercenary love of chorus girls and with ephemeral unions with women of easy virtue whom he met at house parties. He had always taken care to avoid any attachment that might endanger his freedom. His only aim in life had been to get as much fun out of it as possible, and where sex was concerned he found every advantage and no inconvenience in ceaseless variety. But he liked women. Even when they were quite old he could not talk to them without a caress in his eyes and a tenderness in his voice. He was prepared to do anything to please them. They were conscious of his interest in them and were agreeably flattered, and they felt, quite mistakenly, that they could trust him never to let them down. He once said a thing that Ashenden thought showed insight:

'You know, any man can get any woman he wants if he tries hard enough, there's nothing in that, but once he's got her, only a man who thinks the world of women can get rid of her without humiliating her.'

It was simply from habit that he began to make love to Ivy Bishop. She was the prettiest and the youngest girl in the sanatorium. She was in point of fact not so young as Ashenden had first thought her, she was twenty-nine, but for the last eight years she had been wandering from one sanatorium to another, in Switzerland, England, and Scotland, and the sheltered invalid life had preserved her youthful appearance so that you might easily have taken her for twenty. All she knew of the world she had learnt in these establishments, so that she combined rather curiously extreme innocence with extreme sophistication. She had seen a number of love affairs run their course. A good many men, of various nationalities, had made love to her; she accepted their attentions with self-possession and humour, but she had at her disposal plenty of firmness when they showed an inclination to go too far. She had a force of character unexpected in anyone who looked so flower-like, and when it came to a show-down knew how to express her meaning in plain, cool, and decisive words. She was quite ready to have a flirtation with George Templeton. It was a game she understood, and though always charming to him, it was with a bantering lightness that showed quite clearly that she had summed him up and had no mind to take the affair more seriously than he did. Like Ashenden, Templeton went to bed every evening at six and dined in his room, so that he saw Ivy only by day. They went for little walks together, but otherwise were seldom alone. At lunch the conversation between the four of them, Ivy, Templeton, Henry Chester, and Ashenden, was general, but it was obvious that it was for neither of the two men that Templeton took so much trouble to be entertaining. It seemed to Ashenden that he was ceasing to flirt with Ivy to pass the time, and that his feeling for her was growing deeper and more sincere; but he could not tell whether she was conscious of it nor whether it meant anything to her. Whenever Templeton hazarded a remark that was more intimate than the occasion warranted she countered it with an ironic one that made them all laugh. But Templeton's laugh was rueful. He was no longer content to have her take him as a play-boy. The more Ashenden knew Ivy Bishop the more he liked her. There was something pathetic in her sick beauty, with that lovely transparent skin, the thin face in which the eyes were so large and so wonderfully blue; and there was something pathetic in her plight, for like so many others in the sanatorium she seemed to be alone in the world. Her mother led a busy social life, her sisters were married; they took but a perfunctory interest in the young woman from whom they had been separated now for eight years. They corresponded, they came to see her occasionally, but there was no longer very much between them. She accepted the situation without bitterness. She was friendly with everyone and prepared always to listen with sympathy to the complaints and the distress of all and sundry. She went out of her way to be nice to Henry Chester and did what she could to cheer him.

'Well, Mr Chester,' she said to him one day at lunch, 'it's the end of the month, your wife will be coming tomorrow. That's something to look forward to.'

'No, she's not coming this month,' he said quietly, looking down at his plate.

'Oh, I am sorry. Why not? The children are all right, aren't they?'

'Dr Lennox thinks it's better for me that she shouldn't come.'

There was a silence. Ivy looked at him with troubled eyes.

'That's tough luck, old man,' said Templeton in his hearty way. 'Why didn't you tell Lennox to go to hell?'

'He must know best,' said Chester.

Ivy gave him another look and began to talk of something else.

Looking back, Ashenden realized that she had at once suspected the truth.

For next day he happened to walk with Chester.

'I'm awfully sorry your wife isn't coming,' he said. 'You'll miss her visit dreadfully.'

'Dreadfully.'

He gave Ashenden a sidelong glance. Ashenden felt that he had something he wanted to say, but could not bring himself to say it. He gave his shoulders an angry shrug.

'It's my fault if she's not coming. I asked Lennox to write and tell her not to. I couldn't stick it any more. I spend the whole month looking forward to her coming and then when she's here I hate her. You see, I resent so awfully having this filthy disease. She's strong and well and full of beans. It maddens me when I see the pain in her eyes. What does it matter to her really? Who cares if you're ill? They pretend to care, but they're jolly glad it's you and not them. I'm a swine, aren't I?'

Ashenden remembered how Mrs Chester had sat on a stone by the side of the road and wept.

'Aren't you afraid you'll make her very unhappy, not letting her come?'

'She must put up with that. I've got enough with my own unhappiness without bothering with hers.'

Ashenden did not know what to say and they walked on in silence. Suddenly Chester broke out irritably.

'It's all very well for you to be disinterested and unselfish, you're going to live. I'm going to die, and God damn it, I don't want to die. Why should I? It's not fair.'

Time passed. In a place like the sanatorium where there was little to occupy the mind it was inevitable that soon everyone should know that George Templeton was in love with Ivy Bishop. But it was not so easy to tell what her feelings were. It was plain that she liked his company, but she did not seek it, and indeed it looked as though she took pains not to be alone with him. One or two of the middle-aged ladies tried to trap her into some compromising admission, but ingenuous as she was, she was easily a match for them. She ignored their hints and met their straight questions with incredulous laughter. She succeeded in exasperating them.

'She can't be so stupid as not to see that he's mad about her.'

'She has no right to play with him like that.'

'I believe she's just as much in love with him as he is with her.'

'Dr Lennox ought to tell her mother.'

No one was more incensed than McLeod.

'Too ridiculous. After all, nothing can come of it. He's riddled with T.B. and she's not much better.'

Campbell on the other hand was sardonic and gross.

'I'm all for their having a good time while they can. I bet there's a bit of hanky-panky going on if one only knew, and I don't blame 'em.'

'You cad,' said McLeod.

'Oh, come off it. Templeton isn't the sort of chap to play bumble-puppy bridge with a girl like that unless he's getting something out of it, and she knows a thing or two, I bet.'

Ashenden, who saw most of them, knew them better than any of the others. Templeton at last had taken him into his confidence. He was rather amused at himself.

'Rum thing at my time of life, falling in love with a decent girl. Last thing I'd ever expected of myself. And it's no good denying it, I'm in it up to the neck; if I were a well man I'd ask her to marry me tomorrow. I never knew a girl could be as nice as that. I've always thought girls, decent girls, I mean, damned bores. But she isn't a bore, she's as clever as she can stick. And pretty too. My God, what a skin! And that hair: but it isn't any of that that's bowled me over like a row of ninepins. D'you know what's got me? Damned ridiculous when you come to think of it. An old rip like me. Virtue. Makes me laugh like a hyena. Last thing I've ever wanted in a woman, but there it is, no getting away from it, she's good, and it makes me feel like a worm. Surprises you, I suppose?'

'Not a bit,' said Ashenden. 'You're not the first rake who's fallen to innocence. It's merely the sentimentality of middle age.'

'Dirty dog,' laughed Templeton.

'What does she say to it?'

'Good God, you don't suppose I've told her. I've never said a word to her that I wouldn't have said before anyone else. I may be dead in six months, and besides, what have I got to offer a girl like that?'

Ashenden by now was pretty sure that she was just as much in love with Templeton as he was with her. He had seen the flush that coloured her cheeks when Templeton came into the dining-room and he had noticed the soft glance she gave him now and then when he was not looking at her. There was a peculiar sweetness in her smile when she listened to him telling some of his old experiences. Ashenden had the impression that she basked comfortably in his love as the patients on the terrace, facing the snow, basked in the hot sunshine; but it might very well be that she was content to leave it at that, and it was certainly no business of his to tell Templeton what perhaps she had no wish that he should know.

Then an incident occurred to disturb the monotony of life. Though McLeod and Campbell were always at odds they played bridge together because, till Templeton came, they were the best players in the sanatorium. They bickered incessantly, their post-mortems were endless, but after so many years each knew the other's game perfectly and they took a keen delight in scoring off one another. As a rule Templeton refused to play with them; though a fine player he preferred to play with Ivy Bishop, and McLeod and Campbell were agreed on this, that she ruined the game. She was the kind of player who, having made a mistake that lost the rubber, would laugh and say: Well, it only made the difference of a trick. But one afternoon, since Ivy was staying in her room with a headache, Templeton consented to play with Campbell and McLeod. Ashenden was the fourth. Though it was the end of March there had been heavy snow for several days, and they played, in a veranda open on three sides to the wintry air, in fur coats and caps, with mittens on their hands. The stakes were too small for a gambler like Templeton to take the game seriously and his bidding was overbold, but he played so much better than the other three that he generally managed to make his contract or at least to come near it. But there was much doubling and redoubling. The cards ran high, so that an inordinate number of small slams were bid; it was a tempestuous game, and McLeod and Campbell lashed one another with their tongues. Half past five arrived and the last rubber was started, for at six the bell rang to send everyone to rest. It was a hard-fought rubber, with sets on both sides, for McLeod and Campbell were opponents and each was determined that the other should not win. At ten minutes to six it was game all and the last hand was dealt. Templeton was McLeod's partner and Ashenden Campbell's. The bidding started with two clubs from McLeod; Ashenden said nothing; Templeton showed that he had substantial help, and finally McLeod called a grand slam. Campbell doubled and McLeod redoubled. Hearing this, the players at other tables who had broken off gathered round and the hands were played in deadly silence to a little crowd of onlookers. McLeod's face was white with excitement and there were beads of sweat on his brow. His hands trembled. Campbell was very grim. McLeod had to take two finesses and they both came off. He finished with a squeeze and got the last of the thirteen tricks. There was a burst of applause from the onlookers. McLeod, arrogant in victory, sprang to his feet. He shook his clenched fist at Campbell.

'Play that off on your blasted fiddle,' he shouted. 'Grand slam doubled and redoubled. I've wanted to get it all my life and now I've got it. By God. By God.'

He gasped. He staggered forward and fell across the table. A stream of blood poured from his mouth. The doctor was sent for. Attendants came. He was dead.

He was buried two days later, early in the morning so that the patients should not be disturbed by the sight of a funeral. A relation in black came from Glasgow to attend it. No one had liked him. No one regretted him. At the end of a week so far as one could tell, he was forgotten. The Indian Civilian took his place at the principal table and Campbell moved into the room he had so long wanted.

'Now we shall have peace,' said Dr Lennox to Ashenden. 'When you think that I've had to put up with the quarrels and complaints of those two men for years and years . . . Believe me, one has to have patience to run a sanatorium. And to think that after all the trouble he's given me he had to end up like that and scare all those people out of their wits.'

'It was a bit of a shock, you know,' said Ashenden.

'He was a worthless fellow and yet some of the women have been quite upset about it. Poor little Miss Bishop cried her eyes out.'

'I suspect that she was the only one who cried for him and not for herself.'

But presently it appeared that there was one person who had not forgotten him. Campbell went about like a lost dog. He wouldn't play bridge. He wouldn't talk. There was no doubt about it, he was moping for McLeod. For several days he remained in his room, having his meals brought to him, and then went to Dr Lennox and said he didn't like it as well as his old one and wanted to be moved back. Dr Lennox lost his temper, which he rarely did, and told him he had been pestering him to give him that room for years and now he could stay there or get out of the sanatorium. He returned to it and sat gloomily brooding.

'Why don't you play your violin?' the matron asked him at length. 'I haven't heard you play for a fortnight.'

'I haven't.'

'Why not?'

'It's no fun any more. I used to get a kick out of playing because I knew it maddened McLeod. But now nobody cares if I play or not. I shall never play again.'

Nor did he for all the rest of the time that Ashenden was at the sanatorium. It was strange, now that McLeod was dead, life had lost its savour for him. With no one to quarrel with, no one to infuriate, he had lost his incentive and it was plain that it would not be long before he followed his enemy to the grave.

But on Templeton McLeod's death had another effect, and one which was soon to have unexpected consequences. He talked to Ashenden about it in his cool, detached way.

'Grand, passing out like that in his moment of triumph. I can't make out why everyone got in such a state about it. He'd been here for years, hadn't he?'

'Eighteen, I believe.'

'I wonder if it's worth it. I wonder if it's not better to have one's fling and take the consequences.'

'I suppose it depends on how much you value life.'

'But is this life?'

Ashenden had no answer. In a few months he could count on being well, but you only had to look at Templeton to know that he was not going to recover. The death-look was on his face.

'D'you know what I've done?' asked Templeton. 'I've asked Ivy to marry me.'

Ashenden was startled.

'What did she say?'

'Bless her little heart, she said it was the most ridiculous idea she'd ever heard in her life and I was crazy to think of such a thing.'

'You must admit she was right.'

'Quite. But she's going to marry me.'

'It's madness.'

'I dare say it is; but anyhow, we're going to see Lennox and ask him what he thinks about it.'

The winter had broken at last; there was still snow on the hills, but in the valleys it was melted and on the lower slopes the birch-trees were in bud all ready to burst into delicate leaf. The enchantment of spring was in the air. The sun was hot. Everyone felt alert and some felt happy. The old stagers who came only for the winter were making their plans to go south. Templeton and Ivy went to see Dr Lennox together. They told him what they had in mind. He examined them; they were X-rayed and various tests were taken. Dr Lennox fixed a day when he would tell them the results and in the light of this discuss their proposal. Ashenden saw them just before they went to keep the appointment. They were anxious, but did their best to make a joke of it. Dr Lennox showed them the results of his examinations and explained to them in plain language what their condition was.

'All that's very fine and large,' said Templeton then, 'but what we want to know is whether we can get married.'

'It would be highly imprudent.'

'We know that, but does it matter?'

'And criminal if you had a child.'

'We weren't thinking of having one,' said Ivy.

'Well, then I'll tell you in very few words how the matter stands. Then you must decide for yourselves.'

Templeton gave Ivy a little smile and took her hand. The doctor went on.

'I don't think Miss Bishop will ever be strong enough to lead a normal life, but if she continues to live as she has been doing for the last eight years . . .'

'In sanatoriums?'

'Yes. There's no reason why she shouldn't live very comfortably, if not to a ripe old age, as long as any sensible person wants to live. The disease is quiescent. If she marries, if she attempts to live an ordinary life, the foci of infection may very well light up again, and what the results of that may be no one can foretell. So far as you are concerned, Templeton, I can put it even more shortly. You've seen the X-ray photos yourself. Your lungs are riddled with tubercle. If you marry you'll be dead in six months.'

'And if I don't how long can I live?'

The doctor hesitated.

'Don't be afraid. You can tell me the truth.'

'Two or three years.'

'Thank you, that's all we wanted to know.'

They went as they had come, hand in hand; Ivy was crying softly. No one knew what they said to one another; but when they came in to luncheon they were radiant. They told Ashenden and Chester that they were going to be married as soon as they could get a licence. Then Ivy turned to Chester.

'I should so much like your wife to come up for my wedding. D'you think she would?'

'You're not going to be married here?'

'Yes. Our respective relations will only disapprove, so we're not going to tell them until it's all over. We shall ask Dr Lennox to give me away.'

She looked mildly at Chester, waiting for him to speak, for he had not answered her. The other two men watched him. His voice shook a little when he spoke.

'It's very kind of you to want her. I'll write and ask her.'

When the news spread among the patients, though everyone congratulated them, most of them privately told one another that it was very injudicious; but when they learnt, as sooner or later everything that happened in the sanatorium was learnt, that Dr Lennox had told Templeton that if he married he would be dead in six months, they were awed to silence. Even the dullest were moved at the thought of these two persons who loved one another so much that they were prepared to sacrifice their lives. A spirit of kindliness and good will descended on the sanatorium: people who hadn't been speaking spoke to one another again; others forgot for a brief space their own anxieties. Everyone seemed to share in the happiness of the happy pair. And it was not only the spring that filled those sick hearts with new hope, the great love that had taken possession of the man and the girl seemed to spread its effulgence on all that came near them. Ivy was quietly blissful; the excitement became her and she looked younger and prettier. Templeton seemed to walk on air. He laughed and joked as if he hadn't a care in the world. You would have said that he looked forward to long years of uninterrupted felicity. But one day he confided in Ashenden.

'This isn't a bad place, you know,' he said. 'Ivy's promised me that when I hand in my checks she'll come back here. She knows the people and she won't be so lonely.'

'Doctors are often mistaken,' said Ashenden. 'If you live reasonably I don't see why you shouldn't go on for a long time yet.'

'I'm only asking for three months. If I can have that it'll be worth it.'

Mrs Chester came up two days before the wedding. She had not seen her husband for several months and they were shy with one another. It was easy to guess that when they were alone they felt awkward and constrained. Yet Chester did his best to shake off the depression that was now habitual and at all events at meal-times showed himself the jolly, hearty little fellow that he must have been before he fell ill. On the eve of the wedding day they all dined together, Templeton and Ashenden both sitting up for dinner; they drank champagne and stayed up till ten joking, laughing, and enjoying themselves. The wedding took place next morning in the kirk. Ashenden was best man. Everyone in the sanatorium who could stand on his feet attended it. The newly married couple were setting out by car immediately after lunch. Patients, doctors, and nurses assembled to see them off. Someone had tied an old shoe on the back of the car, and as Templeton and his wife came out of the door of the sanatorium rice was flung over them. A cheer was raised as they drove away, as they drove away to love and death. The crowd separated slowly. Chester and his wife went silently side by side. After they had gone a little way he shyly took her hand. Her heart seemed to miss a beat. With a sidelong glance she saw that his eyes were wet with tears.

'Forgive me, dear,' he said. 'I've been very unkind to you.'

'I knew you didn't mean it,' she faltered.

'Yes, I did. I wanted you to suffer because I was suffering. But not any more. All this about Templeton and Ivy Bishop–I don't know how to put it, it's made me see everything differently. I don't mind dying any more. I don't think death's very important, not so important as love. And I want you to live and be happy. I don't grudge you anything any more and I don't resent anything. I'm glad now it's me that must die and not you. I wish for you everything that's good in the world. I love you.'

The
Social Sense

◆

I do not like long-standing engagements. How can you tell whether on a certain day three or four weeks ahead you will wish to dine with a certain person? The chances are that in the interval something will turn up that you would much sooner do and so long a notice presages a large and formal party. But what help is there? The date has been fixed thus far away so that the guests bidden may be certainly disengaged and it needs a very adequate excuse to prevent your refusal from seeming churlish. You accept, and for a month the engagement hangs over you with gloomy menace. It interferes with your cherished plans. It disorganizes your life. There is really only one way to cope with the situation and that is to put yourself off at the last moment. But it is one that I have never had the courage or the want of scruple to adopt.

It was with a faint sense of resentment then that one June evening towards half past eight I left my lodging in Half Moon Street to walk round the corner to dine with the Macdonalds. I liked them. Many years ago I made up my mind not to eat the food of persons I disliked or despised, and though I have on this account enjoyed the hospitality of far fewer people than I otherwise should have done I still think the rule a good one. The Macdonalds were nice, but their parties were a toss-up. They suffered from the delusion that if they asked six persons to dine with them who had nothing in the world to say to one another the party would be a failure, but if they multiplied it by three and asked eighteen it must be a success. I arrived a little late, which is almost inevitable when you live so near the house you are going to that it is not worth while to take a taxi, and the room into which I was shown was filled with people. I knew few of them and my heart sank as I saw myself laboriously making conversation through a long dinner with two total strangers. It was a relief to me when I saw Thomas and Mary Warton come in and an unexpected pleasure when I found on going in to dinner that I had been placed next to Mary.

Thomas Warton was a portrait-painter who at one time had had considerable success, but he had never fulfilled the promise of his youth and had long ceased to be taken seriously by the critics. He made an adequate income, but at the Private View of the Royal Academy no one gave more than a passing glance at the dull but conscientious portraits of fox-hunting squires and prosperous merchants which with unfailing regularity he sent to the annual exhibition. One would have liked to admire his work because he was an amiable and kindly man. If you happened to be a writer he was so genuinely enthusiastic over anything you had done, so charmed with any success you might have had, that you wished your conscience would allow you to speak with decent warmth of his own productions. It was impossible and you were driven to the last refuge of the portrait painter's friend.

'It looks as if it were a marvellous likeness,' you said.

Mary Warton had been in her day a well-known concert singer and she had still the remains of a lovely voice. She must in her youth have been very handsome. Now, at fifty-three, she had a haggard look. Her features were rather mannish and her skin was weather-beaten; but her short grey hair was thick and curly and her fine eyes were bright with intelligence. She dressed picturesquely rather than fashionably and she had a weakness for strings of beads and fantastic ear-rings. She had a blunt manner, a quick sense of human folly, and a sharp tongue, so that many people did not like her. But no one could deny that she was clever. She was not only an accomplished musician, but she was a great reader and she was passionately interested in painting. She had a very rare feeling for art. She liked the modern, not from pose but from natural inclination, and she had bought for next to nothing the pictures of unknown painters who later became famous. You heard at her house the most recent and difficult music and no poet or novelist in Europe could offer the world something new and strange without her being ready to fight on his behalf the good fight against the philistines. You might say she was a highbrow; she was; but her taste was almost faultless, her judgement sound, and her enthusiasm honest.

No one admired her more than Thomas Warton. He had fallen in love with her when she was still a singer and had pestered her to marry him. She had refused him half a dozen times and I had a notion that she had married him in the end with hesitation. She thought that he would become a great painter and when he turned out to be no more than a decent craftsman, without originality or imagination, she felt that she had been cheated. She was mortified by the contempt with which the connoisseurs regarded him. Thomas Warton loved his wife. He had the greatest respect for her judgement and would sooner have had a word of praise from her than columns of eulogy in all the papers in London. She was too honest to say what she did not think. It wounded him bitterly that she held his work in such poor esteem, and though he pretended to make a joke of it you could see that at heart he resented her outspoken comments. Sometimes his long, horse-like face grew red with the anger he tried to control and his eyes dark with hatred. It was notorious among their friends that the couple did not get on. They had the distressing habit of fripping in public. Warton never spoke to others of Mary but with admiration, but she was less discreet and her confidants knew how exasperating she found him. She admitted his goodness, his generosity, his unselfishness; she admitted them ungrudgingly; but his defects were of the sort that make a man hard to live with, for he was narrow, argumentative, and conceited. He was not an artist and Mary Warton cared more for art than for anything in the world. It was a matter on which she could not compromise. It blinded her to the fact that the faults in Warton that maddened her were due in large part to his hurt feelings. She wounded him continually and he was dogmatic and intolerant in self-protection. There cannot be anything much worse than to be despised by the one person whose approval is all in all to you; and though Thomas Warton was intolerable it was impossible not to feel sorry for him. But if I have given the impression that Mary was a discontented, rather tiresome, pretentious woman I have been unjust to her. She was a loyal friend and a delightful companion. You could talk to her of any subject under the sun. Her conversation was humorous and witty. Her vitality was immense.

She was sitting now on the left hand of her host and the talk around her was general. I was occupied with my next-door neighbour, but I guessed by the laughter with which Mary's sallies were greeted that she was at her brilliant best. When she was in the vein no one could approach her.

'You're in great form tonight,' I remarked, when at last she turned to me.

'Does it surprise you?'

'No, it's what I expect of you. No wonder people tumble over one another to get you to their houses. You have the inestimable gift of making a party go.'

'I do my little best to earn my dinner.'

'By the way, how's Manson? Someone told me the other day that he was going into a nursing-home for an operation. I hope it's nothing serious.'

Mary paused for a moment before answering, but she still smiled brightly.

'Haven't you seen the paper tonight?'

'No, I've been playing golf. I only got home in time to jump into a bath and change.'

'He died at two o'clock this afternoon.' I was about to make an exclamation of horrified surprise, but she stopped me. 'Take care. Tom is watching me like a lynx. They're all watching me. They all know I adored him, but they none of them know for certain if he was my lover, even Tom doesn't know; they want to see how I'm taking it. Try to look as if you were talking of the Russian Ballet.'

At that moment someone addressed her from the other side of the table, and throwing back her head a little with a gesture that was habitual with her, a smile on her large mouth, she flung at the speaker so quick and apt an answer that everyone round her burst out laughing. The talk once more became general and I was left to my consternation.

I knew, everyone knew, that for five and twenty years there had existed between Gerrard Manson and Mary Warton a passionate attachment. It had lasted so long that even the more strait-laced of their friends, if ever they had been shocked by it, had long since learnt to accept it with tolerance. They were middle-aged people, Manson was sixty and Mary not much younger, and it was absurd that at their age they should not do what they liked. You met them sometimes sitting in a retired corner of an obscure restaurant or walking together in the Zoo and you wondered why they still took care to conceal an affair that was nobody's business but their own. But of course there was Thomas. He was insanely jealous of Mary. He made many violent scenes and indeed, at the end of one tempestuous period, not so very long ago, he forced her to promise never to see Manson again. Of course she broke the promise, and though she knew that Thomas suspected this, she took precautions to prevent him from discovering it for a fact.

It was hard on Thomas. I think he and Mary would have jogged on well enough together and she would have resigned herself to the fact that he was a second-rate painter if her intercourse with Manson had not embittered her judgement. The contrast between her husband's mediocrity and her lover's brilliance was too galling.

'With Tom I feel as if I were stifling in a closed room full of dusty knick-knacks,' she told me. 'With Gerrard I breathe the pure air of the mountain tops.'

'Is it possible for a woman to fall in love with a man's mind?' I asked in a pure spirit of inquiry.

'What else is there in Gerrard?'

That, I admit, was a poser. For my part I thought, nothing; but the sex is extraordinary and I was quite ready to believe that Mary saw in Gerrard Manson a charm and a physical attractiveness to which most people were blind. He was a shrivelled little man, with a pale intellectual face, faded blue eyes behind his spectacles, and a high dome of shiny bald head. He had none of the appearance of a romantic lover. On the other hand he was certainly a very subtle critic and a felicitous essayist. I resented somewhat his contemptuous attitude towards English writers unless they were safely dead and buried; but this was only to his credit with the intelligentsia, who are ever ready to believe that there can be no good in what is produced in their own country, and with them his influence was great. On one occasion I told him that one had only to put a commonplace in French for him to mistake it for an epigram and he had thought well enough of the joke to use it as his own in one of his essays. He reserved such praise as he was willing to accord his contemporaries to those who wrote in a foreign tongue. The exasperating thing was that no one could deny that he was himself a brilliant writer. His style was exquisite. His knowledge was vast. He could be profound without pomposity, amusing without frivolity, and polished without affectation. His slightest article was readable. His essays were little masterpieces. For my part I did not find him a very agreeable companion. Perhaps I did not get the best out of him. Though I knew him a great many years I never heard him say an amusing thing. He was not talkative and when he made a remark it was oracular. The prospect of spending an evening alone with him would have filled me with dismay. It never ceased to puzzle me that this dull and mannered little man should be able to write with so much grace, wit, and gaiety.

It puzzled me even more that a gallant and vivacious creature like Mary Warton should have cherished for him so consuming a passion. These things are inexplicable and there was evidently something in that odd, crabbed, irascible creature that appealed to women. His wife adored him. She was a fat, frowsy, boring person. She had led Gerrard a dog's life, but had always refused to give him his freedom. She swore to kill herself if he left her and since she was unbalanced and hysterical he was never quite certain that she would not carry out her threat. One day, when I was having tea with Mary, I saw that she was distraught and nervous and when I asked her what was the matter she burst into tears. She had been lunching with Manson and had found him shattered after a terrific scene with his wife.

'We can't go on like this,' Mary cried. 'It's ruining his life. It's ruining all our lives.'

'Why don't you take the plunge?'

'What do you mean?'

'You've been lovers so long, you know the best and the worst of one another by now; you're getting old and you can't count on many more years of life; it seems a pity to waste a love that has endured so long. What good are you doing to Mrs Manson or to Tom? Are they happy because you two are making yourselves miserable?'

'No.'

'Then why don't you chuck everything and just go off together and let come what may?'

Mary shook her head.

'We've talked that over endlessly. We've talked it over for a quarter of a century. It's impossible. For years Gerrard couldn't on account of his daughters. Mrs Manson may have been a very fond mother, but she was a very bad one, and there was no one to see the girls were properly brought up but Gerrard. And now that they're married off he's set in his habits. What should we do? Go to France or Italy? I couldn't tear Gerrard away from his surroundings. He'd be wretched. He's too old to make a fresh start. And besides, though Thomas nags me and makes scenes and we frip and get on one another's nerves, he loves me. When it came to the point I simply shouldn't have the heart to leave him. He'd be lost without me.'

'It's a situation without an issue. I'm dreadfully sorry for you.'

On a sudden Mary's haggard, weather-beaten face was lit by a smile that broke on her large red mouth; and upon my word at that moment she was beautiful.

'You need not be. I was rather low a little while ago, but now I've had a good cry I feel better. Notwithstanding all the pain, all the unhappiness this affair has caused me, I wouldn't have missed it for all the world. For those few moments of ecstasy my love has brought me I would be willing to live all my life over again. And I think he'd tell you the same thing. Oh, it's been so infinitely worth while.'

I could not help but be moved.

'There's no doubt about it,' I said. 'That's love all right.'

'Yes, it's love, and we've just got to go through with it. There's no way out.'

And now with this tragic suddenness the way out had come. I turned a little to look at Mary and she, feeling my eyes upon her, turned too. There was a smile on her lips.

'Why did you come here tonight? It must be awful for you.'

She shrugged her shoulders.

'What could I do? I read the news in the evening paper while I was dressing. He'd asked me not to ring up the nursing-home on account of his wife. It's death to me. Death. I had to come. We'd been engaged for a month. What excuse could I give Tom? I'm not supposed to have seen Gerrard for two years. Do you know that for twenty years we've written to one another every day?' Her lower lip trembled a little, but she bit it and for a moment her face was twisted to a strange grimace; then with a smile she pulled herself together. 'He was everything I had in the world, but I couldn't let the party down, could I? He always said I had a social sense.'

'Happily we shall break up early and you can go home.'

'I don't want to go home. I don't want to be alone. I daren't cry because my eyes will get red and swollen, and we've got a lot of people lunching with us tomorrow. Will you come, by the way? I want an extra man. I must be in good form; Tom expects to get a commission for a portrait out of it.'

'By George, you've got courage.'

'D'you think so? I'm heartbroken, you know. I suppose that's what makes it easier for me. Gerrard would have liked me to put a good face on it. He would have appreciated the irony of the situation. It's the sort of thing he always thought the French novelists described so well.'

The Verger

◆

There had been a christening that afternoon at St Peter's, Neville Square, and Albert Edward Foreman still wore his verger's gown. He kept his new one, its folds as full and stiff as though it were made not of alpaca but of perennial bronze, for funerals and weddings (St Peter's, Neville Square, was a church much favoured by the fashionable for these ceremonies) and now he wore only his second-best. He wore it with complacence, for it was the dignified symbol of his office, and without it (when he took it off to go home) he had the disconcerting sensation of being somewhat insufficiently clad. He took pains with it; he pressed it and ironed it himself. During the sixteen years he had been verger of this church he had had a succession of such gowns, but he had never been able to throw them away when they were worn out and the complete series, neatly wrapped up in brown paper, lay in the bottom drawers of the wardrobe in his bedroom.

The verger busied himself quietly, replacing the painted wooden cover on the marble font, taking away a chair that had been brought for an infirm old lady, and waited for the vicar to have finished in the vestry so that he could tidy up in there and go home. Presently he saw him walk across the chancel, genuflect in front of the high altar, and come down the aisle; but he still wore his cassock.

'What's he 'anging about for?' the verger said to himself. 'Don't 'e know I want my tea?'

The vicar had been but recently appointed, a red-faced energetic man in the early forties, and Albert Edward still regretted his predecessor, a clergyman of the old school who preached leisurely sermons in a silvery voice and dined out a great deal with his more aristocratic parishioners. He liked things in church to be just so, but he never fussed; he was not like this new man who wanted to have his finger in every pie. But Albert Edward was tolerant. St Peter's was in a very good neighbourhood and the parishioners were a very nice class of people. The new vicar had come from the East End and he couldn't be expected to fall in all at once with the discreet ways of his fashionable congregation.

'All this 'ustle,' said Albert Edward. 'But give 'im time, he'll learn.'

When the vicar had walked down the aisle so far that he could address the verger without raising his voice more than was becoming in a place of worship he stopped.

'Foreman, will you come into the vestry for a minute. I have something to say to you.'

'Very good, sir.'

The vicar waited for him to come up and they walked up the church together.

'A very nice christening, I thought, sir. Funny 'ow the baby stopped cryin' the moment you took him.'

'I've noticed they very often do,' said the vicar, with a little smile. 'After all I've had a good deal of practice with them.'

It was a source of subdued pride to him that he could nearly always quiet a whimpering infant by the manner in which he held it and he was not unconscious of the amused admiration with which mothers and nurses watched him settle the baby in the crook of his surpliced arm. The verger knew that it pleased him to be complimented on his talent.

The vicar preceded Albert Edward into the vestry. Albert Edward was a trifle surprised to find the two churchwardens there. He had not seen them come in. They gave him pleasant nods.

'Good afternoon, my lord. Good afternoon, sir,' he said to one after the other.

They were elderly men, both of them, and they had been churchwardens almost as long as Albert Edward had been verger. They were sitting now at a handsome refectory table that the old vicar had brought many years before from Italy and the vicar sat down in the vacant chair between them. Albert Edward faced them, the table between him and them, and wondered with slight uneasiness what was the matter. He remembered still the occasion on which the organist had got into trouble and the bother they had all had to hush things up. In a church like St Peter's, Neville Square, they couldn't afford a scandal. On the vicar's red face was a look of resolute benignity, but the others bore an expression that was slightly troubled.

'He's been naggin' them, he 'as,' said the verger to himself. 'He's jockeyed them into doin' something, but they don't 'alf like it. That's what it is, you mark my words.'

But his thoughts did not appear on Albert Edward's clean-cut and distinguished features. He stood in a respectful but not obsequious attitude. He had been in service before he was appointed to his ecclesiastical office, but only in very good houses, and his deportment was irreproachable. Starting as a page-boy in the household of a merchant-prince, he had risen by due degrees from the position of fourth to first footman, for a year he had been single-handed butler to a widowed peeress, and, till the vacancy occurred at St Peter's, butler with two men under him in the house of a retired ambassador. He was tall, spare, grave, and dignified. He looked, if not like a duke, at least like an actor of the old school who specialized in dukes' parts. He had tact, firmness, and self-assurance. His character was unimpeachable.

The vicar began briskly.

'Foreman, we've got something rather unpleasant to say to you. You've been here a great many years and I think his lordship and the general agree with me that you've fulfilled the duties of your office to the satisfaction of everybody concerned.'

The two churchwardens nodded.

'But a most extraordinary circumstance came to my knowledge the other day and I felt it my duty to impart it to the churchwardens. I discovered to my astonishment that you could neither read nor write.'

The verger's face betrayed no sign of embarrassment.

'The last vicar knew that, sir,' he replied. 'He said it didn't make no difference. He always said there was a great deal too much education in the world for 'is taste.'

'It's the most amazing thing I ever heard,' cried the general. 'Do you mean to say that you've been verger of this church for sixteen years and never learned to read or write?'

'I went into service when I was twelve, sir. The cook in the first place tried to teach me once, but I didn't seem to 'ave the knack for it, and then what with one thing and another I never seemed to 'ave the time. I've never really found the want of it. I think a lot of these young fellows waste a rare lot of time readin' when they might be doin' something useful.'

'But don't you want to know the news?' said the other churchwarden. 'Don't you ever want to write a letter?'

'No, me lord, I seem to manage very well without. And of late years now they've all these pictures in the papers I get to know what's goin' on pretty well. Me wife's quite a scholar and if I want to write a letter she writes it for me. It's not as if I was a bettin' man.'

The two churchwardens gave the vicar a troubled glance and then looked down at the table.

'Well, Foreman, I've talked the matter over with these gentlemen and they quite agree with me that the situation is impossible. At a church like St Peter's, Neville Square, we cannot have a verger who can neither read nor write.'

Albert Edward's thin, sallow face reddened and he moved uneasily on his feet, but he made no reply.

'Understand me, Foreman, I have no complaint to make against you. You do your work quite satisfactorily; I have the highest opinion both of your character and of your capacity; but we haven't the right to take the risk of some accident that might happen owing to your lamentable ignorance. It's a matter of prudence as well as of principle.'

'But couldn't you learn, Foreman?' asked the general.

'No, sir, I'm afraid I couldn't, not now. You see, I'm not as young as I was and if I couldn't seem able to get the letters in me 'ead when I was a nipper I don't think there's much chance of it now.'

'We don't want to be harsh with you, Foreman,' said the vicar. 'But the churchwardens and I have quite made up our minds. We'll give you three months and if at the end of that time you cannot read and write I'm afraid you'll have to go.'

Albert Edward had never liked the new vicar. He'd said from the beginning that they'd made a mistake when they gave him St Peter's. He wasn't the type of man they wanted with a classy congregation like that. And now he straightened himself a little. He knew his value and he wasn't going to allow himself to be put upon.

'I'm very sorry, sir, I'm afraid it's no good. I'm too old a dog to learn new tricks. I've lived a good many years without knowin' 'ow to read and write, and without wishin' to praise myself, self-praise is no recommendation, I don't mind sayin' I've done my duty in that state of life in which it 'as pleased a merciful providence to place me, and if I *could* learn now I don't know as I'd want to.'

'In that case, Foreman, I'm afraid you must go.'

'Yes, sir, I quite understand. I shall be 'appy to 'and in my resignation as soon as you've found somebody to take my place.'

But when Albert Edward with his usual politeness had closed the church door behind the vicar and the two churchwardens he could not sustain the air of unruffled dignity with which he had borne the blow inflicted upon him and his lips quivered. He walked slowly back to the vestry and hung up on its proper peg his verger's gown. He sighed as he thought of all the grand funerals and smart weddings it had seen. He tidied everything up, put on his coat, and hat in hand walked down the aisle. He locked the church door behind him. He strolled across the square, but deep in his sad thoughts he did not take the street that led him home, where a nice strong cup of tea awaited him; he took the wrong turning. He walked slowly along. His heart was heavy. He did not know what he should do with himself. He did not fancy the notion of going back to domestic service; after being his own master for so many years, for the vicar and churchwardens could say what they liked, it was he that had run St Peter's, Neville Square, he could scarcely demean himself by accepting a situation. He had saved a tidy sum, but not enough to live on without doing something, and life seemed to cost more every year. He had never thought to be troubled with such questions. The vergers of St Peter's, like the popes of Rome, were there for life. He had often thought of the pleasant reference the vicar would make in his sermon at evensong the first Sunday after his death to the long and faithful service, and the exemplary character of their late verger, Albert Edward Foreman. He sighed deeply. Albert Edward was a non-smoker and a total abstainer, but with a certain latitude; that is to say he liked a glass of beer with his dinner and when he was tired he enjoyed a cigarette. It occurred to him now that one would comfort him and since he did not carry them he looked about him for a shop where he could buy a packet of Gold Flake. He did not at once see one and walked on a little. It was a long street, with all sorts of shops in it, but there was not a single one where you could buy cigarettes.

'That's strange,' said Albert Edward.

To make sure he walked right up the street again. No, there was no doubt about it. He stopped and looked reflectively up and down.

'I can't be the only man as walks along this street and wants a fag,' he said. 'I shouldn't wonder but what a fellow might do very well with a little shop here. Tobacco and sweets, you know.'

He gave a sudden start.

'That's an idea,' he said. 'Strange 'ow things come to you when you least expect it.'

He turned, walked home, and had his tea.

'You're very silent this afternoon, Albert,' his wife remarked.

'I'm thinkin',' he said.

He considered the matter from every point of view and next day he went along the street and by good luck found a little shop to let that looked as though it would exactly suit him. Twenty-four hours later he had taken it, and when a

month after that he left St Peter's, Neville Square, for ever, Albert Edward
Foreman set up in business as a tobacconist and newsagent. His wife said it was
a dreadful come-down after being verger of St Peter's, but he answered that
you had to move with the times, the church wasn't what it was, and
'enceforward he was going to render unto Caesar what was Caesar's. Albert
Edward did very well. He did so well that in a year or so it struck him that he
might take a second shop and put a manager in. He looked for another long
street that hadn't got a tobacconist in it and when he found it, and a shop to let,
took it and stocked it. This was a success too. Then it occurred to him that if he
could run two he could run half a dozen, so he began walking about London,
and whenever he found a long street that had no tobacconist and a shop to let he
took it. In the course of ten years he had acquired no less than ten shops and he
was making money hand over fist. He went round to all of them himself every
Monday, collected the week's takings, and took them to the bank.

One morning when he was there paying in a bundle of notes and a heavy bag
of silver the cashier told him that the manager would like to see him. He was
shown into an office and the manager shook hands with him.

'Mr Foreman, I wanted to have a talk to you about the money you've got on
deposit with us. D'you know exactly how much it is?'

'Not within a pound or two, sir; but I've got a pretty rough idea.'

'Apart from what you paid in this morning it's a little over thirty thousand
pounds. That's a very large sum to have on deposit and I should have thought
you'd do better to invest it.'

'I wouldn't want to take no risk, sir. I know it's safe in the bank.'

'You needn't have the least anxiety. We'll make you out a list of absolutely
gilt-edged securities. They'll bring you in a better rate of interest than we can
possibly afford to give you.'

A troubled look settled on Mr Foreman's distinguished face. 'I've never 'ad
anything to do with stocks and shares and I'd 'ave to leave it all in your 'ands,'
he said.

The manager smiled. 'We'll do everything. All you'll have to do next time
you come in is just to sign the transfers.'

'I could do that all right,' said Albert uncertainly. 'But 'ow should I know
what I was signin'?'

'I suppose you can read,' said the manager a trifle sharply.

Mr Foreman gave him a disarming smile.

'Well, sir, that's just it. I can't. I know it sounds funny-like, but there it is, I
can't read or write, only me name, an' I only learnt to do that when I went into
business.'

The manager was so surprised that he jumped up from his chair.

'That's the most extraordinary thing I ever heard.'

'You see, it's like this, sir, I never 'ad the opportunity until it was too late and
then some'ow I wouldn't. I got obstinate-like.'

The manager stared at him as though he were a prehistoric monster.

'And do you mean to say that you've built up this important business and
amassed a fortune of thirty thousand pounds without being able to read or
write? Good God, man, what would you be now if you had been able to?'

'I can tell you that, sir,' said Mr Foreman, a little smile on his still aristocratic
features. 'I'd be verger of St Peter's, Neville Square.'

The Taipan

◆

No one knew better than he that he was an important person. He was number one in not the least important branch of the most important English firm in China. He had worked his way up through solid ability and he looked back with a faint smile at the callow clerk who had come out to China thirty years before. When he remembered the modest home he had come from, a little red house in a long row of little red houses, in Barnes, a suburb which, aiming desperately at the genteel, achieves only a sordid melancholy, and compared it with the magnificent stone mansion, with its wide verandas and spacious rooms, which was at once the office of the company and his own residence, he chuckled with satisfaction. He had come a long way since then. He thought of the high tea to which he sat down when he came home from school (he was at St Paul's), with his father and mother and his two sisters, a slice of cold meat, a great deal of bread and butter and plenty of milk in his tea, everybody helping himself, and then he thought of the state in which now he ate his evening meal. He always dressed and whether he was alone or not he expected the three boys to wait at table. His number one boy knew exactly what he liked and he never had to bother himself with the details of housekeeping; but he always had a set dinner with soup and fish, entrée, roast, sweet, and savoury, so that if he wanted to ask anyone in at the last moment he could. He liked his food and he did not see why when he was alone he should have less good a dinner than when he had a guest.

He had indeed gone far. That was why he did not care to go home now, he had not been to England for ten years, and he took his leave in Japan or Vancouver, where he was sure of meeting old friends from the China coast. He knew no one at home. His sisters had married in their own station, their husbands were clerks and their sons were clerks; there was nothing between him and them; they bored him. He satisfied the claims of relationship by sending them every Christmas a piece of fine silk, some elaborate embroidery, or a case of tea. He was not a mean man and as long as his mother lived he had made her an allowance. But when the time came for him to retire he had no intention of going back to England, he had seen too many men do that and he knew how often it was a failure; he meant to take a house near the racecourse in Shanghai: what with bridge and his ponies and golf he expected to get through the rest of his life very comfortably. But he had a good many years before he need think of retiring. In another five or six Higgins would be going home and then he would take charge of the head office in Shanghai. Meanwhile he was very happy where he was, he could save money, which you couldn't do in Shanghai, and have a good time into the bargain. This place had another advantage over Shanghai: he was the most prominent man in the community and what he said went. Even the consul took care to keep on the right side of him. Once a consul and he had been at loggerheads and it was not he who had gone to the wall. The taipan thrust out his jaw pugnaciously as he thought of the incident.

But he smiled, for he felt in an excellent humour. He was walking back to his office from a capital luncheon at the Hong-Kong and Shanghai Bank. They did you very well there. The food was first-rate and there was plenty of liquor. He had started with a couple of cocktails, then he had some excellent sauterne and he had finished up with two glasses of port and some fine old brandy. He felt good. And when he left he did a thing that was rare with him; he walked. His bearers with his chair kept a few paces behind him in case he felt inclined to slip into it, but he enjoyed stretching his legs. He did not get enough exercise these days. Now that he was too heavy to ride it was difficult to get exercise. But if he was too heavy to ride he could still keep ponies, and as he strolled along in the balmy air he thought of the spring meeting. He had a couple of griffins that he had hopes of and one of the lads in his office had turned out a fine jockey (he must see they didn't sneak him away, old Higgins in Shanghai would give a pot of money to get him over there) and he ought to pull off two or three races. He flattered himself that he had the finest stable in the city. He pouted his broad chest like a pigeon. It was a beautiful day, and it was good to be alive.

He paused as he came to the cemetery. It stood there, neat and orderly, as an evident sign of the community's opulence. He never passed the cemetery without a little glow of pride. He was pleased to be an Englishman. For the cemetery stood in a place, valueless when it was chosen, which with the increase of the city's affluence was now worth a great deal of money. It had been suggested that the graves should be moved to another spot and the land sold for building, but the feeling of the community was against it. It gave the taipan a sense of satisfaction to think that their dead rested on the most valuable site on the island. It showed that there were things they cared for more than money. Money be blowed! When it came to 'the things that mattered' (this was a favourite phrase with the taipan), well, one remembered that money wasn't everything.

And now he thought he would take a stroll through. He looked at the graves. They were neatly kept and the pathways were free from weeds. There was a look of prosperity. And as he sauntered along he read the names on the tombstones. Here were three side by side: the captain, the first mate, and the second made of the barque *Mary Baxter*, who had all perished together in the typhoon of 1908. He remembered it well. There was a little group of two missionaries, their wives and children, who had been massacred during the Boxer troubles. Shocking thing that had been! Not that he took much stock in missionaries; but, hang it all, one couldn't have these damned Chinese massacring them. Then he came to a cross with a name on it he knew. Good chap, Edward Mulock, but he couldn't stand his liquor, drank himself to death, poor devil, at twenty-five; the taipan had known a lot of them do that; there were several more neat crosses with a man's name on them and the age, twenty-five, twenty-six, or twenty-seven; it was always the same story: they had come out to China; they had never seen so much money before, they were good fellows and they wanted to drink with the rest: they couldn't stand it, and there they were in the cemetery. You had to have a strong head and a fine constitution to drink drink for drink on the China coast. Of course it was very sad, but the taipan could hardly help a smile when he thought how many of those young fellows he had drunk underground. And there was a death that had been useful, a fellow in his own firm, senior to him and a clever chap too: if that fellow had lived he might not have been taipan now. Truly the ways of fate were inscrutable. Ah, and here was little Mrs Turner, Violet Turner, she had been a pretty little thing, he had had quite an affair with her; he had been devilish cut up when she died. He looked at her age on the tombstone. She'd be no chicken if she were alive now. And as he thought of all those dead people a sense of satisfaction spread through him. He had beaten them all. They were dead and he was alive, and by George he'd scored them off. His eyes collected in one picture all those crowded graves and he smiled scornfully. He very nearly rubbed his hands.

'No one ever thought I was a fool,' he muttered.

He had a feeling of good-natured contempt for the gibbering dead. Then, as he strolled along, he came suddenly upon two coolies digging a grave. He was astonished, for he had not heard that anyone in the community was dead.

'Who the devil's that for?' he said aloud.

The coolies did not even look at him, they went on with their work, standing in the grave, deep down, and they shovelled up heavy clods of earth. Though he had been so long in China he knew no Chinese, in his day it was not thought necessary to learn the damned language, and he asked the coolies in English whose grave they were digging. They did not understand. They answered him in Chinese and he cursed them for ignorant fools. He knew that Mrs Broome's child was ailing and it might have died, but he would certainly have heard of it, and besides, that wasn't a child's grave, it was a man's and a big man's too. It was uncanny. He wished he hadn't gone into that cemetery; he hurried out and stepped into his chair. His good-humour had all gone and there was an uneasy frown on his face. The moment he got back to his office he called to his number two:

'I say, Peters, who's dead, d'you know?'

But Peters knew nothing. The taipan was puzzled. He called one of the native clerks and sent him to the cemetery to ask the coolies. He began to sign his letters. The clerk came back and said the coolies had gone and there was no one to ask. The taipan began to feel vaguely annoyed: he did not like things to happen of which he knew nothing. His own boy would know, his boy always knew everything, and he sent for him; but the boy had heard of no death in the community.

'I knew no one was dead,' said the taipan irritably. 'But what's the grave for?'

He told the boy to go to the overseer of the cemetery and find out what the devil he had dug a grave for when no one was dead.

'Let me have a whisky and soda before you go,' he added, as the boy was leaving the room.

He did not know why the sight of the grave had made him uncomfortable. But he tried to put it out of his mind. He felt better when he had drunk the whisky, and he finished his work. He went upstairs and turned over the pages of *Punch*. In a few minutes he would go to the club and play a rubber or two of bridge before dinner. But it would ease his mind to hear what his boy had to say and he waited for his return. In a little while the boy came back and he brought the overseer with him.

'What are you having a grave dug for?' he asked the overseer point-blank. 'Nobody's dead.'

'I no dig glave,' said the man.

'What the devil do you mean by that? There were two coolies digging a grave this afternoon.'

The two Chinese looked at one another. Then the boy said they had been to the cemetery together. There was no new grave there.

The taipan only just stopped himself from speaking.

'But damn it all, I saw it myself,' were the words on the tip of his tongue.

But he did not say them. He grew very red as he choked them down. The two Chinese looked at him with their steady eyes. For a moment his breath failed him.

'All right. Get out,' he gasped.

But as soon as they were gone he shouted for the boy again, and when he came, maddeningly impassive, he told him to bring some whisky. He rubbed his sweating face with a handkerchief. His hand trembled when he lifted the glass to his lips. They could say what they liked, but he had seen the grave. Why, he could hear still the dull thud as the coolies threw the spadefuls of earth on the ground above them. What did it mean? He could feel his heart beating. He felt strangely ill at ease. But he pulled himself together. It was all nonsense. If there was no grave there it must have been a hallucination. The best thing he could do was to go the club, and if he ran across the doctor he would ask him to give him a look over.

Everyone in the club looked just the same as ever. He did not know why he should have expected them to look different. It was a comfort. These men, living for many years with one another lives that were methodically regulated, had acquired a number of little idiosyncrasies—one of them hummed incessantly while he played bridge, another insisted on drinking beer through a straw—and these tricks which had so often irritated the taipan now gave him a sense of security. He needed it, for he could not get out of his head that strange sight he had seen; he played bridge very badly; his partner was censorious, and the taipan lost his temper. He thought the men were looking at him oddly. He wondered what they saw in him that was unaccustomed.

Suddenly he felt he could not bear to stay in the club any longer. As he went out he saw the doctor reading *The Times* in the reading-room, but he could not bring himself to speak to him. He wanted to see for himself whether that grave was really there, and stepping into his chair he told his bearers to take him to the cemetery. You couldn't have a hallucination twice, could you? And besides, he would take the overseer in with him and if the grave was not there he wouldn't see it, and if it was he'd give the overseer the soundest thrashing he'd ever had.

But the overseer was nowhere to be found. He had gone out and taken the keys with him. When the taipan found he could not get into the cemetery he felt suddenly exhausted. He got back into his chair and told his bearers to take him home. He would lie down for half an hour before dinner. He was tired out. That was it. He had heard that people had hallucinations when they were tired. When his boy came in to put out his clothes for dinner it was only by an effort of will that he got up. He had a strong inclination not to dress that evening, but he resisted it: he made it a rule to dress, he had dressed every evening for twenty years and it would never do to break his rule. But he ordered a bottle of champagne with his dinner and that made him feel more comfortable. Afterwards he told the boy to bring him the best brandy. When he had drunk a couple of glasses of this he felt himself again. Hallucinations be damned! He went to the billiard-room and practised a few difficult shots. There could not be much the matter with him when his eye was so sure. When he went to bed he sank immediately into a sound sleep.

But suddenly he awoke. He had dreamed of that open grave and the coolies digging leisurely. He was sure he had seen them. It was absurd to say it was a hallucination when he had seen them with his own eyes. Then he heard the rattle of the night-watchman going his rounds. It broke upon the stillness of the night so harshly that it made him jump out of his skin. And then terror seized him. He felt a horror of the winding multitudinous streets of the Chinese city, and there was something ghastly and terrible in the convoluted roofs of the temples with their devils grimacing and tortured. He loathed the smells that assaulted his nostrils. And the people. Those myriads of blue-clad coolies, and the beggars in their filthy rags, and the merchants and the magistrates, sleek, smiling, and inscrutable, in their long black gowns. They seemed to press upon him with menace. He hated the country. China. Why had he ever come? He was panic-stricken now. He must get out. He would not stay another year, another month. What did he care about Shanghai?

'Oh, my God,' he cried, 'if I were only safely back in England.'

He wanted to go home. If he had to die he wanted to die in England. He could not bear to be buried among all these yellow men, with their slanting eyes and their grinning faces. He wanted to be buried at home, not in that grave he had seen that day. He could never rest there. Never. What did it matter what people thought? Let them think what they liked. The only thing that mattered was to get away while he had the chance.

He got out of bed and wrote to the head of the firm and said he had discovered he was dangerously ill. He must be replaced. He could not stay longer than was absolutely necessary. He must go home at once.

They found the letter in the morning clenched in the taipan's hand. He had slipped down between the desk and the chair. He was stone dead.

The Consul

◆

Mr Pete was in a state of the liveliest exasperation. He had been in the consular service for more than twenty years and he had had to deal with all manner of vexatious people, officials who would not listen to reason, merchants who took the British Government for a debt-collecting agency, missionaries who resented as gross injustice any attempt at fair play; but he never recollected a case which had left him more completely at a loss. He was a mild-mannered man, but for no reason he flew into a passion with his writer and he very nearly sacked the Eurasian clerk because he had wrongly spelt two words in a letter placed before him for his official signature. He was a conscientious man and he could not persuade himself to leave his office before the clock struck four; the moment it did he jumped up and called for his hat and stick. Because his boy did not bring them at once he abused him roundly. They say that the consuls all grow a little odd; and the merchants who can live for thirty-five years in China without learning enough of the language to ask their way in the street say that it is because they have to study Chinese; and there was no doubt that Mr Pete was decidedly odd. He was a bachelor and on that account had been sent to a series of posts which by reason of their isolation were thought unsuited to married men. He had lived so much alone that his natural tendency to eccentricity had developed to an extravagant degree, and he had habits which surprised the stranger. He was very absent-minded. He paid no attention to his house, which was always in great disorder, nor to his food; his boys gave him to eat what they liked and for everything he had made him pay through the nose. He was untiring in his efforts to suppress the opium traffic, but he was the only person in the city who did not know that his servants kept opium in the consulate itself, and a busy traffic in the drug was openly conducted at the back door of the compound. He was an ardent collector and the house provided for him by the government was filled with the various things which he had collected one after the other, pewter, brass, carved wood; these were his more legitimate enterprises; but he also collected stamps, birds' eggs, hotel labels, and postmarks: he boasted that he had a collection of postmarks which was unequalled in the Empire. During his long sojourning in lonely places he had read a great deal, and though he was no sinologue he had a greater knowledge of China, its history, literature, and people, than most of his colleagues; but from his wide reading he had acquired not toleration but vanity. He was a man of a singular appearance. His body was small and frail and when he walked he gave you the idea of a dead leaf dancing before the wind; and then there was something extraordinarily odd in the small Tyrolese hat, with a cock's feather in it, very old and shabby, which he wore perched rakishly on the side of his large head. He was exceedingly bald. You saw that his eyes, blue and pale, were weak behind the spectacles, and a drooping, ragged, dingy moustache did not hide the peevishness of his mouth. And now, turning out of the street in which was the consulate, he made his way on to the city wall, for there only in the multitudinous city was it possible to walk with comfort.

He was a man who took his work hardly, worrying himself to death over every trifle, but as a rule a walk on the wall soothed and rested him. The city stood in the midst of a great plain and often at sundown from the wall you could see in the distance the snow-capped mountains, the mountains of Tibet; but now he walked quickly, looking neither to the right nor to the left, and his fat spaniel frisked about him unobserved. He talked to himself rapidly in a low monotone. The cause of his irritation was a visit that he had that day received from a lady who called herself Mrs Yü and whom he with a consular passion for precision insisted on calling Miss Lambert. This in itself sufficed to deprive their intercourse of amenity. She was an Englishwoman married to a Chinese. She had arrived two years before with her husband from England, where he had been studying at the University of London; he had made her believe that he was a great personage in his own country and she had imagined herself to be coming to a gorgeous palace and a position of consequence. It was a bitter surprise when she found herself brought to a shabby Chinese house crowded with people: there was not even a foreign bed in it, nor a knife or fork: everything seemed to her very dirty and smelly. It was a shock to find that she had to live with her husband's father and mother and he told her that she must do exactly what his mother bade her; but in her complete ignorance of Chinese it was not till she had been two or three days in the house that she realized that she was not her husband's only wife. He had been married as a boy before he left his native city to acquire the knowledge of the barbarians. When she bitterly upbraided him for deceiving her he shrugged his shoulders. There was nothing to prevent a Chinese from having two wives if he wanted them and, he added with some disregard to truth, no Chinese woman looked upon it as a hardship. It was upon making this discovery that she paid her first visit to the consul. He had already heard of her arrival—in China everyone knows everything about everyone—and he received her without surprise. Nor had he much sympathy to show her. That a foreign woman should marry a Chinese at all filled him with indignation, but that she should do so without making proper inquiries vexed him like a personal affront. She was not at all the sort of woman whose appearance led you to imagine that she would be guilty of such a folly. She was a solid, thick-set, young person, short, plain, and matter-of-fact. She was cheaply dressed in a tailor-made suit and she wore a tam-o'-shanter. She had bad teeth and a muddy skin. Her hands were large and red and ill-cared-for. You could tell that she was not unused to hard work. She spoke English with a cockney whine.

'How did you meet Mr Yü?' asked the consul frigidly.

'Well, you see, it's like this,' she answered.'Dad was in a very good position, and when he died mother said: "Well, it seems a sinful waste to keep all these rooms empty, I'll put a card in the window."'

The consul interrupted her.

'He had lodgings with you?'

'Well, they weren't exactly lodgings,' she said.

'Shall we say apartments then?' replied the consul, with his thin, slightly vain smile.

That was generally the explanation of these marriages. Then because he thought her a very foolish vulgar woman he explained bluntly that according to English law she was not married to Yü and that the best thing she could do was to go back to England at once. She began to cry and his heart softened a little to her. He promised to put her in the charge of some missionary ladies who would look after her on the long journey, and indeed, if she liked, he would see if meanwhile she could not live in one of the missions. But while he talked Miss Lambert dried her tears.

'What's the good of going back to England?' she said at last. 'I'aven't got nowhere to go to.'

'You can go to your mother.'

'She was all against my marrying Mr Yü. I should never hear the last of it if I was to go back now.'

The consul began to argue with her, but the more he argued the more determined she became, and at last he lost his temper.

'If you like to stay here with a man who isn't your husband it's your own look-out, but I wash my hands of all responsibility.'

Her retort had often rankled.

'Then you've got no cause to worry,' she said, and the look on her face returned to him whenever he thought of her.

That was two years ago and he had seen her once or twice since then. It appeared that she got on very badly both with her mother-in-law and with her husband's other wife, and she had come to the consul with preposterous questions about her rights according to Chinese law. He repeated his offer to get her away, but she remained steadfast in her refusal to go, and their interview always ended in the consul's flying into a passion. He was almost inclined to pity the rascally Yü who had to keep the peace between three warring women. According to his English wife's account he was not unkind to her. He tried to act fairly by both his wives. Miss Lambert did not improve. The consul knew that ordinarily she wore Chinese clothes, but when she came to see him she put on European dress. She had become extremely blowsy. Her health suffered from the Chinese food she ate and she was beginning to look wretchedly ill. But really he was shocked when she had been shown into his office that day. She wore no hat and her hair was dishevelled. She was in a highly hysterical state.

'They're trying to poison me,' she screamed and she put before him a bowl of some foul-smelling food. 'It's poisoned,' she said. 'I've been ill for the last ten days, it's only by a miracle I've escaped.'

She gave him a long story, circumstantial and probable enough, enough to convince him: after all, nothing was more likely than that the Chinese women should use familiar methods to get rid of an intruder who was hateful to them.

'Do they know you've come here?'

'Of course they do; I told them I was going to show them up.'

Now at last was the moment for decisive action. The consul looked at her in his most official manner.

'Well, you must never go back there. I refuse to put up with your nonsense any longer. I insist on your leaving this man who isn't your husband.'

But he found himself helpless against the woman's insane obstinacy. He repeated all the arguments he had used so often, but she would not listen, and as usual he lost his temper. It was then, in answer to his final, desperate question, that she had made the remark which had entirely robbed him of his calm.

'But what on earth makes you stay with the man?' he cried.

She hesitated for a moment and a curious look came into her eyes.

'There's something in the way his hair grows on his forehead that I can't help liking,' she answered.

The consul had never heard anything so outrageous. It really was the last straw. And now while he strode along, trying to walk off his anger, though he was not a man who often used bad language he really could not restrain himself, and he said fiercely:

'Women are simply bloody.'

A Friend in Need

◆

For thirty years now I have been studying my fellow-men. I do not know very much about them. I should certainly hesitate to engage a servant on his face, and yet I suppose it is on the face that for the most part we judge the persons we meet. We draw our conclusions from the shape of the jaw, the look in the eyes, the contour of the mouth. I wonder if we are more often right than wrong. Why novels and plays are so often untrue to life is because their authors, perhaps of necessity, make their characters all of a piece. They cannot afford to make them self-contradictory, for then they become incomprehensible, and yet self-contradictory is what most of us are. We are a haphazard bundle of inconsistent qualities. In books on logic they will tell you that it is absurd to say that yellow is tubular or gratitude heavier than air; but in that mixture of incongruities that makes up the self yellow may very well be a horse and cart and gratitude the middle of next week. I shrug my shoulders when people tell me that their first impressions of a person are always right. I think they must have small insight or great vanity. For my own part I find that the longer I know people the more they puzzle me: my oldest friends are just those of whom I can say that I don't know the first thing about them.

These reflections have occurred to me because I read in this morning's paper that Edward Hyde Burton had died at Kobe. He was a merchant and he had been in business in Japan for many years. I knew him very little, but he interested me because once he gave me a great surprise. Unless I had heard the story from his own lips I should never have believed that he was capable of such an action. It was more startling because both in appearance and manner he suggested a very definite type. Here if ever was a man all of a piece. He was a tiny little fellow, not much more than five feet four in height, and very slender, with white hair, a red face much wrinkled, and blue eyes. I suppose he was about sixty when I knew him. He was always neatly and quietly dressed in accordance with his age and station.

Though his offices were in Kobe, Burton often came down to Yokohama. I happened on one occasion to be spending a few days there, waiting for a ship, and I was introduced to him at the British Club. We played bridge together. He played a good game and a generous one. He did not talk very much, either then or later when we were having drinks, but what he said was sensible. He had a quiet, dry humour. He seemed to be popular at the club and afterwards, when he had gone, they described him as one of the best. It happened that we were both staying at the Grand Hotel and next day he asked me to dine with him. I met his wife, fat, elderly, and smiling, and his two daughters. It was evidently a united and affectionate family. I think the chief thing that struck me about Burton was his kindliness. There was something very pleasing in his mild blue eyes. His voice was gentle; you could not imagine that he could possibly raise it in anger; his smile was benign. Here was a man who attracted you because you felt in him a real love for his fellows. He had charm. But there was nothing mawkish in him: he liked his game of cards and his cocktail, he could tell with point a good and spicy story, and in his youth he had been something of an athlete. He was a rich man and he had made every penny himself. I suppose one thing that made you like him was that he was so small and frail; he aroused your instincts of protection. You felt that he could not bear to hurt a fly.

One afternoon I was sitting in the lounge of the Grand Hotel. This was before the earthquake and they had leather arm-chairs there. From the windows you had a spacious view of the harbour with its crowded traffic. There were great liners on their way to Vancouver and San Francisco or to Europe by way of Shanghai, Hong-Kong, and Singapore; there were tramps of all nations, battered and sea-worn, junks with their high sterns and great coloured sails, and innumerable sampans. It was a busy, exhilarating scene, and yet, I know not why, restful to the spirit. Here was romance and it seemed that you had but to stretch out your hand to touch it.

Burton came into the lounge presently and caught sight of me. He seated himself in the chair next to mine.

'What do you say to a little drink?'

He clapped his hands for a boy and ordered two gin fizzes. As the boy brought them a man passed along the street outside and seeing me waved his hand.

'Do you know Turner?' said Burton as I nodded a greeting.

'I've met him at the club. I'm told he's a remittance man.'

'Yes, I believe he is. We have a good many here.'

'He plays bridge well.'

'They generally do. There was a fellow here last year, oddly enough a namesake of mine, who was the best bridge player I ever met. I suppose you never came across him in London. Lenny Burton he called himself. I believe he'd belonged to some very good clubs.'

'No, I don't believe I remember the name.'

'He was quite a remarkable player. He seemed to have an instinct about the cards. It was uncanny. I used to play with him a lot. He was in Kobe for some time.'

Burton sipped his gin fizz.

'It's rather a funny story,' he said. 'He wasn't a bad chap. I liked him. He was always well-dressed and smart-looking. He was handsome in a way with curly hair and pink-and-white cheeks. Women thought a lot of him. There was no harm in him, you know, he was only wild. Of course he drank too much. Those sort of fellows always do. A bit of money used to come in for him once a quarter and he made a bit more by card-playing. He won a good deal of mine, I know that.'

Burton gave a kindly chuckle. I knew from my own experience that he could lose money at bridge with a good grace. He stroked his shaven chin with his thin hand; the veins stood out on it and it was almost transparent.

'I suppose that is why he came to me when he went broke, that and the fact that he was a namesake of mine. He came to see me in my office one day and asked me for a job. I was rather surprised. He told me that there was no more money coming from home and he wanted to work. I asked him how old he was.

'"Thirty-five," he said.

'"And what have you been doing hitherto?" I asked him.

'"Well, nothing very much," he said.

'I couldn't help laughing.

'"I'm afraid I can't do anything for you just yet," I said. "Come back and see me in another thirty-five years, and I'll see what I can do."

'He didn't move. He went rather pale. He hesitated for a moment and then he told me that he had had bad luck at cards for some time. He hadn't been willing to stick to bridge, he'd been playing poker, and he'd got trimmed. He hadn't a penny. He'd pawned everything he had. He couldn't pay his hotel bill and they wouldn't give him any more credit. He was down and out. If he couldn't get something to do he'd have to commit suicide.

'I looked at him for a bit. I could see now that he was all to pieces. He'd been drinking more than usual and he looked fifty. The girls wouldn't have thought so much of him if they'd seen him then.

'"Well, isn't there anything you can do except play cards?" I asked him.

'"I can swim," he said.

'"Swim!"

'I could hardly believe my ears; it seemed such an insane answer to give.

'"I swam for my university."

'I got some glimmering of what he was driving at, I've known too many men who were little tin gods at their university to be impressed by it.

'"I was a pretty good swimmer myself when I was a young man," I said.

'Suddenly I had an idea.'

Pausing in his story, Burton turned to me.

'Do you know Kobe?' he asked.

'No,' I said, 'I passed through it once, but I only spent a night there.'

'Then you don't know the Shioya Club. When I was a young man I swam from there round the beacon and landed at the creek of Tarumi. It's over three miles and it's rather difficult on account of the currents round the beacon. Well, I told my young namesake about it and I said to him that if he'd do it I'd give him a job.

'I could see he was rather taken aback.

'"You say you're a swimmer," I said.

'"I'm not in very good condition," he answered.

'I didn't say anything. I shrugged my shoulders. He looked at me for a moment and then he nodded.

'"All right," he said. "When do you want me to do it?"

'I looked at my watch. It was just after ten.

' "The swim shouldn't take you much over an hour and a quarter. I'll drive round to the creek at half past twelve and meet you. I'll take you back to the club to dress and then we'll have lunch together."

' "Done," he said.

'We shook hands. I wished him good luck and he left me. I had a lot of work to do that morning and I only just managed to get to the creek at Tarumi at half past twelve. But I needn't have hurried; he never turned up.'

'Did he funk it at the last moment?' I asked.

'No, he didn't funk it. He started all right. But of course he'd ruined his constitution by drink and dissipation. The currents round the beacon were more than he could manage. We didn't get the body for about three days.'

I didn't say anything for a moment or two. I was a trifle shocked. Then I asked Burton a question.

'When you made him that offer of a job, did you know he'd be drowned?'

He gave a little mild chuckle and he looked at me with those kind and candid blue eyes of his. He rubbed his chin with his hand.

'Well, I hadn't got a vacancy in my office at the moment.'

The
Round Dozen

◆

I like Elsom. It is a seaside resort in the South of England, not very far from
Brighton, and it has something of the late Georgian charm of that agreeable
town. But it is neither bustling nor garish. Ten years ago, when I used to go there
not infrequently, you might still see here and there an old house, solid and
pretentious in no unpleasing fashion (like a decayed gentlewoman of good
family whose discreet pride in her ancestry amuses rather than offends you),
which was built in the reign of the First Gentleman in Europe and where a
courtier of fallen fortunes may well have passed his declining years. The main
street had a lackadaisical air and the doctor's motor seemed a trifle out of place.
The housewives did their housekeeping in a leisurely manner. They gossiped
with the butcher as they watched him cut from his great joint of South Down a
piece of the best end of the neck, and they asked amiably after the grocer's wife
as he put half a pound of tea and a packet of salt into their string bag. I do not
know whether Elsom was ever fashionable: it certainly was not so then; but it
was respectable and cheap. Elderly ladies, maiden and widowed, lived there,
Indian Civilians and retired soldiers: they looked forward with little shudders
of dismay to August and September which would bring holiday-makers; but
did not disdain to let them their houses and on the proceeds spend a few
worldly weeks in a Swiss pension. I never knew Elsom at that hectic time when
the lodging-houses were full and young men in blazers sauntered along the
front, when Pierrots performed on the beach and in the billiard-room at the
Dolphin you heard the click of balls till eleven at night. I only knew it in winter.
Then in every house on the seafront, stucco houses with bow-windows built a
hundred years ago, there was a sign to inform you that apartments were to let;
and the guests of the Dolphin were waited on by a single waiter and the boots.
At ten o'clock the porter came into the smoking-room and looked at you in so

marked a manner that you got up and went to bed. Then Elsom was a restful place and the Dolphin a very comfortable inn. It was pleasing to think that the Prince Regent drove over with Mrs Fitzherbert more than once to drink a dish of tea in its coffee-room. In the hall was a framed letter from Mr Thackeray ordering a sitting-room and two bedrooms overlooking the sea and giving instructions that a fly should be sent to the station to meet him.

One November, two or three years after the war, having had a bad attack of influenza, I went down to Elsom to regain my strength. I arrived in the afternoon and when I had unpacked my things went for a stroll on the front. The sky was overcast and the calm sea grey and cold. A few seagulls flew close to the shore. Sailing-boats, their masts taken down for the winter, were drawn up high on the shingly beach, and the bathing-huts stood side by side in a long, grey, and tattered row. No one was sitting on the benches that the town council had put here and there, but a few people were trudging up and down for exercise. I passed an old colonel with a red nose who stamped along in plus-fours followed by a terrier, two elderly women in short skirts and stout shoes, and a plain girl in a tam-o'-shanter. I had never seen the front so deserted. The lodging-houses looked like bedraggled old maids waiting for lovers who would never return, and even the friendly Dolphin seemed wan and desolate. My heart sank. Life on a sudden seemed very drab. I returned to the hotel, drew the curtains of my sitting-room, poked the fire, and with a book sought to dispel my melancholy. But I was glad enough when it was time to dress for dinner. I went into the coffee-room and found the guests of the hotel already seated. I gave them a casual glance. There was one lady of middle age by herself and there were two elderly gentlemen, golfers probably, with red faces and baldish heads, who ate their food in moody silence. The only other persons in the room were a group of three who sat in the bow-window, and they immediately attracted my surprised attention. The party consisted of an old gentleman and two ladies, one of whom was old and probably his wife, while the other was younger and possibly his daughter. It was the old lady who first excited my interest. She wore a voluminous dress of black silk and a black lace cap; on her wrists were heavy gold bangles and round her neck a substantial gold chain from which hung a large gold locket; at her neck was a large gold brooch. I did not know that anyone still wore jewellery of that sort. Often, passing second-hand jewellers and pawnbrokers, I had lingered for a moment to look at these strangely old-fashioned articles, so solid, costly, and hideous, and thought with a smile in which there was a tinge of sadness, of the women long since dead who had worn them. They suggested the period when the bustle and the flounce were taking the place of the crinoline and the pork-pie hat was ousting the poke-bonnet. The British people liked things solid and good in those days. They went to church on Sunday morning and after church walked in the Park. They gave dinner-parties of twelve courses where the master of the house carved the beef and the chickens, and after dinner the ladies who could play favoured the company with Mendelssohn's *Songs without Words* and the gentleman with the fine baritone voice sang an old English ballad.

The younger woman had her back turned to me and at first I could see only that she had a slim and youthful figure. She had a great deal of brown hair which seemed to be elaborately arranged. She wore a grey dress. The three of them were chatting in low tones and presently she turned her head so that I saw her profile. It was astonishingly beautiful. The nose was straight and delicate, the line of the cheek exquisitely modelled; I saw then that she wore her hair after the manner of Queen Alexandra. The dinner proceeded to its close and the party got up. The old lady sailed out of the room, looking neither to the right nor to the left, and the young one followed her. Then I saw with a shock that she was old. Her frock was simple enough, the skirt was longer than was at that time worn, and there was something slightly old-fashioned in the cut, I dare say the waist was more clearly indicated than was then usual, but it was a girl's frock. She was tall, like a heroine of Tennyson's, slight, with long legs and a graceful carriage. I had seen the nose before, it was the nose of a Greek goddess, her mouth was beautiful, and her eyes were large and blue. Her skin was of course a little tight on the bones and there were wrinkles on her forehead and about her eyes, but in youth it must have been lovely. She reminded you of those Roman ladies with features of an exquisite regularity whom Alma-Tadema used to paint, but who, notwithstanding their antique dress, were so stubbornly English. It was a type of cold perfection that one had not seen for five-and-twenty years. Now it is as dead as the epigram. I was like an archaeologist who finds some long-buried statue and I was thrilled in so unexpected a manner to hit upon this survival of a past era. For no day is so dead as the day before yesterday.

The gentleman rose to his feet when the two ladies left, and then resumed his chair. A waiter brought him a glass of heavy port. He smelt it, sipped it, and rolled it round his tongue. I observed him. He was a little man, much shorter than his imposing wife, well-covered without being stout, with a fine head of curling grey hair. His face was much wrinkled and it bore a faintly humorous expression. His lips were tight and his chin was square. He was, according to our present notions, somewhat extravagantly dressed. He wore a black velvet jacket, a frilled shirt with a low collar and a large black tie, and very wide evening trousers. It gave you vaguely the effect of costume. Having drunk his port with deliberation, he got up and sauntered out of the room.

When I passed through the hall, curious to know who these singular people were, I glanced at the visitors' book. I saw written in an angular feminine hand, the writing that was taught to young ladies in modish schools forty years or so ago, the names: Mr and Mrs Edwin St Clair and Miss Porchester. Their address was given as 68 Leinster Square, Bayswater, London. These must be the names and this the address of the persons who had so much interested me. I asked the manageress who Mr St Clair was and she told me that she believed he was something in the City. I went into the billiard-room and knocked the balls about for a little while and then on my way upstairs passed through the lounge. The two red-faced gentlemen were reading the evening paper and the elderly lady was dozing over a novel. The party of three sat in a corner. Mrs St Clair was knitting, Miss Porchester was busy with embroidery, and Mr St Clair was reading aloud in a discreet but resonant tone. As I passed I discovered that he was reading *Bleak House*.

I read and wrote most of the next day, but in the afternoon I went for a walk and on my way home I sat down for a little on one of those convenient benches on the sea-front. It was not quite so cold as the day before and the air was pleasant. For want of anything better to do I watched a figure advancing towards me from a distance. It was a man and as he came nearer I saw that it was rather a shabby little man. He wore a thin black greatcoat and a somewhat battered bowler. He walked with his hands in his pockets and looked cold. He gave me a glance as he passed by, went on a few steps, hesitated, stopped and turned back. When he came up once more to the bench on which I sat he took a hand out of his pocket and touched his hat. I noticed that he wore shabby black gloves, and surmised that he was a widower in straitened circumstances. Or he might have been a mute recovering, like myself, from influenza.

'Excuse me, sir,' he said, 'but could you oblige me with a match?'

'Certainly.'

He sat down beside me and while I put my hand in my pocket for matches he hunted in his for cigarettes. He took out a small packet of Gold Flake and his face fell.

'Dear, dear, how very annoying! I haven't got a cigarette left.'

'Let me offer you one,' I replied, smiling.

I took out my case and he helped himself.

'Gold?' he asked, giving the case a tap as I closed it. 'Gold? That's a thing I never could keep. I've had three. All stolen.'

His eyes rested in a melancholy way on his boots, which were sadly in need of repair. He was a wizened little man with a long thin nose and pale-blue eyes. His skin was sallow and he was much lined. I could not tell what his age was; he might have been five-and-thirty or he might have been sixty. There was nothing remarkable about him except his insignificance. But though evidently poor he was neat and clean. He was respectable and he clung to respectability. No, I did not think he was a mute, I thought he was a solicitor's clerk who had lately buried his wife and been sent to Elsom by an indulgent employer to get over the first shock of his grief.

'Are you making a long stay, sir?' he asked me.

'Ten days or a fortnight.'

'Is this your first visit to Elsom, sir?'

'I have been here before.'

'I know it well, sir. I flatter myself there are very few seaside resorts that I have not been to at one time or another. Elsom is hard to beat, sir. You get a very nice class of people here. There's nothing noisy or vulgar about Elsom, if you understand what I mean. Elsom has very pleasant recollections for me, sir. I knew Elsom well in bygone days. I was married in St Martin's Church, sir.'

'Really,' I said feebly.

'It was a very happy marriage, sir.'

'I'm very glad to hear it,' I returned.

'Nine months, that one lasted,' he said reflectively.

Surely the remark was a trifle singular. I had not looked forward with any enthusiasm to the probability which I so clearly foresaw that he would favour me with an account of his matrimonial experiences, but now I waited if not with eagerness at least with curiosity for a further observation. He made none. He sighed a little. At last I broke the silence.

'There don't seem to be very many people about,' I remarked.

'I like it so. I'm not one for crowds. As I was saying just now, I reckon I've spent a good many years at one seaside resort after the other, but I never came in the season. It's the winter I like.'

'Don't you find it a little melancholy?'

He turned towards me and placed his black-gloved hand for an instant on my arm.

'It is melancholy. And because it's melancholy a little ray of sunshine is very welcome.'

The remark seemed to me perfectly idiotic and I did not answer. He withdrew his hand from my arm and got up.

'Well, I mustn't keep you, sir. Pleased to have made your acquaintance.'

He took off his dingy hat very politely and strolled away. It was beginning now to grow chilly and I thought I would return to the Dolphin. As I reached its broad steps a landau drove up, drawn by two scraggy horses, and from it stepped Mr St Clair. He wore a hat that looked like the unhappy result of a union between a bowler and a top-hat. He gave his hand to his wife and then to his niece. The porter carried in after them rugs and cushions. As Mr St Clair paid the driver I heard him tell him to come at the usual time next day and I understood that the St Clairs took a drive every afternoon in a landau. It would not have surprised me to learn that none of them had ever been in a motor-car.

The manageress told me that they kept very much to themselves and sought no acquaintance among the other persons staying at the hotel. I rode my imagination on a loose rein. I watched them eat three meals a day. I watched Mr and Mrs St Clair sit at the top of the hotel steps in the morning. He read *The Times* and she knitted. I suppose Mrs St Clair had never read a paper in her life, for they never took anything but *The Times* and Mr St Clair of course took it with him every day to the City. At about twelve Miss Porchester joined them.

'Have you enjoyed your walk, Eleanor?' asked Mrs St Clair.

'It was very nice, Aunt Gertrude,' answered Miss Porchester.

And I understand that just as Mrs St Clair took 'her drive' every afternoon Miss Porchester took 'her walk' every morning.

'When you have come to the end of your row, my dear,' said Mr St Clair, with a glance at his wife's knitting, 'we might go for a constitutional before luncheon.'

'That will be very nice,' answered Mrs St Clair. She folded up her work and gave it to Miss Porchester. 'If you're going upstairs, Eleanor, will you take my work?'

'Certainly, Aunt Gertrude.'

'I dare say you're a little tired after your walk, my dear.'

'I shall have a little rest before luncheon.'

Miss Porchester went into the hotel and Mr and Mrs St Clair walked slowly along the sea-front, side by side, to a certain point, and then walked slowly back.

When I met one of them on the stairs I bowed and received an unsmiling, polite bow in return, and in the morning I ventured upon a 'good day' but there the matter ended. It looked as though I should never have a chance to speak to any of them. But presently I thought that Mr St Clair gave me now and then a glance, and thinking he had heard my name I imagined, perhaps vainly, that he looked at me with curiosity. And a day or two after that I was sitting in my room when the porter came in with a message.

'Mr St Clair presents his compliments and could you oblige him with the loan of *Whitaker's Almanack.*'

I was astonished.

'Why on earth should he think that I have a *Whitaker's Almanack?*'

'Well, sir, the manageress told him you wrote.'

I could not see the connexion.

'Tell Mr St Clair that I'm very sorry that I haven't got a *Whitaker's Almanack,* but if I had I would very gladly lend it to him.'

Here was my opportunity. I was by now filled with eagerness to know these fantastic persons more closely. Now and then in the heart of Asia I have come upon a lonely tribe living in a little village among an alien population. No one knows how they came there or why they settled in that spot. They live their own lives, speak their own language, and have no communication with their neighbours. No one knows whether they are the descendants of a band that was left behind when their nation swept in a vast horde across the continent or whether they are the dying remnant of some great people that in that country once held empire. They are a mystery. They have no future and no history. This odd little family seemed to me to have something of the same character. They were of an era that is dead and gone. They reminded me of persons in one of those leisurely, old-fashioned novels that one's father read. They belonged to the eighties and they had not moved since then. How extraordinary it was that they could have lived through the last forty years as though the world stood still! They took me back to my childhood and I recollected people who are long since dead. I wonder if it is only distance that gives me the impression that they were more peculiar than anyone is now. When a person was described then as 'quite a character,' by heaven, it meant something.

So that evening after dinner I went into the lounge and boldly addressed Mr St Clair.

'I'm sorry I haven't got a *Whitaker's Almanack*,' I said, 'but if I have any other book that can be of service to you I shall be delighted to lend it to you.'

Mr St Clair was obviously startled. The two ladies kept their eyes on their work. There was an embarrassed hush.

'It does not matter at all, but I was given to understand by the manageress that you were a novelist.'

I racked my brain. There was evidently some connexion between my profession and *Whitaker's Almanack* that escaped me.

'In days gone by Mr Trollope used often to dine with us in Leinster Square and I remember him saying that the two most useful books to a novelist were the Bible and *Whitaker's Almanack*.'

'I see that Thackeray once stayed in this hotel,' I remarked, anxious not to let the conversation drop.

'I never very much cared for Mr Thackeray, though he dined more than once with my wife's father, the late Mr Sargeant Saunders. He was too cynical for me. My niece has not read *Vanity Fair* to this day.'

Miss Porchester blushed slightly at this reference to herself. A waiter brought in the coffee and Mrs St Clair turned to her husband.

'Perhaps, my dear, this gentleman would do us the pleasure to have his coffee with us.'

Although not directly addressed I answered promptly:

'Thank you very much.'

I sat down.

'Mr Trollope was always my favourite novelist,' said Mr St Clair. 'He was so essentially a gentleman. I admire Charles Dickens. But Charles Dickens could never draw a gentleman. I am given to understand that young people nowadays find Mr Trollope a little low. My niece, Miss Porchester, prefers the novels of Mr William Black.'

'I'm afraid I've never read any,' I said.

'Ah, I see that you are like me; you are not up to date. My niece once persuaded me to read a novel by a Miss Rhoda Broughton, but I could not manage more than a hundred pages of it.'

'I did not say I liked it, Uncle Edwin,' said Miss Porchester, defending herself, with another blush, 'I told you it was rather fast, but everybody was talking about it.'

'I'm quite sure it is not the sort of book your Aunt Gertrude would have wished you to read, Eleanor.'

'I remember Miss Broughton telling me once that when she was young people said her books were fast and when she was old they said they were slow, and it was very hard since she had written exactly the same sort of book for forty years.'

'Oh, did you know Miss Broughton?' asked Miss Porchester, addressing me for the first time. 'How very interesting! And did you know Ouida?'

'My dear Eleanor, what will you say next! I'm quite sure you've never read anything by Ouida.'

'Indeed, I have, Uncle Edwin. I've read *Under Two Flags* and I liked it very much.'

'You amaze and shock me. I don't know what girls are coming to nowadays.'

'You always said that when I was thirty you gave me complete liberty to read anything I liked.'

'There is a difference, my dear Eleanor, between liberty and licence,' said Mr St Clair, smiling a little in order not to make his reproof offensive, but with a certain gravity.

I do not know if in recounting this conversation I have managed to convey the impression it gave me of a charming and old-fashioned air. I could have listened all night to them discussing the depravity of an age that was young in the eighteen-eighties. I would have given a good deal for a glimpse of their large and roomy house in Leinster Square. I should have recognized the suite covered in red brocade that stood stiffly about the drawing-room, each piece in its appointed place; and the cabinets filled with Dresden china would have brought me back my childhood. In the dining-room, where they habitually sat, for the drawing-room was used only for parties, was a Turkey carpet and a vast mahogany sideboard 'groaning' with silver. On the walls were the pictures that had excited the admiration of Mrs Humphrey Ward and her uncle Matthew in the Academy of eighteen-eighty.

Next morning, strolling through a pretty lane at the back of Elsom, I met Miss Porchester, who was taking 'her walk'. I should have liked to go a little way with her, but felt certain that it would embarrass this maiden of fifty to saunter alone with a man even of my respectable years. She bowed as I passed her and blushed. Oddly enough, a few yards behind her I came upon the funny shabby little man in black gloves with whom I had spoken for a few minutes on the front. He touched his old bowler hat.

'Excuse me, sir, but could you oblige me with a match?' he said.

'Certainly,' I retorted, 'but I'm afraid I have no cigarettes on me.'

'Allow me to offer you one of mine,' he said, taking out the paper case. It was empty. 'Dear, dear, I haven't got one either. What a curious coincidence!'

He went on and I had a notion that he a little hastened his steps. I was beginning to have my doubts about him. I hoped he was not going to bother Miss Porchester. For a moment I thought of walking back, but I did not. He was a civil little man and I did not believe he would make a nuisance of himself to a single lady.

I saw him again that very afternoon. I was sitting on the front. He walked towards me with little, halting steps. There was something of a wind and he looked like a dried leaf being driven before it. This time he did not hesitate, but sat down beside me.

'We meet again, sir. The world is a small place. If it will not inconvenience you perhaps you will allow me to rest a few minutes. I am a wee bit tired.'

'This is a public bench, and you have just as much right to sit on it as I.'

I did not wait for him to ask me for a match, but at once offered him a cigarette.

'How very kind of you, sir! I have to limit myself to so many cigarettes a day, but I enjoy those I smoke. As one grows older the pleasures of life diminish, but my experience is that one enjoys more those that remain.'

'That is a very consoling thought.'

'Excuse me, sir, but am I right in thinking that you are the well-known author?'

'I am an author,' I replied. 'But what made you think it?'

'I have seen your portrait in the illustrated papers. I suppose you don't recognize me?'

I looked at him again, a weedy little man in neat but shabby black clothes, with a long nose and watery blue eyes.

'I'm afraid I don't.'

'I dare say I've changed,' he sighed. 'There was a time when my photograph was in every paper in the United Kingdom. Of course, those press photographers never do you justice. I give you my word, sir, that if I hadn't seen my name underneath I should never have guessed that some of them were meant for me.'

He was silent for a while. The tide was out and beyond the shingle of the beach was a strip of yellow mud. The breakwaters were half buried in it like the backbones of prehistoric beasts.

'It must be a wonderfully interesting thing to be an author, sir. I've often thought I had quite a turn for writing myself. At one time and another I've done a rare lot of reading. I haven't kept up with it much lately. For one thing my eyes are not so good as they used to be. I believe I could write a book if I tried.'

'They say anybody can write one,' I answered.

'Not a novel, you know. I'm not much of a one for novels; I prefer histories and that-like. But memoirs. If anybody was to make it worth my while I wouldn't mind writing my memoirs.'

'It's very fashionable just now.'

'There are not many people who've had the experiences I've had in one way and another. I did write to one of the Sunday papers about it some little while back, but they never answered my letter.'

He gave me a long, appraising look. He had too respectable an air to be about to ask me for half a crown.

'Of course you don't know who I am, sir, do you?'

'I honestly don't.'

He seemed to ponder for a moment, then he smoothed down his black gloves on his fingers, looked for a moment at a hole in one of them, and then turned to me not without self-consciousness.

'I am the celebrated Mortimer Ellis,' he said.

'Oh?'

I did not know what other ejaculation to make, for to the best of my belief I had never heard the name before. I saw a look of disappointment come over his face, and I was a trifle embarrassed.

'Mortimer Ellis,' he repeated. 'You're not going to tell me you don't know.'

'I'm afraid I must. I'm very often out of England.'

I wondered to what he owed his celebrity. I passed over in my mind various possibilities. He could never have been an athlete, which alone in England gives a man real fame, but he might have been a faith-healer or a champion billiard-player. There is of course no one so obscure as a Cabinet Minister out of office and he might have been the President of the Board of Trade in a defunct administration. But he had none of the look of a politician.

'That's fame for you,' he said bitterly. 'Why, for weeks I was the most talked-about man in England. Look at me. You must have seen my photograph in the papers. Mortimer Ellis.'

'I'm sorry,' I said, shaking my head.

He paused a moment to give his disclosure effectiveness.

'I am the well-known bigamist.'

Now what are you to reply when a person who is practically a stranger to you informs you that he is a well-known bigamist? I will confess that I have sometimes had the vanity to think that I am not as a rule at a loss for a retort, but here I found myself speechless.

'I've had eleven wives, sir,' he went on.

'Most people find one about as much as they can manage.'

'Ah, that's want of practice. When you've had eleven there's very little you don't know about women.'

'But why did you stop at eleven?'

'There now, I knew you'd say that. The moment I set eyes on you I said to myself, he's got a clever face. You know, sir, that's the thing that always grizzles me. Eleven does seem a funny number, doesn't it? There's something unfinished about it. Now three anyone might have, and seven's all right, they say nine's lucky, and there's nothing wrong with ten. But eleven! That's the one thing I regret. I shouldn't have minded anything if I could have brought it up to the Round Dozen.'

He unbuttoned his coat and from an inside pocket produced a bulging and very greasy pocket-book. From this he took a large bundle of newspaper cuttings; they were worn and creased and dirty. But he spread out two or three.

'Now just you look at those photographs. I ask you, are they like me? It's an outrage. Why, you'd think I was a criminal to look at them.'

The cuttings were of imposing length. In the opinion of sub-editors Mortimer Ellis had obviously been a news item of value. One was headed, A Much Married Man; another, Heartless Ruffian Brought to Book; a third, Contemptible Scoundrel Meets his Waterloo.

'Not what you would call a good press,' I murmured.

'I never pay any attention to what the newspapers say,' he answered, with a shrug of his thin shoulders. 'I've known too many journals myself for that. No, it's the judge I blame. He treated me shocking and it did him no good, mind you; he died within the year.'

I ran my eyes down the report I held.

'I see he gave you five years.'

'Disgraceful, I call it, and see what it says.' He pointed to a place with his forefinger. '"Three of his victims pleaded for mercy to be shown to him." That shows what they thought of me. And after that he gave me five years. And just look what he called me, a heartless scoundrel—me, the best-hearted man that ever lived—a pest of society and a danger to the public. Said he wished he had the power to give me the cat. I don't so much mind his giving me five years, though you'll never get me to say it wasn't excessive, but I ask you, had he the right to talk to me like that? No, he hadn't, and I'll never forgive him, not if I live to be a hundred.'

The bigamist's cheeks flushed and his watery eyes were filled for a moment with fire. It was a sore subject with him.

'May I read them?' I asked him.

'That's what I gave them you for. I want you to read them, sir. And if you can read them without saying that I'm a much wronged man, well, you're not the man I took you for.'

As I glanced through one cutting after another I saw why Mortimer Ellis had so wide an acquaintance with the seaside resorts of England. They were his hunting-ground. His method was to go to some place when the season was over and take apartments in one of the empty lodging-houses. Apparently it did not take him long to make acquaintance with some woman or other, widow or spinster, and I noticed that their ages at the time were between thirty-five and fifty. They stated in the witness-box that they had met him first on the sea-front. He generally proposed marriage to them within a fortnight of this and they were married shortly after. He induced them in one way or another to entrust him with their savings and in a few months, on the pretext that he had to go to London on business, he left them never to return. Only one had ever seen him again till, obliged to give evidence, they saw him in the dock. They were women of a certain respectability; one was the daughter of a doctor and another of a clergyman; there was a lodging-house keeper, there was the widow of a commercial traveller, and there was a retired dressmaker. For the most part, their fortunes ranged from five hundred to a thousand pounds, but whatever the sum the misguided women were stripped of every penny. Some of them told really pitiful stories of the destitution to which they had been reduced. But they all acknowledged that he had been a good husband to them. Not only had three actually pleaded for mercy to be shown him, but one said in the witness-box that, if he was willing to come, she was ready to take him back. He noticed that I was reading this.

'And she'd have worked for me,' he said, 'there's no doubt about that. But I said, better let bygones be bygones. No one likes a cut off the best end of the neck better than I do, but I'm not much of a one for cold roast mutton, I will confess.'

It was only by an accident that Mortimer Ellis did not marry his twelfth wife and so achieve the Round Dozen which I understand appealed to his love of symmetry. For he was engaged to be married to a Miss Hubbard—'two thousand pounds she had, if she had a penny, in war-loan,' he confided to me—and the banns had been read, when one of his former wives saw him, made inquiries, and communicated with the police. He was arrested on the very day before his twelfth wedding.

'She was a bad one, she was,' he told me. 'She deceived me something cruel.'

'How did she do that?'

'Well, I met her at Eastbourne, one December it was, on the pier, and she told me in course of conversation that she'd been in the millinery business and had retired. She said she'd made a tidy bit of money. She wouldn't say exactly how much it was, but she gave me to understand it was something like fifteen hundred pounds. And when I married her, would you believe it, she hadn't got three hundred. And that's the one who gave me away. And mind you, I'd never blamed her. Many a man would have cut up rough when he found out he'd been made a fool of. I never showed her that I was disappointed even, I just went away without a word.'

'But not without the three hundred pounds, I take it.'

'Oh come, sir, you must be reasonable,' he returned in an injured tone. 'You can't expect three hundred pounds to last for ever and I'd been married to her for months before she confessed the truth.'

'Forgive my asking,' I said, 'and pray don't think my question suggests a disparaging view of your personal attractions, but–why did they marry you?'

'Because I asked them,' he answered, evidently very much surprised at my inquiry.

'But did you never have any refusals?'

'Very seldom. Not more than four or five in the whole course of my career. Of course I didn't propose till I was pretty sure of my ground and I don't say I didn't draw a blank sometimes. You can't expect to click every time, if you know what I mean, and I've often wasted several weeks making up to a woman before I saw there was nothing doing.'

I surrendered myself for a time to my reflections. But I noticed presently that a broad smile spread over the mobile features of my friend.

'I understand what you mean,' he said. 'It's my appearance that puzzles you. You don't know what it is they see in me. That's what comes of reading novels and going to the pictures. You think what women want is the cowboy type, or the romance of old Spain touch, flashing eyes, an olive skin, and a beautiful dancer. You make me laugh.'

'I'm glad,' I said.

'Are you a married man, sir?'

'I am. But I only have one wife.'

'You can't judge by that. You can't generalize from a single instance, if you know what I mean. Now, I ask you, what would you know about dogs if you'd never had anything but one bull-terrier?'

The question was rhetorical and I felt sure did not require an answer. He paused for an effective moment and went on.

'You're wrong, sir. You're quite wrong. They may take a fancy to a good-looking young fellow, but they don't want to marry him. They don't really care about looks.'

'Douglas Jerrold, who was as ugly as he was witty, used to say that if he was given ten minutes' start with a woman he could cut out the handsomest man in the room.'

'They don't want wit. They don't want a man to be funny; they think he's not serious. They don't want a man who's too handsome; they think he's not serious either. That's what they want, they want a man who's serious. Safety first. And then–attention. I may not be handsome and I may not be amusing, but believe me, I've got what every woman wants. Poise. And the proof is, I've made every one of my wives happy.'

'It certainly is much to your credit that three of them pleaded for mercy to be shown to you and that one was willing to take you back.'

'You don't know what an anxiety that was to me all the time I was in prison. I thought she'd be waiting for me at the gate when I was released and I said to the Governor: "For God's sake, sir, smuggle me out so as no one can see me."'

He smoothed his gloves again over his hands and his eye once more fell upon the hole in the first finger.

'That's what comes of living in lodgings, sir. How's a man to keep himself neat and tidy without a woman to look after him? I've been married too often to be able to get along without a wife. There are men who don't like being married. I can't understand them. The fact is, you can't do a thing really well unless you've got your heart in it, and I like being a married man. It's no difficulty to me to do the little things that women like and that some men can't be bothered with. As I was saying just now, it's attention a woman wants. I never went out of the house without giving my wife a kiss and I never came in without giving her another. And it was very seldom I came in without bringing her some chocolates or a few flowers. I never grudged the expense.'

'After all, it was her money you were spending,' I interposed.

'And what if it was? It's not the money that you've paid for a present that signifies, it's the spirit you give it in. That's what counts with women. No, I'm not one to boast, but I will say this of myself, I am a good husband.'

I looked desultorily at the reports of the trial which I still held.

'I'll tell you what surprises me,' I said. 'All these women were very respectable, of a certain age, quiet, decent persons. And yet they married you without any inquiry after the shortest possible acquaintance.'

He put his hand impressively on my arm.

'Ah, that's what you don't understand, sir. Women have got a craving to be married. It doesn't matter how young they are or how old they are, if they're short or tall, dark or fair, they've all got one thing in common: they want to be married. And mind you, I married them in church. No woman feels really safe unless she's married in church. You say I'm no beauty, well, I never thought I was, but if I had one leg and a hump on my back I could find any number of women who'd jump at the chance of marrying me. It's a mania with them. It's a disease. Why, there's hardly one of them who wouldn't have accepted me the second time I saw her only I like to make sure of my ground before I commit myself. When it all came out there was a rare to-do because I'd married eleven times. Eleven times? Why, it's nothing, it's not even a Round Dozen. I could have married thirty times if I'd wanted to. I give you my word, sir, when I consider my opportunities, I'm astounded at my moderation.'

'You told me you were very fond of reading history.'

'Yes, Warren Hastings said that, didn't he? It struck me at the time I read it. It seemed to fit me like a glove.'

'And you never found these constant courtships a trifle monotonous?'

'Well, sir, I think I've got a logical mind, and it always gave me a rare lot of pleasure to see how the same effects followed on the same causes, if you know what I mean. Now, for instance, with a woman who'd never been married before I always passed myself off as a widower. It worked like a charm. You see, a spinster likes a man who knows a thing or two. But with a widow I always said I was a bachelor: a widow's afraid a man who's been married before knows too much.'

I gave him back his cuttings; he folded them up neatly and replaced them in his greasy pocket-book.

'You know, sir, I always think I've been misjudged. Just see what they say about me: a pest of society, unscrupulous villain, contemptible scoundrel. Now just look at me. I ask you, do I look that sort of man? You know me, you're a judge of character, I've told you all about myself; do you think me a bad man?'

'My acquaintance with you is very slight,' I answered with what I thought considerable tact.

'I wonder if the judge, I wonder if the jury, I wonder if the public ever thought about my side of the question. The public booed me when I was taken into the court and the police had to protect me from their violence. Did any of them think what I'd done for these women?'

'You took their money.'

'Of course I took their money. I had to live the same as anybody has to live. But what did I give them in exchange for their money?'

This was another rhetorical question and though he looked at me as though he expected an answer I held my tongue. Indeed I did not know the answer. His voice was raised and he spoke with emphasis. I could see that he was serious.

'I'll tell you what I gave them in exchange for their money. Romance. Look at this place.' He made a wide, circular gesture that embraced the sea and the horizon. 'There are a hundred places in England like this. Look at that sea and that sky; look at these lodging-houses; look at that pier and the front. Doesn't it make your heart sink? It's dead as mutton. It's all very well for you who come down here for a week or two because you're run down. But think of all those women who live here from one year's end to another. They haven't a chance. They hardly know anyone. They've just got enough money to live on and that's all. I wonder if you know how terrible their lives are. Their lives are just like the front, a long, straight, cemented walk that goes on and on from one seaside resort to another. Even in the season there's nothing for them. They're out of it. They might as well be dead. And then I come along. Mind you, I never made advances to a woman who wouldn't have gladly acknowledged to thirty-five. And I give them love. Why, many of them had never known what it was to have a man do them up behind. Many of them had never known what it was to sit on a bench in the dark with a man's arm round their waist. I bring them change and excitement. I give them a new pride in themselves. They were on the shelf and I come along quite quietly and I deliberately take them down. A little ray of sunshine in those drab lives, that's what I was. No wonder they jumped at me, no wonder they wanted me to go back to them. The only one who gave me away was the milliner; she said she was a widow, my private opinion is that she'd never been married at all. You say I did the dirty on them; why, I brought happiness and glamour into eleven lives that never thought they had even a dog's chance of it again. You say I'm a villain and a scoundrel, you're wrong. I'm a philanthropist. Five years, they gave me; they should have given me the medal of the Royal Humane Society.'

He took out his empty packet of Gold Flake and looked at it with a melancholy shake of the head. When I handed him my cigarette case he helped himself without a word. I watched the spectacle of a good man struggling with his emotion.

'And what did I get out of it, I ask you?' he continued presently. 'Board and lodging and enough to buy cigarettes. But I never was able to save, and the proof is that now, when I'm not so young as I was, I haven't got half a crown in my pocket.' He gave me a sidelong glance. 'It's a great come-down for me to find myself in this position. I've always paid my way and I've never asked a friend for a loan in all my life. I was wondering, sir, if you could oblige me with a trifle. It's humiliating to me to have to suggest it, but the fact is, if you could oblige me with a pound it would mean a great deal to me.'

Well, I had certainly had a pound's worth of entertainment out of the bigamist and I dived for my pocket-book.

'I shall be very glad,' I said.

He looked at the notes I took out.

'I suppose you couldn't make it two, sir?'

'I think I could.'

I handed him a couple of pound notes and he gave a little sigh as he took them.

'You don't know what it means to a man who's used to the comforts of home life not to know where to turn for a night's lodging.'

'But there is one thing I should like you to tell me,' I said. 'I shouldn't like you to think me cynical, but I had a notion that women on the whole take the maxim, "It is more blessed to give than to receive," as applicable exclusively to our sex. How did you persuade these respectable, and no doubt thrifty, women to entrust you so confidently with all their savings?'

An amused smile spread over his undistinguished features.

'Well, sir, you know what Shakespeare said about ambition o'erleaping itself. That's the explanation. Tell a woman you'll double her capital in six months if she'll give it you to handle and she won't be able to give you the money quick enough. Greed, that's what it is. Just greed.'

It was a sharp sensation, stimulating to the appetite (like hot sauce with ice cream), to go from this diverting ruffian to the respectability, all lavender bags and crinolines, of the St Clairs and Miss Porchester. I spent every evening with them now. No sooner had the ladies left him than Mr St Clair sent his compliments to my table and asked me to drink a glass of port with him. When we had finished it we went into the lounge and drank coffee. Mr St Clair enjoyed his glass of old brandy. The hour I thus spent with them was so exquisitely boring that it had for me a singular fascination. They were told by the manageress that I had written plays.

'We used often to go to the theatre when Sir Henry Irving was at the Lyceum,' said Mr St Clair. 'I once had the pleasure of meeting him. I was taken to supper at the Garrick Club by Sir Everard Millais and I was introduced to Mr Irving, as he then was.'

'Tell him what he said to you, Edwin,' said Mrs St Clair.

Mr St Clair struck a dramatic attitude and gave not at all a bad imitation of Henry Irving.

'"You have the actor's face, Mr St Clair," he said to me. "If you ever think of going on the stage, come to me and I will give you a part."' Mr St Clair resumed his natural manner. 'It was enough to turn a young man's head.'

'But it didn't turn yours,' I said.

'I will not deny that if I had been otherwise situated I might have allowed myself to be tempted. But I had my family to think of. It would have broken my father's heart if I had not gone into the business.'

'What is that?' I asked.

'I am a tea merchant, sir. My firm is the oldest in the City of London. I have spent forty years of my life in combating to the best of my ability the desire of my fellow-countrymen to drink Ceylon tea instead of the China tea which was universally drunk in my youth.'

I thought it charmingly characteristic of him to spend a lifetime in persuading the public to buy something they didn't want rather than something they did.

'But in his younger days my husband did a lot of amateur acting and he was thought very clever,' said Mrs St Clair.

'Shakespeare, you know, and sometimes *The School for Scandal.* I would never consent to act trash. But that is a thing of the past. I had a gift, perhaps it was a pity to waste it, but it's too late now. When we have a dinner-party I sometimes let the ladies persuade me to recite the great soliloquies of Hamlet. But that is all I do.'

Oh! Oh! Oh! I thought with shuddering fascination of those dinner-parties and wondered whether I should ever be asked to one of them. Mrs St Clair gave me a little smile, half shocked, half prim.

'My husband was very Bohemian as a young man,' she said.

'I sowed my wild oats. I knew quite a lot of painters and writers, Wilkie Collins, for instance, and even men who wrote for the papers. Watts painted a portrait of my wife, and I bought a picture of Millais. I knew a number of the Pre-Raphaelites.'

'Have you a Rossetti?' I asked.

'No. I admired Rossetti's talent, but I could not approve of his private life. I would never buy a picture by an artist whom I should not care to ask to dinner at my house.'

My brain was reeling when Miss Porchester, looking at her watch, said: 'Are you not going to read to us tonight, Uncle Edwin?'

I withdrew.

It was while I was drinking a glass of port with Mr St Clair one evening that he told me the sad story of Miss Porchester. She was engaged to be married to a nephew of Mrs St Clair, a barrister, when it was discovered that he had had an intrigue with the daughter of his laundress.

'It was a terrible thing,' said Mr St Clair. 'A terrible thing. But of course my niece took the only possible course. She returned him his ring, his letters, and his photograph, and said that she could never marry him. She implored him to marry the young person he had wronged and said she would be a sister to her. It broke her heart. She has never cared for anyone since.'

'And did he marry the young person?'

Mr St Clair shook his head and sighed.

'No, we were greatly mistaken in him. It has been a sore grief to my dear wife to think that a nephew of hers should behave in such a dishonourable manner. Some time later we heard that he was engaged to a young lady in a very good position with ten thousand pounds of her own. I considered it my duty to write to her father and put the facts before him. He answered my letter in a most insolent fashion. He said he would much rather his son-in-law had a mistress before marriage than after.'

'What happened then?'

'They were married and now my wife's nephew is one of His Majesty's Judges of the High Court, and his wife is My Lady. But we've never consented to receive them. When my wife's nephew was knighted Eleanor suggested that we should ask them to dinner, but my wife said that he should never darken our doors and I upheld her.'

'And the laundress's daughter?'

'She married in her own class of life and has a public-house at Canterbury. My niece, who has a little money of her own, did everything for her and is godmother to her eldest child.'

Poor Miss Porchester. She had sacrificed herself on the altar of Victorian morality and I am afraid the consciousness that she had behaved beautifully was the only benefit she had got from it.

'Miss Porchester is a woman of striking appearance,' I said. 'When she was younger she must have been perfectly lovely. I wonder she never married somebody else.'

'Miss Porchester was considered a great beauty. Alma-Tadema admired her so much that he asked her to sit as a model for one of his pictures, but of course we couldn't very well allow that.' Mr St Clair's tone conveyed that the suggestion had deeply outraged his sense of decency. 'No, Miss Porchester never cared for anyone but her cousin. She never speaks of him and it is now thirty years since they parted, but I am convinced that she loves him still. She is a true woman, my dear sir, one life, one love, and though perhaps I regret that she has been deprived of the joys of marriage and motherhood I am bound to admire her fidelity.'

But the heart of woman is incalculable and rash is the man who thinks she will remain in one stay. Rash, Uncle Edwin. You have known Eleanor for many years, for when, her mother having fallen into a decline and died, you brought the orphan to your comfortable and even luxurious house in Leinster Square, she was but a child; but what, when it comes down to brass tacks, Uncle Edwin, do you really know of Eleanor?

It was but two days after Mr St Clair had confided to me the touching story which explained why Miss Porchester had remained a spinster that, coming back to the hotel in the afternoon after a round of golf, the manageress came up to me in an agitated manner.

'Mr St Clair's compliments and will you go up to number twenty-seven the moment you come in.'

'Certainly. But why?'

'Oh, there's a rare upset. They'll tell you.'

I knocked at the door. I heard a 'Come in, come in,' which reminded me that Mr St Clair had played Shakespearean parts in probably the most refined amateur dramatic company in London. I entered and found Mrs St Clair lying on the sofa with a handkerchief soaked in eau-de-Cologne on her brow and a bottle of smelling-salts in her hand. Mr St Clair was standing in front of the fire in such a manner as to prevent anyone else in the room from obtaining any benefit from it.

'I must apologize for asking you to come up in this unceremonious fashion, but we are in great distress, and we thought you might be able to throw some light on what has happened.'

His perturbation was obvious.

'What *has* happened?'

'Our niece, Miss Porchester, has eloped. This morning she sent in a message to my wife that she had one of her sick headaches. When she has one of her sick headaches she likes to be left absolutely alone and it wasn't till this afternoon that my wife went to see if there was anything she could do for her. The room was empty. Her trunk was packed. Her dressing-case with silver fittings was gone. And on the pillow was a letter telling us of her rash act.'

'I'm very sorry,' I said. 'I don't know exactly what I can do.'

'We were under the impression that you were the only gentleman at Elsom with whom she had any acquaintance.'

His meaning flashed across me.

'I haven't eloped with her,' I said. 'I happen to be a married man.'

'I see you haven't eloped with her. At the first moment we thought perhaps . . .

but if it isn't you, who is it?'

'I'm sure I don't know.'

'Show him the letter, Edwin,' said Mrs St Clair from the sofa.

'Don't move, Gertrude. It will bring on your lumbago.'

Miss Porchester had 'her' sick headaches and Mrs St Clair had 'her' lumbago. What had Mr St Clair? I was willing to bet a fiver that Mr St Clair had 'his' gout. He gave me the letter and I read it with an air of decent commiseration.

Dearest Uncle Edwin and Aunt Gertrude

When you receive this I shall be far away. I am going to be married this morning to a gentleman who is very dear to me. I know I am doing wrong in running away like this, but I was afraid you would endeavour to set obstacles in the way of my marriage and since nothing would induce me to change my mind I thought it would save us all much unhappiness if I did it without telling you anything about it. My fiancé is a very retiring man, owing to his long residence in tropical countries not in the best of health, and he thought it much better that we should be married quite privately. When you know how radiantly happy I am I hope you will forgive me. Please send my box to the luggage office at Victoria Station.

Your loving niece,
Eleanor

'I will never forgive her,' said Mr St Clair as I returned him the letter. 'She shall never darken my doors again. Gertrude, I forbid you ever to mention Eleanor's name in my hearing.'

Mrs St Clair began to sob quietly.

'Aren't you rather hard?' I said. 'Is there any reason why Miss Porchester shouldn't marry?'

'At her age,' he answered angrily. 'It's ridiculous. We shall be the laughing-stock of everyone in Leinster Square. Do you know how old she is? She's fifty-one.'

'Fifty-four,' said Mrs St Clair through her sobs.

'She's been the apple of my eye. She's been like a daughter to us. She's been an old maid for years. I think it's positively improper for her to think of marriage.'

'She was always a girl to us, Edwin,' pleaded Mrs St Clair.

'And who is this man she's married? It's the deception that rankles. She must have been carrying on with him under our very noses. She does not even tell us his name. I fear the very worst.'

Suddenly I had an inspiration. That morning after breakfast I had gone out to buy myself some cigarettes and at the tobacconist's I ran across Mortimer Ellis. I had not seen him for some days.

'You're looking very spruce,' I said.

His boots had been repaired and were neatly blacked, his hat was brushed, he was wearing a clean collar and new gloves. I thought he had laid out my two pounds to advantage.

'I have to go to London this morning on business,' he said.

I nodded and left the shop.

I remembered that a fortnight before, walking in the country, I had met Miss Porchester and, a few yards behind, Mortimer Ellis. Was it possible that they had been walking together and he had fallen back as they caught sight of me? By heaven, I saw it all.

'I think you said that Miss Porchester had money of her own,' I said.

'A trifle. She has three thousand pounds.'

Now I was certain. I looked at them blankly. Suddenly Mrs St Clair, with a cry, sprang to her feet.

'Edwin, Edwin, supposing he doesn't marry her?'

Mr St Clair at this put his hand to his head and in a state of collapse sank into a chair.

'The disgrace would kill me,' he groaned.

'Don't be alarmed,' I said. 'He'll marry her all right. He always does. He'll marry her in church.'

They paid no attention to what I said. I suppose they thought I'd suddenly taken leave of my senses. I was quite sure now. Mortimer Ellis had achieved his ambition after all. Miss Porchester completed the Round Dozen.

The
Human
Element

◆

I seem never to find myself in Rome but at the dead season. I pass through in August or September on my way somewhere or other and spend a couple of days revisiting places or pictures that are endeared to me by old associations. It is very hot then and the inhabitants of the city spend their day interminably strolling up and down the Corso. The Caffé Nazionale is crowded with people sitting at little tables for long hours with an empty cup of coffee in front of them and a glass of water. In the Sistine Chapel you see blond and sunburned Germans, in knickerbockers and shirts open at the neck, who have walked down the dusty roads of Italy with knapsacks on their shoulders; and in St Peter's little groups of the pious, tired but eager, who have come on pilgrimage (at an inclusive rate) from some distant country. They are under the charge of a priest and they speak strange tongues. The Hotel Plaza then is cool and restful. The public rooms are dark, silent and spacious. In the lounge at tea-time the only persons are a young, smart officer and a woman with fine eyes, drinking iced lemonade, and they talk intimately, in low tones, with the unwearying fluency of their race. You go up to your room and read and write letters and come down again two hours later and they are still talking. Before dinner a few people saunter into the bar, but for the rest of the day it is empty and the barman has time to tell you of his mother in Switzerland and his experiences in New York. You discuss life and love and the high cost of liquor.

And on this occasion too I found that I had the hotel almost to myself. When the reception clerk took me to my room he told me that they were pretty full, but when, having bathed and changed, I came down again to the hall, the liftman, an old acquaintance, informed me that there were not more than a dozen people staying there. I was tired after a long and hot journey down Italy and had made up my mind to dine quietly in the hotel and go to bed early. It was late when I went into the dining-room, vast and brightly lit, but not more than three or four tables were occupied. I looked round me with satisfaction. It is very agreeable to find yourself alone in a great city which is yet not quite strange to you and in a large empty hotel. It gives you a delectable sense of freedom. I felt the wings of my spirit give a little flutter of delight. I had paused for ten minutes in the bar and had a dry Martini. I ordered myself a bottle of good red wine. My limbs were weary, but my soul responded wonderfully to food and drink and I began to feel a singular lightness of heart. I ate my soup and my fish and pleasant thoughts filled my mind. Scraps of dialogue occurred to me and my fancy played happily with the persons of a novel I was then at work on. I rolled a phrase on my tongue and it tasted better than the wine. I began to think of the difficulty of describing the looks of people in such a way as to make the reader see them as you see them. To me it has always been one of the most difficult things in fiction. What does the reader really get when you describe a face feature by feature? I should think nothing. And yet the plan some writers adopt of taking a salient characteristic, a crooked smile or shifty eyes, and emphasizing that, though effective, avoids rather than solves the problem. I looked about me and wondered how I would describe the people at the tables round me. There was one man by himself just opposite and for practice I asked myself in what way I should treat him. He was a tall, spare fellow, and what I believe is generally called loose-limbed. He wore a dinner jacket and a boiled shirt. He had a rather long face and pale eyes; his hair was fairish and wavy, but it was growing thin, and the baldness of his temples gave him a certain nobility of brow. His features were undistinguished. His mouth and nose were like everybody else's; he was clean-shaven; his skin was naturally pale, but at the moment sunburned. His appearance suggested an intellectual but slightly commonplace distinction. He looked as though he might have been a lawyer or a don who played a pretty game of golf. I felt that he had good taste and was well-read and would be a very agreeable guest at a luncheon-party in Chelsea. But how the devil one was to describe him so as in a few lines to give a vivid, interesting, and accurate picture I could not imagine. Perhaps it would be better to let all the rest go and dwell only on that rather fatigued distinction which on the whole was the most definite impression he gave. I looked at him reflectively. Suddenly he leaned forwards and gave me a stiff but courtly little bow. I have a ridiculous habit of flushing when I am taken aback and now I felt my cheeks redden. I was startled. I had been staring at him for several minutes as though he were a dummy. He must have thought me extremely rude. I nodded with a good deal of embarrassment and looked away. Fortunately at that moment the waiter was handing me a dish. To the best of my belief I had never seen the fellow before. I asked myself whether his bow was due to my insistent stare, which made him think that he had met me somewhere, or whether I had really run across him and completely forgotten. I have a bad memory for faces and I had in this case the excuse that he looked exactly like a great many other people. You saw a dozen of him at every golf course round London on a fine Sunday.

He finished his dinner before me. He got up, but on his way out stopped at my table. He stretched out his hand.

'How d'you do?' he said. 'I didn't recognize you when you first came in. I wasn't meaning to cut you.'

He spoke in a pleasant voice with the tones cultivated at Oxford and copied by many who have never been there. It was evident that he knew me and evident too that he had no notion that I did not also know him. I had risen and since he was a good deal taller than I he looked down on me. He held himself with a sort of languor. He stooped a little, which added to the impression he gave me of having about him an air that was vaguely apologetic. His manner was a trifle condescending and at the same time a trifle shy.

'Won't you come and have your coffee with me?' he said. 'I'm quite alone.'

'Yes, I shall be glad to.'

He left me and I still had no notion who he was or where I had met him. I had noticed one curious thing about him. Not once during the few sentences we exchanged, when we shook hands, or when with a nod he left me, did even the suspicion of a smile cross his face. Seeing him more closely I observed that he was in his way good-looking; his features were regular, his grey eyes were handsome, he had a slim figure; but it was a way that I found uninteresting. A silly woman would say he looked romantic. He reminded you of one of the knights of Burne-Jones though he was on a larger scale and there was no suggestion that he suffered from the chronic colitis that afflicted those unfortunate creatures. He was the sort of man whom you expected to look wonderful in fancy dress till you saw him in it and then you found that he looked absurd.

Presently I finished my dinner and went into the lounge. He was sitting in a large arm-chair and when he saw me he called a waiter. I sat down. The waiter came up and he ordered coffee and liqueurs. He spoke Italian very well. I was wondering by what means I could find out who he was without offending him. People are always a little disconcerted when you do not recognize them, they are so important to themselves, it is a shock to discover of what small importance they are to others. The excellence of his Italian recalled him to me. I remembered who he was and remembered at the same time that I did not like him. His name was Humphrey Carruthers. He was in the Foreign Office and he had a position of some importance. He was in charge of I know not what department. He had been attached to various embassies and I supposed that a sojourn in Rome accounted for his idiomatic Italian. It was stupid of me not to have seen at once that he was connected with the diplomatic service. He had all the marks of the profession. He had the supercilious courtesy that is so well calculated to put up the backs of the general public and the aloofness due to the consciousness the diplomat has that he is not as other men are, joined with the shyness occasioned by his uneasy feeling that other men do not quite realize it. I had known Carruthers for a good many years, but had met him infrequently, at luncheon-parties where I said no more than how do you do to him and at the opera where he gave me a cool nod. He was generally thought intelligent; he was certainly cultured. He could talk of all the right things. It was inexcusable of me not to have remembered him, for he had lately acquired a very considerable reputation as a writer of short stories. They had appeared first in one or other of those magazines that are founded now and then by well-disposed persons to give the intelligent reader something worthy of his attention and that die when their proprietors have lost as much money as they want to; and in their discreet and handsomely printed pages had excited as much attention as an exiguous circulation permitted. Then they were published in book form. They created a sensation. I have seldom read such unanimous praise in the weekly papers. Most of them gave the book a column and the Literary Supplement of *The Times* reviewed it not among the common ruck of novels but in a place by itself cheek by jowl with the memoirs of a distinguished statesman. The critics welcomed Humphrey Carruthers as a new star in the firmament. They praised his distinction, his subtlety, his delicate irony, and his insight. They praised his style, his sense of beauty, and his atmosphere. Here at last was a writer who had raised the short story from the depths into which in English-speaking countries it had fallen and here was work to which an Englishman could point with pride; it bore comparison with the best compositions in this manner of Finland, Russia, and Czecho-Slovakia.

Three years later Humphrey Carruthers brought out his second book and the critics commented on the interval with satisfaction. Here was no hack prostituting his talent for money! The praise it received was perhaps a little cooler than that which welcomed his first volume, the critics had had time to collect themselves, but it was enthusiastic enough to have delighted any common writer who earns his living by his pen and there was no doubt that his position in the world of letters was secure and honourable. The story that attracted most commendation was called *The Shaving Mop* and all the best critics pointed out with what beauty the author in three or four pages had laid bare the tragic soul of a barber's assistant.

But his best-known story, which was also his longest, was called *Week End.* It gave its title to his first book. It narrated the aventures of a number of people who left Paddington Station on Saturday afternoon to stay with friends at Taplow and on Monday morning returned to London. It was so delicate that it was a little difficult to know exactly what happened. A young man, parliamentary secretary to a Cabinet Minister, very nearly proposed to a baronet's daughter, but didn't. Two or three others went on the river in a punt. They all talked a great deal in an allusive way, but none of them ever finished a sentence and what they meant was very subtly indicated by dots and dashes. There were a good many descriptions of flowers in the garden and a sensitive picture of the Thames under the rain. It was all seen through the eyes of the German governess and everyone agreed that Carruthers had conveyed her outlook on the situation with quite delicious humour.

I read both Hmphrey Carruthers's books. I think it part of the writer's business to make himself aware of what is being written by his contemporaries. I am very willing to learn and I thought I might discover in them something that would be useful to me. I was disappointed. I like a story to have a beginning, a middle, and an end. I have a weakness for a point. I think atmosphere is all very well, but atmosphere without anything else is like a frame without a picture; it has not much significance. But it may be that I could not see the merit of Humphrey Carruthers on account of defects in myself, and if I have described his two most successful stories without enthusiasm the cause perhaps lies in my own wounded vanity. For I was perfectly conscious that Humphrey Carruthers looked upon me as a writer of no account. I am convinced that he had never read a word I had written. The popularity I enjoyed was sufficient to persuade him that there was no occasion for him to give me any of his attention. For a moment, such was the stir he created, it looked as though he might himself be faced with that ignominy, but it soon appeared that his exquisite work was above the heads of the public. One can never tell how large the intelligentsia is, but one can tell fairly well how many of its members are prepared to pay money to patronize the arts they cherish. The plays that are of too fine a quality to attract the patrons of the commercial theatre can count on an audience of ten thousand, and the books that demand from their readers more comprehension than can be expected from the common herd sell twelve hundred copies. For the intelligentsia, notwithstanding their sensitiveness to beauty, prefer to go to the theatre on the nod and to get a book from the library.

I am sure this did not distress Carruthers. He was an artist. He was also a clerk in the Foreign Office. His reputation as a writer was distinguished; he was not interested in the vulgar, and to sell well would possibly have damaged his career. I could not surmise what had induced him to invite me to have coffee with him. It is true he was alone, but I should have supposed he found his thoughts excellent company, and I could not believe he imagined that I had anything to say that would interest him. Nevertheless I could not but see that he was doing his dreary best to be affable. He reminded me of where we had last met and we talked for a moment of common friends in London. He asked me how I came to be in Rome at this season and I told him. He volunteered the information that he had arrived that morning from Brindisi. Our conversation did not go easily and I made up my mind that as soon as I civilly could I would get up and leave him. But presently I had an odd sensation, I hardly know what caused it, that he was conscious of this and was desperately anxious not to give me the opportunity. I was surprised. I gathered my wits about me. I noticed that whenever I paused he broke in with a new topic. He was trying to find something to interest me so that I should stay. He was straining every nerve to be agreeable. Surely he could not be lonely; with his diplomatic connexions he must know plenty of people with whom he could have spent the evening. I wondered indeed that he was not dining at the Embassy; even though it was summer there must be someone there he knew. I noticed also that he never smiled. He talked with a sort of harsh eagerness as though he were afraid of a moment's silence and the sound of his voice shut out of his mind something that tortured him. It was very strange. Though I did not like him, though he meant nothing to me and to be with him irked me somewhat, I was against my will a trifle interested. I gave him a searching glance. I wondered if it was my fancy that I saw in those pale eyes of his the cowed look of a hunted dog and, notwithstanding his neat features and his expression so civilly controlled, in his aspect something that suggested the grimace of a soul in pain. I could not understand. A dozen absurd notions flashed through my mind. I was not particularly sympathetic: like an old war horse scenting the fray I roused myself. I had been feeling very tired, but now I grew alert. My sensibilities put out tentacles. I was suddenly alive to every expression of his face and every gesture. I put aside the thought that had come to me that he had written a play and wanted my advice. These exquisite persons succumb strangely to the glamour of the footlights and they are not averse from getting a few tips from the craftsman whose competence they superciliously despise. No, it was not that. A single man in Rome, of aesthetic leanings, is liable to get into trouble, and I asked myself whether Carruthers had got into some difficulty to extricate himself from which the Embassy was the last place he could go to. The idealist, I have noticed, is apt at times to be imprudent in the affairs of the flesh. He sometimes finds love in places which the police inconveniently visit. I tittered in my heart. Even the gods laugh when a prig is caught in an equivocal situation.

Suddenly Carruthers said something that staggered me.

'I'm so desperately unhappy,' he muttered.

He said it without warning. He obviously meant it. There was in his tone a sort of gasp. It might very well have been a sob. I cannot describe what a shock it was to me to hear him say those words. I felt as you do when you turn a corner of the street and on a sudden a great blast of wind meets you, takes your breath away, and nearly blows you off your feet. It was so unexpected. After all I hardly knew the fellow. We were not friends. I did not like him; he did not like me. I have never looked on him as quite human. It was amazing that a man so self-controlled, so urbane, accustomed to the usages of polite society, should break in upon a stranger with such a confession. I am naturally reticent. I should be ashamed, whatever I was suffering, to disclose my pain to another. I shivered. His weakness outraged me. For a moment I was filled with a passion of anger. How dared he thrust the anguish of his soul on me? I very nearly cried: 'What the hell do I care?'

But I didn't. He was sitting huddled up in the big arm-chair. The solemn nobility of his features, which reminded one of the marble statue of a Victorian statesman, had strangely crumpled and his face sagged. He looked almost as though he were going to cry. I hesitated. I faltered. I had flushed when he spoke and now I felt my face go white. He was a pitiable object.

'I'm awfully sorry,' I said.

'Do you mind if I tell you about it?'

'No.'

It was not the moment for many words. I suppose Carruthers was in the early forties. He was a well-made man, athletic in his way, and with a confident bearing. Now he looked twenty years older and strangely shrivelled. He reminded me of the dead soldiers I had seen during the war and how oddly small death had made them. I was embarrassed and looked away, but I felt his eyes claiming mine and I looked back.

'Do you know Betty Welldon-Burns?' he asked me.

'I used to meet her sometimes in London years ago. I've not seen her lately.'

'She lives in Rhodes now, you know. I've just come from there. I've been staying with her.'

'Oh?'

He hesitated.

'I'm afraid you'll think it awfully strange of me to talk to you like this. I'm at the end of my tether. If I don't talk to somebody I shall go off my head.'

He had ordered double brandies with the coffee and now calling the waiter he ordered himself another. We were alone in the lounge. There was a little shaded lamp on the table between us. Because it was a public room he spoke in a low voice. The place gave one oddly enough a sense of intimacy. I cannot repeat all that Carruthers said to me in the words he said it; it would be impossible for me to remember them; it is more convenient for me to put it in my own fashion. Sometimes he could not bring himself to say a thing right out and I had to guess at what he meant. Sometimes he had not understood, and it seemed to me that in certain ways I saw the truth more clearly than he. Betty Welldon-Burns had a very keen sense of humour and he had none. I perceived a good deal that had escaped him.

I had met her a good many times, but I knew her chiefly from hearsay. In her day she had made a great stir in the little world of London and I had heard of her often before I met her. This was at a dance in Portland Place soon after the war. She was then already at the height of her celebrity. You could not open an illustrated paper without seeing in it a portrait of her, and her mad pranks were a staple of conversation. She was twenty-four. Her mother was dead, her father, the Duke of St Erth, old and none too rich, spent most of the year in his

Cornish castle and she lived in London with a widowed aunt. At the outbreak of the war she went to France. She was just eighteen. She was a nurse in a hospital at the Base and then drove a car. She acted in a theatrical tour designed to amuse the troops; she posed in *tableaux* at home for charitable purposes, held auctions for this object and that, and sold flags in Piccadilly. Every one of her activities was widely advertised and in every new role she was profusely photographed. I suppose that she managed to have a very good time. But now that the war was over she was having her fling with a vengeance. Just then everybody a little lost his head. The young, relieved of the burden that for five years had oppressed them, indulged in one wild escapade after another. Betty took part in them all. Sometimes, for one reason or another, an account of them found its way into the newspapers and her name was always in the headlines. At that time night clubs were in the first flush of their success and she was to be seen at them every night. She lived a life of hectic gaiety. It can only be described in a hackneyed phrase, because it was a hackneyed thing. The British public in its odd way took her to its heart and Lady Betty was a sufficient description of her throughout the British islands. Women mobbed her when she went to a wedding and the gallery applauded her at first nights as though she were a popular actress. Girls copied the way she did her hair and manufacturers of soap and face cream paid her money to use her photograph to advertise their wares.

Of course dull, stodgy people, the people who remembered and regretted the old order, disapproved of her. They sneered at her constant appearance in the limelight. They said she had an insane passion for self-advertisement. They said she was fast. They said she drank too much. They said she smoked too much. I will admit that nothing I had heard of her had predisposed me to think very well of her. I held cheap the women who seemed to look upon the war as an occasion to enjoy themselves and be talked about. I am bored by the papers in which you see photographs of persons in society walking in Cannes or playing golf at St Andrews. I have always found the Bright Young People extremely tedious. The gay life seems dull and stupid to the onlooker, but the moralist is unwise to judge it harshly. It is as absurd to be angry with the young things who lead it as with a litter of puppies scampering aimlessly around, rolling one another over and chasing their tails. It is well to bear it with fortitude if they cause havoc in the flower beds or break a piece of china. Some of them will be drowned because their points are not up to the mark and the rest will grow up into well-behaved dogs. Their unruliness is due only to the vitality of youth.

And it was vitality that was Betty's most shining characteristic. The urge of life flowed through her with a radiance that dazzled you. I do not think I shall ever forget the impression she made on me at the party at which I first saw her. She was like a maenad. She danced with an abandon that made you laugh, so obvious was her intense enjoyment of the music and the movement of her young limbs. Her hair was brown, slightly disordered by the vigour of her gestures, but her eyes were deep blue, and her skin was milk and roses. She was a great beauty, but she had none of the coldness of great beauty. She laughed constantly and when she was not laughing she smiled and her eyes danced with the joy of living. She was like a milkmaid on the farmstead of the gods. She had the strength and health of the people; and yet the independence of her bearing, a sort of noble frankness of carriage, suggested the great lady. I do not quite know how to put the feeling she gave me, that though so simple and unaffected she was not unconscious of her station. I fancied that if occasion arose she could get on her dignity and be very grand indeed. She was charming to everybody because, probably without being quite aware of it, in the depths of her heart she felt that the rest of the world was perfectly insignificant. I understood why the factory girls in the East End adored her and why half a million people who had never seen her except in a photograph looked upon her with the intimacy of personal friendship. I was introduced to her and she spent a few minutes talking to me. It was extraordinarily flattering to see the interest she showed in you; you knew she could not really be so pleased to meet you as she seemed or so delighted with what you said, but it was very attractive. She had the gift of being able to jump over the first difficult phases of acquaintance and you had not known her for five minutes before you felt you had known her all her life. She was snatched away from me by someone who wanted to dance with her and she surrendered herself to her partner's arms with just the same eager happiness as she had shown when she sank into a chair by my side. I was surprised when I met her at luncheon a fortnight later to find that she remembered exactly what we had talked about during those noisy ten minutes at the dance. A young woman with all the social graces.

I mentioned the incident to Carruthers.

'She was no fool,' he said. 'Very few people knew how intelligent she was. She wrote some very good poetry. Because she was so gay, because she was so reckless and never cared a damn for anybody, people thought she was scatterbrained. Far from it. She was as clever as a monkey. You would never have thought she'd had the time to read all the things she had. I don't suppose anyone knew that side of her as well as I did. We used to take walks together, in the country at week-ends, and in London we'd drive out to Richmond Park and walk there, and talk. She loved flowers and trees and grass. She was interested in everything. She had a lot of information and a lot of sense. There was nothing she couldn't talk about. Sometimes when we'd been for a walk in the afternoon and we met at a night club and she'd had a couple of glasses of champagne, that was enough to make her completely buffy, you know, and she was the life and soul of the party, I couldn't help thinking how amazed the rest of them would be if they knew how seriously we'd been talking only a few hours before. It was an extraordinary contrast. There seemed to be two entirely different women in her.'

Carruthers said all this without a smile. He spoke with the melancholy he might have used if he had been speaking of some person snatched from the pleasant company of the living by untimely death. He gave a deep sigh.

'I was madly in love with her. I proposed to her half a dozen times. Of course I knew I hadn't a chance. I was only a very junior clerk at the F.O., but I couldn't help myself. She refused me, but she was always frightfully nice about it. It never made any difference to our friendship. You see, she really liked me. I gave her something that other people didn't. I always thought that she was really fonder of me than of anybody. I was crazy about her.'

'I don't suppose you were the only one,' I said, having to say something.

'Far from it. She used to get dozens of love letters from men she'd never seen or heard of, farmers in Africa, miners, and policemen in Canada. All sorts of people proposed to her. She could have married anyone she liked.'

'Even royalty, one heard.'

'Yes, she said she couldn't stand the life. And then she married Jimmie Welldon-Burns.'

'People were rather surprised, weren't they?'

'Did you ever know him?'

'No, I don't think so. I may have met him, but he left no impression on me.'

'He wouldn't. He was the most insignificant fellow that ever breathed. His father was a big manufacturer up in the North. He'd made a lot of money during the war and bought a baronetcy. I believe he hadn't an aitch to his name. Jimmy was at Eton with me, they'd tried hard to make a gentleman of him, and in London after the war he was about a good deal. He was always willing to throw a party. No one ever paid any attention to him. He just paid the bill. He was the most crashing bore. You know, rather prim, terribly polite; he made you rather uncomfortable because he was so anxious not to do the wrong thing. He always wore his clothes as though he'd just put them on for the first time and they were a little too tight for him.'

When Carruthers innocently opened his *Times* one morning and casting his eyes down the fashionable intelligence of the day saw that a marriage had been arranged between Elizabeth, only daughter of the Duke of St Erth, and James, eldest son of Sir John Welldon-Burns, Bart, he was dumbfounded. He rang Betty up and asked if it was true.

'Of course,' she said.

He was so shocked that for the moment he found nothing to say. She went on speaking.

'He's bringing his family to luncheon today to meet father. I dare say it'll be a bit grim. You might stand me a cocktail at Claridge's to fortify me, will you?'

'At what time?' he asked.

'One.'

'All right. I'll meet you there.'

He was waiting for her when she came in. She walked with a sort of spring as though her eager feet itched to break into a dance. She was smiling. Her eyes shone with the joy that suffused her because she was alive and the world was such a pleasant place to live in. People recognizing her whispered to one another as she came in. Carruthers really felt that she brought sunshine and the scent of flowers into the sober but rather overwhelming splendour of Claridge's lounge. He did not wait to say how do you do to her.

'Betty, you can't do it,' he said. 'It's simply out of the question.'

'Why?'

'He's awful.'

'I don't think he is. I think he's rather nice.'

A waiter came up and took their order. Betty looked at Carruthers with those beautiful blue eyes of hers that managed to be at the same time so gay and so tender.

'He's such a frightful bounder, Betty.'

'Oh, don't be so silly, Humphrey. He's just as good as anybody else. I think you're rather a snob.'

'He's so dull.'

'No, he's rather quiet. I don't know that I want a husband who's too brilliant. I think he'll make a very good background. He's quite good-looking and he has nice manners.'

'My God, Betty.'

'Oh, don't be idiotic, Humphrey.'

'Are you going to pretend you're in love with him?'

'I think it would be tactful, don't you?'

'Why are you going to marry him?'

She looked at him coolly.

'He's got pots of money. I'm nearly twenty-six.'

There was nothing much more to be said. He drove her back to her aunt's house. She had a very grand marriage, with dense crowds lining the approach to St Margaret's, Westminster, presents from practically all the royal family, and the honeymoon was passed on the yacht her father-in-law had lent them. Carruthers applied for a post abroad and was sent to Rome (I was right in guessing that he had thus acquired his admirable Italian) and later to Stockholm. Here he was counsellor and here he wrote the first of his stories.

Perhaps Betty's marriage had disappointed the British public who expected much greater things of her, perhaps only that as a young married woman she no longer appealed to the popular sense of romance; the fact was plain that she soon lost her place in the public eye. You ceased to hear very much about her. Not long after the marriage it was rumoured that she was going to have a baby and a little later that she had had a miscarriage. She did not drop out of society, I suppose she continued to see her friends, but her activities were no longer spectacular. She was certainly but seldom seen any more in those raffish assemblies where the members of a tarnished aristocracy hob-nob with the hangers-on of the arts and flatter themselves that they are being at once smart and cultured. People said she was settling down. They wondered how she was getting on with her husband and no sooner did they do this than they concluded that she was not getting on very well. Presently gossip said that Jimmie was drinking too much and then, a year or two later, one heard that he had contracted tuberculosis. The Welldon-Burnses spent a couple of winters in Switzerland. Then the news spread that they had separated and Betty had gone to live in Rhodes. An odd place to choose.

'It must be deadly,' her friends said.

A few of them went to stay with her now and then and came back with reports of the beauty of the island and the leisurely charm of the life. But of course it was very lonely. It seemed strange that Betty, with her brilliance and her energy, should be content to settle there. She had bought a house. She knew no one but a few Italian officials, there was indeed no one to know; but she seemed perfectly happy. Her visitors could not make it out. But the life of London is busy and memories are short. People ceased to concern themselves with her. She was forgotten. Then, a few weeks before I met Humphrey Carruthers in Rome, *The Times* announced the death of Sir James Welldon-Burns, second baronet. His younger brother succeeded him in the title. Betty had never had a child.

Carruthers continued to see her after the marriage. Whenever he came to London they lunched together. She had the ability to take up a friendship after a long separation as though no passage of time had intervened, so that there was never any strangeness in their meetings. Sometimes she asked him when he was going to marry.

'You're getting on, you know, Humphrey. If you don't marry soon you'll get rather old-maidish.'

'D'you recommend marriage?'

It was not a very kindly thing to say, because like everyone else he had heard that she was not getting on too well with her husband, but her remark piqued him.

'On the whole. I think probably an unsatisfactory marriage is better than no marriage at all.'

'You know quite well that nothing would induce me to marry and you know why.'

'Oh, my dear, you're not going to pretend that you're still in love with me?'

'I am.'

'You are a damned fool.'

'I don't care.'

She smiled at him. Her eyes always had that look, partly bantering, partly tender, that gave him such a happy pain in his heart. Funny, he could almost localize it.

'You're rather sweet, Humphrey. You know I'm devoted to you, but I wouldn't marry you even if I were free.'

When she left her husband and went to live in Rhodes Carruthers ceased to see her. She never came to England. They maintained an active correspondence. He suggested coming to Rhodes for a few days, but she thought he had better not. He understood why. Everyone knew he had been madly in love with her. Everyone knew he was still. He did not know in what circumstances exactly the Welldon-Burnses had separated. It might be that there had been a good deal of bad feeling. Betty might think that his presence on the island would compromise her.

'She wrote a charming letter to me when my first book came out. You know I dedicated it to her. She was surprised that I had done anything so good. Everyone was very nice about it, and she was delighted with that. I think her pleasure was the chief thing that pleased me. After all I'm not a professional writer, you know: I don't attach much importance to literary success.'

Fool, I thought, and liar. Did he think I had not noticed the self-satisfaction that consumed him on account of the favourable reception of his books? I did not blame him for feeling that, nothing could be more pardonable, but why be at such pains to deny it. But it was doubtless true that it was mostly for Betty's sake that he relished the notoriety they had brought him. He had a positive achievement to offer her. He could lay at her feet now not only his love, but a distinguished reputation. Betty was not very young any more, she was thirty-six; her marriage, her sojourn abroad, had changed things; she was no longer surrounded by suitors; she had lost the halo with which the public admiration had surrounded her. The distance between them was no longer insuperable. He alone had remained faithful through the years. It was absurd that she should continue to bury her beauty, her wit, her social grace in an island in the corner of the Mediterranean. He knew she was fond of him. She could hardly fail to be touched by his long devotion. And the life he had to offer her now was one that he knew would appeal to her. He made up his mind to ask her once more to marry him. He was able to get away towards the end of July. He wrote and said that he was going to spend his leave in the Greek islands and if she would be glad to see him he would stop off at Rhodes for a day or two where he had heard the Italians had opened a very good hotel. He put his suggestion in this casual way out of delicacy. His training at the Foreign Office had taught him to eschew abruptness. He never willingly put himself in a position from which he could not if necessary withdraw with tact. Betty sent him a telegram in reply. She said it was too marvellous that he was coming to Rhodes and of course he must come and stay with her, for at least a fortnight, and he was to wire what boat he was coming by.

He was in a state of wild excitement when at last the ship he had taken at Brindisi steamed, soon after sunrise, into the neat and pretty harbour of Rhodes. He had hardly slept a wink all night and getting up early had watched the island loom grandly out of the dawn and the sun rise over the summer sea. Boats came out as the ship dropped her anchor. The gangway was lowered. Humphrey, leaning over the rail, watched the doctor and the port officials and the hotel couriers swarm up it. He was the only Englishman on board. His nationality was obvious. A man came on deck and immediately walked up to him.

'Are you Mr Carruthers?'

'Yes.'

He was about to smile and put out his hand, but he perceived in the twinkling of an eye that the person who addressed him, an Englishman like himself, was not a gentleman. Instinctively his manner, remaining exceedingly polite, became a trifle stiff. Of course Carruthers did not tell me this, but I see the scene so clearly that I have no hesitation in describing it.

'Her ladyship hopes you don't mind her not coming to meet you, but the boat got in so early and it's more than an hour's drive to where we live.'

'Oh, of course. Her ladyship well?'

'Yes, thank you. Got your luggage ready?'

'Yes.'

'If you'll show me where it is I'll tell one of these fellows to put it in a boat. You won't have any difficulty at the Customs. I've fixed that up all right, and then we'll get off. Have you had breakfast?'

'Yes, thank you.'

The man was not quite sure of his aitches. Carruthers wondered who he was. You could not say he was uncivil, but he was certainly a little offhand. Carruthers knew that Betty had rather a large estate; perhaps he was her agent. He seemed very competent. He gave the porters instructions in fluent Greek and when they got in the boat and the boatmen asked for more money than he gave them, he said something that made them laugh and they shrugged their shoulders satisfied. The luggage was passed through the Customs without examination, Humphrey's guide shaking hands with the officials, and they went into a sunny place where a large yellow car was standing.

'Are you going to drive me?' asked Carruthers.

'I'm her ladyship's chauffeur.'

'Oh, I see. I didn't know.'

He was not dressed like a chauffeur. He wore white duck trousers and espadrilles on his bare feet, a white tennis shirt, with no tie and open at the neck, and a straw hat. Carruthers frowned. Betty oughtn't to let her chauffeur drive the car like that. It was true that he had had to get up before daybreak and it looked like being a hot drive up to the villa. Perhaps under ordinary conditions he wore uniform. Though not so tall as Carruthers, who was six feet one in his socks, he was not short; but he was broad-shouldered and squarely built, so that he looked stocky. He was not fat, but plump rather; he looked as though he had a hearty appetite and ate well. Young still, thirty perhaps or thirty-one, he had already a massive look and one day would be very beefy. Now he was a hefty fellow. He had a broad face deeply sun-burned, a short thickish nose, and a somewhat sullen look. He wore a short fair moustache. Oddly enough Carruthers had a vague feeling that he had seen him before.

'Have you been with her ladyship long?' he asked.

'Well, I have, in a manner of speaking.'

Carruthers became a trifle stiffer. He did not quite like the manner in which the chauffeur spoke. He wondered why he did not say 'sir' to him. He was afraid Betty had let him get a little above himself. It was like her to be a bit careless about such things. But it was a mistake. He'd give her a hint when he got a chance. Their eyes met for an instant and he could have sworn that there was a twinkle of amusement in the chauffeur's. Carruthers could not imagine why. He was not aware that there was anything amusing in him.

'That, I suppose, is the old city of the Knights,' he said distantly, pointing to the battlemented walls.

'Yes. Her ladyship'll take you over. We get a rare lot of tourists here in the season.'

Carruthers wished to be affable. He thought it would be nicer of him to offer to sit by the chauffeur rather than behind by himself and was just going to suggest it when the matter was taken out of his hands. The chauffeur told the porters to put Carruthers' bags at the back, and settling himself at the wheel said:

'Now if you'll hop in we'll get along.'

Carruthers sat down beside him and they set off along a white road that ran by the sea. In a few minutes they were in the open country. They drove in silence. Carruthers was a little on his dignity. He felt that the chauffeur was inclined to be familiar and he did not wish to give him occasion to be so. He flattered himself that he had a manner with him that puts his inferiors in their place. He thought with sardonic grimness that it would not be long before the chauffeur would be calling him 'sir'. But the morning was lovely; the white road ran between olive groves and the farmhouses they passed now and then, with their white walls and flat roofs, had an Oriental look that took the fancy. And Betty was waiting for him. The love in his heart disposed him to kindliness towards all men and lighting himself a cigarette he thought it would be a generous act to offer the chauffeur one too. After all, Rhodes was very far away from England and the age was democratic. The chauffeur accepted the gift and stopped the car to light up.

'Have you got the baccy?' he asked suddenly.

'Have I got what?'

The chauffeur's face fell.

'Her ladyship wired to you to bring two pounds of Player's Navy Cut. That's why I fixed it up with the Customs people not to open your luggage.'

'I never got the wire.'

'Damn!'

'What on earth does her ladyship want with two pounds of Player's Navy Cut?'

He spoke with hauteur. He did not like the chauffeur's exclamation. The fellow gave him a sidelong glance in which Carruthers read a certain insolence.

'We can't get it here,' he said briefly.

He threw away with what looked very like exasperation the Egyptian cigarette Carruthers had given him and started off again. He looked sulky. He said nothing more. Carruthers felt that his efforts at sociability had been a mistake. For the rest of the journey he ignored the chauffeur. He adopted the frigid manner that he had used so successfully as secretary at the Embassy when a member of the British public came to him for assistance. For some time they had been running up hill and now they came to a long low wall and then to an open gate. The chauffeur turned in.

'Have we arrived?' cried Carruthers.

'Sixty-five kilometres in fifty-seven minutes,' said the chauffeur, a smile suddenly showing his fine white teeth. 'Not so bad considering the road.'

He sounded his klaxon shrilly. Carruthers was breathless with excitement. They drove up a narrow road through an olive grove, and came to a low, white, rambling house. Betty was standing at the door. He jumped out of the car and kissed her on both cheeks. For a moment he could not speak. But subconsciously he noticed that at the door stood an elderly butler in white ducks and a couple of footmen in the fustanellas of their country. They were smart and picturesque. Whatever Betty permitted her chauffeur it was evident that the house was run in the civilized style suited to her station. She led him through the hall, a large apartment with whitewashed walls in which he was vaguely conscious of handsome furniture, into the drawing-room. This was also large and low, with the same whitewashed walls, and he had immediately an impression of comfort and luxury.

'The first thing you must do is to come and look at my view,' she said.

'The first thing I must do is to look at you.'

She was dressed in white. Her arms, her face, her neck, were deeply burned by the sun; her eyes were bluer than he had ever seen them and the whiteness of her teeth was startling. She looked extremely well. She was very trim and neat. Her hair was waved, her nails were manicured; he had had a moment's anxiety that in the easy life she led on this romantic isle she had let herself go.

'Upon my word you look eighteen, Betty. How do you manage it?'

'Happiness,' she smiled.

It gave him a momentary pang to hear her say this. He did not want her to be too happy. He wanted to give her happiness. But now she insisted on taking him out on the terrace. The drawing-room had five long windows that led out to it and from the terrace the olive-clad hill tumbled steeply to the sea. There was a tiny bay below in which a white boat, mirrored on the calm water, lay at anchor. On a further hill, round the corner, you saw the white houses of a Greek village and beyond it a huge grey crag surmounted by the battlements of a medieval castle.

'It was one of the strongholds of the Knights,' she said. 'I'll take you up there this evening.'

The scene was quite lovely. It took your breath away. It was peaceful and yet it had a strange air of life. It moved you not to contemplation, but stirred you to activity.

'You've got the tobacco all right, I suppose.'

He started.

'I'm afraid I haven't. I never got your wire.'

'But I wired to the Embassy and I wired to the Excelsior.'

'I stayed at the Plaza.'

'What a bore! Albert'll be furious.'

'Who is Albert?'

'He drove you out. Player's is the only tobacco he likes and he can't get it here.'

'Oh, the chauffeur.' He pointed to the boat that lay gleaming beneath them. 'Is that the yacht I've heard about?'

'Yes.'

It was a large caïque that Betty had bought, fitted with a motor auxiliary and smartened up. In it she wandered about the Greek islands. She had been as far north as Athens and as far south as Alexandria.

'We'll take you for a trip if you can spare the time,' she said. 'You ought to see Cos while you're here.'

'Who runs it for you?'

'Of course I have a crew, but Albert chiefly. He's very clever with motors and all that.'

He did not know why it gave him a vague discomfort to hear her speak of the chauffeur again. Carruthers wondered if she did not leave too much in his hands. It was a mistake to give a servant too much leeway.

'You know, I couldn't help thinking I'd seen Albert before somewhere. But I can't place him.'

She smiled brightly, her eyes shining, with that sudden gaiety of hers that gave her face its delightful frankness.

'You ought to remember him. He was the second footman at Aunt Louise's. He must have opened the door to you hundreds of times.'

Aunt Louise was the aunt with whom Betty had lived before her marriage.

'Oh, is that who he is? I suppose I must have seen him there without noticing him. How does he happen to be here?'

'He comes from our place at home. When I married he wanted to come with me, so I took him. He was Jimmie's valet for some time and then I sent him to some motor works, he was mad about cars, and eventually I took him on as my chauffeur. I don't know what I should do without him now.'

'Don't you think it's rather a mistake to get too dependent on a servant?'

'I don't know. It never occurred to me.'

Betty showed him the rooms that had been got ready for him, and when he had changed they strolled down to the beach. A dinghy was waiting for them and they rowed out to the caïque and bathed from there. The water was warm and they sunned themselves on the deck. The caïque was roomy, comfortable, and luxurious. Betty showed him over and they came upon Albert tinkering with the engines. He was in filthy overalls, his hands were black and his face was smeared with grease.

'What's the matter, Albert?' said Betty.

He raised himself and faced her respectfully.

'Nothing, m'lady. I was just 'aving a look round.'

'There are only two things Albert loves in the world. One is the car and the other's the yacht. Isn't that true, Albert?'

She gave him a gay smile and Albert's rather stolid face lit up. He showed his beautiful white teeth.

'That's true, m'lady.'

'He sleeps on board, you know. We rigged up a very nice cabin for him aft.'

Carruthers fell into the life very easily. Betty had bought the estate from a Turkish pasha exiled to Rhodes by Abdul Hamid and she had added a wing to the picturesque house. She had made a wild garden of the olive grove that surrounded it. It was planted with rosemary and lavender and asphodel, broom that she had sent from England and the roses for which the island was famous. In the spring, she told him, the ground was carpeted with anemones. But when she showed him her property, telling him her plans and what alterations she had in mind, Carruthers could not help feeling a little uneasy.

'You talk as though you were going to live here all your life,' he said.

'Perhaps I am,' she smiled.

'What nonsense! At your age.'

'I'm getting on for forty, old boy,' she answered lightly.

He discovered with satisfaction that Betty had an excellent cook and it gratified his sense of propriety to dine with her in the splendid dining-room, with its Italian furniture, and be waited on by the dignified Greek butler and the two handsome footmen in their flamboyant uniforms. The house was furnished with taste; the rooms contained nothing that was not essential, but every piece was good. Betty lived in considerable state. When, the day after his arrival, the Governor with several members of his staff came over to dinner she displayed all the resources of the household. The Governor entering the house passed between a double row of flunkeys magnificent in their starched petticoats, embroidered jackets, and velvet caps. It was almost a bodyguard. Carruthers liked the grand style. The dinner-party was very gay. Betty's Italian was fluent and Carruthers spoke it perfectly. The young officers in the Governor's suite were uncommonly smart in their uniforms. They were very attentive to Betty and she treated them with easy cordiality. She chaffed them. After dinner the gramophone was turned on and they danced with her one after the other.

When they were gone Carruthers asked her:

'Aren't they all madly in love with you?'

'I don't know about that. They hint occasionally at alliances permanent or otherwise, but they take it very good-naturedly when I decline with thanks.'

They were not serious. The young ones were callow and the not so young were fat and bald. Whatever they might feel about her Carruthers could not for a moment believe that Betty would make a fool of herself with a middle-class Italian. But a day or two later a curious thing happened. He was in his rooms dressing for dinner; he heard a man's voice outside in the passage, he could not hear what was said or what language was spoken, and then ringing out suddenly Betty's laughter. It was a charming laugh, rippling and gay, like a young girl's, and it had a joyous abandon that was infectious. But whom could she be laughing with? It was not the way you would laugh with a servant. It had a curious intimacy. It may seem strange that Carruthers read all this into a peal of laughter, but it must be remembered that Carruthers was very subtle. His stories were remarkable for such touches.

When they met presently on the terrace and he was shaking a cocktail he sought to gratify his curiosity.

'What were you laughing your head off over just now? Has anyone been here?'

'No.'

She looked at him with genuine surprise.

'I thought one of your Italian officers had come to pass the time of day.'

'No.'

Of course the passage of years had had its effect on Betty. She was beautiful, but her beauty was mature. She had always had assurance, but now she had repose; her serenity was a feature, like her blue eyes and her candid brow, that was part of her beauty. She seemed to be at peace with all the world; it rested you to be with her as it rested you to lie among the olives within sight of the wine-coloured sea. Though she was as gay and witty as ever, the seriousness which once he had been alone to know was now patent. No one could accuse her any longer of being scatter-brained; it was impossible not to perceive the fineness of her character. It had even nobility. That was not a trait it was usual to find in the modern woman and Carruthers said to himself that she was a throwback; she reminded him of the great ladies of the eighteenth century. She had always had a feeling for literature, the poems she wrote as a girl were graceful and melodious, and he was more interested than surprised when she told him that she had undertaken a solid historical work. She was getting materials together for an account of the Knights of St John in Rhodes. It was a story of romantic incidents. She took Carruthers to the city and showed him the noble battlements and together they wandered through austere and stately buildings. They strolled up the silent Street of the Knights with the lovely stone façades and the great coats of arms that recalled a dead chivalry. She had a surprise for him there. She had bought one of the old houses and with affectionate care had restored it to its old state. When you entered the little courtyard, with its carved stone stairway, you were taken back into the middle ages. It had a tiny walled garden in which a fig-tree grew and roses. It was small and secret and silent. The old knights had been in contact with the East long enough to have acquired Oriental ideas of privacy.

'When I'm tired of the villa I come here for two or three days and picnic. It's a relief sometimes not to be surrounded by people.'

'But you're not alone here?'

'Practically.'

There was a little parlour austerely furnished.

'What is this?' said Carruthers pointing with a smile to a copy of the *Sporting Times* that lay on a table.

'Oh, that's Albert's. I suppose he left it here when he came to meet you. He has the *Sporting Times* and the *News of the World* sent him every week. That is how he keeps abreast of the great world.'

She smiled tolerantly. Next to the parlour was a bedroom with nothing much in it but a large bed.

'The house belonged to an Englishman. That's partly why I bought it. He was a Sir Giles Quern, and one of my ancestors married a Mary Quern who was a cousin of his. They were Cornish people.'

Finding that she could not get on with her history without such a knowledge of Latin as would enable her to read the medieval documents with ease, Betty had set about learning the classical language. She troubled to acquire only the elements of grammar and then started, with a translation by her side, to read the authors that interested her. It is a very good method of learning a language and I have often wondered that it is not used in schools. It saves all the endless turning over of dictionaries and the fumbling search for meaning. After nine months Betty could read Latin as fluently as most of us can read French. It seemed a trifle ridiculous to Carruthers that this lovely, brilliant creature should take her work so seriously and yet he was moved; he would have liked to snatch her in his arms and kiss her, not at that moment as a woman, but as a precocious child whose cleverness suddenly enchants you. But later he reflected upon what she had told him. He was of course a very clever man, otherwise he could not have attained the position he held in the Foreign Office, and it would be silly to claim that those two books of his could have made so much stir without some merit; if I have made him look a bit of a fool it is only because I did not happen to like him, and if I have derided his stories it is merely because stories of that sort seem to me rather silly. He had tact and insight. He had a conviction that there was but one way to win her. She was in a groove and happy in it, her plans were definite; but her life at Rhodes was so well-ordered, so complete and satisfying, that for that very reason its hold over her could be combated. His chance was to arouse in her the restlessness that lies deep in the heart of the English. So he talked to Betty of England and London, their common friends and the painters, writers, and musicians with whom his literary success had brought him acquaintance. He talked of the Bohemian parties in Chelsea, and of the opera, of trips to Paris *en bande* for a fancy-dress ball, or to Berlin to see the new plays. He recalled to her imagination a life rich and easy, varied, cultured, intelligent, and highly civilized. He tried to make her feel that she was stagnating in a backwater. The world was hurrying on, from one new and interesting phase to another, and she was standing still. They were living in a thrilling age and she was missing it. Of course he did not tell her this; he left her to infer it. He was amusing and spirited, he had an excellent memory for a good story, he was whimsical and gay. I know I have not made Humphrey Carruthers witty any more than I have shown Lady Betty brilliant. The reader must take my word for it that they were. Carruthers was generally reckoned an entertaining companion, and that is half the battle; people were willing to find him amusing and they vowed the things he said were marvellous. Of course his wit was social. It needed a particular company, who understood his allusions and shared his exclusive sense of humour. There are a score of journalists in Fleet Street who could knock spots off the most famous of the society wits; it is their business to be witty and brilliance is in their day's work. There are a few of the society beauties whose photographs appear in the papers who could get a job at three pounds a week in the chorus of a song-and-dance show. Amateurs must be judged with tolerance. Carruthers knew that Betty enjoyed his society. They laughed a great deal together. The days passed in a flash.

'I shall miss you terribly when you go,' she said in her frank way. 'It's been a treat having you here. You are a sweet, Humphrey.'

'Have you only just discovered it?'

He patted himself on the back. His tactics had been right. It was interesting to see how well his simple plan had worked. Like a charm. The vulgar might laugh at the Foreign Office, but there was no doubt it taught you how to deal with difficult people. Now he had but to choose his opportunity. He felt that Betty had never been more attached to him. He would wait till the end of his visit. Betty was emotional. She would be sorry that he was going. Rhodes would seem very dull without him. Whom would she have to talk to when he was gone? After dinner they usually sat on the terrace looking at the starry sea; the air was warm and balmy and vaguely scented: it was then he would ask her to marry him, on the eve of his departure. He felt it in his bones that she would accept him.

One morning when he had been in Rhodes a little over a week, he happened to be coming upstairs as Betty was walking along the passage.

'You've never shown me your room, Betty,' he said.

'Haven't I? Come in and have a look now. It's rather nice.'

She turned back and he followed her in. It was over the drawing-room and nearly as large. It was furnished in the Italian style, and as is the present way more like a sitting-room than a bedroom. There were fine Paninis on the walls and one or two handsome cabinets. The bed was Venetian and beautifully painted.

'That's a couch of rather imposing dimensions for a widow lady,' he said facetiously.

'It is enormous, isn't it? But it was so lovely, I had to buy it. It cost a fortune.'

His eye took in the bed-table by the side. There were two or three books on it, a box of cigarettes, and on an ash-tray a briar pipe. Funny! What on earth had

Betty got a pipe by her bed for?

'Do look at this *cassone*. Isn't the painting marvellous? I almost cried when I found it.'

'I suppose that cost a fortune too.'

'I daren't tell you what I paid.'

When they were leaving the room he cast another glance at the bed-table. The pipe had vanished.

It was odd that Betty should have a pipe in her bedroom, she certainly didn't smoke one herself, and if she had would have made no secret of it, but of course there were a dozen reasonable explanations. It might be a present she was making to somebody, one of the Italians or even Albert, he had not been able to see if it was new or old, or it might be a pattern that she was going to ask him to take home to have others of the same sort sent out to her. After the moment's perplexity, not altogether unmingled with amusement, he put the matter out of his mind. They were going for a picnic that day, taking their luncheon with them, and Betty was driving him herself. They had arranged to go for a cruise of a couple of days before he left so that he should see Patmos and Cos, and Albert was busy with the engines of the caïque. They had a wonderful day. They visited a ruined castle and climbed a mountain on which grew asphodel, hyacinth, and narcissus, and returned dead beat. They separated not long after dinner and Carruthers went to bed. He read for a little and then turned out his light. But he could not sleep. It was hot under his mosquito-net. He turned and tossed. Presently he thought he would go down to the little beach at the foot of the hill and bathe. It was not more than three minutes' walk. He put on his espadrilles and took a towel. The moon was full and he saw it shining on the sea through the olive-trees. But he was not alone to have thought that this radiant night would be lovely to bathe in, for just before he came out on to the beach sounds reached his ears. He muttered a little damn of vexation, some of Betty's servants were bathing, and he could not very well disturb them. The olive-trees came almost to the water's edge and undecided he stood in their shelter. He heard a voice that gave him a sudden start.

'Where's my towel?'

English. A woman waded out of the water and stood for a moment at its edge. From the darkness a man came forward with nothing but a towel round his loins. The woman was Betty. She was stark naked. The man wrapped a bath-robe round her and began drying her vigorously. She leaned on him while she put on first one shoe and then the other and to support her he placed his arm round her shoulders. The man was Albert.

Carruthers turned and fled up the hill. He stumbled blindly. Once he nearly fell. He was gasping like a wounded beast. When he got into his room he flung himself on the bed and clenched his fists and the dry, painful sobs that tore his chest broke into tears. He evidently had a violent attack of hysterics. It was all clear to him, clear with the ghastly vividness with which on a stormy night a flash of lightning can disclose a ravaged landscape, clear, horribly clear. The way the man had dried her and the way she leaned against him pointed not to passion, but to a long-continued intimacy, and the pipe by the bedside, the pipe had a hideously conjugal air. It suggested the pipe a man might smoke while he was reading in bed before going to sleep. The *Sporting Times*! That was why she had that little house in the Street of the Knights, so that they could spend two or three days together in domestic familiarity. They were like an old married couple. Humphrey asked himself how long the hateful thing had lasted and suddenly he knew the answer: for years. Ten, twelve, fourteen; it had started when the young footman first came to London, he was a boy then and it was obvious enough that it was not he who had made the advances; all through those years when she was the idol of the British public, when everyone adored her and she could have married anyone she liked, she was living with the second footman at her aunt's house. She took him with her when she married. Why had she made that surprising marriage? And the still-born child that came before its time. Of course that was why she had married Jimmie Welldon-Burns, because she was going to have a child by Albert. Oh, shameless, shameless! And then, when Jimmie's health broke down she had made him take Albert as his valet. And what had Jimmie known and what had he suspected? He drank, that was what had started his tuberculosis; but why had he started drinking? Perhaps it was to still a suspicion that was so ugly that he could not face it. And it was to live with Albert that she had left Jimmie and it was to live with Albert that she had settled in Rhodes. Albert, his hands with their broken nails stained by his work on the motors, coarse of aspect and stocky, rather like a butcher with his high colour and clumsy strength, Albert not even very young any more and running to fat, uneducated and vulgar, with his common way of speaking. Albert, Albert, how could she?

Carruthers got up and drank some water. He threw himself into a chair. He could not bear his bed. He smoked cigarette after cigarette. He was a wreck in the morning. He had not slept at all. They brought him in his breakfast; he drank the coffee but could eat nothing. Presently there was a brisk knock on his door.

'Coming down to bathe, Humphrey?'

That cheerful voice sent the blood singing through his head. He braced himself and opened the door.

'I don't think I will today. I don't feel very well.'

She gave him a look.

'Oh, my dear, you look all in. What's the matter with you?'

'I don't know. I think I must have got a touch of the sun.'

His voice was dead and his eyes were tragic. She looked at him more closely. She did not say anything for a moment. He thought she went pale. He *knew*. Then a faintly mocking smile crossed her eyes; she thought the situation comic.

'Poor old boy, go and lie down, I'll send you in some aspirin. Perhaps you'll feel better at luncheon.'

He lay in his darkened room. He would have given anything to get away then so that he need not set eyes on her again, but there was no means of that, the ship that was to take him back to Brindisi did not touch at Rhodes till the end of the week. He was a prisoner. And the next day they were to go to the islands. There was no escape from her there; in the caïque they would be in one another's pockets all day long. He couldn't face that. He was so ashamed. But she wasn't ashamed. At that moment when it had been plain to her that nothing was hidden from him any longer she had smiled. She was capable of telling him all about it. He could not bear that. That was too much. After all she couldn't be certain that he knew, at best she could only suspect; if he behaved as if nothing had happened, if at luncheon and during the days that remained he was as gay and jolly as usual she would think she had been mistaken. It was enough to know what he knew, he would not suffer the crowning humiliation of hearing from her own lips the disgraceful story. But at luncheon the first thing she said was:

'Isn't it a bore. Albert says something's gone wrong with the motor, we shan't be able to go on our trip after all. I daren't trust to sail at this time of the year.'

We might be becalmed for a week.'

She spoke lightly and he answered in the same casual fashion.

'Oh, I'm sorry, but still I don't really care. It's so lovely here, I really didn't much want to go.'

He told her that the aspirin had done him good and he felt much better; to the Greek butler and the two footmen in fustanellas it must have seemed that they talked as vivaciously as usual. That night the British consul came to dinner and the night after some Italian officers. Carruthers counted the days, he counted the hours. Oh, if the moment would only come when he could step on the ship and be free from the horror that every moment of the day obsessed him! He was growing so tired. But Betty's manner was so self-possessed that sometimes he asked himself if she really knew that he was aware of her secret. Was it the truth that she had told about the caïque and not, as had at once struck him, an excuse; and was it an accident that a succession of visitors prevented them from ever being alone together? The worst of having so much tact was that you never quite knew whether other people were acting naturally or being tactful too. When he looked at her, so easy and calm, so obviously happy, he could not believe the odious truth. And yet he had seen with his own eyes. And the future. What would her future be? It was horrible to think of. Sooner or later the truth must become notorious. And to think of Betty a mock and an outcast, in the power of a coarse and common man, growing older, losing her beauty; and the man was five years younger that she. One day he would take a mistress, one of her own maids, perhaps, with whom he would feel at home as he had never felt with the great lady, and what could she do then? What humiliation then must she be prepared to put up with! He might be cruel to her. He might beat her. Betty. Betty.

Carruthers wrung his hands. And on a sudden an idea came to him that filled him with a painful exaltation; he put it away from him, but it returned; it would not let him be. He must save her, he had loved her too much and too long to let her sink, sink as she was sinking; a passion of self-sacrifice welled up in him. Notwithstanding everything, though his love now was dead and he felt for her an almost physical repulsion, he would marry her. He laughed mirthlessly. What would his life be? He couldn't help that. He didn't matter. It was the only thing to do. He felt wonderfully uplifted, and yet very humble, for he was awed at the thoughts of the heights which the divine spirit of man could reach.

His ship was to sail on Saturday and on Thursday when the guests who had been dining left them, he said:

'I hope we're going to be alone tomorrow.'

'As a matter of fact I've asked some Egyptians who spend the summer here. She's a sister of the ex-Khedive and very intelligent. I'm sure you'll like her.'

'Well, it's my last evening. Couldn't we spend it alone?'

She gave him a glance. There was a faint amusement in her eyes, but his were grave.

'If you like. I can put them off.'

'Then do.'

He was to start early in the morning and his luggage was packed. Betty had told him not to dress, but he had answered that he preferred to. For the last time they sat down to dinner facing one another. The dining-room, with its shaded lights, was bare and formal, but the summer night flooding in through the great open windows gave it a sober richness. It had the effect of the private refectory in a convent to which a royal lady had retired in order to devote the remainder of her life to a piety not too austere. They had their coffee on the terrace. Carruthers drank a couple of liqueurs. He was feeling very nervous.

'Betty, my dear, I've got something I want to say to you,' he began.

'Have you? I wouldn't say it if I were you.'

She answered gently. She remained perfectly calm, watching him shrewdly, but with the glimmer of a smile in her blue eyes.

'I must.'

She shrugged her shoulders and was silent. He was conscious that his voice trembled a little and he was angry with himself.

'You know I've been madly in love with you for many years. I don't know how many times I've asked you to marry me. But, after all, things change and people change too, don't they? We're neither of us so young as we were. Won't you marry me now, Betty?'

She gave him the smile that had always been such an attractive thing in her; it was so kindly, so frank, and still, still so wonderfully innocent.

'You're very sweet, Humphrey. It's awfully nice of you to ask me again. I can't tell you how touched I am. But you know, I'm a creature of habit, I've got in the habit of saying no to you now, and I can't change it.'

'Why not?'

There was something aggressive in his tone, something almost ominous, that made her give him a quick look. Her face blanched with sudden anger, but she immediately controlled herself.

'Because I don't want to,' she smiled.

'Are you going to marry anyone else?'

'I? No. Of course not.'

For a moment she seemed to draw herself up as though a wave of ancestral pride swept through her and then she began to laugh. But whether she laughed at the thought that had passed through her mind or because something in Humphrey's proposal had amused her none but she could have told.

'Betty. I implore you to marry me.'

'Never.'

'You can't go on living this life.'

He put into his voice all the anguish of his heart and his face was drawn and tortured. She smiled affectionately.

'Why not? Don't be such a donkey. You know I adore you, Humphrey, but you are rather an old woman.'

'Betty. Betty.'

Did she not see that it was for her sake that he wanted it? It was not love that made him speak, but human pity and shame. She got up.

'Don't be tiresome, Humphrey. You'd better go to bed, you know you have to be up with the lark. I shan't see you in the morning. Good-bye and God bless you. It's been wonderful having you here.'

She kissed him on both cheeks.

Next morning, early, for he had to be on board at eight, when Carruthers stepped out of the front door he found Albert waiting for him in the car. He wore a singlet, duck trousers, and a beret basque. Carruthers' luggage was in the back. He turned to the butler.

'Put my bags beside the chauffeur,' he said. 'I'll sit behind.'

Albert made no remark. Carruthers got in and they drove off. When they arrived at the harbour, porters ran up. Albert got out of the car. Carruthers looked down at him from his greater height.

'You need not see me on board. I can manage perfectly well by myself. Here's a tip for you.'

He gave him a five-pound note. Albert flushed. He was taken aback, he would have liked to refuse it, but did not know how to and the servility of years asserted itself. Perhaps he did not know what he said.

'Thank you, sir.'

Carruthers gave him a curt nod and walked away. He had forced Betty's lover to call him 'sir'. It was as though he had struck her a blow across that smiling mouth of hers and flung in her face an opprobrious word. It filled him with a bitter satisfaction.

He shrugged his shoulders and I could see that even this small triumph now seemed vain. For a little while we were silent. There was nothing for me to say. Then he began again.

'I dare say you think it's very strange that I should tell you all this. I don't care. You know, I feel as if nothing mattered any more. I feel as if decency no longer existed in the world. Heaven knows, I'm not jealous. You can't be jealous unless you love and my love is dead. It was killed in a flash. After all those years. I can't think of her now without horror. What destroys me, what makes me so frightfully unhappy is to think of her unspeakable degradation.'

So it has been said that it was not jealousy that caused Othello to kill Desdemona, but an agony that the creature that he believed angelic should be proved impure and worthless. What broke his noble heart was that virtue should so fall.

'I thought there was no one like her. I admired her so much. I admired her courage and her frankness, her intelligence and her love of beauty. She's just a sham and she's never been anything else.'

'I wonder if that's true. Do you think any of us are all of a piece? Do you know what strikes me? I should have said that Albert was only the instrument, her toll to the solid earth, so to speak; that left her soul at liberty to range the empyrean. Perhaps the mere fact that he was so far below her gave her a sense of freedom in her relations with him that she would have lacked with a man of her own class. The spirit is very strange, it never soars so high as when the body has wallowed for a period in the gutter.'

'Oh, don't talk such rot,' he answered angrily.

'I don't think it is rot. I don't put it very well, but the idea's sound.'

'Much good it does me. I'm broken and done for. I'm finished.'

'Oh, nonsense. Why don't you write a story about it?'

'I?'

'You know, that's the great pull a writer has over other people. When something has made him terribly unhappy, and he's tortured and miserable, he can put it all into a story and it's astonishing what a comfort and relief it is.'

'It would be monstrous. Betty was everything in the world to me. I couldn't do anything so caddish.'

He paused for a little and I saw him reflect. I saw that notwithstanding the horror that my suggestion caused him he did for one minute look at the situation from the standpoint of the writer. He shook his head.

'Not for her sake, for mine. After all I have some self-respect. Besides, there's no story there.'

Jane

♦

I remember very well the occasion on which I first saw Jane Fowler. It is indeed only because the details of the glimpse I had of her then are so clear that I trust my recollection at all, for, looking back, I must confess that I find it hard to believe that it has not played me a fantastic trick. I had lately returned to London from China and was drinking a dish of tea with Mrs Tower. Mrs Tower had been seized with the prevailing passion for decoration; and with the ruthlessness of her sex had sacrificed chairs in which she had comfortably sat for years, tables, cabinets, ornaments on which her eyes had dwelt in peace since she was married, pictures that had been familiar to her for a generation; and delivered herself into the hands of an expert. Nothing remained in her drawing-room with which she had any association, or to which any sentiment was attached; and she had invited me that day to see the fashionable glory in which she now lived. Everything that could be pickled was pickled and what couldn't be pickled was painted. Nothing matched, but everything harmonized.

'Do you remember that ridiculous drawing-room suite that I used to have?' asked Mrs Tower.

The curtains were sumptuous yet severe; the sofa was covered with Italian brocade; the chair on which I sat was in *petit point*. The room was beautiful, opulent without garishness, and original without affectation; yet to me it lacked something; and while I praised with my lips I asked myself why I so much preferred the rather shabby chintz of the despised suite, the Victorian watercolours that I had known so long, and the ridiculous Dresden china that had adorned the chimney-piece. I wondered what it was that I missed in all these rooms that the decorators were turning out with a profitable industry. Was it heart? But Mrs Tower looked about her happily.

'Don't you like my alabaster lamps?' she said. 'They give such a soft light.'
'Personally I have a weakness for a light that you can see by,' I smiled.

'It's so difficult to combine that with a light that you can't be too much seen by,' laughed Mrs Tower.

I had no notion what her age was. When I was quite a young man she was a married woman a good deal older than I, but now she treated me as her contemporary. She constantly said that she made no secret of her age, which was forty, and then added with a smile that all women took five years off. She never sought to conceal the fact that she dyed her hair (it was a very pretty brown with reddish tints), and she said she did this because hair was hideous while it was going grey; as soon as hers was white she would cease to dye it.

'Then they'll say what a young face I have.'

Meanwhile it was painted, though with discretion, and her eyes owed not a little of their vivacity to art. She was a handsome woman, exquisitely gowned, and in the sombre glow of the alabaster lamps did not look a day more than the forty she gave herself.

'It is only at my dressing-table that I can suffer the naked brightness of a thirty-two-candle electric bulb,' she added with smiling cynicism. 'There I need it to tell me the first hideous truth and then to enable me to take the necessary steps to correct it.'

We gossiped pleasantly about our common friends and Mrs Tower brought me up to date in the scandal of the day. After roughing it here and there it was very agreeable to sit in a comfortable chair, the fire burning brightly on the hearth, charming tea-things set out on a charming table, and talk with this amusing, attractive woman. She treated me as a prodigal returned from his husks and was disposed to make much of me. She prided herself on her dinner-parties; she took no less trouble to have her guests suitably assorted than to give them excellent food; and there were few persons who did not look upon it as a treat to be bidden to one of them. Now she fixed a date and asked me whom I would like to meet.

'There's only one thing I must tell you. If Jane Fowler is still here I shall have to put it off.'

'Who is Jane Fowler?' I asked.

Mrs Tower gave a rueful smile.

'Jane Fowler is my cross.'

'Oh!'

'Do you remember a photograph that I used to have on the piano before I had my room done, of a woman in a tight dress with tight sleeves and a gold locket, with her hair drawn back from a broad forehead and her ears showing and spectacles on a rather blunt nose? Well, that was Jane Fowler.'

'You had so many photographs about the room in your unregenerate days,' I said, vaguely.

'It makes me shudder to think of them. I've made them into a huge brown-paper parcel and hidden them in an attic.'

'Well, who is Jane Fowler?' I asked again, smiling.

'She's my sister-in-law. She was my husband's sister and she married a manufacturer in the North. She's been a widow for many years, and she's very well-to-do.'

'And why is she your cross?'

'She's worthy, she's dowdy, she's provincial. She looks twenty years older than I do and she's quite capable of telling anyone she meets that we were at school together. She has an overwhelming sense of family affection and because I am her only living connexion she's devoted to me. When she comes to London it never occurs to her that she should stay anywhere but here–she thinks it would hurt my feelings–and she'll pay me visits of three or four weeks. We sit here and she knits and reads. And sometimes she insists on taking me to dine at Claridge's and she looks like a funny old charwoman and everyone I particularly don't want to be seen by is sitting at the next table. When we are driving home she says she loves giving me a little treat. With her own hands she makes me tea-cosies that I am forced to use when she is here and doilies and centrepieces for the dining-room table.'

Mrs Tower paused to take breath.

'I should have thought a woman of your tact would find a way to deal with a situation like that.'

'Ah, but don't you see, I haven't a chance. She's so immeasurably kind. She has a heart of gold. She bores me to death, but I wouldn't for anything let her suspect it.'

'And when does she arrive?'

'Tomorrow.'

But the answer was hardly out of Mrs Tower's mouth when the bell rang. There were sounds in the hall of a slight commotion and in a minute or two the butler ushered in an elderly lady.

'Mrs Fowler,' he announced.

'Jane,' cried Mrs Tower, springing to her feet. 'I wasn't expecting you today.'

'So your butler has just told me. I certainly said today in my letter.'

Mrs Tower recovered her wits.

'Well, it doesn't matter. I'm very glad to see you whenever you come. Fortunately I'm doing nothing this evening.'

'You mustn't let me give you any trouble. If I can have a boiled egg for my dinner, that's all I shall want.'

A faint grimace for a moment distorted Mrs Tower's handsome features. A boiled egg!

'Oh, I think we can do a little better than that.'

I chuckled inwardly when I recollected that the two ladies were contemporaries. Mrs Fowler looked a good fifty-five. She was a rather big woman; she wore a black straw hat with a wide brim and from it a black lace veil hung over her shoulders, a cloak that oddly combined severity with fussiness, a long black dress, voluminous as though she wore several petticoats under it, and stout boots. She was evidently short-sighted, for she looked at you through large gold-rimmed spectacles.

'Won't you have a cup of tea?' asked Mrs Tower.

'If it wouldn't be too much trouble. I'll take off my mantle.'

She began by stripping her hands of the black gloves she wore, and then took off her cloak. Round her neck was a solid gold chain from which hung a large gold locket in which I felt certain was a photograph of her deceased husband. Then she took off her hat and placed it neatly with her gloves and cloak on the sofa corner. Mrs Tower pursed her lips. Certainly those garments did not go very well with the austere but sumptuous beauty of Mrs Tower's redecorated drawing-room. I wondered where on earth Mrs Fowler had found the extraordinary clothes she wore. They were not old and the materials were expensive. It was astounding to think that dressmakers still made things that had not been worn for a quarter of a century. Mrs Fowler's grey hair was very plainly done, showing all her forehead and her ears, with a parting in the middle. It had evidently never known the tongs of Monsieur Marcel. Now her eyes fell on the tea-table with its teapot of Georgian silver and its cups in Old Worcester.

'What have you done with the tea-cosy I gave you last time I came up, Marion?' she asked. 'Don't you use it?'

'Yes, I used it every day, Jane,' answered Mrs Tower glibly. 'Unfortunately we had an accident with it a little while ago. It got burnt.'

'But the last one I gave you got burnt.'

'I'm afraid you'll think us very careless.'

'It doesn't really matter,' smiled Mrs Fowler. 'I shall enjoy making you another. I'll go to Liberty's tomorrow and buy some silks.'

Mrs Tower kept her face bravely.

'I don't deserve it, you know. Doesn't your vicar's wife need one?'

'Oh, I've just made her one,' said Mrs Fowler brightly.

I noticed that when she smiled she showed white, small, and regular teeth. They were a real beauty. Her smile was certainly very sweet.

But I felt it high time for me to leave the two ladies to themselves, so I took my leave.

Early next morning Mrs Tower rang me up and I heard at once from her voice that she was in high spirits.

'I've got the most wonderful news for you,' she said. 'Jane is going to be married.'

'Nonsense.'

'Her fiancé is coming to dine here tonight to be introduced to me and I want you to come too.'

'Oh, but I shall be in the way.'

'No, you won't. Jane suggested herself that I should ask you. Do come.'

She was bubbling over with laughter.

'Who is he?'

'I don't know. She tells me he's an architect. Can you imagine the sort of man Jane would marry?'

I had nothing to do and I could trust Mrs Tower to give me a good dinner.

When I arrived Mrs Tower, very splendid in a tea-gown a little too young for her, was alone.

'Jane is putting the finishing touches to her appearance. I'm longing for you to see her. She's all in a flutter. She says he adores her. His name is Gilbert and when she speaks of him her voice gets all funny and tremulous. It makes me want to laugh.'

'I wonder what he's like.'

'Oh, I'm sure I know. Very big and massive, with a bald head and an immense gold chain across an immense tummy. A large, fat, clean-shaven, red face and a booming voice.'

Mrs Fowler came in. She wore a very stiff black silk dress with a wide skirt and a train. At the neck it was cut into a timid V and the sleeves came down to the elbows. She wore a necklace of diamonds set in silver. She carried in her hands a long pair of black gloves and a fan of black ostrich feathers. She managed (as so few people do) to look exactly what she was. You could never have thought her anything in the world but the respectable relict of a North-country manufacturer of ample means.

'You've really got quite a pretty neck, Jane,' said Mrs Tower with a kindly smile.

It was indeed astonishingly young when you compared it with her weather-beaten face. It was smooth and unlined and the skin was white. And I noticed then that her head was very well placed on her shoulders.

'Has Marion told you my news?' she said, turning to me with that really charming smile of hers as if we were already old friends.

'I must congratulate you,' I said.

'Wait to do that till you've seen my young man.'

'I think it's too sweet to hear you talk of your young man,' smiled Mrs Tower.

Mrs Fowler's eyes certainly twinkled behind her preposterous spectacles.

'Don't expect anyone too old. You wouldn't like me to marry a decrepit old gentleman with one foot in the grave, would you?'

This was the only warning she gave us. Indeed there was no time for any further discussion, for the butler flung open the door and in a loud voice announced:

'Mr Gilbert Napier.'

There entered a youth in a very well-cut dinner jacket. He was slight, not very tall, with fair hair in which there was a hint of a natural wave, clean-shaven, and blue-eyed. He was not particularly good-looking, but he had a pleasant, amiable face. In ten years he would probably be wizened and sallow; but now, in extreme youth, he was fresh and clean and blooming. For he was certainly not more than twenty-four. My first thought was that this was the son of Jane Fowler's fiancé (I had not known he was a widower) come to say that his father was prevented from dining by a sudden attack of gout. But his eyes fell immediately on Mrs Fowler, his face lit up, and he went towards her with both hands outstretched. Mrs Fowler gave him hers, a demure smile on her lips, and turned to her sister-in-law.

'This is my young man, Marion,' she said.

He held out his hand.

'I hope you'll like me, Mrs Tower,' he said. 'Jane tells me you're the only relation she has in the world.'

Mrs Tower's face was wonderful to behold. I saw then to admiration how bravely good breeding and social usage could combat the instincts of the natural woman. For the astonishment and then the dismay that for an instant she could not conceal were quickly driven away, and her face assumed an expression of affable welcome. But she was evidently at a loss for words. It was not unnatural if Gilbert felt a certain embarrassment and I was too busy preventing myself from laughing to think of anything to say. Mrs Fowler alone kept perfectly calm.

'I know you'll like him, Marion. There's no one enjoys good food more than he does.' She turned to the young man. 'Marion's dinners are famous.'

'I know,' he beamed.

Mrs Tower made some quick rejoinder and we went downstairs. I shall not soon forget the exquisite comedy of that meal. Mrs Tower could not make up her mind whether the pair of them were playing a practical joke on her or whether Jane by wilfully concealing her fiancé's age had hoped to make her look foolish. But then Jane never jested and she was incapable of doing a malicious thing. Mrs Tower was amazed, exasperated, and perplexed. But she had recovered her self-control, and for nothing would she have forgotten that she was a perfect hostess whose duty it was to make her party go. She talked vivaciously; but I wondered if Gilbert Napier saw how hard and vindictive was the expression of her eyes behind the mask of friendliness that she turned to him. She was measuring him. She was seeking to delve into the secret of his soul. I could see that she was in a passion, for under her rouge her cheeks glowed with an angry red.

'You've got a very high colour, Marion,' said Jane, looking at her amiably through her great round spectacles.

'I dressed in a hurry. I dare say I put on too much rouge.'

'Oh, is it rouge? I thought it was natural. Otherwise I shouldn't have mentioned it.' She gave Gilbert a shy little smile. 'You know, Marion and I were at school together. You would never think it to look at us now, would you? But of course I've lived a very quiet life.'

I do not know what she meant by these remarks; it was almost incredible that she made them in complete simplicity; but anyhow they goaded Mrs Tower to such a fury that she flung her own vanity to the winds. She smiled brightly.

'We shall neither of us see fifty again, Jane,' she said.

If the observation was meant to discomfit the widow it failed.

'Gilbert says I mustn't acknowledge to more than forty-nine for his sake,' she answered blandly.

Mrs Tower's hands trembled slightly, but she found a retort.

'There is of course a certain disparity of age between you,' she smiled.

'Twenty-seven years,' said Jane. 'Do you think it's too much? Gilbert says I'm very young for my age. I told you I shouldn't like to marry a man with one foot in the grave.'

I was really obliged to laugh and Gilbert laughed too. His laughter was frank and boyish. It looked as though he were amused at everything Jane said. But Mrs Tower was almost at the end of her tether and I was afraid that unless relief came she would for once forget that she was a woman of the world. I came to the rescue as best I could.

'I suppose you're very busy buying your trousseau,' I said.

'No. I wanted to get my things from the dressmaker in Liverpool I've been to ever since I was first married. But Gilbert won't let me. He's very masterful, and of course he has wonderful taste.'

She looked at him with a little affectionate smile, demurely, as though she were a girl of seventeen.

Mrs Tower went quite pale under her make-up.

'We're going to Italy for our honeymoon. Gilbert has never had a chance of studying Renaissance architecture and of course it's important for an architect to see things for himself. And we shall stop in Paris on the way and get my clothes there.'

'Do you expect to be away long?'

'Gilbert has arranged with his office to stay away for six months. It will be such a treat for him, won't it? You see, he's never had more than a fortnight's holiday before.'

'Why not?' asked Mrs Tower in a tone that no effort of will could prevent from being icy.

'He's never been able to afford it, poor dear.'

'Ah!' said Mrs Tower, and into the exclamation put volumes.

Coffee was served and the ladies went upstairs. Gilbert and I began to talk in the desultory way in which men talk who have nothing whatever to say to one another; but in two minutes a note was brought in to me by the butler. It was from Mrs Tower and ran as follows:

Come upstairs quickly and then go as soon as you can. Take him with you. Unless I have it out with Jane at once I shall have a fit.

I told a facile lie.

'Mrs Tower has a headache and wants to go to bed. I think if you don't mind we'd better clear out.'

'Certainly,' he answered.

We went upstairs and five minutes later were on the doorstep. I called a taxi and offered the young man a lift.

'No, thanks,' he answered. 'I'll just walk to the corner and jump on a bus.'

Mrs Tower sprang to the fray as soon as she heard the front door close behind us.

'Are you crazy, Jane?' she cried.

'Not more than most people who don't habitually live in a lunatic asylum, I trust,' Jane answered blandly.

'May I ask why you're going to marry this young man?' asked Mrs Tower with formidable politeness.

'Partly because he won't take no for an answer. He's asked me five times. I grew positively tired of refusing him.'

'And why do you think he's so anxious to marry you?'

'I amuse him.'

Mrs Tower gave an exclamation of annoyance.

'He's an unscrupulous rascal. I very nearly told him so to his face.'

'You would have been wrong, and it wouldn't have been very polite.'

'He's penniless and you're rich. You can't be such a besotted fool as not to see that he's marrying you for your money.'

Jane remained perfectly composed. She observed her sister-in-law's agitation with detachment.

'I don't think he is, you know,' she replied. 'I think he's very fond of me.'

'You're an old woman, Jane.'

'I'm the same age as you are, Marion,' she smiled.

'I've never let myself go. I'm very young for my age. No one would think I was more than forty. But even I wouldn't dream of marrying a boy twenty years younger than myself.'

'Twenty-seven,' corrected Jane.

'Do you mean to tell me that you can bring yourself to believe that it's possible for a young man to care for a woman old enough to be his mother?'

'I've lived very much in the country for many years. I dare say there's a great deal about human nature that I don't know. They tell me there's a man called Freud, an Austrian, I believe . . .'

But Mrs Tower interrupted her without any politeness at all.

'Don't be ridiculous, Jane. It's so undignified. It's so ungraceful. I always thought you were a sensible woman. Really you're the last person I should ever have thought likely to fall in love with a boy.'

'But I'm not in love with him. I've told him that. Of course I like him very much or I wouldn't think of marrying him. I thought it only fair to tell him quite plainly what my feelings were towards him.'

Mrs Tower gasped. The blood rushed to her head and her breathing oppressed her. She had no fan, but she seized the evening paper and vigorously fanned herself with it.

'If you're not in love with him why do you want to marry him?'

'I've been a widow a very long time and I've led a very quiet life. I thought I'd like a change.'

'If you want to marry just to be married why don't you marry a man of your own age?'

'No man of my own age has asked me five times. In fact no man of my own age has asked me at all.'

Jane chuckled as she answered. It drove Mrs Tower to the final pitch of frenzy.

'Don't laugh, Jane, I won't have it. I don't think you can be right in your mind. It's dreadful.'

It was altogether too much for her and she burst into tears. She knew that at her age it was fatal to cry, her eyes would be swollen for twenty-four hours and she would look a sight. But there was no help for it. She wept. Jane remained perfectly calm. She looked at Marion through her large spectacles and reflectively smoothed the lap of her black silk dress.

'You're going to be so dreadfully unhappy,' Mrs Tower sobbed, dabbing her eyes cautiously in the hope that the black on her lashes would not smudge.

'I don't think so, you know,' Jane answered in those equable, mild tones of hers, as if there were a little smile behind the words. 'We've talked it over very thoroughly. I always think I'm a very easy person to live with. I think I shall make Gilbert very happy and comfortable. He's never had anyone to look after him properly. We're only marrying after mature consideration. And we've decided that if either of us wants his liberty the other will place no obstacles in the way of his getting it.'

Mrs Tower had by now recovered herself sufficiently to make a cutting remark.

'How much has he persuaded you to settle on him?'

'I wanted to settle a thousand a year on him, but he wouldn't hear of it. He was quite upset when I made the suggestion. He says he can earn quite enough for his own needs.'

'He's more cunning than I thought,' said Mrs Tower acidly.

Jane paused a little and looked at her sister-in-law with kindly but resolute eyes.

'You see, my dear, it's different for you,' she said. 'You've never been so very much a widow, have you?'

Mrs Tower looked at her. She blushed a little. She even felt slightly uncomfortable. But of course Jane was much too simple to intend an innuendo. Mrs Tower gathered herself together with dignity.

'I'm so upset that I really must go to bed,' she said. 'We'll resume the conversation tomorrow morning.'

'I'm afraid that won't be very convenient, dear. Gilbert and I are going to get the licence tomorrow morning.'

Mrs Tower threw up her hands in a gesture of dismay, but she found nothing more to say.

The marriage took place at a registrar's office. Mrs Tower and I were the witnesses. Gilbert in a smart blue suit looked absurdly young and he was obviously nervous. It is a trying moment for any man. But Jane kept her admirable composure. She might have been in the habit of marrying as frequently as a woman of fashion. Only a slight colour on her cheeks suggested that beneath her calm was some faint excitement. It is a thrilling moment for any woman. She wore a very full dress of silvery grey velvet in the cut of which I recognized the hand of the dressmaker in Liverpool (evidently a widow of unimpeachable character) who had made her gowns for so many years; but she had so far succumbed to the frivolity of the occasion as to wear a large picture hat covered with blue ostrich feathers. Her gold-rimmed spectacles made it extraordinarily grotesque. When the ceremony was over the registrar (somewhat taken aback, I thought, by the difference of age between the pair he was marrying) shook hands with her, tendering his strictly official congratulations; and the bridegroom, blushing slightly, kissed her. Mrs Tower, resigned but implacable, kissed her; and then the bride looked at me expectantly. It was evidently fitting that I should kiss her too. I did. I confess that I felt a little shy as we walked out of the registrar's office past loungers who waited cynically to see the bridal pairs, and it was with relief that I stepped into Mrs Tower's car. We drove to Victoria Station, for the happy couple were to go over to Paris by the two o'clock train, and Jane had insisted that the wedding-breakfast should be eaten at the station restaurant. She said it always made her nervous not to be on the platform in good time. Mrs Tower, present only from a strong sense of family duty, was able to do little to make the party go off well; she ate nothing (for which I could not blame her, since the food was execrable, and anyway I hate champagne at luncheon) and talked in a strained voice. But Jane went through the menu conscientiously.

'I always think one should make a hearty meal before starting out on a journey,' she said.

We saw them off, and I drove Mrs Tower back to her house.

'How long do you give it?' she said. 'Six months?'

'Let's hope for the best,' I smiled.

'Don't be so absurd. There can be no "best". You don't think he's marrying her for anything but her money, do you? Of course it can't last. My only hope is that she won't have to go through as much suffering as she deserves.'

I laughed. The charitable words were spoken in such a tone as to leave me in small doubt of Mrs Tower's meaning.

'Well, if it doesn't last you'll have the consolation of saying: "I told you so",' I said.

'I promise you I'll never do that.'

'Then you'll have the satisfaction of congratulating yourself on your self-control in not saying: "I told you so".'

'She's old and dowdy and dull.'

'Are you sure she's dull?' I said. 'It's true she doesn't say very much, but when she says anything it's very much to the point.'

'I've never heard her make a joke in my life.'

I was once more in the Far East when Gilbert and Jane returned from their honeymoon and this time I remained away for nearly two years. Mrs Tower was a bad correspondent and though I sent her an occasional picture-postcard I received no news from her. But I met her within a week of my return to London; I was dining out and found that I was seated next to her. It was an immense party, I think we were four-and-twenty, like the blackbirds in the pie, and, arriving somewhat late, I was too confused by the crowd in which I found myself to notice who was there. But when we sat down, looking round the long table I saw that a good many of my fellow-guests were well known to the public from their photographs in the illustrated papers. Our hostess had a weakness for the persons technically known as celebrities and this was an unusually brilliant gathering. When Mrs Tower and I had exchanged the conventional remarks that two people make when they have not seen one another for a couple of years I asked about Jane.

'She's very well,' said Mrs Tower with a certain dryness.

'How has the marriage turned out?'

Mrs Tower paused a little and took a salted almond from the dish in front of her.

'It appears to be quite a success.'

'You were wrong then?'

'I said it wouldn't last and I still say it won't last. It's contrary to human nature.'

'Is she happy?'

'They're both happy.'

'I suppose you don't see very much of them.'

'At first I saw quite a lot of them. But now . . .' Mrs Tower pursed her lips a little. 'Jane is becoming very grand.'

'What *do* you mean?' I laughed.

'I think I should tell you that she's here tonight.'

'Here?'

I was startled. I looked round the table again. Our hostess was a delightful and an entertaining woman, but I could not imagine that she would be likely to invite to a dinner such as this the elderly and dowdy wife of an obscure architect. Mrs Tower saw my perplexity and was shrewd enough to see what was in my mind. She smiled thinly.

'Look on the left of our host.'

I looked. Oddly enough the woman who sat there had by her fantastic appearance attracted my attention the moment I was ushered into the crowded drawing-room. I thought I noticed a gleam of recognition in her eye, but to the best of my belief I had never seen her before. She was not a young woman, for her hair was iron-grey; it was cut very short and clustered thickly round her well-shaped head in tight curls. She made no attempt at youth, for she was conspicuous in that gathering by using neither lipstick, rouge, nor powder. Her face, not a particularly handsome one, was red and weather-beaten; but because it owed nothing to artifice had a naturalness that was very pleasing. It contrasted oddly with the whiteness of her shoulders. They were really magnificent. A woman of thirty might have been proud of them. But her dress was extraordinary. I had not often seen anything more audacious. It was cut very low, with short skirts, which were then the fashion, in black and yellow; it had almost the effect of fancy-dress and yet so became her that though on anyone else it would have been outrageous, on her it had the inevitable simplicity of nature. And to complete the impression of an eccentricity in which there was no pose and of an extravagance in which there was no ostentation she wore, attached by a broad black ribbon, a single eyeglass.

'You're not going to tell me *that* is your sister-in-law,' I gasped.

'That is Jane Napier,' said Mrs Tower icily.

At that moment she was speaking. Her host was turned towards her with an anticipatory smile. A baldish white-haired man, with a sharp, intelligent face, who sat on her left, was leaning forward eagerly, and the couple who sat opposite, ceasing to talk with one another, listened intently. She said her say and they all, with a sudden movement, threw themselves back in their chairs and burst into vociferous laughter. From the other side of the table a man addressed Mrs Tower: I recognized a famous statesman.

'Your sister-in-law has made another joke, Mrs Tower,' he said.

Mrs Tower smiled.

'She's priceless, isn't she?'

'Let me have a long drink of champagne and then for heaven's sake tell me all about it,' I said.

Well, this is how I gathered it had all happened. At the beginning of their honeymoon Gilbert took Jane to various dressmakers in Paris and he made no objection to her choosing a number of 'gowns' after her own heart; but he persuaded her to have a 'frock' or two made according to his own design. It appeared that he had a knack for that kind of work. He engaged a smart French maid. Jane had never had such a thing before. She did her own mending and when she wanted 'doing up' was in the habit of ringing for the housemaid. The dresses Gilbert had devised were very different from anything she had worn before; but he had been careful not to go too far too quickly, and because it pleased him she persuaded herself, though not without misgivings, to wear them in preference to those she had chosen herself. Of course she could not wear them with the voluminous petticoats she had been in the habit of using, and these, though it cost her an anxious moment, she discarded.

'Now if you please,' said Mrs Tower, with something very like a sniff of disapproval, 'she wears nothing but thin silk tights. It's a wonder to me she doesn't catch her death of cold at her age.'

Gilbert and the French maid taught her how to wear her clothes, and, unexpectedly enough, she was very quick at learning. The French maid was in raptures over Madame's arms and shoulders. It was a scandal not to show anything so fine.

'Wait a little, Alphonsine,' said Gilbert. 'The next lot of clothes I design for Madame we'll make the most of her.'

The spectacles of course were dreadful. No one could look really well in gold-rimmed spectacles. Gilbert tried some with tortoiseshell rims. He shook his head.

'They'd look all right on a girl,' he said. 'You're too old to wear spectacles, Jane.' Suddenly he had an inspiration. 'By George, I've got it. You must wear an eyeglass.'

'Oh, Gilbert, I couldn't.'

She looked at him and his excitement, the excitement of the artist, made her smile. He was so sweet to her she wanted to do what she could to please him.

'I'll try,' she said.

When they went to an optician and, suited with the right size, she placed an eyeglass jauntily in her eye Gilbert clapped his hands. There and then, before the astonished shopman, he kissed her on both cheeks.

'You look wonderful,' he cried.

So they went down to Italy and spent happy months studying Renaissance and Baroque architecture. Jane not only grew accustomed to her changed appearance, but found she liked it. At first she was a little shy when she went into the dining-room of an hotel and people turned round to stare at her, no one had ever raised an eyelid to look at her before, but presently she found that the sensation was not disagreeable. Ladies came up to her and asked her where she got her dress.

'Do you like it?' she answered demurely. 'My husband designed it for me.'

'I should like to copy it if you don't mind.'

Jane had certainly for many years lived a very quiet life, but she was by no means lacking in the normal instincts of her sex. She had her answer ready.

'I'm so sorry, but my husband's very particular and he won't hear of anyone copying my frocks. He wants me to be unique.'

She had an idea that people would laugh when she said this, but they didn't; they merely answered:

'Oh, of course I quite understand. You *are* unique.'

But she saw them making mental notes of what she wore, and for some reason this quite 'put her about'. For once in her life that she wasn't wearing what everybody else did, she reflected, she didn't see why everybody else should want to wear what she did.

'Gilbert,' said she, quite sharply for her, 'next time you're designing dresses for me I wish you'd design things that people *can't* copy.'

'The only way to do that is to design things that only you can wear.'

'Can't you do that?'

'Yes, if you'll do something for me.'

'What is it?'

'Cut off your hair.'

I think this was the first time that Jane jibbed. Her hair was long and thick and as a girl she had been quite vain of it; to cut it off was a very drastic proceeding. This really was burning her boats behind her. In her case it was not the first step that cost so much, it was the last; but she took it ('I know Marion will think me a perfect fool, and I shall *never* be able to go to Liverpool again,' she said), and when they passed through Paris on their way home Gilbert led her (she felt quite sick, her heart was beating so fast) to the best hairdresser in the world. She came out of this shop with a jaunty, saucy, impudent head of crisp grey curls. Pygmalion had finished his fantastic masterpiece: Galatea was come to life.

'Yes,' I said, 'but that isn't enough to explain why Jane is here tonight amid this crowd of duchesses, Cabinet Ministers, and suchlike; nor why she is sitting on one side of her host with an Admiral of the Fleet on the other.'

'Jane is a humorist,' said Mrs Tower. 'Didn't you see them all laughing at what she said?'

There was no doubt now of the bitterness in Mrs Tower's heart.

'When Jane wrote and told me they were back from their honeymoon I thought I must ask them both to dinner. I didn't much like the idea, but I felt it had to be done. I knew the party would be deadly and I wasn't going to sacrifice any of the people who really mattered. On the other hand I didn't want Jane to think I hadn't any nice friends. You know I never have more than eight, but on this occasion I thought it would make things go better if I had twelve. I'd been too busy to see Jane until the evening of the party. She kept us all waiting a little–that was Gilbert's cleverness–and at last she sailed in. You could have knocked me down with a feather. She made the rest of the women look dowdy and provincial. She made me feel like a painted old trollop.'

Mrs Tower drank a little champagne.

'I wish I could describe the frock to you. It would have been quite impossible on anyone else; on her it was perfect. And the eyeglass! I'd known her for thirty-five years and I'd never seen her without spectacles.'

'But you knew she had a good figure.'

'How should I? I'd never seen her except in the clothes you first saw her in. Did *you* think she had a good figure? She seemed not to be unconscious of the sensation she made but to take it as a matter of course. I thought of my dinner and I heaved a sigh of relief. Even if she was a little heavy in hand, with that appearance it didn't so very much matter. She was sitting at the other end of the table and I heard a good deal of laughter. I was glad to think that the other people were playing up well; but after dinner I was a good deal taken aback when no less than three men came up to me and told me that my sister-in-law was priceless, and did I think she would allow them to call on her? I didn't quite know whether I was standing on my head or my heels. Twenty-four hours later our hostess of tonight rang me up and said she had heard my sister-in-law was in London and she was priceless and would I ask her to luncheon to meet her? She has an infallible instinct, that woman: in a month everyone was talking about Jane. I am here tonight, not because I've known our hostess for twenty years and have asked her to dinner a hundred times, but because I'm Jane's sister-in-law.'

Poor Mrs Tower. The position was galling, and though I could not help being amused, for the tables were turned on her with a vengeance, I felt that she deserved my sympathy.

'People never can resist those who make them laugh,' I said, trying to console her.

'She never makes *me* laugh.'

Once more from the top of the table I heard a guffaw and guessed that Jane had said another amusing thing.

'Do you mean to say that you are the only person who doesn't think her funny?' I asked, smiling.

'Had it struck *you* that she was a humorist?'

'I'm bound to say it hadn't.'

'She says just the same things as she's said for the last thirty-five years, I laugh when I see everyone else does because I don't want to seem a perfect fool, but I am not amused.'

'Like Queen Victoria,' I said.

It was a foolish jest and Mrs Tower was quite right sharply to tell me so. I tried another tack.

'Is Gilbert here?' I asked, looking down the table.

'Gilbert was asked because she won't go out without him, but tonight he's at a dinner of the Architects' Institute or whatever it's called.'

'I'm dying to renew my acquaintance with her.'

'Go and talk to her after dinner. She'll ask you to her Tuesdays.'

'Her Tuesdays?'

'She's at home every Tuesday evening. You'll meet there everyone you ever heard of. They're the best parties in London. She's done in one year what I've failed to do in twenty.'

'But what you tell me is really miraculous. How has it been done?'

Mrs Tower shrugged her handsome but adipose shoulders.

'I shall be glad if you'll tell me,' she replied.

After dinner I tried to make my way to the sofa on which Jane was sitting, but I was intercepted and it was not till a little later that my hostess came up to me and said:

'I must introduce you to the star of my party. Do you know Jane Napier? She's priceless. She's much more amusing than your comedies.'

I was taken up to the sofa. The admiral who had been sitting beside her at dinner was with her still. He showed no sign of moving and Jane, shaking hands with me, introduced me to him.

'Do you know Sir Reginald Frobisher?'

We began to chat. It was the same Jane as I had known before, perfectly simple, homely and unaffected, but her fantastic appearance certainly gave a peculiar savour to what she said. Suddenly I found myself shaking with laughter. She had made a remark, sensible and to the point, but not in the least witty, which her manner of saying and the bland look she gave me through her eyeglass made perfectly irresistible. I felt light-hearted and buoyant. When I left her she said to me:

'If you've got nothing better to do, come and see us on Tuesday evening. Gilbert will be so glad to see you.'

'When he's been a month in London he'll know that he *can* have nothing better to do,' said the admiral.

So, on Tuesday but rather late, I went to Jane's. I confess I was a little surprised at the company. It was quite a remarkable collection of writers, painters and politicians, actors, great ladies and great beauties: Mrs Tower was right, it was a grand party; I had seen nothing like it in London since Stafford House was sold. No particular entertainment was provided. The refreshments were adequate without being luxurious. Jane in her quiet way seemed to be enjoying herself; I could not see that she took a great deal of trouble with her guests, but they seemed to like being there and the gay, pleasant party did not break up till two in the morning. After that I saw much of her. I not only went often to her house, but seldom went out to luncheon or to dinner without meeting her. I am an amateur of humour and I sought to discover in what lay her peculiar gift. It was impossible to repeat anything she said, for the fun, like certain wines, would not travel. She had no gift for epigram. She never made a brilliant repartee. There was no malice in her remarks nor sting in her rejoinders. There are those who think that impropriety, rather than brevity, is the soul of wit; but she never said a thing that could have brought a blush to a Victorian cheek. I think her humour was unconscious and I am sure it was unpremeditated. It flew like a butterfly from flower to flower, obedient only to its own caprice and pursuivant of neither method nor intention. It depended on the way she spoke and on the way she looked. Its subtlety gained by the flaunting and extravagant appearance that Gilbert had achieved for her; but her appearance was only an element in it. Now of course she was the fashion and people laughed if she but opened her mouth. They no longer wondered that Gilbert had married a wife so much older than himself. They saw that Jane was a woman with whom age did not count. They thought him a devilish lucky young fellow. The admiral quoted Shakespeare to me: 'Age cannot wither her, nor custom stale her infinite variety.' Gilbert was delighted with her success. As I came to know him better I grew to like him. It was quite evident that he was neither a rascal nor a fortune-hunter. He was not only immensely proud of Jane but genuinely devoted to her. His kindness to her was touching. He was a very unselfish and sweet-tempered young man.

'Well, what do you think of Jane now?' he said to me once, with boyish triumph.

'I don't know which of you is more wonderful,' I said. 'You or she.'

'Oh, I'm nothing.'

'Nonsense. You don't think I'm such a fool as not to see that it's you, and you only, who've made Jane what she is.'

'My only merit is that I saw what was there when it wasn't obvious to the naked eye,' he answered.

'I can understand your seeing that she had in her the possibility of that remarkable appearance, but how in the world have you made her into a humorist?'

'But I always thought the things she said a perfect scream. She was always a humorist.'

'You're the only person who ever thought so.'

Mrs Tower, not without magnanimity, acknowledged that she had been mistaken in Gilbert. She grew quite attached to him. But notwithstanding appearances she never faltered in her opinion that the marriage could not last. I was obliged to laugh at her.

'Why, I've never seen such a devoted couple,' I said.

'Gilbert is twenty-seven now. It's just the time for a pretty girl to come along. Did you notice the other evening at Jane's that pretty little niece of Sir Reginald's? I thought Jane was looking at them both with a good deal of attention, and I wondered to myself.'

'I don't believe Jane fears the rivalry of any girl under the sun.'

'Wait and see,' said Mrs Tower.

'You gave it six months.'

'Well, now I give it three years.'

When anyone is very positive in an opinion it is only human nature to wish him proved wrong. Mrs Tower was really too cocksure. But such a satisfaction was not mine, for the end that she had always and confidently predicted to the ill-assorted match did in point of fact come. Still, the fates seldom give us what we want in the way we want it, and though Mrs Tower could flatter herself that she had been right, I think after all she would sooner have been wrong. For things did not happen at all in the way she expected.

One day I received an urgent message from her and fortunately went to see her at once. When I was shown into the room Mrs Tower rose from her chair and came towards me with the stealthy swiftness of a leopard stalking his prey. I saw that she was excited.

'Jane and Gilbert have separated,' she said.

'Not really? Well, you were right after all.'

Mrs Tower looked at me with an expression I could not understand.

'Poor Jane,' I muttered.

'Poor Jane!' she repeated, but in tones of such derision that I was dumbfounded.

She found some difficulty in telling me exactly what had occurred.

Gilbert had left her a moment before she leaped to the telephone to summon me. When he entered the room, pale and distraught, she saw at once that something terrible had happened. She knew what he was going to say before he said it.

'Marion, Jane has left me.'

She gave him a little smile and took his hand.

'I knew you'd behave like a gentleman. It would have been dreadful for her for people to think that *you* had left her.'

'I've come to you because I knew I could count on your sympathy.'

'Oh, I don't blame you, Gilbert,' said Mrs Tower, very kindly. 'It was bound to happen.'

He sighed.

'I suppose so. I couldn't hope to keep her always. She was too wonderful and I'm a perfectly commonplace fellow.'

Mrs Tower patted his hand. He was really behaving beautifully.

'And what's going to happen now?'

'Well, she's going to divorce me.'

'Jane always said she'd put no obstacle in your way if ever you wanted to marry a girl.'

'You don't think it's likely I should ever be willing to marry anyone else after being Jane's husband,' he answered.

Mrs Tower was puzzled.

'Of course you mean that *you've* left Jane.'

'I? That's the last thing I should ever do.'

'Then why is she divorcing you?'

'She's going to marry Sir Reginald Frobisher as soon as the decree is made absolute.'

Mrs Tower positively screamed. Then she felt so faint that she had to get her smelling salts.

'After all you've done for her?'

'I've done nothing for her.'

'Do you mean to say you're going to allow yourself to be made use of like that?'

'We arranged before we married that if either of us wanted his liberty the other should put no hindrance in the way.'

'But that was done on your account. Because you were twenty-seven years younger that she was.'

'Well, it's come in very useful for her,' he answered bitterly.

Mrs Tower expostulated, argued, and reasoned; but Gilbert insisted that no rules applied to Jane, and he must do exactly what she wanted. He left Mrs Tower prostrate. It relieved her a good deal to give me a full account of this interview. It pleased her to see that I was as surprised as herself and if I was not so indignant with Jane as she was she ascribed that to the criminal lack of morality incident to my sex. She was still in a state of extreme agitation when the door was opened and the butler showed in—Jane herself. She was dressed in black and white as no doubt befitted her slightly ambiguous position, but in a dress so original and fantastic, in a hat so striking, that I positively gasped at the sight of her. But she was as ever bland and collected. She came forward to kiss Mrs Tower, but Mrs Tower withdrew herself with icy dignity.

'Gilbert has been here,' she said.

'Yes, I know,' smiled Jane. 'I told him to come and see you. I'm going to Paris tonight and I want you to be very kind to him while I'm away. I'm afraid just at first he'll be rather lonely and I shall feel more comfortable if I can count on your keeping an eye on him.'

Mrs Tower clasped her hands.

'Gilbert has just told me something that I can hardly bring myself to believe. He tells me that you're going to divorce him to marry Reginald Frobisher.'

'Don't you remember, before I married Gilbert you advised me to marry a man of my own age? The admiral is fifty-three.'

'But, Jane, you owe everything to Gilbert,' said Mrs Tower indignantly.

'You wouldn't exist without him. Without him to design your clothes, you'll be nothing.'

'Oh, he's promised to go on designing my clothes,' Jane answered blandly.

'No woman could want a better husband. He's always been kindness itself to you.'

'Oh, I know he's been sweet.'

'How *can* you be so heartless?'

'But I was never in love with Gilbert,' said Jane. 'I always told him that. I'm beginning to feel the need of the companionship of a man of my own age. I think I've probably been married to Gilbert long enough. The young have no conversation.' She paused a little and gave us both a charming smile. 'Of course I shan't lose sight of Gilbert. I've arranged that with Reginald. The admiral has a niece that would just suit him. As soon as we're married we'll ask them to stay with us at Malta—you know that the admiral is to have the Mediterranean Command—and I shouldn't be at all surprised if they fell in love with one another.'

Mrs Tower gave a little sniff.

'And have you arranged with the admiral that if you want your liberty neither should put any hindrance in the way of the other?'

'I suggested it,' Jane answered with composure. 'But the admiral says he knows a good thing when he sees it and he won't want to marry anyone else, and if anyone wants to marry me—he has eight twelve-inch guns on his flagship and he'll discuss the matter at short range.' She gave us a look through her eyeglass which even the fear of Mrs Tower's wrath could not prevent me from laughing at. 'I think the admiral's a very passionate man.'

Mrs Tower gave me an angry frown.

'I never thought you funny, Jane,' she said. 'I never understood why people laughed at the things you said.'

'I never thought I was funny myself, Marion,' smiled Jane, showing her bright, regular teeth. 'I am glad to leave London before too many people come round to our opinion.'

'I wish you'd tell me the secret of your astonishing success,' I said.

She turned to me with that bland, homely look I knew so well.

'You know, when I married Gilbert and settled in London and people began to laugh at what I said no one was more surprised than I was. I'd said the same things for thirty years and no one ever saw anything to laugh at. I thought it must be my clothes or my bobbed hair or my eyeglass. Then I discovered it was because I spoke the truth. It was so unusual that people thought it humorous. One of these days someone else will discover the secret and when people habitually tell the truth of course there'll be nothing funny in it.'

'And why am I the only person not to think it funny?' asked Mrs Tower.

Jane hesitated a little as though she were honestly searching for a satisfactory explanation.

'Perhaps you don't know the truth when you see it, Marion dear,' she answered in her mild good-natured way.

It certainly gave her the last word. I felt that Jane would always have the last word. She *was* priceless.

Footprints
in the Jungle

◆

There is no place in Malaya that has more charm than Tanah Merah. It lies on the sea, and the sandy shore is fringed with casuarinas. The government offices are still in the old Raad Huis that the Dutch built when they owned the land, and on the hill stand the grey ruins of the fort by aid of which the Portuguese maintained their hold over the unruly natives. Tanah Merah has a history and in the vast labyrinthine houses of the Chinese merchants, backing on the sea so that in the cool of the evening they may sit in their loggias and enjoy the salt breeze, families dwell that have been settled in the country for three centuries. Many have forgotten their native language and hold intercourse with one another in Malay and pidgin English. The imagination lingers here gratefully, for in the Federated Malay States the only past is within the memory for the most part of the fathers of living men.

Tanah Merah was for long the busiest mart of the Middle East and its harbour was crowded with shipping when the clipper and the junk still sailed the China seas. But now it is dead. It has the sad and romantic air of all places that have once been of importance and live now on the recollection of a vanished grandeur. It is a sleepy little town and strangers that come to it, losing their native energy, insensibly drop into its easy and lethargic ways. Successive rubber booms bring it no prosperity and the ensuing slumps hasten its decay.

The European quarter is very silent. It is trim and neat and clean. The houses of the white men—government servants and agents of companies—stand round an immense padang, agreeable and roomy bungalows shaded by great cassias, and the padang is vast and green and well cared for, like the lawn of a cathedral close, and indeed there is in the aspect of this corner of Tanah Merah something quiet and delicately secluded that reminds you of the precincts of Canterbury.

The club faces the sea; it is a spacious but shabby building; it has an air of neglect and when you enter you feel that you intrude. It gives you the impression that it is closed really, for alterations and repairs, and that you have taken indiscreet advantage of an open door to go where you are not wanted. In the morning you may find there a couple of planters who have come in from their estates on business and are drinking a gin-sling before starting back again; and latish in the afternoon a lady or two may perhaps be seen looking with a furtive air through old numbers of the *Illustrated London News*. At nightfall a few men saunter in and sit about the billiard-room watching the play and drinking sukas. But on Wednesdays there is a little more animation. On that day the gramophone is set going in the large room upstairs and people come in from the surrounding country to dance. There are sometimes no less than a dozen couples and it is even possible to make up two tables of bridge.

It was on one of these occasions that I met the Cartwrights. I was staying with a man called Gaze who was head of the police and he came into the billiard-room, where I was sitting, and asked me if I would make up a four. The Cartwrights were planters and they came in to Tanah Merah on Wednesdays because it gave their girl a chance of a little fun. They were very nice people, said Gaze, quiet and unobtrusive, and played a very pleasant game of bridge. I followed Gaze into the card-room and was introduced to them. They were already seated at a table and Mrs Cartwright was shuffling the cards. It inspired me with confidence to see the competent way in which she did it. She took half the pack in each hand, and her hands were large and strong, deftly inserted the corners of one half under the corners of the other, and with a click and a neat bold gesture cascaded the cards together.

It had all the effect of a conjuring trick. The card-player knows that it can be done perfectly only after incessant practice. He can be fairly sure that anyone who can so shuffle a pack of cards loves cards for their own sake.

'Do you mind if my husband and I play together?' asked Mrs Cartwright. 'It's no fun for us to win one another's money.'

'Of course not.'

We cut for deal and Gaze and I sat down.

Mrs Cartwright drew an ace and while she dealt, quickly and neatly, chatted with Gaze of local affairs. But I was aware that she took stock of me. She looked shrewd, but good-natured.

She was a woman somewhere in the fifties (though in the East, where people age quickly, it is difficult to tell their ages), with white hair very untidily arranged, and a constant gesture with her was an impatient movement of the hand to push back a long wisp of hair that kept falling over her forehead. You wondered why she did not, by the use of a hairpin or two, save herself so much trouble. Her blue eyes were large, but pale and a little tired; her face was lined and sallow; I think it was her mouth that gave it the expression which I felt was characteristic of caustic but tolerant irony. You saw that here was a woman who knew her mind and was never afraid to speak it. She was a chatty player (which some people object to strongly, but which does not disconcert me, for I do not see why you should behave at the card-table as though you were at a memorial service) and it was soon apparent that she had an effective knack of badinage. It was pleasantly acid, but it was amusing enough to be offensive only to a fool. If now and then she uttered a remark so sarcastic that you wanted all your sense of humour to see the fun in it, you could not but quickly see that she was willing to take as much as she gave. Her large, thin mouth broke into a dry smile and her eyes shone brightly when by a lucky chance you brought off a repartee that turned the laugh against her.

I thought her a very agreeable person. I liked her frankness. I liked her quick wit. I liked her plain face. I never met a woman who obviously cared so little how she looked. It was not only her head that was untidy, everything about her was slovenly; she wore a high-necked silk blouse, but for coolness had unbuttoned the top buttons and showed a gaunt and withered neck; the blouse was crumpled and none too clean, for she smoked innumerable cigarettes and covered herself with ash. When she got up for a moment to speak to somebody I saw that her blue skirt was rather ragged at the hem and badly needed a brush, and she wore heavy, low-heeled boots. But none of this mattered. Everything she wore was perfectly in character.

And it was a pleasure to play bridge with her. She played very quickly, without hesitation, and she had not only knowledge but flair. Of course she knew Gaze's game, but I was a stranger and she soon took my measure. The team-work between her husband and herself was admirable; he was sound and cautious, but knowing him, she was able to be bold with assurance and brilliant with safety. Gaze was a player who founded a foolish optimism on the hope that his opponents would not have the sense to take advantage of his errors, and the pair of us were no match for the Cartwrights. We lost one rubber after another, and there was nothing to do but smile and look as if we liked it.

'I don't know what's the matter with the cards,' said Gaze at last, plaintively. 'Even when we have every card in the pack we go down.'

'It can't be anything to do with your play,' answered Mrs Cartwright, looking him full in the face with those pale blue eyes of hers, 'it must be bad luck pure and simple. Now if you hadn't had your hearts mixed up with your diamonds in that last hand you'd have saved the game.'

Gaze began to explain at length how the misfortune, which had cost us dear, occurred, but Mrs Cartwright, with a deft flick of the hand, spread out the cards in a great circle so that we should cut for deal. Cartwright looked at the time.

'This will have to be the last, my dear,' he said.

'Oh, will it?' She glanced at her watch and then called to a young man who was passing through the room. 'Oh, Mr Bullen, if you're going upstairs tell Olive that we shall be going in a few minutes.' She turned to me. 'It takes us the best part of an hour to get back to the estate and poor Theo has to be up at the crack of dawn.'

'Oh, well, we only come in once a week,' said Cartwright, 'and it's the one chance Olive gets of being gay and abandoned.'

I thought Cartwright looked tired and old. He was a man of middle height, with a bald, shiny head, a stubbly grey moustache, and gold-rimmed spectacles. He wore white ducks and a black-and-white tie. He was rather neat and you could see he took much more pains with his clothes than his untidy wife. He talked little, but it was plain that he enjoyed his wife's caustic humour and sometimes he made quite a neat retort. They were evidently very good friends. It was pleasing to see so solid and tolerant an affection between two people who were almost elderly and must have lived together for so many years.

It took but two hands to finish the rubber and we had just ordered a final gin and bitters when Olive came down.

'Do you really want to go already, Mumsey?' she asked.

Mrs Cartwright looked at her daughter with fond eyes.

'Yes, darling. It's nearly half past eight. It'll be ten before we get our dinner.'

'Damn our dinner,' said Olive gaily.

'Let her have one more dance before we go,' suggested Cartwright.

'Not one. You must have a good night's rest.'

Cartwright looked at Olive with a smile.

'If your mother has made up her mind, my dear, we may just as well give in without any fuss.'

'She's a determined woman,' said Olive, lovingly stroking her mother's wrinkled cheek.

Mrs Cartwright patted her daughter's hand, and kissed it.

Olive was not very pretty, but she looked extremely nice. She was nineteen or twenty, I suppose, and she had still the plumpness of her age; she would be more attractive when she had fined down a little. She had none of the determination that gave her mother's face so much character, but resembled her father; she had his dark eyes and slightly aquiline nose, and his look of rather weak good nature. It was plain that she was strong and healthy. Her cheeks were red and her eyes bright. She had a vitality that he had long since lost. She seemed to be the perfectly normal English girl, with high spirits, a great desire to enjoy herself, and an excellent temper.

When we separated, Gaze and I set out to walk to his house.

'What did you think of the Cartwrights?' he asked me.

'I liked them. They must be a great asset in a place like this.'

'I wish they came oftener. They live a very quiet life.'

'It must be dull for the girl. The father and mother seem very well satisfied with one another's company.'

'Yes, it's been a great success.'

'Olive is the image of her father, isn't she?'

Gaze gave me a sidelong glance.

'Cartwright isn't her father. Mrs Cartwright was a widow when he married her. Olive was born four months after her father's death.'

'Oh!'

I drew out the sound in order to put in it all I could of surprise, interest, and curiosity. But Gaze said nothing and we walked the rest of the way in silence. The boy was waiting at the door as we entered the house and after a last gin pahit we sat down to dinner.

At first Gaze was inclined to be talkative. Owing to the restriction of the output of rubber there had sprung up a considerable activity among the smugglers and it was part of his duty to circumvent their knavishness. Two junks had been captured that day and he was rubbing his hands over his success. The go-downs were full of confiscated rubber and in a little while it was going to be solemnly burnt. But presently he fell into silence and we finished without a word. The boys brought in coffee and brandy and we lit our cheroots. Gaze leaned back in his chair. He looked at me reflectively and then looked at his brandy. The boys had left the room and we were alone.

'I've known Mrs Cartwright for over twenty years,' he said slowly. 'She wasn't a bad-looking woman in those days. Always untidy, but when she was young it didn't seem to matter so much. It was rather attractive. She was married to a man called Bronson. Reggie Bronson. He was a planter. He was manager of an estate up in Selantan and I was stationed at Alor Lipis. It was a much smaller place than it is now; I don't suppose there were more than twenty people in the whole community, but they had a jolly little club, and we used to have a very good time. I remember the first time I met Mrs Bronson as though it was yesterday. There were no cars in those days and she and Bronson had ridden in on their bicycles. Of course then she didn't look so determined as she looks now. She was much thinner, she had a nice colour, and her eyes were very pretty—blue, you know—and she had a lot of dark hair. If she'd only taken more trouble with herself she'd have been rather stunning. As it was she was the best-looking woman there.'

I tried to construct in my mind a picture of what Mrs Cartwright—Mrs Bronson as she was then—looked like from what she was now and from Gaze's not very graphic description. In the solid woman, with her well-covered bones, who sat rather heavily at the bridge-table, I tried to see a slight young thing with buoyant movements and graceful, easy gestures. Her chin now was square and her nose decided, but the roundness of youth must have masked this: she must have been charming with a pink-and-white skin and her hair, carelessly dressed, brown and abundant. At that period she wore a long skirt, a tight waist, and a picture hat. Or did women in Malaya still wear the topees that you see in old numbers of the illustrated papers?

'I hadn't seen her for—oh, nearly twenty years,' Gaze went on. 'I knew she was living somewhere in the F.M.S., but it was a surprise when I took this job and came here to run across her in the club just as I had up in Selantan so many years before. Of course she's an elderly woman now and she's changed out of all recognition. It was rather a shock to see her with a grown-up daughter, it made me realize how the time had passed; I was a young fellow when I met her last and now, by Jingo, I'm due to retire on the age limit in two or three years. Bit thick, isn't it?'

Gaze, a rueful grin on his ugly face, looked at me with faint indignation, as though I could help the hurrying march of the years as they trod upon one another's heels.

'I'm no chicken myself,' I replied.

'You haven't lived out East all your life. It ages one before one's time. One's an elderly man at fifty and at fifty-five one's good for nothing but the scrap-heap.'

But I did not want Gaze to wander off into a disquisition on old age.

'Did you recognize Mrs Cartwright when you saw her again?' I asked.

'Well, I did and I didn't. At the first glance I thought I knew her, but couldn't quite place her. I thought perhaps she was someone I'd met on board ship when I was going on leave and had known only by sight. But the moment she spoke I remembered at once. I remembered the dry twinkle in her eyes and the crisp sound of her voice. There was something in her voice that seemed to mean: You're a bit of a damned fool, my lad, but you're not a bad sort and upon my soul I rather like you.'

'That's a good deal to read into the sound of a voice,' I smiled.

'She came up to me in the club and shook hands with me. "How do you do, Major Gaze? Do you remember me?" she said.

'"Of course I do."

'"A lot of water has passed under the bridge since we met last. We're none of us as young as we were. Have you seen Theo?"

'For a moment I couldn't think whom she meant. I suppose I looked rather stupid, because she gave a little smile, that chaffing smile that I knew so well, and explained.

'"I married Theo, you know. It seemed the best thing to do. I was lonely and he wanted it."

'"I heard you married him," I said. "I hope you've been very happy."

'"Oh, very. Theo's a perfect duck. He'll be here in a minute. He'll be so glad to see you."

'I wondered. I should have thought I was the last man Theo would wish to see. I shouldn't have thought she would wish it very much either. But women are funny.'

'Why shouldn't she wish to see you?' I asked.

'I'm coming to that later,' said Gaze. 'Then Theo turned up. I don't know why I call him Theo; I never called him anything but Cartwright, I never thought of him as anything but Cartwright. Theo was a shock. You know what he looks like now; I remembered him as a curly-headed youngster, very fresh and clean-looking. He was always neat and dapper, he had a good figure, and he held himself well, like a man who's used to taking a lot of exercise. Now I come to think of it he wasn't bad-looking, not in a big, massive way, but graceful, you know, and lithe. When I saw this bowed, cadaverous, bald-headed old buffer with spectacles I could hardly believe my eyes. I shouldn't have known him from Adam. He seemed pleased to see me, at least, interested; he wasn't effusive, but he'd always been on the quiet side and I didn't expect him to be.

'"Are you surprised to find us here?" he asked me.

'"Well, I hadn't the faintest notion where you were."

'"We've kept track of your movements more or less. We've seen your name in the paper every now and then. You must come out one day and have a look at our place. We've been settled there a good many years, and I suppose we shall stay there till we go home for good. Have you ever been back to Alor Lipis?"

'"No, I haven't," I said.

'"It was a nice little place. I'm told it's grown. I've never been back."

'"It hasn't got the pleasantest recollections for us," said Mrs Cartwright.

'I asked them if they'd have a drink and we called the boy. I dare say you noticed that Mrs Cartwright likes her liquor; I don't mean that she gets tight or anything like that, but she drinks her stengah like a man. I couldn't help looking at them with a certain amount of curiosity. They seemed perfectly happy; I gathered that they hadn't done at all badly, and I found out later that they were quite well off. They had a very nice car, and when they went on leave they denied themselves nothing. They were on the best of terms with one another. You know how jolly it is to see two people who've been married a great many years obviously better pleased with their own company than anyone else's. Their marriage had evidently been a great success. And they were both of them devoted to Olive and very proud of her. Theo especially.'

'Although she was only his step-daughter?' I said.

'Although she was only his step-daughter,' answered Gaze. 'You'd think that she would have taken his name. But she hadn't. She called him Daddy, of course, he was the only father she'd ever known, but she signed her letters, Olive Bronson.'

'What was Bronson like, by the way?'

'Bronson? He was a great big fellow, very hearty, with a loud voice and a bellowing laugh, beefy, you know, and a fine athlete. There was not very much to him, but he was as straight as a die. He had a red face and red hair. Now I come to think of it I remember that I never saw a man sweat as much as he did. Water just poured off him, and when he played tennis he always used to bring a towel on the court with him.'

'It doesn't sound very attractive.'

'He was a handsome chap. He was always fit. He was keen on that. He hadn't much to talk about but rubber and games, tennis, you know, and golf and shooting; and I don't suppose he read a book from year's end to year's end. He was the typical public-school boy. He was about thirty-five when I first knew him, but he had the mind of a boy of eighteen. You know how many fellows when they come out East seem to stop growing.'

I did indeed. One of the most disconcerting things to the traveller is to see stout, middle-aged gentlemen, with bald heads, speaking and acting like schoolboys. You might almost think that no idea has entered their heads since they first passed through the Suez Canal. Though married and the fathers of children, and perhaps in control of a large business, they continue to look upon life from the standpoint of the sixth form.

'But he was no fool,' Gaze went on. 'He knew his work from A to Z. His estate was one of the best managed in the country and he knew how to handle his labour. He was a damned good sort, and if he did get on your nerves a little you couldn't help liking him. He was generous with his money, and always ready to do anybody a good turn. That's how Cartwright happened to turn up in the first instance.'

'Did the Bronsons get on well together?'

'Oh, yes, I think so. I'm sure they did. He was good-natured and she was very jolly and gay. She was very outspoken, you know. She can be damned amusing when she likes even now, but there's generally a sting lurking in the joke; when she was a young woman and married to Bronson it was just pure fun. She had high spirits and liked having a good time. She never cared a hang what she said, but it went with her type, if you understand what I mean; there was something so open and frank and careless about her that you didn't care what she said to you. They seemed very happy.

'Their estate was about five miles from Alor Lipis. They had a trap and they used to drive in most evenings about five. Of course it was a very small community and men were in the majority. There were only about six women. The Bronsons were a god-send. They bucked things up the moment they arrived. We used to have very jolly times in that little club. I've often thought of them since and I don't know that on the whole I've ever enjoyed myself more than I did when I was stationed there. Between six and eight-thirty the club at Alor Lipis twenty years ago was about as lively a place as you could find between Aden and Yokohama.

'One day Mrs Bronson told us that they were expecting a friend to stay with them and a few days later they brought Cartwright along. It appeared that he was an old friend of Bronson's, they'd been at school together, Marlborough, or some place like that, and they'd first come out East on the same ship. Rubber had taken a toss and a lot of fellows had lost their jobs. Cartwright was one of them. He'd been out of work for the greater part of a year and he hadn't anything to fall back on. In those days planters were even worse paid than they are now and a man had to be very lucky to put by something for a rainy day. Cartwright had gone to Singapore. They all go there when there's a slump, you know. It's awful then, I've seen it; I've known of planters sleeping in the street because they hadn't the price of a night's lodging. I've known them stop strangers outside the Europe and ask for a dollar to get a meal, and I think Cartwright had had a pretty rotten time.

'At last he wrote to Bronson and asked him if he couldn't do something for him. Bronson asked him to come and stay till things got better, at least it would be free board and lodging, and Cartwright jumped at the chance, but Bronson had to send him the money to pay his railway fare. When Cartwright arrived at Alor Lipis he hadn't ten cents in his pocket. Bronson had a little money of his own, two or three hundred a year, I think, and though his salary had been cut, he'd kept his job, so that he was better off than most planters. When Cartwright came Mrs Bronson told him that he was to look upon the place as his home and stay as long as he liked.'

'It was very nice of her, wasn't it?' I remarked.

'Very.'

Gaze lit himself another cheroot and filled his glass. It was very still and but for the occasional croak of the chik-chak the silence was intense. We seemed to be alone in the tropical night and heaven only knows how far from the habitations of men. Gaze did not speak for so long that at last I was forced to say something.

'What sort of a man was Cartwright at that time?' I asked. 'Younger, of course, and you told me rather nice-looking; but in himself?'

'Well, to tell you the truth, I never paid much attention to him. He was pleasant and unassuming. He's very quiet now, as I dare say you noticed; well, he wasn't exactly lively then. But he was perfectly inoffensive. He was fond of reading and he played the piano rather nicely. You never minded having him about, he was never in the way, but you never bothered very much about him. He danced well and the women rather liked that, but he also played billiards quite decently and he wasn't bad at tennis. He fell into our little groove very naturally. I wouldn't say that he ever became wildly popular, but everyone liked him. Of course we were sorry for him, as one is for a man who's down and out, but there was nothing we could do, and, well, we just accepted him and then forgot that he hadn't always been there. He used to come in with the Bronsons every evening and pay for his drinks like everyone else, I suppose Bronson had lent him a bit of money for current expenses, and he was always very civil. I'm rather vague about him, because really he didn't make any particular impression on me; in the East one meets such a lot of people, and he seemed very much like anybody else. He did everything he could to get something to do, but he had no luck; the fact is, there were no jobs going, and sometimes he seemed rather depressed about it. He was with the Bronsons for over a year. I remember his saying to me once:

'"After all I can't live with them for ever. They've been most awfully good to me, but there are limits."

'"I should think the Bronsons would be very glad to have you," I said. "It's not particularly gay on a rubber estate, and as far as your food and drink go, it must make precious little difference if you're there or not."'

Gaze stopped once more and looked at me with a sort of hesitation.

'What's the matter?' I asked.

'I'm afraid I'm telling you this story very badly,' he said. 'I seem to be just rambling on. I'm not a damned novelist, I'm a policeman, and I'm just telling you the facts as I saw them at the time; and from my point of view all the circumstances are important; it's important, I mean, to realize what sort of people they were.'

'Of course. Fire away.'

'I remember someone, a woman, I think it was, the doctor's wife, asking Mrs Bronson if she didn't get tired sometimes of having a stranger in the house. You know, in places like Alor Lipis there isn't very much to talk about, and if you didn't talk about your neighbours there'd be nothing to talk about at all.'

'"Oh, no," she said, "Theo's no trouble." She turned to her husband, who was sitting there mopping his face. "We like having him, don't we?"

'"He's all right," said Bronson.

'"What does he do with himself all day long?"

'"Oh, I don't know," said Mrs Bronson. "He walks round the estate with Reggie sometimes, and he shoots a bit. He talks to me."

'"He's always glad to make himself useful," said Bronson. "The other day when I had a go of fever, he took over my work and I just lay in bed and had a good time."'

'Hadn't the Bronsons any children?' I asked.

'No,' Gaze answered. 'I don't know why, they could well have afforded it.'

Gaze leant back in his chair. He took off his glasses and wiped them. They were very strong and hideously distorted his eyes. Without them he wasn't so homely. The chik-chak on the ceiling gave its strangely human cry. It was like the cackle of an idiot child.

'Bronson was killed,' said Gaze suddenly.

'Killed?'

'Yes, murdered. I shall never forget that night. We'd been playing tennis, Mrs Bronson and the doctor's wife, Theo Cartwright and I; and then we played bridge. Cartwright had been off his game and when we sat down at the bridge-table Mrs Bronson said to him: "Well, Theo, if you play bridge as rottenly as you played tennis we shall lose our shirts."

'We'd just had a drink, but she called the boy and ordered another round.

'"Put that down your throat," she said to him, "and don't call without top honours and an outside trick."

'Bronson hadn't turned up, he'd cycled in to Kabulong to get the money to pay his coolies their wages and was to come along to the club when he got back. The Bronsons' estate was nearer Alor Lipis than it was to Kabulong, but Kabulong was a more important place commercially, and Bronson banked there.

'"Reggie can cut in when he turns up," said Mrs Bronson.

'"He's late, isn't he?" said the doctor's wife.

'"Very. He said he wouldn't get back in time for tennis, but would be here for a rubber. I have a suspicion that he went to the club at Kabulong instead of coming straight home and is having drinks, the ruffian."

'"Oh, well, he can put away a good many without their having much effect on him," I laughed.

'"He's getting fat, you know. He'll have to be careful."

'We sat by ourselves in the card-room and we could hear the crowd in the billiard-room talking and laughing. They were all on the merry side. It was getting on to Christmas Day and we were all letting ourselves go a little. There was going to be a dance on Christmas Eve.

'I remembered afterwards that when we sat down the doctor's wife asked Mrs Bronson if she wasn't tired.

'"Not a bit," she said. "Why should I be?".

'I didn't know why she flushed.

'"I was afraid the tennis might have been too much for you," said the doctor's wife.

'"Oh, no," answered Mrs Bronson, a trifle abruptly, I thought, as though she didn't want to discuss the matter.

'I didn't know what they meant, and indeed it wasn't till later that I remembered the incident.

'We played three or four rubbers and still Bronson didn't turn up.

'"I wonder what's happened to him," said his wife. "I can't think why he should be so late."

'Cartwright was always silent, but this evening he had hardly opened his mouth. I thought he was tired and asked him what he'd been doing.

'"Nothing very much," he said. "I went out after tiffin to shoot pigeon.'

'"Did you have any luck?" I asked.

'"Oh, I got half a dozen. They were very shy."

'But now he said: "If Reggie got back late, I dare say he thought it wasn't worth while to come here. I expect he's had a bath and when we get in we shall find him asleep in his chair."

'"It's a good long ride from Kabulong," said the doctor's wife.

'"He doesn't take the road, you know," Mrs Bronson explained. "He takes the short cut through the jungle."

'"Can he get along on his bicycle?" I asked.

'"Oh, yes, it's a very good track. It saves about a couple of miles."

'We had just started another rubber when the bar-boy came in and said there was a police-sergeant outside who wanted to speak to me.

'"What does he want?" I asked.

'The boy said he didn't know, but he had two coolies with him.

'"Curse him," I said. "I'll give him hell if I find he's disturbed me for nothing."

'I told the boy I'd come and I finished playing the hand. Then I got up.

'"I won't be a minute," I said. "Deal for me, will you?" I added to Cartwright.

'I went out and found the sergeant with two Malays waiting for me on the steps. I asked him what the devil he wanted. You can imagine my consternation when he told me that the Malays had come to the police-station and said there was a white man lying dead on the path that led through the jungle to Kabulong. I immediately thought of Bronson.

'"Dead?" I cried.

'"Yes, shot. Shot through the head. A white man with red hair."

'Then I knew it was Reggie Bronson, and indeed, one of them naming his estate said he'd recognized him as the man. It was an awful shock. And there was Mrs Bronson in the card-room waiting impatiently for me to sort my cards and make a bid. For a moment I really didn't know what to do. I was frightfully upset. It was dreadful to give her such a terrible and unexpected blow without a word of preparation, but I found myself quite unable to think of any way to soften it. I told the sergeant and the coolies to wait and went back into the club. I tried to pull myself together. As I entered the card-room Mrs Bronson said: "You've been an awful long time." Then she caught sight of my face. "Is anything the matter?" I saw her clench her fists and go white. You'd have thought she had a presentiment of evil.

'"Something dreadful has happened," I said, and my throat was all closed up so that my voice sounded even to myself hoarse and uncanny. "There's been an accident. Your husband's been wounded."

'She gave a long gasp, it was not exactly a scream, it reminded me oddly of a piece of silk torn in two.

'"Wounded?"

'She leapt to her feet and with her eyes starting from her head stared at Cartwright. The effect on him was ghastly, he fell back in his chair and went as white as death.

'"Very, very badly, I'm afraid," I added.

'I knew that I must tell her the truth, and tell it then, but I couldn't bring myself to tell it all at once.

'"Is he," her lips trembled so that she could hardly form the words, "is he–conscious?"

'I looked at her for a moment without answering. I'd have given a thousand pounds not to have to.

'"No, I'm afraid he isn't."

'Mrs Bronson stared at me as though she were trying to see right into my brain.

'"Is he dead?"

'I thought the only thing was to get it out and have done with it.

'"Yes, he was dead when they found him."

'Mrs Bronson collapsed into her chair and burst into tears.

'"Oh, my God," she muttered. "Oh, my God."

'The doctor's wife went to her and put her arms round her. Mrs Bronson with her face in her hands swayed to and fro weeping hysterically. Cartwright, with that livid face, sat quite still, his mouth open, and stared at her. You might have thought he was turned to stone.

'"Oh, my dear, my dear," said the doctor's wife, "you must try and pull yourself together." Then, turning to me, "Get her a glass of water and fetch Harry."

'Harry was her husband and he was playing billiards. I went in and told him what had happened.

'"A glass of water be damned," he said. "What she wants is a good long peg of brandy."

'We took it in to her and forced her to drink it and gradually the violence of her emotion exhausted itself. In a few minutes the doctor's wife was able to take her into the ladies' lavatory to wash her face. I'd made up my mind now what had better be done. I could see that Cartwright wasn't good for much; he was all to pieces. I could understand that it was a fearful shock to him, for after all Bronson was his greatest friend and had done everything in the world for him.

'"You look as though you'd be all the better for a drop of brandy yourself, old man," I said to him.

'He made an effort.

'"It's shaken me, you know," he said. "I . . . I didn't . . ." He stopped as though his mind was wandering; he was still fearfully pale; he took out a packet of cigarettes and struck a match, but his hand was shaking so that he could hardly manage it.

'"Yes, I'll have a brandy."

'"Boy," I shouted, and then to Cartwright: "Now, are you fit to take Mrs Bronson home?"

'"Oh, yes," he answered.

'"That's good. The doctor and I will go along with the coolies and some police to where the body is."

'"Will you bring him back to the bungalow?" asked Cartwright.

'"I think he'd better be taken straight to the mortuary," said the doctor before I could answer. "I shall have to do a P.M."

'When Mrs Bronson, now so much calmer that I was amazed, came back, I told her what I suggested. The doctor's wife, kind woman, offered to go with her and spend the night at the bungalow, but Mrs Bronson wouldn't hear of it. She said she would be perfectly all right, and when the doctor's wife insisted—you know how bent some people are on forcing their kindness on those in trouble—she turned on her almost fiercely.

'"No, no, I must be alone," she said. "I really must. And Theo will be there."

'They got into the trap. Theo took the reins and they drove off. We started after them, the doctor and I, while the sergeant and the coolies followed. I had sent my seis to the police-station with instructions to send two men to the place where the body was lying. We soon passed Mrs Bronson and Cartwright.

'"All right?" I called.

'"Yes," he answered.

'For some time the doctor and I drove without saying a word; we were both of us deeply shocked. I was worried as well. Somehow or other I'd got to find the murderers and I foresaw that it would be no easy matter.

'"Do you suppose it was gang robbery?" said the doctor at last.

'He might have been reading my thoughts.

'"I don't think there's a doubt of it," I answered. "They knew he'd gone into Kabulong to get the wages and lay in wait for him on the way back. Of course he should never have come alone through the jungle when everyone knew he had a packet of money with him."

'"He'd done it for years," said the doctor. "And he's not the only one."

'"I know. The question is, how we're going to get hold of the fellows that did it."

'"You don't think the two coolies who say they found him could have had anything to do with it?"

'"No. They wouldn't have the nerve. I think a pair of Chinks might think out a trick like that, but I don't believe Malays would. They'd be much too frightened. Of course we'll keep an eye on them. We shall soon see if they seem to have any money to fling about."

'"It's awful for Mrs Bronson," said the doctor. "It would have been bad enough at any time, but now she's going to have a baby . . ."

'"I didn't know that," I said, interrupting him.

'"No, for some reason she wanted to keep it dark. She was rather funny about it, I thought."

'I recollected then that little passage between Mrs Bronson and the doctor's wife. I understood why that good woman had been so anxious that Mrs Bronson should not overtire herself.

'"It's strange her having a baby after being married so many years."

'"It happens, you know. But it was a surprise to her. When first she came to see me and I told her what was the matter she fainted, and then she began to cry. I should have thought she'd be as pleased as Punch. She told me that Bronson didn't like children and he'd be awfully bored at the idea, and she made me promise to say nothing about it till she had had a chance of breaking it to him gradually."

'I reflected for a moment.

'"He was the kind of breezy, hearty cove whom you'd expect to be as keen as mustard on having kids."

'"You never can tell. Some people are very selfish and just don't want the bother."

'"Well, how did he take it when she did tell him? Wasn't he rather bucked?"

'"I don't know that she ever told him. Though she couldn't have waited much longer; unless I'm very much mistaken she ought to be confined in about five months."

'"Poor devil," I said. "You know, I've got a notion that he'd have been most awfully pleased to know."

'We drove in silence for the rest of the way and at last came to the point at which the short cut to Kabulong branched off from the road. Here we stopped and in a minute or two my trap, in which were the police-sergeant and the two Malays, came up. We took the head-lamps to light us on our way. I left the doctor's seis to look after the ponies and told him that when the policemen came they were to follow the path till they found us. The two coolies, carrying the lamps, walked ahead, and we followed them. It was a fairly broad track, wide enough for a small cart to pass, and before the road was built it had been the highway between Kabulong and Alor Lipis. It was firm to the foot and good walking. The surface here and there was sandy and in places you could see quite plainly the mark of a bicycle wheel. It was the track Bronson had left on his way to Kabulong.

'We walked twenty minutes, I should think, in single file, and on a sudden the coolies, with a cry, stopped sharply. The sight had come upon them so abruptly that notwithstanding they were expecting it they were startled. There, in the middle of the pathway lit dimly by the lamps the coolies carried, lay Bronson; he'd fallen over his bicycle and lay across it in an ungainly heap. I was too shocked to speak, and I think the doctor was, too. But in our silence the din of the jungle was deafening; those damned cicadas and the bull-frogs were making enough row to wake the dead. Even under ordinary circumstances the noise of the jungle at night is uncanny; because you feel that at that hour there should be utter silence it has an odd effect on you, that ceaseless and invisible uproar that beats upon your nerves. It surrounds you and hems you in. But just then, believe me, it was terrifying. That poor fellow lay dead and all round him the restless life of the jungle pursued its indifferent and ferocious course.

'He was lying face downwards. The sergeant and the coolies looked at me as though awaiting an order. I was a young fellow then and I'm afraid I felt a little frightened. Though I couldn't see the face I had no doubt that it was Bronson, but I felt that I ought to turn the body over to make sure. I suppose we all have our little squeamishnesses; you know, I've always had a horrible distaste for touching dead bodies. I've had to do it fairly often now, but it still makes me feel slightly sick.

'"It's Bronson, all right," I said.

'The doctor—by George, it was lucky for me he was there—the doctor bent down and turned the head. The sergeant directed the lamp on the dead face.

'"My God, half his head's been shot away," I cried.

'"Yes."

'The doctor stood up straight and wiped his hands on the leaves of a tree that grew beside the path.

'"Is he quite dead?" I asked.

'"Oh, yes. Death must have been instantaneous. Whoever shot him must have fired at pretty close range."

'"How long has he been dead, d'you think?"

'"Oh, I don't know, several hours."

'"He would have passed here about five o'clock, I suppose, if he was expecting to get to the club for a rubber at six."

'"There's no sign of any struggle," said the doctor.

'"No, there wouldn't be. He was shot as he was riding along."

'I looked at the body for a little while. I couldn't help thinking how short a time ago it was since Bronson, noisy and loud-voiced, had been so full of hearty life.

'"You haven't forgotten that he had the coolies' wages on him," said the doctor.

'"No, we'd better search him."

'"Shall we turn him over?"

'"Wait a minute. Let us just have a look at the ground first."

'I took the lamp and as carefully as I could looked all about me. Just where he had fallen the sandy pathway was trodden and confused; there were our footprints and the footprints of the coolies who had found him. I walked two or three paces and then saw quite clearly the mark of his bicycle wheels; he had been riding straight and steadily. I followed it to the spot where he had fallen, to just before that, rather, and there saw very distinctly the prints on each side of the wheels of his heavy boots. He had evidently stopped there and put his feet to the ground, then he'd started off again, there was a great wobble of the wheel, and he'd crashed.

'"Now let's search him," I said.

'The doctor and the sergeant turned the body over and one of the coolies dragged the bicycle away. They laid Bronson on his back. I supposed he would have had the money partly in notes and partly in silver. The silver would have been in a bag attached to the bicycle and a glance told me that it was not there. The notes he would have put in a wallet. It would have been a good thick bundle. I felt him all over, but there was nothing; then I turned out the pockets, they were all empty except the right trouser pocket, in which there was a little small change.

'"Didn't he always wear a watch?" asked the doctor.

'"Yes, of course he did."

'I remembered that he wore the chain through the buttonhole in the lapel of his coat and the watch and some seals and things in his handkerchief pocket. But watch and chain were gone.

'"Well, there's not much doubt now, is there?" I said.

'It was clear that he had been attacked by gang robbers who knew he had money on him. After killing him they had stripped him of everything. I suddenly remembered the footprints that proved that for a moment he had stood still. I saw exactly how it had been done. One of them had stopped him on some pretext and then, just as he started off again, another, slipping out of the jungle behind him, had emptied the two barrels of a gun into his head.

'"Well," I said to the doctor, "it's up to me to catch them, and I'll tell you what, it'll be a real pleasure to me to see them hanged."

'Of course there was an inquest. Mrs Bronson gave evidence, but she had nothing to say that we didn't know already. Bronson had left the bungalow about eleven, he was to have tiffin at Kabulong and was to be back between five and six. He asked her not to wait for him, he said he would just put the money in the safe and come straight to the club. Cartwright confirmed this. He had lunched alone with Mrs Bronson and after a smoke had gone out with a gun to shoot pigeon. He had got in about five, a little before perhaps, had a bath and changed to play tennis. He was shooting not far from the place where Bronson was killed, but never heard a shot. That, of course, meant nothing; what with the cicadas and the frogs and the other sounds of the jungle, he would have had to be very near to hear anything; and besides, Cartwright was probably back in the bungalow before Bronson was killed. We traced Bronson's movements. He had lunched at the club, he had got money at the bank just before it closed, had gone back to the club and had one more drink, and then started off on his bicycle. He had crossed the river by the ferry; the ferryman remembered distinctly seeing him, but was positive that no one else with a bicycle had crossed. That looked as though the murderers were not following, but lying in wait for him. He rode along the main road for a couple of miles and then took the path which was a short cut to his bungalow.

'It looked as though he had been killed by men who knew his habits, and suspicion, of course, fell immediately on the coolies of his estate. We examined them all–pretty carefully–but there was not a scrap of evidence to connect any of them with the crime. In fact, most of them were able satisfactorily to account for their actions and those who couldn't seemed to me for one reason and another out of the running. There were a few bad characters among the Chinese at Alor Lipis and I had them looked up. But somehow I didn't think it was the work of the Chinese; I had a feeling that Chinese would have used revolvers and not a shotgun. Anyhow, I could find out nothing there. So then we offered a reward of a thousand dollars to anyone who could put us in the way of discovering the murderers. I thought there were a good many people to whom it would appeal to do a public service and at the same time earn a tidy sum. But I knew that an informer would take no risks, he wouldn't want to tell what he knew till he knew he could tell it safely, and I armed myself with patience. The reward had brightened the interest of my police and I knew they would use every means they had to bring the criminals to trial. In a case like this they could do more than I.

'But it was strange, nothing happened; the reward seemed to tempt no one. I cast my net a little wider. There were two or three kampongs along the road and I wondered if the murderers were there; I saw the headmen, but got no help from them. It was not that they would tell me nothing, I was sure they had nothing to tell. I talked to the bad hats, but there was absolutely nothing to connect them with the murder. There was not the shadow of a clue.

'"Very well, my lads," I said to myself, as I drove back to Alor Lipis, "there's no hurry; the rope won't spoil by keeping."

'The scoundrels had got away with a considerable sum, but money is no good unless you spend it. I felt I knew the native temperament enough to be sure that the possession of it was a constant temptation. The Malays are an extravagant race, and a race of gamblers, and the Chinese are gamblers, too; sooner or later someone would start flinging his money about, and then I should want to know where it came from. With a few well-directed questions I thought I could put the fear of God into the fellow and then, if I knew my business, it shouldn't be hard to get a full confession.

'The only thing now was to sit down and wait till the hue and cry had died down and the murderers thought the affair was forgotten. The itch to spend those ill-gotten dollars would grow more and more intolerable till at last it could be resisted no longer. I would go about my business, but I meant never to relax my watch, and one day, sooner or later, my time must come.

'Cartwright took Mrs Bronson down to Singapore. The company Bronson had worked for asked him if he would care to take Bronson's place, but he said, very naturally, that he didn't like the idea of it; so they put another man in and told Cartwright that he could have the job that Bronson's successor had vacated. It was the management of the estate that Cartwright lives on now. He moved in at once. Four months after this Olive was born at Singapore, and a few months later, when Bronson had been dead just over a year, Cartwright and Mrs Bronson were married. I was surprised; but on thinking it over I couldn't help confessing that it was very natural. After the trouble Mrs Bronson had leant much on Cartwright and he had arranged everything for her; she must have been lonely, and rather lost, and I dare say she was grateful for his kindness, he did behave like a brick; and so far as he was concerned I imagined he was sorry for her, it was a dreadful position for a woman, she had nowhere to go, and all they'd gone through must have been a tie between them. There was every reason for them to marry and it was probably the best thing for them both.

'It looked as though Bronson's murderers would never be caught, for that plan of mine didn't work; there was no one in the district who spent more money than he could account for, and if anyone had that hoard buried away under his floor he was showing a self-control that was superhuman. A year had passed and to all intents and purposes the thing was forgotten. Could anyone be so prudent as after so long not to let a little money dribble out? It was incredible. I began to think that Bronson had been killed by a couple of wandering Chinese who had got away, to Singapore perhaps, where there would be small chance of catching them. At last I gave it up. If you come to think of it, as a rule, it's just those crimes, crimes of robbery, in which there is least chance of getting the culprit; for there's nothing to attach suspicion to him, and if he's caught it can only be by his own carelessness. It's different with crimes of passion or vengeance, then you can find out who had a motive to put the victim out of the way.

'It's no use grizzling over one's failures, and bringing my common sense to bear I did my best to put the matter out of my mind. No one likes to be beaten, but beaten I was and I had to put as good a face on it as I could. And then a Chinaman was caught trying to pawn poor Bronson's watch.

'I told you that Bronson's watch and chain had been taken, and of course Mrs Bronson was able to give us a fairly accurate description of it. It was a half-hunter, by Benson, there was a gold chain, three or four seals, and a sovereign purse. The pawnbroker was a smart fellow and when the Chinaman brought the watch he recognized it at once. On some pretext he kept the man waiting and sent for a policeman. The man was arrested and immediately brought to me. I greeted him like a long-lost brother. I was never so pleased to see anyone in my life. I have no feeling about criminals, you know; I'm rather sorry for them, because they're playing a game in which their opponents hold all the aces and kings; but when I catch one it gives me a little thrill of satisfaction, like bringing off a neat finesse at bridge. At last the mystery was going to be cleared up, for if the Chinaman hadn't done the thing himself we were pretty sure through him to trace the murderers. I beamed on him.

'I asked him to account for his possession of the watch. He said he had bought it from a man he didn't know. That was very thin. I explained the circumstances briefly and told him he would be charged with murder. I meant to frighten him and I did. He said then that he'd found the watch.

'"Found it?" I said. "Fancy that. Where?"

'His answer staggered me; he said he'd found it in the jungle. I laughed at him; I asked him if he thought watches were likely to be left lying about in the jungle; then he said he'd been coming along the pathway that led from Kabulong to Alor Lipis, and had gone into the jungle and caught sight of something gleaming and there was the watch. That was odd. Why should he have said he found the watch just there? It was either true or excessively astute. I asked him where the chain and the seals were, and he produced them immediately. I'd got him scared, and he was pale and shaking; he was a knock-kneed little fellow and I should have been a fool not to see that I hadn't got hold of the murderer there. But his terror suggested that he knew something.

'I asked him when he'd found the watch.

'"Yesterday," he said.

'I asked him what he was doing on the short-cut from Kabulong to Alor Lipis. He said he'd been working in Singapore and had gone to Kabulong because his father was ill, and that he himself had come to Alor Lipis to work. A friend of his father, a carpenter by trade, had given him a job. He gave me the name of the man with whom he had worked in Singapore and the name of the man who had engaged him at Alor Lipis. All he said seemed plausible and could so easily be verified that it was hardly likely to be false. Of course it occurred to me that if he had found the watch as he said, it must have been lying in the jungle for more than a year. It could hardly be in very good condition; I tried to open it, but couldn't. The pawnbroker had come to the police-station and was waiting in the next room. Luckily he was also something of a watch-maker. I sent for him and asked him to look at the watch; when he opened it he gave a little whistle, the works were thick with rust.

'"This watch no good," he said, shaking his head. "Him never go now."

'I asked him what had put it in such a state, and without a word from me he said that it had been long exposed to wet. For the moral effect I had the prisoner put in a cell and I sent for his employer. I sent a wire to Kabulong and another to Singapore. While I waited I did my best to put two and two together. I was inclined to believe the man's story true; his fear might be ascribed to no more guilt than consisted in his having found something and tried to sell it. Even quite innocent persons are apt to be nervous when they're in the hands of the police; I don't know what there is about a policeman, people are never very much at their ease in his company. But if he really had found the watch where he said, someone had thrown it there. Now that was funny. Even if the murderers had thought the watch a dangerous thing to possess, one would have expected them to melt down the gold case; that would be a very simple thing for any native to do; and the chain was of so ordinary a pattern they could hardly have thought it possible to trace that. There were chains like it in every jeweller's shop in the country. Of course there was the possibility that they had plunged into the jungle and having dropped the watch in their hurry had been afraid to go back and look for it. I didn't think that very likely: the Malays are used to keeping things tucked away in their sarongs, and the Chinese have pockets in their coats. Besides, the moment they got into the jungle they knew there was no hurry; they probably waited and divided the swag then and there.

'In a few minutes the man I had sent for came to the police-station and confirmed what the prisoner had said, and in an hour I got an answer from Kabulong. The police had seen his father, who told them that the boy had gone to Alor Lipis to get a job with a carpenter. So far everything he had said seemed true. I had him brought in again, and told him I was going to take him to the place where he said he had found the watch and he must show me the exact spot. I handcuffed him to a policeman, though it was hardly necessary, for the poor devil was shaking with fright, and took a couple of men besides. We drove out to where the track joined the road and walked along it; within five yards of the place where Bronson was killed the Chinaman stopped.

'"Here," he said.

'He pointed to the jungle and we followed him in. We went in about ten yards and he pointed to a chink between two large boulders and said that he found the watch there. It could only have been by the merest chance that he noticed it, and if he really had found it there it looked very much as though someone had put it there to hide it.'

Gaze stopped and gave me a reflective look.

'What would you have thought then?' he asked.

'I don't know,' I answered.

'Well, I'll tell you what I thought. I thought that if the watch was there the money might be there, too. It seemed worth while having a look. Of course, to look for something in the jungle makes looking for a needle in a bundle of hay a drawing-room pastime. I couldn't help that. I released the Chinaman, I wanted all the help I could get, and set him to work. I set my three men to work, and I started in myself. We made a line—there were five of us—and we searched from the road; for fifty yards on each side of the place at which Bronson was murdered and for a hundred yards in we went over the ground foot by foot. We routed among dead leaves and peered in bushes, we looked under boulders and in the hollows of trees. I knew it was a foolish thing to do, for the chances against us were a thousand to one; my only hope was that anyone who had just committed a murder would be rattled and if he wanted to hide anything would hide it quickly; he would choose the first obvious hiding-place that offered itself. That is what he had done when he hid the watch. My only reason for looking in so circumscribed an area was that as the watch had been found so near the road, the person who wanted to get rid of the things must have wanted to get rid of them quickly.

'We worked on. I began to grow tired and cross. We were sweating like pigs. I had a maddening thirst and nothing in the world to drink. At last I came to the conclusion that we must give it up as a bad job, for that day at least, when suddenly the Chinaman—he must have had sharp eyes, that young man—uttered a guttural cry. He stooped down and from under the winding root of a tree drew out a messy, mouldering, stinking thing. It was a pocket-book that had been out in the rain for a year, that had been eaten by ants and beetles and God knows what, that was sodden and foul, but it was a pocket-book all right, Bronson's, and inside were the shapeless, mushed-up, fetid remains of the Singapore notes he had got from the bank at Kabulong. There was still the silver and I was convinced that it was hidden somewhere about, but I wasn't going to bother about that. I had found out something very important; whoever had murdered Bronson had made no money out of it.

'Do you remember my telling you that I'd noticed the print of Bronson's feet on each side of the broad line of the pneumatic tyre, where he had stopped, and presumably spoken to someone? He was a heavy man and the prints were well marked. He hadn't just put his feet on the soft sand and taken them off, but must have stopped at least for a minute or two. My explanation was that he had stopped to chat with a Malay or a Chinaman, but the more I thought of it the less I liked it. Why the devil should he? Bronson wanted to get home, and though a jovial chap, he certainly was not hail-fellow-well-met with the natives. His relations towards them were those of master and servants. Those footprints had always puzzled me. And now the truth flashed across me. Whoever had murdered Bronson hadn't murdered him to rob and if he'd stopped to talk with someone it could only be with a friend. I knew at last who the murderer was.'

I have always thought the detective story a most diverting and ingenious variety of fiction, and have regretted that I never had the skill to write one, but I have read a good many, and I flatter myself it is rarely that I have not solved the mystery before it was disclosed to me; and now for some time I had foreseen what Gaze was going to say, but when at last he said it I confess that it gave me, notwithstanding, somewhat of a shock.

'The man he met was Cartwright. Cartwright was pigeon-shooting. He stopped and asked him what sport he had had, and as he rode on Cartwright raised his gun and discharged both barrels into his head. Cartwright took the money and the watch in order to make it look like the work of gang robbers and hurriedly hid them in the jungle, then made his way along the edge till he got to the road, went back to the bungalow, changed into his tennis things, and drove with Mrs Bronson to the club.

'I remembered how badly he'd played tennis, and how he'd collapsed when, in order to break the news more gently to Mrs Bronson, I said Bronson was wounded and not dead. If he was only wounded he might have been able to speak. By George, I bet that was a bad moment. The child was Cartwright's. Look at Olive: why, you saw the likeness yourself. The doctor had said that Mrs Bronson was upset when he told her she was going to have a baby and made him promise not to tell Bronson. Why? Because Bronson knew that he couldn't be the father of the child.'

'Do you think that Mrs Bronson knew what Cartwright had done?' I asked.

'I'm sure of it. When I look back on her behaviour that evening at the club I am convinced of it. She was upset, but not because Bronson was killed; she was upset because I said he was wounded; on my telling her that he was dead when they found him she burst out crying, but from relief. I know that woman. Look at that square chin of hers and tell me that she hasn't got the courage of the devil. She has a will of iron. She made Cartwright do it. She planned every detail and every move. He was completely under her influence; he is now.'

'But do you mean to tell me that neither you nor anyone else ever suspected that there was anything between them?'

'Never. Never.'

'If they were in love with one another and knew that she was going to have a baby, why didn't they just bolt?'

'How could they? It was Bronson who had the money; she hadn't a bean and neither had Cartwright. He was out of a job. Do you think he would have got another with that story round his neck? Bronson had taken him in when he was starving and he'd stolen his wife from him. They wouldn't have had a dog's chance. They couldn't afford to let the truth come out, their only chance was to get Bronson out of the way, and they got him out of the way.'

'They might have thrown themselves on his mercy.'

'Yes, but I think they were ashamed. He'd been so good to them, he was such a decent chap, I don't think they had the heart to tell him the truth. They preferred to kill him.'

There was a moment's silence while I reflected over what Gaze said.

'Well, what did you do about it?' I asked.

'Nothing. What was there to do? What was the evidence? That the watch and notes had been found? They might easily have been hidden by someone who was afterwards afraid to come and get them. The murderer might have been quite content to get away with the silver. The footprints? Bronson might have stopped to light a cigarette or there might have been a tree-trunk across the path and he waited while the coolies he met there by chance moved it away. Who could prove that the child that a perfectly decent, respectable woman had had four months after her husband's death was not his child? No jury would have convicted Cartwright. I held my tongue and the Bronson murder was forgotten.'

'I don't suppose the Cartwrights have forgotten,' I suggested.

'I shouldn't be surprised. Human memory is astonishingly short and if you want my professional opinion I don't mind telling you that I don't believe remorse for a crime ever sits very heavily on a man when he's absolutely sure he'll never be found out.'

I thought once more of the pair I had met that afternoon, the thin, elderly, bald man with gold-rimmed spectacles, and that white-haired untidy woman with her frank speech and kindly, caustic smile. It was almost impossible to imagine that in the distant past they had been swayed by so turbulent a passion, for that alone made their behaviour explicable, that it had brought them in the end to such a pass that they could see no other issue than a cruel and cold-blooded murder.

'Doesn't it make you feel a little uncomfortable to be with them?' I asked Gaze. 'For, without wishing to be censorious, I'm bound to say that I don't think they can be very nice people.'

'That's where you're wrong. They are very nice people; they're about the pleasantest people here. Mrs Cartwright is a thoroughly good sort and a very amusing woman. It's my business to prevent crime and to catch the culprit when crime is committed, but I've known far too many criminals to think that on the whole they're worse than anybody else. A perfectly decent fellow may be driven by circumstances to commit a crime and if he's found out he's punished; but he may very well remain a perfectly decent fellow. Of course society punishes him if he breaks its laws, and it's quite right, but it's not always his actions that indicate the essential man. If you'd been a policeman as long as I have, you'd know it's not what people do that really matters, it's what they are. Luckily a policeman has nothing to do with their thoughts, only with their deeds; if he had, it would be a very different, a much more difficult matter.'

Gaze flicked the ash from his cheroot and gave me his wry, sardonic, but agreeable smile.

'I'll tell you what, there's one job I *shouldn't* like,' he said.

'What is that?' I asked.

'God's at the Judgement Day,' said Gaze. 'No, sir.'

The
Door
of Opportunity

◆

They got a first-class carriage to themselves. It was lucky, because they were taking a good deal in with them, Alban's suit-case and a hold-all, Anne's dressing-case and her hat-box. They had two trunks in the van, containing what they wanted immediately, but all the rest of their luggage Alban had put in the care of an agent who was to take it up to London and store it till they had made up their minds what to do. They had a lot, pictures and books, curios that Alban had collected in the East, his guns and saddles. They had left Sondurah for ever. Alban, as was his way, tipped the porter generously and then went to the bookstall and bought papers. He bought the *New Statesman* and the *Nation,* and the *Tatler* and the *Sketch,* and the last number of the *London Mercury.* He came back to the carriage and threw them on the seat.

'It's only an hour's journey,' said Anne.

'I know, but I wanted to buy them. I've been starved so long. Isn't it grand to think that tomorrow morning we shall have tomorrow's *Times,* and the *Express* and the *Mail?*'

She did not answer and he turned away, for he saw coming towards them two persons, a man and his wife, who had been fellow-passengers from Singapore.

'Get through the Customs all right?' he cried to them cheerily.

The man seemed not to hear, for he walked straight on, but the woman answered.

'Yes, they never found the cigarettes.'

She saw Anne, gave her a friendly little smile, and passed on. Anne flushed.

'I was afraid they'd want to come in here,' said Alban. 'Let's have the carriage to ourselves if we can.'

She looked at him curiously.

'I don't think you need worry,' she answered. 'I don't think anyone will come in.'

He lit a cigarette and lingered at the carriage door. On his face was a happy smile. When they had passed through the Red Sea and found a sharp wind in the Canal, Anne had been surprised to see how much the men who had looked presentable enough in the white ducks in which she had been accustomed to see them, were changed when they left them off for warmer clothes. They looked like nothing on earth then. Their ties were awful and their shirts all wrong. They wore grubby flannel trousers and shabby old golf-coats that had too obviously been bought off the nail, or blue serge suits that betrayed the provincial tailor. Most of the passengers had got off at Marseilles, but a dozen or so, either because after a long period in the East they thought the trip through the Bay would do them good, or, like themselves, for economy's sake, had gone all the way to Tilbury, and now several of them walked along the platform. They wore solar topees or double-brimmed terais, and heavy greatcoats, or else shapeless soft hats or bowlers, not too well brushed, that looked too small for them. It was a shock to see them. They looked suburban and a trifle second-rate. But Alban had already a London look. There was not a speck of dust on his smart greatcoat, and his black Homburg hat looked brand-new. You would never have guessed that he had not been home for three years. His collar fitted closely round his neck and his foulard tie was neatly tied. As Anne looked at him she could not but think how good-looking he was. He was just under six feet tall, and slim, and he wore his clothes well, and his clothes were well cut. He had fair hair, still thick, and blue eyes and the faintly yellow skin common to men of that complexion after they have lost the pink-and-white freshness of early youth. There was no colour in his cheeks. It was a fine head, well-set on rather a long neck, with a somewhat prominent Adam's apple; but you were more impressed with the distinction than with the beauty of his face. It was because his features were so regular, his nose so straight, his brow so broad that he photographed so well. Indeed, from his photographs you would have thought him extremely handsome. He was not that, perhaps because his eyebrows and his eyelashes were pale, and his lips thin, but he looked very intellectual. There was refinement in his face and a spirituality that was oddly moving. That was how you thought a poet should look; and when Anne became engaged to him she told her girl friends who asked her about him that he looked like Shelley. He turned to her now with a little smile in his blue eyes. His smile was very attractive.

'What a perfect day to land in England!'

It was October. They had steamed up the Channel on a grey sea under a grey sky. There was not a breath of wind. The fishing boats seemed to rest on the placid water as though the elements had for ever forgotten their old hostility: The coast was incredibly green, but with a bright cosy greenness quite unlike the luxuriant, vehement verdure of Eastern jungles. The red towns they passed here and there were comfortable and homelike. They seemed to welcome the exiles with a smiling friendliness. And when they drew into the estuary of the Thames they saw the rich levels of Essex and in a little while Chalk Church on the Kentish shore, lonely in the midst of weather-beaten trees, and beyond it the woods of Cobham. The sun, red in a faint mist, set on the marshes, and night fell. In the station the arc-lamps shed a light that spotted the darkness with cold hard patches. It was good to see the porters lumbering about in their grubby uniforms and the station-master fat and important in his bowler hat.

The station-master blew a whistle and waved his arm. Alban stepped into the carriage and seated himself in the corner opposite to Anne. The train started.

'We're due in London at six-ten,' said Alban. 'We ought to get to Jermyn Street by seven. That'll give us an hour to bath and change and we can get to the Savoy for dinner by eight-thirty. A bottle of pop tonight, my pet, and a slap-up dinner.' He gave a chuckle. 'I heard the Strouds and the Maundrys arranging to meet at the Trocadero Grill-Room.'

He took up the papers and asked if she wanted any of them. Anne shook her head.

'Tired?' he smiled.

'No.'

'Excited?'

In order not to answer she gave a little laugh. He began to look at the papers, starting with the publishers' advertisements, and she was conscious of the intense satisfaction it was to him to feel himself through them once more in the middle of things. They had taken in those same papers in Sondurah, but they arrived six weeks old, and though they kept them abreast of what was going on in the world that interested them both, they emphasized their exile. But these were fresh from the press. They smelt different. They had a crispness that was almost voluptuous. He wanted to read them all at once. Anne looked out of the window. The country was dark, and she could see little but the lights of their carriage reflected on the glass, but very soon the town encroached upon it, and then she saw little sordid houses, mile upon mile of them, with a light in a window here and there, and the chimneys made a dreary pattern against the sky. They passed through Barking and East Ham and Bromley—it was silly that the name on the platform as they went through the station should give her such a tremor—and then Stepney. Alban put down his papers.

'We shall be there in five minutes now.'

He put on his hat and took down from the racks the things the porter had put in them. He looked at her with shining eyes and his lips twitched. She saw that he was only just able to control his emotion. He looked out of the window, too, and they passed over brightly lighted thoroughfares, close packed with tram-cars, buses, and motor-vans, and they saw the streets thick with people. What a mob! The shops were all lit up. They saw the hawkers with their barrows at the kerb.

'London,' he said.

He took her hand and gently pressed it. His smile was so sweet that she had to say something. She tried to be facetious.

'Does it make you feel all funny inside?'

'I don't know if I want to cry or if I want to be sick.'

Fenchurch Street. He lowered the window and waved his arm for a porter. With a grinding of brakes the train came to a standstill. A porter opened the door and Alban handed him out one package after another. Then in his polite way, having jumped out, he gave his hand to Anne to help her down to the platform. The porter went to fetch a barrow and they stood by the pile of their luggage. Alban waved to two passengers from the ship who passed them. The man nodded stiffly.

'What a comfort it is that we shall never have to be civil to those awful people any more,' said Alban lightly.

Anne gave him a quick glance. He was really incomprehensible. The porter came back with his barrow, the luggage was put on, and they followed him to collect their trunks. Alban took his wife's arm and pressed it.

'The smell of London. By God, it's grand.'

He rejoiced in the noise and the bustle, and the crowd of people who jostled them; the radiance of the arc-lamps and the black shadows they cast, sharp but full-toned, gave him a sense of elation. They got out into the street and the porter went off to get them a taxi. Alban's eyes glittered as he looked at the buses and the policemen trying to direct the confusion. His distinguished face bore a look of something like inspiration. The taxi came. Their luggage was stowed away and piled up beside the driver, Alban gave the porter half-a-crown, and they drove off. They turned down Gracechurch Street and in Cannon Street were held up by a block in the traffic. Alban laughed out loud.

'What's the matter?' said Anne.

'I'm so excited.'

They went along the Embankment. It was relatively quiet there. Taxis and cars passed them. The bells of the trams were music in his ears. At Westminster Bridge they cut across Parliament Square and drove through the green silence of St James's Park. They had engaged a room at a hotel just off Jermyn Street. The reception clerk took them upstairs and a porter brought up their luggage. It was a room with twin beds and a bathroom.

'This looks all right,' said Alban. 'It'll do us till we can find a flat or something.'

He looked at his watch.

'Look here, darling, we shall only fall over one another if we try to unpack together. We've got oodles of time and it'll take you longer to get straight and dress than me. I'll clear out. I want to go to the club and see if there's any mail for me. I've got my dinner jacket in my suit-case and it'll only take me twenty minutes to have a bath and dress. Does that suit you?'

'Yes. That's all right.'

'I'll be back in an hour.'

'Very well.'

He took out of his pocket the little comb he always carried and passed it through his long fair hair. Then he put on his hat. He gave himself a glance in the mirror.

'Shall I turn on the bath for you?'

'No, don't bother.'

'All right. So long.'

He went out.

When he was gone Anne took her dressing-case and her hat-box and put them on the top of her trunk. Then she rang the bell. She did not take off her hat. She sat down and lit a cigarette. When a servant answered the bell she asked for the porter. He came. She pointed to the luggage.

'Will you take those things and leave them in the hall for the present. I'll tell you what to do with them presently.'

'Very good, ma'am.'

She gave him a florin. He took the trunk out and the other packages and closed the door behind him. A few tears slid down Anne's cheeks, but she shook herself; she dried her eyes and powdered her face. She needed all her calm. She was glad that Alban had conceived the idea of going to his club. It made things easier and gave her a little time to think them out.

Now that the moment had come to do what she had for weeks determined, now that she must say the terrible things she had to say, she quailed. Her heart sank. She knew exactly what she meant to say to Alban, she had made up her mind about that long ago, and had said the very words to herself a hundred times, three or four times a day every day of the long journey from Singapore, but she was afraid that she would grow confused. She dreaded an argument. The thought of a scene made her feel slightly sick. It was something at all events to have an hour in which to collect herself. He would say she was heartless and cruel and unreasonable. She could not help it.

'No, no, no,' she cried aloud.

She shuddered with horror. And all at once she saw herself again in the bungalow, sitting as she had been sitting when the whole thing started. It was getting on towards tiffin time and in a few minutes Alban would be back from the office. It gave her pleasure to reflect that it was an attractive room for him to come back to, the large veranda which was their parlour, and she knew that though they had been there eighteen months he was still alive to the success she had made of it. The jalousies were drawn now against the midday sun, and the mellowed light filtering through them gave an impression of cool silence. Anne was house-proud, and though they were moved from district to district according to the exigencies of the Service and seldom stayed anywhere very long, at each new post she started with new enthusiasm to make their house cosy and charming. She was very modern. Visitors were surprised because there were no knick-knacks. They were taken aback by the bold colour of her curtains and could not at all make out the tinted reproductions of pictures by Marie Laurencin and Gauguin in silvered frames which were placed on the walls with such cunning skill. She was conscious that few of them quite approved, and the good ladies of Port Wallace and Pemberton thought such arrangements odd, affected, and out of place; but this left her calm. They would learn. It did them good to get a bit of a jolt. And now she looked round the long, spacious veranda with the complacent sigh of the artist satisfied with his work. It was gay. It was bare. It was restful. It refreshed the spirit and gently excited the fancy. Three immense bowls of yellow cannas completed the colour scheme. Her eyes lingered for a moment on the book-shelves filled with books; that was another thing that disconcerted the colony, all the books they had, and strange books too, heavy they thought them for the most part and she gave them a little affectionate look as though they were living things. Then she gave the piano a glance. A piece of music was still open on the rack, it was something of Debussy, and Alban had been playing it before he went to the office.

Her friends in the colony had condoled with her when Alban was appointed D.O. at Daktar, for it was the most isolated district in Sondurah. It was connected with the town which was the headquarters of the Government neither by telegraph nor telephone. But she liked it. They had been there for some time and she hoped they would remain till Alban went home on leave in another twelve months. It was as large as an English county, with a long coast-line, and the sea was dotted with little islands. A broad, winding river ran through it, and on each side of this stretched hills densely covered with virgin forest. The station, a good way up the river, consisted of a row of Chinese shops and a native village nestling amid coconut trees, the District Office, the D.O.'s bungalow, the clerk's quarters, and the barracks. Their only neighbours were the manager of a rubber estate a few miles up the river, and the manager and his assistant, Dutchmen both, of a timber camp on one of the river's tributaries. The rubber estate's launch went up and down twice a month and was their only means of regular communication with the outside world. But though they were lonely they were not dull. Their days were full. Their ponies waited for them at dawn and they rose while the day was still fresh and in the bridle-paths through the jungle lingered the mystery of the tropical night. They came back, bathed, changed, and had breakfast, and Alban went to the office. Anne spent the morning writing letters and working. She had fallen in love with the country from the first day she arrived in it and had taken pains to master the common language spoken. Her imagination was inflamed by the stories she heard of love and jealousy and death. She was told romantic tales of a time that was only just past. She sought to steep herself in the lore of those strange people. Both she and Alban read a great deal. They had for the country a considerable library and new books came from London by nearly every mail. Little that was noteworthy escaped them. Alban was fond of playing the piano. For an amateur he played very well. He had studied rather seriously, and he had an agreeable touch and a good ear; he could read music with ease, and it was always a pleasure to Anne to sit by him and follow the score when he tried something new. But their great delight was to tour the district. Sometimes they would be away for a fortnight at a time. They would go down the river in a prahu and then sail from one little island to another, bathe in the sea, and fish, or else row upstream till it grew shallow and the trees on either bank were so close to one another that you only saw a slim strip of sky between. Here the boatmen had to pole and they would spend the night in a native house. They bathed in a river pool so clear that you could see the sand shining silver at the bottom; and the spot was so lovely, so peaceful and remote, that you felt you could stay there for ever. Sometimes, on the other hand, they would tramp for days along the jungle paths, sleeping under canvas, and notwithstanding the mosquitoes that tormented them and the leeches that sucked their blood, enjoy every moment. Whoever slept so well as on a camp bed? And then there was the gladness of getting back, the delight in the comfort of the well-ordered establishment, the mail that had arrived with letters from home and all the papers, and the piano.

Alban would sit down to it then, his fingers itching to feel the keys, and in what he played, Stravinsky, Ravel, Darius Milhaud, she seemed to feel that he put in something of his own, the sounds of the jungle at night, dawn over the estuary, the starry nights, and the crystal clearness of the forest pools.

Sometimes the rain fell in sheets for days at a time. Then Alban worked at Chinese. He was learning it so that he could communicate with the Chinese of the country in their own language, and Anne did the thousand-and-one things for which she had not had time before. Those days brought them even more closely together; they always had plenty to talk about, and when they were occupied with their separate affairs they were pleased to feel in their bones that they were near to one another. They were wonderfully united. The rainy days that shut them up within the walls of the bungalow made them feel as if they were one body in face of the world.

On occasion they went to Port Wallace. It was a change, but Anne was always glad to get home. She was never quite at her ease there. She was conscious that none of the people they met liked Alban. They were very ordinary people, middle-class and suburban and dull, without any of the intellectual interests that made life so full and varied to Alban and her, and many of them were narrow-minded and ill-natured; but since they had to pass the better part of their lives in contact with them, it was tiresome that they should feel so unkindly towards Alban. They said he was conceited. He was always very pleasant with them, but she was aware that they resented his cordiality. When he tried to be jovial they said he was putting on airs, and when he chaffed them they thought he was being funny at their expense.

Once they stayed at Government House, and Mrs Hannay, the Governor's wife, who liked her, talked to her about it. Perhaps the Governor had suggested that she should give Anne a hint.

'You know, my dear, it's a pity your husband doesn't try to be more come-hither with people. He's very intelligent; don't you think it would be better if he didn't let others see he knows it quite so clearly? My husband said to me only yesterday: Of course I know Alban Torel is the cleverest young man in the Service, but he does manage to put my back up more than anyone I know. I am the Governor, but when he talks to me he always gives me the impression that he looks upon me as a damned fool.'

The worst of it was that Anne knew how low an opinion Alban had of the Governor's parts.

'He doesn't mean to be superior,' Anne answered, smiling. 'And he really isn't in the least conceited. I think it's only because he has a straight nose and high cheek-bones.'

'You know, they don't like him at the club. They call him Powder-Puff Percy.'

Anne flushed. She had heard that before and it made her very angry. Her eyes filled with tears.

'I think it's frightfully unfair.'

Mrs Hannay took her hand and gave it an affectionate little squeeze.

'My dear, you know I don't want to hurt your feelings. Your husband can't help rising very high in the Service. He'd make things so much easier for himself if he were a little more human. Why doesn't he play football?'

'It's not his game. He's always only too glad to play tennis.'

'He doesn't give that impression. He gives the impression that there's no one here who's worth his while to play with.'

'Well, there isn't,' said Anne, stung.

Alban happened to be an extremely good tennis-player. He had played a lot of tournaments in England and Anne knew that it gave him a grim satisfaction to knock those beefy, hearty men all over the court. He could make the best of them look foolish. He could be maddening on the tennis court and Anne was aware that sometimes he could not resist the temptation.

'He does play to the gallery, doesn't he?' said Mrs Hannay.

'I don't think so. Believe me, Alban has no idea he isn't popular. As far as I can see he's always pleasant and friendly with everybody.'

'It's then he's most offensive,' said Mrs Hannay dryly.

'I know people don't like us very much,' said Anne, smiling a little. 'I'm very sorry, but really I don't know what we can do about it.'

'Not you, my dear,' cried Mrs Hannay. 'Everybody adores you. That's why they put up with your husband. My dear, who could help liking you?'

'I don't know why they should adore me,' said Anne.

But she did not say it quite sincerely. She was deliberately playing the part of the dear little woman and within her she bubbled with amusement. They disliked Alban because he had such an air of distinction, and because he was interested in art and literature; they did not understand these things and so thought them unmanly; and they disliked him because his capacity was greater than theirs. They disliked him because he was better bred than they. They thought him superior; well, he was superior, but not in the sense they meant.

They forgave her because she was an ugly little thing. That was what she called herself, but she wasn't that, or if she was it was with an ugliness that was most attractive. She was like a little monkey, but a very sweet little monkey and very human. She had a neat figure. That was her best point. That and her eyes. They were very large, of a deep brown, liquid and shining; they were full of fun, but they could be tender on occasion with a charming sympathy. She was dark, her frizzy hair was almost black, and her skin was swarthy; she had a small fleshy nose, with large nostrils, and much too big a mouth. But she was alert and vivacious. She could talk with a show of real interest to the ladies of the colony about their husbands and their servants and their children in England, and she could listen appreciatively to the men who told her stories that she had often heard before. They thought her a jolly good sort. They did not know what clever fun she made of them in private. It never occurred to them that she thought them narrow, gross, and pretentious. They found no glamour in the East because they looked at it vulgarly with material eyes. Romance lingered at their threshold and they drove it away like an importunate beggar. She was aloof. She repeated to herself Landor's line:

'*Nature I loved, and next to nature, art.*'

She reflected on her conversation with Mrs Hannay, but on the whole it left her unconcerned. She wondered whether she should say anything about it to Alban; it had always seemed a little odd to her that he should be so little aware of his unpopularity; but she was afraid that if she told him of it he would become self-conscious. He never noticed the coldness of the men at the club. He made them feel shy and therefore uncomfortable. His appearance then caused a sort of awkwardness, but he, happily insensible, was breezily cordial to all and sundry. The fact was that he was strangely unconscious of other people. She was in a class by herself, she and a little group of friends they had in London, but he could never quite realize that the people of the colony, the government officials and the planters and their wives, were human beings. They were to him like pawns in a game. He laughed with them, chaffed them, and was amiably tolerant of them; with a chuckle Anne told herself that he was rather like the master of a preparatory school taking little boys out on a picnic and anxious to give them a good time.

She was afraid it wasn't much good telling Alban. He was incapable of the dissimulation which, she happily realized, came so easily to her. What was one to do with these people? The men had come out to the colony as lads from second-rate schools, and life had taught them nothing. At fifty they had the outlook of hobbledehoys. Most of them drank a great deal too much. They read nothing worth reading. Their ambition was to be like everybody else. Their highest praise was to say that a man was a damned good sort. If you were interested in the things of the spirit you were a prig. They were eaten up with envy of one another and devoured by petty jealousies. And the women, poor things, were obsessed by petty rivalries. They made a circle that was more provincial than any in the smallest town in England. They were prudish and spiteful. What did it matter if they did not like Alban? They would have to put up with him because his ability was so great. He was clever and energetic. They could not say that he did not do his work well. He had been successful in every post he had occupied. With his sensitiveness and his imagination he understood the native mind and he was able to get the natives to do things that no one in his position could. He had a gift for languages, and he spoke all the local dialects. He not only knew the common tongue that most of the government officials spoke, but was acquainted with the niceties of the language and on occasion could make use of a ceremonial speech that flattered and impressed the chiefs. He had a gift for organization. He was not afraid of responsibility. In due course he was bound to be made a Resident. Alban had some interest in England; his father was a brigadier-general killed in the war, and though he had no private means he had influential friends. He spoke of them with pleasant irony.

'The great advantage of democratic government,' he said, 'is that merit, with influence to back it, can be pretty sure of receiving its due reward.'

Alban was so obviously the ablest man in the Service that there seemed no reason why he should not eventually be made Governor. Then, thought Anne, his air of superiority, of which they complained, would be in place. They would accept him as their master and he would know how to make himself respected and obeyed. The position she foresaw did not dazzle her. She accepted it as a right. It would be fun for Alban to be Governor and for her to be the Governor's wife. And what an opportunity! They were sheep, the government servants and the planters; when Government House was the seat of culture they would soon fall into line. When the best way to the Governor's favour was to be intelligent, intelligence would become the fashion. She and Alban would cherish the native arts and collect carefully the memorials of a vanished past. The country would make an advance it had never dreamed of. They would develop it, but along lines of order and beauty. They would instil into their subordinates a passion for that beautiful land and a loving interest in these romantic races. They would make them realize what music meant. They would cultivate literature. They would create beauty. It would be the golden age.

Suddenly she heard Alban's footstep. Anne awoke from her day-dream. All that was far away in the future. Alban was only a District Officer yet and what was important was the life they were living now. She heard Alban go into the bath-house and splash water over himself. In a minute he came in. He had changed into a shirt and shorts. His fair hair was still wet.

'Tiffin ready?' he asked.

'Yes.'

He sat down at the piano and played the piece that he had played in the morning. The silvery notes cascaded coolly down the sultry air. You had an impression of a formal garden with great trees and elegant pieces of artificial water and of leisurely walks bordered with pseudo-classical statues. Alban played with a peculiar delicacy. Lunch was announced by the head boy. He rose from the piano. They walked into the dining-room hand in hand. A punkah lazily fanned the air. Anne gave the table a glance. With its bright-coloured tablecloth and the amusing plates it looked very gay.

'Anything exciting at the office this morning?' she asked.

'No, nothing much. A buffalo case. Oh, and Prynne has sent along to ask me to go up to the estate. Some coolies have been damaging the trees and he wants me to come along and look into it.'

Prynne was manager of the rubber estate up the river and now and then they spent a night with him. Sometimes when he wanted a change he came down to dinner and slept at the D.O.'s bungalow. They both liked him. He was a man of five-and-thirty, with a red face, with deep furrows in it, and very black hair. He was quite uneducated, but cheerful and easy, and being the only Englishman within two days' journey they could not but be friendly with him. He had been a little shy of them at first. News spreads quickly in the East and long before they arrived in the district he heard that they were highbrows. He did not know what he would make of them. He probably did not know that he had charm, which makes up for many more commendable qualities, and Alban with his almost feminine sensibilities was peculiarly susceptible to this. He found Alban much more human than he expected, and of course Anne was stunning. Alban played ragtime for him, which he would not have done for the Governor, and played dominoes with him. When Alban was making his first tour of the district with Anne, and suggested that they would like to spend a couple of nights on the estate, he had thought it as well to warn him that he lived with a native woman and had two children by her. He would do his best to keep them out of Anne's sight, but he could not send them away, there was nowhere to send them. Alban laughed.

'Anne isn't that sort of woman at all. Don't dream of hiding them. She loves children.'

Anne quickly made friends with the shy, pretty little native woman and soon was playing happily with the children. She and the girl had long confidential chats. The children took a fancy to her. She brought them lovely toys from Port Wallace. Prynne, comparing her smiling tolerance with the disapproving acidity of the other white women of the colony, described himself as knocked all of a heap. He could not do enough to show his delight and gratitude.

'If all highbrows are like you,' he said, 'give me highbrows every time.'

He hated to think that in another year they would leave the district for good and the chances were that, if the next D.O. was married, his wife would think it dreadful that, rather than live alone, he had a native woman to live with him and, what was more, was much attached to her.

But there had been a good deal of discontent on the estate of late. The coolies were Chinese and infected with communist ideas. They were disorderly. Alban had been obliged to sentence several of them for various crimes to terms of imprisonment.

'Prynne tells me that as soon as their term is up he's going to send them all back to China and get Javanese instead,' said Alban. 'I'm sure he's right. They're much more amenable.'

'You don't think there's going to be any serious trouble?'

'Oh, no. Prynne knows his job and he's a pretty determined fellow. He wouldn't put up with any nonsense and with me and our policemen to back him up I don't imagine they'll try any monkey tricks.' He smiled. 'The iron hand in the velvet glove.'

The words were barely out of his mouth when a sudden shouting arose. There was a commotion and the sound of steps. Loud voices and cries.

'Tuan, Tuan.'

'What the devil's the matter?'

Alban sprang from his chair and went swiftly on to the veranda. Anne followed him. At the bottom of the steps was a group of natives. There was the sergeant, and three or four policemen, boatmen, and several men from the kampong.

'What is it?' called Alban.

Two or three shouted back in answer. The sergeant pushed others aside and Alban saw lying on the ground a man in a shirt and khaki shorts. He ran down the steps. He recognized the man as the assistant manager of Prynne's estate. He was a half-caste. His shorts were covered with blood and there was clotted blood all over one side of his face and head. He was unconscious.

'Bring him up here,' called Anne.

Alban gave an order. The man was lifted up and carried on to the veranda. They laid him on the floor and Anne put a pillow under his head. She sent for water and for the medicine-chest in which they kept things for emergency.

'Is he dead?' asked Alban.

'No.'

'Better try to give him some brandy.'

The boatmen brought ghastly news. The Chinese coolies had risen suddenly and attacked the manager's office. Prynne was killed, and the assistant manager, Oakley by name, had escaped only by the skin of his teeth. He had come upon the rioters when they were looting the office, he had seen Prynne's body thrown out of the window, and had taken to his heels. Some of the Chinese saw him and gave chase. He ran for the river and was wounded as he jumped into the launch. The launch managed to put off before the Chinese could get on board and they had come down-stream for help as fast as they could go. As they went they saw flames rising from the office buildings. There was no doubt that the coolies had burned down everything that would burn.

Oakley gave a groan and opened his eyes. He was a little, dark-skinned man, with flattened features and thick coarse hair. His great native eyes were filled with terror.

'You're all right,' said Anne. 'You're quite safe.'

He gave a sigh and smiled. Anne washed his face and swabbed it with antiseptics. The wound on his head was not serious.

'Can you speak yet?' said Alban.

'Wait a bit,' she said. 'We must look at his leg.'

Alban ordered the sergeant to get the crowd out of the veranda. Anne ripped up one leg of the shorts. The material was clinging to the coagulated wound.

'I've been bleeding like a pig,' said Oakley.

It was only a flesh wound. Alban was clever with his fingers, and though the blood began to flow again they staunched it. Alban put on a dressing and a bandage. The sergeant and a policeman lifted Oakley on to a long chair. Alban gave him a brandy and soda, and soon he felt strong enough to speak. He knew no more than the boatmen had already told. Prynne was dead and the estate was in flames.

'And the girl and the children?' asked Anne.

'I don't know.'

'Oh, Alban.'

'I must turn out the police. Are you sure Prynne is dead?'

'Yes, sir. I saw him.'

'Have the rioters got fire-arms?'

'I don't know, sir.'

'How d'you mean, you don't know?' Alban cried irritably. 'Prynne had a gun, hadn't he?'

'Yes, sir.'

'There must have been more on the estate. You had one, didn't you? The head overseer had one.'

The half-caste was silent. Alban looked at him sternly.

'How many of those damned Chinese are there?'

'A hundred and fifty.'

Anne wondered that he asked so many questions. It seemed waste of time. The important thing was to collect coolies for the transport up-river, prepare the boats, and issue ammunition to the police.

'How many policemen have you got, sir?' asked Oakley.

'Eight and the sergeant.'

'Could I come too? That would make ten of us. I'm sure I shall be all right now I'm bandaged.'

'I'm not going,' said Alban.

'Alban, you must,' cried Anne. She could not believe her ears.

'Nonsense. It would be madness. Oakley's obviously useless. He's sure to have a temperature in a few hours. He'd only be in the way. That leaves nine guns. There are a hundred and fifty Chinese and they've got fire-arms and all the ammunition in the world.'

'How do' you know?'

'It stands to reason they wouldn't have started a show like this unless they had. It would be idiotic to go.'

Anne stared at him with open mouth. Oakley's eyes were puzzled.

'What are you going to do?'

'Well, fortunately we've got the launch. I'll send it to Port Wallace with a request for reinforcements.'

'But they won't be here for two days at least.'

'Well, what of it? Prynne's dead and the estate burned to the ground. We couldn't do any good by going up now. I shall send a native to reconnoitre so that we can find out exactly what the rioters are doing.' He gave Anne his charming smile. 'Believe me, my pet, the rascals won't lose anything by waiting a day or two for what's coming to them.'

Oakley opened his mouth to speak, but perhaps he hadn't the nerve. He was a half-caste assistant manager and Alban, the D.O., represented the power of the Government. But the man's eyes sought Anne's and she thought she read in them an earnest and personal appeal.

'But in two days they're capable of committing the most frightful atrocities,' she cried. 'It's quite unspeakable what they may do.'

'Whatever damage they do they'll pay for. I promise you that.'

'Oh, Alban, you can't sit still and do nothing. I beseech you to go yourself at once.'

'Don't be so silly. I can't quell a riot with eight policemen and a sergeant. I haven't got the right to take a risk of that sort. We'd have to go in boats. You don't think we could get up unobserved. The lalang along the banks is perfect cover and they could just take pot shots at us as we came along. We shouldn't have a chance.'

'I'm afraid they'll only think it weakness if nothing is done for two days, sir,' said Oakley.

'When I want your opinion I'll ask for it,' said Alban acidly. 'So far as I can see when there was danger the only thing you did was to cut and run. I can't persuade myself that your assistance in a crisis would be very valuable.'

The half-caste reddened. He said nothing more. He looked straight in front of him with troubled eyes.

'I'm going down to the office,' said Alban. 'I'll just write a short report and send it down the river by launch at once.'

He gave an order to the sergeant, who had been standing all this time stiffly at the top of the steps. He saluted and ran off. Alban went into a little hall they had to get his topee. Anne swiftly followed him.

'Alban, for God's sake listen to me a minute,' she whispered.

'I don't want to be rude to you, darling, but I am pressed for time. I think you'd much better mind your own business.'

'You can't do nothing, Alban. You must go. Whatever the risk.'

'Don't be such a fool,' he said angrily.

He had never been angry with her before. She seized his hand to hold him back.

'I tell you I can do no good by going.'

'You don't know. There's the woman and Prynne's children. We must do something to save them. Let me come with you. They'll kill them.'

'They've probably killed them already.'

'Oh, how can you be so callous! If there's a chance of saving them it's your duty to try.'

'It's my duty to act like a reasonable human being. I'm not going to risk my life and my policemen's for the sake of a native woman and her half-caste brats. What sort of a damned fool do you take me for?'

'They'll say you were afraid.'

'Who?'

'Everyone in the colony.'

He smiled disdainfully.

'If you only knew what a complete contempt I have for the opinion of everyone in the colony.'

She gave him a long searching look. She had been married to him for eight years and she knew every expression of his face and every thought in his mind. She stared into his blue eyes as if they were open windows. She suddenly went quite pale. She dropped his hand and turned away. Without another word she went back on to the veranda. Her ugly little monkey face was a mask of horror.

Alban went to his office, wrote a brief account of the facts, and in a few minutes the motor launch was pounding down the river.

The next two days were endless. Escaped natives brought them news of happenings on the estate. But from their excited and terrified stories it was impossible to get an exact impression of the truth. There had been a good deal of bloodshed. The head overseer had been killed. They brought wild tales of cruelty and outrage. Anne could hear nothing of Prynne's woman and the two children. She shuddered when she thought of what might have been their fate. Alban collected as many natives as he could. They were armed with spears and swords. He commandeered boats. The situation was serious, but he kept his head. He felt that he had done all that was possible and nothing remained but for him to carry on normally. He did his official work. He played the piano a great deal. He rode with Anne in the early morning. He appeared to have forgotten that they had had the first serious difference of opinion in the whole of their married life. He took it that Anne had accepted the wisdom of his decision. He was as amusing, cordial, and gay with her as he had always been. When he spoke of the rioters it was with grim irony: when the time came to settle matters a good many of them would wish they had never been born.

'What'll happen to them?' asked Anne.

'Oh, they'll hang.' He gave a shrug of distaste. 'I hate having to be present at executions. It always makes me feel rather sick.'

He was very sympathetic to Oakley, whom they had put to bed and whom Anne was nursing. Perhaps he was sorry that in the exasperation of the moment he had spoken to him offensively, and he went out of his way to be nice to him.

Then on the afternoon of the third day, when they were drinking their coffee after luncheon, Alban's quick ears caught the sound of a motor boat approaching. At the same moment a policeman ran up to say that the government launch was sighted.

'At last,' cried Alban.

He bolted out of the house. Anne raised one of the jalousies and looked out at the river. Now the sound was quite loud and in a moment she saw the boat come round the bend. She saw Alban on the landing-stage. He got into a prahu and as the launch dropped her anchor he went on board. She told Oakley that the reinforcements had come.

'Will the D.O. go up with them when they attack?' he asked her.

'Naturally,' said Anne coldly.

'I wondered.'

Anne felt a strange feeling in her heart. For the last two days she had had to exercise all her self-control not to cry. She did not answer. She went out of the room.

A quarter of an hour later Alban returned to the bungalow with the captain of constabulary who had been sent with twenty Sikhs to deal with the rioters. Captain Stratton was a little red-faced man with a red moustache and bow legs, very hearty and dashing, whom she had met often at Port Wallace.

'Well, Mrs Torel, this is a pretty kettle of fish,' he cried, as he shook hands with her, in a loud jolly voice. 'Here I am, with my army all full of pep and ready for a scrap. Up, boys, and at 'em. Have you got anything to drink in this benighted place?'

'Boy,' she cried, smiling.

'Something long and cool and faintly alcoholic, and then I'm ready to discuss the plan of campaign.'

His breeziness was very comforting. It blew away the sullen apprehension that had seemed ever since the disaster to brood over the lost peace of the bungalow. The boy came in with a tray and Stratton mixed himself a stengah. Alban put him in possession of the facts. He told them clearly, briefly, and with precision.

'I must say I admire you,' said Stratton. 'In your place I should never have been able to resist the temptation to take my eight cops and have a whack at the blighters myself.'

'I thought it was a perfectly unjustifiable risk to take.'

'Safety first, old boy, eh, what?' said Stratton jovially. 'I'm jolly glad you didn't. It's not often we get the chance of a scrap. It would have been a dirty trick to keep the whole show to yourself.'

Captain Stratton was all for steaming straight up the river and attacking at once, but Alban pointed out to him the inadvisability of such a course. The sound of the approaching launch would warn the rioters. The long grass at the river's edge offered them cover and they had enough guns to make a landing difficult. It seemed useless to expose the attacking force to their fire. It was silly to forget that they had to face a hundred and fifty desperate men and it would be easy to fall into an ambush. Alban expounded his own plan. Stratton listened to it. He nodded now and then. The plan was evidently a good one. It would enable them to take the rioters in the rear, surprise them, and in all probability finish the job without a single casualty. He would have been a fool not to accept it.

'But why didn't you do that yourself?' asked Stratton.

'With eight men and a sergeant?'

Stratton did not answer.

'Anyhow, it's not a bad idea and we'll settle on it. It gives us plenty of time, so with your permission, Mrs Torel, I'll have a bath.'

They set out at sunset, Captain Stratton and his twenty Sikhs, Alban with his policemen and the natives he had collected. The night was dark and moonless. Trailing behind them were the dug-outs that Alban had gathered together and into which after a certain distance they proposed to transfer their force. It was important that no sound should give warning of their approach. After they had gone for about three hours by launch they took to the dug-outs and in them silently paddled up-stream. They reached the border of the vast estate and landed. Guides led them along a path so narrow that they had to march in single file. It had been long unused and the going was heavy. They had twice to ford a stream. The path led them circuitously to the rear of the coolie lines, but they did not wish to reach them till nearly dawn and presently Stratton gave the order to halt. It was a long cold wait. At last the night seemed to be less dark; you did not see the trunks of the trees, but were vaguely sensible of them against its darkness. Stratton had been sitting with his back to a tree. He gave a whispered order to a sergeant and in a few minutes the column was once more on the march. Suddenly they found themselves on a road. They formed fours. The dawn broke and in the ghostly light the surrounding objects were wanly visible. The column stopped on a whispered order. They had come in sight of the coolie lines. Silence reigned in them. The column crept on again and again halted. Stratton, his eyes shining, gave Alban a smile.

'We've caught the blighters asleep.'

He lined up his men. They inserted cartridges in their guns. He stepped forward and raised his hand. The carbines were pointed at the coolie lines.

'Fire.'

There was a rattle as the volley of shots rang out. Then suddenly there was a tremendous din and the Chinese poured out, shouting and waving their arms, but in front of them, to Alban's utter bewilderment, bellowing at the top of his voice and shaking his fists at them, was a white man.

'Who the hell's that?' cried Stratton.

A very big, very fat man, in khaki trousers and a singlet, was running towards them as fast as his fat legs would carry him and as he ran shaking both fists at them and yelling:

'*Smerige flikkers! Vervloekte ploerten!*'

'My God, it's Van Hasseldt,' said Alban.

This was the Dutch manager of the timber camp which was situated on a considerable tributary of the river about twenty miles away.

'What the hell do you think you're doing?' he puffed as he came up to them.

'How the hell did you get here?' asked Stratton in turn.

He saw that the Chinese were scattering in all directions and gave his men instructions to round them up. Then he turned again to Van Hasseldt.

'What's it mean?'

'Mean? Mean?' shouted the Dutchman furiously. 'That's what I want to know. You and your damned policemen. What do you mean by coming here at this hour in the morning and firing a damned volley. Target practice? You might have killed me. Idiots!'

'Have a cigarette,' said Stratton.

'How did you get here, Van Hasseldt?' asked Alban again, very much at sea. 'This is the force they've sent from Port Wallace to quell the riot.'

'How did I get here? I walked. How did you think I got here? Riot be damned. I quelled the riot. If that's what you came for you can take your damned policemen home again. A bullet came within a foot of my head.'

'I don't understand,' said Alban.

'There's nothing to understand,' spluttered Van Hasseldt, still fuming. 'Some coolies came to my estate and said the Chinks had killed Prynne and burned the bally place down, so I took my assistant and my head overseer and a Dutch friend I had staying with me and came over to see what the trouble was.'

Captain Stratton opened his eyes wide.

'Did you just stroll in as if it was a picnic?' he asked.

'Well, you don't think after all the years I've been in this country I'm going to let a couple of hundred Chinks put the fear of God into me? I found them all scared out of their lives. One of them had the nerve to pull a gun on me and I blew his bloody brains out. And the rest surrendered. I've got the leaders tied up. I was going to send a boat down to you this morning to come up and get them.'

Stratton stared at him for a minute and then burst into a shout of laughter. He laughed till the tears ran down his face. The Dutchman looked at him angrily, then began to laugh too; he laughed with the big belly laugh of a very fat man and his coils of fat heaved and shook. Alban watched them sullenly. He was very angry.

'What about Prynne's girl and the kids?' he asked.

'Oh, they got away all right.'

It just showed how wise he had been not to let himself be influenced by Anne's hysteria. Of course the children had come to no harm. He never thought they would.

Van Hasseldt and his little party started back for the timber camp, and as soon after as possible Stratton embarked his twenty Sikhs and leaving Alban with his sergeant and his policemen to deal with the situation departed for Port Wallace. Alban gave him a brief report for the Governor. There was much for him to do. It looked as though he would have to stay for a considerable time; but since every house on the estate had been burned to the ground and he was obliged to install himself in the coolie lines he thought it better that Anne should not join him. He sent her a note to that effect. He was glad to be able to reassure her of the safety of poor Prynne's girl. He set to work at once to make his preliminary inquiry. He examined a host of witnesses. But a week later he received an order to go to Port Wallace at once. The launch that brought it was to take him and he was able to see Anne on the way down for no more than an hour. Alban was a trifle vexed.

'I don't know why the Governor can't leave me to get things straight without dragging me off like this. It's extremely inconvenient.'

'Oh, well, the Government never bothers very much about the convenience of its subordinates, does it?' smiled Anne.

'It's just red-tape. I would offer to take you along, darling, only I shan't stay a minute longer than I need. I want to get my evidence together for the Sessions Court as soon as possible. I think in a country like this it's very important that justice should be prompt.'

When the launch came in to Port Wallace one of the harbour police told him that the harbour-master had a chit for him. It was from the Governor's secretary and informed him that His Excellency desired to see him as soon as convenient after his arrival. It was ten in the morning. Alban went to the club, had a bath and shaved, and then in clean ducks, his hair neatly brushed, he called a rickshaw and told the boy to take him to the Governor's office. He was at once shown in to the secretary's room. The secretary shook hands with him.

'I'll tell H.E. you're here,' he said. 'Won't you sit down?'

The secretary left the room and in a little while came back.

'H.E. will see you in a minute. Do you mind if I get on with my letters?'

Alban smiled. The secretary was not exactly come-hither. He waited, smoking a cigarette, and amused himself with his own thoughts. He was making a good job of the preliminary inquiry. It interested him. Then an orderly came in and told Alban that the Governor was ready for him. He rose from his seat and followed him into the Governor's room.

'Good morning, Torel.'

'Good morning, sir.'

The Governor was sitting at a large desk. He nodded to Alban and motioned to him to take a seat. The Governor was all grey. His hair was grey, his face, his eyes; he looked as though the tropical suns had washed the colour out of him; he had been in the country for thirty years and had risen one by one through all the ranks of the Service; he looked tired and depressed. Even his voice was grey. Alban liked him because he was quiet; he did not think him clever, but he had an unrivalled knowledge of the country, and his great experience was a very good substitute for intelligence. He looked at Alban for a full moment without speaking and the odd idea came to Alban that he was embarrassed. He very nearly gave him a lead.

'I saw Van Hasseldt yesterday,' said the Governor suddenly.

'Yes, sir?'

'Will you give me your account of the occurrences at the Alud Estate and of the steps you took to deal with them.'

Alban had an orderly mind. He was self-possessed. He marshalled his facts well and was able to state them with precision. He chose his words with care and spoke them fluently.

'You had a sergeant and eight policemen. Why did you not immediately go to the scene of the disturbance?'

'I thought the risk was unjustifiable.'

A thin smile was outlined on the Governor's grey face.

'If the officers of this Government had hesitated to take unjustifiable risks it would never have become a province of the British Empire.'

Alban was silent. It was difficult to talk to a man who spoke obvious nonsense.

'I am anxious to hear your reasons for the decision you took.'

Alban gave them coolly. He was quite convinced of the rightness of his action. He repeated, but more fully, what he had said in the first place to Anne. The Governor listened attentively.

'Van Hasseldt, with his manager, a Dutch friend of his, and a native overseer, seems to have coped with the situation very efficiently,' said the Governor.

'He had a lucky break. That doesn't prevent him from being a damned fool. It was madness to do what he did.'

'Do you realize that by leaving a Dutch planter to do what you should have done yourself, you have covered the Government with ridicule?'

'No, sir.'

'You've made yourself a laughing-stock in the whole colony.'

Alban smiled.

'My back is broad enough to bear the ridicule of persons to whose opinion I am entirely indifferent.'

'The utility of a government official depends very largely on his prestige, and I'm afraid his prestige is likely to be inconsiderable when he lies under the stigma of cowardice.'

Alban flushed a little.

'I don't quite know what you mean by that, sir.'

'I've gone into the matter very carefully. I've seen Captain Stratton, and Oakley, poor Prynne's assistant, and I've seen Van Hasseldt. I've listened to your defence.'

'I didn't know that I was defending myself, sir.'

'Be so good as not to interrupt me. I think you committed a grave error of judgement. As it turns out, the risk was very small, but whatever it was, I think you should have taken it. In such matters promptness and firmness are essential. It is not for me to conjecture what motive led you to send for a force of constabulary and do nothing till they came. I am afraid, however, that I consider that your usefulness in the Service is no longer very great.'

Alban looked at him with astonishment.

'But would you have gone under the circumstances?' he asked him.

'I should.'

Alban shrugged his shoulders.

'Don't you believe me?' rapped out the Governor.

'Of course I believe you, sir. But perhaps you will allow me to say that if you had been killed the colony would have suffered an irreparable loss.'

The Governor drummed on the table with his fingers. He looked out of the window and then looked again at Alban. When he spoke it was not unkindly.

'I think you are unfitted by temperament for this rather rough-and-tumble life, Totel. If you'll take my advice you'll go home. With your abilities I feel sure that you'll soon find an occupation much better suited to you.'

'I'm afraid I don't understand what you mean, sir.'

'Oh, come, Torel, you're not stupid. I'm trying to make things easy for you. For your wife's sake as well as for your own I do not wish you to leave the colony with the stigma of being dismissed from the Service for cowardice. I'm giving you the opportunity of resigning.'

'Thank you very much, sir. I'm not prepared to avail myself of the opportunity. If I resign I admit that I committed an error and that the charge you make against me is justified. I don't admit it.'

'You can please yourself. I have considered the matter very carefully and I have no doubt about it in my mind. I am forced to discharge you from the Service. The necessary papers will reach you in due course. Meanwhile you will return to your post and hand over to the officer appointed to succeed you on his arrival.'

'Very good, sir,' replied Alban, a twinkle of amusement in his eyes. 'When do you desire me to return to my post?'

'At once.'

'Have you any objection to my going to the club and having tiffin before I go?'

The Governor looked at him with surprise. His exasperation was mingled with an unwilling admiration.

'Not at all. I'm sorry, Torel, that this unhappy incident should have deprived the Government of a servant whose zeal has always been so apparent and whose tact, intelligence, and industry seemed to point him out in the future for very high office.'

'Your Excellency does not read Schiller, I suppose. You are probably not acquainted with his celebrated line: *mit der Dummheit kämpfen die Götter selbst vergebens.*'

'What does it mean?'

'Roughly: Against stupidity the gods themselves battle in vain.'

'Good morning.'

With his head in the air, a smile on his lips, Alban left the Governor's office. The Governor was human, and he had the curiosity to ask his secretary later in the day if Alban Torel had really gone to the club.

'Yes, sir. He had tiffin there.'

'It must have wanted some nerve.'

Alban entered the club jauntily and joined the group of men standing at the bar. He talked to them in the breezy, cordial tone he always used with them. It was designed to put them at their ease. They had been discussing him ever since Stratton had come back to Port Wallace with his story, sneering at him and laughing at him, and all who had resented his superciliousness, and they were the majority, were triumphant because his pride had had a fall. But they were so taken aback at seeing him now, so confused to find him as confident as ever, that it was they who were embarrassed.

One man, though he knew perfectly, asked him what he was doing in Port Wallace.

'Oh, I came about the riot on the Alud Estate. H.E. wanted to see me. He does not see eye to eye with me about it. The silly old ass has fired me. I'm going home as soon as he appoints a D.O. to take over.'

There was a moment of awkwardness. One, more kindly disposed than the others, said:

'I'm awfully sorry.'

Alban shrugged his shoulders.

'My dear fellow, what can you do with a perfect damned fool? The only thing is to let him stew in his own juice.'

When the Governor's secretary had told his chief as much of this as he thought discreet, the Governor smiled.

'Courage is a queer thing. I would rather have shot myself than go to the club just then and face all those fellows.'

A fortnight later, having sold to the incoming D.O. all the decorations that Anne had taken so much trouble about, with the rest of their things in packing-cases and trunks, they arrived at Port Wallace to await the local steamer that was to take them to Singapore. The padre's wife invited them to stay with her, but Anne refused; she insisted that they should go to the hotel. An hour after their arrival she received a very kind little letter from the Governor's wife asking her to go and have tea with her. She went. She found Mrs Hannay alone, but in a minute the Governor joined them. He expressed his regret that she was leaving and told her how sorry he was for the cause.

'It's very kind of you to say that,' said Anne, smiling gaily, 'but you mustn't think I take it to heart. I'm entirely on Alban's side. I think what he did was absolutely right and if you don't mind my saying so I think you've treated him most unjustly.'

'Believe me, I hated having to take the step I took.'

'Don't let's talk about it,' said Anne.

'What are your plans when you get home? asked Mrs Hannay.

Anne began to chat brightly. You would have thought she had not a care in the world. She seemed in great spirits at going home. She was jolly and amusing and made little jokes. When she took leave of the Governor and his wife she thanked them for all their kindness. The Governor escorted her to the door.

The next day but one, after dinner, they went on board the clean and comfortable little ship. The padre and his wife saw them off. When they went into their cabin they found a large parcel on Anne's bunk. It was addressed to Alban. He opened it and saw that it was an immense powder-puff.

'Hullo, I wonder who sent us this,' he said, with a laugh. 'It must be for you, darling.'

Anne gave him a quick look. She went pale. The brutes! How could they be so cruel? She forced herself to smile.

'It's enormous, isn't it? I've never seen such a large powder-puff in my life.'

But when he had left the cabin and they were out at sea, she threw it passionately overboard.

And now, now that they were back in London and Sondurah was nine thousand miles away, she clenched her hands as she thought of it. Somehow, it seemed the worst thing of all. It was so wantonly unkind to send that absurd object to Alban, Powder-Puff Percy; it showed such a petty spite. Was that their idea of humour? Nothing had hurt her more and even now she felt that it was only by holding on to herself that she could prevent herself from crying. Suddenly she started, for the door opened and Alban came in. She was still sitting in the chair in which he had left her.

'Hullo, why haven't you dressed?' He looked about the room. 'You haven't unpacked.'

'No.'

'Why on earth not?'

'I'm not going to unpack. I'm not going to stay here. I'm leaving you.'

'What are you talking about?'

'I've stuck it out till now. I made up my mind I would till we got home. I set my teeth, I've borne more than I thought it possible to bear, but now it's finished. I've done all that could be expected of me. We're back in London now and I can go.'

He looked at her in utter bewilderment.

'Are you mad, Anne?'

'Oh, my God, what I've endured! The journey to Singapore, with all the officers knowing, and even the Chinese stewards. And at Singapore, the way people looked at us at the hotel, and the sympathy I had to put up with, the bricks they dropped and their embarrassment when they realized what they'd done. My God, I could have killed them. That interminable journey home. There wasn't a single passenger on the ship who didn't know. The contempt they had for you and the kindness they went out of their way to show me. And you so self-complacent and so pleased with yourself, seeing nothing, feeling nothing. You must have the hide of a rhinoceros. The misery of seeing you so chatty and agreeable. Pariahs, that's what we were. You seemed to ask them to snub you. How can anyone be so shameless?'

She was flaming with passion. Now that at last she need not wear the mask of indifference and pride that she had forced herself to assume she cast aside all reserve and all self-control. The words poured from her trembling lips in a virulent stream.

'My dear, how can you be so absurd?' he said good-naturedly, smiling. 'You must be very nervous and high-strung to have got such ideas in your head. Why didn't you tell me? You're like a country bumpkin who comes to London and thinks everyone is staring at him. Nobody bothered about us, and if they did what on earth did it matter? You ought to have more sense than to bother about what a lot of fools say. And what do you imagine they were saying?'

'They were saying you'd been fired.'

'Well, that was true,' he laughed.

'They said you were a coward.'

'What of it?'

'Well, you see, that was true too.'

He looked at her for a moment reflectively. His lips tightened a little.

'And what makes you think so?' he asked acidly.

'I saw it in your eyes, that day the news came, when you refused to go to the estate and I followed you into the hall when you went to fetch your topee. I begged you to go, I felt that whatever the danger you must take it, and suddenly I saw the fear in your eyes. I nearly fainted with the horror.'

'I should have been a fool to risk my life to no purpose. Why should I? Nothing that concerned me was at stake. Courage is the obvious virtue of the stupid. I don't attach any particular importance to it.'

'How do you mean that nothing that concerned you was at stake? If that's true then your whole life is a sham. You've given away everything you stood for, everything we both stand for. You've let all of us down. We did set ourselves up on a pinnacle, we did think ourselves better than the rest of them because we loved literature and art and music, we weren't content to live a life of ignoble jealousies and vulgar tittle-tattle, we did cherish the things of the spirit, and we loved beauty. It was our food and drink. They laughed at us and sneered at us. That was inevitable. The ignorant and the common naturally hate and fear those who are interested in things they don't understand. We didn't care. We called them Philistines. We despised them and we had a right to despise them. Our justification was that we were better and nobler and wiser and braver than they were. And you weren't better, you weren't nobler, you weren't braver. When the crisis came you slunk away like a whipped cur with his tail between his legs. You of all people hadn't the right to be a coward. They despise *us* now and they have the right to despise us. Us and all we stood for. Now they can say that art and beauty are all rot; when it comes to a pinch people like us always let you down. They never stopped looking for a chance to turn and rend us and you gave it to them. They can say that they always expected it. It's a triumph for them. I used to be furious because they called you Powder-Puff Percy. Did you know they did?'

'Of course. I thought it very vulgar, but it left me entirely indifferent.'

'It's funny that their instinct should have been so right.'

'Do you mean to say you've been harbouring this against me all these weeks? I should never have thought you capable of it.'

'I couldn't let you down when everyone was against you. I was too proud for that. Whatever happened I swore to myself that I'd stick to you till we got home. It's been torture.'

'Don't you love me any more?'

'Love you? I loathe the very sight of you.'

'Anne!'

'God knows I loved you. For eight years I worshipped the ground you trod on. You were everything to me. I believed in you as some people believe in God. When I saw the fear in your eyes that day, when you told me that you weren't going to risk your life for a kept woman and her half-caste brats, I was shattered. It was as though someone had wrenched my heart out of my body and trampled on it. You killed my love there and then, Alban. You killed it stone-dead. Since then when you've kissed me I've had to clench my hands so as not to turn my face away. The mere thought of anything else makes me feel physically sick. I loathe your complacence and your frightful insensitiveness. Perhaps I could have forgiven it if it had been just a moment's weakness and if afterwards you'd been ashamed. I should have been miserable, but I think my love was so great that I should only have felt pity for you. But you're incapable of shame. And now I believe in nothing. You're only a silly, pretentious, vulgar poseur. I would rather be the wife of a second-rate planter so long as he had the common human virtues of a man than the wife of a fake like you.'

He did not answer. Gradually his face began to discompose. Those handsome, regular features of his horribly distorted and suddenly he broke out into loud sobs. She gave a little cry.

'Don't Alban, don't.'

'Oh, darling, how can you be so cruel to me? I adore you. I'd give my whole life to please you. I can't live without you.'

She put out her arms as though to ward off a blow.

'No, no, Alban, don't try to move me. I can't. I must go. I can't live with you any more. It would be frightful. I can never forget. I must tell you the truth, I have only contempt for you and repulsion.'

He sank down at her feet and tried to cling to her knees. With a gasp she sprang up and he buried his head in the empty chair. He cried painfully with sobs that tore his chest. The sound was horrible. The tears streamed from Anne's eyes and, putting her hands to her ears to shut out that dreadful, hysterical sobbing, blindly stumbling she rushed to the door and ran out.

The Book-Bag

◆

Some people read for instruction, which is praiseworthy, and some for pleasure, which is innocent, but not a few read from habit, and I suppose that this is neither innocent nor praiseworthy. Of that lamentable company am I. Conversation after a time bores me, games tire me, and my own thoughts, which we are told are the unfailing resource of a sensible man, have a tendency to run dry. Then I fly to my book as the opium-smoker to his pipe. I would sooner read the catalogue of the Army and Navy Stores or Bradshaw's *Guide* than nothing at all, and indeed I have spent many delightful hours over both these works. At one time I never went out without a second-hand bookseller's list in my pocket. I know no reading more fruity. Of course to read in this way is as reprehensible as doping, and I never cease to wonder at the impertinence of great readers who, because they are such, look down on the illiterate. From the standpoint of what eternity is it better to have read a thousand books than to have ploughed a million furrows? Let us admit that reading with us is just a drug that we cannot do without—who of this band does not know the restlessness that attacks him when he has been severed from reading too long, the apprehension and irritability, and the sigh of relief which the sight of a printed page extracts from him?—and so let us be no more vainglorious than the poor slaves of the hypodermic needle or the pint-pot.

And like the dope-fiend who cannot move from place to place without taking with him a plentiful supply of his deadly balm I never venture far without a sufficiency of reading matter. Books are so necessary to me that when in a railway train I have become aware that fellow-travellers have come away without a single one I have been seized with a veritable dismay. But when I am starting on a long journey the problem is formidable. I have learnt my lesson. Once, imprisoned by illness for three months in a hill-town in Java, I came to the end of all the books I had brought with me, and knowing no Dutch was obliged to buy the schoolbooks from which intelligent Javanese, I suppose, acquired knowledge of French and German. So I read again after five-and-twenty years the frigid plays of Goethe, the fables of La Fontaine, and the tragedies of the tender and exact Racine. I have the greatest admiration for Racine, but I admit that to read his plays one after the other requires a certain effort in a person who is suffering from colitis. Since then I have made a point of travelling with the largest sack made for carrying soiled linen and filling it to the brim with books to suit every possible occasion and every mood. It weighs a ton and strong porters reel under its weight. Custom-house officials look at it askance, but recoil from it with consternation when I give them my word that it contains nothing but books. Its inconvenience is that the particular work I suddenly hanker to read is always at the bottom and it is impossible for me to get it without emptying the book-bag's entire contents upon the floor. Except for this, however, I should perhaps never have heard the singular history of Olive Hardy.

I was wandering about Malaya, staying here and there, a week or two if there was a rest-house or a hotel, and a day or so if I was obliged to inflict myself on a planter or a District Officer whose hospitality I had no wish to abuse; and at the moment I happened to be at Penang. It is a pleasant little town, with a hotel that has always seemed to me very agreeable, but the stranger finds little to do there and time hung a trifle heavily on my hands. One morning I received a letter from a man I knew only by name. This was Mark Featherstone. He was Acting Resident, in the absence on leave of the Resident, at a place called Tenggarah. There was a sultan there and it appeared that a water festival of some sort was to take place which Featherstone thought would interest me. He said that he would be glad if I would come and stay with him for a few days. I wired to tell him that I should be delighted and next day took the train to Tenggarah. Featherstone met me at the station. He was a man of about thirty-five, I should think, tall and handsome, with fine eyes and a strong, stern face. He had a wiry black moustache and bushy eyebrows. He looked more like a soldier than a government official. He was very smart in white ducks, with a white topee, and he wore his clothes with elegance. He was a little shy, which seemed odd in a strapping fellow of resolute mien, but I surmised that this was only because he was unused to the society of that strange fish, a writer, and I hoped in a little to put him at his ease.

'My boys'll look after your barang,' he said. 'We'll go down to the club. Give them your keys and they'll unpack before we get back.'

I told him that I had a good deal of luggage and thought it better to leave everything at the station but what I particularly wanted. He would not hear of it.

'It doesn't matter a bit. It'll be safer at my house. It's always better to have one's barang with one.'

'All right.'

I gave my keys and the ticket for my trunk and my book-bag to a Chinese boy who stood at my host's elbow. Outside the station a car was waiting for us and we stepped in.

'Do you play bridge?' asked Featherstone.

'I do.'

'I thought most writers didn't.'

'They don't,' I said. 'It's generally considered among authors a sign of deficient intelligence to play cards.'

The club was a bungalow, pleasing but unpretentious; it had a large reading-room, a billiard-room with one table, and a small card-room. When we arrived it was empty but for one or two persons reading the English weeklies, and we walked through to the tennis courts, where a couple of sets were being played. A number of people were sitting on the veranda, looking on, smoking, and sipping long drinks. I was introduced to one or two of them. But the light was failing and soon the players could hardly see the ball. Featherstone asked one of the men I had been introduced to if he would like a rubber. He said he would. Featherstone looked about for a fourth. He caught sight of a man sitting a little by himself, paused for a second, and went up to him. The two exchanged a few words and then came towards us. We strolled in to the card-room. We had a very nice game. I did not pay much attention to the two men who made up the four. They stood me drinks and I, a temporary member of the club, returned the compliment. The drinks were very small, quarter whiskies, and in the two hours we played each of us was able to show his open-handedness without an excessive consumption of alcohol. When the advancing hour suggested that the next rubber must be the last we changed from whisky to gin pahits. The rubber came to an end. Featherstone called for the book and the winnings and losings of each one of us were set down. One of the men got up.

'Well, I must be going,' he said.

'Going back to the estate?' asked Featherstone.

'Yes,' he nodded. He turned to me. 'Shall you be here tomorrow?'

'I hope so.'

He went out of the room.

'I'll collect my mem and get along home to dinner,' said the other.

'We might be going too,' said Featherstone.

'I'm ready whenever you are,' I replied.

We got into the car and drove to his house. It was a longish drive. In the darkness I could see nothing much, but presently I realized that we were going up a rather steep hill. We reached the Residency.

It had been an evening like any other, pleasant, but not at all exciting, and I had spent I don't know how many just like it. I did not expect it to leave any sort of impression on me.

Featherstone led me into his sitting-room. It looked comfortable, but it was a trifle ordinary. It had large basket arm-chairs covered with cretonne and on the walls were a great many framed photographs; the tables were littered with papers, magazines, and official reports, with pipes, yellow tins of straight-cut cigarettes, and pink tins of tobacco. In a row of shelves were untidily stacked a good many books, their bindings stained with damp and the ravages of white ants. Featherstone showed me my room and left me with the words:

'Shall you be ready for a gin pahit in ten minutes?'

'Easily,' I said.

I had a bath and changed and went downstairs. Featherstone, ready before me, mixed our drinks as he heard me clatter down the wooden staircase. We dined. We talked. The festival which I had been invited to see was the next day but one, but Featherstone told me he had arranged for me before that to be received by the Sultan.

'He's a jolly old boy,' he said. 'And the palace is a sight for sore eyes.'

After dinner we talked a little more, Featherstone put on the gramophone, and we looked at the latest illustrated papers that had arrived from England.

Then we went to bed. Featherstone came to my room to see that I had everything I wanted.

'I suppose you haven't any books with you,' he said. 'I haven't got a thing to read.'

'Books?' I cried.

I pointed to my book-bag. It stood upright, bulging oddly, so that it looked like a humpbacked gnome somewhat the worse for liquor.

'Have you got books in there? I thought that was your dirty linen or a camp-bed or something. Is there anything you can lend me?'

'Look for yourself.'

Featherstone's boys had unlocked the bag, but quailing before the sight that then discovered itself had done no more. I knew from long experience how to unpack it. I threw it over on its side, seized its leather bottom and, walking backwards, dragged the sack away from its contents. A river of books poured on to the floor. A look of stupefaction came upon Featherstone's face.

'You don't mean to say you travel with as many books as that? By George, what a snip!'

He bent down and turning over rapidly looked at the titles. There were books of all kinds. Volumes of verse, novels, philosophical works, critical studies (they say books about books are profitless, but they certainly make very pleasant reading), biographies, history; there were books to read when you were ill and books to read when your brain, all alert, craved for something to grapple with; there were books that you had always wanted to read, but in the hurry of life at home had never found time to; there were books to read at sea when you were meandering through narrow waters on a tramp steamer, and there were books for bad weather when your whole cabin creaked and you had to wedge yourself in your bunk in order not to fall out; there were books chosen solely for their length, which you took with you when on some expedition you had to travel light, and there were the books you could read when you could read nothing else. Finally Featherstone picked out a life of Byron that had recently appeared.

'Hullo, what's this?' he said. 'I read a review of it some time ago.'

'I believe it's very good,' I replied. 'I haven't read it yet.'

'May I take it? It'll do me for tonight at all events.'

'Of course. Take anything you like.'

'No, that's enough. Well, good night. Breakfast at eight-thirty.'

When I came down next morning the head boy told me that Featherstone, who had been at work since six, would be in shortly. While I waited for him I glanced at his shelves.

'I see you've got a grand library of books on bridge,' I remarked as we sat down to breakfast.

'Yes, I get every one that comes out. I'm very keen on it.'

'That fellow we were playing with yesterday plays a good game.'

'Which? Hardy?'

'I don't know. Not the one who said he was going to collect his wife. The other.'

'Yes, that was Hardy. That was why I asked him to play. He doesn't come to the club very often.'

'I hope he will tonight.'

'I wouldn't bank on it. He has an estate about thirty miles away. It's a longish ride to come just for a rubber of bridge.'

'Is he married?'

'No. Well, yes. But his wife is in England.'

'It must be awfully lonely for those men who live by themselves on those estates,' I said.

'Oh, he's not so badly off as some. I don't think he much cares about seeing people. I think he'd be just as lonely in London.'

There was something in the way Featherstone spoke that struck me as a little strange. His voice had what I can only describe as a shuttered tone. He seemed suddenly to have moved away from me. It was as though one were passing along a street at night and paused for a second to look in at a lighted window that showed a comfortable room and suddenly an invisible hand pulled down a blind. His eyes, which habitually met those of the person he was talking to with frankness, now avoided mine, and I had a notion that it was not only my fancy that read in his face an expression of pain. It was drawn for a moment as it might be by a twinge of neuralgia. I could not think of anything to say and Featherstone did not speak. I was conscious that his thoughts, withdrawn from me and what we were about, were turned upon a subject unknown to me. Presently he gave a little sigh, very slight, but unmistakable, and seemed with a deliberate effort to pull himself together.

'I'm going down to the office immediately after breakfast,' he said. 'What are you going to do with yourself?'

'Oh, don't bother about me. I shall slack around. I'll stroll down and look at the town.'

'There's not much to see.'

'All the better. I'm fed up with sights.'

I found that Featherstone's veranda gave me sufficient entertainment for the morning. It had one of the most enchanting views I had seen in the F.M.S. The Residency was built on the top of a hill and the garden was large and well cared for. Great trees gave it almost the look of an English park. It had vast lawns and there Tamils, black and emaciated, were scything with deliberate and beautiful gestures. Beyond and below, the jungle grew thickly to the bank of a broad, winding, and swiftly flowing river, and on the other side of this, as far as the eye could reach, stretched the wooded hills of Tenggarah. The contrast between the trim lawns, so strangely English, and the savage growth of the jungle beyond pleasantly titillated the fancy. I sat and read and smoked. It is my business to be curious about people and I asked myself how the peace of this scene, charged nevertheless with a tremulous and dark significance, affected Featherstone who lived with it. He knew it under every aspect: at dawn when the mist rising from the river shrouded it with a ghostly pall; in the splendour of noon; and at last when the shadowy gloaming crept softly out of the jungle, like an army making its way with caution in unknown country, and presently enveloped the green lawns and the great flowering trees and the flaunting cassias in the silent night. I wondered whether, unbeknownst to him, the tender and yet strangely sinister aspect of the scene, acting on his nerves and his loneliness, imbued him with some mystical quality so that the life he led, the life of the capable administrator, the sportsman, and the good fellow, on occasion seemed to him not quite real. I smiled at my own fancies, for certainly the conversation we had had the night before had not indicated in him any stirrings of the soul. I had thought him quite nice. He had been at Oxford and was a member of a good London club. He seemed to attach a good deal of importance to social things. He was a gentleman and slightly conscious of the fact that he belonged to a better class than most of the Englishmen his life had brought him in contact with. I gathered from the various silver pots that adorned his dining-room that he excelled in games. He played tennis and billiards. When he went on leave he hunted and, anxious to keep his weight down, he dieted carefully. He talked a good deal of what he would do when he retired. He hankered after the life of a country gentleman. A little house in Leicestershire, a couple of hunters, and neighbours to play bridge with. He would have his pension and he had a little money of his own. But meanwhile he worked hard and did his work, if not brilliantly, certainly with competence. I have no doubt that he was looked upon by his superiors as a reliable officer. He was cut upon a pattern that I knew too well to find very interesting. He was like a novel that is careful, honest, and efficient, yet a little ordinary, so that you seem to have read it all before, and you turn the pages listlessly, knowing that it will never afford you a surprise or move you to excitement.

But human beings are incalculable and he is a fool who tells himself that he knows what a man is capable of.

In the afternoon Featherstone took me to see the Sultan. We were received by one of his sons, a shy, smiling youth who acted as his A.D.C. He was dressed in a neat blue suit, but round his waist he wore a sarong, white flowers on a yellow ground, on his head a red fez, and on his feet knobby American shoes. The palace, built in the Moorish style, was like a very big doll's house and it was painted bright yellow, which is the royal colour. We were led into a spacious room, furnished with the sort of furniture you would find in an English lodging-house at the seaside, but the chairs were covered with yellow silk. On the floor was a Brussels carpet and on the walls photographs in very grand gilt frames of the Sultan at various state functions. In a cabinet was a large collection of all kinds of fruit done entirely in crochet work. The Sultan came in with several attendants. He was a man of fifty, perhaps, short and stout, dressed in trousers and tunic of a large white-and-yellow check; round his middle he wore a very beautiful yellow sarong and on his head a white fez. He had large handsome friendly eyes. He gave us coffee to drink, sweet cakes to eat, and cheroots to smoke. Conversation was not difficult, for he was affable, and he told me that he had never been to a theatre or played cards, for he was very religious, and he had four wives and twenty-four children. The only bar to the happiness of his life seemed to be that common decency obliged him to divide his time equally between his four wives. He said than an hour with one was a month and with another five minutes. I remarked that Professor Einstein – or was it Bergson? – had made similar observations upon time and indeed on this question had given the world much to ponder over. Presently we took our leave and the Sultan presented me with some beautiful white Malaccas.

In the evening we went to the club. One of the men we had played with the day before got up from his chair as we entered.

'Ready for a rubber?' he said.

'Where's our fourth?' I asked.

'Oh, there are several fellows here who'll be glad to play.'

'What about that man we played with yesterday?' I had forgotten his name.

'Hardy? He's not here.'

'It's not worth while waiting for him,' said Featherstone.

'He very seldom comes to the club. I was surprised to see him last night.'

I did not know why I had the impression that behind the very ordinary words of these two men there was an odd sense of embarrassment. Hardy had made no impression on me and I did not even remember what he looked like. He was just a fourth at the bridge table. I had a feeling that they had something against him. It was no business of mine and I was quite content to play with a man who at that moment joined us. We certainly had a more cheerful game than before. A good deal of chaff passed from one side of the table to the other. We played less serious bridge. We laughed. I wondered if it was only that they were less shy of the stranger who had happened in upon them or if the presence of Hardy had caused in the other two a certain constraint. At half past eight we broke up and Featherstone and I went back to dine at his house.

After dinner we lounged in arm-chairs and smoked cheroots. For some reason our conversation did not flow easily. I tried topic after topic, but could not get Featherstone to interest himself in any of them. I began to think that in the last twenty-four hours he had said all he had to say. I fell somewhat discouraged into silence. It prolonged itself, and again, I did not know why, I had a faint sensation that it was charged with a significance that escaped me. I felt slightly uncomfortable. I had that queer feeling that one sometimes has when sitting in an empty room that one is not by oneself. Presently I was conscious that Featherstone was steadily looking at me. I was sitting by a lamp, but he was in shadow so that the play of his features was hidden from me. But he had very large brilliant eyes and in the half darkness they seemed to shine dimly. They were like new boot-buttons that caught reflected light. I wondered why he looked at me like that. I gave him a glance and catching his eyes insistently fixed upon me faintly smiled.

'Interesting book that one you lent me last night,' he said suddenly, and I could not help thinking his voice did not sound quite natural. The words issued from his lips as though they were pushed from behind.

'Oh, the *Life of Byron*?' I said breezily. 'Have you read it already?'

'A good deal of it. I read till three.'

'I've heard it's very well done. I'm not sure that Byron interests me so much as all that. There was so much in him that was so frightfully second-rate. It makes one rather uncomfortable.'

'What do you think is the real truth of that story about him and his sister?'

'Augusta Leigh? I don't know very much about it. I've never read *Astarte*.'

'Do you think they were really in love with one another?'

'I suppose so. Isn't it generally believed that she was the only woman he ever genuinely loved?'

'Can you understand it?'

'I can't really. It doesn't particularly shock me. It just seems to me very unnatural. Perhaps "unnatural" isn't the right word. It's incomprehensible to me. I can't throw myself into the state of feeling in which such a thing seems possible. You know, that's how a writer gets to know the people he writes about, by standing himself in their shoes and feeling with their hearts.'

I know I did not make myself very clear, but I was trying to describe a sensation, an action of the subconscious, which from experience was perfectly familiar to me, but which no words I knew could precisely indicate. I went on:

'Of course she was only his half-sister, but just as habit kills love I should have thought habit would prevent its arising. When two persons have known one another all their lives and lived together in close contact I can't imagine how or why that sudden spark should flash that results in love. The probabilities are that they would be joined by mutual affection and I don't know anything that is more contrary to love than affection.'

I could just see in the dimness the outline of a smile flicker for a moment on my host's heavy, and it seemed to me then, somewhat saturnine face.

'You only believe in love at first sight?'

'Well, I suppose I do, but with the proviso that people may have met twenty times before seeing one another. "Seeing" has an active side and a passive one. Most people we run across mean so little to us that we never bestir ourselves to look at them. We just suffer the impression they make on us.'

'Oh, but one's often heard of couples who've known one another for years and it's never occurred to one they cared two straws for each other and suddenly they go and get married. How do you explain that?'

'Well, if you're going to bully me into being logical and consistent, I should suggest that their love is of a different kind. After all, passion isn't the only reason for marriage. It may not even be the best one. Two people may marry because they're lonely or because they're good friends or for convenience sake. Though I said that affection was the greatest enemy of love, I would never deny that it's a very good substitute. I'm not sure that a marriage founded on it isn't the happiest.'

'What did you think of Tim Hardy?'

I was a little surprised at the sudden question, which seemed to have nothing to do with the subject of our conversation.

'I didn't think of him very much. He seemed quite nice. Why?'

'Did he seem to you just like everybody else?'

'Yes. Is there anything peculiar about him? If you'd told me that, I'd have paid more attention to him.'

'He's very quiet, isn't he? I suppose no one who knew nothing about him would give him a second thought.'

I tried to remember what he looked like. The only thing that had struck me when we were playing cards was that he had fine hands. It passed idly through my mind that they were not the sort of hands I should have expected a planter to have. But why a planter should have different hands from anybody else I did not trouble to ask myself. His were somewhat large, but very well formed with peculiarly long fingers, and the nails were of an admirable shape. They were virile and yet oddly sensitive hands. I noticed this and thought no more about it. But if you are a writer instinct and the habit of years enable you to store up impressions that you are not aware of. Sometimes of course they do not correspond with the facts and a woman for example may remain in your subconsciousness as a dark, massive, and ox-eyed creature when she is indeed rather small and of a nondescript colouring. But that is of no consequence. The impression may very well be more exact than the sober truth. And now, seeking to call up from the depths of me a picture of this man I had a feeling of some ambiguity. He was clean-shaven and his face, oval but not thin, seemed strangely pale under the tan of long exposure to the tropical sun. His features were vague. I did not know whether I remembered it or only imagined now that his rounded chin gave one the impression of a certain weakness. He had thick brown hair, just turning grey, and a long wisp fell down constantly over his forehead. He pushed it back with a gesture that had become habitual. His brown eyes were rather large and gentle, but perhaps a little sad; they had a melting softness which, I could imagine, might be very appealing.

After a pause Featherstone continued:

'It's rather strange that I should run across Tim Hardy here after all these years. But that's the way of the F.M.S. People move about and you find yourself in the same place as a man you'd known years before in another part of the country. I first knew Tim when he had an estate near Sibuku. Have you ever been there?'

'No. Where is it?'

'Oh, it's up north. Towards Siam. It wouldn't be worth your while to go. It's just like every other place in the F.M.S. But it was rather nice. It had a very jolly little club and there were some quite decent people. There was the schoolmaster and the head of the police, the doctor, the padre, and the government engineer. The usual lot, you know. A few planters. Three or four women. I was A.D.O. It was one of my first jobs. Tim Hardy had an estate about twenty-five miles away. He lived there with his sister. They had a bit of money of their own and he'd bought the place. Rubber was pretty good then and he wasn't doing at all badly. We rather cottoned on to one another. Of course it's a toss-up with planters. Some of them are very good fellows, but they're not exactly . . .' he sought for a word or a phrase that did not sound snobbish. 'Well, they're not the sort of people you'd be likely to meet at home. Tim and Olive were of one's own class, if you understand what I mean.'

'Olive was the sister?'

'Yes. They'd had a rather unfortunate past. Their parents had separated when they were quite small, seven or eight, and the mother had taken Olive and the father had kept Tim. Tim went to Clifton, they were West Country people, and only came home for the holidays. His father was a retired naval man who lived at Fowey. But Olive went with her mother to Italy. She was educated in Florence; she spoke Italian perfectly and French too. For all those years Tim and Olive never saw one another once, but they used to write to one another regularly. They'd been very much attached when they were children. As far as I could understand, life when their people were living together had been rather stormy with all sorts of scenes and upsets, you know the sort of thing that happens when two people who are married don't get on together, and that had thrown them on their own resources. They were left a good deal to themselves. Then Mrs Hardy died and Olive came home to England and went back to her father. She was eighteen then and Tim was seventeen. A year later the war broke out. Tim joined up and his father, who was over fifty, got some job at Portsmouth. I take it he had been a hard liver and a heavy drinker. He broke down before the end of the war and died shortly after a lingering illness. They don't seem to have had any relations. They were the last of a rather old family; they had a fine old house in Dorsetshire that had belonged to them for a good many generations, but they had never been able to afford to live in it and it was always let. I remember seeing photographs of it. It was very much a gentleman's house, of grey stone and rather stately, with a coat of arms carved over the front door, and mullioned windows. Their great ambition was to make enough money to be able to live in it. They used to talk about it a lot. They never spoke as though either of them would marry, but always as though it were a settled thing that they would remain together. It was rather funny considering how young they were.'

'How old were they then?' I asked.

'Well, I suppose he was twenty-five or twenty-six and she was a year older. They were awfully kind to me when I first went up to Sibuku. They took a fancy to me at once. You see, we had more in common than most of the people there. I think they were glad of my company. They weren't particularly popular.'

'Why not?' I asked.

'They were rather reserved and you couldn't help seeing that they liked their own society better than other people's. I don't know if you've noticed it, but that always seems to put people's backs up. They resent it somehow if they have a feeling that you can get along very well without them.'

'It's tiresome, isn't it?' I said.

'It was rather a grievance to the other planters that Tim was his own master and had private means. They had to put up with an old Ford to get about in, but Tim had a real car. Tim and Olive were very nice when they came to the club and they played in the tennis tournaments and all that sort of thing, but you had an impression that they were always glad to get away again. They'd dine out with people and make themselves very pleasant, but it was pretty obvious that they'd just as soon have stayed at home. If you had any sense you couldn't blame them. I don't know if you've been much to planters' houses. They're a bit dreary. A lot of gimcrack furniture and silver ornaments and tiger skins. And the food's uneatable. But the Hardys had made their bungalow rather nice. There was nothing very grand in it; it was just easy and homelike and comfortable. Their living-room was like a drawing-room in an English country house. You felt that their things meant something to them and that they had had them a long time. It was a very jolly house to stay at. The bungalow was in the middle of the estate, but it was on the brow of a little hill and you looked right over the rubber trees to the sea in the distance. Olive took a lot of trouble with her garden and it was really topping. I never saw such a show of cannas. I used to go there for weekends. It was only about half an hour's drive to the sea and we'd take our lunch with us and bathe and sail. Tim kept a small boat there. Those days were grand. I never knew one could enjoy oneself so much. It's a beautiful bit of coast and it was really extraordinarily romantic. Then in the evenings we'd play patience and chess or turn on the gramophone. The cooking was damned good too. It was a change from what one generally got. Olive had taught their cook to make all sorts of Italian dishes and we used to have great wallops of macaroni and risotto and gnocchi and things like that. I couldn't help envying them their life, it was so jolly and peaceful, and when they talked of what they'd do when they went back to England for good I used to tell them they'd always regret what they'd left.

'"We've been very happy here," said Olive.

'She had a way of looking at Tim, with a slow, sidelong glance from under her long eyelashes, that was rather engaging.

'In their own house they were quite different from what they were when they went out. They were so easy and cordial. Everybody admitted that and I'm bound to say that people enjoyed going there. They often asked people over. They had the gift of making you feel at home. It was a very happy house, if you know what I mean. Of course no one could help seeing how attached they were to one another. And whatever people said about their being stand-offish and self-centred, they were bound to be rather touched by the affection they had for one another. People said they couldn't have been more united if they had been married, and when you saw how some couples got on you couldn't help thinking they made most marriages look rather like a wash-out. They seemed to think the same things at the same time. They had little private jokes that made them laugh like children. They were so charming with one another, so gay and happy, that really to stay with them was, well, a spiritual refreshment. I don't know what else you could call it. When you left them, after a couple of days at the bungalow, you felt you'd absorbed some of their peace and their sober gaiety. It was as though your soul had been sluiced with cool clear water. You felt strangely purified.'

It was singular to hear Featherstone talking in this exalted strain. He looked so spruce in his smart white coat, technically known as a bum-freezer, his moustache was so trim, his thick curly hair so carefully brushed, that his high-flown language made me a trifle uncomfortable. But I realized that he was trying to express in his clumsy way a very sincerely felt emotion.

'What was Olive Hardy like?' I asked.

'I'll show you. I've got quite a lot of snapshots.'

He got up from his chair and going to a shelf brought me a large album. It was the usual thing, indifferent photographs of people in groups and unflattering likenesses of single figures. They were in bathing dress or in shorts or tennis things, generally with their faces screwed up because the sun blinded them, or puckered by the distortion of laughter. I recognized Hardy, not much changed after ten years, with his wisp of hair hanging across his forehead. I remembered him better now that I saw the snapshots. In them he looked nice and fresh and young. He had an alertness of expression that was attractive and that I certainly had not noticed when I saw him. In his eyes was a sort of eagerness for life that danced and sparkled through the fading print. I glanced at the photographs of his sister. Her bathing dress showed that she had a good figure, well-developed, but slender; and her legs were long and slim.

'They look rather alike,' I said.

'Yes, although she was a year older they might have been twins, they were so much alike. They both had the same oval face and that pale skin without any colour in the cheeks, and they both had those soft brown eyes, very liquid and appealing, so that you felt whatever they did you could never be angry with them. And they both had a sort of careless elegance that made them look charming whatever they wore and however untidy they were. He's lost that now, I suppose, but he certainly had it when I first knew him. They always rather reminded me of the brother and sister in *Twelfth Night.* You know whom I mean.'

'Viola and Sebastian.'

'They never seemed to belong quite to the present. There was something Elizabethan about them. I don't think it was only because I was very young then that I couldn't help feeling they were strangely romantic somehow. I could see them living in Illyria.'

I gave one of the snapshots another glance.

'The girl looks as though she had a good deal more character than her brother,' I remarked.

'She had. I don't know if you'd have called Olive beautiful, but she was awfully attractive. There was something poetic in her, a sort of lyrical quality, as it were, that coloured her movements, her acts, and everything about her. It seemed to exalt her above common cares. There was something so candid in her expression, so courageous and independent in her bearing, that—oh, I don't know, it made mere beauty just fall flat and dull.'

'You speak as if you'd been in love with her,' I interrupted.

'Of course I was. I should have thought you'd guessed that at once. I was frightfully in love with her.'

'Was it love at first sight?' I smiled.

'Yes, I think it was, but I didn't know it for a month or so. When it suddenly struck me that what I felt for her—I don't know how to explain it, it was a sort of shattering turmoil that affected every bit of me – that that was love, I knew I'd felt it all along. It was not only her looks, though they were awfully alluring, the smoothness of her pale skin and the way her hair fell over her forehead and the grave sweetness of her brown eyes, it was more than that; you had a sensation of well-being when you were with her, as though you could relax and be quite natural and needn't pretend to be anything you weren't. You felt she was incapable of meanness. It was impossible to think of her as envious of other people or catty. She seemed to have a natural generosity of soul. One could be silent with her for an hour at a time and yet feel that one had had a good time.'

'A rare gift,' I said.

'She was a wonderful companion. If you made a suggestion to do something she was always glad to fall in with it. She was the least exacting girl I ever knew. You could throw her over at the last minute and however disappointed she was it made no difference. Next time you saw her she was just as cordial and serene as ever.'

'Why didn't you marry her?'

Featherstone's cheroot had gone out. He threw the stub away and deliberately lit another. He did not answer for a while. It may seem strange to persons who live in a highly civilized state that he should confide these intimate things to a stranger; it did not seem strange to me. I was used to it. People who live so desperately alone, in the remote places of the earth, find it a relief to tell someone whom in all probability they will never meet again the story that has burdened perhaps for years their waking thoughts and their dreams at night. And I have an inkling that the fact of your being a writer attracts their confidence. They feel that what they tell you will excite your interest in an impersonal way that makes it easier for them to discharge their souls. Besides, as we all know from our own experience, it is never unpleasant to talk about oneself.

'Why didn't you marry her?' I had asked him.

'I wanted to badly enough,' Featherstone answered at length. 'But I hesitated to ask her. Although she was always so nice to me and so easy to get on with, and we were such good friends, I always felt that there was something a little mysterious in her. Although she was so simple, so frank and natural, you never quite got over the feeling of an inner kernel of aloofness, as if deep in her heart she guarded, not a secret, but a sort of privacy of the soul that not a living person would ever be allowed to know. I don't know if I make myself clear.'

'I think so.'

'I put it down to her upbringing. They never talked of their mother, but somehow I got the impression that she was one of those neurotic, emotional women who wreck their own happiness and are a pest to everyone connected with them. I had a suspicion that she'd led rather a hectic life in Florence and it struck me that Olive owed her beautiful serenity to a disciplined effort of her own will, and that her aloofness was a sort of citadel she'd built to protect herself from the knowledge of all sorts of shameful things. But of course that aloofness was awfully captivating. It was strangely exciting to think that if she loved you, and you were married to her, you would at last pierce right into the hidden heart of that mystery; and you felt that if you could share that with her it would be as it were a consummation of all you'd ever desired in your life. Heaven wouldn't be in it. You know, I felt about it just like Bluebeard's wife about the forbidden chamber in the castle. Every room was open to me, but I should never rest till I had gone into that last one that was locked against me.'

My eye was caught by a chik-chak, a little brown house lizard with a large head, high up on the wall. It is a friendly little beast and it is good to see it in a house. It watched a fly. It was quite still. On a sudden it made a dart and then as the fly flew away fell back with a sort of jerk into a strange immobility.

'And there was another thing that made me hesitate. I couldn't bear the thought that if I proposed to her and she refused me she wouldn't let me come to the bungalow in the same old way. I should have hated that, I enjoyed going there so awfully. It made me so happy to be with her. But you know, sometimes one can't help oneself. I did ask her at last, but it was almost by accident. One evening, after dinner, when we were sitting on the veranda by ourselves, I took her hand. She withdrew it at once.

'"Why did you do that?" I asked her.

'"I don't very much like being touched," she said. She turned her head a little and smiled. "Are you hurt? You mustn't mind, it's just a funny feeling I have. I can't help it."

'"I wonder if it's ever occurred to you that I'm frightfully fond of you," I said.

'I expect I was terribly awkward about it, but I'd never proposed to anyone before.' Featherstone gave a little sound that was not quite a chuckle and not quite a sigh. 'For the matter of that, I've never proposed to anyone since. She didn't say anything for a minute. Then she said:

'"I'm very glad, but I don't think I want you to be anything more than that."

'Why not?" I asked.

'"I could never leave Tim."

'"But supposing he marries?"

'"He never will."

'I'd gone so far then that I thought I'd better go on. But my throat was so dry that I could hardly speak. I was shaking with nervousness.

'"I'm frightfully in love with you, Olive. I want to marry you more than anything in the world."

'She put her hand very gently on my arm. It was like a flower falling to the ground.

'"No, dear, I can't," she said.

'I was silent. It was difficult for me to say what I wanted to. I'm naturally rather shy. She was a girl. I couldn't very well tell her that it wasn't quite the same thing living with a husband and living with a brother. She was normal and healthy; she must want to have babies; it wasn't reasonable to starve her natural instincts. It was such a waste of her youth. But it was she who spoke first.

'"Don't let's talk about this any more," she said. "D'you mind? It did strike me one or twice that perhaps you cared for me. Tim noticed it. I was sorry because I was afraid it would break up our friendship. I don't want it to do that, Mark. We do get on so well together, the three of us, and we have such jolly times. I don't know what we should do without you now."

'"I thought of that too," I said.

'"D'you think it need?" she asked me.

'"My dear, I don't want it to," I said. "You must know how much I love coming here. I've never been so happy anywhere before!"

'"You're not angry with me?"

'"Why should I be? It's not your fault. It only means that you're not in love with me. If you were you wouldn't care a hang about Tim."

'"You are rather sweet," she said.

'She put her arm around my neck and kissed me lightly on the cheek. I had a notion that in her mind it settled our relation. She adopted me as a second brother.

'A few weeks later Tim went back to England. The tenant of their house in Dorset was leaving and though there was another in the offing, he thought he ought to be on the spot to conduct negotiations. And he wanted some new machinery for the estate. He thought he'd get it at the same time. He didn't expect to be gone more than three months and Olive made up her mind not to go. She knew hardly anyone in England, and it was practically a foreign country to her, she didn't mind being left alone, and she wanted to look after the estate. Of course they could have put a manager in charge, but that wasn't the same thing. Rubber was falling and in case of accidents it was just as well that one or other of them should be there. I promised Tim I'd look after her and if she wanted me she could always call me up. My proposal hadn't changed anything. We carried on as though nothing had happened. I don't know whether she'd told Tim. He made no sign that he knew. Of course I loved her as much as ever, but I kept it to myself. I have a good deal of self-control, you know. I had a sort of feeling I hadn't a chance. I hoped eventually my love would change into something else and we could just be wonderful friends. It's funny, it never has, you know. I suppose I was hit too badly ever to get quite over it.

'She went down to Penang to see Tim off and when she came back I met her at the station and drove her home. I couldn't very well stay at the bungalow while Tim was away, but I went over every Sunday and had tiffin and we'd go down to the sea and have a bathe. People tried to be kind to her and asked her to stay with them, but she wouldn't. She seldom left the estate. She had plenty to do. She read a lot. She was never bored. She seemed quite happy in her own company, and when she had visitors it was only from a sense of duty. She didn't want them to think her ungracious. But it was an effort and she told me she heaved a sigh of relief when she saw the last of them and could again enjoy without disturbance the peaceful loneliness of the bungalow. She was a very curious girl. It was strange that at her age she should be so indifferent to parties and the other small gaieties the station afforded. Spiritually, if you know what I mean, she was entirely self-supporting. I don't know how people found out that I was in love with her; I thought I'd never given myself away in anything, but I had hints here and there that they knew. I gathered they thought Olive hadn't gone home with her brother on my account. One woman, a Mrs Sergison, the policeman's wife, actually asked me when they were going to be able to congratulate me. Of course I pretended I didn't know what she was talking about, but it didn't go down very well. I couldn't help being amused. I meant so little to Olive in that way that I really believe she'd entirely forgotten that I'd asked her to marry me. I can't say she was unkind to me, I don't think she could have been unkind to anyone; but she treated me with just the casualness with which a sister might treat a younger brother. She was two or three years older than I. She was always terribly glad to see me, but it never occurred to her to put herself out for me; she was almost amazingly intimate with me, but unconsciously, you know, as you might be with a person you'd known so well all your life that you never thought of putting on frills with him. I might not have been a man at all, but an old coat that she wore all the time because it was easy and comfortable and she didn't mind what she did in it. I should have been crazy not to see that she was a thousand miles away from loving me.

'Then one day, three or four weeks before Tim was due back, when I went to the bungalow I saw she'd been crying. I was startled. She was always so composed. I'd never seen her upset over anything.

'"Hullo, what's the matter?" I said.

'"Nothing."

'"Come off it, darling," I said. "What have you been crying about?"

'She tried to smile.

'"I wish you hadn't got such sharp eyes," she said. "I think I'm being silly. I've just had a cable from Tim to say he's postponed his sailing."

'"Oh, my dear, I am sorry," I said. "You must be awfully disappointed."

'"I've been counting the days. I want him back so badly."

'"Does he say why he's postponing?" I asked.

'"No, he says he's writing. I'll show you the cable."

'I saw that she was very nervous. Her slow quiet eyes were filled with apprehension and there was a little frown of anxiety between her brows. She went into her bedroom and in a moment came back with the cable. I felt she was watching me anxiously as I read. So far as I remember it ran:

Darling, I cannot sail on the seventh after all. Please forgive me. Am writing fully. Fondest love. Tim.

'"Well, perhaps the machinery he wanted isn't ready and he can't bring himself to sail without it," I said.

'"What could it matter if it came by a later ship? Anyhow, it'll be hung up at Penang."

'"It may be something about the house."

'"If it is why doesn't he say so? He must know how frightfully anxious I am."

'"It wouldn't occur to him," I said. "After all, when you're away you don't realize that the people you've left behind don't know something that you take as a matter of course."

'She smiled again, but now more happily.

'"I dare say you're right. In point of fact Tim is a little like that. He's always been rather slack and casual. I dare say I've been making a mountain out of a molehill. I must just wait patiently for his letter."

'Olive was a girl with a lot of self-control and I saw her by an effort of will pull herself together. The little line between her eyebrows vanished and she was once more her serene, smiling, and kindly self. She was always gentle: that day she had a mildness so heavenly that it was shattering. But for the rest of the time I could see that she kept her restlessness in check only by the deliberate exercise of her common sense. It was as though she had a foreboding of ill. I was with her the day before the mail was due. Her anxiety was all the more pitiful to see because she took such pains to hide it. I was always busy on mail day, but I promised to get up to the estate later on and hear the news. I was just thinking of starting when Hardy's seis came along in the car with a message from the amah asking me to go at once to her mistress. The amah was a decent, elderly woman to whom I had given a dollar or two and said that if anything went wrong on the estate she was to let me know at once. I jumped into my car. When I arrived I found the amah waiting for me on the steps.

'"A letter came this morning," she said.

'I interrupted her. I ran up the steps. The sitting-room was empty.

'"Olive," I called.

'I went into the passage and suddenly I heard a sound that froze my heart. The amah had followed me and now she opened the door of Olive's room. The sound I had heard was the sound of Olive crying. I went in. She was lying on her bed, on her face, and her sobs shook her from head to foot. I put my hand on her shoulder.

'"Olive, what is it?" I asked.

'"Who's that?" she cried. She sprang to her feet suddenly, as though she were scared out of her wits. And then: "Oh, it's you," she said. She stood in front of me, with her head thrown back and her eyes closed, and the tears streamed from them. It was dreadful. "Tim's married," she gasped, and her face screwed up in a sort of grimace of pain.

'I must admit that for one moment I had a thrill of exultation, it was like a little electric shock tingling through my heart; it struck me that now I had a chance, she might be willing to marry me; I know it was terribly selfish of me; you see, the news had taken me by surprise; but it was only for a moment, after that I was melted by her awful distress and the only thing I felt was deep sorrow because she was unhappy. I put my arm round her waist.

'"Oh, my dear, I'm sorry,' I said. "Don't stay here. Come into the sitting-room and sit down and we'll talk about it. Let me give you something to drink."

'She let me lead her into the next room and we sat down on the sofa. I told the amah to fetch the whisky and syphon and I mixed her a good strong stengah and made her drink a little. I took her in my arms and rested her head on my shoulder. She let me do what I liked with her. The great tears streamed down her poor face.

'"How could he?" she moaned. "How could he?"

'"My darling," I said, "it was bound to happen sooner or later. He's a young man. How could you expect him never to marry? It's only natural."

'"No, no, no," she gasped.

'Tight-clenched in her hand I saw that she had a letter and I guessed that it was Tim's.

'"What does he say?" I asked.

'She gave a frightened movement and clutched the letter to her heart as though she thought I would take it from her.

'"He says he couldn't help himself. He says he had to. What does it mean?"

'"Well, you know, in his way he's just as attractive as you are. He has so much charm. I suppose he just fell madly in love with some girl and she with him."

'"He's so weak," she moaned.

'"Are they coming out?" I asked.

'"They sailed yesterday. He says it won't make any difference. He's insane. How *can* I stay here?"

'She began to cry hysterically. It was torture to see that girl, usually so calm, utterly shattered by her emotion. I had always felt that her lovely serenity masked a capacity for deep feeling. But the abandon of her distress simply broke me up. I held her in my arms and kissed her, her eyes and her wet cheek and her hair. I don't think she knew what I was doing. I was hardly conscious of it myself. I was so deeply moved.

'"What shall I do?" she wailed.

'"Why won't you marry me?" I said.

'She tried to withdraw herself from me, but I wouldn't let her go.

'"After all, it would be a way out," I said.

'"How can I marry you?" she moaned. "I'm years older than you are."

'"Oh, what nonsense, two or three. What do I care?"

'"No, no."

'"Why not?" I said.

'"I don't love you," she said.

'"What does that matter? I love you."

'I don't know what I said. I told her that I'd try to make her happy. I said I'd never ask anything from her but what she was prepared to give me. I talked and talked. I tried to make her see reason. I felt that she didn't want to stay there, in the same place as Tim, and I told her that I'd be moved soon to some other district. I thought that might tempt her. She couldn't deny that we'd always got on awfully well together. After a time she did seem to grow a little quieter. I had a feeling that she was listening to me. I had even a sort of feeling that she knew that she was lying in my arms and that it comforted her. I made her drink a drop more whisky. I gave her a cigarette. At last I thought I might be just mildly facetious.

'"You know, I'm not a bad sort really," I said. "You might do worse."

'"You don't know me," she said. "You know nothing whatever about me."

'"I'm capable of learning," I said.

'She smiled a little.

'"You're awfully kind, Mark," she said.

'"Say yes, Olive," I begged.

'She gave a deep sigh. For a long time she stared at the ground. But she did not move and I felt the softness of her body in my arms. I waited. I was frightfully nervous and the minutes seemed endless.

'"All right," she said at last, as though she were not conscious that any time had passed between my prayer and her answer.

'I was so moved that I had nothing to say. But when I wanted to kiss her lips, she turned her face away, and wouldn't let me. I wanted us to be married at once, but she was quite firm that she wouldn't. She insisted on waiting till Tim came back. You know how sometimes you see so clearly into people's thoughts that you're more certain of them than if they'd spoken them; I saw that she couldn't quite believe that what Tim had written was true and that she had a sort of miserable hope that it was all a mistake and he wasn't married after all. It gave me a pang, but I loved her so much, I just bore it. I was willing to bear anything. I adored her. She wouldn't even let me tell anyone that we were engaged. She made me promise not to say a word till Tim's return. She said she couldn't bear the thought of the congratulations and all that. She wouldn't even let me make any announcement of Tim's marriage. She was obstinate about it. I had a notion that she felt if the fact were spread about it gave it a certainty that she didn't want it to have.

'But the matter was taken out of her hands. News travels mysteriously in the East. I don't know what Olive had said in the amah's hearing when first she received the news of Tim's marriage; anyhow, the Hardys' seis told the Sergisons and Mrs Sergison attacked me the next time I went into the club.

'"I hear Tim Hardy's married," she said.

'"Oh?" I answered, unwilling to commit myself.

'She smiled at my blank face, and told me that her amah having told her the rumour she had rung up Olive and asked her if it was true. Olive's answer had been rather odd. She had not exactly confirmed it, but said that she had received a letter from Tim telling her he was married.

'"She's a strange girl," said Mrs Sergison. "When I asked her for details she said she had none to give and when I said: 'Aren't you thrilled?' she didn't answer."

"'Olive's devoted to Tim, Mrs Sergison,' I said. "His marriage has naturally been a shock to her. She knows nothing about Tim's wife. She's nervous about her."

"'And when are you two going to be married?" she asked me abruptly.

"':What an embarrassing question!" I said, trying to laugh it off.

'She looked at me shrewdly.

"'Will you give me your word of honour that you're not engaged to her?"

'I didn't like to tell her a deliberate lie, nor to ask her to mind her own business, and I'd promised Olive faithfully that I would say nothing till Tim got back. I hedged.

"'Mrs Sergison,' I said, "when there's anything to tell I promise that you'll be the first person to hear it. All I can say to you now is that I do want to marry Olive more than anything in the world."

"'I'm very glad that Tim's married," she answered. "And I hope she'll marry you very soon. It was a morbid and unhealthy life that they led up there, those two, they kept far too much to themselves and they were far too much absorbed in one another."

'I saw Olive practically every day. I felt that she didn't want me to make love to her, and I contented myself with kissing her when I came and when I went. She was very nice to me, kindly and thoughtful; I knew she was glad to see me and sorry when it was time for me to go. Ordinarily, she was apt to fall into silence but during this time she talked more than I had ever heard her talk before. But never of the future and never of Tim and his wife. She told me a lot about her life in Florence and her mother. She had led a strange lonely life, mostly with servants and governesses, while her mother, I suspected, engaged in one affair after another with vague Italian counts and Russian princes. I guessed that by the time she was fourteen there wasn't much she didn't know. It was natural for her to be quite unconventional: in the only world she knew till she was eighteen conventions weren't mentioned because they didn't exist. Gradually, Olive seemed to regain her serenity and I should have thought that she was beginning to accustom herself to the thought of Tim's marriage if it hadn't been that I couldn't but notice how pale and tired she looked. I made up my mind that the moment he arrived I'd press her to marry me at once. I could get short leave whenever I asked for it, and by the time that was up I thought I could manage a transfer to some other post. What she wanted was change of air and fresh scenes.

'We knew, of course, within a day when Tim's ship would reach Penang, but it was a question whether she'd get in soon enough for him to catch the train and I wrote to the P. & O. agent asking him to telegraph as soon as he had definite news. When I got the wire and took it up to Olive I found that she'd just received one from Tim. The ship had docked early and he was arriving next day. The train was supposed to get in at eight o'clock in the morning, but it was liable to be anything from one to six hours late, and I bore with me an invitation from Mrs Sergison asking Olive to come back with me to stay the night with her so that she would be on the spot and need not go to the station till the news came through that the train was coming.

'I was immensely relieved. I thought that when the blow at last fell Olive wouldn't feel it so much. She had worked herself up into such a state that I couldn't help thinking that she must have a reaction now. She might take a fancy to her sister-in-law. There was no reason why they shouldn't all three get on very well together. To my surprise Olive said she wasn't coming down to the station to meet him.

'"They'll be awfully disappointed," I said.

'"I'd rather wait here," she answered. She smiled a little. "Don't argue with me, Mark, I've quite made up my mind."

'"I've ordered breakfast in my house," I said.

'"That's all right. You meet them and take them to your house and give them breakfast, and then they can come along here afterwards. Of course I'll send the car down."

'"I don't suppose they'll want to breakfast if you're not there," I said.

'"Oh, I'm sure they will. If the train gets in on time they wouldn't have thought of breakfasting before it arrived and they'll be hungry. They won't want to take this long drive without anything to eat."

'I was puzzled. She had been looking forward so intensely to Tim's coming, it seemed strange that she should want to wait all by herself while the rest of us were having a jolly breakfast. I supposed she was nervous and wanted to delay as long as possible meeting the strange woman who had come to take her place. It seemed unreasonable, I couldn't see that an hour sooner or an hour later could make any difference, but I knew women were funny, and anyhow I felt Olive wasn't in the mood for me to press it.

'"Telephone when you're starting so that I shall know when to expect you," she said.

'"All right," I said, "but you know I shan't be able to come with them. It's my day for going to Lahad."

'This was a town that I had to go to once a week to take cases. It was a good way off and one had to ferry across a river, which took some time, so that I never got back till late. There were a few Europeans there and a club. I generally had to go on there for a bit to be sociable and see that things were getting along all right.

'"Besides," I added, "with Tim bringing his wife home for the first time I don't suppose he'll want me about. But if you'd like to ask me to dinner I'll be glad to come to that."

'Olive smiled.

'"I don't think it'll be my place to issue any more invitations, will it?" she said. "You must ask the bride."

'She said this so lightly that my heart leaped. I had a feeling that at last she had made up her mind to accept the altered circumstances and, what was more, was accepting them with cheerfulness. She asked me to stay to dinner. Generally I left about eight and dined at home. She was very sweet, almost tender, and I was happier than I'd been for weeks. I had never been more desperately in love with her. I had a couple of gin pahits and I think I was in rather good form at dinner. I know I made her laugh. I felt that at last she was casting away the load of misery that had oppressed her. That was why I didn't let myself be very much disturbed by what happened at the end.

'"Don't you think it's about time you were leaving a presumably maiden lady?" she said.

'She spoke in a manner that was so quietly gay that I answered without hesitation:

'"Oh, my dear, if you think you've got a shred of reputation left you deceive yourself. You're surely not under the impression that the ladies of Sibuku don't know that I've been coming to see you every day for a month. The general feeling is that if we're not married it's high time we were. Don't you think it would be just as well if I broke it to them that we're engaged?"

'"Oh, Mark, you mustn't take our engagement very seriously," she said.

'I laughed.

'"How else do you expect me to take it? It is serious."

'She shook her head a little.

'"No. I was upset and hysterical that day. You were being very sweet to me. I said yes because I was too miserable to say no. But now I've had time to collect myself. Don't think me unkind. I made a mistake. I've been very much to blame. You must forgive me."

'"Oh, darling, you're talking nonsense. You've got nothing against me."

'She looked at me steadily. She was quite calm. She had even a little smile at the back of her eyes.

'"I can't marry you. I can't marry anyone. It was absurd of me ever to think I could."

'I didn't answer at once. She was in a queer state and I thought it better not to insist.

'"I suppose I can't drag you to the altar by main force," I said.

'I held out my hand and she gave me hers. I put my arm round her, and she made no attempt to withdraw. She suffered me to kiss her as usual on her cheek.

'Next morning I met the train. For once in a way it was punctual. Tim waved to me as his carriage passed the place where I was standing, and by the time I had walked up he had already jumped out and was handing down his wife. He grasped my hand warmly.

'"Where's Olive?" he said, with a glance along the platform. "This is Sally."

'I shook hands with her and at the same time explained why Olive was not there.

'"It was frightfully early, wasn't it?" said Mrs Hardy.

'I told them that the plan was for them to come and have a bit of breakfast at my house and then drive home.

'"I'd love a bath," said Mrs Hardy.

'"You shall have one," I said.

'She was really an extremely pretty little thing, very fair, with enormous blue eyes and a lovely little straight nose. Her skin, all milk and roses, was exquisite. A little of the chorus girl type, of course, and you may happen to think that rather namby-pamby, but in that style she was enchanting. We drove to my house, they both had a bath and Tim a shave; I just had two minutes alone with him. He asked me how Olive had taken his marriage. I told him she'd been upset.

'"I was afraid so," he said, frowning a little. He gave a short sigh. "I couldn't do anything else."

'I didn't understand what he meant. At that moment Mrs Hardy joined us and slipped her arm through her husband's. He took her hand in his and gently pressed it. He gave her a look that had in it something pleased and humorously affectionate, as though he didn't take her quite seriously, but enjoyed his sense of proprietorship and was proud of her beauty. She really was lovely. She was not at all shy, she asked me to call her Sally before we'd known one another ten minutes, and she was quick in the uptake. Of course, just then she was excited at arriving. She'd never been East and everything thrilled her. It was quite obvious that she was head over heels in love with Tim. Her eyes never left him and she hung on his words. We had a jolly breakfast and then we parted. They got into their car to go home and I into mine to go to Lahad. I promised to go straight to the estate from there and in point of fact it was out of my way to pass by my house. I took a change with me. I didn't see why Olive shouldn't like Sally very much, she was frank and gay, and ingenuous; she was extremely young, she couldn't have been more than nineteen, and her wonderful prettiness couldn't fail to appeal to Olive. I was just as glad to have had a reasonable excuse to leave the three of them by themselves for the day, but as I started out from Lahad I had a notion that by the time I arrived they would all be pleased to see me. I drove up to the bungalow and blew my horn two or three times, expecting someone to appear. Not a soul. The place was in total darkness. I was surprised. It was absolutely silent. I couldn't make it out. They must be in. Very odd, I thought. I waited a moment, then got out of the car and walked up the steps. At the top of them I stumbled over something. I swore and bent down to see what it was; it had felt like a body. There was a cry and I saw it was the amah. She shrank back cowering as I touched her and broke into loud wails.

'"What the hell's the matter?" I cried, and then I felt a hand on my arm and heard a voice: Tuan, Tuan. I turned and in the darkness recognized Tim's head boy. He began to speak in little frightened gasps. I listened to him with horror. What he told me was unspeakable. I pushed him aside and rushed into the house. The sitting-room was dark. I turned on the light. The first thing I saw was Sally huddled up in an arm-chair. She was startled by my sudden appearance and cried out. I could hardly speak. I asked her if it was true. When she told me it was I felt the room suddenly going round and round me. I had to sit down. As the car that bore Tim and Sally drove up the road that led to the house and Tim sounded the klaxon to announce their arrival and the boys and the amah ran out to greet them there was the sound of a shot. They ran to Olive's room and found her lying in front of the looking-glass in a pool of blood. She had shot herself with Tim's revolver.

'"Is she dead?" I said.

'"No, they sent for the doctor, and he took her to the hospital."

'I hardly knew what I was doing. I didn't even trouble to tell Sally where I was going. I got up and staggered to the door. I got into the car and told my seis to drive like hell to the hospital. I rushed in. I asked where she was. They tried to bar my way, but I pushed them aside. I knew where the private rooms were. Someone clung to my arm, but I shook him off. I vaguely understood that the doctor had given instructions that no one was to go into the room. I didn't care about that. There was an orderly at the door; he put out his arm to prevent me from passing. I swore at him and told him to get out of my way. I suppose I made a row, I was beside myself; the door opened and the doctor came out.

'"Who's making all this noise?" he said. "Oh, it's you. What do you want?"

'"Is she dead?" I asked.

'"No. But she's unconscious. She never regained consciousness. It's only a matter of an hour or two."

'"I want to see her."

'"You can't."

'"I'm engaged to her."

'"You?" he cried, and even at that moment I was aware that he looked at me strangely. "That's all the more reason."

'I didn't know what he meant. I was stupid with horror.

'"Surely you can do something to save her," I cried.

'He shook his head.

'"If you saw her you wouldn't wish it," he said.

'I stared at him aghast. In the silence I heard a man's convulsive sobbing.

'"Who's that?" I asked.

'"Her brother."

'Then I felt a hand on my arm. I looked round and saw it was Mrs Sergison.

'"My poor boy," she said, "I'm so sorry for you."

'"What on earth made her do it?" I groaned.

'"Come away, my dear," said Mrs Sergison. "You can do no good here."

'"No, I must stay," I said.

'"Well, go and sit in my room," said the doctor.

'I was so broken that I let Mrs Sergison take me by the arm and lead me into the doctor's private room. She made me sit down. I couldn't bring myself to realize that it was true. I thought it was a horrible nightmare from which I must awake. I don't know how long we sat there. Three hours. Four hours. At last the doctor came in.

'"It's all over," he said.

'Then I couldn't help myself, I began to cry. I didn't care what they thought of me. I was so frightfully unhappy.

'We buried her next day.

'Mrs Sergison came back to my house and sat with me for a while. She wanted me to go to the club with her. I hadn't the heart. She was very kind, but I was glad when she left me by myself. I tried to read, but the words meant nothing to me. I felt dead inside. My boy came in and turned on the lights. My head was aching like mad. Then he came back and said that a lady wished to see me. I asked who it was. He wasn't quite sure, but he thought it must be the new wife of the tuan at Putatan. I couldn't imagine what she wanted. I got up and went to the door. He was right. It was Sally. I asked her to come in. I noticed that she was deathly white. I felt sorry for her. It was a frightful experience for a girl of that age and for a bride a miserable homecoming. She sat down. She was very nervous. I tried to put her at her ease by saying conventional things. She made me very uncomfortable because she stared at me with those enormous blue eyes of hers, and they were simply ghastly with horror. She interrupted me suddenly.

'"You're the only person here I know," she said. "I had to come to you. I want you to get me away from here."

'I was dumbfounded.

'"What *do* you mean?" I said.

'"I don't want you to ask me any questions. I just want you to get me away. At once. I want to go back to England!"

'"But you can't leave Tim like that just now," I said. "My dear, you must pull yourself together. I know it's been awful for you. But think of Tim. If you have any love for him the least you can do is try and make him a little less unhappy."

'"Oh, you don't know," she cried. "I can't tell you. It's too horrible. I beseech you to help me. If there's a train tonight let me get on it. If I can only get to Penang I can get a ship. I can't stay in this place another night. I shall go mad."

'I was absolutely bewildered.

'"Does Tim know?" I asked her.

'"I haven't seen Tim since last night. I'll never see him again. I'd rather die."

'I wanted to gain a little time.

'"But how can you go without your things? Have you got any luggage?"

'"What does that matter?" she cried impatiently. "I've got what I want for the journey."

'"Have you any money?"

'"Enough. Is there a train tonight?"

'"Yes," I said. "It's due just after midnight."

'"Thank God. Will you arrange everything? Can I stay here till then?"

'"You're putting me in a frightful position," I said. "I don't know what to do for the best. You know, it's an awfully serious step you're taking."

'"If you knew everything you'd know it was the only possible thing to do."

'"It'll create an awful scandal here. I don't know what people'll say. Have you thought of the effect on Tim?" I was worried and unhappy. "God knows I don't want to interfere in what isn't my business. But if you want me to help you I ought to know enough to feel justified in doing so. You must tell me what's happened."

'"I can't. I can only tell you that I know everything."

'She hid her face with her hands and shuddered. Then she gave herself a shake as though she were recoiling from some frightful sight.

'"He had no right to marry me. It was monstrous."

'And as she spoke her voice rose shrill and piercing. I was afraid she was going to have an attack of hysterics. Her pretty doll-like face was terrified and her eyes stared as though she could never close them again.

'"Don't you love him any more?" I asked.

'"After that?"

'"What will you do if I refuse to help you?" I said.

'"I suppose there's a clergyman here or a doctor. You can't refuse to take me to one of them."

'"How did you get here?"

'"The head boy drove me. He got a car from somewhere."

'"Does Tim know you've gone?"

'"I left a letter for him."

'"He'll know you're here."

'"He won't try to stop me. I promise you that. He daren't. For God's sake don't you try either. I tell you I shall go mad if I stay here another night."

'I sighed. After all she was of an age to decide for herself.'

I, the writer of this, hadn't spoken for a long time.

'Did you know what she meant?' I asked Featherstone.

He gave me a long, haggard look.

'There was only one thing she could mean. It was unspeakable. Yes, I knew all right. It explained everything. Poor Olive. Poor sweet. I suppose it was unreasonable of me, at that moment I only felt a horror of that little pretty fair-haired thing with her terrified eyes. I hated her. I didn't say anything for a while. Then I told her I'd do as she wished. She didn't even say thank you. I think she knew what I felt about her. When it was dinner-time I made her eat something and then she asked me if there was a room she could go and lie down in till it was time to go to the station. I showed her into my spare room and left her. I sat in the sitting-room and waited. My God, I don't think the time has ever passed so slowly for me. I thought twelve would never strike. I rang up the station and was told the train wouldn't be in till nearly two. At midnight she came back to the sitting-room and we sat there for an hour and a half. We had nothing to say to one another and we didn't speak. Then I took her to the station and put her on the train.'

'Was there an awful scandal?'

Featherstone frowned.

'I don't know. I applied for short leave. After that I was moved to another post. I heard that Tim had sold his estate and bought another. But I didn't know where. It was a shock to me at first when I found him here.'

Featherstone, getting up, went over to a table and mixed himself a whisky and soda. In the silence that fell now I heard the monotonous chorus of the croaking frogs. And suddenly the bird that is known as the fever-bird, perched in a tree close to the house, began to call. First, three notes in a descending, chromatic scale, then five, then four. The varying notes of the scale succeeded one another with maddening persistence. One was compelled to listen and to count them, and because one did not know how many there would be it tortured one's nerves.

'Blast that bird,' said Featherstone. 'That means no sleep for me tonight.'

French Joe

◆

It was Captain Bartlett who told me of him. I do not think that many people have been to Thursday Island. It is in the Torres Straits and is so called because it was discovered on a Thursday by Captain Cook. I went there since they told me in Sydney that it was the last place God ever made. They said there was nothing to see and warned me that I should probably get my throat cut. I had come up from Sydney in a Japanese tramp and they put me ashore in a small boat. It was the middle of the night and there was not a soul on the jetty. One of the sailors who landed my kit told me that if I turned to the left I should presently come to a two-storey building and this was the hotel. The boat pushed off and I was left alone. I do not much like being separated from my luggage, but I like still less to pass the night on a jetty and sleep on hard stones; so I shouldered a bag and set out. It was pitch dark. I seemed to walk much more than a few hundred yards which they had spoken of and was afraid I had missed my way, but at last saw dimly a building which seemed to be important enough to suggest that it might be the hotel. No light showed, but my eyes by now were pretty well accustomed to the darkness and I found a door. I struck a match, but could see no bell. I knocked; there was no reply; I knocked again, with my stick, as loudly as I could, then a window above me was opened and a woman's voice asked me what I wanted.

'I've just got off the *Shika Maru*,' I said. 'Can I have a room?'

'I'll come down.'

I waited a little longer, and the door was opened by a woman in a red flannel dressing-gown. Her hair was hanging over her shoulders in long black wisps. In her hand she held a paraffin lamp. She greeted me warmly, a little stoutish woman, with keen eyes and a nose suspiciously red, and bade me come in. She took me upstairs and showed me a room.

'Now you sit down,' she said, 'and I'll make up the bed before you can say Jack Robinson. What will you 'ave? A drop of whisky would do you good, I should think. You won't want to be washing at this time of night, I'll bring you a towel in the morning.'

And while she made the bed she asked me who I was and what I had come to Thursday Island for. She could see I wasn't a sea-faring man—all the pilots came to this hotel and had done for twenty years—and she didn't know what business could have brought me. I wasn't that fellow as was coming to inspect the Customs was I? She'd 'eard they were sending someone from Sydney. I asked her if there were any pilots staying there then. Yes, there was one, Captain Bartlett, did I know him? A queer fish he was and no mistake. Hadn't got a hair on his head, but the way he could put his liquor away, well, it was a caution. There, the bed was ready and she expected I'd sleep like a top and one thing she could say was, the sheets were clean. She lit the end of a candle and bade me good night.

Captain Bartlett certainly was a queer fish, but he is of no moment to my present purpose; I made his acquaintance at dinner next day—before I left Thursday Island I had eaten turtle soup so often that I ceased to look upon it as a luxury—and it was because in the course of conversation I mentioned that I spoke French that he asked me to go and see French Joe.

'It'll be a treat to the old fellow to talk his own lingo for a bit. He's ninety-three, you know.'

For the last two years, not because he was ill but because he was old and destitute, he had lived in the hospital and it was here that I visited him. He was lying in bed, in flannel pyjamas much too large for him, a little shrivelled old man with vivacious eyes, a short white beard, and bushy black eyebrows. He was glad to speak French with me, which he spoke with the marked accent of his native isle, for he was a Corsican, but he had dwelt so many years among English-speaking people that he no longer spoke his mother tongue with accuracy. He used English words as though they were French, making verbs of them with French terminations. He talked very quickly, with broad gestures, and his voice for the most part was clear and strong; but now and then it seemed suddenly to fade away so that it sounded as though he spoke from the grave. The hushed and hollow sound gave me an eerie feeling. Indeed I could not look upon him still as of this world. His real name was Joseph de Paoli. He was a nobleman and a gentleman. He was of the same family as the general we have all read of in Boswell's Johnson, but he showed no interest in his famous ancestor.

'We have had so many generals in our family,' he said. 'You know, of course, that Napoleon Bonaparte was a connexion of mine. No, I have never read Boswell. I have not read books. I have lived.'

He had entered the French army in 1851. Seventy-five years ago. It is terrifying. As a lieutenant of artillery ('like my cousin Bonaparte,' he said) he had fought the Russians in the Crimea and as a captain the Prussians in 1870. He showed me a scar on his bald pate from an Uhlan's lance and then with a dramatic gesture told how he had thrust his sword in the Uhlan's body with such violence that he could not withdraw it. The Uhlan fell dead and the sword remained in the body. But the Empire perished and he joined the communists. For six weeks he fought against the government troops under Monsieur Thiers. To me Thiers is but a shadowy figure, and it was startling and even a trifle comic to hear French Joe speak with passionate hatred of a man who has been dead for half a century. His voice rose into a shrill scream as he repeated the insults, Oriental in their imagery, which in the council he had flung at the head of this mediocre statesman. French Joe was tried and sentenced to five years in New Caledonia.

'They should have shot me,' he said, 'but, dirty cowards, they dared not.'

Then came the long journey in a sailing vessel, and the antipodes, and his wrath flamed out again when he spoke of the indignity thrust upon him, a political prisoner, when they herded him with vulgar criminals. The ship put in at Melbourne, and one of the officers, a fellow-Corsican, enabled him to slip over the side. He swam ashore and, taking his friend's advice, went straight to the police-station. No one there could understand a word he said, but an interpreter was sent for, his dripping papers were examined, and he was told that so long as he did not set foot on a French ship he was safe.

'Freedom,' he cried to me. 'Freedom.'

Then came a long series of adventures. He cooked, taught French, swept streets, worked in the gold mines, tramped, starved, and at last found his way to New Guinea. Here he underwent the most astonishing of his experiences, for drifting into the savage interior, and they are cannibals there still, after a hundred desperate adventures and hair-breadth escapes he made himself king of some wild tribe.

'Look at me, my friend,' he said, 'I who lie here on a hospital bed, the object of charity, have been monarch of all I surveyed. Yes, it is something to say that I have been a king.'

But eventually he came into collision with the British, and his sovereignty passed from him. He fled the country and started life once more. It is clear that he was a fellow of resource for eventually he came to own a fleet of pearling luggers on Thursday Island. It looked as though at last he had reached a haven of peace and, an elderly man now, he looked forward to a prosperous and even respectable old age. A hurricane destroyed his boats and ruin fell upon him. He never recovered. He was too old to make a fresh start, and since then had earned as best he could a precarious livelihood till at last, beaten, he had accepted the hospital's kindly shelter.

'But why did you not go back to France or Corsica? An amnesty was granted to the communists a quarter of a century ago.'

'What are France and Corsica to me after fifty years? A cousin of mine seized my land. We Corsicans never forget and never forgive. If I had gone back I should have had to kill him. He had his children.'

'Funny old French Joe,' smiled the nurse who stood at the end of the bed.

'At all events you have had a fine life,' I said.

'Never. Never. I have had a frightful life. Misfortune has followed me wherever I turned my steps and look at me now. I am rotten, fit for nothing but the grave. I thank God that I had no children to inherit the curse that is upon me.'

'Why, Joe, I thought you didn't believe in God,' said the nurse.

'It is true. I am a sceptic. I have never seen a sign that there is in the scheme of things an intelligent purpose. If the universe is the contrivance of some being, that being can only be a criminal imbecile.' He shrugged his shoulders. 'Anyhow, I have not got much longer in this filthy world and then I shall go and see for myself what is the real truth of the whole business.'

The nurse told me it was time to leave the old man and I took his hand to bid him farewell. I asked him if there was anything I could do for him.

'I want nothing,' he said. 'I only want to die.' His black shining eyes twinkled. 'But meanwhile I should be grateful for a packet of cigarettes.'

The
Four Dutchmen

◆

The Van Dorth Hotel at Singapore was far from grand. The bedrooms were dingy and the mosquito nets patched and darned; the bath-houses, all in a row and detached from the bedrooms, were dank and smelly. But it had character. The people who stayed there, masters of tramps whose round ended at Singapore, mining engineers out of a job, and planters taking a holiday, to my mind bore a more romantic air than the smart folk, globe-trotters, government officials and their wives, wealthy merchants, who gave luncheon-parties at the Europe and played golf and danced and were fashionable. The Van Dorth had a billiard-room, with a table with a threadbare cloth, where ships' engineers and clerks in insurance offices played snooker. The dining-room was large and bare and silent. Dutch families on the way to Sumatra ate solidly through their dinner without exchanging a word with one another, and single gentlemen on a business trip from Batavia devoured a copious meal while they intently read their paper. On two days a week there was rijstafel and then a few residents of Singapore who had a fancy for this dish came for tiffin. The Van Dorth Hotel should have been a depressing place, but somehow it wasn't; its quaintness saved it. It had a faint aroma of something strange and half-forgotten. There was a scrap of garden facing the street where you could sit in the shade of trees and drink cold beer. In that crowded and busy city, though motors whizzed past and rickshaws passed continuously, the coolies' feet pattering on the road and their bells ringing, it had the remote peacefulness of a corner of Holland. It was the third time I had stayed at the Van Dorth. I had been told about it first by the skipper of a Dutch tramp, the S.S. *Utrecht*, on which I had travelled from Merauke in New Guinea to Macassar. The journey took the best part of a month, since the ship stopped at a number of islands in the Malay Archipelago, the Aru and the Kei Islands, Banda-Neira, Amboina, and others of which I have even forgotten the names, sometimes for an hour or two, sometimes for a day, to take on or discharge cargo. It was a charming, monotonous and diverting trip. When we dropped anchor, the agent came out in his launch, and generally the Dutch Resident, and we gathered on deck under the awning and the captain ordered beer. The news of the island was exchanged for the news of the world. We brought papers and mail. If we were staying long enough the Resident asked us to dinner and, leaving the ship in charge of the second officer, we all (the captain, the chief officer, the engineer, the supercargo, and I) piled into the launch and went ashore. We spent a merry evening. These little islands, one so like another, allured my fancy just because I knew that I should never see them again. It made them strangely unreal, and as we sailed away and they vanished into the sea and sky it was only by an effort of the imagination that I could persuade myself that they did not with my last glimpse of them cease to exist.

But there was nothing illusive, mysterious, or fantastic about the captain, the chief officer, the chief engineer, and the supercargo. Their solidity was amazing. They were the four fattest men I ever saw. At first I had great difficulty in telling them apart, for though one, the supercargo, was dark and the others were fair, they looked astonishingly alike. They were all big, with large round bare red faces, with large fat arms and large fat legs and large fat bellies. When they went ashore they buttoned up their stengah-shifters and then their great double chins bulged over the collars and they looked as though they would choke. But generally they wore them unbuttoned. They sweated freely and wiped their shiny faces with bandanas and vigorously fanned themselves with palm-leaf fans.

It was a treat to see them at tiffin. Their appetites were enormous. They had rijstafel every day, and each seemed to vie with the other how high he could pile his plate. They loved it hot and strong.

'In dis country you can't eat a ting onless it's tasty,' said the skipper.

'De only way to keep yourself up in dis country is to eat hearty,' said the chief.

They were the greatest friends, all four of them; they were like schoolboys together, playing absurd little pranks with one another. They knew each other's jokes by heart and no sooner did one of them start the familiar lines than he would splutter with laughter so violently, the heavy shaking laughter of the fat man, that he could not go on. And then the others began to laugh too. They rolled about in their chairs, and grew redder and redder, hotter and hotter, till the skipper shouted for beer, and each, gasping but happy, drank his bottle in one enchanted draught. They had been on this run together for five years and when, a little time before, the chief officer had been offered a ship of his own he refused it. He would not leave his companions. They had made up their minds that when the first of them retired they would all retire.

'All friends and a good ship. Good grub and good beer. Vot can a sensible man vant more?'

At first they were a little stand-offish with me. Although the ship had accommodation for half a dozen passengers, they did not often get any, and never one whom they did not know. I was a stranger and a foreigner. They liked their bit of fun and did not want anyone to interfere with it. But they were all of them very fond of bridge, and on occasion the chief and the engineer had duties that prevented one or the other playing. They were willing to put up with me when they discovered that I was ready to make a fourth whenever I was wanted.

Their bridge was as incredibly fantastic as they were. They played for infinitesimal stakes, five cents a hundred: they did not want to win one another's money, they said, it was the game they liked. But what a game! Each was wildly determined to play the hand and hardly one was dealt without at least a small slam being declared. The rule was that if you could get a peep at somebody else's cards you did, and if you could get away with a revoke you told your partner when there was no danger it could be claimed and you both roared with laughter till the tears rolled down your fat cheeks. But if your partner had insisted on taking the bid away from you and had called a grand slam on five spades to the queen, whereas you were positive on your seven little diamonds you could have made it easily, you could always score him off by redoubling without a trick in your hand. He went down two or three thousand and the glasses on the table danced with the laughter that shook your opponents.

I could never remember their difficult Dutch names, but knowing them anonymously as it were, only by the duties they performed, as one knows the characters Pantaloon, Harlequin, and Punchinello, of the old Italian comedy, added grotesquely to their drollery. The mere sight of them, all four together, set you laughing, and I think they got a good deal of amusement from the astonishment they caused in strangers. They boasted that they were the four most famous Dutchmen in the East Indies. To me not the least comic part of them was their serious side. Sometimes late at night, when they had given up all pretence of still wearing their uniforms, and one or the other of them lay by my side on a long chair in a pyjama jacket and a sarong, he would grow sentimental. The chief engineer, due to retire soon, was meditating marriage with a widow whom he had met when last he was home and spending the rest of his life in a little town with old red-brick houses on the shores of the Zuyder Zee. But the captain was very susceptible to the charms of the native girls and his thick English became almost unintelligible from emotion when he described to me the effect they had on him. One of these days he would buy himself a house on the hills in Java and marry a pretty little Javanese. They were so small and so gentle and they made no noise, and he would dress her in silk sarongs and give her gold chains to wear round her neck and gold bangles to put on her arms. But the chief mocked him.

'Silly all dat is. Silly. She goes mit all your friends and de house boys and everybody. By de time you retire, my dear, vot you'll vant vill be a nurse, not a vife.'

'Me?' cried the skipper. 'I shall want a vife ven I'm eighty!'

He had picked up a little thing last time the ship was at Macassar and as we approached that port he began to be all of a flutter. The chief officer shrugged fat and indulgent shoulders. The captain was always losing his head over one brazen hussy after another, but his passion never survived the interval between one stop at a port and the next, and then the chief was called in to smooth out the difficulties that ensued. And so it would be this time.

'De old man suffers from fatty degeneration of de heart. But so long as I'm dere to look after him not much harm comes of it. He vastes his money and dat's a pity, but as long as he's got it to vaste, why shouldn't he?'

The chief officer had a philosophic soul.

At Macassar then I disembarked, and bade farewell to my four fat friends.

'Make another journey with us,' they said. 'Come back next year or the year after. You'll find us all here just the same as ever.'

A good many months had passed since then and I had wandered through more than one strange land. I had been to Bali and Java and Sumatra; I had been to Cambodia and Annam; and now, feeling as though I were home again, I sat in the garden of the Van Dorth Hotel. It was cool in the very early morning and having had breakfast I was looking at back numbers of the *Straits Times* to find out what had been happening in the world since last I had been within reach of papers. Nothing very much. Suddenly my eyes caught a headline: *The* Utrecht *Tragedy. Supercargo and Chief Engineer. Not Guilty.* I read the paragraph carelessly and then I sat up. The *Utrecht* was the ship of my four fat Dutchmen and apparently the supercargo and the chief engineer had been on trial for murder. It couldn't be my two fat friends. The names were given, but the names meant nothing to me. The trial had taken place in Batavia. No details were given in this paragraph; it was only a brief announcement that after the judges had considered the speeches of the prosecution and of the defence their verdict was as stated. I was astounded. It was incredible that the men I knew could have committed a murder. I could not find out who had been murdered. I looked through back numbers of the paper. Nothing.

I got up and went to the manager of the hotel, a genial Dutchman, who spoke admirable English, and showed him the paragraph.

'That's the ship I sailed on. I was in her for nearly a month. Surely these fellows aren't the men I knew. The men I knew were enormously fat.'

'Yes, that's right,' he answered. 'They were celebrated all through the Dutch East Indies, the four fattest men in the service. It's been a terrible thing. It made a great sensation. And they were friends. I knew them all. The best fellows in the world.'

'But what happened?'

He told me the story and answered my horrified questions. But there were things I wanted to know that he couldn't tell me. It was all confused. It was unbelievable. What actually had happened was only conjecture. Then someone claimed the manager's attention and I went back to the garden. It was getting hot now and I went up to my room. I was strangely shattered.

It appeared that on one of the trips the captain took with him a Malay girl that he had been carrying on with and I wondered if it was the one he had been so eager to see when I was on board. The other three had been against her coming–what did they want with a woman in the ship? it would spoil everything–but the captain insisted and she came. I think they were all jealous of her. On that journey they didn't have the fun they generally had. When they wanted to play bridge the skipper was dallying with the girl in his cabin; when they touched at a port and went ashore the time seemed long to him till he could get back to her. He was crazy about her. It was the end of all their larks. The chief officer was more bitter against her than anybody: he was the captain's particular chum, they had been shipmates ever since they first came out from Holland; more than once high words passed between them on the subject of the captain's infatuation. Presently those old friends spoke to one another only when their duties demanded it. It was the end of the good fellowship that had so long obtained between the four fat men. Things went from bad to worse. There was a feeling among the junior officers that something untoward was pending. Uneasiness. Tension. Then one night the ship was aroused by the sound of a shot and the screams of the Malay girl. The supercargo and the chief engineer tumbled out of their bunks and they found the captain, a revolver in his hand, at the door of the chief officer's cabin. He pushed past them and went on deck.

They entered and found the chief officer dead and the girl cowering behind the door. The captain had found them in bed together and had killed the chief. How he had discovered what was going on didn't seem to be known, nor what was the meaning of the intrigue. Had the chief induced the girl to come to his cabin in order to get back on the captain, or had she, knowing his ill-will and anxious to placate him, lured him to become her lover? It was a mystery that would never be solved. A dozen possible explanations flashed across my mind. While the engineer and the supercargo were in the cabin, horror-struck at the sight before them, another shot was heard. They knew at once what had happened. They rushed up the companion. The captain had gone to his cabin and blown his brains out. Then the story grew dark and enigmatic. Next morning the Malay girl was nowhere to be found and when the second officer, who had taken command of the ship, reported this to the supercargo, the supercargo said: 'She's probably jumped overboard. It's the best thing she could have done. Good riddance to bad rubbish.' But one of the sailors on the watch, just before dawn, had seen the supercargo and the chief engineer carry something up on deck, a bulky package, about the size of the native woman, look about them to see that they were unobserved, and drop it overboard; and it was said all over the ship that these two to avenge their friends had sought the girl out in her cabin and strangled her and flung her body into the sea. When the ship arrived at Macassar they were arrested and taken to Batavia to be tried for murder. The evidence was flimsy and they were acquitted. But all through the East Indies they knew that the supercargo and the chief engineer had executed justice on the trollop who had caused the death of the two men they loved.

And thus ended the comic and celebrated friendship of the four fat Dutchmen.

The
Back of Beyond

◆

George Moon was sitting in his office. His work was finished, and he lingered there because he hadn't the heart to go down to the club. It was getting on towards tiffin time, and there would be a good many fellows hanging about the bar. Two or three of them would offer him a drink. He could not face their heartiness. Some he had known for thirty years. They had bored him, and on the whole he disliked them, but now that he was seeing them for the last time it gave him a pang. Tonight they were giving him a farewell dinner. Everyone would be there and they were presenting him with a silver tea-service that he did not in the least want. They would make speeches in which they would refer eulogistically to his work in the colony, express their regret at his departure, and wish him long life to enjoy his well-earned leisure. He would reply suitably. He had prepared a speech in which he surveyed the changes that had taken place in the F.M.S. since first, a raw cadet, he had landed at Singapore. He would thank them for their loyal cooperation with him during the term which it had been his privilege to serve as Resident at Timbang Belud, and draw a glowing picture of the future that awaited the country as a whole and Timbang Belud in particular. He would remind them that he had known it as a poverty-stricken village with a few Chinese shops and left it now a prosperous town with paved streets down which ran trams, with stone houses, a rich Chinese settlement, and a clubhouse second in splendour only to that of Singapore. They would sing 'For he's a jolly good fellow' and 'Auld Lang Syne'. Then they would dance and a good many of the younger men would get drunk. The Malays had already given him a farewell party and the Chinese an interminable feast. Tomorrow a vast concourse would see him off at the station and that would be the end of him. He wondered what they would say of him. The Malays and the Chinese would say he had been stern, but acknowledge that he had been just. The planters had not liked him. They thought him hard because he would not let them ride roughshod over their labour. His subordinates had feared him. He drove them. He had no patience with slackness or inefficiency. He had never spared himself and saw no reason why he should spare others. They thought him inhuman. It was true that there was nothing come-hither in him. He could not throw off his official position when he went to the club and laugh at bawdy stories, chaff and be chaffed. He was conscious that his arrival cast a gloom, and to play bridge with him (he liked to play every day from six to eight) was looked upon as a privilege rather than an entertainment. When at some other table a young man's four as the evening wore on grew hilarious, he caught glances thrown in his direction and sometimes an older member would stroll up to the noisy ones and in an undertone advise them to be quiet. George Moon sighed a little. From an official standpoint his career had been a success, he had been the youngest Resident ever appointed in the F.M.S., and for exceptional services a C.M.G. had been conferred upon him; but from the human it had perhaps been otherwise. He had earned respect, respect for his ability, industry, and trustworthiness, but he was too clear-sighted to think for a moment that he had inspired affection. No one would regret him. In a few months he would be forgotten.

He smiled grimly. He was not sentimental. He had enjoyed his authority, and it gave him an austere satisfaction to know that he had kept everyone up to the mark. It did not displease him to think that he had been feared rather than loved. He saw his life as a problem in higher mathematics, the working-out of which had required intense application of all his powers, but of which the result had not the least practical consequence. Its interest lay in its intricacy and its beauty in its solution. But like pure beauty it led nowhither. His future was blank. He was fifty-five, and full of energy, and to himself his mind seemed as alert as ever, his experience of men and affairs was wide: all that remained to him was to settle down in a country town in England or in a cheap part of the Riviera and play bridge with elderly ladies and golf with retired colonels. He had met, when on leave, old chiefs of his, and had observed with what difficulty they adapted themselves to the change in their circumstances. They had looked forward to the freedom that would be theirs when they retired and had pictured the charming uses to which they would put their leisure. Mirage. It was not very pleasant to be obscure after having dwelt in a spacious Residency, to make do with a couple of maids when you had been accustomed to the service of half a dozen Chinese boys and, above all, it was not pleasant to realize that you did not matter a row of beans to anyone when you had grown used to the delicate flattery of knowing that a word of praise could delight and a frown humiliate all sorts and conditions of men.

George Moon stretched out his hand and helped himself to a cigarette from the box on his desk. As he did so he noticed all the little lines on the back of his hand and the thinness of his shrivelled fingers. He frowned with distaste. It was the hand of an old man. There was in his office a Chinese mirror-picture that he had bought long ago and that he was leaving behind. He got up and looked at himself in it. He saw a thin yellow face, wrinkled and tight-lipped, thin grey hair, and grey tired eyes. He was tallish, very spare, with narrow shoulders, and he held himself erect. He had always played polo and even now could beat most of the younger men at tennis. When you talked to him he kept his eyes fixed on your face, listening attentively, but his expression did not change, and you had no notion what effect your words had on him. Perhaps he did not realize how disconcerting this was. He seldom smiled.

An orderly came in with a name written on a chit. George Moon looked at it and told him to show the visitor in. He sat down once more in his chair and looked with his cold eyes at the door through which in a moment the visitor would come. It was Tom Saffary, and he wondered what he wanted. Presumably something to do with the festivity that night. It had amused him to hear that Tom Saffary was the head of the committee that had organized it, for their relations during the last year had been far from cordial. Saffary was a planter and one of his Tamil overseers had lodged a complaint against him for assault. The Tamil had been grossly insolent to him and Saffary had given him a thrashing. George Moon realized that the provocation was great, but he had always set his face against the planters taking the law in their own hands, and when the case was tried he sentenced Saffary to a fine. But when the court rose, to show that there was no ill feeling he asked Saffary to luncheon: Saffary, resentful of what he thought an unmerited affront, curtly refused and since then had declined to have any social relations with the Resident. He answered when George Moon, casually, but resolved not to be affronted, spoke to him; but would neither play bridge nor tennis with him. He was manager of the largest rubber estate in the district, and George Moon asked himself sardonically whether he had arranged the dinner and collected subscriptions for the presentation because he thought his dignity required it or whether, now that his Resident was leaving, it appealed to his sentimentality to make a noble gesture. It tickled George Moon's frigid sense of humour to think that it would fall to Tom Saffary to make the principal speech of the evening, in which he would enlarge upon the departing Resident's admirable qualities and voice the community's regret at their irreparable loss.

Tom Saffary was ushered in. The Resident rose from his chair, shook hands with him and thinly smiled.

'How do you do? Sit down. Won't you have a cigarette?'

'How do you do?'

Saffary took the chair to which the Resident motioned him, and the Resident waited for him to state his business. He had a notion that his visitor was embarrassed. He was a big, burly, stout fellow, with a red face and a double chin, curly black hair, and blue eyes. He was a fine figure of a man, strong as a horse, but it was plain he did himself too well. He drank a good deal and ate too heartily. But he was a good business man and a hard worker. He ran his estate efficiently. He was popular in the community. He was generally known as a good chap. He was free with his money and ready to lend a helping hand to anyone in distress. It occurred to the Resident that Saffary had come in order before the dinner to compose the difference between them. The emotion that might have occasioned such a desire excited in the Resident's sensibility a very faint, good-humoured contempt. He had no enemies because individuals did not mean enough to him for him to hate any of them, but if he had, he thought, he would have hated them to the end.

'I dare say you're a bit surprised to see me here this morning, and I expect, as it's your last day and all that, you're pretty busy.'

George Moon did not answer, and the other went on.

'I've come on rather an awkward business. The fact is that my wife and I won't be able to come to the dinner tonight, and after that unpleasantness we had together last year I thought it only right to come and tell you that it has nothing to do with that. I think you treated me very harshly; it's not the money I minded, it was the indignity, but bygones are bygones. Now that you're leaving I don't want you to think that I bear any more ill-feeling towards you.'

'I realized that when I heard that you were chiefly responsible for the send-off you're giving me,' answered the Resident civilly. 'I'm sorry that you won't be able to come tonight.'

'I'm sorry, too. It's on account of Knobby Clarke's death,' Saffary hesitated for a moment. 'My wife and I were very much upset by it.'

'It was very sad. He was a great friend of yours, wasn't he?'

'He was the greatest friend I had in the colony.'

Tears shone in Tom Saffary's eyes. Fat men were very emotional, thought George Moon.

'I quite understand that in that case you should have no heart for what looks like being a rather uproarious party,' he said kindly. 'Have you heard anything of the circumstances?'

'No, nothing but what appeared in the paper.'

'He seemed all right when he left here.'

'As far as I know he'd never had a day's illness in his life.'

'Heart, I suppose. How old was he?'

'Same age as me. Thirty-eight.'

'That's young to die.'

Knobby Clarke was a planter and the estate he managed was next door to Saffary's. George Moon had liked him. He was a rather ugly man, sandy, with high cheek-bones and hollow temples, large pale eyes in deep sockets and a big mouth. But he had an attractive smile and an easy manner. He was amusing and could tell a good story. He had a careless good-humour that people found pleasing. He played games well. He was no fool. George Moon would have said he was somewhat colourless. In the course of his career he had known a good many men like him. They came and went. A fortnight before, he had left for England on leave and the Resident knew that the Saffarys had given a large dinner-party on his last night. He was married and his wife of course went with him.

'I'm sorry for her,' said George Moon. 'It must have been a terrible blow. He was buried at sea, wasn't he?'

'Yes. That's what it said in the paper.'

The news had reached Timbang the night before. The Singapore papers arrived at six, just as people were getting to the club, and a good many men waited to play bridge or billiards till they had had a glance at them. Suddenly one fellow had called out:

'I say, do you see this? Knobby's dead.'

'Knobby who? Not Knobby Clarke?'

There was a three-line paragraph in a column of general intelligence:

Messrs Star, Mosley and Co. have received a cable informing them that Mr Harold Clarke of Timbang Batu died suddenly on his way home and was buried at sea.

A man came up and took the paper from the speaker's hand, and incredulously read the note for himself. Another peered over his shoulder. Such as happened to be reading the paper turned to the page in question and read the three indifferent lines.

'By George,' cried one.

'I say, what tough luck,' said another.

'He was as fit as a fiddle when he left here.'

A shiver of dismay pierced those hearty, jovial, careless men, and each one for a moment remembered that he too was mortal. Other members came in and as they entered, braced by the thought of the six o'clock drink, and eager to meet their friends, they were met by the grim tidings.

'I say, have you heard? Poor Knobby Clarke's dead.'

'No? I say, how awful!'

'Rotten luck, isn't it?'

'Rotten.'

'Damned good sort.'

'One of the best.'

'It gave me quite a turn when I saw it in the paper just by chance.'

'I don't wonder.'

One man with the paper in his hand went into the billiard-room to break the news. They were playing off the handicap for the Prince of Wales's Cup. That august personage had presented it to the club on the occasion of his visit to Timbang Belud. Tom Saffary was playing against a man called Douglas, and the Resident, who had been beaten in the previous round, was seated with about a dozen others watching the game. The marker was monotonously calling out the score. The newcomer waited for Saffary to finish his break and then he called out to him.

'I say, Tom, Knobby's dead.'

'Knobby? It's not true.'

The other handed him the paper. Three or four gathered round to read with him.

'Good God!'

There was a moment's awed silence. The paper was passed from hand to hand. It was odd that none seemed willing to believe till he saw it for himself in black and white.

'Oh, I am sorry.'

'I say, it's awful for his wife,' said Tom Saffary. 'She was going to have a baby. My poor missus'll be upset.'

'Why, it's only a fortnight since he left here.'

'He was all right then.'

'In the pink.'

Saffary, his fat red face sagging a little, went over to a table and, seizing his glass, drank deeply.

'Look here, Tom,' said his opponent, 'would you like to call the game off?'

'Can't very well do that.' Saffary's eye sought the score board and he saw that he was ahead. 'No, let's finish. Then I'll go home and break it to Violet.'

Douglas had his shot and made fourteen. Tom Saffary missed an easy in-off, but left nothing. Douglas played again, but did not score and again Saffary missed a shot that ordinarily he could have been sure of. He frowned a little. He knew his friends had betted on him pretty heavily and he did not like the idea of failing them. Douglas made twenty-two. Saffary emptied his glass and by an effort of will that was quite patent to the sympathetic onlookers settled down to concentrate on the game. He made a break of eighteen and when he just failed to do a long Jenny they gave him a round of applause. He was sure of himself now and began to score quickly. Douglas was playing well too, and the match grew exciting to watch. The few minutes during which Saffary's attention wandered had allowed his opponent to catch up with him, and now it was anybody's game.

'Spot two hundred and thirty-five,' called the Malay, in his queer clipped English. 'Plain two hundred and twenty-eight. Spot to play.'

Douglas made eight, and then Saffary, who was plain, drew up to two hundred and forty. He left his opponent a double balk. Douglas hit neither ball, and so gave Saffary another point.

'Spot two hundred and forty-three,' called the marker. 'Plain two hundred and forty-one. Plain to play.'

Saffary played three beautiful shots off the red and finished the game.

'A popular victory,' the bystanders cried.

'Congratulations, old man,' said Douglas.

'Boy,' called Saffary, 'ask these gentlemen what they'll have. Poor old· Knobby.'

He sighed heavily. The drinks were brought and Saffary signed the chit. Then he said he'd be getting along. Two others had already begun to play.

'Sporting of him to go on like that,' said someone when the door was closed on Saffary.

'Yes, it shows grit.'

'For a while I thought his game had gone all to pieces.'

'He pulled himself together in grand style. He knew there were a lot of bets on him. He didn't want to let his backers down.'

'Of course it's a shock, a thing like that.'

'They were great pals. I wonder what he died of.'

'Good shot, sir.'

George Moon, remembering this scene, thought it strange that Tom Saffary, who on hearing of his friend's death had shown such self-control, should now apparently take it so hard. It might be that just as in the war a man when hit often did not know it till some time afterwards, Saffary had not realized how great a blow to him Harold Clarke's death was till he had had time to think it over. It seemed to him, however, more probable that Saffary, left to himself, would have carried on as usual, seeking sympathy for his loss in the company of his fellows, but that his wife's conventional sense of propriety had insisted that it would be bad form to go to a party when the grief they were suffering from made it only decent for them to eschew for a little festive gatherings. Violet Saffary was a nice little woman, three or four years younger than her husband; not very pretty, but pleasant to look at and always becomingly dressed; amiable, ladylike, and unassuming. In the days when he had been on friendly terms with the Saffarys the Resident had from time to time dined with them. He had found her agreeable, but not very amusing. They had never talked but of commonplace things. Of late he had seen little of her. When they chanced to meet she always gave him a friendly smile, and on occasion he said one or two civil words to her. But it was only by an effort of memory that he distinguished her from half a dozen of the other ladies in the community whom his official position brought him in contact with.

Saffary had presumably said what he had come to say and the Resident wondered why he did not get up and go. He sat heaped up in his chair oddly, so that it gave you the feeling that his skeleton had ceased to support him and his considerable mass of flesh was falling in on him. He looked dully at the desk that separated him from the Resident. He sighed deeply.

'You must try not to take it too hard, Saffary,' said George Moon. 'You know how uncertain life is in the East. One has to resign oneself to losing people one's fond of.'

Saffary's eyes slowly moved from the desk, and he fixed them on George Moon's. They stared unwinking. George Moon liked people to look him in the eyes. Perhaps he felt that when he thus held their vision he held them in his power. Presently two tears formed themselves in Saffary's blue eyes and slowly ran down his cheeks. He had a strangely puzzled look. Something had frightened him. Was it death? No. Something that he thought worse. He looked cowed. His mien was cringing so that he made you think of a dog unjustly beaten.

'It's not that,' he faltered. 'I could have borne that.'

George Moon did not answer. He held that big, powerful man with his cold level gaze and waited. He was pleasantly conscious of his absolute indifference. Saffary gave a harassed glance at the papers on the desk.

'I'm afraid I'm taking up too much of your time.'

'No, I have nothing to do at the moment.'

Saffary looked out of the window. A little shudder passed between his shoulders. He seemed to hesitate.

'I wonder if I might ask your advice,' he said at last.

'Of course,' said the Resident, with the shadow of a smile, 'that's one of the things I'm here for.'

'It's a purely private matter.'

'You may be quite sure that I shan't betray any confidence you place in me.'

'No, I know you wouldn't do that, but it's rather an awkward thing to speak about, and I shouldn't feel very comfortable meeting you afterwards. But you're going away tomorrow, and that makes it easier, if you understand what I mean.'

'Quite.'

Saffary began to speak, in a low voice, sulkily, as though he were ashamed, and he spoke with the awkwardness of a man unused to words. He went back and said the same thing over again. He got mixed up. He started a long, elaborate sentence and then broke off abruptly because he did not know how to finish it. George Moon listened in silence, his face a mask, smoking, and he only took his eyes off Saffary's face to reach for another cigarette from the box in front of him and light it from the stub of that which he was just finishing. And while he listened he saw, as it were a background, the monotonous round of the planter's life. It was like an accompaniment of muted strings that threw into sharper relief the calculated dissonances of an unexpected melody.

With rubber at so low a price every economy had to be exercised and Tom Saffary, notwithstanding the size of the estate, had to do work which in better times he had had an assistant for. He rose before dawn and went down to the lines where the coolies were assembled. When there was just enough light to see he read out the names, ticking them off according to the answers, and assigned the various squads to their work. Some tapped, some weeded, and others tended the ditches. Saffary went back to his solid breakfast, lit his pipe, and sallied forth again to inspect the coolies' quarters. Children were playing and babies sprawling here and there. On the sidewalks Tamil women cooked their rice. Their black skins shone with oil. They were draped about in dull red cotton and wore gold ornaments in their hair. There were handsome creatures among them, upright of carriage, with delicate features and small, exquisite hands; but Saffary looked upon them only with distaste. He set out on his rounds. On his well-grown estate the trees planted in rows gave one a charming feeling of the prim forest of a German fairy-tale. The ground was thick with dead leaves. He was accompanied by a Tamil overseer, his long black hair done in a chignon, barefooted, in sarong and baju, with a showy ring on his finger. Saffary walked hard, jumping the ditches when he came to them, and soon he dripped with sweat. He examined the trees to see that they were properly tapped, and when he came across a coolie at work looked at the shavings and if they were too thick swore at him and docked him half a day's pay. When a tree was not to be tapped any more he told the overseer to take away the cup and the wire that held it to the trunk. The weeders worked in gangs.

At noon Saffary returned to the bungalow and had a drink of beer which, because there was no ice, was luke-warm. He stripped off the khaki shorts, the flannel shirt, the heavy boots and stockings in which he had been walking, and shaved and bathed. He lunched in a sarong and baju. He lay off for half an hour, and then went down to his office and worked till five; he had tea and went to the club. About eight he started back for the bungalow, dined, and half an hour after went to bed.

But last night he went home immediately he had finished his match. Violet had not accompanied him that day. When the Clarkes were there they had met at the club every afternoon, but now they had gone home she came less often. She said there was no one there who much amused her and she had heard everything everyone had to say till she was fed to the teeth. She did not play bridge and it was dull for her to wait about while he played. She told Tom he need not mind leaving her alone. She had plenty of things to do in the house.

As soon as she saw him back so early she guessed that he had come to tell her that he had won his match. He was like a child in his self-satisfaction over one of these small triumphs. He was a kindly, simple creature and she knew that his pleasure at winning was not only on his own account, but because he thought it must give her pleasure too. It was rather sweet of him to hurry home in order to tell her all about it without delay.

'Well, how did your match go?' she said as soon as he came lumbering into the sitting-room.

'I won.'

'Easily?'

'Well, not as easily as I should have. I was a bit ahead, and then I stuck, I couldn't do a thing, and you know what Douglas is, not at all showy, but steady, and he pulled up with me. Then I said to myself, well, if I don't buck up I shall get a licking. I had a bit of luck here and there, and then, to cut a long story short, I beat him by seven.'

'Isn't that splendid? You ought to win the cup now, oughtn't you?'

'Well, I've got three matches more. If I can get into the semi-finals I ought to have a chance.'

Violet smiled. She was anxious to show him that she was as much interested as he expected her to be.

'What made you go to pieces when you did?'

His face sagged.

'That's why I came back at once. I'd have scratched only I thought it wasn't fair on the fellows who'd backed me. I don't know how to tell you, Violet.'

She gave him a questioning look.

'Why, what's the matter? Not bad news?'

'Rotten. Knobby's dead.'

For a full minute she stared at him, and her face, her neat friendly little face, grew haggard with horror. At first it seemed as though she could not understand.

'What *do* you mean?' she cried.

'It was in the paper. He died on board. They buried him at sea.'

Suddenly she gave a piercing cry and fell headlong to the floor. She had fainted dead away.

'Violet,' he cried, and threw himself down on his knees and took her head in his arms. 'Boy, boy.'

A boy, startled by the terror in his master's voice, rushed in, and Saffary shouted him to bring brandy. He forced a little between Violet's lips. She opened her eyes, and as she remembered they grew dark with anguish. Her face was screwed up like a little child's when it is just going to burst into tears. He lifted her up in his arms and laid her on the sofa. She turned her head away.

'Oh, Tom, it isn't true. It can't be true.'

'I'm afraid it is.'

'No, no, no.'

She burst into tears. She wept convulsively. It was dreadful to hear her. Saffary did not know what to do. He knelt beside her and tried to soothe her. He sought to take her in his arms, but with a sudden gesture she repelled him.

'Don't touch me,' she cried, and she said it so sharply that he was startled. He rose to his feet.

'Try not to take it too hard, sweetie,' he said. 'I know it's been an awful shock. He was one of the best.'

She buried her face in the cushions and wept despairingly. It tortured him to see her body shaken by those uncontrollable sobs. She was beside herself. He put his hand gently on her shoulder.

'Darling, don't give way like that. It's so bad for you.'

She shook herself free from his hand.

'For God's sake leave me alone,' she cried. 'Oh, Hal, Hal.' He had never heard her call the dead man that before. Of course his name was Harold, but everyone called him Knobby. 'What shall I do?' she wailed. 'I can't bear it. I can't bear it.'

Saffary began to grow a trifle impatient. So much grief did seem to him exaggerated. Violet was not normally so emotional. He supposed it was the damned climate. It made women nervous and high-strung. Violet hadn't been home for four years. She was not hiding her face now. She lay, almost falling off the sofa, her mouth open in the extremity of her pain, and the tears streamed from her staring eyes. She was distraught.

'Have a little more brandy,' he said. 'Try to pull yourself together, darling. You can't do Knobby any good by getting in such a state.'

With a sudden gesture she sprang to her feet and pushed him aside. She gave him a look of hatred.

'Go away, Tom. I don't want your sympathy. I want to be left alone.'

She walked swiftly over to an arm-chair and threw herself down in it. She flung back her head and her poor white face was wrenched into a grimace of agony.

'Oh, it's not fair,' she moaned. 'What's to become of me now? Oh, God, I wish I were dead.'

'Violet.'

His voice quavered with pain. He was very nearly crying too. She stamped her foot impatiently.

'Go away, I tell you. Go away.'

He started. He stared at her and suddenly gasped. A shudder passed through his great bulk. He took a step towards her and stopped, but his eyes never left her white, tortured face; he stared as though he saw in it something that appalled him. Then he dropped his head and without a word walked out of the room. He went into a little sitting-room they had at the back, but seldom used, and sank heavily into a chair. He thought. Presently the gong sounded for dinner. He had not had his bath. He gave his hands a glance. He could not be bothered to wash them. He walked slowly into the dining-room. He told the boy to go and tell Violet that dinner was ready. The boy came back and said she did not want any.

'All right. Let me have mine then,' said Saffary.

He sent Violet in a plate of soup and a piece of toast, and when the fish was served he put some on a plate for her and gave it to the boy. But the boy came back with it at once.

'Mem, she say no wantchee,' he said.

Saffary ate his dinner alone. He ate from habit, solidly, through the familiar courses. He drank a bottle of beer. When he had finished the boy brought him a cup of coffee and he lit a cheroot. Saffary sat still till he had finished it. He thought. At last he got up and went back into the large veranda which was where they always sat. Violet was still huddled in the chair in which he had left her. Her eyes were closed, but she opened them when she heard him come. He took a light chair and sat down in front of her.

'What *was* Knobby to you, Violet?' he said.

She gave a slight start. She turned away her eyes, but did not speak.

'I can't quite make out why you should have been so frightfully upset by the news of his death.'

'It was an awful shock.'

'Of course. But it seems very strange that anyone should go simply to pieces over the death of a friend.'

'I don't understand what you mean,' she said.

She could hardly speak the words and he saw that her lips were trembling.

'I've never heard you call him Hal. Even his wife called him Knobby.'

She did not say anything. Her eyes, heavy with grief, were fixed on vacancy.

'Look at me, Violet.'

She turned her head slightly and listlessly gazed at him.

'Was he your lover?'

She closed her eyes and tears flowed from them. Her mouth was strangely twisted.

'Haven't you got anything to say at all?'

She shook her head.

'You must answer me, Violet.'

'I'm not fit to talk to you now,' she moaned. 'How can you be so heartless?'

'I'm afraid I don't feel very sympathetic at the moment. We must get this straight now. Would you like a drink of water?'

'I don't want anything.'

'Then answer my question.'

'You have no right to ask it. It's insulting.'

'Do you ask me to believe that a woman like you who hears of the death of someone she knew is going to faint dead away and then, when she comes to, is going to cry like that? Why, one wouldn't be so upset over the death of one's only child. When we heard of your mother's death you cried of course, anyone would, and I know you were utterly miserable, but you came to me for comfort and you said you didn't know what you'd have done without me.'

'This was so frightfully sudden.'

'Your mother's death was sudden, too.'

'Naturally I was very fond of Knobby.'

'How fond? So fond that when you heard he was dead you didn't know and you didn't care what you said? Why did you say it wasn't fair? Why did you say, "What's going to become of me now?"?'

She sighed deeply. She turned her head this way and that like a sheep trying to avoid the hands of the butcher.

'You musn't take me for an utter fool, Violet. I tell you it's impossible that you should be so shattered by the blow if there hadn't been something between you.'

'Well, if you think that, why do you torture me with questions?'

'My dear, it's no good shilly-shallying. We can't go on like this. What d'you think I'm feeling?'

She looked at him when he said this. She hadn't thought of him at all. She had been too much absorbed in her own misery to be concerned with his.

'I'm so tired,' she sighed.

He leaned forward and roughly seized her wrist.

'Speak,' he cried.

'You're hurting me.'

'And what about me? D'you think you're not hurting me? How can you have the heart to let me suffer like this?'

He let go of her arm and sprang to his feet. He walked to the end of the room and back again. It looked as though the movement had suddenly roused him to fury. He caught her by the shoulders and dragged her to her feet. He shook her.

'If you don't tell me the truth I'll kill you,' he cried.

'I wish you would,' she said.

'He was your lover?'

'Yes.'

'You swine.'

With one hand still on her shoulder so that she could not move he swung back his other arm and with a flat palm struck her repeatedly, with all his strength, on the side of her face. She quivered under the blows, but did not flinch or cry out. He struck her again and again. All at once he felt her strangely inert, he let go of her and she sank unconscious to the floor. Fear seized him. He bent down and touched her, calling her name. She did not move. He lifted her up and put her back into the chair from which a little while before he had pulled her. The brandy that had been brought when first she fainted was still in the room and he fetched it and tried to force it down her throat. She choked and it spilt over her chin and neck. One side of her pale face was livid from the blows of his heavy hand. She sighed a little and opened her eyes. He held the glass again to her lips, supporting her head, and she sipped a little of the neat spirit. He looked at her with penitent, anxious eyes.

'I'm sorry, Violet. I didn't mean to do that. I'm dreadfully ashamed of myself. I never thought I could sink so low as to hit a woman.'

Though she was feeling very weak and her face was hurting, the flicker of a smile crossed her lips. Poor Tom. He did say things like that. He felt like that. And how scandalized he would be if you asked him why a man shouldn't hit a woman. But Saffary, seeing the wan smile, put it down to her indomitable courage. By God, she's a plucky little woman, he thought. Game isn't the word.

'Give me a cigarette,' she said.

He took one out of his case and put it in her mouth. He made two or three ineffectual attempts to strike his lighter. It would not work.

'Hadn't you better get a match?' she said.

For the moment she had forgotten her heart-rending grief and was faintly amused at the situation. He took a box from the table and held the lighted match to her cigarette. She inhaled the first puff with a sense of infinite relief.

'I can't tell you how ashamed I am, Violet,' he said. 'I'm disgusted with myself. I don't know what came over me.'

'Oh, that's all right. It was very natural. Why don't you have a drink? It'll do you good.'

Without a word, his shoulders all hunched up as though the burden that oppressed him were material, he helped himself to a brandy and soda. Then, still silent, he sat down. She watched the blue smoke curl into the air.

'What are you going to do?' she said at last.

He gave a weary gesture of despair.

'We'll talk about that tomorrow. You're not in a fit state tonight. As soon as you've finished your cigarette you'd better go to bed.'

'You know so much, you'd better know everything.'

'Not now, Violet.'

'Yes, now.'

She began to speak. He heard her words, but could hardly make sense of them. He felt like a man who has built himself a house with loving care and thought to live in it all his life, and then, he does not understand why, sees the housebreakers come and with their picks and heavy hammers destroy it room by room, till what was a fair dwelling-place is only a heap of rubble. What made it so awful was that it was Knobby Clarke who had done this thing. They had come to the F.M.S. on the same ship and had worked at first on the same estate. They call the young planter a creeper and you can tell him in the streets of Singapore by his double felt hat and his khaki coat turned up at the wrists. Callow youths who saunter about staring and are inveigled by wily Chinese into buying worthless truck from Birmingham which they send home as Eastern curios, sit in the lounges of cheap hotels drinking innumerable stengahs, and after an evening at the pictures get into rickshaws and finish the night in the Chinese quarter. Tom and Knobby were inseparable. Tom, a big, powerful fellow, simple, very honest, hard-working; and Knobby, ungainly, but curiously attractive, with his deep-set eyes, hollow cheeks, and large humorous mouth. It was Knobby who made the jokes and Tom who laughed at them. Tom married first. He met Violet when he went on leave. The daughter of a doctor killed in the war, she was governess in the house of some people who lived in the same place as his father. He fell in love with her because she was alone in the world, and his tender heart was touched by the thought of the drab life that lay before her. But Knobby married, because Tom had and he felt lost without him, a girl who had come East to spend the winter with relations. Enid Clarke had been very pretty then in her blonde way, and full-face she was pretty still, though her skin, once so clear and fresh, was already faded; but she had a very weak, small, insignificant chin and in profile reminded you of a sheep. She had pretty flaxen hair, straight, because in the heat it would not keep its wave, and china-blue eyes. Though but twenty-six, she had already a tired look. A year after marriage she had a baby, but it died when only two years old.

It was after this that Tom Saffary managed to get Knobby the post of manager of the estate next his own. The two men pleasantly resumed their old familiarity, and their wives, who till then had not known one another very well, soon made friends. They copied one another's frocks and lent one another servants and crockery when they gave a party. The four of them met every day. They went everywhere together. Tom Saffary thought it grand.

The strange thing was that Violet and Knobby Clarke lived on those terms of close intimacy for three years before they fell in love with one another. Neither saw love approaching. Neither suspected that in the pleasure each took in the other's company there was anything more than the casual friendship of two persons thrown together by the circumstances of life. To be together gave them no particular happiness, but merely a quiet sense of comfort. If by chance a day passed without their meeting they felt unaccountably bored. That seemed very natural. They played games together. They danced together. They chaffed one another. The revelation came to them by what looked like pure accident. They had all been to a dance at the club and were driving home in Saffary's car. The Clarkes's estate was on the way and he was dropping them at their bungalow. Violet and Knobby sat in the back. He had had a good deal to drink, but was not drunk; their hands touched by chance, and he took hers and held it. They did not speak. They were all tired. But suddenly the exhilaration of the champagne left him and he was cold sober. They knew in a flash that they were madly in love with one another and at the same moment they realized they had never been in love before. When they reached the Clarkes's Tom said:

'You'd better hop in beside me, Violet.'

'I'm too exhausted to move,' she said.

Her legs seemed so weak that she thought she would never be able to stand.

When they met next day neither referred to what had happened, but each knew that something inevitable had passed. They behaved to one another as they had always done, they continued to behave so for weeks, but they felt that everything was different. At last flesh and blood could stand it no longer and they became lovers. But the physical tie seemed to them the least important element in their relation, and indeed their way of living made it impossible for them, except very seldom, to enjoy any intimate connexion. It was enough that they saw one another, though in the company of others, every day; a glance, a touch of the hand, assured them of their love, and that was all that mattered. The sexual act was no more than an affirmation of the union of their souls.

They very seldom talked of Tom or Enid. If sometimes they laughed together at their foibles it was not unkindly. It might have seemed odd to them to realize how completely these two people whom they saw so constantly had ceased to matter to them if they had given them enough thought to consider the matter. Their relations with them fell into the routine of life that nobody notices, like shaving oneself, dressing, and eating three meals a day. They felt tenderly towards them. They even took pains to please them, as you would with a bed-ridden invalid, because their own happiness was so great that in charity they must do what they could for others less fortunate. They had no scruples. They were too much absorbed in one another to be touched even for a moment by remorse. Beauty now excitingly kindled the pleasant humdrum life they had led so long.

But then an event took place that filled them with consternation. The company for which Tom worked entered into negotiations to buy extensive rubber plantations in British North Borneo and invited Tom to manage them. It was a better job than his present one, with a higher salary, and since he would have assistants under him he would not have to work so hard. Saffary welcomed the offer. Both Clarke and Saffary were due for leave and the two couples had arranged to travel home together. They had already booked their passages. This changed everything. Tom would not be able to get away for at least a year. By the time the Clarkes came back the Saffarys would be settled in Borneo. It did not take Violet and Knobby long to decide that there was only one thing to do. They had been willing enough to go on as they were, notwithstanding the hindrance to the enjoyment of their love, when they were certain of seeing one another continually; they felt that they had endless time before them and the future was coloured with a happiness that seemed to have no limit; but neither could suffer for an instant the thought of separation. They made up their minds to run away together, and then it seemed to them on a sudden that every day that passed before they could be together always and all the time was a day lost. Their love took another guise. It flamed into a devouring passion that left them no emotion to waste on others. They cared little for the pain they must cause Tom and Enid. It was unfortunate, but inevitable. They made their plans deliberately. Knobby on the pretence of business would go to Singapore and Violet, telling Tom that she was going to spend a week with friends on an estate down the line, would join him there. They would go over to Java and thence take ship to Sydney. In Sydney Knobby would look for a job. When Violet told Tom that the Mackenzies had asked her to spend a few days with them, he was pleased.

'That's grand. I think you want a change, darling,' he said. 'I've fancied you've been looking a bit peaked lately.'

He stroked her cheek affectionately. The gesture stabbed her heart.

'You've always been awfully good to me, Tom,' she said, her eyes suddenly filled with tears.

'Well, that's the least I could be. You're the best little woman in the world.'

'Have you been happy with me these eight years?'

'Frightfully.'

'Well, that's something, isn't it? No one can ever take that away from you.'

She told herself that he was the kind of man who would soon console himself. He liked women for themselves and it would not be long after he had regained his freedom before he found someone that he would wish to marry. And he would be just as happy with his new wife as he had been with her. Perhaps he would marry Enid. Enid was one of those dependent little things that somewhat exasperated her and she did not think her capable of deep feeling. Her vanity would be hurt; her heart would not be broken. But now that the die was cast, everything settled and the day fixed, she had a qualm. Remorse beset her. She wished that it had been possible not to cause those two people such fearful distress. She faltered.

'We've had a very good time here, Tom,' she said. 'I wonder if it's wise to leave it all. We're giving up a certainty for we don't know what.'

'My dear child, it's a chance in a million and much better money.'

'Money isn't everything. There's happiness.'

'I know that, but there's no reason why we shouldn't be just as happy in B.N.B. And besides, there was no alternative. I'm not my own master. The directors want me to go and I must, and that's all there is to it.'

She sighed. There was no alternative for her either. She shrugged her shoulders. It was hateful to cause others pain; sometimes you couldn't help yourself. Tom meant no more to her than the casual man on the voyage out who was civil to you: it was absurd that she should be asked to sacrifice her life for him.

The Clarkes were due to sail for England in a fortnight and this determined the date of their elopement. The days passed. Violet was restless and excited. She looked forward with a joy that was almost painful to the peace that she anticipated when they were once on board the ship and could begin the life which she was sure would give her at last perfect happiness.

She began to pack. The friends she was supposed to be going to stay with entertained a good deal and this gave her an excuse to take quite a lot of luggage. She was starting next day. It was eleven o'clock in the morning and Tom was making his round of the estate. One of the boys came to her room and told her that Mrs Clarke was there and at the same moment she heard Enid calling her. Quickly closing the lid of her trunk, she went out on to the veranda. To her astonishment Enid came up to her, flung her arms round her neck and kissed her eagerly. She looked at Enid and saw her cheeks, usually pale, were flushed and that her eyes were shining. Enid burst into tears.

'What on earth's the matter, darling?' she cried.

For one moment she was afraid that Enid knew everything. But Enid was flushed with delight and not with jealousy or anger.

'I've just seen Dr Harrow,' she said. 'I didn't want to say anything about it. I've had two or three false alarms, but this time he says it's all right.'

A sudden coldness pierced Violet's heart.

'What do you mean? You're not going to . . .'

She looked at Enid and Enid nodded.

'Yes, he says there's no doubt about it at all. He thinks I'm at least three months gone. Oh, my dear, I'm so wildly happy.'

She flung herself again into Violet's arms and clung to her, weeping.

'Oh, darling, don't.'

Violet felt herself grow pale as death and knew that if she didn't keep a tight hold of herself she would faint.

'Does Knobby know?'

'No, I didn't say a word. He was so disappointed before. He was so frightfully cut up when baby died. He's wanted me to have another so badly.'

Violet forced herself to say the things that were expected of her, but Enid was not listening. She wanted to tell the whole story of her hopes and fears, of her symptoms, and then of her interview with the doctor. She went on and on.

'When are you going to tell Knobby?' Violet asked at last. 'Now, when he gets in?'

'Oh, no, he's tired and hungry when he gets back from his round. I shall wait until tonight after dinner.'

Violet repressed a movement of exasperation; Enid was going to make a scene of it and was choosing her moment; but after all, it was only natural. It was lucky, for it would give her the chance to see Knobby first. As soon as she was rid of her she rang him up. She knew that he always looked in at his office on his way home, and she left a message asking him to call her. She was only afraid that he would not do so till Tom was back, but she had to take a chance of that. The bell rang and Tom had not come in.

'Hal?'

'Yes.'

'Will you be at the hut at three?'

'Yes. Has anything happened?'

'I'll tell you when I see you. Don't worry.'

She rang off. The hut was a little shelter on Knobby's estate which she could get to without difficulty and where they occasionally met. The coolies passed it while they worked and it had no privacy; but it was a convenient place for them without exciting comment to exchange a few minutes' conversation. At three Enid would be resting and Tom at work in his office.

When Violet walked up Knobby was already there. He gave a gasp.

'Violet, how white you are.'

She gave him her hand. They did not know what eyes might be watching them and their behaviour here was always such as anyone could observe.

'Enid came to see me this morning. She's going to tell you tonight. I thought you ought to be warned. She's going to have a baby.'

'Violet!'

He looked at her aghast. She began to cry. They had never talked of the relations they had, he with his wife and she with her husband. They ignored the subject because it was to each horribly painful. Violet knew what her own life was; she satisfied her husband's appetite, but, with a woman's strange nonchalance, because to do so gave her no pleasure, attached no importance to it; but somehow she had persuaded herself that with Hal it was different. He felt now instinctively how bitterly what she had learned wounded her. He tried to excuse himself.

'Darling, I couldn't help myself.'

She cried silently and he watched her with miserable eyes.

'I know it seems beastly,' he said, 'but what could I do? It wasn't as if I had any reason to . . .'

She interrupted him.

'I don't blame you. It was inevitable. It's only because I'm stupid that it gives me such a frightful pain in my heart.'

'Darling!'

'We ought to have gone away together two years ago. It was madness to think we could go on like this.'

'Are you sure Enid's right? She thought she was in the family way three or four years ago.'

'Oh, yes, she's right. She's frightfully happy. She says you wanted a child so badly.'

'It's come as such an awful surprise. I don't seem able to realize it yet.'

She looked at him. He was staring at the leaf-strewn earth with harassed eyes. She smiled a little.

'Poor Hal.' She sighed deeply. 'There's nothing to be done about it. It's the end of us.'

'What do you mean?' he cried.

'Oh, my dear, you can't very well leave her now, can you? It was all right before. She would have been unhappy, but she would have got over it. But now it's different. It's not a very nice time for a woman anyhow. For months she feels more or less ill. She wants affection. She wants to be taken care of. It would be frightful to leave her to bear it all alone. We couldn't be such beasts.'

'Do you mean to say you want me to go back to England with her?'

She nodded gravely.

'It's lucky you're going. It'll be easier when you get away and we don't see one another every day.'

'But I can't live without you now.'

'Oh, yes, you can. You must. I can. And it'll be worse for me, because I stay behind and I shall have nothing.'

'Oh, Violet, it's impossible.'

'My dear, it's no good arguing. The moment she told me I saw it meant that. That's why I wanted to see you first. I thought the shock might lead you to blurt out the whole truth. You know I love you more than anything in the world. She's never done me any harm. I couldn't take you away from her now. It's bad luck on both of us, but there it is, I simply wouldn't dare to do a filthy thing like that.'

'I wish I were dead,' he moaned.

'That wouldn't do her any good, or me either,' she smiled.

'What about the future? Have we got to sacrifice our whole lives?'

'I'm afraid so. It sounds rather grim, darling, but I suppose sooner or later we shall get over it. One gets over everything.'

She looked at her wrist-watch.

'I ought to be getting back. Tom will be in soon. We're all meeting at the club at five.'

'Tom and I are supposed to be playing tennis.' He gave her a pitiful look. 'Oh, Violet, I'm so frightfully unhappy.'

'I know. So am I. But we shan't do any good by talking about it.'

She gave him her hand, but he took her in his arms and kissed her, and when she released herself her cheeks were wet with his tears. But she was so desperate she could not cry.

Ten days later the Clarkes sailed.

While George Moon was listening to as much of this story as Tom Saffary was able to tell him, he reflected in his cool, detached way how odd it was that these commonplace people, leading lives so monotonous, should have been convulsed by such a tragedy. Who would have thought that Violet Saffary, so neat and demure, sitting in the club reading the illustrated papers or chatting with her friends over a lemon squash, should have been eating her heart out for love of that ordinary man? George Moon remembered seeing Knobby at the club the evening before he sailed. He seemed in great spirits. Fellows envied him because he was going home. Those who had recently come back told him by no means to miss the show at the Pavilion. Drink flowed freely. The Resident had not been asked to the farewell party the Saffarys gave for the Clarkes, but he knew very well what it had been like, the good cheer, the cordiality, the chaff, and then after dinner the gramophone turned on and everyone dancing. He wondered what Violet and Clarke had felt as they danced together. It gave him an odd sensation of dismay to think of the despair that must have filled their hearts while they pretended to be so gay.

And with another part of his mind George Moon thought of his own past. Very few knew that story. After all, it happened twenty-five years ago.

'What are you going to do now, Saffary?' he asked.

'Well, that's what I wanted you to advise me about. Now that Knobby's dead I don't know what's going to happen to Violet if I divorce her. I was wondering if I oughtn't to let her divorce me.'

'Oh, you want to divorce?'

'Well, I must.'

George Moon lit another cigarette and watched for a moment the smoke that curled away into the air.

'Did you ever know that I'd been married?'

'Yes, I think I'd heard. You're a widower, aren't you?'

'No, I divorced my wife. I have a son of twenty-seven. He's farming in New Zealand. I saw my wife the last time I was home on leave. We met at a play. At first we didn't recognize one another. She spoke to me. I asked her to lunch at the Berkeley.'

George Moon chuckled to himself. He was alone. It was a musical comedy. He found himself sitting next to a large fat dark woman whom he vaguely thought he had seen before, but the play was just starting and he did not give her a second look. When the curtain fell after the first act she looked at him with bright eyes and spoke.

'How are you, George?'

It was his wife. She had a bold, friendly manner and was very much at her ease.

'It's a long time since we met,' she said.

'It is.'

'How has life been treating you?'

'Oh, all right.'

'I suppose you're a Resident now. You're still in the Service, aren't you?'

'Yes. I'm retiring soon, worse luck.'

'Why? You look very fit.'

'I'm reaching the age limit. I'm supposed to be an old buffer and no good any more.'

'You're lucky to have kept so thin. I'm terrible, aren't I?'

'You don't look as though you were wasting away.'

'I know. I'm stout and I'm growing stouter all the time. I can't help it and I love food. I can't resist cream and bread and potatoes.'

George Moon laughed, but not at what she said; at his own thoughts. In years gone by it had sometimes occurred to him that he might meet her, but he had never thought that the meeting would take this turn. When the play was ended and with a smile she bade him good night, he said:

'I suppose you wouldn't lunch with me one day?'

'Any day you like.'

They arranged a date and duly met. He knew that she had married the man on whose account he had divorced her, and he judged by her clothes that she was in comfortable circumstances. They drank a cocktail. She ate the *hors-d'œuvre* with gusto. She was fifty if she was a day, but she carried her years with spirit. There was something jolly and careless about her, she was quick on the uptake, chatty, and she had the hearty, infectious laugh of the fat woman who has let herself go. If he had not known that her family had for a century been in the Indian Civil Service he would have thought that she had been a chorus girl. She was not flashy, but she had a sort of flamboyance of nature that suggested the stage. She was not in the least embarrassed.

'You never married again, did you?' she asked.

'No.'

'Pity. Because it wasn't a success the first time there's no reason why it shouldn't have been the second.'

'There's no need for me to ask if you've been happy.'

'I've got nothing to complain of. I think I've got a happy nature. Jim's always been very good to me; he's retired now, you know, and we live in the country, and I adore Betty.'

'Who's Betty?'

'Oh, she's my daughter. She got married two years ago. I'm expecting to be a grandmother almost any day.'

'That ages us a bit.'

She gave a laugh.

'Betty's twenty-two. It was nice of you to ask me to lunch, George. After all, it would be silly to have any feelings about something that happened so long ago as all that.'

'Idiotic.'

'We weren't fitted to one another and it's lucky we found it out before it was too late. Of course I was foolish, but then I was very young. Have you been happy too?'

'I think I can say I've been a success.'

'Oh, well, that's probably all the happiness you were capable of.'

He smiled in appreciation of her shrewdness. And then, putting the whole matter aside easily, she began to talk of other things. Though the courts had given him custody of their son, he, unable to look after him, had allowed his mother to have him. The boy had emigrated at eighteen and was now married. He was a stranger to George Moon, and he was aware that if he met him in the street he would not recognize him. He was too sincere to pretend that he took much interest in him. They talked of him, however, for a while, and then they talked of actors and plays.

'Well,' she said at last, 'I must be running away. I've had a lovely lunch. It's been fun meeting you, George. Thanks so much.'

He put her into a taxi and taking off his hat walked down Piccadilly by himself. He thought her quite a pleasant, amusing woman: he laughed to think that he had ever been madly in love with her. There was a smile on his lips when he spoke again to Tom Saffary.

'She was a damned good-looking girl when I married her. That was the trouble. Though, of course, if she hadn't been I'd never have married her. They were all after her like flies round a honey-pot. We used to have awful rows. And at last I caught her out. Of course I divorced her.'

'Of course.'

'Yes, but I know I was a damned fool to do it.' He leaned forward. 'My dear Saffary, I know now that if I'd had any sense I'd have shut my eyes. She'd have settled down and made me an excellent wife.'

He wished he were able to explain to his visitor how grotesque it had seemed to him when he sat and talked with that jolly, comfortable, and good-humoured woman that he should have made so much fuss about what now seemed to him to matter so little.

'But one has one's honour to think of,' said Saffary.

'Honour be damned. One has one's happiness to think of. Is one's honour really concerned because one's wife hops into bed with another man? We're not crusaders, you and I, or Spanish grandees. I *liked* my wife. I don't say I haven't had other women. I have. But she had just that something that none of the others could give me. What a fool I was to throw away what I wanted more than anything in the world because I couldn't enjoy exclusive possession of it!'

'You're the last man I should ever have expected to hear speak like that.'

George Moon smiled thinly at the embarrassment that was so clearly expressed on Saffary's fat troubled face.

'I'm probably the first man you've heard speak the naked truth,' he retorted.

'Do you mean to say that if it were all to do over again you would act differently?'

'If I were twenty-seven again I suppose I should be as big a fool as I was then. But if I had the sense I have now I'll tell you what I'd do if I found my wife had been unfaithful to me. I'd do just what you did last night: I'd give her a damned good hiding and let it go at that.'

'Are you asking me to forgive Violet?'

The Resident shook his head slowly and smiled.

'No. You've forgiven her already. I'm merely advising you not to cut off your nose to spite your face.'

Saffary gave him a worried look. It disconcerted him to know that this cold precise man should see in his heart emotions which seemed so unnatural to himself that he thrust them out of his consciousness.

'You don't know the circumstances,' he said. 'Knobby and I were almost like brothers. I got him his job. He owed everything to me. And except for me Violet might have gone on being a governess for the rest of her life. It seemed such a waste; I couldn't help feeling sorry for her. If you know what I mean, it was pity that first made me take any notice of her. Don't you think it's a bit thick that when you've been thoroughly decent with people they should go out of their way to do the dirty on you? It's such awful ingratitude.'

'Oh, my dear boy, one mustn't expect gratitude. It's a thing that no one has a right to. After all, you do good because it gives you pleasure. It's the purest form of happiness there is. To expect thanks for it is really asking too much. If you get it, well, it's like a bonus on shares on which you've already received a dividend; it's grand, but you mustn't look upon it as your due.'

Saffary frowned. He was perplexed. He could not quite make it out that George Moon should think so oddly about things that it had always seemed to him there were no two ways of thinking about. After all there were limits. I mean, if you had any sense of decency you had to behave like a tuan. There was your own self-respect to think of. It was funny that George Moon should give reasons that looked so damned plausible for doing something that, well, damn it, you had to admit you'd be only too glad to do if you could see your way to it. Of course George Moon was queer. No one ever quite understood him.

'Knobby Clarke is dead, Saffary. You can't be jealous of him any more. No one knows a thing except you and me and your wife, and tomorrow I'm going away for ever. Why don't you let bygones be bygones?'

'Violet would only despise me.'

George Moon smiled and, unexpectedly on that prim, fastidious face, his smile had a singular sweetness.

'I know her very little. I always thought her a very nice woman. Is she as detestable as that?'

Saffary gave a start and reddened to his ears.

'No, she's an angel of goodness. It's me who's detestable for saying that of her.' His voice broke and he gave a little sob. 'God knows I only want to do the right thing.'

'The right thing is the kind thing.'

Saffary covered his face with his hands. He could not curb the emotion that shook him.

'I seem to be giving, giving all the time, and no one does a God-damned thing for me. It doesn't matter if my heart is broken, I must just go on.' He drew the back of his hand across his eyes and sighed deeply. 'I'll forgive her.'

George Moon looked at him reflectively for a little.

'I wouldn't make too much of a song and dance about it, if I were you,' he said. 'You'll have to walk warily. She'll have a lot to forgive too.'

'Because I hit her, you mean? I know, that was awful of me.'

'Not a bit. It did her a power of good. I didn't mean that. You're behaving generously, old boy, and, you know, one needs a devil of a lot of tact to get people to forgive one one's generosity. Fortunately women are frivolous and they very quickly forget the benefits conferred upon them. Otherwise, of course, there'd be no living with them.'

Saffary looked at him open-mouthed.

'Upon my word you're a rum 'un, Moon,' he said. 'Sometimes you seem as hard as nails and then you talk so that one thinks you're almost human, and then, just as one thinks one's misjudged you and you have a heart after all, you come out with something that just shocks one. I suppose that's what they call a cynic.'

'I haven't deeply considered the matter,' smiled George Moon, 'but if to look truth in the face and not resent it when it's unpalatable, and take human nature as you find it, smiling when it's absurd and grieved without exaggeration when it's pitiful, is to be cynical, then I suppose I'm a cynic. Mostly human nature is both absurd and pitiful, but if life has taught you tolerance you find in it more to smile at than to weep.'

When Tom Saffary left the room the Resident lit himself with deliberation the last cigarette he meant to smoke before tiffin. It was a new role for him to reconcile an angry husband with an erring wife and it caused him a discreet amusement. He continued to reflect upon human nature. A wintry smile hovered upon his thin and pallid lips. He recalled with what interest in the dry creeks of certain places along the coast he had often stood and watched the Jumping Johnnies. There were hundreds of them sometimes, from little things of a couple of inches long to great fat fellows as long as your foot. They were the colour of the mud they lived in. They sat and looked at you with large round eyes and then with a sudden dash buried themselves in their holes. It was extraordinary to see them scudding on their flappers over the surface of the mud. It teemed with them. They gave you a fearful feeling that the mud itself was mysteriously become alive and an atavistic terror froze your heart when you remembered that such creatures, but gigantic and terrible, were once the only inhabitants of the earth. There was something uncanny about them, but something amusing too. They reminded you very much of human beings. It was quite entertaining to stand there for half an hour and observe their gambols.

George Moon took his topee off the peg and not displeased with life stepped out into the sunshine.

P. & O.

◆

Mrs Hamlyn lay on her long chair and lazily watched the passengers come along the gangway. The ship had reached Singapore in the night, and since dawn had been taking on cargo; the winches had been grinding away all day, but by now her ears were accustomed to their insistent clamour. She had lunched at the Europe, and for lack of anything better to do had driven in a rickshaw through the gay, multitudinous streets of the city. Singapore is the meeting-place of many races. The Malays, though natives of the soil, dwell uneasily in towns, and are few; and it is the Chinese, supple, alert, and industrious, who throng the streets; the dark-skinned Tamils walk on their silent, naked feet, as though they were but brief sojourners in a strange land, but the Bengalis, sleek and prosperous, are easy in their surroundings, and self-assured; the sly and obsequious Japanese seem busy with pressing and secret affairs; and the English in their topees and white ducks, speeding past in motor-cars or at leisure in their rickshaws, wear a nonchalant and careless air. The rulers of these teeming peoples take their authority with a smiling unconcern. And now, tired and hot, Mrs Hamlyn waited for the ship to set out again on her long journey across the Indian Ocean.

She waved a rather large hand, for she was a big woman, to the doctor and Mrs Linsell as they came on board. She had been on the ship since she left Yokohama, and had watched with acid amusement the intimacy which had sprung up between the two. Linsell was a naval officer who had been attached to the British Embassy at Tokio, and she had wondered at the indifference with which he took the attentions that the doctor paid his wife. Two men came along the gangway, new passengers, and she amused herself by trying to discover from their demeanour whether they were single or married. Close by, a group of men were sitting together on rattan chairs, planters she judged by their khaki suits and wide-brimmed double felt hats, and they kept the deck-steward busy with their orders. They were talking loudly and laughing, for they had all drunk enough to make them somewhat foolishly hilarious, and they were evidently giving one of their number a send-off; but Mrs Hamlyn could not tell which it was that was to be a fellow-passenger. The time was growing short. More passengers arrived, and then Mr Jephson with dignity strolled up the gangway. He was a consul and was going home on leave. He had joined the ship at Shanghai and had immediately set about making himself agreeable to Mrs Hamlyn. But just then she was disinclined for anything in the nature of a flirtation. She frowned as she thought of the reason which was taking her back to England. She would be spending Christmas at sea, far from anyone who cared two straws about her, and for a moment she felt a little twist of her heartstrings; it vexed her that a subject which she was so resolute to put away from her should so constantly intrude on her unwilling mind.

But a warning bell clanged loudly, and there was a general movement among the men who sat beside her.

'Well, if we don't want to be taken on we'd better be toddling,' said one of them.

They rose and walked towards the gangway. Now that they were all shaking hands she saw who it was that they had come to see the last of. There was nothing very interesting about the man on whom Mrs Hamlyn's eyes rested, but because she had nothing better to do she gave him more than a casual glance. He was a big fellow, well over six feet high, broad and stout; he was dressed in a bedraggled suit of khaki drill and his hat was battered and shabby. His friends left him, but they bandied chaff from the quay, and Mrs Hamlyn noticed that he had a strong Irish brogue; his voice was full, loud, and hearty.

Mrs Linsell had gone below and the doctor came and sat down beside Mrs Hamlyn. They told one another their small adventures of the day. The bell sounded again and presently the ship slid away from the wharf. The Irishman waved a last farewell to his friends, and then sauntered towards the chair on which he had left papers and magazines. He nodded to the doctor.

'Is that someone you know?' asked Mrs Hamlyn.

'I was introduced to him at the club before tiffin. His name is Gallagher. He's a planter.'

After the hubbub of the port and the noisy bustle of departure, the silence of the ship was marked and grateful. They steamed slowly past green-clad, rocky cliffs (the P. & O. anchorage was in a charming and secluded cove), and came out into the main harbour. Ships of all nations lay at anchor, a great multitude, passenger boats, tugs, lighters, tramps; and beyond, behind the breakwater, you saw the crowded masts, a bare straight forest, of the native junks. In the soft light of the evening the busy scene was strangely touched with mystery, and you felt that all those vessels, their activity for the moment suspended, waited for some event of a peculiar significance.

Mrs Hamlyn was a bad sleeper and when the dawn broke she was in the habit of going on deck. It rested her troubled heart to watch the last faint stars fade before the encroaching day, and at that early hour the sea had often an immobility which seemed to make all earthly sorrows of little consequence. The light was wan, and there was a pleasant shiver in the air. But next morning, when she went to the end of the promenade deck, she found that someone was up before her. It was Mr Gallagher. He was watching the low coast of Sumatra which the sunrise like a magician seemed to call forth from the dark sea. She was startled and a little vexed, but before she could turn away he had seen her and nodded.

'Up early,' he said. 'Have a cigarette?'

He was in pyjamas and slippers. He took his case from his coat pocket and handed it to her. She hesitated. She had on nothing but a dressing gown and a little lace cap which she had put over her tousled hair, and she knew that she must look a sight; but she had her reasons for scourging her soul.

'I suppose a woman of forty has no right to mind how she looks,' she smiled, as though he must know what vain thoughts occupied her. She took the cigarette. 'But you're up early too.'

'I'm a planter. I've had to get up at five in the morning for so many years that I don't know how I'm going to get out of the habit.'

'You'll not find it will make you very popular at home.'

She saw his face better now that it was not shadowed by a hat. It was agreeable without being handsome. He was of course much too fat, and his features, which must have been good enough when he was a young man, were thickened. His skin was red and bloated. But his dark eyes were merry; and though he could not have been less than five and forty his hair was black and thick. He gave you the impression of great strength. He was a heavy, ungraceful, commonplace man, and Mrs Hamlyn, except for the promiscuity of ship-board, would never have thought it worth while to talk to him.

'Are you going home on leave?' she hazarded.

'No, I'm going home for good.'

His black eyes twinkled. He was of a communicative turn, and before it was time for Mrs Hamlyn to go below in order to have her bath he had told her a good deal about himself. He had been in the Federated Malay States for twenty-five years, and for the last ten had managed an estate in Selatan. It was a hundred miles from anything that could be described as civilization and the life had been lonely; but he had made money; during the rubber boom he had done very well, and with an astuteness which was unexpected in a man who looked so happy-go-lucky he had invested his savings in government stock. Now that the slump had come he was prepared to retire.

'What part of Ireland do you come from?' asked Mrs Hamlyn.

'Galway.'

Mrs Hamlyn had once motored through Ireland and she had a vague recollection of a sad and moody town with great stone warehouses, deserted and crumbling, which faced the melancholy sea. She had a sensation of greenness and of soft rain, of silence and of resignation. Was it here that Mr Gallagher meant to spend the rest of his life? He spoke of it with boyish eagerness. The thought of his vitality in that grey world of shadows was so incongruous that Mrs Hamlyn was intrigued.

'Does your family live there?' she asked.

'I've got no family. My mother and father are dead. So far as I know I haven't a relation in the world.'

He had made all his plans, he had been making them for twenty-five years, and he was pleased to have someone to talk to of all these things that he had been obliged for so long only to talk to himself about. He meant to buy a house and he would keep a motor-car. He was going to breed horses. He didn't much care about shooting; he had shot a lot of big game during his first years in the F.M.S.; but now he had lost his zest. He didn't see why the beasts of the jungle should be killed; he had lived in the jungle so long. But he could hunt.

'Do you think I'm too heavy?' he asked.

Mrs Hamlyn, smiling, looked him up and down with appraising eyes.

'You must weigh a ton,' she said.

He laughed. The Irish horses were the best in the world, and he'd always kept pretty fit. You had a devil of a lot of walking exercise on a rubber estate and he'd played a good deal of tennis. He'd soon get thin in Ireland. Then he'd marry. Mrs Hamlyn looked silently at the sea coloured now with the tenderness of the sunrise. She sighed.

'Was it easy to drag up all your roots? Is there no one you regret leaving behind? I should have thought after so many years, however much you'd looked forward to going home, when the time came at last to go it must have given you a pang.'

'I was glad to get out. I was fed up. I never want to see the country again or anyone in it.'

One or two early passengers now began to walk round the deck and Mrs Hamlyn, remembering that she was scantily clad, went below.

During the next day or two she saw little of Mr Gallagher, who passed his time in the smoking-room. Owing to a strike the ship was not touching at Colombo and passengers settled down to a pleasant voyage across the Indian Ocean. They played deck games, they gossiped about one another, they flirted. The approach of Christmas gave them an occupation, for someone had suggested that there should be a fancy-dress dance on Christmas Day, and the ladies set about making their dresses. A meeting was held of the first-class passengers to decide whether the second-class passengers should be invited, and notwithstanding the heat the discussion was animated. The ladies said that the second-class passengers would only feel ill-at-ease. On Christmas Day it was expected that they would drink more than was good for them and un-pleasantness might ensue. Everyone who spoke insisted that there was in his (or her) mind no idea of class distinction, no one would be so snobbish as to think there was any difference between first- and second-class passengers as far as that went, but it would really be kinder to the second-class passengers not to put them in a false position. They would enjoy themselves much more if they had a party of their own in the second-class cabin. On the other hand, no one wanted to hurt their feelings, and of course one had to be more democratic nowadays (this was in reply to the wife of a missionary in China who said she had travelled on the P. & O. for thirty-five years and she had never heard of the second-class passengers being invited to a dance in the first-class saloon) and even though they wouldn't enjoy it, they might like to come. Mr Gallagher, dragged unwillingly from the card-table, because it had been foreseen that the voting would be close, was asked his opinion by the consul. He was taking home in the second-class a man who had been employed on his estate. He raised his massive bulk from the couch on which he sat.

'As far as I'm concerned I've only got this to say: I've got the man who was looking after our engines with me. He's a rattling good fellow, and he's just as fit to come to your party as I am. But he won't come because I'm going to make him so drunk on Christmas Day that by six o'clock he'll be fit for nothing but to be put to bed.'

Mr Jephson, the consul, gave a distorted smile. On account of his official position, he had been chosen to preside at the meeting and he wished the matter to be taken seriously. He was a man who often said that if a thing was worth doing it was worth doing well.

'I gather from your observations,' he said, not without acidity, 'that the question before the meeting does not seem to you of great importance.'

'I don't think it matters a tinker's curse,' said Gallagher, with twinkling eyes.

Mrs Hamlyn laughed. The scheme was at last devised to invite the second-class passengers, but to go to the captain privily and point out to him the advisability of withholding his consent to their coming into the first-class saloon. It was on the evening of the day on which this happened that Mrs Hamlyn, having dressed for dinner, came on deck at the same time as Mr Gallagher.

'Just in time for a cocktail, Mrs Hamlyn,' he said jovially.

'I'd like one. To tell you the truth I need cheering up.'

'Why?' he smiled.

Mrs Hamlyn thought his smile attractive, but she did not want to answer his question.

'I told you the other morning,' she answered cheerfully. 'I'm forty.'

'I never met a woman who insisted on the fact so much.'

They went into the lounge and the Irishman ordered a dry Martini for her and a gin pahit for himself. He had lived too long in the East to drink anything else.

'You've got hiccups,' said Mrs Hamlyn.

'Yes, I've had them all the afternoon,' he answered carelessly. 'It's rather funny, they came on just as we got out of sight of land.'

'I daresay they'll pass off after dinner.'

They drank, the second bell rang, and they went into the dining-saloon.

'You don't play bridge?' he said, as they parted.

'No.'

Mrs Hamlyn did not notice that she saw nothing of Gallagher for two or three days. She was occupied with her own thoughts. They crowded upon her when she was sewing; they came between her and the novel with which she sought to cheat their insistence. She had hoped that as the ship took her further away from the scene of her unhappiness, the torment of her mind would be eased; but contrariwise, each day that brought her nearer England increased her distress. She looked forward with dismay to the bleak emptiness of the life that awaited her; and then, turning her exhausted wits from a prospect that made her flinch, she considered, as she had done she knew not how many times before, the situation from which she had fled.

She had been married for twenty years. It was a long time and of course she could not expect her husband to be still madly in love with her; she was not madly in love with him; but they were good friends and they understood one another. Their marriage, as marriages go, might very well have been looked upon as a success. Suddenly she discovered that he had fallen in love. She would not have objected to a flirtation, he had had those before, and she had chaffed him about them; he had not minded that, it somewhat flattered him, and they had laughed together at an inclination which was neither deep nor serious. But this was different. He was in love as passionately as a boy of eighteen. He was fifty-two. It was ridiculous. It was indecent. And he loved without sense or prudence; by the time the hideous fact was forced upon her all the foreigners in Yokohama knew it. After the first shock of astonished anger, for he was the last man from whom such a folly might have been expected, she tried to persuade herself that she could have understood, and so have forgiven, if he had fallen in love with a girl. Middle-aged men often make fools of themselves with flappers, and after twenty years in the Far East she knew that the fifties were the dangerous age for men. But he had no excuse. He was in love with a woman eight years older than herself. It was grotesque, and it made her, his wife, perfectly absurd. Dorothy Lacom was hard on fifty. He had known her for eighteen years, for Lacom, like her own husband, was a silk merchant in Yokohama. Year in, year out, they had seen one another three or four times a week, and once, when they happened to be in England together, had shared a house at the seaside. But nothing! Not till a year ago had there been anything between them but a chaffing friendship. It was incredible. Of course Dorothy was a handsome woman; she had a good figure, over-developed, perhaps, but still comely; with bold black eyes and a red mouth and lovely hair; but all that she had had years before. She was forty-eight. Forty-eight!

Mrs Hamlyn tackled her husband at once. At first he swore that there was not a word of truth in what she accused him of, but she had her proofs; he grew sulky; and at last he admitted what he could no longer deny. Then he said an astonishing thing.

'Why should you care?' he asked.

It maddened her. She answered him with angry scorn. She was voluble, finding in the bitterness of her heart wounding things to say. He listened to her quietly.

'I've not been such a bad husband to you for the twenty years we've been married. For a long time now we've only been friends. I have a great affection for you, and this hasn't altered it in the very smallest degree. I'm giving Dorothy nothing that I take away from you.'

'But what have you to complain of in me?'

'Nothing. No man could want a better wife.'

'How can you say that when you have the heart to treat me so cruelly?'

'I don't want to be cruel to you. I can't help myself.'

'But what on earth made you fall in love with her?'

'How can I tell? You don't think I wanted to, do you?'

'Couldn't you have resisted?'

'I tried. I think we both tried.'

'You talk as though you were twenty. Why, you're both middle-aged people. She's eight years older than I am. It makes me look such a perfect fool.'

He did not answer. She did not know what emotions seethed in her heart. Was it jealousy that seemed to clutch at her throat, anger, or was it merely wounded pride?

'I'm not going to let it go on. If only you and she were concerned I would divorce you, but there's her husband, and then there are the children. Good heavens, does it occur to you that if they were girls instead of boys she might be a grandmother by now?'

'Easily.'

'What a mercy that we have no children!'

He put out an affectionate hand as though to caress her, but she drew back with horror.

'You've made me the laughing stock of all my friends. For all our sakes I'm willing to hold my tongue, but only on the condition that everything stops now, at once, and for ever.'

He looked down and played reflectively with a Japanese knick-knack that was on the table.

'I'll tell Dorothy what you say,' he replied at last.

She gave him a little bow, silently, and walked past him out of the room. She was too angry to observe that she was somewhat melodramatic.

She waited for him to tell the result of his interview with Dorothy Lacom, but he made no further reference to the scene. He was quiet, polite, and silent; and at last she was obliged to ask him.

'Have you forgotten what I said to you the other day?' she inquired, frigidly.

'No. I talked to Dorothy. She wished me to tell you that she is desperately sorry that she has caused you so much pain. She would like to come and see you, but she is afraid you wouldn't like it.'

'What decision have you come to?'

He hesitated. He was very grave, but his voice trembled a little.

'I'm afraid there's no use in our making a promise we shouldn't be able to keep.'

'That settles it then,' she answered.

'I think I should tell you that if you brought an action for divorce we should have to contest it. You would find it impossible to get the necessary evidence and you would lose your case.'

'I wasn't thinking of doing that. I shall go back to England and consult a lawyer. Nowadays these things can be managed fairly easily, and I shall throw myself on your generosity. I dare say you will enable me to get my freedom without bringing Dorothy Lacom into the matter.'

He sighed.

'It's an awful muddle, isn't it? I don't want you to divorce me, but of course I'll do anything I can to meet your wishes.'

'What on earth do you expect me to do?' she cried, her anger rising again. 'Do you expect me to sit still and be made a damned fool of?'

'I'm awfully sorry to put you in a humiliating position.' He looked at her with harassed eyes. 'I'm quite sure we didn't want to fall in love with one another. We're both of us very conscious of our age. Dorothy, as you say, is old enough to be a grandmother and I'm a baldish, stoutish gentleman of fifty-two. When you fall in love at twenty you think your love will last for ever, but at fifty you know so much, about life and about love, and you know that it will last so short a time.' His voice was low and rueful. It was as though before his mind's eye he saw the sadness of autumn and the leaves falling from the trees. He looked at her gravely. 'And at that age you feel that you can't afford to throw away the chance of happiness which a freakish destiny has given you. In five years it will certainly be over, and perhaps in six months. Life is rather drab and grey, and happiness is so rare. We shall be dead so long.'

It gave Mrs Hamlyn a bitter sensation of pain to hear her husband, a matter-of-fact and practical man, speak in a strain which was quite new to her. He had gained on a sudden a wistful and tragic personality of which she knew nothing. The twenty years during which they had lived together had no power over him and she was helpless in face of his determination. She could do nothing but go, and now, resentfully determined to get the divorce with which she had threatened him, she was on her way to England.

The smooth sea, upon which the sun beat down so that it shone like a sheet of glass, was as empty and hostile as life in which there was no place for her. For three days no other craft had broken in upon the solitariness of that expanse. Now and again its even surface was scattered for the twinkling of an eye by the scurry of flying fish. The heat was so great that even the most energetic of

passengers had given up deck games, and now (it was after luncheon) such as
were not resting in their cabins lay about on chairs. Linsell strolled towards her
and sat down.

'Where's Mrs Linsell?' asked Mrs Hamlyn.

'Oh, I don't know. She's about somewhere.'

His indifference exasperated her. Was it possible that he did not see that his
wife and the surgeon were falling in love with one another? Yet, not so very long
ago, he must have cared. Their marriage had been romantic. They had become
engaged when Mrs Linsell was still at school and he little more than a boy.
They must have been a charming, handsome pair, and their youth and their
mutual love must have been touching. And now, after so short a time, they were
tired of one another. It was heartbreaking. What had her husband said?

'I suppose you're going to live in London when you get home?' asked Linsell
lazily, for something to say.

'I suppose so,' said Mrs Hamlyn.

It was hard to reconcile herself to the fact that she had nowhere to go, and
where she lived mattered not in the least to anyone alive. Some association of
ideas made her think of Gallagher. She envied the eagerness with which he was
returning to his native land, and she was touched, and at the same time amused,
when she remembered the exuberant imagination he showed in describing the
house he meant to live in and the wife he meant to marry. Her friends in
Yokohama, apprised in confidence of her determination to divorce her
husband, had assured her that she would marry again. She did not much want
to enter a second time upon a state which had once so disappointed her, and
besides, most men would think twice before they suggested marriage to a
woman of forty. Mr Gallagher wanted a buxom young person.

'Where is Mr Gallagher?' she asked the submissive Linsell. 'I haven't seen
him for the last day or two.'

'Didn't you know? He's ill.'

'Poor thing. What's the matter with him?'

'He's got hiccups.'

Mrs Hamlyn laughed.

'Hiccups don't make one ill, do they?'

'The surgeon is rather worried. He's tried all sorts of things, but he can't stop
them.'

'How very odd.'

She thought no more about it, but next morning, chancing upon the surgeon,
she asked him how Mr Gallagher was. She was surprised to see his boyish,
cheerful face darken and grow perplexed.

'I'm afraid he's very bad, poor chap.'

'With hiccups?' she cried in amazement.

It was a disorder that really it was impossible to take seriously.

'You see, he can't keep any food down. He can't sleep. He's fearfully
exhausted. I've tried everything I can think of.' He hesitated. 'Unless I can stop
them soon–I don't quite know what'll happen.'

Mrs Hamlyn was startled.

'But he's so strong. He seemed so full of vitality.'

'I wish you could see him now.'

'Would he like me to go and see him?'

'Come along.'

Gallagher had been moved from his cabin into the ship's hospital, and as they approached it they heard a loud hiccup. The sound, perhaps owing to its connexion with insobriety, had in it something ludicrous. But Gallagher's appearance gave Mrs Hamlyn a shock. He had lost flesh and the skin hung about his neck in loose folds; under the sunburn his face was pale. His eyes, before full of fun and laughter, were haggard and tormented. His great body was shaken incessantly by the hiccups and now there was nothing ludicrous in the sound; to Mrs Hamlyn, for no reason that she knew, it seemed strangely terrifying. He smiled when she came in.

'I'm sorry to see you like this,' she said.

'I shan't die of it, you know,' he gasped. 'I shall reach the green shores of Erin all right.'

There was a man sitting beside him and he rose as they entered.

'This is Mr Pryce,' said the surgeon. 'He was in charge of the machinery on Mr Gallagher's estate.'

Mrs Hamlyn nodded. This was the second-class passenger to whom Gallagher had referred when they had discussed the party which was to be given on Christmas Day. He was a very small man, but sturdy, with a pleasantly impudent countenance and an air of self-assurance.

'Are you glad to be going home?' asked Mrs Hamlyn.

'You bet I am, lady,' he answered.

The intonation of the few words told Mrs Hamlyn that he was a cockney and, recognizing the cheerful, sensible, good-humoured, and careless type, her heart warmed to him.

'You're not Irish?' she smiled.

'Not me, miss. London's my 'ome and I shan't be sorry to see it again, I can tell you.'

Mrs Hamlyn never thought it offensive to be called miss.

'Well, sir, I'll be getting along,' he said to Gallagher, with the beginning of a gesture as though he were going to touch a cap which he hadn't got on.

Mrs Hamlyn asked the sick man whether she could do anything for him and in a minute or two left him with the doctor. The little cockney was waiting outside the door.

'Can I speak to you a minute or two, miss?' he asked.

'Of course.'

The hospital cabin was aft and they stood, leaning against the rail, and looked down on the well-deck where lascars and stewards off duty were lounging about on the covered hatches.

'I don't know exactly 'ow to begin,' said Pryce, uncertainly, a serious look strangely changing his lively, puckered face. 'I've been with Mr Gallagher for four years now and a better gentleman you wouldn't find in a week of Sundays.'

He hesitated again.

'I don't like it and that's the truth.'

'What don't you like?'

'Well, if you ask me 'e's for it, and the doctor don't know it. I told 'im, but 'e won't listen to a word I say.'

'You mustn't be too depressed, Mr Pryce. Of course the doctor's young, but I think he's quite clever, and people don't die of hiccups, you know. I'm sure Mr Gallagher will be all right in a day or two.'

'You know when it came on? Just as we was out of sight of land. She said 'e'd never see 'is 'ome.'

Mrs Hamlyn turned and faced him. She stood a good three inches taller than he.

'What do you mean?'

'My belief is, it's a spell been put on 'im, if you understand what I mean. Medicine's going to do 'im no good. You don't know them Malay women like what I do.'

For a moment Mrs Hamlyn was startled, and because she was startled she shrugged her shoulders and laughed.

'Oh, Mr Pryce, that's nonsense.'

'That's what the doctor said when I told 'im. But you mark my words,'e'll die before we see land again.'

The man was so serious that Mrs Hamlyn, vaguely uneasy, was against her will impressed.

'Why should anyone cast a spell on Mr Gallagher?' she asked.

'Well, it's a bit awkward speakin' of it to a lady.'

'Please tell me.'

Pryce was so embarrassed that at another time Mrs Hamlyn would have had difficulty in concealing her amusement.

'Mr Gallagher's lived a long time up-country, if you understand what I mean, and of course it's lonely, and you know what men are, miss.'

'I've been married for twenty years,' she replied, smiling.

'I beg your pardon, ma'am. The fact is he had a Malay girl living with him. I don't know 'ow long, ten or twelve years, I think. Well, when 'e made up 'is mind to come 'ome for good she didn't say nothing. She just sat there. He thought she'd carry on no end, but she didn't. Of course 'e provided for 'er all right, 'e gave 'er a little 'ouse for herself, an' 'e fixed it up so as so much should be paid 'er every month. 'E wasn't mean, I will say that for 'im, an' she knew all along as 'e'd be going some time. She didn't cry or anything. When 'e packed up all 'is things and sent them off, she just sat there an' watched 'em go. And when 'e sold 'is furniture to the Chinks she never said a word. He'd give 'er all she wanted. And when it was time for 'im to go so as to catch the boat she just kep' on sitting on the steps of the bungalow, you know, and she just looked an' said nothing. He wanted to say good-bye to 'er, same as anyone would, an', would you believe it? she never even moved. "Aren't you going to say good-bye to me?" he says. A rare funny look come over 'er face. And do you know what she says? "You go," she says; they 'ave a funny way of talking, them natives, not like we 'ave, "you go," she says, "but I tell you that you will never come to your own country. When the land sinks into the sea, death will come upon you, an' before them as goes with you sees the land again, death will have took you." It gave me quite a turn.'

'What did Mr Gallagher say?' asked Mrs Hamlyn.

'Oh, well, you know what 'e is. He just laughed. "Always merry and bright," 'e says and 'e jumps into the motor, an' off we go.'

Mrs Hamlyn saw the bright and sunny road that ran through the rubber estates, with their trim green trees, carefully spaced, and their silence, and then wound its way up hill and down through the tangled jungle. The car raced on, driven by a reckless Malay, with its white passengers, past Malay houses that stood away from the road among the coconut trees, sequestered and taciturn, and through busy villages where the market-place was crowded with dark-skinned little people in gay sarongs. Then towards evening it reached the trim, modern town, with its clubs and its golf links, its well-ordered rest-house, its white people, and its railway-station, from which the two men could take the train to Singapore. And the woman sat on the steps of the bungalow, empty till the new manager moved in, and watched the road down which the car had panted, watched the car as it sped on, and watched till at last it was lost in the shadow of the night.

'What was she like?' Mrs Hamlyn asked.

'Oh, well, to my way of thinking them Malay women are all very much alike, you know,' Pryce answered. 'Of course she wasn't so young any more, and you know what they are, them natives, they run to fat something terrible.'

'Fat?'

The thought, absurdly enough, filled Mrs Hamlyn with dismay.

'Mr Gallagher was always one to do himself well, if you understand what I mean.'

The idea of corpulence at once brought Mrs Hamlyn back to common sense. She was impatient with herself because for an instant she had seemed to accept the little cockney's suggestion.

'It's perfectly absurd, Mr Pryce. Fat women can't throw spells on people at a distance of a thousand miles. In fact life is very difficult for a fat woman anyway.'

'You can laugh, miss, but unless something's done, you mark my words, the governor's for it. And medicine ain't goin' to save him, not white man's medicine.'

'Pull yourself together, Mr Pryce. This fat lady had no particular grievance against Mr Gallagher. As these things are done in the East he seems to have treated her very well. Why should she wish him any harm?'

'We don't know 'ow they look at things. Why, a man can live there for twenty years with one them natives, and d'you think 'e knows what's goin' on in that black heart of hers? Not 'im!'

She could not smile at his melodramatic language, for his intensity was impressive. And she knew, if anyone did, that the hearts of men, whether their skins are yellow or white or brown, are incalculable.

'But even if she felt angry with him, even if she hated him and wanted to kill him, what could she do?' It was strange that Mrs Hamlyn with her questions was trying now, unconsciously, to reassure herself. 'There's no poison that could start working after six or seven days.'

'I never said it was poison.'

'I'm sorry, Mr Pryce,' she smiled, 'but I'm not going to believe in a magic spell, you know.'

'You've lived in the East?'

'Off and on for twenty years.'

'Well, if you can say what they can do and what they can't, it's more than I can.' He clenched his fist and beat it on the rail with sudden, angry violence. 'I'm fed up with the bloody country. It's got on my nerves, that's what it is. We're no match for them, us white men, and that's a fact. If you'll excuse me I think I'll go an' 'ave a tiddley. I've got the jumps.'

He nodded abruptly and left her. Mrs Hamlyn watched him, a sturdy, shuffling little man in a shabby khaki, slither down the companion into the waist of the ship, walk across it with bent head, and disappear into the second-class saloon. She did not know why he left with her a vague uneasiness. She could not get out of her mind that picture of a stout woman, no longer young, in a sarong, a coloured jacket, and gold ornaments, who sat on the steps of a bungalow looking at an empty road. Her heavy face was painted, but in her large, tearless eyes there was no expression. The men who drove in the car were like schoolboys going home for the holidays. Gallagher gave a sigh of relief. In the early morning, under the bright sky, his spirits bubbled. The future was like a sunny road that wandered through a wide-flung, wooded plain.

Later in the day Mrs Hamlyn asked the doctor how his patient did. The doctor shook his head.

'I'm done. I'm at the end of my tether.' He frowned unhappily. 'It's rotten luck, striking a case like this. It would be bad enough at home, but on board ship . . .'

He was an Edinburgh man, but recently qualified, and he was taking his voyage as a holiday before settling down to practice. He felt himself aggrieved. He wanted to have a good time and, faced with this mysterious illness, he was worried to death. Of course he was inexperienced, but he was doing everything that could be done and it exasperated him to suspect that the passengers thought him an ignorant fool.

'Have you heard what Mr Pryce thinks?' asked Mrs Hamlyn.

'I never heard such rot. I told the captain and he's right up in the air. He doesn't want it talked about. He thinks it'll upset the passengers.'

'I'll be as silent as the grave.'

The surgeon looked at her sharply.

'Of course you don't believe that there can be any truth in nonsense of that sort?' he asked.

'Of course not.' She looked out at the sea, which shone, blue and oily and still, all round them. 'I've lived in the East a long time,' she added. 'Strange things happen there.'

'This is getting on my nerves,' said the doctor.

Near them two little Japanese gentlemen were playing deck quoits. They were trim and neat in their tennis shirts, white trousers, and buckram shoes. They looked very European, they even called the score to one another in English, and yet somehow to look at them filled Mrs Hamlyn at that moment with a vague disquiet. Because they seemed to wear so easily a disguise there was about them something sinister. Her nerves too were on edge.

And presently, no one quite knew how, the notion spread through the ship that Gallagher was bewitched. While the ladies sat about on their deck-chairs, stitching away at the costumes they were making for the fancy-dress party on Christmas Day, they gossiped about it in undertones, and the men in the smoking-room talked of it over their cocktails. A good many of the passengers had lived long in the East and from the recesses of their memory they produced strange and inexplicable stories. Of course it was absurd to think seriously that Gallagher was suffering from a malignant spell, such things were impossible, and yet this and that was a fact and no one had been able to explain it. The doctor had to confess that he could suggest no cause for Gallagher's condition, he was able to give a physiological explanation, but why these terrible spasms should have suddenly assailed him he did not say. Feeling vaguely to blame, he tried to defend himself.

'Why, it's the sort of case you might never come across in the whole of your practice,' he said. 'It's rotten luck.'

He was in wireless communication with passing ships, and suggestions for treatment came from here and there.

'I've tried everything they tell me,' he said irritably. 'The doctor of the Japanese boat advised adrenalin. How the devil does he expect me to have adrenalin in the middle of the Indian Ocean?'

There was something impressive in the thought of this ship speeding through a deserted sea, while to her from all parts came unseen messages. She seemed at that moment strangely alone and yet the centre of the world. In the lazaret the sick man, shaken by the cruel spasms, gasped for life. Then the passengers became conscious that the ship's course was altered, and they heard that the captain had made up his mind to put in at Aden. Gallagher was to be landed there and taken to the hospital, where he could have attention which on board was impossible. The chief engineer received orders to force his engines. The ship was an old one and she throbbed with the greater effort. The passengers had grown used to the sound and feel of her engines, and now the greater vibration shook their nerves with a new sensation. It would not pass into each one's unconsciousness, but beat on their sensibilities so that each felt a personal concern. And still the wide sea was empty of traffic, so they seemed to traverse an empty world. And now the uneasiness which had descended upon the ship, but which no one had been willing to acknowledge, became a definite malaise. The passengers grew irritable, and people quarrelled over trifles which at another time would have seemed insignificant. Mr Jephson made his hackneyed jokes, but no one any longer repaid him with a smile. The Linsells had an altercation, and Mrs Linsell was heard late at night walking round the deck with her husband and uttering in a low, tense voice a stream of vehement reproaches. There was a violent scene in the smoking-room one night over a game of bridge, and the reconciliation which followed it was attended with general intoxication. People talked little of Gallagher, but he was seldom absent from their thoughts. They examined the route map. The doctor said now that Gallagher could not live more than three or four days, and they discussed acrimoniously what was the shortest time in which Aden could be reached. What happened to him after he was landed was no affair of theirs; they did not want him to die on board.

Mrs Hamlyn saw Gallagher every day. With the suddenness with which after tropical rain in the spring you seem to see the herbage grow before your very eyes, she saw him go to pieces. Already his skin hung loosely on his bones, and his double chin was like the wrinkled wattle of a turkey-cock. His cheeks were sunken. You saw now how large his frame was, and through the sheet under which he lay his bony structure was like the skeleton of a prehistoric giant. For the most part he lay with his eyes closed, torpid with morphia, but shaken still with terrible spasms, and when now and again he opened his eyes they were preternaturally large; they looked at you vaguely, perplexed and troubled, from the depths of their bony sockets. But when, emerging from his stupor, he recognized Mrs Hamlyn, he forced a gallant smile to his lips.

'How are you, Mr Gallagher?' she said.

'Getting along, getting along. I shall be all right when we get out of this confounded heat. Lord, how I look forward to a dip in the Atlantic. I'd give anything for a good long swim. I want to feel the cold grey sea of Galway beating against my chest.'

Then the hiccup shook him from the crown of his head to the sole of his feet. Mr Pryce and the stewardess shared the care of him. The little cockney's face wore no longer its look of impudent gaiety, but instead was sullen.

'The captain sent for me yesterday,' he told Mrs Hamlyn when they were alone. 'He gave me a rare talking to.'

'What about?'

'He said 'e wouldn't 'ave all this hoodoo stuff. He said it was frightening the passengers and I'd better keep a watch on me tongue or I'd 'ave 'im to reckon with. It's not my doing. I never said a word except to you and the doctor.'

'It's all over the ship.'

'I know it is. D'you think it's only me that's saying it? All them Lascars and the Chinese, they all know what's the matter with him. You don't think you can teach them much, do you? They know it ain't a natural illness.'

Mrs Hamlyn was silent. She knew through the amahs of some of the passengers that there was no one on the ship, except the whites, who doubted that the woman whom Gallagher had left in distant Selantan was killing him with her magic. All were convinced that as they sighted the barren rocks of Arabia his soul would be parted from his body.

'The captain says if he hears of me trying any hanky-panky he'll confine me to my cabin for the rest of the voyage,' said Pryce, suddenly, a surly frown on his puckered face.

'What do you mean by hanky-panky?'

He looked at her for a moment fiercely as though she too were an object of the anger he felt against the captain.

'The doctor's tried every damned thing he knows, and he's wirelessed all over the place, and what good 'as 'e done? Tell me that. Can't 'e see the man's dying? There's only one way to save him now.'

'What do you mean?'

'It's magic what's killing 'im, and it's only magic what'll save him. Oh, don't say it can't be done. I've seen it with me own eyes.' His voice rose, irritable and shrill. 'I've seen a man dragged from the jaws of death, as you might say, when they got in a *pawang*, what we call a witch-doctor, an' 'e did 'is little tricks. I seen it with me own eyes, I tell you.'

Mrs Hamlyn did not speak. Pryce gave her a searching look.

'One of them Lascars on board, he's a witch-doctor, same as the *pawang* that we 'ave in the F.M.S. An' 'e says he'll do it. Only he must 'ave a live animal. A cock would do.'

'What do you want a live animal for?' Mrs Hamlyn asked, frowning a little.

The cockney looked at her with quick suspicion.

'If you take my advice you won't know anything about it. But I tell you what, I'm going to leave no stone unturned to save my governor. An' if the captain 'ears of it and shuts me up in me cabin, well, let 'im.'

At that moment Mrs Linsell came up and Pryce with his quaint gesture of salute left them. Mrs Linsell wanted Mrs Hamlyn to fit the dress she had been making herself for the fancy-dress ball, and on the way down to the cabin she spoke to her anxiously of the possibility that Mr Gallagher might die on Christmas Day. They could not possibly have the dance if he did. She had told the doctor that she would never speak to him again if this happened, and the doctor had promised her faithfully that he would keep the man alive over Christmas Day somehow.

'It would be nice for him, too,' said Mrs Linsell.

'For whom?' asked Mrs Hamlyn.

'For poor Mr Gallagher. Naturally no one likes to die on Christmas Day. Do they?'

'I don't really know,' said Mrs Hamlyn.

That night, after she had been asleep a little while, she awoke weeping. It dismayed her that she should cry in her sleep. It was as though then the weakness of the flesh mastered her, and, her will broken, she were defenceless against a natural sorrow. She turned over in her mind, as so often before, the details of the disaster which had so profoundly affected her; she repeated the conversations with her husband, wishing she had said this and blaming herself because she had said the other. She wished with all her heart that she had remained in comfortable ignorance of her husband's infatuation, and asked herself whether she would not have been wiser to pocket her pride and shut her eyes to the unwelcome truth. She was a woman of the world, and she knew too well how much more she lost in separating herself from her husband than his love; she lost the settled establishment and the assured position, the ample means and the support of a recognized background. She had known of many separated wives, living equivocally on smallish incomes, and knew how quickly their friends found them tiresome. And she was lonely. She was as lonely as the ship that throbbed her hasting way through an unpeopled sea, and lonely as the friendless man who lay dying in the ship's lazaret. Mrs Hamlyn knew that her thoughts had got the better of her now and that she would not easily sleep again. It was very hot in her cabin. She looked at the time; it was between four and half past; she must pass two mortal hours before broke the reassuring day.

She slipped into a kimono and went on deck. The night was sombre and although the sky was unclouded no stars were visible. Panting and shaking, the old ship under full steam lumbered through the darkness. The silence was uncanny. Mrs Hamlyn with bare feet groped her way slowly along the deserted deck.

It was so black that she could see nothing. She came to the end of the promenade deck and leaned against the rail. Suddenly she started and her attention was fixed, for on the lower deck she caught a fitful glow. She leaned forward cautiously. It was a little fire, and she saw only the glow because the naked backs of men, crouched round, hid the flame. At the edge of the circle she divined, rather than saw, a stocky figure in pyjamas. The rest were natives, but this was a European. It must be Pryce and she guessed immediately that some dark ceremony of exorcism was in progress. Straining her ears she heard a low voice muttering a string of secret words. She began to tremble. She was aware that they were too intent upon their business to think that anyone was watching them, but she dared not move. Suddenly, rending the sultry silence of the night like a piece of silk violently torn in two, came the crowing of a cock. Mrs Hamlyn almost shrieked. Mr Pryce was trying to save the life of his friend and master by a sacrifice to the strange gods of the East. The voice went on, low and insistent. Then in the dark circle there was a movement, something was happening, she knew not what; there was a cluck-cluck from the cock, angry and frightened, and then a strange, indescribable sound; the magician was cutting the cock's throat; then silence; there were vague doings that she could not follow, and in a little while it looked as though someone were stamping out the fire. The figures she had dimly seen were dissolved in the night and all once more was still. She heard again the regular throbbing of the engines.

Mrs Hamlyn stood still for a little while, strangely shaken, and then walked slowly along the deck. She found a chair and lay down in it. She was trembling still. She could only guess what had happened. She did not know how long she lay there, but at last she felt that the dawn was approaching. It was not yet day, and it was no longer night. Against the darkness of the sky she could now see the ship's rail. Then she saw a figure come towards her. It was a man in pyjamas.

'Who's that?' she cried nervously.

'Only the doctor,' came a friendly voice.

'Oh! What are you doing here at this time of night?'

'I've been with Gallagher.' He sat down beside her and lit a cigarette. 'I've given him a good strong hypodermic and he's quiet now.'

'Has he been very ill?'

'I thought he was going to pass out. I was watching him, and suddenly he started up on his bed and began to talk Malay. Of course I couldn't understand a thing. He kept on saying one word over and over again.'

'Perhaps it was a name, a woman's name.'

'He wanted to get out of bed. He's a damned powerful man even now. By George, I had a struggle with him. I was afraid he'd throw himself overboard. He seemed to think someone was calling him.'

'When was that?' asked Mrs Hamlyn slowly.

'Between four and half past. Why?'

'Nothing.'

She shuddered.

Later in the morning when the ship's life was set upon its daily round, Mrs Hamlyn passed Pryce on the deck, but he gave her a brief greeting and walked on with quickly averted gaze. He looked tired and overwrought. Mrs Hamlyn thought again of the fat woman, with golden ornaments in her thick, black hair, who sat on the steps of the deserted bungalow and looked at the road which ran through the trim lines of the rubber trees.

It was fearfully hot. She knew now why the night had been so dark. The sky was no longer blue, but a dead, level white; its surface was too even to give the effect of cloud; it was as though in the upper air the heat hung like a pall. There was no breeze, and the sea, as colourless as the sky, was smooth and shining like the dye in a dyer's vat. The passengers were listless, when they walked round the deck they panted, and beads of sweat broke out on their foreheads. They spoke in undertones. Something uncanny and disquieting brooded over the ship, and they could not bring themselves to laugh. A feeling of resentment arose in their hearts; they were alive and well, and it exasperated them that, so near, a man should be dying and by the fact (which was after all no concern of theirs) so mysteriously affect them. A planter in the smoking-room over a gin sling said brutally what most of them felt, though none had confessed.

'Well, if he's going to peg out,' he said, 'I wish he'd hurry up and get it over. It gives me the creeps.'

The day was interminable. Mrs Hamlyn was thankful when the dinner hour arrived. So much time, at all events, was passed. She sat at the doctor's table.

'When do we reach Aden?' she asked.

'Some time tomorrow. The captain says we shall sight land between five and six in the morning.'

She gave him a sharp look. He stared at her for a moment, then dropped his eyes and reddened. He remembered that the woman, the fat woman sitting on the bungalow steps, had said that Gallagher would never see the land. Mrs Hamlyn wondered whether he, the sceptical, matter-of-fact young doctor, was wavering at last. He frowned a little and then, as though he sought to pull himself together, looked at her once more.

'I shan't be sorry to hand over my patient to the hospital people at Aden, I can tell you,' he said.

Next day was Christmas Eve. When Mrs Hamlyn awoke from a troubled sleep the dawn was breaking. She looked out of her port-hole and saw that the sky was clear and silvery; during the night the haze had melted, and the morning was brilliant. With a lighter heart she went on deck. She walked as far forward as she could go. A late star twinkled palely close to the horizon. There was a shimmer on the sea as though a loitering breeze passed playful fingers over its surface. The light was wonderfully soft, tenuous like a budding wood in spring, and crystalline so that it reminded you of the bubbling of water in a mountain brook. She turned to look at the sun rising rosy in the east, and saw coming towards her the doctor. He wore his uniform; he had not been to bed all night; he was dishevelled and he walked, with bowed shoulders, as though he were dog-tired. She knew at once that Gallagher was dead. When he came up to her she saw that he was crying. He looked so young then that her heart went out to him. She took his hand.

'You poor dear,' she said. 'You're tired out.'

'I did all I could,' he said. 'I wanted so awfully to save him.'

His voice shook and she saw that he was almost hysterical.

'When did he die?' she asked.

He closed his eyes, trying to control himself, and his lips trembled.

'A few minutes ago.'

Mrs Hamlyn sighed. She found nothing to say. Her gaze wandered across the calm, dispassionate, and ageless sea. It stretched on all sides of them as infinite as human sorrow. But on a sudden her eyes were held, for there, ahead of them, on the horizon was something which looked like a precipitous and massy cloud. But its outline was too sharp to be a cloud's. She touched the doctor on the arm.

'What's that?'

He looked at it for a moment and under his sunburn she saw him grow white.

'Land.'

Once more Mrs Hamlyn thought of the fat Malay woman who sat silent on the steps of Gallagher's bungalow. Did she know?

They buried him when the sun was high in the heavens. They stood on the lower deck and on the hatches, the first- and second-class passengers, the white stewards and the European officers. The missionary read the burial service.

'Man that is born of a woman hath but a short time to live, and is full of misery. He cometh up, and is cut down, like a flower; he fleeth as it were a shadow, and never continueth in one stay.'

Pryce looked down at the deck with knit brows. His teeth were tight clenched. He did not grieve, for his heart was hot with anger. The doctor and the consul stood side by side. The consul bore to a nicety the expression of an official regret, but the doctor, clean-shaven now, in his neat fresh uniform and his gold braid, was pale and harassed. From him Mrs Hamlyn's eyes wandered to Mrs Linsell. She was pressed against her husband, weeping, and he was holding her hand tenderly. Mrs Hamlyn did not know why this sight singularly affected her. At that moment of grief, her nerves distraught, the little woman went by instinct to the protection and support of her husband. But then Mrs Hamlyn felt a little shudder pass through her and she fixed her eyes on the seams in the deck, for she did not want to see what was toward. There was a pause in the reading. There were various movements. One of the officers gave an order. The missionary's voice continued:

'Forasmuch as it has pleased Almighty God of his great mercy to take unto himself the soul of our dear brother here departed: we therefore commend his body to the deep, to be turned into corruption, looking for the resurrection of the body when the sea shall give up its dead.'

Mrs Hamlyn felt the hot tears flow down her cheeks. There was a dull splash. The missionary's voice went on.

When the service was finished the passengers scattered; the second-class passengers returned to their quarters and a bell rang to summon them to luncheon. But the first-class passengers sauntered aimlessly about the promenade deck. Most of the men made for the smoking-room and sought to cheer themselves with whiskies and sodas and with gin slings. But the consul put up a notice on the board outside the dining-saloon summoning the passengers to a meeting. Most of them had an idea for what purpose it was called, and at the appointed hour they assembled. They were more cheerful than they had been for a week and they chattered with a gaiety which was only subdued by a mannerly reserve. The consul, an eyeglass in his eye, said that he had gathered them together to discuss the question of the fancy-dress dance on the following day. He knew they all had the deepest sympathy for Mr Gallagher and he would have proposed that they should combine to send an appropriate message to the deceased's relatives, but his papers had been examined by the purser and no trace could be found of any relative or friend with whom it was possible to communicate. The late Mr Gallagher appeared to be quite alone in the world. Meanwhile he (the consul) ventured to offer his sincere sympathy to the doctor, who, he was quite sure, had done everything that was possible in the circumstances.

'Hear, hear,' said the passengers.

They had all passed through a very trying time, proceeded the consul, and to some it might seem that it would be more respectful to the deceased's memory if the fancy-dress ball were postponed till New Year's Eve. This, however, he told them frankly was not his view, and he was convinced that Mr Gallagher himself would not have wished it. Of course it was a question for the majority to decide. The doctor got up and thanked the consul and the passengers for the kind things that had been said of him, it had of course been a very trying time, but he was authorized by the captain to say that the captain expressly wished that all the festivities to be carried out on Christmas Day as though nothing had happened. He (the doctor) told them in confidence that the captain felt the passengers had got into a rather morbid state, and thought it would do them all good if they had a jolly good time on Christmas Day. Then the missionary's wife rose and said they mustn't think only of themselves; it had been arranged by the Entertainment Committee that there should be a Christmas Tree for the children, immediately after the first-class passengers' dinner, and the children had been looking forward to seeing everyone in fancy-dress; it would be too bad to disappoint them; she yielded to no one in her respect for the dead, and she sympathized with anyone who felt too sad to think of dancing just then, her own heart was very heavy, but she did feel it would be merely selfish to give way to a feeling which could do no good to anyone. Let them think of the little ones. This very much impressed the passengers. They wanted to forget the brooding terror which had hung over the boat for so many days, they were alive and they wanted to enjoy themselves; but they had an uneasy notion that it would be decent to exhibit a certain grief. It was quite another matter if they could do as they wished from altruistic motives. When the consul called for a show of hands everyone but Mrs Hamlyn, and one old lady who was rather rheumatic, held up an eager arm.

'The ayes have it,' said the consul. 'And I venture to congratulate the meeting on a very sensible decision.'

It was just going to break up when one of the planters got on his feet and said he wished to offer a suggestion. Under the circumstances didn't they think it would be as well to invite the second-class passengers? They had all come to the funeral that morning. The missionary jumped up and seconded the motion. The events of the last few days had drawn them all together, he said, and in the presence of death all men were equal. The consul again addressed them. This matter had been discussed at a previous meeting and the conclusion had been reached that it would be pleasanter for the second-class passengers to have their own party, but circumstances alter cases, and he was distinctly of opinion that their previous decision should be reversed.

'Hear, hear,' said the passengers.

A wave of democratic feeling swept over them and the motion was carried by acclamation. They separated light-heartedly, they felt charitable and kindly. Everyone stood everyone else drinks in the smoking-room.

And so, on the following evening, Mrs Hamlyn put on her fancy-dress. She had no heart for the gaiety before her, and for a moment had thought of feigning illness, but she knew no one would believe her, and was afraid to be thought affected. She was dressed as Carmen and she could not resist the vanity of making herself as attractive as possible. She darkened her eyelashes and rouged her cheeks. The costume suited her. When the bugle sounded and she went into the saloon she was received with flattering surprise. The consul (always a humorist) was dressed as a ballet-girl and was greeted with shouts of delighted laughter. The missionary and his wife, self-conscious but pleased with themselves, were very grand as Manchus. Mrs Linsell, as Columbine, showed all that was possible of her very pretty legs. Her husband was an Arab sheik and the doctor was a Malay sultan.

A subscription had been collected to provide champagne at dinner and the meal was hilarious. The company had provided crackers in which were paper hats of various shapes and these the passengers put on. There were paper streamers too which they threw at one another and little balloons which they beat from one to the other across the room. They laughed and shouted. They were very gay. No one could say that they were not having a good time. As soon as dinner was finished they went into the saloon, where the Christmas Tree, with candles lit, was ready, and the children were brought in, shrieking with delight, and given presents. Then the dance began. The second-class passengers stood about shyly round the part of the deck reserved for dancing and occasionally danced with one another.

'I'm glad we had them,' said the consul, dancing with Mrs Hamlyn. 'I'm all for democracy, and I think they're very sensible to keep themselves to themselves.'

But she noticed that Pryce was not to be seen, and when an opportunity presented asked one of the second-class passengers where he was.

'Blind to the world,' was the answer. 'We put him to bed in the afternoon and locked him up in his cabin.'

The consul claimed her for another dance. He was very facetious. Suddenly Mrs Hamlyn felt that she could not bear it any more, the noise of the amateur band, the consul's jokes, the gaiety of the dancers. She knew not why, but the merriment of those people passing on their ship through the night and the solitary sea affected her on a sudden with horror. When the consul released her she slipped away and, with a look to see that no one had noticed her, ascended the companion to the boat deck. Here everything was in darkness. She walked softly to a spot where she knew she would be safe from all intrusion. But she heard a faint laugh and she caught sight in a hidden corner of a Columbine and a Malay sultan. Mrs Linsell and the doctor had resumed already the flirtation which the death of Gallagher had interrupted.

Already all those people had put out of their minds with a kind of ferocity the thought of that poor lonely man who had so strangely died in their midst. They felt no compassion for him but resentment rather, because on his account they had been ill-at-ease. They seized upon life avidly. They made their jokes, they flirted, they gossiped. Mrs Hamlyn remembered what the consul had said, that among Mr Gallagher's papers no letters could be found, not the name of a single friend to whom the news of his death might be sent, and she knew not why this seemed to her unbearably tragic. There was something mysterious in a man who could pass through the world in such solitariness. When she remembered how he had come on deck in Singapore, so short a while since, in such rude health, full of vitality, and his arrogant plans for the future, she was seized with dismay. Those words of the burial service filled her with a solemn awe: *Man that is born of a woman hath but a short time to live, and is full of misery. He cometh up, and is cut down, like a flower . . .* Year in, year out, he had made his plans for the future, he wanted to live so much and he had so much to live for, and then just when he stretched out his hand—oh, it was pitiful; it made all the other distresses of the world of small account. Death with its mystery was the only thing that really mattered. Mrs Hamlyn leaned over the rail and looked at the starry sky. Why did people make themselves unhappy? Let them weep for the death of those they loved, death was terrible always, but for the rest, was it worth while to be wretched, to harbour malice, to be vain and uncharitable? She thought again of herself and her husband and the woman he so strangely loved. He too had said that we live to be happy so short a time and we are so long dead. She pondered long and intently, and suddenly, as summer lightning flashes across the darkness of the night, she made a discovery which filled her with tremulous surprise; for she found that in her heart was no longer anger with her husband nor jealousy of her rival. A notion dawned on some remote horizon of her consciousness and like the morning sun suffused her soul with a tender, blissful glow. Out of the tragedy of that unknown Irishman's death she gathered elatedly the courage for a desperate resolution. Her heart beat quickly, she was impatient to carry it into effect. A passion for self-sacrifice seized her.

The music had stopped, the ball was over; most of the passengers would have gone to bed and the rest would be in the smoking-room. She went down to her cabin and met no one on the way. She took her writing pad and wrote a letter to her husband:

My dear,
It is Christmas Day and I want to tell you that my heart is filled with kindly thoughts towards both of you. I have been foolish and unreasonable. I think we should allow those we care for to be happy in their own way, and we should care for them enough not to let it make us unhappy. I want you to know that I grudge you none of the joy that has so strangely come into your life. I am no longer jealous, nor hurt, nor vindictive. Do not think I shall be unhappy or lonely. If ever you feel that you need me, come to me, and I will welcome you with a cheerful spirit and without reproach or ill-will.

I am most grateful for all the years of happiness and of tenderness that you gave me, and in return I wish to offer you an affection which makes no claim on you and is, I hope, utterly disinterested. Think kindly of me and be happy, happy, happy.

She signed her name and put the letter into an envelope. Though it would not go till they reached Port Said she wanted to place it at once in the letter-box. When she had done this, beginning to undress, she looked at herself in the glass. Her eyes were shining and under her rouge her colour was bright. The future was no longer desolate, but bright with a fair hope. She slipped into bed and fell at once into a sound and dreamless sleep.

Episode

◆

It was quite a small party, because our hostess liked general conversation; we never sat down to dinner more than eight, and generally only six, and after dinner when we went up to the drawing-room the chairs were so arranged that it was impossible for two persons to go into a huddle in a corner and so break things up. I was glad on arriving to find that I knew everyone. There were two nice clever women besides our hostess and two men besides myself. One was my friend Ned Preston. Our hostess made it a point never to ask wives with their husbands, because she said each cramped the other's style and if they didn't like to come separately they needn't come at all. But since her food and her wine were good and the talk almost always entertaining they generally came. People sometimes accused her of asking husbands more often than wives, but she defended herself by saying that she couldn't possibly help it because more men were husbands than women were wives.

Ned Preston was a Scot, a good-humoured, merry soul, with a gift for telling a story, sometimes too lengthily, for he was uncommonly loquacious, but with dramatic intensity. He was a bachelor with a small income which sufficed for his modest needs, and in this he was lucky since he suffered from that form of chronic tuberculosis which may last for years without killing you, but which prevents you from working for your living. Now and then he would be ill enough to stay in bed for two or three weeks, but then he would get better and be as gay, cheerful, and talkative as ever. I doubt whether he had enough money to live in an expensive sanatorium and he certainly hadn't the temperament to suit himself to its life. He was worldly. When he was well he liked to go out, out to lunch, out to dinner, and he liked to sit up late into the night smoking his pipe and drinking a good deal of whisky. If he had been content to live the life of an invalid he might have been alive now, but he wasn't; and who can blame him?

He died at the age of fifty-five of a haemorrhage which he had one night after coming home from some house where, he may well have flattered himself, he was the success of the party.

He had that febrile vitality that some consumptives have, and was always looking for an occupation to satisfy his desire for activity. I don't know how he heard that at Wormwood Scrubs they were in want of prison visitors, but the idea took his fancy so he went to the Home Office and saw the official in charge of prisons to offer his services. The job is unpaid, and though a number of persons are willing to undertake it, either from compassion or curiosity, they are apt to grow tired of it, or find it takes up too much time, and the prisoners whose problems, interests and future they have been concerned with are left somewhat in the lurch. The Home Office people consequently are wary of taking on anyone who does not look as if he would persevere, and they make careful inquiries into the applicant's antecedents, character, and general suitability. Then he is given a trial, is discreetly watched, and if the impression is unfavourable is politely thanked and told that his services are no longer required. But Ned Preston satisfied the dour and shrewd official who interviewed him that he was in every way reliable, and from the beginning he got on well with the governor, the warders, and the prisoners. He was entirely lacking in class-consciousness, so prisoners, whatever their station in life, felt at ease with him. He neither preached nor moralized. He had never done a criminal, or even a mean, thing in his life, but he treated the crime of the prisoners he had to deal with as though it were an illness like his own tuberculosis which was a nuisance you had to put up with, but which it did no good to talk about.

Wormwood Scrubs is a first offenders' prison and it is a building, grim and cold, of forbidding appearance. Ned took me over it once and I had goose-flesh as the gates were unlocked for us and we went in. We passed through the halls in which the men were working.

'If you see any pals of yours take no notice of them,' Ned said to me. 'They don't like it.'

'Am I likely to see any pals of mine?' I asked drily.

'You never can tell. I shouldn't be surprised if you had had friends who'd passed bad cheques once too often or were caught in a compromising situation in one of the parks. You'd be surprised how often I run across chaps I've met out at dinner.'

One of Ned's duties was to see prisoners through the first difficult days of their confinement. They were often badly shaken by their trial and sentence; and when, after the preliminary proceedings they had to go through on entering the jail, the stripping, the bath, the medical examination and the questioning, the getting into prison clothes, they were led into a cell and locked up, they were apt to break down. Sometimes they cried hysterically; sometimes they could neither eat nor sleep. Ned's business then was to cheer them, and his breezy manner, his natural kindliness, often worked wonders. If they were anxious about their wives and children he would go to see them and if they were destitute provide them with money. He brought them news so that they might get over the awful feeling that they were shut away from the common interests of their fellow-men. He read the sporting papers to be able to tell them what horse had won an important race or whether the champion had won his fight. He would advise them about their future, and when the time approached for their release see what jobs they were fitted for and then persuade employers to give them a chance to make good.

Since everyone is interested in crime it was inevitable that sooner or later, with Ned there, the conversation should turn upon it. It was after dinner and we were sitting comfortably in the drawing-room with drinks in our hands.

'Had any interesting cases at the Scrubs lately, Ned?' I asked him.

'No, nothing much.'

He had a high, rasping voice and his laugh was a raucous cackle. He broke into it now.

'I went to see an old girl today who was a packet of fun. Her husband's a burglar. The police have known about him for years, but they've never been able to get him till just now. Before he did a job he and his wife concocted an alibi, and though he's been arrested three or four times and sent up for trial, the police have never been able to break it and he's always got off. Well, he was arrested again a little while ago, but he wasn't upset, the alibi he and his wife had made up was perfect and he expected to be acquitted as he'd been before. His wife went into the witness-box and to his utter amazement she didn't give the alibi and he was convicted. I went to see him. He wasn't so much worried at being in gaol as puzzled by his wife not having spoken up, and he asked me to go and see her and ask what the game was. Well I went, and d'you know what she said to me? She said: "Well, sir, it's like this; it was such a beautiful alibi I just couldn't bear to waste it."'

Of course we all laughed. The story-teller likes an appreciative audience, and Ned Preston was never disinclined to hold the floor. He narrated two or three more anecdotes. They tended to prove a point he was fond of making, that in what till we all got democratic in England were called the lower orders there was more passion, more romance, more disregard of consequences than could ever be found in the well-to-do and presumably educated classes, whom prudence has made timid and convention inhibited.

'Because the working man doesn't read much,' he said, 'because he has no great gift for expressing himself, you think he has no imagination. You're wrong. He's extravagantly imaginative. Because he's a great husky brute you think he has no nerves. You're wrong again. He's a bundle of nerves.'

Then he told us a story which I shall tell as best I can in my own words.

Fred Manson was a good-looking fellow, tall, well-made, with blue eyes, good features, and a friendly, agreeable smile, but what made him remarkable so that people turned round in the streets to stare at him was that he had a thick head of hair, with a great wave in it, of a deep rich red. It was really a great beauty. Perhaps it was this that gave him so sensual a look. His maleness was like a heady perfume. His eyebrows were thick, only a little lighter that his hair, and he was lucky enough not to have the ugly skin that so disfigures red-heads. His was a smooth olive. His eyes were bold, and when he smiled or laughed, which in the healthy vitality of his youth he did constantly, his expression was wonderfully alluring. He was twenty-two and he gave you the rather pleasant impression of just loving to be alive. It was inevitable that with such looks and above all with that troubling sexuality he should have success with women. He was charming, tender, and passionate, but immensely promiscuous. He was not exactly callous or brazen, he had a kindly nature, but somehow or other he made it quite clear to the objects of his passing fancy that all he wanted was a little bit of fun and it was impossible for him to remain faithful to anyone.

Fred was a postman. He worked in Brixton. It is a densely populated part of London, and has the curious reputation of harbouring more criminals than any other suburb because trams run to it from across the river all night long, so that when a man has done a job of housebreaking in the West End he can be sure of getting home without difficulty. Fred liked his job. Brixton is a district of innumerable streets lined with little houses inhabited by the people who work in the neighbourhood and also by clerks, shop-assistants, skilled workers of one sort or another whose jobs take them every day across the river. He was strong and healthy and it was a pleasure to him to walk from street to street delivering the letters. Sometimes there would be a postal packet to hand in or a registered letter that had to be signed for, and then he would have the opportunity of seeing people. He was a sociable creature. It was never long before he was well known on whatever round he was assigned to. After a time his job was changed. His duty then was to go to the red pillar-boxes into which the letters were put, empty them, and take the contents to the main post-office of the district. His bag would be pretty heavy sometimes by the time he was through, but he was proud of his strength and the weight only made him laugh.

One day he was emptying a box in one of the better streets, a street of semi-detached houses, and had just closed his bag when a girl came running along.

'Postman,' she cried, 'take this letter, will you. I want it to go by this post most particularly.'

He gave her his good-natured smile.

'I never mind obliging a lady,' he said, putting down his bag and opening it.

'I wouldn't trouble you, only it's urgent,' she said as she handed him the letter she had in her hand.

'Who is it to—a feller?' he grinned.

'None of your business.'

'All right, be haughty. But I tell you this, he's no good. Don't you trust him.'

'You've got a nerve,' she said.

'So they tell me.'

He took off his cap and ran his hand through his mop of curling red hair. The sight of it made her gasp.

'Where d'you get your perm?' she asked with a giggle.

'I'll show you one of these days if you like.'

He was looking down at her with his amused eyes, and there was something about him that gave her a funny little feeling in the pit of her stomach.

'Well, I must be on my way,' he said. 'If I don't get on with the job pretty damn quick I don't know what'll happen to the country.'

'I'm not detaining you,' she said coolly.

'That's where you make a mistake,' he answered.

He gave her a look that made her heart beat nineteen to the dozen and she felt herself blushing all over. She turned away and ran back to the house. Fred noticed it was four doors away from the pillar-box. He had to pass it and as he did so he looked up. He saw the net curtains twitch and knew she was watching. He felt pleased with himself. During the next few days he looked at the house whenever he passed it, but never caught a glimpse of the girl. One afternoon he ran across her by chance just as he was entering the street in which she lived.

'Hullo,' he said, stopping.

'Hullo.'

She blushed scarlet.

'Haven't seen you about lately.'

'You haven't missed much.'

'That's what you think.'

She was prettier than he remembered, dark-haired, dark-eyed, rather tall, slight, with a good figure, a pale skin, and very white teeth.

'What about coming to the pictures with me one evening?'

'Taking a lot for granted, aren't you?'

'It pays,' he said with his impudent, charming grin.

She couldn't help laughing.

'Not with me, it doesn't.'

'Oh, come on. One's only young once.'

There was something so attractive in him that she couldn't bring herself to give him a saucy answer.

'I couldn't really. My people wouldn't like me going out with a fellow I don't know. You see, I'm the only one they have and they think a rare lot of me. Why, I don't even know your name.'

'Well, I can tell you, can't I? Fred. Fred Manson. Can't you say you're going to the pictures with a girl friend?'

She had never felt before what she was feeling then. She didn't know if it was pain or pleasure. She was strangely breathless.

'I suppose I could do that.'

They fixed the night, the time, and the place. Fred was waiting for her and they went in, but when the picture started and he put his arm round her waist, without a word, her eyes fixed on the screen, she quietly took it away. He took hold of her hand, but she withdrew it. He was surprised. That wasn't the way girls usually behaved. He didn't know what one went to the pictures for if it wasn't to have a bit of a cuddle. He walked home with her after the show. She told him her name. Grace Carter. Her father had a shop of his own in the Brixton Road, he was a draper and he had four assistants.

'He must be doing well,' said Fred.

'He doesn't complain.'

Gracie was a student at London University. When she got her degree she was going to be a school teacher.

'What d'you want to do that for when there's a good business waiting for you?'

'Pa doesn't want me to have anything to do with the shop–not after the education he's given me. He wants me to better myself, if you know what I mean.'

Her father had started life as an errand boy, then became a draper's assistant, and because he was hard-working, honest, and intelligent was now owner of a prosperous little business. Success had given him grand ideas for his only child. He didn't want her to have anything to do with trade. He hoped she'd marry a professional man perhaps, or at least someone in the City. Then he'd sell the business and retire, and Gracie would be quite the lady.

When they reached the corner of her street Gracie held out her hand.

'You'd better not come to the door,' she said.

'Aren't you going to kiss me good night?'

'I am not.'

'Why?'

'Because I don't want to.'

'You'll come to the pictures again, won't you?'

'I think I'd better not.'

'Oh, come on.'

There was such a warm urgency in his voice that she felt as though her knees would give way.

'Will you behave if I do?' He nodded. 'Promise?'

'Swop me bob.'

He scratched his head when he left her. Funny girl. He'd never met anyone quite like her. Superior, there was no doubt about that. There was something in her voice that got you. It was warm and soft. He tried to think what it was like. It was like as if the words kissed you. Sounded silly, that did, but that's just what it was like.

From then on they went to the pictures once or twice a week. After a while she allowed him to put his arm round her waist and to hold her hand, but she never let him go farther than that.

'Have you ever been kissed by a fellow?' he asked her once.

'No, I haven't,' she said simply. 'My ma's funny, she says you've got to keep a man's respect.'

'I'd give anything in the world just to kiss you, Gracie.'

'Don't be so silly.'

'Won't you let me just once?' She shook her head. 'Why not?'

'Because I like you too much,' she said hoarsely, and then walked quickly away from him.

It gave him quite a turn. He wanted her as he'd never wanted a woman before. What she'd said finished him. He'd been thinking of her a lot, and he'd looked forward to the evenings they spent together as he'd never looked forward to anything in his life. For the first time he was uncertain of himself. She was above him in every way, what with her father making money hand over fist and her education and everything, and him only a postman. They had made a date for the following Friday night and he was in a fever of anxiety lest she shouldn't come. He repeated to himself over and over again what she'd said: perhaps it meant that she'd made up her mind to drop him. When at last he saw her walking along the street he almost sobbed with relief. That evening he neither put his arm round her nor took her hand and when he walked her home he never said a word.

'You're very quiet tonight, Fred,' she said at last. 'What's the matter with you?'

He walked a few steps before he answered.

'I don't like to tell you.'

She stopped suddenly and looked up at him. There was terror on her face.

'Tell me whatever it is,' she said unsteadily.

'I'm gone, I can't help myself, I'm so stuck on you I can't see straight. I didn't know what it was to love like I love you.'

'Oh, is that all? You gave me such a fright. I thought you were going to say you were going to be married.'

'Me? Who d'you take me for? It's you I want to marry.'

'Well, what's to prevent you, silly?'

'Gracie! D'you mean it?'

He flung his arms round her and kissed her full on the mouth. She didn't resist. She returned his kiss and he felt in her a passion as eager as his own.

They arranged that Gracie should tell her parents that she was engaged to him and that on the Sunday he should come and be introduced to them. Since the shop stayed open late on Saturday and by the time Mr Carter got home he was tired out, it was not till after dinner on Sunday that Gracie broke her news. George Carter was a brisk, not very tall man, but sturdy, with a high colour, who with increasing prosperity had put on weight. He was more than rather bald and he had a bristle of grey moustache. Like many another employer who had risen from the working class he was a slave-driver and he got as much work out of his assistants for as little money as was possible. He had an eye for every thing and he wouldn't put up with any nonsense, but he was reasonable and even kindly, so that they did not dislike him. Mrs Carter was a quiet, nice woman, with a pleasant face and the remains of good looks. They were both in the early fifties, for they had married late after 'walking out' for nearly ten years.

They were very much surprised when Gracie told them what she had to tell, but not displeased.

'You're a sly one,' said her father. 'Why, I never suspected for a minute you'd taken up with anyone. Well, I suppose it had to come sooner or later. What's his name?'

'Fred Manson.'

'A fellow you met at college?'

'No. You must have seen him about. He clears our pillar-box. He's a postman.'

'Oh, Gracie,' cried Mrs Carter, 'you can't mean it. You can't marry a common postman, not after all the education we've given you.'

For an instant Mr Carter was speechless. He got redder in the face than ever.

'Your ma's right, my girl,' he burst out now. 'You can't throw yourself away like that. Why, it's ridiculous.'

'I'm not throwing myself away. You wait till you see him.'

Mrs Carter began to cry.

'It's such a come-down. It's such a humiliation. I shall never be able to hold up my head again.'

'Oh, Ma, don't talk like that. He's a nice fellow and he's got a good job.'

'You don't understand,' she moaned.

'How d'you get to know him?' Mr Carter interrupted. 'What sort of family's he got?'

'His pa drives one of the post-office vans,' Gracie answered defiantly.

'Working-class people.'

'Well, what of it? His pa's worked twenty-four years for the post-office and they think a lot of him.'

Mrs Carter was biting the corner of her handkerchief.

'Gracie, I want to tell you something. Before your pa and me got married I was in domestic service. He wouldn't ever let me tell you because he didn't want you to be ashamed of me. That's why we was engaged all those years. The lady I was with said she'd leave me something in her will if I stayed with her till she passed away.'

'It was that money that gave me my start,' Mr Carter broke in. 'Except for that I'd never have been where I am today. And I don't mind telling you you're ma's the best wife a man ever had.'

'I never had a proper education,' Mrs Carter went on, 'but I always was ambitious. The proudest moment of my life was when your pa said we could afford a girl to help me and he said then: "The time'll come when you have a cook *and* a house-maid," and he's been as good as his word, and now you're going back to what I come from. I'd set my heart on your marrying a gentleman.'

She began crying again. Gracie loved her parents and couldn't bear to see them so distressed.

'I'm sorry, Ma, I knew it would be a disappointment to you, but I can't help it, I can't really. I love him so. I love him so terribly. I'm sure you'll like him when you see him. We're going for a walk on the Common this afternoon. Can't I bring him back to supper?'

Mrs Carter gave her husband a harassed look. He sighed.

'I don't like it and it's no good pretending I do, but I suppose we'd better have a look at him.'

Supper passed off better than might have been expected. Fred wasn't shy, and he talked to Gracie's parents as though he had known them all his life. If to be waited on by a maid, if to sup in a dining-room furnished in solid mahogany and afterwards to sit in a drawing-room that had a grand piano in it was new to him, he showed no embarrassment. After he had gone and they were alone in their bedroom Mr and Mrs Carter talked him over.

'He is handsome, you can't deny that,' she said.

'Handsome is as handsome does. D'you think he's after her money?'

'Well, he must know that you've got a tidy little bit tucked away somewhere, but he's in love with her all right.'

'Oh, what makes you think that?'

'Why, you've only got to see the way he looks at her.'

'Well, that's something at all events.'

In the end the Carters withdrew their opposition on the condition that the young things shouldn't marry until Gracie had taken her degree. That would give them a year, and at the back of their minds was the hope that by then she would have changed her mind. They saw a good deal of Fred after that. He spent every Sunday with them. Little by little they began quite to like him. He was so easy, so gay, so full of high spirits, and above all so obviously head over ears in love with Gracie, that Mrs Carter soon succumbed to his charm, and after a while even Mr Carter was prepared to admit that he didn't seem a bad fellow. Fred and Gracie were happy. She went to London every day to attend lectures and worked hard. They spent blissful evenings together. He gave her a very nice engagement ring and often took her out to dinner in the West End and to a play. On fine Sundays he drove her out into the country in a car that he said a friend had lent him. When she asked him if he could afford all the money he spent on her he laughed, and said a chap had given him a tip on an outsider and he'd made a packet. They talked interminably of the little flat they would have when they were married and the fun it would be to furnish it. They were more in love with one another than ever.

Then the blow fell. Fred was arrested for stealing money from the letters he collected. Many people, to save themselves the trouble of buying postal orders, put notes in their envelopes, and it wasn't difficult to tell that they were there. Fred went up for trial, pleaded guilty, and was sentenced to two years' hard labour. Gracie went to the trial. Up to the last moment she had hoped that he would be able to prove his innocence. It was a dreadful shock to her when he pleaded guilty. She was not allowed to see him. He went straight from the dock to the prison van. She went home and, locking herself up in her bedroom, threw herself on the bed and wept. When Mr Carter came back from the shop Gracie's mother went up to her room.

'Gracie, you're to come downstairs,' she said. 'Your father wants to speak to you.'

Gracie got up and went down. She did not trouble to dry her eyes.

'Seen the paper?' he said, holding out to her the *Evening News.*

She didn't answer.

'Well, that's the end of that young man,' he went on harshly.

They too, Gracie's parents, had been shocked when Fred was arrested, but she was so distressed, she was so convinced that everything could be explained, that they hadn't had the heart to tell her that she must have nothing more to do with him. But now they felt it time to have things out with her.

'So that's where the money came from for those dinners and theatres. And the car. I thought it funny he should have a friend who'd lend him a car on Sundays when he'd be wanting it himself. He hired it, didn't he?'

'I suppose so,' she answered miserably. 'I just believed what he told me.'

'You've had a lucky escape, my girl, that's all I can say.'

'He only did it because he wanted to give me a good time. He didn't want me to think I couldn't have everything as nice when I was with him as what I've been used to at home.'

'You're not going to make excuses for him, I hope. He's a thief, that's what he is.'

'I don't care,' she said sullenly.

'You don't care? What d'you mean by that?'

'Exactly what I say. I'm going to wait for him and the moment he comes out I'm going to marry him.'

Mrs Carter gave a gasp of horror.

'Gracie, you can't do a thing like that,' she cried. 'Think of the disgrace. And what about us? We've always held our heads high. He's a thief, and once a thief always a thief.'

'Don't go on calling him a thief,' Gracie shrieked, stamping her foot with rage. 'What he did he did just because he loved me. I don't care if he is a thief. I love him more than I ever loved him. You don't know what love is. You waited ten years to marry Pa just so as an old woman should leave you some money. D'you call that love?'

'You leave your ma out of this,' Mr Carter shouted. Then an idea occurred to him and he gave a piercing glance. 'Have you *got* to marry the feller?'

Gracie blushed furiously.

'No. There's never been anything of that sort. And not through any fault of mine either. He loved me too much. He didn't want to do anything perhaps he'd regret afterwards.'

Often on summer evenings in the country when they'd been lying in a field in one another's arms, mouth to mouth, her desire had been as intense as his. She knew how much he wanted her and she was ready to give him what he asked. But when things got too desperate he'd suddenly jump up and say:

'Come on, let's walk.'

He'd drag her to her feet. She knew what was in his mind. He wanted to wait till they were married. His love had given him a delicacy of sentiment that he'd never known before. He couldn't make it out himself, but he had a funny sort of feeling about her, he felt that if he had her before marriage it would spoil things. Because she guessed what was in his heart she loved him all the more.

'I don't know what's come over you,' moaned Mrs Carter. 'You was always such a good girl. You've never given us a day's uneasiness.'

'Stop it, Ma,' said Mr Carter violently. 'We've got to get this straight once and for all. You've got to give up this man, see? I've got me own position to think of and if you think I'm going to have a gaol-bird for a son-in-law you'd better think again. I've had enough of this nonsense. You've got to promise me that you'll have nothing more to do with the feller ever.'

'D'you think I'm going to give him up now? How often d'you want me to tell you I'm going to marry him the moment he gets out?'

'All right, then you can get out of my house and get out pretty damn quick. And stay out.'

'Pa!' cried Mrs Carter.

'Shut up.'

'I'll be glad to go,' said Gracie.

'Oh, will you? And how d'you think you're going to live?'

'I can work, can't I? I can get a job at Payne and Perkins. They'll be glad to have me.'

'Oh, Gracie, you couldn't go and work in a shop, you can't demean yourself like that,' said Mrs Carter.

'Will you shut up, Ma,' shouted Mr Carter, beside himself now with rage. 'Work, will you? You that's never done a stroke of work in your life except that tomfoolery at the college. Bright idea it was of your ma's to give you an education. Fat lot of good it'll be to you when you've got to stand on your feet for hours and got to be civil and pleasant to a lot of old trouts who just try and give you all the trouble they can just to show how superior they are. I bet you'll like it when you're bawled out by the manageress because you're not bright and snappy. All right, marry your gaol-bird. I suppose you know you'll have to keep him too. You don't think anyone's going to give him a job, do you, not with his record. Get out, get out, get out.'

He had worked himself up to such a pitch of fury that he sank panting into a chair. Mrs Carter, frightened, poured out a glass of water and gave him some to drink. Gracie slipped out of the room.

Next day, when her father had gone to work and her mother was out shopping, she left the house with such effects as she could get into a suit-case. Payne and Perkins was a large department store in the Brixton Road, and with her good appearance and pleasant manner she found no difficulty in getting taken on. She was put in the ladies' lingerie. For a few days she stayed at the Y.W.C.A. and then arranged to share a room with one of the girls who worked with her.

Ned Preston saw Fred in the evening of the day he went to gaol. He found him shattered, but only because of Gracie. He took his thieving very lightly.

'I had to do the right thing by her, didn't I? Her people, they didn't think I was good enough for her; I wanted to show them I was just as good as they were. When we went up to the West End I couldn't give her a sandwich and half of bitter in a pub, why, she's never been in a pub in her life, I *had* to take her to a restaurant. If people are such fools as to put money in letters, well, they're just asking for it.'

But he was frightened. He wasn't sure that Gracie would see it like that.

'I've got to know what she's going to do. If she chucks me now—well, it's the end of everything for me, see? I'll find some way of doing meself in, I swear to God I will.'

He told Ned the whole story of his love for Gracie.

'I could have had her over and over again if I'd wanted to. And I did want to and so did she. I knew that. But I respected her, see? She's not like other girls. She's one in a thousand, I tell you.'

He talked and talked. He stormed, he wept. From that confused torrent of words emerged one thing very clearly. A passionate, a frenzied love. Ned promised that he would see the girl.

'Tell her I love her, tell her that what I did I just did because I wanted her to have the best of everything, and tell her I just can't live without her.'

As soon as he could find time Ned Preston went to the Carters' house, but when he asked for Gracie the maid who opened the door told him that she didn't live there any more. Then he asked to see her mother.

'I'll go and see if she's in.'

He gave the maid his card, thinking the name of his club engraved in the corner would impress Mrs Carter enough to make her willing to see him. The maid left him at the door, but in a minute or two asked him to come in. He was shown into the stiff and little-used sitting-room. Mrs Carter kept him waiting for some time and when she came in, holding his card in the tips of her fingers, he guessed it was because she had thought fit to change her dress. The black silk she wore was evidently a dress for occasions. He told her his connexion with Wormwood Scrubs and said that he had to do with a man named Frederick Manson. The moment he mentioned the name Mrs Carter assumed a hostile attitude.

'Don't speak to me of that man,' she cried. 'A thief, that's what he is. The trouble he's caused us. They ought to have given him five years, they ought.'

'I'm sorry he's caused you trouble,' said Ned mildly. 'Perhaps if you'd give me a few facts I might help to straighten things out.'

Ned Preston certainly had a way with him. Perhaps Mrs Carter was impressed because he was a gentleman. 'Class he is,' she probably said to herself. Anyhow it was not long before she was telling him the whole story. She grew upset as she told it and began to cry.

'And now she's gone and left us. Run away. I don't know how she could bring herself to do a thing like that. God knows, we love her. She's all we've got and we done everything in the world for her. Her pa never meant it when he told her to get out of the house. Only she was so obstinate. He got in a temper, he always was a quick-tempered man, he was just as upset as I was when we found she'd gone. And d'you know what she's been and gone and done? Got herself a job at Payne and Perkins. Mr Carter can't abide them. Cutting prices all the time they are. Unfair competition, he calls it. And to think of our Gracie working with a lot of shop-girls–oh, it's so humiliating.'

Ned made a mental note of the store's name. He hadn't been at all sure of getting Gracie's address out of Mrs Carter.

'Have you seen her since she left you?' he asked.

'Of course I have. I knew they'd jump at her at Payne and Perkins, a superior girl like that, and I went there, and there she was, sure enough–in the ladies' lingerie. I waited outside till closing time and then I spoke to her. I asked her to come home. I said her pa was willing to let bygones be bygones. And d'you know what she said? She said she'd come home if we never said a word against Fred and if we was prepared to have her marry him as soon as ever he got out. Of course I had to tell her pa. I never saw him in such a state, I thought he was going to have a fit, he said he'd rather see her dead at his feet than married to that gaol-bird.'

Mrs Carter again burst into tears and as soon as he could Ned Preston left her. He went to the department store, up to the ladies' lingerie, and asked for Grace Carter. She was pointed out to him and he went up to her.

'Can I speak to you for a minute? I've come from Fred Manson.'

She went deathly white. For a moment it seemed that she could not utter a word.

'Follow me, please.'

She took him into a passage smelling of disinfectants which seemed to lead to the lavatories. They were alone. She stared at him anxiously.

'He sends you his love. He's worried about you. He's afraid you're awfully unhappy. What he wants to know really is if you're going to chuck him.'

'Me?' Her eyes filled with tears, but on her face was a look of ecstasy. 'Tell him that nothing matters to me as long as he loves me. Tell him I'd wait twenty years for him if I had to. Tell him I'm counting the days till he gets out so as we can get married.'

For fear of the manageress she couldn't stay away from her work for more than a minute or two. She gave Ned all the loving messages she could get into the time to give Fred Manson. Ned didn't get to the Scrubs till nearly six. The prisoners are allowed to put down their tools at five-thirty and Fred had just put his down. When Ned entered the cell he turned pale and sank on to the bed as though his anxiety was such that he didn't trust his legs. But when Ned told him his news he gave a gasp of relief. For a while he couldn't trust himself to speak.

'I knew you'd seen her the moment you came in. I smelt her.'

He sniffed as though the smell of her body were strong in his nostrils, and his face was as it were a mask of desire. His features on a sudden seemed strangely blurred.

'You know, it made me feel quite uncomfortable so that I had to look the other way,' said Ned Preston when he told us this, with a cackle of his shrill laughter. 'It was sex in its nakedness all right.'

Fred was an exemplary prisoner. He worked well, he gave no trouble. Ned suggested books for him to read and he took them out of the library, but that was about as far as he got.

'I can't get on well with them somehow,' he said. 'I start reading and then I begin thinking of Gracie. You know, when she kisses you ordinary-like–oh, it's so sweet, but when she kisses you really, my God, it's lovely.'

Fred was allowed to see Gracie once a month, but their meetings, with a glass screen between, under the eyes of a warder, were so painful that after several visits they agreed it would be better if she didn't come any more. A year passed. Owing to his good behaviour he could count on a remittance of his sentence and so would be free in another six months. Gracie had saved every penny she could out of her wages and now as the time approached for Fred's release she set about getting a home ready for him. She took two rooms in a house and furnished them on the hire purchase system. One room of course was to be their bedroom and the other the living-room and kitchen. There was an old-fashioned range in it and this she had taken out and replaced by a gas-stove. She wanted everything to be nice and new and clean and comfortable. She took pains to make the two little rooms bright and pretty. To do all this she had to go without all the barest necessities of existence and she grew thin and pale. Ned suspected that she was starving herself and when he went to see her took a box of chocolates or a cake so that she should have at least something to eat. He brought the prisoner news of what Gracie was doing and she made him promise to give him accurate accounts of every article she bought. He took fond, more than fond, passionate messages from one to the other. He was convinced that Fred would go straight in future and he got him a job as commissionaire from a firm that had a chain of restaurants in London. The wages were good and by calling taxis or fetching cars he would be able to make money on the side. He was to start work as soon as he came out of gaol. Gracie took the necessary steps so that they could get married at once. The eighteen months of Fred's imprisonment were drawing to an end. Gracie was in a fever of excitement.

It happened then that Ned Preston had one of his periodical bouts of illness and was unable to go to the prison for three weeks. It bothered him, for he didn't like to abandon his prisoners, so as soon as he could get out of bed he went to the Scrubs. The chief warder told him that Manson had been asking for him.

'I think you'd better go and see him. I don't know what's the matter with him. He's been acting rather funny since you've been away.'

It was just a fortnight before Fred was due to be released. Ned Preston went to his cell.

'Well, Fred, how are you?' he asked. 'Sorry I haven't been able to come and see you. I've been ill, and I haven't been able to see Gracie either. She must be all of a dither by now.'

'Well, I want you to go and see her.'

His manner was so surly that Ned was taken aback. It was unlike him to be anything but pleasant and civil.

'Of course I will.'

'I want you to tell her that I'm not going to marry her.'

Ned was so astounded that for a minute he could only stare blankly at Fred Manson.

'What on earth d'you mean?'

'Exactly what I say.'

'You can't let her down now. Her people have thrown her out. She's been working all this time to get a home ready for you. She's got the licence and everything.'

'I don't care. I'm not going to marry her.'

'But why, why, why?'

Ned was flabbergasted. Fred Manson was silent for a bit. His face was dark and sullen.

'I'll tell you. I've thought about her night and day for eighteen months and now I'm sick to death of her.'

When Ned Preston reached this point of his story our hostess and our fellow guests broke into loud laughter. He was plainly taken aback. There was some little talk after that and the party broke up. Ned and I, having to go in the same direction, walked along Piccadilly together. For a time we walked in silence.

'I noticed you didn't laugh with the others,' he said abruptly.

'I didn't think it funny.'

'What d'you make of it?'

'Well, I can see his point, you know. Imagination's an odd thing, it dries up; I suppose, thinking of her incessantly all that time he'd exhausted every emotion she could give him, and I think it was quite literally true, he'd just got sick to death of her. He'd squeezed the lemon dry and there was nothing to do but throw away the rind.'

'I didn't think it funny either. That's why I didn't tell them the rest of the story. I wouldn't accept it at first. I thought it was just hysteria or something. I went to see him two or three days running. I argued with him. I really did my damnedest. I thought if he'd only see her it would be all right, but he wouldn't even do that. He said he hated the sight of her. I couldn't move him. At last I had to go and tell her.'

We walked on a little longer in silence.

'I saw her in that beastly, stinking corridor. She saw at once there was something the matter and she went awfully white. She wasn't a girl to show much emotion. There was something gracious and rather noble about her face. Tranquil. Her lips quivered a bit when I told her and she didn't say anything for a minute. When she spoke it was quite calmly, as though—well, as though she'd just missed a bus and would have to wait for another. As though it was a nuisance, you know, but nothing to make a song and dance about. "There's nothing for me to do now but put my head in the gas-oven,' she said.

'And she did.'

The Kite

◆

I know this is an odd story. I don't understand it myself and if I set it down in black and white it is only with a faint hope that when I have written it I may get a clearer view of it, or rather with the hope that some reader, better acquainted with the complications of human nature than I am, may offer me an explanation that will make it comprehensible to me. Of course the first thing that occurs to me is that there is something Freudian about it. Now, I have read a good deal by Freud, and some books by his followers, and intending to write this story I have recently flipped through again the volume published by the Modern Library which contains his basic writings. It was something of a task, for he is a dull and verbose writer, and the acrimony with which he claims to have originated such and such a theory shows a vanity and a jealousy of others working in the same field which somewhat ill become the man of science. I believe, however, that he was a kindly and benign old party. As we know, there is often a great difference between the man and the writer. The writer may be bitter, harsh, and brutal, while the man may be so meek and mild that he wouldn't say boo to a goose. But that is neither here nor there. I found nothing in my re-reading of Freud's works that cast any light on the subject I had in mind. I can only relate the facts and leave it at that.

First of all I must make it plain that it is not my story and that I knew none of the persons with whom it is concerned. It was told me one evening by my friend Ned Preston, and he told it me because he didn't know how to deal with the circumstances and he thought, quite wrongly as it happened, that I might be able to give him some advice that would help him. In a previous story I have related what I thought the reader should know about Ned Preston, and so now I need only remind him that my friend was a prison visitor at Wormwood Scrubs. He took his duties very seriously and made the prisoners' troubles his own. We had been dining together at the Café Royal in that long, low room with its absurd and charming decoration which is all that remains of the old Café Royal that painters have loved to paint; and we were sitting over our coffee and liqueurs and, so far as Ned was concerned against his doctor's orders, smoking very long and very good Havanas.

'I've got a funny chap to deal with at the Scrubs just now,' he said, after a pause, 'and I'm blowed if I know how to deal with him.'

'What's he in for?' I asked.

'He left his wife and the court ordered him to pay so much a week in alimony and he's absolutely refused to pay it. I've argued with him till I was blue in the face. I've told him he's only cutting off his nose to spite his face. He says he'll stay in jail all his life rather than pay her a penny. I tell him he can't let her starve, and all he says is: "Why not?" He's perfectly well behaved, he's no trouble, he works well, he seems quite happy, he's just getting a lot of fun out of thinking what a devil of a time his wife is having.'

'What's he got against her?'

'She smashed his kite.'

'She did what?' I cried.

'Exactly that. She smashed his kite. He says he'll never forgive her for that till his dying day.'

'He must be crazy.'

'No, he isn't, he's a perfectly reasonable, quite intelligent, decent fellow.'

Herbert Sunbury was his name, and his mother, who was very refined, never allowed him to be called Herb or Bertie, but always Herbert, just as she never called her husband Sam but only Samuel. Mrs Sunbury's first name was Beatrice, and when she got engaged to Mr Sunbury and he ventured to call her Bea she put her foot down firmly.

'Beatrice I was christened,' she said, 'and Beatrice I always have been and always shall be, to you and to my nearest and dearest.'

She was a little woman, but strong, active, and wiry, with a sallow skin, sharp, regular features, and small beady eyes. Her hair, suspiciously black for her age, was always very neat, and she wore it in the style of Queen Victoria's daughters, which she had adopted as soon as she was old enough to put it up and had never thought fit to change. The possibility that she did something to keep her hair its original colour was, if such was the case, her only concession to frivolity, for, far from using rouge or lipstick, she had never in her life so much as passed a powder-puff over her nose. She never wore anything but black dresses of good material, but made (by that little woman round the corner) regardless of fashion after a pattern that was both serviceable and decorous. Her only ornament was a thin gold chain from which hung a small gold cross.

Samuel Sunbury was a little man too. He was as thin and spare as his wife, but he had sandy hair, gone very thin now so that he had to wear it very long on one side and brushed it carefully over the large bald patch. He had pale blue eyes and his complexion was pasty. He was a clerk in a lawyer's office and had worked his way up from office boy to a respectable position. His employer called him Mr Sunbury and sometimes asked him to see an unimportant client. Every morning for twenty-four years Samuel Sunbury had taken the same train to the City, except of course on Sundays and during his fortnight's holiday at the seaside, and every evening he had taken the same train back to the suburb in which he lived. He was neat in his dress; he went to work in quiet grey trousers, a black coat, and a bowler hat, and when he came home he put on his slippers and a black coat which was too old and shiny to wear at the office; but on Sundays when he went to the chapel he and Mrs Sunbury attended he wore a morning coat with his bowler. Thus he showed his respect for the day of rest and at the same time registered a protest against the ungodly who went bicycling or lounged about the streets until the pubs opened. On principle the Sunburys were total abstainers, but on Sundays, when to make up for the frugal lunch, consisting of a scone and butter with a glass of milk, which Samuel had during the week, Beatrice gave him a good dinner of roast beef and Yorkshire pudding, for his health's sake she liked him to have a glass of beer. Since she wouldn't for the world have kept liquor in the house, he sneaked out with a jug after morning service and got a quart from the pub round the corner; but nothing would induce him to drink alone, so, just to be sociable-like, she had a glass too.

Herbert was the only child the Lord had vouchsafed to them, and this certainly through no precaution on their part. It just happened that way. They doted on him. He was a pretty baby and then a good-looking child. Mrs Sunbury brought him up carefully. She taught him to sit up at table and not put his elbows on it, and she taught him how to use his knife and fork like a little gentleman. She taught him to stretch out his little finger when he took his tea-cup to drink out of it and when he asked why, she said:

'Never you mind. That's how it's done. It shows you know what's what.'

In due course Herbert grew old enough to go to school. Mrs Sunbury was anxious because she had never let him play with the children in the street.

'Evil communications corrupt good manners,' she said. 'I always have kept myself to myself and I always shall keep myself to myself.'

Although they had lived in the same house ever since they were married she had taken care to keep her neighbours at a distance.

'You never know who people are in London,' she said. 'One thing leads to another, and before you know where you are you're mixed up with a lot of riff-raff and you can't get rid of them.'

She didn't like the idea of Herbert being thrown into contact with a lot of rough boys at the County Council school and she said to him:

'Now, Herbert, do what I do; keep yourself to yourself and don't have anything more to do with them than you can help.'

But Herbert got on very well at school. He was a good worker and far from stupid. His reports were excellent. It turned out that he had a good head for figures.

'If that's a fact,' said Samuel Sunbury, 'he'd better be an accountant. There's always a good job waiting for a good accountant.'

So it was settled there and then that this was what Herbert was to be. He grew tall.

'Why, Herbert,' said his mother, 'soon you'll be as tall as your dad.'

By the time he left school he was two inches taller, and by the time he stopped growing he was five feet ten.

'Just the right height,' said his mother. 'Not too tall and not too short.'

He was a nice-looking boy, with his mother's regular features and dark hair, but he had inherited his father's blue eyes, and though he was rather pale his skin was smooth and clear. Samuel Sunbury had got him into the office of the accountants who came twice a year to do the accounts of his own firm and by the time he was twenty-one he was able to bring back to his mother every week quite a nice little sum. She gave him back three half-crowns for his lunches and ten shillings for pocket money, and the rest she put in the Savings Bank for him against a rainy day.

When Mr and Mrs Sunbury went to bed on the night of Herbert's twenty-first birthday, and in passing I may say that Mrs Sunbury never went to bed, she retired, but Mr Sunbury, who was not quite so refined as his wife, always said: 'Me for Bedford,'–when then Mr and Mrs Sunbury went to bed, Mrs Sunbury said:

'Some people don't know how lucky they are; thank the Lord, I do. No one's ever had a better son than our Herbert. Hardly a day's illness in his life and he's never given me a moment's worry. It just shows if you bring up somebody right they'll be a credit to you. Fancy him being twenty-one, I can hardly believe it.'

'Yes, I suppose before we know where we are he'll be marrying and leaving us.'

'What should he want to do that for?' asked Mrs Sunbury with asperity. 'He's got a good home here, hasn't he? Don't you go putting silly ideas into his head, Samuel, or you and me'll have words and you know that's the last thing I want. Marry indeed! He's got more sense than that. He knows when he's well off. He's got sense, Herbert has.'

Mr Sunbury was silent. He had long ago learnt that it didn't get him anywhere with Beatrice to answer back.

'I don't hold with a man marrying till he knows his own mind,' she went on. 'And a man doesn't know his own mind till he's thirty or thirty-five.'

'He was pleased with his presents,' said Mr Sunbury to change the conversation.

'And so he ought to be,' said Mrs Sunbury still upset.

They had in fact been handsome. Mr Sunbury had given him a silver wrist-watch, with hands that you could see in the dark, and Mrs Sunbury had given him a kite. It wasn't by any means the first one she had given him. That was when he was seven years old, and it happened this way. There was a large common near where they lived and on Saturday afternoons when it was fine Mrs Sunbury took her husband and son for a walk there. She said it was good for Samuel to get a breath of fresh air after being cooped up in a stuffy office all the week. There were always a lot of people on the common, but Mrs Sunbury who liked to keep herself to herself kept out of their way as much as possible.

'Look at them kites, Mum,' said Herbert suddenly one day.

There was a fresh breeze blowing and a number of kites, small and large, were sailing through the air.

'*Those*, Herbert, not them,' said Mrs Sunbury.

'Would you like to go and see where they start, Herbert?' asked his father.

'Oh, yes, Dad.'

There was a slight elevation in the middle of the common and as they approached it they saw boys and girls and some men racing down it to give their kites a start and catch the wind. Sometimes they didn't and fell to the ground, but when they did they would rise, and as the owner unravelled his string go higher and higher. Herbert looked with ravishment.

'Mum, can I have a kite?' he cried.

He had already learnt that when he wanted anything it was better to ask his mother first.

'Whatever for?' she said.

'To fly it, Mum.'

'If you're so sharp you'll cut yourself,' she said.

Mr and Mrs Sunbury exchanged a smile over the little boy's head. Fancy him wanting a kite. Growing quite a little man he was.

'If you're a good boy and wash your teeth regular every morning without me telling you I shouldn't be surprised if Santa Claus didn't bring you a kite on Christmas Day.'

Christmas wasn't far off and Santa Claus brought Herbert his first kite. At the beginning he wasn't very clever at managing it, and Mr Sunbury had to run down the hill himself and start it for him. It was a very small kite, but when Herbert saw it swim through the air and felt the little tug it gave his hand he was thrilled; and then every Saturday afternoon, when his father got back from the City, he would pester his parents to hurry over to the common. He quickly learnt how to fly it, and Mr and Mrs Sunbury, their hearts swelling with pride, would watch him from the top of the knoll while he ran down and as the kite caught the breeze lengthened the cord in his hand.

It became a passion with Herbert, and as he grew older and bigger his mother bought him larger and larger kites. He grew very clever at gauging the winds and could do things with his kite you wouldn't have thought possible. There were other kite-flyers on the common, not only children, but men, and since nothing brings people together so naturally as a hobby they share it was not long before Mrs Sunbury, notwithstanding her exclusiveness, found that she, her Samuel, and her son were on speaking terms with all and sundry. They would compare their respective kites and boast of their accomplishments. Sometimes Herbert, a big boy of sixteen now, would challenge another kite-flyer. Then he would manoeuvre his kite to windward of the other fellow's, allow his cord to drift against his, and by a sudden jerk bring the enemy kite down. But long before this Mr Sunbury had succumbed to his son's enthusiasm and he would often ask to have a go himself. It must have been a funny sight to see him running down the hill in his striped trousers, black coat, and bowler hat. Mrs Sunbury would trot sedately behind him and when the kite was sailing free would take the cord from him and watch it as it soared. Saturday afternoon became the great day of the week for them, and when Mr Sunbury and Herbert left the house in the morning to catch their train to the City the first thing they did was to look up at the sky to see if it was flying weather. They liked best of all a gusty day, with uncertain winds, for that gave them the best chance to exercise their skill. All through the week, in the evenings, they talked about it. They were contemptuous of smaller kites than theirs and envious of bigger ones. They discussed the performances of other flyers as hotly, and as scornfully, as boxers or football-players discuss their rivals. Their ambition was to have a bigger kite than anyone else and a kite that would go higher. They had long given up a cord, for the kite they gave Herbert on his twenty-first birthday was seven feet high, and they used piano wire wound round a drum. But that did not satisfy Herbert. Somehow or other he had heard of a box-kite which had been invented by somebody, and the idea appealed to him at once. He thought he could devise something of the sort himself and since he could draw a little he set about making designs of it. He got a small model made and tried it out one afternoon, but it wasn't a success. He was a stubborn boy and he wasn't going to be beaten. Something was wrong, and it was up to him to put it right.

Then an unfortunate thing happened. Herbert began to go out after supper. Mrs Sunbury didn't like it much, but Mr Sunbury reasoned with her. After all, the boy was twenty-two, and it must be dull for him to stay home all the time. If he wanted to go for a walk or see a movie there was no great harm. Herbert had fallen in love. One Saturday evening, after they'd had a wonderful time on the common, while they were at supper, out of a clear sky he said suddenly:

'Mum, I've asked a young lady to come in to tea tomorrow. Is that all right?'

'You done what?' said Mrs Sunbury, for a moment forgetting her grammar.

'You heard, Mum.'

'And may I ask who she is and how you got to know her?'

'Her name's Bevan, Betty Bevan, and I met her first at the pictures one Saturday afternoon when it was raining. It was an accident-like. She was sitting next to me and she dropped her bag and I picked it up and she said thank you and so naturally we got talking.'

'And d'you mean to tell me you fell for an old trick like that? Dropped her bag indeed!'

'You're making a mistake, Mum, she's a nice girl, she is really and well educated too.'

'And when did all this happen?'

'About three months ago.'

'Oh, you met her three months ago and you've asked her to come to tea tomorrow?'

'Well, I've seen her since of course. That first day, after the show, I asked her if she'd come to the pictures with me on the Tuesday evening, and she said she didn't know, perhaps she would and perhaps she wouldn't. But she came all right.'

'She would. I could have told you that.'

'And we've been going to the pictures about twice a week ever since.'

'So that's why you've taken to going out so often?'

'That's right. But, look, I don't want to force her on you, if you don't want her to come to tea I'll say you've got a headache and take her out.'

'Your mum will have her to tea all right,' said Mr Sunbury. 'Won't you, dear? It's only that your mum can't abide strangers. She never has liked them.'

'I keep myself to myself,' said Mrs Sunbury gloomily. 'What does she do?'

'She works in a typewriting office in the City and she lives at home, if you call it home; you see, her mum died and her dad married again, and they've got three kids and she doesn't get on with her step-ma. Nag, nag, nag all the time, she says.'

Mrs Sunbury arranged the tea very stylishly. She took the knick-knacks off the little table in the sitting room, which they never used, and put a tea-cloth on it. She got out the tea-service and the plated tea-kettle which they never used either, and she made scones, baked a cake, and cut thin bread-and-butter.

'I want her to see that we're not just nobody,' she told her Samuel.

Herbert went to fetch Miss Bevan, and Mr Sunbury intercepted them at the door in case Herbert should take her into the dining-room where normally they ate and sat. Herbert gave the tea-table a glance of surprise as he ushered the young woman into the sitting-room.

'This is Betty, Mum,' he said.

'Miss Bevan, I presume,' said Mrs Sunbury.

'That's right, but call me Betty, won't you?'

'Perhaps the acquaintance is a bit short for that,' said Mrs Sunbury with a gracious smile. 'Won't you sit down, Miss Bevan?'

Strangely enough, or perhaps not strangely at all, Betty Bevan looked very much as Mrs Sunbury must have looked at her age. She had the same sharp features and the same rather small beady eyes, but her lips were scarlet with paint, her cheeks lightly rouged, and her short black hair permanently waved. Mrs Sunbury took in all this at a glance, and she reckoned to a penny how much her smart rayon dress had cost, her extravagantly high-heeled shoes, and the saucy hat on her head. Her frock was very short and she showed a good deal of flesh-coloured stocking. Mrs Sunbury, disapproving of her make-up and of her apparel, took an instant dislike to her, but she had made up her mind to behave like a lady, and if she didn't know how to behave like a lady nobody did, so that at first things went well. She poured out tea and asked Herbert to give a cup to his lady friend.

'Ask Miss Bevan if she'll have some bread-and-butter or a scone, Samuel, my dear.'

'Have both,' said Samuel, handing round the two plates, in his coarse way. 'I like to see people eat hearty.'

Betty insecurely perched a piece of bread-and-butter and a scone on her saucer and Mrs Sunbury talked affably about the weather. She had the satisfaction of seeing that Betty was getting more and more ill-at-ease. Then she cut the cake and pressed a large piece on her guest. Betty took a bite at it and when she put it in her saucer it fell to the ground.

'Oh, I am sorry,' said the girl, as she picked it up.

'It doesn't matter at all, I'll cut you another piece,' said Mrs Sunbury.

'Oh, don't bother, I'm not particular. The floor's clean.'

'I hope so,' said Mrs Sunbury with an acid smile, 'but I wouldn't dream of letting you eat a piece of cake that's been on the floor. Bring it here, Herbert, and I'll give Miss Bevan some more.'

'I don't want any more, Mrs Sunbury, I don't really.'

'I'm sorry you don't like my cake. I made it specially for you.' She took a bit. 'It tastes all right to me.'

'It's not that, Mrs Sunbury, it's a beautiful cake, it's only that I'm not hungry.'

She refused to have more tea and Mrs Sunbury saw she was glad to get rid of the cup. 'I expect they have their meals in the kitchen,' she said to herself. Then Herbert lit a cigarette.

'Give us a fag, Herb,' said Betty. 'I'm simply dying for a smoke.'

Mrs Sunbury didn't approve of women smoking, but she only raised her eyebrows slightly.

'We prefer to call him Herbert, Miss Bevan,' she said.

Betty wasn't such a fool as not to see that Mrs Sunbury had been doing all she could to make her uncomfortable, and now she saw a chance to get back on her.

'I know,' she said. 'When he told me his name was Herbert I nearly burst out laughing. Fancy calling anyone Herbert. A scream, I call it.'

'I'm sorry you don't like the name my son was given at his baptism. I think it's a very nice name. But I suppose it all depends on what sort of class of people one is.'

Herbert stepped in to the rescue.

'At the office they call me Bertie, Mum.'

'Then all I can say is, they're a lot of very common men.'

Mrs Sunbury lapsed into a dignified silence and the conversation, such as it was, was maintained by Mr Sunbury and Herbert. It was not without satisfaction that Mrs Sunbury perceived that Betty was offended. She also perceived that the girl wanted to go, but didn't quite know how to manage it.

She was determined not to help her. Finally Herbert took the matter into his own hands.

'Well, Betty, I think it's about time we were getting along,' he said. 'I'll walk back with you.'

'Must you go already?' said Mrs Sunbury, rising to her feet. 'It's been a pleasure, I'm sure.'

'Pretty little thing,' said Mr Sunbury tentatively after the young things had left.

'Pretty my foot. All that paint and powder. You take my word for it, she'd look very different with her face washed and without a perm. Common, that's what she is, common as dirt.'

An hour later Herbert came back. He was angry.

'Look here, Mum, what d'you mean by treating the poor girl like that? I was simply ashamed of you.'

'Don't talk to your mother like that, Herbert,' she flared up. 'You didn't ought to have brought a woman like that into my house. Common, she is, common as dirt.'

When Mrs Sunbury got angry not only did her grammar grow shaky, but she wasn't quite safe on her aitches. Herbert took no notice of what she said.

'She said she'd never been so insulted in her life. I had a rare job pacifying her.'

'Well, she's never coming here again, I tell you that straight.'

'That's what you think. I'm engaged to her, so put that in your pipe and smoke it.'

Mrs Sunbury gasped.

'You're not?'

'Yes, I am. I've been thinking about it for a long time, and then she was so upset tonight I felt sorry for her, so I popped the question and I had a rare job persuading her, I can tell you.'

'You fool,' screamed Mrs Sunbury. 'You fool.'

There was quite a scene then. Mrs Sunbury and her son went at it hammer and tongs, and when poor Samuel tried to intervene they both told him roughly to shut up. At last Herbert flung out of the room and out of the house and Mrs Sunbury burst into angry tears.

No reference was made next day to what had passed. Mrs Sunbury was frigidly polite to Herbert and he was sullen and silent. After supper he went out. On Saturday he told his father and mother that he was engaged that afternoon and wouldn't be able to come to the common with them.

'I dare say we shall be able to do without you,' said Mrs Sunbury grimly.

It was getting on to the time for their usual fortnight at the seaside. They always went to Herne Bay, because Mrs Sunbury said you had a nice class of people there, and for years they had taken the same lodgings. One evening, in as casual a way as he could, Herbert said:

'By the way, Mum, you'd better write and tell them I shan't be wanting my room this year. Betty and me are getting married and we're going to Southend for the honeymoon.'

For a moment there was dead silence in the room.

'Bit sudden-like, isn't it, Herbert?' said Mr Sunbury uneasily.

'Well, they're cutting down at Betty's office and she's out of a job, so we thought we'd better get married at once. We've taken two rooms in Dabney Street and we're furnishing out of my Savings Bank money.'

Mrs Sunbury didn't say a word. She went deathly pale and tears rolled down her thin cheeks.

'Oh, come on, Mum, don't take it so hard,' said Herbert. 'A fellow has to marry sometime. If Dad hadn't married you, I shouldn't be here now, should I?'

Mrs Sunbury brushed her tears away with an impatient hand.

'Your dad didn't marry me; I married 'im. I knew he was steady and respectable. I knew he'd make a good 'usband and father. I've never 'ad cause to regret it and no more 'as your dad. That's right, Samuel, isn't it?'

'Right as rain, Beatrice,' he said quickly.

'You know, you'll like Betty when you get to know her. She's a nice girl, she is really. I believe you'd find you had a lot in common. You must give her a chance, Mum.'

'She's never going to set foot in this house only over my dead body.'

'That's absurd, Mum. Why, everything'll be just the same if you'll only be reasonable. I mean, we can go flying on Saturday afternoons same as we always did. Just this time I've been engaged it's been difficult. You see, she can't see what there is in kite-flying, but she'll come round to it, and after I'm married it'll be different, I mean I can come and fly with you and Dad; that stands to reason.'

'That's what you think. Well, let me tell you that if you marry that woman you're not going to fly my kite. I never gave it you, I bought it out of the housekeeping money, and it's mine, see.'

'All right then, have it your own way. Betty says it's a kid's game anyway and I ought to be ashamed of myself, flying a kite at my age.'

He got up and once more stalked angrily out of the house. A fortnight later he was married. Mrs Sunbury refused to go to the wedding and wouldn't let Samuel go either. They went for their holiday and came back. They resumed their usual round. On Saturday afternoons they went to the common by themselves and flew their enormous kite. Mrs Sunbury never mentioned her son. She was determined not to forgive him. But Mr Sunbury used to meet him on the morning train they both took and they chatted a little when they managed to get into the same carriage. One morning Mr Sunbury looked up at the sky.

'Good flying weather today,' he said.

'D'you and Mum still fly?'

'What do you think? She's getting as clever as I am. You should see her with her skirts pinned up running down the hill. I give you my word, I never knew she had it in her. Run? Why, she can run better than what I can.'

'Don't make me laugh, Dad!'

'I wonder you don't buy a kite of your own, Herbert. You've been always so keen on it.'

'I know I was. I did suggest it once, but you know what women are, Betty said: "Be your age," and oh, I don't know what all. I don't want a kid's kite, of course, and them big kites cost money. When we started to furnish Betty said it was cheaper in the long run to buy the best and so we went to one of them hire purchase places and what with paying them every month and the rent, well, I haven't got any more money than just what we can manage on. They say it doesn't cost any more to keep two than one, well, that's not my experience so far.'

'Isn't she working?'

'Well, no, she says after working for donkeys' years as you might say, now she's married she's going to take it easy, and of course someone's got to keep the place clean and do the cooking.'

So it went on for six months, and then one Saturday afternoon when the Sunburys were as usual on the common Mrs Sunbury said to her husband:

'Did you see what I saw, Samuel?'

'I saw Herbert, if that's what you mean. I didn't mention it because I thought it would only upset you.'

'Don't speak to him. Pretend you haven't seen him.'

Herbert was standing among the idle lookers-on. He made no attempt to speak to his parents, but it did not escape Mrs Sunbury that he followed with all his eyes the flight of the big kite he had flown so often. It began to grow chilly and the Sunburys went home. Mrs Sunbury's face was brisk with malice.

'I wonder if he'll come next Saturday,' said Samuel.

'If I didn't think betting was wrong I'd bet you sixpence he will, Samuel. I've been waiting for this all along.'

'You have?'

'I knew from the beginning he wouldn't be able to keep away from it.'

She was right. On the following Saturday and on every Saturday after that when the weather was fine Herbert turned up on the common. No intercourse passed. He just stood there for a while looking on and then strolled away. But after things had been going on like this for several weeks, the Sunburys had a surprise for him. They weren't flying the big kite which he was used to, but a new one, a box-kite, a small one, on the model for which he had made the designs himself. He saw it was creating a lot of interest among the other kite-flyers; they were standing round it and Mrs Sunbury was talking volubly. The first time Samuel ran down the hill with it the thing didn't rise, but flopped miserably on the ground, and Herbert clenched his hands and ground his teeth. He couldn't bear to see it fail. Mr Sunbury climbed up the little hill again, and the second time the box-kite took the air. There was a cheer among the bystanders. After a while Mr Sunbury pulled it down and walked back with it to the hill. Mrs Sunbury went up to her son.

'Like to have a try, Herbert?'

He caught his breath.

'Yes, Mum, I should.'

'It's just a small one because they say you have to get the knack of it. It's not like the old-fashioned sort. But we've got specifications for a big one, and they say when you get to know about it and the wind's right you can go up to two miles with it.'

Mr Sunbury joined them.

'Samuel, Herbert wants to try the kite.'

Mr Sunbury handed it to him, a pleased smile on his face, and Herbert gave his mother his hat to hold. Then he raced down the hill, the kite took the air beautifully, and as he watched it rise his heart was filled with exultation. It was grand to see that little black thing soaring so sweetly, but even as he watched it he thought of the great big one they were having made. They'd never be able to manage that. Two miles in the air, mum had said. Whew!

'Why don't you come back and have a cup of tea, Herbert,' said Mrs Sunbury, 'and we'll show you the designs for the new one they want to build for us. Perhaps you could make some suggestions.'

He hesitated. He'd told Betty he was just going for a walk to stretch his legs, she didn't know he'd been coming to the common every week, and she'd be waiting for him. But the temptation was irresistible.

'I don't mind if I do,' he said.

After tea they looked at the specifications. The kite was huge, with gadgets he had never seen before, and it would cost a lot of money.

'You'll never be able to fly it by yourselves,' he said.

'We can try.'

'I suppose you wouldn't like me to help you just at first?' he asked uncertainly.

'Mightn't be a bad idea,' said Mrs Sunbury.

It was late when he got home, much later than he thought, and Betty was vexed.

'Wherever have you been, Herb? I thought you were dead. Supper's waiting and everything.'

'I met some fellows and got talking.'

She gave him a sharp look, but didn't answer. She sulked.

After supper he suggested they should go to a movie, but she refused.

'You go if you want to,' she said. 'I don't care to.'

On the following Saturday he went again to, the common and again his mother let him fly the kite. They had ordered the new one and expected to get it in three weeks. Present his mother said to him:

'Elizabeth is here.'

'Betty?'

'Spying on you.'

It gave him a nasty turn, but he put on a bold front.

'Let her spy. I don't care.'

But he was nervous and wouldn't go back to tea with his parents. He went straight home. Betty was waiting for him.

'So that's the fellows you got talking to. I've been suspicious for some time, you going for a walk on Saturday afternoon, and all of a sudden I tumbled to it. Flying a kite, you, a grown man. Contemptible I call it.'

'I don't care what you call it. I like it, and if you don't like it you can lump it.'

'I won't have it and I tell you that straight. I'm not going to have you make a fool of yourself.'

'I've flown a kite every Saturday afternoon ever since I was a kid, and I'm going to fly a kite as long as ever I want to.'

'It's that old bitch, she's just trying to get you away from me. I know her. If you were a man you'd never speak to her again, not after the way she's treated me.'

'I won't have you call her that. She's my mother and I've got the right to see her as often as ever I want to.'

The quarrel went on hour after hour. Betty screamed at him and Herbert shouted at her. They had had trifling disagreements before, because they were both obstinate, but this was the first serious row they had had. They didn't speak to one another on the Sunday, and during the rest of the week, though outwardly there was peace between them, their ill-feeling rankled. It happened that the next two Saturdays it poured with rain. Betty smiled to herself when she saw the downpour, but if Herbert was disappointed he gave no sign of it. The recollection of their quarrel grew dim. Living in two rooms as they did, sleeping in the same bed, it was inevitable that they should agree to forget their differences. Betty went out of her way to be nice to her Herb, and she thought that now she had given him a taste of her tongue and he knew she wasn't going to be put upon by anyone, he'd be reasonable. He was a good husband in his way, generous with his money and steady. Give her time and she'd manage him all right.

But after a fortnight of bad weather it cleared.

'Looks as if we're going to have good flying weather tomorrow,' said Mr Sunbury as they met on the platform to await their morning train. 'The new kite's come.'

'It has?'

'Your mum says of course we'd like you to come and help us with it, but no one's got the right to come between a man and his wife, and if you're afraid of Betty, her kicking up a rumpus, I mean, you'd better not come. There's a young fellow we've got to know on the common who's just mad about it, and he says he'll get it to fly if anybody can.'

Herbert was seized with a pang of jealousy.

'Don't you let any strangers touch our kite. I'll be there all right.'

'Well, you think it over, Herbert, and if you don't come we shall quite understand.'

'I'll come,' said Herbert.

So next day when he got back from the City he changed from his business clothes into slacks and an old coat. Betty came into the bedroom.

'What are you doing?'

'Changing,' he answered gaily. He was so excited, he couldn't keep the secret to himself. 'Their new kite's come and I'm going to fly it.'

'Oh, no, you're not,' she said. 'I won't have it.'

'Don't be a fool, Betty. I'm going, I tell you, and if you don't like it you can do the other thing.'

'I'm not going to let you, so that's that.'

She shut the door and stood in front of it. Her eyes flashed and her jaw was set. She was a little thing and he was a tall strong man. He took hold of her two arms to push her out of the way, but she kicked him violently on the shin.

'D'you want me to give you a sock on the jaw?'

'If you go you don't come back,' she shouted.

He caught her up, though she struggled and kicked, threw her on to the bed and went out.

If the small box-kite had caused an excitement on the common it was nothing to what the new one caused. But it was was difficult to manage, and though they ran and panted and other enthusiastic flyers helped them Herbert couldn't get it up.

'Never mind,' he said, 'we'll get the knack of it presently. The wind's not right today, that's all.'

He went back to tea with his father and mother and they talked it over just as they had talked in the old days. He delayed going because he didn't fancy the scene Betty would make him, but when Mrs Sunbury went into the kitchen to get supper ready he had to go home. Betty was reading the paper. She looked up.

'Your bag's packed,' she said.

'My what?'

'You heard what I said. I said if you went you needn't come back. I forgot about your things. Everything's packed. It's in the bedroom.'

He looked at her for a moment with surprise. She pretended to be reading again. He would have liked to give her a good hiding.

'All right, have it your own way,' he said.

He went into the bedroom. His clothes were packed in a suitcase, and there was a brown-paper parcel in which Betty had put whatever was left over. He took the bag in one hand, the parcel in the other, walked through the sitting-room without a word and out of the house. He walked to his mother's and rang the bell. She opened the door.

'I've come home, Mum,' he said.

'Have you, Herbert? Your room's ready for you. Put your things down and come in. We were just sitting down to supper.' They went into the dining-room. 'Samuel, Herbert's come home. Run out and get a quart of beer.'

Over supper and during the rest of the evening he told them the trouble he had had with Betty.

'Well, you're well out of it, Herbert,' said Mrs Sunbury when he had finished. 'I told you she was no wife for you. Common she is, common as dirt, and you who's always been brought up so nice.'

He found it good to sleep in his own bed, the bed he'd been used to all his life, and to come down to breakfast on the Sunday morning, unshaved and unwashed, and read the *News of the World.*

'We won't go to chapel this morning,' said Mrs Sunbury. 'It's been an upset to you, Herbert; we'll all take it easy today.'

During the week they talked a lot about the kite, but they also talked a lot about Betty. They discussed what she would do next.

'She'll try and get you back,' said Mrs Sunbury.

'A fat chance she's got of doing that,' said Herbert.

'You'll have to provide for her,' said his father.

'Why should he do that?' cried Mrs Sunbury. 'She trapped him into marrying her and now she's turned him out of the home he made for her.'

'I'll give her what's right as long as she leaves me alone.'

He was feeling more comfortable every day, in fact he was beginning to feel as if he's never been away, he settled in like a dog in its own particular basket; it was nice having his mother to brush his clothes and mend his socks; she gave him the sort of things he'd always eaten and liked best; Betty was a scrappy sort of cook, it had been fun just at first, like picnicking, but it wasn't the sort of eating a man could get his teeth into, and he could never get over his mother's idea that fresh food was better than the stuff you bought in tins. He got sick of the sight of tinned salmon. Then it was nice to have space to move about in rather than be cooped up in two small rooms, one of which had to serve as a kitchen as well.

'I never made a bigger mistake in my life than when I left home, Mum,' he said to her once.

'I know that, Herbert, but you're back now and you've got no cause ever to leave it again.'

His salary was paid on Friday and in the evening when they had just finished supper the bell rang.

'That's her,' they said with one voice.

Herbert went pale. His mother gave him a glance.

'You leave it to me,' she said. 'I'll see her.'

She opened the door. Betty was standing on the threshold. She tried to push her way in, but Mrs Sunbury prevented her.

'I want to see Herb.'

'You can't. He's out.'

'No, he isn't. I watched him go in with his dad and he hasn't come out again.'

'Well, he doesn't want to see you, and if you start making a disturbance I'll call the police.'

'I want my week's money.'

'That's all you've ever wanted of him.' She took out her purse. 'There's thirty-five shillings for you.'

'Thirty-five shillings? The rent's twelve shillings a week.'

'That's all you're going to get. He's got to pay his board here, hasn't he?'

'And then there's the instalments on the furniture.'

'We'll see about that when the time comes. D'you want the money or don't you?'

Confused, unhappy, browbeaten, Betty stood irresolutely. Mrs Sunbury thrust the money in her hand and slammed the door in her face. She went back to the dining-room.

'I've settled her hash all right,' she said.

The bell rang again, it rang repeatedly, but they did not answer it, and presently it stopped. They guessed that Betty had gone away.

It was fine next day, with just the right velocity in the wind, and Herbert, after failing two or three times, found he had got the knack of flying the big box-kite. It soared into the air and up and up as he unreeled the wire.

'Why, it's a mile up if it's a yard,' he told his mother excitedly.

He had never had such a thrill in his life.

Several weeks passed by. They concocted a letter for Herbert to write in which he told Betty that so long as she didn't molest him or members of his family she would receive a postal order for thirty-five shillings every Saturday morning and he would pay the instalments on the furniture as they came due. Mrs Sunbury had been much against this, but Mr Sunbury, for once at variance with her, and Herbert agreed that it was the right thing to do. Herbert by then had learnt the ways of the new kite and was able to do great things with it. He no longer bothered to have contests with the other kite-flyers. He was out of their class. Saturday afternoons were his moments of glory. He revelled in the admiration he aroused in the bystanders and enjoyed the envy he knew he excited in the less fortunate flyers. Then one evening when he was walking back from the station with his father Betty waylaid him.

'Hullo, Herb,' she said.

'Hullo.'

'I want to talk to my husband alone, Mr Sunbury.'

'There's nothing you've got to say to me that my dad can't hear,' said Herbert sullenly.

She hesitated. Mr Sunbury fidgeted. He didn't know whether to stay or go.

'All right, then,' she said. 'I want you to come back home, Herb. I didn't mean it that night when I packed your bag. I only did it to frighten you. I was in a temper. I'm sorry for what I did. It's all so silly, quarrelling about a kite.'

'Well, I'm not coming back, see. When you turned me out you did me the best turn you ever did me.'

Tears began to trickle down Betty's cheeks.

'But I love you, Herb. If you want to fly your silly old kite, you fly it, I don't care so long as you come back.'

'Thank you very much, but it's not good enough. I know when I'm well off and I've had enough of married life to last me a lifetime. Come on, Dad.'

They walked on quickly and Betty made no attempt to follow them. On the following Sunday they went to chapel and after dinner Herbert went to the coal-shed where he kept the kite to have a look at it. He just couldn't keep away from it. He doted on it. In a minute he rushed back, his face white, with a hatchet in his hand.

'She's smashed it up. She did it with this.'

The Sunburys gave a cry of consternation and hurried to the coal-shed. What Herbert had said was true. The kite, the new expensive kite, was in fragments. It had been savagely attacked with the hatchet, the woodwork was all in pieces, the reel was hacked to bits.

'She must have done it while we were at chapel. Watched us go out, that's what she did.'

'But how did she get in?' asked Mr Sunbury.

'I had two keys. When I came home I noticed one was missing, but I didn't think anything about it.'

'You can't be sure she did it, some of them fellows on the common have been very snooty, I wouldn't put it past them to have done this.'

'Well, we'll soon find out,' said Herbert. 'I'll go and ask her, and if she did it I'll kill her.'

His rage was so terrible that Mrs Sunbury was frightened.

'And get yourself hung for murder? No, Herbert, I won't let you go. Let your dad go, and when he comes back we'll decide what to do.'

'That's right, Herbert, let me go.'

They had a job to persuade him, but in the end Mr Sunbury went. And in half an hour he came back.

'She did it all right. She told me straight out. She's proud of it. I won't repeat her language, it fair startled me, but the long and short of it was she was jealous of the kite. She said Herbert loved the kite more than he loved her and so she smashed it up and if she had to do it again she'd do it again.'

'Lucky she didn't tell me that. I'd have wrung her neck even if I'd had to swing for it. Well, she never gets another penny out of me, that's all.'

'She'll sue you,' said his father.

'Let her.'

'The instalment on the furniture is due next week, Herbert,' said Mrs Sunbury quietly. 'In your place I wouldn't pay it.'

'Then they'll just take it away,' said Samuel, 'and all the money he's paid on it so far will be wasted.'

'Well, what of it?' she answered. 'He can afford it. He's rid of her for good and all and we've got him back and that's the chief thing.'

'I don't care twopence about the money,' said Herbert. 'I can see her face when they come to take the furniture away. It meant a lot to her, it did, and the piano, she set a rare store on that piano.'

So on the following Friday he did not send Betty her weekly money, and when she sent him on a letter from the furniture people to say that if he didn't pay the instalment due by such and such a date they would remove it, he wrote back and said he wasn't in a position to continue the payments and they could remove the furniture at their convenience. Betty took to waiting for him at the station, and when he wouldn't speak to her followed him down the street screaming curses at him. In the evenings she would come to the house and ring the bell till they thought they would go mad, and Mr and Mrs Sunbury had the greatest difficulty in preventing Herbert from going out and giving her a sound thrashing. Once she threw a stone and broke the sitting-room window. She wrote obscene and abusive postcards to him at his office. At last she went to the magistrate's court and complained that her husband had left her and wasn't providing for her support. Herbert received a summons. They both told their story and if the magistrate thought it a strange one he didn't say so. He tried to effect a reconciliation between them, but Herbert resolutely refused to go back to his wife. The magistrate ordered him to pay Betty twenty-five shillings a week. He said he wouldn't pay it.

'Then you'll go to prison,' said the magistrate. 'Next case.'

But Herbert meant what he said. On Betty's complaint he was brought once more before the magistrate, who asked him what reason he had for not obeyng the order.

'I said I wouldn't pay her and I won't, not after she smashed my kite. And if you send me to prison I'll go to prison.'

The magistrate was stern with him this time.

'You're a very foolish young man,' he said. 'I'll give you a week to pay the arrears, and if I have any more nonsense from you you'll go to prison till you come to your senses.'

Herbert didn't pay, and that is how my friend Ned Preston came to know him and I heard the story.

'What d'you make of it?' asked Ned as he finished. 'You know, Betty isn't a bad girl. I've seen her several times, there's nothing wrong with her except her insane jealousy of Herbert's kite; and he isn't a fool by any means. In fact he's smarter than the average. What d'you suppose there is in kite-flying that makes the damned fool so mad about it?'

'I don't know,' I answered. I took my time to think. 'You see, I don't know a thing about flying a kite. Perhaps it gives him a sense of power as he watches it soaring towards the clouds and of mastery over the elements as he seems to bend the winds of heaven to his will. It may be that in some queer way he identifies himself with the kite flying so free and so high above him, and it's as it were an escape from the monotony of life. It may be that in some dim, confused way it represents an ideal of freedom and adventure. And you know, when a man once gets bitten with the virus of the ideal not all the King's doctors and not all the King's surgeons can rid him of it. But all this is very fanciful and I dare say it's just stuff and nonsense. I think you'd better put your problem before someone who knows a lot more about the psychology of the human animal than I do.'

A Woman of Fifty

◆

My friend Wyman Holt is a professor of English Literature in one of the smaller universities of the Middle West, and hearing that I was speaking in a near-by city–near-by as distances go in the vastness of America–he wrote to ask me if I would come and give a talk to his class. He suggested that I should stay with him for a few days so that he could show me something of the surrounding country. I accepted the invitation, but told him that my engagements would prevent me from spending more than a couple of nights with him. He met me at the station, drove me to his house, and after we had had a drink we walked over to the campus. I was somewhat taken aback to find so many people in the hall in which I was to speak, for I had not expected more than twenty at the outside and I was not prepared to give a solemn lecture, but only an informal chat. I was more than a little intimidated to see a number of middle-aged and elderly persons, some of whom I suspected were members of the faculty, and I was afraid they would find what I had to say very superficial. However, there was nothing to do but to start and, after Wyman had introduced me to the audience in a manner that I very well knew I couldn't live up to, that is what I did. I said my say, I answered as best I could a number of questions, and then I retired with Wyman into a little room at the back of the stage from which I had spoken.

Several people came in. They said the usual kindly things to me that are said on these occasions, and I made the usual polite replies. I was thirsting for a drink. Then a woman came in and held out her hand to me.

'How very nice it is to see you again,' she said. 'It's years since we last met.'

To the best of my belief I'd never set eyes on her before. I forced a cordial smile to my tired, stiff lips, shook her proffered hand effusively and wondered who the devil she was. My professor must have seen from my face that I was trying to place her, for he said:

'Mrs Greene is married to a member of our faculty and she gives a course on the Renaissance and Italian literature.'

'Really,' I said. 'Interesting.'

I was no wiser than before.

'Has Wyman told you that you're dining with us tomorrow night?'

'I'm very glad,' I said.

'It's not a party. Only my husband, his brother, and my sister-in-law. I suppose Florence has changed a lot since then.'

'Florence?' I said to myself. 'Florence?'

That was evidently where I'd known her. She was a woman of about fifty with grey hair simply done and marcelled without exaggeration. She was a trifle too stout and she was dressed neatly enough, but without distinction, in a dress that I guessed had been bought ready-made at the local branch of a big store. She had rather large eyes of a pale blue and a poor complexion; she wore no rouge and had used a lipstick but sparingly. She seemed a nice creature. There was something maternal in her demeanour, something placid and fulfilled, which I found appealing. I supposed that I had run across her on one of my frequent visits to Florence and because it was perhaps the only time she had been there our meeting made more of an impression on her than on me. I must confess that my acquaintance with the wives of members of a faculty is very limited, but she was just the sort of person I should have expected the wife of a professor to be, and picturing her life, useful but uneventful, on scanty means, with its little social gatherings, its bickerings, its gossip, its busy dullness, I could easily imagine that her trip to Florence must linger with her as a thrilling and unforgettable experience.

On the way back to his house Wyman said to me:

'You'll like Jasper Greene. He's clever.'

'What's he a professor of?'

'He's not a professor; he's an instructor. A fine scholar. He's her second husband. She was married to an Italian before.'

'Oh?' That didn't chime in with my ideas at all. 'What was her name?'

'I haven't a notion. I don't believe it was a great success.' Wyman chuckled. 'That's only a deduction I draw from the fact that she hasn't a single thing in the house to suggest that she ever spent any time in Italy. I should have expected her to have at least a refectory table, an old chest or two, and an embroidered cope hanging on the wall.'

I laughed. I knew those rather dreary pieces that people buy when they're in Italy, the gilt wooden candlesticks, the Venetian glass mirrors, and the high-backed, comfortless chairs. They look well enough when you see them in the crowded shops of the dealers in antiques, but when you bring them to another country they're too often a sad disappointment. Even if they're genuine, which they seldom are, they look ill-at-ease and out of place.

'Laura has money,' Wyman went on. 'When they married she furnished the house from cellar to attic in Chicago. It's quite a show place; it's a little masterpiece of hideousness and vulgarity. I never go into the living-room without marvelling at the unerring taste with which she picked out exactly what you'd expect to find in the bridal suite of a second-class hotel in Atlantic City.'

To explain this irony I should state that Wyman's living-room was all chromium and glass, rough modern fabrics, with a boldly Cubist rug on the floor, and on the walls Picasso prints and drawings by Tchelicheff. However, he gave me a very good dinner. We spent the evening chatting pleasantly about things that mutually interested us and finished it with a couple of bottles of beer. I went to bed in a room of somewhat aggressive modernity. I read for a while and then putting out the light composed myself to sleep.

'Laura?' I said to myself. 'Laura what?'

I tried to think back. I thought of all the people I knew in Florence, hoping that by association I might recall when and where I had come in contact with Mrs Greene. Since I was going to dine with her I wanted to recall something that would prove that I had not forgotten her. People look upon it as a slight if you don't remember them. I suppose we all attach a sort of importance to ourselves, and it is humiliating to realize that we have left no impression at all upon the persons we have associated with. I dozed off, but before I fell into the blessedness of deep sleep, my subconscious, released from the effort of striving at recollection, I suppose, grew active and I was suddenly wide awake, for I remembered who Laura Greene was. It was no wonder that I had forgotten her, for it was twenty-five years since I had seen her, and then only haphazardly during a month I spent in Florence.

It was just after the First World War. She had been engaged to a man who was killed in it and she and her mother had managed to get over to France to see his grave. They were San Francisco people. After doing their sad errand they had come down to Italy and were spending the winter in Florence. At that time there was quite a large colony of English and Americans. I had some American friends, a Colonel Harding and his wife, colonel because he had occupied an important position in the Red Cross, who had a handsome villa in the Via Bolognese, and they asked me to stay with them. I spent most of my mornings sightseeing and met my friends at Doney's in the Via Tornabuoni round about noon to drink a cocktail. Doney's was the gathering-place of everybody one knew, Americans, English, and such of the Italians as frequented their society. There you heard all the gossip of the town. There was generally a lunch-party either at a restaurant or at one or other of the villas with their fine old gardens a mile or two from the centre of the city. I had been given a card to the Florence Club, and in the afternoon Charley Harding and I used to go there to play bridge or a dangerous game of poker with a pack of thirty-two cards. In the evening there would be a dinner-party with more bridge perhaps and often dancing. One met the same people all the time, but the group was large enough, the people sufficiently various, to prevent it from being tedious. Everyone was more or less interested in the arts, as was only right and proper in Florence, so that, idle as life seemed, it was not entirely frivolous.

Laura and her mother, Mrs Clayton, a widow, lived in one of the better boarding-houses. They appeared to be comfortably off. They had come to Florence with letters of introduction and soon made many friends. Laura's story appealed to their sympathies, and people were glad on that account to do what they could for the two women, but they were in themselves nice and quickly became liked for themselves. They were hospitable and gave frequent lunches at one or other of the restaurants where one ate macaroni and the inevitable scaloppini, and drank Chianti. Mrs Clayton was perhaps a little lost in this cosmopolitan society, where matters that were strange to her were seriously or gaily talked about, but Laura took to it as though it were her native element. She engaged an Italian woman to teach her the language and soon was reading the *Inferno* with her; she devoured books on the art of the Renaissance and on Florentine history, and I sometimes came across her,

Baedeker in hand, at the Uffizzi or in some church studiously examining works
of art.

She was twenty-four or twenty-five then and I was well over forty, so that
though we often met we became cordially acquainted rather than intimate. She
was by no means beautiful, but she was comely in rather an unusual way; she
had an oval face with bright blue eyes and very dark hair which she wore very
simply, parted in the middle, drawn over her ears and tied in a chignon low on
the nape of her neck. She had a good skin and naturally high colour; her
features were good without being remarkable, and her teeth were even, small,
and white; but her chief asset was her easy grace of movement, and I was not
surprised when they told me that she danced 'divinely'. Her figure was very
good, somewhat fuller than was the fashion of the moment; and I think what
made her attractive was the odd mingling in her appearance of the Madonna in
an altar-piece by one of the later Italian painters and a suggestion of sensuality.
It certainly made her very alluring to the Italians who gathered at Doney's in
the morning or were occasionally invited to lunch or dinner in the American or
English villas. She was evidently accustomed to dealing with amorous young
men, for though she was charming, gracious, and friendly with them she kept
them at their distance. She quickly discovered that they were all looking for an
American heiress who would restore the family fortunes, and with a demure
amusement which I found admirable made them delicately understand that she
was far from rich. They sighed a little and turned their attentions at Doney's,
which was their happy hunting-ground, to more likely objects. They continued
to dance with her, and to keep their hand in flirted with her, but their
aspirations ceased to be matrimonial.

But there was one young man who persisted. I knew him slightly because he
was one of the regular poker-players at the club. I played occasionally. It was
impossible to win and the disgruntled foreigners used sometimes to say that the
Italians ganged up on us, but it may be only that they knew the particular game
they played better than we did. Laura's admirer, Tito di San Pietro, was a bold
and even reckless player and would often lose sums he could ill afford. (That
was not his real name, but I call him that since his own is famous in Florentine
history.) He was a good-looking youth, neither short nor tall, with fine black
eyes, thick black hair brushed back from his forehead and shining with oil, an
olive skin, and features of classical regularity. He was poor and he had some
vague occupation, which did not seem to interfere with his amusements, but he
was always beautifully dressed. No one quite knew where he lived, in a
furnished room perhaps or in the attic of some relation; and all that remained of
his ancestors' great possessions was a Cinquecento villa about thirty miles from
the city. I never saw it, but I was told that it was of amazing beauty, with a great
neglected garden of cypresses and live oaks, overgrown borders of box,
terraces, artificial grottoes, and crumbling statues. His widowed father, the
count, lived there alone and subsisted on the wine he made from the vines
of the small property he still owned and the oil from his olive trees. He seldom
came to Florence, so I never met him, but Charley Harding knew him fairly
well.

'He's a perfect specimen of the Tuscan nobleman of the old school,' he said.
'He was in the diplomatic service in his youth and he knows the world. He has
beautiful manners and such an air, you almost feel he's doing you a favour when
he says how d'you do to you. He's a brilliant talker. Of course he hasn't a penny,
he squandered the little he inherited on gambling and women, but he bears his

poverty with great dignity. He acts as though money were something beneath his notice.'

'What sort of age is he?' I asked.

'Fifty, I should say, but he's still the handsomest man I've ever seen in my life.'

'Oh?'

'You describe him, Bessie. When he first came here he made a pass at Bessie. I've never been quite sure how far it went.'

'Don't be a fool, Charley,' Mrs Harding laughed.

She gave him the sort of look a woman gives her husband when she has been married to him many years and is quite satisfied with him.

'He's very attractive to women and he knows it,' she said. 'When he talks to you he gives you the impression that you're the only woman in the world and of course it's flattering. But it's only a game and a woman would have to be a perfect fool to take him seriously. He *is* very handsome. Tall and spare and he holds himself well. He has great dark liquid eyes, like the boy's; his hair is snow-white, but very thick still, and the contrast with his bronzed, young face is really breath-taking. He has a ravaged, rather battered look, but at the same time a look of such distinction, it's really quite incredibly romantic.'

'He also has his great dark liquid eyes on the main chance,' said Charley Harding dryly. 'And he'll never let Tito marry a girl who has no more money than Laura.'

'She has about five thousand dollars a year of her own,' said Bessie. 'And she'll get that much more when her mother dies.'

'Her mother can live for another thirty years, and five thousand a year won't go far to keep a husband, a father, and two or three children, and restore a ruined villa with practically not a stick of furniture in it.'

'I think the boy's desperately in love with her.'

'How old is he?' I asked.

'Twenty-six.'

A few days after this Charley, on coming back to lunch, since for once we were lunching by ourselves, told me that he had run across Mrs Clayton in the Via Tornabuoni and she had said that she and Laura were driving out that afternoon with Tito to meet his father and see the villa.

'What d'you suppose that means?' asked Bessie.

'My guess is that Tito is taking Laura to be inspected by his old man, and if he approves he's going to ask her to marry him.'

'And will he approve?'

'Not on your life.'

But Charley was wrong. After the two women had been shown over the house they were taken for a walk round the garden. Without exactly knowing how it had happened Mrs Clayton found herself alone in an alley with the old count. She spoke no Italian, but he had been an attaché in London and his English was tolerable.

'Your daughter is charming, Mrs Clayton,' he said. 'I am not surprised that my Tito has fallen in love with her.'

Mrs Clayton was no fool and it may be that she too had guessed why the young man had asked them to go and see the ancestral villa.

'Young Italians are very impressionable. Laura is sensible enough not to take their attention too seriously.'

'I was hoping she was not quite indifferent to the boy.'

'I have no reason to believe that she likes him any more than any other of the young men who dance with her,' Mrs Clayton answered somewhat coldly. 'I think I should tell you at once that my daughter has a very moderate income and she will have no more till I die.'

'I will be frank with you. I have nothing in the world but this house and the few acres that surround it. My son could not afford to marry a penniless girl, but he is not a fortune-hunter and he loves your daughter.'

The count had not only the grand manner, but a great deal of charm and Mrs Clayton was not insensible to it. She softened a little.

'All that is neither here nor there. We don't arrange our children's marriages in America. If Tito wants to marry her, let him ask her, and if she's prepared to marry him she'll presumably say so.'

'Unless I am greatly mistaken that is just what he is doing now. I hope with all my heart that he will be successful.'

They strolled on and presently saw walking towards them the two young people hand in hand. It was not difficult to guess what had passed. Tito kissed Mrs Clayton's hand and his father on both cheeks.

'Mrs Clayton, Papa, Laura has consented to be my wife.'

The engagement made something of a stir in Florentine society and a number of parties were given for the young couple. It was quite evident that Tito was very much in love, but less so that Laura was. He was good-looking, adoring, high-spirited, and gay; it was likely enough that she loved him; but she was a girl who did not display emotion and she remained what she had always been, somewhat placid, amiable, serious but friendly, and easy to talk to. I wondered to what extent she had been influenced to accept Tito's offer by his great name, with its historical associations, and the sight of that beautiful house with its lovely view and the romantic garden.

'Anyhow there's no doubt about its being a love match on his side,' said Bessie Harding, when we were talking it over. 'Mrs Clayton tells me that neither Tito nor his father has shown any desire to know how much Laura has.'

'I'd bet a million dollars that they know to the last cent what she's got and they've calculated exactly how much it comes to in *lire*,' said Harding with a grunt.

'You're a beastly old man, darling,' she answered.

He gave another grunt.

Shortly after that I left Florence. The marriage took place from the Hardings' house and a vast crowd came to it, ate their food and drank their champagne. Tito and his wife took an apartment on the Lungarno and the old count returned to his lonely villa in the hills. I did not go to Florence again for three years and then only for a week. I was staying once more with the Hardings. I asked about my old friends and then remembered Laura and her mother.

'Mrs Clayton went back to San Francisco,' said Bessie, 'and Laura and Tito live at the villa with the count. They're very happy.'

'Any babies?'

'No.'

'Go on,' said Harding.

Bessie gave her husband a look.

'I cannot imagine why I've lived thirty years with a man I dislike so much,' she said. 'They gave up the apartment on the Lungarno. Laura spent a good deal of money doing things to the villa, there wasn't a bathroom in it, she put in central heating, and she had to buy a lot of furniture to make it habitable, and then Tito lost a small fortune playing poker and poor Laura had to pay up.'

'Hadn't he got a job?'

'It didn't amount to anything and it came to an end.'

'What Bessie means by that is that he was fired,' Harding put in.

'Well, to cut a long story short, they thought it would be more economical to live at the villa and Laura had the idea that it would keep Tito out of mischief. She loves the garden and she's made it lovely. Tito simply worships her and the old count's taken quite a fancy to her. So really it's all turned out very well.'

'It may interest you to know that Tito was in last Thursday,' said Harding. 'He played like a madman and I don't know how much he lost.'

'Oh, Charley. He promised Laura he'd never play again.'

'As if a gambler ever kept a promise like that. It'll be like last time. He'll burst into tears and say he loves her and it's a debt of honour and unless he can get the money he'll blow his brains out. And Laura will pay as she paid before.'

'He's weak, poor dear, but that's his only fault. Unlike most Italian husbands he's absolutely faithful to her and he's kindness itself.' She looked at Harding with a sort of humorous grimness. 'I've yet to find a husband who was perfect.'

'You'd better start looking around pretty soon, dear, or it'll be too late,' he retorted with a grin.

I left the Hardings and returned to London. Charley Harding and I corresponded in a desultory sort of way, and about a year later I got a letter from him. He told me as usual what he had been doing in the interval, and mentioned that he had been to Montecatini for the baths and had gone with Bessie to visit friends in Rome; he spoke of the various people I knew in Florence, So-and-so had just bought a Bellini and Mrs Such-and-such had gone to America to divorce her husband. Then he went on: 'I suppose you've heard about the San Pietros. It's shaken us all and we can talk of nothing else. Laura's terribly upset, poor thing, and she's going to have a baby. The police keep on questioning her and that doesn't make it any easier for her. Of course we brought her to stay here. Tito comes up for trial in another month.'

I hadn't the faintest notion what all this was about. So I wrote at once to Harding asking him what it meant. He answered with a long letter. What he had to tell me was terrible. I will relate the bare and brutal facts as shortly as I can. I learned them partly from Harding's letter and partly from what he and Bessie told me when two years later I was with them once more.

The count and Laura took to one another at once and Tito was pleased to see how quickly they had formed an affectionate friendship, for he was as devoted to his father as he was in love with his wife. He was glad that the count began to come more often to Florence than he had been used to. They had a spare room in the apartment and on occasion he spent two or three nights with them. He and Laura would go bargain-hunting in the antique shops and buy old pieces to put in the villa. He had tact and knowledge and little by little the house, with its spacious rooms and marble floors, lost its forlorn air and became a friendly place to live in. Laura had a passion for gardening and she and the count spent long hours together planning and then supervising the workmen who were restoring the gardens to their ancient, rather stately, beauty.

Laura made light of it when Tito's financial difficulties forced them to give up the apartment in Florence; she had had enough of Florentine society by then and was not displeased to live altogether in the grand house that had belonged to his ancestors. Tito liked city life and the prospect dismayed him, but he could not complain since it was his own folly that had made it necessary for them to cut down expenses. They still had the car and he amused himself by taking long drives while his father and Laura were busy, and if they knew that now and then he went into Florence to have a flutter at the club they shut their eyes to it. So a year passed. Then, he hardly knew why, he was seized with a vague misgiving. He couldn't put his finger on anything; he had an uneasy feeling that perhaps Laura didn't care for him so much as she had at first; sometimes it seemed to him that his father was inclined to be impatient with him; they appeared to have a great deal to say to one another, but he got the impression that he was being edged out of their conversation, as though he were a child who was expected to sit still and not interrupt while his elders talked of things over his head; he had a notion that often his presence was unwelcome to them and that they were more at their ease when he was not there. He knew his father, and his reputation, but the suspicion that rose in him was so horrible that he refused to entertain it. And yet sometimes he caught a look passing between them that disconcerted him, there was a tender possessiveness in his father's eyes, a sensual complacency in Laura's, which, if he had seen it in others, would have convinced him that they were lovers. But he couldn't, he wouldn't believe that there was anything between them. The count couldn't help making love to a woman and it was likely enough that Laura felt his extraordinary fascination, but it was shameful to suppose for a moment that they, these two people he loved, had formed a criminal, almost an incestuous, connexion. He was sure that Laura had no idea that there was anything more in her feeling than the natural affection of a young, happily married woman for her father-in-law. Notwithstanding he thought it better that she should not remain in everyday contact with his father, and one day he suggested that they should go back to live in Florence. Laura and the count were astonished that he should propose such a thing and would not hear of it. Laura said that, having spent so much money on the villa, she couldn't afford to leave it, now that Laura had made it so comfortable, to live in a wretched apartment in the city. An argument started and Tito got rather excited. He took some remark of Laura's to mean that if she lived at the villa it was to keep him out of temptation. This reference to his losses at the poker-table angered him.

'You always throw your money in my face,' he said passionately. 'If I'd wanted to marry money I'd have had the sense to marry someone who had a great deal more than you.'

Laura went very pale and glanced at the count.

'You have no right to speak to Laura like that,' he said. 'You are an ill-mannered oaf.'

'I shall speak to my wife exactly as I choose.'

'You are mistaken. So long as you are in my house you will treat her with the respect which is her right and your duty.'

'When I want lessons in behaviour from you, Father, I will let you know.'

'You are very impertinent, Tito. You will kindly leave the room.'

He looked very stern and dignified, and Tito, furious and yet slightly intimidated, leapt to his feet and stalked out slamming the door behind him. He took the car and drove in to Florence. He won quite a lot of money that day (lucky at cards, unlucky in love) and to celebrate his winnings got more than a little drunk. He did not go back to the villa till the following morning. Laura was as friendly and placid as ever, but his father was somewhat cool. No reference was made to the scene. But from then on things went from bad to worse. Tito was sullen and moody, the count critical and on occasion sharp words passed between them. Laura did not interfere, but Tito gained the impression that after a dispute that had been more than acrimonious Laura interceded with his father, for the count thenceforward, refusing to be annoyed, began to treat him with the tolerant patience with which you would treat a wayward child. He convinced himself that they were acting in concert and his suspicions grew formidable. They even increased when Laura in her good-natured way, saying that it must be very dull for him to remain so much in the country, encouraged him to go more often to Florence to see his friends.

He jumped to the conclusion that she said this only to be rid of him. He began to watch them. He would enter suddenly a room in which he knew they were, expecting to catch them in a compromising position, or silently follow them to a secluded part of the garden. They were chatting unconcernedly of trivial things. Laura greeted him with a pleasant smile. He could put his finger on nothing to confirm his torturing suspicions. He started to drink. He grew nervous and irritable. He had no proof, no proof whatever, that there was anything between them, and yet in his bones he was certain that they were grossly, shockingly deceiving him. He brooded till he felt he was going mad. A dark aching fire within him consumed his being. On one of his visits to Florence he bought a pistol. He made up his mind that if he could have proof of what in his heart he was certain of, he would kill them both.

I don't know what brought on the final catastrophe. All that came out at the trial was that, driven beyond endurance, Tito had gone one night to his father's room to have it out with him. His father mocked and laughed at him. They had a furious quarrel and Tito took out his pistol and shot the count dead. Then he collapsed and fell, weeping hysterically, on his father's body; the repeated shots brought Laura and the servants rushing in. He jumped up and grabbed the pistol, to shoot himself he said afterwards, but he hesitated or they were too quick for him, and they snatched it out of his hand. The police were sent for. He spent most of his time in prison weeping; he would not eat and had to be forcibly fed; he told the examining magistrate that he had killed his father because he was his wife's lover. Laura, examined and examined again, swore that there had never been anything between the count and herself but a natural affection. The murder filled the Florentine public with horror. The Italians were convinced of her guilt, but her friends, English and American, felt that she was incapable of the crime of which she was accused. They went about saying that Tito was neurotic and insanely jealous and in his stupid way had mistaken her American freedom of behaviour for a criminal passion. On the face of it Tito's charge was absurd. Carlo di San Pietro was nearly thirty years older than she, an elderly man with white hair; who could suppose that there would have been anything between her and her father-in-law, when her husband was young, handsome, and in love with her?

It was in Harding's presence that she saw the examining magistrate and the lawyers who had been engaged to defend Tito. They had decided to plead insanity. Experts for the defence examined him and decided that he was insane, experts for the prosecution examined him and decided that he was sane. The fact that he had bought a pistol three months before he committed the dreadful crime went to prove that it was premeditated. It was discovered that he was deeply in debt and his creditors were pressing him; the only means he had of settling with them was by selling the villa, and his father's death put him in possession of it. There is no capital punishment in Italy, but murder with premeditation is punished by solitary confinement for life. On the approach of the trial the lawyers came to Laura and told her that the only way in which Tito could be saved from this was for her to admit in court that the count had been her lover. Laura went very pale. Harding protested violently. He said they had no right to ask her to perjure herself and ruin her reputation to save that shiftless, drunken gambler whom she had been so unfortunate as to marry. Laura remained silent for a while.

'Very well,' she said at last, 'if that's the only way to save him I'll do it.'

Harding tried to dissuade her, but she was decided.

'I should never have a moment's peace if I knew that Tito had to spend the rest of his life alone in a prison cell.'

And that is what happened. The trial opened. She was called and under oath stated that for more than a year her father-in-law had been her lover. Tito was declared insane and sent to an asylum. Laura wanted to leave Florence at once, but in Italy the preliminaries to a trial are endless and by then she was near her time. The Hardings insisted on her remaining with them till she was confined. She had a child, a boy, but it only lived twenty-four hours. Her plan was to go back to San Francisco and live with her mother till she could find a job, for Tito's extravagance, the money she had spent on the villa, and then the cost of the trial had seriously impoverished her.

It was Harding who told me most of this; but one day when he was at the club and I was having a cup of tea with Bessie and we were again talking over these tragic happenings she said to me:

'You know, Charley hasn't told you the whole story because he doesn't know it. I never told him. Men are funny in some ways; they're much more easily shocked than women.'

I raised my eyebrows, but said nothing.

'Just before Laura went away we had a talk. She was very low and I thought she was grieving over the loss of her baby. I wanted to say someting to help her. "You mustn't take the baby's death too hardly," I said. "As things are, perhaps it's better it died." "Why?" she said. "Think what the poor little thing's future would have been with a murderer for his father." She looked at me for a moment in that strange quiet way of hers. And then what d'you think she said?'

'I haven't a notion,' said I.

'She said: "What makes you think his father was a murderer?"

'I felt myself grow as red as a turkey-cock. I could hardly believe my ears. "Laura, what *do* you mean?" I said. "You were in court," she said. "You heard me say Carlo was my lover."'

Bessie Harding stared at me as she must have stared at Laura.

'What did you say then?' I asked.

'What was there for me to say? I said nothing. I wasn't so much horrified, I was bewildered. Laura looked at me and, believe it or not, I'm convinced there was a twinkle in her eyes. I felt a perfect fool.'

'Poor Bessie,' I smiled.

Poor Bessie, I repeated to myself now as I thought of this strange story. She and Charley were long since dead and by their death I had lost good friends. I went to sleep then, and next day Wyman Holt took me for a long drive.

We were to dine with the Greenes at seven and we reached their house on the dot. Now that I had remembered who Laura was I was filled with an immense curiosity to see her again. Wyman had exaggerated nothing. The living-room into which we went was the quintessence of commonplace. It was comfortable enough, but there was not a trace of personality in it. It might have been furnished *en bloc* by a mail-order house. It had the bleakness of a government office. I was introduced first to my host Jasper Greene and then to his brother Emery and to his brother's wife Fanny. Jasper Greene was a large, plump man with a moon face and a shock of black, coarse, unkempt hair. He wore large cellulose-rimmed spectacles. I was staggered by his youth. He could not have been much over thirty and was therefore nearly twenty years younger than Laura. His brother, Emery, a composer and teacher in a New York school of music, might have been seven or eight and twenty. His wife, a pretty little thing, was an actress for the moment out of a job. Jasper Greene mixed us some very adequate cocktails but for a trifle too much vermouth, and we sat down to dinner. The conversation was gay and even boisterous. Jasper and his brother were loud-voiced and all three of them, Jasper, Emery, and Emery's wife, were loquacious talkers. They chaffed one another, they joked and laughed; they discussed art, literature, music, and the theatre. Wyman and I joined in when we had a chance, which was not often; Laura did not try to. She sat at the head of the table, serene, with an amused, indulgent smile on her lips as she listened to their scatter-brained nonsense; it was not stupid nonsense, mind you, it was intelligent and modern, but it was nonsense all the same. There was something maternal in her attitude, and I was reminded oddly of a sleek dachshund lying quietly in the sun while she looks lazily, and yet watchfully, at her litter of puppies romping round her. I wondered whether it crossed her mind that all this chatter about art didn't amount to much when compared with those incidents of blood and passion that she remembered. But did she remember? It had all happened a long time ago and perhaps it seemed no more than a bad dream. Perhaps those commonplace surroundings were part of her deliberate effort to forget, and to be among these young people was restful to her spirit. Perhaps Jasper's clever stupidity was a comfort. After that searing tragedy it might be that she wanted nothing but the security of the humdrum.

Possibly because Wyman was an authority on the Elizabethan drama the conversation at one moment touched on that. I had already discovered that Jasper Greene was prepared to lay down the law on subjects all and sundry, and now he delivered himself as follows:

'Our theatre has gone all to pot because the dramatists of our day are afraid to deal with the violent emotions which are the proper subject matter of tragedy,' he boomed. 'In the sixteenth century they had a wealth of melodramatic and bloody themes to suit their purpose and so they produced great plays. But where can our playwrights look for themes? Our Anglo-Saxon blood is too phlegmatic, too supine, to provide them with material they can make anything of, and so they are condemned to occupy themselves with the trivialities of social intercourse.'

I wondered what Laura thought of this, but I took care not to catch her eye. She could have told them a story of illicit love, jealousy, and parricide which would have been meat to one of Shakespeare's successors, but had he treated it, I suppose he would have felt bound to finish it with at least one more corpse strewn about the stage. The end of her story, as I knew it now, was unexpected certainly, but sadly prosaic and a trifle grotesque. Real life more often ends things with a whimper than with a bang. I wondered too why she had gone out of her way to renew our old acquaintance. Of course she had no reason to suppose that I knew as much as I did; perhaps with a true instinct she was confident that I would not give her away; perhaps she didn't care if I did. I stole a glance at her now and then while she was quietly listening to the excited babbling of the three young people, but her friendly, pleasant face told me nothing. If I hadn't known otherwise I would have sworn that no untoward circumstance had ever troubled the course of her uneventful life.

The evening came to an end and this is the end of my story, but for the fun of it I am going to relate a small incident that happened when Wyman and I got back to his house. We decided to have a bottle of beer before going to bed and went into the kitchen to fetch it. The clock in the hall struck eleven and at that moment the phone rang. Wyman went to answer it and when he came back was quietly chortling to himself.

'What's the joke?' I asked.

'It was one of my students. They're not supposed to call members of the faculty after ten-thirty, but he was all hot and bothered. He asked me how evil had come into the world.'

'And did you tell him?'

'I told him that St Thomas Aquinas had got hot and bothered too about that very question and he'd better worry it out for himself. I said that when he found the solution he was to call me, no matter what time it was. Two o'clock in the morning if he liked.'

'I think you're pretty safe not to be disturbed for many a long night,' I said.

'I won't conceal from you that I have formed pretty much the same impression myself,' he grinned.

The
Lotus Eater

◆

Most people, the vast majority in fact, lead the lives that circumstances have thrust upon them, and though some repine, looking upon themselves as round pegs in square holes, and think that if things had been different they might have made a much better showing, the greater part accept their lot, if not with serenity, at all events with resignation. They are like tram-cars travelling for ever on the selfsame rails. They go backwards and forwards, backwards and forwards, inevitably, till they can go no longer and then are sold as scrap-iron. It is not often that you find a man who has boldly taken the course of his life into his own hands. When you do, it is worth while having a good look at him.

That was why I was curious to meet Thomas Wilson. It was an interesting and a bold thing he had done. Of course the end was not yet and until the experiment was concluded it was impossible to call it successful. But from what I had heard it seemed he must be an odd sort of fellow and I thought I should like to know him. I had been told he was reserved, but I had a notion that with patience and tact I could persuade him to confide in me. I wanted to hear the facts from his own lips. People exaggerate, they love to romanticize, and I was quite prepared to discover that his story was not nearly so singular as I had been led to believe.

And this impression was confirmed when at last I made his acquaintance. It was on the Piazza in Capri, where I was spending the month of August at a friend's villa, and a little before sunset, when most of the inhabitants, native and foreign, gather together to chat with their friends in the cool of the evening. There is a terrace that overlooks the Bay of Naples, and when the sun sinks slowly into the sea the island of Ischia is silhouetted against a blaze of splendour. It is one of the most lovely sights in the world. I was standing there with my friend and host watching it, when suddenly he said:

'Look, there's Wilson.'

'Where?'

'The man sitting on the parapet, with his back to us. He's got a blue shirt on.'

I saw an undistinguished back and a small head of grey hair, short and rather thin.

'I wish he'd turn round,' I said.

'He will presently.'

'Ask him to come and have a drink with us at Morgano's.'

'All right.'

The instant of overwhelming beauty had passed and the sun, like the top of an orange, was dipping into a wine-red sea. We turned round and leaning our backs against the parapet looked at the people who were sauntering to and fro. They were all talking their heads off and the cheerful noise was exhilarating. Then the church bell, rather cracked, but with a fine resonant note, began to ring. The Piazza at Capri, with its clock tower over the footpath that leads up from the harbour, with the church up a flight of steps, is a perfect setting for an opera by Donizetti, and you felt that the voluble crowd might at any moment break out into a rattling chorus. It was charming and unreal.

I was so intent on the scene that I had not noticed Wilson get off the parapet and come towards us. As he passed us my friend stopped him.

'Hullo, Wilson, I haven't seen you bathing the last few days.'

'I've been bathing on the other side for a change.'

My friend then introduced me. Wilson shook hands with me politely, but with indifference; a great many strangers come to Capri for a few days, or a few weeks, and I had no doubt he was constantly meeting people who came and went; and then my friend asked him to come along and have a drink with us.

'I was just going back to supper,' he said.

'Can't it wait?' I asked.

'I suppose it can,' he smiled.

Though his teeth were not very good his smile was attractive. It was gentle and kindly. He was dressed in a blue cotton shirt and a pair of grey trousers, much creased and none too clean, of a thin canvas, and on his feet he wore a pair of very old espadrilles. The get-up was picturesque, and very suitable to the place and the weather, but it did not at all go with his face. It was a lined, long face, deeply sunburned, thin-lipped, with small grey eyes rather close together and tight, neat features. The grey hair was carefully brushed. It was not a plain face, indeed in his youth Wilson might have been good-looking, but a prim one. He wore the blue shirt, open at the neck, and the grey canvas trousers, not as though they belonged to him, but as though, shipwrecked in his pyjamas, he had been fitted out with odd garments by compassionate strangers. Notwithstanding this careless attire he looked like the manager of a branch office in an insurance company, who should by rights be wearing a black coat with pepper-and-salt trousers, a white collar, and an unobjectionable tie. I could very well see myself going to him to claim the insurance money when I had lost a watch, and being rather disconcerted while I answered the questions he put to me by his obvious impression, for all his politeness, that people who made such claims were either fools or knaves.

Moving off, we strolled across the Piazza and down the street till we came to Morgano's. We sat in the garden. Around us people were talking in Russian, German, Italian, and English. We ordered drinks. Donna Lucia, the host's wife, waddled up and in her low, sweet voice passed the time of day with us. Though middle-aged now and portly, she had still traces of the wonderful beauty that thirty years before had driven artists to paint so many bad portraits of her. Her eyes, large and liquid, were the eyes of Hera and her smile was affectionate and gracious. We three gossiped for a while, for there is always a scandal of one sort or another in Capri to make a topic of conversation, but nothing was said of particular interest and in a little while Wilson got up and left us. Soon afterwards we strolled up to my friend's villa to dine. On the way he asked me what I had thought of Wilson.

'Nothing,' I said. 'I don't believe there's a word of truth in your story.'

'Why not?'

'He isn't the sort of man to do that sort of thing.'

'How does anyone know what anyone is capable of?'

'I should put him down as an absolutely normal man of business who's retired on a comfortable income from gilt-edged securities. I think your story's just the ordinary Capri tittle-tattle.'

'Have it your own way,' said my friend.

We were in the habit of bathing at a beach called the Baths of Tiberius. We took a fly down the road to a certain point and then wandered through lemon groves and vineyards, noisy with cicadas and heavy with the hot smell of the sun, till we came to the top of the cliff down which a steep winding path led to the sea. A day or two later, just before we got down my friend said:

'Oh, there's Wilson back again.'

We scrunched over the beach, the only drawback to the bathing-place being that it was shingle and not sand, and as we came along Wilson saw us and waved. He was standing up, a pipe in his mouth, and he wore nothing but a pair of trunks. His body was dark brown, thin, but not emaciated, and, considering his wrinkled face and grey hair, youthful. Hot from our walk, we undressed quickly and plunged at once into the water. Six feet from the shore it was thirty feet deep, but so clear that you could see the bottom. It was warm, yet invigorating.

When I got out Wilson was lying on his belly, with a towel under him, reading a book. I lit a cigarette and went and sat down beside him.

'Had a nice swim?' he asked.

He put his pipe inside his book to mark the place and closing it put it down on the pebbles beside him. He was evidently willing to talk.

'Lovely,' I said. 'It's the best bathing in the world.'

'Of course people think those were the Baths of Tiberius.' He waved his hand towards a shapeless mass of masonry that stood half in the water and half out. 'But that's all rot. It was just one of his villas, you know.'

I did. But it is just as well to let people tell you things when they want to. It disposes them kindly towards you if you suffer them to impart information. Wilson gave a chuckle.

'Funny old fellow, Tiberius. Pity they're saying now there's not a word of truth in all those stories about him.'

He began to tell me all about Tiberius. Well, I had read my Suetonius too and I had read histories of the Early Roman Empire, so there was nothing very new to me in what he said. But I observed that he was not ill-read. I remarked on it.

'Oh, well, when I settled down here I was naturally interested, and I have plenty of time for reading. When you live in a place like this, with all its associations, it seems to make history so actual. You might almost be living in historical times yourself.'

I should remark here that this was in 1913. The world was an easy, comfortable place and no one could have imagined that anything might happen seriously to disturb the serenity of existence.

'How long have you been here?' I asked.

'Fifteen years.' He gave the blue and placid sea a glance, and a strangely tender smile hovered on his thin lips. 'I fell in love with the place at first sight. You've heard, I daresay, of the mythical German who came here on the Naples boat just for lunch and a look at the Blue Grotto and stayed forty years; well, I can't say I exactly did that, but it's come to the same thing in the end. Only it won't be forty years in my case. Twenty-five. Still, that's better than a poke in the eye with a sharp stick.'

I waited for him to go on. For what he had just said looked indeed as though there might be something after all in the singular story I had heard. But at that moment my friend came dripping out of the water very proud of himself because he had swum a mile, and the conversation turned to other things.

After that I met Wilson several times, either in the Piazza or on the beach. He was amiable and polite. He was always pleased to have a talk and I found out that he not only knew every inch of the island but also the adjacent mainland. He had read a great deal on all sorts of subjects, but his speciality was the history of Rome and on this he was very well informed. He seemed to have little imagination and to be of no more than average intelligence. He laughed a good deal, but with restraint, and his sense of humour was tickled by simple jokes. A commonplace man. I did not forget the odd remark he had made during the first short chat we had had by ourselves, but he never so much as approached the topic again. One day on our return from the beach, dismissing the cab at the Piazza, my friend and I told the driver to be ready to take us up to Anacapri at five. We were going to climb Monte Solaro, dine at a tavern we favoured, and walk down in the moonlight. For it was full moon and the views by night were lovely. Wilson was standing by while we gave the cabman instructions, for we had given him a lift to save him the hot dusty walk, and more from politeness than for any other reason I asked him if he would care to join us.

'It's my party,' I said.

'I'll come with pleasure,' he answered.

But when the time came to set out my friend was not feeling well, he thought he had stayed too long in the water, and would not face the long and tiring walk. So I went alone with Wilson. We climbed the mountain, admired the spacious view, and got back to the inn as night was falling, hot, hungry, and thirsty. We had ordered our dinner beforehand. The food was good, for Antonio was an excellent cook, and the wine came from his own vineyard. It was so light that you felt you could drink it like water and we finished the first bottle with our macaroni. By the time we had finished the second we felt that there was nothing much wrong with life. We sat in a little garden under a great vine laden with grapes. The air was exquisitely soft. The night was still and we were alone. The maid brought us *bel paese* cheese and a plate of figs. I ordered coffee and strega, which is the best liqueur they make in Italy. Wilson would not have a cigar, but lit his pipe.

'We've got plenty of time before we need start,' he said, 'the moon won't be over the hill for another hour.'

'Moon or no moon,' I said briskly, 'of course we've got plenty of time. That's one of the delights of Capri, that there's never any hurry.'

'Leisure,' he said. 'If people only knew! It's the most priceless thing a man can have and they're such fools they don't even know it's something to aim at. Work? They work for work's sake. They haven't got the brains to realize that the only object of work is to obtain leisure.'

Wine has the effect on some people of making them indulge in general reflections. These remarks were true, but no one could have claimed that they were original. I did not say anything, but struck a match to light my cigar.

'It was full moon the first time I came to Capri,' he went on reflectively. 'It might be the same moon as tonight.'

'It was, you know,' I smiled.

He grinned. The only light in the garden was what came from an oil lamp that hung over our heads. It had been scanty to eat by, but it was good now for confidences.

'I didn't mean that. I mean, it might be yesterday. Fifteen years it is, and when I look back it seems like a month. I'd never been to Italy before. I came for my summer holiday. I went to Naples by boat from Marseilles and I had a look round, Pompeii, you know, and Paestum and one or two places like that; then I came here for a week. I liked the look of the place right away, from the sea, I mean, as I watched it come closer and closer; and then when we got into the little boats from the steamer and landed at the quay, with all that crowd of jabbering people who wanted to take your luggage, and the hotel touts, and the tumbledown houses on the Marina and the walk up to the hotel, and dining on the terrace–well, it just got me. That's the truth. I didn't know if I was standing on my head or my heels. I'd never drunk Capri wine before, but I'd heard of it; I think I must have got a bit tight. I sat on that terrace after they'd all gone to bed and watched the moon over the sea, and there was Vesuvius with a great red plume of smoke rising up from it. Of course I know now that wine I drank was ink, Capri wine my eye, but I thought it all right then. But it wasn't the wine that made me drunk, it was the shape of the island and those jabbering people, the moon and the sea and the oleander in the hotel garden. I'd never seen an oleander before.'

It was a long speech and it had made him thirsty. He took up his glass, but it was empty. I asked him if he would have another strega.

'It's sickly stuff. Let's have a bottle of wine. That's sound, that is, pure juice of the grape and can't hurt anyone.'

I ordered more wine, and when it came filled the glasses. He took a long drink and after a sigh of pleasure went on.

'Next day I found my way to the bathing-place we go to. Not bad bathing, I thought. Then I wandered about the island. As luck would have it, there was a *festa* up at the Punta di Timberio and I ran straight into the middle of it. An image of the Virgin and priests, acolytes swinging censers, and a whole crowd of jolly, laughing, excited people, a lot of them all dressed up. I ran across an Englishman there and asked him what it was all about. "Oh, it's the feast of the Assumption," he said, "at least that's what the Catholic Church says it is, but that's just their hanky-panky. It's the festival of Venus. Pagan, you know. Aphrodite rising from the sea and all that." It gave me quite a funny feeling to hear him. It seemed to take one a long way back, if you know what I mean. After that I went down one night to have a look at the Faraglioni by moonlight. If the fates had wanted me to go on being a bank manager they oughtn't to have let me take that walk.'

'You were a bank manager, were you?' I asked.

I had been wrong about him, but not far wrong.

'Yes. I was manager of the Crawford Street branch of the York and City. It was convenient for me because I lived up Hendon way. I could get from door to door in thirty-seven minutes.'

He puffed at his pipe and relit it.

'That was my last night, that was. I'd got to be back at the bank on Monday morning. When I looked at those two great rocks sticking out of the water, with the moon above them, and all the little lights of the fishermen in their boats catching cuttlefish, all so peaceful and beautiful, I said to myself, well, after all, why should I go back? It wasn't as if I had anyone dependent on me. My wife had died of bronchial pneumonia four years before and the kid went to live with her grandmother, my wife's mother. She was an old fool, she didn't look after the kid properly and she got blood-poisoning, they amputated her leg, but they couldn't save her and she died, poor little thing.'

'How terrible,' I said.

'Yes, I was cut up at the time, though of course not so much as if the kid had been living with me, but I dare say it was a mercy. Not much chance for a girl with only one leg. I was sorry about my wife too. We got on very well together. Though I don't know if it would have continued. She was the sort of woman who was always bothering about what other people'd think. She didn't like travelling. Eastbourne was her idea of a holiday. D'you know, I'd never crossed the Channel till after her death.'

'But I suppose you've got other relations, haven't you?'

'None. I was an only child. My father had a brother, but he went to Australia before I was born. I don't think anyone could easily be more alone in the world than I am. There wasn't any reason I could see why I shouldn't do exactly what I wanted. I was thirty-four at that time.'

He had told me he had been on the island for fifteen years. That would make him forty-nine. Just about the age I should have given him.

'I'd been working since I was seventeen. All I had to look forward to was doing the same old thing day after day till I retired on my pension. I said to myself, is it worth it? What's wrong with chucking it all up and spending the rest of my life down here? It was the most beautiful place I'd ever seen. But I'd had a business training, I was cautious by nature. "No," I said, "I won't be carried away like this, I'll go tomorrow like I said I would and think it over. Perhaps when I get back to London I'll think quite differently." Damned fool, wasn't I? I lost a whole year that way.'

'You didn't change your mind, then?'

'You bet I didn't. All the time I was working I kept thinking of the bathing here and the vineyards and the walks over the hills and the moon and the sea, and the Piazza in the evening when everyone walks about for a bit of a chat after the day's work is over. There was only one thing that bothered me: I wasn't sure if I was justified in not working like everybody else did. Then I read a sort of history book, by a man called Marion Crawford it was, and there was a story about Sybaris and Crotona. There were two cities; and in Sybaris they just enjoyed life and had a good time, and in Crotona they were hardy and industrious and all that. And one day the men of Crotona came over and wiped Sybaris out, and then after a while a lot of other fellows came over from

somewhere else and wiped Crotona out. Nothing remains of Sybaris, not a
stone, and all that's left of Crotona is just one column. That settled the matter
for me.'

'Oh?'

'It came to the same in the end, didn't it? And when you look back now, who
were the mugs?'

I did not reply and he went on.

'The money was rather a bother. The bank didn't pension one off till after
thirty years' service, but if you retired before that they gave you a gratuity.
With that and what I'd got for the sale of my house and the little I'd managed to
save, I just hadn't enough to buy an annuity to last the rest of my life. It would
have been silly to sacrifice everything so as to lead a pleasant life and not have a
sufficient income to make it pleasant. I wanted to have a little place of my own, a
servant to look after me, enough to buy tobacco, decent food, books now
and then, and something over for emergencies. I knew pretty well how much
I needed. I found I had just enough to buy an annuity for twenty-five years.'

'You were thirty-five at the time?'

'Yes. It would carry me on till I was sixty. After all, no one can be certain of
living longer than that, a lot of men die in their fifties, and by the time a man's
sixty he's had the best of life.'

'On the other hand no one can be sure of dying at sixty,' I said.

'Well, I don't know. It depends on himself, doesn't it?'

'In your place I should have stayed on at the bank till I was entitled to my
pension.'

'I should have been forty-seven then. I shouldn't have been too old to enjoy
my life here, I'm older than that now and I enjoy it as much as I ever did, but I
should have been too old to experience the particular pleasure of a young man.
You know, you can have just as good a time at fifty as you can at thirty, but it's
not the same sort of good time. I wanted to live the perfect life while I still had
the energy and the spirit to make the most of it. Twenty-five years seemed a
long time to me, and twenty-five years of happiness seemed worth paying
something pretty substantial for. I'd made up my mind to wait a year and I
waited a year. Then I sent in my resignation and as soon as they paid me my
gratuity I bought the annuity and came on here.'

'An annuity for twenty-five years?'

'That's right.'

'Have you never regretted?'

'Never. I've had my money's worth already. And I've got ten years more.
Don't you think after twenty-five years of perfect happiness one ought to be
satisfied to call it a day?'

'Perhaps.'

He did not say in so many words what he would do then, but his intention
was clear. It was pretty much the story my friend had told me, but it sounded
different when I heard it from his own lips. I stole a glance at him. There was
nothing about him that was not ordinary. No one, looking at that neat, prim
face, could have thought him capable of an unconventional action. I did not
blame him. It was his own life that he had arranged in this strange manner, and
I did not see why he should not do what he liked with it. Still, I could not
prevent the little shiver that ran down my spine.

'Getting chilly?' he smiled. 'We might as well start walking down. The
moon'll be up by now.'

Before we parted Wilson asked me if I would like to go and see his house one day; and two or three days later, finding out where he lived, I strolled up to see him. It was a peasant's cottage, well away from the town, in a vineyard, with a view of the sea. By the side of the door grew a great oleander in full flower. There were only two small rooms, a tiny kitchen, and a lean-to in which firewood could be kept. The bedroom was furnished like a monk's cell, but the sitting-room, smelling agreeably of tobacco, was comfortable enough, with two large arm-chairs that he had brought from England, a large roll-top desk, a cottage piano, and crowded bookshelves. On the walls were framed engravings of pictures by G. F. Watts and Lord Leighton. Wilson told me that the house belonged to the owner of the vineyard who lived in another cottage higher up the hill, and his wife came in every day to do the rooms and the cooking. He had found the place on his first visit to Capri, and taking it on his return for good had been there ever since. Seeing the piano and music open on it, I asked him if he would play.

'I'm no good, you know, but I've always been fond of music and I get a lot of fun out of strumming.'

He sat down at the piano and played one of the movements from a Beethoven sonata. He did not play very well. I looked at his music, Schumann and Schubert, Beethoven, Bach, and Chopin. On the table on which he had his meals was a greasy pack of cards. I asked him if he played patience.

'A lot.'

From what I saw of him then and from what I heard from other people I made for myself what I think must have been a fairly accurate picture of the life he had led for the last fifteen years. It was certainly a very harmless one. He bathed; he walked a great deal, and he seemed never to lose his sense of the beauty of the island which he knew so intimately; he played the piano and he played patience; he read. When he was asked to a party he went and, though a trifle dull, was agreeable. He was not affronted if he was neglected. He liked people, but with an aloofness that prevented intimacy. He lived thriftily, but with sufficient comfort. He never owed a penny. I imagine he had never been a man whom sex had greatly troubled, and if in his younger days he had had now and then a passing affair with a visitor to the island whose head was turned by the atmosphere, his emotion, while it lasted, remained, I am pretty sure, well under his control. I think he was determined that nothing should interfere with his independence of spirit. His only passion was for the beauty of nature, and he sought felicity in the simple and natural things that life offers to everyone. You may say that it was a grossly selfish existence. It was. He was of no use to anybody, but on the other hand he did nobody any harm. His only object was his own happiness, and it looked as though he had attained it. Very few people know where to look for happiness; fewer still find it. I don't know whether he was a fool or a wise man. He was certainly a man who knew his own mind. The odd thing about him to me was that he was so immensely commonplace. I should never have given him a second thought but for what I knew, that on a certain day, ten years from then, unless a chance illness cut the thread before, he must deliberately take leave of the world he loved so well. I wondered whether it was the thought of this, never quite absent from his mind, that gave him the peculiar zest with which he enjoyed every moment of the day.

I should do him an injustice if I omitted to state that he was not at all in the habit of talking about himself. I think the friend I was staying with was the only person in whom he had confided. I believe he only told me the story because he suspected I already knew it, and on the evening on which he told it me he had drunk a good deal of wine.

My visit drew to a close and I left the island. The year after, war broke out. A number of things happened to me, so that the course of my life was greatly altered, and it was thirteen years before I went to Capri again. My friend had been back some time, but he was no longer so well off, and had moved into a house that had no room for me; so I was putting up at the hotel. He came to meet me at the boat and we dined together. During dinner I asked him where exactly his house was.

'You know it,' he answered. 'It's the little place Wilson had. I've built on a room and made it quite nice.'

With so many other things to occupy my mind I had not given Wilson a thought for years; but now, with a little shock, I remembered. The ten years he had before him when I made his acquaintance must have elapsed long ago.

'Did he commit suicide as he said he would?'

'It's rather a grim story.'

Wilson's plan was all right. There was only one flaw in it and this, I suppose, he could not have foreseen. It had never occurred to him that after twenty-five years of complete happiness, in this quiet backwater, with nothing in the world to disturb his serenity, his character would gradually lose its strength. The will needs obstacles in order to exercise its power; when it is never thwarted, when no effort is needed to achieve one's desires, because one has placed one's desires only in the things that can be obtained by stretching out one's hand, the will grows impotent. If you walk on a level all the time the muscles you need to climb a mountain will atrophy. These observations are trite, but there they are. When Wilson's annuity expired he had no longer the resolution to make the end which was the price he had agreed to pay for that long period of happy tranquillity. I do not think, as far as I could gather, both from what my friend told me and afterwards from others, that he wanted courage. It was just that he couldn't make up his mind. He put it off from day to day.

He had lived on the island for so long and had always settled his accounts so punctually that it was easy for him to get credit; never having borrowed money before, he found a number of people who were willing to lend him small sums when now he asked for them. He had paid his rent regularly for so many years that his landlord, whose wife Assunta still acted as his servant, was content to let things slide for several months. Everyone believed him when he said that a relative had died and that he was temporarily embarrassed because owing to legal formalities he could not for some time get the money that was due to him. He managed to hang on after this fashion for something over a year. Then he could get no more credit from the local tradesmen, and there was no one to lend him any more money. His landlord gave him notice to leave the house unless he paid up arrears of rent before a certain date.

The day before this he went into his tiny bedroom, closed the door and the window, drew the curtain, and lit a brazier of charcoal. Next morning when Assunta came to make his breakfast she found him insensible but still alive. The room was draughty, and though he had done this and that to keep out the fresh air he had not done it very thoroughly. It almost looked as though at the last moment, and desperate though his situation was, he had suffered from a certain infirmity of purpose. Wilson was taken to the hospital, and though very ill for some time he at last recovered. But as a result either of the charcoal poisoning or of the shock he was no longer in complete possession of his faculties. He was not insane, at all events not insane enough to be put in an asylum, but he was quite obviously no longer in his right mind.

'I went to see him,' said my friend. 'I tried to get him to talk, but he kept looking at me in a funny sort of way, as though he couldn't quite make out where he'd seen me before. He looked rather awful lying there in bed, with a week's growth of grey beard on his chin; but except for that funny look in his eyes he seemed quite normal.'

'What funny look in his eyes?'

'I don't know exactly how to describe it. Puzzled. It's an absurd comparison, but suppose you threw a stone up into the air and it didn't come down but just stayed there . . .'

'It would be rather bewildering,' I smiled.

'Well, that's the sort of look he had.'

It was difficult to know what to do with him. He had no money and no means of getting any. His effects were sold, but for too little to pay what he owed. He was English, and the Italian authorities did not wish to make themselves responsible for him. The British Consul in Naples had no funds to deal with the case. He could of course be sent back to England, but no one seemed to know what could be done with him when he got there. Then Assunta, the servant, said that he had been a good master and a good tenant, and as long as he had the money had paid his way; he could sleep in the woodshed in the cottage in which she and her husband lived, and he could share their meals. This was suggested to him. It was difficult to know whether he understood or not. When Assunta came to take him from the hospital he went with her without remark. He seemed to have no longer a will of his own. She had been keeping him now for two years.

'It's not very comfortable, you know,' said my friend. 'They've rigged him up a ramshackle bed and given him a couple of blankets, but there's no window, and it's icy cold in winter and like an oven in summer. And the food's pretty rough. You know how these peasants eat: macaroni on Sundays and meat once in a blue moon.'

'What does he do with himself all the time?'

'He wanders about the hills. I've tried to see him two or three times, but it's no good; when he sees you coming he runs like a hare. Assunta comes down to have a chat with me now and then and I give her a bit of money so that she can buy him tobacco, but God knows if he ever gets it.'

'Do they treat him all right?' I asked.

'I'm sure Assunta's kind enough. She treats him like a child. I'm afraid her husband's not very nice to him. He grudges the cost of his keep. I don't believe he's cruel or anything like that, but I think he's a bit sharp with him. He makes him fetch water and clean the cow-shed and that sort of thing.'

'It sounds pretty rotten,' I said.

'He brought it on himself. After all, he's only got what he deserved.'

'I think on the whole we all get what we deserve,' I said. 'But that doesn't prevent its being rather horrible.'

Two or three days later my friend and I were taking a walk. We were strolling along a narrow path through an olive grove.

'There's Wilson,' said my friend suddenly. 'Don't look, you'll only frighten him. Go straight on.'

I walked with my eyes on the path, but out of the corners of them I saw a man hiding behind an olive tree. He did not move as we approached, but I felt that he was watching us. As soon as we had passed I heard a scamper. Wilson, like a hunted animal, had made for safety. That was the last I ever saw of him.

He died last year. He had endured that life for six years. He was found one morning on the mountainside lying quite peacefully as though he had died in his sleep. From where he lay he had been able to see those two great rocks called the Faraglioni which stand out of the sea. It was full moon and he must have gone to see them by moonlight. Perhaps he died of the beauty of that night.

The Wash-Tub

◆

Positano stands on the side of a steep hill, a disarray of huddled white houses, their tiled roofs washed pale by the suns of a hundred years; but unlike many of these Italian towns perched out of harm's way on a rocky eminence it does not offer you at one delightful glance all it has to give. It has quaint streets that zig-zag up the hill, and battered, painted houses in the baroque style, but very late, in which Neapolitan noblemen led for a season lives of penurious grandeur. It is indeed almost excessively picturesque and in winter its two or three modest hotels are crowded with painters, male and female, who in their different ways acknowledge by their daily labours the emotion it has excited in them. Some take infinite pains to place on canvas every window and every tile their peering eyes can discover and doubtless achieve the satisfaction that rewards honest industry. 'At all events it's sincere,' they say modestly when they show you their work. Some, rugged and dashing, in a fine frenzy attack their canvas with a pallet knife charged with a wad of paint, and they say: 'You see, what I was trying to bring out was my personality.' They slightly close their eyes and tentatively murmur: 'I think it's rather me, don't you?' And there are some who give you highly entertaining arrangements of spheres and cubes and utter sombrely: 'That's how I see it!' These for the most part are strong silent men who waste no words.

But Positano looks full south and the chances are that in summer you will have it to yourself. The hotel is clean and cool and there is a terrace, overhung with vines, where you can sit at night and look at the sea bespangled with dim stars. Down at the Marine, on the quay, is a little tavern where you can dine under an archway off anchovies and ham, macaroni and fresh-caught mullet, and drink cold wine. Once a day the steamer from Naples comes in, bringing the mail, and for a quarter of an hour gives the beach (there is no port and the passengers are landed in small boats) an air of animation.

One August, tiring of Capri where I had been staying, I made up my mind to spend a few days at Positano, so I hired a fishing-boat and rowed over. I stopped on the way in a shady cove to bathe and lunch and sleep, and did not arrive till evening. I strolled up the hill, my two bags following me on the heads of two sturdy women, to the hotel, and was surprised to learn that I was not its only guest. The waiter, whose name was Giuseppe, was an old friend of mine, and at that season he was boots, porter, chambermaid, and cook as well. He told me that an American *signore* had been staying there for three months.

'Is he a painter or writer or something?' I asked.

'No, *Signore*, he's a gentleman.'

Odd, I thought. No foreigners came to Positano at that time of year but German *Wandervogel*, looking hot and dusty, with satchels on their backs, and they only stayed overnight. I could not imagine anyone wishing to spend three months there; unless of course he were hiding. And since all London had been excited by the flight earlier in the year of an eminent, but dishonest, financier, the amusing thought occurred to me that this mysterious stranger was perhaps he. I knew him slightly and trusted that my sudden arrival would not disconcert him.

'You'll see the *Signore* at the Marina,' said Giuseppe, as I was setting out to go down again. 'He always dines there.'

He was certainly not there when I arrived. I asked what there was for dinner and drank an americano, which is by no means a bad substitute for a cocktail. In a few minutes, however, a man walked in who could be no other than my fellow-guest at the hotel and I had a moment's disappointment when I saw that it was not the absconding financier. A tall, elderly man, bronzed after his summer on the Mediterranean, with a handsome, thin face. He wore a very neat, even smart, suit of cream-coloured silk and no hat. His grey hair was cut very short, but was still thick. There was ease in his bearing, and elegance. He looked round the half-dozen tables under the archway at which the natives of the place were playing cards or dominoes and his eyes rested on me. They smiled pleasantly. He came up.

'I hear you have just arrived at the hotel. Giuseppe suggested that as he couldn't come down here to effect an introduction you wouldn't mind if I introduced myself. Would it bore you to dine with a total stranger?'

'Of course not. Sit down.'

He turned to the maid who was laying a cover for me and in beautiful Italian told her that I would eat with him. He looked at my americano.

'I have got them to stock a little gin and French vermouth for me. Would you allow me to mix you a very dry Martini?'

'Without hesitation.'

'It gives an exotic note to the surroundings which brings out the local colour.'

He certainly made a very good cocktail and with added appetite we ate the ham and anchovies with which our dinner began. My host had a pleasant humour and his fluent conversation was agreeable.

'You must forgive me if I talk too much,' he said presently. 'This is the first chance I've had to speak English for three months. I don't suppose you will stay here long and I mean to make the most of it.'

'Three months is a long time to stay at Positano.'

'I've hired a boat and I bathe and fish. I read a great deal. I have a good many books here and if there's anything I can lend you I shall be very glad.'

'I think I have enough reading matter. But I should love to look at what you have. It's always fun looking at other people's books.'

He gave me a sharp look and his eyes twinkled.

'It also tells you a good deal about them,' he murmured.

When we finished dinner we went on talking. The stranger was well-read and interested in a diversity of topics. He spoke with so much knowledge of painting that I wondered if he was an art critic or a dealer. But then it appeared that he had been reading Suetonius and I came to the conclusion that he was a college professor. I asked him his name.

'Barnaby,' he answered.

'That's a name that has recently acquired an amazing celebrity.'

'Oh, how so?'

'Have you never heard of the celebrated Mrs Barnaby? She's a compatriot of yours.'

'I admit that I've seen her name in the papers rather frequently of late. Do you know her?'

'Yes, quite well. She gave the grandest parties all last season and I went to them whenever she asked me. Everyone did. She's an astounding woman. She came to London to do the season, and, by George, she did it. She just swept everything before her.'

'I understand she's very rich?'

'Fabulously, I believe, but it's not that that has made her success. Plenty of American women have money. Mrs Barnaby has got where she has by sheer force of character. She never pretends to be anything but what she is. She's natural. She's priceless. You know her history, of course?'

My friend smiled.

'Mrs Barnaby may be a great celebrity in London, but to the best of my belief in America she is almost inconceivably unknown.'

I smiled also, but within me; I could well imagine how shocked this distinguished and cultured man would be by the rollicking humour, the frankness, with its tang of the soil, and the rich and vital experience of the amazing Mrs Barnaby.

'Well, I'll tell you about her. Her husband appears to be a very rough diamond; he's a great hulking fellow, she says, who could fell a steer with his fist. He's known in Arizona as One-Bullet Mike.'

'Good gracious! Why?'

'Well, years ago in the old days he killed two men with a single shot. She says he's handier with his gun even now than any man West of the Rockies. He's a miner, but he's been a cowpuncher, a gun-runner, and God knows what in his day.'

'A thoroughly Western type,' said my professor a trifle acidly, I thought.

'Something of a desperado, I imagine. Mrs Barnaby's stories about him are a real treat. Of course everyone's been begging her to let him come over, but she says he'd never leave the wide open spaces. He struck oil a year or two ago and now he's got all the money in the world. He must be a great character. I've heard her keep the whole dinner-table spellbound when she's talked of the old days when they roughed it together. It gives you quite a thrill when you see this grey-haired woman, not at all pretty, but exquisitely dressed, with the most wonderful pearls, and hear her tell how she washed the miners' clothes and cooked for the camp. Your American women have an adaptability that's really stupendous. When you see Mrs Barnaby sitting at the head of her table, perfectly at home with princes of the blood, ambassadors, cabinet ministers, and the duke of this and the duke of that, it seems almost incredible that only a few years ago she was cooking the food of seventy miners.'

'Can she read or write?'

'I suppose her invitations are written by her secretary, but she's by no means an ignorant woman. She told me she used to make a point of reading for an hour every night after the fellows in camp had gone to bed.'

'Remarkable!'

'On the other hand One-Bullet Mike only learnt to write his name when he suddenly found himself under the necessity of signing cheques.'

We walked up the hill to our hotel and before separating for the night arranged to take our luncheon with us next day and row over to a cove that my friend had discovered. We spent a charming day bathing, reading, eating, sleeping, and talking, and we dined together in the evening. The following morning, after breakfast on the terrace, I reminded Barnaby of his promise to show me his books.

'Come right along.'

I accompanied him to his bedroom, where Giuseppe, the waiter, was making his bed. The first thing I caught sight of was a photograph in a gorgeous frame of the celebrated Mrs Barnaby. My friend caught sight of it too and suddenly turned pale with anger.

'You fool, Giuseppe. Why have you taken that photograph out of my wardrobe? Why the devil did you think I put it away?'

'I didn't know, Signore. That's why I put it back on the Signore's table. I thought he liked to see the portrait of his *signora*.'

I was staggered.

'Is my Mrs Barnaby your wife?' I cried.

'She is.'

'Good Lord, are you One-Bullet Mike?'

'Do I look it?'

I began to laugh.

'I'm bound to say you don't.'

I glanced at his hands. He smiled grimly and held them out.

'No, sir. I have never felled a steer with my naked fist.'

For a moment we stared at one another in silence.

'She'll never forgive me,' he moaned. 'She wanted me to take a false name, and when I wouldn't she was quite vexed with me. She said it wasn't safe. I said it was bad enough to hide myself in Positano for three months, but I'd be damned if I'd use any other name than my own.' He hesitated. 'I throw myself on your mercy. I can do nothing but trust to your generosity not to disclose a secret that you have discovered by the most unlikely chance.'

'I will be as silent as the grave, but honestly I don't understand. What does it all mean?'

'I am a doctor by profession and for the last thirty years my wife and I have lived in Pennsylvania. I don't know if I have struck you as a roughneck, but I venture to say that Mrs Barnaby is one of the most cultivated women I have ever known. Then a cousin of hers died and left her a very large fortune. There's no mistake about that. My wife is a very, very rich woman. She has always read a great deal of English fiction and her one desire was to have a London season and entertain and do all the grand things she had read about in books. It was her money and although the prospect did not particularly tempt me, I was very glad that she should gratify her wish. We sailed last April. The young Duke and Duchess of Hereford happened to be on board.'

'I know. It was they who first launched Mrs Barnaby. They were crazy about her. They've boomed her like an army of press-agents.'

'I was ill when we sailed, I had a carbuncle which confined me to my stateroom, and Mrs Barnaby was left to look after herself. Her deck-chair happened to be next the duchess's, and from a remark she overheard it occurred to her that the English aristocracy were not so wrapped up in our social leaders as one might have expected. My wife is a quick little woman and she remarked to me that if you had an ancestor who signed Magna Carta perhaps you were not excessively impressed because the grandfather of one of your acquaintances sold skunks and the grandfather of another ran ferryboats. My wife has a very keen sense of humour. Getting into conversation with the duchess, she told her a little Western anecdote, and to make it more interesting told it as having happened to herself. Its success was immediate. The duchess begged for another and my wife ventured a little further. Twenty-four hours later she had the duke and duchess eating out of her hand. She used to come down to my stateroom at intervals and tell me of her progress. In the innocence of my heart, I was tickled to death and since I had nothing else to do, I sent to the library for the works of Bret Harte and primed her with effective touches.'

I slapped my forehead.

'We said she was as good as Bret Harte,' I cried.

'I had a grand time thinking of the consternation of my wife's friends when at the end of the voyage I appeared and we told them the truth. But I reckoned without my wife. The day before we reached Southampton Mrs Barnaby told me that the Herefords were arranging parties for her. The duchess was crazy to introduce her to all sorts of wonderful people. It was a chance in a thousand; but of course I should spoil everything, she admitted that she had been forced by the course of events to represent me as very different from what I was. I did not know that she had already transformed me into One-Bullet Mike, but I had a shrewd suspicion that she had forgotten to mention that I was on board. Well, to make a long story short, she asked me to go to Paris for a week or two till she had consolidated her position. I didn't mind that. I was much more inclined to do a little work at the Sorbonne than to go to parties in Mayfair, and so leaving her to go on to Southampton, I got off at Cherbourg. But when I had been in Paris ten days she flew over to see me. She told me that her success had exceeded her wildest dreams: it was ten times more wonderful than any of the novels; but my appearance would ruin it all. Very well, I said, I would stay in Paris. She didn't like the idea of that; she said she'd never have a moment's peace so long as I was so near and I might run across someone who knew me. I suggested Vienna or Rome. They wouldn't do either, and at last I came here and here have I been hiding like a criminal for three interminable months.'

'Do you mean to say you never killed the two gamblers, shooting one with your right hand and the other with your left?'

'Sir, I have never fired a pistol in my life.'

'And what about the attack on your log-cabin by the Mexican bandits when your wife loaded your guns for you and you stood the siege for three days till the Federal troops rescued you?'

Mr Barnaby smiled grimly.

'I never heard that one. Isn't it a trifle crude?'

'Crude! It was as good as any Wild West picture.'

'If I may venture a guess, that is where my wife in all probability got the idea.'

'But the wash-tub. Washing the miners' clothes and all that. You don't know how she made us roar with that story. Why, she swam into London Society in her wash-tub.'

I began to laugh.

'She's made the most gorgeous fools of us all,' I said.

'She's made a pretty considerable fool of me, I would have you observe,' remarked Mr Barnaby.

'She's a marvellous woman and you're right to be proud of her. I always said she was priceless. She realized the passion for romance that beats in every British heart and she's given us exactly what we wanted. I wouldn't betray her for worlds.'

'It's all very fine for you, sir. London may have gained a wonderful hostess, but I'm beginning to think that I have lost a perfectly good wife.'

'The only place for One-Bullet Mike is the great open West. My dear Mr Barnaby, there is only one course open to you now. You must continue to disappear.'

'I'm very much obliged to you.'

I thought he replied with a good deal of acidity.

A
Man
with a Conscience

♦

St Laurent de Maroni is a pretty little place. It is neat and clean. It has an Hôtel de Ville and a Palais de Justice of which many a town in France would be proud. The streets are wide, and the fine trees that border them give a grateful shade. The houses look as though they had just had a coat of paint. Many of them nestle in little gardens, and in the gardens are palm trees and flame of the forest; cannas flaunt their bright colours and crotons their variety; the bougainvillaeas, purple or red, riot profusely, and the elegant hibiscus offers its gorgeous flowers with a negligence that seems almost affected. St Laurent de Maroni is the centre of the French penal settlements of Guiana, and a hundred yards from the quay at which you land is the great gateway of the prison camp. These pretty little houses in their tropical gardens are the residence of the prison officials, and if the streets are neat and clean it is because there is no lack of convicts to keep them so. One day, walking with a casual acquaintance, I came upon a young man, in the round straw hat and the pink and white stripes of the convict's uniform, who was standing by the road-side with a pick. He was doing nothing.

'Why are you idling?' my companion asked him.

The man gave his shoulders a scornful shrug.

'Look at the blade of grass there,' he answered. 'I've got twenty years to scratch it away.'

St Laurent de Maroni exists for the group of prison camps of which it is the centre. Such trade as it has depends on them; its shops, kept by Chinese, are there to satisfy the wants of the warders, the doctors, and the numerous officials who are connected with the penal settlements. The streets are silent and deserted. You pass a convict with a dispatch-case under his arm; he has some job in the administration; or another with a basket; he is a servant in somebody's house. Sometimes you come upon a little group in the charge of a warder; often you see them strolling to or from the prison unguarded. The prison gates are open all day long and the prisoners freely saunter in and out. If you see a man not in the prison uniform he is probably a freed man who is condemned to spend a number of years in the colony and who, unable to get work, living on the edge of starvation, is drinking himself to death on the cheap strong rum which is called tafia.

There is an hotel at St Laurent de Maroni and here I had my meals. I soon got to know by sight the habitual frequenters. They came in and sat each at his little table, ate their meals in silence, and went out again. The hotel was kept by a coloured woman, and the man she lived with, an ex-convict, was the only waiter. But the Governor of the colony, who lives at Cayenne, had put at my disposal his own bungalow and it was there I slept. An old Arab looked after it; he was a devout Mahommedan, and at intervals during the day I heard him say his prayers. To make my bed, keep my rooms tidy, and run errands for me, the commandant of the prison had assigned me another convict. Both were serving life sentences for murder; the commandant told me that I could place entire confidence in them; they were as honest as the day, and I could leave anything about without the slightest risk. But I will not conceal from the reader that when I went to bed at night I took the precaution to lock my door and to bolt my shutters. It was foolish no doubt, but I slept more comfortably.

I had come with letters of introduction, and both the governor of the prison settlements and the commandant of the camp at St Laurent did everything they could to make my visit agreeable and instructive. I will not here narrate all I heard and saw. I am not a reporter. It is not my business to attack or to defend the system which the French have thought fit to adopt in regard to their criminals. Besides, the system is now condemned; prisoners will soon cease to be sent out to French Guiana, to suffer the illnesses incidental to the climate and the work in malarial jungles to which so many are relegated, to endure nameless degradations, to lose hope, to rot, to die. I will only say that I saw no physical cruelty. On the other hand I saw no attempt to make the criminal on the expiration of his sentence a useful citizen. I saw nothing done for his spiritual welfare. I heard nothing of classes that he could attend in order to improve his education or organized games that might distract his mind. I saw no library where he could get books to read when his day's work was done. I saw a condition of affairs that only the strongest character could hope to surmount. I saw a brutishness that must reduce all but a very few to apathy and despair.

All this has nothing to do with me. It is vain to torment oneself over sufferings that one cannot alleviate. My object here is to tell a story. As I am well aware, one can never know everything there is to be known about human nature. One can be sure only of one thing, and that is that it will never cease to have a surprise in store for you. When I had got over the impression of bewilderment, surprise, and horror to which my first visit to the prison camp gave rise, I bethought myself that there were certain matters that I was interested to inquire into. I should inform the reader that three-quarters of the convicts at St Laurent de Maroni are there for murder. This is not official information and it may be that I exaggerate; every prisoner has a little book in which are set down his crime, his sentence, his punishments, and whatever else the authorities think necessary to keep note of; and it was from an examination of a considerable number of these that I formed my estimate. It gave me something of a shock to realize that in England far, far the greater number of these men whom I saw working in shops, lounging about the verandas of their dormitories, or sauntering through the streets would have suffered capital punishment. I found them not at all disinclined to speak of the crime for which they had been convicted, and in pursuance of my purpose I spent the better part of one day inquiring into crimes of passion. I wanted to know exactly what was the motive that had made a man kill his wife or his girl. I had a notion that jealousy and wounded honour might not perhaps tell the whole story. I got some curious replies, and among them one that was not to my mind lacking in humour. This was from a man working in the carpenter's shop who had cut his wife's throat; when I asked him why he had done it, he answered with a shrug of the shoulders: *Manque d'entente.* His casual tone made the best translation of this: We didn't get on very well. I could not help observing that if men in general looked upon this as an adequate reason for murdering their wives, the mortality in the female sex would be alarming. But after putting a good many questions to a good many men I arrived at the conclusion that at the bottom of nearly all these crimes was an economic motive; they had killed their wives or mistresses not only from jealousy, because they were unfaithful to them, but also because somehow it affected their pockets. A woman's infidelity was sometimes an occasion of financial loss, and it was this in the end that drove a man to his desperate act; or, himself in need of money to gratify other passions, he murdered because his victim was an obstacle to his exclusive possession of it. I do not conclude that a man never kills his woman because his love is spurned or his honour tarnished, I only offer my observation on these particular cases as a curious sidelight on human nature. I should not venture to deduce from it a general rule.

I spent another day inquiring into the matter of conscience. Moralists have sought to persuade us that it is one of the most powerful agents in human behaviour. Now that reason and pity have agreed to regard hell-fire as a hateful myth, many good men have seen in conscience the chief safeguard that shall induce the human race to walk in the way of righteousness. Shakespeare has told us that it makes cowards of us all. Novelists and playwrights have described for us the pangs that assail the wicked; they have vividly pictured the anguish of a stricken conscience and the sleepless nights it occasions; they have shown it poisoning every pleasure till life is so intolerable that discovery and punishment come as a welcome relief. I had often wondered how much of all this was true. Moralists have an axe to grind; they must draw a moral. They think that if they say a thing often enough people will believe it. They are apt to state that a thing is so when they consider it desirable that it should be. They tell us that the wages of sin is death; we know very well that it is not always. And so far as the authors of fiction are concerned, the playwrights and the novelists, when they get hold of an effective theme they are disposed to make use of it without bothering very much whether it agrees with the facts of life. Certain statements about human nature become, as it were, common property, and so are accepted as self-evident. In the same way painters for ages painted shadows black, and it was not till the impressionists looked at them with unprejudiced eyes and painted what they saw that we discovered that shadows were coloured. It had sometimes struck me that perhaps conscience was the expression of a high moral development, so that its influence was strong only in those whose virtue was so shining that they were unlikely to commit any action for which they could seriously reproach themselves. It is generally accepted that murder is a shocking crime, and it is the murderer above all other criminals who is supposed to suffer remorse. His victim, we have been led to believe, haunts his dreams in horrifying nightmares, and the recollection of his dreadful deed tortures his waking hours. I could not miss the opportunity to inquire into the truth of this. I had no intention of insisting if I encountered reticence or distress, but I found in none of those with whom I talked any such thing. Some said that in the same circumstances they would do as they had done before. Determinists without knowing it, they seemed to look upon their action as ordained by a fate over which they had no control. Some appeared to think that their crime was committed by someone with whom they had no connexion.

'When one's young, one's foolish,' they said, with a careless gesture or a deprecating smile.

Others told me that if they had known what the punishment was they would suffer, they would certainly have held their hands. I found in none any regret for the human being they had violently bereft of life. It seemed to me that they had no more feeling for the creature they had killed than if it had been a pig whose throat they had cut in the way of business. Far from feeling pity for their victim, they were more inclined to feel anger because he had been the occasion of their imprisonment in that distant land. In only one man did I discern anything that might appropriately be called a conscience, and his story was so remarkable that I think it well worth narrating. For in this case it was, so far as I can understand, remorse that was the motive of the crime. I noticed the man's number, which was printed on the chest of the pink and white pyjamas of his prison uniform, but I have forgotten it. Anyhow it is of no consequence. I never knew his name. He did not offer to tell me and I did not like to ask it. I will call him Jean Charvin.

I met him on my first visit to the camp with the commandant. We were walking through a courtyard round which were cells, not punishment cells, but individual cells which are given to well-behaved prisoners who ask for them. They are sought after by those to whom the promiscuity of the dormitories is odious. Most of them were empty, for their occupants were engaged in their various employments. Jean Charvin was at work in his cell, writing at a small table, and the door was open. The commandant called him and he came out. I looked into the cell. It contained a fixed hammock, with a dingy mosquito-net; by the side of this was a small table on which were his bits and pieces, a shaving-mop and a razor, a hairbrush and two or three battered books. On the walls were photographs of persons of respectable appearance and illustrations from picture papers. He had been sitting on his bed to write and the table on which he had been writing was covered with papers. They looked like accounts. He was a handsome man, tall, erect, and lean, with flashing dark eyes and clean-cut, strong features. The first thing I noticed about him was that he had a fine head of long, naturally-waving dark brown hair. This at once made him look different from the rest of the prisoners, whose hair is close-cropped, but cropped so badly, in ridges, that it gives them a sinister look. The commandant spoke to him of some official business, and then as we were leaving added in a friendly way:

'I see your hair is growing well.'

Jean Charvin reddened and smiled. His smile was boyish and engaging.

'It'll be some time yet before I get it right again.'

The commandant dismissed him and we went on.

'He's a very decent fellow,' he said. 'He's in the accountant's department, and he's had leave to let his hair grow. He's delighted.'

'What is he here for?' I asked.

'He killed his wife. But he's only got six years. He's clever and a good worker. He'll do well. He comes from a very decent family and he's had an excellent education.'

I thought no more of Jean Charvin, but by chance I met him next day on the road. He was coming towards me. He carried a black dispatch-case under his arm, and except for the pink and white stripes of his uniform and the ugly round straw hat that concealed his handsome head of hair, you might have taken him for a young lawyer on his way to court. He walked with a long, leisurely stride, and he had an easy, you might almost say a gallant, bearing. He recognized me, and taking off his hat bade me good morning. I stopped, and for something to say asked him where he was going. He told me he was taking some papers from the governor's office to the bank. There was a pleasing frankness in his face, and his eyes, his really beautiful eyes, shone with good will. I supposed that the vigour of his youth was such that it made life, notwithstanding his position and his surroundings, more than tolerable, even pleasant. You would have said that here was a young man without a care in the world.

'I hear you're going to St Jean tomorrow,' he said.

'Yes. It appears I must start at dawn.'

St Jean is a camp seventeen kilometres from St Laurent, and it is here that are interned the habitual criminals who have been sentenced to transportation after repeated terms of imprisonment. They are petty thieves, confidence men, forgers, tricksters, and suchlike; the prisoners of St Laurent, condemned for more serious offences, look upon them with contempt.

'You should find it an interesting experience,' Jean Charvin said, with his frank and engaging smile. 'But keep your pocket-book buttoned up, they'd steal the shirt off your back if they had half a chance. They're a dirty lot of scoundrels!'

That afternoon, waiting till the heat of the day was less, I sat on the veranda outside my bedroom and read: I had drawn the jalousies and it was tolerably cool. My old Arab came up the stairs on his bare feet, and in his halting French told me that there was a man from the commandant who wanted to see me.

'Send him up,' I said.

In a moment the man came, and it was Jean Charvin. He told me that the commandant had sent him to give me a message about my excursion next day to St Jean. When he had delivered it I asked him if he would not sit down and have a cigarette with me. He wore a cheap wrist-watch and he looked at it.

'I have a few minutes to spare. I should be glad to.' He sat down and lit the cigarette I offered him. He gave me a smiling look of his soft eyes. 'Do you know, this is the first time I've ever been asked to sit down since I was sentenced.' He inhaled a long whiff of his cigarette. 'Egyptian. I haven't smoked an Egyptian cigarette for three years.'

The convicts make their own cigarettes out of a coarse, strong tobacco that is sold in square blue packets. Since one is not allowed to pay them for the services they may render you, but may give them tobacco, I had bought a good many packets of this.

'How does it taste?'

'One gets accustomed to everything and, to tell you the truth, my palate is so vitiated, I prefer the stuff we get here.'

'I'll give you a couple of packets.'

I went into my room and fetched them. When I returned he was looking at some books that were lying on the table.

'Are you fond of reading?' I asked.

'Very. I think the want of books is what I most suffer from now. The few I can get hold of I'm forced to read over and over again.'

To so great a reader as myself no deprivation seems more insupportable than the lack of books.

'I have several French ones in my bag. I'll look them out and if you care to have them I'll give them to you if you can come along again.'

My offer was due only in part to kindness; I wanted to have another chance of a talk with him.

'I should have to show them to the commandant. He would only let me keep them if there was no doubt they couldn't possibly corrupt my morals. But he's a good-natured man, I don't think he'll make any difficulties.'

There was a hint of slyness in the smile with which he said this, and I suspected that he had taken the measure of the well-meaning conscientious chief of the camp and knew pretty well how to get on the right side of him. It would have been unjust to blame him if he exercised tact, and even cunning, to render his lot as tolerable as might be.

'The commandant has a very good opinion of you.'

'He's a fine man. I'm very grateful to him, he's done a great deal for me. I'm an accountant by profession and he's put me in the accountant's department. I love figures, it gives me an intense satisfaction to deal with them, they're living things to me, and now that I can handle them all day long I feel myself again.'

'And are you glad to have a cell of your own?'

'It's made all the difference. To be herded with fifty men, the scum of the earth, and never to be alone for a minute—it was awful. That was the worst of all. At home, at Le Havre, that is where I lived, I had an apartment, modest of course, but my own, and we had a maid who came in by the day. We lived decently. It made it ten times harder for me than for the rest, most of them, who have never known anything but squalor, filth, and promiscuity.'

I had asked him about the cell in the hope that I could get him to talk about the life that is led in those vast dormitories in which the men are locked from five in the evening till five next morning. During these twelve hours they are their own masters. A warder can enter, they told me, only at the risk of his life. They have no light after eight o'clock, but from sardine-tins, a little oil, and a rag they make lamps by the light of which they can see enough to play cards. They gamble furiously, not for love, but for the money they keep secreted on their bodies; they are unscrupulous ruthless men, and naturally enough bitter quarrels often arise. They are settled with knives. Often in the morning, when the dormitory is opened, a man is found dead, but no threats, no promises, will induce anyone to betray the slayer. Other things Jean Charvin told me which I cannot narrate. He told me of one young fellow who had come out from France on the same ship with himself and with whom he had made friends. He was a good-looking boy. One day he went to the commandant and asked him if he could have a cell to himself. The commandant asked him why he wanted one. He explained. The commandant looked through his list and told him that at the moment all were occupied, but that as soon as there was a vacancy he should have one. Next morning when the dormitory was opened, he was found dead on his hammock with his belly ripped open to the breast-bone.

'They're savage brutes, and if one isn't a brute by the time one arrives only a miracle can save one from becoming as brutal as the rest.'

Jean Charvin looked at his watch and got up. He walked away from me and then, with his charming smile, turned and faced me.

'I must go now. If the commandant gives me permission I will come and get the books you were kind enough to offer me.'

In Guiana you do not shake hands with a convict, and a tactful man, taking leave of you, puts himself in such a position that there can be no question of your offering him your hand or of refusing his should he, forgetting for a moment, instinctively tender it. Heaven knows, it would have meant nothing to me to shake hands with Jean Charvin; it gave me a pang to see the care he had taken to spare me embarrassment.

I saw him twice more during my stay at St Laurent. He told me his story, but I will tell it now in my words rather than in his, for I had to piece it together from what he said at one time and another, and what he left out I have had to supply out of my own imagination. I do not believe it has led me astray. It was as though he had given me three letters out of a number of five-letter words; the chances are that I have guessed most of the words correctly.

Jean Charvin was born and bred in the great seaport of Le Havre. His father had a good post in the Customs. Having finished his education, he did his military service, and then looked about for a job. Like a great many other young Frenchmen he was prepared to sacrifice the hazardous chance of wealth for a respectable security. His natural gift for figures made it easy for him to get a place in the accountant's department of a large exporting house. His future was assured. He could look forward to earning a sufficient income to live in the modest comfort of the class to which he belonged. He was industrious and well-behaved. Like most young Frenchmen of his generation he was athletic. He swam and played tennis in summer, and in winter he bicycled. On two evenings a week to keep himself fit he spent a couple of hours in a gymnasium. Through his childhood, his adolescence, and his young manhood, he lived in the constant companionship of a boy called, shall we say for the purposes of this narrative, Henri Renard, whose father was also an official in the Customs. Jean and Riri went to school together, played together, worked for their examinations together, spent their holidays together, for the two families were intimate, had their first affairs with girls together, partnered one another in the local tennis tournaments, and did their military service together. They never quarrelled. They were never so happy as in one another's society. They were inseparable. When the time came for them to start working they decided that they would go into the same firm; but that was not so easy; Jean tried to get Riri a job in the exporting house that had engaged him, but could not manage it, and it was not till a year later that Riri got something to do. But by then trade was as bad at Le Havre as everywhere else, and in a few months he found himself once more without employment.

Riri was a light-hearted youth, and he enjoyed his leisure. He danced, bathed, and played tennis. It was thus that he made the acquaintance of a girl who had recently come to live at Le Havre. Her father had been a captain in the colonial army and on his death her mother had returned to Le Havre, which was her native place. Marie-Louise was then eighteen. She had spent almost all her life in Tonkin. This gave her an exotic attraction for the young men who had never been out of France in their lives, and first Riri, then Jean, fell in love with her. Perhaps that was inevitable: it was certainly unfortunate. She was a well-brought-up girl, an only child, and her mother, besides her pension, had a little money of her own. It was evident that she could be pursued only with a view of marriage. Of course Riri, dependent for the while entirely on his father, could not make an offer that there was the least chance of Madame Meurice, Marie-Louise's mother, accepting; but having the whole day to himself he was able to see a great deal more of Marie-Louise than Jean could. Madame Meurice was something of an invalid, so that Marie-Louise had more liberty than most French girls of her age and station. She knew that both Riri and Jean were in love with her, she liked them both and was pleased by their attentions, but she gave no sign that she was in love with either. It was impossible to tell which she preferred. She was well aware that Riri was not in a position to marry her.

'What did she look like?' I asked Jean Charvin.

'She was small, with a pretty little figure, with large grey eyes, a pale skin, and soft, mouse-coloured hair. She was rather like a little mouse. She was not beautiful, but pretty, in a quaint demure way; there was something very appealing about her. She was easy to get on with. She was simple and unaffected. You couldn't help feeling that she was reliable and would make anyone a good wife.'

Jean and Riri hid nothing from one another and Jean made no secret of the fact that he was in love with Marie-Louise, but Riri had met her first and it was an understood thing between them that Jean should not stand in his way. At length she made her choice. One day Riri waited for Jean to come away from his office and told him that Marie-Louise had consented to marry him. They had arranged that as soon as he got a job his father should go to her mother and make the formal offer. Jean was hard hit. It was not easy to listen with eager sympathy to the plans that the excitable and enchanted Riri made for the future. But he was too much attached to Riri to feel sore with him; he knew how lovable he was and he could not blame Marie-Louise. He tried with all his might to accept honestly the sacrifice he made on the altar of friendship.

'Why did she choose him rather than you?' I asked.

'He had immense vitality. He was the gayest, most amusing lad you ever met. His high spirits were infectious. You couldn't be dull in his company.'

'He had pep,' I smiled.

'And an incredible charm.'

'Was he good-looking?'

'No, not very. He was shorter than me, slight and wiry; but he had a nice, good-humoured face.' Jean Charvin smiled rather pleasantly. 'I think without any vanity I can say that I was better-looking than Riri.'

But Riri did not get a job. His father, tired of keeping him in idleness, wrote to everyone he could think of, the members of his family and his friends in various parts of France, asking them if they could not find something, however modest, for Riri to do; and at last he got a letter from a cousin in Lyons who was in the silk business to say that his firm were looking for a young man to go out to Phnom-Penh, in Cambodia, where they had a branch, to buy native silk for them. If Riri was willing to take the job he could get it for him.

Though like all French parents Riri's hated him to emigrate, there seemed no help for it, and it was determined, although the salary was small, that he must go. He was not disinclined. Cambodia was not so far from Tonkin, and Marie-Louise must be familiar with the life. She had so often talked of it that he had come to the conclusion that she would be glad to go back to the East. To his dismay she told him that nothing would induce her to. In the first place she could not desert her mother, whose health was obviously declining; and then, after having at last settled down in France, she was determined never again to leave it. She was sympathetic to Riri, but resolute. With nothing else in prospect his father would not hear of his refusing the offer; there was no help for it, he had to go. Jean hated losing him, but from the moment Riri told him his bad news, he had realized with an exulting heart that fate was playing into his hands. With Riri out of his way for five years at least, and unless he were incompetent with the probability that he would settle in the East for good, Jean could not doubt that after a while Marie-Louise would marry him. His circumstances, his settled, respectable position in Le Havre, where she could be near her mother, would make her think it very sensible; and when she was no longer under the spell of Riri's charm there was no reason why her great liking for him should not turn to love. Life changed for him. After months of misery he was happy again, and though he kept them to himself he too now made great plans for the future. There was no need any longer to try not to love Marie-Louise.

Suddenly his hopes were shattered. One of the shipping firms at Le Havre had a vacancy, and it looked as though the application that Riri had quickly made would be favourably considered. A friend in the office told him that it was a certainty. It would settle everything. It was an old and conservative house, and it was well known that when you once got into it you were there for life. Jean Charvin was in despair, and the worst of it was that he had to keep his anguish to himself. One day the director of his own firm sent for him.

When he reached this point Jean stopped. A harassed look came into his eyes.

'I'm going to tell you something now that I've never told to anyone before. I'm an honest man, a man of principle; I'm going to tell you of the only discreditable action I've ever done in my life.'

I must remind the reader here that Jean Charvin was wearing the pink and white stripes of the convict's uniform, with his number stencilled on his chest, and that he was serving a term of imprisonment for the murder of his wife.

'I couldn't imagine what the director wanted with me. He was sitting at his desk when I went into his office, and he gave me a searching look.

'"I want to ask you a question of great importance," he said. "I wish you to treat it as confidential. I shall of course treat your answer as equally so."

'I waited. He went on:

'"You've been with us for a considerable time. I am very well satisfied with you, there is no reason why you shouldn't reach a very good position in the firm. I put implicit confidence in you."

'"Thank you, sir," I said. "I will always try to merit your good opinion."

'"The question at issue is this. Monsieur Untel is proposing to engage Henri Renard. He is very particular about the character of his employees, and in this case it is essential that he shouldn't make a mistake. Part of Henri Renard's duties would be to pay the crews of the firm's ships, and many hundreds of thousand francs will pass through his hands. I know that Henri Renard is your great friend and that your families have always been very intimate. I put you on your honour to tell me whether Monsieur Untel would be justified in engaging this young man."

'I saw at once what the question meant. If Riri got the job he would stay and marry Marie-Louise, if he didn't he would go out to Cambodia and I should marry her. I swear to you it was not I who answered, it was someone who stood in my shoes and spoke with my voice, I had nothing to do with the words that came from my mouth.

'"*Monsieur le directeur*," I said, "Henri and I have been friends all our lives. We have never been separated for a week. We went to school together; we shared our pocket-money and our mistresses when we were old enough to have them; we did our military service together."

'"I know. You know him better than anyone in the world. That is why I ask you these questions."

'"It is not fair, *Monsieur le directeur*. You are asking me to betray my friend. I cannot, and I will not answer your questions."

'The director gave me a shrewd smile. He thought himself much cleverer than he really was.

'"Your answer does you credit, but it has told me all I wished to know." Then he smiled kindly. I suppose I was pale, I dare say I was trembling a little. "Pull yourself together, my dear boy; you're upset and I can understand it. Sometimes in life one is faced by a situation where honesty stands on the one side and loyalty on the other. Of course one mustn't hesitate, but the choice is bitter. I shall not forget your behaviour in this case and on behalf of Monsieur Untel I thank you."

'I withdrew. Next morning Riri received a letter informing him that his services were not required, and a month later he sailed for the Far East.'

Six months after this Jean Charvin and Marie-Louise were married. The marriage was hastened by the increasing gravity of Madame Meurice's illness. Knowing that she could not live long, she was anxious to see her daughter settled before she died. Jean wrote to Riri telling him the facts and Riri wrote back warmly congratulating him. He assured him that he need have no compunctions on his behalf; when he had left France he realized that *he* could never marry Marie-Louise, and he was glad that Jean was going to. He was finding consolation at Phnom-Penh. His letter was very cheerful. From the beginning Jean had told himself that Riri, with his mercurial temperament, would soon forget Marie-Louise, and his letter looked as if he had already done so. He had done him no irreparable injury. It was a justification. For if *he* had lost Marie-Louise he would have died; with him it was a matter of life and death.

For a year Jean and Marie-Louise were extremely happy. Madame Meurice died, and Marie-Louise inherited a couple of hundred thousand francs; but with the depression and the unstable currency they decided not to have a child till the economic situation was less uncertain. Marie-Louise was a good and frugal housekeeper. She was an affectionate, amiable, and satisfactory wife. She was placid. This before he married her had seemed to Jean a rather charming trait, but as time wore on it was borne in upon him that her placidity came from a certain lack of emotional ardour. It concealed no depth. He had always thought she was like a little mouse; there was something mouse-like in her furtive reticences; she was oddly serious about trivial matters and could busy herself indefinitely with things that were of no consequence. She had her own little set of interests and they left no room in her pretty sleek head for any others. She sometimes began a novel, but seldom cared to finish it. Jean was obliged to admit to himself that she was rather dull. The uneasy thought came to him that perhaps it had not been worth while to do a dirty trick for her sake. It began to worry him. He missed Riri. He tried to persuade himself that what was done was done and that he had really not been a free agent, but he could not quite still the prickings of his conscience. He wished now that when the director of his firm spoke to him he had answered differently.

Then a terrible thing happened. Riri contracted typhoid fever and died. It was a frightful shock for Jean. It was a shock to Marie-Louise too; she paid Riri's parents the proper visit of condolence, but she neither ate less heartily nor slept less soundly. Jean was exasperated by her composure.

'Poor chap, he was always so gay,' she said, 'he must have hated dying. But why did he go out there? I told him the climate was bad; it killed my father and I knew what I was talking about.'

Jean felt that he had killed him. If he had told the director all the good he knew of Riri, knew as no one else in the world did, he would have got the post and would now be alive and well.

'I shall never forgive myself,' he thought. 'I shall never be happy again. Oh, what a fool I was, and what a cad!'

He wept for Riri. Marie-Louise sought to comfort him. She was a kind little thing and she loved him.

'You mustn't take it too hardly. After all, you wouldn't have seen him for five years, and you'd have found him so changed that there wouldn't have been anything between you any more. He would have been a stranger to you. I've seen that sort of thing happen so often. You'd have been delighted to see him, and in half an hour you'd have discovered that you had nothing to say to one another.'

'I dare say you're right,' he sighed.

'He was too scatter-brained ever to have amounted to anything very much. He never had your firmness of character and your clear, solid intellect.'

He knew what she was thinking. What would have been her position now if she had followed Riri to Indo-China and found herself at twenty-one a widow with nothing but her own two hundred thousand francs to live on? It was a lucky escape and she congratulated herself on her good sense. Jean was a husband of whom she could be proud. He was earning good money. Jean was tortured by remorse. What he had suffered before was nothing to what he suffered now. The anguish that the recollection of his treachery caused him was worse than a physical pain gnawing at his vitals. It would assail him suddenly when he was in the middle of his work and twist his heartstrings with a violent pang. His agony was such that he craved for relief, and it was only by an effort of all his will that he prevented himself from making a full confession to Marie-Louise. But he knew how she would take it; she would not be shocked, she would think it rather a clever trick and be even subtly flattered that for her sake he had been guilty of a despicable act. She could not help him. He began to dislike her. For it was for her that he had done the shameful thing, and what was she? An ordinary, commonplace, rather calculating little woman.

'What a fool I've been,' he repeated.

He did not even find her pretty any more. He knew now that she was terribly stupid. But of course she was not to blame for that, she was not to blame because he had been false to his friend; and he forced himself to be as sweet and tender to her as he had always been. He did whatever she wanted. She had only to express a wish for him to fulfil it if it was in his power. He tried to pity her, he tried to be tolerant; he told himself that from her own petty standpoint she was a good wife, methodical, saving, and in her manner, dress, and appearance a credit to a respectable young man. All that was true; but it was on her account that Riri had died, and he loathed her. She bored him to distraction. Though he said nothing, though he was kind, amiable, and indulgent, he could often have killed her. When he did, however, it was almost without meaning to. It was ten months after Riri's death, and Riri's parents, Monsieur and Madame Renard, gave a party to celebrate the engagement of their daughter. Jean had seen little of them since Riri's death and he did not want to go. But Marie-Louise said they must; he had been Riri's greatest friend and it would be a grave lack of politeness on Jean's part not to attend an important celebration in the family. She had a keen sense of social obligation.

'Besides, it'll be a distraction for you. You've been in poor spirits for so long, a little amusement will do you good. There'll be champagne, won't there? Madame Renard doesn't like spending money, but on an occasion like this she'll have to sacrifice herself.'

Marie-Louise chuckled slyly when she thought what a wrench it would be to Madame Renard to unloose her purse-strings.

The party had been very gay. It gave Jean a nasty turn when he found that they were using Riri's old room for the women to put their wraps in and the men their coats. There was plenty of champagne. Jean drank a great deal to drown the bitter remorse that tormented him. He wanted to deaden the sound in his ears of Riri's laugh and to shut his eyes to the good-humour of his shining glance. It was three o'clock when they got home. Next day was Sunday, so Jean had no work to go to. They slept late. The rest I can tell in Jean Charvin's own words.

'I had a headache when I woke. Marie-Louise was not in bed. She was sitting at the dressing-table brushing her hair. I've always been very keen on physical culture, and I was in the habit of doing exercises every morning. I didn't feel very much inclined to do them that morning, but after all that champagne I thought I'd better. I got out of bed and took up my Indian clubs. Our bedroom was fairly large and there was plenty of room to swing them between the bed and the dressing-table where Marie-Louise was sitting. I did my usual exercises. Marie-Louise had started a little while before having her hair cut differently, quite short, and I thought it repulsive. From the back she looked like a boy, and the stubble of cropped hair on her neck made me feel rather sick. She put down her brushes and began to powder her face. She gave a nasty little laugh.

'"What are you laughing at?" I asked.

'"Madame Renard. That was the same dress she wore at our wedding, she'd had it dyed and done over; but it didn't deceive me. I'd have known it anywhere."

'It was such a stupid remark, it infuriated me. I was seized with rage, and with all my might I hit her over the head with my Indian club. I broke her skull, apparently, and she died two days later in hospital without recovering consciousness.'

He paused for a moment. I handed him a cigarette and lit another myself.

'I was glad she did. We could never have lived together again, and it would have been very hard to explain my action.'

'Very.'

'I was arrested and tried for murder. Of course I swore it was an accident, I said the club had slipped out of my hand, but the medical evidence was against me. The prosecution proved that such an injury as Marie-Louise had suffered could only have been caused by a violent and deliberate blow. Fortunately for me they could find no motive. The public prosecutor tried to make out that I had been jealous of the attentions some man had paid her at the party and that we had quarrelled on that account, but the man he mentioned swore that he had done nothing to arouse my suspicions and others at the party testified that we had left the best of friends. They found on the dressing-table an unpaid dressmaker's bill and the prosecutor suggested that we had quarrelled about that, but I was able to prove that Marie-Louise paid for her clothes out of her own money, so that the bill could not possibly have been the cause of a dispute. Witnesses came forward and said that I had always been kind to Marie-Louise. We were generally looked upon as a devoted couple. My character was excellent and my employer spoke in the highest terms of me. I was never in danger of losing my head, and at one moment I thought I had a chance of getting off altogether. In the end I was sentenced to six years. I don't regret what I did, for from that day, all the time I was in prison awaiting my trial, and since, while I've been here, I've ceased to worry about Riri. If I believed in ghosts I'd be inclined to say that Marie-Louise's death had laid Riri's. Anyhow, my conscience is at rest, and after all the torture I suffered I can assure you that everything I've gone through since is worth it; I feel I can now look the world in the face again.'

I know that this is a fantastic story; I am by way of being a realist, and in the stories I write I seek verisimilitude. I eschew the bizarre as scrupulously as I avoid the whimsical. If this had been a tale that I was inventing I would certainly have made it more probable. As it is, unless I had heard it with my own ears I am not sure that I should believe it. I do not know whether Jean Charvin told me the truth, and yet the words with which he closed his final visit to me had a convincing ring. I had asked him what were his plans for the future.

'I have friends working for me in France,' he answered. 'A great many people thought at the time that I was the victim of a grave miscarriage of justice; the director of my firm is convinced that I was unjustly condemned; and I may get a reduction of my sentence. Even if I don't, I think I can count upon getting back to France at the end of my six years. You see, I'm making myself useful here. The accounts were very badly kept when I took them over, and I've got them in apple-pie order. There have been leakages, and I'm convinced that if they'll give me a free hand, I can stop them. The commandant likes me and I'm certain that he'll do everything he can for me. At the worst I shan't be much over thirty when I get back.'

'But won't you find it rather difficult to get work?'

'A clever accountant like me, and a man who's honest and industrious, can always get work. Of course I shan't be able to live in Le Havre, but the director of my firm has business connexions at Lille and Lyons and Marseilles. He's promised to do something for me. No, I look forward to the years to come with a good deal of confidence. I shall settle down somewhere, and as soon as I'm comfortably fixed up I shall marry. After what I've been through I want a home.'

We were sitting in one of the corners of the veranda that surrounded my house in order to get any draught there might be, and on the north side I had left a jalousie undrawn. The strip of sky you saw with a single coconut tree on one side, its green foliage harsh against the blue, looked like an advertisement for a tropical cruise. Jean Charvin's eyes searched the distance as though he sought to see the future.

'But next time I marry,' he said thoughtfully, 'I shan't marry for love, I shall marry for money.'

Winter
Cruise

◆

Captain Erdmann knew Miss Reid very little till the *Friedrich Weber* reached Haiti. She came on board at Plymouth, but by then he had taken on a number of passengers, French, Belgian, and Haitian, many of whom had travelled with him before, and she was placed at the chief engineer's table. The *Friedrich Weber* was a freighter sailing regularly from Hamburg to Cartagena on the Colombian coast and on the way touching at a number of islands in the West Indies. She carried phosphates and cement from Germany and took back coffee and timber; but her owners, the Brothers Weber, were always willing to send her out of her route if a cargo of any sort made it worth their while. The *Friedrich Weber* was prepared to take cattle, mules, potatoes, or anything else that offered the chance of earning an honest penny. She carried passengers. There were six cabins on the upper deck and six below. The accommodation was not luxurious, but the food was good, plain, and abundant, and the fares were cheap. The round trip took nine weeks and was not costing Miss Reid more than forty-five pounds. She looked forward not only to seeing many interesting places, with historical associations, but also to acquiring a great deal of information that would enrich her mind.

The agent had warned her that till the ship reached Port au Prince in Haiti she would have to share a cabin with another woman. Miss Reid did not mind that, she liked company, and when the steward told her that her companion was Madame Bollin she thought at once that it would be a very good opportunity to rub up her French. She was only very slightly disconcerted when she found that Madame Bollin was coal-black. She told herself that one had to accept the rough with the smooth and that it takes all sorts to make a world. Miss Reid was a good sailor, as indeed was only to be expected since her grandfather had been a naval officer, but after a couple of roughish days the weather was fine and in a very short while she knew all her fellow-passengers. She was a good mixer. That was one of the reasons why she had made a success of her business; she owned a tea room at a celebrated beauty spot in the west of England and she always had a smile and a pleasant word for every customer who came in; she closed down in the winter and for the last four years had taken a cruise. You met such interesting people, she said, and you always learnt something. It was true that the passengers on the *Friedrich Weber* weren't of quite so good a class as those she had met the year before on her Mediterranean cruise, but Miss Reid was not a snob, and though the table manners of some of them shocked her somewhat, determined to look upon the bright side of things she decided to make the best of them. She was a great reader and she was glad, on looking at the ship's library, to find that there were a lot of books by Phillips Oppenheim, Edgar Wallace, and Agatha Christie; but with so many people to talk to she had no time for reading and she made up her mind to leave them till the ship emptied herself at Haiti.

'After all,' she said, 'human nature is more important than literature.'

Miss Reid had always had the reputation of being a good talker and she flattered herself that not once during the many days they were at sea had she allowed the conversation at table to languish. She knew how to draw people out, and whenever a topic seemed to be exhausted she had a remark ready to revive it or another topic waiting on the tip of her tongue to set the conversation off again. Her friend Miss Prince, daughter of the late Vicar of Campden, who had come to see her off at Plymouth, for she lived there, had often said to her:

'You know, Venetia, you have a mind like a man. You're never at a loss for something to say.'

'Well, I think if you're interested in everyone, everyone will be interested in you,' Miss Reid answered modestly. 'Practice makes perfect, and I have the infinite capacity for taking pains which Dickens said was genius.'

Miss Reid was not really called Venetia, her name was Alice, but disliking it she had, when still a girl, adopted the poetic name which she felt so much better suited to her personality.

Miss Reid had a great many interesting talks with her fellow-passengers and she was really sorry when the ship at length reached Port au Prince and the last of them disembarked. The *Friedrich Weber* stopped two days there, during which she visited the town and the neighbourhood. When they sailed she was the only passenger. The ship was skirting the coast of the island stopping off at a variety of ports to discharge or to take on cargo.

'I hope you will not feel embarrassed alone with so many men, Miss Reid,' said the captain heartily as they sat down to midday dinner.

She was placed on his right hand and at table besides sat the first mate, the chief engineer, and the doctor.

'I'm a woman of the world, Captain. I always think if a lady is a lady gentlemen will be gentlemen.'

'We're only rough sailor men, madam, you mustn't expect too much.'

'Kind hearts are more than coronets and simple faith than Norman blood, Captain,' answered Miss Reid.

He was a short, thick-set man, with a clean-shaven head and a red, clean-shaven face. He wore a white stengah-shifter, but except at meal-times unbuttoned at the neck and showing his hairy chest. He was a jovial fellow. He could not speak without bellowing. Miss Reid thought him quite an eccentric, but she had a keen sense of humour and was prepared to make allowances for that. She took the conversation in hand. She had learnt a great deal about Haiti on the voyage out and more during the two days she had spent there, but she knew that men liked to talk rather than to listen, so she put them a number of questions to which she already knew the answers; oddly enough they didn't. In the end she found herself obliged to give quite a little lecture, and before dinner was over, *Mittag Essen* they called it in their funny way, she had imparted to them a great deal of interesting information about the history and economic situation of the Republic, the problems that confronted it, and its prospects for the future. She talked rather slowly, in a refined voice, and her vocabulary was extensive.

At nightfall they put in at a small port where they were to load three hundred bags of coffee, and the agent came on board. The captain asked him to stay to supper and ordered cocktails. As the steward brought them Miss Reid swam into the saloon. Her movements were deliberate, elegant, and self-assured. She always said that you could tell at once by the way she walked if a woman was a lady. The captain introduced the agent to her and she sat down.

'What is that you men are drinking?' she asked.

'A cocktail. Will you have one, Miss Reid?'

'I don't mind if I do.'

She drank it and the captain somewhat doubtfully asked her if she would have another.

'Another? Well, just to be matey.'

The agent, much whiter than some, but a good deal darker than many, was the son of a former minister of Haiti to the German court, and having lived for many years in Berlin spoke good German. It was indeed on this account that he had got a job with a German shipping firm. On the strength of this Miss Reid, during supper, told them all about a trip down the Rhine that she had once taken. Afterwards she and the agent, the skipper, the doctor, and the mate sat around a table and drank beer. Miss Reid made it her business to draw the agent out. The fact that they were loading coffee suggested to her that he would be interested in learning how they grew tea in Ceylon, yes, she had been to Ceylon on a cruise, and the fact that his father was a diplomat made it certain that he would be interested in the royal family of England. She had a very pleasant evening. When she at last retired to rest, for she would never have thought of saying she was going to bed, she said to herself:

'There's no doubt that travel is a great education.'

It was really an experience to find herself alone with all those men. How they would laugh when she told them all about it when she got home! They would say that things like that only happened to Venetia. She smiled when she heard the captain on deck singing with that great booming voice of his. Germans were so musical. He had a funny way of strutting up and down on his short legs singing Wagner tunes to words of his own invention. It was *Tannhäuser* he was singing now (that lovely thing about the evening star) but knowing no German Miss Reid could only wonder what absurd words he was putting to it. It was as well.

'Oh, what a bore that woman is, I shall certainly kill her if she goes on much longer.' Then he broke into Siegfried's martial strain. 'She's a bore, she's a bore, she's a bore. I shall throw her into the sea.'

And that of course is what Miss Reid was. She was a crashing, she was a stupendous, she was an excruciating bore. She talked in a steady monotone, and it was no use to interrupt her because then she started again from the beginning. She had an insatiable thirst for information and no casual remark could be thrown across the table without her asking innumerable questions about it. She was a great dreamer and she narrated her dreams at intolerable length. There was no subject upon which she had not something prosy to say. She had a truism for every occasion. She hit on the commonplace like a hammer driving a nail into the wall. She plunged into the obvious like a clown in a circus jumping through a hoop. Silence did not abash her. Those poor men far away from their homes and the patter of little feet, and with Christmas coming on, no wonder they felt low; she redoubled her efforts to interest and amuse them. She was determined to bring a little gaiety into their dull lives. For that was the awful part of it: Miss Reid meant well. She was not only having a good time herself, but she was trying to give all of them a good time. She was convinced that they liked her as much as she liked them. She felt that she was doing her bit to make the party a success and she was naïvely happy to think that she was succeeding. She told them all about her friend Miss Price and how often she had said to her: Venetia, no one ever has a dull moment in your company. It was the captain's duty to be polite to a passenger and however much he would have liked to tell her to hold her silly tongue he could not, but even if he had been free to say what he liked, he knew that he could not have brought himself to hurt her feelings. Nothing stemmed the torrent of her loquacity. It was as irresistible as a force of nature. Once in desperation they began talking German, but Miss Reid stopped this at once.

'Now I won't have you saying things I don't understand. You ought all to make the most of your good luck in having me all to yourselves and practise your English.'

'We were talking of technical matters that would only bore you, Miss Reid,' said the captain.

'I'm never bored. That's why, if you won't think me a wee bit conceited to say so, I'm never boring. You see, I like to know things. Everything interests me and you never know when a bit of information won't come in useful.'

The doctor smiled dryly.

'The captain was only saying that because he was embarrassed. In point of fact he was telling a story that was not fit for the ears of a maiden lady.'

'I may be a maiden lady but I'm also a woman of the world, I don't expect sailors to be saints. You need never be afraid of what you say before me, Captain, I shan't be shocked. I should love to hear your story.'

The doctor was a man of sixty with thin grey hair, a grey moustache, and small bright blue eyes. He was a silent, bitter man, and however hard Miss Reid tried to bring him into the conversation it was almost impossible to get a word out of him. But she wasn't a woman who would give in without a struggle, and one morning when they were at sea and she saw him sitting on deck with a book, she brought her chair next to his and sat down beside him.

'Are you fond of reading, Doctor?' she said brightly.

'Yes.'

'So am I. And I suppose like all Germans you're musical.'

'I'm fond of music.'

'So am I. The moment I saw you I thought you looked clever.'

He gave her a brief look and pursing his lips went on reading. Miss Reid was not disconcerted.

'But of course one can always read. I always prefer a good talk to a good book. Don't you?'

'No.'

'How very interesting. Now do tell me why?'

'I can't give you a reason.'

'That's very strange, isn't it? But then I always think human nature is strange. I'm terribly interested in people, you know. I always like doctors, they know so much about human nature, but I could tell you some things that would surprise even you. You learn a great deal about people if you run a tea-shop like I do, that's to say if you keep your eyes open.'

The doctor got up.

'I must ask you to excuse me, Miss Reid. I have to go and see a patient.'

'Anyhow I've broken the ice now,' she thought, as he walked away. 'I think he was only shy.'

But a day or two later the doctor was not feeling at all well. He had an internal malady that troubled him now and then, but he was used to it and disinclined to talk about it. When he had one of his attacks he only wanted to be left alone. His cabin was small and stuffy, so he settled himself on a long chair on deck and lay with his eyes closed. Miss Reid was walking up and down to get the half-hour's exercise she took morning and evening. He thought that if he pretended to be asleep she would not disturb him. But when she had passed him half a dozen times she stopped in front of him and stood quite still. Though he kept his eyes closed he knew that she was looking at him.

'Is there anything I can do, Doctor?' she said.

He started.

'Why, what should there be?'

He gave her a glance and saw that her eyes were deeply troubled.

'You look dreadfully ill,' she said.

'I'm in great pain.'

'I know. I can see that. Can't something be done?'

'No, it'll pass off presently.'

She hesitated for a moment then went away. Presently she returned.

'You look so uncomfortable with no cushions or anything. I've brought you my own pillow that I always travel with. Do let me put it behind your head.'

He felt at that moment too ill to remonstrate. She lifted his head gently and put the soft pillow behind it. It really did make him feel more comfortable. She passed her hand across his forehead and it was cool and soft.

'Poor dear,' she said. 'I know what doctors are. They haven't the first idea how to take care of themselves.'

She left him, but in a minute or two returned with a chair and a bag. The doctor when he saw her gave a twitch of anguish.

'Now I'm not going to let you talk, I'm just going to sit beside you and knit. I always think it's a comfort when one isn't feeling very well to have someone near.'

She sat down and taking an unfinished muffler out of her bag began busily to ply her needles. She never said a word. And strangely enough the doctor found her company a solace. No one else on board had even noticed that he was ill, he had felt lonely, and the sympathy of that crashing bore was grateful to him. It soothed him to see her silently working and presently he fell asleep. When he awoke she was still working. She gave him a little smile, but did not speak. His pain had left him and he felt much better.

He did not go into the saloon till late in the afternoon. He found the captain and Hans Krause, the mate, having a glass of beer together.

'Sit down, Doctor,' said the captain. 'We're holding a council of war. You know that the day after tomorrow is Sylvester Abend.'

'Of course.'

Sylvester Abend, New Year's Eve, is an occasion that means a great deal to a German, and they had all been looking forward to it. They had brought a Christmas tree all the way from Germany with them.

'At dinner today Miss Reid was more talkative than ever. Hans and I have decided that something must be done about it.'

'She sat with me for two hours this morning in silence. I suppose she was making up for lost time.'

'It's bad enough to be away from one's home and family just now anyway and all we can do is to make the best of a bad job. We want to enjoy our Sylvester Abend, and unless something is done about Miss Reid we haven't a chance.'

'We can't have a good time if she's with us,' said the mate. 'She'll spoil it as sure as eggs is eggs.'

'How do you propose to get rid of her, short of throwing her overboard?' smiled the doctor. 'She's not a bad old soul; all she wants is a lover.'

'At her age?' cried Hans Krause.

'Especially at her age. That inordinate loquacity, that passion for information, the innumerable questions she asks, her prosiness, the way she goes on and on—it is all a sign of her clamouring virginity. A lover would bring her peace. Those jangled nerves of hers would relax. At least for an hour she would have lived. The deep satisfaction which her being demands would travel through those exacerbated centres of speech, and we should have quiet.'

It was always a little difficult to know how much the doctor meant what he said and when he was having a joke at your expense. The captain's blue eyes, however, twinkled mischievously.

'Well, Doctor, I have great confidence in your powers of diagnosis. The remedy you suggest is evidently worth trying, and since you are a bachelor it is clear that it is up to you to apply it.'

'Pardon me, Captain, it is my professional duty to prescribe remedies for the patients under my charge in this ship, but not to administer them personally. Besides, I am sixty.'

'I am a married man with grown-up children,' said the captain. 'I am old and fat and asthmatic, it is obvious that I cannot be expected to undertake a task of this kind. Nature cut me out for the role of a husband and father, not for that of a lover.'

'Youth in these matters is essential and good looks are advantageous,' said the doctor gravely.

The captain gave a great bang on the table with his fist.

'You are thinking of Hans. You're quite right. Hans must do it.'

The mate sprang to his feet.

'Me? Never.'

'Hans, you are tall, handsome, strong as a lion, brave, and young. We have twenty-three days more at sea before we reach Hamburg, you wouldn't desert your trusted old captain in an emergency or let down your good friend the doctor?'

'No, Captain, it's asking too much of me. I have been married less than a year and I love my wife. I can hardly wait to get back to Hamburg. She is yearning for me as I am yearning for her. I will not be unfaithful to her, especially with Miss Reid.'

'Miss Reid's not so bad,' said the doctor.

'Some people might call her even nice-looking,' said the captain.

And indeed when you took Miss Reid feature by feature she was not in fact a plain woman. True, she had a long stupid face, but her brown eyes were large and she had very thick lashes; her brown hair was cut short and curled rather prettily over her neck; she hadn't a bad skin, and she was neither too fat nor too thin. She was not old as people go nowadays, and if she had told you that she was forty you would have been quite willing to believe it. The only thing against her was that she was drab and dull.

'Must I then for twenty-three mortal days endure the prolixity of that tedious woman? Must I for twenty-three mortal days answer her inane questions and listen to her fatuous remarks? Must I, an old man, have my Silvester Abend, the jolly evening I was looking forward to, ruined by the unwelcome company of that intolerable virgin? And all because no one can be found to show a little gallantry, a little human kindness, a spark of charity to a lonely woman. I shall wreck the ship.'

'There's always the radio-operator,' said Hans.

The captain gave a loud shout.

'Hans, let the ten thousand virgins of Cologne arise and call you blessed. Steward,' he bellowed, 'tell the radio-operator that I want him.'

The radio-operator came into the saloon and smartly clicked his heels together. The three men looked at him in silence. He wondered uneasily whether he had done something for which he was to be hauled over the coals. He was above the middle height, with square shoulders and narrow hips, erect and slender, his tanned, smooth skin looked as though a razor had never touched it, he had large eyes of a startling blue and a mane of curling golden hair. He was a perfect specimen of young Teutonic manhood. He was so healthy, so vigorous, so much alive that even when he stood some way from you, you felt the glow of his vitality.

'Aryan, all right,' said the captain. 'No doubt about that. How old are you, my boy?'

'Twenty-one, sir.'

'Married?'

'No, sir.'

'Engaged?'

The radio-operator chuckled. There was an engaging boyishness in his laugh.

'No, sir.'

'You know that we have a female passenger on board?'

'Yes, sir.'

'Do you know her?'

'I've said good morning to her when I've seen her on deck.'

The captain assumed his most official manner. His eyes, which generally twinkled with fun, were stern and he got a sort of bark into his rich, fruity voice.

'Although this is a cargo-boat and we carry valuable freight, we also take such passengers as we can get, and this is a branch of our business that the company is anxious to encourage. My instructions are to do everything possible to promote the happiness and comfort of the passengers. Miss Reid needs a lover. The doctor and I have come to the conclusion that you are well suited to satisfy Miss Reid's requirements.'

'Me, sir?'

The radio-operator blushed scarlet and then began to giggle, but quickly composed himself when he saw the set faces of the three men who confronted him.

'But she's old enough to be my mother.'

'That at your age is a matter of no consequence. She is a woman of the highest distinction and allied to all the great families of England. If she were German she would be at least a countess. That you should have been chosen for this responsible position is an honour that you should greatly appreciate. Furthermore, your English is halting and this will give you an excellent opportunity to improve it.'

'That of course is something to be thought of,' said the radio-operator. 'I know that I want practice.'

'It is not often in this life that it is possible to combine pleasure with intellectual improvement, and you must congratulate yourself on your good fortune.'

'But if I may be allowed to put the question, sir, why does Miss Reid want a lover?'

'It appears to be an old English custom for unmarried women of exalted rank to submit themselves to the embraces of a lover at this time of year. The company is anxious that Miss Reid should be treated exactly as she would be on an English ship, and we trust that if she is satisfied, with her aristocratic connexions she will be able to persuade many of her friends to take cruises in the line's ships.'

'Sir, I must ask to be excused.'

'It is not a request that I am making, it is an order. You will present yourself to Miss Reid, in her cabin, at eleven o'clock tonight.'

'What shall I do when I get there?'

'Do?' thundered the captain. 'Do? Act naturally.'

With a wave of the hand he dismissed him. The radio-operator clicked his heels, saluted, and went out.

'Now let us have another glass of beer,' said the captain.

At supper that evening Miss Reid was at her best. She was verbose. She was playful. She was refined. There was not a truism that she failed to utter. There was not a commonplace that she forebore to express. She bombarded them with foolish questions. The captain's face grew redder and redder as he sought to contain his fury; he felt that he could not go on being polite to her any longer and if the doctor's remedy did not help, one day he would forget himself and give her, not a piece, but the whole of his mind.

'I shall lose my job,' he thought, 'but I'm not sure that it wouldn't be worth it.'

Next day they were already sitting at table when she came in to dinner.

'Sylvester Abend tomorrow,' she said, brightly. That was the sort of thing she would say. She went on: 'Well, what have you all been up to this morning?'

Since they did exactly the same thing every day, and she knew very well what that was, the question was enraging. The captain's heart sank. He briefly told the doctor what he thought of him.

'Now, no German, please,' said Miss Reid archly. 'You know I don't allow that, and why, Captain, did you give the poor doctor that sour look? It's Christmas time, you know; peace and goodwill to all men. I'm so excited about tomorrow evening, and will there be candles on the Christmas tree?'

'Naturally.'

'How thrilling! I always think a Christmas tree without candles isn't a Christmas tree. Oh, d'you know, I had such a funny experience last night. I can't understand it at all.'

A startled pause. They all looked intently at Miss Reid. For once they hung on her lips.

'Yes,' she went on in that monotonous, rather finicking way of hers, 'I was just getting into bed last night when there was a knock at my door. "Who is it?" I said. "It's the radio-operator," was the answer. "What is it?" I said. "Can I speak to you?" he said.'

They listened with rapt attention.

'"Well, I'll just pop on a dressing-gown," I said, "and open the door." So I popped on a dressing-gown and opened the door. The radio-operator said: "Excuse me, miss, but do you want to send a radio?" Well, I did think it was funny his coming at that hour to ask me if I wanted to send a radio, I just laughed in his face, it appealed to my sense of humour if you understand what I mean, but I didn't want to hurt his feelings so I said: "Thank you so much, but I don't think I want to send a radio." He stood there, looking so funny, as if he was quite embarrassed, so I said: "Thank you all the same for asking me," and then I said "Good night, pleasant dreams", and shut the door.'

'The damned fool,' cried the captain.

'He's young, Miss Reid,' the doctor put in. 'It was excess of zeal. I suppose he thought you would want to send a New Year's greeting to your friends and he wished you to get the advantage of the special rate.'

'Oh, I didn't mind at all. I like these queer little things that happen to one when one's travelling. I just get a good laugh out of them.'

As soon as dinner was over and Miss Reid had left them the captain sent for the radio-operator.

'You idiot, what in heaven's name made you ask Miss Reid last night whether she wanted to send a radio?'

'Sir, you told me to act naturally. I am a radio-operator. I thought it natural to ask her if she wanted to send a radio. I didn't know what else to say.'

'God in heaven,' shouted the captain, 'when Siegfried saw Brunhilde lying on her rock and cried: *Das ist kein Mann*,' (the captain sang the words, and being pleased with the sound of his voice, repeated the phrase two or three times before he continued), 'did Siegfried when she awoke ask her if she wished to send a radio, to announce to her papa, I suppose, that she was sitting up after her long sleep and taking notice?'

'I beg most respectfully to draw your attention to the fact that Brunhilde was Siegfried's aunt. Miss Reid is a total stranger to me.'

'He did not reflect that she was his aunt. He knew only that she was a beautiful and defenceless woman of obviously good family and he acted as any gentleman would have done. You are young, handsome, Aryan to the tips of your fingers, the honour of Germany is in your hands.'

'Very good, sir. I will do my best.'

That night there was another knock on Miss Reid's door.

'Who is it?'

'The radio-operator. I have a radio for you, Miss Reid.'

'For me?' She was surprised, but it at once occurred to her that one of her fellow-passengers who had got off at Haiti had sent her New Year's greetings. 'How very kind people are,' she thought. 'I'm in bed. Leave it outside the door.'

'It needs an answer. Ten words prepaid.'

Then it couldn't be a New Year's greeting. Her heart stopped beating. It could only mean one thing; her shop had been burned to the ground. She jumped out of bed.

'Slip it under the door and I'll write the answer and slip it back to you.'

The envelope was pushed under the door and as it appeared on the carpet it had really a sinister look. Miss Reid snatched it up and tore the envelope open. The words swam before her eyes and she couldn't for a moment find her spectacles. This is what she read:

'Happy New Year. Stop. Peace and goodwill to all men. Stop. You are very beautiful. Stop. I love you. Stop. I must speak to you. Stop. Signed: Radio Operator.'

Miss Reid read this through twice. Then she slowly took off her spectacles and hid them under a scarf. She opened the door.

'Come in,' she said.

Next day was New Year's Eve. The officers were cheerful and a little sentimental when they sat down to dinner. The stewards had decorated the saloon with tropical creepers to make up for holly and mistletoe, and the Christmas tree stood on a table with the candles ready to be lit at supper time. Miss Reid did not come in till the officers were seated, and when they bade her good morning she did not speak but merely bowed. They looked at her curiously. She ate a good dinner, but uttered never a word. Her silence was uncanny. At last the captain could stand it no longer, and he said:

'You're very quiet today, Miss Reid.'

'I'm thinking,' she remarked.

'And will you not tell us your thoughts, Miss Reid?' the doctor asked playfully.

She gave him a cool, you might almost have called it a supercilious, look.

'I prefer to keep them to myself, Doctor. I will have a little more of that hash, I've got a very good appetite.'

They finished the meal in a blessed silence. The captain heaved a sigh of relief. That was what meal-time was for, to eat, not to chatter. When they had finished he went up to the doctor and wrung his hand.

'Something has happened, Doctor.'

'It has happened. She's a changed woman.'

'But will it last?'

'One can only hope for the best.'

Miss Reid put on an evening dress for the evening's celebration, a very quiet black dress, with artificial roses at her bosom and a long string of imitation jade round her neck. The lights were dimmed and the candles on the Christmas tree were lit. It felt a little like being in church. The junior officers were supping in the saloon that evening and they looked very smart in their white uniforms. Champagne was served at the company's expense and after supper they had a *Maibowle.* They pulled crackers. They sang songs to the gramophone, *Deutschland, Deutschland über Alles, Alt Heidelberg,* and *Auld Lang Syne.* They shouted out the tunes lustily, the captain's voice rising loud above the others, and Miss Reid joining in with a pleasing contralto. The doctor noticed that Miss Reid's eyes from time to time rested on the radio-operator, and in them he read an expression of some bewilderment.

'He's a good-looking fellow, isn't he?' said the doctor.

Miss Reid turned round and looked at the doctor coolly.

'Who?'

'The radio-operator. I thought you were looking at him.'

'Which is he?'

'The duplicity of women,' the doctor muttered, but with a smile he answered: 'He's sitting next to the chief engineer.'

'Oh, of course, I recognize him now. You know, I never think it matters what a man looks like. I'm so much more interested in a man's brains than in his looks.'

'Ah,' said the doctor.

They all got a little tight, including Miss Reid, but she did not lose her dignity and when she bade them good night it was in her best manner.

'I've had a very delightful evening. I shall never forget my New Year's Eve on a German boat. It's been very interesting. Quite an experience.'

She walked steadily to the door, and this was something of a triumph, for she had drunk drink for drink with the rest of them through the evening.

They were all somewhat jaded next day. When the captain, the mate, the doctor, and the chief engineer came down to dinner they found Miss Reid already seated. Before each place was a small parcel tied up in pink ribbon. On each was written: Happy New Year. They gave Miss Reid a questioning glance.

'You've all been so very kind to me I thought I'd like to give each of you a little present. There wasn't much choice at Port au Prince, so you mustn't expect too much.'

There was a pair of briar pipes for the captain, half a dozen silk handkerchiefs for the doctor, a cigar-case for the mate, and a couple of ties for the chief engineer. They had dinner and Miss Reid retired to her cabin to rest. The officers looked at one another uncomfortably. The mate fiddled with the cigar-case she had given him.

'I'm a little ashamed of myself,' he said at last.

The captain was pensive and it was plain that he too was a trifle uneasy.

'I wonder if we ought to have played that trick on Miss Reid,' he said. 'She's a good old soul and she's not rich; she's a woman who earns her own living. She must have spent the best part of a hundred marks on these presents. I almost wish we'd left her alone.'

The doctor shrugged his shoulders.

'You wanted her silenced and I've silenced her.'

'When all's said and done, it wouldn't have hurt us to listen to her chatter for three weeks more,' said the mate.

'I'm not happy about her,' added the captain. 'I feel there's something ominous in her quietness.'

She had spoken hardly a word during the meal they had just shared with her. She seemed hardly to listen to what they said.

'Don't you think you ought to ask her if she's feeling quite well, doctor?' suggested the captain.

'Of course she's feeling quite well. She's eating like a wolf. If you want inquiries made you'd much better make them of the radio-operator.'

'You may not be aware of it, Doctor, but I am a man of great delicacy.'

'I am a man of heart myself,' said the doctor.

For the rest of the journey those men spoilt Miss Reid outrageously. They treated her with the consideration they would have shown to someone who was convalescent after a long and dangerous illness. Though her appetite was excellent they sought to tempt her with new dishes. The doctor ordered wine and insisted on her sharing his bottle with him. They played dominoes with her. They played chess with her. They played bridge with her. They engaged her in conversation. But there was no doubt about it, though she responded to their advances with politeness, she kept herself to herself. She seemed to regard them with something very like disdain; you might almost have thought that she looked upon those men and their efforts to be amiable as pleasantly ridiculous. She seldom spoke unless spoken to. She read detective stories and at night sat on deck looking at the stars. She lived a life of her own.

At last the journey drew to its close. They sailed up the English Channel on a still grey day; they sighted land. Miss Reid packed her trunk. At two o'clock in the afternoon they docked at Plymouth. The captain, the mate, and the doctor came along to say good-bye to her.

'Well, Miss Reid,' said the captain in his jovial way, 'we're sorry to lose you, but I suppose you're glad to be getting home.'

'You've been very kind to me, you've all been very kind to me, I don't know what I've done to deserve it. I've been very happy with you. I shall never forget you.'

She spoke rather shakily, she tried to smile, but her lips quivered, and tears ran down her cheeks. The captain got very red. He smiled awkwardly.

'May I kiss you, Miss Reid?'

She was taller than he by half a head. She bent down and he planted a fat kiss on one wet cheek an a fat kiss on the other. She turned to the mate and the doctor. They both kissed her.

'What an old fool I am,' she said. 'Everybody's so good.'

She dried her eyes and slowly, in her graceful, rather absurd way, walked down the companion. The captain's eyes were wet. When she reached the quay she looked up and waved to someone on the boat deck.

'Who's she waving to?' asked the captain.

'The radio-operator.'

Miss Price was waiting on the quay to welcome her. When they had passed the Customs and got rid of Miss Reid's heavy luggage they went to Miss Price's house and had an early cup of tea. Miss Reid's train did not start till five. Miss Price had much to tell Miss Reid.

'But it's too bad of me to go on like this when you've just come home. I've been looking forward to hearing all about your journey.'

'I'm afraid there's not very much to tell.'

'I can't believe that. Your trip was a success, wasn't it?'

'A distinct success. It was very nice.'

'And you didn't mind being with all those Germans?'

'Of course they're not like English people. One has to get used to their ways. They sometimes do things that—well, that English people wouldn't do, you know. But I always think that one has to take things as they come.'

'What sort of things do you mean?'

Miss Reid looked at her friend calmly. Her long, stupid face had a placid look, and Miss Price never noticed that in the eyes was a strangely mischievous twinkle.

'Things of no importance really. Just funny, unexpected, rather nice things. There's no doubt that travel is a wonderful education.'

A Marriage of Convenience

◆

I left Bangkok on a shabby little ship of four or five hundred tons. The dingy saloon, which served also as dining-room, had two narrow tables down its length with swivel chairs on both sides of them. The cabins were in the bowels of the ship and they were extremely dirty. Cockroaches walked about on the floor and however placid your temperament it is difficult not to be startled when you go to the wash-basin to wash your hands and a huge cockroach stalks leisurely out.

We dropped down the river, broad and lazy and smiling, and its green banks were dotted with little huts on piles standing at the water's edge. We crossed the bar; and the open sea, blue and still, spread before me. The look of it and the smell of it filled me with elation.

I had gone on board early in the morning and soon discovered that I was thrown amid the oddest collection of persons I had ever encountered. There were two French traders and a Belgian colonel, an Italian tenor, the American proprietor of a circus with his wife, and a retired French official with his. The circus proprietor was what is termed a good mixer, a type which according to your mood you fly from or welcome, but I happened to be feeling much pleased with life and before I had been on board an hour we had shaken for drinks, and he had shown me his animals. He was a very short fat man, and his stengah-shifter, white but none too clean, outlined the noble proportions of his abdomen, but the collar was so tight that you wondered he did not choke. He had a red, clean-shaven face, a merry blue eye, and short, untidy sandy hair. He wore a battered topee well on the back of his head. His name was Wilkins and he was born in Portland, Oregon. It appears that the Oriental has a passion for the circus and Mr Wilkins for twenty years had been travelling up and down the East from Port Said to Yokohama (Aden, Bombay, Madras, Calcutta, Rangoon,

Singapore, Penang, Bangkok, Saigon, Huë, Hanoi, Hong-Kong, Shanghai, their names roll on the tongue savourily, crowding the imagination with sunshine and strange sounds and a multicoloured activity) with his menagerie and his merry-go-rounds. It was a strange life he led, unusual, and one that, one would have thought, must offer the occasion for all sorts of curious experiences, but the odd thing about him was that he was a perfectly common-place little man and you would have been prepared to find him running a garage or keeping a third-rate hotel in a second-rate town in California. The fact is, and I have noticed it so often that I do not know why it should always surprise me, that the extraordinariness of a man's life does not make him extraordinary, but contrariwise if a man is extraordinary he will make extraordinariness out of a life as humdrum as that of a country curate. I wish I could feel it reasonable to tell here the story of the hermit I went to see on an island in the Torres Straits, a shipwrecked mariner who had lived there alone for thirty years, but when you are writing a book you are imprisoned by the four walls of your subject and though for the entertainment of my own digressing mind I set it down now I should be forced in the end, by my sense of what is fit to go between two covers and what is not, to cut it out. Anyhow, the long and short of it is that notwithstanding his long and intimate communion with nature and his thoughts the man was as dull, insensitive, and vulgar an oaf at the end of this experience as he must have been at the beginning.

The Italian singer passed us, and Mr Wilkins told me that he was a Neapolitan who was on his way to Hong-Kong to rejoin his company, which he had been forced to leave owing to an attack of malaria in Bangkok. He was an enormous fellow, and very fat, and when he flung himself into a chair it creaked with dismay. He took off his topee, displayed a great head of long, curly, greasy hair, and ran podgy and beringed fingers through it.

'He ain't very sociable,' said Mr Wilkins. 'He took the cigar I gave him, but he wouldn't have a drink. I shouldn't wonder if there wasn't somethin' rather queer about him. Nasty-lookin' guy, ain't he?'

Then a little fat woman in white came on deck holding by the hand a Wa-Wa monkey. It walked solemnly by her side.

'This is Mrs Wilkins,' said the circus proprietor, 'and our youngest son. Draw up a chair, Mrs Wilkins, and meet this gentleman. I don't know his name, but he's already paid for two drinks for me and if he can't shake any better than he has yet he'll pay for one for you too.'

Mrs Wilkins sat down with an abstracted serious look, and with her eyes on the blue sea suggested that she did not see why she shouldn't have a lemonade.

'My, it's hot,' she murmured, fanning herself with the topee which she took off.

'Mrs Wilkins feels the heat,' said her husband. 'She's had twenty years of it now.'

'Twenty-two and a half,' said Mrs Wilkins, still looking at the sea.

'And she's never got used to it.'

'Nor never shall and you know it,' said Mrs Wilkins.

She was just the same size as her husband and just as fat, and she had a round red face like his and the same sandy, untidy hair. I wondered if they had married because they were so exactly alike, or if in the course of years they had acquired this astonishing resemblance. She did not turn her head but continued to look absently at the sea.

'Have you shown him the animals?' she asked.

'You bet your life I have.'

'What did he think of Percy?'

'Thought him fine.'

I could not but feel that I was being unduly left out of a conversation of which I was at all events partly the subject, so I asked:

'Who's Percy?'

'Percy's our eldest son. There's a flyin'-fish, Elmer. He's the orang-utan. Did he eat his food well this morning?'

'Fine. He's the biggest orang-utan in captivity. I wouldn't take a thousand dollars for him.'

'And what relation is the elephant?' I asked.

Mrs Wilkins did not look at me, but with her blue eyes still gazed indifferently at the sea.

'He's no relation,' she answered. 'Only a friend.'

The boy brought lemonade for Mrs Wilkins, a whisky and soda for her husband, and a gin and tonic for me. We shook dice and I signed the chit.

'It must come expensive if he always loses when he shakes,' Mrs Wilkins murmured to the coast-line.

'I guess Egbert would like a sip of your lemonade, my dear,' said Mr Wilkins.

Mrs Wilkins slightly turned her head and looked at the monkey sitting on her lap.

'Would you like a sip of mother's lemonade, Egbert?'

The monkey gave a little squeak and putting her arm round him she handed him a straw. The monkey sucked up a little lemonade and having drunk enough sank back against Mrs Wilkins's ample bosom.

'Mrs Wilkins thinks the world of Egbert,' said her husband. 'You can't wonder at it, he's her youngest.'

Mrs Wilkins took another straw and thoughtfully drank her lemonade.

'Egbert's all right,' she remarked. 'There's nothin' wrong with Egbert.'

Just then the French official, who had been sitting down, got up and began walking up and down. He had been accompanied on board by the French minister at Bangkok, one or two secretaries, and a prince of the royal family. There had been a great deal of bowing and shaking of hands and as the ship slipped away from the quay much waving of hats and handkerchiefs. He was evidently a person of consequence. I had heard the captain address him as Monsieur le Gouverneur.

'That's the big noise on this boat,' said Mr Wilkins. 'He was Governor of one of the French colonies and now he's makin' a tour of the world. He came to see my circus at Bangkok. I guess I'll ask him what he'll have. What shall I call him, my dear?'

Mrs Wilkins slowly turned her head and looked at the Frenchman, with the rosette of the Legion of Honour in his buttonhole, pacing up and down.

'Don't call him anythin',' she said. 'Show him a hoop and he'll jump right through it.'

I could not but laugh. Monsieur le Gouverneur was a little man, well below the average height, and smally made, with a very ugly little face and thick, almost negroid features; and he had a bushy grey head, bushy grey eyebrows, and a bushy grey moustache. He did look a little like a poodle and he had the poodle's soft, intelligent and shining eyes. Next time he passed us Mr Wilkins called out:

'*Monsoo. Qu'est-ce que vous prenez?*' I cannot reproduce the eccentricities of his accent. '*Une petite verre de porto.*' He turned to me. 'Foreigners, they all drink porto. You're always safe with that.'

'Not the Dutch,' said Mrs Wilkins, with a look at the sea. 'They won't touch nothin' but Schnapps.'

The distinguished Frenchman stopped and looked at Mr Wilkins with some bewilderment. Whereupon Mr Wilkins tapped his breast and said:

'*Moa, proprietarre Cirque. Vous avez visité.*'

Then, for a reason that escaped me, Mr Wilkins made his arms into a hoop and outlined the gestures that represented a poodle jumping through it. Then he pointed at the Wa-Wa that Mrs Wilkins was still holding on her lap.

'*La petit fils de mon femme,*' he said.

Light broke upon the Governor and he burst into a peculiarly musical and infectious laugh. Mr Wilkins began laughing too.

'*Oui, oui,*' he cried. '*Moa,* circus proprietor. *Une petite verre de porto. Oui. Oui. N'est-ce-pas?*'

'Mr Wilkins talks French like a Frenchman,' Mrs Wilkins informed the passing sea.

'*Mais très volontiers,*' said the Governor, still smiling. I drew him up a chair and he sat down with a bow to Mrs Wilkins.

'Tell poodle-face his name's Egbert,' she said, looking at the sea.

I called the boy and we ordered a round of drinks.

'You sign the chit, Elmer,' she said. 'It's not a bit of good Mr What's-his-name shakin' if he can't shake nothin' better than a pair of treys.'

'*Vous comprenez le français, madame?*' asked the Governor politely.

'He wants to know if you speak French, my dear.'

'Where does he think I was raised? Naples?'

Then the Governor, with exuberant gesticulation, burst into a torrent of English so fantastic that it required all my knowledge of French to understand what he was talking about.

Presently Mr Wilkins took him down to look at his animals and a little later we assembled in the stuffy saloon for luncheon. The Governor's wife appeared and was put on the captain's right. The Governor explained to her who we all were and she gave us a gracious bow. She was a large woman, tall and of a robust build, of fifty-five perhaps, and she was dressed somewhat severely in black silk. On her head she wore a huge round topee. Her features were so large and regular, her form so statuesque, that you were reminded of the massive females who take part in processions. She would have admirably suited the role of Columbia or Britannia in a patriotic demonstration. She towered over her diminutive husband like a skyscraper over a shack. He talked incessantly, with vivacity and wit, and when he said anything amusing her heavy features relaxed into a large fond smile.

'*Que tu es bête, mon ami,*' she said. She turned to the captain. 'You must not pay any attention to him. He is always like that.'

We had indeed a very amusing meal and when it was over we separated to our various cabins to sleep away the heat of the afternoon. In such a small ship having once made the acquaintance of my fellow passengers, it would have been impossible, even had I wished it, not to pass with them every moment of the day that I was not in my cabin. The only person who held himself aloof was the Italian tenor. He spoke to no one, but sat by himself as far forward as he could get, twanging a guitar in an undertone so that you had to strain your ears to catch the notes. We remained in sight of land and the sea was like a pail of milk. Talking of one thing and another we watched the day decline, we dined, and then we sat out again on deck under the stars. The two traders played picquet in the hot saloon, but the Belgian colonel joined our little group. He was shy and fat and opened his mouth only to utter a civility. Soon, influenced perhaps by the night and encouraged by the darkness that gave him, up there in the bows, the sensation of being alone with the sea, the Italian tenor, accompanying himself on his guitar, began to sing, first in a low tone, and then a little louder, till presently, his music captivating him, he sang with all his might. He had the real Italian voice, all macaroni, olive oil, and sunshine, and he sang the Neapolitan songs that I had heard in my youth in the Piazza San Ferdinando, and fragments from *La Bohème*, and *Traviata*, and *Rigoletto*. He sang with emotion and false emphasis and his tremolo reminded you of every third-rate Italian tenor you had ever heard, but there in the openness of that lovely night his exaggerations only made you smile and you could not but feel in your heart a lazy sensual pleasure. He sang for an hour, perhaps, and we all fell silent; then he was still, but he did not move and we saw his huge bulk dimly outlined against the luminous sky.

I saw that the little French Governor had been holding the hand of his large wife and the sight was absurd and touching.

'Do you know that this is the anniversary of the day on which I first saw my wife?' he said, suddenly breaking the silence which had certainly weighed on him, for I had never met a more loquacious creature. 'It is also the anniversary of the day on which she promised to be my wife. And, which will surprise you, they were one and the same.'

'*Voyons, mon ami*,' said the lady, 'you are not going to bore our friends with that old story. You are really quite insupportable.'

But she spoke with a smile on her large, firm face, and in a tone that suggested that she was quite willing to hear it again.

'But it will interest them, *mon petit chou*.' It was in this way that he always addressed his wife and it was funny to hear this imposing and even majestic lady thus addressed by her small husband. 'Will it not, monsieur?' he asked me. 'It is a romance, and who does not like romance, especially on such a night as this?'

I assured the Governor that we were all anxious to hear and the Belgian colonel took the opportunity once more to be polite.

'You see, ours was a marriage of convenience pure and simple.'

'*C'est vrai*,' said the lady. 'It would be stupid to deny it. But sometimes love comes after marriage and not before, and then it is better. It lasts longer.'

I could not but notice that the Governor gave her hand an affectionate little squeeze.

'You see, I had been in the navy, and when I retired I was forty-nine. I was strong and active and I was very anxious to find an occupation. I looked about; I pulled all the strings I could. Fortunately I had a cousin who had some political importance. It is one of the advantages of democratic government that if you have sufficient influence, merit, which otherwise might pass unnoticed, generally receives its due reward.'

'You are modesty itself, *mon pauvre ami*,' said she.

'And presently I was sent for by the Minister to the Colonies and offered the post of Governor in a certain colony. It was a very distant spot that they wished to send me to and a lonely one, but I had spent my life wandering from port to port, and that was not a matter that troubled me. I accepted with joy. The minister told me that I must be ready to start in a month. I told him that would be easy for an old bachelor who had nothing much in the world but a few clothes and a few books.

'"*Comment, mon lieutenant,*" he cried. "You are a bachelor?"

'"Certainly," I answered. "And I have every intention of remaining one."

'"In that case I am afraid I must withdraw my offer. For this position it is essential that you should be married."

'It is too long a story to tell you, but the gist of it was that owing to the scandal my predecessor, a bachelor, had caused by having native girls to live in the Residency and the consequent complaints of the white people, planters and the wives of functionaries, it had been decided that the next Governor must be a model of respectability. I expostulated. I argued. I recapitulated my services to the country and the services my cousin could render at the next elections. Nothing would serve. The minister was adamant.

'"But what can I do?" I cried with dismay.

'"You can marry," said the minister.

'"*Mais voyons, monsieur le ministre,* I do not know any women. I am not a lady's man and I am forty-nine. How do you expect me to find a wife?"

'"Nothing is more simple. Put an advertisement in the paper."

'I was confounded. I did not know what to say.

'"Well, think it over," said the minister. "If you can find a wife in a month you can go, but no wife no job. That is my last word." He smiled a little, to him the situation was not without humour. "And if you think of advertising I recommend the *Figaro.*"

'I walked away from the ministry with death in my heart. I knew the place to which they desired to appoint me and I knew it would suit me very well to live there; the climate was tolerable and the Residency was spacious and comfortable. The notion of being a Governor was far from displeasing me and, having nothing much but my pension as a naval officer, the salary was not to be despised. Suddenly I made up my mind. I walked to the offices of the *Figaro,* composed an advertisement, and handed it in for insertion. But I can tell you, when I walked up the Champs Elysées afterwards my heart was beating much more furiously than it had ever done when my ship was stripped for action.'

The Governor leaned forward and put his hand impressively on my knee.

'*Mon cher monsieur,* you will never believe it, but I had four thousand three hundred and seventy-two replies. It was an avalanche. I had expected half-a-dozen; I had to take a cab to take the letters to my hotel. My room was swamped with them. There were four thousand three hundred and seventy-two women who were willing to share my solitude and be a Governor's lady. It was staggering. They were of all ages from seventeen to seventy. There were maidens of irreproachable ancestry and the highest culture, there were unmarried ladies who had made a little slip at one period of their career and now desired to regularize their situation; there were widows whose husbands had died in the most harrowing circumstances; and there were widows whose children would be a solace to my old age. They were blonde and dark, tall and short, fat and thin; some could speak five languages and others could play the piano. Some offered me love and some craved for it; some could only give me solid friendship but mingled with esteem; some had a fortune and others golden prospects. I was overwhelmed. I was bewildered. At last I lost my temper, for I am a passionate man, and I got up and I stamped on all those letters and all those photographs and I cried: I will marry none of them. It was hopeless, I had less than a month now and I could not see over four thousand aspirants to my hand in that time. I felt that if I did not see them all, I should be tortured for the rest of my life by the thought that I had missed the one woman the fates had destined to make me happy. I gave it up as a bad job.

'I went out of my room hideous with all those photographs and littered papers and to drive care away went on to the boulevard and sat down at the Café de la Paix. After a time I saw a friend passing and he nodded to me and smiled. I tried to smile but my heart was sore. I realized that I must spend the years that remained to me in a cheap *pension* at Toulon or Brest as an *officier de marine en retraite. Zut!* My friend stopped and coming up to me sat down.

'"What is making you look so glum, *mon cher?*" he asked me. "You who are the gayest of mortals."

'I was glad to have someone in whom I could confide my troubles and told him the whole story. He laughed consumedly. I have thought since that perhaps the incident had its comic side, but at the time, I assure you, I could see in it nothing to laugh at. I mentioned the fact to my friend not without asperity and then, controlling his mirth as best he could, he said to me: "But, my dear fellow, do you really want to marry?" At this I entirely lost my temper.

'"You are completely idiotic," I said. "If I did not want to marry, and what is more marry at once, within the next fortnight, do you imagine that I should have spent three days reading love letters from women I have never set eyes on?"

'"Calm yourself and listen to me," he replied. "I have a cousin who lives in Geneva. She is Swiss, *du reste*, and she belongs to a family of the greatest respectability in the republic. Her morals are without reproach, she is of a suitable age, a spinster, for she has spent the last fifteen years nursing an invalid mother who has lately died, she is well educated and *pardessus le marché* she is not ugly."

'"It sounds as though she were a paragon," I said.

'"I do not say that, but she has been well brought up and would become the position you have to offer her."

'"There is one thing you forget. What inducement would there be for her to give up her friends and her accustomed life to accompany in exile a man of forty-nine who is by no means a beauty?"'

Monsieur le Gouverneur broke off his narrative and shrugging his shoulders so emphatically that his head almost sank between them, turned to us.

'I am ugly. I admit it. I am of an ugliness that does not inspire terror or respect, but only ridicule, and that is the worst ugliness of all. When people see me for the first time they do not shrink with horror, there would evidently be something flattering in that, they burst out laughing. Listen, when the admirable Mr Wilkins showed me his animals this morning, Percy, the orang-utan, held out his arms and but for the bars of the cage would have clasped me to his bosom as a long lost brother. Once indeed when I was at the Jardin des Plantes in Paris and was told that one of the anthropoid apes had escaped I made my way to the exit as quickly as I could for fear that, mistaking me for the refugee, they would seize me and, notwithstanding my expostulations, shut me up in the monkey house.'

'*Voyons, mon ami,*' said Madame his wife, in her deep slow voice, 'you are talking even greater nonsense than usual. I do not say that you are an Apollo, in your position it is unnecessary that you should be, but you have dignity, you have poise, you are what any woman would call a fine man.'

'I will resume my story. When I made this remark to my friend he replied: "One can never tell with women. There is something about marriage that wonderfully attracts them. There would be no harm in asking her. After all it is regarded as a compliment by a woman to be asked in marriage. She can but refuse."

'"But I do not know your cousin and I do not see how I am to make her acquaintance. I cannot go to her house, ask to see her and when I am shown into the drawing-room say: *Voilà*, I have come to ask you to marry me. She would think I was a lunatic and scream for help. Besides, I am a man of an extreme timidity, and I could never take such a step."

'"I will tell you what to do," said my friend. "Go to Geneva and take her a box of chocolates from me. She will be glad to have news of me and will receive you with pleasure. You can have a little talk and then if you do not like the look of her you take your leave and no harm is done. If on the other hand you do, we can go into the matter and you can make a formal demand for her hand."

'I was desperate. It seemed the only thing to do. We went to a shop at once and bought an enormous box of chocolates and that night I took the train to Geneva. No sooner had I arrived than I sent her a letter to say that I was the bearer of a gift from her cousin and much wished to give myself the pleasure of delivering it in person. Within an hour I received her reply to the effect that she would be pleased to receive me at four o'clock in the afternoon. I spent the interval before my mirror and seventeen times I tied and retied my tie. As the clock struck four I presented myself at the door of her house and was immediately ushered into the drawing-room. She was waiting for me. Her cousin said she was not ugly. Imagine my surprise to see a young woman, *enfin* a woman still young, of a noble presence, with the dignity of Juno, the features of Venus, and in her expression the intelligence of Minerva.'

'You are too absurd,' said Madame. 'But by now these gentlemen know that one cannot believe all you say.'

'I swear to you that I do not exaggerate. I was so taken aback that I nearly dropped the box of chocolates. But I said to myself: *La garde meurt mais ne se rend pas.* I presented the box of chocolates. I gave her news of her cousin. I found her amiable. We talked for a quarter of an hour. And then I said to myself: *Allons-y.* I said to her:

'"Mademoiselle, I must tell you that I did not come here merely to give you a box of chocolates."

'She smiled and remarked that evidently I must have had reasons to come to Geneva of more importance than that.

'"I came to ask you to do me the honour of marrying me." She gave a start.

'"But, *monsieur*, you are mad," she said.

'"I beseech you not to answer till you have heard the facts," I interrupted, and before she could say another word I told her the whole story. I told her about my advertisement in the *Figaro* and she laughed till the tears ran down her face. Then I repeated my offer.

'"You are serious?" she asked.

'"I have never been more serious in my life."

'"I will not deny that your offer has come as a surprise. I had not thought of marrying, I have passed the age; but evidently your offer is not one that a woman should refuse without consideration. I am flattered. Will you give me a few days to reflect?"

'"*Mademoiselle*, I am absolutely desolated," I replied. "But I have not time.

If you will not marry me I must go back to Paris and resume my perusal of the fifteen or eighteen hundred letters that still await my attention."

'"It is quite evident that I cannot possibly give you an answer at once. I had not set eyes on you a quarter of an hour ago. I must consult my friends and my family."

'"What have they got to do with it? You are of full age. The matter is pressing. I cannot wait. I have told you everything. You are an intelligent woman. What can prolonged reflection add to the impulse of the moment?"

'"You are not asking me to say yes or no this very minute? That is outrageous."

'"That is exactly what I am asking. My train goes back to Paris in a couple of hours."

'She looked at me reflectively.

'"You are quite evidently a lunatic. You ought to be shut up both for your own safety and that of the public."

'"Well, which is it to be?" I said. "Yes or no?"

'She shrugged her shoulders.

'"*Mon Dieu.*" She waited a minute and I was on tenterhooks. "Yes."

The Governor waved his hand towards his wife.

'And there she is. We were married in a fortnight and I became Governor of a colony. I married a jewel, my dear sirs, a woman of the most charming character, one in a thousand, a woman of masculine intelligence and a feminine sensibility, an admirable woman.'

'But hold your tongue, *mon ami,*' his wife said. 'You are making me as ridiculous as yourself.'

He turned to the Belgian colonel.

'Are you a bachelor, *mon colonel*? If so I strongly recommend you to go to Geneva. It is a nest (*une pépinière* was the word he used) of the most adorable young women. You will find a wife there as nowhere else. Geneva is besides a charming city. Do not waste a minute, but go there and I will give you a letter to my wife's nieces.'

It was she who summed up the story.

'The fact is that in a marriage of convenience you expect less and so you are less likely to be disappointed. As you do not make senseless claims on one another there is no reason for exasperation. You do not look for perfection and so you are tolerant to one another's faults. Passion is all very well, but it is not a proper foundation for marriage. *Voyez-vous,* for two people to be happy in marriage they must be able to respect one another, they must be of the same condition, and their interests must be alike; then if they are decent people and are willing to give and take, to live and let live, there is no reason why their union should not be as happy as ours.' She paused. 'But, of course, my husband is a very, very remarkable man.'

Mirage

◆

I had been wandering about the East for months and at last reached Haiphong.
It is a commercial town and a dull one, but I knew that from there I could find a
ship of sorts to take me to Hong-Kong. I had some days to wait and nothing to
do. It is true that from Haiphong you can visit the Bay of Along, which is one of
the *Sehenswurdigkeiten* of Indo-China, but I was tired of sights. I contented myself with sitting in the cafés, for here it was none too warm and I was glad to get
out of tropical clothes, and reading back numbers of *L'Illustration,* or for the
sake of exercise taking a brisk walk along straight, wide streets. Haiphong is
traversed by canals and sometimes I got a glimpse of a scene which in its varied
life, with all the native craft on the water, was multicoloured and charming.
There was one canal, with tall Chinese houses on each side of it, that had a
pleasant curve. The houses were whitewashed, but the whitewash was
discoloured and stained; with their grey roofs they made an agreeable
composition against the pale sky. The picture had the faded elegance of an old
water-colour. There was nowhere an emphatic note. It was soft and a little
weary and inspired one with a faint melancholy. I was reminded I scarcely
know why of an old maid I knew in my youth, a relic of the Victorian age, who
wore black silk mittens and made crochet shawls for the poor, black for widows
and white for married women. She had suffered in her youth, but whether from
ill-health or unrequited love, no one exactly knew.

But there was a local paper at Haiphong, a small dingy sheet with stubby type
the ink of which came off on your fingers, and it gave you a political article, the
wireless news, advertisements, and local intelligence. The editor, doubtless
hard pressed for matter, printed the names of the persons, Europeans, natives
of the country, and Chinese, who had arrived at Haiphong or left it, and mine
was put in with the rest. On the morning of the day before that on which the old

tub I was taking was to sail for Hong-Kong I was sitting in the café of the hotel drinking a Dubonnet before luncheon when the boy came in and said that a gentleman wished to see me. I did not know a soul in Haiphong and asked who it was. The boy said he was an Englishman and lived there, but he could not tell me his name. The boy spoke very little French and it was hard for me to understand what he said. I was mystified, but told him to show the visitor in. A moment later he came back followed by a white man and pointed me out to him. The man gave me a look and walked towards me. He was a very tall fellow, well over six feet high, rather fat and bloated, with a red, clean-shaven face and extremely pale blue eyes. He wore very shabby khaki shorts and a stengah-shifter unbuttoned at the neck, and a battered helmet. I concluded at once that he was a stranded beachcomber who was going to touch me for a loan and wondered how little I could hope to get off for.

He came up to me and held out a large red hand with broken, dirty nails.

'I don't suppose you remember me,' he said. 'My name's Grosely. I was at St Thomas's Hospital with you. I recognized your name as soon as I saw it in the paper and I thought I'd look you up.'

I had not the smallest recollection of him, but I asked him to sit down and offered him a drink. By his appearance I had first thought he would ask me for ten piastres and I might have given him five, but now it looked more likely that he would ask for a hundred and I should have to think myself lucky if I could content him with fifty. The habitual borrower always asks twice what he expects to get and it only dissatisfies him to give him what he has asked since then he is vexed with himself for not having asked more. He feels you have cheated him.

'Are you a doctor?' I asked.

'No, I was only at the bloody place a year.'

He took off his sun-helmet and showed me a mop of grey hair, which much needed a brush. His face was curiously mottled and he did not look healthy. His teeth were badly decayed and at the corners of his mouth were empty spaces. When the boy came to take the orders he asked for brandy.

'Bring the bottle,' he said. '*La bouteille.* Savvy?' He turned to me. 'I've been living here for the last five years, but I can't get along with the French somehow. I talk Tonkinese.' He leaned his chair back and looked at me. 'I remember you, you know. You used to go about with those twins. What was their name? I expect I've changed more than you have. I've spent the best part of my life in China. Rotten climate, you know. It plays hell with a man.'

I still had not the smallest recollection of him. I thought it best to say so.

'Were you the same year as I was?' I asked.

'Yes. '92.'

'It's a devil of a long time ago.'

About sixty boys and young men entered the hospital every year; they were most of them shy and confused by the new life they were entering upon; many had never been in London before; and to me at least they were shadows that passed without any particular rhyme or reason across a white sheet. During the first year a certain number for one reason or another dropped out, and in the second year those that remained gained by degrees the beginnings of a personality. They were not only themselves, but the lectures one had attended with them, the scone and coffee one had eaten at the same table for luncheon, the dissection one had done at the same board in the same dissecting room, and

The Belle of New York one had seen together from the pit of the Shaftesbury Theatre.

The boy brought the bottle of brandy, and Grosely, if that was really his name, pouring himself out a generous helping drank it down at a gulp without water or soda.

'I couldn't stand doctoring,' he said. 'I chucked it. My people got fed up with me and I went out to China. They gave me a hundred pounds and told me to shift for myself. I was damned glad to get out, I can tell you. I guess I was just about as much fed up with them as they were with me. I haven't troubled them much since.'

Then from somewhere in the depths of my memory a faint hint crept into the rim, as it were, of consciousness, as on a rising tide the water slides up the sand and then withdraws to advance with the next wave in a fuller volume. I had first an inkling of some shabby little scandal that had got into the papers. Then I saw a boy's face, and so gradually the facts recurred to me; I remembered him now. I didn't believe he was called Grosely then, I think he had a one-syllabled name, but that I was uncertain of. He was a very tall lad (I began to see him quite well), thin, with a slight stoop, he was only eighteen and had grown too fast for his strength, he had curly, shining brown hair, rather large features (they did not look so large now, perhaps because his face was fat and puffy) and a peculiarly fresh complexion, very pink and white, like a girl's. I imagine people, women especially, would have thought him a very handsome boy, but to us he was only a clumsy, shuffling lout. Then I remembered that he did not often come to lectures, no, it wasn't that I remembered, there were too many students in the theatre to recollect who was there and who wasn't. I remembered the dissecting room. He had a leg at the next table to the one I was working at and he hardly ever touched it; I forget why the men who had other parts of the body complained of his neglecting the work, I suppose somehow it interfered with them. In those days a good deal of gossip went on over the dissection of a 'part' and out of the distance of thirty years some of it came back to me. Someone started the story that Grosely was a very gay dog. He drank like a fish and was an awful womanizer. Most of those boys were very simple, and they had brought to the hospital the notions they had acquired at home and at school. Some were prudish and they were shocked; others, those who worked hard, sneered at him and asked how he could hope to pass his exams; but a good many were excited and impressed, he was doing what they would have liked to do if they had had the courage. Grosely had his admirers and you could often see him surrounded by a little band listening open-mouthed to stories of his adventures. Recollections now were crowding upon me. In a very little while he lost his shyness and assumed the airs of a man of the world. They must have looked absurd on this smooth-cheeked boy with his pink and white skin. Men (so they called themselves) used to tell one another of his escapades. He became quite a hero. He would make caustic remarks as he passed the museum and saw a pair of earnest students going over their anatomy together. He was at home in the public-houses of the neighbourhood and was on familiar terms with the barmaids. Looking back, I imagine that, newly arrived from the country and the tutelage of parents and schoolmasters, he was captivated by his freedom and the thrill of London. His dissipations were harmless enough. They were due only to the urge of youth. He lost his head.

But we were all very poor and we did not know how Grosely managed to pay for his garish amusements. We knew his father was a country doctor and I think we knew exactly how much he gave his son a month. It was not enough to pay for the harlots he picked up on the promenade at the Pavilion and for the drinks he stood his friends in the Criterion Bar. We told one another in awe-struck tones that he must be getting fearfully into debt. Of course he could pawn things, but we knew by experience that you could not get more than three pounds for a microscope and thirty shillings for a skeleton. We said he must be spending at least ten pounds a week. Our ideas were not very grand and this seemed to us the wildest pitch of extravagance. At last one of his friends disclosed the mystery: Grosely had discovered a wonderful system for making money. It amused and impressed us. None of us would have thought of anything so ingenious or have had the nerve to attempt it if he had. Grosely went to auctions, not Christie's, of course, but auctions in the Strand and Oxford Street, and in private houses, and bought anything portable that was going cheap. Then he took his purchase to a pawnbroker's and pawned it for ten shillings or a pound more than he had paid. He was making money, four or five pounds a week, and he said he was going to give up medicine and make a regular business of it. Not one of us had ever made a penny in his life and we regarded Grosely with admiration.

'By Jove, he's clever,' we said.

'He's just about as sharp as they make them.'

'That's the sort that ends up as a millionaire.'

We were all very worldly-wise and what we didn't know about life at eighteen we were pretty sure wasn't worth knowing. It was a pity that when an examiner asked us a question we were so nervous that the answer often flew straight out of our head and when a nurse asked us to post a letter we blushed scarlet. It became known that the Dean had sent for Grosely and hauled him over the coals. He had threatened him with sundry penalties if he continued systematically to neglect his work. Grosely was indignant. He'd had enough of that sort of thing at school, he said, he wasn't going to let a horse-faced eunuch treat him like a boy. Damn it all, he was getting on for nineteen and there wasn't much you could teach him. The Dean had said he heard he was drinking more than was good for him. Damned cheek. He could carry his liquor as well as any man of his age, he'd been blind last Saturday and he meant to get blind next Saturday, and if anyone didn't like it he could do the other thing. Grosely's friends quite agreed with him that a man couldn't let himself be insulted like that.

But the blow fell at last and now I remembered quite well the shock it gave us all. I suppose we had not seen Grosely for two or three days, but he had been in the habit of coming to the hospital more and more irregularly, so if we thought anything about it, I imagine we merely said that he was off on one of his bats. He would turn up again in a day or so, rather pale, but with a wonderful story of some girl he had picked up and the time he had had with her. The anatomy lecture was at nine in the morning and it was a rush to get there in time. On this particular day little attention was paid to the lecturer, who, with a visible pleasure in his limpid English and admirable elocution, was describing I know not what part of the human skeleton, for there was much excited whispering along the benches and a newspaper was surreptitiously passed from hand to hand. Suddenly the lecturer stopped. He had a pedagogic sarcasm. He affected not to know the names of his students.

'I am afraid I am disturbing the gentleman who is reading the paper.

Anatomy is a very tedious science and I regret that the regulations of the Royal College of Surgeons oblige me to ask you to give it enough of your attention to pass an examination in it. Any gentleman, however, who finds this impossible is at liberty to continue his perusal of the paper outside.'

The wretched boy to whom this reproof was addressed reddened to the roots of his hair and in his embarrassment tried to stuff the newspaper in his pocket. The professor of anatomy observed him coldly.

'I am afraid, sir, that the paper is a little too large to go into your pocket,' he remarked. 'Perhaps you would be good enough to hand it down to me?'

The newspaper was passed from row to row to the well of the theatre, and, not content with the confusion to which he had put the poor lad, the eminent surgeon, taking it, asked:

'May I inquire what it is in the paper that the gentleman in question found of such absorbing interest?'

The student who gave it to him without a word pointed out the paragraph that we had all been reading. The professor read it and we watched him in silence. He put the paper down and went on with his lecture. The headline ran *Arrest of a Medical Student.* Grosely had been brought before the police-court magistrate for getting goods on credit and pawning them. It appears that this is an indictable offence and the magistrate had remanded him for a week. Bail was refused. It looked as though his method of making money by buying things at auctions and pawning them had not in the long run proved as steady a source of income as he expected and he had found it more profitable to pawn things that he was not at the expense of paying for. We talked the matter over excitedly as soon as the lecture was over and I am bound to say that, having no property ourselves, so deficient was our sense of its sanctity we could none of us look upon his crime as a very serious one; but with the natural love of the young for the terrible there were few who did not think he would get anything from two years' hard labour to seven years' penal servitude.

I do not know why, but I did not seem to have any recollection of what happened to Grosely. I think he may have been arrested towards the end of a session and his case may have come on again when we had all separated for holidays. I did not know if it was disposed of by the police-court magistrate or whether it went up for trial. I had a sort of feeling that he was sentenced to a short term of imprisonment, six weeks perhaps, for his operations had been pretty extensive; but I knew that he had vanished from our midst and in a little while was thought of no more. It was strange to me that after all these years I should recollect so much of the incident so clearly. It was as though, turning over an album of old snapshots, I saw all at once the photograph of a scene I had quite forgotten.

But of course in that gross elderly man with grey hair and mottled red face I should never have recognized the lanky pink-cheeked boy. He looked sixty, but I knew he must be much less than that. I wondered what he had done with himself in the intervening time. It did not look as though he had excessively prospered.

'What were you doing in China?' I asked him.

'I was a tide-waiter.'

'Oh, were you?'

It is not a position of great importance and I took care to keep out of my tone any note of surprise. The tide-waiters are employees of the Chinese Customs whose duty it is to board the ships and junks at the various treaty ports and I think their chief business is to prevent opium-smuggling. They are mostly retired A.B.s from the Royal Navy and non-commissioned officers who have finished their time. I have seen them come on board at various places up the Yangtse. They hobnob with the pilot and the engineer, but the skipper is a trifle curt with them. They learn to speak Chinese more fluently than most Europeans and often marry Chinese women.

'When I left England I swore I wouldn't go back till I'd made my pile. And I never did. They were glad enough to get anyone to be a tide-waiter in those days, any white man I mean, and they didn't ask questions. They didn't care who you were. I was damned glad to get the job, I can tell you, I was about broke to the wide when they took me on. I only took it till I could get something better, but I stayed on, it suited me, I wanted to make money and I found out that a tide-waiter could make a packet if he knew the right way to go about it. I was with the Chinese Customs for the best part of twenty-five years and when I came away I wouldn't mind betting that lots of commissioners would have been glad to have the money I had.'

He gave me a sly, mean look. I had an inkling of what he meant. But there was a point on which I was willing to be reassured; if he was going to ask me for a hundred piastres (I was resigned to that sum now) I thought I might just as well take the blow at once.

'I hope you kept it,' I said.

'You bet I did. I invested all my money in Shanghai and when I left China I put it all in American railway bonds. Safety first is my motto. I know too much about crooks to take any risks myself.'

I liked that remark, so I asked him if he wouldn't stay and have luncheon with me.

'No, I don't think I will. I don't eat much tiffin and anyway my chow's waiting for me at home. I think I'll be getting along.' He got up and he towered over me. 'But look here, why don't you come along this evening and see my place? I've married a Haiphong girl. Got a baby too. It's not often I get a chance of talking to anyone about London. You'd better not come to dinner. We only eat native food and I don't suppose you'd care for that. Come along about nine, will you?'

'All right,' I said.

I had already told him that I was leaving Haiphong next day. He asked the boy to bring him a piece of paper so that he might write down his address. He wrote laboriously in the hand of a boy of fourteen.

'Tell the porter to explain to your rickshaw boy where it is. I'm on the second floor. There's no bell. Just knock. Well, see you later.'

He walked out and I went in to luncheon.

After dinner I called a rickshaw and with the porter's help made the boy understand where I wanted to go. I found presently that he was taking me along the curved canal the houses of which had looked to me so like a faded Victorian water-colour; he stopped at one of them and pointed to the door. It looked so shabby and the neighbourhood was so squalid that I hesitated, thinking he had made a mistake. It seemed unlikely that Grosely could live so far in the native quarter and in a house so bedraggled. I told the rickshaw boy to wait and pushing open the door saw a dark staircase in front of me. There was no one about and the street was empty. It might have been the small hours of the morning. I struck a match and fumbled my way upstairs; on the second floor I struck another match and saw a large brown door in front of me. I knocked and in a moment it was opened by a little Tonkinese woman holding a candle. She was dressed in the earth-brown of the poorer classes, with a tight little black turban on her head; her lips and the skin round them were stained red with betel and when she opened her mouth to speak I saw that she had the black teeth and black gums that so disfigure these people. She said something in her native language and then I heard Grosely's voice:

'Come along in. I was beginning to think you weren't going to turn up.'

I passed through a little dark ante-chamber and entered a large room that evidently looked on the canal. Grosely was lying on a long chair and he raised his length from it as I came in. He was reading the Hong-Kong papers by the light of a paraffin-lamp that stood on a table by his side.

'Sit down,' he said, 'and put your feet up.'

'There's no reason I should take your chair.'

'Go on. I'll sit on this.'

He took a kitchen chair and sitting on it put his feet on the end of mine.

'That's my wife,' he said pointing with his thumb at the Tonkinese woman who had followed me into the room. 'And over there in the corner's the kid.'

I followed his eyes and against the wall, lying on bamboo mats and covered with a blanket, I saw a child sleeping.

'Lively little beggar when he's awake. I wish you could have seen him. She's going to have another soon.'

I glanced at her and the truth of what he said was apparent. She was very small, with tiny hands and feet, but her face was flat and the skin muddy. She looked sullen, but may only have been shy. She went out of the room and presently came back with a bottle of whisky, two glasses, and a syphon. I looked round. There was a partition at the back of dark unpainted wood, which I suppose shut off another room, and pinned against the middle of this was a portrait cut out of an illustrated paper of John Galsworthy. He looked austere, mild, and gentlemanly, and I wondered what he did there. The other walls were whitewashed, but the whitewash was dingy and stained. Pinned on to them were pages of pictures from the *Graphic* or the *Illustrated London News*.

'I put them up,' said Grosely, 'I thought they made the place look homelike.'

'What made you put up Galsworthy? Do you read his books?'

'No, I didn't know he wrote books. I liked his face.'

There were one or two torn and shabby rattan mats on the floor and in a corner a great pile of the *Hong-Kong Times*. The only furniture consisted of a wash-hand stand, two or three kitchen chairs, a table or two, and a large teak native bed. It was cheerless and sordid.

'Not a bad little place, is it?' said Grosely. 'Suits me all right. Sometimes I've thought of moving, but I don't suppose I ever shall now.' He gave a little chuckle. 'I came to Haiphong for forty-eight hours and I've been here five years. I was on my way to Shanghai really.'

He was silent. Having nothing to say I said nothing. Then the little Tonkinese woman made a remark to him, which I could not of course understand, and he answered her. He was silent again for a minute or two, but I thought he looked at me as though he wanted to ask me something. I did not know why he hesitated.

'Have you ever tried smoking opium on your travels in the East?' he inquired at last, casually.

'Yes, I did once, at Singapore. I thought I'd like to see what it was like.'

'What happened?'

'Nothing very thrilling, to tell you the truth. I thought I was going to have the most exquisite emotions. I expected visions, like de Quincey's, you know. The only thing I felt was a kind of physical well-being, the same sort of feeling that you get when you've had a Turkish bath and are lying in the cooling room, and then a peculiar activity of mind so that everything I thought of seemed extremely clear.'

'I know.'

'I really felt that two and two are four and there could not be the smallest doubt about it. But next morning–oh God! My head reeled. I was as sick as a dog, I was sick all day, I vomited my soul out, and as I vomited I said to myself miserably: And there are people who call this fun.'

Grosely leaned back in his chair and gave a low mirthless laugh.

'I expect it was bad stuff. Or you went at it too hard. They saw you were a mug and gave you dregs that had been smoked already. They're enough to turn anybody up. Would you like to have another try now? I've got some stuff here that I know's good.'

'No, I think once was enough for me.'

'D'you mind if I have a pipe or two? You want it in a climate like this. It keeps you from getting dysentery. And I generally have a bit of a smoke about this time.'

'Go ahead,' I said.

He spoke again to the woman and she, raising her voice, called out something in a raucous tone. An answer came from the room behind the wooden partition and after a minute or two an old woman came out carrying a little round tray. She was shrivelled and old and when she entered gave me an ingratiating smile of her stained mouth. Grosely got up and crossed over to the bed and lay on it. The old woman set the tray down on the bed; on it was a spirit-lamp, a pipe, a long needle, and a little round box of opium. She squatted on the bed and Grosely's wife got on it too and sat, her feet tucked up under her, with her back against the wall. Grosely watched the old woman while she put a little pellet of the drug on the needle, held it over the flame till it sizzled, and then plugged it into the pipe. She handed it to him and with a great breath he inhaled it, he held the smoke for a little while and then blew it out in a thick grey cloud. He handed her back the pipe and she started to make another. Nobody spoke. He smoked three pipes in succession and then sank back.

'By George, I feel better now. I was feeling all in. She makes a wonderful pipe, this old hag. Are you sure you won't have one?'

'Quite.'

'Please yourself. Have some tea then.'

He spoke to his wife, who scrambled off the bed and went out of the room. Presently she came back with a little china pot of tea and a couple of Chinese bowls.

'A lot of people smoke here, you know. It does you no harm if you don't do it to excess. I never smoke more than twenty to twenty-five pipes a day. You can go on for years if you limit yourself to that. Some of the Frenchmen smoke as many as forty or fifty a day. That's too much. I never do that, except now and then when I feel I want a binge. I'm bound to say it's never done me any harm.'

We drank our tea, pale and vaguely scented and clean on the palate. Then the old woman made him another pipe and then another. His wife has got back on to the bed and soon curling herself up at his feet went to sleep. Grosely smoked two or three pipes at a time, and while he was smoking seemed intent upon nothing else, but in the intervals he was loquacious. Several times I suggested going, but he would not let me. The hours wore on. Once or twice while he smoked I dozed. He told me all about himself. He went on and on. I spoke only to give him a cue. I cannot relate what he told me in his own words. He repeated himself. He was very long-winded and he told me his story confusedly, first a late bit, then an early bit, so that I had to arrange the sequence for myself; sometimes I saw that, afraid he had said too much, he held something back; sometimes he lied and I had to make a guess at the truth from the smile he gave me or the look in his eyes. He had not the words to describe what he had felt, and I had to conjecture his meaning from slangy metaphors and hackneyed, vulgar phrases. I kept on asking myself what his real name was, it was on the tip of my tongue and it irritated me not to be able to recall it, though why it should in the least matter to me I did not know. He was somewhat suspicious of me at first and I saw that this escapade of his in London and his imprisonment had been all these years a tormenting secret. He had always been haunted by the fear that sooner or later someone would find out.

'It's funny that even now you shouldn't remember me at the hospital,' he said, looking at me shrewdly. 'You must have a rotten memory.'

'Hang it all, it's nearly thirty years ago. Think of the thousands of people I've met since then. There's no reason why I should remember you any more than you remember me.'

'That's right. I don't suppose there is.'

It seemed to reassure him. At last he had smoked enough and the old woman made herself a pipe and smoked it. Then she went over to the mat on which the child was lying and huddled down beside it. She lay so still that I supposed she had fallen directly asleep. When at last I went I found my boy curled up on the footboard of the rickshaw in so deep a slumber that I had to shake him. I knew where I was and I wanted air and exercise, so I gave him a couple of piastres and told him I would walk.

It was a strange story I carried away with me.

It was with a sort of horror that I had listened to Grosely, telling me of those twenty years he had spent in China. He had made money, I do not know how much, but from the way he talked I should think something between fifteen and twenty thousand pounds, and for a tide-waiter it was a fortune. He could not have come by it honestly, and little as I knew of the details of his trade, by his sudden reticences, by his leers and hints I guessed that there was no base transaction that, if it was made worth his while, he jibbed at. I suppose that nothing paid him better than smuggling opium, and his position gave him the opportunity to do this with safety and profit. I understood that his superior officers had often had their suspicions of him, but had never been able to get such proof of his malpractices as to justify them in taking any steps. They contented themselves with moving him from one port to another, but that did not disturb him; they watched him, but he was too clever for them. I saw that he was divided between the fear of telling me too much to his discredit and the desire to boast of his own astuteness. He prided himself on the confidence the Chinese had placed in him.

'They knew they could trust me,' he said, 'and it gave me a pull. I never double-crossed a Chinaman once.'

The thought filled him with the complacency of the honest man. The Chinese discovered that he was keen on curios and they got in the habit of giving him bits or bringing him things to buy; he never made inquiries how they had come by them and he bought them cheap. When he had got a a good lot he sent them to Peking and sold them at a handsome profit. I remembered how he had started his commercial career by buying things at auctions and pawning them. For twenty years by shabby shift and petty dishonesty he added pound to pound, and everything he made he invested in Shanghai. He lived penuriously, saving half his pay; he never went on leave because he did not want to waste his money, he would not have anything to do with the Chinese women, he wanted to keep himself free from any entanglement; he did not drink. He was consumed by one ambition, to save enough to be able to go back to England and live the life from which he had been snatched as a boy. That was the only thing he wanted. He lived in China as though in a dream; he paid no attention to the life around him; its colour and strangeness, its possibilities of pleasure, meant nothing to him. There was always before him the mirage of London, the Criterion Bar, himself standing with his foot on the rail, the promenade at the Empire and the Pavilion, the picked-up harlot, the serio-comic at the music-hall, and the musical comedy at the Gaiety. This was life and love and adventure. This was romance. This was what he yearned for with all his heart. There was surely something impressive in the way in which during all those years he had lived like an anchorite with that one end in view of leading again a life that was so vulgar. It showed character.

'You see,' he said to me, 'even if I'd been able to get back to England on leave I wouldn't have gone. I didn't want to go till I could go for good. And then I wanted to do the thing in style.'

He saw himself putting on evening clothes every night and going out with a gardenia in his buttonhole, and he saw himself going to the Derby in a long coat and a brown hat and a pair of opera glasses slung over his shoulder. He saw himself giving the girls a look over and picking out the one he fancied. He made up his mind that on the night he arrived in London he would get blind, he hadn't been drunk for twenty years; he couldn't afford to in his job, you had to keep your wits about you. He'd take care not to get drunk on the ship on the way home. He'd wait till he got to London. What a night he'd have! He thought of it for twenty years.

I do not know why Grosely left the Chinese Customs, whether the place was getting too hot for him, whether he had reached the end of his service, or whether he had amassed the sum he had fixed. But at last he sailed. He went second class; he did not intend to start spending money till he reached London. He took rooms in Jermyn Street, he had always wanted to live there, and he went straight to a tailor's and ordered himself an outfit. Slap up. Then he had a look round the town. It was different from how he remembered it, there was much more traffic and he felt confused and a little at sea. He went to the Criterion and found there was no longer a bar where he had been used to lounge and drink. There was a restaurant in Leicester Square where he had been in the habit of dining when he was in funds, but he could not find it; he supposed it had been torn down. He went to the Pavilion, but there were no women there; he was rather disgusted and went on to the Empire, he found they had done away with the Promenade. It was rather a blow. He could not quite make it out. Well, anyhow, he must be prepared for changes in twenty years, and if he couldn't do anything else he could get drunk. He had had fever several times in China and the change of climate had brought it on again, he wasn't feeling any too well, and after four or five drinks he was glad to go to bed.

That first day was only a sample of many that followed it. Everything went wrong. Grosely's voice grew peevish and bitter as he told me how one thing and another had failed him. The old places were gone, the people were different, he found it hard to make friends, he was strangely lonely; he had never expected that in a great city like London. That's what was wrong with it, London had become too big, it wasn't the jolly, intimate place it had been in the early nineties. It had gone to pieces. He picked up a few girls, but they weren't as nice as the girls he had known before, they weren't the fun they used to be, and he grew dimly conscious that they thought him a rum sort of cove. He was only just over forty and they looked upon him as an old man. When he tried to cotton on to a lot of young fellows standing round a bar they gave him the cold shoulder. Anyway, these young fellows didn't know how to drink. He'd show them. He got soused every night, it was the only thing to do in that damned place, but, by Jove, it made him feel rotten next day. He supposed it was the climate of China. When he was a medical student he could drink a bottle of whisky every night and be as fresh as a daisy in the morning. He began to think more about China. All sorts of things that he never knew he had noticed came back to him. It wasn't a bad life he'd led there. Perhaps he'd been a fool to keep away from those Chinese girls, they were pretty little things some of them, and they didn't put on the airs these English girls did. One could have a damned good time in China if one had the money he had. One could keep a Chinese girl and get into the club, and there'd be a lot of nice fellows to drink with and play bridge with and billiards. He remembered the Chinese shops and all the row in the streets and the coolies carrying loads and the ports with the junks in them and the rivers with pagodas on the banks. It was funny, he never thought much of China while he was there and now—well, he couldn't get it out of his mind. It obsessed him. He began to think that London was no place for a white man. It had just gone to the dogs, that was the long and short of it, and one day the thought came to him that perhaps it would be a good thing if he went back to China. Of course it was silly, he'd worked like a slave for twenty years to be able to have a good time in London, and it was absurd to go and live in China. With his money he ought to be able to have a good time anywhere. But somehow he couldn't think of anything else but China. One day he went to the pictures and saw a scene at Shanghai. That settled it. He was fed up with London. He hated it. He was going to get out and this time he'd get out for good. He had been home a year and a half, and it seemed longer to him than all his twenty years in the East. He took a passage on a French boat sailing from Marseilles, and when he saw the coast of Europe sink into the sea he heaved a great sigh of relief. When they got to Suez and he felt the first touch of the East he knew he had done the right thing. Europe was finished. The East was the only place.

He went ashore at Djibouti and again at Colombo and Singapore, but though the ship stopped for two days at Saigon he remained on board there. He'd been drinking a good deal and he was feeling a bit under the weather. But when they reached Haiphong, where they were staying for forty-eight hours, he thought he might just as well have a look at it. That was the last stopping-place before they got to China. He was bound for Shanghai. When he got there he meant to go to a hotel and look around a bit and then get hold of a girl and a place of his own. He would buy a pony or two and race. He'd soon make friends. In the East they weren't so stiff and stand-offish as they were in London. Going ashore, he dined at the hotel and after dinner got into a rickshaw and told the boy he wanted a woman. The boy took him to the shabby tenement in which I had sat for so many hours and there were the old woman and the girl who was now the mother of his child. After a while the old woman asked him if he wouldn't like a smoke. He had never tried opium, he had always been frightened of it, but now he didn't see why he shouldn't have a go. He was feeling good that night and the girl was a jolly cuddlesome little thing; she was rather like a Chinese girl, small and pretty, like an idol. Well, he had a pipe or two, and he began to feel very happy and comfortable. He stayed all night. He didn't sleep. He just lay, feeling very restful, and thought about things.

'I stopped there till my ship went on to Hong-Kong,' he said. 'And when she left I just stopped on.'

'How about your luggage?' I asked.

For I am perhaps unworthily interested in the manner people combine practical details with the ideal aspects of life. When in a novel penniless lovers drive in a long, swift racing car over the distant hills I have always a desire to know how they managed to pay for it; and I have often asked myself how the characters of Henry James in the intervals of subtly examining their situation coped with the physiological necessities of their bodies.

'I only had a trunk full of clothes, I was never one to want much more than I stood up in, and I went down with the girl in a rickshaw to fetch it. I only meant to stay on till the next boat came through. You see, I was so near China here I thought I'd wait a bit and get used to things, if you understand what I mean, before I went on.'

I did. Those last words of his revealed him to me. I knew that on the threshold of China his courage had failed him. England had been such a terrible disappointment that now he was afraid to put China to the test too. If that failed him he had nothing. For years England had been like a mirage in the desert. But when he had yielded to the attraction, those shining pools and the palm trees and the green grass were nothing but the rolling sandy dunes. He had China, and so long as he never saw it again he kept it.

'Somehow I stayed on. You know, you'd be surprised how quickly the days pass. I don't seem to have time to do half the things I want to. After all I'm comfortable here. The old woman makes a damned good pipe, and she's a jolly little girl, my girl, and then there's the kid. A lively young beggar. If you're happy somewhere what's the good of going somewhere else?'

I looked round that large bare sordid room. There was no comfort in it and not one of the little personal things that one would have thought might have given him the feeling of home. Grosely had taken on this equivocal little apartment, which served as a house of assignation and as a place for Europeans to smoke opium in, with the old woman who kept it, just as it was, and he camped, rather than lived, there still as though next day he would pack his traps and go. After a little while he answered my question.

'I've never been so happy in my life. I often think I'll go on to Shanghai some day, but I don't suppose I ever shall. And God knows, I never want to see England again.'

'Aren't you awfully lonely sometimes for people to talk to?'

'No. Sometimes a Chinese tramp comes in with an English skipper or a Scotch engineer, and then I go on board and we have a talk about old times. There's an old fellow here, a Frenchman who was in the Customs, and he speaks English; I go and see him sometimes. But the fact is I don't want anybody very much. I think a lot. It gets on my nerves when people come between me and my thoughts. I'm not a big smoker, you know, I just have a pipe or two in the morning to settle my stomach, but I don't really smoke till night. Then I think.'

'What d'you think about?'

'Oh, all sorts of things. Sometimes about London and what it was like when I was a boy. But mostly about China. I think of the good times I had and the way I made my money, and I remember the fellows I used to know, and the Chinese. I had some narrow squeaks now and then, but I always came through all right. And I wonder what the girls would have been like that I might have had. Pretty little things. I'm sorry now I didn't keep one or two. It's a great country, China; I love those shops, with an old fellow sitting on his heels smoking a water-pipe, and all the shop-signs. And the temples. By George, that's the place for a man to live in. There's life.'

The mirage shone before his eyes. The illusion held him. He was happy. I wondered what would be his end. Well, that was not yet. For the first time in his life perhaps he held the present in his hand.

The Letter

◆

Outside on the quay the sun beat fiercely. A stream of motors, lorries and buses, private cars and hirelings, sped up and down the crowded thoroughfare, and every chauffeur blew his horn; rickshaws threaded their nimble path amid the throng, and the panting coolies found breath to yell at one another; coolies, carrying heavy bales, sidled along with their quick jog-trot and shouted to the passer-by to make way; itinerant vendors proclaimed their wares. Singapore is the meeting-place of a hundred peoples; and men of all colours, black Tamils, yellow Chinks, brown Malays, Armenians, Jews, and Bengalis, called to one another in raucous tones. But inside the office of Messrs Ripley, Joyce, and Naylor it was pleasantly cool; it was dark after the dusty glitter of the street and agreeably quiet after its unceasing din. Mr Joyce sat in his private room, at the table, with an electric fan turned full on him. He was leaning back, his elbows on the arms of the chair, with the tips of the outstretched fingers of one hand resting neatly against the tips of the outstretched fingers of the other. His gaze rested on the battered volumes of the Law Reports which stood on a long shelf in front of him. On the top of a cupboard were square boxes of japanned tin, on which were painted the names of various clients.

There was a knock at the door.

'Come in.'

A Chinese clerk, very neat in his white ducks, opened it.

'Mr Crosbie is here, sir.'

He spoke beautiful English, accenting each word with precision, and Mr Joyce had often wondered at the extent of his vocabulary. Ong Chi Seng was a Cantonese, and he had studied law at Gray's Inn. He was spending a year or two with Messrs Ripley, Joyce, and Naylor in order to prepare himself for practice on his own account. He was industrious, obliging, and of exemplary character.

'Show him in,' said Mr Joyce.

He rose to shake hands with his visitor and asked him to sit down. The light fell on him as he did so. The face of Mr Joyce remained in shadow. He was by nature a silent man, and now he looked at Robert Crosbie for quite a minute without speaking. Crosbie was a big fellow, well over six feet high, with broad shoulders, and muscular. He was a rubber-planter, hard with the constant exercise of walking over the estate, and with the tennis which was his relaxation when the day's work was over. He was deeply sunburned. His hairy hands, his feet in clumsy boots were enormous, and Mr Joyce found himself thinking that a blow of that great fist could easily kill the fragile Tamil. But there was no fierceness in his blue eyes; they were confiding and gentle; and his face, with its big, undistinguished features, was open, frank, and honest. But at this moment it bore a look of deep distress. It was drawn and haggard.

'You look as though you hadn't had much sleep the last night or two,' said Mr Joyce.

'I haven't.'

Mr Joyce noticed now the old felt hat, with its broad double brim, which Crosbie had placed on the table; and then his eyes travelled to the khaki shorts he wore, showing his red hairy thighs, the tennis shirt open at the neck, without a tie, and the dirty khaki jacket with the ends of the sleeves turned up. He looked as though he had just come in from a long tramp among the rubber trees. Mr Joyce gave a slight frown.

'You must pull yourself together, you know. You must keep your head.'

'Oh, I'm all right.'

'Have you seen your wife today?'

'No, I'm to see her this afternoon. You know, it is a damned shame that they should have arrested her.'

'I think they had to do that,' Mr Joyce answered in his level, soft tone.

'I should have thought they'd have let her out on bail.'

'It's a very serious charge.'

'It is damnable. She did what any decent woman would do in her place. Only, nine women out of ten wouldn't have the pluck. Leslie's the best woman in the world. She wouldn't hurt a fly. Why, hang it all, man, I've been married to her for twelve years, do you think I don't know her? God, if I'd got hold of the man I'd have wrung his neck, I'd have killed him without a moment's hesitation. So would you.'

'My dear fellow, everybody's on your side. No one has a good word to say for Hammond. We're going to get her off. I don't suppose either the assessors or the judge will go into court without having already made up their minds to bring in a verdict of not guilty.'

'The whole thing's a farce,' said Crosbie violently. 'She ought never to have been arrested in the first place, and then it's terrible, after all the poor girl's gone through, to subject her to the ordeal of a trial. There's not a soul I've met since I've been in Singapore, man or woman, who hasn't told me that Leslie was absolutely justified. I think it's awful to keep her in prison all these weeks.'

'The law is the law. After all, she confesses that she killed the man. It is terrible, and I'm dreadfully sorry for both you and her.'

'I don't matter a hang,' interrupted Crosbie.

'But the fact remains that murder has been committed, and in a civilized community a trial is inevitable.'

'Is it murder to exterminate noxious vermin? She shot him as she would have shot a mad dog.'

Mr Joyce leaned back again in his chair and once more placed the tips of his ten fingers together. The little construction he formed looked like the skeleton of a roof. He was silent for a moment.

'I should be wanting in my duty as your legal adviser,' he said at last, in an even voice, looking at his client with his cool, brown eyes, 'if I did not tell you that there is one point which causes me just a little anxiety. If your wife had only shot Hammond once, the whole thing would be absolutely plain sailing. Unfortunately she fired six times.'

'Her explanation is perfectly simple. In the circumstances anyone would have done the same.'

'I dare say,' said Mr Joyce, 'and of course I think the explanation is very reasonable. But it's no good closing our eyes to the facts. It's always a good plan to put yourself in another man's place, and I can't deny that if I were prosecuting for the Crown that is the point on which I should centre my inquiry.'

'My dear fellow, that's perfectly idiotic.'

Mr Joyce shot a sharp glance at Robert Crosbie. The shadow of a smile hovered over his shapely lips. Crosbie was a good fellow, but he could hardly be described as intelligent.

'I dare say it's of no importance,' answered the lawyer, 'I just thought it was a point worth mentioning. You haven't got very long to wait now, and when it's all over I recommend you to go off somewhere with your wife on a trip, and forget all about it. Even though we are almost dead certain to get an acquittal, a trial of that sort is anxious work, and you'll both want a rest.'

For the first time Crosbie smiled, and his smile strangely changed his face. You forgot the uncouthness and saw only the goodness of his soul.

'I think I shall want it more than Leslie. She's borne up wonderfully. By God, there's a plucky little woman for you.'

'Yes, I've been very much struck by her self-control,' said the lawyer. 'I should never have guessed that she was capable of such determination.'

His duties as her counsel had made it necessary for him to have a good many interviews with Mrs Crosbie since her arrest. Though things had been made as easy as could be for her, the fact remained that she was in gaol, awaiting her trial for murder, and it would not have been surprising if her nerves had failed her. She appeared to bear her ordeal with composure. She read a great deal, took such exercise as was possible, and by favour of the authorities worked at the pillow lace which had always formed the entertainment of her long hours of leisure. When Mr Joyce saw her, she was neatly dressed in cool, fresh, simple frocks, her hair was carefully arranged, and her nails were manicured. Her manner was collected. She was able even to jest upon the little inconveniences of her position. There was something casual about the way in which she spoke of the tragedy, which suggested to Mr Joyce that only her good breeding prevented her from finding something a trifle ludicrous in a situation which was eminently serious. It surprised him, for he had never thought that she had a sense of humour.

He had known her off and on for a good many years. When she paid visits to Singapore she generally came to dine with his wife and himself, and once or twice she had passed a week-end with them at their bungalow by the sea. His wife had spent a fortnight with her on the estate, and had met Geoffrey

Hammond several times. The two couples had been on friendly, if not on
intimate, terms, and it was on this account that Robert Crosbie had rushed over
to Singapore immediately after the catastrophe and begged Mr Joyce to take
charge personally of his unhappy wife's defence.

The story she told him the first time he saw her she had never varied in the
smallest detail. She told it as coolly then, a few hours after the tragedy, as she
told it now. She told it connectedly, in a level, even voice, and her only sign of
confusion was when a slight colour came into her cheeks as she described one or
two of its incidents. She was the last woman to whom one would have expected
such a thing to happen. She was in the early thirties, a fragile creature, neither
short nor tall, and graceful rather than pretty. Her wrists and ankles were very
delicate, but she was extremely thin, and you could see the bones of her hands
through the white skin, and the veins were large and blue. Her face was
colourless, slightly sallow, and her lips were pale. You did not notice the colour
of her eyes. She had a great deal of light brown hair, and it had a slight natural
wave; it was the sort of hair that with a little touching-up would have been very
pretty, but you could not imagine that Mrs Crosbie would think of resorting to
any such device. She was a quiet, pleasant, unassuming woman. Her manner
was engaging, and if she was not very popular it was because she suffered from a
certain shyness. This was comprehensible enough, for the planter's life is lonely,
and in her own house, with people she knew, she was in her quiet way
charming. Mrs Joyce, after her fortnight's stay, had told her husband that
Leslie was a very agreeable hostess. There was more in her, she said, than
people thought; and when you came to know her you were surprised how much
she had read and how entertaining she could be.

She was the last woman in the world to commit murder.

Mr Joyce dismissed Robert Crosbie with such reassuring words as he could
find and, once more alone in his office, turned over the pages of the brief. But it
was a mechanical action, for all its details were familiar to him. The case was the
sensation of the day, and it was discussed in all the clubs, at all the dinner tables,
up and down the Peninsula, from Singapore to Penang. The facts that Mrs
Crosbie gave were simple. Her husband had gone to Singapore on business,
and she was alone for the night. She dined by herself, late, at a quarter to nine,
and after dinner sat in the sitting-room working at her lace. It opened on the
veranda. There was no one in the bungalow, for the servants had retired to their
own quarters at the back of the compound. She was surprised to hear a step on
the gravel path in the garden, a booted step, which suggested a white man
rather than a native, for she had not heard a motor drive up, and she could not
imagine who could be coming to see her at that time of night. Someone
ascended the few stairs that led up to the bungalow, walked across the veranda,
and appeared at the door of the room in which she sat. At the first moment she
did not recognize the visitor. She sat with a shaded lamp, and he stood with his
back to the darkness.

'May I come in?' he said.

She did not even recognize the voice.

'Who is it?' she asked.

She worked with spectacles, and she took them off as she spoke.

'Geoff Hammond.'

'Of course. Come in and have a drink.'

She rose and shook hands with him cordially. She was a little surprised to see
him, for though he was a neighbour neither she nor Robert had been lately on

very intimate terms with him, and she had not seen him for some weeks. He was the manager of a rubber estate nearly eight miles from theirs, and she wondered why he had chosen this late hour to come and see them.

'Robert's away,' she said. 'He had to go to Singapore for the night.'

Perhaps he thought his visit called for some explanation, for he said:

'I'm sorry. I felt rather lonely tonight, so I thought I'd just come along and see how you were getting on.'

'How on earth did you come? I never heard a car.'

'I left it down the road. I thought you might both be in bed and asleep.'

This was natural enough. The planter gets up at dawn in order to take the roll-call of the workers, and soon after dinner he is glad to go to bed. Hammond's car was in point of fact found next day a quarter of a mile from the bungalow.

Since Robert was away there was no whisky and soda in the room. Leslie did not call the boy, who was probably asleep, but fetched it herself. Her guest mixed himself a drink and filled his pipe.

Geoff Hammond had a host of friends in the colony. He was at this time in the late thirties, but he had come out as a lad. He had been one of the first to volunteer on the outbreak of war, and had done very well. A wound in the knee caused him to be invalided out of the army after two years, but he returned to the Federated Malay States with a D.S.O. and an M.C. He was one of the best billiard-players in the colony. He had been a beautiful dancer and a fine tennis-player, but though able no longer to dance, and his tennis, with a stiff knee, was not so good as it had been, he had the gift of popularity and was universally liked. He was a tall, good-looking fellow, with attractive blue eyes and a fine head of black, curling hair. Old stagers said his only fault was that he was too fond of the girls, and after the catastrophe they shook their heads and vowed that they had always known this would get him into trouble.

He began now to talk to Leslie about the local affairs, the forthcoming races in Singapore, the price of rubber, and his chances of killing a tiger which had been lately seen in the neighbourhood. She was anxious to finish by a certain date a piece of lace on which she was working, for she wanted to send it home for her mother's birthday, and so put on her spectacles again, and drew towards her chair the little table on which stood the pillow.

'I wish you wouldn't wear those great horn-spectacles,' he said. 'I don't know why a pretty woman should do her best to look plain.'

She was a trifle taken aback at this remark. He had never used that tone with her before. She thought the best thing was to make light of it.

'I have no pretensions to being a raving beauty, you know, and if you ask me point-blank, I'm bound to tell you that I don't care two pins if you think me plain or not.'

'I don't think you're plain. I think you're awfully pretty.'

'Sweet of you,' she answered, ironically. 'But in that case I can only think you half-witted.'

He chuckled. But he rose from his chair and sat down in another by her side.

'You're not going to have the face to deny that you have the prettiest hands in the world,' he said.

He made a gesture as though to take one of them. She gave him a little tap.

'Don't be an idiot. Sit down where you were before and talk sensibly, or else I shall send you home.'

He did not move.

'Don't you know that I'm awfully in love with you?' he said.

She remained quite cool.

'I don't. I don't believe it for a minute, and even if it were true I don't want you to say it.'

She was the more surprised at what he was saying, since during the seven years she had known him he had never paid her any particular attention. When he came back from the war they had seen a good deal of one another, and once when he was ill Robert had gone over and brought him back to their bungalow in his car. He had stayed with them for a fortnight. But their interests were dissimilar, and the acquaintance had never ripened into friendship. For the last two or three years they had seen little of him. Now and then he came over to play tennis, now and then they met him at some planter's who was giving a party, but it often happened that they did not set eyes on him for a month at a time.

Now he took another whisky and soda. Leslie wondered if he had been drinking before. There was something odd about him, and it made her a trifle uneasy. She watched him help himself with disapproval.

'I wouldn't drink any more if I were you,' she said, good-humouredly still.

He emptied his glass and put it down.

'Do you think I'm talking to you like this because I'm drunk?' he asked abruptly.

'That is the most obvious explanation, isn't it?'

'Well, it's a lie. I've loved you ever since I first knew you. I've held my tongue as long as I could, and now it's got to come out. I love you, I love you, I love you.'

She rose and carefully put aside the pillow.

'Good night,' she said.

'I'm not going now.'

At last she began to lose her temper.

'But, you poor fool, don't you know that I've never loved anyone but Robert, and even if I didn't love Robert you're the last man I should care for.'

'What do I care? Robert's away.'

'If you don't go away this minute I shall call the boys, and have you thrown out.'

'They're out of earshot.'

She was very angry now. She made a movement as though to go on to the veranda, from which the house-boy would certainly hear her, but he seized her arm.

'Let me go,' she cried furiously.

'Not much. I've got you now.'

She opened her mouth and called 'Boy, boy,' but with a quick gesture he put his hand over it. Then before she knew what he was about he had taken her in his arms and was kissing her passionately. She struggled, turning her lips away from his burning mouth.

'No, no, no,' she cried. 'Leave me alone. I won't.'

She grew confused about what happened then. All that had been said before she remembered accurately, but now his words assailed her ears through a mist of horror and fear. He seemed to plead for her love. He broke into violent protestations of passion. And all the time he held her in his tempestuous embrace. She was helpless, for he was a strong, powerful man, and her arms were pinioned to her sides; her struggles were unavailing, and she felt herself grow weaker; she was afraid she would faint, and his hot breath on her face made her feel desperately sick. He kissed her mouth, her eyes, her cheeks, her hair. The pressure of his arms was killing her. He lifted her off her feet. She tried to kick him, but he only held her more closely. He was carrying her now. He wasn't speaking any more, but she knew that his face was pale and his eyes hot with desire. He was taking her into the bedroom. He was no longer a civilized man, but a savage. And as he ran he stumbled against a table which was in the way. His stiff knee made him a little awkward on his feet, and with the burden of the woman in his arms he fell. In a moment she had snatched herself away from him. She ran round the sofa. He was up in a flash, and flung himself towards her. There was a revolver on the desk. She was not a nervous woman, but Robert was to be away for the night, and she had meant to take it into her room when she went to bed. That was why it happened to be there. She was frantic with terror now. She did not know what she was doing. She heard a report. She saw Hammond stagger. He gave a cry. He said something, she didn't know what. He lurched out of the room on to the veranda. She was in a frenzy now, she was beside herself, she followed him out, yes, that was it, she must have followed him out, though she remembered nothing of it, she followed firing automatically, shot after shot, till the six chambers were empty. Hammond fell down on the floor of the veranda. He crumpled up into a bloody heap.

When the boys, startled by the reports, rushed up, they found her standing over Hammond with the revolver still in her hand and Hammond lifeless. She looked at them for a moment without speaking. They stood in a frightened, huddled bunch. She let the revolver fall from her hand, and without a word turned and went into the sitting-room. They watched her go into her bedroom and turn the key in the lock. They dared not touch the dead body, but looked at it with terrified eyes, talking excitedly to one another in undertones. Then the head-boy collected himself; he had been with them for many years, he was Chinese and a level-headed fellow. Robert had gone into Singapore on his motor-cycle, and the car stood in the garage. He told the seis to get it out; they must go at once to the Assistant District Officer and tell him what had happened. He picked up the revolver and put it in his pocket. The A.D.O., a man called Withers, lived on the outskirts of the nearest town, which was about thirty-five miles away. It took them an hour and a half to reach him. Everyone was asleep, and they had to rouse the boys. Presently Withers came out and they told him their errand. The head-boy showed him the revolver in proof of what he said. The A.D.O. went into his room to dress, sent for his car, and in a little while was following them back along the deserted road. The dawn was just breaking as he reached the Crosbies' bungalow. He ran up the steps of the veranda, and stopped short as he saw Hammond's body lying where he fell. He touched the face. It was quite cold.

'Where's mem?' he asked the house-boy.

The Chinese pointed to the bedroom. Withers went to the door and knocked. There was no answer. He knocked again.

'Mrs Crosbie,' he called.

'Who is it?'

'Withers.'

There was another pause. Then the door was unlocked and slowly opened. Leslie stood before him. She had not been to bed, and wore the tea-gown in which she had dined. She stood and looked silently at the A.D.O.

'Your house-boy fetched me,' he said. 'Hammond. What have you done?'

'He tried to rape me, and I shot him.'

'My God. I say, you'd better come out here. You must tell me exactly what happened.'

'Not now. I can't. You must give me time. Send for my husband.'

Withers was a young man, and he did not know exactly what to do in an emergency which was so out of the run of his duties. Leslie refused to say anything till at last Robert arrived. Then she told the two men the story, from which since then, though she had repeated it over and over again, she had never in the slightest degree diverged.

The point to which Mr Joyce recurred was the shooting. As a lawyer he was bothered that Leslie had fired not once, but six times, and the examination of the dead man showed that four of the shots had been fired close to the body. One might almost have thought that when the man fell she stood over him and emptied the contents of the revolver into him. She confessed that her memory, so accurate for all that had preceded, failed her here. Her mind was blank. It pointed to an uncontrollable fury; but uncontrollable fury was the last thing you would have expected from this quiet and demure woman. Mr Joyce had known her a good many years, and had always thought her an unemotional person; during the weeks that had passed since the tragedy her composure had been amazing.

Mr Joyce shrugged his shoulders.

'The fact is, I suppose,' he reflected, 'that you can never tell what hidden possibilities of savagery there are in the most respectable of women.'

There was a knock at the door.

'Come in.'

The Chinese clerk entered and closed the door behind him. He closed it gently, with deliberation, but decidedly, and advanced to the table at which Mr Joyce was sitting.

'May I trouble you, sir, for a few words' private conversation?' he said.

The elaborate accuracy with which the clerk expressed himself always faintly amused Mr Joyce, and now he smiled.

'It's no trouble, Chi Seng,' he replied.

'The matter on which I desire to speak to you, sir, is delicate and confidential.'

'Fire away.'

Mr Joyce met his clerk's shrewd eyes. As usual Ong Chi Seng was dressed in the height of local fashion. He wore very shiny patent-leather shoes and gay silk socks. In his black tie was a pearl and ruby pin, and on the fourth finger of his left hand a diamond ring. From the pocket of his neat white coat protruded a gold fountain pen and a gold pencil. He wore a gold wrist-watch, and on the bridge of his nose invisible pince-nez. He gave a little cough.

'The matter has to do with the case R. *v.* Crosbie, sir.'

'Yes?'

'A circumstance has come to my knowledge, sir, which seems to me to put a different complexion on it.'

'What circumstance?'

'It has come to my knowledge, sir, that there is a letter in existence from the defendant to the unfortunate victim of the tragedy.'

'I shouldn't be at all surprised. In the course of the last seven years I have no doubt that Mrs Crosbie often had occasion to write to Mr Hammond.'

Mr Joyce had a high opinion of his clerk's intelligence and his words were designed to conceal his thoughts.

'That is very probable, sir. Mrs Crosbie must have communicated with the deceased frequently, to invite him to dine with her for example, or to propose a tennis game. That was my first thought when the matter was brought to my notice. This letter, however, was written on the day of the late Mr Hammond's death.'

Mr Joyce did not flicker an eyelash. He continued to look at Ong Chi Seng with the smile of faint amusement with which he generally talked to him.

'Who has told you this?'

'The circumstances were brought to my knowledge, sir, by a friend of mine.'

Mr Joyce knew better than to insist.

'You will no doubt recall, sir, that Mrs Crosbie has stated that until the fatal night she had had no communication with the deceased for several weeks.'

'Have you got the letter?'

'No, sir.'

'What are its contents?'

'My friend gave me a copy. Would you like to peruse it, sir?'

'I should.'

Ong Chi Seng took from an inside pocket a bulky wallet. It was filled with papers, Singapore dollar notes and cigarette cards. From the confusion he presently extracted a half-sheet of thin notepaper and placed it before Mr Joyce. The letter read as follows:

R. will be away for the night. I absolutely must see you. I shall expect you at eleven. I am desperate, and if you don't come I won't answer for the consequences. Don't drive up.–L.

It was written in the flowing hand which the Chinese were taught at the foreign schools. The writing, so lacking in character, was oddly incongruous with the ominous words.

'What makes you think that this note was written by Mrs Crosbie?'

'I have every confidence in the veracity of my informant, sir,' replied Ong Chi Seng. 'And the matter can very easily be put to the proof. Mrs Crosbie will, no doubt, be able to tell you at once whether she wrote such a letter or not.'

Since the beginning of the conversation Mr Joyce had not taken his eyes off the respectable countenance of his clerk. He wondered now if he discerned in it a faint expression of mockery.

'It is inconceivable that Mrs Crosbie should have written such a letter,' said Mr Joyce.

'If that is your opinion, sir, the matter is of course ended. My friend spoke to me on the subject only because he thought, as I was in your office, you might like to know of the existence of this letter before a communication was made to the Deputy Public Prosecutor.'

'Who has the original?' asked Mr Joyce sharply.

Ong Chi Seng made no sign that he perceived in this question and its manner a change of attitude.

'You will remember, sir, no doubt, that after the death of Mr Hammond it was discovered that he had had relations with a Chinese woman. The letter is at present in her possession.'

That was one of the things which had turned public opinion most vehemently against Hammond. It came to be known that for several months he had had a Chinese woman living in his house.

For a moment neither of them spoke. Indeed everything had been said and each understood the other perfectly.

'I'm obliged to you, Chi Seng. I will give the matter my consideration.'

'Very good, sir. Do you wish me to make a communication to that effect to my friend?'

'I dare say it would be as well if you kept in touch with him,' Mr Joyce answered with gravity.

'Yes, sir.'

The clerk noiselessly left the room, shutting the door again with deliberation, and left Mr Joyce to his reflections. He stared at the copy, in its neat, impersonal writing, of Leslie's letter. Vague suspicions troubled him. They were so disconcerting that he made an effort to put them out of his mind. There must be a simple explanation of the letter, and Leslie without doubt could give it at once, but, by heaven, an explanation was needed. He rose from his chair, put the letter in his pocket, and took his topee. When he went out Ong Chi Seng was busily writing at his desk.

'I'm going out for a few minutes, Chi Seng,' he said.

'Mr George Reed is coming by appointment at twelve o'clock, sir. Where shall I say you've gone?'

Mr Joyce gave him a thin smile.

'You can say that you haven't the least idea.'

But he knew perfectly well that Ong Chi Seng was aware that he was going to the gaol. Though the crime had been committed in Belanda and the trial was to take place at Belanda Bharu, since there was in the gaol no convenience for the detention of a white woman Mrs Crosbie had been brought to Singapore.

When she was led into the room in which he waited she held out her thin, distinguished hand, and gave him a pleasant smile. She was as ever neatly and simply dressed, and her abundant, pale hair was arranged with care.

'I wasn't expecting to see you this morning,' she said, graciously.

She might have been in her own house, and Mr Joyce almost expected to hear her call the boy and tell him to bring the visitor a gin pahit.

'How are you?' he asked.

'I'm in the best of health, thank you.' A flicker of amusement flashed across her eyes. 'This is a wonderful place for a rest cure.'

The attendant withdrew and they were left alone.

'Do sit down,' said Leslie.

He took a chair. He did not quite know how to begin. She was so cool that it seemed almost impossible to say to her the thing he had come to say. Though she was not pretty there was something agreeable in her appearance. She had elegance, but it was the elegance of good breeding in which there was nothing of the artifice of society. You had only to look at her to know what sort of people she had and what kind of surroundings she had lived in. Her fragility gave her a singular refinement. It was impossible to associate her with the vaguest idea of grossness.

'I'm looking forward to seeing Robert this afternoon,' she said, in her good-humoured, easy voice. (It was a pleasure to hear her speak, her voice and her accent were so distinctive of her class.) 'Poor dear, it's been a great trial to his nerves. I'm thankful it'll all be over in a few days.'

'It's only five days now.'

'I know. Each morning when I awake I say to myself, "one less."' She smiled then. 'Just as I used to do at school and the holidays were coming.'

'By the way, am I right in thinking that you had no communication whatever with Hammond for several weeks before the catastrophe?'

'I'm quite positive of that. The last time we met was at a tennis-party at the MacFarrens. I don't think I said more than two words to him. They have two courts, you know, and we didn't happen to be in the same sets.'

'And you haven't written to him?'

'Oh, no.'

'Are you quite sure of that?'

'Oh, quite,' she answered, with a little smile. 'There was nothing I should write to him for except to ask him to dine or to play tennis, and I hadn't done either for months.'

'At one time you'd been on fairly intimate terms with him. How did it happen that you had stopped asking him to anything?'

Mrs Crosbie shrugged her thin shoulders.

'One gets tired of people. We hadn't anything very much in common. Of course, when he was ill Robert and I did everything we could for him, but the last year or two he'd been quite well, and he was very popular. He had a good many calls on his time, and there didn't seem to be any need to shower invitations upon him.'

'Are you quite certain that was all?'

Mrs Crosbie hesitated for a moment.

'Well, I may just as well tell you. It had come to our ears that he was living with a Chinese woman, and Robert said he wouldn't have him in the house. I had seen her myself.'

Mr Joyce was sitting in a straight-backed arm-chair, resting his chin on his hand, and his eyes were fixed on Leslie. Was it his fancy that, as she made this remark, her black pupils were filled on a sudden, for the fraction of a second, with a dull red light? The effect was startling. Mr Joyce shifted in his chair. He placed the tips of his ten fingers together. He spoke very slowly, choosing his words.

'I think I should tell you that there is in existence a letter in your handwriting to Geoff Hammond.'

He watched her closely. She made no movement, nor did her face change colour, but she took a noticeable time to reply.

'In the past I've often sent him little notes to ask him to something or other, or to get me something when I knew he was going to Singapore.'

'This letter asks him to come and see you because Robert was going to Singapore.'

'That's impossible. I never did anything of the kind.'

'You'd better read it for yourself.'

He took it out of his pocket and handed it to her. She gave it a glance and with a smile of scorn handed it back to him.

'That's not my handwriting.'

'I know, it's said to be an exact copy of the original.'

She read the words now, and as she read a horrible change came over her. Her colourless face grew dreadful to look at. It turned green. The flesh seemed on a sudden to fall away and her skin was tightly stretched over the bones. Her lips receded, showing her teeth, so that she had the appearance of making a grimace. She stared at Mr Joyce with eyes that started from their sockets. He was looking now at a gibbering death's head.

'What does it mean?' she whispered.

Her mouth was so dry that she could utter no more than a hoarse sound. It was no longer a human voice.

'That is for you to say,' he answered.

'I didn't write it. I swear I didn't write it.'

'Be very careful what you say. If the original is in your handwriting it would be useless to deny it.'

'It would be a forgery.'

'It would be difficult to prove that. It would be easy to prove that it was genuine.'

A shiver passed through her lean body. But great beads of sweat stood on her forehead. She took a handkerchief from her bag and wiped the palms of her hands. She glanced at the letter again and gave Mr Joyce a sidelong look.

'It's not dated. If I had written it and forgotten all about it, it might have been written years ago. If you'll give me time, I'll try and remember the circumstances.'

'I noticed there was no date. If this letter were in the hands of the prosecution they would cross-examine the boys. They would soon find out whether someone took a letter to Hammond on the day of his death.'

Mrs Crosbie clasped her hands violently and swayed in her chair so that he thought she would faint.

'I swear to you that I didn't write that letter.'

Mr Joyce was silent for a little while. He took his eyes from her distraught face, and looked down on the floor. He was reflecting.

'In these circumstances we need not go into the matter further,' he said slowly, at last breaking the silence. 'If the possessor of this letter sees fit to place it in the hands of the prosecution you will be prepared.'

His words suggested that he had nothing more to say to her, but he made no movement of departure. He waited. To himself he seemed to wait a very long time. He did not look at Leslie, but he was conscious that she sat very still. She made no sound. At last it was he who spoke.

'If you have nothing more to say to me I think I'll be getting back to my office.'

'What would anyone who read the letter be inclined to think that it meant?' she asked then.

'He'd know that you had told a deliberate lie,' answered Mr Joyce sharply.

'When?'

'You have stated definitely that you had had no communication with Hammond for at least three months.'

'The whole thing has been a terrible shock to me. The events of that dreadful night have been a nightmare. It's not very strange if one detail has escaped my memory.'

'It would be unfortunate, when your memory has reproduced so exactly every particular of your interview with Hammond, that you should have forgotten so important a point as that he came to see you in the bungalow on the night of his death at your express desire.'

'I hadn't forgotten. After what happened I was afraid to mention it. I thought you'd none of you believe my story if I admitted that he'd come at my invitation. I dare say it was stupid of me; but I lost my head, and after I'd said once that I'd had no communication with Hammond I was obliged to stick to it.'

By now Leslie had recovered her admirable composure, and she met Mr Joyce's appraising glance with candour. Her gentleness was very disarming.

'You will be required to explain, then, *why* you asked Hammond to come and see you when Robert was away for the night.'

She turned her eyes full on the lawyer. He had been mistaken in thinking them insignificant, they were rather fine eyes, and unless he was mistaken they were bright now with tears. Her voice had a little break in it.

'It was a surprise I was preparing for Robert. His birthday is next month. I knew he wanted a new gun and you know I'm dreadfully stupid about sporting things. I wanted to talk to Geoff about it. I thought I'd get him to order it for me.'

'Perhaps the terms of the letter are not very clear to your recollection. Will you have another look at it?'

'No, I don't want to,' she said quickly.

'Does it seem to you the sort of letter a woman would write to a somewhat distant acquaintance because she wanted to consult him about buying a gun?'

'I dare say it's rather extravagant and emotional. I do express myself like that, you know. I'm quite prepared to admit it's very silly.' She smiled. 'And after all, Geoff Hammond wasn't quite a distant acquaintance. When he was ill I'd nursed him like a mother. I asked him to come when Robert was away, because Robert wouldn't have him in the house.'

Mr Joyce was tired of sitting so long in the same position. He rose and walked once or twice up and down the room, choosing the words he proposed to say; then he leaned over the back of the chair in which he had been sitting. He spoke slowly in a tone of deep gravity.

'Mrs Crosbie, I want to talk to you very, very seriously. This case was comparatively plain sailing. There was only one point which seemed to me to require explanation: as far as I could judge, you had fired no less than four shots into Hammond when he was lying on the ground. It was hard to accept the possibility that a delicate, frightened, and habitually self-controlled woman, of gentle nature and refined instincts, should have surrendered to an absolutely uncontrolled frenzy. But of course it was admissible. Although Geoffrey Hammond was much liked and on the whole thought highly of, I was prepared to prove that he was the sort of man who might be guilty of the crime which in justification of your act you accused him of. The fact, which was discovered after his death, that he had been living with a Chinese woman gave us something very definite to go upon. That robbed him of any sympathy which might have been felt for him. We made up our minds to make use of the odium which such a connexion cast upon him in the minds of all respectable people. I told your husband this morning that I was certain of an acquittal, and I wasn't just telling him that to give him heart. I do not believe the assessors would have left the court.'

They looked into one another's eyes. Mrs Crosbie was strangely still. She was like a little bird paralysed by the fascination of a snake. He went on in the same quiet tones.

'But this letter has thrown an entirely different complexion on the case. I am your legal adviser, I shall represent you in court. I take your story as you tell it me, and I shall conduct your defence according to its terms. It may be that I believe your statements, and it may be that I doubt them. The duty of counsel is to persuade the court that the evidence placed before it is not such as to justify it in bringing in a verdict of guilty, and any private opinion he may have of the guilt or innocence of his client is entirely beside the point.'

He was astonished to see in Leslie's eyes the flicker of a smile. Piqued, he went on somewhat dryly:

'You're not going to deny that Hammond came to your house at your urgent, and I may even say, hysterical invitation?'

Mrs Crosbie, hesitating for an instant, seemed to consider.

'They can prove that the letter was taken to his bungalow by one of the house-boys. He rode over on his bicycle.'

'You mustn't expect other people to be stupider than you. The letter will put them on the track of suspicions which have entered nobody's head. I will not tell you what I personally thought when I saw the copy. I do not wish you to tell me anything but what is needed to save your neck.'

Mrs Crosbie gave a shrill cry. She sprang to her feet, white with terror.

'You don't think they'd hang me?'

'If they came to the conclusion that you hadn't killed Hammond in self-defence, it would be the duty of the assessors to bring in a verdict of guilty. The charge is murder. It would be the duty of the judge to sentence you to death.'

'But what can they prove?' she gasped.

'I don't know what they can prove. You know. I don't want to know. But if their suspicions are aroused, if they begin to make inquiries, if the natives are questioned—what is it that can be discovered?'

She crumpled up suddenly. She fell on the floor before he could catch her. She had fainted. He looked round the room for water, but there was none there, and he did not want to be disturbed. He stretched her out on the floor, and kneeling beside her waited for her to recover. When she opened her eyes he was disconcerted by the ghastly fear that he saw in them.

'Keep quite still,' he said. 'You'll be better in a moment.'

'You won't let them hang me,' she whispered.

She began to cry, hysterically, while in undertones he sought to quieten her.

'For goodness sake pull yourself together,' he said.

'Give me a minute.'

Her courage was amazing. He could see the effort she made to regain her self-control, and soon she was once more calm.

'Let me get up now.'

He gave her his hand and helped her to her feet. Taking her arm, he led her to the chair. She sat down wearily.

'Don't talk to me for a minute or two,' she said.

'Very well.'

When at last she spoke it was to say something which he did not expect. She gave a little sigh.

'I'm afraid I've made rather a mess of things,' she said.

He did not answer, and once more there was a silence.

'Isn't it possible to get hold of the letter?' she said at last.

'I do not think anything would have been said to me about it if the person in whose possession it is was not prepared to sell it.'

'Who's got it?'

'The Chinese woman who was living in Hammond's house.'

A spot of colour flickered for an instant on Leslie's cheek-bones.

'Does she want an awful lot for it?'

'I imagine that she has a very shrewd idea of its value. I doubt if it would be possible to get hold of it except for a very large sum.'

'Are you going to let me be hanged?'

'Do you think it's so simple as all that to secure possession of an unwelcome piece of evidence? It's no different from suborning a witness. You have no right to make any such suggestion to me.'

'Then what is going to happen to me?'

'Justice must take its course.'

She grew very pale. A little shudder passed through her body.

'I put myself in your hands. Of course I have no right to ask you to do anything that isn't proper.'

Mr Joyce had not bargained for the little break in her voice which her habitual self-restraint made quite intolerably moving. She looked at him with humble eyes, and he thought that if he rejected their appeal they would haunt him for the rest of his life. After all, nothing could bring poor Hammond back to life again. He wondered what really was the explanation of that letter. It was not fair to conclude from it that she had killed Hammond without provocation. He had lived in the East a long time and his sense of professional honour was not perhaps so acute as it had been twenty years before. He stared at the floor. He made up his mind to do something which he knew was unjustifiable, but it stuck in his throat and he felt dully resentful towards Leslie. It embarrassed him a little to speak.

'I don't know exactly what your husband's circumstances are?'

Flushing a rosy red, she shot a swift glance at him.

'He has a good many tin shares and a small share in two or three rubber estates. I suppose he could raise money.'

'He would have to be told what it was for.'

She was silent for a moment. She seemed to think.

'He's in love with me still. He would make any sacrifice to save me. Is there any need for him to see the letter?'

Mr Joyce frowned a little, and, quick to notice, she went on.

'Robert is an old friend of yours. I'm not asking you to do anything for me, I'm asking you to save a rather simple, kind man who never did you any harm from all the pain that's possible.'

Mr Joyce did not reply. He rose to go and Mrs Crosbie, with the grace that was natural to her, held out her hand. She was shaken by the scene, and her look was haggard, but she made a brave attempt to speed him with courtesy.

'It's so good of you to take all this trouble for me. I can't begin to tell you how grateful I am.'

Mr Joyce returned to his office. He sat in his own room, quite still, attempting to do no work, and pondered. His imagination brought him many strange ideas. He shuddered a little. At last there was the discreet knock on the door which he was expecting. Ong Chi Seng came in.

'I was just going out to have my tiffin, sir,' he said.

'All right.'

'I didn't know if there was anything you wanted before I went, sir.'

'I don't think so. Did you make another appointment for Mr Reed?'

'Yes, sir. He will come at three o'clock.'

'Good.'

Ong Chi Seng turned away, walked to the door, and put his long slim fingers on the handle. Then, as though on an afterthought, he turned back.

'Is there anything you wish me to say to my friend, sir?'

Although Ong Chi Seng spoke English so admirably he had still a difficulty with the letter R, and he pronounced it 'fliend'.

'What friend?'

'About the letter Mrs Crosbie wrote to Hammond deceased, sir.'

'Oh! I'd forgotten about that. I mentioned it to Mrs Crosbie and she denies having written anything of the sort. It's evidently a forgery.'

Mr Joyce took the copy from his pocket and handed it to Ong Chi Seng. Ong Chi Seng ignored the gesture.

'In that case, sir, I suppose there would be no objection if my fliend delivered the letter to the Deputy Public Prosecutor.'

'None. But I don't quite see what good that would do your friend.'

'My fliend, sir, thought it was his duty in the interests of justice.'

'I am the last man in the world to interfere with anyone who wishes to do his duty, Chi Seng.'

The eyes of the lawyer and of the Chinese clerk met. Not the shadow of a smile hovered on the lips of either, but they understood each other perfectly.

'I quite understand, sir,' said Ong Chi Seng, 'but from my study of the case R. *v.* Crosbie I am of opinion that the production of such a letter would be damaging to our client.'

'I have always had a very high opinion of your legal acumen, Chi Seng.'

'It had occurred to me, sir, that if I could persuade my fliend to induce the Chinese woman who has the letter to deliver it into our hands it would save a great deal of trouble.'

Mr Joyce idly drew faces on his blotting-paper.

'I suppose your friend is a business man. In what circumstances do you think he would be induced to part with the letter?'

'He has not got the letter. The Chinese woman has the letter. He is only a relation of the Chinese woman. She is ignorant woman; she did not know the value of that letter till my friend told her.'

'What value did he put on it?'

'Ten thousand dollars, sir.'

'Good God! Where on earth do you suppose Mrs Crosbie can get ten thousand dollars! I tell you the letter's a forgery.'

He looked up at Ong Chi Seng as he spoke. The clerk was unmoved by the outburst. He stood at the side of the desk, civil, cool, and observant.

'Mr Crosbie owns an eighth share of the Betong Rubber Estate and a sixth share of the Selantan River Rubber Estate. I have a fliend who will lend him the money on the security of his property.'

'You have a large circle of acquaintance, Chi Seng.'

'Yes, sir.'

'Well, you can tell them all to go to hell. I would never advise Mr Crosbie to give a penny more than five thousand for a letter that can be very easily explained.'

'The Chinese woman does not want to sell the letter, sir. My fliend took a long time to persuade her. It is useless to offer her less than the sum mentioned.'

Mr Joyce looked at Ong Chi Seng for at least three minutes. The clerk bore the searching scrutiny without embarrassment. He stood in a respectful attitude with downcast eyes. Mr Joyce knew his man. Clever fellow, Chi Seng, he thought, I wonder how much he's going to get out of it.

'Ten thousand dollars is a very large sum.'

'Mr Crosbie will certainly pay it rather than see his wife hanged, sir.'

Again Mr Joyce paused. What more did Chi Seng know than he had said? He must be pretty sure of his ground if he was obviously so unwilling to bargain. That sum had been fixed because whoever it was that was managing the affair knew it was the largest amount that Robert Crosbie could raise.

'Where is the Chinese woman now?' asked Mr Joyce.

'She is staying at the house of my fliend, sir.'

'Will she come here?'

'I think it more better if you go to her, sir. I can take you to the house tonight and she will give you the letter. She is very ignorant woman, sir, and she does not understand cheques.'

'I wasn't thinking of giving her a cheque. I will bring bank notes with me.'

'It would only be waste of valuable time to bring less than ten thousand dollars, sir.'

'I quite understand.'

'I will go and tell my fliend after I have had my tiffin, sir.'

'Very good. You'd better meet me outside the club at ten o'clock tonight.'

'With pleasure, sir,' said Ong Chi Seng.

He gave Mr Joyce a little bow and left the room. Mr Joyce went out to have luncheon, too. He went to the club and here, as he had expected, he saw Robert Crosbie. He was sitting at a crowded table, and as he passed him, looking for a place, Mr Joyce touched him on the shoulder.

'I'd like a word or two with you before you go,' he said.

'Right you are. Let me know when you're ready.'

Mr Joyce had made up his mind how to tackle him. He played a rubber of bridge after luncheon in order to allow time for the club to empty itself. He did not want on this particular matter to see Crosbie in his office. Presently Crosbie came into the card-room and looked on till the game was finished. The other players went on their various affairs, and the two were left alone.

'A rather unfortunate thing has happened, old man,' said Mr Joyce, in a tone which he sought to render as casual as possible. 'It appears that your wife sent a letter to Hammond asking him to come to the bungalow on the night he was killed.'

'But that's impossible,' cried Crosbie. 'She's always stated that she had had no communication with Hammond. I know from my own knowledge that she hadn't set eyes on him for a couple of months.'

'The fact remains that the letter exists. It's in the possession of the Chinese woman Hammond was living with. Your wife meant to give you a present on your birthday, and she wanted Hammond to help her to get it. In the emotional excitement that she suffered from after the tragedy, she forgot all about it, and having once denied having any communication with Hammond she was afraid to say that she had made a mistake. It was, of course, very unfortunate, but I dare say it was not unnatural.'

Crosbie did not speak. His large, red face bore an expression of complete bewilderment, and Mr Joyce was at once relieved and exasperated by his lack of comprehension. He was a stupid man, and Mr Joyce had no patience with stupidity. But his distress since the catastrophe had touched a soft spot in the lawyer's heart; and Mrs Crosbie had struck the right note when she asked him to help her, not for her sake, but for her husband's.

'I need not tell you that it would be very awkward if this letter found its way into the hands of the prosecution. Your wife has lied, and she would be asked to explain the lie. It alters things a little if Hammond did not intrude, an unwanted guest, but came to your house by invitation. It would be easy to arouse in the assessors a certain indecision of mind.'

Mr Joyce hesitated. He was face to face now with his decision. If it had been a time for humour, he could have smiled at the reflection that he was taking so grave a step, and that the man for whom he was taking it had not the smallest conception of its gravity. If he gave the matter a thought, he probably imagined that what Mr Joyce was doing was what any lawyer did in the ordinary run of business.

'My dear Robert, you are not only my client, but my friend. I think we must get hold of that letter. It'll cost a good deal of money. Except for that I should have preferred to say nothing to you about it.'

'How much?'

'Ten thousand dollars.'

'That's a devil of a lot. With the slump and one thing and another it'll take just about all I've got.'

'Can you get it at once?'

'I suppose so. Old Charlie Meadows will let me have it on my tin shares and on those two estates I'm interested in.'

'Then will you?'

'Is it absolutely necessary?'

'If you want your wife to be acquitted.'

Crosbie grew very red. His mouth sagged strangely.

'But . . .' he could not find words, his face now was purple. 'But I don't understand. She can explain. You don't mean to say they'd find her guilty? They couldn't hang her for putting a noxious vermin out of the way.'

'Of course they wouldn't hang her. They might only find her guilty of manslaughter. She'd probably get off with two or three years.'

Crosbie started to his feet and his red face was distraught with horror.

'Three years.'

Then something seemed to dawn in that slow intelligence of his. His mind was darkness across which shot suddenly a flash of lightning, and though the succeeding darkness was as profound, there remained the memory of something not seen but perhaps just descried. Mr Joyce saw that Crosbie's big red hands, coarse and hard with all the odd jobs he had set them to, trembled.

'What was the present she wanted to make me?'

'She says she wanted to give you a new gun.'

Once more that great red face flushed a deeper red.

'When have you got to have the money ready?'

There was something odd in his voice now. It sounded as though he spoke with invisible hands clutching at his throat.

'At ten o'clock tonight. I thought you could bring it to my office at about six.'

'Is the woman coming to you?'

'No, I'm going to her.'

'I'll bring the money. I'll come with you.'

Mr Joyce looked at him sharply.

'Do you think there's any need for you to do that? I think it would be better if you left me to deal with this matter by myself.'

'It's my money, isn't it? I'm going to come.'

Mr Joyce shrugged his shoulders. They rose and shook hands. Mr Joyce looked at him curiously.

At ten o'clock they met in the empty club.

'Everything all right?' asked Mr Joyce.

'Yes. I've got the money in my pocket.'

'Let's go then.'

They walked down the steps. Mr Joyce's car was waiting for them in the square, silent at that hour, and as they came to it Ong Chi Seng stepped out of the shadow of a house. He took his seat beside the driver and gave him a direction. They drove past the Hotel de l'Europe and turned up by the Sailor's Home to get into Victoria Street. Here the Chinese shops were still open, idlers lounged about, and in the roadway rickshaws and motor-cars and gharries gave a busy air to the scene. Suddenly their car stopped and Chi Seng turned round.

'I think it more better if we walk here, sir,' he said.

They got out and he went on. They followed a step or two behind. Then he asked them to stop.

'You wait here, sir. I go in and speak to my fliend.'

He went into a shop, open to the street, where three or four Chinese were standing behind the counter. It was one of those strange shops where nothing was on view, and you wondered what it was they sold there. They saw him address a stout man in a duck suit with a large gold chain across his breast, and the man shot a quick glance out into the night. He gave Chi Seng a key and Chi Seng came out. He beckoned to the two men waiting and slid into a doorway at the side of the shop. They followed him and found themselves at the foot of a flight of stairs.

'If you wait a minute I will light a match,' he said, always resourceful. 'You come upstairs, please.'

He held a Japanese match in front of them, but it scarcely dispelled the darkness and they groped their way up behind him. On the first floor he unlocked a door and going in lit a gas-jet.

'Come in, please,' he said.

It was a small square room, with one window, and the only furniture consisted of two low Chinese beds covered with matting. In one corner was a large chest, with an elaborate lock, and on this stood a shabby tray with an opium pipe on it and a lamp. There was in the room the faint, acrid scent of the drug. They sat down and Ong Chi Seng offered them cigarettes. In a moment the door was opened by the fat Chinaman whom they had seen behind the counter. He bade them good evening in very good English, and sat down by the side of his fellow-countryman.

'The Chinese woman is just coming,' said Chi Seng.

A boy from the shop brought in a tray with a teapot and cups and the Chinaman offered them a cup of tea. Crosbie refused. The Chinese talked to one another in undertones, but Crosbie and Mr Joyce were silent. At last there was the sound of a voice outside; someone was calling in a low tone; and the Chinaman went to the door. He opened it, spoke a few words, and ushered a woman in. Mr Joyce looked at her. He had heard much about her since Hammond's death, but he had never seen her. She was a stoutish person, not very young, with a broad, phlegmatic face, she was powdered and rouged and her eyebrows were a thin black line, but she gave you the impression of a woman of character. She wore a pale blue jacket and a white skirt, her costume was not quite European nor quite Chinese, but on her feet were little Chinese silk slippers. She wore heavy gold chains round her neck, gold bangles on her wrists, gold ear-rings, and elaborate gold pins in her black hair. She walked in slowly, with the air of a woman sure of herself, but with a certain heaviness of tread, and sat down on the bed beside Ong Chi Seng. He said something to her and nodding she gave an incurious glance at the two white men.

'Has she got the letter?' asked Mr Joyce.

'Yes, sir.'

Crosbie said nothing, but produced a roll of five-hundred-dollar notes. He counted out twenty and handed them to Chi Seng.

'Will you see if that is correct?'

The clerk counted them and gave them to the fat Chinaman.

'Quite correct, sir.'

The Chinaman counted them once more and put them in his pocket. He spoke again to the woman and she drew from her bosom a letter. She gave it to Chi Seng who cast his eyes over it.

'This is the right document, sir,' he said, and was about to give it to Mr Joyce when Crosbie took it from him.

'Let me look at it,' he said.

Mr Joyce watched him read and then held out his hand for it.

'You'd better let me have it.'

Crosbie folded it up deliberately and put it in his pocket.

'No, I'm going to keep it myself. It's cost me enough money.'

Mr Joyce made no rejoinder. The three Chinese watched the little passage, but what they thought about it, or whether they thought, it was impossible to tell from their impassive countenances. Mr Joyce rose to his feet.

'Do you want me any more tonight, sir?' said Ong Chi Seng.

'No.' He knew that the clerk wished to stay behind in order to get his agreed share of the money, and he turned to Crosbie. 'Are you ready?'

Crosbie did not answer, but stood up. The Chinaman went to the door and opened it for them. Chi Seng found a bit of candle and lit it in order to light them down, and the two Chinese accompanied them to the street. They left the woman sitting quietly on the bed smoking a cigarette. When they reached the street the Chinese left them and went once more upstairs.

'What are you going to do with that letter?' asked Mr Joyce.

'Keep it.'

They walked to where the car was waiting for them and here Mr Joyce offered his friend a lift. Crosbie shook his head.

'I'm going to walk.' He hesitated a little and shuffled his feet. 'I went to Singapore on the night of Hammond's death partly to buy a new gun that a man I knew wanted to dispose of. Good night.'

He disappeared quickly into the darkness.

Mr Joyce was quite right about the trial. The assessors went into court fully determined to acquit Mrs Crosbie. She gave evidence on her own behalf. She told her story simply and with straightforwardness. The D.P.P. was a kindly man and it was plain that he took no great pleasure in his task. He asked the necessary questions in a deprecating manner. His speech for the prosecution might really have been a speech for the defence, and the assessors took less than five minutes to consider their popular verdict. It was impossible to prevent the great outburst of applause with which it was received by the crowd that packed the courthouse. The judge congratulated Mrs Crosbie and she was a free woman.

No one had expressed a more violent disapprobation of Hammond's behaviour than Mrs Joyce; she was a woman loyal to her friends and she had insisted on the Crosbies staying with her after the trial, for she in common with everyone else had no doubt of the result, till they could make arrangements to go away. It was out of the question for poor, dear, brave Leslie to return to the bungalow at which the horrible catastrophe had taken place. The trial was over by half past twelve and when they reached the Joyces' house a grand luncheon was awaiting them. Cocktails were ready, Mrs Joyce's million-dollar cocktail was celebrated through all the Malay States, and Mrs Joyce drank Leslie's health. She was a talkative, vivacious woman, and now she was in the highest spirits. It was fortunate, for the rest of them were silent. She did not wonder; her husband never had much to say, and the other two were naturally exhausted from the long strain to which they had been subjected. During luncheon she carried on a bright and spirited monologue. Then coffee was served.

'Now, children,' she said in her gay, bustling fashion, 'you must have a rest and after tea I shall take you both for a drive to the sea.'

Mr Joyce, who lunched at home only by exception, had of course to go back to his office.

'I'm afraid I can't do that, Mrs Joyce,' said Crosbie. 'I've got to get back to the estate at once.'

'Not today?' she cried.

'Yes, now. I've neglected it for too long and I have urgent business. But I shall be very grateful if you will keep Leslie until we have decided what to do.'

Mrs Joyce was about to expostulate, but her husband prevented her.

'If he must go, he must, and there's an end of it.'

There was something in the lawyer's tone which made her look at him quickly. She held her tongue and there was a moment's silence. Then Crosbie spoke again.

'If you'll forgive me, I'll start at once so that I can get there before dark.' He rose from the table. 'Will you come and see me off, Leslie?'

'Of course.'

They went out of the dining-room together.

'I think that's rather inconsiderate of him,' said Mrs Joyce. 'He must know that Leslie wants to be with him just now.'

'I'm sure he wouldn't go if it wasn't absolutely necessary.'

'Well, I'll just see that Leslie's room is ready for her. She wants a complete rest, of course, and then amusement.'

Mrs Joyce left the room and Joyce sat down again. In a short time he heard Crosbie start the engine of his motor-cycle and then noisily scrunch over the gravel of the garden path. He got up and went into the drawing-room. Mrs Crosbie was standing in the middle of it, looking into space, and in her hand was an open letter. He recognized it. She gave him a glance as he came in and he saw that she was deathly pale.

'He knows,' she whispered.

Mr Joyce went up to her and took the letter from her hand. He lit a match and set the paper afire. She watched it burn. When he could hold it no longer he dropped it on the tiled floor and they both looked at the paper curl and blacken. Then he trod it into ashes with his foot.

'What does he know?'

She gave him a long, long stare and into her eyes came a strange look. Was it contempt or despair? Mr Joyce could not tell.

'He knows that Geoff was my lover.'

Mr Joyce made no movement and uttered no sound.

'He'd been my lover for years. He became my lover almost immediately after he came back from the war. We knew how careful we must be. When we became lovers I pretended I was tired of him, and he seldom came to the house when Robert was there. I used to drive out to a place we knew and he met me, two or three times a week, and when Robert went to Singapore he used to come to the bungalow late, when the boys had gone for the night. We saw one another constantly, all the time, and not a soul had the smallest suspicion of it. And then lately, a year ago, he began to change. I didn't know what was the matter. I couldn't believe that he didn't care for me any more. He always denied it. I was frantic. I made him scenes. Sometimes I thought he hated me. Oh, if you knew what agonies I endured. I passed through hell. I knew he didn't want me any more and I wouldn't let him go. Misery! Misery! I loved him. I'd given him everything. He was my life. And then I heard he was living with a Chinese woman. I couldn't believe it. I wouldn't believe it. At last I saw her, I saw her with my own eyes, walking in the village, with her gold bracelets and her necklaces, an old, fat Chinese woman. She was older than I was. Horrible! They all knew in the kampong that she was his mistress. And when I passed her, she looked at me and I knew that she knew I was his mistress too. I sent for him. I told him I must see him. You've read the letter. I was mad to write it. I didn't know what I was doing. I didn't care. I hadn't seen him for ten days. It was a lifetime. And when last we'd parted he took me in his arms and kissed me, and told me not to worry. And he went straight from my arms to hers.'

She had been speaking in a low voice, vehemently, and now she stopped and wrung her hands.

'That damned letter. We'd always been so careful. He always tore up any word I wrote to him the moment he'd read it. How was I to know he'd leave that one? He came, and I told him I knew about the Chinawoman. He denied it. He said it was only scandal. I was beside myself. I don't know what I said to him. Oh, I hated him then. I tore him limb from limb. I said everything I could to wound him. I insulted him. I could have spat in his face. And at last he turned on me. He told me he was sick and tired of me and never wanted to see me again. He said I bored him to death. And then he acknowledged that it was true about the Chinawoman. He said he'd known her for years, before the war, and she was the only woman who really meant anything to him, and the rest was just pastime. And he said he was glad I knew and now at last I'd leave him alone. And then I don't know what happened, I was beside myself, I saw red. I seized the revolver and I fired. He gave a cry and I saw I'd hit him. He staggered and rushed for the veranda. I ran after him and fired again. He fell and then I stood over him and I fired till the revolver went click, click, and I knew there were no more cartridges.'

At last she stopped, panting. Her face was no longer human, it was distorted with cruelty, and rage and pain. You would never have thought that this quiet, refined woman was capable of such fiendish passion. Mr Joyce took a step backwards. He was absolutely aghast at the sight of her. It was not a face, it was a gibbering, hideous mask. Then they heard a voice calling from another room, a loud, friendly, cheerful voice. It was Mrs Joyce.

'Come along, Leslie darling, your room's ready. You must be dropping with sleep.'

Mrs Crosbie's features gradually composed themselves. Those passions, so clearly delineated, were smoothed away as with your hand you would smooth crumpled paper, and in a minute the face was cool and calm and unlined. She was a trifle pale, but her lips broke into a pleasant, affable smile. She was once more the well-bred and even distinguished woman.

'I'm coming, Dorothy dear. I'm sorry to give you so much trouble.'

The Portrait of a Gentleman

♦

I arrived in Seoul towards evening and after dinner, tired by the long railway journey from Peking, to stretch my cramped legs I went for a walk. I wandered at random along a narrow and busy street. The Koreans in their long white gowns and their little white top-hats were amusing to look at and the open shops displayed wares that arrested my foreign eyes. Presently I came to a second-hand bookseller's and catching sight of shelves filled with English books went in to have a look at them. I glanced at the titles and my heart sank. They were commentaries on the Old Testament, treatises on the Epistles of St Paul, sermons and lives of divines doubtless eminent, but whose names were unfamiliar to me; I am an ignorant person. I supposed that this was the library of some missionary whom death had claimed in the midst of his labours and whose books then had been purchased by a Japanese bookseller. The Japanese are astute, but I could not imagine who in Seoul would be found to buy a work in three volumes on the Epistle to the Corinthians. But as I was turning away, between volume two and volume three of this treatise I noticed a little book bound in paper. I do not know what induced me to take it out. It was called *The Complete Poker Player* and its cover was illustrated with a hand holding four aces. I looked at the title-page. The author was Mr John Blackbridge, actuary and counsellor-at-law, and the preface was dated 1879. I wondered how this work happened to be among the books of a deceased missionary and I looked in one or two of them to see if I could find his name. Perhaps it was there only by accident. It may be that it was the entire library of a stranded gambler and had found its way to those shelves when his effects were sold to pay his hotel bill. But I preferred to think that it was indeed the property of the missionary and that when he was weary of reading divinity he rested his mind by the perusal of these lively pages. Perhaps somewhere in Korea, at night and alone in his mission-house, he dealt innumerable poker hands in order to see for himself whether you could really only get a straight flush once in sixty-five thousand hands. But the owner of the shop was looking at me with disfavour so I turned to him and asked the price of the book. He gave it a contemptuous glance and told me I could have it for twenty sen. I put it in my pocket.

I do not remember that for so small a sum I have ever purchased better entertainment. For Mr John Blackbridge in these pages of his did a thing no writer can do who deliberately tries to, but that, if done unconsciously, gives a book a rare and precious savour; he painted a complete portrait of himself. He stands before the reader so vividly that I was convinced that a wood-cut of him figured as a frontispiece and I was surprised to discover, on looking at the book again the other day, that there was nothing of the kind. I see him very distinctly as a man of middle-age, in a black frockcoat and a chimney-pot hat, wearing a black satin stock; he is clean-shaven and his jaw is square; his lips are thin and his eyes wary; his face is sallow and somewhat wrinkled. It is a countenance not without severity, but when he tells a story or makes one of his dry jokes his eyes light up and his smile is winning. He enjoyed his bottle of Burgundy, but I cannot believe that he ever drank enough to confuse his excellent faculties. He was just rather than merciful at the card-table and he was prepared to punish presumption with rigour. He had few illusions, for here are some of the things that life had taught him: 'Men hate those whom they have injured; men love those whom they have benefited; men naturally avoid their benefactors; men are universally actuated by self-interest; gratitude is a lively sense of expected benefits; promises are never forgotten by those to whom they are made, usually by those who make them.'

It may be presumed that he was a Southerner, for while speaking of Jack Pots, which he describes as a frivolous attempt to make the game more interesting, he remarks that they are not popular in the South. 'This last fact,' he says, 'contains much promise, because the South is the conservative portion of the country, and may be relied on as the last resort of good sense in social matters. The revolutionary Kossuth made no progress below Richmond; neither Spiritualism, nor Free Love, nor Communism, has ever been received with the least favour by the Southern mind; and it is for this reason that we greatly respect the Southern verdict upon the Jack Pot.' It was in his day an innovation and he condemned it. 'The time has arrived when all additions to the present standard combinations in Draw Poker must be worthless; the game being complete. The Jack Pot,' he says, 'was invented (in Toledo, Ohio) by reckless players to compensate losses incurred by playing against cautious players; and the principle is the same as if a party should play whist for stakes, and all be obliged every few minutes to stop, and purchase tickets in a lottery; or raffle for a turkey; or share a deal in Keno.'

Poker is a game for gentlemen (he does not hesitate to make frequent use of this abused word; he lived in a day when to be a gentleman had its obligations but also its privileges) and a straight flush is to be respected, not because you make money on it ('I have never seen anyone make much money upon a straight flush,' he says) but 'because it prevents any hand from being *absolutely* the winning hand, and thus relieves gentlemen from the necessity of betting on a certainty. Without the use of straights, and hence without the use of a straight flush, four aces would be a certainty and no gentleman could do more than *call* on them.' This, I confess, catches me on the raw, for once in my life I had a straight flush, and bet on it till I was called.

Mr John Blackbridge had personal dignity, rectitude, humour, and common sense. 'The amusements of mankind,' he says, 'have not as yet received proper recognition at the hands of the makers of the civil law, and of the unwritten social law,' and he had no patience with the persons who condemn the most agreeable pastime that has been invented, namely gambling, because risk is attached to it. Every transaction in life is a risk, he truly observes, and involves the question of loss and gain. 'To retire to rest at night is a practice that is fortified by countless precedents, and it is generally regarded as prudent and necessary. Yet it is surrounded by risks of every kind.' He enumerates them and finally sums up his argument with these reasonable words: 'If social circles welcome the banker and merchant who live by taking fair risks for the sake of profit, there is no apparent reason why they should not at least tolerate the man who at times employs himself in giving and taking fair risks for the sake of amusement.' But here his good sense is obvious. 'Twenty years of experience in the city of New York, both professionally (you must not forget that he is an actuary and counsellor-at-law) and as a student of social life, satisfy me that the average American gentleman in a large city has not over three thousand dollars a year to spend upon amusements. Will it be fair to devote more than one-third of his fund to cards? I do not think that anyone will say that one-third is not ample allowance for a single amusement. Given, therefore, a thousand dollars a year for the purpose of playing Draw Poker, what should be the limit of the stakes, in order that the average American gentleman may play the game with a contented mind, and with the certainty not only that he can pay his losses, but that his winnings will be paid to him?' Mr Blackbridge has no doubt that the answer is two dollars and a half. 'The game of Poker should be intellectual and not emotional; and it is impossible to exclude the emotions from it, if the stakes are so high that the question of loss and gain penetrates to the feelings.' From this quotation it may be seen that Mr Blackbridge looked upon poker as only on the side a game of chance. He considered that it needed as much force of character, mental ability, power of decision, and insight into motive to play poker as to govern a country or to lead an army, and I have an idea that on the whole he would have thought it a more sensible use of a man's faculties.

I am tempted to quote interminably, for Mr Blackbridge seldom writes a sentence that is other than characteristic, and his language is excellent; it is dignified as befits his subject and his condition (he does not forget that he is a gentleman), measured, clear, and pointed. His phrase takes an ample sweep when he treats of mankind and its foibles, but he can be as direct and simple as you please. Could anything be better than this terse but adequate description of a card-sharper? 'He was a very good-looking man of about forty years of age, having the appearance of one who had been leading a temperate and thoughtful life.' But I will content myself with giving a few of his aphorisms and wise saws chosen almost at random from the wealth of his book.

'Let your chips talk for you. A silent player is so far forth, a mystery; and a mystery is always feared.'

'In this game never do anything that you are not compelled to; while cheerfully responding to your obligations.'

'At Draw Poker all statements not called for by the laws of the game, or supported by ocular demonstration, may be set down as fictitious; designed to enliven the path of truth throughout the game, as flowers in summer enliven the margins of the highway.'

'Lost money is never recovered. After losing you may win, but the losing does not bring the winning.'

'No gentleman will ever play any game of cards with the design of habitually winning and never losing.'

'A gentleman is always willing to pay a fair price for recreation and amusement.'

'. . . that habit of mind which continually leads us to undervalue the mental force of other men, while we continually overvalue their good luck.'

'The injury done to your capital by a loss is never compensated by the benefit done to your capital by a gain of the same amount.'

'Players usually straddle when they are in bad luck, upon the principle that bad play and bad luck united will win. A slight degree of intoxication aids to perfect this intellectual deduction.'

'Euchre is a contemptible game.'

'The lower cards as well as the lower classes are only useful in combination or in excess, and cannot be depended upon under any other circumstances.'

'It is a hard matter to hold four Aces as steadily as a pair, but the table will bear their weight with as much equanimity as a pair of deuces.'

Of good luck and bad luck: 'To feel emotions over such incidents is unworthy of a man; and it is much more unworthy to express them. But no words need be wasted over practices which all men despise in others; and, in their reflecting moments, lament in themselves.'

'Endorsing for your friends is a bad habit, but it is nothing to playing Poker on credit. . . . Debit and credit ought never to interfere with the fine intellectual calculations of this game.'

There is a grand ring in his remarks on the player who has trained his intellect to bring logic to bear upon the principles and phenomena of the game. 'He will thus feel a constant sense of security amid all possible fluctuations that occur, and he will also abstain from pressing an ignorant or an intellectually weak opponent, beyond what may be necessary either for the purpose of playing the game correctly, or of punishing presumption.'

I leave Mr John Blackbridge with this last word and I can hear him saying it gently, but with a tolerant smile:

'For we must take human nature as it is.'

Raw
Material

◆

I have long had in mind a novel in which a card-sharper was the principal character; and, going up and down the world, I have kept my eyes open for members of this profession. Because the idea is prevalent that it is a slightly dishonourable one the persons who follow it do not openly acknowledge the fact. Their reticence is such that it is often not till you have become quite closely acquainted with them, or even have played cards with them two or three times, that you discover in what fashion they earn their living. But even then they have a disinclination to enlarge upon the mysteries of their craft. They have a weakness for passing themselves off for cavalrymen, commercial agents, or landed proprietors. This snobbish attitude makes them the most difficult class in the world for the novelist to study. It has been my good fortune to meet a number of these gentlemen, and though I have found them affable, obliging, and debonair, I have no sooner hinted, however discreetly, at my curiosity (after all purely professional) in the technique of their calling than they have grown shy and uncommunicative. An airy reference on my part to stacking the cards has made them assume immediately the appearance of a clam. I am not easily discouraged, and learning by experience that I could hope for no good results from a direct method, I have adopted the oblique. I have been childlike with them and bland. I have found that they gave me their attention and even their sympathy. Though they confessed honestly that they had never read a word I had written they were interested by the fact that I was a writer. I suppose they felt obscurely that I too followed a calling that the Philistine regarded without indulgence. But I have been forced to gather my facts by a bold surmise. It has needed patience and industry.

It may be imagined with what enthusiasm I made the acquaintance a little while ago of two gentlemen who seemed likely to add appreciably to my small store of information. I was travelling from Haiphong on a French liner going East, and they joined the ship at Hong-Kong. They had gone there for the races and were now on their way back to Shanghai. I was going there too, and thence to Peking. I soon learned that they had come from New York for a trip, were bound for Peking also, and by a happy coincidence meant to return to America in the ship in which I had myself booked a passage. I was naturally attracted to them, for they were pleasant fellows, but it was not till a fellow-passenger warned me that they were professional gamblers that I settled down to complete enjoyment of their acquaintance. I had no hope that they would ever discuss with frankness their interesting occupation, but I expected from a hint here, from a casual remark there, to learn some very useful things.

One—Campbell was his name—was a man in the late thirties, small, but so well built as not to look short, slender, with large, melancholy eyes and beautiful hands. But for a premature baldness he would have been more than commonly good-looking. He was neatly dressed. He spoke slowly, in a low voice, and his movements were deliberate. The other was made on another pattern. He was a big, burly man with a red face and crisp black hair, of powerful appearance, strong in the arm and pugnacious. His name was Peterson.

The merits of the combination were obvious. The elegant, exquisite Campbell had the subtle brain, the knowledge of character, and the deft hands; but the hazards of the card-sharper's life are many, and when it came to a scrap Peterson's ready fist must often have proved invaluable. I do not know how it spread through the ship so quickly that a blow of Peterson's would stretch any man out. But during the short voyage from Hong-Kong to Shanghai they never even suggested a game of cards. Perhaps they had done well during the race-week and felt entitled to a holiday. They were certainly enjoying the advantages of not living for the time in a dry country and I do not think I do them an injustice if I say that for the most part they were far from sober. Each one talked little of himself but willingly of the other. Campbell informed me that Peterson was one of the most distinguished mining engineers in New York and Peterson assured me that Campbell was an eminent banker. He said that his wealth was fabulous. And who was I not to accept ingenuously all that was told me? But I thought it negligent of Campbell not to wear jewellery of a more expensive character. It seemed to me that to use a silver cigarette case was rather careless.

I stayed but a day in Shanghai, and though I met the pair again in Peking I was then so much engaged that I saw little of them. I thought it a little odd that Campbell should spend his entire time in the hotel. I do not think he even went to see the Temple of Heaven. But I could quite understand that from his point of view Peking was unsatisfactory and I was not surprised when the pair returned to Shanghai, where, I knew, the wealthy merchants played for big money. I met them again in the ship that was to take us across the Pacific and I could not but sympathize with my friends when I saw that the passengers were little inclined to gamble. There were no rich people among them. It was a dull crowd. Campbell indeed suggested a game of poker, but no one would play more than twenty-dollar table stakes, and Peterson, evidently not thinking it worth while, would not join. Although we played afternoon and evening through the journey he sat down with us only on the last day. I suppose he thought he might just as well make his bar chits, and this he did very satisfactorily in a single sitting. But Campbell evidently loved the game for itself. Of course it is only if you have a passion for the business by which you earn your living that you can make a success of it. The stakes were nothing to him and he played all day and every day. It fascinated me to see the way in which he dealt the cards, very slowly, with his delicate hands. His eyes seemed to bore through the back of each one. He drank heavily, but remained quiet and self-controlled. His face was expressionless. I judged him to be a perfect card-player and I wished that I could see him at work. It increased my esteem for him to see that he could take what was only a relaxation so seriously.

I parted with the pair at Victoria and concluded that I should never see them again. I set about sorting my impressions and made notes of the various points that I thought would prove useful.

When I arrived in New York I found an invitation to luncheon at the Ritz with an old friend of mine. When I went she said to me:

'It's quite a small party. A man is coming whom I think you'll like. He's a prominent banker; he's bringing a friend with him.'

The words were hardly out of her mouth when I saw coming up to us Campbell and Peterson. The truth flashed across me: Campbell really was an opulent banker; Peterson really was a distinguished engineer; they were not card-sharpers at all. I flatter myself I kept my face, but as I blandly shook hands with them I muttered under my breath furiously:

'Impostors!'

Straight Flush

◆

I am not a bad sailor and when under stress of weather the game broke up I did not go below. We were in the habit of playing poker into the small hours, a mild game that could hurt nobody, but it had been blowing all day and with nightfall the wind strengthened to half a gale. One or two of our bunch admitted that they felt none too comfortable and one or two others played with unwonted detachment. But even if you are not sick dirty weather at sea is an unpleasant thing. I hate the fool who tells you he loves a storm and tramping the deck lustily vows that it can never be too rough for him. When the woodwork groans and creaks, glasses crash to the floor and you lurch in your chair as the ship heels over, when the wind howls and the waves thunder against the side, I very much prefer dry land. I think no one was sorry when one of the players said he had had enough, and the last round of jack pots was agreed to without demur. I remained alone in the smoking-room, for I knew I should not easily get to sleep in that racket and I could not read in bed with any comfort when the North Pacific kept dashing itself against my port-holes. I shuffled together the two packs we had been playing with and set out a complicated patience.

I had been playing about ten minutes when the door was opened with a blast of wind that sent my cards flying, and two passengers, rather breathless, slipped into the smoking-room. We were not a full ship and we were ten days out from Hong-Kong, so that I had had time to become acquainted with pretty well everyone on board. I had spoken on several occasions to the pair who now entered, and seeing me by myself they came over to my table.

They were very old men, both of them. That perhaps was what had brought them together, for they had first met when they got on board at Hong-Kong, and now you saw them sitting together in the smoking-room most of the day, not talking very much, but just comfortable to be side by side, with a bottle of

Vichy water between them. They were very rich old men too and that was a bond between them. The rich feel at ease in one another's company. They know that money means merit. Their experience of the poor is that they always want something. It is true that the poor admire the rich and it is pleasant to be admired, but they envy them as well and this prevents their admiration from being quite candid. Mr Rosenbaum was a little hunched-up Jew, very frail in clothes that looked too big for him, and he gave you the impression of hanging on to mortality only by a hair. His ancient, emaciated body looked as though it were already attacked by the corruption of the grave. The only expression his face ever bore was one of cunning, but it was purely habitual, the result of ever so many years' astuteness; he was a kindly, friendly person, very free with his drinks and cigars, and his charity was world-famous. The other was called Donaldson. He was a Scot, but had gone to California as a little boy and made a great deal of money mining. He was short and stout, with a red, clean-shaven, shiny face and no hair but a sickle of silver above his neck, and very gentle eyes. Whatever force he had had to make his way in the world had been worn away by the years and he was now a picture of mild beneficence.

'I thought you'd turned in long ago,' I remarked.

'I should have,' returned the Scot, 'only Mr Rosenbaum kept me up talking of old times.'

'What's the good of going to bed when you can't sleep?' said Mr Rosenbaum.

'Walk ten times round the deck with me tomorrow morning and you'll sleep all right.'

'I've never taken any exercise in my life and I'm not going to begin now.'

'That's foolishness. You'd be twice the man you are now if you'd taken exercise. Look at me. You'd never think I was seventy-nine, would you.'

Mr Rosenbaum looked critically at Mr Donaldson.

'No, I wouldn't. You're very well preserved. You look younger than me and I'm only seventy-six. But then I never had a chance to take care of myself.'

At that moment the steward came up.

'The bar's just going to close, gentlemen. Is there anything I can get you?'

'It's a stormy night,' said Mr Rosenbaum. 'Let's have a bottle of champagne.'

'Small Vichy for me,' said Mr Donaldson.

'Oh, very well, small Vichy for me too.'

The steward went away.

'But mind you,' continued Mr Rosenbaum testily, 'I wouldn't have done without the things you've done without, not for all the money in the world.'

Mr Donaldson gave me his gentle smile.

'Mr Rosenbaum can't get over it because I've never touched a card nor a drop of alcohol for fifty-seven years.'

'Now I ask you, what sort of a life is that?'

'I was a very heavy drinker when I was a young fellow and a desperate gambler, but I had a very terrible experience. It was a lesson to me and I took it.'

'Tell him about it,' said Mr Rosenbaum. 'He's an author. He'll write it up and perhaps he'll be able to make his passage money.'

'It's not a story I like telling very much even now. I'll make it as short as I can. Me and three others had staked out a claim, friends all of us, and the oldest wasn't twenty-five; there was me and my partner and a couple of brothers, McDermott their name was, but they were more like friends than brothers.

What was one's was the other's, and one wouldn't go into town without the other went too, and they were always laughing and joking together. A fine clean pair of boys, over six feet high both of them, and handsome. We were a wild bunch and we had pretty good luck on the whole and when we made money we didn't hesitate to spend it. Well, one night we'd all been drinking very heavily and we started a poker game. I guess we were a good deal drunker than we realized. Anyhow suddenly a row started between the McDermotts. One of them accused the other of cheating. "You take that back," cried Jamie. "I'll see you in hell first," says Eddie. And before me and my partner could do anything Jamie had pulled out his gun and shot his brother dead.'

The ship gave a huge roll and we all clung to our seats. In the steward's pantry there was a great clatter as bottles and glasses slid along a shelf. It was strange to hear that grim little story told by that mild old man. It was a story of another age and you could hardly believe that this fat, red-faced little fellow, with his silver fringe of hair, in a dinner jacket, two large pearls in his shirt-front, had really taken part in it.

'What happened then?' I asked.

'We sobered up pretty quick. At first Jamie couldn't believe Eddie was dead. He took him in his arms and kept calling him. "Eddie," he says, "wake up, old boy, wake up." He cried all night and next day we rode in with him to town, forty miles it was, me on one side of him and my partner on the other, and handed him over to the sheriff. I was crying too when we shook hands with him and said good-bye. I told my partner I'd never touch a card again or drink as long as I lived, and I never have, and I never will.'

Mr Donaldson looked down, and his lips were trembling. He seemed to see again that scene of long ago. There was one thing I should have liked to ask him about, but he was evidently so much moved I did not like to. They seem not to have hesitated, his partner and himself, but delivered up this wretched boy to justice as though it were the most natural thing in the world. It suggested that even in those rough, wild men the respect for the law had somehow the force of an instinct. A little shiver ran through me. Mr Donaldson emptied his glass of Vichy and with a curt good night left us.

'The old fellow's getting a bit childish,' said Mr Rosenbaum. 'I don't believe he was ever very bright.'

'Well, apparently he was bright enough to make an awful lot of money.'

'But how? In those days in California you didn't want brains to make money, you only wanted luck. I know what I'm talking about. Johannesburg was the place where you had to have your wits about you. Joburg in the eighties. It was grand. We were a tough lot of guys, I can tell you. It was each for himself and the devil take the hindmost.'

He took a meditative sip of his Vichy.

'You talk of your cricket and baseball, your golf and tennis and football, you can have them, they're all very well for boys; is it a reasonable thing, I ask you, for a grown man to run about and hit a ball? Poker's the only game fit for a grown man. Then your hand is against every man and every man's hand is against yours. Team-work? Who ever made a fortune by team-work? There's only one way to make a fortune and that's to down the fellow who's up against you.'

'I didn't know you were a poker player,' I interrupted. 'Why don't you take a hand one evening?'

'I don't play any more. I've given it up too, but for the only reason a man should. I can't see myself giving it up because a friend of mine was unlucky enough to get killed. Anyway a man who's damn fool enough to get killed isn't worth having as a friend. But in the old days! If you wanted to know what poker was you ought to have been in South Africa then. It was the biggest game I've ever seen. And they were fine players; there wasn't a crooked dodge they weren't up to. It was grand. Just to give you an example, one night I was playing with some of the biggest men in Johannesburg and I was called away. There was a couple of thousand pounds in the pot! "Deal me a hand, I won't keep you waiting," I said. "All right," they said, "don't hurry." Well, I wasn't gone more than a minute. When I came back I picked up my cards and saw I'd got a straight flush to the queen. I didn't say a word, I just threw in my hand. I knew my company. And do you know, I was wrong.'

'What do you mean? I don't understand.'

'It was a perfectly straight deal and the pot was won on three sevens. But how could I tell that? Naturally I thought someone else had a straight flush to the king. It looked to me just the sort of hand I might lose a hundred thousand pounds on.'

'Too bad,' I said.

'I very nearly had a stroke. And it was on account of another pat straight flush that I gave up playing poker. I've only had about five in my life.'

'I believe the chances are nearly sixty-six thousand to one against.'

'In San Francisco it was, the year before last. I'd been playing in poor luck all the evening. I hadn't lost much money because I never had a chance to play. I'd hardly had a pair and if I got a pair I couldn't improve. Then I got a hand just as bad as the others and I didn't come in. The man next to me wasn't playing either and I showed him my hand. "That's the kind of thing I've been getting all the evening," I said. "How can anyone be expected to play with cards like that?" "Well, I don't know what more you want," he said, as he looked at them. "Most of us would be prepared to come in on a straight flush." "What's that," I cried. I was trembling like a leaf. I looked at the cards again. I thought I had two or three little hearts and two or three little diamonds. It was a straight flush in hearts all right and I hadn't seen it. My eyes, it was. I knew what it meant. Old age. I don't cry much. I'm not that sort of man. But I couldn't help it then. I tried to control myself, but the tears just rolled down my cheeks. Then I got up. "I'm through, gentlemen," I said. "When a man's eyes are so dim that he can't see a straight flush when it's dealt him he has no business to play poker. Nature's given me a hint and I'm taking it. I'll never play poker again as long as I live." I cashed in my chips, all but one, and I left the house. I've never played since.'

Mr Rosenbaum took a chip out of his waistcoat pocket and showed it to me.

'I kept this as a souvenir. I always carry it about with me. I'm a sentimental old fool, I know that, but, you see, poker was the only thing I cared for. Now I've only got one thing left.'

'What is that?' I asked.

A smile flickered across his cunning little face and behind his thick glasses his rheumy eyes twinkled with ironic glee. He looked incredibly astute and malicious. He gave the thin, high-pitched cackle of an old man amused and answered with a single word 'Philanthropy'.

A Casual Affair

♦

I am telling this story in the first person, though I am in no way connected with it, because I do not want to pretend to the reader that I know more about it than I really do. The facts are as I state them, but the reasons for them I can only guess, and it may be that when the reader has read them he will think me wrong. No one can know for certain. But if you are interested in human nature there are few things more diverting than to consider the motives that have resulted in certain actions. It was only by chance that I heard anything of the unhappy circumstances at all. I was spending two or three days on an island on the north coast of Borneo, and the District Officer had very kindly offered to put me up. I had been roughing it for some time and I was glad enough to have a rest. The island had been at one time a place of some consequence, with a Governor of its own, but was so no longer; and now there was nothing much to be seen of its former importance except the imposing stone house in which the Governor had once lived and which now the District Officer, grumblingly because of its unnecessary size, inhabited. But it was a comfortable house to stay in, with an immense drawing-room, a dining-room large enough to seat forty people, and lofty, spacious bedrooms. It was shabby, because the government at Singapore very wisely spent as little money on it as possible; but I rather liked this, and the heavy official furniture gave it a sort of dull stateliness that was amusing. The garden was too large for the District Officer to keep up and it was a wild tangle of tropical vegetation. His name was Arthur Low; he was a quiet, smallish man in the later thirties, married, with two young children. The Lows had not tried to make themselves at home in this great place, but camped there, like refugees from a stricken area, and looked forward to the time when they would be moved to some other post where they could settle down in surroundings more familiar to them.

I took a fancy to them at once. The D.O. had an easy manner and a humorous way with him. I am sure he performed his various duties admirably, but he did everything he could to avoid the official demeanour. He was slangy of speech and pleasantly caustic. It was charming to see him play with the two children. It was quite obvious that he had found marriage a very satisfactory state. Mrs Low was an extremely nice little woman, plump, with dark eyes under fine eyebrows, not very pretty, but certainly attractive. She looked healthy and she had high spirits. They chaffed one another continually and each one seemed to look upon the other as immensely comic. Their jokes were neither very good nor very new, but they thought them so killing that you were obliged to laugh with them.

I think they were glad to see me, especially Mrs Low, for with nothing much to do but keep an eye on the house and the children, she was thrown very much on her own resources. There were so few white people on the island that the social life was soon exhausted; and before I had been there twenty-four hours she pressed me to stay a week, a month, or a year. On the evening of my arrival they gave a dinner-party to which the official population, the government surveyor, the doctor, the schoolmaster, the chief of constabulary, were invited, but on the following evening the three of us dined by ourselves. At the dinner-party the guests had brought their house-boys to help, but that night we were waited on by the Lows' one boy and my travelling servant. They brought in the coffee and left us to ourselves. Low and I lit cheroots.

'You know that I've seen you before,' said Mrs Low.

'Where?' I asked.

'In London. At a party. I heard someone point you out to somebody else. In Carlton House Terrace at Lady Kastellan's.'

'Oh? When was that?'

'Last time we were home on leave. There were Russian dancers.'

'I remember. About two or three years ago. Fancy you being there!'

'That's exactly what we said to one another at the time,' said Low, with a slow, engaging smile. 'We'd never been at such a party in our lives.'

'It made a great splash, you know,' I said. 'It was *the* party of the season. Did you enjoy it?'

'I hated every minute of it,' said Mrs Low.

'Don't let's overlook the fact that you insisted on going, Bee.' said Low. 'I knew we'd be out of it among all those swells. My dress clothes were the same I'd had at Cambridge and they'd never been much of a fit.'

'I bought a frock specially at Peter Robinson's. It looked lovely in the shop. I wished I hadn't wasted so much money when I got there; I never felt so dowdy in my life.'

'Well it didn't much matter. We weren't introduced to anybody.'

I remembered the party quite well. The magnificent rooms in Carlton House Terrace had been decorated with great festoons of yellow roses and at one end of the vast drawing-room a stage had been erected. Special costumes of the Regency period had been designed for the dancers and a modern composer had written the music for the two charming ballets they danced. It was hard to look at it all and not allow the vulgar thought to cross one's mind that the affair must have cost an enormous amount of money. Lady Kastellan was a beautiful woman and a great hostess, but I do not think anyone would have ascribed to her any vast amount of kindliness, she knew too many people to care much for any one in particular, and I couldn't help wondering why she had asked to such a grand party two obscure and quite unimportant little persons from a distant colony.

'Had you known Lady Kastellan long?' I asked.

'We didn't know her at all. She sent us a card and we went because I wanted to see what she was like,' said Mrs Low.

'She's a very able woman,' I said.

'I dare say she is. She hadn't an idea who we were when the butler man announced us, but she remembered at once. "Oh, yes," she said, "you're poor Jack's friends. Do go and find yourselves seats where you can see. You'll adore Lifar, he's too marvellous." And then she turned to say how d'you do to the next people. But she gave me a look. She wondered how much I knew and she saw at once that I knew everything.'

'Don't talk such nonsense, darling,' said Low. 'How could she know all you think she did by just looking at you, and how could you tell what she was thinking?'

'It's true, I tell you. We said everything in that one look, and unless I'm very much mistaken I spoilt her party for her.'

Low laughed and I smiled, for Mrs Low spoke in a tone of triumphant vindictiveness.

'You are terribly indiscreet, Bee.'

'Is she a great friend of yours?' Mrs Low asked me.

'Hardly. I've met her here and there for fifteen years. I've been to a good many parties at her house. She gives very good parties and she always asks you to meet the people you want to see.'

'What d'you think of her?'

'She's by way of being a considerable figure in London. She's amusing to talk to and she's nice to look at. She does a lot for art and music. What do *you* think of her?'

'I think she's a bitch,' said Mrs Low, with cheerful but decided frankness.

'That settles her,' I said.

'Tell him, Arthur.'

Low hesitated for a moment.

'I don't know that I ought to.'

'If you don't, I shall.'

'Bee's got her knife into her all right,' he smiled. 'It was rather a bad business really.'

He made a perfect smoke-ring and watched it with absorption.

'Go on, Arthur,' said Mrs Low.

'Oh, well. It was before we went home last time. I was D.O. in Selangor and one day they came and told me that a white man was dead in a small town a couple of hours up the river. I didn't know there was a white man living there. I thought I'd better go and see about it, so I got in the launch and went up. I made inquiries when I got there. The police didn't know anything about him except that he'd been living there for a couple of years with a Chinese woman in the bazaar. It was rather a picturesque bazaar, tall houses on each side, with a board walk in between, built on piles on the river-bank, and there were awnings above to keep out the sun. I took a couple of policemen with me and they led me to the house. They sold brass-ware in the shop below and the rooms above were let out. The master of the shop took me up two flights of dark, rickety stairs, foul with every kind of Chinese stench, and called out when we got to the top. The door was opened by a middle-aged Chinese woman and I saw that her face was all bloated with weeping. She didn't say anything, but made way for us to pass. It wasn't much more than a cubby-hole under the roof; there was a small window that looked on the street, but the awning that stretched across it dimmed the light. There wasn't any furniture except a deal table and a kitchen chair with a broken back. On a mat against the wall a dead man was lying. The first thing I did was to have the window opened. The room was so frowsty that I retched, and the strongest smell was the smell of opium. There was a small oil-lamp on the table and a long needle, and of course I knew what they were there for. The pipe had been hidden. The dead man lay on his back with nothing on but a sarong and a dirty singlet. He had long brown hair, going grey, and a short beard. He was a white man all right. I examined him as best I could. I had to judge whether death was due to natural causes. There were no signs of violence. He was nothing but skin and bone. It looked to me as though he might very likely have died of starvation. I asked the man of the shop and the woman a number of questions. The policeman corroborated their statements. It appeared that the man coughed a great deal and brought up blood now and then, and his appearance suggested that he might very well have had T.B. The Chinaman said he'd been a confirmed opium smoker. It all seemed pretty obvious. Fortunately cases of that sort are rare, but they're not unheard of—the white man who goes under and gradually sinks to the last stage of degradation. It appeared that the Chinese woman had been fond of him. She'd kept him on her own miserable earnings for the last two years. I gave the necessary instructions. Of course I wanted to know who he was. I supposed he'd been a clerk in some English firm or an assistant in an English store at Singapore or Kuala Lumpur. I asked the Chinese woman if he'd left any effects. Considering the destitution in which they'd lived it seemed a rather absurd question, but she went to a shabby suit-case that lay in a corner, opened it, and showed me a square parcel about the size of two novels put together wrapped in an old newspaper. I had a look at the suit-case. It contained nothing of any value. I took the parcel.'

Low's cheroot had gone out and he leaned over to relight it from one of the candles on the table.

'I opened it. Inside was another wrapping, and on this, in a neat, well-educated writing: To the District Officer, me as it happened, and then the words: please deliver personally to the Viscountess Kastellan, 53 Carlton House Terrace, London, sw. That was a bit of a surprise. Of course I had to examine the contents. I cut the string and the first thing I found was a gold and platinum cigarette-case. As you can imagine I was mystified. From all I'd heard the pair of them, the dead man and the Chinese woman, had scarcely enough to eat, and the cigarette-case looked as if it had cost a packet. Besides the cigarette-case there was nothing but a bundle of letters. There were no envelopes. They were in the same neat writing as the directions and they were signed with the initial J. There were forty of fifty of them. I couldn't read them all there, but a rapid glance showed me that they were a man's love letters to a woman. I sent for the Chinese woman to ask her the name of the dead man. Either she didn't know or wouldn't tell me. I gave orders that he should be buried and got back into the launch to go home. I told Bee.'

He gave her his sweet little smile.

'I had to be rather firm with Arthur,' she said. 'At first he wouldn't let me read the letters, but of course I wasn't going to put up with any nonsense like that.'

'It was none of our business.'

'You had to find out the name if you could.'

'And where exactly did you come in?'

'Oh, don't be so silly,' she laughed. 'I should have gone mad if you hadn't let me read them.'

'And did you find out his name?' I asked.

'No.'

'Was there no address?'

'Yes, there was, and a very unexpected one. Most of the letters were written on Foreign Office paper.'

'That was funny.'

'I didn't quite know what to do. I had half a mind to write to the Viscountess Kastellan and explain the circumstances, but I didn't know what trouble I might be starting; the directions were to deliver the parcel to her personally, so I wrapped everything up again and put it in the safe. We were going home on leave in the spring and I thought the best thing was to leave everything over till then. The letters were by way of being rather compromising.'

'To put it mildly,' giggled Mrs Low. 'The truth is they gave the whole show away.'

'I don't think we need go into that,' said Low.

A slight altercation ensued; but I think on his part it was more for form's sake, since he must have known that his desire to preserve an official discretion stood small chance against his wife's determination to tell me everything. She had a down on Lady Kastellan and didn't care what she said about her. Her sympathies were with the man. Low did his best to tone down her rash assertions. He corrected her exaggerations. He told her that she'd let her imagination run away with her and had read into the letters more than was there. She would have done it. They'd evidently made a deep impression on her, and from her vivid account and Low's interruptions I gained a fairly coherent impression of them. It was plain for one thing that they were very moving.

'I can't tell you how it revolted me, the way Bee gloated over them,' said Low.

'They were the most wonderful letters I've ever read. You never wrote letters like that to me.'

'What a damned fool you would have thought me if I had,' he grinned.

She gave him a charming, affectionate smile.

'I suppose I should, and yet, God knows I was crazy about you, and I'm damned if I know why.'

The story emerged clearly enough. The writer, the mysterious J., presumably a clerk in the Foreign Office, had fallen in love with Lady Kastellan and she with him. They had become lovers and the early letters were passionately lyrical. They were happy. They expected their love to last for ever. He wrote to her immediately after he had left her and told her how much he adored her and how much she meant to him. She was never for a moment absent from his thoughts. It looked as though her infatuation was equal to his, for in one letter he justified himself because she had reproached him for not coming to some place where he knew she would be. He told her what agony it had been to him that a sudden job had prevented him from being with her when he'd so eagerly looked forward to it.

Then came the catastrophe. How it came or why one could only guess. Lord

Kastellan learnt the truth. He not merely suspected his wife's infidelity, he had proofs of it. There was a fearful scene between them, she left him and went to her father's. Lord Kastellan announced his intention of divorcing her. The letters changed in character. J. wrote at once asking to see Lady Kastellan, but she begged him not to come. Her father insisted that they shouldn't meet. J. was distressed at her unhappiness and dismayed by the trouble he had brought upon her, and he was deeply sympathetic because of what she was enduring at home, for her father and mother were furious; but at the same time it was plain that he was relieved that the crisis had come. Nothing mattered except that they loved one another. He said he hated Kastellan. Let him bring his action. The sooner they could get married the better. The correspondence was one-sided, there were no letters from her, and one had to guess from his replies what she said in them. She was obviously frightened out of her wits and nothing that he could say helped. Of course he would have to leave the Foreign Office. He assured her that this meant nothing to him. He could get a job somewhere, in the colonies, where he would earn much more money. He was sure he could make her happy. Naturally there would be a scandal, but it would be forgotten, and away from England people would not bother. He besought her to have courage. Then it looked as though she had written somewhat peevishly. She hated being divorced, Kastellan refused to take the blame on himself and be made respondent, she did not want to leave London, it was her whole life, and bury herself in some God-forsaken place on the other side of nowhere. He answered unhappily. He said he would do anything she wanted. He implored her not to love him less and he was tortured by the thought that this disaster had changed her feelings for him. She reproached him for the mess they had got into; he did not try to defend himself; he was prepared to admit that he alone was to blame. Then it appeared that pressure was being brought to bear on Kastellan from some high quarter and there was even yet a chance that something might be arranged. Whatever she wrote made J., the unknown J., desperate. His letter was almost incoherent. He begged her again to see him, he implored her to have strength, he repeated that she meant everything in the world to him, he was frightened that she would let people influence her, he asked her to burn her boats behind her and bolt with him to Paris. He was frantic. Then it seemed that for some days she did not write to him. He could not understand. He did not know if she was receiving his letters. He was in an agony. The blow fell. She must have written to say that if he would resign from the Foreign Office and leave England her husband was prepared to take her back. His answer was broken-hearted.

'He never saw through her for a moment,' said Mrs Low.

'What was there to see through?' I asked.

'Don't you know what she wrote to him? I do.'

'Don't be such an ass, Bee. You can't possibly know.'

'Ass yourself. Of course I do. She put it up to him. She threw herself on his mercy. She dragged in her father and mother. She brought in her children; I bet that was the first thought she'd given them since they were born. She knew that he loved her so much that he was willing to do everything in the world for her, even lose her. She knew that he was prepared to accept the sacrifice of his love, his life, his career, everything for her sake, and she let him make it. She let the offer come from him. She let him persuade her to accept it.'

I listened to Mrs Low with a smile, but with attention. She was a woman and she felt instinctively how a woman in those circumstances would act. She thought it hateful, but she felt in her bones that in just that way would she herself have acted. Of course it was pure invention, with nothing but J.'s letter as a foundation, but I had an impression that it was very likely.

That was the last letter in the bundle.

I was astonished. I had known Lady Kastellan for a good many years, but only casually; and I knew her husband even less. He was immersed in politics, he was Under-Secretary at the Home Office at the time of the great do to which the Lows and I had been invited; and I never saw him but in his own house. Lady Kastellan had the reputation of being a beauty; she was tall and her figure was good in a massive way. She had a lovely skin. Her blue eyes were large, set rather wide apart and her face was broad. It gave her a slightly cow-like look. She had pretty pale brown hair and she held herself superbly. She was a woman of great self-possession, and it amazed me to learn that she had ever surrendered to such passion as the letters suggested. She was ambitious and there was no doubt that she was very useful to Kastellan in his political life. I should have thought her incapable of indiscretion. Searching my memory I seemed to remember hearing years before that the Kastellans were not getting on very well, but I had never heard any details, and whenever I saw them it looked as though they were on very good terms with one another. Kastellan was a big, red-faced fellow with sleek black hair, jovial and loud-voiced, but with little shrewd eyes that watched and noted. He was industrious, an effective speaker, but a trifle pompous. He was a little too conscious of his own importance. He did not let you forget that he had rank and wealth. He was inclined to be patronizing with people of less consequence than himself.

I could well believe that when he discovered that his wife was having an affair with a junior clerk in the Foreign Office there was a devil of a row. Lady Kastellan's father had been for many years permanent Under-Secretary for Foreign Affairs and it would have been more than usually embarrassing for his daughter to be divorced on account of one of his subordinates. For all I knew Kastellan was in love with his wife and he may have been teased by a very natural jealousy. But he was a proud man, deficient in humour. He feared ridicule. The role of the deceived husband is difficult to play with dignity. I do not suppose he wanted a scandal that might well jeopardize his political future. It may be that Lady Kastellan's advisers threatened to defend the case and the prospect of washing dirty linen in public horrified him. It is likely enough that pressure was brought to bear on him and the solution to forgive and take his wife back if her lover were definitely eliminated may have seemed the best to adopt. I have no doubt Lady Kastellan promised everything she was asked.

She must have had a bad fright. I didn't take such a severe view of her conduct as Mrs Low. She was very young; she was not more than thirty-five now. Who could tell by what accident she had become J.'s mistress? I suspect that love had caught her unawares and that she was in the middle of an affair almost before she knew what she was about. She must always have been a cold, self-possessed woman, but it is just with people like that that nature at times plays strange tricks. I am prepared to believe that she lost her head completely. There is no means of knowing how Kastellan discovered what was going on, but the fact that she kept her lover's letters shows that she was too much in love to be prudent. Arthur Low had mentioned that it was strange to find in the dead man's possession his letters and not hers; but that seemed to me easily explainable. At the time of the catastrophe they were doubtless given back to him in exchange for hers. He very naturally kept them. Reading them again he could relive the love that meant everything in the world to him.

I didn't suppose that Lady Kastellan, devoured by passion, could ever have considered what would happen if she were found out. When the blow fell it is not strange that she was scared out of her wits. She may not have had more to do with her children than most women who live the sort of life she lived, but she may for all that not have wanted to lose them. I did not even know whether she had ever cared for her husband, but from what I knew of her I guessed that she was not indifferent to his name and wealth. The future must have looked pretty grim. She was losing everything, the grand house in Carlton House Terrace, the position, the security; her father could give her no money and her lover had still to find a job. It may not have been heroic that she should yield to the entreaties of her family, but it was comprehensible.

While I was thinking all this Arthur Low went on with his story.

'I didn't quite know how to set about getting in touch with Lady Kastellan,' he said. 'It was awkward not knowing the chap's name. However, when we got home I wrote to her. I explained who I was and said that I'd been asked to give her some letters and a gold and platinum cigarette-case by a man who'd recently died in my district. I said I'd been asked to deliver them to her in person. I thought perhaps she wouldn't answer at all or else communicate with me through a solicitor. But she answered all right. She made an appointment for me to come to Carlton House Terrace at twelve one morning. Of course it was stupid of me, but when finally I stood on the doorstep and rang the bell I was quite nervous. The door was opened by a butler. I said I had an appointment with Lady Kastellan. A footman took my hat and coat. I was led upstairs to an enormous drawing-room.

'"I'll tell her ladyship you're here, sir," the butler said.

'He left me and I sat on the edge of a chair and looked round. There were huge pictures on the walls, portraits you know, I don't know who they were by, Reynolds I should think and Romney, and there was a lot of Oriental china, and gilded consoles and mirrors. It was all terribly grand and it made me feel very shabby and insignificant. My suit smelt of camphor and it was baggy at the knees. My tie felt a bit loud. The butler came in again and asked me to go with him. He opened another door from the one I'd come in by and I found myself in a further room, not so large as the drawing-room, but large all the same and very grand too. A lady was standing by the fireplace. She looked at me as I came in and bowed slightly. I felt frightfully awkward as I walked along the whole length of the room and I was afraid of stumbling over the furniture. I can only hope I didn't look such a fool as I felt. She didn't ask me to sit down.

'"I understand you have some things that you wish to deliver to me personally," she said. "It's very good of you to bother."

'She didn't smile. She seemed perfectly self-possessed, but I had a notion that she was sizing me up. To tell you the truth it put my back up. I didn't much fancy being treated as if I were a chauffeur applying for a situation.

'"Please don't mention it," I said, rather stiffly. "It's all in the day's work."

'"Have you got the things with you?" she asked.

'I didn't answer, but I opened the dispatch-case I'd brought with me and took out the letters. I handed them to her. She accepted them without a word. She gave them a glance. She was very much made up, but I swear she went white underneath. The expression of her face didn't change. I looked at her hands. They were trembling a little. Then she seemed to pull herself together.

'"Oh, I'm so sorry," she said. "Won't you sit down?"

'I took a chair. For a moment she didn't seem to know quite what to do. She held the letters in her hand. I, knowing what they were, wondered what she felt. She didn't give much away. There was a desk beside the chimney-piece and she opened a drawer and put them in. Then she sat down opposite me and asked me to have a cigarette. I handed her the cigarette-case. I'd had it in my breast pocket.

'"I was asked to give you this too," I said.

'She took it and looked at it. For a moment she didn't speak and I waited. I didn't quite know if I ought to get up and go.

'"Did you know Jack well?" she asked suddenly.

'"I didn't know him at all," I answered. "I never saw him until after his death."

'"I had no idea he was dead till I got your note," she said. "I'd lost sight of him for a long time. Of course he was a very old friend of mine."

'I wondered if she thought I hadn't read the letters or if she'd forgotten what sort of letters they were. If the sight of them had given her a shock she had quite got over it by then. She spoke almost casually.

'"What did he die of in point of fact?" she asked.

'"Tuberculosis, opium, and starvation," I answered.

'"How dreadful," she said.

'But she said it quite conventionally. Whatever she felt she wasn't going to let me see. She was as cool as a cucumber, but I fancied, though it may have been only my fancy, that she was watching me, with all her wits about her, and wondering how much I knew. I think she'd have given a good deal to be certain of that.

'"How did you happen to get hold of these things?" she asked me.

'"I took possession of his effects after his death." I explained. "They were done up in a parcel and I was directed to give them to you."

'"Was there any need to undo the parcel?"

'I wish I could tell you what frigid insolence she managed to get into the question. It made me go white and I hadn't any make-up on to hide it. I answered that I thought it my duty to find out if I could who the dead man was. I should have liked to be able to communicate with his relations.

'"I see," she said.

'She looked at me as though that were the end of the interview and she expected me to get up and take myself off. But I didn't. I thought I'd like to get a bit of my own back. I told her how I'd been sent for and how I'd found him. I described the whole thing and I told her how, as far as I knew, there'd been no one at the end to take pity on him but a Chinese woman. Suddenly the door was opened and we both looked round. A big, middle-aged man came in and stopped when he saw me.

'"I beg your pardon," he said, "I didn't know you were busy."

'"Come in," she said, and when he had approached, "This is Mr Low. My husband."

'Lord Kastellan gave me a nod.

'"I just wanted to ask you," he began, and then he stopped.

'His eyes had caught the cigarette-case that was still resting on Lady Kastellan's open hand. I don't know if she saw the look of inquiry in his eyes. She gave him a friendly little smile. She was quite amazingly mistress of herself.

'"Mr Low comes from the Federated Malay States. Poor Jack Almond's dead and he's left me his cigarette-case."

'"Really?" said Lord Kastellan. "When did he die?"

'"About six months ago," I said.

'Lady Kastellan got up.

'"Well, I won't keep you any longer. I dare say you're busy. Thank you so much for carrying out Jack's request."

'"Things are pretty bad just now in the F.M.S. if all I hear is true," said Lord Kastellan.

'I shook hands with them both and Lady Kastellan rang a bell.

'"Are you staying in London?" she asked, as I was going. "I wonder if you'd like to come to a little party I'm giving next week."

'"I have my wife with me," I said.

'"Oh, how very nice. I'll send you a card."

'A couple of minutes later I found myself in the street. I was glad to be alone. I'd had a bad shock. As soon as Lady Kastellan mentioned the name I remembered. It was Jack Almond, the wretched bum I'd found dead in the Chinese house, dead of starvation. I'd known him quite well. It never struck me for a moment that it was he. Why, I'd dined and played cards with him, and we'd played tennis together. It was awful to think of him dying quite near me and me never knowing. He must have known he only had to send me a message and I'd have done something. I made my way into St James's Park and sat down. I wanted to have a good think.'

I could understand that it was a shock to Arthur Low to discover who the dead wastrel had been, for it was a shock to me too. Oddly enough I also had known him. Not intimately, but as a man I met at parties and now and then at a house in the country where we were both passing the week-end. Except that it was years since I had even thought of him it would have been stupid of me not to put two and two together. With his name there flashed back into my memory all my recollections of him. So that was why he had suddenly thrown up a career he liked so much! At that time, it was just after the war, I happened to know several people in the Foreign Office; Jack Almond was thought the cleverest of all the young men attached to it, and the highest posts the Diplomatic Service had to offer were within his reach. Of course it meant waiting. But it did seem absurd for him to fling away his chances in order to go into business in the Far East. His friends did all they could to dissuade him. He said he had had losses and found it impossible to live on his salary. One would have thought he could scrape along till things grew better. I remembered very well what he looked like. He was tall and well-made, a trifle dressy, but he was young enough to carry off his faultless clothes with a dash, with dark brown hair, very neat and sleek, blue eyes with very long lashes, and a fresh brilliant colour. He looked the picture of health. He was amusing, gay, and quick-witted. I never knew anyone who had more charm. It is a dangerous quality and those who have it trade on it. Often they think it enough to get them through life without any further effort. It is well to be on one's guard against it. But with Jack Almond it was the expression of a sweet and generous nature. He delighted because he was delightful. He was entirely without conceit. He had a gift for languages, he spoke French and German without a trace of accent, and his manners were admirable. You felt that when the time came he could play the part of an ambassador to a foreign power in the grand style. No one could fail to like him. It was not strange that Lady Kastellan should have fallen madly in love with him. My fancy ran away with me. What is there more moving than young love? The walks together of that handsome pair in one of the parks in the warm evenings of early summer, the dances they went to where he held her in his arms, the enchantment of the secret they shared when they exchanged glances across a dinner-table, and the passionate encounters, hurried and dangerous, but worth a thousand risks, when at some clandestine meeting-place they could give themselves to the fulfilment of their desire. They drank the milk of Paradise.

How frightful that the end of it all should have been so tragic! 'How did you know him?' I now asked Low.

'He was with Dexter and Farmilow. You know, the shipping people. He had quite a good job. He'd brought letters to the Governor and people like that. I was in Singapore at the time. I think I met him first at the club. He was damned good at games and all that sort of thing. Played polo. He was a fine tennis-player. You couldn't help liking him.'

'Did he drink, or what?'

'No.' Arthur Low was quite emphatic. 'He was one of the best. The women were crazy about him, and you couldn't blame them. He was one of the most decent fellows I've ever met.'

I turned to Mrs Low.

'Did you know him?'

'Only just. When Arthur and I were married we went to Perak. He was sweet, I remember that. He had the longest eyelashes I've ever seen on a man.'

'He was out quite a long time without going home. Five years, I think. I don't want to use hackneyed phrases, but the fact is I can't say it in any other way, he'd won golden opinions. There were a certain number of fellows who'd been rather sick at his being shoved into a damned good job by influence, but they couldn't deny that he'd made good. We knew about his having been in the F.O. and all that, but he never put on any frills.'

'I think what took me,' Mrs Low interrupted, 'was that he was so tremendously alive. It bucked you up just to talk to him.'

'He had a wonderful send-off when he sailed. I happened to have run up to Singapore for a couple of days and I went to the dinner at the Europe the night before. We all got rather tight. It was a grand lark. There was quite a crowd to see him off. He was only going for six months. I think everybody looked forward to his coming back. It would have been better for him if he never had.'

'Why, what happened then?'

'I don't know exactly. I'd been moved again, and I was right away north.'

How exasperating! It is really much easier to invent a story out of your own head than to tell one about real people, of whom you not only must guess the motives, but whose behaviour even at crucial moments you are ignorant of.

'He was a very good chap, but he was never an intimate friend of ours, you know how cliquey Singapore is, and he moved in rather more exalted circles that we did; when we went north I forgot about him. But one day at the club I heard a couple of fellows talking. Walton and Kenning. Walton had just come up from Singapore. There'd been a big polo match.

'"Did Almond play?" asked Kenning.

'"You bet your life he didn't," said Walton. "They kicked him out of the team last season."

'I interrupted.

'"What *are* you talking about?" I said.

'"Don't you know?" said Walton. "He's gone all to pot, poor devil."

'"How?" I asked.

'"Drink."

'"They say he dopes too," said Kenning.

'"Yes, I've heard that," said Walton. "He won't last long at that rate. Opium, isn't it?"

'"If he doesn't look out he'll lose his job." said Kenning.

'I couldn't make it out,' Low went on. 'He was the last man I should ever have expected to go that way. He was so typically English and he was a gentleman and all that. It appeared that Walton had travelled out with him on the same ship when Jack came back from leave. He joined the ship at Marseilles. He was rather low, but there was nothing funny about that; a lot of people don't feel any too good when they're leaving home and have to get back to the mill. He drank a good deal. Fellows do that sometimes too. But Walton said rather a curious thing about him. He said it looked as if the life had gone out of him. You couldn't help noticing it because he'd always had such high spirits. There'd been a general sort of idea that he was engaged to some girl in England and on the ship they jumped to the conclusion that she'd thrown him over.'

'That's what I said when Arthur told me,' said Mrs Low. 'After all, five years is a long time to leave a girl.'

'Anyhow they thought he'd get over it when he got back to work. But he didn't, unfortunately. He went from bad to worse. A lot of people liked him and they did all they could to persuade him to pull himself together. But there was nothing doing. He just told them to mind their own business. He was snappy and rude, which was funny because he'd always been so nice to everybody. Walton said you could hardly believe it was the same man. Government House dropped him and a lot of others followed suit. Lady Ormonde, the Governor's wife, was a snob, she knew he was well-connected and all that, and she wouldn't have given him the cold shoulder unless things had got pretty bad. He was a nice chap, Jack Almond, it seemed a pity that he should make such a mess of things. I was sorry, you know, but of course it didn't impair my appetite or disturb my night's sleep. A few months later I happened to be in Singapore myself, and when I went to the club I asked about him. He'd lost his job all right, it appeared that he often didn't go to the office for two or three days at a time; and I was told that someone had made him manager of a rubber estate in Sumatra in the hope that away from the temptations of Singapore he might pull himself together. You see, everyone had liked him so much, they couldn't bear the thought of his going under without some sort of a struggle. But it was no good. The opium had got him. He didn't keep the job in Sumatra long and he was back again in Singapore. I heard afterwards that you would hardly have recognized him. He'd always been so spruce and smart; he was shabby and unwashed and wild-eyed. A number of fellows at the club got together and arranged something. They felt they had to give him one more chance and they sent him out to Sarawak. But it wasn't any use. The fact is, I think, he didn't want to be helped. I think he just wanted to go to hell in his own way and be as quick as he could about it. Then he disappeared; someone said he'd gone home; anyhow he was forgotten. You know how people drop out in the F.M.S. I suppose that's why when I found a dead man in a sarong, with a beard, lying in a little smelly room in a Chinese house thirty miles from anywhere, it never occurred to me for a moment that it might be Jack Almond. I hadn't heard his name for years.'

'Just think what he must have gone through in that time,' said Mrs Low, and her eyes were bright with tears, for she had a good and tender heart.

'The whole thing's inexplicable,' said Low.

'Why?' I asked.

'Well, if he was going to pieces, why didn't he do it when he first came out? His first five years he was all right. One of the best. If this affair of his had broken him you'd have expected him to break when it was all fresh. All that time he was as gay as a bird. You'd have said he hadn't a care in the world. From all I heard it was a different man who came back from leave.'

'Something happened during those six months in London,' said Mrs Low. 'That's obvious.'

'We shall never know,' sighed Low.

'But we can guess,' I smiled. 'That's where the novelist comes in. Shall I tell you what I think happened?'

'Fire away.'

'Well, I think that during those first five years he was buoyed up by the sacrifice he'd made. He had a chivalrous soul. He had given up everything that made life worth living to him to save the woman he loved better than anything in the world. I think he had an exaltation of spirit that never left him. He loved her still, with all his heart; most of us fall in and out of love; some men can only love once, and I think he was one of them. And in a strange way he was happy because he'd been able to sacrifice his happiness for the sake of someone who was worthy of the sacrifice. I think she was always in his thoughts. Then he went home. I think he loved her as much as ever and I don't suppose he ever doubted that her love was as strong and enduring as his. I don't know what he expected. He may have thought she'd see it was no good fighting her inclination any more and would run away with him. It may have been that he'd have been satisfied to realize that she loved him still. It was inevitable that they should meet; they lived in the same world. He saw that she didn't care a row of pins for him any longer. He saw that the passionate girl had become a prudent, experienced woman of the world, he saw that she'd never loved him as he thought she loved him, and he may have suspected that she'd lured him coldly into making the sacrifice that was to save her. He saw her at parties, self-possessed and triumphant. He knew that the lovely qualities he'd ascribed to her were of his own imagining and she was just an ordinary woman who had been carried away by a momentary infatuation and having got over it had returned to her true life. A great name, wealth, social distinction, worldly success: those were the things that mattered to her. He'd sacrificed everything, his friends, his familiar surroundings, his profession, his usefulness in the world, all that gives value to existence–for nothing. He'd been cheated, and it broke him. Your friend Walton said the true thing, you noticed it yourself, he said it looked as if the life had gone out of him. It had. After that he didn't care any more and perhaps the worst thing was that even with it all, though he knew Lady Kastellan for what she was, he loved her still. I know nothing more shattering than to love with all your heart, than not to be able however hard you try to break yourself of it, someone who you know is worthless. Perhaps that is why he took to opium. To forget and to remember.'

It was a long speech I had made, and now I stopped.

'All that's only fancy,' said Low.

'I know it is,' I answered, 'but it seems to fit the circumstances.'

'There must have been a weak strain in him. Otherwise he could have fought and conquered.'

'Perhaps. Perhaps there is always a certain weakness attached to such great charm as he possessed. Perhaps few people love as wholeheartedly and as devotedly as he loved. Perhaps he didn't want to fight and conquer. I can't bring myself to blame him.'

I didn't add, because I was afraid they would think it cynical, that maybe if only Jack Almond hadn't had those wonderfully long eyelashes he might now have been alive and well, minister to some foreign power and on the high road to the Embassy in Paris.

'Let's go into the drawing-room,' said Mrs Low. 'The boy wants to clear the table.'

And that was the end of Jack Almond.

Neil MacAdam

◆

Captain Bredon was good-natured. When Angus Munro, the Curator of the museum at Kuala Solor, told him that he had advised Neil MacAdam, his new assistant, on his arrival at Singapore to put up at the Van Dyke Hotel, and asked him to see that the lad got into no mischief during the few days he must spend there, he said he would do his best. Captain Bredon commanded the *Sultan Ahmed*, and when he was at Singapore always stayed at the Van Dyke. He had a Japanese wife and kept a room there. It was his home. When he got back after his fortnight's trip along the coast of Borneo the Dutch manager told him that Neil had been there for two days. The boy was sitting in the little dusty garden of the hotel reading old numbers of *The Straits Times*. Captain Bredon took a look at him first and then went up.

'You're MacAdam, aren't you?'

Neil rose to his feet, flushed to the roots of his hair, and answered shyly: 'I am.'

'My name's Bredon. I'm skipper of the *Sultan Ahmed*. You're sailing with me next Tuesday. Munro asked me to look after you. What about a stengah? I suppose you've learned what that means by now.'

'Thank you very much, but I don't drink.'

He spoke with a broad Scots accent.

'I don't blame you. Drink's been the ruin of many a good man in this country.'

He called the Chinese boy and ordered himself a double whisky and a small soda.

'What have you been doing with yourself since you got in?'

'Walking about.'

'There's nothing much to see in Singapore.'

'I've found plenty.'

Of course the first thing he had done was to go to the museum. There was little that he had not seen at home, but the fact that those beasts and birds, those reptiles, moths, butterflies, and insects were native to the country excited him. There was one section devoted to that part of Borneo of which Kuala Solor was the capital, and since these were the creatures that for the next three years would chiefly concern him, he examined them with attention. But it was outside, in the streets, that it was most thrilling, and except that he was a grave and sober young man he would have laughed aloud with joy. Everything was new to him. He walked till he was footsore. He stood at the corner of a busy street and wondered at the long line of rickshaws and the little men between the shafts running with dogged steps. He stood on a bridge over a canal and looked at the sampans wedged up against one another like sardines in a tin. He peered into the Chinese shops in Victoria Road where so many strange things were sold. Bombay merchants, fat and exuberant, stood at their shop doors and sought to sell him silks and tinsel jewellery. He watched the Tamils, pensive and forlorn, who walked with a sinister grace, and the bearded Arabs, in white skull-caps, who bore themselves with scornful dignity. The sun shone upon the varied scene with hard, acrid brilliance. He was confused. He thought it would take him years to find his bearings in this multi-coloured and excessive world.

After dinner that night Captain Bredon asked him if he would like to go round the town.

'You ought to see a bit of life while you're here,' he said.

They stepped into rickshaws and drove to the Chinese quarter. The Captain, who never drank at sea, had been making up for his abstinence during the day. He was feeling good. The rickshaws stopped at a house in a side street and they knocked at the door. It was opened and they passed through a narrow passage into a large room with benches all round it covered with red plush. A number of women were sitting about – French, Italian, and American. A mechanical piano was grinding out harsh music and a few couples were dancing. Captain Bredon ordered drinks. Two or three women, waiting for an invitation, gave them inviting glances.

'Well, young feller, is there anyone you fancy here?' the Captain asked facetiously.

'To sleep with, d'you mean? No.'

'No white girls where you're going, you know.'

'Oh, well.'

'Like to go an' see some natives?'

'I don't mind.'

The Captain paid for the drinks and they strolled on. They went to another house. Here the girls were Chinese, small and dainty, with tiny feet and hands like flowers, and they wore suits of flowered silk. But their painted faces were like masks. They looked at the strangers with black derisive eyes. They were strangely inhuman.

'I brought you here because I thought you ought to see the place,' said Captain Bredon, with the air of a man doing his bounden duty, 'but just look-see is all. They don't like us for some reason. In some of these Chinese joints they won't even let a white man in. Fact is, they say we stink. Funny, ain't it? They say we smell of corpses.'

'We?'

'Give me Japs,' said the Captain. 'They're fine. My wife's a Jap, you know.

You come along with me and I'll take you to a place where they have Japanese girls, and if you don't see something you like there I'm a Dutchman.'

Their rickshaws were waiting and they stepped into them. Captain Bredon gave a direction and the boys started off. They were let into the house by a stout middle-aged Japanese woman, who bowed low as they entered. She took them into a neat, clean room furnished only with mats on the floor; they sat down and presently a little girl came in with a tray on which were two bowls of pale tea. With a shy bow she handed one to each of them. The Captain spoke to the middle-aged woman and she looked at Neil and giggled. She said something to the child, who went out, and presently four girls tripped in. They were sweet in their kimonos, with the shining black hair artfully dressed; they were small and plump, with round faces and laughing eyes. They bowed low as they came in and with good manners murmured polite greetings. Their speech sounded like the twittering of birds. Then they knelt, one on each side of the two men, and charmingly flirted with them. Captain Bredon soon had his arms round two slim waists. They all talked nineteen to the dozen. They were very gay. It seemed to Neil that the Captain's girls were mocking him, for their gleaming eyes were mischievously turned towards him, and he blushed. But the other two cuddled up to him, smiling, and spoke in Japanese as though he understood every word they said. They seemed so happy and guileless that he laughed. They were very attentive. They handed him the bowl so that he should drink his tea, and then took it from him so that he should not have the trouble of holding it. They lit his cigarette for him and one put out a small, delicate hand to take the ash so that it should not fall on his clothes. They stroked his smooth face and looked with curiosity at his large young hands. They were as playful as kittens.

'Well, which is it to be?' said the Captain after a while. 'Made your choice yet?'

'What d'you mean?'

'I'll just wait and see you settled and then I'll fix myself up.'

'Oh, I don't want either of them. I'm going home to bed.'

'Why, what's the matter? You're not scared, are you?'

'No, I just don't fancy it. But don't let me stand in your way. I'll get back to the hotel all right.'

'Oh, if you're not going to do anything I won't either. I only wanted to be matey.'

He spoke to the middle-aged woman and what he said caused the girls to look at Neil with sudden surprise. She answered and the Captain shrugged his shoulders. Then one of the girls made a remark that set them all laughing.

'What does she say?' asked Neil.

'She's pulling your leg,' replied the Captain, smiling.

But he gave Neil a curious look. The girl, having made them laugh once, now said something directly to Neil. He could not understand, but the mockery of her eyes made him blush and frown. He did not like to be made fun of. Then she laughed outright and throwing her arm round his neck lightly kissed him.

'Come on, let's be going,' said the Captain.

When they dismissed their rickshaws and walked into the hotel Neil asked him:

'What was it that girl said that made them all laugh?'

'She said you were a virgin.'

'I don't see anything to laugh at in that,' said Neil, with his slow Scots accent.

'Is it true?'

'I suppose it is.'

'How old are you?'

'Twenty-two.'

'What are you waiting for?'

'Till I marry.'

The Captain was silent. At the top of the stairs he held out his hand. There was a twinkle in his eyes when he bade the lad good night, but Neil met it with a level, candid, and untroubled gaze.

Three days later they sailed. Neil was the only white passenger. When the Captain was busy he read. He was reading again Wallace's *Malay Archipelago*. He had read it as a boy, but now it had a new and absorbing interest for him. When the Captain was at leisure they played cribbage or sat in long chairs on the deck, smoking, and talked. Neil was the son of a country doctor, and he could not remember when he had not been interested in natural history. When he had done with school he went to the University of Edinburgh and there took a B.Sc. with Honours. He was looking out for a job as demonstrator in biology when he chanced to see in *Nature* an advertisement for an assistant curator of the museum at Kuala Solor. The Curator, Angus Munro, had been at Edinburgh with his uncle, a Glasgow merchant, and his uncle wrote to ask him if he would give the boy a trial. Though Neil was especially interested in entomology he was a trained taxidermist, which the advertisement said was essential; he enclosed certificates from Neil's old teachers; he added that Neil had played football for his university. In a few weeks a cable arrived engaging him and a fortnight later he sailed.

'What's Mr Munro like?' asked Neil.

'Good fellow. Everybody likes him.'

'I looked out his papers in the scientific journals. He had one in the last number of *The Ibis* on the Gymnathidæ.'

'I don't know anything about that. I know he's got a Russian wife. They don't like her much.'

'I got a letter from him at Singapore saying they'd put me up for a bit till I could look round and see what I wanted to do.'

Now they were steaming up the river. At the mouth was a straggling fishermen's village standing on piles on the water; on the bank grew thickly nipah palm and the tortured mangrove; beyond stretched the dense green of the virgin forest. In the distance, darkly silhouetted against the blue sky, was the rugged outline of a mountain. Neil, his heart beating with the excitement that possessed him, devoured the scene with eager eyes. He was surprised. He knew his Conrad almost by heart and he was expecting a land of brooding mystery. He was not prepared for the blue milky sky. Little white clouds on the horizon, like sailing boats becalmed, shone in the sun. The green trees of the forest glittered in the brilliant light. Here and there, on the banks, were Malay houses with thatched roofs, and they nestled cosily among fruit trees. Natives in dugouts rowed, standing, up the river. Neil had no feeling of being shut in, nor, in that radiant morning, of gloom, but of space and freedom. The country offered him a gracious welcome. He knew he was going to be happy in it. Captain Bredon from the bridge threw a friendly glance at the lad standing below him. He had taken quite a fancy to him during the four days the journey had lasted. It was true he did not drink, and when you made a joke he was as likely as not to take you seriously, but there was something very taking in his seriousness;

everything was interesting and important to him–that, of course, was why he did not find your jokes amusing; but even though he didn't see them he laughed, because he felt you expected it. He laughed because life was grand. He was grateful for every little thing you told him. He was very polite. He never asked you to pass him anything without saying 'please' and always said 'thank you' when you gave it. And he was a good-looking fellow, no one could deny that. Neil was standing with his hands on the rail, bare-headed, looking at the passing bank. He was tall, six foot two, with long, loose limbs, broad shoulders, and narrow hips; there was something charmingly coltish about him, so that you expected him at any moment to break into a caper. He had brown curly hair with a peculiar shine in it; sometimes when the light caught it, it glittered like gold. His eyes, large and very blue, shone with good-humour. They reflected his happy disposition. His nose was short and blunt and his mouth big, his chin determined; his face was rather broad. But his most striking feature was his skin; it was very white and smooth, with a lovely patch of red on either cheek. It would have been a beautiful skin even for a woman. Captain Bredon made the same joke to him every morning.

'Well, my lad, have you shaved today?'

Neil passed his hand over his chin.

'No, d'you think I need it?'

The Captain always laughed at this.

'Need it? Why, you've got a face like a baby's bottom.'

And invariably Neil reddened to the roots of his hair.

'I shave once a week,' he retorted.

But it wasn't only his looks that made you like him. It was his ingenuousness, his candour, and the freshness with which he confronted the world. For all his intentness and the solemn way in which he took everything, and his inclination to argue upon every point that came up, there was something strangely simple in him that gave you quite an odd feeling. The Captain couldn't make it out.

'I wonder if it's because he's never had a woman,' he said to himself. 'Funny. I should have thought the girls never left him alone. With a complexion like that.'

But the *Sultan Ahmed* was nearing the bend after rounding which Kuala Solor would be in sight and the Captain's reflections were interrupted by the necessities of his work. He rang down to the engine room. The ship slackened to half speed. Kuala Solor straggled along the left bank of the river, a white, neat, and trim little town, and on the right on a hill were the fort and the Sultan's palace. There was a breeze and the Sultan's flag, at the top of a tall staff, waved bravely against the sky. They anchored in mid-stream. The doctor and a police officer came on board in the government launch. They were accompanied by a tall thin man in white ducks. The Captain stood at the head of the gangway and shook hands with them. Then he turned to the last comer.

'Well, I've brought you your young hopeful safe and sound.' And a glance at Neil: 'This is Munro.'

The tall thin man held out his hand and gave Neil an appraising look. Neil flushed a little and smiled. He had beautiful teeth.

'How do you do, sir?'

Munro did not smile with his lips, but faintly with his grey eyes. His cheeks were hollow and he had a thin aquiline nose and pale lips. He was deeply sunburned. His face looked tired, but his expression was very gentle, and Neil immediately felt confidence in him. The Captain introduced him to the doctor and the policeman and suggested that they should have a drink. When they sat down and the boy brought bottles of beer Munro took off his topee. Neil saw that he had close-cropped brown hair turning grey. He was a man of forty, quiet, self-possessed in manner, with an intellectual air that distinguished him from the brisk little doctor and the heavy swaggering police officer.

'MacAdam doesn't drink,' said the Captain when the boy poured out four glasses of beer.'

'All the better,' said Munro. 'I hope you haven't been trying to lure him into evil ways.'

'I tried to in Singapore,' returned the Captain, with a twinkle in his eyes, 'but there was nothing doing.'

When he had finished his beer Munro turned to Neil.

'Well, we'll be getting ashore, shall we?'

Neil's baggage was put in charge of Munro's boy and the two men got into a sampan. They landed.

'Do you want to go straight up to the bungalow or would you like to have a look round first? We've got a couple of hours before tiffin.'

'Couldn't we go to the museum?' said Neil.

Munro's eyes smiled gently. He was pleased. Neil was shy and Munro not by nature talkative, so they walked in silence. By the river were the native huts, and here, living their immemorial lives, dwelt the Malays. They were busy, but without haste, and you were conscious of a happy, normal activity. There was a sense of the rhythm of life of which the pattern was birth and death, love, and the affairs common to mankind. They came to the bazaars, narrow streets with arcades, where the teeming Chinese, working and eating, noisily talking, as is their way, indefatigably strove with eternity.

'It's not much after Singapore,' said Munro, 'but I always think it's rather picturesque.'

He spoke with an accent less broad than Neil's but the Scots burr was there and it put Neil at his ease. He could never quite get it out of his head that the English of English people was affected.

The museum was a handsome stone building and as they entered its portals Munro instinctively straightened himself. The attendant at the door saluted and Munro spoke to him in Malay, evidently explaining who Neil was, for the attendant gave him a smile and saluted again. It was cool in there in comparison with the heat without and the light was pleasant after the glare of the street.

'I'm afraid you'll be disappointed,' said Munro. 'We haven't got half the things we ought to have, but up to now we've been handicapped by lack of money. We've had to do the best we could. So you must make allowances.'

Neil stepped in like a swimmer diving confidently into a summer sea. The specimens were admirably arranged. Munro had sought to please as well as to instruct, and birds and beasts and reptiles were presented, as far as possible in their natural surroundings, in such a way as to give a vivid impression of life. Neil lost his shyness and began with boyish enthusiasm to talk of this and that. He asked an infinity of questions. He was excited. Neither of them was conscious of the passage of time, and when Munro glanced at his watch he was surprised to see what the hour was. They got into rickshaws and drove to the bungalow.

Munro led the young man into a drawing-room. A woman was lying on a sofa reading a book and as they came in she slowly rose.

'This is my wife. I'm afraid we're dreadfully late, Darya.'

'What does it matter?' she smiled. 'What is more unimportant than time?'

She held out her hand, a rather large hand, to Neil and gave him a long, reflective, but friendly look.

'I suppose you've been showing him the museum.'

She was a woman of five-and-thirty, of medium height, with a pale brown face of a uniform colour and pale blue eyes. Her hair, parted in the middle and wound into a knot on the nape of her neck, was untidy; it had a moth-like quality and was of a curious pale brown. Her face was broad, with high cheek-bones, and she had a rather fleshy nose. She was not a pretty woman, but there was in her slow movements a sensual grace and in her manner as it were a physical casualness that only very dull people could have failed to find interesting. She wore a frock of green cotton. She spoke English perfectly, but with a slight accent.

They sat down to tiffin. Neil was overcome once more with shyness, but Darya did not seem to notice it. She talked freely and easily. She asked him about his journey and what he had thought of Singapore. She told him about the people he would have to meet. That afternoon Munro was to take him to call on the Resident, the Sultan being away, and later they would go to the club. There he would see everybody.

'You will be popular,' she said, her pale blue eyes resting on him with attention. A man less ingenuous than Neil might have noticed that she took stock of his size and youthful virility, his shiny curling hair and his lovely skin. 'They don't think much of us.'

'Oh, nonsense, Darya. You're too sensitive. They're English, that's all.'

'They think it's rather funny of Angus to be a scientist and they think it's rather vulgar of me to be a Russian. I don't care. They're fools. They're the most commonplace, the most narrow-minded, the most conventional people it has ever been my misfortune to live amongst.'

'Don't put MacAdam off the moment he arrives. He'll find them kind and hospitable.'

'What is your first name?' she asked the boy.

'Neil.'

'I shall call you by it. And you must call me Darya. I hate being called Mrs Munro. It makes me feel like a minister's wife.'

Neil blushed. He was embarrassed that she should ask him so soon to be so familiar. She went on.

'Some of the men are not bad.'

'They do their job competently and that's what they're here for,' said Munro.

'They shoot. They play football and tennis and cricket. I get on with them quite well. The women are intolerable. They are jealous and spiteful and lazy. They can talk of nothing. If you introduce an intellectual subject they look down their noses as though you were indecent. What can they talk about now? They're interested in nothing. If you speak of the body they think you improper, and if you speak of the soul they think you priggish.'

'You mustn't take what my wife says too literally,' smiled Munro, in his gentle, tolerant way. 'The community here is just like any other in the East, neither very clever, nor very stupid, but amiable and kindly. And that's a good deal.'

'I don't want people to be amiable and kindly. I want them to be vital and passionate. I want them to be interested in mankind. I want them to attach more importance to the things of the spirit than to a gin pahit or a curry tiffin. I want art to matter to them, and literature.' She addressed herself abruptly to

Neil: 'Have you got a soul?'

'Oh, I don't know. I don't know exactly what you mean.'

'Why do you blush when I ask you? Why should you be ashamed of your soul? It is what is important in you. Tell me about it. I am interested in you and I want to know.'

It seemed very awkward to Neil to be tackled in this way by a perfect stranger. He had never met anyone like this. But he was a serious young man and when he was asked a question straight out he did his best to answer it. It was Munro's presence that embarrassed him.

'I don't know what you mean by the soul. If you mean an immaterial or spiritual entity, separately produced by the creator, in temporary conjunction with the material body, then my answer is in the negative. It seems to me that such a radically dualistic view of human personality cannot be defended by anyone who is able to take a calm view of the evidence. If, on the other hand, you mean by soul the aggregate of psychic elements which form what we know as the personality of the individual, then, of course, I have.'

'You're very sweet and you're wonderfully handsome,' she said, smiling. 'No, I mean the heart with its longings and the body with its desires and the infinite in us. Tell me, what did you read on the journey, or did you only play deck tennis?'

Neil was taken aback at the inconsequence of her reply. He would have been a little affronted except for the good-humour in her eyes and the naturalness in her manner. Munro smiled quietly at the young man's bewilderment. when he smiled the lines that ran from the wings of his nostrils to the corners of his mouth became deep furrows.

'I read a lot of Conrad.'

'For pleasure or to improve your mind?'

'Both. I admire him awfully.'

Darya threw up her arms in an extravagant gesture of protest.

'That Pole,' she cried. 'How can you English ever have let yourselves be taken in by that wordy mountebank? He was all the superficiality of his countrymen. That stream of words, those involved sentences, the showy rhetoric, that affection of profundity: when you get through all that to the thought at the bottom, what do you find but a trivial commonplace? He was like a second-rate actor who puts on a romantic dress and declaims a play by Victor Hugo. For five minutes you say this is heroic, and then your whole soul revolts and you cry, no, this is false, false, false.'

She spoke with a passion that Neil had never known anyone show when speaking of art or literature. Her cheeks, usually colourless, flushed and her pale eyes glowed.

'There's no one who got atmosphere like Conrad,' said Neil. 'I can smell and see and feel the East when I read him.'

'Nonsense. What do you know about the East? Everyone will tell you that he made the grossest blunders. Ask Angus.'

'Of course he was not always accurate,' said Munro, in his measured, reflective way. 'The Borneo he described is not the Borneo we know. He saw it from the deck of a merchant-vessel and he was not an acute observer even of what he saw. But does it matter? I don't know why fiction should be hampered by fact. I don't think it's a mean achievement to have created a country, a dark, sinister, romantic, and heroic country of the soul.'

'You're a sentimentalist, my poor Angus.' And then again to Neil: 'You must read Turgenev, you must read Tolstoy, you must read Dostoyevsky.'

Neil did not in the least know what to make of Darya Munro. She skipped over the first stages of acquaintance and treated him at once like someone she had known intimately all her life. It puzzled him. It seemed so reckless. When he met anyone his own instinct was to go cautiously. He was amiable, but he did not like to step too far before he saw his way before him. He did not want to give anyone his confidence before he thought himself justified. But with Darya you could not help yourself; she forced your confidence. She poured out the feelings and thoughts that most people keep to themselves like a prodigal flinging gold pieces to a scrambling crowd. She did not talk, she did not act, like anyone he had ever known. She did not mind what she said. She would speak of the natural functions of the human animal in a way that brought the blushes coursing to his cheeks. They excited her ridicule.

'Oh, what a prig you are! What is there indecent in it? When I'm going to take a purge, why shouldn't I say so, and when I think you want one, why shouldn't I tell you?'

'Theoretically I dare say you're right,' said Neil, always judicious and reasonable.

She made him tell her of his father and mother, his brothers, his life at school and at the university. She told him about herself. Her father was a general killed in the war and her mother a Princess Lutchkov. They were in Eastern Russia when the Bolsheviks seized power, and fled to Yokohama. Here they had subsisted miserably on the sale of their jewels and such objects of art as they had been able to save, and here she married a fellow-exile. She was unhappy with him and in two years divorced him. Her mother died and, penniless, she was driven to earn her living as best she could. She was employed by an American relief organization. She taught in a mission school. She worked in a hospital. She made Neil's blood boil, and at the same time embarrassed him very much, when she spoke of the men who tried to take advantage of her defencelessness and her poverty. She spared him no details.

'Brutes,' he said.

'Oh, all men are like that,' she replied, with a shrug of her shoulders.

She told him how once she protected her virtue at the point of her revolver.

'I swore I'd kill him if he took another step, and if he had I'd have shot him like a dog.'

'Gosh!' said Neil.

It was at Yokohama that she met Angus. He was spending his leave in Japan. She was captivated by his straightforwardness, the decency which was so obvious in him, his tenderness and his consideration. He was not a business man; he was a scientist, and science is milk-brother to art. He offered her peace. He offered her security. And she was tired of Japan. Borneo was a land of mystery. They had been married for five years.

She gave Neil the Russian novelists to read. She gave him *Fathers and Sons*, *Anna Karenina*, and *The Brothers Karamazov*.

'Those are the three peaks of our literature. Read them. They are the greatest novels the world has ever seen.'

Like many of her countrymen she talked as though no other literature counted, and as though a few novels and stories, some indifferent poetry, and half a dozen good plays had made whatever else the world has produced negligible. Neil was fascinated and overwhelmed.

'You're rather like Alyosha yourself, Neil,' she said, looking at him with eyes that were now so soft and tender, 'an Alyosha with a Scotch dourness, suspicious and prudent, that will not let the soul in you, the spiritual beauty, come out.'

'I'm not a bit like Alyosha,' he answered self-consciously.

'You don't know what you're like. You don't know anything about yourself. Why are you a naturalist? Is it for money? You could have made much more money by going into your uncle's office in Glasgow. I feel in you something strange and unearthly. I could bow down at your feet as Father Zossima did to Dimitri.'

'Please don't,' he said, smiling, but flushing a little too.

But the novels he read made her seem a little less strange to him. They gave her an environment and he recognized in her traits which, however unusual in the women he knew in Scotland, his mother and the daughters of his uncle in Glasgow, were common to many of the characters in Russian fiction. He no longer wondered that she should like to sit up so late, drinking innumerable cups of tea, and lie on the sofa nearly all day long reading and incessantly smoking cigarettes. She could do nothing at all for days on end without being bored. She had a curious mixture of languor and zest. She often said, with a shrug of her shoulders, that she was an Oriental, and a European only by chance. She had a feline grace that indeed suggested the Oriental. She was immensely untidy and it did not seem to affect her that cigarette-ends, old papers, and empty tins should lie about their living-room. But he thought she had something of Anna Karenina in her and he transferred to her the sympathy he felt for that pathetic creature. He understood her arrogance. It was not unnatural that she despised the women of the community, whose acquaintance little by little he made; they *were* commonplace; her mind was quicker than theirs, she had a wider culture, and she had above all a sort of tremulous sensitiveness that made *them* extraordinarily colourless. She certainly took no pains to conciliate them. Though at home she slopped about in a sarong and baju, when she and Angus went out to dinner she dressed with a splendour that was somewhat out of place. She liked to display her ample bosom and her shapely back. She painted her cheeks and made up her eyes like an actress for the footlights. Though it made Neil angry to see the amused or outraged glances that her appearance provoked, he could not in his heart but think it a pity that she should make such an object of herself. She looked grand, of course, but if you hadn't known who she was you would have thought she wasn't respectable. There were things about her that he could never get over. She had an enormous appetite and it fashed him that she ate more than he and Angus together. He could never quite get used to the bluntness with which she discussed sexual matters. She took it for granted that at home and in Edinburgh he had had affairs with a host of women. She pressed him for details of his adventures. His Scotch pawkiness helped him to parry her thrusts and he evaded her questions with native caution. She laughed at his reticence.

Sometimes she shocked him. He grew accustomed to the frankness with which she admired his looks, and when she told him that he was as beautiful as a young Norse god he did not turn a hair. Flattery fell off him like water from a duck's back. But he did not like it when she ran her hand, though large, very soft, with caressing fingers, through his curly hair or, a smile on her lips, stroked his smooth face. He couldn't bear being mussed about. One day she wanted a drink of tonic water and began pouring some out in a glass that stood on the table.

'That's my glass,' he said quickly. 'I've just been drinking out of it.'

'Well, what of it? You haven't got syphilis, have you?'

'I hate drinking out of other people's glasses myself.'

She was funny about cigarettes too. Once, when he hadn't been there very long, he had just lit one, when she passed and said:

'I want that.'

She took it out of his mouth and began to smoke it. After two or three puffs, she said she did not want any more and handed it back to him. The end she had had in her mouth was red from the rouge on her lips, and he didn't want to go on smoking it at all. But he was afraid she would think it rude if he threw it away. It somewhat disgusted him. Often she would ask him for a cigarette and when he handed it to her, say:

'Oh, light it for me, will you?'

When he did so, and held it out to her, she opened her mouth so that he should put it in. He hadn't been able to help wetting the end a little. He wondered she could bear to put it in her mouth after it had been in his. The whole thing seemed to him awfully familiar. He was sure Munro wouldn't like it. She had even done this once or twice at the club. Neil had felt himself go purple. He wished she hadn't got these rather unpleasant habits, but he supposed that they were Russian, and one couldn't deny that she was wonderfully good company. Her conversation was very stimulating. It was like champagne (which Neil had tasted once and thought wretched stuff), 'metaphorically speaking'. There was nothing she couldn't talk about. She didn't talk like a man; with a man you generally knew what he would say next, but with her you never did; her intuition was quite remarkable. She gave you ideas. She enlarged your mind and excited your imagination. Neil felt alive as he had never felt alive before. He seemed to walk on mountain peaks, and the horizons of the spirit were unbounded. Neil felt a certain complacency when he stopped to reflect on what an exalted plane his mind communed with hers. Such conversations made very small beer of the vaunted pleasure of sense. She was in many ways (he was of a cautious nature and seldom made a statement even to himself that he did not qualify) the most intelligent woman he had ever met. And besides, she was Angus Munro's wife.

For, whatever Neil's reservations were about Darya, he had none about Munro, and she would have had to be a much less remarkable woman not to profit by the enormous admiration he conceived for her husband. With him Neil let himself go. He felt for him what he had never felt for anyone before. He was so sane, so balanced, so tolerant. This was the sort of man he would himself like to be when he was older. He talked little, but when he did, with good sense. He was wise. He had a dry humour that Neil understood. It made the hearty English fun of the men at the club seem inane. He was kind and patient. He had a dignity that made it impossible to conceive anyone taking a liberty with him, but he was neither pompous nor solemn. He was honest and absolutely truthful. But Neil admired him no less as a scientist than as a man. He had imagination. He was careful and painstaking. Though his interest was in research he did the routine work of the museum conscientiously. He was just then much interested in stick-insects and intended to write a paper on their powers of parthenogenetic reproduction. An incident occurred in connexion with the experiments he was making that made a great impression on Neil. One day, a little captive gibbon escaped from its chain and ate up all the larvae and so destroyed the whole of Munro's evidence. Neil nearly cried. Angus Munro took the gibbon in his arms and, smiling, stroked it.

'Diamond, Diamond,' he said, quoting Sir Isaac Newton, 'you little know the damage you have done.'

He was also studying mimicry and instilled into Neil his absorbed interest in this controversial subject. They had interminable talks about it. Neil was astonished at the Curator's wonderful knowledge. It was encyclopaedic, and he was abashed at his own ignorance. But it was when Munro spoke of the trips into the country to collect specimens that his enthusiasm was most contagious. That was the perfect life, a life of hardship, difficulty, often of privation and sometimes of danger, but rewarded by the thrill of finding a rare, or even a new, species, by the beauty of the scenery, and the intimate observation of nature, and above all the sense of freedom from every tie. It was for this part of the work that Neil had been chiefly engaged. Munro was occupied in research work that made it difficult for him to be away from home for several weeks at a time, and Darya had always refused to accompany him. She had an unreasoning fear of the jungle. She was terrified of wild beasts, snakes, and venomous insects. Though Munro had told her over and over again that no animal hurt you unless you molested or frightened it, she could not get over her instinctive horror. He did not like leaving her. She cared little for the local society and with him away he realized that life for her must be intolerably dull. But the Sultan was keenly interested in natural history and was anxious that the museum should be completely representative of the country's fauna. One expedition Munro and Neil were to make together, so that Neil should learn how to go to work, and the plans for this were discussed by them for months. Neil looked forward to it as he had never looked forward to anything in his life.

Meanwhile he learned Malay and acquired a smattering of the dialects that would be useful to him on future journeys. He played tennis and football. He soon knew everyone in the community. On the football field he threw off his absorption in science and his interest in Russian fiction and gave himself up to the pleasure of the game. He was strong, quick, and active. After it was all over it was grand to have a sluice down and a long tonic with a slice of lemon and go over it all with the other fellows. It had never been intended that Neil should live permanently with the Munros. There was a roomy rest-house at Kuala Solor, but the rule was that no one should stay in it for more than a fortnight and such of the bachelors as had no official quarters clubbed together and took a house between them. When Neil arrived it so happened that there was no vacancy in any of these messes. One evening, however, when he had been about four months in the colony, two men, Waring and Jonson, when they were sitting together after a game of tennis, told him that one member of their mess was going home and if he would like to join them they would be glad to have him. They were young fellows of his own age, in the football team, and Neil liked them both. Waring was in the Customs and Jonson in the police. He jumped at the suggestion. They told him how much it would cost and fixed a day, a fortnight later, when it would be convenient for him to move in.

At dinner he told the Munros.

'It's been awfully good of you to let me stay so long. It's made me very uncomfortable planting myelf on you like this, I've been quite ashamed, but now there's no excuse for me.'

'But we like having you here,' said Darya. 'You don't need an excuse.'

'I can hardly go on staying here indefinitely.'

'Why not? Your salary's miserable, what's the use of wasting it on board and lodging? You'd be bored stiff with Jonson and Waring. Stupids. They haven't an idea in their heads outside playing the gramophone and knocking balls about.'

It was true that it had been very convenient to live free of cost. He had saved the greater part of his salary. He had a thrifty soul and had never been used to spending money when it wasn't necessary, but he was proud. He could not go on living at other people's expense. Darya looked at him with her quiet, observant eyes.

'Angus and I have got used to you now. I think we'd miss you. If you like, you can pay us for your board. You don't cost anything, but if it'll make you easier I'll find out exactly what difference you make in cookie's book and you can pay that.'

'It must be an awful nuisance having a stranger in the house,' he answered uncertainly.

'It'll be miserable for you there. Good heavens, the filth they eat.'

It was true also that at the Munros you ate better than anywhere else at Kuala Solor. He had dined out now and then, and even at the Resident's you didn't get a very good dinner. Darya liked her food and kept the cook up to the mark. He made Russian dishes which were a fair treat. That cabbage soup of Darya's was worth walking five miles for. But Munro hadn't said anything.

'I'd be glad if you'd stay here,' he said now. 'It's very convenient to have you on the spot. If anything comes up we can talk it over there and then. Waring and Jonson are very good fellows, but I dare say you'd find them rather limited after a bit.'

'Oh, well, then I'll be very pleased. Heaven knows, I couldn't want anything better than this. I was only afraid I was in the way.'

Next day it was raining cats and dogs and it was impossible to play tennis or football, but towards six Neil put on a mackintosh and went to the club. It was empty but for the Resident, who was sitting in an arm-chair reading *The Fortnightly*. His name was Trevelyan, and he claimed to be related to the friend of Byron. He was a tall fat man, with close-cropped white hair and the large red face of a comic actor. He was fond of amateur theatricals and specialized in cynical dukes and facetious butlers. He was a bachelor, but generally supposed to be fond of the girls, and he liked his gin pahit before dinner. He owed his position to the Sultan's friendship. He was a slack, complacent man, a great talker, not very fond of work, who wanted everything to go smoothly and no one to give trouble. Though not considered especially competent he was popular in the community because he was easy-going and hospitable, and he certainly made life more comfortable than if he had been energetic and efficient. He nodded to Neil.

'Well, young fellow, how are bugs today?'

'Feeling the weather, sir,' said Neil gravely.

'Hi-hi.'

In a few minutes Waring, Jonson, and another man, called Bishop, came in. He was in the Civil Service. Neil did not play bridge, so Bishop went up to the Resident.

'Would you care to make a fourth, sir?' he asked him. 'There's nobody much in the club today.'

The Resident gave the others a glance.

'All right. I'll just finish this article and join you. Cut for me and deal. I shall only be five minutes.'

Neil went up to the three men.

'Oh, I say, Waring, thanks awfully, but I can't move over to you after all. The Munros have asked me to stay on with them for good.'

A broad smile broke on Waring's face.

'Fancy that.'

'It's awfully nice of them, isn't it? They made rather a point of it. I couldn't very well refuse.'

'What did I tell you?' said Bishop.

'I don't blame the boy,' said Waring.

There was something in their manner that Neil did not like. They seemed to be amused. He flushed.

'What the hell are you talking about?' he cried.

'Oh, come off it,' said Bishop. 'We know our Darya. You're not the first good-looking young fellow she's had a romp with, and you won't be the last.'

The words were hardly out of his mouth before Neil's clenched fist shot out like a flash. He hit Bishop on the face and he fell heavily to the floor. Jonson sprang at Neil and seized him round the middle, for he was beside himself.

'Let me go,' he shouted. 'If he doesn't withdraw that I'll kill him.'

The Resident, startled by the commotion, looked up and rose to his feet. He walked heavily towards them.

'What's this? What's this? What the hell are you boys playing at?'

They were taken aback. They had forgotten him. He was their master. Jonson let go of Neil and Bishop picked himself up. The Resident, a frown on his face, spoke to Neil sharply.

'What's the meaning of this? Did you hit Bishop?'

'Yes, sir.'

'Why?'

'He made a foul suggestion reflecting on a woman's honour,' said Neil, very haughtily, and still white with rage.

The Resident's eyes twinkled, but he kept a grave face.

'What woman?'

'I refuse to answer,' said Neil, throwing back his head and drawing himself up to his full imposing height.

It would have been more effective if the Resident hadn't been a good two inches taller, and very much stouter.

'Don't be a damned young fool.'

'Darya Munro,' said Jonson.

'What did you say, Bishop?'

'I forget the exact words I used. I said she'd hopped into bed with a good many young chaps here, and I supposed she hadn't missed the chance of doing the same with MacAdam.'

'It was a most offensive suggestion. Will you be so good as to apologize and shake hands. Both of you.'

'I've had a hell of a biff, sir. My eye's going to look like the devil. I'm damned if I apologize for telling the truth.'

'You're old enough to know that the fact that your statement is true only makes it more offensive, and as far as your eye is concerned I'm told that a raw beef-steak is very efficacious in these circumstances. Though I put my desire that you should apologize in the form of a request out of politeness, it is in point of fact an order.'

There was a moment's silence. The Resident looked bland.

'I apologize for what I said, sir,' Bishop said sulkily.

'Now then, MacAdam.'

'I'm sorry I hit him, sir. I apologize, too.'

'Shake hands.'

The two young men solemnly did so.

'I shouldn't like this to go any further. It wouldn't be nice for Munro, whom I think we all like. Can I count on you all holding your tongues?'

They nodded.

'Now be off with you. You stay, MacAdam, I want to have a few words with you.'

When the two of them were left alone, the Resident sat down and lit himself a cheroot. He offered one to Neil, but he only smoked cigarettes.

'You're a very violent young man,' said the Resident, with a smile. 'I don't like my officers to make scenes in a public place like this.'

'Mrs Munro is a great friend of mine. She's been kindness itself to me. I won't hear a word said against her.'

'Then I'm afraid you'll have your job cut out for you if you stay here much longer.'

Neil was silent for a moment. He stood, tall and slim, before the Resident, and his grave young face was guileless. He flung back his head defiantly. His emotion made him speak in broader Scots even than usual.

'I've lived with the Munros for four months, and I give you my word of honour that so far as I am concerned there is not an iota of truth in what that beast said. Mrs Munro has never treated me with anything that you could call undue familiarity. She's never by word or deed given me the smallest hint that she had an improper idea in her head. She's been like a mother to me or an elder sister.'

The Resident watched him with ironical eyes.

'I'm very glad to hear it. That's the best thing I've heard about her for a long time.'

'You believe me, sir, don't you?'

'Of course. Perhaps you've reformed her.' He called out, 'Boy. Bring me a gin pahit.' And then to Neil. 'That'll do. You can go now if you want to. But no more fighting, mind you, or you'll get the order of the boot.'

When Neil walked back to the Munros' bungalow the rain had stopped and the velvet sky was bright with stars. In the garden the fire-flies were flitting here and there. From the earth rose a scented warmth and you felt that if you stopped you would hear the growth of that luxuriant vegetation. A white flower of the night gave forth an overwhelming perfume. In the veranda Munro was typing some notes, and Darya, lying at full length on a long chair, was reading. The lamp behind her lit her smoky hair so that it shone like an aureole. She looked up at Neil and, putting down her book, smiled. Her smile was very friendly.

'Where have you been, Neil?'

'At the club.'

'Anybody there?'

The scene was so cosy and domestic, Darya's manner so peaceful and quietly assured, that it was impossible not to be touched. The two of them there, each occupied with his own concerns, seemed so united, their intimacy so natural, that no one could have conceived that they were not perfectly happy in one another. Neil did not believe a single word of what Bishop had said and the

Resident had hinted. It was incredible. After all, he knew that what they had suspected of *him* was untrue, so what reason was there to think that the rest was any truer? They had dirty minds, all those people; because they were a lot of swine they thought everyone else as bad as they were. His knuckle hurt him a little. He was glad he had hit Bishop. He wished he knew who had started that filthy story. He'd wring his neck.

But now Munro fixed a date for the expedition that they had so much discussed, and in his careful way began to make preparations so that at the last moment nothing should be forgotten. The plan was to go as far up the river as possible and then make their way through the jungle and hunt for specimens on the little-known Mount Hitam. They expected to be away two months. As the day on which they were to start grew nearer Munro's spirits rose, and though he did not say very much, though he remained quiet and self-controlled, you could tell by the light in his eyes and the jauntiness of his step how much he looked forward to it. One morning, at the museum, he was almost sprightly.

'I've got some good news for you,' he said suddenly to Neil, after they had been looking at some experiments they were making. 'Darya's coming with us.'

'Is she? That's grand.'

Neil was delighted. That made it perfect.

'It's the first time I've ever been able to induce her to accompany me. I told her she'd enjoy it, but she would never listen to me. Queer cattle, women, I'd given it up and never thought of asking her to come this time, and suddenly, last night, out of a blue sky she said she'd like to.'

'I'm awfully glad,' said Neil.

'I didn't much like the idea of leaving her by herself so long; now we can stay just as long as we want to.'

They started early one morning in four prahus, manned by Malays, and besides themselves the party consisted of their servants and four Dyak hunters. The three of them lay on cushions side by side, under an awning; in the other boats were the Chinese servants and the Dyaks. They carried bags of rice for the whole party, provisions for themselves, clothes, books, and all that was necessary for their work. It was heavenly to leave civilization behind them and they were all excited. They talked. They smoked. They read. The motion of the river was exquisitely soothing. They lunched on a grassy bank. Dusk fell and they moored for the night. They slept at a long house and their Dyak hosts celebrated their visit with arrak, eloquence, and a fantastic dance. Next day the river, narrowing, gave them more definitely the feeling that they were adventuring into the unknown, and the exotic vegetation that crowded the banks to the water's edge, like an excited mob pushed from behind by a multitude, caused Neil a breathless ravishment. O wonder and delight! On the third day, because the water was shallower and the stream more rapid, they changed into lighter boats, and soon it grew so strong that the boatmen could paddle no longer, and they poled against the current with powerful and magnificent gestures. Now and then they came to rapids and had to disembark, unload, and haul the boats through a rock-strewn passage. After five days they reached a point beyond which they could go no further. There was a government bungalow there, and they settled in for a couple of nights while Munro made arrangements for their excursion into the interior. He wanted bearers for their baggage, and men to build a house for them when they reached Mount Hitam. It was necessary for Munro to see the headman of a village in the vicinity, and thinking it would save time if he went himself rather than let the headman come to him, the day after they arrived he set out at dawn with a guide and a couple of Dyaks. He expected to be back in a few hours. When he had seen him off Neil thought he would have a bathe. There was a pool a little way from the bungalow, and the water was so clear that you saw every grain of the sandy bottom. The river was so narrow there that the trees over-arched it. It was a lovely spot. It reminded Neil of the pools in Scotch streams he had bathed in as a boy, and yet it was strangely different. It had an air of romance, a feeling of virgin nature, that filled him with sensations that he found hard to analyse. He tried, of course, but older heads than his have found it difficult to anatomize happiness. A kingfisher was sitting on an overhanging branch and its vivid blue was reflected as bluely in the crystal stream. It flew away with a flashing glitter of jewelled wings when Neil, slipping off his sarong and baju, scrambled down into the water. It was fresh without being cold. He splashed and tumbled about. He enjoyed the movement of his strong limbs. He floated and looked at the blue sky peeping through the leaves and the sun that here and there gilded the water. Suddenly he heard a voice.

'How white your body is, Neil.'

With a gasp he let himself sink and turning round saw Darya standing on the bank.

'I say, I haven't got any clothes on.'

'So I saw. It's much nicer bathing without. Wait a minute, I'll come in, it looks lovely.'

She also was wearing a sarong and a baju. He turned away his head quickly, for he saw that she was taking them off. He heard her splash into the water. He gave two or three strokes in order that she should have room to swim about at a good distance from him, but she swam up to him.

'Isn't the feel of the water on one's body lovely?' she said.

She laughed and opening her hand splashed water in his face. He was so embarrassed he did not know which way to look. In that limpid water it was impossible not to see that she was stark naked. It was not so bad now, but he could not help thinking how difficult it would be to get out. She seemed to be having a grand time.

'I don't care if I do get my hair wet,' she said.

She turned over on her back and with strong strokes swam round the pool. When she wanted to get out, he thought, the best thing would be if he turned his back and when she was dressed she could go and he would get out later. She seemed quite unconscious of the awkwardness of the situation. He was vexed with her. It really was rather tactless to behave like that. She kept on talking to him just as if they were on dry land and properly dressed. She even called his attention to herself.

'Does my hair look awful? It's so fine it gets like rat tails when it's wet. Hold me under the shoulders a moment while I try to screw it up.'

'Oh, it's all right,' he said. 'You'd better leave it now.'

'I'm getting frightfully hungry,' she said presently. 'What about breakfast?'

'If you'll get out first and put on your things, I'll follow you in a minute.'

'All right.'

She swam the two strokes needed to bring her to the side, and he modestly looked away so that he should not see her get out nude from the water.

'I can't get up,' she cried. 'You'll have to help me.'

It had been easy enough to get in, but the bank overhung the water and one had to lift oneself up by the branch of a tree.

'I can't. I haven't got a stitch of clothing on.'

'I know that. Don't be so Scotch. Get up on the bank and give me a hand.'

There was no help for it. Neil swung himself up and pulled her after him. She had left her sarong beside his. She took it up unconcernedly and began to dry herself with it. There was nothing for him but do to the same, but for decency's sake he turned his back on her.

'You really have a most lovely skin,' she said. 'It's as smooth and white as a woman's. It's funny on such a manly virile figure. And you haven't got a hair on your chest.'

Neil wrapped the sarong round him and slipped his arms into the baju.

'Are you ready?'

She had porridge for breakfast, and eggs and bacon, cold meat, and marmalade. Neil was a trifle sulky. She was really almost too Russian. It was stupid of her to behave like that; of course there was no harm in it, but it was just the sort of thing that made people think the things they did about her. The worst of it was that you couldn't give her a hint. She'd only laugh at you. But the fact was that if any of those men at Kuala Solor had seen them bathing like that together, stark naked, nothing would have persuaded them that something improper hadn't happened. In his judicious way Neil admitted to himself that you could hardly blame them. It was too bad of her. She had no right to put a fellow in such a position. He had felt such a fool. And say what you liked, it was indecent.

Next morning, having seen their carriers on the way, a long procession in single file, each man carrying his load in a creel on his back, with their servants, guides, and hunters, they started to walk. The path ran over the foothills of the mountain, through scrub and tall grass, and now and then they came to narrow streams which they crossed by rickety bridges of bamboo. The sun beat on them fiercely. In the afternoon they reached the shade of a bamboo forest, grateful after the glare, and the bamboos in their slender elegance rose to incredible heights, and the green light was like the light under the sea. At last they reached the primeval forest, huge trees swathed in luxuriant creepers, an inextricable tangle, and awe descended upon them. They cut their way through the undergrowth. They walked in twilight and only now and then caught through the dense foliage above them a glimpse of sunshine. They saw neither man nor beast, for the denizens of the jungle are shy and at the first sound of footsteps vanish from sight. They heard birds up high in the tall trees, but saw none save the twittering sunbirds that flew in the underwoods and delicately coquetted with the wild flowers. They halted for the night. The carriers made a floor of branches and on this spread waterproof sheets. The Chinese cook made them their dinner and then they turned in.

It was the first night Neil had ever spent in the jungle and he could not sleep. The darkness was profound. The noise was deafening of innumerable insects, but like the roar of traffic in a great city it was so constant that in a little while it was like an impenetrable silence, and when on a sudden he heard the shriek of a monkey seized by a snake or the scream of a night-bird he nearly jumped out of his skin. He had a mysterious sensation that all around creatures were watching them. Over there, beyond the camp-fires, savage warfare was waged and they three on their bed of branches were defenceless and alone in face of the horror of nature. By his side Munro was breathing quietly in his deep sleep.

'Are you awake, Neil?' Darya whispered.

'Yes. Is anything the matter?'

'I'm terrified.'

'It's all right. There's nothing to be afraid of.'

'The silence is so awful. I wish I hadn't come.'

She lit a cigarette.

Neil, having at last dozed off, was awakened by the hammering of a woodpecker, and its complacent laugh as it flew from one tree to another seemed to mock the sluggards. A hurried breakfast, and the caravan started. The gibbons swung from branch to branch, gathering in the dawn dew from the leaves, and their strange cry was like the call of a bird. The light had driven away Darya's fears, and notwithstanding a sleepless night she was alert and gay. They continued to climb. In the afternoon they reached the spot that the guides had told them would be a good camping place, and here Munro decided to build a house. The men set to work. With their long knives they cut palm leaves and saplings and soon had erected a two-roomed hut raised on piles from the ground. It was neat and fresh and green. It smelt good.

The Munros, he from old habit, she because she had for years wandered about the world and had a catlike knack of making herself comfortable wherever she went, were at home anywhere. In a day they had arranged everything and settled down. Their routine was invariable. Every morning Neil and Munro started out separately, collecting. The afternoon was devoted to pinning insects in boxes, placing butterflies between sheets of paper and skinning birds. When dusk came they caught moths. Darya busied herself with the hut and the servants, sewed and read and smoked innumerable cigarettes. The days passed very pleasantly, monotonous but eventful. Neil was enraptured. He explored the mountain in all directions. One day, to his pride, he found a new species of stick-insect. Munro named it Cuniculina MacAdami. This was fame. Neil (at twenty-two) realized that he had not lived in vain. But another day he only just escaped being bitten by a viper. Owing to its green colour he had not seen it and was only saved from lurching against it by the Dyak hunter who was with him. They killed it and brought it back to camp. Darya shuddered at the sight of it. She had a terror of the wild creatures of the jungle and was almost hysterical. She would never go more than a few yards from the camp for fear of being lost.

'Has Angus ever told you how he was lost?' she asked Neil one evening when they were sitting quietly together after dinner.

'It wasn't a very pleasant experience,' he smiled.

'Tell him, Angus.'

He hesitated a little. It was not a thing he liked to recall.

'It was some years ago, I'd gone out with my butterfly net and I'd been very lucky. I'd got several rare specimens that I'd been looking for a long time. After a while I thought I was getting hungry so I turned back. I walked for some time and it struck me I'd come a good deal farther than I knew. Suddenly I caught sight of an empty match-box. I'd thrown it away when I started to come back; I'd been walking in a circle and was exactly where I was an hour before. I was not pleased. But I had a look round and set off again. It was fearfully hot and I was simply dripping with sweat. I knew more or less the direction the camp was in and I looked about for traces of my passage to see if I had come that way. I thought I found one or two and went on hopefully. I was frightfully thirsty. I walked on and on, picking my way over snags and trailing plants, and suddenly I knew I was lost. I couldn't have gone so far in the right direction without hitting the camp. I can tell you I was startled. I knew I must keep my head, so I sat down and thought the situation over. I was tortured by thirst. It was long past midday and in three or four hours it would be dark. I didn't like the idea of spending a night in the jungle at all. The only thing I could think of was to try and find a stream; if I followed its course, it would eventually bring me to a larger stream and sooner or later to the river. But of course it might take a couple of days. I cursed myself for being such a fool, but there was nothing better to do and I began walking. At all events if I found a stream I should be able to get a drink. I couldn't find a trickle of water anywhere, not the smallest brook that might lead to something like a stream. I began to be alarmed. I saw myself wandering on till at last I fell exhausted. I knew there was a lot of game in the forest and if I came upon a rhino I was done for. The maddening thing was I knew I couldn't be more than ten miles from my camp. I forced myself to keep my head. The day was waning and in the depths of the jungle it was growing dark already. If I'd brought a gun I could have fired it. In the camp they must have realized I was lost and would be looking for me. The undergrowth was so thick that I couldn't see six feet into it and presently, I don't know if it was nerves or not, I had the sensation that some animal was walking stealthily beside me. I stopped and it stopped too. I went on and it went on. I couldn't see it. I could see no movement in the undergrowth. I didn't even hear the breaking of a twig or the brushing of a body through leaves, but I knew how silently those beasts could move, and I was positive something was stalking me. My heart beat so violently against my ribs that I thought it would break. I was scared out of my wits. It was only by the exercise of all the self-control I had that I prevented myself from breaking into a run. I knew if I did that I was lost. I should be tripped up before I had gone twenty yards by a tangle root and when I was down it would spring on me. And if I started to run God knew where I should get to. And I had to husband my strength. I felt very like crying. And that intolerable thirst. I've never been so frightened in my life. Believe me, if I'd had a revolver I think I'd have blown my brains out. It was so awful I just wanted to finish with it. I was so exhausted I could hardly stagger. If I had an enemy who'd done me a deadly injury I wouldn't wish him the agony I endured then. Suddenly I heard two shots. My heart stood still. They were looking for me. Then I did lose my head. I ran in the direction of the sound, screaming at the top of my voice. I fell, I picked myself up again. I ran on, I shouted till I thought my lungs would burst, there was another shot, nearer, I shouted again, I heard answering shouts; there was a scramble of men in the undergrowth. In a minute I was surrounded by Dyak hunters. They wrung and kissed my hands. They laughed and cried. I very nearly cried too. I was down and out, but they gave me a drink. We were only three miles from the camp. It was pitch dark when we got back. By God, it was a near thing.'

A convulsive shudder passed through Darya.

'Believe me, I don't want to be lost in the jungle again.'

'What would have happened if you hadn't been found?'

'I can tell you. I should have gone mad. If I hadn't been stung by a snake or attacked by a rhino I should have gone on blindly till I fell exhausted. I should have starved to death. I should have died of thirst. Wild beasts would have eaten my body and ants cleaned my bones.'

Silence fell upon them.

Then it happened, when they had spent nearly a month on Mount Hitam, that Neil, notwithstanding the quinine Munro had made him take regularly, was stricken with fever. It was not a bad attack, but he felt very sorry for himself and was obliged to stay in bed. Darya nursed him. He was ashamed to give her so much trouble, but she would not listen to his protests. She was certainly very capable. He resigned himself to letting her do things for him that one of the Chinese boys could have done just as well. He was touched. She waited on him hand and foot. But when the fever was at its height and she sponged him all over with cold water, though the comfort was indescribable, he was excessively embarrassed. She insisted on washing him night and morning.

'I wasn't in the British hospital at Yokohama for six months without learning at least the routine of nursing,' she said, smiling.

She kissed him on the lips each time after she had finished. It was friendly and sweet of her. He rather liked it, but attached no importance to it; he even went so far, a rare thing for him, as to be facetious on the subject.

'Did you always kiss your patients at the hospital?' he asked her.

'Don't you like me to kiss you?' she smiled.

'It doesn't do me any harm.'

'It may even hasten your recovery,' she mocked.

One night he dreamt of her. He awoke with a start. He was sweating profusely. The relief was wonderful, and he knew that his temperature had fallen; he was well. He did not care. For what he had dreamt filled him with shame. He was horrified. That he should have such thoughts, even in his sleep, made him feel awful. He must be a monster of depravity. Day was breaking, and he heard Munro getting up in the room next door that he occupied with Darya. She slept late, and he took care not to disturb her. When he passed through Neil's room, Neil in a low voice called him.

'Hullo, are you awake?'

'Yes, I've had the crisis. I'm all right now.'

'Good. You'd better stay in bed today. Tomorrow you'll be as fit as a fiddle.'

'Send Ah Tan to me when you've had your breakfast, will you?'

'Right-ho.'

He heard Munro start out. The Chinese boy came and asked him what he wanted. An hour later Darya awoke. She came in to bid him good morning. He could hardly look at her.

'I'll just have my breakfast and then I'll come in and wash you,' she said.

'I'm washed. I got Ah Tan to do it.'

'Why?'

'I wanted to spare you the trouble.'

'It isn't a trouble. I like doing it.'

She came over to the bed and bent down to kiss him, but he turned away his head.

'Oh, don't.'

'Why not?'

'It's silly.'

She looked at him for a moment, surprised, and then with a slight shrug of the shoulders left him. A little later she came back to see if there was anything he wanted. He pretended to be asleep. She very gently stroked his cheek.

'For God's sake don't do that,' he cried.

'I thought you were sleeping. What's the matter with you today?'

'Nothing.'

'Why are you being horrid to me? Have I done anything to offend you?'

'No.'

'Tell me what it is.'

She sat down on the bed and took his hand. He turned his face to the wall. He was so ashamed he could hardly speak.

'You seem to forget I'm a man. You treat me as if I was a boy of twelve.'

'Oh?'

He was blushing furiously. He was angry with himself and vexed with her. She really should be more tactful. He plucked nervously at the sheet.

'I know it means nothing to you and it ought not to mean anything to me. It doesn't when I'm well and up and about. One can't help one's dreams, but they are an indication of what is going on in the subconscious.'

'Have you been dreaming about me? Well, I don't think there's any harm in that.'

He turned his head and looked at her. Her eyes were gleaming, but his were sombre with remorse.

'You don't know men,' he said.

She gave a little burble of laughter. She bent down and threw her arms round his neck. She had nothing on but her sarong and baju.

'You darling,' she cried. 'Tell me, what did you dream?'

He was startled out of his wits. He pushed her violently aside.

'What are you doing? You're crazy.'

He jumped half out of bed.

'Don't you know that I'm madly in love with you?' she said.

'What *are* you talking about?'

He sat down on the side of the bed. He was frankly bewildered. She chuckled.

'Why do you suppose I came up to this horrible place? To be with you, ducky. Don't you know I'm scared stiff of the jungle? Even in here I'm frightened there'll be snakes or scorpions or something. I adore you.'

'You have no right to speak to me like that,' he said sternly.

'Oh, don't be so prim,' she smiled.

'Let's get out of here.'

He walked out on to the veranda and she followed him. He threw himself into a chair. She knelt by his side and tried to take his hands, but he withdrew them.

'I think you must be mad. I hope to God you don't mean what you say.'

'I do. Every word of it,' she smiled.

It exasperated him that she seemed unconscious of the frightfulness of her confession.

'Have you forgotten your husband?'

'Oh, what does he matter?'

'Darya.'

'I can't be bothered about Angus now.'

'I'm afraid you're a very wicked woman,' he said slowly, a frown darkening his smooth brow.

She giggled.

'Because I've fallen in love with you? Darling, you shouldn't be so absurdly good-looking.'

'For God's sake don't laugh.'

'I can't help it; you're comic—but still adorable. I love your white skin and your shining curly hair. I love you because you're so prim and Scotch and humourless. I love your strength. I love your youth.'

Her eyes glowed and her breath came quickly. She stooped and kissed his naked feet. He drew them away quickly, with a cry of protest, and in the agitation of his gesture nearly overthrew the rickety chair.

'Woman, you're insane. Have you no shame?'

'No.'

'What do you want of me?' he asked fiercely.

'Love.'

'What sort of man do you take me for?'

'A man like any other,' she replied calmly.

'Do you think after all that Angus Munro has done for me I could be such a damned beast as to play about with his wife? I admire him more than any man I've ever known. He's grand. He's worth a dozen of me and you put together. I'd sooner kill myself than betray him. I don't know how you can think me capable of such a dastardly act.'

'Oh, my dear, don't talk such bilge. What harm is it going to do him? You mustn't take that sort of thing so tragically. After all, life is very short; we're fools if we don't take what pleasure we can out of it.'

'You can't make wrong right by talking about it.'

'I don't know about that. I think that's a very controvertible statement.'

He looked at her with amazement. She was sitting at his feet, cool to all appearance and collected, and she seemed to be enjoying the situation. She seemed quite unconscious of its seriousness.

'Do you know that I knocked a fellow down at the club because he made an insulting remark about you?'

'Who?'

'Bishop.'

'Dirty dog. What did he say?'

'He said you'd had affairs with men.'

'I don't know why people won't mind their own business. Anyhow, who cares what they say? I love you. I've never loved anyone like you. I'm absolutely sick with love for you.'

'Be quiet. Be quiet.'

'Listen, tonight when Angus is asleep I'll slip into your room. He sleeps like a rock. There's no risk.'

'You mustn't do that.'

'Why not?'

'No, no, no.'

He was frightened out of his wits. Suddenly she sprang to her feet and went into the house.

Munro came back at noon, and in the afternoon they busied themselves as usual. Darya, as she sometimes did, worked with them. She was in high spirits. She was so gay that Munro suggested that she was beginning to enjoy the life.

'It's not so bad,' she admitted. 'I'm feeling happy today.'

She teased Neil. She seemed not to notice that he was silent and kept his eyes averted from her.

'Neil's very quiet,' said Munro. 'I suppose you're feeling a bit weak still.'

'No. I just don't feel very talkative.'

He was harassed. He was convinced that Darya was capable of anything. He remembered the hysterical frenzy of Nastasya Filipovna in *The Idiot*, and felt that she too could behave with that unfortunate lack of balance. He had seen her more than once fly into a temper with one of the Chinese servants and he knew how completely she could lose her self-control. Resistance only exasperated her. If she did not immediately get what she wanted she would go almost insane with rage. Fortunately she lost interest in a thing with the same suddenness with which she hankered for it, and if you could distract her attention for a minute she forgot all about it. It was in such situations that Neil had most admired Munro's tact. He had often been slyly amused to see with what a pawky and yet tender cunning he appeased her feminine tantrums. It was on Munro's account that Neil's indignation was so great. Munro was a saint, and from what a state of humiliation and penury and random shifts had he not taken her to make her his wife! She owed everything to him. His name protected her. She had respectability. The commonest gratitude should have made it impossible for her to harbour such thoughts as she had that morning expressed. It was all very well for men to make advances, that was what men did, but for women to do so was disgusting. His modesty was outraged. The passion he had seen in her face, and the indelicacy of her gestures, scandalized him.

He wondered whether she would really carry out her threat to come to his room. He didn't think she would dare. But when night came and they all went to bed, he was so terrified that he could not sleep. He lay there listening anxiously. The silence was broken only by the repeated and monotonous cry of an owl. Through the thin wall of woven palm leaves he heard Munro's steady breathing. Suddenly he was conscious that someone was stealthily creeping into his room. He had already made up his mind what to do.

'Is that you, Mr Munro?' he called in a loud voice.

Darya stopped suddenly. Munro awoke.

'There's someone in my room. I thought it was you.'

'It's all right,' said Darya. 'It's only me, I couldn't sleep, so I thought I'd go and smoke a cigarette on the veranda.'

'Oh, is that all?' said Munro. 'Don't catch cold.'

She walked through Neil's room and out. He saw her light a cigarette. Presently she went back and he heard her get into bed.

He did not see her next morning, for he started out collecting before she was up, and he took care not to get in till he was pretty sure Munro would be back. He avoided being alone with her till it was dark and Munro went down for a few minutes to arrange the moth-traps.

'Why did you wake Angus last night?' she said in a low angry whisper.

He shrugged his shoulders and going on with his work did not answer.

'Were you frightened?'

'I have a certain sense of decency.'

'Oh, don't be such a prig.'

'I'd rather be a prig than a dirty swine.'

'I hate you.'

'Then leave me alone.'

She did not answer, but with her open hand smartly slapped his face. He flushed, but did not speak. Munro returned and they pretended to be intent on whatever they were doing.

For the next few days Darya, except at meal-times and in the evenings, never spoke to Neil. Without prearrangement they exerted themselves to conceal from Munro that their relations were strained. But the effort with which Darya roused herself from a brooding silence would have been obvious to anyone more suspicious than Angus, and sometimes she could not help herself from being a trifle sharp with Neil. She chaffed him, but in her chaff was a sting. She knew how to wound and caught him on the raw, but he took care not to let her see it. He had an inkling that the good-humour he affected infuriated her.

Then one day when Neil came back from collecting, though he had delayed till the last possible minute before tiffin, he was surprised to find that Munro had not yet returned. Darya was lying on a mattress on the veranda, sipping a gin pahit and smoking. She did not speak to him when he passed through to wash. In a minute the Chinese boy came into his room and told him that tiffin was ready. He walked out.

'Where's Mr Munro?' he asked.

'He's not coming,' said Darya. 'He sent a message to say that the place he's at is so good he won't come down till night.'

Munro had set out that morning for the summit of the mountain. The lower levels had yielded poor results in the way of mammals, and Munro's idea was, if he could find a good place higher up, with a supply of water, to transfer the camp. Neil and Darya ate their meal in silence. After they had finished he went into the house and came out again with his topee and his collecting gear. It was unusual for him to go out in the afternoon.

'Where are you going?' she asked abruptly.

'Out.'

'Why?'

'I don't feel tired. I've got nothing much else to do this afternoon.'

Suddenly she burst into tears.

'How can you be so unkind to me?' she sobbed. 'Oh, it is cruel to treat me like this.'

He looked down at her from his great height, his handsome, somewhat stolid face bearing a harassed look.

'What have *I* done?'

'You've been beastly to me. Bad as I am I haven't deserved to suffer like this. I've done everything in the world for you. Tell me one single little thing I could do that I haven't done gladly. I'm so terribly unhappy.'

He moved on his feet uneasily. It was horrible to hear her say that. He loathed and feared her, but he had still the respect for her that he had always felt, not only because she was a woman, but because she was Angus Munro's wife. She wept uncontrollably. Fortunately the Dyak hunters had gone that morning with Munro. There was no one about the camp but the three Chinese servants and they, after tiffin, were asleep in their own quarters fifty yards away. They were alone.

'I don't want to make you unhappy. It's all so silly. It's absurd of a woman like you to fall in love with a fellow like me. It makes me look such a fool. Haven't you got any self-control?'

'Oh, God. Self-control!'

'I mean, if you really cared for me you couldn't want me to be such a cad. Doesn't it mean anything to you that your husband trusts us implicitly? The mere fact of his leaving us alone like this puts us on our honour. He's a man who would never hurt a fly. I should never respect myself again if I betrayed his confidence.'

She looked up suddenly.

'What makes you think he would never hurt a fly? Why, all those bottles and cases are full of the harmless animals he's killed.'

'In the interests of science. That's quite another thing.'

'Oh, you fool, you fool.'

'Well, if I am a fool I can't help it. Why do you bother about me?'

'Do you think I wanted to fall in love with you?'

'You ought to be ashamed of yourself.'

'Ashamed? How stupid! My God, what have I done that I should eat my heart out for such a pretentious ass?'

'You talk about what you've done for me. What has Munro done for you?'

'Munro bores me to death. I'm sick of him. Sick to death of him.'

'Then I'm not the first?'

Ever since her amazing avowal he had been tortured by the suspicion that what those men at Kuala Solor had said of her was true. He had refused to believe a word of it, and even now he could not bring himself to think that she could be such a monster of depravity. It was frightful to think that Angus Munro, so trusting and tender, should have lived in a fool's paradise. She could not be as bad as that. But she misunderstood him. She smiled through her tears.

'Of course not. How can you be so silly? Oh, darling, don't be so desperately serious. I love you.'

Then it was true. He had sought to persuade himself that what she felt for him was exceptional, a madness that together they could contend with and vanquish. But she was simply promiscuous.

'Aren't you afraid Munro will find out?'

She was not crying any more. She adored talking about herself, and she had a feeling that she was inveigling Neil into a new interest in her.

'I sometimes wonder if he doesn't know, if not with his mind, then with his heart. He's got the intuition of a woman and a woman's sensitiveness. Sometimes I've been certain he suspected and in his anguish I've sensed a strange, spiritual exaltation. I've wondered if in his pain he didn't find an infinitely subtle pleasure. There are souls, you know, that feel a voluptuous joy in laceration.'

'How horrible!' Neil had no patience with these conceits. 'The only excuse for you is that you're insane.'

She was now much more sure of herself. She gave him a bold look.

'Don't you think I'm attractive? A good many men have. You must have had dozens of women in Scotland who weren't so well made as I am.'

She looked down at her shapely, sensual figure with calm pride.

'I've never had a woman,' he said gravely.

'Why not?'

She was so surprised that she sprang to her feet. He shrugged his shoulders. He could not bring himself to tell her how disgusting the idea of such a thing was to him, and how vile he had thought the haphazard amours of his fellow-students at Edinburgh. He took a mystical joy in his purity. Love was sacred. The sexual act horrified him. Its excuse was the procreation of children and its sanctification marriage. But Darya, her whole body rigid, stared at him, panting; and suddenly, with a sobbing cry in which there was exultation and at the same time wild desire, she flung herself on her knees and seizing his hand passionately kissed it.

'Alyosha,' she gasped. 'Alyosha.'

And then, crying and laughing, she crumpled up in a heap at his feet. Strange, hardly human sounds issued from her throat and convulsive tremors passed through her body so that you would have thought she was receiving one electric shock after another. Neil did not know if it was an attack of hysteria or an epileptic fit.

'Stop it,' he cried. 'Stop it.'

He took her up in his strong arms and laid her in the chair. But when he tried to leave her she would not let him. She flung her arms round his neck and held him. She covered his face with kisses. He struggled. He turned his face away. He put his hand between her face and his to protect himself. Suddenly she dug her teeth into it. The pain was so great that, without thinking, he gave her a great swinging blow.

'You devil,' he cried.

His violent gesture had forced her to release him. He held his hand and looked at it. She had caught him by the fleshy part on the side, and it was bleeding. Her eyes blazed. She was feeling alert and active.

'I've had enough of this. I'm going out,' he said.

She sprang to her feet.

'I'll come with you.'

He put on his topee and, snatching up his collecting gear without a word, turned on his heel. With one stride he leaped down the three steps that led from the floor of the house to the ground. She followed him.

'I'm going into the jungle,' he said.

'I don't care.'

In the ravening desire that possessed her she forgot her morbid fear of the jungle. She recked nothing of snakes and wild beasts. She did not mind the branches that hit her face or the creepers that entangled her feet. For a month Neil had explored all that part of the forest and he knew every yard of it. He told himself grimly that he'd teach her to come with him. He forced his way through the undergrowth with rapid strides; she followed him, stumbling but determined; he crashed on, blind with rage, and she crashed after him. She talked; he did not listen to what she said. She besought him to have pity on her. She bemoaned her fate. She made herself humble. She wept and wrung her hands. She tried to cajole him. The words poured from her lips in an unceasing stream. She was like a mad woman. At last in a little clearing he stopped suddenly and turning round faced her.

'This is impossible,' he cried. 'I'm fed up. When Angus comes back I must tell him I've got to go. I shall go back to Kuala Solor tomorrow morning and go home.'

'He won't let you go, he wants you. He finds you invaluable.'

'I don't care. I'll fake up something.'

'What?'

He mistook her.

'Oh, you needn't be frightened, I shan't tell him the truth. You can break his heart if you want to; I'm not going to.'

'You worship him, don't you? That dull, phlegmatic man.'

'He's worth a hundred of you.'

'It would be rather funny if I told him you'd gone because I wouldn't yield to your advances.'

He gave a slight start and looked at her to see if she was serious.

'Don't be such a fool. You don't think he'd believe that, do you? He knows it would never occur to me.'

'Don't be too sure.'

She had spoken carelessly, with no particular intention other than to continue the argument, but she saw that he was frightened and some instinct of cruelty made her press the advantage.

'Do you expect mercy from me? You've humiliated me beyond endurance. You've treated me like dirt. I swear that if you make any suggestion of going I shall go straight to Angus and say that you took advantage of his absence to try and assault me.'

'I can deny it. After all it's only your word against mine.'

'Yes, but my word'll count. I can prove what I say.'

'What do you mean?'

'I bruise easily. I can show him the bruise where you struck me. And look at your hand.' He turned and gave it a sudden glance. 'How did those teeth marks get there?'

He stared at her stupidly. He had gone quite pale. How could he explain that bruise and that scar? If he was forced to in self-defence he could tell the truth, but was it likely that Angus would believe it? He worshipped Darya. He would take her word against anyone's. What monstrous ingratitude it would seem for all Munro's kindness and what treachery in return for so much confidence! He would think him a filthy skunk and from his standpoint with justice. That was what shattered him, the thought that Munro, for whom he would willingly have laid down his life, should think ill of him. He was so unhappy that tears, unmanly tears that he hated, came to his eyes. Darya saw that he was broken. She exulted. She was paying him back for the misery he had made her suffer. She held him now. He was in her power. She savoured her triumph, and in the midst of her anguish laughed in her heart because he was such a fool. At that moment she did not know whether she loved or despised him.

'Now will you be good?' she said.

He gave a sob and blindly, with a sudden instinct of escape from that abominable woman, took to his heels and ran as hard as he could. He plunged through the jungle, like a wounded animal, not looking where he was going, till he was out of breath. Then, panting, he stopped. He took out his handkerchief and wiped away the sweat that was pouring into his eyes and blinding him. He was exhausted and he sat down to rest.

'I must take care I don't get lost,' he said to himself.

That was the least of his troubles, but all the same he was glad that he had a pocket compass, and he knew in which direction he must go. He heaved a deep sigh and rose wearily to his feet. He started walking. He watched his way and with another part of his mind miserably asked himself what he should do. He was convinced that Darya would do what she had threatened. They were to be another three weeks in that accursed place. He dared not go; he dared not stay. His mind was in a whirl. The only thing was to get back to camp and think it out quietly. In about a quarter of an hour he came to a spot that he recognized. In an hour he was back. He flung himself miserably into a chair. And it was Angus who filled his thoughts. His heart bled for him. Neil saw now all sorts of things that before had been dark to him. They were revealed to him in a flash of bitter insight. He knew why the women at Kuala Solor were so hostile to Darya and why they looked at Angus so strangely. They treated him with a sort of affectionate levity. Neil thought it was because Angus was a man of science and so in their foolish eyes somewhat absurd. He knew now it was because they were sorry for him and at the same time found him ridiculous. Darya had made him the laughing-stock of the community. If ever there was a man who hadn't deserved ill usage at a woman's hands it was he. Suddenly Neil gasped and began to tremble all over. It had suddenly occurred to him that Darya did not know her way through the jungle; in his anguish he had hardly been conscious of where they went. Supposing she could not find her way home? She would be terrified. He remembered the ghastly story Angus had told them of being lost in the forest. His first instinct was to go back and find her, and he sprang to his feet. Then a fierce anger seized him. No, let her shift for herself. She had gone of her own free will. Let her find her own way back. She was an abominable woman and deserved all that might come to her. Neil threw back his head defiantly, a frown of indignation on his smooth young brow, and clenched his hands. Courage. He made up his mind. It would be better for Angus if she never returned. He sat down and began trying to mount a skin of a Mountain Trogon. But the Trogon has a skin like wet tissue-paper and his hands trembled. He tried to apply his mind to the work he was doing, but his thoughts fluttered desperately, like moths in a trap, and he could not control them. What was happening over there in the jungle? What had she done when he suddenly bolted? Every now and then, against his will, he looked up. At any moment she might appear in the clearing and walk calmly up to the house. He was not to blame. It was the hand of God. He shuddered. Storm clouds were gathering in the sky and night fell quickly.

Just after dusk Munro arrived.

'Just in time,' he said. 'There's going to be a hell of a storm.'

He was in great spirits. He had come upon a fine plateau, with lots of water, from which there was a magnificent view to the sea. He had found two or three rare butterflies and a flying squirrel. He was full of plans to move the camp to his new place. All about it he had seen abundant evidence of animal life. Presently he went into the house to take off his heavy walking boots. He came out at once.

'Where's Darya?'

Neil stiffened himself to behave with naturalness.

'Isn't she in her room?'

'No. Perhaps she's gone down to the servants' quarters for something.'

He walked down the steps and strolled a few yards.

'Darya,' he called. 'Darya.' There was no answer. 'Boy.'

A Chinese servant came running up and Angus asked him where his mistress was. He did not know. He had not seen her since tiffin.

'Where can she be?' asked Munro, coming back, puzzled.

He went to the back of the house and shouted.

'She can't have gone out. There's nowhere to go. When did you see her last, Neil?'

'I went out collecting after tiffin. I'd had a rather unsatisfactory morning and I thought I'd try my luck again.'

'Strange.'

They hunted everywhere round the camp. Munro thought she might have made herself comfortable somewhere and gone to sleep.

'It's too bad of her to frighten one like this.'

The whole party joined in the search. Munro began to grow alarmed.

'It's not possible that she should have gone for a stroll in the jungle and lost her way. She's never moved more than a hundred yards from the house to the best of my knowledge since we've been here.'

Neil saw the fear in Munro's eyes and looked down.

'We'd better get everyone along and start hunting. There's one thing, she can't be far. She knows that if you get lost the best thing is to stay where you are and wait for people to come and find you. She'll be scared out of her wits, poor thing.'

He called out the Dyak hunters and told the Chinese servants to bring lanterns. He fired his gun as a signal. They separated into two parties, one under Munro, the other under Neil, and went down the two rough paths that in the course of the month they had made in their comings and goings. It was arranged that whoever found Darya should fire three shots in quick succession. Neil walked with his face stern and set. His conscience was clear. He seemed to bear in his hands the decree of immanent justice. He knew that Darya would never be found. The two parties met. It was not necessary to look at Munro's face. He was distracted. Neil felt like a surgeon who is forced to perform a dangerous operation without assistance or appliances to save the life of someone he loves. It behoved him to be firm.

'She could never have got so far as this,' said Munro. 'We must go back and beat the jungle within the radius of a mile from the house inch by inch. The only explanation is that she was frightened by something or fainted or was stung by a snake.'

Neil did not answer. They started out again and, making lines, combed the undergrowth. They shouted. Every now and then they fired a gun and listened for a faint call in answer. Birds of the night flew with a whirring of wings, frightened, as they advanced with their lanterns; and now and then they half saw, half guessed at an animal, deer, boar, or rhino, that fled at their approach. The storm broke suddenly. A great wind blew and then the lightning rent the darkness, like a scream of a woman in pain, and the tortured flashes, quick, quick, one on the heels of the other, like demon dancers in a frantic reel, wriggled down the night. The horror of the forest was revealed in an unearthly day. The thunder crashed down the sky in huge rollers, peal upon peal, like vast, primeval waves dashing against the shores of eternity. That fearful din hurtled through space as though sound had size and weight. The rain pelted in fierce torrents. Rocks and gigantic trees came tumbling down the mountain. The tumult was awful. The Dyak hunters cowered, gibbering in terror of the angry spirits who spoke in the storm, but Munro urged them on. The rain fell all night, with lightning and thunder, and did not cease till dawn. Wet through and shivering they returned to the camp. They were exhausted. When they had eaten Munro meant to resume the desperate search. But he knew that it was hopeless. They would never see her alive again. He flung himself down wearily. His face was tired and white and anguished.

'Poor child. Poor child.'

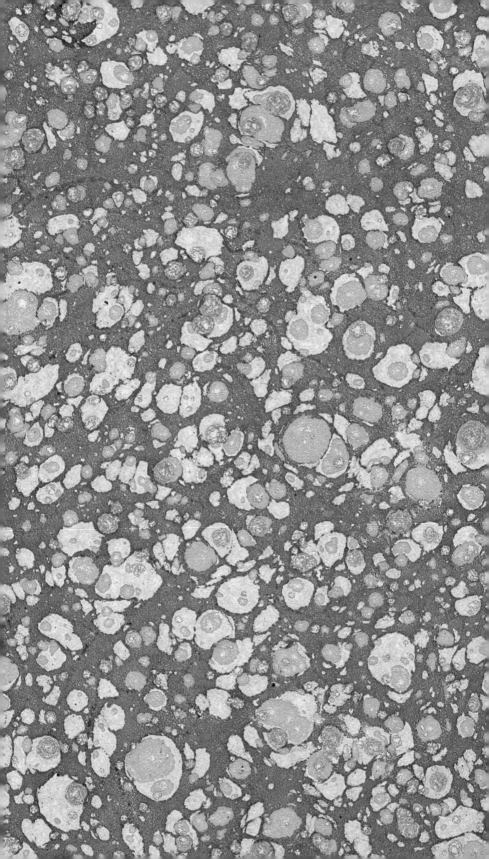